THREE COMPLETE NOVELS

HAROLD ROBBINS

THREE COMPLETE NOVELS

HAROLD ROBBINS

THE CARPETBAGGERS
79 PARK AVENUE
A STONE FOR DANNY FISHER

WINGS BOOKS
NEW YORK • AVENEL, NEW JERSEY

This 1994 edition is published by Wings Books, distributed by Outlet Book Company, Inc., a Random House Company, 40 Engelhard Avenue, Avenel, New Jersey 07001, by arrangement with Simon and Schuster Inc.

Random House
New York • Toronto • London • Sydney • Auckland

Printed and bound in the United States of America

Library of Congress Cataloging-in-Publication Data

Robbins, Harold, 1912–
  [Novels, Selections]
  Three complete novels / Harold Robbins.
    p. cm.
  Contents: The carpetbaggers—79 Park Avenue—A stone for Danny Fisher.
  ISBN 0-517-10071-1
  I. Title.
PS3568.0224A6   1994
813'.54—dc20
                                                                    94-4235
                                                                      CIP

8 7 6 5 4 3 2 1

CONTENTS

THE CARPETBAGGERS

For PAUL GITLIN
as a small appreciation
of his friendship
and guidance
across the years

CONTENTS

PREFACE

. . . And behind the Northern Armies came another army of men. They came by the hundreds, yet each traveled alone. They came on foot, by mule, on horseback, on creaking wagons or riding in handsome chaises. They were of all shapes and sizes and descended from many nationalities. They wore dark suits, usually covered with the gray dust of travel, and dark, broad-brimmed hats to shield their white faces from the hot, unfamiliar sun. And on their back, or across their saddle, or on top of their wagon was the inevitable faded multicolored bag made of worn and ragged remnants of carpet into which they had crammed all their worldly possessions. It was from these bags that they got their name. The Carpetbaggers.

. . . And they strode the dusty roads and streets of the exhausted Southlands, their mouths tightening greedily, their eyes everywhere, searching, calculating, appraising the values that were left behind in the holocaust of war.

. . . Yet not all of them were bad, just as not all men are bad. Some of them even learned to love the land they came to plunder and stayed and became respected citizens.

JONAS – 1925
Book One

CHAPTER ONE

THE SUN WAS BEGINNING TO FALL FROM THE SKY INTO THE WHITE Nevada desert as Reno came up beneath me. I banked the Waco slowly and headed due east. I could hear the wind pinging the biplane's struts and I grinned to myself. The old man would really hit the roof when he saw this plane. But he wouldn't have anything to complain about. It didn't cost him anything. I won it in a crap game.

I moved the stick forward and came down slowly to fifteen hundred feet. I was over Route 32 now and the desert on either side of the road was a rushing blur of sand. I put her nose on the horizon and looked over the side. There it was, about eight miles in front of me. Like a squat, ugly toad in the desert. The factory.

CORD EXPLOSIVES

I eased the stick forward again and by the time I shot past, I was only about a hundred feet over it. I went into an Immelmann and looked back.

They were at the windows already. The dark Mexican and Indian girls in their brightly colored dresses and the men in their faded blue work clothes. I could almost see the whites of their frightened eyes looking after me. I grinned again. Their life was dull enough. Let them have a real thrill.

I pulled out at the top of the Immelmann and went on to twenty-five hundred feet. Then I hit the stick and dove right for the tar-pitched roof.

The roar from the big Pratt & Whitney engine crescendoed and deafened my ears and the wind tore at my eyes and face. I narrowed my lids and drew my lips back across my teeth. I could feel the blood racing in my veins, my heart pounding and the juices of life starting up in my gut.

Power, power, power! Up here where the world was like a toy beneath me. Where I held the stick like my cock in my hands and there was no one, not even my father, to say me no!

The black roof of the plant lay on the white sand like a girl on the white sheets of a bed, the dark pubic patch of her whispering its invitation into the dimness of the night. My breath caught in my throat. Mother. I didn't want to turn away. I wanted to go home.

Ping! One of the thin wire struts snapped clean. I blinked my eyes and licked my lips. The salty taste of the tears touched my tongue. I could see the faint gray pebbles in the black tar of the roof now. I eased back on the stick and began to come out of the dive. At eight hundred feet, I leveled. off and went into a wide turn that would take me to the field behind the factory. I headed into the wind and made a perfect three-point landing. Suddenly I was tired. It had been a long flight up from Los Angeles.

Nevada Smith was walking across the field toward me as the plane rolled to a stop. I cut the switches and the engine died, coughing the last drop of fuel out of its carburetor lungs. I looked out at him.

Nevada never changed. From the time I was five years old and I first saw him walking up to the front porch, he hadn't changed. The tight, rolling, bowlegged walk, as if he'd never got used to being off a horse, the tiny white weather crinkles in the leathery skin at the corner of his eyes. That was sixteen years ago. It was 1909.

I was playing around the corner of the porch and my father was reading the weekly Reno paper on the big rocker near the front door. It was about eight o'clock in the morning and the sun was already high in the sky. I heard the clip-clop of a horse and came around to the front to see.

A man was getting off his horse. He moved with a deceptively slow grace. He threw the reins over the hitching post and walked toward the house. At the foot of the steps, he stopped and looked up.

My father put the paper down and got to his feet. He was a big man. Six two. Beefy. Ruddy face that burned to a crisp in the sun. He looked down.

Nevada squinted up at him. "Jonas Cord?"

My father nodded. "Yes."

The man pushed his broad-brimmed cowboy hat back on his head, revealing the crow-black hair. "I hear tell you might be looking for a hand."

My father never said yes or no to anything. "What can you do?" he asked.

The man's smile remained expressionless. He glanced slowly across the front of the house and out on the desert. He looked back at my father. "I could ride herd but you ain't got no cattle. I can mend fence, but you ain't got none of them, either."

My father was silent for a moment. "You any good with that?" he asked.

For the first time, I noticed the gun on the man's thigh. He wore it real low and tied down. The handle was black and worn and the hammer and metal shone dully with oil.

"I'm alive," he answered.

"What's your name?"

"Nevada."

"Nevada what?"

The answer came without hesitation. "Smith. Nevada Smith."

My father was silent again. This time the man didn't wait for him to speak.

He gestured toward me. "That your young 'un?"

My father nodded.

"Where's his mammy?"

My father looked at him, then picked me up. I fit real good in the crook of his arm. His voice was emotionless. "She died a few months back."

The man stared up at us. "That's what I heard."

My father stared back at him for a moment. I could feel the muscles in his arm tighten under my behind. Then before I could catch my breath, I was flying through the air over the porch rail.

The man caught me with one arm and rolled me in close to him as he went down on one knee to absorb the impact. The breath whooshed out of me and before I could begin to cry, my father spoke again.

A faint smile crossed his lips. "Teach him how to ride," he said. He picked up his paper and went into the house without a backward glance.

Still holding me with one hand, the man called Nevada began to rise again. I looked down. The gun in his other hand was like a live black snake, pointed at my father. While I was looking, the gun disappeared back in the holster. I looked up into Nevada's face.

His face broke into a warm, gentle smile. He set me down on the ground carefully. "Well, Junior," he said. "You heard your pappy. Come on."

I looked up at the house but my father had already gone inside. I didn't know it then but that was the last time my father ever held me in his arms. From that time on, it was almost as if I were Nevada's boy.

I had one foot over the side of the cockpit by the time Nevada came up. He squinted up at me. "You been pretty busy."

I dropped to the ground beside him and looked down at him. Somehow I never could get used to that. Me being six two like my father and Nevada still the same five nine. "Pretty busy," I admitted.

Nevada stretched and looked into the rear cockpit. "Neat," he said. "How d'ja get it?"

I smiled. "I won it in a crap game."

He looked at me questioningly.

"Don't worry," I added quickly. "I let him win five hundred dollars afterward."

He nodded, satisfied. That, too, was one of the things Nevada taught me. Never walk away from the table after you win a man's horse without letting him win back at least one stake for tomorrow. It didn't diminish your winnings by much and at least the sucker walked away feeling he'd won something.

I reached into the rear cockpit and pulled out some chocks. I tossed one to Nevada and walked around and set mine under a wheel. Nevada did the same on the other side.

"Your pappy ain't gonna like it. You messed up production for the day."

I straightened up. "I don't guess it will matter much." I walked around the prop toward him. "How'd he hear about it so soon?"

Nevada's lips broke into the familiar mirthless smile. "You took the girl to the hospital. They sent for her folks. She told them before she died."

"How much do they want?"

"Twenty thousand."

"You can buy 'em for five."

He didn't answer. Instead, he looked down at my feet. "Get your shoes on and come on," he said. "Your father's waiting."

He started back across the field and I looked down at my feet. The warm earth felt good against my naked toes. I wriggled them in the sand for a moment, then went back to the cockpit and pulled out a pair of Mexican huaraches. I slipped into them and started out across the field after Nevada.

I hate shoes. They don't let you breathe.

CHAPTER TWO

I KEPT RAISING SMALL CLOUDS OF SAND WITH THE HUARACHES AS I WALKED toward the factory. The faint clinical smell of the sulphur they used in making gunpowder came to my nose. It was the same kind of smell that was in the hospital the night I took her there. It wasn't at all the kind of smell there was the night we made the baby.

It was cool and clean that night. And there was the smell of the ocean and the surf that came in through the open windows of the small cottage I kept out at Malibu. But in the room there was nothing but the exciting scent of the girl and her wanting.

We had gone into the bedroom and stripped with the fierce urgency in our vitals. She was quicker than I and now she was on the bed, looking up at me as I opened the dresser drawer and took out a package of rubbers.

Her voice was a whisper in the night. "Don't, Joney. Not this time."

I looked at her. The bright Pacific moon threw its light in the window. Only her face was in shadows. Somehow, what she said brought the fever up.

The bitch must have sensed it. She reached for me and kissed me. "I hate those damn things, Joney. I want to feel you inside me."

I hesitated a moment. She pulled me down on top of her. Her voice whispered in my ear. "Nothing will happen, Joney. I'll be careful."

Then I couldn't wait any longer and her whisper changed into a sudden cry of pain. I couldn't breathe and she kept crying in my ear, "I love you, Joney. I love you, Joney."

She loved me all right. She loved me so good that five weeks later she tells me we got to get married. We were sitting in the front seat of my car this time, driving back from the football game.

I looked over at her. "What for?"

She looked up at me. She wasn't frightened, not then. She was too sure of herself. Her voice was almost flippant. "The usual reason. What other reason does a fellow and a girl get married for?"

My voice turned bitter. I knew when I'd been taken. "Sometimes it's because they want to get married."

"Well, I want to get married." She moved closer to me.

I pushed her back on the seat. "Well, I don't."

She began to cry then. "But you said you loved me."

I didn't look at her. "A man says a lot of things when he's humping." I pulled the car over against the curb and parked. I turned to her. "I thought you said you'd be careful."

She was wiping at her tears with a small, ineffectual handkerchief. "I love you, Joney. I wanted to have your baby."

For the first time since she told me, I began to feel better. That was one of the troubles with being Jonas Cord, Jr. Too many girls, and their mothers, too, thought that spelled money. Big money. Ever since the war, when my father built an empire on gunpowder.

I looked down at her. "Then it's simple. Have it."

Her expression changed. She moved toward me. "You mean—you mean— we'll get married?"

The faint look of triumph in her eyes faded quickly when I shook my head. "Uh-uh. I meant have the baby if you want it that bad."

She pulled away again. Suddenly, her face was set and cold. Her voice was calm and practical. "I don't want it that bad. Not without a ring on my finger. I'll have to get rid of it."

I grinned and offered her a cigarette. "Now you're talking, little girl."

She took the cigarette and I lit it for her. "But it's going to be expensive," she said.

"How much?" I asked.

She drew in a mouthful of smoke. "There's a doctor in Mexican Town. The girls say he's very good." She looked at me questioningly. "Two hundred?"

"O.K., you got it," I said quickly. It was a bargain. The last one cost me three fifty. I flipped my cigarette over the side of the car and started the motor. I pulled the car out into traffic and headed toward Malibu.

"Hey, where you going?" she asked.

I looked over at her. "To the beach house," I answered. "We might as well make the most of the situation."

She began to laugh and drew closer to me. She looked up into my face. "I wonder what Mother would say if she knew just how far I went to get you. She told me not to miss a trick."

I laughed. "You didn't."

She shook her head. "Poor Mother. She had the wedding all planned."

Poor Mother. Maybe if the old bitch had kept her mouth shut, her daughter might have been alive today.

It was the night after that, about eleven thirty, that my telephone began to ring. I had just about fogged off and I cursed, reaching for the phone.

Her voice came through in a scared whisper. "Joney, I'm bleeding."

The sleep shot out of my head like a bullet. "What's the matter?"

"I went down to Mexican Town this afternoon and now something's wrong. I haven't stopped bleeding and I'm frightened."

I sat up in bed. "Where are you?"

"I checked into the Westwood Hotel this afternoon. Room nine-o-one."

"Get back into bed. I'll be right down."

"Please hurry, Joney. Please."

The Westwood is a commercial hotel in downtown L.A. Nobody even looked twice when I went up in the elevator without announcing myself at the desk. I stopped in front of Room 901 and tried the door. It was unlocked. I went in.

I never saw so much blood in my life. It was all over the cheap carpeting on the floor, the chair in which she had sat when she called me, the white sheets on the bed.

She was lying on the bed and her face was as white as the pillow under her head. Her eyes had been closed but they flickered open when I came over. Her lips moved but no sound came out.

I bent over her. "Don't try to talk, baby. I'll get a doctor. You're gonna be all right."

She closed her eyes and I went over to the phone. There was no use in just calling a doctor. My father wasn't going to be happy if I got our name into the papers again. I called McAllister. He was the attorney who handled the firm's business in California.

His butler called him to the phone. I tried to keep my voice calm. "I need a doctor and an ambulance quick."

In less than a moment, I understood why my father used Mac. He didn't waste any time on useless questions. Just where, when and who. No why. His voice was precise. "A doctor and an ambulance will be there in ten minutes. I advise you to leave now. There's no point in your getting any more involved than you are."

I thanked him and put down the phone. I glanced over at the bed. Her eyes were closed and she appeared to be sleeping. I started for the door and her eyes opened.

"Don't go, Joney. I'm afraid."

I went back to the bed and sat down beside it. I took her hand and she closed her eyes again. The ambulance was there in ten minutes. And she didn't let go of my hand until we'd reached the hospital.

CHAPTER THREE

I WALKED INTO THE FACTORY AND THE NOISE AND THE SMELL CLOSED IN ON me like a cocoon. I could feel the momentary stoppage of work as I walked by and I could hear the subdued murmur of voices following me.

"El hijo."

The son. That was how they knew me. They spoke of me with a fondness and a pride, as their ancestors had of the children of their patrones. It gave them a sense of identity and belonging that helped make up for the meager way in which they had to live.

I walked past the mixing vats, the presses and the molds and reached the back stairway to my father's office. I started up the steps and looked back at them. A hundred faces smiled up at me. I waved my hand and smiled back at them in the same way I had always done, ever since I first climbed those steps when I was a kid.

I went through the door at the top of the stairway and the noise was gone as soon as the door closed behind me. I walked down the short corridor and into my father's outer office.

Denby was sitting at his desk, scribbling a note in his usual fluttery fashion. A girl sat at a desk across from him, beating hell out of a typewriter. Two other persons were seated on the visitor's couch. A man and a woman.

The woman was dressed in black and she was twisting a small white handkerchief in her hands. She looked up at me as I stood in the doorway. I didn't have to be told who she was. The girl looked enough like her mother. I met her eyes and she turned her head away.

Denby got up nervously. "Your father's waiting."

I didn't answer. He opened the door to my father's office and I walked through. He closed the door behind me. I looked around the office.

Nevada was leaning against the left wall bookcase, his eyes half closed in that deceptive manner of alertness peculiar to him. McAllister was seated in a chair across from my father. He turned his head to look at me. My father sat behind the immense old oak desk and glared. Outside of that, the office was just as I remembered it.

The dark oak-paneled walls, the heavy leather chairs. The green velvet drapes on the windows and the picture of my father and President Wilson on the wall behind the desk. At my father's side was the telephone table with the three telephones and right next to it was the table with the ever present carafe of water, bottle of bourbon whisky and two glasses. The whisky bottle was about one-third filled. That made it about three o'clock. I checked my watch. It was ten after three. My father was a bottle-a-day man.

I crossed the office and stopped in front of him. I looked down and met his angry glare. "Hello, Father."

His ruddy face grew even redder. The cords on his neck stood out as he shouted, "Is that all you got to say after ruining a day's production and scaring the shit out of half the help with your crazy stunts?"

"Your message was to get down here in a hurry. I got here as quickly as I could, sir."

But there was no stopping him now. He was raging. My father had that kind of a temper. One moment he would be still and quiet, and the next, higher than a kite.

"Why the hell didn't you get out of that hotel room when McAllister told you? What did you go to the hospital for? Do you know what you've done? Left yourself wide open for criminal charges as an accomplice abetting an abortion."

I was angry now. I had every bit as much of a temper as my father. "What was I supposed to do? The girl was bleeding to death and afraid. Was I supposed to just walk out of there and leave her to die alone?"

"Yes. If you had any brains at all, that's just what you'd have done. The girl died, anyway, and your staying there didn't make any difference. Now those goddam bastards outside want twenty thousand dollars or they'll call for the police! You think I've got twenty thousand dollars for every bitch you plug? This is the third girl in a year you got caught with!"

It didn't make any difference to him that the girl had died. It was the twenty grand. But then I realized it wasn't the money, either. It went far deeper than that.

The bitterness that had crept into his voice was the tip-off. I looked at him with a sudden understanding. My father was getting old and it was eating out his gut. Rina must have been at him again. More than a year had passed since the big wedding in Reno and nothing had happened.

I turned and started for the door without speaking. Father yelled after me. "Where do you think you're going?"

I looked back at him. "Back to L.A. You don't need me to make up your mind. You're either going to pay them off or you're not. It doesn't make any difference to me. Besides, I got a date."

He came around the desk after me. "What for?" he shouted. "To knock up another girl?"

I faced him squarely. I had enough of his crap. "Stop complaining, old man. You ought to be glad that someone in your family still has balls. Otherwise, Rina might think there was something wrong with all of us!"

His face twisted with rage. He lifted both hands as if to strike me. His lips drew back tightly across his teeth in a snarl, the veins in his forehead stood out in red, angry welts. Then, suddenly, as an electric switch cuts off the light, all expression on his face vanished. He staggered and pitched forward against me.

By reflex, my arms came out and I caught him. For a brief moment, his eyes were clear, looking into mine. His lips moved. "Jonas—my son."

Then his eyes clouded and his full weight came on me and he slid to the floor. I looked down at him. I knew he was dead even before Nevada rolled him over and tore open his shirt.

Nevada was kneeling on the floor beside my father's body, McAllister was on the telephone calling for a doctor and I was picking up the bottle of Jack Daniel's when Denby came in through the door.

He shrank back against the door, the papers in his hand trembling. "My God, Junior," he said in a horrified voice. His eyes lifted from the floor to me. "Who's going to sign the German contracts?"

I glanced over at McAllister. He nodded imperceptibly. "I am," I answered.

Down on the floor, Nevada was closing my father's eyes. I put down the bottle of whisky unopened and looked back at Denby.

"And stop calling me Junior," I said.

CHAPTER FOUR

BY THE TIME THE DOCTOR CAME, WE HAD LIFTED MY FATHER'S BODY TO the couch and covered it with a blanket. The doctor was a thin, sturdy man, bald, with thick glasses. He lifted the blanket and looked. He dropped the blanket. "He's dead, all right."

I didn't speak. It was McAllister who asked the question while I swung to and fro in my father's chair. "Why?"

The doctor came toward the desk. "Encephalic embolism. Stroke. Blood clot hit the brain, from the looks of him." He looked at me. "You can be thankful it was quick. He didn't suffer."

It was certainly quick. One minute my father was alive, the next moment he was nothing, without even the power to brush off the curious fly that was crawling over the edge of the blanket onto his covered face. I didn't speak.

The doctor sat down heavily in the chair opposite me. He took out a pen and a sheet of paper. He laid the paper on the desk. Upside down, I could read the heading across the top in bold type. DEATH CERTIFICATE. The pen began to scratch across the paper. After a moment, he looked up. "O.K. if I put down embolism as the cause of death or do you want an autopsy?"

I shook my head. "Embolism's O.K. An autopsy wouldn't make any difference now."

The doctor wrote again. A moment later, he had finished and he pushed the certificate over to me. "Check it over and see if I got everything right."

I picked it up. He had everything right. Pretty good for a doctor who had never seen any of us before today. But everybody in Nevada knew everything about the Cords. Age 67. Survivors: Wife, Rina Marlowe Cord; Son, Jonas Cord, Jr. I slid it back across the desk to him. "It's all right."

He picked it up and got to his feet. "I'll file it and have my girl send you copies." He stood there hesitantly, as if trying to make up his mind as to whether he should offer some expression of sympathy. Evidently, he decided against it, for he went out the door without another word.

Then Denby came in again. "What about those people outside? Shall I send them away?"

I shook my head. They'd only come back again. "Send them in."

They came in the door, the girl's father and mother, their faces wearing a fixed expression that was a strange mixture of grief and sympathy.

Her father looked at me. "I'm sorry we couldn't meet under happier circumstances, Mr. Cord."

I looked at him. The man's face was honest. I believe he really meant it. "I am, too," I said.

His wife immediately broke into sobs. "It's terrible, terrible," she wailed, looking at my father's covered body on the couch.

I looked at her. Her daughter had resembled her but the resemblance stopped at the surface. The kid had had a refreshing honesty about her; this woman was a born harpy.

"What are you crying about?" I asked. "You never even knew him before today. And only then to ask him for money."

She stared at me in shock. Her voice grew shrill. "How can you say such a thing? Your own father lying there on the couch and after what you did to my daughter."

I got to my feet. The one thing I can't stand is a phony. "After what I did to your daughter?" I shouted. "I didn't do anything to your daughter that she didn't want me to. Maybe if you hadn't told her to stop at nothing to catch me, she'd be alive today. But no, you told her to get Jonas Cord, Jr., at any cost. She told me you were already planning the wedding!"

Her husband turned to her. His voice was trembling. "You mean to tell me you knew she was pregnant?"

She looked at him, frightened. "No, Henry, no. I didn't know. I only said to her it would be nice if she could marry him, that's all I said."

His lips tightened, and for a second I thought he was about to strike her. But he didn't. Instead, he turned back to me. "I'm sorry, Mr. Cord. We won't trouble you any more."

He started proudly for the door. His wife hurried after him. "But, Henry," she cried. "Henry."

"Shut up!" he snapped, opening the door and almost pushing her through it in front of him. "Haven't you said enough already?"

The door closed behind them and I turned to McAllister. "I'm not in the clear yet, am I?"

He shook his head.

I thought for a moment. "Better go down to see him tomorrow at his place of business. I think he'll give you a release now. He seems like an honest man."

McAllister smiled slowly. "And that's how you figure an honest man will act?"

"That's one thing I learned from my father." Involuntarily I glanced at the couch. "He used to say every man has his price. For some it's money, for some it's women, for others glory. But the honest man you don't have to buy—he winds up costing you nothing."

"Your father was a practical man," McAllister said.

I stared at the lawyer. "My father was a selfish, greedy son of a bitch who wanted to grab everything in the world," I said. "I only hope I'm man enough to fill his shoes."

McAllister rubbed his chin thoughtfully. "You'll do all right."

I gestured toward the couch. "I won't always have him there to help me."

McAllister didn't speak. I glanced over at Nevada. He had been leaning against the wall silently all the time. His eyes flickered under the veiled lids. He took out a pack of makin's and began to roll a cigarette. I turned back to McAllister. "I'm going to need a lot of help," I said.

McAllister showed his interest with his eyes. He didn't speak.

"I'll need an adviser, a consultant and a lawyer," I continued. "Are you available?"

He spoke slowly. "I don't know whether I can find the time, Jonas," he said. "I've got a pretty heavy practice."

"How heavy?"

"I gross about sixty thousand a year."

"Would a hundred thousand move you to Nevada?"

His answer came quick. "If you let me draw the contract."

I took out a pack of cigarettes and offered him one. He took it and I stuck one in my mouth. I struck a match and held it for him. "O.K.," I said.

He stopped in the middle of the light. He looked at me quizzically. "How do you know you can afford to pay me that kind of money?"

I lit my own cigarette and smiled. "I didn't know until you took the job. Then I was sure."

A returning smile flashed across his face and vanished. Then he was all business. "The first thing we have to do is call a meeting of the board of directors and have you officially elected president of the company. Do you think there might be any trouble on that score?"

I shook my head. "I don't think so. My father didn't believe in sharing. He kept ninety per cent of the stock in his own name and according to his will, it comes to me on his death."

"Do you have a copy of the will?"

"No," I answered. "But Denby must. He has a record of everything my father ever did."

I hit the buzzer and Denby came in.

"Get me a copy of my father's will," I ordered.

A moment later, it was on the desk—all official, with a blue lawyer's binding. I pushed it over to McAllister. He flipped through it quickly.

"It's in order," he said. "The stock is yours all right. We better get it probated right away."

I turned to Denby questioningly. Denby couldn't wait to answer. The words came tumbling out. "Judge Haskell in Reno has it on file."

"Call him and tell him to move on it right away," I said. Denby started out. I stopped him. "And when you get through with him, call the directors and tell him I'm having a special meeting of the board at breakfast tomorrow. At my house."

Denby went out and I turned back to McAllister. "Is there anything else I ought to do, Mac?"

He shook his head slowly. "No, not right now. There's only the German contract. I don't know too much about it but I heard your father say it was a great opportunity. It's got something to do with a new kind of product. Plastics, I think he called it."

I ground out my cigarette in the ash tray on the desk. "Have Denby give you the file on it. You look at it tonight and give me a breakdown tomorrow morning before the board meeting. I'll be up at five o'clock."

A strange look began to come over McAllister's face. For a moment, I didn't know what it was, then I recognized it. Respect. "I'll be there at five, Jonas."

He got up and started for the door. I called to him before he reached it. "While you're at it, Mac, have Denby give you a list of the other stockholders in the company. I think I ought to know their names before the meeting."

The look of respect on his face grew deeper. "Yes, Jonas," he said, going out the door.

I swung around to Nevada and looked up at him. "What do you think?" I asked.

He waited a long moment before he answered. Then he spit away a piece of cigarette paper that clung to his lip. "I think your old man is resting real easy."

That reminded me. I had almost forgotten. I got up from the chair and walked around the desk and over to the couch. I picked up the blanket and looked down at him.

His eyes were closed and his mouth was grim. There was a slightly blue stain under the skin of his right temple, going on up into the hairline. That must be the embolism, I thought.

Somehow, deep inside of me, I wanted some tears to come out for him. But there weren't any. He had abandoned me too long ago—that day on the porch when he threw me to Nevada.

I heard the door behind me open and I dropped the blanket back and turned around. Denby was standing in the doorway.

"Jake Platt wants to see you, sir."

Jake was the plant manager. He kept the wheels turning. He also listened to the wind and by now the word must be racing all over the plant.

"Send him in," I said.

He appeared in the doorway beside Denby as soon as the words were out of my mouth. He was a big, heavy man. He even walked heavy. He came into the office, his hand outstretched. "I just heard the sad news." He crossed over to the couch and looked down at my father's body, his face assuming his best Irish-wake air. "It's a sad loss, indeed. Your father was a great man." He shook his head mournfully. "A great man."

I walked back behind the desk. And you're a great actor, Jake Platt, I thought. Aloud I said, "Thank you, Jake."

He turned to me, his face brightening at the thought of his act going over. "And I want you to know if there's anything you want of me, anything at all, just call on me."

"Thank you, Jake," I said again. "It's good to know there are men like you in my corner."

He preened almost visibly at my words. His voice lowered to a confidential tone. "The word's all over the plant now. D'ya think I ought to say something to them? You know them Mexicans and Indians. They're a might touchy and nervous and need a little calming down."

I looked at him. He was probably right. "That's a good idea, Jake. But I think it would seem better if I talk to them myself."

Jake had to agree with me whether he liked it or not. That was his policy. Not to disagree with the boss. "That's true, Jonas," he said, masking his disappointment. "If you feel up to it."

"I feel up to it," I said, starting for the door.

Nevada's voice came after me. "What about him?"

I turned back and followed his glance to the couch. "Call the undertakers and have them take care of him. Tell them we want the best casket in the state."

Nevada nodded.

"Then meet me out in front with the car and we'll go home." I went out the door without waiting for his reply. Jake trotted after me as I turned down the back corridor and went out onto the stairway leading to the plant.

Every eye in the factory turned toward me as I came through that doorway onto the little platform at the top of the staircase. Jake held up his hands and quiet began to fall in the factory. I waited until every machine in the place had come to a stop before I spoke. There was something eerie about it. It was the first time I had ever heard the factory completely silent. I began to speak and my voice echoed crazily through the building.

"*Mi padre ha muerto.*" I spoke in Spanish. My Spanish wasn't very good but it was their language and I continued in it. "But I, his son, am here and hope to continue in his good work. It is indeed too bad that my father is not here to express his appreciation to all you good workers himself for everything you have done to make this company a success. I hope it is enough for you to know that just before he passed away, he authorized a five-per-cent increase in wages for every one of you who work in the plant."

Jake grabbed my arm frantically. I shook his hand off and continued. "It is my earnest wish that I continue to have the same willing support that you gave to my father. I trust you will be patient with me for I have much to learn. Many thanks and may you all go with God."

I started down the steps and Jake came after me. The workers made a path as I walked through. They were silent for the most part; occasionally, one would touch me reassuringly as I passed by. Twice I saw tears in someone's eyes. At least my father didn't go uncried for. Even if they were tears in the eyes of someone who didn't know him.

I came out of the factory into the daylight and blinked my eyes. The sun was still in the sky. I had almost forgotten it was there, it seemed so long ago.

The big Pierce-Arrow was right in front of the door, with Nevada at the wheel. I started across toward it. Jake's hand on my arm stopped me. I turned toward him.

His voice was half whining. "What did you have to go and do that for, Jonas? You don't know them bastards like I do. Give 'em an inch, they'll want your arm. Your father was always after me to keep the pay scale down."

I stared at him coldly. Some people didn't learn fast enough. "Did you hear what I said in there, Jake?"

"I heard what you said, Jonas. That's what I'm talking about. I—"

I cut him off. "I don't think you did, Jake," I said softly. "My first words were *'Mi padre ha muerto.'* My father is dead."

"Yes, but—"

"That means exactly what it says, Jake. He's dead. But I'm not. I'm here and the only thing you better remember is that I'm exactly like him in just one way. I'll take no crap from anyone who works for me, and anyone who doesn't like what I do can get the hell out!"

Jake learned fast. He was at the car door, holding it open for me. "I didn't mean anything, Jonas. I only—"

There was no use explaining to him that if you pay more, you get more. Ford had proved that when he gave his workers raises the year before. He more than tripled production. I got into the car and looked back at the factory. The black, sticky tar on the roof caught my eye. I remembered it from the plane.

"Jake," I said. "See that roof?"

He turned toward it and peered at it. His voice was puzzled. "Yes, sir?"

Suddenly I was very tired. I leaned back against the cushions and closed my eyes. "Paint it white," I said.

CHAPTER FIVE

I DOZED AS THE BIG PIERCE ATE UP THE TWENTY MILES BETWEEN MY FATH-er's new house and the factory. Every once in a while, I would open my eyes and catch a glimpse of Nevada watching me in the rear-view mirror, then my eyes would close again as if weighted down by lead.

I hate my father and I hate my mother and if I had had sisters and brothers, I would hate them, too. No, I didn't hate my father. Not any more. He was dead. You don't hate the dead. You only remember them. And I didn't hate my mother. She wasn't my mother, anyway. I had a stepmother. And I didn't hate her. I loved her.

That was why I had brought her home. I wanted to marry her. Only, my father said I was too young. Nineteen was too young, he had said. But he wasn't too young. He married her a week after I had gone back to college.

I met Rina at the country club two weeks before vacation was over. She came from back East, someplace in Massachusetts called Brookline, and she was like no one I had ever met before. All the girls out here are dark and tanned from the sun, they walk like men, talk like men, even ride like men. The only time you can be sure they are something else is in the evenings, when they wear skirts instead of Levi's, for even at the swimming pool, according to the fashion, they look like boys. Flat-chested and slim-hipped.

But Rina was a girl. You couldn't miss that. Especially in a bathing suit, the way she was the first time I saw her. She was slim, all right, and her shoulders were broad, maybe too broad for a woman. But her breasts were strong and full, jutting rocks against the silk-jersey suit that gave the lie to the fashion. You could not look at them without tasting the milk and honey of their sweetness in your mouth. They rested easy on a high rib cage that melted down into a narrow waist that in turn flared out into slim but rounded hips and buttocks.

Her hair was a pale blond that she wore long, tied back behind her head, again contrary to fashion. Her brow was high, her eyes wide apart and slightly slanted, the blue of them reflecting a glow beneath their ice. Her nose was straight and not too thin, reflecting her Finnish ancestry. Perhaps her only flaw was her mouth. It was wide—not generous-wide, because her lips were not full enough. It was a controlled mouth that set firmly on a tapered, determined chin.

She had gone to Swiss finishing schools, was slow to laughter and reserved in her manner. In two days, she had me swinging from the chandeliers. Her voice was soft and low and had a faintly foreign sound that bubbled in your ear.

It was about ten days later, at the Saturday-night dance at the club, that I first knew how much I wanted her. It was a slow, tight waltz and the lights were down low and blue. Suddenly she missed half a step. She looked up at me and smiled that slow smile.

"You're very strong," she said and pressed herself back against me.

I could feel the heat from her loins pouring into me as we began to dance again. At last, I couldn't stand it any more. I took her arm and started from the dance floor.

She followed me silently out to the car. We climbed into the big Duesenberg roadster and I threw it into gear and we raced down the highway. The night air on the desert was warm. I looked at her out of the corner of my eyes. Her head was back against the seat, her eyes closed to the wind.

I turned off into a date grove and cut the motor. She was still leaning back against the seat. I bent over and kissed her mouth.

Her mouth neither gave nor took. It was like a well on an oasis in the desert. It was there for when you needed it. I reached for her breast. Her hand caught mine and held it.

I lifted my head and looked at her. Her eyes were open and yet they were guarded. I could not see into them. "I want you," I said.

Her eyes did not change expression. I could hardly hear her voice. "I know."

I moved toward her again. This time, her hand against my chest, stopped me. "Lend me your handkerchief," she said, taking it from my breast pocket.

It fluttered whitely in the night, then dropped from sight with her hands. She didn't raise her head from the back of the seat, she didn't speak, she just watched me with those guarded eyes.

I felt her searching fingers and I leaned toward her but somehow she kept me from getting any closer to her. Then suddenly, I felt an exquisite pain rushing from the base of my spine and I almost climbed halfway out of the seat.

I took out a cigarette and lit it with trembling fingers as she crumpled the handkerchief into a small ball and threw it over the side of the car. Then she took the cigarette from my mouth and placed it between her lips.

"I still want you," I said.

She gave the cigarette back to me and shook her head.

"Why?" I asked.

She turned her face toward me. It shone palely in the dark. "Because in two days I'm going home. Because in the stockmarket crash of twenty-three, my father lost everything. Because I must find and marry a rich husband. I must do nothing to endanger that."

I stared at her for a moment, then started the engine. I backed the car out of the date grove and set it on the road for home. I didn't say anything but I had all the answers for her. I was rich. Or I would be someday.

I left Rina in the parlor and went into my father's study. As usual, he was working at his desk, the single lamp throwing its light down on the papers. He looked up as I came in.

"Yes?" he asked, as if I were someone in his office who had intruded in the midst of a problem.

I hit the wall switch and flooded the room with light. "I want to get married," I said.

He looked at me for a moment as if he was far away. He had been, but he came back fast. "You're crazy," he said unemotionally. He looked down at his desk again. "Go to bed and don't bother me."

I stood there. "I mean it, Dad," I said. It was the first time I had called him that since I was a kid.

He got to his feet slowly. "No," he said. "You're too young."

That was all he said. It would never occur to him to ask who, what, why. No, only I was too young. "All right, Father," I said, turning toward the door. "Remember I asked you."

"Wait a minute," he said. I stopped, my hand on the doorknob. "Where is she?"

"Waiting in the parlor," I answered.

He looked at me shrewdly. "When did you decide?"

"Tonight," I answered. "Just tonight."

"I suppose she's one of those silly little girls who show up at the club dance and she's waiting on pins and needles to meet the old man?" he asked.

I rose to her defense. "She's not like that at all. As a matter of fact, she doesn't even know that I'm in here asking you."

"You mean you haven't even asked her yet?"

"I don't have to," I answered, with the supreme confidence of my years. "I know her answer."

My father shook his head. "Just for the record, don't you think you had better ask her?"

I went out and brought Rina back into the room. "Rina, this is my father; Father, this is Rina Marlowe."

Rina nodded politely. For all you could tell from her manner, it could have been high noon instead of two o'clock in the morning.

Father looked at her thoughtfully. There was a curious expression on his face

I had never seen before. He came around his desk and held out his hand to her. "How do you do, Miss Marlowe?" he said in a soft voice. I stared at him. I had never seen him do that with any of my friends before.

She took his hand. "How do you do?"

Still holding her hand, he let his voice fall into a semi-amused tone. "My son thinks he wants to marry you, Miss Marlowe, but I think he's too young. Don't you?"

Rina looked at me. For a moment, I could see into her eyes. They were bright and shining, then they were guarded again.

She turned to Father. "This is very embarrassing, Mr. Cord. Would you please take me home?"

Stunned, unable to speak, I watched my father take her arm and walk out of the room with her. A moment later, I heard the roar of the Duesenberg and angrily I looked around for something to vent my spleen on. The only thing available was the lamp on the table. I smashed it against the wall.

Two weeks later, at college, I got a telegram from my father.

RINA AND I WERE MARRIED THIS MORNING. WE ARE AT THE WALDORF-ASTORIA, NEW YORK. LEAVING TOMORROW ON LEVIATHAN FOR EUROPEAN HONEYMOON.

I picked up the telephone and called him.

"There's no fool like an old fool!" I shouted across the three thousand miles of wire between us. "Don't you know the only reason she married you was for your money?"

Father didn't even get angry. He even chuckled. "You're the fool. All she wanted was a man, not a boy. She even insisted that we sign a premarital property agreement before she would marry me."

"Oh, yeah?" I asked. "Who drew the agreement? Her lawyer?"

Father chuckled again. "No. Mine." His voice changed abruptly. It grew heavy and coarse with meaning. "Now get back to your studies, son, and don't meddle in things that don't concern you. It's midnight here and I'm just about to go to bed."

The telephone went dead in my hands. I stared at it for a moment, then slowly put it down. I couldn't sleep that night. Across my mind's eye unreeled pornographic pictures of Rina and my father in wild sexual embrace. Several times, I woke up in a cold sweat.

A hand was shaking me gently. Slowly I opened my eyes. The first thing I saw was Nevada's face. "Wake up, Jonas," he said. "We're home."

I blinked my eyes to clear the sleep from them.

The last piece of sun was going down behind the big house. I shook my head and stepped out of the car. I looked up at the house. Strange house. I don't think I'd spent more than two weeks in it since my father had it built and now it was mine. Like everything else my father had done.

I started for the steps. Rina had thought of everything. Except this. My father was dead. And I was going to tell her.

CHAPTER SIX

THE FRONT DOOR OPENED AS I CROSSED THE VERANDA. MY FATHER HAD built a traditional Southern plantation house, and to run it, he had brought Robair up from New Orleans. Robair was a Creole butler in the full tradition.

He was a giant of a man, towering a full head over me, and as gentle and efficient as he was big. His father and grandfather had been butlers before him and even though they had been slaves, they had instilled in him a pride in his work. He had a sixth sense for his duties. Somehow, he was always there when he was wanted.

He stepped aside to let me enter. "Hello, Master Cord." He greeted me in his soft Creole English.

"Hello, Robair," I said, turning to him as he closed the door. "Come with me."

He followed me silently into my father's study. His face impassive, he closed the door behind him. "Yes, Mr. Cord?"

It was the first time he had called me Mister, instead of Master. I looked at him. "My father is dead," I said.

"I know," he said. "Mr. Denby called."

"Do the others know?" I asked.

He shook his head. "I told Mr. Denby that Mrs. Cord was out and I haven't said anything to the other servants."

There was a faint sound outside the closed door. Robair continued speaking as he moved swiftly toward it. "I figured you would want to break the sad news yourself." He threw the door open.

There was no one there. He stepped quickly out the door. I followed him. A figure was hurrying up the long staircase that curved around the entrance hall to the upper floor.

Robair's voice was low but held the whip of authority. "Louise!"

The figure stopped. It was Rina's personal maid.

"Come down here," he commanded.

Louise came down the steps hesitantly. I could see the terrified look on her face as she approached. "Yes, Mr. Robair?" Her voice was frightened, too.

For the first time, Robair let me see how he kept the servants in line. He moved almost lazily but his hand met her face with the impact of a pistol shot. His voice was filled with contempt. "How many times do I tell you not to listen at doors?"

She stood holding her hand to her face. The tears began to run down her cheeks.

"Now you get back to the kitchen. I'll deal with you later."

She ran toward the kitchen, still holding her face. Robair turned back to me. "I apologize for her, Mr. Cord," he said, his voice once more deep and soft.

"Ordinarily, my servants don't do such a thing, but that one is pretty hard to keep in her place."

I took out a cigarette and almost before I had it in my mouth, Robair struck a match and held it for me. I dragged deep. "That's all right, Robair. I don't think she'll be with us much longer."

Robair put out the match and carefully deposited it in an ash tray. "Yes, sir."

I looked at the staircase speculatively. Oddly enough, I hesitated.

Robair's voice came over my shoulder. "Mrs. Cord is in her room."

I looked at him. His face was an impenetrable butler's mask. "Thank you, Robair. I'll go up and tell her."

I started up the staircase. His voice held me. "Mr. Cord?" I turned and looked down at him.

His black face gleamed. "What time shall I serve dinner, sir?"

I thought for a moment. "About eight o'clock," I answered.

"Thank you, sir," he said and started for the kitchen.

I knocked softly at Rina's door. There was no answer. I opened it and walked in. Her voice came from the bathroom.

"Louise, bring me a bath towel."

I walked into the bathroom and took a large towel from the stack on the shelf over her dressing table. I started for the enclosed bathtub just as she slid back the glass door.

She was gold and white and gleaming with the water running down her body. She stood there for a moment surprised. Most women would have tried to cover themselves. But not Rina. She held out a hand for the towel.

She wrapped it around her expertly and stepped from the tub. "Where's Louise?" she asked, sitting down at the dressing table.

"Downstairs," I answered.

She began to dry her face with another towel. "Your father wouldn't like this."

"He'll never know," I answered.

"How do you know I won't tell him?"

"You won't," I said definitely.

It was then that she began to sense something was wrong. She looked up at me in the mirror. Her face was suddenly serious. "Did something happen between you and your father, Jonas?"

She watched me for a moment; there was still a puzzled look in her eyes. She gave me a small towel. "Be a good boy, will you, Jonas, and dry my back? I can't reach it." She smiled up into the mirror. "You see, I really do need Louise."

I took the towel and moved closer to her. She let the big bath towel slide down from her shoulders. I patted the beads of moisture from her flawless skin. The scent of her perfume came up to me, pungent from her bath warmth.

I pressed my lips to her neck. She turned toward me in surprise. "Stop that, Jonas! Your father said this morning you were a sex maniac but you don't have to try to prove it!"

I stared into her eyes. There was no fear in them. She was very sure of herself. I smiled slowly. "Maybe he was right," I said. "Or maybe he just forgot what it was like to be young."

I pulled her off the seat toward me. The towel fell still further until it hung only by the press of our bodies. I covered her mouth with mine and reached for her breast. It was hard and firm and strong and I could feel her heart beating wildly beneath it.

Maybe I was wrong but for a moment, I thought I could feel the fires in her reaching toward me. Then, angrily, she tore herself from me. The towel lay unheeded on the floor now. "Have you gone crazy?" she spit at me, her breast heaving. "You know at any minute now he could come walking through that door."

I stood very still for a second, then let the built-up pressure in my lungs escape in a slow sigh. "He'll never come through that door again," I said.

The color began to drain from her face slowly. "What—what do you mean?" she stammered.

My eyes went right into hers. For the first time, I could see into them. She was afraid. Just like everyone else that had to look into an unknown future. "Mrs. Cord," I said slowly, "your husband is dead."

Her pupils dilated wildly for a moment and she sank slowly back onto the seat. By reflex, she picked up the towel and placed it around her again. "I can't believe it," she said dully.

"What is it that you can't believe, Rina?" I asked cruelly. "That he's dead or that you were wrong when you married him instead of me?"

I don't think she even heard me. She looked up at me, her eyes dry, but there was a gentle sorrow in them—a compassion I never knew she was capable of. "Was there any pain?" she asked.

"No," I answered. "It was quick. A stroke. One minute he was as big as life and roaring like a lion, and the next—" I snapped my fingers. "It was like that."

Her eyes were still on mine. "I'm glad for his sake," she said softly. "I wouldn't have wanted him to suffer."

She got to her feet slowly. The veil came down over her eyes again. "I think you'd better go now," she said.

This was the familiar Rina, the one I wanted to take apart. The distant one, the unattainable one, the calculating one. "No," I said. "I haven't finished yet."

She started past me. "What is there to finish?"

I seized her arm and pulled her back toward me. "We're not finished," I said into her upturned face. "You and me. I brought you home one night because I wanted you. But you chose my father because he represented a quicker return for you. I think I've waited long enough!"

She stared back at me. She wasn't afraid now. This was the ground she was used to fighting on. "You wouldn't dare!"

For an answer, I pulled the towel from her. She turned to run from the room but I caught her arm and pulled her back to me. With my other hand, I caught her hair and pulled her head back so that her face turned up to mine. "No?"

"I'll scream," she gasped hoarsely. "The servants will come running!"

I grinned. "No, they won't. They'll only think it a cry of grief. Robair's got them in the kitchen and not one will come up unless I send for her."

"Wait!" she begged. "Please wait. For your father's sake?"

"Why should I?" I asked. "He didn't wait for me." I picked her up and carried her into the bedroom. Her fists and hands scratched at my face and beat against my chest.

I threw her on the bed, the white satin cover still on it. She tried to roll off on the other side. I grabbed her shoulder and spun her back. She bit my hand

and tried to scramble away when I pulled it back. I placed my knee across her thighs and slapped viciously at her face. The blow knocked her back on the pillow. I could see the white marks left by my fingers.

She closed her eyes for a moment and when she opened them, they were clouded and there was a wildness in them that I had never seen before. She smiled and her arms went up around my neck, pulling me down to her. Her mouth fastened against mine. I could feel her body begin to move under me.

"Do it to me, Jonas!" she breathed into my mouth. "Now! I can't wait any more. I've waited so long." Her searching fingers ran down my hip and found my core. She turned her face into the pillow, her movements becoming more frenetic. I could hardly hear her fierce, urgent whisper. "Hurry, Jonas. Hurry!"

I started to get up but she couldn't wait for me to get my clothing off. She pulled me down again and took me inside her. She was like a burning bed of coals. She drew my head down to her neck.

"Make me pregnant, Jonas," she whispered into my ear. "Make me pregnant like you did to those three girls in Los Angeles. Put your life into me!"

I looked into her face. Her eyes were clear and there was a taunting triumph in them. They reflected none of the passion of the body beneath me. Her arms and legs tightened around me.

She smiled, her eyes looking into mine. "Make me pregnant, Jonas," she whispered. "Like your father never would. He was afraid someone would take something away from you!"

"What—what?" I tried to get up but she was like a bottomless well that I couldn't get out of.

"Yes, Jonas," she said, still smiling, her body devouring me. "Your father never took any chances. That's why he made me sign that agreement before we got married. He wanted everything for his precious son!"

I tried to get up but she had moved her legs in some mysterious manner. Laughing, triumphant, she said, "But you'll make me pregnant, won't you, Jonas? Who will know but us? You will share your fortune with your child even if the whole world believes it to be your father's."

She rose beneath me, seeking and demanding my life force. In a sudden frenzy, I tore myself from her, just as my strength drained from me. I fell across the bed near her feet.

The agony passed and I opened my eyes. Her head was turned into the pillow and she was crying. Silently I got to my feet and left the room.

All the way down the hall to my room, I kept thinking, my father cared, he really cared. Even if I didn't see it, he loved me.

He loved me. But never enough to show it.

By the time I got to my room, the tears were rolling down my cheeks.

CHAPTER SEVEN

I WAS ON THE TINY INDIAN PINTO THAT I HAD WHEN I WAS TEN YEARS OLD, galloping insanely across the dunes. The panic of flight rose within me but I didn't know what I was running from. I looked back over my shoulder.

My father was following me on the big strawberry roan. His jacket was open and blowing in the wind and I could see the heavy watch chain stretched tight across his chest. I heard his voice, weird and eerie in the wind. "Come back here, Jonas. Damn you, come back!"

I turned and urged the pinto to even greater speed. I used my bat unmercifully and there were tiny red welts on the horse's side from where I had hit him. Gradually, I began to pull away.

Suddenly, as if from nowhere, Nevada was beside me, riding easily on his big black horse. He looked across at me calmly. His voice was low. "Go back, Jonas. It's your father calling you. What kind of a son are you, anyway?"

I didn't answer, just kept urging my horse on. I looked back again over my shoulder.

My father was pulling his horse to a stop. His face was very sad. "Look after him, Nevada." I could hear him only faintly, for there was a great distance between us. "Look after him, for I haven't the time." He turned the strawberry roan around and began to gallop away.

I stopped my pony and turned to look after him. He was already growing smaller in the distance. Even his outline was fading in the sudden tears that leapt to my eyes. I wanted to cry out after him, "Don't go, Father." But the words stuck in my throat.

I sat up in bed, my skin wet with perspiration. I shook my head to get the echo of the dream out of it. Through the open window I could hear the sound of horses coming from the corral in back of the house.

I went over to the window and looked out. The sun was at five o'clock and casting a long morning shadow. Down in the corral, several of the hands were leaning against the fence, watching a rider trying to break a wiry bay colt. I squinted my eyes against the sun.

I turned from the window quickly. That was the kind of medicine I needed. Something that would jar the empty feeling out of me, that would clean the bitter taste from my mouth. I pulled on a pair of Levi's and an old blue shirt and started from the room.

I headed down the corridor to the back stairs. I met Robair just as I came to them. He was carrying a tray with a glass of orange juice and a pot of steaming coffee. He looked at me without surprise.

"Good morning, Mr. Jonas."

"Good morning, Robair," I replied.

"Mr. McAllister is here to see you. I showed him into the study."

I hesitated a moment. The corral would have to wait. There were more important things I had to do. "Thank you, Robair," I said, turning for the front staircase.

"Mr. Jonas," he called after me.

I stopped and looked back at him.

"If you're goin' to talk business, Mr. Jonas, I find you always talk better if you got something in your stomach."

I looked at him, then at the tray. I nodded and sat down on the top step. Robair set the tray down beside me. I picked up the glass of orange juice and drained it. Robair poured the coffee and lifted the cover from the toast. I sipped at the coffee. Robair was right. The empty feeling was in my stomach. It was going away now. I picked up a slice of toast.

If McAllister noticed the way I was dressed, he made no comment about it. He came directly to the point. "The ten per cent of minority stock is divided as follows," he said, spreading some papers on the desk. "Two and one half per cent each, Rina Cord and Nevada Smith; two per cent each, Judge Samuel Haskell and Peter Commack, president of the Industrial Bank of Reno; and one per cent to Eugene Denby."

I looked at him. "What's the stock worth?"

"On what basis?" he asked. "Earnings or net worth?"

"Both," I answered.

He looked down at his papers again. "On the basis of average earnings the past five years, the minority stock is worth forty-five thousand dollars; on the basis of net worth maybe sixty thousand dollars." He lit a cigarette. "The earning potential of the corporation has been declining since the war."

"What does that mean?"

"There just isn't the demand for our product in peacetime that there is in war," he answered.

I took out a cigarette and lit it. I began to have doubts about the hundred thousand a year I was paying him. "Tell me something I don't know," I said.

He looked down at the papers again, then up at me. "Commack's bank turned down the two-hundred-thousand-dollar loan your father wanted to finance the German contract you signed yesterday."

I put the cigarette out slowly in the ash tray. "I guess that leaves me a little short, doesn't it?"

McAllister nodded. "Yes."

My next question took him by surprise. "Well, what did you do about it?"

He stared at me as if I were psychic. "What makes you think that I did?"

"You were in my father's office when I got there and I know he wouldn't call you just to settle with that girl's parents. He could have done that himself. And you took the job. That meant you were sure of getting your money."

He began to smile. "I arranged another loan at the Pioneer National Trust Company in Los Angeles. I made it for three hundred thousand, just to be on the safe side."

"Good," I said. "That will give me the money I need to buy out the minority stockholders."

He was still staring at me with that look of surprise in his eyes when I dropped into the chair beside him. "Now," I said, "tell me everything you've been able to find out about this new thing my father was so hot about. What was it you called it? Plastics?"

CHAPTER EIGHT

R OBAIR SERVED A RANCH-STYLE BREAKFAST: STEAK AND EGGS, HOT BIS-cuits. I looked around the table. The last plate had been cleared away and now Robair discreetly withdrew, closing the big doors behind him. I drained my coffee cup and got to my feet.

"Gentlemen," I said, "I know I don't have to tell you what a shock it was yesterday to find myself suddenly with the responsibility of a big company like Cord Explosives. That's why I asked you gentlemen here this morning to help me decide what's best for the company."

Commack's thin voice reached across the table. "You can count on us to do what's right, son."

"Thank you, Mr. Commack," I said. "It seems to me that the first thing we have to do is elect a new president. Someone who will devote himself to the company the same way my father did."

I looked around the table. Denby sat at the end, scribbling notes in a pad. Nevada was rolling a cigarette. He glanced up at me, his eyes smiling. McAllister sat quietly next to him. Haskell and Commack were silent. I waited for the silence to grow heavy. It did. I didn't have to be told who were my friends.

"Do you have any suggestions, gentlemen?" I asked.

Commack looked up at me. "Do you?"

"I thought so yesterday," I said. "But I slept on it and this morning I came to the conclusion that it's a pretty big nut to crack for someone with my experience."

For the first time that morning, Haskell, Commack and Denby brightened. They exchanged quick looks. Commack spoke up. "That's pretty sensible of you, son," he said. "What about Judge Haskell here? He's retired from the bench but I think he might take the job on to help you out."

I turned to the Judge. "Would you, Judge?"

The Judge smiled slowly. "Only to help you out, boy," he said. "Only to help you out."

I looked over at Nevada. He was smiling broadly now. I smiled back at him, then turned to the others. "Shall we vote on it, gentlemen?"

For the first time, Denby spoke up. "According to the charter of this company, a president can only be elected by a meeting of the stockholders. And then only by a majority of the stock outstanding."

"Let's have a stockholder's meeting, then," Commack said. "The majority of stock is represented here."

"That's a good idea," I said. I turned to the Judge, smiling. "That is if I can vote my stock," I added.

"You sure can, boy," the Judge boomed, taking a paper from his pocket and handing it to me. "It's there in your father's will. I had it admitted to probate this morning. It's all legally yours now."

I took the will and continued. "All right, then, the director's meeting is adjourned and the stockholder's meeting is called to order. The first item on the agenda is to elect a president and treasurer of the company to replace the late Jonas Cord."

Commack smiled. "I nominate Judge Samuel Haskell."

Denby spoke quickly. Too quickly. "Second the nomination."

I nodded. "The nomination of Judge Haskell is noted. Any further nominations before the slate is closed?"

Nevada got to his feet. "I nominate Jonas Cord, Junior," he drawled.

I smiled at him. "Thank you." I turned to the Judge and my voice went hard and flat. "Do I hear the nomination seconded?"

The Judge's face was flushed. He glanced at Commack, then at Denby. Denby's face was white.

"Do I hear the nomination seconded?" I repeated coldly.

He knew I had them. "Second the nomination," the Judge said weakly.

"Thank you, Judge," I said.

It was easy after that. I bought their stock for twenty-five thousand dollars and the first thing I did was fire Denby.

If I was going to have a secretary, I didn't want a prissy little sneak like him. I wanted one with tits.

Robair came into the study, where McAllister and I were working. I looked up. "Yes, Robair?"

He bowed his head respectfully. "Miss Rina would like to see you in her room, suh."

I got to my feet and stretched. This sitting at a desk for half a day was worse than anything I'd ever done. "O.K., I'll go right up."

McAllister looked at me questioningly.

"Wait for me," I said. "I won't be long."

Robair held the door for me and I went up the stairs to Rina's room. I knocked on the door.

"Come in," she called.

She was sitting at her table in front of a mirror. Louise was brushing her hair with a big white brush. Rina's eyes looked up at me in the mirror.

"You wanted to see me?" I asked.

"Yes," she answered. She turned to Louise. "That's all for now," she said. "Leave us."

The girl nodded silently and started for the door. Rina's voice reached after her. "And wait downstairs. I'll call when I want you."

Rina looked at me and smiled. "She has a habit of listening at keyholes."

"I know," I said, closing the door behind me. "What is it you wanted to see me about?"

Rina got to her feet. Her black negligee swirled around her. Through it I could see she was wearing black undergarments, also. Her eyes caught mine. She smiled again. "What do you think of my widow's weeds?"

"Very merry-widowish," I answered. "But that isn't what you asked me up for."

She took a cigarette and lit it. "I want to get out of here right after the funeral."

"What for?" I asked. "It's your house. He left it to you."

Her eyes met mine through a cloud of smoke she blew out. "I want you to buy the house from me."

"What'll I use for money?"

"You'll get it," she said flatly. "Your father always got it for the things he wanted."

I studied her. She seemed to know exactly what she was doing. "How much do you want?" I asked cautiously.

"One hundred thousand dollars," she said calmly.

"What?" I exclaimed. "It isn't worth more than fifty-five."

"I know," she said. "But I'm throwing in something else—my stock in the Cord Explosives Company."

"The stock isn't worth the difference!" I exploded. "I just bought twice as much this morning for twenty-five thousand!"

She got to her feet and walked over to me. Her eyes stared coldly up at me. "Look, Jonas," she said coldly, "I'm being nice about it. Under the Nevada law, I'm entitled to one third your father's estate, will or no will. I could break the probate of the will just like that if I wanted to. And even if I couldn't, I could tie you up in court for five years. What would happen to all your plans then?"

I stared at her silently.

"If you don't believe me, why don't you ask your lawyer friend downstairs?" she added.

"You already checked?" I guessed.

"Damn right I did!" she snapped. "Judge Haskell called me as soon as he got back to his office!"

I drew in my breath. I should have known the old bastard wouldn't let go that easy. "I haven't got that kind of money," I said. "Neither has the company."

"I know that," she said. "But I'm willing to be reasonable about it. I'll take fifty thousand the day after the funeral and your note endorsed by the company for ten thousand a year for the next five years."

I didn't need a lawyer to tell me she'd had good advice. "O.K.," I said, starting for the door. "Come on downstairs. I'll have McAllister prepare the papers."

She smiled again. "I couldn't do that."

"Why not?" I demanded.

"I'm in mourning," she said. "How would it look for the widow of Jonas Cord to come downstairs to transact business?" She went back to her vanity table and sat down. "When the papers are ready, send them up."

CHAPTER NINE

IT WAS FIVE O'CLOCK WHEN WE GOT OUT OF THE TAXI IN FRONT OF THE BANK building in downtown Los Angeles. We went through the door and walked back to the executive offices in the rear of the bank. McAllister led me through another door marked PRIVATE. It was a reception room.

A secretary looked up. "Mr. McAllister." She smiled. "We thought you were in Nevada."

"I was," he replied. "Is Mr. Moroni in?"

"Let me check," she said. "Sometimes he has a habit of leaving the office without telling me." She disappeared through another door.

I looked at McAllister. "That's the kind of secretary I want. She's got brains and a nice pair of boobs to go with them."

He smiled. "A girl like that gets seventy-five, eighty dollars a week. They don't come cheap."

"Yuh gotta pay for anything that's good," I said.

The secretary appeared in the doorway, smiling at us. "Mr. Moroni will see you now, Mr. McAllister."

I followed him into the inner office. It was large, with dark, wood-paneled walls. There was a big desk spang in the middle of it and a small man with iron-gray hair and shrewd dark eyes sitting behind it. He got up as we came into the room.

"Mr. Moroni," McAllister said, "this is Jonas Cord."

Moroni put out his hand. I took it. It wasn't the usual soft banker's hand. This one was hard and callused and the grip was strong. There were many years of labor contained in that hand and most of them had not been behind a desk. "It's good to meet you, Mr. Cord," he said with a faint trace of an Italian accent.

"My pleasure, sir," I said respectfully.

He waved us to the chairs in front of his desk and we sat down. McAllister came right to the point. When he had finished, Moroni leaned forward across his desk and looked at me. "I'm sorry to hear about your loss," he said. "From everything I've heard, he was a very unusual man."

I nodded. "He was, sir."

"You realize, of course, this makes quite a difference?"

I looked at him. "Without trying to stand on a technicality, Mr. Moroni, I thought the loan was being made to the Cord Explosives Company, not to either my father or me."

Moroni smiled. "A good banker makes loans to companies but he always looks at the man behind the company."

"My experience is limited, sir, but I thought the first objective of a good banker was to achieve adequate collateralization for a loan. I believe that was inherent in the loan agreement that Mr. McAllister made with you."

Moroni smiled. He leaned back in his chair and took out a cigar. He lit it and looked at me through a cloud of smoke. "Mr. Cord, tell me what you believe the primary responsibility of the borrower is."

I looked at him. "To make a profit on his loan."

"I said the borrower, Mr. Cord, not the lender."

"I know you did, Mr. Moroni," I said. "But if I didn't feel I would make a profit on the money you're going to lend me, there'd be no point in my taking it."

"Just how do you expect to make that profit?" he asked. "How well do you know your business, Mr. Cord?"

"Not as well as I should, Mr. Moroni. Certainly not as well as I will next week, next month, next year. But this much I do know. Tomorrow is coming and a whole new world with it. There'll be opportunities to make money that never existed in my father's time. And I'll take advantage of them."

"I presume you're referring to this new product you're acquiring by the German contract?"

"That's part of it," I said, even if I hadn't thought of it until he mentioned it.

"Just how much do you know about plastics?" he asked.

"Very little," I admitted.

"Then what makes you so sure it's worth anything?"

"Du Pont and Eastman's interest in the American rights. Anything they're interested in has to be worth something. And, your agreement to lend us the money to acquire those rights. As soon as I clear up a few things here, I intend to spend two or three months in Germany learning everything there is to know about plastics."

"Who will run the company while you're away?" Moroni asked. "A great deal can happen in three months."

"Mr. McAllister, sir," I said. "He's already agreed to join the company."

A kind of respect came into the banker's face. "I know my directors may not agree with me, Mr. Cord, but I've decided to give you your loan. It has certain elements of speculation that may not conform to what they consider sound banking practices, but the Pioneer National Trust Company was built on loans like this. We were the first bank to lend money to the producers of motion pictures and there's nothing quite as speculative as that."

"Thank you, Mr. Moroni," I said.

He picked up the telephone on his desk. "Bring in the Cord loan agreement and the check."

"You will note," he said, "that although the loan is for three hundred thousand dollars, we have extended your credit under this agreement to a maximum of five hundred thousand dollars." He smiled at me. "One of my principles of banking, Mr. Cord. I don't believe in budgeting my clients too closely. Sometimes a few dollars more make the difference between success and failure."

Suddenly I liked this man. It takes one crap-shooter to recognize another. And this man had it. I smiled at him. "Thanks, Mr. Moroni. Let's hope I make a lot of money for both of us." I leaned over and signed the loan application.

"I'm sure you will," Moroni said and pushed the check across the desk at me.

I picked it up and gave it to McAllister without looking at it. I got to my feet. "Thank you again, Mr. Moroni. I'm sorry I have to run but we have to get back to Nevada tonight."

"Tonight? But there aren't any trains until morning."

"I have my own plane, Mr. Moroni. That's how we came up. We'll be home by nine o'clock."

Moroni came around his desk. There was a look of concern on his face. "Better fly low, Mr. Cord," he said. "After all, we just gave you a lot of money."

I laughed aloud. "Don't worry, Mr. Moroni. It's as safe as an automobile. Besides, if anything happens to us on the way down, just stop payment on the check."

They both laughed. I could see the look of nervousness cross McAllister's face, but to his credit, he didn't say anything.

We shook hands and Moroni walked us to the door. "Good luck," he said as we walked out into the reception room.

A man was sitting on the couch. He got to his feet slowly. I recognized Buzz Dalton, the pilot whose plane I had won in a crap game. "Hey, Buzz," I called. "Don't you say hello to your friends?"

A smile broke over his face. "Jonas!" he exclaimed. "What the hell are you doin' here?"

"Diggin' for a little scratch," I said, taking his hand. "You?"

"The same," he answered, a dejected look coming over his face again. "But no luck so far."

"Why?" I asked.

Buzz shrugged. "I got a mail contract. L.A. to Frisco. Twelve months guaranteed at ten thousand a month. But I guess I'll have to pass it up. I can't get the dough to buy the three planes I need. Banks think it's too risky."

"How much do you have to borrow?"

"About twenty-five grand," he said. "Twenty for the planes and five to keep them flying until the first check comes in."

"Yuh got the contract?"

"In my pocket," he said, taking it out.

I looked at it. "It sounds like a good deal to me."

"It is," he answered. "I got it all worked out. I can net five grand a month after expenses and amortization. Here's the paper I worked out on that."

The figures seemed right to me. I had a good idea what it cost to run a plane. I turned around and looked at Moroni. "You meant what you said in there? About my additional credit? There's no strings on it?"

He smiled. "No strings at all."

I turned back to Buzz. "You got your money on two conditions," I said. "I get fifty per cent of the stock in your company and chattel mortgage on your planes amortized over twelve months, both payable to the Cord Explosives Company.

Buzz's face broke into a grin. "Man, you got yourself a deal!"

"O.K.," I said. I turned to Mr. Moroni. "Would you be kind enough to arrange the details for me? I have to be back tonight."

"I'll be glad to, Mr. Cord." He smiled.

"Make the loan for thirty thousand dollars," I said.

"Hey, wait a minute," Buzz interrupted. "I only asked for twenty-five."

"I know," I said, turning back to him with a smile. "But I learned something today."

"What's that?" Buzz asked.

"It's bad business to lend a guy just enough money to give him the shorts. That's takin' a chance and you both can lose. If you really want him to make it, lend him enough to make sure he can do the job."

❖ ❖ ❖

My father had the biggest funeral ever held in this part of the state. Even the Governor came down. I had closed the plant and the little church was packed to the rafters, with the overflow spilling out into the street.

Rina and I stood alone in the small pew down in front. She stood straight and tall in her black dress, her blond hair and her face hidden by the black veil. I looked down at the new black shoes on my feet. They were my father's shoes and they hurt. At the last minute, I'd discovered I didn't have anything in the house except huaraches. Robair had brought the shoes down from my father's closet. He had never worn them. I promised myself I would never wear them again, either.

I heard a sigh run through the congregation and looked up. They were closing my father's coffin. I had a last quick glimpse of his face, then it was gone and there was a curious kind of blankness in my mind and for a moment I couldn't even remember what he looked like.

Then the sound of weeping came to my ears and I looked around out of the corners of my eyes. The Mex women from the plant were crying. I heard a snuffle behind me. I half turned. It was Jake Platt, tears in his whisky eyes.

I looked at Rina standing next to me. I could see her eyes through the dark veil. They were clear and calm. From the congregation behind us came the sound of many people weeping for my father.

But Rina, his wife, didn't weep. And neither did I, his son.

CHAPTER TEN

IT WAS A WARM NIGHT, EVEN WITH THE BREEZE THAT CAME IN THROUGH THE open windows from across the desert. I tossed restlessly on the bed and pushed the sheets down from me. It had been a long day, starting with the funeral and then going over plans with McAllister until it was time for him to leave. I was tired but I couldn't sleep. Too many thoughts were racing through my mind. I wondered if that was the reason I used to hear my father pacing up and down in his room long after the rest of the house had gone to bed.

There was a sound at the door. I sat up in bed. My voice jarred the stillness. "Who is it?"

The door opened farther and I could see her face; the rest of her dissolved into the darkness along with the black negligee. Her voice was very low as she closed the door behind her. "I thought you might be awake, Jonas. I couldn't sleep, either."

"Worried about your money?" I asked sarcastically. "The check's over there on the dresser along with the notes. Just sign the release and it's yours."

"It isn't the money," she said, coming still further into the room.

"What is it, then?" I asked coldly. "You came to say you're sorry? To express your sympathy? Is this a condolence call?"

She was standing next to the bed now and looked down at me. "You don't have to say things like that, Jonas," she said simply. "Even if he was your father, I was his wife. Yes, I came to say I'm sorry."

But I wasn't satisfied with that. "Sorry about what?" I flung at her. "Sorry he didn't give you more than he did? Sorry that you didn't marry me instead of him?" I laughed bitterly. "You didn't love him."

"No, I didn't love him," she said tightly. "But I respected him. He was more a man than anyone I ever met."

I didn't speak.

Suddenly she was crying. She sat down on the edge of the bed and hid her face in her hands.

"Cut it out," I said roughly. "It's too late for tears."

She put her hands down and stared at me. In the darkness, I could see the wet silver sparkle rolling down her cheeks. "What do you know it's too late for?" she cried. "Too late to love him? It isn't that I didn't try. It's just that I'm not capable of love. I don't know why. It's the way I am, that's all. Your father knew that and understood it. That's why I married him. Not for his money. He knew that, too. And he was content with what I gave him."

"If that's the truth," I said, "then what are you crying for?"

"Because I'm frightened," she said.

"Frightened?" I laughed. It just didn't fit her. "What are you afraid of?"

She took a cigarette from somewhere in her negligee and put it in her mouth unlit. Her eyes shone at me like a panther's eyes must in a desert campfire at night. "Men," she said shortly.

"Men?" I repeated. "You—afraid of men? Why, you're the original teasing—"

"That's right, you stupid fool!" she said angrily. "I'm afraid of men, listening to their demands, putting up with their lecherous hands and one-track minds. And hearing them disguise their desire with the words of love when all they want is just one thing. To get inside me!"

"You're crazy!" I said angrily. "That's not the only thing we think of!"

"No?" she asked. I heard the rasp of a match and the flame broke the darkness. She looked down at me. "Then look at yourself, Jonas. Look at yourself lusting for your father's wife!"

I didn't have to look to know she was right. I knocked the match angrily from her hand.

Then, all at once, she was clinging to me, her lips placing tiny kisses on my face and chin, her body trembling with her fears. "Jonas, Jonas. Please let me stay with you. Just for tonight," she cried. "I'm afraid to be alone!"

I raised my hands to push her away. She was naked beneath the black negligee. Her flesh was cool and soft as the summer desert breeze and her thrusting nipples rasped across the palms of my rising hands.

I froze, staring at her in the darkness. There was only her face before me, then the taste of her salty tears on her lips and mine. The anger inside me washed away in the cascading torrent of desire. And with only my devil to guide us, together we plunged into the fiery pleasures of our own particular hell.

❖ ❖ ❖

I awoke and glanced at the window. The first flicker of dawn was spilling into the room. I turned to look at Rina. She was lying on my pillow, her arm flung across her eyes. I touched her shoulder lightly.

She took away her arm. Her eyes were open; they were clear and calm.

She got out of bed in a smooth, fluid motion. Her body shone with a young, golden translucence. She picked up her black negligee from the foot of the bed and slipped into it. I sat there watching her as she walked over to the dresser.

"There's a pen in the top right drawer," I said.

She took out the pen and signed the release.

"Aren't you going to read it?" I asked.

She shook her head. "What for? You can't get any more than I agreed to give you."

She was right. She had forgone all rights to any further claims in the estate. Picking up the check and the notes, she walked to the door. She turned there and looked back at me.

"I won't be here when you get back from the plant."

I looked at her for a moment. "You don't have to go," I said.

Her eyes met mine. I thought I caught a hint of sadness in them. "No, Jonas," she said softly. "It wouldn't work out."

"Maybe," I said.

"No, Jonas," she said. "It's time you got out from under the shadow of your father. He was a great man but so will you be. In your own way."

I reached for a cigarette on the bedside table and lit it without speaking. The smoke burned into my lungs.

"Good-by, Jonas," she said. "Good luck."

I stared at her for a moment, then I spoke. My voice was husky from the cigarette. "Thank you," I said. "Good-by, Rina."

The door opened and shut quickly and she was gone. I got out of bed and walked over to the window. The first morning red of the sun was on the horizon. It was going to be a scorcher.

I heard the door open behind me and my heart leaped inside my breast. She had come back. I turned around.

Robair came into the room carrying a tray. His white teeth flashed in a gentle smile. "I thought you might do with a cup of coffee."

When I got down to the plant, Jake Platt had a gang of men up on the roof, painting it white. I grinned to myself and went inside.

That first day was hectic. It seemed that nothing went right. The detonator caps we had sent to Endicott Mines were faulted and we had to rush-ship replacements. For the third time that year, Du Pont underbid us on a government contract for pressed cordite.

I spent half the day going over the figures and it finally boiled down to our policy on percentage of profit. When I suggested that we'd better re-examine our policy if it was going to cost us business, Jake Platt protested. My father, he said, claimed it didn't pay them to operate on a basis of less than twelve per cent. I blew up and told Jake Platt that I was running the factory now and what my father had done was his own business. On the next bid, I'd damn sure make certain we underbid Du Pont by at least three cents a pound.

By that time, it was five o'clock and the production foreman came in with the production figures. I'd just started to go over them when Nevada interrupted me.

"Jonas," he said.

I looked up. He had been there in the office all day but he was quiet and sat in a corner and I had even forgotten that he was there. "Yes?" I answered.

"Is it all right if I leave a little early?" he asked. "I got some things to do."

"Sure," I said, looking down at the production sheets again. "Take the Duesenberg. I'll get Jake to drive me home."

"I won't need it," he said. "I left my own car in the lot."

"Nevada," I called after him. "Tell Robair I'll be home for dinner at eight o'clock."

There was a moment's hesitation, then I heard his reply. "Sure thing, Jonas. I'll tell him."

I was through earlier than I had expected and pulled the Duesenberg up in front of the house at seven thirty, just as Nevada came down the steps with a valise in each hand.

He stared at me in a kind of surprise. "You're home early."

"Yeah," I answered. "I finished sooner than I thought."

"Oh," he said and continued down the steps to his car. He put the valises in the back.

I followed him down and I could see the back of his car was filled with luggage. "Where you going with all that stuff, Nevada?"

"It's mine," he said gruffly.

"I didn't say it wasn't," I said. "I just asked where you were going."

"I'm leavin'."

"On a hunting trip?" I asked. This was the time of the year Nevada and I always used to go up into the mountains when I was a kid.

"Nope," he said. "Fer good."

"Wait a minute," I said. "You just can't walk out like that."

His dark eyes bore into mine. "Who says I can't?"

"I do," I said. "How'm I going to get along without you?"

He smiled slowly. "Real good, I reckon. You don't need me to wet-nurse you no more. I been watchin' you the last few days."

"But—but," I protested.

Nevada smiled slowly. "All jobs got to end sometime, Jonas. I put about sixteen years into this one and now there's nothing left for me to do. I don't like the idea of drawing a salary with no real way to earn it."

I stared at him for a moment. He was right. There was too much man in him to hang around being a flunky. "You got enough money?"

He nodded. "I never spent a cent of my own in sixteen years. Your pappy wouldn't let me."

"What are you going to do?"

"Join up with a couple of old buddies. We're takin' a Wild West show up the coast to California. Expect to have a real big time."

We stood around awkwardly for a moment, then Nevada put out his hand. "So long, Jonas."

I held onto his hand. I could feel the tears hovering just beneath my eyelids. "So long, Nevada."

He walked around the car and got in behind the wheel. Starting the motor he shifted into gear. He raised his hand in farewell just as he began to roll.

"Keep in touch, Nevada," I yelled after him, and watched until he was out of sight.

I walked back into the house and went into the dining room. I sat down at the empty table.

Robair came in with an envelope in his hand. "Mr. Nevada left this for you," he said.

Numbly I opened it and took out a note written laboriously in pencil:

DEAR SON,

I ain't much of a man for good-bys, so this is it. There ain't nothing any more for me to do around here so I figure it's time I went. All my life I wanted to give you something for your birthday but your pappy always beat me to it. Your pappy gave you everything. So until now there was nothing you ever wanted that I could give you. In this envelope you will find something you really want. You don't have to worry about it. I went to a lawyer in Reno and signed it all over good and proper.

Happy birthday.

Your friend,
Nevada Smith

I looked at the other papers in the envelope. They were Cord Explosives Company stock certificates endorsed over to my name.

I put them down on the table and a lump began to come up in my throat. Suddenly, the house was empty. Everybody was gone. My father, Rina, Nevada. Everybody. The house began to echo with memories.

I remembered what Rina had said, about getting out from under the shadow of my father. She was right. I couldn't live in this house. It wasn't mine. It was his. For me, it would always be his house.

My mind was made up. I'd find an apartment in Reno. There wouldn't be any memories in an apartment. I'd turn the house over to McAllister. He had a family and it would save him the trouble of looking for one.

I looked down at Nevada's note again. The last line hit me. Happy birthday. A pain began to tie up my gut. I had forgotten and Nevada had been the only one left to remember.

Today was my birthday.

I was twenty-one.

THE STORY OF NEVADA SMITH
Book Two

CHAPTER ONE

IT WAS AFTER NINE O'CLOCK WHEN NEVADA PULLED THE CAR OFF THE HIGH-way onto the dirt road that led to the ranch. He stopped the car in front of the main house and got out. He stood there listening to the sounds of laughter coming from the casino.

A man came out on the porch and looked down at him. "Hello, Nevada."

Nevada answered without turning around. "Hello, Charlie. It sounds like the divorcees are having themselves a high ol' time."

Charlie smiled. "Why shouldn't they? Divorcin' is a pretty good piece of business for most of 'em."

Nevada turned and looked up at him. "I guess it is. Only, I can't get used to the idea of ranchin' women instead of cattle."

"Now, mebbe, you'll get used to it," Charlie said. "After all, you own fifty per cent of this spread. Time you settled down and got to work on it."

"I don't know," Nevada said. "I kinda got me the travelin' itch. I figger I been in one place long enough."

"Where you goin' to travel?" Charlie asked. "There ain't no place left. The country's all used up with roads going to every place. You're thirty years late."

Nevada nodded silently. Charlie was right but the strange thing was he didn't feel thirty years late. He felt the same as he always did. Right for now.

"I put the woman in your cabin," Charlie said. "Martha and I been waitin' supper for you."

Nevada got back into the car. "Then I better go an' get her. We'll be back as soon as I git washed up."

Charlie nodded and went back inside as the car started off. At the door, he turned and looked after it as it wound its way up the small hill toward the back of the ranch. He shook his head and went inside.

Martha was waiting for him. "How is he?" she asked anxiously.

"I don't know," he answered, shaking his head again. "He seems kinda mixed up an' lost to me. I just don't know."

The cabin was dark when Nevada went in. He reached for the oil lamp beside the door and put it on a table. He struck a match and held it to the wick. The wick sputtered a moment then burst into flame. He put the chimney back on and replaced the lamp on the shelf.

Rina's voice came from behind him. "Why didn't you turn on the electricity, Nevada?"

"I like lamp light," he said simply. "Electric light ain't natural. It's wearin' on the eyes."

She was sitting in a chair facing the door, her face pale and luminous. She was wearing a heavy sweater that came down over the faded blue jeans covering her legs.

"You cold?" he asked. "I'll start a fire."

She shook her head. "I'm not cold."

He stood there silent for a moment, then spoke. "I'll bring in my things an' wash up. Charlie and Martha waited supper for us."

"I'll help you bring them in."

"O.K."

They came out into the night. The stars were deep in the black velvet and the sound of music and laughter came faintly to them from down the hill.

She looked down toward the casino. "I'm glad I'm not one of them."

He handed her a suitcase. "You never could be. You ain't the type."

"I thought of divorcing him," she said. "But something inside me kept me from it even though I knew it was wrong from the beginning."

"A deal's a deal," he said shortly as he turned back into the cabin, his arms full.

"I guess that's it."

They made two more trips silently and then she sat down on the edge of the bed as he stripped off his shirt and turned to the washbasin in the corner of the small bedroom.

The muscles rippled under his startlingly white skin. The hair covering his chest was like a soft black down as it fell toward his flat, hard stomach. He covered his face and neck with soap and then splashed water over it. He reached for a towel blindly.

She gave it to him and he rubbed vigorously. He put down the towel and reached for a clean shirt. He slipped into it and began to button it.

"Wait a minute," she said suddenly. "Let me do that for you."

Her fingers were quick and light. He felt their touch against his skin like a whisper of air. She looked up into his face, her eyes wondering. "How old are you, Nevada? Your skin is like a young boy's."

He smiled suddenly.

"How old?" she persisted.

"I was born in eighty-two, according to my reckoning," he said. "My mother was a Kiowa and they didn't keep such good track of birthdays. That makes me forty-three." He finished tucking the shirt into his trousers.

"You don't look more than thirty."

He laughed, pleased despite himself. "Let's go and git some grub."

She took his arm. "Let's," she said. "Suddenly, I'm starving."

It was after midnight when they got back to the cabin. He opened the door and let her enter before him. He crossed to the fireplace and set a match to the kindling. She came up behind him and he looked up.

"You go on to bed," he said.

Silently she walked into the bedroom and he fanned the kindling. The wood caught and leaped into flame. He put a few logs over it and got up and crossed the room to a cupboard. He took down a bottle of bourbon and a glass and sat down in front of the fire.

He poured a drink and looked at the whisky in the glass. The fire behind it gave it a glowing heat. He drank the whisky slowly.

When he had finished, he put the empty glass down and began to strip off his boots. He left them beside the chair and walked over to the couch and stretched out. He had just lighted a cigarette when her voice came from the bedroom door.

"Nevada?"

He sat up and turned toward her. "Yeah?"

"Did Jonas say anything about me?"

"No."

"He gave me a hundred thousand dollars for the stock and the house."

"I know," he replied.

She hesitated a moment, then came farther into the room. "I don't need all that money. If you need any—"

He laughed soundlessly. "I'm O.K. Thanks, anyway."

"Sure?"

He chuckled again, wondering what she would say if she knew about the six-thousand-acre ranch he had in Texas, about the half interest in the Wild-West show. He, too, had learned a great deal from the old man. Money was only good when it was working for you.

"Sure," he said. He got to his feet and walked toward her. "Now go to bed, Rina. You're out on your feet."

He followed her into the bedroom and took a blanket from the closet as she got into bed. She caught his hands as he walked by the bed. "Talk to me while I fall asleep."

He sat down on the side of the bed. "What about?" he asked.

She still held onto his hand. "About yourself. Where you were born, where you came from—anything."

He smiled into the dark. "Ain't very much to tell," he said. "As far as I know, I was born in West Texas. My father was a buffalo-hunter named John Smith and my mother was a Kiowa princess named—"

"Don't tell me," she interrupted sleepily. "I know her name. Pocahontas."

He laughed softly. "Somebody told you," he said in mock reproach. "Pocahontas. That was her name."

"Nobody told me," she whispered faintly. "I read it someplace."

Her hand slipped slowly from his and he looked down. Her eyes were closed and she was fast asleep.

Quietly he got up and straightened the blanket around her, then turned and walked into the other room. He spread a blanket on the couch and undressed quickly. He stretched out and wrapped the blanket around him.

John Smith and Pocahontas. He wondered how many times he had mockingly told that story. But the truth was stranger still. And probably, no one would believe it.

It was so long ago that there were times he didn't believe it himself any more. His name wasn't Nevada Smith then, it was Max Sand.

And he was wanted for armed robbery and murder in three different states.

CHAPTER TWO

IT WAS IN MAY OF 1882 THAT SAMUEL SAND CAME INTO THE SMALL CABIN that he called home and sat down heavily on a box that served him for a chair. Silently his squaw woman heated some coffee and placed it before him. She moved heavily, being swollen with child.

He sat there for a long time, his coffee growing cold before him. Occasionally, he would look out the door toward the prairie, with its faint remnant patches of snow still hidden in the corners of rises.

The squaw began to cook the evening meal. Beans and salt buffalo meat. It was still early in the day to cook the meal, because the sun had not yet reached the noon, but she felt vaguely disturbed and had to do something. Now and then, she would glance at Sam out of the corners of her eyes but he was lost in a troubled world that women were not allowed to enter. So she kept stirring the beans and meat in the pot and waited for his mood and the day to pass.

Kaneha was sixteen that spring and it was only the summer before that the buffalo-hunter had come to the tepees of her tribe to purchase a wife. He had come on a black horse, leading a mule that was burdened heavily with pack.

The chief and the council of braves came out to greet him. They sat down in a circle of peace around the fire with the pot of stew cooking over it. The chief took out the pipe and Sam took out a bottle of whisky. Silently the chief held the pipe to the glowing coals and then, when it was lit, held it to his mouth and puffed deeply. He passed it to Sam, who puffed and in turn passed it to the brave seated next to him in the circle.

When the pipe came back to the chief, Sam opened the bottle of whisky. He wiped the rim of it carefully and tilted it to his lips, then offered it to the chief. The chief did the same and took a large swallow of the whisky. It burned his throat and his eyes watered and he wanted to cough, but he choked back the cough and passed the bottle to the brave seated next to him.

When the bottle came back to Sam, he placed it on the ground in front of the chief. He leaned forward and took a piece of meat out of the pot. He chewed elaborately on the fatty morsel with much smacking of his lips and then swallowed it.

He looked at the chief. "Good dog."

The chief nodded. "We cut out its tongue and kept it tied to a stake that it would be properly fat."

They were silent for a moment and the chief reached again for the bottle of whisky. Sam knew it was then time for him to speak.

"I am a mighty hunter," he boasted. "My gun has slain thousands of buffalo. My prowess is known all across the plains. There is no brave who can feed as many as I."

The chief nodded solemnly. "The deeds of Red Beard are known to us. It is an honor to welcome him to our tribe."

"I have come to my brothers for the maiden known as Kaneha," Sam said. "I want her for my squaw."

The chief sighed slowly in relief. Kaneha was the youngest of his daughters and the least favored. For she was tall for a maiden, almost as tall as the tallest brave, and thin, her waist so thin that two hands could span it. There was not enough room inside her for a child to grow, and her face and features were straight and flat, not round and fat, as a maiden's should be. The chief sighed again in relief. Kaneha would be no problem now.

"It is a wise choice," he said aloud. "The maiden Kaneha is ripe for child-bearing. Already her blood floods thickly to the ground when the moon is high."

Sam got to his feet and walked over to the mule. He opened one of the packs and took out six bottles of whisky and a small wooden box. He carried them back to the circle and placed them on the ground before him. He sat down again.

"I have brought gifts to my brothers, the Kiowa," he said. "In appreciation of the honor they show me when they allow me to sit in their council."

He placed the whisky bottles in front of the chief and opened the little box. It was filled with gaily colored beads and trinkets. He held the box so that all could see and then placed it, too, before the chief.

The chief nodded again. "The Kiowa is grateful for the gifts of Red Beard. But the loss of the maiden Kaneha will be a difficult one for her tribe to bear. Already she has won her place among us by her skills in her womanly crafts. Her cooking and sewing, her artistry in leather-making."

"I am aware of the high regard in which the Kiowa hold their daughter Kaneha," Sam said formally. "And I came prepared to compensate them for their loss."

He got to his feet again. "For the loss of her aid in feeding the tribe, I pledge the meat of two buffalo," he said, looking down at them. "For the loss of her labor, I give to my brothers this mule which I have brought with me. And to compensate them for the loss of her beauty, I bring them—"

He paused dramatically and walked back to his mule. Silently he untied the heavy rolled pack on its back. He carried the pack back to the seated council and laid it on the ground before them. Slowly he unrolled it.

A sigh of awe came unbidden from the circle. The chief's eyes glittered.

" . . . the hide of the sacred white buffalo," Sam said. He looked around the circle. Their eyes were fixed on the beautiful white skin that shone before them like snow on the ground.

The albino buffalo was a rarity. The chief that could be laid to rest on such a sacred hide was assured that his spirit would enter the happy hunting grounds. To the skin-traders, it might be worth almost as much as ten ordinary hides. But Sam knew what he wanted.

He wanted a woman. For five years, he had lived on these plains and had been able only to share the services of a whore once a year at trading time in the small room back of the skin-trader's post. It was time he had a woman of his own.

The chief, so impressed with the munificence of Sam's offer that he forgot to bargain further, looked up. "It is with honor that we give the mighty hunter Red Beard the woman Kaneha to be his squaw."

He rose to his feet as a sign that the council was over.

"Prepare my daughter Kaneha for her husband," he said. He turned and walked toward his tent and Sam followed him.

In another tent, Kaneha sat waiting. Somehow, she had known that Red Beard had come for her. In keeping with maidenly modesty, she had gone into the waiting tent so that she might not hear the bargaining. She sat there calmly, for she was not afraid of Red Beard. She had looked into his face many times when he had come to visit her father.

Now there was the sound of babbling women coming toward the tent. She looked toward the flap. The bargaining was over. She only hoped that Red Beard had at least offered one buffalo for her. The women burst into the tent. They were all talking at once. No bride had ever brought greater gifts. The mule. Beads. Whisky. The hide of a sacred white buffalo. Two buffalo for meat.

Kaneha smiled proudly to herself. In that moment, she knew that Red Beard loved her. From outside the tent came the sound of the drums beginning to beat out the song of marriage. The women gathered in a circle around her, their feet stamping in time to the drums.

She dropped her shift to the ground and the women came close. One on each side of her began to unplait the long braid that hung past her shoulders. Two others began to cover her body with grease from the bear, which was to make her fertile. At last, all was done and they stepped back.

She stood there naked in the center of the tent, facing the flap. Her body shone with the grease and she was straight and tall, her breasts high and her stomach flat, her legs straight and long.

The flap opened and the medicine man entered. In one hand he carried the devil wand, in the other the marriage stick. He shook the devil wand in the four corners of the tent and sprang twice into the air to make sure there were no devils hovering over them, then he advanced toward her. He held the marriage stick over her head.

She looked up at it. It was made of highly polished wood, carved into the shape of an erect phallus and testes. Slowly he lowered it until it rested on her forehead. She closed her eyes because it was not seemly for a maiden to look so deeply into the source of a warrior's strength.

The medicine man began to dance around her, springing high into the air and mumbling incantations over her. He pressed the stick to her breasts, to her stomach, to her back and buttocks, to her cheeks and to her eyes, until now it was covered with the bear grease from her body. Finally, he leaped into the air with a horrible shriek and when his feet touched the earth again, everything was silent, even the drums.

As in a trance, she took the marriage stick from the medicine man. Silently she held it to her face, then her breasts, then her stomach.

The drums began again, beating slowly. In time with their rhythm, she lowered the stick between her legs. Her feet began to move in time to the drums, slowly at first, then faster as the drums picked up tempo. Her long black hair, which hung to her buttocks, began to flare out wildly as she began to move around the circle of women, holding out the marriage stick for their blessing and cries of envy.

The circle completed, she once more stood alone in its center, her feet moving in time with the drums. Holding the marriage stick between her legs, she began to crouch slightly, lowering herself onto it.

"Ai-ee," the women sighed as they swayed to the tempo of the drums.

"Ai-ee," they sighed again in approbation as she lifted herself from the stick. It was not seemly for a maiden to be too eager to swallow up her husband.

Now they held their breath as once more the stick began to enter her. Each was reminded of her own marriage, when she, too, had looked up at the circle of women, her eyes pleading for help. But none dared move forward. This the bride must do for herself.

Through Kaneha's pain, the drums began to throb. Her lips grew tight together. This was her husband, Red Beard, the mighty hunter. She must not disgrace him here in the tent of women. When he himself came into her, instead of his spirit, the way for him must be easy and quick.

She closed her eyes and made a sudden convulsive movement. The hymen ruptured and she staggered as a wave of pain washed over her. The drums were wilder now. Slowly she straightened up and removed the marriage stick. She held it out proudly toward the medicine man.

He took it and quickly left the tent. Silently the women formed a circle around her. Naked, in its center so she would be shielded from other eyes, she walked to the tent of the chief.

The women stood aside as she entered. In the dim light, the chief and Sam looked up at her. She stood there proudly, her head raised, her eyes respectfully looking over their heads. Her breasts heaved and her legs trembled slightly. She prayed that Red Beard would be pleased with what he saw.

The chief spoke first, as was the custom. "See how profusely she bleeds," he said. "She will bear you many sons."

"Aye, she will bear me many sons," Sam said, his eyes on her face. "And because I am pleased with her, I pledge my brothers the meat of an additional buffalo."

Kaneha smiled quickly and left the tent to go down to the river to bathe. Her prayers had been answered. Red Beard was pleased with her.

Now she moved heavily, swollen with his child, as he sat at the table wondering why the buffalo didn't come. Something inside him told him they would never come again. Too many had been slain in the last few years.

At last, he looked up from the table. "Git the gear together," he said. "We're moving out of here."

Kaneha nodded and obediently began to gather up the household things while he went out and hitched the mules to the cart. Finished, he came back to the cabin.

Kaneha picked up the first bundle and started for the door when the pain seized her. The bundle fell from her hands and she doubled over. She looked up at him, her eyes filled with meaning.

"You mean now?" Sam asked, almost incredulously.

She nodded.

"Here, let me help you."

She straightened up, the seizure leaving her. "No," she said firmly in Kiowa. "This is for a woman, not for a brave."

Sam nodded. He walked to the door. "I'll be outside."

It was two o'clock in the morning when he first heard the cry of a baby from inside the cabin. He had been half dozing and the sound brought him awake into a night filled with stars. He sat there tensely, listening.

About twenty minutes passed, then the door of the cabin opened and Kaneha stood there. He struggled to his feet and went into the cabin.

In the corner on a blanket in front of the fire lay the naked baby. Sam stood there, looking down.

"A son," Kaneha said proudly.

"Well, I'll be damned." Sam touched it and the baby squalled, opening its eyes. "A son," Sam said. "How about that?" He bent over, looking closely.

His beard tickled the baby and it screamed again. Its skin was white and the eyes were blue like the father's, but the hair was black and heavy on his little head.

The next morning they left the cabin.

CHAPTER THREE

THEY SETTLED DOWN ABOUT TWENTY MILES OUTSIDE OF DODGE CITY AND Sam started to haul freight for the stage lines. Being the only man in the area with mules, he found himself in a fairly successful business.

They lived in a small cabin and it was there Max began to grow up. Kaneha was very happy with her son. Occasionally, she would wonder why the spirits had not given her more children but she did not worry about it. Because she was Indian, they kept to themselves.

Sam liked it that way, too. Basically, he was a very shy man and his years alone on the plains had not helped cure his shyness. He developed a reputation in the town for being taciturn and stingy. There were rumors floating around that actually he had a hoard of gold cached out on his place from the years he was a buffalo-hunter.

By the time Max was eleven years old, he was as lithe and quick on his feet as his Indian forebears. He could ride any horse he chose without a saddle and could shoot the eye out of a prairie gopher at a hundred yards with his .22. His black hair hung straight and long, Indian fashion, and his eyes were dark blue, almost black in his tanned face.

They were seated at the table one night, eating supper, when Sam looked over at his son. "They're startin' up a school in Dodge," he said.

Max looked up at his father as Kaneha came to the table from the stove. He didn't know whether he was supposed to speak or not. He kept eating silently.

"I signed you up for it," Sam said. "I paid ten dollars."

Now Max felt it was time for him to speak. "What fer?"

THE CARPETBAGGERS ❖ 55

"To have them learn you to read an' write," his father answered.

"What do I have to know that fer?" Max asked.

"A man should know them things," Sam said.

"You don't," Max said with the peculiar logic of children. "And it don't bother you none."

"Times is different now," Sam said. "When I was a boy, there warn't no need for such things. Now ever'thing is readin' or writin'."

"I don't want to go."

"You're goin'," Sam said, roaring suddenly. "I already made arrangements. You can sleep in the back of Olsen's Livery Stable durin' the week."

Kaneha wasn't quite sure she understood what her husband was saying. "What is this?" she asked in Kiowa.

Sam answered in the same language. "A source of big knowledge. Without it, our son can never be a great chief among the White Eyes."

This was enough reason for Kaneha. "He will go," she said simply. Big knowledge meant big medicine. She went back to her stove.

The next Monday, Sam brought Max over to the school. The teacher, an impoverished Southern lady, came to the door and smiled at Sam.

"Good morning, Mr. Sand," she said.

"Good mornin', ma'am. I brought my son to school."

The teacher looked at him, then at Max, then around the yard in front of the school cabin. "Where is he?" she asked in a puzzled voice.

Sam pushed Max forward. Max stumbled slightly and looked up at the teacher. "Say howdy to yer teacher," Sam said.

Max, uncomfortable in his clean buckskin shirt and leggings, dug his bare feet into the dirt and spoke shyly. "Howdy, ma'am."

The teacher looked down at him in stunned surprise. Her nose wrinkled up in disgust. "Why, he's an Indian!" she cried. "We don't take Indians in this school."

Sam stared at her. "He's my son, ma'am."

The teacher curled her lip cuttingly. "We don't take halfbreeds in this school, either. This school is for white children only." She began to turn her back.

Sam's voice stopped her. It was icy cold as he made probably the longest speech he ever made in his life. "I don't know nothin' about your religion, ma'am, nor do I mind how you believe. All I do know is you're two thousand miles from Virginia an' you took my ten dollars to teach my boy the same as you took the money from ever'body else at the meetin' in the general store. If you're not goin' to learn him the way you agreed, you better take the next stage back East."

The teacher stared at him indignantly. "Mr. Sand, how dare you talk to me like that? Do you think the parents of the other children would want them to attend school with your son?"

"They were all at that meetin'," Sam said. "I didn't hear none of them say no."

The teacher looked at him. Sam could see the fight go out of her. "I'll never understand you Westerners," she said helplessly.

She looked down at Max disapprovingly. "At any rate, we can't have him in school in those clothes. He'll have to wear proper clothes like the other children."

"Yes, ma'am," Sam said. He turned to Max. "Come on," he said. "We're goin' to the store to get you regular clothes."

"While you're at it," she said, "get him a haircut. That way, he won't seem any different from the others."

Sam nodded. He knew what she meant. "I will, ma'am," he said. "Thank you, ma'am."

Max trotted along beside him as they strode down toward the general store. He looked up at his father. It was the first time he had thought about it. "Am I different than the others, Pa?"

Sam looked down at him. It was the first time he'd thought about it, too. A sudden sadness came into him. He knelt down in the dust of the street beside his son. He spoke with the sudden knowledge that came from living off the earth.

"Of course you're different," he said, looking into Max's eyes. "Everybody in this world is different, like there are no two buffalo alike or no two mules. Everybody is alike an' yet everybody is different."

By the end of Max's first year in school, the teacher was very proud of him. Much to her surprise, he had turned out to be her best pupil. His mind was quick and bright and he learned easily. When the term ended, she made sure to get Sam's promise that his son would return in the fall.

When the school closed down for the summer, Max brought his clothing back from Olsens' and settled down. During that first week, he was kept busy repairing all the damage done to the cabin by the winter.

One evening, after Max had gone to bed, Kaneha turned to her husband. "Sam," she said in English.

Sam almost dropped the leather harness on which he had been working. It was the first time in all their years together that she had called him by name.

Kaneha felt the blood rush into her face. She wondered at her temerity. Squaws never spoke to their husband except in reply. She looked down at the floor in front of her. "It is true that our son has done well in the school of the White Eyes?"

She could feel his gaze boring into her. "It's true," she heard his voice reply.

"I am proud of our son," she said, lapsing into Kiowa. "And I am grateful to his father, who is a mighty hunter and great provider."

"Yes?" Sam asked, still watching.

"While it is true that our son learns many things in the school of the White Eyes that make mighty medicine, there are things also that he learns that disturb him greatly."

"Such as?" Sam asked gently.

She looked up into his face proudly. "There are some among the White Eyes who say to our son that he is less than they, that his blood does not run red like theirs."

Sam's lips tightened. He wondered how she would know this. She never came into town, she never left the place. He felt a vague guilt stir inside him. "They are stupid children," he said.

"I know," she said simply.

He reached out his hand and touched her cheek gratefully. She caught his hand and held it to her cheek. "I think it is time we send our son to the tents of the mighty chief, his grandfather, so that he may learn the true strength of his blood."

Sam looked into her face. In many ways, it was a wise suggestion. In one summer with the Kiowa, Max would learn all the things he needed to survive in this land. He would also learn that he came from a family that could trace its blood further back than any of the jackals who tormented him. He nodded. "I will take our son to the tents of my brothers, the Kiowa," he said.

He looked at her again. He was now fifty-two and she was little more than half his age. She was still straight and slim and strong; she had never run to fat the way Indian women usually did. He felt his heart begin to swell inside him.

He let the harness drop from his hand and he drew her head down to his chest. His hand stroked her hair gently. Suddenly he knew what he had felt deep inside him all these years. He turned her face up to him. "I love you, Kaneha," he said.

Her eyes were dark and filled with tears. "I love you, my husband."

And for the first time, he kissed her on the mouth.

CHAPTER FOUR

IT WAS ABOUT TWO O'CLOCK ON A SATURDAY AFTERNOON THREE SUMMERS later when Max stood on a wagon in the yard back of Olsen's Livery Stable, pitching hay up into the open loft over his head. He was naked above his buckskin breeches and his body was burnt a coppery black by the blazing sun that hung overhead. The muscles rippled easily in his back as be forked the hay up from the wagon.

The three men came riding into the yard and pulled their horses up near the wagon. They did not dismount but sat there, looking at him.

Max did not interrupt his work and after a moment, one of them spoke. "Hey, Injun," he said. "Where is the Sand boy?"

Max threw another forkful into the loft. Then he sank the pitchfork into the hay and looked down at them. "I'm Max Sand," he said easily, resting on the fork handle.

The men exchanged meaningful looks. "We're lookin' fer yer pappy," the man who had spoken before said.

Max stared at them without answering. His blue eyes were dark and unreadable.

"We were over at the stage line but the place was closed. There was a sign there that said your pappy hauled freight."

"That's right," Max said. "But this is Saturday afternoon an' he's gone home."

One of the others pushed forward. "We got a wagonload of freight we got to get over to Virginia City," he said. "We're in a hurry. We'd like to talk to him."

Max picked up the pitchfork again. He tossed another forkful of hay into the loft. "I'll tell him when I get home tonight."

"We cain't wait that long," the first man said. "We want to make the deal and get on out of here tonight. How do we find your place?"

Max looked at them curiously. They didn't look like settlers or miners or the usual run of people that had freight for his father to haul. They looked more like gunmen or drifters, the way they sat there with their guns tied low on their legs, their hats shading their faces.

"I'll be th'ough here in a couple of hours," Max said. "I'll take you out there."

"I said we was in a hurry, boy. Your pappy won't like it none if he hears we gave our load to somebody else."

Max shrugged his shoulders. "Follow the north road out about twenty miles."

Without another word the three turned their horses around and began to ride out of the yard. Their voices floated back on the lazy breeze.

"Yuh'd think with all the dough ol' Sand's got buried, he'd do better than bein' a squaw man," one of them said.

Max heard the others laugh as he angrily pitched hay up into the loft.

It was Kaneha who heard them first. Her ears were turned to the road every Saturday afternoon for it was then that Max came home from school. She went to the door and opened it. "Three men come," she said, looking out.

Sam got up from the table and walked behind her and looked out. "Yeah," he said, "I wonder what they want."

Kaneha had a premonition of danger. "Bolt the door and do not let them enter," she said. "They ride silently like Apache on the warpath, not open like honest men."

Sam laughed. "You're just not used to seein' people," he said. "They're probably jus' lookin' for the way to town."

"They come from the direction of town," Kaneha said. But it was too late. He was already outside the door.

"Howdy," he called as they pulled their horses up in front of the cabin.

"You Sam Sand?" the one in the lead asked.

Sam nodded. "That's me. Whut kin I do for you gents?"

"We got a load we want hauled up to Virginia City," the man said. He took off his hat and wiped his face on his sleeve. "It's pow'ful hot today."

"It shore is," Sam nodded. "Come on inside and cool off a bit while we talk about it."

The men dismounted and Sam walked into the cabin.

"Fetch a bottle of whisky," he said to Kaneha. He turned back to the men. "Set yourself down. What kind'a freight yuh got?"

"Gold."

"Gold?" Sam asked. "They ain't enough gold out heah to haul in a wagon."

"That ain't what we hear," one of the men said. Suddenly there were guns in their hands. "We hear you got enough gold buried out heah to fill up a wagon."

Sam stared at them for a moment, then he laughed. "Put your guns away, gents," he said. "Yuh don' believe that crazy yarn, do yuh?"

The first man came slowly toward him. His arm flashed and the gun whipped across Sam's face. Sam fell backward against the wall. He stared up at the man incredulously.

"Yuh'll tell us where it is befo' we through," the man said tightly.

The air in the cabin was almost unbearably hot. The three men had drawn off into a corner and were whispering among themselves. Occasionally they would glance across the room at their captives.

Sam hung limply, tied to the support post in the center of the cabin. His head sagged down on his naked chest and the blood dropped down his face, matting on the graying red hair of his beard and chest. His eyes were swollen and almost closed, his nose broken and squashed against his cheek.

Kaneha was tied in a chair. Her eyes were fixed unblinkingly on her husband. She strained to turn her head to hear what the men were saying behind her but she could not move, she was bound too tightly.

"Mebbe he ain't really got the gold," one of the men whispered.

"He's got it all right," the first one said. "He's jus' tough. Yuh don' know them ol' buffalo hunters like I do."

"Well, you ain't never goin' to make him talk the way yuh're goin'," the short man said. "He's gonna die first."

"He'll talk," the first man answered. He went to the stove and took a burning coal from it with a pair of fire tongs. He walked back to Sam and pulled his head back against the post by his hair. He held the tongs in front of Sam's face. "Wheah's the gold?"

Sam's eyes were open. His voice was a husky croak. "They ain't none. For God's sake wouldn't I tell yuh if they was?"

The man pressed the burning coal against Sam's neck and shoulder. Sam screamed in pain. "They ain't no gold!" His head fell sideways. The man withdrew the burning coal and the blood welled up beneath the scorched flesh and ran down his chest and arm.

The man picked up a bottle of whisky from the table and took a swig from it. "Th'ow some water on him," he said. "If'n he won't talk for hisself, mebbe he'll talk for his squaw."

The youngest man picked up a pail and threw water over Sam. Sam shook his head and opened his eyes. He stared at them.

The oldest man put the bottle down and walked over to Kaneha. He took a hunting knife from his belt. The other men's eyes followed him. He cut the rope that bound her to the chair. "On yer feet," he said harshly.

Silently Kaneha rose. The man's knife moved quickly behind her and her shift fell to the floor. She stood there naked before them. The youngest man licked his lips. He reached for the whisky and took a drink, his eyes never leaving her.

Holding Kaneha by the hair, his knife to her back, the oldest man pushed her over toward Sam. They stopped in front of him.

"It's been fifteen years since I skinned an Injun, squaw man," he said. "But I ain't fergot how." He moved swiftly around in front of her, his knife moving lightly up and down her skin.

A faint thin line of blood appeared where the knife had traced from under her chin down her throat through the valley between her breasts across her stomach and coming to a stop in the foliage of her pubis.

Sam began to cry, his own pain forgotten, his body wracked with bitter sobs. "Leave her be," he pleaded. "Please leave her be. They ain't no gold."

Kaneha reached out her hand. She touched her husband's face gently. "I am not afraid, my husband," she said in Kiowa. "The spirits will return evil to those who bring it."

Sam's face fell forward, the tears running down from his eyes across his bearded and bleeding cheeks. "I am sorry, my dear one," he said in Kiowa.

"Tie her hands to the legs of that table," the older man commanded.

It was done quickly and he knelt over her, his knife poised at her throat. He looked back up toward Sam. "The gold?" he asked.

Sam shook his head. He could not speak any more.

"My God," the youngest man said in a wondering voice. "I'm gittin' a hard on."

"That's an idee," the man with the knife said. He looked up at Sam. "I'm shoah the man wouldn' min' if'n we used his squaw a little bit before we skinned her. Injuns are downright hospitable that way."

He got to his feet. He put the knife on the table and unbuckled his gun belt. Kaneha drew back her legs and kicked at him.

He swore softly. "Hold her laigs," he said. "I'll go first."

It was almost seven o'clock when Max rode up to the cabin on the bay horse that Olsen lent him. The cabin was still and there was no smoke coming from the chimney. That was strange. Usually, his mother would be cooking when he got home.

He swung down off the horse and started for the cabin. He stopped suddenly, staring at it. The door was open and moved lazily in the thin breeze. An inexplicable fear came into him and he broke into a run.

He burst through the door and came to a stop in surprised shock, his eyes widening in horror. His father hung tied to the center post, his mouth and eyes open in death, the back of his head blown away by the .45 that had been placed in his mouth and fired.

Slowly Max's eyes went down to the floor. There was a shapeless mass lying in a pool of blood, which bore the outline of what once had been his mother.

The paralysis left him at the same moment he started to scream, but the vomit that rose in his throat choked off the sound. Again and again he gagged until there was no more inside him. He clung weakly to the side of the door, the sour stench from his stomach all around.

He turned and staggered blindly out of the cabin. He sank to the ground outside and began to cry. After a while, his tears were gone. He rose to his feet wearily and walked around to the back of the house to the watering trough.

He plunged his head in and washed the vomit from his face and clothing. Then, still dripping, he straightened up and looked around.

His father's horse was gone but the six mules were browsing unconcernedly in the corral and the wagon was still under the lean-to in back of the cabin. The four sheep and the chickens of which his mother had been so proud were still in the pen.

He wiped his arms across his eyes. He had to do something, he thought vaguely. But he couldn't bring himself to bury what was in the cabin. They weren't his mother and father; his parents could never look like that. There was only one thing to do.

He walked over to the stack of firewood and gathered up an armful. Then he walked back into the house and put it down on the floor. It took him almost a half hour until firewood lay covering the floor like a blanket, three layers thick. He looked at it thoughtfully for a moment then turned and went outside again.

He took the harness down from the lean-to wall and hitched the mules up to the wagon. He picked up a crate and went through the pen, throwing all the chickens into it. He placed the crate in the wagon. Then one by one, he lifted the sheep into the wagon and tied them to the floor rings.

He led the team of mules and the wagon around to the front of the cabin and tied the bay horse's lead to the back of the wagon. Then he walked them all to the road about two hundred yards from the house and tethered the team to a small scrub tree and went back to the house.

He picked up the pitch bucket and went inside. Slowly he smeared the pitch over the firewood that lay on the floor. He kept his eyes down and away from the bodies of his parents. He stopped at the door and smeared the last of the pitch on that.

He hesitated a moment, then remembering something, he went back into the cabin. He reached up on the shelf where his father had kept his rifle and pistol but they were not there. He pushed his hand farther along the shelf and felt something soft. He took it down.

It was a new buckskin shirt and breeches his mother had made for him. It was bright and soft and clean-chamois colored. Again his eyes filled with sudden tears. He rolled it up under his arm and went back to the door.

He held a match to the pitch stick until it was blazing brightly. After holding it for a second more to make sure, he threw it into the cabin and stepped back from the open door.

He looked up at the sky in sudden surprise. The sun had just gone down and night had fallen in quick anger. The stars stared balefully down on him.

A cloud of heavy, billowing smoke poured out of the doorway. Suddenly, there was a crack like thunder and a flame leaped through the doorway as the tinder-dry wood caught fire.

He walked down to the road and got up on the wagon and began to drive to town. He did not look back until three miles later, when he reached the top of a small rise.

There was a bright-orange flame reaching high into the sky where his home had been.

CHAPTER FIVE

HE DROVE THE WAGON INTO THE YARD BEHIND OLSEN'S LIVERY STABLE. Then he got down and walked across to the house that stood next to it. He climbed up the back steps and knocked at the door.

"Mister Olsen," he called out.

A shadow darkened the light of the window. The door opened and Olsen stood there. "Max!" he said. "What you doin' back here?"

Max stared up into Olsen's face. "They killed my ma and pa," he said.

"Killed? " Olsen exclaimed in surprise. "Who killed?"

Attracted by the sound of her husband's voice, Mrs. Olsen appeared in the doorway behind him.

"The three men," Max said. "They asked me an' I gave them the directions to my house. An' they killed 'em." He hesitated a moment and his voice almost broke. "An' they stole Pa's hoss an' took his rifle an' pistol, too."

Mrs. Olsen saw into the shock that lay behind the boy's façade of calm. She pushed her husband out of the way and reached out to Max. "You come inside an' let me fix you somethin' hot to drink," she said.

He looked into her eyes. "They ain't time, ma'am," he said. "I got to be gettin' after them." He turned to Olsen. "I got the mules an' the wagon an' four sheep an' sixteen chickens outside in the yard. Would you give me a hundred dollars an' the pinto for 'em?"

Olsen nodded. "Why, sure, boy," he said. The mules and the wagon alone were worth three times that. "I'll even give you the big bay if you want. He's a better hoss. An' I'll throw in a saddle, too."

Max shook his head. "No, thank you, Mr. Olsen. I want a pony I can ride without a saddle an' one that's used to the plains. He won't have as much to tote an' I'll move faster that way."

"All right, if that's the way you want it."

"Can I have the money now?" Max asked.

"Sure, boy," Olsen answered. He turned back into the room.

Mrs. Olsen's voice stopped him. "Oh, no, you're not," she said. She drew Max into the house firmly. "First, he's goin' to eat something. Then he's goin' to sleep. Time enough in the morning for him to start."

"But they'll be further away by then," Max protested.

"No they won't," she said with woman's logic. "They got to stop to sleep, too. They won't be any further ahead of you then than they are right now."

She closed the door behind him and led him over to the table. She pushed him into a chair and placed a plate of soup in front of him. Automatically he began to eat.

"I'll go outside an' unhitch the team," Mr. Olsen said.

When he came back into the house, Max was sleeping, his head resting in his crossed arms on the table.

Mrs. Olsen gestured her husband to silence. "You just can't let him go after those men by himself," she whispered.

"I got to go, ma'am." Max's voice came over her shoulder.

She turned around and looked at him. "You can't," she cried out. "They're grown men an' they'll hurt you. Why, you're just a boy!"

He looked up into her face and she was aware for the first time of the pride that glowed deep in those dark-blue eyes. "They hurt me all they're goin' to, ma'am," he said. "I'm 'bout sixteen, an' with my mother's people, a boy ain't a boy no more once he's sixteen. He's a man."

On his second day out of Dodge, he slowed his pinto to a walk and studied the side of the road carefully. After a few minutes, he stopped and dismounted. He looked along the edge of the road carefully.

The four horses had stopped here. They had milled around for a little while and then two of them had gone back onto the road toward Virginia City. The other two had gone eastward across the plains.

He remounted and rode along the plains, his eyes searching out the trail until he found what he was looking for. One of the horses had been his father's. He recognized the shoe marking in the soft earth. It was lighter than the other marking, which meant he was not being ridden, but led. It also meant that the man up ahead must have been the leader, otherwise they wouldn't have let him take the horse, which was the most valuable thing they had stolen.

A few miles farther along the trail, he saw some horse droppings. He stopped his horse and jumped down. He kicked at the dung with his foot. It was not more than seven hours old. They had wasted more time along the trail than he'd thought they would. He got back on the pinto and pushed on.

He rode most of that night, following the trail in the bright moonlight. By the evening of the next day, he was less than an hour behind his quarry.

He looked up at the sky. It was about seven o'clock and would be dark soon. The man would be stopping to make camp if he hadn't already. Max got off his horse and waited for night to fall.

While he sat there, he cut a forked branch from a scrub tree and fitted a round stone onto it. Then he bound the stone to the crotch with thin strips of leather, winding them down the branch to make a handle. When he was finished, he had a war club as good as any he'd learned to make the summer he spent with the Kiowa.

It was dark then and he got to his feet, fastening the club to his belt. He took the horse by the halter and started forward cautiously on foot.

He walked slowly, his ears alert for any strange sound, his nostrils sniffing at the breeze for the scent of a campfire.

He was in luck, for he caught the scent of the campfire from about a quarter mile away. He tied the pinto to a bush and pulled the rifle from the pack on the horse's back. Silently he moved forward.

The whinny of a horse came to his ears and he dropped to the ground and peered forward. He figured the horses were tied about three hundred yards ahead of him. He looked for the campfire but couldn't find it.

Cautiously he made his way downwind from the horses in a wide circle. The smell of the campfire was strong in his nostrils now. He raised his head from the tall plain grass. The campfire was about two hundred yards in front of him. He could see the man, sitting hunched over it, eating from a frying pan. The man was no fool. He had picked a camp site between two rocks. That way, he could be approached only from in front.

Max sank back into the grass. He would have to wait until the man was asleep. He stretched out and looked up at the sky. When the moon was up, a few hours from now, it would be time for him to move. Until then, it would do no harm for him to rest. He closed his eyes. In a moment, he was sleeping soundly.

His eyes opened suddenly and he stared straight up at the moon. It hung white and high in the sky over him. He sat up slowly and peered over the grass.

The campfire was glowing faintly now, dying slowly. He could see the shadow of the man lying near the rocks. He started to inch forward. The man snored lightly and turned in his sleep. Max froze for a moment, then the figure was still again and Max inched forward a little farther. He could see the man's outstretched hand, a gun at the tip of the fingers.

He crawled around behind and picked up a small pebble from the ground beside him. Silently he took the war club from his belt and got up into a half crouch. Holding his breath in tightly, he threw the stone near the man's feet.

With a muttered curse, he sat up, looking forward, his gun in his hand. He never knew what hit him as Max brought the war club down on his head from behind.

Max came back with the pinto about the time that dawn was breaking in the east. He tied his horse to the scrub near the others and walked back to look at the man.

His eyes were still closed. He was breathing evenly though there was a smear of blood along his cheek and ear where the club had caught him. He lay naked on his back on the ground, his arms and legs outstretched tautly, staked to the ground.

Max sat down on the rock and began to whet his knife along its smooth surface. When the sun came up, the man opened his eyes. They were dull at first, then gradually they began to clear. He tried to sit up and became aware that he was tied down. He twisted his head and looked at Max.

"What's the idee?" he asked.

Max stared at him. He didn't stop whetting his knife. "I'm Max Sand," he said. "Remember me?"

Max walked over to him. He stood there looking down, the knife held loosely in his hand. There was a sick feeling inside him as he looked at the man and pictured what must have happened in the cabin. The image chased the feeling from him. When he spoke, his voice was calm and emotionless. "Why did you kill my folks?"

"I didn't do nothing to them," the man said, his eyes watching the knife.

"You got my pa's hoss out there."

"He sol' it to me," the man replied.

"Pa wouldn' sell the on'y hoss he had," Max said.

"Let me up outa here," the man screamed suddenly.

Max held the knife to the man's throat. "You want to tell me what happened?"

"The others did it!" the man screamed. "I had nothin' to do with it. They wanted the gold!" His eyes bugged out hysterically. In his fear, he began to urinate, the water trickling down his bare legs. "Le' me go, you crazy Injun bastard!" he screamed.

Max moved swiftly now. All the hesitation that he had felt was gone. He was the son of Red Beard and Kaneha and inside him was the terrible vengeance of the Indian. His knife flashed bright in the morning sun and when he straightened up the man was silent.

Max looked down impassively. The man had only fainted, even though his eyes stared upward, open and unseeing. His eyelids had been slit so they could never again be closed and the flesh hung like strips of ribbon down his body from his shoulders to his thighs.

Max turned and walked until he found an anthill. He scooped the top of it up in his hands and went back to the man. Carefully he set it down on the man's pubis. In a moment, the tiny red ants were everywhere on the man. They ran into all the blood-sweetened crevices of his body, up across his eyes and into his open mouth and nostrils.

The man began to cough and moan. His body stirred. Silently Max watched him. This was the Indian punishment for a thief, rapist and murderer.

It took the man three days to die. Three days of the blazing sun burning into his open eyes and blistering his torn flesh while the ants industriously foraged his body. Three days of screaming for water and three nights of agony as insects and mosquitoes, drawn by the scent of blood, came to feast upon him.

At the end, he was out of his mind, and on the fourth morning, when Max came down to look at him, he was dead. Max stared at him for a moment, then took out his knife and lifted his scalp.

He went back to the horses and mounted his pinto. Leading the other two animals, he turned and rode north toward the land of the Kiowa.

The old chief, his grandfather, came out of his tepee to watch him as he dismounted. He waited silently until Max came up to him.

Max looked into the eyes of the old man. "I come in sadness to the tents of my people," he said in Kiowa.

The chief did not speak.

"My father and mother are dead," he continued.

The chief still did not speak.

Max reached to his belt and took off the scalp that hung there. He threw it down in front of the chief. "I have taken the scalp of one of the murderers," he said. "And I come to the tent of my grandfather, the mighty chief, to spend the time of my sorrow."

The chief looked down at the scalp, then up at Max. "We are no longer free to roam the plains," he said. "We live on the land that the White Eyes allow us. Have any of them seen you as you approached?"

"None saw me," Max answered. "I came from the hills behind them."

The chief looked down at the scalp again. It had been a long time since the scalp of an enemy hung from the post before his tepee. His heart swelled with pride. He looked at Max. The White Eyes could imprison the bodies but they could not imprison the spirit. He picked up the scalp and hung it from the post then turned back to Max.

"A tree has many branches," he said slowly. "And when some branches fall or are cut down, other branches must be grown to take their place so their spirits may find where to live."

He took a feather from his headdress and held it toward Max. "There is a maiden whose brave was killed in a fall from his horse two suns ago. She had already taken the marriage stick and now must live alone in a tent by the river until his spirit is replaced in her. Go now and take her."

Max stared at him. "Now?" he asked.

The chief thrust the feather into his hand. "Now," he said, with the knowledge of all his years. "It is the best time, while the spirit of war and vengeance still rages like a torrent in your blood. It is the best time to take a woman."

Max turned and picked up the lead and walked down through the camp with the horses. The Indians watched him silently as he passed by. He walked slowly with his head held high. He reached the bank of the small river and followed it around a bend.

A single tent stood there, out of sight of the rest of the camp. Max walked toward it. He tied the horses to some shrubs and lifted the flap of the tent and walked in.

The tent was empty. He lifted the flap again and looked out. There was no one in sight. He let the flap down. He walked to the back of the tent and sat down on a bed of skins stretched out on the floor.

A moment later the girl came in. Her hair and body were wet from the river and her dress clung to her. Her eyes went wide as she saw him. She stood there poised for flight.

She wasn't much more than a child, Max saw. Fourteen, maybe fifteen at the most. Suddenly he knew why the chief had sent him down here. He picked up the feather and held it toward her. "Don't be afraid," he said gently. "The mighty chief has put us together so that we may drive the devils from each other."

CHAPTER SIX

ASTRIDE THE WIRY PINTO, MAX CAME DOWN THE RAMP FROM THE RAIL-road car behind the last of the cattle. He waited a moment until the last steer had entered the stockyard and then dropped the gate behind it. He took off his hat and wiped the sweat from his forehead on his sleeve and looked up at the sun.

It hung almost overhead, white hot, baking into the late spring dust of the yards. The cattle lowed softly as if somehow they, too, knew they had come to the end of the road. The long road that led up from Texas, to a railroad that took them to Kansas City, and their impending doom.

Max put the hat back on his head and squinted down the fence to where the boss sat with the cattle-buyers. He rode down toward them.

Farrar turned as he stopped his horse beside them. "They all in?"

"They all in, Mr. Farrar," Max answered.

"Good," Farrar said. He turned to one of the cattle-buyers. "The count O.K.? Eleven hundred and ten head I make it."

"I make it the same," the buyer said.

Farrar got down from the fence. "I'll come over to your office this afternoon to pick up the check."

The buyer nodded. "It'll be ready."

Farrar got up on his horse. "C'mon, kid," he said over his shoulder. "Let's get over to the hotel and wash some of this steer-shit stink off'n us."

"Man," Farrar said, after a bath. "I feel twenty pounds lighter."

Max straightened up from putting on his boots and turned around. "Yeah," he said. "Me, too."

Farrar's eyes widened and he whistled. Max had on an almost white buckskin shirt and breeches. His high-heeled cowboy boots were polished to a mirror-like sheen and the kerchief around his throat was like a sparkle of yellow gold against his dark, sun-stained skin. His hair, almost blue black, hung long to his shoulders.

Farrar whistled again. "Man, where'd you get them clothes?"

Max smiled. "It was the last set my ma made for me."

Farrar laughed. "Well, you shore enough look Injun with them on."

Max smiled with him. "I am Indian," he said quietly.

Farrar's laughter disappeared quickly. "Half Indian, kid," he said. "Your pappy was white and he was a good man. I hunted with Sam Sand too many years to hear you not proud of him."

"I am proud of him, Mr. Farrar," Max said. "But I still remember it was white men killed him an' Ma."

He picked his gun belt up from the chair and strapped it on. Farrar watched him bend over to tie the holster to his thigh. "You still ain't give up lookin' for them?" he asked.

Max looked up. "No, sir, I ain't."

"Kansas City's a big place," Farrar said. "How you know you'll find him here?"

"If he's here, I'll find him," Max answered. "This is where he's supposed to be. Then I'll go down into West Texas an' get the other one."

Farrar was silent for a moment. "Well, dressed like that, you better look out he don't recognize you and find you first."

"I'm hopin' he does," Max said quietly. "I want him to know what he's dyin' for."

Farrar turned away from the bleak look in the boy's eyes and picked up a shirt. Max waited quietly for him to finish dressing. "I'll pick up my time now, Mr. Farrar," he said when the man had pulled on his trousers.

Farrar walked over to the dresser and picked up his poke. "There you are," he said. "Four months' pay—eighty dollars—an' the sixty dollars you won at poker."

Max put the money in a back pocket without counting it. "Thanks, Mr. Farrar."

"Sure I can't talk you into comin' back with me?" Farrar asked.

"No, thank you, Mr. Farrar."

"You can't keep all that hate in your soul, boy," the older man said. "It ain't healthy. You'll only wind up harmin' yourself."

"I can't help that, Mr. Farrar," Max said slowly. His eyes were empty and cold. "I can't ferget it's the same breast that fed me that bastard's usin' to keep his tobacco in."

The door closed behind him and Farrar stood there staring at it.

Mary Grady smiled at the boy. "Finish your whisky," she said, "while I get my dress off."

The boy watched her for a moment, then drank the whisky quickly. He coughed as he went over to the edge of the bed and sat down.

Mary looked over at him as she slipped the dress up over her head. "How are you feelin'?"

The boy looked at her. She could see the vagueness already in his eyes. "All ri', I guess," he answered. "I ain' used to drinkin' so much."

She came over and stood looking down at him, her dress over her arm. "Stretch out and shut your eyes. You'll be all right in a few minutes."

He looked up at her dumbly, without response.

She put out her hand and pushed his shoulder. A hint of awareness sparked in his eyes. He tried to get to his feet, his hand locked around the butt of his gun, but the effort was too much. He collapsed, falling sideways across the bed.

Expertly Mary bent over him and lifted his eyelid. The boy was out cold. She smiled to herself and crossing to the window, looked out into the street.

Her pimp was standing across the street in front of a saloon. She raised and lowered the shade twice in the agreed signal and he started toward the hotel.

She was dressed by the time he got up to the room. "You took long enough gettin' him up here," he said surlily.

"What could I do?" she said. "He wouldn't drink. He's just a kid."

"How much did he have on him?" the pimp asked.

"I don't know," Mary answered. "The money's in his back pocket Get it an' let's get out of here. This hotel always gives me the creeps."

The pimp crossed to the bed and pulled the money out of the boy's back pocket. He counted it swiftly. "A hundred and thirty dollars," he said.

Mary went over to him and put her arms around him. "A hundred and thirty dollars. Maybe we can take the night off now," she said, kissing his chin. "We could go over to my place and have a whole night together."

The pimp looked down at her. "What? Are you crazy?" he rasped. "It's only eleven o'clock. You can turn three more tricks tonight."

He turned to look down at the boy while she picked up her pocketbook. "Don't forget the bottle of whisky," he said over his shoulder.

"I won't," she answered.

"He don't look like no cowboy," he said. "He looks more like an Indian to me."

"He is," she said. "He was looking for some guy who had a tobacco pouch made from an Indian woman's skin." She laughed. "I don't think he even wanted to get laid. I got him up here by lettin' him think I knew who he was lookin' for."

The pimp looked down thoughtfully. "He's carryin' a gun, too. It should be worth somethin' to the guy he's lookin' for to know about him."

"You know who he's lookin' for?"

"Maybe," the pimp said. "C'mon."

It was almost two o'clock in the morning before the pimp found the man he was looking for. He was playing cards in the back of the Golden Eagle.

The pimp touched him on the shoulder cautiously. "Mr. Dort," he whispered.

"What the hell do you want?"

The pimp licked his lips nervously. "I'm sorry, Mr. Dort," he apologized quickly. "I got some information that I think you ought to have."

The pimp looked around the table nervously. The other men stared at him. "Maybe it's better private like, Mr. Dort," he said. "It's about that tobacco pouch."

He pointed to the table where it lay.

Dort laughed. "My Injun-tit tobacco pouch? Somebody's allus tryin' to buy it. It ain't for sale."

"It's not that, Mr. Dort," the pimp whispered.

Dort turned his back to him. "What the hell are you tryin' to tell me?"

"I figger it's worth somethin'—"

Dort rose swiftly. He grabbed the pimp's jacket and slammed him tightly against the wall. "What should I know?" he asked.

"It should be worth something, Mr. Dort," the pimp said, his eyes wide in fright. Dort was one of the worst killers in town.

"It'll be worth something," Dort said menacingly. "If you don't talk real quick—"

"There's an Indian kid in town lookin' for you," the pimp said in terror. "He's packin' a gun."

"An Injun kid?" Dort questioned. Slowly his grip relaxed. "What did he look like?"

Quickly the pimp described Max.

"His eyes, was they blue?" Dort asked harshly.

The pimp nodded. "Yeah. I saw them when he picked one of my girls up in the saloon. That's how come I didn't know he was Indian at first. You know him?"

Dort nodded without thinking. "I know him," he said. "That was his mother's."

All their eyes were on the tobacco pouch now. Dort picked it up and put it in his pocket.

"What're you goin' to do?" the pimp asked.

"Do?" Dort repeated dully. He looked at the pimp, then at the table of men around him. He couldn't run away now. If he did, everything would be gone. His reputation, his position in this oblique society.

"Do?" he said again, this time with growing strength and conviction. "I aim to do what I shoulda done a year ago. Kill him." He turned back to the pimp. "Where is he?"

"I'll take you to him," the pimp said eagerly.

The others at the table looked at each other for a moment, then silently got to their feet. "Wait for us, Tom," one of them called. "This oughta be some fun."

When they got to the hotel, Max had already left. But the hotel clerk told them where they could find him tomorrow. At the stockyards at two o'clock. The clerk was supposed to meet him there and collect a dollar for the room.

Dort threw a silver dollar on the counter. "There's your dollar," he said. "I'll collect it for you."

Farrar leaned against the fence, watching Max cut the prime steers into the feed pen. A man was leaning on the fence next to him. "That boy's got a sixth sense with a horse," Farrar said, without looking at him.

The man's voice was noncommittal. "Yeah." He finished rolling a cigarette and stuck it in his mouth. "Got a match?"

"Why, sure," Farrar said, reaching into his pocket. He struck a match and held it toward the man. His hand froze as he saw the tobacco pouch in his hand.

The man followed his gaze. "What you lookin' at?"

"That tobacco pouch," Farrar said. "I ain't seen nothin' like it."

The man laughed. "Ain't nothin' but an ol' squaw tit," he said. "They the best things for keepin' tobacco moist an' fresh. They ain't much for wear, though. This one's gettin' awful thin."

Suddenly, Farrar turned from the fence to signal Max. "I wouldn't do that if I were you," the man said.

There was a rustle of movement behind him and Farrar became aware of the other men. He watched helplessly as Max dropped the gate on the last of the steers and rode over to them.

Max got off his horse and tied it to a post. "All finished, Mr. Farrar," he said with a smile.

"That was good ridin', boy," the man said. He threw the tobacco pouch to Max. "Here, have yourself a smoke."

Max caught it easily. "Thanks, mister," he said. He looked down at the pouch to open it. He looked up at the man, then down at the pouch again, his face going pale.

The pouch fell from his fingers and the tobacco spilled onto the ground. He stared up at the man. "I never would've known you, you hadn't done that," he said softly.

Dort laughed harshly. "It's the beard, I reckon."

Max started to back away slowly. "You're one of them, all right. Now I recognize you."

"I'm one of them," Dort said, his hand hovering over his gun. "What're you goin' to do about it?"

Unconsciously Farrar and the others moved to the side. "Don't do anything, Max," Farrar called hoarsely. "That's Tom Dort. You got no idea how fast he is."

Max didn't take his eyes from Dort's face. "It don't make no difference how fast he is, Mr. Farrar," he said. "I'm goin' to kill him."

"Go for your gun, Injun," Dort said heavily.

"I'll wait," Max said softly. "I want you to die slow, like my ma."

Dort's face was turning red and flushed in the hot sun. "Draw," he said hoarsely. "Draw, you goddam half-breed son of a two-bit Injun whore. Draw, damn you!"

"I ain' in no hurry to kill you," Max answered softly. "I ain' even goin' for your head or heart. I'm goin' to shoot you in the balls first, then a couple of times in the belly. I wanna watch you die."

Dort began to feel fear growing in him. Out of the corner of his eye, he saw the watching men. He stared at Max. The boy's face shone with hatred; his lips were drawn back tightly across his teeth.

Now, Dort thought, now. I might just as well get it over with. His hand moved suddenly toward his gun.

Farrar saw the movement but fast as he shifted his eyes, it wasn't quick enough to see Max's gun leap into his hand. It roared almost before Dort's gun had cleared its holster.

The gun fell from Dort's hand and he sank to his knees in the dirt, his hands grabbing at his crotch.

Max started walking toward him slowly.

Dort kneeled there for a moment in almost a praying position, then lifted his hand and looked at it. The blood ran down from his fingers. He stared up at Max. "You son of a bitch!" he screamed and grabbed for the gun in the dirt beside him.

Max waited until Dort lifted the muzzle toward him, then he fired twice again.

The bullets threw Dort over backward and he lay on the ground, his body twitching slightly. Max walked closer and stood over him, looking down, the smoking gun still in his hand.

Two days later, Max was given his choice of joining the Army or standing trial. There was a lot of talk about a war with Cuba and the judge was very patriotic. The chances were Max could have got off on self-defense, but he didn't dare take the chance even with witnesses.

He had a date he had to keep, with a man whose name he didn't even know.

CHAPTER SEVEN

NEVADA STIRRED RESTLESSLY, WITH THE VAGUE FEELING THAT SOMEONE else was in the room with him. Automatically he reached for a cigarette, and when his hand hit empty air and fell downward against the side of the couch, he came awake.

It was a moment before he remembered where he was, then he swung his legs off the couch and reached for his pants. The cigarettes were in the right-hand pocket. He put one in his mouth and struck a match.

The flame flared in the darkness and he saw Rina sitting in the deep chair, looking at him. He drew deeply on the cigarette and blew out the match. "Why ain't you sleeping?" he asked.

She took a deep breath. "I couldn't sleep," she said. "I'm afraid."

He looked at her quizzically. "Afraid, Rina? Afraid of what?"

She didn't move in the chair. "I'm afraid of what will happen to me."

He laughed quietly, reassuringly. "You're all set and you're young. You got your whole life in front of you."

Her face was a luminous shadow in the darkness. "I know," she whispered. "That's what I tell myself. But the trouble is I can't make myself believe it."

Suddenly, she was on her knees on the floor in front of him. "You've got to help me, Nevada!"

He reached out and stroked her hair. "Things take time, Rina," he said.

Her hands caught at his. "You don't understand, Nevada," she said harshly. "I've always felt like this. Before I married Cord, before I ever came out here. Even when I was a little girl."

"I reckon, sometime or other, everyone's afraid, Rina."

Her voice was still hoarse with terror. "But not like me! I'm different. I'm going to die young of some horrible disease. I know that, Nevada. I feel it inside."

Nevada sat there quietly, his hand absently stroking her head as she cried. "Things'll be different once you get back East," he said softly. "There'll be young men there an—"

She raised her hand and looked up at him. The first faint flicker of morning light illuminated her features. Her eyes were wide and shining with her tears. "Young men, Nevada?" she asked and her voice seemed to fill with scorn. "They're one of the things I'm afraid of. Don't you think if I weren't, I'd have married Jonas instead of his father?"

He didn't answer.

"Young men are all alike," she continued. "They only want one thing from me." Her lips drew back across her white teeth and she spat the words out at him. "To fuck! To do nothing but fuck, fuck, fuck!"

He stared at her, a kind of shock running through him at hearing her clear and venomously ladylike articulation of the so familiar word. Then it was gone and he smiled.

"What do you expect, Rina?" he asked. "Why are you tellin' me all this?"

Her eyes looked into his face. "Because I want you to know me," she said. "I want you to understand what I'm like. No man ever has."

The cigarette scorched his lips. He put it out quickly. "Why me?"

"Because you're not a boy." The answer came quickly. "You're a grown man."

"An' you, Rina?" he asked.

Her eyes became almost defiant but her voice betrayed her unsureness. "I think I'm a lesbian."

He laughed.

"Don't laugh!" she said quickly. "It's not so crazy. I've been with girls and I've been with men. And I've never made it with a man, not with any man like I have with a girl." She laughed bitterly. "Men are such fools. It's so easy to make them believe what they want to. And I know all the tricks."

His male vanity was aroused. "Maybe that's because you ain't never come up against a real man."

A challenging note came into her voice. "Oh, no?" He felt her fingers lightly search his thighs beneath the blanket and find his phallus. Quickly she threw the blanket aside and pressed her head into his lap. He felt the movement of her lips, and suddenly he was angry.

He pulled her head back by the hair. "What're you tryin' to prove?" he asked harshly.

Her breath came hard and uneven. "That you're the man," she whispered. "The one man that can make me feel."

He stared at her, not answering.

"You are the one, Nevada," she whispered. "I know it. I can feel it down inside me. You can make me whole again. I'll never be afraid any more."

She turned her head again but his hand held her firm. Her eyes were wide and desperate. "Please, Nevada, please. Let me prove how I can love you!" She began to cry again.

Suddenly, he got to his feet and went over to the fireplace. He stirred the coals alive, fed them kindling and another log. A moment later, a crackling heat came sparkling into the room. He turned to look at her. She was still sitting on the floor in front of the couch, watching him.

Slowly he walked back toward her. "When I asked you up here, Rina, I thought I was doin' the right thing." He sat down and reached for a cigarette.

Before he could light it, she held a match for him. "Yes, Nevada?" she questioned softly.

The flame glowed in his eyes and died as the match went out. "I ain't the man you're lookin' for, Rina."

Her fingers touched lightly on his cheek. "No, Nevada," she said quickly. "That's not true."

"Mebbe not," he said and a slow smile came over his lips. "But I figger I'm too young. You see, all I want to do with you is—fuck, fuck, fuck!"

She stared at him for a moment and then she began to smile. She got up quickly and took the cigarette from his mouth. Her lips brushed fleetingly against his for a moment, then she walked to the fire and turned to face him. She put the cigarette between her lips and inhaled deeply.

Then she made a slight movement and the robe fell to the floor. The leaping fire turned her naked body into red gold. Swiftly she threw the cigarette into the fireplace behind her and started back toward him.

"Maybe it's better this way," she said, coming down into his outstretched arms. "Now we can be friends."

CHAPTER EIGHT

"THE SHOW'S IN TROUBLE," THE CASHIER SAID. Nevada glanced at Rina. She was looking out the window of the ticket wagon, watching the last act of the Wild-West show going on in the arena. The faint sounds of the whooping and yelling drifted back to them on the still, warm air.

"How much trouble?" Nevada asked, his eyes coming back from her.

"Enough," the cashier said flatly. "We're booked in a week behind Buffalo Bill Cody's show for the whole summer. If these two weeks are any indication, we'll drop forty thousand this season."

A bugle sounding a charge hung in the air. Nevada shifted in his uncomfortable wooden chair and began to roll a cigarette. The performance was almost over now. The cavalry was coming to the rescue of the beleaguered pioneers. He stuck the cigarette in his mouth.

"How'd you let a stupid thing like that happen?" he asked, the cigarette dangling unlit from his lips.

"Wasn't my fault, Nevada," the cashier answered quickly. "I think the agent sold us out."

Nevada didn't answer. He lit the cigarette.

"What you going to do?" the cashier asked worriedly.

Nevada filled his lungs with smoke. "Play out the season."

"For forty grand?" The cashier's voice was shocked. "We can't afford to lose that much money!"

Nevada studied him. The cashier's face was flushed and embarrassed. He wondered why the man seemed so upset. It wasn't his money that was going to be lost.

"We can't afford not to," Nevada said. "We fold up, we lose all our top hands. They won't sign with us for next year if we dump 'em now."

Nevada got to his feet, walked over to the window and looked out. The Indians were riding out of the arena with the whooping cavalry hot after them. He turned back to the cashier. "I'm takin' Mrs. Cord down to the railroad station. I'll drop in at the agent's office after that. You wait for me here. I'll be back."

"O.K., Nevada," the cashier answered.

Nevada took Rina's arm as they went down the wagon steps. They cut across the field to his car. All around them hustled performers, hurrying their horses to the corral, racing to their wagons to change clothes, yelling to each other about their plans for the evening.

Rina turned to him as they reached the car. "Let me stay with you, Nevada, please."

He smiled slowly. "I thought we had that settled."

"But, Nevada," Her eyes grew serious. "There's nothing for me back East. Really. Here, at least, I can feel alive, excitement—"

"Stop actin' like a kid," he said. "You're a grown woman now. This ain't no life for you. You'd be sick of it in a week."

"I'll buy half your losses this season if you let me stay," she said quickly.

He looked at her sharply. He thought she hadn't even heard the conversation back in the wagon, she had seemed so engrossed in the show. "You can't afford it," he said.

"And you can?" she countered.

"Better'n you," he said quickly. "I got more'n just the one thing goin' for me."

She stared at him for a moment, then got into the car. She didn't speak until they were at the station and she was ready to board the train.

"You'll write me, Nevada?" she asked.

"I ain't much for writin'," he said.

"But you'll keep in touch?" she persisted. "You'll answer if I write you?"

He nodded.

"You'll let me come and visit you sometimes?" she asked. "If I'm lonely and frightened?"

"That's what friends're for," he said.

A hint of moisture came into her eyes. "You've been a good friend, Nevada," she said seriously.

She kissed him on the cheek and climbed up the steps of the Pullman car. At the door, she turned and waved brightly, then disappeared inside. He saw her face appear in the window for a moment as the train began to move. Then she was gone and he turned and walked out of the station.

He walked up a rickety flight of stairs that led into a dust-ridden corridor. The paint on the door was scratched and worn, the lettering simple and faded.

DANIEL PIERCE—BOOKING AGENT

The office lived up to the reputation of the corridor outside. A girl looked up at him from a littered desk. Her hair bore traces of its last henna rinse, the gum cracked in her mouth as she asked, almost hostilely, "What d'ya want?"

"Dan Pierce in?" he asked.

She studied Nevada for a moment, her eyes taking in his worn leather jacket, the faded Levi's, the wide-brimmed cowboy hat. "If you're lookin' for a job," she said, "there ain't any."

"I'm not lookin' for a job," he said quickly. "I'm lookin' for Mr. Pierce."

"You got an appointment?"

Nevada shook his head. "No."

"He don't see nobody without an appointment," she said brusquely.

"I'm from the Wild-West show," Nevada said. "He'll see me."

A spark of interest appeared on her face. "The Buffalo Bill show?"

Nevada shook his head. "No. The Great Southwest Rodeo."

"Oh." The interest vanished from her face. "The other one."

Nevada nodded. "Yeah, the other one."

"Well, he ain't here," she said.

"Where can I find him?" he asked.

"I don't know. He went out to a meeting."

Nevada's voice was insistent. "Where?"

Something in his eyes made her answer. "He went over to Norman Pictures. He's on the back lot trying to sell them some client for a Western."

"How do I get there?"

"It's out on Lankershim Boulevard, past Universal, past Warner's."

"Thanks," he said and walked out.

He saw the big billboard in front of Universal as soon as he turned onto Lankershim.

UNIVERSAL PICTURES
THE HOME OF TOM MIX AND TONY
SEE
RIDERS OF THE PURPLE SAGE
A UNIVERSAL PICTURE

A few minutes later, he passed another sign in front of Warner Bros.

WARNER BROS. PRESENT
MILTON SILLS
IN
THE SEA HAWK
A VITAGRAPH PICTURE

The Norman studio was about five miles farther down the road. The usual billboard was out in front.

BERNARD B. NORMAN PRODUCTIONS
PRESENT
THE SHERIFF OF PEACEFUL VILLAGE
WITH AN ALL-STAR CAST

He turned in at the big gate where a gateman stopped him.

"Is Dan Pierce here?" Nevada asked.

"Just a moment, I'll see." The guard went back into his booth and checked a sheet of paper. "You must be the man he's expecting," he said. "He's on the back lot. Follow the road there right out. You can't miss it."

Nevada thanked him and put the car into gear. He drove slowly, for the road was filled with people. Some were actors in varying costumes but most seemed ordinary working men, wearing overalls and work clothes. He rolled past some very large buildings and after a few minutes was out in the clear. Here there was nothing but scrub grass and hills.

He came to another sign as he reached the foot of the first hill.

PEACEFUL SET
PARK CARS HERE

He followed the arrow. Just off the side of the road were a number of cars and trucks. He pulled in next to one of them and got out.

"Dan Pierce up there?" Nevada asked a man sitting in one of the trucks.

"Is he with the *Peaceful* crew?" the driver asked.

"I reckon," Nevada said.

"They're just over the hill."

At the crest of the hill, Nevada paused and looked down. A little below was a knot of people.

"Roll 'em, they're coming!" a heavy voice shouted.

Suddenly a stagecoach came roaring along the dirt road below him. Just as it took the curve, Nevada saw the driver jump off and roll to the side of the road. A moment later, the horses broke free of their traces and the coach tilted off the side of the road and went tumbling down the hill.

The dust had scarcely subsided when a voice shouted, "Cut! Cut! God damn it, Russell. You jumped too soon. The stage didn't go over the hill for a full forty frames after you!"

The driver got up from the side of the road and walked slowly toward the group of men, dusting his jeans with his hat.

Nevada started down the hill. He searched the crowd for Pierce, but didn't see him anywhere.

A man walked past, carrying a can of film. "Is Dan Pierce around?" Nevada asked.

The man shrugged his shoulders. "I dunno. Ask him," he said, pointing at a young man wearing knickers.

"Is Dan Pierce around?"

The young man looked up. "He had to go up to the front office for a phone call."

"Thanks," Nevada said. "I'll wait for him." He began to roll a cigarette.

The stentorian voice was shouting again. "Is Pierce back with that goddam stunt man yet?"

"He went to phone him," the young man said. A startled look came to his face as he looked at Nevada again. "Wait a minute, sir," he yelled and started toward Nevada. "You the guy Pierce was expecting?"

"I guess so."

"Come with me," the young man said.

Nevada followed him into the group of men clustered around a tall man next to the camera.

The young man stopped in front of him. "This is the man Pierce was expecting, sir."

The man turned and looked at Nevada, then pointed at a cliff on the next hill. Below the cliff flowed a wide stream of water. "Could you jump a horse off that cliff into the water?"

Nevada followed the pointing finger. It was about a sixty-foot drop and the horse would have to leap out at least fifteen feet to land in the water.

"We have the stream dug twenty-five feet deep right there," the director said.

Nevada nodded. That was deep enough. "I reckon it can be done," he said.

The director broke into a smile. "Well, I'll be goddamned!" he roared. "We finally found us a man with balls." He clapped Nevada on the back. "You go over there and the wrangler will give you the horse. We'll be ready just as soon as we get this shot here."

He turned back to the cameraman. Nevada tapped him on the shoulder. "I said I reckon it can be done," he said. "I didn't say I'd do it."

The director stared at him curiously. "We're paying triple the stunt rate; isn't ninety dollars enough for you? O.K., I'll make it a hundred."

Nevada smiled. "You got me wrong. I came out here lookin' for Dan Pierce. I ain't no stunt-rider."

The director's mouth twisted contemptuously. "You cowboys are all alike. All talk and no guts."

Nevada stared at him for a minute. He felt the hard knot of anger tightening inside him. He was tired of this, of the runaround he'd been getting ever since Pierce's office. His voice went cold. "It'll cost you five hundred dollars for me to take a horse off that cliff."

The director stared at him, then broke into a smile. "You must've heard that every man in Hollywood turned that jump down."

Nevada didn't answer.

"O.K. Five hundred it is," the director said casually and turned back to the cameraman.

Nevada stood near the horse's head, feeding him an occasional lump of sugar. The horse nuzzled his hand. He patted the horse's neck. It was a good horse. The animal responded quickly and there wasn't a frightened bone in his body.

"We're about ready," the director said. "I've got cameras covering you from every angle, so you don't have to worry which way to look. You go when I give the signal."

Nevada nodded and mounted the horse. The director stood limned against the edge of the cliff, his hand raised in the air. Suddenly, his hand dropped and Nevada dug his spurs into the horse. The animal leaped forward in almost a full gallop. Nevada gave him his head and led him into the jump.

Nevada took him high and the horse started down, his legs stiff, braced for a short fall. Nevada felt the great beast's heart suddenly pound between his legs as his hoofs didn't meet the expected ground.

The animal writhed in sudden panic as it began to tumble forward. Quickly Nevada kicked free of the stirrups and threw himself over the horse's side. He saw the water rushing up toward him and hoped he had jumped far enough so that the horse didn't land on top of him.

He hit the water in a clean dive and let the momentum carry him deep. He felt an explosion in the water near him. That would be the horse. His lungs were burning but he stayed down as long as he could.

At last, he had to come up. It seemed like forever till he broke the surface, gasping. He turned his head and saw the horse floating on its side, its head twisted in a peculiar manner. There was a look of great agony in its eyes.

He turned and swam quickly toward the bank. Angrily he strode toward the director.

The director was smiling. "That was great. The greatest shot ever made!"

"That hoss's back is probably broke!" Nevada said. He turned and looked out at the horse again. The animal was struggling to keep its head above water. "Why don't somebody shoot the poor son of a bitch?" Nevada demanded.

"We already sent for the wrangler to bring a rifle. He's back on the other hill."

"That hoss'll be drowned before he gets here," Nevada snapped. "Hasn't anybody got a gun?"

"Sure, but nobody could hit him. A revolver's no good at that distance."

Nevada stared at the director. "Give me a gun."

Nevada took the gun and hefted it in his hand. He spun the cylinder. "These are blanks," he said. Someone gave him bullets. He reloaded the gun quickly and walked over to the side of the stream. He fired at a piece of wood in the water. The gun dragged a little to the left. He waited a moment until the horse raised its head again, then shot the animal between the eyes.

Nevada walked back and gave the director the gun. Silently the big man took it and held out a pack of cigarettes. Nevada took one and the director held the match for him. Nevada let the smoke fill his lungs.

A man came running up, gasping and short of breath. "I'm sorry, Mr. Von Elster," he said hoarsely. "I just can't locate that stunt man anywhere. But I'll get you another one tomorrow."

"Didn't anybody tell you? He showed up already, Pierce. We just made the shot."

Pierce stared at him. "How could he? I just left him back at—"

The director stepped to one side, revealing Nevada. "Here he is. See for yourself."

Pierce looked at Nevada, then at the director. "That's not the one. That's Nevada Smith. He owns the Great Southwest Rodeo and Wild-West Show." He turned back to Nevada and stuck his hand out. "Good to see you, Nevada." He smiled. "What brings you out here?"

Nevada glared at him. The anger bubbled up again inside him. He lashed out, quickly and Pierce hit the ground in shocked surprise. He stared up at Nevada. "What's got into you, Nevada?"

"What I want to know is how much the Cody show got into you!"

Von Elster stepped between them. "I've been looking for someone like you a long time, Smith," he said. "Sell your show and come to work for us. I'll pay you two fifty a week to start."

Pierce's voice came up from the ground. "Oh, no you don't, Von Elster. A thousand a week or nothing!"

Nevada started to speak. "You shut up!" Dan Pierce told him authoritatively. "I'm your agent and don't you forget it!" He turned back to Von Elster. "This stunt will be all over Hollywood in an hour," he said. "I could take him down the line to Universal or Warner's. They'd snap him up like that."

Von Elster stared at the agent. "Five hundred," he snapped. "And that's my last offer."

Pierce grabbed Nevada's arm. "Come on, Nevada. We'll go over to Warner's. Every studio's looking for somebody to give Tom Mix a little competition."

"Seven fifty," Von Elster said.

"For six months, then a thousand a week and corresponding increases semi-annually thereafter."

"It's a deal," Von Elster said. He shook hands with Pierce and then turned to Nevada. He smiled and held out his hand. "What did you say your name was?"

"Smith, Nevada Smith."

They shook hands. "And how old are you, young fellow?"

Pierce answered before Nevada could speak. "He's thirty, Mr. Von Elster."

Nevada started to open his mouth in protest but the pressure of Pierce's hand on his arm kept him silent.

"We'll make that twenty-nine for publicity." Von Elster smiled. "Now, you two come on with me down to the front office. I want to tell Norman we finally found the Sheriff of Peaceful Village!"

Nevada turned away to hide a smile. He wondered what the men down on the prison farm so many years ago would have said had they known he'd finally turned up wearing a badge. Even if it was only in the movies.

CHAPTER NINE

"MY GOD!" THE WARDEN HAD SAID WHEN THEY BROUGHT MAX INTO his office. "What do they think they're doin' down there? This is a prison, not a reform school!"

"Don't let his looks fool you none, Warden," the tobacco-chewing deputy said, throwing the papers on the desk for the warden to sign. "He's a mean one, all right. He killed a man down in New Orleans."

The warden picked up the papers. "What's he up for? Murder?"

"Nope," the deputy replied. "Unlawful use of a weapon. He beat the murder rap—self-defense." He let go a wad into the spittoon. "This guy caught him in some fancy lady's bedroom."

"I was the lady's bodyguard, Warden," Max said.

The warden looked up at him shrewdly. "That didn't give you the right to kill a man."

"I had to, Warden," Max said. "He was comin' at me with a knife an' I had to defend myself. I had no clothes on."

"That's right, Warden." The deputy cackled lewdly. "Naked as a jaybird he was."

"Sounds like a genuine case of self-defense to me," the warden said. "How come they hang a bum one like this on him?"

"It was a cousin of the Darcys he croaked," the deputy said quickly.

"Oh," the warden said. That explained everything. The Darcys were pretty important people in New Orleans. "In that case, you're lucky you didn't get the book." He signed the papers and pushed them across the desk. "Here y'are, Deputy."

The deputy picked up the papers and unlocked Max's handcuffs. "So long, rooster."

The warden got to his feet heavily. "How old are you, boy?"

"'Bout nineteen, I reckon," Max answered.

"That's kinda young to be bodyguardin' one of them fancy women down in New Orleans," the warden said. "How'd you come to that?"

"I needed a job when I got out of the Army," Max answered. "An' she wanted someone who was fast with a gun. I was fast enough, I reckon."

"Too fast," the warden said. He walked around the desk. "I'm a fair man but I don't hold with no trouble-makers. You all just get up every mornin', do your work like you're tol' an' you'll have no trouble with me."

"I understand, Warden," Max said.

The warden walked to the door of his office. "Mike!" he roared.

A giant Negro trusty stuck his head in the door. "Yassuh, Warden."

"Take this new man out and give him ten lashes."

The surprise showed on Max's face.

"There's nothin' personal in it," the warden said quickly. "An ounce of prevention, I always say. It kinda sticks in your mind if you ever think about makin' any trouble." He walked back around his desk.

"C'mon, boy," the Negro said.

The door closed behind them and they started down the corridor. The trusty's voice was warm and comforting. "Don' you worry none about them lashes, boy," he said. "I knocks you out with the first one an' you never feels the other nine!"

Max had reached New Orleans about Mardi Gras time early that year. The streets were filled with laughing, shoving people and somehow he absorbed the warmth of their mood. Something about the whole town got inside him and he decided to stay over a day or two before riding on to West Texas.

He put his horse in a livery stable, checked into a small hotel and went down into the Latin Quarter, looking for excitement.

Six hours later, he threw down a pair of tens to three sevens and that was that. He had lost his money, his horse, everything but the clothes on his back. He pushed his chair back and got to his feet.

"That cleans me, gents," he said. "I'll go roun' to the stable an' fetch my hoss."

One of the gamblers looked up at him. "May I be so bold as to inquire, suh, what you intend to do after that?" he asked in his soft Southern accent.

Max shrugged and grinned. "I dunno. Get a job, I reckon."

"What kind of job?"

"Any kind. I'm pretty good with hosses. Punch cattle. Anything."

The gambler gestured at Max's gun. "Any good with that?"

"Some."

The gambler got to his feet casually. "Lady Luck wasn't very kind to you tonight."

"You didn' help her much," Max said.

The gambler's hand streaked toward his coat. He froze, staring into the muzzle of Max's gun. It had come out so fast that he hadn't even sensed the motion.

"A man can get killed doin' foolish things like that," Max said softly.

The gambler's face relaxed into a smile. "You are good," he said respectfully.

Max slipped his gun back into the holster. "I think I've got a job for you," the gambler said. "That is if you don't mind working for a lady."

"A job's a job," Max said. "This ain't no time to be gettin' choosy."

The next morning, Max and the gambler sat in the parlor of the fanciest house in New Orleans. A Creole maid came into the room. "Miss Pluvier will see you now." She curtsied. "If you will please follow me."

They followed her up a long, gracious staircase. The maid opened a door and curtsied as they walked through, then closed the door after them. Max took two steps into the room and stopped in his tracks, gawking.

He had never seen a room like this. Everything was white. The silk-covered walls, the drapes at the windows, the woodwork, the furniture, the canopy of shimmering silk over the bed. Even the carpet that spread lushly over the floor was white.

"Is this the young man?" a soft voice asked.

Max turned in the direction of the voice. The woman surprised him even more than the room. She was tall, almost as tall as he was, and her face was young, very young; but her hair was what did it more than anything else. It was long, almost to her waist, and white, blue-white like strands of glistening satin.

The gambler spoke in a respectful voice. "Miss Pluvier, may I present Max Sand."

Miss Pluvier studied Max for a moment. "How do you do?"

Max nodded his head. "Ma'am."

Miss Pluvier walked around him, looking at him from all angles. "He seems rather young," she said doubtfully.

"He's extremely capable, I assure you," the gambler said. "He's a veteran of the recent war with Spain."

She raised her hand carelessly, interrupting his speech. "I'm sure his qualifications are satisfactory if you recommend him," she said. "But he does seem rather dirty."

"I just rode in from Florida, ma'am," Max said, finding his voice.

"His figure is rather good, though." She continued as if he hadn't spoken. She walked around him again. "Very broad shoulders, almost no hips at all. He should wear clothes well. I think he'll do."

She walked back to the dressing table where she had been standing. She turned to face them. "Young man," she asked, "do you know what you're supposed to do?"

Max shook his head. "No, ma'am."

"You're to be my bodyguard," she said matter-of-factly. "I have a rather large establishment here. Downstairs, we have several gaming rooms for gentlemen. Of course, we provide other discreet entertainments. Our house enjoys the highest reputation in the South and as a result, many people are envious of us. Sometimes, these people go to extremes in their desire to cause trouble. My friends have persuaded me to seek protection."

"I see, ma'am," Max said.

Her voice became more businesslike. "My hours will be your hours," she said, "and you will live here with us. Your wages will be a hundred dollars a month. Twenty dollars a month will be deducted for room and board. And under no circumstances are you to have anything to do with any of the young ladies who reside here."

Max nodded. "Yes, ma'am."

Miss Pluvier smiled. She turned to the gambler. "Now, if you will be kind enough to take him to your tailor and have six suits made for him—three white and three black—I think everything will be in order."

The gambler smiled. "I'll attend to it right away."

Max followed him. At the door, he stopped and looked back. She was seated at the dressing table in front of the mirror, brushing her hair. Her eyes glanced up and caught his. "Thank you, ma'am," he said.

"Please call me Miss Pluvier," she said coldly.

❄   ❄   ❄

It was after three o'clock one morning when Max came into the foyer from the gaming rooms on his nightly tour of inspection. Already, the cleaning women were busy in the downstairs rooms. He paused at the front door.

"Everythin' locked up, Jacob?" he asked the tall Negro doorman.

"Tighter'n a drum, Mistuh Sand."

"Good," Max smiled as he started for the staircase, then stopped and looked back. "Did Mr. Darcy leave?"

"No, suh," the Negro replied. "He spendin' the night with Miss Eleanor. You don' have to worry, though. I move 'em to the gol' room."

Max nodded and started up the staircase. Darcy had been his only problem the last few months. The young man was determined not to be satisfied until he had spent a night with the mistress of the house. And tonight he had been rather unpleasant about it.

Max stopped at the top of the stairway. He knocked at a door and went in. His employer was seated at her dressing table, a maid brushing her hair. Her eyes met his in the mirror.

"Everythin's locked up, Miss Pluvier," he said.

Her eyebrows raised questioningly. "Darcy?"

"In the gold room with Eleanor at the other end of the house."

"*Bon.*" She nodded.

Max stood there looking at her, his face troubled. She saw his expression in the mirror and waved the maid from the room. "You are disturbed, *chéri?*"

He nodded. "It's Darcy," he admitted. "I don't like the way he's actin'. I think we ought to bar him."

"La." She laughed. "We can't do that. The family is too important."

She laughed again happily and came toward him. She placed her arms around his neck and kissed him. "My young *Indien* is jealous." She smiled. "Do not worry about him. He will forget about it soon. All young men do. I have seen it happen before."

A little while later, he lay beside her on the big white bed, his eyes delighting in the wonder of her lovely body. He felt her fingers stroking him gently, reawakening the fires inside him. He closed his eyes.

He felt her soft lips brushing his flesh; her whispering voice seemed to float upward to him. "*Mon coeur, mon indien, mon chéri.*" He heard the soft sounds of her pleasure as she raised her lips from him. Through his almost closed lids he could see the blurred sensuality of her face.

"The weapon you carry has turned into a cannon," she murmured, her fingers still stroking him gently.

His hand reached out and stroked her hair. An expression of almost frightened ecstasy came into her face and he closed his eyes. He could feel the trembling begin deep inside him. How could a woman know so much? From what deep spring could such a fountain of pleasure come? He caught his breath. It was almost unbearable, this strange delight. It was like nothing he had ever known.

There was a soft sound at the door. He turned his head slightly, wondering what it could be. Suddenly, the door burst open and Darcy was there in the room.

He felt her roll away from him as he sat up; then her voice from the foot of the bed: "Get out of here, you damned idiot!"

Darcy stared at her stupidly. He weaved slightly, his eyes bewildered. His hand came out of his pocket and a shower of bills fell to the floor. "See, I brought a thousand dollars with me," he said drunkenly.

She got out of the bed. She stormed toward him regally, unaware of her nudity. She raised a hand, pointing to the door. "Get out, I said!"

Darcy just stood there staring at her. "My God," he mumbled huskily. "I want you."

Max finally found his voice. "You heard Miss Pluvier," he said. "Get out."

For the first time, Darcy became aware of him. His face began to flush with anger. "You," he said thickly. "You! All the time I was begging, pleading, it was you. You were laughing at me all the time!"

A knife appeared in his hand suddenly. He thrust quickly and Max rolled off the bed to the floor as the knife stabbed the satin sheets. Max snatched a pillow from the bed and held it in front of him as he backed toward the chair from which his gun hung.

Darcy's eyes were glazed with rage. "You were laughing all the time," he mumbled. "Every time you did it you were laughing at me."

"You better get out of here before you get hurt," Max said.

Darcy shook his head. "And have you laugh at me some more? Oh, no. This time I'm going to do the laughing."

He lunged with the knife again. This time it caught in the pillow and he fell against Max, who was shoved against the wall. The gun went off, and a look of surprise came over Darcy's face as he slumped to his knees, then sprawled out on the floor. The naked woman stared at Max. Quickly she knelt beside Darcy. She reached for his pulse, then dropped his hand. "You didn't have to kill him, you fool!" she said angrily.

Max looked at her. Her breasts heaved excitedly and there was a fine moisture in the valley between them. He had never seen her look so beautiful. "What was I supposed to do?" he asked. "He was comin' at me with a knife!"

"You could have knocked him out!" she snapped.

"What was I supposed to hit him with?" he snapped back, feeling the anger rise in him. "My cannon?"

She stood very still for a moment, staring at him. Then she turned and walked to the door. She looked out into the hallway. The house was quiet. The shot had been muffled by the pillow. Slowly she closed the door and came back toward him.

He stood there watching the blurred, sensual look come back into her face. She sank to her knees before him, and he felt her lips press against his thighs. "Do not be angry with Anne-Louise, my stalwart, wild stallion," she whispered. "Make love to me."

He reached down to lift her to the bed. But she held his arms. "No," she said, pulling him down to the floor beside her. "Here."

They made love for the last time on the floor, lying next to a dead man. In the morning, Anne-Louise Pluvier calmly turned him over to the police.

CHAPTER TEN

THE EAST, WEST AND SOUTH OF THE PRISON WAS BOUNDED BY A SWAMP, along which the cypresses rose high and spilled their leaves onto the murky surface of the water. The only way out was to the north, across the rice paddies tended by Cajun tenant farmers. There was a small village eighteen miles north of the prison and it was here that most prisoners trying to escape were caught and brought back to the prison by the Cajuns for the ten-dollar bounty offered by the state. Those who were not caught were presumed dead in the swamp. There had been only two such cases reported in the prison's twenty years of operation.

One morning in May, after Max had been there a few months, the guard checking out his hut reported to one of the trusties the absence of a prisoner named Jim Reeves.

The trusty looked around. "He ain't here?"

"He ain't out in the latrines, neither," the guard said. "I looked."

"He's gone, then," the trusty said. "I reckon he went over the wall in the night."

"That Jim Reeves sure is a fool," the guard said softly. He turned on his heel. "I better go tell the warden."

They were lined up in front of the kitchen, getting their coffee and grits, when Max saw one of the guards ride out of the prison and start up the road toward the village.

He sat down against the wall of one of the huts and watched the guard disappear up the road while he ate. Mike, the giant Negro trusty who had given him ten lashes the day he arrived, came over and sat down beside him.

Max looked over at the trusty. "That all the fuss they make over a man gettin' out?"

Mike nodded, his mouth filled with grits. "What you expec' them to do?" he asked. "They'll git him back. You wait and see."

He was right. The next morning, while they were at breakfast again, Jim Reeves came back. He was sitting in a wagon between two Cajuns, who carried their long rifles in the crooks of their arms. The prisoners looked up at him silently as he rode by.

When they came back from their work in the evening, Jim Reeves was tied naked to the whipping post. Silently the trusties led the prisoners to the compound, so that they could view the punishment before they had their meal.

The warden stood there until all the prisoners were in line. "You men know the penalty for attempted escape—ten lashes and fifteen days in the cage for each day out." He turned to Mike, standing next to him. "I don't want him knocked out. He must be conscious so he can rue the folly of his action."

Mike nodded stolidly and stepped forward. The muscles along his back rippled and the long snake wrapped itself lightly around the prisoner. It seemed to caress him almost gently, but when Mike lifted it from the victim's back, a long red welt of blood bubbled and rose to the surface.

A moment later, the prisoner screamed. The snake rippled around him again. This time, his scream was pure agony. The prisoner fainted three times before the lashing was completed. Each time, the warden stepped forward and had a pail of water thrown into his face to revive him, then ordered the lashing continued.

At the end, Jim Reeves hung there from the post, unconscious. Blood dripped down his back from his shoulders, across his buttocks and the top of his thighs.

"Cut him down and put him in the cage," the warden said.

Silently the men broke ranks and formed a food line. Max looked at the cage as he got on the line. The cage was exactly that—steel bars forming a four-foot cubicle. There was room to neither walk, stand or even stretch out full length. There was only space enough to sit or crouch on all fours like an animal. There was no shelter from the sun or the elements.

For the next thirty days, Jim Reeves would live there like an animal—without clothing, without medical attention, with only bread and water for his food. He would live there in the midst of his pain and his excrement and there was no one who would speak to him or dare give him aid, under penalty of the same punishment.

Max took his plate of meat and beans around to the side of the hut, where he would not have to look at the cage. He sank to the ground and began to eat slowly.

Mike sat down next to him. The big Negro's face was sweating. He began to eat silently. Max looked at him and couldn't eat any more. He pushed his plate away from him, rolled a cigarette and lit it.

"You ain't hungry, man?" Mike asked. "I'll eat that there food."

Max stared at him for a moment, then silently turned the plate over, spilling the contents on the ground.

Mike stared at him in surprise. "What for you do that, man?" he asked.

"Now I know why you stay here as a trusty instead of leavin' like you should," Max said. "You're evenin' up with the whole world when you swing that snake."

A look of understanding came into the trusty's eyes. "So that's what you' thinkin'," he said softly.

"That's what I'm thinkin'," Max said coldly.

The Negro looked into Max's eyes. "You don' know nothin'," he said slowly. "Years ago, when I first got here, I seen a man git a beatin' like that. When they cut him down, he was all tore up, front an' back. He died less'n two days after. Ain't a man died since I took the rope. Tha's more'n twelve years now. An' if you looked close, you would have seen they ain't a mark on the front of him, nor one lash laid over the other. I know they's lots of things wrong about my job, but somebody's gotta do it. An' it mought as well be me, because I don' like hurtin' folks. Not even pricks like Jim Reeves."

Max stared down at the ground, thinking about what he had just heard. A glimmer of understanding began to lighten the sourness in his stomach. Silently he pushed his sack of makings toward the trusty. Without speaking, Mike took it and rolled himself a cigarette. Quietly the two men leaned their heads back against the hut, smoking.

❖ ❖ ❖

Jim Reeves came into the hut. It was a month since he had been carried out of the cage, encrusted in his own filth, bent over, his eyes wild like an animal's. Now his eyes searched the dark, then he came over to the bunk where Max lay stretched out and tapped him on the shoulder. Max sat up.

"I got to get outa here," he said.

Max stared at him in the dark. "Don't we all?"

"Don't joke with me, Injun," Reeves said harshly. "I mean it."

"I mean it, too," Max said. "But ain't nobody made it yet."

"I got a way figured out," Reeves said. "But it takes two men to do it. That's why I come to you."

"Why me?" Max asked. "Why not one of the men on a long stretch?"

"Because most of them are city men," Reeves said, "and we wouldn' last two days in the swamp."

Max swung into a sitting position. "Now I know you're crazy," he said. "Nobody can get th'ough that swamp. It's forty miles of quicksand, alligators, moccasins an' razorbacks. The only way is north, past the village."

A bitter smile crossed Reeves's face. "That's what I thought," he said. "It was easy, over the fence and up the road. Easy, I thought. They didn' even call out the dogs. They didn' have to. Every damn Cajun in the neighborhood was out lookin' for me."

He knelt by the side of Max's bunk. "The swamp," he said. "That's the only way. I got it figured out. We get a boat an'—"

"A boat!" Max said. "Where in hell we goin' to get a boat?"

"It'll take time," Reeves said cautiously. "But ricin' time is comin' up. Warden leases us out to the big planters then. Prison labor is cheap an' the warden pockets the money. Them rice paddies is half filled with water. There's always boats around."

"I don't know," Max said doubtfully.

Reeves's eyes were glowing like an animal's. "You want to lose two whole years of your life in this prison, boy? You got that much time just to throw away?"

"Let me think about it," Max said hesitantly. "I'll let you know."

Reeves slipped away in the dark as Mike came into the hut. The trusty made his way directly to Max's bunk. "He been at you to go th'ough the swamp with him?" he asked.

The surprise showed in Max's voice. "How'd you know?"

"He's been at ev'ybody in the place an' they all turned him down. I figgered he'd be gettin' to you soon."

"Oh," Max said.

"Don' do it, boy," the giant trusty said softly. "No matter how good it looks, don' do it. Reeves is so full of hate, he don' care who gets hurt so long as he gets out."

Max stretched out on the bunk. His eyes stared up into the dark. The only thing that made sense in what Reeves had said was the two years. Max didn't have two years to throw away. Why, in two years, he'd be twenty-one.

CHAPTER ELEVEN

"MAN, THIS IS REAL FOOD," MIKE SAID ENTHUSIASTICALLY AS HE SAT down beside Max, his plate piled high with fat back, chitterlings, collard greens and potatoes.

Max looked over at him wearily. Stolidly he pushed the food into his mouth. It was better than the prison food, all right. They didn't see as much meat in a week as they had on their plates right now. But he wasn't hungry. He was tired, bent-over tired from pulling at the rice all day. He didn't think he'd ever straighten out.

Reeves and another prisoner sat down on the other side of him. Reeves looked over his plate at him, his mouth working over the fat meat. "Picked yourself a gal yet, boy?"

Max shook his head. They were there all right. Cajun girls, young and strong, with their short skirts and muscular thighs and legs. Plenty of them, all over the fields, working side by side with the men, their hair flying and their teeth flashing and the female smell of them always in your nostrils. It didn't seem to matter to them that the men were prisoners. Only that they were men and for once there were enough of them to go around.

"I'm too tired," Max said. He put his plate down and rubbed his ankle. It was sore from the leg iron and walking in the water all day.

"I'm not," the prisoner next to Reeves said. "I been savin' up my hump a whole year for this week. I'm gonna git me enough to last me till nex' yeah."

"Better not pass it up, Injun," Reeves said. "There ain't nothin' in this world like Cajun girls."

"Man, that's the truth," the other prisoner said excitedly.

"You got one picked out?" Reeves asked across Max to Mike. His eyes were cold and baleful.

Mike didn't answer. He just kept eating.

Reeves's face darkened. "I seen you out there on the field. Walkin' up an' down with that rifle in your hands. Showin' the girls what you got in them tight pants."

Mike still didn't reply. He began to wipe up the gravy in his plate with pieces of bread.

Reeves's laugh was nasty. "There's always some half-wit girl lookin' for a big buck nigger with a cock as long as my arm. An' I bet you just can't wait to stick it into some white girl. That's all you niggers think of, stickin' it in white women."

Mike stuck the last piece of bread into his mouth and swallowed it. Regretfully he looked down at the empty plate and got to his feet. "Man, that was sho' good."

"I'm talkin' to you, nigger," Reeves said.

For the first time, Mike looked down at him. Almost lazily he bent over Max and with one hand picked Reeves up by the throat. He held him writhing in the air at the level of his head. "You talkin' to me, jailbird?"

Reeves quaked, his voice choking in his throat.

Mike began to shake Reeves gently. "Remember one thing, jailbird," he said. "I'm a trusty an' you' jus' a prisoner. You likes stayin' healthy, you better learn to shut you' mouth."

Reeves's arms flailed helplessly in the air. His face was almost purple. Mike shook him a few more times, then casually flung him at the wall of the bunkhouse, about five feet away.

Reeves crashed against the wall and slid down it to the floor. His eyes glared at Mike. His lips moved but no sound escaped them.

Mike smiled at him. "You' learnin', jailbird," he said. "You' learnin'." He picked up his empty plate. "I'm goin' see if I can't scrounge me some more of these eats. I swear if they ain't the best I ever tasted."

Reeves struggled to his feet as the trusty walked away. "I'll kill him!" he swore tightly. "Honest to God, someday before I get out of here, I'll kill that nigger!"

There was an air of expectancy in the bunkhouse that night. Max was stretched out on his bunk and the feeling was contagious. Suddenly, he wasn't tired any more. He couldn't sleep.

The guard had come and checked the leg irons, fastening each man to the bed post. He had gone to the door and stood there for a moment. Then he laughed into the dark and went out.

Almost immediately, Max heard the scratch of a match, then a faint glow spread through the darkness. Max turned toward the light. Somehow one of the men had got a candle. It burned almost gaily at the head of his bed.

There was a subdued sound of laughter in the room. Max heard a voice say, "At leas' this time we can see what they look like."

"I don't care what they look like," another voice answered quickly, "as long as they got big tits."

Still another voice said raucously, "Your pecker won't know what to do, it's so used to yoh lily-white hand."

A soft laughter rippled through the room. About a half hour passed. Max could hear the sounds of restless movements, men twisting anxiously in their bunks.

"You reckon maybe they won't show up?" a voice asked nervously.

"They'll show up, all right," another prisoner replied. "They been waitin' for this as long as we have."

"Sweet Jesus." An anguished voice came from the far end of the room. "I can't hold it no more. All day long I been thinkin' about them women, about tonight—" His voice trailed off in a hoarse moan.

For a moment, the room filled with the sounds of the men turning restlessly in their bunks. Max felt the sweat come out on his forehead and his heart began to beat heavily. He rolled over on his stomach, feeling the sweet, heavy warmth suddenly spread into his loins. For a moment he writhed, caught in the fire of a wild desire, then angrily he forced himself to turn over. He rolled a cigarette with trembling fingers. He felt shreds of the tobacco fall around him but he finally lit it and dragged the smoke deep into his lungs.

"They ain't comin'," a voice cried, almost on the verge of tears.

"They ain't nothin' but a bunch of cock-teasers!" another voice said angrily. "T' hell with them."

Max lay quietly in his bunk, letting the smoke trickle through his nostrils. The candle sputtered and flickered out and now the bunkhouse was pitch black. Mike's voice came softly from the next bunk. "How you doin', boy?"

"All right."

"Gimme a drag of that there butt."

Their hands touched briefly as Max silently held the cigarette out. The cigarette glowed and cast a faint shine over Mike's face as he dragged on it.

"Don' worry, boy." His voice was soft and reassuring. "They'll show up any moment now the candle's out. What those damn fools can't seem to understan' is them women don' want to see 'em, anymore'n they want theyselves to be seen."

A moment later, the bunkhouse door opened and the women began to come in. They entered silently, their bare feet making the faintest whisper on the floor.

Max turned in his bunk, hoping he could catch a glimpse of the one that would come to him. But all he could see were shadows that entered and then were lost in the dark. A hand touched his face. He started.

"Are you young or old?" a voice whispered.

"Young," he whispered back.

Her hand found his and brought it to her cheek. For a moment, his fingers explored her face gently. Her skin was soft and warm. He felt her lips tremble beneath his fingers. "Do you want me to stay with you?" she whispered.

"Yes."

Swiftly she came into the bunk beside him and he buried his head in the softness of her bosom. A great warmth and gentleness welled up inside him.

As if from a great distance, he heard a man across the room begin to cry softly. "My darling," he said, "my darling wife. You don't know how I've missed you."

Max turned his face up to the woman. As she bent to kiss his lips, he felt the tears rolling down her cheeks and he knew that she also had heard.

He closed his eyes. How could he tell this woman he couldn't even see what he felt? How could he tell her she brought kindness and love into this room?

"Thank you," he whispered gratefully. "Thank you, thank you, thank you."

On the fourth day at the rice fields, Reeves came over to him. "I been wanting to talk to you," he said quickly. "But I had to wait until that damn nigger wasn't around. I got a boat!"

"What?"

"Keep yer voice down," Reeves said harshly. "It's all arranged. It'll be in that big clump of cypresses south of the prison the day after we get back."

"How d'you know?"

"I got it fixed with my girl," Reeves said.

"You sure she ain't jobbin' you?"

"I'm sure," Reeves answered quickly. "These Cajun girls all want the same thing. I told her I'd take her to New Orleans with me if she helped me escape. The boat'll be there. Her place is out in the middle of nowhere. It'll be a perfect place to hide out until they stop lookin' for us."

He glanced up quickly and began to move off.

That evening, Mike sat down next to Max at chow. For a long time, there were only the sounds of eating, the scraping of spoons on plates.

"You goin' with Reeves now that he got his boat?" Mike asked suddenly.

Max stared at him. "You know that already?"

Mike smiled. "Ain' no secrets in a place like this."

"I don' know," Max said.

"Believe me, boy," the Negro said sincerely, "thirty days in the cage is a lot longer than the year an' a half you got to go."

"But maybe we'll make it."

"You won't make it," Mike said sadly. "Fust thing the warden does is get out the dogs. They don' get you, the swamp will."

"How would he know we went by the swamp?" Max asked quickly. "You wouldn' tell him?"

The Negro's eyes had a hurt expression. "You knows better'n that, boy. I may be a trusty, but I ain't no fink. The warden's gonna know all by himself. One man allus goes by the road. Two men allus goes by the swamp. It's like it was the rule."

Max was silent as he dragged on his cigarette.

"Please don' go, boy," Mike said. "Don' do nothin' to make me have to hurt you. I want to be you' friend."

Max looked at him, then smiled slowly. He reached out his hand and rested it on the big man's shoulder. "No matter what," he said seriously, "you're my friend."

"You goin'," Mike said. "You' mind's made up." Mike got to his feet and walked off slowly.

Max looked after him, puzzled. How could Mike know what he himself didn't know? He got to his feet and scraped off his plate.

But it wasn't until he was over the fence the next night and racing madly toward the clump of cypresses with Reeves at his side that he knew how right Mike had been.

Then Reeves was scrambling around at the foot of the cypresses, sunk half to his knees in the murky swamp water, swearing, "The bitch! The no-good lying Cajun whore!"

There was no boat there.

CHAPTER TWELVE

THEY PUSHED THEIR WAY THROUGH THE REEDS, SLOSHING IN THE WATER up to their waist, and up onto a hummock. They sank to their haunches, their chests heaving, their lungs gulping in great mouthfuls of air. From a great distance, they could hear the baying of a hound.

Reeves slapped at the insects around his head. "They're gaining on us," he mumbled through swollen lips.

Max looked at his companion. Reeves's face was swollen and distorted from insect bites, his clothing torn. Reeves stared back at him balefully. "How do you know we ain't been goin' in circles? Three days now and we ain't seen nothing."

"That's how I know. If we was goin' in circles, we woulda run into them sure."

"I can't keep this up much longer," Reeves said. "I'm goin' crazy from bug bites. I'm ready to let 'em take me."

"Maybe you are," Max said, "but I ain't. I ain't got this far to go back an' sit in a cage." He got to his feet. "Come on. We rested enough."

Reeves looked over at him. "How come them bugs don't bother you?" he asked resentfully. "It mus' be your Injun blood or somethin'."

"Might be," Max said. "Also might be that I don't scratch at 'em. Come on."

"Can't we stay here for the night?" Reeves complained.

"Uh-uh," Max said. "We got another two hours of daylight. That's another mile. Let's go."

He pushed off into the water. He didn't look back, but a moment later, he heard Reeves splash into the water behind him. It was almost dark when he found another hummock.

Reeves sprawled flat on the ground. Max looked down at him. For a moment, he felt almost sorry for him, then he remembered the fierce hatreds that flamed in Reeves and he wasn't sorry any more. He'd known what he was doing.

Max took out his knife and hacked swiftly at one of the long canes. He sharpened the end to a pointed spear. Then he sloshed out into the water. He stood there motionlessly for almost fifteen minutes, until he saw an indistinct shape swimming under the surface. He held his breath, waiting for it to come closer. It did and he moved swiftly. The spear flashed into the water.

He felt the pull against his arms as he lifted the spear free of the water. A large, squirming catfish was impaled on the tip.

"We got a good one this time," he said, returning to Reeves. He squatted down beside him and began to skin the fish.

Reeves sat up. "Start a fire," he said. "We'll cook this one."

Max was already chewing on a piece. He shook his head. "The smell of a fire carries for miles."

Reeves got to his feet angrily. "I don't give a damn," he snarled, his face flushing. "I ain't no damn Injun like you. I'm cookin' my fish."

He scrambled around, gathering twigs. At last, he had enough to start a small fire. His hand groped in his pocket for matches. He found one and scraped it on a log. It didn't light. Angrily he scraped it again. He stared at the match. "They're still wet," he said.

"Yeah," Max answered, still chewing stolidly on the fish. It was rubbery and oily but he chewed it slowly, swallowing only a little at a time.

"You c'n start a fire," Reeves snapped.

Max looked up at him. "How?"

"Injun style," Reeves said, "rubbin' two sticks together."

Max laughed. "It won't work. The wood's too damp." He picked up a piece of the fish and held it up toward Reeves. "Here, eat it. It ain't so bad if you chew it slow."

Reeves took the fish and squatted down beside Max, then began to chew on it. After a moment, he spat it out. "I can't eat it." He was silent for a moment, his arms wrapped around himself. "It's gettin' damn cold out here," he said, shivering slightly.

Max looked at him. It wasn't that cold. Faint beads of perspiration stood out on Reeves's face and he was beginning to tremble.

"Lay down," Max said. "I'll cover you with grass—that'll keep you warm."

Reeves stretched out and Max bent down and touched his face. It was hot with fever. Max straightened up slowly and went to cut some more grass.

It was a hell of a time for Reeves to come down with malaria. Reluctantly he took one of his matches from its oilskin wrapping and lighted a fire.

❖   ❖   ❖

Reeves continued to shake spastically beneath the blanket of swamp grass and moan through his chattering teeth. Max glanced up at the sky. The night was almost gone. Unconsciously he sighed. He wondered how long it would take for the warden to catch up with them now.

He dozed, swaying slightly, as he sat. A strange sound hit his subconscious and suddenly he was awake.

He reached for his fishing spear and crouched down. The sound came again. Whatever it was, it was large. He heard the sound again, closer this time. His legs drew up beneath him. He was set to lunge the spear. It wasn't much but it was the only weapon he had.

Then Mike was standing there casually, his rifle crooked in his arm. "You' a damn fool, boy," he said. "Shoulda knowed better'n to light a fire out here."

Max got to his feet. He could feel fatigue spread over him now that it was over. He gestured to the sick man. "He got the fever."

Mike walked over to Reeves. "Sure 'nough," he said, his voice marveling. "That warden, he was right. He figgered Reeves would get it after three days in the swamp."

Mike sat down next to the fire and warmed his hands. "Man but that fire sure do feel good," he said. "You should'n'a waited aroun'."

"What else could I do?"

"He would'n'a waited if it was you."

"But it wasn' me," Max said.

The Negro looked down at the ground. "Maybe you better git goin' now, boy."

Max stared at him. "What do you mean?"

"Git goin'," Mike said harshly.

"But the rest of the posse?"

"They won' catch up fo' a couple of hours," Mike said. "They be satisfied catchin' Reeves."

Max stared at him, then looked off into the swamp. After a moment, he shook his head. "I can't do it," he said.

"You' a bigger fool than I thought, boy," Mike said heavily. "'Twas him, he'd be off in the swamp now."

"We busted out together," Max answered. "It's only fittin' we go back together."

"All right, boy," Mike said in a resigned voice. He got to his feet. "Drown that fire."

Max kicked the fire into the water, where it sputtered and died. He glanced back and saw Mike pick up Reeves as if he were a baby and sling him over his shoulder. Max started back into the swamp toward the prison.

"Where at you goin', boy?" Mike's voice came from behind him.

Max turned around and stared.

Mike pointed in the opposite direction. "The end o' the swamp about twenty-fi' miles that way."

Sudden comprehension came to Max. "You can't do it, Mike. You ain't even officially a prisoner no more."

The big man's head nodded. "You' right, boy. I ain't a prisoner. That means I kin go where I wants an' if I don't want to go back, they can't say nothin' about it."

"But it's different if they catch you helpin' me."

"If they catch us, they catch us," Mike said simply. "Anyway, I don't wanta be the one who lays the snake on you. I can't do it. You see, we's really frien's."

Eight days later, they came out of the swamp. They stretched out on the hard, dry ground, gasping for breath. Max raised his head. Far in the distance, he could see smoke rising on the horizon.

"There's a town there," he said excitedly, scrambling to his feet. "We'll be able to git some decent grub."

"Not so fast," Reeves said, pulling him down. Reeves was still yellow from the fever but it had passed. "If it's a town, there's a general store. We'll hit it tonight. No use takin' any chances. They might be expectin' us."

Max looked over at Mike. The big Negro nodded.

They hit the store at two in the morning. When they came out, they all wore fresh clothing, had guns tucked in their belt and almost eighteen dollars they had found in the till.

Max wanted to steal three horses from the livery stable and ride out. "Ain't that just like an Injun?" Reeves said sarcastically. "They'll trace horses faster'n us. We'll keep off the road two or three days, then we'll worry about horses."

Two days later, they had their horses. Four days later, they knocked off a bank in a small town and came out with eighteen hundred dollars. Ten minutes later, they were on their way to Texas.

CHAPTER THIRTEEN

MAX CAME INTO FORT WORTH TO MEET THE TRAIN THAT WAS TO BRING Jim Reeves's daughter from New Orleans. He sat in the barber chair and stared at himself in the mirror. The face that looked back was no longer the face of a boy. The trim black beard served to disguise the high cheekbones. He no longer looked like an Indian.

Max got out of the chair. "How much do I owe you?"

"Fifty cents for the haircut, two bits for the beard trim."

Max threw him a silver dollar.

Mike came off the side of the building against which he had been leaning and fell into step. "It's about time fer the train to be comin' in," Max said. "I reckon we might as well walk down to the station."

Three and a half years before, they had come into Fort Worth one night with seven thousand dollars in their saddlebags. Behind them they had left two empty banks and two dead men. But they had been lucky. Not one of them had been identified as other than an unknown person.

"This looks like a good town," Max had said enthusiastically. "I counted two banks comin' in."

Reeves had looked up at him from a chair in the cheap hotel room. "We're through with that," he said.

Max stared at him. "Why? They look like setups."

Reeves shook his head. "That's where I made my mistake last time. I didn't know when to quit." He stuck a cigarette in his mouth.

"What we goin' to do, then?" Max asked.

Reeves lit the cigarette. "Look aroun' for a good legitimate business. There's lots of opportunity out here. Land is cheap and Texas is growin'."

Reeves found the business he was looking for in a little town sixty-five miles south of Fort Worth. A saloon and gambling hall. In less than two years, he had become the most important man in town. Then he started a bank in a corner of the gambling house and, a little time later, began to acquire land. There was even talk of electing him mayor.

He bought a small ranch outside of town, fixed up the house and moved out of the rooms over the saloon. A little while after that, he moved the bank out of the saloon, which Max then operated, and ensconced it in a small building on the main street. In less than a year, people began to forget that he had ever owned the saloon and began to think of him as the town banker. He began to grow quietly rich.

He needed but one thing more to complete his guise of respectability. A family. He sent discreet inquiries back to New Orleans. He learned that his wife was dead and his daughter was living with her mother's relatives. He sent her a telegram and received one in return, saying that she would arrive at Fort Worth on the fifth of March.

Max stood looking down the platform at the disembarking passengers. "You know what she looks like?" Mike asked.

"Just what Jim tol' me and it's been ten years since he saw her."

Little by little, the passengers walked away until the only one left was a young woman, surrounded by several valises and a small trunk. She kept looking up and down the platform. Mike looked at Max questioningly. "You reckon that might be her?"

Max shrugged his shoulders.

They walked down to the young woman. Max took off his Stetson. "Miss Reeves?"

A smile of relief appeared on the young woman's face. "I declare, I'm glad to see you," she said warmly. "I was beginnin' to think Daddy never received my telegram."

Max returned her smile. "I'm Max Sand," he said. "Your father sent me to meet you."

A fleeting shadow crossed the girl's face. "I half expected that," she said. "Daddy's been too busy to come home for ten years."

Max guessed that she didn't know her father had been in prison. "Come," he said gently. "I've got a room for you over at the Palace Hotel. You can clean up and sleep there tonight. We got a two-day trip home, so we won't start till morning."

By the time they reached the hotel, twenty minutes later, Max was in love for the first time in his life.

❖　❖　❖

Max tied his horse to the hitching post in front of the Reeves ranch house. He climbed up the steps and knocked at the door. When Reeves's daughter opened it, her face looked tired and strained, as if she'd been weeping. "Oh, it's you," she said in a low voice. "Come in."

He followed her into the parlor. He reached for her, suddenly concerned. "Betty, what's wrong?"

She slipped away from his hands. "Why didn't you tell me you were an escaped convict?" she asked, not looking at him.

His face settled into cold lines. "Would it have made any diff'rence?"

She met his look honestly. "Yes," she said. "I'd never have let myself get this involved if I'd known."

"Now that you do know," he persisted. "Does it matter?"

"Yes," she said again. "Oh, don't ask me. I'm so confused!"

"What else did your father tell you?"

She looked down at her hands. "He said I couldn't marry you. Not only because of that but because you're—you're half Indian!"

"An' just because of that, you stopped lovin' me?"

She stared down at her twisting hands without answering. "I don't know how I feel," she said finally.

He reached out and pulled her toward him. "Betty, Betty," he said huskily. "Las' night at the dance, you kissed me. You said you loved me. I haven't changed since then."

For a moment, she stood quietly, then pulled herself away from him. "Don't touch me!" she said quickly.

Max stared at her curiously. "You don' have to be afraid of me."

She shrank from his hand. "Don't touch me," she said, and this time the fear in her voice was much too familiar for Max not to recognize it. Without another word, he turned and left the room.

He rode straight into town to the bank and walked into the back room that served Reeves as an office.

Reeves looked up from the big roll-top desk. "What the hell do you mean bustin' in here like this?" he demanded.

Max stared at him. "Don't try to bull-shit me, Reeves. You already done a good job on your daughter."

Reeves leaned back in his chair and laughed. "Is that all?" he asked.

"It's enough," Max said. "Las' night she promised to marry me."

Reeves leaned forward. "I gave you credit for more brains'n that, Max."

"It don't matter now, Reeves. I'm movin' on."

Reeves stared at him for a moment. "You mean that?"

Max nodded. "I mean it."

"You takin' the nigger with you?"

"Yeah," Max said. "When I get our share of the money."

Reeves swung his chair around and took some bills from the safe behind him. He threw them down on the desk in front of Max. "There it is."

Max looked down at it, then at Reeves. He picked up the money and counted it. "There's only five hundred dollars here," he said.

"What did you expect?" Reeves asked.

"We came into Fort Worth with seven thousand. My share of that alone was twenty-three hundred an' we ain't been exactly losin' money in the saloon." Max took a ready-made from Reeves's desk and lit it. "I figger Mike an' me's due at least five thousand."

Reeves shrugged. "I won't argue," he said. "After all, we been through a lot together, you an' me. If that's what you figure, that's what you get."

He counted the money out on the desk. Max picked it up and put it in his pocket. "I didn't think you'd part with it so easy," he said.

He was halfway to the saloon when someone hailed him from the rear. He turned around slowly.

The sheriff and two deputies advanced on him, their guns drawn. Reeves was with them.

"What's up, Sheriff?" Max asked.

"Search him," Reeves said excitedly. "You'll find the money he stole right on him."

"Stole?" Max said. "He's crazy! That money's mine. He owed it to me."

"Keep your hand away from your gun," the sheriff said, moving forward cautiously. He stuck his hand in Max's pocket. It came out with a sheaf of bills.

"See!" Reeves yelled. "What did I tell you?"

"You son of a bitch!" Max exploded. He flung himself toward Reeves. Before he could reach him, the sheriff brought his gun butt down along the side of Max's head. It was just at that moment that Mike looked out the window of the room over the saloon.

Reeves walked over to Max and looked down at him. "I shoulda known better than to trust a half-breed."

"Pick him up, boys, an' tote him over to the jail," the sheriff said.

"Better get over to the saloon and get his nigger friend, too," Reeves said. "He was probably in on it."

Mike saw the sheriff look over at the saloon, then begin to walk toward it. He didn't wait any longer. He went down the back stairs and got the hell out of town.

Reeves rode along the road to his ranch, half humming to himself. He was feeling good. For the first time, he was secure. Max wouldn't dare talk; it would only make it worse for him. And the nigger was gone. Leave it to a nigger to run when things got rough. He was so wrapped up in his thoughts that he never heard the crack of the snake as it whipped out from behind the trees and dragged him down off his horse.

He scrambled to his feet and reached for his gun but the next crack of the snake tore it from his fingers. Mike walked slowly toward him, the big whip coiling slowly back up his arm.

Reeves screamed in terror.

The big snake cracked again and Reeves spun around and tumbled over backward into the dust. He got to his hands and knees and began to crawl, then scrambled to his feet and tried to run. The snake ran down the road after him and crept between his legs, throwing him to the ground. He turned his head and saw Mike's arm go up into the air, the long black whip rising with it.

He screamed as the snake tore into him again.

* * *

Sometime early the next morning, the sheriff and his deputies came across a body lying at the side of the road. During the night, someone had torn the bars from the window of the jail's only cell and Max had escaped.

One of the deputies saw the body first. He wheeled his horse over beside it and looked down.

The sheriff and the other deputy wheeled their horses. For a long while, they stared down at the mutilated body. Then one of them took off his hat and wiped the cold, beaded sweat from his forehead. "That looks like Banker Reeves."

The sheriff turned and looked at him. "That *was* Banker Reeves," he said. He, too, took off his hat and wiped his face. "Funny," he added. "The only thing I know of that can do that to a man is a Louisiana prison snake."

CHAPTER FOURTEEN

THE NAME OF THE VILLAGE IN SPANISH WAS VERY LONG AND DIFFICULT for Americans to pronounce, so after a while they gave it their own name. Hideout. It was a place to go when there was nowhere else to turn, when the law was hot on your neck and you were tired of sleeping nights on the cold prairie and eating dry beef and cold beans from a can. It was expensive but it was worth it. Four miles over the border and the law could not reach you.

And it was the only place in Mexico where you could always get American whisky. Even if you had to pay four times the price for it.

The *alcalde* sat at his table in the rear of the cantina and watched the two *americanos* come in. They sat down at the table near the door. The smaller one ordered tequila.

The *alcalde* watched the two with interest. Soon they would be going away. It was always like that. When first they came, they'd have nothing but the best. The finest whisky, the best rooms, the most expensive girls. Then their money would run short and they'd begin to reduce their expenses. First, the room would be changed for a cheaper one; next, the girls would go. Last, the whisky. When they got down to drinking tequila, it meant that before long, they'd be moving on.

He lifted his glass and drank his tequila quickly. That was the way of the world. He looked at the smaller man again. There was something about him that had caught his eye. He sighed, thinking of his youth. Juárez would have liked this one: the Indian blood in the *Jefe* told him instinctively which ones were the warriors. He sighed again. Poor Juárez, he wanted so much for the people and got so little. He wondered if before the *Jefe* died, he had realized that the only reason for his failure was that the people didn't want as much for themselves as he had wanted for them. He stared at the *americanos*, remembering the first time he had seen them. It was almost three years ago.

They had come into the cantina quietly, weary and covered with the dust of their travels. Then, as now, they had sat at the table near the door.

The bottle and glasses were on the table when the big man at the bar had come over to them. He spoke to the smaller man, ignoring the other. "We don't allow niggers in this here saloon."

The smaller man didn't even look up. He filled his friend's glass first, then his own. He lifted it to his lips.

The glass shattered against the floor and silence abruptly fell across the cantina. "Get your nigger outa here," the big man said. He stared at them for a moment, then turned and strode back to the bar.

The Negro started to rise but the smaller man stopped him with a gesture from his eyes. Slowly the Negro sank back into his chair.

It was only when the smaller man left the table to go to the bar that the *alcalde* realized that he wasn't as small as he had first thought. It was only by comparison to the Negro that he seemed small.

"Who makes the rules here?" he asked the bartender.

The bartender gestured toward the rear. "The *alcalde, señor.*"

The *americano* turned and came toward the table. His eyes surprised the *alcalde*; they were a hard, dark blue. He spoke in Spanish, with a trace of Cuban accent. "Does the swine speak the truth, *señor?*"

"No, *señor,*" the *alcalde* replied. "All are welcome here who have the money to pay their way."

The man nodded and returned to the bar. He stopped in front of the man who had come over to his table. "The *alcalde* tells me my friend can stay," he said.

The man turned to him angrily. "Who the hell cares what that greaser thinks? Just because we're across the border, doesn't mean I have to drink with niggers!"

The smaller man's voice was cold. "My friend eats with me, drinks with me, sleeps with me, and he's not goin'." He turned his back calmly and went back to his table.

He was just seating himself again when the angry *americano* started for him. "If you like niggers so much, nigger-lover, see how you like sleepin' with a dead one!" he shouted, pulling his gun.

The smaller *americano* seemed scarcely to move but the gun was in his hand, smoke rising from its barrel, the echo of a shot fading away in the rafters of the cantina. And the loud-mouthed one lay dead on the floor in front of the bar.

"I apologize for the disturbance we have made against the hospitality of your village," he said in his strange Spanish.

The *alcalde* looked down at the man on the floor, and shrugged. "*De nada,*" he said. "It is nothing. You were right. The swine had no grace."

Now, almost three years later, the *alcalde* sighed, remembering. The little one had grace, much grace—natural like a panther. And the gun. *Caramba!* There had never been anything so fast. It seemed almost to have a life of its own. What a *pistolera* this one would have made. Juárez would have been proud of him.

Several times each year, the two friends would quietly disappear from the village and as quietly reappear—several weeks, sometimes several months later. And each time they came back, they had money to pay for their rooms, their women, their whisky.

But each time, the *alcalde* could sense a deeper solitude in them, a greater aloneness. There were times he felt a strange kind of pity for them. They were not like the others that came to the village. This way of life held no pleasure for them.

And now they were drinking tequila again. How many times before they would go out like this and never return? Not only to this village but to nowhere on this earth.

Max swallowed the tequila and bit into the lime. The tart juice burst into his throat, giving his mouth a clean, fresh feeling. He looked at Mike. "How much we got left?"

Mike thought for a moment. "Maybe three more weeks."

Max rolled a cigarette and lit it. "What we gotta do is make a big hit. Then maybe we could go up into California or Nevada or someplace where they don' know us an' git ourselves straightened out. Money shore don' last long around this place."

The Negro nodded. "It sho' don'," he agreed. "But that ain' the answer. We gotta split up. They lookin' for us together. When they see me, it's like you carryin' a big ol' sign with you' name on it."

Max filled his glass again. "Tryin' to get rid of me?" He smiled, throwing the liquor down his throat and reaching for the lime.

Mike said seriously, "Maybe 'thout me, you could settle down someplace an' make a life fo' yourself. You won' have to run no mor'."

Max spit out a lime seed. "We made us a deal to stick together. We get enough money this time, we'll head for California."

The door opened and a tall, redheaded cowboy came in. He walked over to their table and dropped into an empty chair. "Ol' Charlie Dobbs got here in the nick o' time, I reckon." He laughed. "That there tequila'll eat the linin' off your stomach sure as hell. Bartender, bring us a bottle of whisky."

The bartender put whisky and glasses on the table and walked away. Charlie filled the glasses and they drank.

"What brings you back, Charlie?" Max asked. "I thought you were headin' up Reno way."

"I was. But I run into the biggest thing ever I saw. It was too good to pass up."

"What kinda job?" Max asked, leaning across the table.

Charlie lowered his voice. "A new bank. You remember I tol' you I heard las' year they were minin' for oil up in Texas? I decided to pay them diggin's a visit on my way north." He poured another drink and swallowed it quickly. "Well, they found it all right. It's the craziest thing you ever saw. They sink a well down in the groun' an' instead of water, up comes oil. Then they pipe it off, barrel it an' ship it east. There's oil all over the place an' that bank's just bustin' with money."

"Sounds good to me," Max said. "What's the deal?"

"A local man set up the job but he needs help. He wants two shares, we get one share each."

"Fair enough," Max said. He turned to Mike. "What do you think?"

Mike nodded. "When we pull the job?" he asked.

Charlie looked at him. "Right after the new year. The bank is gettin' in a lot of money then for new diggin'." He refilled all the glasses. "We'll have to start tomorrow. It took me three weeks to ride down here."

CHAPTER FIFTEEN

MAX PUSHED HIS WAY INTO THE SALOON BEHIND CHARLIE DOBBS. IT WAS crowded with oil-miners and cowboys and the dice table and faro layouts were working full blast. Men were standing three deep around them waiting for a chance at the games.

"What'd I tell you?" Charlie chortled. "This is a real boom town all right." He led the way down the bar to where a man was standing by himself.

The man turned and looked at him. "You took long enough gettin' here," he said in a low voice.

"It's a long ride, Ed," Charlie said.

"Meet me outside," Ed said, throwing a silver dollar on the bar and walking out. He glanced quickly at Max as he passed.

Max caught a glimpse of pale gimlet eyes without expression. The man seemed to be in his late forties, with a long, sandy mustache trailing across his lip. There was something familiar about him but Max couldn't place it. There was only the feeling that he had seen him before.

The man was waiting outside the saloon for them. He walked ahead and they followed him into a dark alley. He turned to face them. "I said we needed four men," he said angrily.

"There's another man, Ed," Charlie said quickly. "He's layin' up just outside of town."

"All right. You got here just in time. Tomorrow night—that's Friday night— the president and the cashier of the bank work late makin' up the riggin' crews' payrolls for Saturday. They usually get through about ten o'clock. We get them as they come out the door an' hustle them back inside. That way, they can open the safe for us; we don't have to blow it."

"All right with me," Charlie said. "What do you think, Max?"

Max looked at Ed. "They carry guns?"

"I reckon. You afraid of gunplay?"

Max shook his head. "No. I jus' like to know what to expect."

"How much you think we'll get?" Charlie interjected.

"Fifty thousand, maybe more."

Charlie whistled. "Fifty thousand!"

"You'll drift over here one at a time. Quiet. I don't want no one to be lookin' at us. We'll meet in back of the bank at nine thirty sharp." Ed looked at them and they nodded again. He started to walk away, then came back. He peered at Max. "Ain't I seen you someplace before?"

Max shrugged his shoulders. "Mebbe. I been aroun'. You look familiar to me, too."

"Maybe it'll come to me tomorrow night." He started to walk down the alley.

Max watched him until he turned into the street. He turned slowly to Charlie. "There's somethin' about that man. I got the feelin' I should know who he is."

Charlie laughed. "Let's go. Mike'll be wonderin' what happened to us."

"Set yourself!" Ed whispered hoarsely. "They're comin'!"

Max pressed tightly against the wall near the door. On the other side of the doorway, Ed and Charlie were waiting. He could hear the sound of two men's voices as they approached the door inside the bank.

They all moved at once as the door opened, pushing it inward with sudden force.

"What the hell's goin'—" a voice said from the darkness inside. It was followed by a thud, then the sound of a body falling.

"You keep your mouth shet, mister, if you want to keep livin'!" There was a frightened gasp, then silence. "Git them into the back room." Ed's voice came harshly.

Max bent swiftly and pulled the fallen man along the floor toward the back. There was the sound of a match behind him and then a lamp cast a tiny glow in the back room. He pulled the man into the room. He slumped and lay still when Max let him go.

"Check the front door!" Ed hissed.

Max ran back to the door and peeped out. The street was quiet and deserted. "No one out there," he said.

"Good," Ed said. "Let's get to work." He turned to the other of the two men. "Open the safe."

The man was in his late fifties. He was staring at the man on the floor with a horror-stricken look. "I—I can't," he said. "Only Mr. Gordon can. He's the president, the only one who knows the combination."

Ed turned to Max. "Wake him up."

Max knelt beside the man. He turned his face. The head looked peculiar, the jaw hung slack. Max looked up at Ed. "Ain't nothin' goin' to wake him up. You caved his head in."

"My God!" the other man said. He seemed almost ready to faint.

Ed stepped around in front of him. "I reckon you're goin' to have to open the safe, after all."

"B—but I can't," the bank clerk said. "I don't know the combination."

Ed hit him viciously across the face. The man fell against a desk. "Well, learn it, then!"

"Honest, mister," he sobbed. "I don't know it. Mr. Gordon was the only one. He was—"

Ed hit him again. "Open that safe!"

"Look, mister," the man begged. "There's over four thousand dollars in that desk there! Take it and don't hit me any more, please. I don't know the combination—"

Ed moved around the desk and opened the center drawer. He took out a package of bills and stuffed it into his jacket. He walked around the desk and stood in front of the kneeling bank clerk. "Now, open the safe!" he said, hitting the man again.

The man sprawled out on the floor. " I don't know, mister, I don't know!"

When Ed drew his foot back to kick him, Max touched his shoulder. "Maybe he's tellin' the truth."

Ed stared at him for a moment, then lowered his foot. "Maybe. I know how we can find out fast." He gestured at Max. "Get back on the door."

Max walked back through the bank to the front door and looked out again. The street was still deserted. He stood there, quietly alert.

Ed's voice came to him from the back room. "Tie the bastard to the chair."

"What are you gonna do?" the bank clerk protested in a weak voice.

Max walked back and looked in the room. Ed was kneeling in front of the potbellied stove, stirring the poker in the live coals. Charlie straightened up from tying the clerk and looked at Ed curiously. "What're you doin'?"

"He'll talk if this red-hot poker gits close enough to his eyes," Ed said grimly.

"Wait a minute," Charlie protested. "You think the guy is lyin', kill him."

Ed got to his feet and turned on Charlie angrily. "That's the trouble with you young ones nowadays. You got no guts, you're too squeamish. He can't open no safe if he's dead!"

"He can't open it if he don't know the combination, either!"

"You don't like it, scram!" Ed said savagely. "There's fifty thousand bucks in that there safe. I'm goin' to git it!"

Max turned from the door and started back toward the front of the bank. He had taken about two steps when he was stopped by Ed's voice, coming from the back room.

"This'll work, believe me," Ed was saying. "'Bout ten, twelve years back, Rusty Harris, Tom Dort an' me gave the treatment to an ol' buffalo-skinner an' his squaw—"

Max felt his stomach heave and he reached for the wall to keep from falling. He closed his eyes for a moment and the scene in the cabin came back to him— his father hanging lifelessly, his mother crumpled on the floor, the orange glow of the fire against the night sky.

His head began to clear. He shook it. A cold, dead feeling replaced the nausea. He turned toward the back room.

Ed was still kneeling in front of the stove. Charlie stood across the room, his face white and sick. "The ol' miser had gold stashed somewhere aroun' the place. Everybody in Dodge knew it—" Ed looked up and saw Max, who had crossed the room and was standing over him. "What're you doin' here? I tol' you to cover the door!"

Max looked down at him. His voice was hollow. "Did you ever git that gold?"

A puzzled look crossed Ed's face.

"You didn't," Max said, "because there wasn't any to start with."

Ed stared at him. "How do you know?"

"I know," Max said slowly. "I'm Max Sand."

Recognition leaped into Ed's face. He went for his gun, rolling sideways away from Max. Max kicked the gun from his hand and Ed scrambled after it as Max pulled the white-hot poker from the fire. Ed turned, raising the gun toward Max, just as the poker lunged at his eyes.

He screamed in agony as the white metal burned its way through his flesh.

The gun went off, the bullet going wild into the ceiling above him, then it fell from his hand.

Max stood there a moment, looking down. The stench of burned flesh reached up to his nostrils. It was over. Twelve years and it was over.

He turned dully as Charlie pulled at his arm. "Let's git outa here!" Charlie shouted. "The whole town'll be down on us in a minute!"

"Yeah," Max said slowly. He let the poker fall from his hand and started for the door. Mike was holding the horses and they leaped into the saddle. They rode out of town in a hail of bullets with a posse less than thirty minutes behind them.

Three days later, they were holed up in a small cave in the foothills. Max came back from the entrance and looked down at his friend. "How you doin', Mike?"

Mike's usually shiny black face was drawn and gray. "Poorly, boy, poorly."

Max bent over and wiped his face. "I'm sorry," he said. "We ain't got no more water."

Mike shook his head. "It don' really matter, boy. I got it good this time. I's th'ough travelin'."

Charlie's voice came from the back of the cave. "It'll be dawn in another hour. We better git movin'."

"You go, Charlie. I'm stayin' here with Mike."

Mike pushed himself to a sitting position, his back against the wall of the cave. "Don' be a fool, boy," he said.

Max shook his head. "I'm stayin' with you."

Mike smiled. His hand reached for Max's and squeezed it gently. "We's friends, boy, ain't we? Real friends?"

Max nodded.

"An' I never steered you bad, did I?" Mike asked. "I'm goin' to die an' they's nothin' you can do about it."

Max rolled a cigarette, lit it and stuck it in Mike's mouth. "Shut up an' rest."

"Open my belt."

Max leaned across his friend and pulled the buckle. Mike groaned as the belt slid off. "Tha's better," he said. "Now look inside that belt."

Max turned it over. There was a money pouch taped to the inner surface.

Mike smiled. "They's five thousand dollars in that pouch. I been holdin' out for the right time—now. It was for the day we lef' this business."

Max rolled another cigarette and lit it. He watched his friend silently. Mike coughed. "You was born thirty years too late for this business. They ain't no mo' room in this worl' for a gun fighter. We come in at the tail end with nothin' but the leavin's."

Max still sat silently, his eyes on Mike's face. "I'm still not goin'."

Mike looked up at him. "Don' make me feel like I picked the wrong one back there in that prison," he said. "Not now when I'm a dyin' man."

Max's face broke into a sudden smile. "You're full of shit, Mike."

Mike grinned up at him. "I kin hold the posse off all day. By then, you'll be so far no'th, they'll never catch up to you." He started to laugh and suddenly stopped as he began to cough blood. He reached up a hand to Max. "He'p me to my feet, boy."

Max reached out and pulled Mike up. The big man leaned against him as they moved toward the mouth of the cave. They came out into the night and there was a small breeze just picking up at the edge of the cliffs.

For a moment they stood there, savoring the physical closeness of each other, the small things of love that men can share, then slowly Max lowered his friend to the ground.

Mike looked down the ridge. "I can hol' them here forever," he said. "Now,'member what I said, boy. Go straight. No more thievin'. No more gun fightin'. I got you' word, boy?"

"You got my word, Mike."

"If you breaks it, I sure's hell'll come back an' haunt you!" the big man said. He turned his head away and looked down the ridge. "Now git, boy," he said huskily. "Dawn is breakin'." He reached for the rifle at his side.

Max turned and walked over to his horse. He mounted and sat there for a moment, looking back at Mike. The big colored man never turned to look back. Max dug his spurs into his horse and it leaped away.

It wasn't until an hour later, when the sun was bright and Max was on the next ridge, that he began to wonder about the quiet. By this time, there should have been the sound of gunfire behind him.

He never knew that Mike had died the moment he was out of sight.

He felt naked at first without his beard. Rubbing his fingers over his cleanly shaven face, he walked into the kitchen.

Charlie looked up from the kitchen table. "My God," he exclaimed. "I never would've known you!"

Martha, his wife, turned from the stove. She smiled suddenly. "You're much younger than I thought. And handsomer, too."

Max felt a flush of color run up into his cheeks. Awkwardly he sat down. "I figgered it's time for me to be movin' on."

Charlie and his wife exchanged quick looks.

"Why?" Charlie asked. "You own half this spread. You just can't go off an' leave it."

Max studied him. He rolled a cigarette and lit it. "We been here three months now. Let's stop kiddin' ourselves. This place can't carry the both of us."

They were silent. Max was right. Even though he had advanced the money to buy the ranch, there wasn't enough in it yet for all of them.

"What if somebody recognizes you?" Martha asked. "Your poster's in every sheriff's office in the southwest."

Max smiled and rubbed his chin again. "They won't recognize me. Not without the beard."

"You better think up a new name for yourself," Charlie said.

Max blew out a cloud of smoke. "Yeah. I reckon so. It's time. Everything's gotta change."

But the name hadn't come to him until the day he stood in the hot Nevada sun looking up at old man Cord and young Jonas. Then it came easy. As if it had been his own all his life.

Smith. Nevada Smith.

It was a good name. It told nothing about him.

He looked down at the little boy staring up at him with frightened eyes, then at the cold black gun in his other hand. He saw the child follow his eyes. He dropped the gun back into his holster. He smiled slowly.

"Well, Junior," he said. "You heard your pappy."

He turned to his horse and led it around to the bunkhouse, the boy trotting obediently behind him. The bunkhouse was empty. The boy's voice piped up behind him. "Are you going to live here with Wong Toy?"

He smiled again. "I reckon so."

He picked out one of the bunks and spread his bedroll on it. Quickly he put his things away. When he turned around, the boy was still watching him with wide eyes.

"You're really goin' to stay?" the child asked.

"Uh-huh."

"Really?" the boy insisted. "Forever?" His voice caught slightly. "You're not goin' to go away like the others? Like Mommy did?"

Something in the child's eyes caught inside him. He knelt beside the boy. "I'll stay jest as long as you want me to."

Suddenly, the boy flung his arms around Nevada's neck and pressed his cheek close to his face. His breath was soft and warm. "I'm glad," he said. "Now you can learn me to ride."

Nevada straightened up, the boy still clinging to his legs. He walked outside and put the boy up on the saddle of his horse. He started to climb up behind him when suddenly the gun was heavy against his thigh.

"I'll be back in a minute," he said, and went back into the bunkhouse. Quickly he pulled the tie strings and unbuckled the gun belt. He hung it on a nail over his bunk and went out again into the white sunlight.

And he never strapped the gun on again.

CHAPTER SIXTEEN

RINA STEPPED DOWN FROM THE TRAIN INTO THE BRIGHT, FLASHING SHADows of afternoon sun lacing the platform. A tall uniformed chauffeur stepped forward and touched his hand to his cap. "Miss Marlowe?" Rina nodded.

"Mr. Smith sends his apologies for not being able to meet you, ma'am. He's tied up at meetings at the studio. He says he'll see you for cocktails."

"Thank you," Rena said. She turned her face away for a moment to hide her disappointment. Three years was a long time.

The chauffeur picked up her valises. "If you'll follow me to the car, ma'am?"

Rina nodded again. She followed the tall uniform through the station to a shining black Pierce-Arrow limousine. Quickly the chauffeur stowed the bags up front and opened the door for her. The tiny gold insignia emblazoned over the handle shone up at her.

N
—
S

She settled back and reached for a cigarette. The chauffeur's voice through the speaker startled her. "You'll find them in the container near your right hand, ma'am."

She caught a glimpse of the man's quick smile in the rearview mirror as he started the big motor. She lit a cigarette and studied the interior of the car. The gold insignia was everywhere, even woven into the upholstery.

She leaned her head back. She didn't know why she should be surprised. She had read enough in the newspapers about him. The forty-acre ranch, and the thirty-room mansion he had built right in the middle of Beverly Hills. But reading about it never made it seem real. She closed her eyes so she could remember how it had become a reality for her.

It had been about five months after she'd come back East. She'd gone down to New York for a week of shopping and a banker friend of her father's had asked her to attend the premiere of a motion picture produced by a company in which he had a substantial interest.

"What's it called?" she had asked.

"*The Sheriff of Peaceful Village*," the banker had answered. "It's a Norman picture. Bernie Norman says it's the greatest Western ever made."

"Westerns bore me," she'd answered. "I had enough of that when I was out there myself."

"Norman says he has a new star in the man that's playing the lead. Nevada Smith. He says he'll be the biggest—"

"What was that name?" she interrupted. She couldn't have heard right.

"Nevada Smith," the banker repeated. "An odd name but these movie actors always have fancy names."

"I'll go," she had said quickly.

She remembered walking into the theater—the crowds, the bright lights outside, the well-groomed men and bejeweled women. And then that world seemed to vanish with the magic of the image on the screen.

It was near the end of the picture now and alone in a dreary room, the sheriff of Peaceful Village was putting on his gun, the gun he had sworn never to touch again.

The camera moved in close to his face, so close that she could almost see the tiny pores in his skin, feel his warm breath. He raised the gun and looked at it.

She could feel the weariness in him, see the torture of decision tighten his lips, set his square jaw, flatten the high, Indian-like cheekbones into the thin lines that etched their way into his cheeks. But his eyes were what held her.

They were the eyes of a man who had known death. Not once but many times. The eyes of a man who understood its futility, who felt its pain and sorrow.

Slowly the sheriff walked to the door and stepped outside. The bright sunlight came down and hit his face. He pulled his dark hat down over his eyes to shield them from the glare and began to walk down the lonely street. Faces of the townspeople peeked out at him from behind shutters and windows and curtains. He didn't return their glances, just walked forward stolidly, his faded shirt beginning to show the sweat pouring from him in the heat, his patched jeans looking threadbare against his lean, slightly bowed legs. The bright metal of his badge shone on his breast.

Death wore soft, expensive clothing. No dust marred the shine of his boots, the gleaming ivory handle of his gun. There was hatred in his face, the pleasurable lust to kill in his eyes, and his hand hovered like a rattlesnake above his holster.

They looked deep into each other's eyes for a moment. Death's eyes glittered with the joy of combat. The sheriff's were weary with sadness.

Death moved first, his hand speeding to his gun, but with a speed almost too quick for the eye to follow, the sheriff's gun seemed to leap into his hand. Death was flung violently backward to the ground, his gun falling from his hand, his eyes already glazing. His body twitched as two more bullets tore in him, and then he lay still.

The sheriff stood there for a moment, then slowly put his gun back into the holster. He turned his back on the dead man and began to walk down the street.

People began to flock out of the buildings. They watched the sheriff, their faces bright with battle lust. He did not return their glances.

The girl came out onto a porch. The sheriff stopped in front of her.

The girl's eyes were dim with tears.

The sheriff's were wide and unblinking. An expression of contempt suddenly came into his face. Disgust with her demand for blood, disgust for a town full of people who wanted nothing but their own form of sacrifice.

His hand moved up to his shirt and tore off the badge. He flung it into the dirt at her feet and turned away.

The girl looked down at the badge in shock, then up at the sheriff's retreating back. She started to move after him, then stopped.

Far down the street, the sheriff was mounting his horse. He turned it toward the hills. His shoulders slumping and head bowed, wearily he moved out of their lives and into the bright, glaring sunlight, as the screen began to fade.

There was silence as the lights came up in the theater. Rina turned to the banker, who smiled embarrassedly at her and cleared his throat. "That's the first time a movie ever did this to me."

Oddly enough, she felt a lump in her own throat. "Me, too," she said huskily.

He took her arm. "There's Bernie Norman over there. I want to go over and congratulate him."

They pushed their way through a crowd of enthusiastic well-wishers. Norman was a heavy-set man with dark jowls; his eyes were bright and elated. "How about that guy, Nevada Smith?" he asked. "Did you ever see anything like it? Still want me to get Tom Mix for a picture?"

The banker laughed and Rina looked up at him. He didn't laugh very often. "Tom Mix?" He chortled. "Who's he?"

Norman hit the banker on the back. "This picture will net two million," he said happily. "And I got Nevada Smith starting another picture right away!"

The limousine turned into a driveway at the foot of the hill. It passed under an iron gateway over which the now familiar insignia was emblazoned and began to wind its way up the narrow roadway to the top of the hill. Rina looked out the window and saw the huge house, its white roof turning blood orange in the falling sun.

She began to feel strange. What was she doing here? This wasn't the Nevada she knew. Suddenly, frantically, she opened her purse and began to search through it for Nevada's cablegram. Then it was in her hand and she felt calmer as she read it.

She remembered sending him a wire from Switzerland last month. It had been three years since she had heard from him. Three years in which she had kept on running. The first six months she spent in Boston, then boredom set in. New York was next, then London, Paris, Rome, Madrid, Constantinople, Berlin. There were the parties, the hungers, the fierce affairs, the passionate men, the voracious women. And the more she ran, the more frightened and alone she became.

And then came the morning in Zurich when she awoke with the sun shining in her eyes. She lay naked in bed, a white sheet thrown over her. Her mouth was dry and parched; she felt as if she hadn't had a drink of water in months. She reached for the carafe on the night table and when it wasn't there, she first realized she wasn't in her own room.

She sat up in a room that was furnished in expensive European fashion but wasn't familiar at all. She looked around for her robe but there wasn't a single item of her clothing anywhere. Vaguely she wondered where she was. There were cigarettes and matches on the night table and she lit one. The acrid smoke bit into her lungs as the door opened.

An attractive dark-haired woman came into the room. She paused when she saw Rina sitting up in bed. A smile came to her lips. She came over to the bed. "Ah, you are awake, *ma chérie*," she said softly, bending and kissing Rina on the mouth.

Rina stared up at her, her eyes wide. "Who are you?"

"Ah, my love, you do not remember me?"

Rina shook her head.

"Maybe this will refresh your memory, my darling," the woman said, dropping her gown and pressing Rina's head to her naked full bosom. "There now, do you remember how much we loved each other?" Her hand caressed Rina's face. Angrily Rina pushed it away.

The door opened again and a man came in. He held a bottle of champagne in one hand and was completely nude. He smiled at them. "Ah," he said. "We are all awake once again. The party was getting dull."

He crossed the room and held the champagne bottle out to Rina. "Have some wine, darling," he said. "The trouble is—one wakes up with such a terrible thirst, no?"

Rina held her hands to her temples. She felt the throbbing pulse beneath her fingers. It was a nightmare. This wasn't real. It couldn't be.

The man stroked her head solicitously. "A headache, no? I will bring some aspirin."

He turned and left the room. Terrified, Rina looked up at the woman. "Please," she begged. "I think I'm going out of my mind. Where are we?"

"In Zurich, of course, at Philippe's place."

"In Zurich?" Rina questioned. "Philippe?" She looked up at the woman. "Was that Philippe?"

"*Mais non*, of course not. That was Karl, my husband. Don't you remember?"

Rina shook her head. "I don't remember anything."

"We met at the races three weeks ago in Paris," the woman said. "You were alone in the box next to Philippe's. Your friend could not come, remember?"

Rina closed her eyes. She was beginning to remember. She had placed a bet on the beautiful red roan and the man in the adjoining box had leaned over. "A very wise choice," he had said. "That is my horse. I am Le Comte de Chaen."

"The count in the next box!" Rina exclaimed.

The woman nodded. She smiled again. "You remember," she said in a pleased voice. "The party began in Paris but it was too warm there, so we drove here to Philippe's chalet. That was almost two weeks ago."

"Two weeks?"

The woman nodded. "It has been a wonderful party," she said. She sat down on the bed next to Rina. "You're a very beautiful girl."

Rina stared at her, speechless. The door opened again and Karl came in, a bottle of aspirin in one hand, the champagne in the other. A tall blond man wearing a dressing robe followed him. He threw some photographs down on the bed. "How do you like them, Rina?"

She stared down at the pictures. A sick feeling began to come up into her throat. This could not be her. Not like this. Nude. With that woman and those men. She looked up at them helplessly.

The count was smiling. "I should have done better," he said apologetically. "But I think there was something the matter with the timer."

The woman picked them up. "I think you did well enough, Philippe." She laughed. "It was so funny. Making love with that little bulb in your hand so you could take the picture."

Rina was still silent.

Karl bent over her. "Our little *Américaine* is still sick," he said gently. He held out two aspirins to her. "Here, take these. You will feel better."

Rina stared up at the three of them. "I'd like to get dressed, please," she said in a weak voice.

The woman nodded. "But of course," she said. "Your clothes are in the closet." They turned and left the room.

Rina got out of bed and washed her face quickly. She debated over taking a bath but decided against it. She was in too much of a hurry to leave. She dressed and walked out into the other room.

The woman was still in her peignoir, but the men had changed to soft shirts and white flannels. She started to walk out without looking at them. The man named Karl called, "Mrs. Cord, you forgot your purse."

Silently she turned to take it from him, her eyes avoiding his face.

"I put in a set of the photographs as a memento of our party."

She opened the bag. The pictures stared obscenely up at her. "I don't want them," she said, holding them out.

He waved them aside. "Keep them. We can always make more copies from the negatives."

Slowly she lifted her eyes to his face. He was smiling. "Perhaps you would like a cup of coffee while we talk business?" he asked politely.

The negatives cost her ten thousand dollars and she burned them in an ash tray before she left the room. She sent the cable to Nevada from the hotel, as soon as she had checked in.

I'M LONELY AND MORE FRIGHTENED THAN I EVER WAS BEFORE. ARE YOU
STILL MY FRIEND?

His reply reached her the next day, with a credit for five thousand dollars and
confirmed reservations from Zurich through to California.

She crinkled the cablegram in her fingers as she read it once more while the
limousine climbed to the top of the hill. The cable was typical of the Nevada she
remembered. But it didn't seem at all like the Nevada she was coming to see.

I AM STILL YOUR FRIEND.

It was signed "Nevada."

CHAPTER SEVENTEEN

NEVADA LEANED BACK IN HIS CHAIR AND LOOKED AROUND THE LARGE
office. An aura of tension had crept into the room. Dan Pierce's face was
bland and smiling. "It isn't the money this time, Bernie," he said. "It's
just that we feel the time is right. Let's do a picture about the West as it really
was and skip the hokum that we've been turning out for years."

Norman looked down at his desk for a moment, his hand toying with the blue-
covered script. He assumed an earnest expression. "It isn't the script, believe me,
Dan," he said, turning to Von Elster for assurance. "We think it's great, don't
we?"

The lanky, bald director nodded. "It's one of the greatest I ever read."

"Then why the balk?" the agent asked.

Norman shook his head. "The time isn't right. The industry is too upset. Warner's has a talking picture coming out soon. *The Lights of New York*. Some people
think that when it comes out, silent movies will be finished."

Dan Pierce laughed. "Malarkey! Movies are movies. If you want to hear actors
talk, go to the theater, that's where talk belongs."

Norman turned to Nevada, his voice taking on a fatherly tone. "Look, Nevada,
have we ever steered you wrong? From the day you first came here, we've
treated you right. If it's a question of money, that's no problem. Just name the
figure."

Nevada smiled at him. "It isn't the money, Bernie. You know that. Ten thousand a week is enough for any man, even if income taxes have gone up to seven
per cent. It's this script. It's the first real story I've ever read out here."

Norman reached for a cigar. Nevada leaned back in his chair. He remembered
when he had first heard of the script. It was last year, when he was making
Gunfire at Sundown.

One of the writers, a young man with glasses and a very pale skin, had come over to him. "Mr. Smith," he asked diffidently. "Can I trouble you for a minute?"

Nevada turned from the make-up man. "Why, sure—" He hesitated.

"Mark Weiss," the writer said quickly.

Nevada smiled. "Sure, Mark, what can I do for you?"

"I've got a script I'd like you to read," Weiss said quickly. "I spent two years researching it. It's about one of the last gun fighters in the Southwest. I think it's different from anything that's ever been made." ▾

"I'd be glad to read it." That was one of the hazards of being a star. Everyone had a script they wanted you to read and each was the greatest ever written. "What's it called?"

"*The Renegade.*" He held out a blue-covered script.

The script felt heavy in his hand. He opened it to the last page and looked at the writer doubtfully. The script was three times standard length. "Pretty long, isn't it?"

Weiss nodded. "It is long but there was no way I could see to cut it. Everything in there is true. I spent the last two years checking old newspaper files through the entire Southwest."

Nevada turned back to the make-up man, the script still in his hand. "What happened to him?" he asked over his shoulder.

"Nobody seems to know. One day he just disappeared and nothing was ever heard about him again. There was a posse after him, and they think he died there in the mountains."

"A new story's always good," Nevada said. "People are getting tired of the same old heroes. What do you call this guy?"

The writer's voice seemed to hang in the air. "Sand," he said. "Max Sand."

The script slipped from Nevada's fingers. He felt the blood rush from his face. "What did you say?" he asked hollowly.

Weiss stared at him. "Max Sand. We can change it but that was his real name."

Nevada shook his head and looked down at the script. It lay there in the dust. Weiss knelt swiftly and picked it up. "Are you all right, Mr. Smith?" he asked in a concerned voice.

Nevada took a deep breath. He felt his self-control returning. He took the script from the outstretched hand and forced a smile.

A look of relief came into Weiss's face. "Thanks, Mr. Smith," he said gratefully. "I really appreciate this. Thanks very much."

For a week, Nevada couldn't bring himself to read it. In some strange way, he felt that if he did, he'd be exposing himself. Then one evening, he came into the library after dinner, where Von Elster was waiting, and found him deeply engrossed in this script.

"How long have you been sitting on this?" the director asked.

Nevada shrugged. "About a week. You know how it is. These writers are always coming up with scripts. Is it any good?"

Von Elster put it down slowly. "It's more than good. It's great. I want to be the director if you do it."

Late that night, the lamp still burning near his bed, Nevada realized what the director meant. Weiss had given depth and purpose to his portrait of a man who lived alone and developed a philosophy born of pain and sadness. There was no glamour in his crimes, only the desperate struggle for survival.

Nevada knew as he read it that the picture would be made. The script was too good to be passed up. For his own self-protection, he had to make the picture. If it escaped into someone else's hands, there was no telling how much further they'd delve into the life of Max Sand.

He bought the script from Weiss the next morning for one thousand dollars.

Nevada returned to the present suddenly. "Let's hold it for a year," Bernie Norman was saying. "By then, we'll know which way to jump."

Dan Pierce looked across at him. Nevada knew the look. It meant that Pierce felt he'd gone as far as he could.

"Chaplin and Pickford had the right idea in forming United Artists," Nevada said. "I guess that's the only way a star can be sure of making the pictures he wants."

Norman's eyes changed subtly. "They haven't had a good year since," he said. "They've dropped a bundle."

"Mebbe," Nevada said. "Only time will tell. It's still a new company."

Norman looked at Pierce for a moment, then back to Nevada. "O.K.," he said. "I'll make a deal with you. We'll put up a half million toward the picture, you guarantee all the negative cost over that."

"That's a million and a half more!" Pierce answered. "Where's Nevada going to get that kind of money?"

Norman smiled. "The same place we do. At the bank. He won't have any trouble. I'll arrange it. You'll own the picture one hundred per cent. All we'll get is distribution fees and our money back. That's a better deal than United Artists can give. That shows you how much we want to go along with you, Nevada. Fair enough?"

Nevada had no illusions. If the picture didn't make it, his name would be on the notes at the bank, not Norman's. He'd lose everything he had and more. He looked down at the blue-covered script. A resolution began to harden inside him.

Jonas' father had said to him once that it wasn't any satisfaction to win or lose if it wasn't your own money, and you'd never make it big playing for table stakes. This picture just couldn't miss. He knew it. He could feel it inside him.

He looked up at Norman again. "O.K., Bernie," he said. "It's a deal."

When they came out into the fading sunlight in front of Norman's bungalow office, Nevada looked at the agent. Pierce's face was glum. "Maybe you better come down to my office," he muttered. "We got a lot of talking to do."

"It can keep till tomorrow," Nevada said. "I got company from the East waitin' for me at home."

"You just bit off a big nut," the agent said.

They started toward their cars. "I reckon it's about time," Nevada said confidently. "The only way to make real money is to gamble big money."

"You can also lose big that way," Pierce said dourly.

Nevada paused beside his white Stutz Bearcat. He put his hand affectionately on the door, much in the same manner he did with his horses. "We won't lose."

The agent squinted at him. "I hope you know what you're doing. I just don't like it when Norman comes in so fast and promises us all the profits. There's a monkey somewhere."

Nevada smiled. "The trouble with you, Dan, is you're an agent. All agents are suspicious. Bernie came in because he had to. He didn't want to take any chances on losin' me." He opened the door and got into the car. "I'll be down at your office at ten tomorrow morning."

"O.K.," the agent said. He started toward his own car, then stopped and came back. "This talking-picture business bothers me. A couple of other companies have announced they're going to make talkies."

"Let 'em," Nevada said. "It's their headache." He turned the key, pressed the starter and the big motor sprang into life with a roar. "It's a novelty," he shouted to the agent over the noise. "By the time our picture comes out people will have forgotten all about talkies."

The telephone on the small table near the bed rang softly. Rina walked over and picked it up. It was one of those new French telephones, the first she'd seen since she'd returned from Europe. The now familiar insignia was in the center of the dial, where the number usually was printed. "Hello."

Nevada's familiar voice was in her ear. "Howdy, friend. You all settled in?"

"Nevada!" she exclaimed.

"You got other friends?"

She laughed. "I'm unpacked," she said. "And amazed."

"At what?"

"Everything. This place. It's fabulous. I never saw anything like it."

His voice was a quiet whisper in her ear. "It's not very much. Paltry little spread, but I call it home."

"Oh, Nevada," she laughed. "I still can't believe it. Why did you ever build such a fantastic house? It's not like you at all."

"It's part of the act, Rina," he said. "Like the big white hat, the fancy shirts and the colored boots. You're not really a star unless you have the trappings."

"With N Bar S on everything?" she asked.

"With N Bar S on everything," he repeated. "But don't let it throw you. There are crazier things in Hollywood."

"I've got so much to tell you," she said. "What time will you be home?"

"Home?" He laughed. "I am home. I'm down in the bar, waiting for you."

"I'll be down in a minute," she said, then hesitated. "But, Nevada, how will I find the bar? This place is so immense."

"We got Indian guides just for occasions like this," he said. "I'll send one up after you."

She put down the telephone and went over to the mirror. By the time she had finished applying lipstick to her mouth, there was a soft knock at the door.

She crossed the room and opened it.

Nevada stood there, smiling. "Beg pardon, ma'am," he said with mock formality. "I jes' checked the entire joint an' you won't believe it, but I was the only Indian around!"

"Oh, Nevada!" she said softly.

Then suddenly she was in his arms, her face buried against the hard muscles of his chest, her tears staining the soft white front of his fancy shirt.

JONAS – 1930
Book Three

CHAPTER ONE

THE LIGHTS OF LOS ANGELES CAME UP UNDER THE RIGHT WING. I LOOKED over at Buzz, sitting next to me in the cockpit. "We're almost home."

His pug-nosed face crinkled in a smile. He looked at his watch. "I think we got us a new record, too."

"The hell with the record," I said. "All I want is that mail contract."

He nodded. "We'll get it now for sure." He reached over and patted the dashboard. "This baby insured that for us."

I swung wide over the city, heading for Burbank. If we got the airmail contract, Chicago to Los Angeles, it wouldn't be long before Inter-Continental would span the country. From Chicago east to New York would be the next step.

"I see in the papers that Ford has a tri-motor job on the boards that will carry thirty-two passengers," Buzz said.

"When will it be ready?"

"Two, maybe three years," he answered. "That's the next step."

"Yeah," I said. "But we can't afford to wait for Ford. It could take five years before something practical came from them. We gotta be ready in two years."

Buzz stared at me. "Two years? How are we gonna do it? It's impossible."

I glanced at him. "How many mail planes are we flying now?"

"About thirty-four," he said.

"And if we get the new mail contract?"

"Double, maybe triple that many," he said. He looked at me shrewdly. "What're you gettin' at?"

"The manufacturers of those planes are making more out of our mail contracts than we are," I said.

"If you're talkin' about buildin' our own planes, you're nuts!" Buzz said. "It would take us two years just to set up a factory."

"Not if we bought one that was already in business," I answered.

He thought for a moment. "Lockheed, Martin, Curtiss-Wright, they're all too busy. They wouldn't sell. The only one who might is Winthrop. They're layin' off since they lost that Army contract."

I smiled at him. "You're thinkin' good, Buzz."

He stared at me in the dim light. "Oh, no. I worked for old man Winthrop. He swore he'd never—"

We were over Burbank airport now. I swung wide to the south end of the field where the Winthrop plant stood. I banked the plane so Buzz could see from his side. "Look down there."

Up through the darkness, illuminated by two searchlights, rose the giant white letters painted on the black tarred roof.

CORD AIRCRAFT, INC.

The reporters clustered around us as soon as we hit the ground. Their flash bulbs kept hitting my eyes and I blinked. "You tired, Mr. Cord?" one of them yelled.

I rubbed my unshaven cheeks and grinned. "Fresh as a daisy," I said. A stone on the field cut into my foot. I turned back to the plane and yelled up to Buzz. "Hey, throw me my shoes, will you?"

He laughed and threw them down and the reporters made a great fuss about taking my picture while I was putting them on.

Buzz climbed down beside me. They took some more pictures and we started to walk toward the hangar. "How does it feel to be home?" another reporter yelled.

"Good."

"Real good," Buzz added.

We meant it. Five days ago, we took off from Le Bourget in Paris. Newfoundland, New York, Chicago, Los Angeles—five days.

A reporter came running up, waving a sheet of paper. "You just broke the Chicago-to-L.A. record!" he said. "That makes five records you broke on this flight!"

"One for each day." I grinned. "That's nothin' to complain about."

"Does that mean you'll get the mail contract?" a reporter asked.

Behind them, at the entrance to the hangar, I could see McAllister waving frantically. "That's the business end," I said. "I leave that to my partner, Buzz. He'll fill you gentlemen in on it."

I cut away from them quickly, leaving them to surround Buzz while I walked over to McAllister. His face wore a harassed expression. "I thought you'd never get here on time."

"I said I'd be in by nine o'clock."

He took my arm. "I've got a car waiting," he said. "We'll go right to the bank from here. I told them I'd bring you down."

"Wait a minute," I said, shaking my arm free. "Told who?"

"The syndication group that agreed to meet your price for the sublicensing of the high-speed injection mold. Even Du Pont's coming in with them now." He took my arm again and began to hurry me to the car.

I pulled free again. "Wait a minute." I said. "I haven't been near a bed for five days and I'm beat. I'll see them tomorrow."

"Tomorrow?" he yelled. "They're waiting down there now!"

"I don't give a damn," I said. "Let 'em wait."

"But they're giving you ten million dollars!"

"They're giving me nothing," I said. "They had the same chance to buy that patent we did. They were all in Europe that year but they were too tight. Now they need it, they can wait until tomorrow."

I got into the car. "The Beverly Hills Hotel."

McAllister climbed in beside me. He looked distraught. "Tomorrow?" he said. "They don't want to wait."

The chauffeur started the car. I looked over at McAllister and grinned. I began to feel a little sorry for him. I knew it hadn't been an easy deal to swing.

"Tell you what," I said gently. "Let me get six hours' shut-eye and then we can meet."

"That will be three o'clock in the morning!" Max exclaimed.

I nodded. "Bring them to my suite in the hotel. I'll be ready for them then."

Monica Winthrop was waiting in the suite. She got up from the couch and put out her cigarette as I came in. She ran over and kissed me. "Oh, what a beard!" she exclaimed in mock surprise.

"What're you doin' here?" I asked. "I was looking for you at the airport."

"I would have been there but I was afraid Daddy would show up," she said quickly.

She was right. Amos Winthrop was too much of a heller not to recognize the symptoms. The trouble was he couldn't divide his time properly. He let women interfere with his work and work interfere with his women. But Monica was his only daughter and, like all rakes, he thought of her as something special. Which she was. But not in the way he thought.

"Mix me a drink," I said, walking past her to the bedroom. "I'm going to slip into a hot tub. I smell so loud I can hear myself."

She picked up a tumbler filled with bourbon and ice and followed me into the bedroom. "I had your drink ready," she said. "And the tub is full."

I took the drink from her hand. "How'd you know when I got here?"

She smiled again. "I heard it on the radio."

I sipped at the drink as she came over to me. "You don't have to take a bath on my account," she said. "That smell is kind of exciting."

I put the drink down and walked into the bathroom, taking off my shirt. When I turned to close the door, she was right behind me. "Don't get into the tub yet," she said. "It's a shame to waste all that musky maleness."

She put her arms around my neck and pressed her body against me. I sought her lips but she turned her face away and buried it in my shoulder. I felt her take a deep, shuddering breath. She moaned softly and the heat came out of her body like steam from an oven.

I turned her face up to me with my hand. Her eyes were almost closed. She moaned again, her body writhing. I tugged at my belt and my trousers fell to the floor. I kicked them aside and backed her toward the vanity table along the wall. Her eyes were still closed as she leaped up on me like a monkey climbing a coconut tree.

"Breathe slow, baby," I said as she began to scream in a tortured half whisper. "I may not smell as good as this for years."

The water was soft and hot, and weariness washed in and out as it rippled against me. I reached behind me, trying to get to my back with the soap. I couldn't make it.

"Let me do that," she said.

I looked up at her as she took the washcloth from my hand and began to rub my back. The slow, circular motion was soothing and I leaned forward and closed my eyes. "Don't stop," I said. "That feels good."

"You're just like a baby. You need someone to take care of you.

I opened my eyes and looked up at her again. "I been thinkin' that, too," I said. "I think I'll get a Jap houseboy."

"A Jap houseboy won't do this," she said. I felt her tap my shoulder. "Lean back. I want to rinse the soap off."

I leaned back in the water, my eyes still closed. She moved the washcloth over my chest and then down. I opened my eyes. She was staring down at me.

"It looks so small and helpless," she whispered.

"That wasn't what you said a little while ago."

"I know," she said, still in that whisper, the foggy look coming back into her eyes.

I knew the look. I reached up and put my arm around her neck and pulled her down on the edge of the tub. I felt her hand go down and cover me with the washcloth as we kissed. "You're growing strong," she whispered, her mouth moving against mine.

I laughed and just then the telephone rang. We turned quickly, startled, and the water splashed up and drenched the front of her dress. Silently she took the phone from the vanity and gave it to me. "Yes?" I growled into it.

It was McAllister. He was down in the lobby.

"I said three o'clock," I snapped.

"It is three o'clock," he answered. "Can we come up? Winthrop's with us, too. He said he has to see you."

I looked over at Monica. That was all I needed. To have her father come up and find her in my room. "No," I said quickly. "I'm still in the tub. Take 'em into the bar and buy 'em a drink."

"The bars are all closed."

"O.K., then, I'll meet you in the lobby," I said.

"The lobby's no place to close this deal. There's no privacy. They won't like it at all. I don't understand why we can't come up."

"Because I got a broad up here."

"So what?" he answered. "They're all broad-minded." He laughed at his pun.

"The girl's Monica Winthrop."

There was silence on the other end of the telephone. Then I heard him sigh wearily. "Christ!" he said. "Your father was right. You just never stop, do you?"

"Time enough for me to stop when I'm your age."

"I don't know," he said wearily. "They won't like the idea of meeting in the lobby."

"If it's privacy they want," I said, "I know just the place."

"Where?"

"The men's room, just off the elevators. I'll meet you there in five minutes. That'll be private enough!"

I put down the phone and got to my feet. I looked at Monica. "Hand me a towel," I said. "I gotta go downstairs and see your father."

CHAPTER TWO

I CAME INTO THE MEN'S ROOM, RUBBING MY CHEEK. I STILL HAD THE FIVE-day beard. I hadn't had time to shave. I grinned at the sight of them, all engrossed in their duties, not even looking around as I entered.

"The meeting will come to order, gentlemen," I said.

They looked over their shoulders at me, a startled expression on their faces. I heard one of them mutter a faint damn under his breath and wondered what minor tragedy brought that out.

McAllister came over to me. "I must say, Jonas," he said rather pompously. "You have a rather peculiar choice of meeting place."

I stared at him. I knew he was talking for the benefit of the others, so I didn't really mind. I looked down at his trousers. "Aw, Mac," I said. "Button your fly before you start talking." His face grew red and his hand dropped quickly to his trouser front.

I laughed and turned to the others. "I'm sorry to put you to this inconvenience, gentlemen," I said. "But I have a space problem up in my room. I've got a box up there that takes up almost the whole place."

The only one who got it was Amos Winthrop. I saw a knowing grin appear on his face. I wondered what his expression would be if he knew it was his daughter I was talking about.

By this time, Mac had recovered his aplomb and stepped in to take over. There were introductions all around and then we got down to business. As Mac explained to me, the three big chemical corporations had set up a separate company to sublicense from me. It was this company which would make the first payment and guarantee the royalties.

I had only one question to ask. "Who guarantees the money?"

Mac indicated one of the men. "Sheffield here," he said. "Mr. Sheffield is one of the partners of George Stewart, Inc."

I looked at Sheffield. Stewart, Morgan, Lehman were all good names down on the Street. I couldn't ask for better people financially. There was something about the man's face that seemed familiar. I searched my memory. Then I had it.

F. Martin Sheffield. New York, Boston, Southampton, Palm Beach. Harvard School of Business, summa cum laude, before the war. Major, U.S. Army, 1917–18. Three decorations for bravery under fire. Ten-goal polo-player. Society. Age now—from his appearance, about thirty-five; from the record, forty-two.

I remembered he'd come to visit my father about ten years ago. He'd wanted then to float a public issue for the company. My father had turned him down.

"No matter how good they make it sound, Junior," my father had said, "never let 'em get their hooks into you. Because then they run your business, not you. All they can give you is money when the only thing that counts is power. And that they always keep for themselves."

I stared at Sheffield. "How're you goin' to guarantee the payments?"

His dark, deep-set eyes glittered behind the pince-nez bifocals. "We're on the contract with the others, Mr. Cord," he said.

His voice was surprisingly deep for a slight man. And very sure of itself. It was as if he did not deign to answer my question, as if everybody knew that Stewart's name on a contract was guarantee enough.

Maybe it was, but something about him rankled deep inside me. "You didn't answer my question, Mr. Sheffield," I said politely. "I asked how the money was to be guaranteed. I'm not a banker or a Wall Street man, I'm just a poor boy who had to leave school and go to work because his pappy died. I don't understand these things. I know when I go into a bank and they ask me to guarantee something, I have to put up collateral—like land, mortgages, bonds, something of value—before they give me anything. That's what I mean."

A faintly cold smile came to his thin lips. "Surely, Mr. Cord, you don't mean to imply that all these companies might not be good for the amount promised?"

I kept my voice bland. "I didn't mean anything like that, Mr. Sheffield. It's just that men who have had more experience than I, men who are older and know more, tell me that these are unsettled times. The market's broke and banks are failing all over the country. There's no telling what might happen next. I'd like to know how I'm goin' to be paid, that's all."

"Your money will be guaranteed out of income that the new company will earn," Sheffield said, still patiently explaining.

"I see," I said, nodding my head. "You mean I'll be paid out of money you earn if I grant you the license?"

"That's about it," he said.

I took a cigarette from my pocket and lit it. "I still don't understand. Why can't they pay me all at once?"

"Ten million dollars is a large amount of cash, even for these companies," he said. "They have many demands on their capital. That's why we're in the picture."

"Oh," I said, still playing it dumb. "You mean you're going to advance the money?"

"Oh, no," he said quickly. "That's not it at all. We're simply underwriting the stock, providing the organizational capital to make the new company possible. That alone will come to several million dollars."

"Including your brokerage fees?"

"Of course," he answered. "That's quite customary."

"Of course."

He shot a shrewd look at me. "Mr. Cord, you object to our position?"

I shrugged my shoulders. "Not at all. Why should I? It's not my place to tell other people how to run their business. I have enough trouble with my own."

"But you do seem to have some doubts about our proposition."

"I do," I said. "I was under the impression I was to receive ten million dollars for these rights. Now I find I'm only *guaranteed* ten million dollars. There's a difference between the two. In one case, I'm paid outright, in the other, I'm an accidental participant in your venture, subject to the same risks that you are but with a limitation put upon the extent of my participation."

"Do you object to that kind of deal?"

"Not at all. It's just that I like to know where I stand."

"Good. Then we can get down to signing the papers." Sheffield smiled in relief.

"Not yet," I said and his smile vanished as quickly as it had come. "I'm willing to become a participant in the manner suggested but if I'm to take that risk, I feel I should be guaranteed fifteen million, not ten."

For a moment, there was a shocked silence, then everybody began to talk at once. "But you already agreed to ten!" Sheffield protested.

I stared at him. "No, I didn't. This is the first time we met."

Mac was blowing a gasket. "Wait a minute, Jonas. You led me to believe you'd listen to an offer of ten million dollars!"

"Well, I listened."

For the first time, I saw his lawyer's calm ruffled. "I acted in good faith on your behalf. I won't be a party to this kind of underhanded negotiation. If this deal doesn't go through as agreed, I'm through! I'm resigning!"

I stared at him impassively. "Suit yourself."

Mac raged. "Your trouble is you're getting too big for your breeches! I remember when you were still wet behind the ears—"

I was angry now; my voice went icy cold. "The trouble is you're just the lawyer and it's my property you're dealing with. I'll make the decision as to what I do with it—sell it or give it away, whatever I want to do. It's mine, I own it and you work for me. Remember that!"

Mac's face went white. I could see it all working around in his mind. The hundred thousand a year I was paying him. The bonus participation in profits. The house he lived in. The schools his kids were going to. His position in society. I wondered if at that moment he wasn't regretting the sixty-thousand-a-year practice he'd given up to come to me.

But I couldn't bring myself to feel sorry for him. He knew what he was doing. He even wrote his own contract, on his own terms. He wanted money and he got it. It was too late now for him to start complaining.

I looked at the others. They were staring at us. I knew then, sorry for Mac or not, I had to give him a leg up. "Aw, come off it, Mac," I said, making my voice warm and friendly. "We're too close to let a stupid thing like this come between us. Forget it. There'll be other deals. The important thing to do is to get your new contract signed so that I can be sure none of these other pirates steal you away from me."

I saw the look of relief flood into his face. "Sure, Jonas," he said. He hesitated. "I guess we're both a little bit overtired. Me with the negotiation, you with that record-breaking flight. I guess I just misunderstood what you told me."

He turned to the others. "I'm sorry, gentlemen," he said smoothly, himself once more. "It's my fault. I didn't mean to mislead you but I misunderstood Mr. Cord. My apologies."

An awkward silence fell in the room. For a moment nobody spoke, then I grinned and walked over to the urinal. "This is just so we don't have to write this meeting off as a total loss," I said over my shoulder.

It was Sheffield who made the first break. I heard him whispering hurriedly to the others. When I turned around, he looked at me. "Split it with you," he said. "Twelve five."

They wanted it real bad if they came up that quickly. At first, I shook my head, then I had an idea. "I heard a great deal about you from my father," I said. "He said you were a real sportsman, that you'd gamble on anything."

A smile appeared on his thin lips. "I've been known to wager a bit at times," he admitted.

"For two and a half million dollars, I'll bet you can't pee into that far urinal from where you're standing," I said, pointing to the one about four feet from him. "If you do, the deal is yours for twelve five. If you don't, I get fifteen."

His mouth hung open, his eyes staring behind their glasses. "Mr. Cord!" he sputtered.

"You can call me Jonas," I said. "Remember it's for two and a half million dollars."

He looked at the others. They stared back at him. Then at me. Finally the Mahlon Chemical man spoke up. "It's two and a half million dollars, Martin. I'd take a shot at it for that kind of money!"

Sheffield hesitated a moment. He looked at Mac but Mac wouldn't meet his gaze. Then he turned toward the urinal, his hand going to his fly. He looked at me. I nodded. Nothing happened. Nothing at all. He just stood there, a red flush creeping up his collar into his face. A moment passed, another moment. His face was red now.

I broke the silence. "All right, Mr. Sheffield," I said with a straight face. "I concede. You win the bet. The deal is for twelve five."

He stared at me, trying to read my mind. I kept my expression blank. I held out my hand toward him. He hesitated a moment, then took it.

"May I call you Martin?" I asked.

He nodded, a faint smile appearing on his thin lips. "Please do."

I shook his hand. "Martin," I said solemnly. "Your fly is open!"

CHAPTER THREE

MCALLISTER MADE THE NECESSARY CHANGES IN THE CONTRACTS AND we signed them right there. It was after four thirty when we came out into the lobby. I started for the elevator when Amos Winthrop tapped me on the shoulder.

I didn't want to talk to him. "Can it keep until morning, Amos?" I asked. "I gotta get some sleep."

His face crinkled in a knowing smile. He hit me on the shoulder jovially. "I know the kind of sleepin' you want to do, boy, but this is important."

"Nothing can be that important."

The elevator door opened and I stepped into it. Amos was right beside me. The operator started to close the doors. "Just a minute," I said.

The doors rolled open again and I stepped out. "All right, Amos," I asked. "What is it?"

We walked over to a couch and sat down. "I need another ten thousand," he said.

I stared at him. No wonder he was always broke. He spent it faster than they could print it. "What happened to all the cash you got for your stock?"

An embarrassed expression crossed his face. "It's gone," he said. "You know how much I owed."

I knew. He owed everybody. By the time he got through with his creditors and his ex-wives, I could see where the fifty grand had gone. I was beginning to feel sorry I'd included him in the deal but I'd thought he'd be able to contribute something to the company. At one time, he was one of the best designers of aircraft in the country.

"Your contract doesn't provide for advances like that," I said.

"I know," he answered. "But this is important. It won't happen again, I promise. It's for Monica."

"Monica?" I looked at him. This was going to be good. "What about her?"

He shook his head. "I want to send her to her mother in England. She's too much for me. I can't control her any more. She's seeing some guy on the sly and I have a feeling if she isn't balling him already, she soon will be."

For a moment, I stared at him. I wondered if this wasn't a gentle form of blackmail. It could be that he already knew and was taking this way of letting me know. "Do you know the guy?"

He shook his head. "If I did, I'd kill him," he said vehemently. "A nice sweet innocent kid like her."

I kept my face impassive. Love is blind but parents are blinder. Even a cheater like Amos, with all his knowledge, was no smarter than Joe Doakes in Pomona. "You talk to her?"

He shook his head again. "I tried but she won't listen. You know how kids are nowadays. They learn everything in school; you can't teach them anything. When she was sixteen, I found a package of Merry Widows in her pocketbook."

He should have stopped her then. He was about three years too late. She was nineteen now and carried her own brass ring. "Guys like you never learn."

"What was I supposed to do?" he asked truculently. "Keep her locked in her room?"

I shook my head. "You could have tried being her father."

"What makes you such an expert?" he snapped. "You won't talk like that after you have kids of your own."

I could have told him. I had a father who was too busy with his own life, too. But I was tired. I got to my feet.

"What about the money?" he asked anxiously.

"I'll give it to you," I said. A feeling of disgust suddenly came up in me. What did I need guys like this around me for? They were like leeches. Once they got into you, they never let go. "As a matter of fact, I'll give you twenty-five thousand."

An expression of surprised relief flooded across his face. "You will, Jonas?"

I nodded. "On one condition."

For the first time, caution came into his eyes. "What do you mean?"

"I want your resignation."

"From Winthrop Aircraft?" His voice was incredulous.

"From Cord Aircraft," I said pointedly.

The color began to drain from his face. "But—but I started the company. I know everything about it. I was just planning a new plane that the Army will sure as hell go for—"

"Take the money, Amos," I said coldly. "You've had it." I started for the ele-vator. I stepped inside and the boy closed the doors in his face. "Going up, Mr. Cord?" he asked.

I stared at him. That was a stupid question. What other way was there to go? "All the way," I said wearily.

Monica was lying across the bed in the tops of my pajamas, half asleep. She opened her eyes and looked at me. "Everything go all right?"

I nodded.

She watched me as I threw my shirt across a chair. "What did Daddy want?"

I stepped out of my trousers and caught the pajama bottoms she threw at me. "He just turned in his resignation," I said, kicking off my shorts and getting into the pajamas.

She sat up in bed, her brown eyes widening in surprise. "He did?"

I nodded.

"I wonder why?"

I looked at her. "He said it had something to do with you. That he wanted more time to be your father."

She stared at me for a moment, then began to laugh. "Well, I'll be damned," she said. "All my life I wanted him to pay some kind of attention to me and now, when I don't need him any more, he suddenly wants to play daddy."

"Don't need him any more?"

She nodded. "Not any more. Ever," she said slowly. She came off the bed and laid her head against my chest. Her voice was a childlike whisper of confidence. "Not now that I have you. You're everything to me—father, brother, lover."

I stroked her soft brown hair slowly. Suddenly, a surge of sympathy came up inside me. I knew how alone you could be when you were nineteen.

Her eyes were closed and there were faintly blue weary hollows in the soft white flesh beneath them. I pressed my lips lightly to her forehead. "Come to bed, child," I said gently. "It's almost morning."

She was asleep in a moment, her head resting on my shoulder, her neck in the crook of my arm. For a long time, I couldn't fall asleep. I lay there looking down at her quiet face as the sun came up and light spilled into the room.

Damn Amos Winthrop! Damn Jonas Cord! I cursed all men who were too busy and self-centered to be fathers to their children.

I began to feel weariness seep through me. Half asleep, I felt her move beside me and the warmth of her long, graceful body flowed down along my side. Then sleep came. The dark, starless night of wonderful sleep.

We were married the next evening at the Little Chapel in Reno.

CHAPTER FOUR

I SAW THE GLEAMING PHOSPHORESCENCE MOVING IN THE WATER AND flicked the fly gaily across the stream just over the trout. The instinct came up in me. I knew I had him. Everything was right. The water, the flickering shadows from the trees lining the bank, the bottle-blue, green and red tail of the fly at the end of my line. Another moment and the bastard would strike. I set myself when I heard Monica's voice from the bank behind me.

"Jonas!"

Her voice shattered the stillness and the trout dived for the bottom of the stream. The fly began to drag and before I turned around, I knew the honeymoon was over.

"What is it?" I growled.

She stood there in a pair of shorts, her knees red and her nose peeling. "There's a telephone call for you. From Los Angeles."

"Who?"

"I don't know," she answered. "It's a woman. She didn't give her name."

I looked back at the stream. There were no lights in the water. The fish were gone. That was the end of it. The fishing was over for the day.

I started toward the bank. "Tell her to hold on," I said. "I'll be up there in a minute."

She nodded and started back to the cabin. I began to reel in the line. I wondered who could be calling me. Not many people knew about the cabin in the hills.

When I was a kid, I used to come up here with Nevada. My father always intended to come along but he never did make it.

I came out of the stream and trudged up the path. It was late in the afternoon and the evening sounds were just beginning. Through the trees I could hear the crickets beginning their song.

I laid the rod alongside the outside wall of the cabin and went inside. Monica was sitting in a chair near the telephone, turning the pages of a magazine. I picked up the phone. "Hello."

"Mr. Cord?"

"Yes."

"Just a moment," the operator sang. "Los Angeles, your party is on the wire."

I heard a click, then a familiar voice. "Jonas?"

"Rina?"

"Yes," she said. "I've been trying to get you for three days. Nobody would tell me where you were, then I thought of the cabin."

"Great," I said, looking over the telephone at Monica. She was looking down at the magazine but I knew she was listening.

"By the way," Rina said in that low, husky voice. "Congratulations. I hope you'll be very happy. Your bride's a very pretty girl."

"You know her?"

"No," Rina answered quickly. "I saw the pictures in the papers."

"Oh," I said. "Thanks. But that isn't why you called."

"No, it's not," she said with her usual directness. "I need your help."

"If it's another ten you need, I can always let you have it."

"It's for more money than that. Much more."

"How much more?"

"Two million dollars."

"What?" I all but yelled. "What the hell do you need that much money for?"

"It's not for myself," she said. Her voice sounded very upset. "It's for Nevada. He's in a bind. He's about to lose everything he's got."

"But I thought he was doing great. The papers say he's making a half million dollars a year."

"He is," Rina said. "But—"

"But what?" I pulled out a cigarette and fished around for a match. I knew Monica saw me but she kept her nose buried in the magazine. "I'm listening," I said, dragging on the cigarette.

"Nevada's hocked everything he has to make a picture. He's been working on it for over a year and now everything's gone wrong and they don't want to release it."

"Why?" I asked. "Is it a stinker?"

"No," she said quickly. "It's not that. It's great. But only talking pictures are going. That's all the theaters will play."

"Why didn't he make a talking picture to start with?" I asked.

"He started it more than a year ago. Nobody expected talkies to come in the way they did," she answered. "Now the bank's calling his loan and Norman won't advance any more money. He claims he's stuck with his own pictures."

"I see," I said.

"You've got to help him, Jonas. His whole life is wrapped up in this picture. If he loses it, he'll never get over it."

"Nevada never cared that much about money," I said.

"It isn't the money," she said quickly. "It's the way he feels about this picture. He believes in it. For once, he had a chance to show what the West was really like."

"Nobody gives a damn what the West was really like."

"Did you ever see one of his pictures?" she asked.

"No."

A shade of disbelief crept into her voice. "Weren't you curious to see what he looked like on the screen?"

"Why should I be?" I asked. "I know what he looks like."

Her voice went flat. "Are you going to help?"

"That's a lot of dough," I said. "Why should I?"

"I remember when you wanted something real bad and he gave it to you."

I knew what she was talking about. Nevada's stock interest in Cord Explosives. "It didn't cost him two million bucks," I said.

"It didn't?" she asked. "What's it worth now?"

That stopped me for a moment. Maybe it wasn't yet, but in five more years it would be.

"If he's in that much of a jam," I said, "why didn't he call me himself?"

"Nevada's a proud man," she said. "You know that."

"How come you're so interested?"

"Because he's my friend," she said quickly. "When I needed help, he didn't ask any questions."

"I'm not promising anything," I said. "But I'll fly down to L.A. tonight. Where can I reach you?"

"I'm staying at Nevada's," she said. "But you better let me meet you someplace. I don't want him to know I called you."

"O.K.," I said. "I'll be at the Beverly Hills Hotel about midnight."

I put down the telephone. "Who was that?" Monica asked.

"My father's widow," I said, walking past her toward the bedroom. "Pack your bags. I'm taking you back to the ranch. I have to go down to L.A. on business tonight."

"But it's only been five days," she said. "You promised we'd have a two-week honeymoon."

"This is an emergency."

She followed me into the bedroom as I sat down on the bed and pulled off my waders. "What will people think if we come back from our honeymoon after only five days?" she said.

I stared up at her. "What the hell do I care what they think?"

She began to cry. "I won't go," she said, stamping her foot.

I got to my feet and started out. "Then stay!" I said angrily. "I'm going down the hill to get the car. If you're not ready when I get back, I'm leaving without you!"

What was it with dames, anyway? You stood in front of some two-bit preacher for five lousy minutes and when you walked away, everything was turned inside out.

Before you were married, it was great. You were the king. She stood there with one hand on your cock to let you know she wanted it, and with the other, tried to light your cigarette, wash your back, feed your face and smooth your pillow all at the same time.

Then come the magic words and you got to beg for it. You got to go by the book. Play with it, warm it up, treat it gentle. You got to rest on your elbows and light her cigarettes and carry her wrap and open doors. You even have to thank her when she lets you have it, the same piece she couldn't stop offering you before.

I pulled the car up in front of the cabin and tooted the horn. Monica came out carrying a small bag and stood there waiting for me to open the car door. After a moment, she opened the door and got in with a grieved expression. And she wore the same expression for the two hours it took us to drive back to the ranch.

It was nine o'clock when I pulled up in front of the house. As usual, Robair was at the door. His expression didn't change when I stayed in the car after he took out Monica's valise. His eyes flicked across my face as he turned and bowed to Monica. "Evenin', Miz Cord," he said. "Ah have you' room all tidied up an' ready for you." Robair looked at me again and turned and went back up the steps.

When Monica spoke, her voice was low and taut as a bowstring. "How long will you be gone?"

I shrugged. "As long as it takes for me to finish my business." Then I felt a softening inside me. What the hell, after all we'd only been married for five days. "I'll get back as quick as I can."

"Don't hurry back!" she said and stalked up the steps and into the house without a backward glance.

I swore angrily and threw the car into gear, then started up the road to the plant. I kept the old Waco in the field behind it. I was still angry when I climbed into the cockpit and I didn't begin to feel better until I was twenty-five hundred feet up and heading toward Los Angeles.

CHAPTER FIVE

I LOOKED DOWN AT THE BLUE-COVERED SCRIPT IN MY HAND, THEN BACK UP at Rina. Time hadn't taken anything away from her. She was still slim and strong and her breasts jutted like rocks at the canyon edge and I knew they would be just as hard to the touch. The only things that had changed were her eyes. There was a sureness in them that hadn't been there before.

"I'm not much for reading," I said.

"I thought that was what you'd say," she said. "So I arranged with the studio to screen the picture for you. They're waiting down there right now."

"How long you been out here?"

"About a year and a half. Ever since I came back from Europe."

"Staying at Nevada's all this time?"

She nodded.

"You sleeping with him?"

She didn't evade. "Yes. He's very good for me."

"Are you good for him?" I asked.

Her eyes were still on mine. "I hope so," she said quietly. "But that doesn't really matter. You don't give a damn whether I am or I'm not."

"I was just curious," I said, getting to my feet and dropping the script on the chair. "I was just wondering what it takes to keep you."

"It's not what you think," she said quickly.

"What is it, then?" I shot back. "Money?"

"No." She shook her head. "A man. A real man. I never could make it with boys."

That touched home. "Maybe I'll make it in time," I said.

"You just got married five days ago."

I stared at her for a moment. I could feel all the old familiar excitement climbing up in me. "Let's go," I said tersely. "I haven't got all night."

I sat in the darkened projection room with Rina on one side of me and Von Elster, the director, on the other.

Rina hadn't lied. The picture was great, but for only one reason. Nevada. He held the picture together with an innate core of strength that somehow illuminated the screen.

It was the strength I had always felt in him but up there it was larger, more purposeful, and no one could escape it. He started out on that screen as a sixteen-year-old boy and rode off into the hills in the end as a twenty-five-year-old man. Not once during the whole picture was I ever aware of his real age.

I leaned back in my chair with a sigh as the lights came up. I reached for a cigarette, still feeling the excitement of the screen. I lit the cigarette and dragged on it. The surging reached down into my loins. There was still something missing, I felt vaguely. Then I felt the heat in my thighs and I knew what it was.

I looked at Von Elster. "Outside of that small bit about the madam in New Orleans and the convict's daughter in the cow town, there aren't any women in the picture."

Von Elster smiled. "There are some things you don't do in a Western. Women is one of them."

"Why?"

"Because the industry feels that the image of the clean, strong man must be preserved. The hero can be guilty of any crime but fornication."

I laughed and got to my feet. "Forgive the question," I said. "But why can't you just add voices the way you did the music? Why make the whole thing over?"

"I wish we could," Von Elster said. "But the projection speed of silent film is different from sound film. Talking film is projected at the speed of speech, while silent film moves much faster, depending on dialogue cards and broader action to carry the story."

I nodded. Mechanically, what he said made sense. Like everything else in this world, there was a technology to this business and it was beginning to interest me. Without mechanics, the whole thing would be impossible.

"Come back to the hotel with me. I'd like to talk some more about this."

I saw a sudden look of caution come into Rina's eyes. She glanced at Von Elster, then turned to me. "It's almost four o'clock," she said quickly. "And I think we've gone about as far as we can without Nevada."

"O.K.," I said easily. "You bring him up to the hotel in the morning. Eight o'clock, all right?"

"Eight o'clock will be fine."

"I can drop you off at your hotel, Mr. Cord," Von Elster said eagerly.

I glanced at Rina. She shook her head imperceptibly. "Thanks," I said. "Rina can drop me on her way home."

Rina didn't speak until the car pulled to a stop in front of the hotel. "Von Elster is on the make," she said. "He's worried. He's never made a talking picture before and he wants to do this one. It's a big picture and if it comes off, he'll be in solid again."

"You mean he's shaky?" I asked.

"Everybody in Hollywood is. From Garbo and Gilbert on down. No one is sure just what talking pictures are going to do to their career. I hear John Gilbert's voice is so bad that MGM won't even pencil him in for another picture."

"What about Nevada's voice?"

"It's good," she said. "Very good. We made a sound test the other day."

"Well, that's one less thing to worry about."

"Are you going to do it?" she asked.

"What's in it for me if I do?" I countered.

"You could make a lot of money," she said.

"I don't need it," I said. "I'll make a lot of money, anyway."

Her eyes turned to me, her voice was cold. "You haven't changed, have you?"

I shook my head. "No. Why should I? Does anybody? Did you?" I reached for her hand. It was cold as ice. "Just how much are you willing to give to bail Nevada out?"

Her eyes were steady on mine. "I'd give everything I've got if it would help."

I felt a kind of sadness creeping into me. I wondered how many people would say that for me. Right then, I couldn't think of one. I let go of her hand and got out of the car.

She leaned toward me. "Well, Jonas, have you made up your mind?"

"Not yet," I said slowly. "There's a lot more I have to know about."

"Oh." She leaned back disappointedly.

"But don't you worry," I said. "If I do it, you'll be the first one I come to for payment."

She signaled the chauffeur. He put the car into gear. "Knowing you," she said quietly, "I never expected anything else."

The limousine rolled away and I turned and walked into the hotel. I went up to my room and opened up the script. It took about an hour and a half to go through it. It was almost six o'clock before I closed my eyes.

CHAPTER SIX

THE TELEPHONE KEPT BANGING AWAY AT MY HEAD. I SHOOK MY HEAD TO clear it and looked at my watch. It was a few minutes past seven. I picked up the phone.

"Mr. Cord? Von Elster here. I'm sorry to bother you so early, but I'm down in the lobby with Mr. Norman. It's very important we see you before you meet with Nevada."

"Who's Norman?" I asked, still trying to clear my head.

"Bernard B. Norman of Norman Pictures. That's the company releasing the picture. Mr. Norman feels he can be of help to you in making the right kind of deal with Nevada."

"Why should I need any help?" I asked. "I've known Nevada all my life."

His voice grew confidential. "Nevada's all right, Mr. Cord. But his agent, Dan Pierce, is a very sharp man. Mr. Norman just wants to give you a few pointers before you tangle with him."

I reached for a cigarette. Von Elster hadn't lost any time. He'd run right back to his boss the minute he smelled my money. I didn't know what they wanted but I was damn sure it boded no good for Nevada.

"Wait down there until I can get dressed. I'll call you."

I put down the phone and finished lighting the cigarette. The blue cover of the script caught my eye. I picked up the telephone again. I gave the operator Tony Moroni's home number out in the valley.

"Sorry to wake you up, Tony," I said. "This is Jonas."

His soft voice chuckled over the phone. "That's all right, Jonas. I get up early, anyway. By the way, congratulations on your marriage."

"Thanks," I said automatically, suddenly remembering I hadn't even thought about Monica since I came to town. "Did you bank Nevada Smith's new picture?"

"*The Renegade?*"

"Yeah."

"Yes, we did," he answered.

"What's the story on it?" I asked.

"It's a good picture," he said. "It would have a better chance if it were a talkie, but it's a good picture."

"If you think it's good, why are you calling your loan?"

"Let me ask a question first, Jonas," he said. "Exactly what is your interest?"

"I don't know yet," I said frankly. "Nevada's my friend. I want to find out what's happening. Why are you calling the loan?"

"You know how we work," he explained. "We made the loan to Smith on his collateral plus the guarantee of the Norman Pictures Company. Now Bernie Norman needs credit to remake some of his own pictures, so he's withdrawing his guarantee. Automatically, that means we have to call in the loan."

No wonder Von Elster and Bernie Norman were down in the lobby waiting to see me. They didn't want anybody to interfere with their fingering Nevada.

"Exactly what happens to Nevada?" I asked.

"If he can't pay the loan, we foreclose on the picture, then all his collateral goes into an escrow account. Then we liquidate until we recover."

"What do you do with the picture then?" I asked. "Junk it?"

"Oh, no." He laughed softly. "Then we turn it over to Norman to release. That gives Bernie a chance to get his money out. He has about four hundred thousand in it. After he recovers, the overage is paid to us. When our loan is paid off, we turn over what's left to Smith."

The whole thing was beginning to make sense. By the time any money got to Nevada, he'd have had it. "What's the chances on any overage?" I asked.

"Not very good," Tony answered. "Under the present deal, the distribution fees are very low and Nevada Smith's money comes out first. When we take over, the fees will triple and his share will come out last."

"Who gets the fees—the bank?"

He laughed again. "Of course not. Bernie does. He's the distributor."

Now I had it. The boys downstairs were going to make it real big. Screw Nevada. That way, they could grab themselves off a big one for practically nothing. I wondered just how smart Nevada's agent could be if he let him stick his head into a trap like that.

"One more question, Tony," I said, "and I'll stop bothering you. How much more money should it take to make *The Renegade* over as a talkie?"

He was silent for a moment. "Let's see," he said. "The sets are still standing, they have all the costumes. That's about half the cost. Maybe another million; less, if they're lucky."

"Is it worth it?"

He hesitated. "I usually don't venture opinions on pictures. Too many things can happen."

"This time, venture," I said. "I need an opinion from somebody who hasn't any ax to grind."

"From every report I've had, it could be a very good gamble."

"Thanks," I said. "Now do me a favor. Hold off any action on the loan until I talk to you later in the day. Maybe I'll come in on the guarantee in place of Norman."

"You'll still need another million after that."

"I know," I answered. "But my writing hand's still good. I can always sign another note."

Moroni laughed pleasantly as we said our good-bys. He wasn't worried. He knew I could cover the money easily out of the advance I got from the syndicate that leased the patents on my plastic mold. Bankers always were ready to lend you as much money as you wanted, so long as you could put up collateral.

I looked down at my watch as I put down the phone. It was almost seven thirty and I felt fuzzy. I started to pick up the phone, then changed my mind. The hell with them. Let them wait if they wanted to see me. I turned and went into the bathroom to take a shower.

The telephone rang three different times while I was under the shower. I stood there letting the hot water soak into my skin and wash away the weariness. It was almost eight o'clock when I came out of the bathroom and the telephone began ringing again.

It was Von Elster again. His voice was low and conspiratorial. "Nevada, his agent and Rina are on their way up," he whispered. "They didn't see us."

"Good," I said.

"But how are we going to meet?"

"I guess it's too late now," I said easily. "I'll just have to take my chances with Nevada's agent, I guess. Tell your Mr. Norman I appreciate his offer, though. If there's anything I need, I'll call him."

I heard his gasp of shock as I hung up. I laughed and wondered how he was going to explain that to his boss. I climbed into my trousers and was reaching for a shirt when a knock came at the door.

"Come in," I yelled from the bedroom. I heard the door open and finished buttoning up my shirt. I looked for my shoes but they were over on the other side of the bed. It wasn't worth walking over to get them so I came out in my bare feet.

Rina was already seated on the big couch. Nevada and another man were standing in the middle of the room. A slow smile came over Nevada's face. He held out his hand. "Jonas," he said warmly.

I took his hand awkwardly. It seemed funny to shake hands with him as one would with a stranger. "Nevada."

There were faint lines of strain in the corners of his eyes, but for a moment they disappeared as he looked up into my face. "You're lookin' more like your pappy every day, son."

"You're lookin' pretty good yourself. Where'd you get them duds?"

A faint tinge of sheepishness came into his face. "That's part of the act," he said. "I got to wear 'em. The kids expect it." He fished in his pocket with that familiar gesture and came up with a package of makin's. He began to roll a cigarette. "I been readin' a lot about you in the papers. Flyin' from Paris to Los Angeles, gettin' married an' all. Your wife with you?"

I shook my head.

He glanced at me shrewdly. In that moment, I knew he knew how it was with Monica and me. He could read me like a book. I could never hide anything from him. "Too bad," he said. "I'd like to have met her."

I looked at the other man to change the subject. Nevada caught himself quickly. "Oh, this is Dan Pierce, my agent."

We shook hands and I came right to the point. "I saw your picture last night," I said. "I liked it. Too bad you have to make it over."

"I thought talking pictures wouldn't last," Nevada said.

"That's not the whole story, Nevada," Pierce broke in angrily. He turned to me. "Nevada wanted the picture silent, sure, but by the time we'd started shooting, he saw he was wrong. We tried then to turn it into a talkie but we couldn't."

"Why?"

"Norman wouldn't let us," Pierce said. "He only had one sound stage at that time and he was using it for one of his own pictures. He insisted we start shooting right away or he'd withdraw his guarantee."

The picture was clear now. The whole thing had been a sucker play from the start. I looked at Nevada. I didn't understand it. He was a better poker player than that.

Nevada read me again. "I know what you're thinkin', boy," he said quickly. "But I wanted to make this picture. It said something that none of the other phonies I'd been in even came close to."

"What about Norman?" I asked. "How come they won't advance you the money to shoot it over?"

"They've run out of credit," Nevada said. "That's why the bank is calling the loan."

"That's a lot of crap!" Pierce exploded again. "We're caught in a squeeze play. Bernie Norman makes the bank call our loan and the bank turns the picture back to him. He gets it for peanuts—about a third what it would have cost him to make it."

"How much would it take to make the picture over?" I asked.

Nevada looked at me. "About a million bucks."

"Plus the loan the bank is calling," Pierce added quickly.

I turned to him. "Would you still have Norman release the picture?"

He nodded. "Sure. They've got ten thousand contracts on it an' if it's a talkie, not a theater will cancel out."

"If it's silent?"

"We'll be lucky to get fifteen hundred," he said. "They all want talkies."

"What do you think I should do?"

Nevada hesitated a moment, then his eyes came squarely on mine. "I wouldn't do it if I was you," he said frankly. "You could blow the whole bundle."

I saw the look that Pierce threw him. It was filled with anger but also with a peculiar sort of respect. To Pierce I was just another sucker. But to his credit, he recognized that I was something more to Nevada.

I stared at him for a moment, then turned and looked down at Rina, sitting on the couch. Her face was impassive. Only her eyes were pleading.

I turned back to Nevada. "I'll take the shot," I said. "But only on one condition. I'll buy you out and it will be my picture. And when we make it again, we'll make it the way I want it. There'll be no arguments; everybody will do as they're told. You included. If I'm going to lose the hand, at least I want to deal the cards."

Nevada nodded. He'd heard my father say the same words often enough. And he'd been the one who taught me always to reach for the deal when the stakes were high.

"But what do you know about making pictures?" Pierce asked.

"Nothing," I said. "But how many people do you know who have made a talking picture?"

That stopped him. I could see the comprehension come into his eyes. What I had said was true. It was a new business. There were no veterans any more. I turned back to Nevada. "Well?"

"I don't know," he said slowly. "I'm lettin' you take the whole risk. I can't lose anything."

"You're wrong!" Pierce said quickly. "If it's a stinker, your career is shot!"

Nevada smiled at him. "I got along pretty good before," he said. "I'm a little old to worry about anything I fell into by accident."

"Well, Nevada?"

He stuck out his hand and the worry lines around his eyes lifted suddenly and he was young again. "It's a deal, Junior."

I took his hand and then went over to the telephone. I called Moroni at the bank. "Make arrangements to transfer the loan to Cord Explosives," I said.

"Good luck, Jonas," he said with a chuckle. "I had the feeling you were going to do it."

"Then you knew more than I did."

"That's what makes a good banker," he said.

I hung up and turned back to the others. "Now, the first thing I do is fire Von Elster."

Nevada's face was shocked. "But Von is one of the best in the business," he protested. "He's directed every picture I ever made. He discovered me."

"He's a lousy little shit," I said. "The minute he thought you were in trouble, he tried to sell you out. He had Bernie Norman up here at seven o'clock this morning. They wanted to give me some free advice. I didn't talk to them."

"Now maybe you'll believe me when I say Bernie was behind the squeeze," Pierce said.

"Like it or not, Nevada," I said, "we made a deal. It's my picture and what I say goes."

He nodded silently.

"The next thing I want is for Pierce to arrange for me to see as many of the talkies as possible in the next three days. Then, next weekend, I'll fly you all to New York. We're goin' to spend three or four days goin' to the theater. We might even pick up a stage director while we're there. We'll see." I paused to light a cigarette and saw a sudden look come over Nevada's face. "What are you smiling at?"

"Like I said, you're gettin' more like your pappy every day."

I grinned back at him. Just then, the waiter came in with breakfast. Nevada and Pierce went into the bathroom to wash up and Rina and I were left alone.

There was a gentle look on her face. "If you'd only let yourself go, Jonas," she said softly, "I think you might become a human being."

I looked into her eyes. "Don't try to con me," I said. "We both know why I did it. You and I made our deal last night."

The gentle look faded from her face. "Do you want me to blow you right now?" she asked.

I knew I had hit her from the way she spoke. I smiled. "I can wait."

"So can I," she replied. "Forever, if I have to."

Just then the telephone rang. "Get it," I said.

Rina picked it up and I heard a voice crackle for a moment, then she handed the phone to me. "Your wife."

"Hello, Monica."

Her voice was filled with anger. "Business!" she shrieked. "And when I call you up, some cheap whore answers. I suppose you're going to tell me it's your stepmother!"

"That's right!"

There was an angry click and the phone went dead in my hands. I looked down at it for a moment, then began to laugh. Everything was so right. And so wrong.

CHAPTER SEVEN

I LOOKED OUT THE WINDOW AT THE FIELD. THERE WERE SEVERAL PLANES warming up on the line, the red, white and blue ICA gleaming in the circle along their sides and under their wings. I looked down at the planning board, then up at the designer.

Morrissey was young, even younger than I. He had graduated from M.I.T., where he'd majored in aeronautical engineering and design. He wasn't a flier; he was of a new generation that walked on the sky. What he proposed was radical. A single-wing, two-motor plane that would outlift anything in the air.

He set his glasses lower on his nose. "The way I see it, Mr. Cord," he said in his precise manner, "is that by deepening the wings, we get all the lift we need and also increase our fuel capacity. Plus which, we have the added advantage of keeping our pilot in direct visual control."

"What I'm interested in is the payload and speed," I said.

"If my calculations are correct," Morrissey said, "we should be able to carry twenty passengers in addition to the pilot and copilot at a cruising speed of about two fifty. It should fly for about six hours before refueling."

"You mean we could fly from here to New York with only one stopover in Chicago?" Buzz asked skeptically. "I don't believe it!"

"That's what my calculations show, Mr. Dalton," Morrissey said politely.

Buzz looked at me. "You can throw away your money on fool schemes like this," he said, "but not me. I've been through too many of these pipe dreams."

"About how much would it take to build the first one?" I asked Morrissey.

"Four hundred, maybe five hundred thousand. After we get rid of the bugs, we can produce them for about a quarter of a million."

Dalton laughed raucously. "A half million bucks for one airplane? That's crazy. We'll never get our money out."

First-class passage coast to coast by train was over four hundred dollars. It took almost four full days. Plus meals, it came to more than five hundred bucks per passenger. A plane like this would have a payload of seven grand a trip, plus the mail franchise, which would bring it up to about eighty-five hundred dollars. Flying five trips a week, in less than twenty weeks we could get all our costs back, plus operating expenses. From there on in, it would be gravy. Why, we could even afford to throw in free meals on the flight.

I looked down at my watch. It was almost nine o'clock. I got to my feet. "I have to get down to the studio. They're shooting the first scene today."

Dalton's face turned red with anger. "Come off it, Jonas. Get down to business. For the past month and a half, all you been doin' is spending time at that goddam studio. While you're jerkin' off with that lousy picture, we got to find ourselves a plane to build. If we don't, the whole industry will get ahead of us."

I stared at him, unsmiling. "As far as I'm concerned," I said, "we have one."

"You're not—" he said incredulously, "you don't mean you're goin' to take a chance with this?"

I nodded, then turned to Morrissey. "You can start building the plane right away."

"Wait a minute," Dalton snapped. "If you think ICA is going to foot the bill, you're crazy. Don't forget I own half of the stock."

"And Cord Explosives owns the other half," I said. "Cord Explosives also holds over half a million dollars of mortgages on ICA planes, most of which are past due right now. If I foreclosed on them, I'd wind up owning all of Intercontinental Airlines."

He stared at me angrily for a moment, then his face relaxed into a grin. "I shoulda known better, Jonas. I shoulda learned my lesson when I lost that Waco to you in the poker game."

I smiled back. "You're a great flier, Buzz. You stick to flying and leave the business end to me. I'll make a rich man out of you yet."

He reached for a cigarette. "O.K.," he said easily. "But I still think you're nuts to build this plane. We could lose our shirt on it."

I didn't answer as we walked out to my car. There was no use explaining to Buzz the simple rules of credit. ICA would order twenty of these planes from Cord Aircraft. The two companies would then give chattel mortgages on them to Cord Explosives. And Cord Explosives would discount those mortgages at the banks, even before the planes were built. The worst that could happen, if the plane was no good, was that Cord Explosives would end up with a whopping tax deduction.

I got into the car. "Good luck with the picture!" Buzz yelled after me as I pulled away.

I turned into the main gate at the Norman studios. The guard looked out and waved me on. "Good morning, Mr. Cord," he called. "Good luck, sir."

I smiled and drove toward the parking lot. There was a small marker with my name on it. MR. CORD. They didn't miss a trick when it came to sucking ass. There was a reserved table with my name on it in the executive dining room. I also had a private bungalow with a suite of offices and two secretaries, a liquor cabinet stocked to the brim, an electric refrigerator, a private can and shower, a dressing room, a conference room and two secretarial offices in addition to my own.

I went through the back door of my bungalow and directly into my office. I wasn't at the desk more than a moment when one of the secretaries came in.

She stood in front of the desk, looking very efficient with her notebook and pencil. "Good morning, Mr. Cord," she said brightly. "Any dictation?"

I shook my head. You'd think by this time she'd know better. For the past five weeks, this had been going on every morning. I never write anything—messages, memos, instructions. If I want anything written, I call McAllister. That's what lawyers are for.

The telephone on my desk buzzed. She picked it up. "Mr. Cord's office." She listened a moment, then turned to me. "They've completed rehearsal on Stage Nine. And they're ready for their first take. They want to know if you'd like to come down."

I got up. "Tell them I'm on my way."

Stage Nine was at the far end of the lot. We built the New Orleans set there because we figured it was quieter and there wouldn't be any interfering sounds coming across from the other stages. I began to hurry along the brick paths, cursing the distance, until I saw a messenger's bicycle leaning against one of the executive bungalows. A moment later, I was pedaling like mad down the path. I heard the messenger start yelling behind me.

I pulled around in front of Stage Nine and almost crashed into a man opening the door. He stood there and looked at me in shocked surprise. It was Bernie Norman. "Why, Mr. Cord," he said. "You didn't have to do that. You could have called for a car to bring you down here."

I leaned the bike against the wall. "I didn't have time, Mr. Norman," I said. "They said they were ready to start. It's my money and my time they're spending in there."

They were ready to play the first scene, the one where Max, as a young man, is having his first interview with the madam of the fancy house. That wasn't the opening of the picture, but that's the way they shoot them. They make all the interior scenes first, then the exteriors. When it's all finished, an editor splices it together in its proper sequence.

The actress playing the madam was Cynthia Randall, Norman's biggest female star. She was supposed to be the sexiest thing in the movies. Personally, she didn't do a thing for me. I like my women with tits. Two make-up men and a hairdresser were hovering over her as she sat in front of the dressing table that was part of the set.

Nevada was standing over in the other corner, his back to me, talking to Rina. He turned around as I came up and a chill ran through me as memory dragged up a picture of him from my childhood. He looked even younger than he did when I first saw him. I don't know how he did it; even his eyes were the eyes of a young man.

He smiled slowly. "Well, Junior. Here we go."

I nodded, still staring at him. "Yeah," I said. "Here we go."

Somebody yelled, "Places, everybody!"

"I guess that means me," Nevada said.

Rina's face was turned toward the set, a rapt expression in her eyes. A man pushed past carrying a cable. I turned away from him and almost bumped into another man. I decided to get out of the way before I did any damage.

I wound up near the sound booth. From there I could see and hear everything. Now I knew why pictures cost so much money. We were on our eleventh take of that same scene when I noticed the sound man in the booth. He was bent over the control board, his earphones tight to his head, twisting the dials crazily.

Every other moment, I could see his lips move in silent curses, then he would spin the dials again.

"Something wrong with the machine?" I asked.

He looked up at me. I could tell from his look he didn't know who I was. "There's nothing wrong with the machine," he said.

"Something's bothering you?"

"Look, buddy," he said. "We both need our jobs, right?"

I nodded.

"When the boss tells yuh to make somebody look good, yuh do what he says— yuh don't ask no questions. Right?"

"Right," I said.

"Well, I'm doin' my best. But I ain't God. I can't change the sound of voices."

I stared at him, a kind of dismay creeping over me. I had only Rina's word that Nevada's voice test had been O.K. "You mean Nevada Smith?"

He shook his head. "Naah," he said contemptuously. "He's O.K. It's the dame. She comes over so nasal it sounds like her voice is coming out of her eyeballs."

The sound man turned back to his machine. I reached over and snatched the earphones off his head. He turned angrily. "What the hell's the idea?"

But I had them on by then and there was nothing he could do but stand there. Nevada was speaking. His voice came through fine—there was a good sound to it. Then Cynthia Randall began to speak and I didn't know whether to believe my eyes or my ears.

Her voice had all the irritating qualities of a cat wailing on the back fence, with none of the sexual implications. It shivered its way down my spine. A voice like that could put an end to sex, even in the fanciest house in New Orleans. I ripped the earphones from my head and thrust them into the sound man's astonished hands. I started out on the set. A man grabbed at me but I angrily pushed him aside.

A voice yelled, "Cut!" and a sudden silence fell over the set. Everyone was staring at me with strangely startled expressions.

I was seething. All I knew was that someone had played me for a patsy and I didn't like it. I think the girl knew why I was there. A look of caution appeared in her eyes, even as she tried to bring a smile to her lips.

Bernie Norman hurried onto the set. A flicker of relief showed in her face and I knew the whole story. She reached for Bernie's arm as he turned toward me. "Mr. Cord," he asked, "is anything wrong?"

"Yeah," I said grimly. "Her. Get her off the set. She's fired!"

"You just can't do that, Mr. Cord!" he exclaimed. "She has a contract for this picture!"

"Maybe she has," I admitted, "but not with me. It wasn't my pen she squeezed the last drop of ink out of."

Bernie stared at me, the pale coming up underneath his tan. He knew what I was talking about. "This is highly irregular," he protested. "Miss Randall is a very important star."

"I don't care if she's the Mother of God," I interrupted. I held out my wrist and looked down at the watch and then back up at him. "You've got exactly five minutes to get her off this set or I'll close down this picture and hit you with the biggest lawsuit you ever had!"

❖   ❖   ❖

I sat down on the canvas chair with my name on it and looked around the now deserted set. Only a few people hovered about, moving like disembodied ghosts at a banquet. I looked over at the sound man hunched over his control board, his earphones still glued to his head. I closed my eyes wearily. It was after ten o'clock at night.

I heard footsteps approaching and opened my eyes. It was Dan Pierce. He'd been on the phone trying to borrow a star from one of the other studios. "Well?" I asked.

He shook his head negatively. "No dice. MGM wouldn't lend us Garbo. They're planning a talking picture for her themselves."

"What about Marion Davies?"

"I just hung up on her. She loves the part but it isn't the kind of thing she feels she can do. Maybe we should've stuck with Cynthia Randall. It's costing you thirty grand a day to sit around like this."

I lit the cigarette and stared up at him. "I'd rather drop it now than be laughed out of the theater and lose it all later."

"Maybe we could bring an actress in from New York?"

"We haven't the time," I said. "Ten days, three hundred grand."

Just then, Rina came up with some sandwiches. "I thought you'd be hungry," she said, "so I sent out for these."

I took one and bit into it somberly. She turned and gave one to the second man. "Thanks, Miss Marlowe."

"You're welcome," she said and walked back to where she'd been sitting with Nevada.

"Too bad you can't find one that sounds like her," the sound man mumbled through a mouthful of sandwich.

I looked at him. "What do you mean?"

"She's got somethin' in her voice that gets yuh," he said. "If it came through on the sound track like that, you'd have them falling out of the balconies."

I stared at him now. "You mean Rina?"

He nodded and swallowed his mouthful. "Yeah." A slow, meaningful grin came to his lips. "An' if I ain't crazy, she'd photograph like a roll in the hay, too. She's all woman."

I turned to Dan. "What do you think?"

"It's possible," he admitted cautiously.

"Then, let's go," I said, getting to my feet. "Thirty grand a day is a lot of money."

Rina took it as a big joke when I asked her to speak a few of the lines into the microphone. She still didn't think I meant it when I called the crew back for a full-scale screen test. I don't think she took me seriously at all until we sat in the screening room at two that morning and watched her and Nevada play one scene.

I'd never seen anything like her on the screen before. Whatever it was she had, it was twice as strong up there on the screen. She just plain made your mouth water.

I turned to her. "Go home and go to bed. I want you in wardrobe at six o'clock tomorrow morning. We start shooting at nine."

She shook her head. "Uh-uh, Jonas. The joke's gone far enough. I won't have any part of it."

"You be on that set ready to shoot at nine!" I said grimly. "You're the one who called, not me, remember?"

I looked at Nevada. There was a puzzled expression on his face. And something about the clear innocence in his eyes hit me wrong. "And you better see to it that she shows up!" I said angrily.

I turned and stormed out of the projection room, leaving them staring after me with shocked faces.

CHAPTER EIGHT

I OPENED ONE EYE SLOWLY AND PEERED AT MY WRIST WATCH. TWO O'CLOCK! I sat up quickly and the pain almost split my skull. I groaned out loud and the door opened.

It was Dan, already dressed in cream-colored slacks and a loud sports shirt. He held a glass of what looked like tomato juice. "Here," he said. "Drink it down, pal. It'll wash the fuzz away."

I lifted the glass to my lips. It tasted awful going down but he was right. A moment later, my head began to clear. I looked around the bedroom. It was a shambles. "Where are the girls?" I asked.

"I paid them off an' sent them home."

"Good." I got to my feet woozily. "I gotta get down to the studio. They were going to start shooting at nine."

Dan smiled. "I called and told them you were tied up but would get down there this afternoon. I figured it was better if you got some sleep. That was a hectic night."

I grinned at him. It sure was.

Dan and I had really tied one on the night before. I'd met him coming off the set and offered to give him a lift downtown. But on the way we'd decided to stop and eat. I was wound up tighter than a dollar watch and he'd offered to help me unwind. Steaks at a spot he knew, which ought to have been closed but wasn't, along with bourbon and later the works. The works came out of his little black book, which all agents seem to carry. I'd unwound all right but now I wondered if they'd ever be able to wind me up again.

His Jap houseboy had shirred eggs and sausages ready when I came out of the shower. I was starved. I ate six eggs and about a dozen of the little bangers. When I put down my fourth cup of coffee Dan smiled and asked, "How are yuh feeling now?"

I grinned back at him. "I never felt better in my life." It was true. For once I felt relaxed and loose. There wasn't the usual tightening in my gut as I thought about the day. "You said something about getting down to business?"

We'd talked the night before, more than I usually did with a stranger. But Dan Pierce was different. He was a type I hadn't encountered before and he fascinated me. He was tough, shrewd and knew what he wanted. I was in over my head and I knew it. I wouldn't be for long, but until I got the hang of it I could use someone like Dan Pierce.

"I sold my agency this morning to MCA."

"What for?"

"Because I'm coming in with you."

"Aren't you jumping the gun a little?" I asked. "I'm only in for this one picture. What'll you do after that?"

Dan smiled. "That's what you say. It even might be what you really believe, right now. But I know different. You got a feel for this business—a natural feel for it that not many people have. And there's a challenge that you can't resist. You just found another gambling game. You'll stick."

I sipped at the coffee. It was strong and black, just the way I liked it. "And just how do you figure you can help?" I asked.

"Because I know all the angles in this business, all the dirty tricks it would take you a long time to find out about. You're a busy man and time's the most valuable thing you've got. I wouldn't be worth half as much if motion pictures were your only business. But it's not. And it never will be. It's just another game of craps."

I stared at him. "Give me a free sample."

"For one thing," he said quickly, "I wouldn't have started the picture until I'd had a sound test on everyone."

"That's something I already learned. I want a sample of what I don't know."

He reached around behind him for a blue-covered script. "If Rina comes off on the screen like that test indicates, we can make a few changes in this and save ourselves four hundred thousand dollars."

"How?"

"By building up her story and confining more of the picture to the New Orleans episode. It'll save five weeks of exteriors and nobody knows yet how good those microphones work outside."

I reached for a cigarette. "If we did that," I said slowly, "what happens to Nevada? His part would be cut way down."

Dan's eyes met mine steadily. "Nevada's not my problem any more, he's MCA's. I'm workin' for you now an' I figure you already used up all the sentiment you're entitled to on this picture. This is just like any other kind of business. The big thing is to make money."

I dragged on the butt and sipped at the coffee. For the first time since Rina called, I was back to normal. For a while, she'd had me spinning like a top. I didn't know whether I was coming or going. I felt different now. "What kind of deal do you have in mind?"

"No salary. Just a ten-per-cent piece of the action and an expense account."

I laughed. "I thought you said you sold your agency."

"That's the only way I can figure my compensation without adding to your overhead."

"Don't kid me," I said. "You'd be living off the expense account."

"Sure I will. But even with a salary, I would. How do you expect me to do a job for you if I can't spend money? Money is the only thing in this town nobody talks back to."

"I'll give you a ten-per-cent participation in profits. But no stock interest."

He studied me for a moment. "What about the expense account?"

"That's O.K."

He stuck out his hand. "It's a deal."

It was after three o'clock when we walked onto Stage Nine. The place was jumping, a mumble of buzzing, efficient noise, as they got ready for the next take. Nevada was standing on the edge of the set; Rina wasn't anywhere in sight. I stopped near the sound man. "How's it coming?"

He looked up at me and grinned. "Sounds great," he said, tapping his earphones.

I smiled and walked over to Nevada. He was talking to the director and they both turned as I came up. "How's she doing?"

The new director shrugged. "She was a little nervous at first but she's settling down. She'll be O.K."

"She'll be great," Nevada said warmly. "I never figured all the times she cued me on the script that it would come in handy for her too."

One of the assistant directors hurried up. "We're ready now, Mr. Carrol."

The director nodded and the assistant turned around and yelled, "Places, everybody!"

The director walked over to the camera as Nevada moved out on the set. I turned and saw Rina entering from the side. I stared, unable to believe my eyes. Her long, white-blond hair was tied up on top of her head and they'd bound her breasts so tight she looked like a boy. Her mouth was painted in a tiny Cupid's bow and her eyebrows were penciled to a thin, unnatural line. She was no longer a woman—she was a caricature of every ad in *Vanity Fair*.

Dan's face was impassive. He stared at me, his eyes unrevealing. "They did a good job," he said. "She's right in the image."

"She don't look like a woman."

"That's what they go for."

"I don't give a damn what they go for! I don't like it. Broads that look like that are a dime a dozen in this town."

A faint smile came into Dan's eyes. "You don't like it, change it," he said. "You're the boss. It's your picture."

I stared at him for a moment. I felt like walking out onto the set and blowing a fuse. But instinct held me back. I knew one more display like yesterday's would demoralize the whole crew. "Tell Carrol I want to see him," I said to Dan.

He nodded approvingly. "Smart," he said. "That's the right way to do it. You may need me even less than I thought!" He walked over to the director.

A moment later, the director called a ten-minute break. He came over to me and I could see he was nervous. "What seems to be the trouble, Mr. Cord?"

"Who O.K.'d that make-up and costume?"

The director looked at me, then over his shoulder at Rina. "I'm sure it was approved by wardrobe and make-up," he said. "Nevada told them to give her the full treatment."

"Nevada?"

He nodded. I looked at Dan. "I want everybody concerned in my office in ten minutes," I said.

"Right, Jonas."

I turned and walked out of the building.

CHAPTER NINE

I LOOKED AROUND THE OFFICE. I GUESS THE STUDIO KNEW WHAT THEY WERE doing after all. It was just large enough to hold all of us.

Dan sat in an easy chair to the left of my desk, Carrol, the new director, beside him. Rina and Nevada were on the couch, and across the room from them was the cameraman. On the other side of the room were the make-up man and the head of the wardrobe department, a slim woman of indeterminate age, with a young face and prematurely-gray hair, wearing a simple tailored dress. Finally, my secretary was on my right, with the inevitable pencil poised over her pad.

I lit a cigarette. "All of you saw that test last night," I said. "It was great. How come that girl wasn't on the set this afternoon?"

Nobody answered. "Rina, stand up." Silently she got to her feet and stood there looking at me. I glanced around the room again. "What's her name?"

The director coughed and laughed nervously. "Mr. Cord, everybody knows her name."

"Yeah? What is it?"

"Rina Marlowe."

"Then why don't she look like Rina Marlowe instead of an ass-end combination of Clara Bow, Marion Davies and Cynthia Randall? She sure as hell doesn't look like Rina Marlowe!"

"I'm afraid you don't understand, Mr. Cord."

I looked around. "What's your name?"

She stared right back at me. "I'm Ilene Gaillard," she said. "I'm the costume designer."

"All right, Miss Gaillard. Suppose you tell me what I don't understand."

"Miss Marlowe has to be dressed in the very forefront of fashion," she said calmly. "You see, Mr. Cord, though we make certain concessions to the period in which the picture takes place, the fundamental design must carry forward the latest in high fashion. That's what most women go to the movies to see. Motion pictures set the style."

I squinted at her. "Style or no style, Miss Gaillard, it doesn't make sense that a girl should have to look like a boy to be in fashion. No man in his right mind could be interested in a figure like that."

"Don't blame Miss Gaillard, Jonas. I told her to do it."

I turned to Nevada. "You told her?"

He nodded.

Sooner or later, it was bound to happen. I let my voice grow cold. "It's my money that's on the line now and the deal was that I'm the boss. So from now on, you worry about your acting. Everything else is my headache."

Nevada's lips tightened and deep in his eyes I could see the hurt. I turned away so that I wouldn't have to see it. Rina was watching with a curious kind of detachment.

"Rina!" She turned to me, an impassive mask dropping quickly over her eyes. "Go into the bathroom and wash all that muck off your face. Put on your usual make-up."

Rina left the room silently and I went back behind my desk and sat down. Nobody said a word until she came back into the room, her mouth wide again, her lips full and her eyebrows flowing into the natural curve of her brow. Her hair spilled like white shimmering gold down to her shoulders. But there was still something wrong. Underneath the negligee, her body was still a straight line.

"Go back in there and get out of that harness you're wearing."

Still silent, she did as I told her. And this time when she came out, she moved. Nobody could miss the fact that there was a woman underneath that negligee.

"That's more like it," I said. "We'll shoot those scenes again now."

Rina nodded and turned away. Miss Gaillard's voice stopped her. "We can't photograph her like that."

I looked at the designer. "What did you say?"

Miss Gaillard stood up. "We can't shoot her like that. Her bust bounces."

I laughed. "What's the matter with that? Tits should bounce."

"Of course," the designer said quickly. "But on the screen everything is exaggerated." She looked at the cameraman. "Isn't that right, Lee?"

The cameraman nodded. "That's right, Mr. Cord. They won't look natural at all."

"We'll have to put some kind of brassière on her," Miss Gaillard said.

"O.K. Go see what you can do."

A moment later, Rina and the designer came out of the bathroom. They walked toward me. It was better than the original harness but they didn't look as good as they did without restraint. It just didn't look right to me.

I got up from the desk and walked over to Rina. "Let me see."

Rina looked at me, her eyes deliberately distant. Impassively she dropped the negligee from her shoulders, holding it to her by the crook of her elbows. "Turn right," I said. "Now left."

I stepped back and looked at Rina. I knew what it was now. Whenever she turned, the brassière pulled and flattened, which was what gave her breasts that unnatural look. I looked at the designer. "Maybe if we took off the shoulder straps?"

Ilene Gaillard shrugged. "We can try." She reached over and pushed down the straps.

Rina stood there, her eyes fixed on some distant point over my shoulder. "Now turn." The brassière still cut into her breasts. "Unhh-unhh," I said. "I still don't like it."

"There's one other thing I can try."

"O.K.," I said.

A few minutes later, they came out again. Rina wore a wire-ribbed contraption almost like a small corset, except it didn't come down over her hips. And when she moved, her breasts didn't. You could see them all right, but they looked as if they had been molded out of plaster of Paris.

I looked at the designer. "Isn't there some way we can cut out some of those wires?"

"I think that looks fine, Mr. Cord. Anyway, I don't see why you're so worried about her bustline. Her legs are good and you'll see plenty of them."

"Miss Gaillard, since you're not a man, I don't expect you to understand what

I'm getting at. I can see all the legs I want to see just walking down the street. Just answer my question, please."

"No, we can't cut the wires, Mr. Cord," she replied, equally polite. "If we do, she might as well be wearing nothing. There wouldn't be enough rigidity to support her."

"Maybe if I show you what I want, you can do it. Take it off, Rina," I said, walking over to her.

Impassively Rina turned aside for a moment. When she turned around again, the contraption was in one hand and with the other she held the top of the negligee closed.

I took it and tossed in onto my desk. I put my hands to the top of Rina's negligee and pushed it down until it formed a square across her breast just above the nipples. Her breasts rose like twin white moons against my dark, clenched fists. I looked back at the designer. "See what I mean?"

Maybe she didn't but there wasn't a man in the room whose eyes weren't popping out of his head.

"What you want is impossible, Mr. Cord. Rina's a big girl. Thirty-eight C. There isn't a brassière made that could support her bust like that. I'm a designer, Mr. Cord, not a structural engineer."

I let go of Rina's negligee and turned to Miss Gaillard. "Thank you," I said, going over to the telephone. "That's the first constructive idea I've heard since this meeting started."

Morrissey was there in less than twenty minutes.

"I've got a little problem, Morrissey. I need your help."

His nervousness disappeared slightly and he looked around shyly. "Anything I can do, Mr. Cord."

"Stand up, Rina," I said. Slowly she got to her feet and walked around us. Morrissey's eyes widened behind his glasses. I was glad to see that other things could occupy his mind besides airplanes.

"There isn't a brassière made that can keep them from jiggling," I said. "And still look natural. I want you to design one that will."

He turned back to me, an expression of shock on his face. "You're joking, Mr. Cord!"

"I was never more serious in my life."

"But—but I don't know anything about brassières. I'm an aeronautical engineer," he stammered, blushing a bright pink.

"That's why I called you," I said calmly. "I figured if you can design planes that have to withstand thousands of pounds of stress you ought to be able to come up with something that would hold up a little thing like a pair of tits." I turned to the costume designer. "Fill him in on what he needs to know."

Miss Gaillard looked at me, then at Morrissey. "Perhaps it would be better if we worked in my office in Wardrobe. I have everything there you might need."

Morrissey had been staring at Rina's breasts while the designer spoke. For a moment, I thought he was paralyzed, then he turned around. "I think I might be able to do something."

"I knew you could," I said, smiling.

"I'm not promising anything, of course. But it's a very intriguing problem."

I kept a straight face. "Very," I said solemnly.

Morrissey turned to the designer. "Do you happen to have a pair of calipers?"

"Calipers? What do we need calipers for?"

Morrissey looked at her in amazement. "How else would we be able to measure the depth and the circumference?"

She stared at him blankly for a moment, then, taking his arm, began to walk him toward the door. "I'm sure we can get a pair from Engineering. You'd better come with us, Rina."

Morrissey was back in a little over an hour. He came in waving a sheet of paper. "I think we've got it! It was really very simple once we found the point of stress. The weight of each breast pulls to either side. That means the origin of stress falls between them, right in the center of the cleavage."

I stared at him. His language was a curious mixture of engineering and wardrobe design. But he was too wrapped up in his explanation to pay attention to my look. "The whole thing then became a problem of compensation. We had to find a way to utilize the stress to hold the breasts steady. I inserted a V-shaped wire in the cleavage using the suspension principle. Understand?"

I shook my head. "You went way past me."

"You know the principle used in a suspension bridge?"

"Vaguely," I said.

"Under that principle, the more pressure the mass exerts against itself, the more pressure is created to hold it in place."

I nodded. I still didn't understand it completely. But I had all I needed for now. What I wanted to know was would it work?

I didn't have long to wait for the answer. Rina came into the office shortly after that with Ilene Gaillard. Deliberately she let the wrap fall to the floor and stood there in the repaired negligee.

"Walk toward Mr. Cord," the designer said.

Slowly Rina walked toward me. I couldn't take my eyes from her. The sweetest pair of knockers a man ever put his head down on. She stopped in front of my desk and looked down at me. For the first time that afternoon, she spoke. "Well?"

I was conscious of the effort it took to raise my eyes and look up into her face. Her eyes were cold and calculating. The bitch was always exactly aware of the effect she had on me. She started to turn away. "One more thing, Miss Gaillard," I said. "Tomorrow when we start shooting, I want her in a black negligee, instead of that white one. I want everybody to know she's a whore, not a virgin bride."

"Yes, Mr. Cord." Ilene came up to my desk, her eyes shining. "I really think we're going to set a new style with Miss Marlowe. Unless I'm completely mistaken, women all over the world will be trying for her style once this picture comes out."

I grinned at her. "We didn't set the fashion, Miss Gaillard," I said. "Women looked like women long before either of us was born."

She nodded and started out. I looked around the room. The meeting was over and everybody was getting stiffly to his feet. Nevada was the last one out and I called him back.

He came back to my desk. I turned and looked at my secretary. She was still sitting there, her book filled with shorthand notes. "What've you got there?" I asked.

"The minutes of the meeting."

"What for?"

"It's a company rule," she said. "Minutes of all executive meetings are recorded and copies circulated."

"Give me that book." I held it over the wastebasket and set a match to it. When the flame caught, I dropped it into the basket and looked up at her.

She was staring at me with an expression of horror.

"Now trot your fat little ass out of here," I said. "And if I ever hear of any minutes of meetings in this office ever showing up outside these walls, you'll be looking for another job."

Nevada was smiling as I turned back to him. "I'm sorry I had to speak the way I did, Nevada."

"That's all right, Junior. I shouldn't have shot my mouth off."

"There's a lot of people in this town think I'm a sucker and that I got conned into a bum deal. You and I know that's not true but I have to stop that kind of talk. I can't afford it."

"I understand, Junior. Your pappy was the same way. There was only one boss when he was around."

Suddenly, I realized how far apart we'd grown. For a moment, I had a wave of nostalgia for my childhood, when I could always reach out to Nevada for assurance. It wasn't that way any more. It was exactly the opposite. Nevada was leaning on me. "Thanks, Nevada," I said, forcing a smile to my lips. "And don't worry. Everything'll turn out all right now."

He turned and I watched him walk out of the office. Shortly after he left Dan Pierce came into the office. I reached for a cigarette and lit it. "About what you said this morning. I think we ought to change the script. You better send for the writers right away."

He grinned knowingly. "I already did."

CHAPTER TEN

WE COMPLETED THE PICTURE IN FOUR WEEKS. NEVADA KNEW WHAT was happening but he never said a word. Two weeks after that, we held the first sneak preview at a theater out in the valley.

I got there late and the studio publicity man let me in. "There are only a few seats left on the side, Mr. Cord," he apologized.

I looked down at the orchestra. There was a section roped off in the center for studio guests. It was jammed. Everybody at the studio from Norman on down was there. They were all waiting for me to fall on my ass.

I went up into the balcony just as the lights went down and the picture came on. I found my way in the dark to a seat in the middle of a bunch of youngsters and looked up at the screen.

My name looked funny up there.

JONAS CORD PRESENTS—

But the feeling left when the credits were over and the picture began. After ten minutes had passed I started to sense a restlessness in the kids around me. "Aw, shit," I heard one of them whisper. "I thought this was gonna be somethin' different. It's just another friggin' Western."

Then Rina came on screen. Five minutes later, when I looked around me, the kids' faces were staring up at the screen, their mouths partly open, their expressions rapt. There wasn't a sound except their breathing. Next to me sat a boy holding a girl's hand tightly in his lap. When Rina finally pulled Nevada down onto the bed with her, I could feel the kid squirm. He whispered, "Jesus!"

I reached for a cigarette and began to smile. Nobody had to tell me this picture was box office. When I came down into the lobby after it was over, Nevada was standing in the corner surrounded by kids and signing autographs. I looked for Rina. She was at the other end of the lobby surrounded by reporters. Bernie Norman was hovering over her like a proud father.

Dan was standing in the center of a circle of men. He looked up as I came over. "You were right, Jonas," he cried jubilantly. "She creamed 'em. We'll gross ten million dollars!"

I gestured and he followed me out to my car. "When this is over," I said, "bring Rina to my hotel."

He stared at me. "It's still eating yuh, isn't it?"

"Don't lecture me, just do as I say!"

"What if she won't come?"

"She'll come," I said grimly. "Just tell her it's collection day!"

It was one o'clock in the morning and I was halfway through a bottle of bourbon when the knock came on the door. I went over and opened it.

Rina walked into the room and I closed the door. She turned to face me. "Well?"

I gestured toward the bedroom. She looked at me for a moment, then shrugged her shoulders and nonchalantly started for the bedroom. "I told Nevada I was coming here," she said over her shoulder.

I spun her around violently. "What the hell did you do a damn fool thing like that for?"

Her eyes appraised me calmly. "Nevada and I are going to get married. I told him I wanted to be the first to tell you."

I couldn't believe my ears. "No!" I shouted hoarsely. "You can't. I won't let you. He's an old man, he's through. You'll be the biggest star in the business when this picture comes out."

"I know."

"If you know, then why? You don't need him. You don't need anybody."

"Because when I needed him, he helped me," she said evenly. "Now it's my turn. He needs me."

"He needs you? Why? Because he was too proud to do his own crawling?"

"That's not true and you know it!"

"Making you a star was my idea!"

"I didn't ask you for it," Rina said angrily. "I didn't even want it. Don't think I didn't see what you were doing. Cutting down his part in his own picture, building me up as a monument to your own ego while you were ruining him!"

"I didn't see you trying to stop me," I said. "We both know he's on the way out. There's a new kind of cowboy over at one of the studios. A singing cowboy. He uses a guitar instead of a gun!"

"You know everything, don't you!" Her hand slashed angrily out at my face. I could feel its sting even as she spoke. "That's why he needs me more than ever!"

I exploded and grabbed her by the shoulders, shaking her violently. "What about me? Why do you think I went into this? Not for Nevada. For you! Did you ever stop to think that when I came rushing up here to see you, that maybe I needed you?"

She stared into my eyes angrily.

"You'll never need anybody, Jonas, only yourself. Otherwise, you wouldn't have left your wife down there all by herself. If you had any feelings at all, even pity, you'd have gone down there, or had her come up here."

"You leave my wife out of this!"

She turned to pull away and the front of her dress tore down to her waist. I stared at her. Her breasts rose and fell and I could feel the fever climb up in me. "Rina!" I crushed my mouth down on hers. "Rina, please."

Her mouth moved for a moment as she struggled to get away from me, then she was pressing herself closer and closer, her arms around my neck. That's the way we were when the door behind me opened. "Get outa here!" I said hoarsely, without bothering to turn around.

"Not this time, Jonas!"

I gave Rina a shove toward the bedroom, then turned around slowly to face my father-in-law and another man. Behind them was Monica, standing in the doorway. I stared at her. She had a belly way out to here.

The hollow echo of triumph was in Amos Winthrop's voice as he spoke. "Ten grand was too much to give me to send her away before." He chuckled quietly. "How much do you think it'll cost you to get rid of her now?"

As I stared at Monica, I began to curse myself silently. No wonder Amos Winthrop could laugh. I'd known Monica for less than a month before we got married. Even to my untrained eyes, she was at least five months' pregnant. That meant she was two months gone when she married me.

I cursed myself again. There's no fool like a young fool—my old man always used to say. And, as usual, my father was right.

That wasn't my cake she was baking in her oven.

THE STORY OF RINA MARLOWE
Book Four

CHAPTER ONE

CAREFULLY RINA CLOSED THE MAGAZINE, TURNING DOWN THE CORNER of the page that she had been reading, and let it drop on the white sheet that covered her.

"Did you want something, dear?" Ilene's voice came from the deep armchair near the bed.

Rina turned to look at her. Ilene's face was thinned by concern. "No," Rina said. "What time is it?"

Ilene looked down at her watch. "Three o'clock."

"Oh," Rina said. "What time did the doctor say he'd come?"

"Four," Ilene answered. "There's nothing I can get for you?"

Rina shook her head. "No, thanks. I'm fine." She picked up the magazine again, riffled through the pages, then threw it back on the coverlet. "I wish to hell they'd let me out of here!"

Ilene was out of the chair now. She looked down at Rina from the side of the bed. "Don't fret," she said quickly. "You'll be out soon enough. Then you'll wish you were still here. I heard that the studio's just waiting for you to get out so they can put you to work in *Madame Pompadour*."

Rina sighed. "Not that old chestnut again. Every time they get stuck for a picture, they take that one down off the shelf and dust it off. Then they make a big announcement and as soon as they get all the trade stories and publicity they can, back it goes on the shelf."

"Not this time," Ilene said earnestly. "I spoke to Bernie Norman in New York yesterday. He has a new writer on it and said the script was shaping up great. He says it's got social significance now."

Rina smiled. "Social significance? Who's writing it—Eugene O'Neill?"

Ilene stared at her. "You knew all the time."

Rina shook her head. "No, I didn't. It was just a wild guess. Has Bernie really got O'Neill?"

Ilene nodded. "He expects to have a copy of the script sent over to you as soon as O'Neill is finished."

Despite herself, Rina was impressed. Maybe this time, Bernie really meant it. She felt a surge of excitement flow into her. O'Neill was a writer, not an ordinary Hollywood hack. He could make something of the story. Then the excitement drained out of her, leaving her even more weary than before. Social significance. Everything that was done these days bore the tag. Ever since Roosevelt took office.

"What time is it?"

"Ten after three," Ilene answered.

Rina leaned back against the pillow. "Why don't you go out and get a cup of coffee?"

Ilene smiled. "I'm all right."

"You've been here all day."

"I want to be here," Ilene answered.

"You go." Rina closed her eyes. "I think I'll take a little nap before the doctor comes."

Ilene stood there for a moment, until she heard the soft, shallow breath of rest. Then gently she straightened the covers and looked into Rina's face. The large eyes were closed, the cheeks thin and drawn tightly across the high cheekbones. There was a faintly blue pallor beneath the California tan. She reached down and brushed the white-blond hair back from Rina's forehead, then quickly kissed the tired mouth and left the room.

The nurse seated in the outer room looked up. "I'm going down for a cup of coffee," Ilene said. "She's sleeping."

The nurse smiled with professional assurance. "Don't worry, Miss Gaillard," she said. "Sleep is the best thing for her."

Ilene nodded and went out into the corridor. She felt the tightness in her chest, the mist that constantly had pressed against her eyes these last few weeks. She came out of the elevator and started for the coffee shop.

Still lost in her thoughts, she didn't hear the doctor until her hand was on the door. "Miss Gaillard?" For a moment, she had no voice. She could only nod dumbly. "Mind if I join you?"

"Not at all," she said.

He smiled and held the door open for her. They went inside to a corner table. The doctor waved his hand and two cups of coffee appeared before them. "How about a bun?" he asked. "You look as if you could use a little food." He laughed in his professional manner. "There's no sense in having another patient just now."

"No, thank you," she said. "The coffee will do fine."

The doctor put down his coffee cup. "Good coffee."

She nodded. "Rina is sleeping." She said the first thing that came into her mind.

"Good." The doctor nodded, looking at her. His dark eyes shone brightly through the bifocals. "Does Miss Marlowe have any relatives out here?"

"No," Ilene answered quickly. Then the implication hit her. She stared at him. "You mean . . ." Her voice trailed off.

"I don't mean anything," the doctor said. "It's just that in cases like this, we like to know the names of the next of kin in case something does happen."

"Rina has no relatives that I know of."

The doctor looked at her curiously. "What about her husband?"

"Who?" Ilene's voice was puzzled.

"Isn't she married to Nevada Smith?" the doctor asked.

"She was," Ilene answered. "But they were divorced three years ago. She's been married since then to Claude Dunbar, the director."

"That ended in divorce, too?"

"No," Ilene answered tersely. Her lips tightened. "He committed suicide, after they'd been married a little over a year."

"Oh," the doctor said. "I'm sorry. I guess I haven't had much time these last few years to keep up with things."

"If there's anything special that needs to be done, I guess I'm the one who could do it," she said. "I'm her closest friend. She gave me power of attorney."

The doctor stared at her silently. She could read what was in his mind behind those shining bifocals. She drew her head up proudly. What did it matter what he thought? What did it matter what anyone thought now?

"Did you get the results from the blood tests?"

The doctor nodded.

She tried to keep her voice from shaking. "Is it leukemia?"

"No," he said. He could see the hope spring up in her eyes. Quickly he spoke to avoid the pain of disappointment. "It was what we thought. Encephalitis." He noted her puzzled expression. "Sometimes it's called sleeping sickness."

The hope in Ilene refused to die. "Then she has a chance?"

"A very small one," the doctor said, still watching her carefully. "But if she lives, there's no telling what she'll be like."

"What do you mean?" Ilene asked harshly.

"Encephalitis is a virus that settles in the brain," he explained slowly. "For the next four or five days, as the virus builds up in intensity, she will be subject to extraordinary high fevers. During these fevers, the virus will attack the brain. It is only after the fever breaks that we'll be able to tell how much damage she has sustained."

"You mean her mind will be gone?" Ilene's eyes were large with horror.

"I don't know," the doctor said. "The damage can take many forms. Her mind; perhaps she'll be paralyzed or partly so; she may know her own name, she may not. The residual effects are similar to a stroke. It depends on what part of the brain has been damaged."

The sick fear came up inside her. Quickly she caught her breath against it, her face paling. "Breathe deeply and sip a little water," the doctor said.

She did as he commanded and the color flooded back into her face. "Is there anything we can do? Anything at all?"

"We're doing everything we can. We know so little about the disease; how it's transmitted. In its more common form, in tropical countries, it's supposed to be carried by insects and transmitted by their bite. But many cases, in the United States and elsewhere, just appear, with no apparent causation at all."

"We just got back from Africa three months ago," Ilene said. "We made a picture there."

"I know," the doctor said. "Miss Marlowe told me about it. That was what first made me suspicious."

"But no one else is sick," Ilene said. "And we were all out there for three months, living exactly the same way, in the same places."

The doctor shrugged. "As I said, we aren't really sure what causes it."

Ilene stared at him. A note of bewilderment crept into her voice. "Why couldn't it be me?" she asked. "She has so much to live for."

The doctor reached across the table and patted her hand. With that one warm gesture, she no longer resented him, as she did most men. "How many times in my life have I heard that question? And I'm no closer to the answer now than when I first began to practice."

She looked at him gratefully. "Do you think we should say anything to her?"

His dark eyes grew large behind his glasses. "What purpose would it serve?" he asked. "Let her have her dreams."

Rina heard the dim voices outside the door. She was tired, weary and tired, and everything was a soft, blurred haze. Vaguely she wondered if the dream would come again. The thin edges of it poked at her mind. Good. It was coming.

Softly, comfortably now, she let herself slip down into it. Further and further she felt herself dropping into the dream. She smiled unconsciously and turned her face against the pillow. Now she was surrounded by her dream. The dream of death she had dreamed ever since she was a little girl.

CHAPTER TWO

IT WAS COOL IN THE YARD BENEATH THE SHADE OF THE GIANT OLD APPLE trees. Rina sat in the grass and arranged the dolls around the small wooden plank that served as a table.

"Now, Susie," she said to the little dark-haired doll. "You must not gulp your food."

The black eyes of the doll stared unwinkingly back at her.

"Oh, Susie!" she said in imaginary concern. "You spilled it all over your dress! Now I'll have to change you again."

She picked up the doll and undressed it quickly. She washed the clothes in an imaginary tub, then ironed them. "Now you stay clean," she exclaimed in pretended anger.

She turned to the other doll. "Are you enjoying your breakfast, Mary?" She smiled. "Eat it all up. It'll make you big and strong."

Occasionally, she would glance toward the big house. She was happy to be left alone. It wasn't very often that she was. Usually, one or the other of the servants would be calling her to come back in. Then her mother would scold her and tell her that she was not to play in the yard, that she must stay near the kitchen door at the far side of the house.

But she didn't like it there. It was hot and there was no grass, only dirt. Besides, it was near the stables and the smell of the horses. She didn't understand why her mother always made such a fuss. Mr. and Mrs. Marlowe never said anything when they found her there. Once, Mr. Marlowe even had picked her up and swung her high over his head, tickling her with his mustache until she almost burst with hysterical laughter.

But when she'd come inside, her mother had been angry and had spanked her bottom and made her go up to their room and stay there all afternoon. That was the worst punishment of all. She loved to be in the kitchen while her mother cooked the dinner. Everything smelled so good. Everybody always said her mother was the best cook the Marlowes had ever had.

She heard footsteps and looked up. Ronald Marlowe threw himself to the ground beside her. She looked down again and finished feeding Susie, then said in a matter-of-fact voice, "Would you like some dinner, Laddie?"

He sniffed disdainfully from the superiority of his lofty eight years. "I don't see anything to eat."

She turned toward him. "You're not looking," she said. She forced a doll's plate into his hand. "Eat it. It's very good for you."

Reluctantly he pretended to eat. After a moment, he was bored and got to his feet. "I'm hungry," he said. "I'm going in and get some real food."

"You won't get any," she said.

"Why not?"

"Because my mommy's still sick and nobody cooked."

"I'll get something," he said confidently.

She watched him walk away and turned back to her dolls. It was turning dusk when Molly, the upstairs maid, came out looking for her. The girl's face was red from crying. "Come, macushla," she said, sweeping Rina up in her arms. "It's your mither that wants to set eyes on ye again."

Peters, the coachman, was there, as was Mary, the downstairs maid, and Annie, the scullery helper. They were standing around her mother's bed and they made way for her as she came over. There was also a man in a black suit, holding a cross in his hand.

She stood very still near the bed, looking at her mother solemnly. Her mother looked beautiful, her face so white and calm, her white-blond hair brushed back softly from her forehead. Rina moved closer to the bed.

Her mother's lips moved but Rina couldn't hear what she was saying. The man in the black suit picked her up. "Kiss your mother, child," he said.

Obediently Rina kissed her mother's cheek. It was cool to her lips. Her mother smiled again and closed her eyes, then suddenly opened them and looked upward unseeingly. Quickly the man shifted Rina to his other arm. He reached down and closed her mother's eyes.

Molly held out her arms and the man gave Rina to her. Rina looked back at her mother. She was sleeping now. She looked beautiful, just as she did in the early mornings when Rina would awaken and stare at her over the edge of the bed.

Rina looked around the room at the others. The girls were crying, and even Peters, the coachman, had tears in his eyes. She looked up into Molly's face. "Why are you crying?" she asked solemnly. "Is my mommy dead?"

The tears came afresh in the girl's eyes. She hugged Rina closely to her. "Hush, child," she whispered. "We're crying because we love her."

She started out of the room with Rina in her arms. The door closed behind them and Rina looked up into her face. "Will Mommy be up in time to make breakfast tomorrow?"

Molly stared at her in sudden understanding. Then she sank to her knees in the hallway at the top of the back stairs. She rocked back and forth with the child in her arms. "Oh, my poor little child, my poor little orphan child," she cried.

Rina looked up at her and after a moment, the tears became contagious and she, too, began to cry. But she didn't quite know why.

Peters came into the kitchen while the servants were eating supper. Rina looked up at him and smiled. "Look, Mr. Peters." She laughed happily. "I had three desserts!"

Molly looked down at her. "Hush, child," she said quickly, the tears coming again to her eyes. "Finish your ice cream."

Rina stared at her thoughtfully and lifted the spoon again to her mouth. She couldn't understand why the girls began to cry every time they spoke to her. The home-made vanilla ice cream tasted cool and sweet. She took another spoonful.

"I just spoke to the master," Peters said. "He said it would be all right if we laid her out in my room over the stable. And Father Nolan said we could bury her from St. Thomas'."

"But how can we?" Molly cried, "when we don't even know if she was a Catholic? Not once in the three years she's been here did she go to Mass."

"What difference does that make?" Peters asked angrily. "Did she not make her confession to Father Nolan? Did she not receive the last rites from him and take the Holy Sacraments? Father Nolan is satisfied that she was a Catholic."

Mary, the downstairs maid, who was the oldest of the three girls, nodded her head in agreement. "I think Father Nolan is right," she said. "Maybe she'd done something and was afraid to go to Mass, but the important thing was that she came back to the church in the end."

Peters nodded his head emphatically. "It's settled, then," he said, starting for the door. He stopped and looked back at them. "Molly, take the child to sleep with you tonight. I'm goin' down to the saloon and get sivral of the boys to help me move her tonight. Father Nolan said he'd send Mr. Collins over to fix her up. He told me the church would pay for it."

"Oh, the good Father," Mary said.

"Bless him," Annie said, crossing herself.

"Can I have some more ice cream?" Rina asked.

There was a knock at the door and Molly opened it quickly. "Oh, it's you, mum," she exclaimed in a whisper.

"I came to see if the child was all right," Geraldine Marlowe said.

The girl stepped back. "Won't you come in, mum?"

Mrs. Marlowe looked over at the bed. Rina was sleeping soundly, her dolls, Susie and Mary, on either side of her. Her white-blond hair hung in tiny ringlets around her head. "How is she?"

"Fine, mum." The girl bobbed her head. "The poor darlin' was so exhausted with the excitement, she dropped off like that. Mercifully she doesn't understand. She's too young."

Geraldine Marlowe looked at the child again. For a moment, she thought of how it would be if she were the one to go, leaving her Laddie alone and motherless. Though, in a way, that was different, for Laddie would still have his father.

She remembered the day she had hired Rina's mother. Her references were very good although she had not worked for several years. "I have a child, ma'am," she'd said in her peculiarly precise schoolbook English. "A little girl, two years old."

"What about your husband, Mrs. Osterlaag?"

"He went down with his ship. He and the child never saw each other." She'd looked down at the floor for a moment. "We had the child late in life, ma'am. We Finns don't marry young; we wait until we can afford it. I lived on our savings as long as I could. I must go back to work."

Mrs. Marlowe had hesitated. A two-year-old child might turn out to be an annoyance.

"Rina would be no problem, ma'am. She's a good child and very quiet. She can sleep in my room and I'd be willing to have you take out of my wages for her board."

Mrs. Marlowe had always wanted a little girl but after Laddie was born, the doctor had told her there would be no more children. It would be good for Laddie to have someone to play with. He was getting entirely too spoiled.

She'd smiled suddenly. "There will be no deduction from your wages, Mrs. Osterlaag. After all, how much can a little girl eat?"

That had been almost three years ago. And Rina's mother had been right. Rina had been no trouble at all.

"What will happen to the child, mum?" Molly whispered.

Mrs. Marlowe turned to the servant girl. "I don't know," she said, thinking about it for the first time. "Mr. Marlowe is going to inquire in town tomorrow about her relatives."

The servant girl shook her head. "He won't find any, mum," she said positively. "I often heard the mither say there was no family at all." Her eyes began to fill with tears. "Oh, the poor, poor darlin'. Now she'll have to go to the county home."

Mrs. Marlowe felt a lump come up in her throat. She looked down at Rina, sleeping peacefully in the bed. She could feel the tears stirring behind her own eyes. "Stop your crying, Molly," she said sharply. "I'm sure she won't have to go to the county home. Mr. Marlowe will locate her family."

"But what if he doesn't?"

"Then we'll think of something," she said. She crossed the room and stepped quickly out into the narrow hallway. There was a scuffling sound behind her. She turned around.

"Aisy now, boys!" She heard Peters' voice. Then he appeared, backing through the doorway across the hall. She pressed herself back to let them pass.

"Beggin' your pardon, mum," he said, his face flushed with exertion. "A sad, sad thing."

They went past with their shrouded burden, impregnating the still, warm air with a faint but unmistakable odor of beer. She wondered if she had done the right thing when she'd persuaded her husband to allow them to use the apartment over the stables. An Irish wake could well turn into a shambles.

She heard their heavy footsteps on the stairs as they carried Bertha Osterlaag, born in a small fishing village in Finland, down to her eventual funeral in a strange church, and her grave in a strange land.

CHAPTER THREE

ARRISON MARLOWE COULD SEE HIS WIFE'S HEAD BENT OVER HER EM-
broidery from the doorway. He crossed the room quietly, and bending
over the back of her chair, quickly kissed her cheek. His wife's voice
held the usual delightful shock. "Oh, Harry! What if the servants are watching?"

"Not tonight." He laughed. "They're all thinking about their party. I see Mary's
all dressed up."

A tone of reproach came into his wife's voice. "You know it's not a party they're
having."

He crossed in front of her, still smiling. "That's not what they call it," he said.
"But leave it to the Irish to make a party out of anything." He walked over to
the sideboard. "A little sherry before dinner?"

"I think I'd like a Martini tonight, if you don't mind, dear," Geraldine said
hesitantly.

He turned in half surprise. When they had been in Europe on their honeymoon
a bartender in Paris had introduced them to the new drink and ever since, it had
served as a sort of signal between them.

"Of course, my dear," he said. He pulled at the bell rope. Mary appeared in
the doorway. "Some cracked ice, please, Mary."

The girl curtseyed and disappeared. He turned back to the sideboard and took
down a bottle of gin, the French vermouth and a tiny bottle of orange bitters.
Using a measuring jigger, he carefully poured three jiggers of gin into the cocktail
shaker and one of vermouth. Then ceremoniously he allowed four drops of bitters
to trickle into the shaker. By this time, the ice was already on the sideboard
beside him and he filled the shaker to the brim with ice. Carefully he put the
top on the shaker and began to shake vigorously.

At last, the drink was cold enough. He unscrewed the cap and carefully poured
the contents into glasses. The shaker empty, he dropped a green olive into each
glass, then stood back and surveyed them with approval. Each glass was filled to
the brim—one more drop and it would overflow, one drop less and it would not
be full.

Geraldine Marlowe lifted hers to her lips. She wrinkled her nose in approval.
"It's delicious."

"Thank you," he said, lifting his own glass. "Your good health, my dear."

He put his glass down wonderingly and looked at his wife. Perhaps what he
had heard was true—that women didn't really bloom until they were older, and
then their desire increased. He calculated swiftly. He was thirty-four; that made
Geraldine thirty-one. They had been married seven years and with the exception
of their honeymoon, their life had assumed a pattern of regularity. But now, twice
in less than a week. Perhaps it was true.

If it was, it was all right with him. He loved his wife. That was the only reason he went down to that house on South Street. To spare her the humiliation of having to endure him more than she wanted. He lifted his drink again.

"Did you find out anything about Bertha's family today?" she asked.

Harrison Marlowe shook his head. "There's no family anywhere. Perhaps in Europe, but we don't even know what town she came from."

Geraldine looked down at her drink. Its pale golden color glowed in the glass. "How terrible," she said quietly. "What will happen to the child now?"

Harrison shrugged his shoulders. "I don't know. I suppose I'll have to notify the authorities. She'll probably go to the county orphanage."

"We can't let that happen!" The words burst from Geraldine's lips involuntarily.

Harrison stared at her in surprise. "Why not?" he asked. "I don't see what else we can do."

"Why can't we just keep her?"

"You just can't," he said. "There are certain legalities involved. An orphaned child isn't like a chattel. You can't keep her because she happens to be left at your house."

"You can speak to the authorities," Geraldine said. "I'm sure they would prefer to leave her with us rather than have her become a public charge."

"I don't know," Harrison said. "They might want us to adopt her to make sure that she doesn't become a charge."

"Harry, what a wonderful idea!" Geraldine smiled and got out of her chair, then walked to her husband. "Now, why didn't I think of that?"

"Think of what?"

"Adopting Rina," Geraldine said. "I'm so proud of you. You have such a wonderful mind. You think of everything."

He stared at her speechlessly.

She placed her arms around his neck. "But then you always wanted a little girl around the house, didn't you? And Laddie would be so happy to have a little sister."

He felt the soft press of her body against him and the answering surge of warmth well up inside him.

She kissed him quickly on the lips, then, as quickly, turned her face away from him almost shyly as she felt his immediate response.

"Suddenly, I'm so excited," she whispered meaningfully, her face half hidden against his shoulder. "Do you think it would be all right if we had another Martini?"

Dandy Jim Callahan stood in the middle of his office, looking at them. He rubbed his chin thoughtfully. "I don't know," he said slowly. "It's a difficult thing you ask."

"But, surely, Mr. Mayor," Geraldine Marlowe said quickly, "you can do it."

The mayor shook his head. "It's not so easy as you think, my dear lady. You forget the church has something to say about this, too. After all, the mother was Catholic and you just can't take a Catholic child and turn it over to a Protestant family. At least, not in Boston. They'd never stand for it."

Geraldine turned away, the disappointment showing clearly in her face. It was then for the first time that she saw her husband as something other than the nice young Harvard boy she had married.

He stepped forward and there appeared in his voice a quality of strength that she had never heard before. "The church would like it even less if I were to prove that the mother was never a Catholic. They'd look pretty foolish then, wouldn't they?"

The mayor turned to him. "You have such proof?"

"I have," Marlowe said. He took a sheet of paper out of his pocket. "The mother's passport and the child's birth certificate. Both clearly state they were Protestant."

Dandy Jim took the papers from him and studied them. "If you had these, why didn't you stop them?"

"How could I?" Marlowe asked. "I didn't receive them until today. The servants and Father Nolan made all the arrangements last night. Besides, what difference does it make to the poor woman? She's getting a Christian burial."

Dandy Jim nodded and gave the papers back. "This will be very embarrassing to Father Nolan," he said. "A young priest with his first church making a mistake like that. The Bishop won't like it at all."

"The Bishop need never know," Marlowe said.

Dandy Jim stared at him thoughtfully but didn't speak.

Marlowe pressed. "There's an election coming up next year."

Dandy Jim nodded, "There's always an election."

"That's true," Marlowe said. "There will be other elections and campaigns. A candidate needs contributions almost as much as he needs votes."

Dandy Jim smiled. "Did I ever tell you I met your father?"

Marlowe smiled back. "No, you didn't. But my father often mentioned it. He told me many times how he threw you out of his office."

Dandy Jim nodded. "That's true. Your father has a wild temper. One would almost take him for an Irishman. And all I did was ask him for a small campaign contribution. That was about twenty years ago. I was running for City Council then. Do you know what he said to me then?"

Marlowe shook his head.

"He swore that if ever I was so much as elected to the post of dog-catcher, he'd take his family and move out." Dandy Jim was smiling. "He won't like it when he hears you've contributed to my campaign fund."

Marlowe stood his ground. "My father is my father and I respect him very much," he said, "but what I do with my money and my politics is my concern, not his."

"You have other children?" Dandy Jim asked.

"A boy," Geraldine answered quickly. "Laddie is eight."

Dandy Jim smiled. "I don't know," he said. "Someday women will have the vote and if that little girl is brought up on the hill, that's one vote I may never get."

"I promise you this, Mr. Mayor," Geraldine said quickly. "If that day ever comes, the women of my household will always vote for you!"

Dandy Jim's smile grew broader. He made a courtly bow. "It is a weakness of politicians to always be making deals."

The next day, Timothy Kelly, the mayor's secretary, appeared at Marlowe's office in the bank and picked up a check for five hundred dollars. He suggested that Marlowe talk to a certain judge in the municipal court.

It was there the adoption was made. Quickly, quietly and legally. When Marlowe departed the judge's chambers, he left with the judge a birth certificate for one white female child named Katrina Osterlaag.

In his pocket was a birth certificate in the name of his daughter, Rina Marlowe.

CHAPTER FOUR

UNDERNEATH THE OVERSIZED UMBRELLA PLANTED IN THE SAND, GERaldine Marlowe sat in a canvas chair, her parasol at her side. Slowly she moved her fan back and forth.

"I can't remember a summer as hot as this," she said breathlessly. "It must be over ninety here in the shade."

Her husband grunted from the chair next to hers, his head still immersed in the Boston newspaper, which arrived on the Cape one day late.

"What did you say, Harry?"

He folded his paper and looked at his wife. "That Wilson's a damn fool!"

Geraldine was still looking at the ocean. "What makes you say that, dear?"

He tapped the paper vigorously. "That League of Nations thing. Now he says he's going to Europe and see to it that peace is insured."

Geraldine looked at him. "I think that's a wonderful idea," she said mildly. "After all, we were lucky this time. Laddie was too young to go. The next time, it may be different."

He snorted again. "There won't be a next time. Germany is through forever. Besides, what can they do to us? They're on the other side of the ocean. We can just sit back and let them kill each other off if they want to start another war."

Geraldine shrugged her shoulders. "You better move in closer under the umbrella, dear," she said. "You know how red you get in the sun."

Harrison Marlowe got up and moved his chair farther under the umbrella. He settled back in the chair with a sigh and buried himself in the newspaper once more.

Rina appeared suddenly in front of her mother. "It's been an hour since I had lunch, Mother," she said. "Can I go into the water now?"

"May I," Geraldine corrected automatically. She looked at Rina. She had grown up this summer. It was hard to believe she was only thirteen.

She was tall for her age, almost five three, only one inch shorter than Laddie, who was three years older. Her hair was bleached completely white from the sun and her skin was deeply tanned, so dark that her almond-shaped eyes seemed light by comparison. Her legs were long and graceful, her hips just beginning to round a little and her breasts came full and round against her little girl's bathing suit, more like a sixteen-year-old's.

"May I, Mother?" Rina asked.

"You may," Geraldine nodded. "But be careful, dear, don't swim too far out. I don't want you to tire yourself."

But Rina was already gone. Geraldine Marlowe half smiled to herself. Rina was like that; she was like none of the other girls Geraldine knew. Rina didn't play like a girl. She could swim and outrun any of the boys that Laddie played with and they knew it. She didn't pretend to be afraid of the water or hide from the sun. She just didn't care whether her skin was soft and white.

Harrison Marlowe looked up from his paper. "I have to go up to the city tomorrow. We're closing the Standish loan."

"Yes, dear." The faint, shrill voices of the children floated lazily back toward them. "We'll have to do something about Rina," she said thoughtfully.

"Rina?" he questioned. "What about Rina?"

She turned to him. "Haven't you noticed? Our little girl's growing up."

He cleared his throat. "Umm—yes. But she's still a baby."

Geraldine Marlowe smiled. It was true what they said about fathers. They spoke more about their sons but secretly they delighted in their daughters. "She's become a woman in the past year," she said.

His face flushed and he looked down at his paper. In a vague way, he had realized it, but this was the first time they had spoken about it openly. He looked toward the water, trying to find Rina in the screaming, splashing crowd. "Don't you think we ought to call her back? It's dangerous for her to be so far out in the deep water."

Geraldine smiled at him. Poor Harrison. She could read him like a book. It wasn't the water he was afraid of, it was the boys. She shook her head. "No. She's perfectly safe out there. She can swim like a fish."

His embarrassed gaze met her own. "Don't you think you ought to have a little talk with her? Maybe explain some things to her. You know, like I did with Laddie two years ago?"

Geraldine's smile turned mischievous. She loved to see her husband, who was usually so sure of himself, positive about his tiniest conviction, flounder around like this. "Don't be silly, Harry." She laughed. "There's nothing I have to explain to her now. When a thing like that happens, it's just natural to tell her everything she should know."

"Oh," he said in a relieved voice.

She turned thoughtful again. "I think Rina's going to be one of those lucky children who make the transition from adolescence without any of the embarrassing stages," she said. "There's not the slightest trace of gawkiness about her and her skin is as clear as a bell. Not a sign of a blemish or a pimple. Not like Laddie at all."

She turned back toward the ocean. "Just the same, I think we'd better do something about Rina. I'd better get her some brassières."

Marlowe didn't speak.

She turned to him again. "I honestly think her bust is as large as mine already. I do hope it doesn't get too big. She's going to be a very beautiful girl."

He smiled slowly. "Why shouldn't she be?"

She reached for his hand, quietly returning his smile. They both knew what he meant. Neither of them ever thought of Rina as anything but their own natural child.

"Would you mind very much if I came into town with you tonight?" she asked softly. "It would be nice to stay in a hotel for one evening."

He pressed her hand. "I think it would be very nice."

"Molly could look after the children," she said. "And I'd have time to do a little shopping tomorrow before we return."

He looked at her and grinned. "I agree with you," he said in a mock-solemn voice. "The cottage down here is a little crowded. I'll call the hotel and make sure they have a shakerful of Martinis waiting for us the moment we arrive."

She dropped his hand. "You lecher!" she exclaimed, laughing.

Rina swam with easy, purposeful strokes, her eyes fixed on the diving raft out past the rolling surf. Laddie should be out there with his friend Tommy Randall. She came up out of the water almost at their feet. The boys were stretched out on their backs, faces up to the sun, and they sat up as Rina began to climb the ladder.

Laddie's face showed his annoyance at her invasion of their sanctum. "Why don't you stay back there with the girls?"

"I've got as much right out here as you have," she retorted, after catching her breath, straightening the shoulder straps of her too-small bathing suit.

"Aw, go on," Tommy said, looking up. "Let her stay."

Rina glanced at him swiftly from the corners of her eyes and saw his gaze fixed on her partly revealed breasts. It was at that exact moment that she began to turn into a woman.

Now even Laddie was staring at her with a curious look she had never before noticed in his eyes. Instinctively she let her hands fall to her sides. If that was all it took to make them accept her, let them look. She sat down opposite them, still feeling their gaze on her.

A dull ache began to throb in her breasts and she looked down at herself. Her nipples were clearly limned against the black jersey of her bathing suit. She looked up again at the boys. They were staring at her quite openly now.

"What are you looking at?"

The two boys exchanged quick, embarrassed glances and immediately looked away. Tommy fixed his eyes out over the water and Laddie looked down at the raft.

She stared at Laddie. "Well?"

The red flush crept up from Laddie's throat.

"I saw you. You both were looking at my chest!" she said accusingly.

The boys again exchanged quick glances. Laddie got to his feet. "Come on, Tommy," he said. "It's getting too crowded out here!"

He dove from the raft and a moment later, his friend followed. Rina watched them swimming toward the shore for a moment, then stretched back on the raft and stared up into the bright sky. Boys were strange creatures, she thought.

The tight bathing suit cut into her breasts. She shrugged her shoulders and her breasts leaped free of the encumbering suit. She looked down at herself.

They were white against the dark tan of her arms and throat and the nipples were flushed and pink and fuller than she had ever seen them before. Tentatively she touched them with her fingertips. They were hard as tiny pebbles and a warm, pleasant kind of pain flashed through them.

The warmth of the sun began to fill them with a sweet, gentle ache. Slowly she began to massage the ache away and gradually the warmth spilled from her breasts down into her body. She felt herself go hazy with a contentment she had never known before.

CHAPTER FIVE

RINA STOOD IN FRONT OF THE MIRROR AND ADJUSTED THE STRAPS ON THE brassière. She took a deep breath. She turned to her mother, sitting on the bed behind her.

"There, Mother," she said proudly. "How does it look?"

Geraldine looked at her daughter doubtfully. "Perhaps if you moved it to the last hook," she said hesitantly and delicately.

"I tried, Mother," Rina answered. "But I can't wear it like that. It cuts into me."

Geraldine nodded. Next time, she would get a larger size but who ever would have thought a thirty-four would be so tight on such a slender frame?

Rina turned back to the mirror and looked at herself with satisfaction. Now she was beginning to look outside more like she felt inside. She noticed her mother watching her in the mirror.

"Do you think I could get some new bathing suits too, Mother?" she asked. "The ones I have are too small for me."

"I was just thinking that," her mother answered. "And some new dresses, too. Maybe Daddy will drive us down to Hyannis Port after breakfast."

Rina flashed a happy grin and ran to her mother. She threw her arms around her. "Oh, thank you, Mother!" she cried happily.

Geraldine drew Rina's head down to her breast. She kissed the top of the white-blond head and turned the child's tanned face up to hers. She looked down into Rina's eyes, her fingers lightly stroking her daughter's cheek. "What is happening to my little girl?" she asked almost sadly.

Rina caught her mother's hand and kissed her open palm. "Nothing, Mother," she said with the sureness and confidence that was to become an integral part of her. "Nothing but what you told me. I'm growing up."

Geraldine looked down into her daughter's face. A sudden mist came into her eyes.

"Don't be in too much of a hurry, my baby," she said, pressing Rina's head closely to her bosom. "We have too few years for childhood."

But Rina scarcely heard her. And if she had, it was doubtful that the words would carry any meaning. For they were only words and words were as futile against the strong forces awakening inside her as the waves breaking fruitlessly against the shore outside the window.

Laddie turned and swiftly threw the ball to first base. The runner spun and slid back toward safety, his heels kicking up a fine spray of dust. When the dust cleared, they could hear the umpire call, "Yer out!" and the game was over.

The boys clustered about him, pounding his back happily. "Swell game,

Laddie!" "Good pitching!" Then they dispersed and he and Tommy were alone, threading their way back to the beach.

"What yuh doin' this afternoon?" Tommy asked.

Laddie shrugged his shoulders. "Nothin'." He was still thinking about that wild pitch that Mahoney hit for a home run. He should never have let the ball get away from him like that. He had to do better if he wanted to make the varsity team at Barrington the next spring. He made up his mind to spend an hour every afternoon pitching into a barrel. They said that was how Walter Johnson had developed his control.

"The Bijou's got a new Hoot Gibson picture," Tommy said.

"I saw it back in Boston." Laddie looked at his friend. "When's Joan coming down again?"

"My cousin?" Tommy asked.

"Yuh know anyone else by that name?" Laddie asked sarcastically.

"Maybe this weekend," Tommy answered.

"Then maybe we'll take her to the movies," Laddie said.

"Big deal!" Tommy snorted. "It's O.K. for you but what about me? It's no fun sitting next to you and watching you cop feels. Who'm I goin' to take?"

"I don't know," Laddie answered.

Tommy walked along for a moment, then snapped his fingers. "I got it!" he said excitedly.

"Who?"

"Your sister. Rina."

"Rina?" Laddie said. "She's just a kid."

Tommy laughed. "She ain't such a kid. They're really poppin' out on her. They look even bigger lately than when we seen 'em on the raft a couple weeks ago."

"But she's only thirteen," Laddie said.

"My cousin Joan's only fourteen now. She was thirteen last summer when you were nuzzlin' her on the back porch."

Laddie looked at him. Maybe Tommy was right. Rina was growing up. He shrugged his shoulders. "O.K.," he said finally. "You ask her. It won't do any good, though. I don't think my mother will let her go."

"She will if you ask her," Tommy said surely.

"I'm goin' in to shower an' put on my suit," Laddie said. "I'll meet yuh on the beach."

"O.K.," Tommy answered. "See yuh."

The cottage was cool and silent after the heat and noise at the game. Slowly Laddie walked through to the kitchen. "Molly?" he called.

There was no answer and he remembered it was Thursday, Molly's day off. He heard a noise upstairs and walked over to the staircase. "Mother?"

Rina's voice came down to him. "They drove down to Hyannis Port to have dinner with some people."

"Oh," he said. He went back into the kitchen and opened the icebox. He took out a bottle of milk and a piece of chocolate cake and put them on the table. He drank the milk from the bottle and ate the cake with his fingers. It wasn't until after he had finished that he remembered he'd promised himself he wouldn't touch any sweets in hopes that his skin would clear up.

He sat there in a kind of lethargy. He heard the bathroom door slam and footsteps leading back to Rina's room. Idly he wondered what she was doing home at this time of the afternoon. Usually she was down at the beach already with her giggling bunch of silly girl friends.

Maybe Tommy was right. She was growing up. Certainly the way she brazenly sat there on the raft with her boobs half hanging out and letting them goggle at her didn't make her seem like a kid. Tommy was right about one thing, though. They were bigger than his cousin's.

A picture of Rina sitting on the raft flashed through his mind: the way she looked at them while they looked at her; her hair falling wet and straight to her shoulders, her lower lip pouting and kind of heavy.

He felt a familiar heat surge through him. He half groaned aloud. Oh, no, not again. He'd promised himself after the last time, he'd stop. He got to his feet abruptly. He wouldn't do it this time. He picked up the empty plate and put it in the sink, then walked out of the kitchen and started up the stairs. He'd grab a cold shower and then beat it out to the beach.

Rina's room was opposite the head of the staircase and the door was partly open. He was almost halfway up when the light spilling from her room caught his eye. There was a movement inside the room and he stopped on the staircase, his heart pounding. Slowly he sank to his knees so that only his eyes were above the top of the landing.

Rina had just crossed the room and was standing in front of the mirror, her back to the door, clad only in a brassière and a pair of bloomers. While he watched, she reached behind her and unfastened the brassière, then, half turning, stepped out of the bloomers. Holding them in her hand, she crossed the room and came back in a moment, carrying a bathing suit. She paused again in front of the mirror and stepped into the suit. Slowly she pulled it up over her breasts and straightened the shoulder straps.

He felt faint beads of perspiration across his forehead. This was the first time he had ever seen a grown-up girl completely naked. He had never thought they could be so beautiful and exciting.

Walking quietly, he passed her room and went into his own. He closed the door and sank, still trembling, to the bed. For a long moment, he sat there, the pain of the heat surging inside him bending him almost double.

Slowly he reasoned with himself. No. He mustn't. Not again. If he gave in to it now, he would always give in to it. At last, he began to feel better. He wiped his forehead with his arm and got to his feet.

All you needed was a little self-control and determination. He began to feel proud of himself. What he had to do was remove himself from all kinds of temptation. That meant everything. Even the French pictures he had bought from the candy store down in Lobstertown.

Quickly he opened a dresser drawer and burrowing underneath a broken slat, came out with the pictures. He placed them on the dresser drawer face down. He wouldn't even look at them one last time. He'd flush them down the toilet when he went in to take his shower.

He undressed rapidly and put on his bathrobe. He walked back to the dresser and caught a glimpse of his face in the mirror. It was filled with a noble resolve. It was amazing how quickly resolution could reflect itself. He turned and left the room, forgetting the pictures that lay on the dresser.

He was drying himself in front of the mirror when he heard her footsteps turn down the hall to his room. Suddenly, he froze as he remembered. The pictures were still on the dresser. He grabbed for the bathrobe on the door behind him.

It was too late. When he got to his room, she was standing near the dresser, the pictures in her hand. She looked up at him in surprise. "Laddie, where did you get these pictures?" she asked, a curious excitement in her voice.

"Give them to me!" he demanded, walking toward her.

"I will not!" she retorted, turning her back to him. "I haven't finished looking at them yet."

Lithely she spun away from his outstretched hand, across the room to the far side of the bed. "Let me finish," she said calmly. "Then you can have them back."

"No!" he shouted hoarsely, flinging himself across the bed at her.

She turned to avoid his grasp but his hand caught her shoulder. The pictures flew from her hand as she fell to the bed beside him. She reached for the pictures. His hand caught at her shoulder strap to keep her from getting them, and the strap broke in his hand. He froze suddenly, staring at one white breast that had escaped the bathing suit.

"You broke my strap," she said quietly, making no move to cover herself, her eyes watching his face.

He didn't answer.

She smiled slowly and raised her hand to her breast, rubbing her palm gently across the nipple. "I'm just as pretty as any of the girls in those pictures, aren't I?"

He was fascinated, unable to speak, his eyes following the deliberate movement of her hand. "Aren't I?" she asked again. "You can tell me. I won't tell anyone. Why do you think I let you watch while I was undressing?"

"You knew I was watching?" he asked in surprise.

She laughed. "Of course, stupid. I could see you in the mirror. I almost burst out laughing. I thought your eyes would pop out of your head."

He could feel the tension begin to build up inside him. "I don't think that's funny."

"Look at me," she said. "I like you to look at me. I wish everybody could."

"That's not right," he said.

"Why isn't it?" she demanded. "What's wrong with it? I like to look at you, why shouldn't you look at me?"

"But you never did," he said quickly.

A secret smile came to her lips. "Oh, yes I did."

"You did? When?"

"The other afternoon when you came back from the beach. There was no one home and I watched you through the bathroom window. I saw everything you did."

"Everything?" The word escaped from him in a groan of dismay.

"Everything," she said smugly. "You were exercising your muscle." Her eyes looked into his. "I never knew it could get so big. I always thought it was little and kind of droopy like it was when you were a little boy."

There was a tightness in his throat and he could hardly speak. He began to get up from the bed. "I think you better get out of here," he said hoarsely.

She looked up at him, still smiling. "Would you like to look at me again?"

He didn't answer.

Her hand reached up and took down the other shoulder strap. She wriggled out of her bathing suit. He stared down at her naked body, feeling his legs begin to tremble. He saw her eyes move down over him. His bathrobe hung open. He looked at her again.

"Now take off your bathrobe and let me see all of you," she said.

As if in a daze, he let the bathrobe slip to the floor. With a groan, he sank to his knees beside the bed, holding himself.

Quickly she rolled across the bed and looked down at him. A faint sound of triumph came into her voice. "Now," she said, "you can do it for me."

His hand reached up to touch her breast. She let it rest there for a moment, then suddenly moved away from him. "No!" she said sharply. "Don't touch me!"

He stared at her dumbly, the agony pouring through him in waves.

Her heavy-lidded eyes watched him.

"Do it for me," she said in a husky voice. "And I'll do it for you. But don't touch me!"

CHAPTER SIX

ALL THROUGH THE MOVIE, LADDIE COULD HEAR THEM GIGGLING AND whispering. He could imagine what they were doing in the darkened theater, even though he couldn't see. His mind flamed with visions.

Now Tommy was offering Rina a gumdrop. He could see him casually holding the bag toward her, the back of his hand seemingly accidentally pressing against her breast. Laddie shifted restlessly in his seat, trying to pierce the dark out of the corner of his eye, but it was a waste of time. He couldn't see anything.

"May I have some candy?" Joan's voice came from the darkness.

"What?" he asked, startled for a moment. "Yeah. Sure." He held the bag toward her.

She turned as she helped herself from the bag and he felt the soft press of her breasts. But it served only to remind him of Rina. He sank back into his seat unhappily.

They stopped in front of Tommy's cottage on the way home. "How about some pop?" Joan asked. "We've got a big bottle in the icebox."

Laddie shook his head. "No, thanks," he said quickly. "It's almost eight o'clock and I promised Mother we'd be home before dark."

Rina didn't say anything.

"Maybe you could come over later?" Joan asked. "After you've taken Rina home?"

Rina looked at him. He flushed. "I don't think so," he answered. "I'm pretty tired. I wanted to get to bed early."

Joan shot a curious look at him, then silently turned and walked into the cottage. There was an awkward moment until Tommy spoke. "Well, good night, then," he said. "See yuh on the beach tomorrow."

They walked the rest of the way home in silence. It was already dark when they climbed up the steps to the porch. He opened the screen door and held it for her.

She started to enter the house, then stopped when she saw he made no move to follow her. "Aren't you coming in?"

He shook his head. "Not right now. I think I'll stay out for a little while."

"I think I will, too," she said quickly, stepping back onto the porch.

He let the screen door swing shut. Its clatter echoed through the house. "Is that you, children?" Geraldine Marlowe called.

"Yes, Mother," Rina answered. She glanced quickly at Laddie. "Can we stay outside for a little while, Mother? It's so hot tonight."

"All right. But only for half an hour, Rina. I want you in bed by eight thirty."

"O.K., Mother."

Laddie crossed the porch and sat down on the large wicker chaise. Rina followed and sat down beside him. "Why did Joan want you to come back?" she asked suddenly.

He didn't look at her. "I dunno."

"Did she want you to do it for her?"

"Of course not!" he said indignantly.

"I don't like Joan," she said suddenly. "She's a—she's a hyp—a hypo—"

"A hypocrite." He supplied the word for her, surprised by the unexpected depth of her perception. "What makes you say that?"

"Tommy wanted me to touch him in the movies, but when I wouldn't, he took Joan's hand and she did."

"No!" The word escaped him involuntarily. Rina was right. The little bitch *was* a hypocrite.

"And she never even looked at him once," Rina continued. "She was always looking at the screen and once she even asked you for some candy."

He stared at her wonderingly.

"I wonder if they're doing it now," she said thoughtfully.

A picture of Joan and Tommy flashed through his mind. He began to get excited.

"I'm not a hypocrite, am I?" she asked. A slow smile came to her lips. She moved and he felt her fingers brush across his thigh. She looked into his face. "Would you like to do it now?" she whispered.

"Now?" he said in a stunned voice. He glanced over his shoulder back to the house.

"They won't come out," she said quietly. "Father is reading his newspaper and Mother is knitting. I saw them through the doorway."

"But—" he stammered. "But—how?"

She smiled again, her fingers taking the handkerchief from his breast pocket.

Geraldine looked up at the mantel clock. It was just eight thirty. She heard the screen door slam and Rina came into the room. Her daughter's eyes were bright and shining and her face wore a happy smile. The smile was infectious and Geraldine smiled back at her.

"Did you have a good time at the movies, dear?"

Rina nodded. "A wonderful time, Mother," she said excitedly. "It was such fun. You don't know how great it is to be able to see a picture without all those brats squalling and running up and down the aisles like they do in the afternoons."

Geraldine laughed. "It was only yesterday that you were one of those brats."

Rina's face suddenly turned serious. "But I'm not any more, am I, Mother?"

Geraldine nodded her head gently. "No, darling. You're quite grown up now."

Rina spun around happily. "That's right, Mother," she said gaily. "I'm quite grown up now."

Geraldine laughed. "Now up to bed with you, young lady. You still need your rest."

"O.K., Mother." Rina bent over her and quickly kissed her cheek. "Good night."

She crossed the room and kissed her father's cheek. "Good night, Father."

She ran out of the room and they could hear her feet running up the stairs. Harrison Marlowe lowered his paper. "She seems quite happy."

"Why shouldn't she be?" Geraldine said. "Her first date. Every girl is excited after her first date."

He put down the paper. "What do you say we go out on the porch for a bit of air?"

They came out into the night. "Laddie?" she called.

"Over here, Mother."

She turned and saw him rising from the chaise. "Did you have a good time?"

"All right," he said shortly.

"Rina wasn't any bother, was she?"

"No."

"You don't sound happy about having to take her with you."

"It was O.K., Mother," he said tensely.

"Sometimes, son," his father said, "we have to do things even if we don't like it. One of them is looking after your sister. That's a brother's job."

"I said it was all right, Father," he snapped.

"Laddie!" his mother exclaimed in surprise.

Laddie looked down at the floor. "I'm sorry, Father," he said in a low voice.

She moved over and looked into his face. "Are you feeling all right, Laddie?" she asked with concern. "You look flushed and warm to me and your face is all perspired. Here, let me wipe it for you." Her hand sought his breast-pocket handkerchief. "Why, Laddie, what happened to your handkerchief? I saw it in your pocket when you left."

For a moment there was something in his eyes that reminded her of a stricken animal, then it was gone. "I—I guess I lost it," he stammered.

She touched his forehead. "Are you sure you haven't a fever?"

"I think you'd better go up to bed, son," his father said.

"Yes, Father." He turned to his mother and kissed her. "Good night," he said and went quickly into the house.

"I wonder what's the matter with him?"

Harrison Marlowe snorted. "I know what's the matter with him."

"You do?"

He nodded. "He's spoiled, that's what. He's so used to having everything the way he wants it, he sulks when he has to do a little thing like chaperon his sister. He's angry because he couldn't sit over in the Randall's yard and spoon with Tommy's cousin Joan."

"Harry, you're being horrid!"

"No I'm not," he said. "Take it from me. I know boys. What he needs is a little discipline." He began to pack his pipe. "And you're doing the same with Rina. Giving her everything she wants. She'll be spoiled soon, too."

"I know what's bothering you," she said. "You just don't like the idea of them growing up. You'd like to keep them children forever."

"No. But you have to admit they are spoiled."

"Maybe they are a little," she admitted.

He smiled. "Well, anyway, it's a good thing they'll be going back to school next month. Barrington's good for Laddie."

"Yes," she agreed. "And I'm glad Rina's been accepted at Jane Vincent's school. They'll make a little lady out of her."

For Laddie, it was a summer of pain and torture, of wild physical sensation and excruciating, conscience-stricken agonies. He couldn't sleep, he couldn't eat, he was afraid to look at her in the mornings and then, when he saw her, he couldn't bear to let her out of his sight. Jealous tortures flamed inside him when he saw her smiling or talking to other boys. Visions born of his knowledge of her would fill his mind and he could see them with her the way he had been. An uneasy, frightened contentment would steal through him when they were together.

And lurking all the while in the deep recesses of his mind was the fear—the fear of discovery, the fear of seeing the hurt and shock and loathing come to the faces of his parents once they knew.

But when she looked at him, smiled at him, touched him, all that was suddenly gone and he would do anything in the world to please her. He abased himself, groveled before her, wept with the agony of his self-flagellation. Then the fear would return. Because there was no escaping the fact. She was his sister. It was wrong.

It was with a feeling of relief that he saw the crazy summer come to an end. It was over, he thought. Away from her, he would be able to find himself again, to control the fevers that she set raging in his blood. When they would come again to the beach next summer, it would be different. He would be different, she would be different.

No more, he would say to her. No more. It's wrong.

That was what he believed when he returned to school at the end of that summer.

CHAPTER SEVEN

"**I**'M PREGNANT," SHE SAID. "I'M GOING TO HAVE A BABY." Laddie felt a dull ache spread over him. Somehow, this was the way he'd always known it would turn out. Ever since that first summer two years ago. He looked up at her, squinting his eyes against the sun. "How do you know?"

She spoke quietly, as if she were just talking about the weather. "I'm late," she said simply. "I've never been late before."

He looked down at his hands. They were sun-darkened against the white sand. "What are you going to do?"

"I don't know," she answered. Her white-blond hair glittered in the sunlight as she turned and looked out at the ocean. "If nothing happens by tomorrow, I guess I'll have to tell Mother."

"Will you—will you tell her about us?"

"No," she said swiftly, in a low voice. She picked the next question from his lips. "I'll tell her it was Tommy, or Bill, or Joe," she answered, still not looking at him.

Despite himself, he felt a twinge of jealousy. "Did you—with all of them?" he asked hesitantly.

Her dark eyes fixed on his own now. "No," she said emphatically. "Of course not. Only with you."

"What if she talks to them? Then she'll know you're lying."

"She won't," Rina said positively. "Especially when I tell her I don't know which one it was."

He stared at her. In so many ways, she was older than he. "What do you think she'll do?"

Rina shrugged her shoulders. "I don't know. There's not very much she can do, I guess."

He watched her walk down the beach to meet some friends, then rolled over in the sand and placed his head on his arms. He groaned aloud. It had happened. Somewhere in the back of his mind he had always known it would. He remembered the night just a few short weeks ago.

They had come down to the beach that summer as they did every year. But this time, it was going to be different. He had sworn it to himself. And he had told her, too.

"No more," he said. "It's stupid, it's kid stuff. You stick to your friends and I'll stick to mine. We'll only get in trouble if we keep it up."

She had agreed. Even promised. And he had to admit she had kept her word. It was he who had broken his vow. And all because of that damned bottle of orange pop.

It had been a rainy afternoon and they were alone in the cottage. It was hot and humid and the air clung heavily to his body, sheathing it in an invisible choking blanket. His shirt and trousers were wringing with perspiration when he went into the kitchen. He opened the icebox but the usual bottle of orange pop he kept there was gone. He closed the icebox door angrily.

He went upstairs and past her open door before his mind absorbed what his eyes had seen. He walked back and stood in the open doorway. She was naked on the bed, half reclining, the bottle of orange pop in her hand. She was staring at it intently.

He felt the pulse begin to hammer in his head, the perspiration break out anew beneath his clothing. "What are you doing with my orange pop?" he asked. He knew he sounded stupid, even as he spoke.

She moved her head slightly on the pillow and looked at him. Her eyes were heavy-lidded and hazy. "Drinking it," she answered huskily, putting it to her mouth. "What do you think?"

The soda overflowed her mouth and ran in orange driblets down her cheeks, across her breasts to the convex of her belly and onto the white sheet. She smiled at him and held out the bottle. "Want some?"

As if he were someone else, he saw himself cross the room and lift the bottle to his lips. It was warm from her touch. He felt the sweetness of the liquid spill into his mouth. He looked down at her.

She was smiling up at him. "You're excited," she said softly. "And you said you wouldn't be any more. But you are."

Some of the orange soda spilled down across his shirt as he suddenly realized he had betrayed himself. He turned to go but her hand caught him around the thigh. He almost screamed with the sudden inflaming agony of her touch.

"Just this once more," she whispered. "And then never again."

He stood frozen, afraid to move, afraid he would stumble and fall because of the trembling within him. "No," he said hoarsely.

"Please," she whispered, her fingers opening, searching.

He stood there as if paralyzed. An anguished moan came from deep within him. There would be no more of this, no more humiliation, no more groveling before her. This time she would learn to leave him alone.

With one hand, he seized her wrists and bent her back to the bed. Her eyes were still confident, still unafraid as they watched him. Suddenly, he pressed his lips to hers. Her mouth was warm and moist and still tasted of the orange soda. Then he moved his head and his lips were traveling down her body, across her throat, over her breasts.

It was then she began to fight him. "No!" she whispered, writhing away from him. "No! Don't touch me!"

But he didn't even hear her. He could feel the red rage pumping in his temples; there was a congestion in his chest. He felt her hand pull loose and rake his chest, leaving a clean, hot path of pain in its wake. Bewildered, he looked down at himself and saw the bloody traces of her fingernails on his flesh. A terrible anger rose up in him.

"You cock-teaser!" he yelled, swinging his free hand. The blow caught her on the side of her face, knocking her back against the bed. She stared up at him with frightened eyes.

"You bitch!" he said, tearing his belt from his trousers. He raised her arms over her head and lashed her wrists to the iron bedpost. He picked up the half-empty bottle from the bed where it had fallen. "Still thirsty?"

She shook her head.

He tilted the bottle and began to laugh as the orange soda ran down over her. "Drink!" he said. "Drink all you can!"

The bottle flew from his hands as she kicked it away. He caught at her legs and pinned them against the bed with his knees. He laughed wildly. "Now, my darling little sister, there'll be no more games."

"No more games," she gasped, staring up into his eyes. His face came down and his mouth covered hers. She felt herself begin to relax.

Then the fierce, sharp pain penetrated her body. She screamed. His hand came down heavily over her mouth, as again and again the pain ripped through her.

And all that was left was the sound of her voice, screaming silently in the confines of her throat, and the ugliness and horror of his body on her own.

Laddie rolled over on the sand. It was all over now. Tomorrow his mother would know. And it would be his fault. They would blame him and they would be right.

No matter what, he shouldn't have let it happen. A shadow fell across him and he looked up.

Rina was standing there. She dropped to the sand beside him. "What are we going to do?"

"I don't know," he said dully.

She reached a hand out to his. "I shouldn't have let you do it," she whispered.

"You couldn't have stopped me," he said. "I must have been crazy." He looked at her. "If we were anybody else, we could run away and get married."

"I know."

His voice turned bitter. "It isn't as if we were really brother and sister. If only they hadn't adopted—"

"But they did," Rina said quickly, and with a sure knowledge. "Besides, we can't blame it on them. It wasn't their fault." She felt the tears come into her eyes. She sat there silently as they rolled down her cheeks.

"Don't cry."

"I—I can't help it," she whispered. "I'm scared."

"I am, too," he said. "But crying won't help."

The tears kept rolling silently down her cheeks. After a moment, she heard his voice. She looked at him. His lips moved awkwardly. "Even if you are my sister, you know that I love you?"

She didn't answer.

"I've always loved you, I guess. I couldn't help it. Somehow, the other girls were nothing when I compared them with you."

"I guess the reason I was so bad was because I was jealous of the girls you went with," she confessed. "I didn't want them to have you. That's why I did what I did. I couldn't let any other boy touch me. I couldn't stand them."

His hand tightened on her fingers. "Maybe it'll turn out all right yet," he said, trying for reassurance.

"Maybe," she said, a dull hopelessness in her voice.

Then they ran out of language and they turned and watched the surf run away with their childhood.

Laddie sat at the helm of his small sailboat and watched his mother in the bow. He felt a gust of wind take the sail and automatically he compensated for the drift while scanning the sky. There were squall clouds coming up ahead. Time to head for the dock. Slowly he began to come about.

"Turning back?" he heard his mother call.

"Yes, Mother," he replied. It seemed strange to have her aboard. But she had wanted to come. It was almost as if she had sensed there was something troubling him.

"You've been pretty quiet this morning," she said.

He didn't meet her gaze. "I have to concentrate on the boat, Mother."

"I don't know what's the matter with you children," she said. "You're both so moody lately."

He didn't answer. He kept his eyes on the squall clouds up ahead. He thought about Rina. Then himself. Then his parents. A sorrow began to well up inside him. He felt his eyes begin to burn and smart.

His mother's voice was shocked. "Why, Laddie, you're crying!"

Then the dam broke and the sobs racked his chest. He felt his mother's hand draw his head down to her breast as she had done so often when he was a baby. "What's the matter, Laddie? What's wrong?" she asked softly.

"Nothing," he gasped, trying to choke back the tears. "Nothing."

She stroked his head gently. "Something is wrong," she said softly. "I know there is. You can tell me, Laddie. Whatever it is, you can tell me. I'll understand and try to help."

"There's nothing you can do," he cried. "Nothing anybody can do now!"

"Try me and see." He didn't speak, his eyes searching her face for something, she didn't know what. A curious dread came into her. "Has it—is it something to do with Rina?"

It was as if the muscles that held his face together all dissolved at once. "Yes, yes!" he cried. "She's going to have a baby! My baby, Mother," he added through tight lips. "I raped her, she's going to have my baby!"

"Oh, no!"

"Yes, Mother," he said, his face suddenly stony.

The tears sprang to her eyes and she covered her face with her hands. This couldn't happen to her children. Not her children. She had wanted everything for them, given them everything. After a moment, she regained control of herself. "I think we'd better turn back," she managed to say quietly.

"We are, Mother," he said. He looked down at his hands on the tiller. The words slipped from him now. "I don't know what got into me, Mother." He stared at her with agonized eyes, his voice strained and tense. "But growing up isn't what it's cracked up to be, it's not what it says in books. Growing up's such a crock of shit!"

He stopped in shock at his own language. "I'm sorry, Mother."

"It's all right, son."

They were silent for a moment and the waves slapped wildly against the hull of the boat. "You mustn't blame Rina, Mother," he said, raising his voice. "She's only a kid. Whatever happened was my fault."

She looked up at her son. A glimmer of intuition pierced the gray veil that seemed to have fallen in front of her eyes. "Rina's a very beautiful girl, Laddie," she said. "I think anyone would find it difficult not to love your sister."

Laddie met his mother's eyes. "I love her, Mother," he said quietly. "And she really isn't my sister."

Geraldine didn't speak.

"Is it terribly wrong to say that, Mother?" he asked. "I don't love her like a sister. I love her"—he searched for a word—"different."

Different, Geraldine thought. It was as good a word as any.

"Is it terribly wrong, Mother?" Laddie asked again.

She looked at her son, feeling a sorrow for him that she could not explain. "No, Laddie," she said quietly. "It's just one of those things that can't be helped."

He took a deep breath, beginning to feel better. At least she understood, she hadn't condemned him. "What are we going to do, Mother?" he asked.

She looked into his eyes. "The first thing we have to do is let Rina know we understand. The poor child must be frightened out of her mind."

He reached forward and took his mother's hand, pressing it to his lips. "You're so good to us, Mother," he whispered, looking gratefully into her eyes.

They were the last words he ever spoke. For just at that moment, the squall came roaring in from the starboard side and capsized the boat.

❖   ❖   ❖

Rina watched stolidly as the lobstermen brought the pitifully small bodies to the shore and laid them on the beach. She looked down at them. Laddie and Mother. A vague spinning began to roar inside her. A cramp suddenly seized her groin and she doubled over, sinking to her knees in the sand beside the still figures. She closed her eyes, weeping as a terrible moisture began to seep from her.

CHAPTER   EIGHT

M ARGARET BRADLEY LOOKED DOWN WEARILY AT THE PAPERS ON HER desk. They were covered with the hen-tracked hieroglyphics of the girls who trooped through her science classes. Abruptly she pushed them to one side and got to her feet. She walked over to the window and looked out restlessly. She was bored, tired of the never-ending, day-in, day-out routine.

Looking out into the gray dusk of evening, she wondered why Sally's letter hadn't arrived yet. It had been more than two weeks since she'd heard from her and usually letters came regularly twice a week. Could it be that Sally had found someone else? Another friend with whom she could share those *intime* whispered secrets?

There was a hesitant knock at the door and she turned toward it. "Yes?"

"A special-delivery letter for you, Miss Bradley." It was the quavering voice of Thomas, the porter.

Quickly she opened the door and took the letter. "Thank you very much, Thomas," she said, closing the door.

She leaned against it, looking down at the letter in her hand. She began to feel brighter. It was Sally's handwriting. She crossed to her desk and rapidly tore open the envelope.

Dear Peggy,
    Yesterday I was married. . . .

The knock at the door was so low that at first she did not hear it. It came again, a little louder this time. She raised her head from the desk. "Who is it?" she called in her husky voice.

"Rina Marlowe, Miss Bradley. May I see you for a moment?"

Wearily the teacher got to her feet. "Just a moment," she called.

She walked into the bathroom and looked at herself in the mirror. Her eyes were red-rimmed and swollen, her lipstick slightly smeared. She looked older than her twenty-six years. She turned on the tap and cleaned the make-up from her face with a washcloth. She stared at herself. For ten years, she and Sally had been inseparable. Now it was over.

She replaced the washcloth on the rack and walked out to the door. "Come in," she said, opening it.

Rina looked into the teacher's face. Miss Bradley looked as if she had been crying. "I'm sorry if I disturbed you," she said. "I can come back later if you like."

The teacher shook her head. "No, that's all right," she answered. She crossed to the small desk and sat down behind it. "What is it?"

Rina shut the door behind her slowly. "I was wondering if I could be excused from the dance Saturday night?"

Margaret Bradley stared at her. For a moment, she couldn't believe her ears. Missing the monthly dance was considered the ultimate punishment. The girls would do anything rather than lose that privilege. It was the only time boys were allowed within the confines of the school. "I don't understand," she said.

Rina looked down at the floor. "I just don't want to go, that's all."

It wasn't because the boys didn't like her. The teacher knew it was quite the opposite. The slim, blond sixteen-year-old standing before her was surrounded by boys at every dance. She came from a good family. The Marlowes were well known in Boston. Her father was a banker, a widower.

"That's a rather strange request," she said. "You must have a reason.

Rina still looked down at the floor. She didn't answer.

Margaret Bradley forced a smile to her lips. "Come now," she said in a friendly voice. "You can talk to me. I'm not that much older than you that I wouldn't understand."

Rina looked up at her and she was surprised by the deep revelation of fear in the girl's eyes. Then it was gone and she looked down at the floor again.

The teacher got up and walked around the desk. She took Rina's hand and led her to a seat. "You're afraid of something," she said gently.

"I can't stand them touching me," she whispered.

"Them?" Margaret Bradley asked, her voice puzzled. "Who?"

"Boys. They all want to touch me and my skin creeps." Rina looked up suddenly. "It would be all right if they just wanted to dance or to talk but they're always trying to get you alone someplace."

"What boys?" The teacher's voice was suddenly harsh. "We'll soon put a stop to their coming here."

Rina got up suddenly. "I'd better go," she said nervously. "I didn't think it would work, anyway."

She started for the door. "Wait a minute!" Margaret Bradley's voice was commanding. Rina turned and looked back at her. "Did any of them do more than— than just touch you?"

Rina shook her head.

"How old are you?"

"Sixteen," Rina answered.

"I guess by now you know that boys are always like that."

Rina nodded.

"I felt the same way when I was your age."

"You did?" Rina asked. A note of relief came into her voice. "I thought I was the only one. None of the other girls feel the way I do."

"They're fools!" The teacher's voice was full of a harsh anger, but she checked herself sharply. There was no sense in allowing her bitterness to expose her. "I was just going to make myself a cup of tea," she said. "Would you care to join me?"

Rina hesitated. "If it wouldn't be too much trouble."

"It won't be any trouble at all," Margaret Bradley said. "Now, you just sit down and make yourself comfortable. I'll have the tea ready in a minute."

She went into the small kitchenette. To her surprise, she found herself humming as she turned on the burner beneath the teakettle.

"I think a summer in Europe between now and the time she goes to Smith in the fall would be of great benefit to her," Margaret Bradley said.

Harrison Marlowe leaned back in his chair and looked at the teacher across the white expanse of the dinner table, then at Rina, seated opposite her. What he saw inspired a kind of confidence in him. A plain, not unattractive young woman in her late twenties, he imagined. She wore simple, tailored clothes, almost mannish in their effect, that seemed to proclaim her profession. She had none of the foolish mannerisms that so many of the young women had today. There was nothing of the flapper about her. She was very serious and business-like.

"Her mother and I often spoke about Rina going to Europe," he began tentatively.

"No girl is considered quite finished if she hasn't spent some time there," the teacher said assuredly.

Marlowe nodded slowly. It was a great responsibility bringing up a daughter. Somehow he had never realized it until several months ago, when he had come into the parlor and found Rina there.

She was wearing a dark-blue dress that somehow made her seem older than her years. Her white-blond hair shone in the semidimness.

"Hello, Father."

"Rina!" he exclaimed. "What are you doing home?"

"I got to thinking how awful it must be for you to come into this great big empty house and find yourself all alone," she said, "so I thought I'd take a few days off from school."

"But—but what about your studies?" he asked.

"I can make them up easily enough."

"But—"

"Aren't you glad to see me, Father?" she asked, interrupting.

"Of course I am," he said quickly.

"Then why don't you kiss me?" She turned her cheek toward him. He kissed her cheek. As he straightened up, she held him with her arm. "Now I'll kiss you."

She kissed him on the mouth and her lips were warm. Then she laughed suddenly. "Your mustache tickles!"

He smiled down at her. "You always said that," he said fondly. "Ever since you were a little girl."

"But I'm not a little girl any longer, am I, Father?"

He looked at her, beautiful, almost a woman in her dark-blue dress. "I guess not," he said.

She turned to the sideboard. "I thought you might like a drink before dinner." The bottles of liquor were all ready for him. He walked over to the sideboard.

She even had cracked ice in the bucket. "What's for dinner?" he asked.

"I had Molly make your favorite. Roast chicken, *rissolé* potatoes."

"Good," he said, reaching for a bottle of whisky. Her voice stopped his hand. "Wouldn't you like a Martini? You haven't had one for a long time."

He hesitated a moment, then reached for the bottle of gin. It wasn't until he turned around that he realized there were two cocktails in his hand. Habit was a strange commander. He turned to put one of them back on the sideboard.

"May I, Father? I'm past sixteen. There are many girls at school whose parents allow them a cocktail at dinner."

He stared at her, then poured half of one drink back into the shaker. He gave her the half-filled glass. He raised his glass in a toast.

She smiled, sipping delicately at her glass. "This is delicious," she said, in exactly the same words and tone of voice he had so often heard his wife use.

He felt the hot, uncontrollable tears leap into his eyes and turned away swiftly so that she would not see. Her hand caught at his sleeve and he turned back to her. Her eyes were deep with sympathy. He let her draw him down slowly to the couch beside her.

And then, for a moment, he wasn't her father. He was just a lonely man weeping against the breast of his mother, his wife, his daughter. He felt her young, strong arms around his shoulders, her fingers lightly brushing his hair. He heard the rumble of her whispered voice within her chest. "Poor Daddy, poor Daddy."

As suddenly as it had come, the moment was gone and he was aware only of the firm, taut breasts against his cheek. Self-consciously he raised his head. "I guess I made a fool of myself," he said awkwardly.

"No, Father," she said quietly. "For the first time in my life, I didn't feel like a child any more. I felt grown up and needed."

He forced a tired smile to his lips. "There's time enough for you to grow up."

Later that night, after dinner, she came over and sat on the arm of his chair. "I'm not going back to school any more," she said. "I'm going to stay home and keep house for you."

He smiled. "You'd get bored with that quickly enough," he said. "You'd miss the excitement of school, of boyfriends—"

"Boys!" she said scornfully. "I can do without them. They're a bunch of grubby little animals always mooning after you. I can't stand them."

"You can't, eh?" he said quizzically. "Just what kind of man would please your majesty?"

She looked down at him seriously. "I think an older man," she said. "Someone like you, maybe. Someone who makes me feel safe and secure and needed. Boys are always trying to get something from you, show that they're stronger, more important."

He laughed. "That's only because they're young."

"I know," she answered, still serious. "That's why they frighten me. They're only interested in what they want; they don't care about me." She leaned over and kissed the top of his head. "Your hair is so nice with that touch of gray in it." A note of regret came into her voice. "Too bad I can't marry you. I love you, Father."

"No!" he said sharply, so sharply that he surprised even himself with the inexplicable violence of his reaction.

"No what, Father?" she asked, startled.

He got to his feet and stared down at her. "No, you're not staying home. You're going back to school tomorrow. I'll have Peters drive you up."

She stared up at him and her eyes began to well with tears. Suddenly, she was a little girl again. "Don't you love me, Father?" she cried. "Don't you want me to stay with you?"

He stared at her for a moment, then compassion filled him. "Of course I love you, darling," he said quietly. "But don't you see, we can't put ourselves in a shell to protect ourselves from the world around us."

"But all I want is to be with you, Daddy!"

"No, child, no," he said patiently. "I know that's the way you feel now but someday, when you're older, and maybe married with children of your own, you'll understand."

She tore herself from his arms and faced him angrily. "No!" she stormed. "I'll never get married! I'll never have children! I'll never let some boy get his dirty hands on me!"

"Rina!" he exclaimed in a shocked voice.

She stared at him dumbly, then her face dissolved into tears again. "Oh, Father!" she cried in a hurt, broken voice. "Can't you see? It's not I, it's you who don't understand!"

"Rina, darling," he said, reaching for her. But she had already fled the room. He heard her running footsteps on the staircase, then her door slammed.

He came back to the present slowly, looking down the long dining table at the teacher, then at Rina. Her eyes were shining, brightly expectant.

"I am sure that if Rina's mother were alive, Miss Bradley," Marlowe said in his oddly formal manner, "she would be as happy as I am to entrust our daughter to your very capable hands."

Margaret Bradley looked quickly down at her soup, so that he could not see the sudden triumph in her eyes. "Thank you, Mr. Marlowe," she said demurely.

CHAPTER NINE

THEY STAYED ON DECK UNTIL THEY HAD PASSED THE STATUE OF LIBERTY and Ellis Island, until the water was a bottle green beneath the ship and they could no longer see the shore.

"Excited?" Margaret Bradley asked.

Rina's eyes were sparkling. "It's like a dream."

Margaret smiled. "It will get better and better. Right now we'd best go down to our cabin and rest up a bit before dinner."

"But I'm not the least bit tired," Rina protested.

"You will be," Margaret said firmly but pleasantly. "We'll be aboard the *Leviathan* for six days. You'll have plenty of time to see everything."

She nodded in silent approval as they entered their cabin. Harrison Marlowe wasn't cheap when he did something for his daughter. It was a first-class cabin, with twin beds and private bath. He hadn't hesitated, either, when she'd suggested that Rina would need a new wardrobe. Instead, he'd simply written a check for a thousand dollars and told her that if it wasn't sufficient, she should let him know.

They had got only a few things in New York; the rest they would get in Paris. But without saying anything to Rina, she had ordered several things and had them sent directly to the ship. She couldn't wait to see the expression on Rina's face when she saw them.

The boxes were on the bed but she did not call attention to them. She wanted the moment to be just right. She took off her light spring coat and sank into a deep, comfortable chair. Opening her purse, she took out a package of cigarettes. It wasn't until after she had lit one that she became aware that Rina was staring at her. Then she realized that Rina had never seen her smoke.

She held out the package. "Have one?"

Rina hesitated.

"Go ahead," she urged. "It's all right. You'll find most European women smoke; they're not so provincial as we are."

She watched Rina light a cigarette and laughed as she coughed. "Don't swallow the smoke."

Rina held the smoke in her mouth and let it out slowly. "How's that?"

Margaret smiled. "Fine."

"This is fun, Miss Bradley."

Margaret looked at her. "Now that we're really on our way, I think we can dispense with formalities. From now on, you may call me Peggy." She got to her feet. "Would you like to bathe first, Rina?"

Rina shook her head. "No, Miss Bradley, you can go first if you like."

Margaret shook her head, smiling. "Peggy."

"I mean Peggy."

"That's better," Margaret said.

She looked up as Rina came out of the bathroom, tying the belt of her robe. Her long blond hair fell to her shoulders, looking even more silvery against her dark tan. There was a low knock at the door. Rina looked at her questioningly.

"I ordered sherry," she explained. "It's good for your appetite the first day at sea. I find it helps prevent *mal de mer*."

She took the tray from the steward and gave one glass to Rina. "Cheers," she said, smiling and sipping the wine slowly.

"It's nice," Rina said.

"I'm glad you like it."

Rina put the glass down. "Shall I wear my new blue suit tonight?"

Margaret assumed a shocked expression. "First-class dining is formal, Rina."

"I have a few of my party dresses," Rina said. "I can wear one of them."

"Not those horrible dresses they wear at the school dances?"

A hurt expression appeared on Rina's face. "I thought they were very pretty."

Margaret laughed. "For children, perhaps. But not for a young lady going to Europe."

"I don't know what to wear, then," Rina said helplessly.

She had teased Rina enough. "Those boxes on the bed are yours," she said casually. "I think you might find something to wear in one of them."

The expression on Rina's face as she opened the boxes was all that Margaret had hoped for. Rina put on a stark black cocktail gown that clung to her figure, revealing her naked shoulders. As they walked into the dining salon, an hour later, every male eye followed them.

Possessively Margaret reached across the table and patted Rina's hand. "You look lovely, my dear."

Margaret put down the towel and turned to look at herself in the full-length mirror. Pleased with her reflection, she ran her hands down along her sides, then stretched luxuriously. Her small breasts with their tiny nipples were no larger than many men's, and her hips were flat and her legs straight.

She slipped into the silk pajamas, quickly buttoning the fly front of the long, man-tailored trousers, then fastening the tightly fitting bolero jacket. She brushed her dark hair straight back and pinned it. Once more, she glanced at the mirror. At a quick glance, few could tell her from a male.

Pleased, she left the bathroom and entered the stateroom. "You can go in now, Rina."

Rina stared at her in amazement. "Miss Bradley—Peggy, I mean—those pajamas!"

Margaret smiled at her. "Like them?"

Rina nodded.

Margaret was pleased. "They're made of genuine Chinese brocade. A friend sent me the material from San Francisco. I designed them myself." One thing she could always say for Sally—she had good taste. Of all the things she had ever given her, these pajamas were her favorite.

Rina got out of her chair and took a cotton nightgown from the bureau. She started for the bathroom.

"Wait a minute," Margaret said. She went to her bureau and took out a small box. "While I was at it," she said, "I also bought you a few nightgowns."

She watched Rina's face as she opened the box. "They're real silk!"

"I was afraid that all you had were those horrible school shifts."

Rina looked down at the box. "There's a different color for every night in the week," she said. "They're all so beautiful, I don't know which to wear first."

Margaret smiled again. "Why don't you wear the white one tonight?"

"O.K.," Rina said. She picked it up and started again for the bathroom. She stopped at the door. "I don't know how to thank you, Peggy," she said gratefully. "You make everything seem so wonderful."

Margaret laughed happily. "That's just the way I want it to be for you," she said. She looked at Rina as if the idea had just come to her. "What do you say we celebrate tonight? While you're changing, I'll order a bottle of champagne. We'll have a little party all by ourselves."

"That would be fun." Rina smiled. "I always wanted to drink champagne but Father would never let me."

"Well, this will be a secret between us." Margaret laughed, reaching for the telephone. "I promise I won't tell him."

❖ ❖ ❖

Rina put down her glass and began to giggle.

Margaret leaned back in her chair, still holding hers by its fragile stem. "What's funny?"

"My nightgown crinkles and gives off tiny sparks when I move."

"That's static electricity," Margaret said. "Silk is a very good conductor."

"I know," Rina answered quickly. "I remember that from your class." She ran her hand down along the gown. "It gives off tiny blue sparks. Can you see them?"

"No."

Rina leaped to her feet. "I'll turn off the lights," she said. "You'll be able to see them then."

She turned off the lights and stood in front of Margaret. "Watch," she said. She ran her hands down the sides of her gown. There was a faint crackling and tiny sparks appeared at her fingertips. Rina picked up her glass and emptied it. She held the glass toward Margaret. "May I have some more, Peggy?"

"Of course," Margaret answered, refilling her glass.

Rina held it to her lips and sipped. "Champagne is nothing but pop made from wine," she said seriously. "But it tastes better. It's not as sweet."

"It's getting warmer in here, don't you think?"

"It is getting warmer," Rina answered. "Do you want me to turn on the fan?"

"Oh, no," Margaret said quickly. "We'd only catch cold in the draft. I'll just slip off my jacket."

She felt Rina's eyes on her small bosom and she picked up her glass quickly. "Do you mind?"

Rina shook her head. She lifted her glass and took another sip. "Do you hear music?"

Margaret nodded. "It's the orchestra from the ballroom. They're playing a waltz."

Rina got to her feet. She swayed in time to the music. "I love to dance," she said. She glided lightly around the room, the white gown flaring out as she turned, showing her long, tanned legs.

Margaret felt a weakness in the pit of her stomach as she got to her feet. "I love to dance, too," she said, making a mock bow. "May I have this dance, Miss Marlowe?"

Rina looked at her, smiling. "Just this one. All the others are taken, Miss Bradley."

Margaret shook a reproachful finger at Rina. "Mr. Bradley, if you please."

Rina laughed. "Of course. Just this one, Mr. Bradley."

Margaret put her arm around Rina's waist. They both laughed as the tiny blue sparks crackled from Rina's gown. Margaret felt her legs tremble as the warmth from Rina's breasts came through the gown. Holding the young girl firmly, she led her into the dance. They spun furiously in a circle as the music reached a crescendo, then abruptly halted.

Rina looked up into her face. Margaret smiled at her. "We'd better have some more champagne." She poured Rina a glass and picked up her own. "You're a very good dancer, Rina."

"Thank you. You lead better than any of the boys that ever came to the school dances. You do everything so well." Rina swayed slightly. "The dancing made me dizzy."

"Perhaps you'd better lie down on your bed for a moment."

Rina shook her head. "And break up our party?"

"Lie down for a minute. You won't break up the party. I'll come and sit on the bed."

"O.K.," Rina said. She walked over to the bed and put her glass on the night table, then stretched out on the white sheet.

Margaret sat down beside her. "Feel better?"

"The room is still spinning," Rina said.

Margaret bent over her and stroked her forehead lightly. "Close your eyes for a moment."

Obediently Rina closed her eyes. They were silent for a moment while Margaret continued to stroke her forehead. "That's better," Rina said softly. "The spinning has gone."

Margaret didn't answer, but kept stroking her head lightly. Rina opened her eyes and looked at her. Margaret reached for her glass. "A little more champagne?"

Rina nodded. She sipped and handed it back to Margaret, who smiled at her, then put the glass down.

"I'm glad we're going to Europe together," Rina said suddenly. "I've never really had a close girl friend before. The girls at school always seemed such ninnies to me. Always talking about boys."

"They're nothing but silly children, most of them," Margaret said. "That's why I liked you the moment you came into my room that night. I knew you were different, more mature."

"Ever since Laddie died, I couldn't stand boys," Rina said.

"Laddie?"

"My brother," Rina explained. "He and my father are the only two men that I ever really liked."

"He must have been very nice," Margaret said.

"He was." Rina turned her head away. "I think I was in love with him."

"That's nothing," Margaret said quickly. "All girls love their brothers."

"He really wasn't my brother, you know. I was adopted."

"How do you know you loved him?" Margaret asked, faint jealousy stirring within her.

"I know," Rina answered. "And I think he loved me, too."

"You do?" Margaret asked, the jealousy stronger. "Did he—did you?"

Rina looked away. "I never spoke to anyone about it before."

"You can talk to me," Margaret said. "I'm your friend. We have no secrets between us."

"You won't be angry with me?"

"I won't be angry with you," Margaret said almost sharply. "Tell me!"

Rina's voice was muffled by the pillow. "I wouldn't let him touch me because I was afraid of what would happen. Then one day, he came into my room and tied my hands to the bed with his belt and he did it to me. He hurt me so bad!"

"He couldn't have loved you so much if he hurt you."

"But he did!" Rina said wildly. "Don't you see, Peggy? I wanted him to. All the time I kept daring him and when he did, I knew I loved him. But he went out in the boat with Mother and they died." She began to sob. "It was my fault because I wanted him to. Can't you see that I was the one who was supposed to die, not Mother? She took my place in the dream. Now I don't even dream the dream any more."

"You'll dream your dreams again," Margaret said slowly, holding Rina's head against her bosom.

"No, I won't!"

"Yes, you will," Margaret said firmly. "Tell me about it and I'll help you."

Rina stopped sobbing. "Do you think you could?" she asked, her eyes searching Margaret's face.

"Tell me and we'll see."

Rina took a deep breath. "I dreamed that I was dead and everybody was around my bed, crying. I could feel how much they loved me and wanted me because they kept begging me not to die. But I couldn't do anything about it. I was dead."

Margaret felt a cold shiver of excitement tremble through her. Slowly she got to her feet. "Close your eyes, Rina," she said quietly, "and we'll act out your dream. Whom do you want me to be?"

Rina looked up at her shyly. "Will you be Laddie?"

"I'll be Laddie," Margaret answered. "Now you close your eyes."

Margaret looked down at the girl. Suddenly her eyes began to fill with tears. A sudden fear began to tear through her. Rina was dead. Rina was really dead. "Rina!" she cried hoarsely. "Please don't die! Please!"

Rina did not move and Margaret fell to her knees beside the bed. "Please, Rina. I can't live without you." She leaned over the bed and covered Rina's face with kisses.

Rina opened her eyes suddenly, a small, proud smile on her face. "You're really crying," she said, her fingers touching Margaret's cheek. She closed her eyes again contentedly.

Slowly Margaret slipped the nightgown off. "You're beautiful," she whispered. "You're the most beautiful woman in the world. You're much too beautiful to die."

Rina looked up at her. "Do you really think I'm beautiful?"

Margaret nodded. She ripped off her pajama bottoms and let them fall to the floor. "All you have to do is look at me to see how beautiful you really are." She caught Rina's hand and pressed it to her breasts, then down across her stomach to her thighs. "Feel how flat I am, just like a man?"

Slowly she sank down onto the bed beside Rina, gently caressing her breasts, pressing her lips to the soft, cool cheeks.

"I feel so safe with you, so good," Rina whispered. "You're not like the other boys, I don't like them to touch me. I'm afraid of them. But I'm not afraid of you."

With a cry of agony, Margaret rolled, her knees forcing Rina's legs apart. "I love you, Rina! Please don't die!"

She pressed her mouth against Rina's. For a moment, she felt the fire of her tongue and then she heard Rina's voice whispering huskily. "Laddie, fuck me, fuck me! I love you, Laddie!"

CHAPTER TEN

RINA LOOKED DOWN AT HER WATCH. IT WAS HALF PAST TWO. "I REALLY must be going," she said.

"To hurry after such a lunch?" Jacques Deschamps spread his hands. "It is sacrilege. You must have a liqueur before you go."

Rina smiled at the slim, graying *avocat*. "But—I—"

"You have been in Paris for more than a year," Jacques interrupted, "and you still have not learned that one does not hurry after a meal. Whatever it is, it will wait." He hissed at a passing waiter. "Psst!"

The waiter stopped and bowed respectfully. "Monsieur?"

Rina sank back into her chair. Jacques looked at her questioningly. "Pernod. Over ice."

He shuddered. "Over ice," he repeated to the waiter. "You heard mademoiselle."

The waiter looked at her quickly with that glance of appraisal that all Frenchmen seemed to share. "Over ice, monsieur," he said. "The usual for you?"

Jacques nodded and the waiter left. He turned back to Rina. "And how does the painting go?" he asked. "You are making progress?"

Rina laughed. "You know better than that. I'm afraid I'll never be a painter."

"But you are having fun?"

She turned and looked out at the street. The faint smell of May that came only to Paris was in the air. The truck drivers were already in their shirt sleeves and the women had long since begun to abandon their drab gray and black winter coats.

"You do not answer," he said.

She turned back to him as the waiter came with their drinks. "I'm having fun," she said, picking up her drink.

"You are not sure?" he persisted.

She smiled suddenly. "Of course I'm sure."

He lifted his glass. "À *votre santé*."

"À *votre santé*," she echoed.

He put his glass down. "And your friend?" he asked. "How is she?"

"Peggy's fine," Rina said automatically. She looked at him steadily. "Peggy is very good to me. I don't know what I'd do without her."

"How do you know?" he said quickly. "You have never tried. You could be many things. You are young, beautiful. You could marry, have children, you could even—"

"Be your mistress?" She smiled, interrupting.

He nodded and smiled. "Even be my mistress. That is not the worst thing that could happen. But you remember my terms."

She looked into his face. "You're a very kind man, Jacques," she said, remembering the afternoon she had first heard them.

She and Peggy had been in Paris a few months and had just found their apartment, after her father had given his permission for her to stay in Paris for a year. Peggy had taken her to a party given by a professor at the University, where she had just begun to work.

Rina felt very alone at the party. Her French was not good enough to let her mix easily and she had retreated to a corner. She was leafing through a magazine when she heard a voice. "Miss *Américaine?*"

She looked up. A slim, dark man with a touch of gray at his temples was standing there. He was smiling gently.

"*Non parle fran—*"

"I speak English," he said quickly.

She smiled.

"And what is a pretty girl like you doing all alone with a magazine?" he asked. "Who is fool enough to bring you to a party like this and then—" He gestured expressively.

"My friend brought me," Rina said, indicating Peggy. "She has just got a job at the University."

Peggy was talking animatedly with one of the professors. She looked very attractive in her slim, tailored suit. "Oh," he said, a strangely quizzical look on his face.

"And whom did you bring?"

"No one." He shrugged. "Actually. I came in the hopes of meeting you."

She glanced at his hands and saw that he wore a wedding ring, as so many Frenchmen did. "You don't expect me to believe that?" she said. "What would your wife say?"

He smiled and laughed with her. "My wife would be very understanding. She could not come with me. She is very, very pregnant." He held his arms out in an exaggerated circle in front of him.

She laughed again and just then, Peggy's voice came over her shoulder. "Having fun, darling?"

Some weeks later, she was alone in the apartment one afternoon when the telephone rang. It was Jacques and she met him for lunch. And several times after that.

Then one afternoon—it had been a day just like this one—they sat dawdling over their liqueurs. "Why are you so afraid of men?" he asked her suddenly.

She felt the red fire creep up into her throat and over her face. "What makes you say that?"

"I have the feeling," he said. "Inside. I know."

She looked down at her drink. She didn't speak.

"Your friend is not the answer," he said.

She looked up at him. "Peggy has nothing to do with it. She's a good friend, no more."

He smiled knowingly. "You are in France, remember? There is nothing wrong, we understand such things. But I do not understand you. You are not the usual kind who lives like that."

She could feel her face flaming now. "I don't think that's very nice of you."

He laughed. "It is not," he admitted frankly. "But I do not like to see you waste yourself."

"You'd like it better if I went to sleep with some clumsy fool who knows nothing and cares less about the way I feel?" she said angrily.

He shook his head. "No. I would not like that at all. I would like you to come to bed with me."

"What makes you think it would be any different with you?"

He looked into her eyes. "Because I am a man, not a boy. Because I would want to please you. Boys are like bulls; they think only of themselves. In this you are right. But because of this, do not think that it is only women who know how to make love. There are men also who are aware of the sensitivities."

"Like yourself?" she asked sarcastically.

"Like myself. Do you think I see you again and again only because I have a purely intellectual interest in you?"

She laughed suddenly. "At least you are honest."

"I am a great believer in the truth."

A few months later, on a rainy afternoon, she went to his apartment and it was just as he said. He was kind and gentle and she did not hurt at all. And all the while, she felt the power in her, the power to bring him to a point of ecstasy from which he would never return, a power that could never turn into terror for her because she could always control it or him.

She watched him buttoning his shirt in front of the mirror. "Jacques."

He turned. "What is it, my sweet?"

She held out her arms to him. "Come here, Jacques."

He came over to the bed. He bent swiftly and kissed her naked breast. "When you make love, my darling," he said, "your nipples are full like bursting purple plums. Now they are like little pink poppies."

"It was like you said it would be, Jacques."

"I am glad."

She took his strong brown hands in her own and looked down at them. His gold wedding ring shone up at her. She looked up into his face. "I think I would like to be your mistress," she said softly.

"*Bon*," he said. "I had hoped you would say that. That is why I took this little apartment. You can move in tonight."

She was surprised. "Move in here?"

He nodded. "If you do not like this place, I will get another."

"But I can't do that! What about Peggy?"

"What about her?" He shrugged. "It is *fini*."

"Can't we just go on like this? I'll meet you here whenever you like."

"You mean you will not move in?"

She shook her head. "I can't. What would Peggy do? She needs my help to keep the apartment. Besides, if my father ever found out, he'd kill me."

"But he does not worry about your living with that—that *lesbienne*?" he said bitterly.

"You don't know my father. Back in Boston, they don't ever think about things like that."

"What does he think she is?"

"What she has always been," she answered. "My teacher, my companion."

He laughed shortly. "She has been your teacher, yes."

"Oh, Jacques," she said in a hurt voice. "Don't spoil everything now. Why can't we go on like this?"

He looked at her. "Then you won't move in here?"

"I can't," she said. "Don't you understand, I can't."

He got to his feet, and walked back to the dresser. He finished buttoning his shirt and picked up his tie.

"I don't see what difference it would make. After all, you're married. How much time do you think you could spend here, anyway?"

He studied her. "That is different," he said coldly.

"Different?" she shouted in anger. "Why is it different for you and not for me?"

He stared at her. "A man may be unfaithful to his wife, as she may to him if she is so minded. But a man is never unfaithful to his mistress, nor is a woman unfaithful to her lover."

"But Peggy is not a man!"

"No, she is not," he said grimly. "She is something worse than a man."

Rina looked at him for a moment. She drew her head up proudly. "Those are your terms?" she asked quietly.

She sat there proudly, her back straight, her naked breasts magnificent over her deep chest. He could see the outlines of her ribs against her flesh as they rose and fell with her breath. Never in my life have I known so much beauty, he thought. Aloud he said, "If that's the way you put it, those are my terms."

She didn't answer.

"I just don't understand," she said. She looked up at him. "You had better hand me my dress."

That had been many months ago and oddly enough, they still remained friends. She raised the Pernod to her lips and emptied her glass. "And now I really must go," she said. "I promised Pavan I would be at his studio by three o'clock."

He raised an eyebrow. "Pavan? You have taken up sculpting?"

She shook her head. "No, I'm modeling for him."

Jacques knew how Pavan worked. He used many models for just one statue. He was always trying to create the ideal. He would never succeed.

She felt his quizzical gaze sweep down to her breasts. She laughed. "No, it's not what you think."

"No?" he asked. "Why not?"

"He says they're too large."

"He is mad," Jacques said quickly. "But then, all artists are mad. What is it, then?"

She got to her feet. "My pubis," she said.

For the first time since she had known him, he was speechless.

She laughed.

He found his voice. "But why?"

"Because it's the highest mountain any man will ever climb, he says, and more men will die trying to climb it than ever fell from Mount Everest." She smiled and bent over him. "But we won't tell him that you survived the ascent, will we, Jacques?"

She kissed his cheek quickly and turned and walked out onto the sidewalk. He watched her until she was lost in the crowded street, then turned back to the waiter. "Psst!" he said. "I think I will have another drink!"

CHAPTER ELEVEN

S HE HURRIED PAST THE POLITE GREETING OF THE CONCIERGE, UP THE three narrow flights of the staircase. She'd stayed at the studio later than she thought. There would be just enough time to prepare dinner before Peggy got home.

Rina went through the tiny living room into the kitchen. Swiftly she lit the gas under the hot-water heater for the tub and with the same match, the oven, leaving the flame low. She took the small, browned chicken she'd just purchased, already cooked, at the corner rotisserie and put it into a pan and into the oven to keep warm. Rapidly she sliced bread from a long loaf, arranged it next to a large piece of cheese and began to set the table. In a few minutes, she was finished.

She looked down at her watch. There would even be time enough for a bath if the water was hot enough. She walked over and felt the tank. It was lukewarm. There would be enough if she didn't fill the tub more than half full.

She walked back into the living room on her way to the bathroom, her fingers already busy with the buttons of her blouse. The door opened and she turned toward it. "You're early," she said.

Peggy looked at her coldly and without answering, she closed the door behind her. Rina shrugged her shoulders. Peggy had these moods. One moment, she'd be bright, warm and gay, the next cold, even sullen. It would pass. "There's some wine and cheese on the table if you'd like something before dinner," she said, starting for the bathroom again.

Peggy's hand spun her around. "I thought I told you not to see Deschamps again!"

Rina stared at her. So that was it. Someone must have seen them at the restaurant and told Peggy. Strange that of all the men they knew, Peggy was jealous of none except Jacques. The younger men never upset her, but Jacques, with his curious, confident smile and the bright-gray hair at his temples, always managed to upset her.

"I just ran into him and he invited me to lunch," she said. It wasn't that she was afraid of Peggy's jealous rages but she didn't feel like having a quarrel. "I just couldn't be rude."

"Then where were you all afternoon?" Peggy demanded. "You weren't at art school, you weren't home. I kept calling both places until I became frantic with worry."

"I didn't feel like going to school," she said.

Peggy's eyes squinted at her. "You didn't walk over to his apartment, by any chance?"

Rina stared back at her. "No, I didn't."

"He was seen entering his apartment with a blonde about four o'clock."

Rina raised an eyebrow. Jacques hadn't wasted any time. "I'm not the only blonde in Paris," she said.

"He didn't answer his phone," Peggy said accusingly.

Rina smiled. "I can't say that I blame him, do you?"

Peggy's hand slashed across Rina's face. "You're lying!"

Rina's hand flew to her cheek. She stared at Peggy.

The other side of her face flamed as Peggy slapped her again. She grabbed Rina's shoulders and began to shake her. "Now I want the truth!"

"I told you the truth!" Rina screamed. She struck out at Peggy wildly.

Peggy fell back in surprise at the sudden onslaught. A hurt expression came over her face. "Why do you do these things to me when you know I love you so much?"

Rina stared at her. For the first time, a feeling of revulsion swept over her. First for Peggy, then for herself.

Almost instantly, Peggy threw herself to her knees, her arms clasped around Rina's thighs. "Please, please, darling, don't look at me like that. Don't be angry with me. I'm sorry. I was crazy jealous."

Rina's face ached where it had been slapped. Suddenly, she was tired. "Don't do that again—ever," she said wearily.

"I won't, I won't," Peggy promised wildly. "It's just that I can't bear to think of that lecher getting his filthy hands on you again."

"He's not a lecher, he's a man," Rina said. She looked down at Peggy. A faint note of contempt came into her voice. "A real man. Not an imitation!"

"I have shown you more than you would learn from all the men in the world."

A sudden knowledge came to Rina—the first faint revelation of self-truth. A cold fright ran through her. She looked down at the dark-brown head pressed against the front of her skirt.

"That's what's wrong. You're so anxious to show me love, to teach me love. But it's all from the outside in. Why can't you teach me to feel love, to give love?" Slowly she pushed Peggy away from her. And then, for the lack of a better place to do it, she dropped to her knees and turned her face into Peggy's bosom and began to cry.

"Cry, lover, cry," Peggy whispered. "Cry it all out. I'll always take care of you. That's what love is for."

It was early when Amru Singh arrived at the party that Pavan was giving to celebrate the unveiling of his master statue. It was about six o'clock when Amru Singh made his obeisance to his host, politely refused a drink and took his usual place against the wall in the empty room.

As was his habit, he took off his shirt and folded it neatly and placed it on the floor. Then he took off his shoes—he wore no socks—and placed them next to the shirt. He took a very deep breath and placing his back against the wall, slid down until he was seated squarely on the shirt with his legs crossed beneath him.

It was thus that he could observe, without turning his head, the actions of every person in the room. It was also from this position that he could most easily fill his mind. He thought about many things, but mostly about the vanities and ambitions of man. Amru Singh was seeking a man whose vanities and ambitions transcended the personal, aspiring only to the glory that had been buried by the centuries deep in the human spirit. That he had not yet found such a man did not discourage him.

He felt his muscles lock in the familiar tension which was at the same time relaxed and comforting; he felt his breathing become slower, shallower. He closed off a corner of his mind for a few minutes, though his eyes remained open and alert. It could be any night, perhaps tonight, that his search would be ended.

But he could already feel the evil spirit of the goddess Kali unleashed in the room. With an inward shrug of his shoulders, he cast from him the feeling of disappointment. There were so many little people in the room.

On the floor, in the corner behind the big sofa, a man and a woman were committing an act of fornication, hidden, or so they thought, from the others. He thought of the positions of obscenity carved high into the walls of the temple of the goddess and felt a distaste seep through him. This ugly copulation, which he could observe through the space between the high Regency legs of the couch, was not justified by even a holy worship of the evil one.

In a niche near the door, with a single light shining down on it from above, stood the draped statue on a pedestal. It stood there very still, like a corpse in a shroud, and did not even stir when the door opened for two newly entered guests. Without moving his eyes, Amru knew them. The blond American girl and her friend, the dark woman. He closed his mind to them as the clock began to toll the hour and Pavan began his speech.

It was nothing but a repetition of what he had been saying all evening, and many times before, but at its finish, he suddenly began to weep. He was very drunk and he almost fell as, with a quick gesture, he tore the covering from the statue.

There was a silence in the room as all looked at the cold marble form of the statue. It was scaled to two-thirds life size and carved from a rose-blush Italian marble that took on a soft hue of warm life from the light in the room. The figure stood poised on tiptoe, the hands held over her upturned face, reaching for her lover, the sun.

Then the silence was broken as all at once began to comment and congratulate the sculptor. That is all except one. He was Leocadia, the art dealer. A small, gray man with the thin, pursed lips of the money-changer.

In the end, no matter what anyone said, his was the final judgment. It was he who determined its value. It did not matter that the price he set might forever prohibit a sale; his evaluation was the recognition of art.

Pavan approached him anxiously. "Well, monsieur?" he asked. "What do you think?"

Leocadia did not look at Pavan. He never looked at anyone while he spoke to him. The artists claimed that he could not meet their gaze because he was a parasite living better from the proceeds of their life's blood than they themselves did. "The market for sculpture is very weak," he said.

"Bah!" Pavan snorted. "I do not ask about the market. I ask about my work!"

"Your work is as always," the dealer said evasively.

Pavan turned and gestured, his arm outflung toward the silent statue. "Look at those breasts. I took them from different girls to achieve the symmetry that nature did not provide. And the face. Flawless! Notice the brow, the eyes, the cheekbones, the nose!" He was suddenly silent, staring up at the statue. "The nose," he said, almost whispering.

He turned toward the models, huddling against the wall. "Bring monsieur a bottle of wine! The nose, monsieur," he said accusingly. "Why did you not tell me about the nose?"

Leocadia was silent. This was no time to tell Pavan he had found nothing at fault with the nose. He had a reputation to maintain.

"My chisel!" Pavan roared. He climbed upon a chair and positioned the chisel delicately. He scraped the stone slightly, then polished the surface with his sleeve. The marble shone once more and he stepped down and looked.

Suddenly he screamed in frustrated agony. "It's wrong!" he cried. "It's all wrong! Why didn't you tell me, monsieur? Why did you let me make a fool of myself?"

Leocadia still did not speak.

Pavan stared dumbly at the dealer, tears coming to his eyes, then he turned and violently swung the mallet at the statue's head. The marble cracked and the head fell into fragments on the floor. Pavan began to swing wildly at the rest of the statue. The arms fell, then a shoulder; a crack appeared across the bust and that, too, shattered. The statue rocked crazily on its pedestal, then crashed forward.

Pavan knelt over the pieces, swinging his mallet like a man possessed. "I loved you!" he screamed, tears streaming down his cheeks. "I loved you and you betrayed me!" At last, he sank exhausted to the floor, amidst the debris.

As suddenly as they had come, the tears stopped and Pavan began searching frantically among the pieces of shattered marble. At last, he found what he sought. He got to his feet. Holding the fragment in his hand, he weaved unsteadily toward the art dealer. Cupping the marble in his hands, he held it out. "I see now where I went wrong, monsieur," he said. "Do you?"

Leocadia looked at the piece of stone. He didn't even know what it was intended to be. But again, this was no time for him to speak. He nodded cautiously.

"Thank God!" Pavan cried. "Thank the good Lord that I did not destroy the sole thing of beauty in the stupidity of my disappointment!"

The crowd pushed forward to see what Pavan held in his hand. It seemed to be only a piece of broken marble. "What is it?" one of them whispered to another.

"You stupid fools! Do you not recognize where you come from? The soul itself of a woman's beauty?" Pavan roared.

He got to his feet and stared at them balefully. "This is fit only for the gods themselves to lie upon!" He looked down at the stone in his hands and a tender look came over his face.

"Now I see my error," he said. "It is around this tiny core that I will carve into stone the perfect Woman!" He looked around at them dramatically.

Leocadia looked at the piece of marble again. So that was what it was. Almost immediately, he thought of the fat young Egyptian prince who had come into the gallery. This was something he would appreciate. "A thousand francs," he said.

Pavan looked at the dealer, his confidence suddenly restored. "A thousand francs!" he said scornfully.

"Fifteen hundred, then," Leocadia murmured.

Pavan was caught up now in the never-ending struggle between artist and dealer. He turned to his fellow artists. "Only fifteen hundred francs he offers me!"

He whirled back to the dealer. "Not a centime less than twenty-five hundred and a commission to do the sculpture of the woman from whom this was taken!" he shouted.

Leocadia looked down at the floor. "How can I undertake such a commission when I do not know the model?"

Pavan spun around. The models looked at each other curiously, wondering which of them had posed for that particular portion of the statue. But it was none of them. Suddenly, Pavan's arm shot out. "You!" he shouted, pointing. "Come here!"

They turned and followed his pointing finger. Rina stood frozen to the spot. Her face began to flame, then hands pulled her forward, propelling her toward the sculptor.

Pavan seized her hand and turned toward the dealer. For once, Leocadia looked. Almost immediately, he looked away again. "Agreed!" he murmured.

A deep bellow of triumph arose from the sculptor's throat. He lifted Rina into his arms and kissed her excitedly on both cheeks. "You will live forever, my lovely one!" he cried proudly. "I will carve your beauty into the stone for all eternity to worship!"

Rina began to laugh. It was crazy. They were all crazy. Pavan began to sing lustily, dragging her with him in an erratic dance. He lifted her up onto the pedestal where the statue formerly stood. She felt hands tugging at her dress, at her clothing. She reached out her arms to brace herself, to keep from falling. Then she was completely nude on the pedestal. A strange hush fell over the room.

It was Pavan himself who led her down. He threw a cloth around her as she started to walk toward the bathroom. One of the models handed her her torn clothing. Rina took it and closed the door behind her. A moment later, she reappeared.

Peggy was waiting for her. She half led, half dragged Rina toward the door. The door slammed behind them.

Suddenly, one of the curtains in the mind of Amru Singh lifted. Through the thin wooden partition behind his head, he could hear dim voices.

"Are you crazy?"

"It wasn't that important, Peggy."

"What if it gets into the papers? The next thing you know, it will be picked up and spread all over the front pages in Boston!"

Rina's laughter echoed gaily. "I can just see the headline now," she said. "Boston girl chosen as most beautiful cunt in Paris!"

"You sound as if you're proud of it."

"Why shouldn't I be? It's the only thing I've ever done for myself."

"Once it gets around, every man in Paris will be after you. I suppose you'd like that."

"Maybe I would. It's time I began to grow up, stopped taking your word for everything."

There was the sound of a vicious slap, then an angry voice. "You're a whore, a cheap whore, and that's how a whore should be treated!"

There was a moment's silence. "I told you never to do that again!"

He heard the sound of another slap. "Whore, bitch! That's the only language you understand!" There was a pause, then "Rina!" The hidden sound of fear was in the voice. Amru Singh thought it sounded much like the trainer of the tiger who steps into the cage only to find his kitten has become a full-grown cat. "What are you doing? Put down that shoe!"

Then there was a half-pitched scream and the sound of a body falling, tumbling erratically down the long, steep stair well. And for the first time in the memory of anyone there, Amru Singh left a party before the last guest had departed.

Rina was standing at the railing, her face ashen, looking down the stair well. Her sharp-pointed high-heeled shoe was still in her hand. He took the shoe from her fingers and bending down, slipped it on her foot.

"I never even touched her!"

"I know," Amru Singh said quietly.

She collapsed suddenly against him. He could feel the wild, frightened beating of her heart against his chest. "She slipped and fell over the railing!"

"Don't say anything to anyone!" he whispered commandingly. "Leave the talking to me!"

Then the door behind them opened and two departing guests came out into the hall. Amru Singh turned toward them, his hand pressing Rina's face against his chest so that she could scarcely breathe, let alone speak. "There's been an accident," he said calmly. "Call a doctor."

He felt Rina begin to cry against his shoulder. He looked down at the shining blond head. A strange satisfied look came into his dark, deep-set eyes.

His portent had come true. The evil goddess, Kali, had struck. But this time, she was not to receive the innocent as a further sacrifice to her power, no matter how carefully she had contrived to plant the guilt.

CHAPTER TWELVE

RINA WAS STANDING ON HER HEAD, THE LENGTH OF HER BODY AGAINST the wall, when Jacques entered the apartment. He stood there for a moment, looking at her slim body, sheathed in the tight black leotard, her hair shining as it spilled over on the floor.

"What are you doing?" he asked politely.

She smiled an upside-down smile at him. "Standing on my head."

"I can see that," he answered. "But why?"

"Amru Singh says it is very good for the brain. The blood washes the brain and a new perspective is given to the world. He is right, too. You just don't know how different everything looks upside down."

"Did Amru Singh also tell you how one goes about kissing a girl who is standing on her head?" he asked with a smile.

"No," she answered. A mischievous smile came over her face. "I thought of that myself!" She arched her back quickly and moved her legs.

He laughed aloud. There was no mistaking the invitation of the Y she made against the wall. He bent forward quickly, placing his head between her outstretched legs, and kissed her.

She collapsed on the floor in laughter. "It is good to hear you laugh," he said. "You did not laugh much at first."

"I wasn't happy at first."

"And you are happy now?" he asked.

The laughter was still in her eyes as she looked up at him. "Very happy." She was a very different person from the dazed girl he had seen that night several months ago. He remembered the telephone ringing beside his bed.

"Monsieur Deschamps?" a deep, quiet voice had asked.

"*Oui?*" he replied, still half asleep.

"My apologies for disturbing your rest," the voice continued, in French with a peculiar British and yet not quite British accent. "My name is Amru Singh. I am with a friend of yours, Mademoiselle Rina Marlowe. She needs your help."

He was awake now. "Is it serious?"

"Quite serious," Amru Singh replied. "Mademoiselle Bradley had an accident. She was killed in a fall and the police are being very difficult."

"Let me speak with Mademoiselle Marlowe."

"Unfortunately, she is in no position to come to the telephone. She is in a state of complete shock."

"Where are you?"

"At the studio of Monsieur Pavan, the sculptor. You know the place?"

"Yes," Jacques answered quickly. "I will be there in half an hour. In the meanwhile, do not let her talk to anyone."

"I have already seen to that," Amru Singh said. "She will not speak with anyone until you arrive."

Jacques did not quite understand what Amru Singh had meant until he saw Rina's ashen face and the blank look in her eyes. The police had efficiently isolated her in the small dressing room of the studio.

"Your friend seems to be in a very bad state of shock, monsieur," the Inspector said when Jacques introduced himself. "I have sent for a doctor."

Jacques bowed. "You are very kind, Inspector. Perhaps you can tell me what happened? I just arrived, in response to a telephone call from a mutual friend."

The Inspector gestured broadly. "It is nothing but routine, Monsieur. Mademoiselle Bradley fell down the stairs. We require only a statement from Mademoiselle Marlowe, who was the only person with her at the time."

Jacques nodded. There must be more to it than that, he thought. Or why would Amru Singh have sent for him? "May I go into the dressing room?"

The Inspector bowed. "Of course, monsieur."

Jacques entered the small room. Rina was seated on a small chair, half hidden behind a tall man wearing a turban.

"Monsieur Deschamps?"

Jacques bowed. "At your service, Monsieur Singh." He glanced at Rina. She didn't seem to see him.

When Amru Singh spoke, his voice was soft, as if he were speaking to a child. "Your friend Monsieur Deschamps is here, mademoiselle."

Rina looked up, her eyes blank, unrecognizing.

Jacques looked at Amru Singh questioningly. The man's dark eyes were inscrutable. "I was at the scene of the accident, Monsieur Deschamps. She was very upset and seemed under a compulsion to accept blame for her friend's accident."

"Did she have anything to do with it?" Jacques asked.

"As I already explained to the police," Amru Singh said blandly, "nothing I saw led me to think so."

"What did she say to them?"

"I thought it best that she not speak with them," Amru Singh replied.

"Are you a doctor?"

"I am a student, monsieur," Amru Singh replied.

Jacques looked up at him. "Then how were you able to keep her from speaking to the police?"

Amru Singh's face was impassive. "I told her not to."

"And she obeyed?" Jacques asked.

Amru Singh nodded. "There was little else she could do."

"May I speak to her?"

"If you wish," Amru Singh answered. "But I suggest someplace other than here. They would perhaps misconstrue what she might say."

"But the police have already sent for a doctor," Jacques said. "Will he not—"

Amru Singh smiled. "The doctor will merely confirm that she is in shock."

Which was exactly what the doctor did. Jacques turned to the Inspector. "If you will permit me, Inspector, I shall escort Mademoiselle Marlowe to her home. I will bring her down to your office tomorrow afternoon, after her own physician has attended her, to make a statement."

The Inspector bowed.

In the taxi, Jacques leaned forward and gave the driver Rina's address.

"I think it would be better if Mademoiselle Marlowe were not to go to her own apartment," Amru Singh said quickly. "There is much there to remind her of her late friend."

Jacques thought for a moment, then gave the driver his other address.

Amru Singh walked into the apartment and Rina followed him docilely. Jacques closed the door behind them. Amru Singh led her to a chair. He gestured and she sat down. "I have taken away my shoulder," he said quietly. "I can no longer speak for you. You must speak now for yourself."

Rina raised her head slowly. Her eyes were blinking as if she were awakening from a deep sleep. Then she saw him.

Instantly, the tears rushed to her eyes. She flung herself into his arms. "Jacques! Jacques!" she cried. "I knew you would come!"

She began to sob, her body trembling against him. The words kept tumbling from her lips in wild, disjointed sentences.

"Shh," he whispered soothingly, holding her. "Don't be afraid. Everything will be all right."

He heard the door open and close behind him. He turned his head slightly. Amru Singh was gone.

The following day, they went to the Inspector's office. From there, they went to her flat and moved her things to his apartment. Two nights later, when he had come into the apartment unexpectedly, Amru Singh rose from a chair.

"Amru Singh is my friend," Rina said hesitantly.

Jacques looked at her, then at the Indian. He stepped forward quickly, his hand outstretched. "If he is your friend," he said, "then he is my friend, also."

The Indian's white teeth flashed in a smile as their hands met in a warm clasp. From that time until now, the three of them had dinner together at least once a week.

❖ ❖ ❖

Jacques turned the key in the door. He stepped aside to let Rina enter, then followed her into the bedroom. As soon as she entered, she kicked off her shoes. She sat down on the edge of the bed, rubbing her feet. "Ah, that feels good."

He knelt in front of her and massaged her foot. He smiled up at her. "You were very beautiful tonight."

She looked at him mischievously. "*Monsieur le Ministre* thought so," she teased. "He said if I should ever consider another liaison, to keep him in mind."

"The old lecher!" Jacques swore. "He must be all of eighty years old—and at the Opera, too!"

She got up from the bed and took her dress off, then seated herself, yoga fashion, on the floor. Her legs were crossed under her, her arms formed a square in front of her chest.

"What are you doing?" he asked in surprise.

"Preparing for meditation," she answered. "Amru Singh says that five minutes' meditation before going to sleep relieves the mind and the body of all its tensions."

He removed the studs from his shirt and placed them on the dresser. He watched her in the mirror. "It would be very easy for me to become jealous of Amru Singh."

"That would make me very unhappy," she said seriously. "For then I would have to stop seeing Amru."

"You would do that for me?"

"Of course," she said. "I love you. He is only my friend, my teacher."

"He is my friend, too," he said, as seriously. "I would be very unhappy if you let a jesting remark disturb that relationship."

She smiled. He smiled back at her and turned back to the dresser. He began to take off his shirt. "And what have you learned from our friend today?"

"There is a good possibility that I may soon be free of the death wish that has governed many of my actions since I was a child," she answered.

"Good," Jacques said. "And how is this to come about?"

"He is teaching me the yoga exercises for childbearing. It will give me control over my entire body."

"I don't see how that will help. The exercises are important only when having a child."

"I know," she said.

Something in her voice made him look at her in the mirror. Her face was impassive as she held the position of meditation. "What brought that subject up?" he asked.

Her eyes flicked up at him. "You," she said. "Doctor Fornay says that you have made me *enceinte*."

Suddenly, he was on the floor beside her, holding her in his arms and kissing her, talking of divorcing his wife so that the child would be born at the family villa in the south of France.

She placed a finger on his lips. It seemed to him as if she had suddenly become older than he. "Come, now," she said gently. "You are acting like an American, with stupid, provincial ideas. We both know that a divorce would ruin your career, so speak no more about it. I will have the child and we will go on as we are."

"But what if your father finds out?"

She smiled. "There is no need for him to know. When I go home for a visit, I will merely say I made an unfortunate marriage and no one will be the wiser."

She laughed and pushed him toward the bathroom. "Now go. Take your bath. You have had enough excitement for one day. Did you get the Boston papers for me?"

"They're in my brief case."

He sank into the tub. The water was warm and relaxing and gradually he could feel the excited tempo of his heart return to something that approximated normal. Slowly and with a feeling of great strength and luxury, he began to lather himself.

He came out of the bathroom, tying his robe. Rina wasn't in the bedroom and he walked through into the living room. Something in the way she was sitting at the table, staring down at the newspaper, sent a frightened chill racing through his body. "Rina!"

She turned toward him. Slowly her eyes lifted. He had never seen such depths of torture in his life. It was as if she had lost all hope of redemption. "I can't have the baby, Jacques," she whispered in an empty voice.

His voice grated in his throat. "What?"

The tears were beginning to well into her eyes. "I must go home," she whispered.

"Why?" he cried, the hurt already beginning.

She gestured to the paper, and he walked over and looked down over her shoulder.

A banner headline streamed across the entire page:

HARRISON MARLOWE INDICTED
FIFTH-GENERATION BOSTON BANKER
CRIMINALLY IMPLICATED IN FAILURE
OF FAMILY BANK

Below was a three-column picture of Harrison Marlowe.

He caught her shoulders. "Oh, my darling!" he said.

He could barely hear her whispered, "And I wanted this baby so."

He knew better than to argue with her. One thing he understood as a Frenchman—filial duty. "We'll have another baby," he said. "When this is over, you'll return to France."

He could feel her move within the circle of his arms. "No," she cried, "Doctor Fornay told me there will never be another child!"

CHAPTER THIRTEEN

THE LARGE OVERHEAD FAN DRONED ON AND THE AUGUST HEAT LAY HEAVY and humid in the Governor's office. The slightly built, nervous male secretary showed Rina to a chair in front of the massive desk.

She sat down and watched the young man, standing nervously next to the Governor, pick up sheet after sheet of paper as the Governor signed each one. At last he was finished and the secretary picked up the last sheet of paper and hurried out, closing the door behind him.

She looked at the Governor as he reached across the desk and took a cigar from a humidor. For a moment, she caught a glimpse of piercing dark eyes, set deep in a handsome face. His voice was slightly husky. "Do you mind if I smoke, Miss Marlowe?"

She shook her head.

He smiled, taking a small knife and carefully trimming the end of the cigar. He placed it in his mouth and struck a match. The flame burned brightly yellow, large and small, with his breath as he drew on the cigar. She was conscious of the faintly pleasant smell of Havana leaf as he dropped the match into an ash tray.

He smiled again. "One of the few pleasures my physician still allows me," he said. He had a simple yet extraordinary clear voice that easily filled the room, though he spoke quietly, like an actor trained to have his whispers heard in the far reaches of the second balcony. He leaned across the desk, his voice lowering to a confidential whisper. "You know, I expect to live to be a hundred and twenty-five and even my physician thinks I might make it if I cut down on my smoking."

She felt the convincing warmth and intensity flow toward her and for the moment, she believed it, too. "I'm sure you will, Governor."

He leaned back in his chair, a faintly pleased look on his face. "Just between us, I don't really care whether I live that long or not," he said. "It's just that when I die, I don't want to leave any enemies, and I figure the only way I'll ever do that is to outlive them all."

He laughed and she joined him, for the moment forgetting her reason for being there. There was something incredibly young and vital about him that belied the already liberal sprinkling of gray in his thick, lustrous black hair.

He looked across the massive desk at her, feeling once again the rushing of time against him. He drew on his cigar and let the smoke out slowly. He liked what he saw. None of this modern nonsense about dieting and boyish bobs for her. Her hair fell long and full to her shoulders.

He looked up and suddenly met her eyes. Almost instantly, he knew that she had been aware that he was studying her. He smiled without embarrassment. "You were a child when I approved your adoption papers."

Her words put him at ease. "My mother and father often told me how kind you were and how you made it possible for them to adopt me."

He nodded slowly. It was smart of them to tell her the truth. Sooner or later, she'd have found out, anyway. "You're eighteen now?"

"Nineteen next month," she said quickly.

"You've grown a little since I saw you." Then his face turned serious as he placed the cigar carefully in the ash tray. "I know why you've come to see me," he said in his resonant voice. "And I'd like to express my sympathy for the predicament your father is in."

"Have you studied the charges that are being made against him?" Rina asked quickly.

"I've looked over the papers," he admitted.

"Do you think he's guilty?"

The Governor looked at her. "Banking is like politics," he said. "There are many things which are morally right and legally wrong. That they may be one and the same thing doesn't matter. Judgment is rendered only on the end result."

"You mean," she said quickly, "the trick is—not to get caught!"

He felt a glow of satisfaction. He liked quick, bright people, he liked the free exchange of ideas that came from them. Too bad that politics attracted so few of that kind. "I wouldn't be cynical," he said quietly. "It isn't as simple as that. The law is not an inflexible thing. It is alive and reflects the hopes and desires of the people. That's why laws are so often changed or amended. In the long run, we trust that eventually the legal and the moral will come together like parallel lines which meet in infinity."

"Infinity is a long time for a man my father's age to wait," she said. "No one has that much time. Not even you if you live to the hundred and twenty-five."

"Unfortunately, decision will always remain the greatest hazard of leadership," he answered. "Your father assumed that hazard when he authorized those loans. He justified it to himself because without them, certain mills might be forced to close, throwing many people out of work, and causing others to lose their investment or principal means of support. So your father was completely right morally in what he did.

"But legally, it's another story. A bank's principal obligation is to its depositors. The law takes this into account and the state has rules governing such loans. Under the law, your father should never have made those loans because they were inadequately collateralized. Of course, if the mills hadn't closed and the loans had been repaid, he'd have been called a public benefactor, a farseeing businessman. But the opposite happened and now these same people who might have praised him are screaming for his head."

"Doesn't it make any difference that he lost his entire fortune trying to save the bank?" Rina asked.

The Governor shook his head. "Unfortunately, no."

"Then, is there nothing you can do for him?" she asked desperately.

"A good politician doesn't go against the tide of public opinion," he said slowly. "And right now the public is yelling for a scapegoat. If your father puts up a defense, he'll lose and get ten to fifteen years. In that case, I'd be long out of office before he was eligible for parole."

He picked up the cigar from the ash tray and rolled it gently between his strong white fingers. "If you could convince your father to plead guilty and waive jury trial, I'll arrange for a judge to give him one to three years. In fifteen months, I'll grant him a pardon."

She stared at him. "But what if something happens to you?"

He smiled. "I'm going to live to be a hundred and twenty-five, remember? But even if I weren't around, your father couldn't lose. He'd still be eligible for parole in twenty months."

Rina got to her feet and held out her hand. "Thank you very much for seeing me," she said, meeting his eyes squarely. "No matter what happens, I hope you live to be a hundred and twenty-five."

From her side of the wire partition, she watched her father walk toward her. His eyes were dull, his hair had gone gray, even his face seemed to have taken on a grayish hue that blended softly into the drab gray prison uniform.

"Hello, Father," she said softly as he slipped into the chair opposite her.

He forced a smile. "Hello, Rina."

"Is it all right, Father?" she asked anxiously. "Are they—"

"They're treating me fine," he said quickly. "I have a job in the library. I'm in charge of setting up a new inventory control. They have been losing too many books."

She glanced at him. Surely he was joking.

An awkward silence came over them. "I received a letter from Stan White," he said finally. "They have an offer of sixty thousand dollars for the house."

Stan White was her father's lawyer. "That's good," she said. "From what they told me, I didn't think we'd get that much. Big houses are a glut on the market."

"Some Jews want it," he said without rancor. "That's why they'll pay that much."

"It was much too big for us and we wouldn't live there when you come home, anyway."

He looked at her. "There won't be very much left. Perhaps ten thousand after we take care of the creditors and Stan."

"We won't need very much," she said. "We'll manage until you're active again."

This time his voice was bitter. "Who would take a chance on me? I'm not a banker any more, I'm a convict."

"Don't talk like that!" she said sharply. "Everyone knows that what happened wasn't your fault. They know you took nothing for yourself."

"That makes it even worse," he said wryly. "It's one thing to be condemned for a thief, quite another for being a fool."

"I shouldn't have gone to Europe. I should have stayed at home with you. Then perhaps none of this would have happened."

"It was I who failed in my obligation to you."

"You never did that, Father."

"I've had a lot of time to think up here. I lay awake nights wondering what you're going to do now."

"I'll manage, Father," she said. "I'll get a job."

"Doing what?"

"I don't know," she replied quickly. "I'll find something."

"It's not as easy as that. You're not trained for anything." He looked down at his hands. "I've even spoiled your chances for a good marriage."

She laughed. "I wasn't thinking of getting married. All the young men in Boston are just that—young men. They seem like boys to me; I haven't the patience for them. When I get married, it will be to a mature man, like you."

"What you need is a vacation," he said. "You look tired and drawn."

"We'll both take a vacation when you come home," she said. "We'll go to Europe. I know a place on the Riviera where we could live a whole year on less than two thousand dollars."

"That's still a long way off," he said. "You need a vacation now."

"What are you getting at, Father?" she asked.

"I wrote to my cousin Foster," he said. "He and his wife, Betty, want you to come out and stay with them. They say it's beautiful out there and you could stay with them until I could come out to join you."

"But then I wouldn't be able to visit you," she said quickly, reaching for his hands in the narrow space beneath the bars.

He pressed her fingers. "It will be better that way. Both of us will have less painful things to remember."

"But, Father—" she began to protest.

The guard started over and her father got to his feet. "I've already given Stan White instructions," he said. "Now, you do as I say and go out there."

He turned away and she watched him walk off through eyes that were beginning to mist over with tears. She didn't see him again until many months later, when she was on her way to Europe again on her honeymoon. She brought her husband out to the prison.

"Father," she said, almost shyly, "this is Jonas Cord."

What Harrison Marlowe saw was a man his own age, perhaps even older, but with a height and youthful vitality that seemed characteristic of the Westerner.

"Is there anything we can get you, Father?" she asked.

"Anything we can do at all, Mr. Marlowe?" Jonas Cord added.

"No, No, thank you."

Cord looked at him and Harrison Marlowe caught a glimpse of deep-set, penetrating blue eyes. "My business is expanding, Mr. Marlowe," he said. "Before you make any plans after leaving here, I'd appreciate your speaking with me. I need a man with just your experience to help me in refinancing my expansion."

"You're very kind, Mr. Cord."

Jonas Cord turned to Rina. "If you'll excuse me," he said, "I know you want some time alone with your father. I'll be waiting outside."

Rina nodded and the two men said good-by. For a short time, father and daughter looked at each other, then Rina spoke. "What do you think of him, Father?"

"Why, he's as old as I am!"

Rina smiled. "I told you I'd marry a mature man, Father. I never could stand boys."

"But—but—" her father stammered. "You're a young woman. You have your whole life ahead of you. Why did you marry him?"

Rina smiled gently. "He's an extremely wealthy man, Father," she said softly. "And very lonely."

"You mean you married him for that?" Then suddenly he understood the reason for her husband's offer. "Or so he could take care of me?" he asked.

"No, Father," she said quickly. "That isn't why I married him at all."

"Then why?" he asked. "Why?"

"To take care of me, Father," she said simply.

"But, Rina—" he began to protest.

She cut him off quickly. "After all, Father," she said, "you yourself said there wasn't anything I could do to take care of myself. Wasn't that why you sent me out there?"

He didn't answer. There wasn't anything left for him to say. After a few more awkward moments, they parted. He stretched out on the narrow cot in his cell and stared up at the ceiling. He felt a cold chill creeping through him. He shivered slightly and pulled the thin blanket across his legs. How had he failed her? Where had he gone wrong?

He turned his face into the hard straw pillow and the hot tears began to course down his cheeks. He began to shiver as the chill grew deeper within him. Later that night, they came and took him to the prison hospital, with a fever of a hundred and two. He died of bronchial pneumonia three days later, while Rina and Jonas Cord were still on the high seas.

CHAPTER FOURTEEN

T HE PAIN BEGAN TO ECHO IN HER TEMPLES, CUTTING LIKE A SHARP KNIFE into the dream. She felt it begin to slip away from her, and then the terrible loneliness of awakening. She stirred restlessly. Everyone was fading away, everyone except her. She held her breath for a moment, fighting the return to reality. But it was no use. The last warm traces of the dream were gone. She was awake.

She opened her eyes and stared unrecognizingly for a moment around the hospital room, then she remembered where she was. There were new flowers on the dresser opposite the foot of the bed. They must have brought them in while she slept.

She moved her head slowly. Ilene was dozing in the big easy chair near the window. It was night outside. She must have dozed the afternoon away.

"I have a terrible headache," she whispered softly. "May I have some aspirin, please?"

Ilene's head snapped forward. She looked at Rina questioningly.

Rina smiled. "I've slept away the whole afternoon."

"The whole afternoon?" It was the first time in almost a week that Rina had been conscious. "The whole afternoon," Ilene repeated. "Yes."

"I was so tired," Rina said. "And I always get a headache when I nap during the day. I'd like some aspirin."

"I'll call the nurse."

"Never mind, I'll call her," Rina said quickly. She started to raise her hand to the call button over her head. But she couldn't lift her arm.

She looked down at it. It was strapped to the side of the bed. There was a needle inserted into a vein on her forearm, attached to a long tube which led up to an inverted bottle suspended from a stand. "What's that for?"

"The doctor thought it would be better if they didn't disturb your rest to feed you," Ilene said quickly. She leaned across the bed and pressed the buzzer.

The nurse appeared almost instantly in the doorway. She walked quickly to the bed and stood next to Ilene, looking down at Rina. "Are we awake?" she asked with professional brightness.

Rina smiled slowly. "We're awake," she said faintly. "You're a new one, aren't you? I don't remember you."

The nurse flashed a quick look at Ilene. She had been on duty ever since Rina was checked into the hospital. "I'm the night nurse," she answered calmly. "I've just come on."

"I always get a headache when I sleep in the afternoon," Rina said. "I was wondering if I could have some aspirin?"

"I'll call the doctor," the nurse said.

Rina turned her head. "You must be exhausted," she said to Ilene. "Why don't you go home and get some rest? You've been here all day."

"I'm really not tired. I grabbed forty winks myself this afternoon."

The doctor came into the room just then and Rina turned toward the door. He stood there blinking his eyes behind his shining glasses. "Good evening, Miss Marlowe. Did you have a good rest?"

Rina smiled. "Too much, doctor. It's left me with a headache." Her brows knit. "It's a peculiar kind of a headache, though."

He came over to the side of the bed and put his fingers on her wrist, finding her pulse. "Peculiar?" he asked, looking down at his watch. "How do you mean peculiar?"

"It seems to hurt most when I try to remember names. I know you and I know my friend here"—she gestured to Ilene—"but when I try to say your name, the headache comes and I can't remember."

The doctor laughed as he let go of her wrist. "That's not at all unusual. There are some types of migraine headaches which make people forget their own name. Yours isn't that bad, is it?"

"No, it's not," Rina answered.

The doctor took an ophthalmoscope from his pocket and leaned over. "I'm going to look into your eyes with this," he said. "This makes it possible for me to see behind them and we may find out that your headache is due to nothing but simple eyestrain. Don't be frightened."

"I'm not frightened, doctor," Rina answered. "A doctor in Paris once looked at me with one of those. He thought I was in shock. But I wasn't. I was only hypnotized."

He placed his thumb in a corner of her eye and raised the eyelid. He pressed a button on the instrument and a bright light reflected through the pin-point hole. "What's your name?" he asked casually.

"Katrina Osterlaag," she answered quickly. Then she laughed. "See, doctor, I told you my headache wasn't that bad. I still know my name."

"What's your father's name?" he asked, moving the instrument to the other eye.

"Harrison Marlowe. See, I know that, too."

"What's your name?" he asked again, the light making a half circle in the upper corner of her eye.

"Rina Marlowe," she answered. She laughed aloud. "You can't trick me, doctor."

He turned off the light and straightened up. "No, I can't," he said, smiling down at her.

There was a movement at the door and two attendants wheeled in a large, square machine. They pushed it over to the side of the bed next to the doctor.

"This is an electroencephalograph," the doctor explained quietly. "It's used to measure the electrical impulses emanating from the brain. It's very helpful sometimes in locating the source of headaches so we can treat them."

"It looks very complicated," Rina said.

"It's not," he answered. "It's very simple, really. I'll explain it to you as we go along."

"And I thought all you had to do was take a few aspirins for a headache."

He laughed with her. "Well, you know how we doctors are," he said. "How can we ever justify our fees if all we do is recommend a few pills?"

She laughed again and the doctor turned toward Ilene. He nodded silently at her, his eyes gesturing to the door. He had already turned back to Rina by the time she had opened it.

"You'll come back later, won't you?" Rina asked.

Ilene turned around. The attendants were already plugging in the machine and the nurse was helping the doctor prepare Rina. "I'll be back," Ilene promised. She walked out and closed the door gently behind her.

It was almost an hour later when the doctor came out of the room. He dropped into a chair opposite Ilene, his hand fishing in his pocket. It came out with a crumpled package of cigarettes, which he held out to her. She took one and he struck a match, holding it first for her, then for himself.

"Well?" she asked through stiff lips.

"We'll be able to tell more when we study the electroencephalogram," he said, dragging on his cigarette. "But there are already definite signs of deterioration in certain neural areas."

"Please, doctor," she said. "In words that I can understand."

"Of course," he said. He took a deep breath. "The brain already shows signs of damage in certain nerve areas. It is this damage that makes it difficult for her to remember things—simple, everyday things like names, places, time. Everything in her memory is present, there is no past, perhaps no today. It is an unconscious effort to recall these little things that causes the strain and brings on the headache."

"But isn't that a good sign?" she asked hopefully. "This is the first time in almost a week that she seems partly normal."

"I know how concerned you are," he said cautiously. "And I don't want to appear unduly pessimistic, but the human mechanism is a peculiar machine. It is a tribute to her physical stamina that she's holding up as well as she is. She's going through recurrent waves of extremely high fever, a fever that destroys everything in its path. It's almost a miracle that when it abates slightly, even for a moment, as it just has, she can return to a semblance of lucidity."

"You mean she's slipping back into delirium?"

"I mean that her temperature is beginning to climb again," he answered.

Ilene got to her feet quickly and crossed to the door. "Do you think I can speak to her again before she slips back?"

"I'm sorry," he said, shaking his head. He got to his feet. "Her temperature began to rise about twenty minutes after you left the room. I put her in sedation to ease the pain."

She stared at the doctor. "Oh, my God!" she said in a low voice. "How long, doctor? How long must she suffer like this?"

"I don't know," he said slowly. He took her arm. "Why don't you let me drive you home? There's nothing you can do tonight, believe me. She's asleep."

"I'd—I'd like to look in on her just for a moment," she said hesitantly.

"It's all right, but let me warn you. Do not be upset by her appearance. We had to cut off most of her hair to make the electroencephalogram."

❖   ❖   ❖

Ilene closed the door of her office and crossed to her desk. There were some preliminary sketches of the costumes for a new picture waiting for her approval. She flicked on the light and walked over to the built-in bar.

She took down a bottle of Scotch and filled a glass with ice cubes. Covering the ice with the whisky, she went back to her desk, sat down and picked up the sketches. She sipped at the drink as she studied them.

She pressed a button in the arm of her chair and an overhead spotlight set in the ceiling shone down onto the drawings. She turned her chair toward the pedestal on her left, trying to imagine the dress on the model.

But her eyes kept misting over with tears. The sketches seemed to disappear and all she could see was Rina standing there on the pedestal, the white light shining down on her long blond hair—the white-blond hair that still hung in angry clinging tufts to the pillow under her shorn head.

"Why did you have to do it, God?" she cried aloud angrily at the ceiling. "Why do you always have to destroy the beautiful things? Isn't there enough ugliness in the world?"

The tears kept blurring in her eyes, but through them, she could still see Rina as she stood on the pedestal for the first time, the white silk shimmering down over her body.

It wasn't long ago. Five years. And the white silk was for a wedding gown. It was just before Rina's marriage to Nevada Smith.

CHAPTER FIFTEEN

IT STARTED OUT AS A QUIET WEDDING BUT IT TURNED INTO A CIRCUS, THE biggest publicity stunt ever to come out of Hollywood. And all because David Woolf had finally made it into the bed of the redheaded extra who had a bit-role in *The Renegade*.

Though he was a junior publicist, just one step above the lowest clerk in the department, and made only thirty-five a week, David was a very big man with the girls. This could be explained in one word. Nepotism. Bernie Norman was his uncle.

Not that it did him much good. But the girls didn't know that. How could they know that Norman could scarcely stand the sight of his sister's son and had only given him the job to shut her up? Now, in order to keep his nephew from annoying him, he had given his three secretaries orders to bar David from his office, no matter what the emergency.

This annoyed David, but right now it was far from his mind. He was twenty-three and there were more important considerations at hand. What a difference between the broads out here and those back home. He thought of the usherettes back at the Bijou Theater in New York, the frightened little Italian girls and the big brassy Irish, and the quickies that took place in the deserted second balcony or out on the empty stage in back of the big screen while the picture unfurled itself over their nervous heads. Even back there, Bernie Norman's name had been a help to him. Why else would they take an eighteen-year-old kid off a junk wagon and make him an assistant manager?

The girl was talking. At first David didn't hear her. "What did you say?" he asked.

"I'd like to go to the Nevada Smith wedding."

Her position may have been oblique but her approach wasn't. He recognized it. "It's going to be a small affair," he said.

Her voice was clearer now as she looked up at him. "There'll still be a lot of important people there who'd never see me any other way."

"I'll see what I can do," he said.

It was a little while later, when he was making his third greedy attempt to grab the brass ring, that the idea came to him. "Yeow!" he yelled suddenly as the far-reaching implications unfurled in his mind.

Startled, the girl looked up at him and saw a blindly rapt expression on his face. "Take it easy, honey. You'll wake the neighbors," she whispered softly, thinking he had reached his climax.

And, in a manner of speaking, he had.

Bernie Norman prided himself on being the first executive in the studio each day. Every morning at seven o'clock, his long black chauffeur-driven limousine would swirl through the massive steel gates of the executive entrance and draw to a stop in front of his office building. He liked to get in early, he always said, because it gave him a chance to go through his correspondence, which was at least twice as voluminous as that of anyone else in the studio, before his three secretaries came in. That way, the rest of his day could be left free for anyone who came to his door. His door was always open, he claimed.

Actually, he got there early because he was a born snoop. Though no one ever spoke about it, everyone in the studio knew what he did the moment the front door closed behind him. He would prowl through the silent offices, executive and secretary alike, looking at the papers lying on desks, peeking into whatever desk drawers happened to be unlocked and examining the contents of every letter and memo. It got so that whenever an executive wanted to be sure that something got to Norman's attention, he would leave a rough draft of his message lying innocently on his desk when he went home.

Norman justified this to himself easily. He was merely keeping his finger on the pulse of things. How could one man control so complicated an organization, otherwise?

He arrived at the door to his own private office that morning about eight o'clock, his inspection having taken a little longer than usual. He sighed heavily and opened his door. Problems, always problems.

He started for his desk, then froze with horror. His nephew David was asleep on his couch, sheaves of papers strewn over the floor around him. Bernie could feel the anger bubbling up inside him.

He crossed the room and pulled David from the couch. "What the hell are you doing sleeping in my office, you bum bastard!" he shouted.

David sat up, startled. He rubbed his eyes. "I didn't mean to fall asleep. I was looking at some papers and I must have dozed off."

"Papers!" Norman yelled. "What papers?" Quickly he picked one up. He turned horror-stricken eyes back to his nephew. "The production contract for *The Renegade!*" he accused. "My own confidential file!"

"I can explain," David said quickly, awake now.

"No explanations!" Norman said dramatically. He pointed to the door. "Out! If you're not out of the studio in five minutes, I'll call the guards and have you thrown out. You're through. Fired! *Fartig!* One thing we don't tolerate in this studio—sneaks and spies. My own sister's son! Go."

"Aw, come off it, Uncle Bernie," David said, getting to his feet.

"Come off it, he tells me!" Norman roared. "Half the night his mama keeps me up with telephone calls." His voice unconsciously mimicked his sister's nasal whine. " 'My Duvidele didn't come home yet, all night he didn't come home. Maybe he vass in a accident.' Accident, hah! I should tell her her little Duvidele was fucking all night the redheaded *shiksa* extra from the studio, hah! Get out!"

David stared at his uncle. "How did you know?"

"Know?" his uncle roared. "I know everything that goes on in this studio. You think I built a business like this fucking in furnished rooms all night? No! I worked, I tell you, I worked like a dirty dog. Day and night!"

He walked over to the chair behind his desk and sank into it. He clasped his hand over his heart in an exaggerated gesture. "Aggravation like this, from my own flesh and blood first thing in the morning, I need like another *luch im kopf!*" He unlocked his desk and took out a bottle of pills. Quickly he swallowed two and leaned back in his chair, his eyes closed.

David looked at his uncle. "You all right, Uncle Bernie?"

Slowly Norman opened his eyes. "You still here?" he asked in the voice of a man making a supreme effort to control himself. "Go!" His eyes fell on the papers still on the floor. "First pick up the papers," he added quickly. "Then go!"

"You don't even know why I came here this morning," David said tentatively. "Something very important came up."

His uncle opened his eyes and looked at him. "If it's something important, come to see me like everybody else. You know my door is always open."

"Open?" David laughed sarcastically. "If Christ himself came into this studio, those three harpies wouldn't let him in to see you!"

"Don't bring religion into it!" Norman held up a warning hand. "You know my policy. Everybody's the same as everybody else. Somebody wants to see me, they talk to my number-three girl, she talks to my number-two girl, my number-two girl talks to my number-one girl. My number-one girl thinks it important enough, she talks to me and the next thing you know, you're in my office!" He snapped his fingers. "Like that! But don't come sneaking around in the night, looking at confidential papers! Now go!"

"O.K." David started for the door. He should have known better than to try to do anything for the old bastard. "I'm going," he said bitterly. "But when I walk out this door, you look good—real good, because you're throwing out a million dollars along with me!"

"Wait a minute!" his uncle called after him. "I like to be fair. You said you had something important to tell me? So tell it. I'm listening."

David closed the door. "Next month, before the picture opens, Nevada Smith and Rina Marlowe are getting married," he said.

"You're telling me something?" His uncle glowered. "Who cares? They didn't even invite me to the wedding. Besides, Nevada's finished."

"Maybe," David said. "But the girl isn't. You saw the picture?"

"Of course I saw the picture!" Norman snapped. "We're sneaking it tonight."

"Well, after the sneak, she's going to be the hottest thing in the business."

His uncle looked up at him, a respect dawning in his eyes. "So?"

"From the papers, I see nobody's got her under contract," David said. "You sign her this morning. Then—"

His uncle was already nodding his head.

"Then you tell them you want to give them the wedding. As a present from the studio. We'll make it the biggest thing ever to hit Hollywood. "It'll add five million to the gross."

"So what good does that do us?" Norman asked. "We don't own any of the picture, we don't share in the profits."

"We get a distribution fee, don't we?" David asked, his confidence growing as he saw the intent look on his uncle's face. "Twenty-five per cent of five million is one and a quarter million dollars. Enough to carry half the cost of our whole distribution setup for a whole year. And the beautiful thing about it is we can charge all our expenses for the wedding to publicity and slap the charge right back against the picture. That way, it doesn't cost us one penny. Cord pays everything out of his share of the profit."

Norman got to his feet. There were tears in his eyes. "I knew it! Blood will tell!" he cried dramatically. "From now on you're working for me. You're my assistant! I'll tell the girls to have the office next door made ready for you. More than this I couldn't ask from my own son—if I had a son!"

"There's one more thing."

"There is?" Norman sat down again. "What?"

"I think we should try to make a deal with Cord to do a picture a year for us."

Norman shook his head. "Oh, no! We got enough crazy ones around here without him."

"He's got a feeling for pictures. You can see it in *The Renegade*."

"It was a lucky accident."

"No it wasn't," David insisted. "I was on the set through the whole thing. There wasn't anything in the picture that he didn't have something to do with. If it wasn't for him, Marlowe would never be the star she's going to be. He has the greatest eye for cunt I ever saw in my life."

"He's a *goy*," Norman said deprecatingly. "What do they know about cunt?"

"The *goyim* knew about cunt before Adam led Eve out of the Garden of Eden."

"No," Norman said.

"Why not?"

"That kind of man I don't want around," Norman said. "He won't be satisfied just to make a picture. Pretty soon, he'll want to run the whole thing. He's a *balabuss*, he's not the kind who would work with partners."

He got up and walked around the desk toward his nephew. "No," he said. "Him I won't do business with. But your other ideas I like. This morning we'll go out and get the girl's signature on the contract. Then we'll tell them about the wedding. Nevada won't like it but he'll do it. After all, he's got his own money in the picture and he won't be taking any chances!"

❖   ❖   ❖

David saw to it that a special print of the newsreel of the wedding was sent on to Cord, who was in Europe at the time. When Jonas walked into the small screening room in London, where he had arranged for it to be run off, the lights immediately went down and a blast of music filled the room. On the screen, lettering was coming out of a turning camera until there was nothing else to be seen.

NORMAN NEWSREEL

THE FIRST WITH

THE FINEST IN

PICTURES!

The dramatically somber voice of the narrator came on under a long shot of a church, around which crowds of people swirled.

All Hollywood, all the world, is agog with excitement over the fairy-tale wedding in Hollywood today of Nevada Smith and Rina Marlowe, stars of the forthcoming Bernard B. Norman release The Renegade.

There was a shot of Nevada riding up to the church resplendently dressed in a dark, tailored cowboy suit, astride a snow-white horse.

Here is the groom, the world-famous cowboy Nevada Smith, arriving at the church with his equally famous horse, Whitey.

Nevada walked up the steps and into the church, with the police holding back mobs of screaming people. Then a black limousine drew up. Bernie Norman got out and turned to assist Rina. She stood for a moment, smiling at the crowd, then taking Norman's proffered arm, began to walk into the church, as the camera moved in for a close-up.

And here is the bride, the lovely Rina Marlowe, star of The Renegade, *on the arm of Bernard B. Norman, noted Hollywood producer, who will give the bride away. Miss Marlowe's wedding gown is ivory Alençon lace, designed especially for her by Ilene Gaillard, famous couturière, who also designed the exciting costumes that you will see Miss Marlowe wear in the Bernard B. Norman picture* The Renegade.

The camera then cut to the exterior of Nevada's Beverly Hills home, where there was a tremendous tent with throngs of people milling about it.

Here on the lawn of the palatial home of Nevada Smith is the tent erected by the Bernard B. Norman studio workmen as their tribute to the famous couple. It is large enough to shelter and feed a thousand guests and is the largest of its kind ever set up anywhere in the world. And now let us say hello to some of the famous guests.

The camera rolled down the lawn as the announcer introduced many famous stars and newspaper columnists, who paused in the midst of their obviously carefully posed groups to smile and bow in the direction of the camera. The camera moved on up the steps to the entrance of the house as Nevada and Rina appeared in the doorway. A moment later, Norman stood between them. Rina held a large bouquet of roses and orchids in her arms.

Here again is the happy bride and groom, together with their friend, the famous producer Bernard B. Norman. The bride is about to throw her bouquet to the eagerly waiting crowd.

There was a shot of Rina throwing her bouquet and a scramble of pretty young girls. The flowers were finally caught by a red-haired, sloe-eyed girl and the camera moved in for a quick close-up of her.

The bouquet was caught by Miss Anne Barry, a close friend of the bride's. Miss Barry, a beautiful redhead, also has an important role in The Renegade *and has just been placed under contract by Norman Pictures for her fine portrayal in that part.*

The camera then moved in for a final close-up. Rina, Norman and Nevada smiled into the theater. Norman was standing between them, one arm placed in fatherly fashion around Nevada's shoulder, the other hidden from view behind the bride. They all laughed happily as the scene faded.

Lights in the screening room came up as Jonas got to his feet and, unsmiling, walked out of the room. There was a cold feeling in the pit of his stomach. If that was the way Rina wanted it, she could have it.

But what Jonas didn't see, and neither could anyone else who had been looking at the screen, was Bernie Norman's left hand, hidden behind Rina's back.

It was comfortably and casually exploring the rounded contours of her buttocks.

CHAPTER SIXTEEN

IT HAD BEEN AFTER EIGHT O'CLOCK WHEN ILENE HEARD THE DOOR TO HER outer office open. She put down the small palette and wiped the smudges of paint from her hands on her loose gray smock. She turned toward the door just as Rina came in.

"I'm sorry to hold you up, Ilene," Rina apologized. "We went overtime on the set tonight."

Ilene smiled. "It's O.K. I had some work to finish up, anyway." She looked at Rina. "You look tired. Why don't you sit down and rest a few minutes? I heard from the production office that you'd be late so I ordered coffee and sandwiches."

Rina flashed a grateful smile. "Thanks," she said, dropping onto the big couch and kicking off her shoes. "I am tired."

Ilene pushed a coffee table over to the couch. She opened a small refrigerator and took out a tray of sandwiches, which she set down in front of Rina. Opening a large Thermos of black coffee, quickly she poured a cup for Rina.

Rina held the steaming cup to her lips. "This is good," she said over the rim. She sipped again, then leaned her head against the back of the couch. "I'm really so pooped I'm not even hungry."

"You have a right to be," Ilene answered. "You haven't had a week off in the year since you finished *The Renegade*. Three pictures, one right after the other, and next week you're starting another. It's a wonder you haven't collapsed."

Rina looked at her. "I like to work."

"So do I," Ilene replied quickly. "But there's a point where you have to draw the line."

Rina didn't answer. She sipped at her coffee and picked up a copy of *Variety*.

Idly she turned the page. She stopped at a headline, read for a moment, then held the paper out to Ilene. "Have you seen this?"

Ilene glanced down at the paper. The headline caught her eye. It was typical Varietese:

THE RENEGADE'S BIGGEST HAUL—BOX OFFICE

In a year filled with cries from moaning exhibitors and anguished producers about the seemingly bottomless pit into which motion-picture grosses are falling, it's encouraging to note one ray of sunshine. It was reliably learned from informed sources that the domestic gross of *The Renegade* passed the five-million-dollar mark last week, a little less than one year after release. Based on these figures, the Rina Marlowe vehicle, with many subsequents still to be played in the U.S. and the rest of the world still to be heard from, can be expected to gross at ten million dollars. *The Renegade*, a Norman release, was produced and bankrolled by Jonas Cord, a rich young Westerner better known for his record-breaking flight from Paris to L.A. last year, and also features Nevada Smith.

Ilene looked up from the paper. "I saw it."

"Does that mean everyone got their money back?"

"I guess it does," Ilene said. "That is, if Bernie didn't steal them blind."

Rina smiled. She felt a surge of relief. At least, Nevada didn't have to worry now. She picked up a sandwich and began to eat ravenously. "Suddenly I'm hungry," she said between mouthfuls.

Silently Ilene refilled her coffee cup, then poured one for herself. Rina ate quickly and in a few minutes, she had finished. She took a cigarette from the small box on the table and lit it.

She leaned back and blew the smoke at the ceiling. A faint touch of color came back into her cheeks. "I feel better now. We can try on those costumes as soon as I finish this cigarette."

"No hurry," Ilene said. "I have time."

Rina got to her feet. "We might as well get started," she said, grinding her cigarette out in an ash tray. "I just remembered, I have a breakfast layout to do for *Screen Stars* magazine at six o'clock in the morning."

Ilene walked over to the closet and slid back the doors. Six pairs of circus-style chemise tights, each in a different color, hung there. Rina took one down and turned to Ilene, holding the brief costume in front of her. "They get smaller and smaller."

Ilene smiled. "Bernie himself gave the orders for those. After all, the name of the picture is *The Girl on the Flying Trapeze*."

She took the costume and held it while Rina began to undress. Rina turned her back as she slipped out of her dress and struggled into the tight-fitting costume. "Whew!" she gasped. "Maybe I shouldn't have eaten those sandwiches!"

Ilene stepped back and studied the costume. "Better step up on the pedestal," she said. "There are a few things I'll have to do."

Quickly she chalked out the alterations. "O.K.," she said. "Let's try the next one."

Rina reached behind her to unfasten the hooks. One of them stuck. "You'll have to help me, Ilene. I can't get out of this thing."

Rina stepped down from the pedestal and turned her back to Ilene. Deftly Ilene freed the hook. The cloth parted quickly and her fingers brushed against Rina's naked back. They tingled with the firm, warm touch of her flesh. Ilene felt the rush of blood to her temples. She stepped back quickly as if she had touched a hot iron. Too many times had she been tempted to let a thing like this get her into trouble. It had taken too many years to get this job.

Rina dropped the top of the costume to her waist and struggled to get the tights over her hips. She looked at Ilene. "I'm afraid you'll have to help me again."

Ilene kept her face a mask. "Step back on the pedestal," she said through stiff lips.

Rina got back on the pedestal and turned toward her. Ilene tugged at the garment, her fingers burning where they touched Rina. At last, the tights gave way and Ilene felt Rina shiver as her hand accidentally brushed the soft silken pubis.

"Are you cold?" Ilene asked, stepping back.

Rina stared at her for a moment, then averted her eyes. "No," she answered in a low voice, stepping out of the tights. She picked them up and held them toward Ilene.

Ilene reached for the costume, touched Rina's hand and suddenly couldn't let it go. She looked up at Rina steadily, her heart choking inside her.

Rina shivered again. "No," she whispered, her eyes still looking away. "Please, don't."

Ilene felt as if she were in a dream. Nothing seemed real. "Look at me," she said.

Slowly Rina turned her head. Their eyes met and Ilene could sense her trembling. She saw Rina's nipples burst forth upon her breasts like awakening red flowers on a white field.

She moved toward her and buried her face in the pale soft flax between her hips. They were very still for a moment, then she felt Rina's hand lightly brushing across her hair. She stepped back and Rina came down into her arms.

Ilene felt the hot tears suddenly push their way into her eyes. "Why?" she cried wildly. "Why did you have to marry him?"

As usual, Nevada awoke at four thirty in the morning, pulled on a pair of worn Levi's and went down to the stables. As usual, on his way out, he closed the connecting door between their rooms to let Rina know he had gone out.

The wrangler was waiting with a steaming mug of bitter black range coffee. Their conversation followed the routine morning pattern as Nevada felt the hot coffee scald its way down to his stomach.

The mug empty, and Nevada in the lead, they walked through the stable, looking into each stall. At the end was Whitey's stall. Nevada came to a stop in front of it. "Mornin', boy," he whispered.

The palomino stuck its head over the gate and looked at Nevada with large, intelligent eyes. It nuzzled against Nevada's hand, searching for the lump of sugar it knew would appear there. It wasn't disappointed.

Nevada opened the gate and went into the stall. He ran his hands over the sleek, glistening sides of the animal. "We're gettin' a little fat, boy," he whispered.

"That's because we haven't had much to do lately. I better take you out for a little exercise."

Without speaking, the wrangler handed him the big saddle that lay crosswise on the partition between the stalls. Nevada slung it over the horse's back and cinched it tight. He placed the bit in the mouth and led the animal out of the stable. In front of the white-painted wooden building, he mounted up.

He rode down the riding trail to the small exercise track he had built at the foot of the hill in back of the house. He could see the gray spires of the roof as he rode past. Mechanically he put the horse through its paces.

The item he had read in *Variety* came to his mind. His lip curved at the irony. Here he was with the biggest-grossing picture of the year and not once during that whole period had anyone approached him about beginning another. The day of the big Western movie was over. It was too expensive.

At least he wasn't the only one, he thought. Mix, Maynard, Gibson, Holt— they were all in the same boat. Maynard had tried to fight it. He made a series of quickies for Universal, which took about five days to complete. Nevada had seen one of them. Not for him. The picture was choppy and the sound worse. Half the time, you couldn't even understand what the actors were saying.

Tom Mix had tried something else. He'd taken a Wild-West show to Europe and, if the trade papers were right, he and his horse, Tony, had knocked them dead. Maybe that was worth thinking about. The troop he had on the road was still doing all right. If he went out with it, it would do even better. It was that or take up the guitar.

That was the new Western—a singing cowboy and a guitar. He felt a vague distaste even as he thought about it. That chubby little Gene Autry had made it big. The only problem, he'd heard from one of the wranglers, was to keep him from falling off his horse. Tex Ritter was doing all right at Columbia, too.

Nevada looked up again at the house. That was the biggest stupidity of all—a quarter-million-dollar trap. It took more than twenty servants to keep it running and ate up money like a pack of prairie wolves devouring a stray steer. He quickly reviewed his income.

The cattle ranch in Texas had just started to pay off when the depression hit and now he was lucky if it broke even. His royalties on the sale of Nevada Smith toys and cowboy suits had dwindled as children shifted their fickle loyalties to other stars. All that was left was his share of the Wild-West show and the Nevada divorce ranch. That brought in at most two thousand a month. The house alone cost him six thousand a month just to keep going.

Rina had offered to share the expenses but he'd refused, feeling it was a man's responsibility to pay the bills. But now, even with the bank loans for *The Renegade* paid off, he knew it wouldn't be possible to keep the house going without dipping further into his capital. The sensible thing was to get rid of it.

He'd have to take a loss. Thalberg over at Metro had offered him a hundred and fifty thousand. That way, at least, he'd save the broker's fee.

He made up his mind. There was no use sitting around, waiting for the telephone to ring. He'd go out on the road with the show and sell the house. He began to feel better. He decided to tell Rina when she got back from the studio that night.

The telephone on the pole against the far rail began to ring loudly. He walked his horse over to it. "Yes?"

"Mr. Smith?"

It was the voice of the butler. "Yes, James," he said.

"Mrs. Smith would like you to join her for breakfast in the Sun Room."

Nevada hesitated. Strange how quickly the servants recognized who was important in the family. James now used the same distant formal manner of speaking to him that he had once used in speaking to Rina.

He heard the butler clear his throat. "Shall I tell Mrs. Smith you will be up, sir?" he asked. "I think she's expecting some photographers from *Screen Stars* magazine."

So that was it. Nevada felt a stirring of resentment inside him. This was the first time in months that Rina had called him for breakfast and it took a publicity layout to do it. Almost immediately, he regretted the way he felt. After all, it wasn't her fault. She'd been working day and night for months.

"Tell her I'll be up as soon as I stable the horse," he said.

"Just one more shot of you pouring coffee for Nevada," the photographer said, "and we're finished."

Nevada picked up his cup and extended it across the table to Rina. She lifted the silver coffeepot and poised it over the cup. Professionally and automatically, the smiles came to their lips.

They'd gone through the whole routine. The picture of Rina frying bacon and eggs while he looked over her shoulder at the stove, the burned-toast bit, the popping of food into each other's mouth. Everything the readers of fan magazines had come to expect from movie stars. This was supposed to give them the homey touch.

There was an awkward silence for a moment after the photographers picked up their gear and left. Nevada spoke first. "I'm glad that's over."

"So am I," Rina said. She hesitated, then looked up at the wall clock. "I'd better get started. I'm due in make-up at seven thirty."

She started to get up but the telephone near her began to ring. She sat down again and picked it up. "Hello."

Nevada could hear a voice crackle through the receiver. Rina shot him a funny look, then spoke into the telephone again.

"Good morning, Louella," she said in a sweet voice. "No, you didn't wake me up. Nevada and I were just having breakfast. . . . Yes, that's right—*The Girl on the Flying Trapeze*. It's a wonderful part. . . . No, Norman decided against borrowing Gable from Metro. He says there's only one man who could do the part justice. . . . Of course. Nevada, it's a natural for him. Wait a minute, I'll put him on and let him tell you himself."

She covered the mouthpiece with her hand. "It's Parsons," she whispered quickly. "Bernie decided yesterday he wanted you to play the part of the stunt-rider. Louella's checking on the story."

"What's the matter?" Nevada asked dryly. "Wouldn't MGM lend him Gable?"

"Don't be silly! Get on the phone."

"Hello, Louella."

The familiar, sticky-sweet voice chewed at his ear. "Congratulations, Nevada! I think it's just wonderful that you're to play opposite your lovely wife again!"

"Wait a minute. Louella." He laughed. "Not so fast. I'm not making the picture."

"You're not?" Another Parsons scoop was in the making. "Why?"

"I've already agreed to go out on the road with my Wild-West show," he said. "And that will keep me tied up for at least six months. While I'm away, Rina will look for another house for us. I think we'll both be more comfortable in a smaller place."

Her voice was businesslike now. "You're selling Hilltop?"

"Yes."

"To Thalberg?" she questioned. "I heard he was interested."

"I don't know," he said. "Several people have expressed interest."

"You'll let me know the moment you decide?"

"Of course."

"There's no trouble between you two?" she asked shrewdly.

"Louella!" He laughed. "You know better than that."

"I'm glad! You're both such nice people," she said. She hesitated a moment. "Keep in touch if there's any news."

"I will, Louella."

"Good luck to both of you!"

Nevada put down the telephone and looked across the table. He hadn't meant for it to come out this way, but there was nothing that could be done about it now.

Rina's face was white with anger. "You could have told me about it before you told the whole world!"

"Who had the chance?" he retorted, angry despite himself. "This is the first time we've talked in months. Besides, you might have told me about the picture."

"Bernie tried to get you all day yesterday but you never came to the phone."

"That's a lot of crap," he said. "I was home all day and he never called. Besides, I wouldn't have his handouts—or yours either, for that matter."

"Maybe if you took your nose out of that damn stable once in a while, you'd find out what was going on."

"I know what's going on," he said angrily. "You don't have to start acting like a movie star."

"Oh, what's the use?" she said bitterly. "What did you ever marry me for?"

"Or you me?" he asked, with equal bitterness.

As they stared at each other, the truth suddenly came to both of them. They had married because they both knew they had lost each other and wanted desperately to hold onto what was already gone. With the knowledge, the anger dissipated as quickly as it had come. "I'm sorry," he said.

She looked down at the coffeepot. "I am, too. I told you I was a spoiler, that I wouldn't be any good for you."

"Don't be silly," he said. "It wasn't your fault. It would have happened, anyway. The business is changing."

"I'm not talking about the business," Rina answered. "I'm talking about you and me. You should have married someone who could have given you a family. I've given you nothing."

"You can't take all the blame. We both tried in our own way but neither of us had what the other really needed. We just made a mistake, that's all."

"I won't be able to file for a divorce until after I finish this next picture," she said in a low voice. "It's all right with me if you want to file before then."

"No, I can wait," he said calmly.

She glanced up at the wall clock. "My God! I'm late!" she exclaimed. "I'll have to hurry."

At the door, she stopped and looked back at him. "Are you still my friend?"

He nodded his head slowly and returned her smile, but his voice was serious. "I'll always be your friend."

She stood there for a moment and he could see the sudden rush of tears to her eyes, then she turned and ran from the room.

He walked over to the window, and lifting the curtain, looked out onto the front drive. He saw her come running from the house, saw the chauffeur close the door. The car disappeared down the hill on its way to the studio. He let the curtain fall back into place.

Rina never came back to the house. She stayed that night at Ilene's apartment. The next day, she moved into a hotel and three months later filed for divorce in Reno. The grounds were incompatibility.

And that, except for the legalities, was the way it ended.

CHAPTER SEVENTEEN

DAVID HEARD THE VIOLENT SLAM OF THE DOOR IN HIS UNCLE'S OFFICE. He got to his feet quickly and walked to the connecting door. He opened it and found his uncle Bernie seated in his chair, red faced and angry, gasping for breath. He was trying to shake some pills out of the inverted bottle in his hand.

David quickly filled a glass with water from the carafe on the desk and handed it to Norman. "What happened?"

Norman swallowed the two pills and put down the glass. He looked up at David. "Why didn't I go into the cloak-and-suit business with my brother, your uncle Louie?"

David knew no answer was expected, so he waited patiently until Norman continued. "Fifty, a hundred suits they make a day. Everything is calm, everything is quiet. At night, he goes home. He eats. He sleeps. No worries. No ulcers. No aggravations. That's the way a man should live. Easy. Not like a dog. Not like me."

David asked again, "What happened?"

"As if I haven't got enough troubles," Norman complained, "our stockholders say we're losing too much money. I run to New York to explain. The union threatens to strike the theaters. I sit down and work out a deal that at least they don't close the theaters. Then I get word from Europe that Hitler took over all our German properties, offices, theaters, everything! More than two million dollars the *anti-semiten* stole. Then I get a complaint from the underwriters and bankers, the pictures ain't got no prestige. So I buy the biggest, most artistic hit on Broadway. *Sunspots* the name of it is. It's so artistic, even I don't understand what it's all about.

"Now I'm stuck with an artistic bomb. I talk to all the directors in Hollywood about it. I'm not so dumb altogether that it don't take me long to find out they don't understand it neither, so I hire the director who did the play on the stage, Claude Dunbar, a *faigele* if I ever saw one. But fifty thousand he gets.

"A hundred and fifty I'm in already and no box office. So I call up Louie and say lend me Garbo. He laughs in my face. You ain't got enough money, he says. Besides, we got her in prestige of our own. *Anna Christie* by Eugene O'Neill she's making. Good-by, I says and call up Jack Warner. How about Bette Davis? Wait a minute, he says. I sit on the phone ten minutes.

"The *pisher* thinks I don't know what he's doin'? He's calling his brother Harry in New York, that's what he's doin'. Here I am, sitting on long distance in New York with the charges running up by the minute and he's calling back his brother Harry, who is two blocks away from where I'm sitting. Hang up the phone, I feel like telling him. I can call your brother for only a nickel.

"Finally, Jack gets back on the phone to me ninety-five dollars later. You're lucky, he says. We ain't got her penciled in for nothing until September. You can have her for a hundred and fifty grand. For a hundred and fifty, don't do me no favors, I tell him. The most she's gettin' is thirty, thirty-five a picture, maybe not even that.

"How much you want to pay? he asks. Fifty, I says. Forget it, he says. O.K., then, seventy-five, I says. One and a quarter, he says. One even and it's a deal, I says. It's a deal, he says. I hang up the telephone. A hundred and thirty-five dollars the call costs me to talk two minutes.

"So I go back to Wall Street and tell the underwriters and bankers we now got prestige. This picture is goin' to be so artistic, we'll be lucky if we get anybody into the theater. They're very happy and congratulate me and I get on the train and come back to Hollywood."

Bernie ran out of breath suddenly and picked up the glass of water again and drained it. "Ain't that enough trouble for anyone?"

David nodded.

"So enough troubles I got when I walk into my office this morning, you agree? So who do I find waiting but Rina Marlowe, that *courveh*. 'Rina, darling,' I say to her, 'you look positively gorgeous this morning.' Do I even get a hello? No! She shoves the *Reporter* under my nose and says, 'What's this? Is it true?'

"I look down and see the story about Davis in *Sunspots*. 'What are you getting so excited about, darling?' I say. 'That's not for you, a bomb like that. I got a part for you that will kill the people. *Scheherazade*. Costumes like you never in your life saw before.' And you know what she says to me?" He shook his head sadly.

"What?" David asked.

"After all I done for her, the way she spoke to me!" his uncle said in a hurt voice. " 'Take your hand off my tits,' she says, 'and furthermore, if I don't get that part, you can shove *Scheherazade* up your fat ass!' Then she walks out the door. How do you like that?" Norman asked in an aggrieved voice. "All I was trying to do was calm her down a little. Practically everybody in Hollywood she fucks but me she talks to like that!"

David nodded. He'd heard the stories about her, too. In the year since she had broken up with Nevada, she seemed to have gone suddenly wild. The parties out at her new place in Beverly Hills were said to be orgies. There was even talk about her and Ilene Gaillard, the costume designer. But as long as nothing got into print, they'd looked the other way. What she did was her own business as long as it didn't affect them. "What are you going to do about it?"

"What can I do about it?" Bernie asked. "Give her the part. If she walked out on us, we'd lose twice as much as we're losing right now."

He reached for a cigar. "I'll call her this afternoon and tell her." He stopped in the midst of lighting it. "No, I got a better idea. You go out to her place this afternoon and tell her. I'm damned if I'll let her make it look like I'm kissing her ass."

"O.K.," David said. He started back toward his own office.

"Wait a minute," his uncle called after him.

David turned around.

"You know who I ran into in the Waldorf my last night in New York?" Bernie asked. "Your friend."

"My friend?"

"Yes, you know who. The crazy one. The flier. Jonas Cord."

"Oh," David said. He liked the way his uncle put it, reminding him of the earlier conversation they had had about Cord some years ago. He and Cord had never exchanged so much as a word. He even doubted if Cord knew he was alive. "How did he look?"

"The same," his uncle replied. "Like a bum. Wearing sneakers and no tie. I don't know how he gets away with it. Anybody else they would throw out, but him? Shows you there's nothing like *goyishe* money."

"You talk to him?" David asked curiously.

"Sure," Norman answered. "I read in the papers where he's making another picture. Who knows, I says to myself, the *schnorrer* might get lucky again. Besides, with prestige like we're stuck with, we could use him. We could pay a lot of bills with his money.

"It's two o'clock in the morning and he's got two *courveh* on his arm. I walk over and say, 'Hello, Jonas.' He looks at me like he's never seen me before in his life. 'Remember me,' I says, 'Bernie Norman from Hollywood.' 'Oh, sure,' he says.

"But I can't tell from his face whether he really does or doesn't, he needs a shave so bad. 'These two little girls are actresses,' he says to me, 'but I won't tell you their names. Otherwise, you might sign them up yourself. If I like a girl,' he says, 'I put her under contract to Cord Explosives now. No more do I take any chances and let them get away from me the way you signed that Marlowe dame.' With that, he gives me such a playful shot in the arm that for two hours I can't raise my hand.

"I made myself smile even if I didn't feel like it. 'In our business, you got to move fast,' I says, 'otherwise you get left behind the parade. But that's over and done with. What I want to do is talk to you about this new picture I hear you're makin'. We did a fantastic job for you on your last one and I think we should set up a meetin'.'

"'What's the matter with right now?' he asks. 'It's O.K. with me,' I says. He turns to the girls. 'Wait right here,' he says to them. He turns back to me an' takes my arm. 'Come on,' he says, draggin' me off. 'Come up to my office.'

"I look at him in surprise. 'You got an office here in the Waldorf,' I ask him. 'I got an office in every hotel in the United States,' he says. We get on an elevator an' he says 'Mezzanine, please.' We get off and walk down the hall to a door. I look at the sign. 'Gentlemen,' it says. I look at him. He grins. 'My office,' he says, opening the door. "We go inside an' it's white and empty. There's a table there and a chair for the attendant. He sits down in the chair and suddenly I see he's very sober, he's not smiling now.

" 'I haven't decided yet where I'm going to release the picture,' he says. 'It all depends on where I can get the best deal.' 'That's smart thinking.' I says, 'but I really can't talk until I know what your picture is about.' 'I'll tell you,' he says. 'It's about the fliers in the World War. I bought up about fifty old planes—Spads, Fokkers, Nieuports, De Havillands—and I figger on havin' a ball flyin' the wings off them.'

" 'Oh, a war picture,' I says. 'That's not so good. War pictures is dead since *All Quiet on the Western Front*. Nobody'll come to see them. But since I got experience with you and we was lucky together, I might go along for the ride. What terms you looking for?' He looks me in the eye. 'Studio overhead, ten per cent,' he says. 'Distribution, fifteen per cent with all expenses deducted from the gross before calculating the distribution fees.' 'That's impossible,' I says. 'My overhead runs minimum twenty-five per cent.'

" 'It doesn't,' he says, 'but I won't quibble about it. I just want to point out some simple arithmetic to you. According to your annual report, your overhead during the past few years averaged twenty-one per cent. During that period, *The Renegade* contributed twenty-five per cent of your gross. Deduct that from your gross and you'll find your overhead's up to almost thirty-six per cent. The same thing applies to the studio,' he says. 'Volume governs the percentages and if I supply the volume, I shouldn't be burdened with ordinary percentages. I want some of the gravy, as you picture people call it.'

" 'I couldn't afford it,' I says. 'The way the picture business is going,' he says, 'you can't afford not to.' 'My board of directors would never approve it,' I says. He gets up, smiling. 'They will,' he says. 'Give 'em a couple of years an' they will. Why don't you take a piss long as you're here,' he says. I'm so surprised I walk over to the urinal. When I turn around, he's already gone. The next morning, before I get on the train, I try to locate him but nobody seems to know where he is. His office don't even know he's in New York. He disappeared completely." Bernie looked down at his desk. "A real *meshuggeneh*, I tell you."

David smiled. "I told you he'd learn fast. His arithmetic is right, you know."

His uncle looked up at him. "Don't you think I know it's right?" he asked. "But is he so poor that I have to give him bread from my own mouth?"

"If you'll follow me, sir," the butler said politely. "Miss Marlowe is in the solarium."

David nodded and followed silently up the staircase and to the back of the house. The butler halted before a door and knocked.

"Mr. Woolf is here, mum."

"Tell him to come in," Rina called through the closed door.

The butler held the door open. David blinked as the bright California sun suddenly spilled down on him. The roof of the room was a clear glass dome and the sides were of glass, too.

There was a tall screen at the far end of the room. Rina's voice came from behind it. "Help yourself to a drink from the bar. I'll be out in a minute."

He looked around and located the bar in the corner. There were casual, canvas-covered chairs scattered all about the room and a large white rug over most of the floor.

Ilene Gaillard came out from behind the screen. She was wearing a white shirt with sleeves rolled to just above her elbows, and black man-tailored slacks that clung tightly to her narrow hips. Her white-streaked hair was brushed back in a severe straight line.

"Hello, David. Let me help you."

"Thanks, Ilene."

"Make another Martini for me," Rina called from behind the screen.

Ilene didn't answer. She looked at David. "What will it be?"

"Scotch and water," he answered. "Just a little ice."

"O.K.," she said, her hands already moving deftly behind the bar. She held the drink toward him. "There, how's that?"

He tasted it. "Great."

"Got my Martini ready?" Rina said from behind him.

He turned. She was just coming from behind the screen, tying a white terry-cloth robe around her. From the glimpse he caught of the tanned thigh beneath the robe as she moved, he guessed she was wearing nothing underneath. "Hello, Rina."

"Hello, David," she answered. She looked at Ilene. "Where's my drink?"

"David's obviously here on business," Ilene said. "Why don't you wait until after you've had your talk?"

"Don't be so bossy!" Rina snapped. "Make the drink!" She turned to David. "My father gave me Martinis when I was a child. I can drink them like water. Ilene doesn't seem to understand that."

"Here." Ilene's voice was clipped.

Rina took the Martini from her. "Cheers, David."

"Cheers," David replied.

She belted down half her Martini, then led him to one of the chairs. "Sit down," she said, dropping into another.

"Lovely house you have," he said politely.

"It is nice." she said. "Ilene and I had a wonderful time furnishing it." She reached up and patted Ilene's cheek. "Ilene has the most wonderful sense of color. You should speak to your uncle about letting her try her hand at art direction. I'm sure he'd find out that she could do a terrific job."

"Rina," Ilene said, a happy note in her voice, "I'm sure David didn't come here to talk about me."

"I'll speak to Uncle Bernie," he said politely. "I'm sure she could, too."

"See?" Rina said. "The trouble with Ilene is that she's too modest. She's one of the most talented people I ever met."

She held up her empty glass toward Ilene. "Refill."

David caught a glimpse of her lush, full breasts. It would take more than massage to keep her weight down if she kept on drinking like that.

Rina cut into his thoughts. "Did the old bastard decide to give me that part in *Sunspots?*"

David looked at her. "You have to understand my uncle's point of view, Rina," he said quickly. "You're the most valuable asset the company has. You can't blame him if he doesn't want to put you in a picture that's almost certain to lay an egg."

Rina took the drink from Ilene. "What it all boils down to," she said belligerently, "is that he thinks I can't act. All I'm good for is walking around as near naked as he can get me."

"He thinks you're a fine actress, Rina. But more important, you're the one in a million who is a star. He's just trying to protect you, that's all."

"I'll protect myself," she snapped angrily. "Do I get the part or don't I?"

"You get it."

"Good," she said, sipping her drink. She got out of her chair and he realized that she was slightly drunk. "Tell your uncle for me that I won't wear a brassiere the next time I come to his office."

"I'm sure that will make him very happy." David grinned at her. He put down his drink and got to his feet.

"I think he wants to fuck me," she said, weaving slightly.

He laughed. "Who doesn't?" he asked. "I can name at least sixty million men who've thought about it."

"You don't," she said, her eyes suddenly looking right into his.

"Who says?"

"I do," she said seriously. "You never asked me."

"Remind me to get up my nerve sometime."

"What's the matter with right now?" she asked, pulling at the sash of her robe. It fell open, revealing her nude body. He stared, so surprised that he was unable to speak.

"Go downstairs, Ilene," Rina said without taking her eyes off him. "And see to it that dinner is on time."

David caught a glimpse of Ilene's eyes as she hurried past him and out the door. If he lived to be a hundred years old, he would never forget the depth of the pain and anguish he saw there.

CHAPTER EIGHTEEN

UNTIL HE MET RINA MARLOWE, CLAUDE DUNBAR HAD BEEN IN LOVE with only three things in his life—his mother, himself and the theater—and in that order. His *Hamlet* in modern dress was the most successful Shakespearean production ever played in a New York theater. But it was his direction of *Sunspots*, an otherwise mediocre play, that lifted him to the pinnacle of his career.

Sunspots was a three-character play dealing with two prospectors, living isolated lives at the edge of a great desert, and a young girl, an amnesiac, who wandered into their camp. It develops into a struggle between the men, the younger trying to protect the girl from the lechery of the older, only, after succeeding, to succumb himself to the lechery in the girl.

It was all talk and very little action, and despite a year's run on Broadway, Dunbar had been so surprised when Norman called and told him he had bought the play and wanted him to direct the motion picture that he had agreed without hesitation. It was only after he got to California, however, that he learned who was to play the lead.

"Rina Marlowe!" he'd said to Norman. "But I thought Davis was going to play it."

The producer had stared at him blandly. "Warner screwed me," he said, lowering his voice to a confidential whisper. "So right away I thought of Rina."

"But isn't there anyone else, Mr. Norman?" he'd asked, stammering slightly as he always did when upset. "What about the girl who played it on the stage?"

"No name," Norman said quickly. "This is an important property, this play of yours. We have to protect it with all the box office we can get. Rina never made a picture that didn't make money."

"Maybe," Dunbar admitted. "But can she act?"

"There's no better actress in Hollywood than that girl. You're a director. Go over to her house this afternoon with the script and see for yourself."

"Mr. Norman—"

But Norman had already taken his arm and was leading him to the door. "Be fair, Mr. Dunbar. Give the girl a chance, work with her a little. Then if you still think she can't do it, we'll see."

So efficient had the producer been in getting rid of him that he hadn't been aware of it himself until he stood outside the closed door, with the three secretaries staring at him.

He felt his face flush and to cover his embarrassment, he went over to the girl at the desk nearest the door. "Could you tell me where Miss Marlowe lives?" he asked. "And how to get there?"

The secretary smiled. "I can do better than that, Mr. Dunbar," she said efficiently, picking up the telephone. "I'll arrange for a car to pick you up and take you there."

That afternoon, before he went to Rina's house, Claude Dunbar dropped into a theater that was playing her latest picture. He watched the screen in a kind of fascinated horror. There was no doubt that the girl was beautiful. He could even see that she had a type of animalism that would appeal to a certain type of audience. But she wasn't the kind of girl called for in the play.

The girl in the play was somber, introspective, frightened. As she tried to recapture her memory, she looked as she felt—gaunt, tortured and burned out by the heat of the desert. The fact that she was female caused the desire in the men, not her physical appearance. And it wasn't until the very climax that the play revealed the root of her fears to be her own capacity for lechery.

On the screen, Rina was exciting and bold, aware of her sexuality and continually flaunting it before the audience, but there was no subtlety in her acting. And yet, in all honesty, he felt the surge of vitality flowing from her. When she was on the screen, no matter who else was in the scene, he could not take his eyes off her.

He left the theater and went back to his hotel, where the car was going to pick him up. As was usual whenever he was disturbed, he called his mother. "Do you know who they want to play in the picture, Mother?"

"Who?" his mother asked, with her usual calm.

"Rina Marlowe."

His mother's voice was shocked. "No!"

"Yes, Mother," he said. "Mr. Norman tells me they couldn't get Bette Davis."

"Well, you turn right around and come home," his mother said firmly. "You tell Mr. Norman that you have a reputation to consider, that he promised you Davis and you won't accept that blond creature as a substitute!"

"But I already told Mr. Norman I'd talk to Miss Marlowe. He said if I wasn't satisfied after meeting her, he'd try to get someone else."

"All right," she said. "But remember, your integrity counts far more than anything else. If you're not completely satisfied, you come right home."

"Yes, Mother," he said. "Much love."

"Much love and take care," his mother replied, completing their farewell ritual.

Rina entered the room where he was waiting, wearing a black leotard that covered her body from her feet to her neck. Her pale-blond hair was pulled back straight and tied in a knot behind her head. She wore no make-up.

"Mr. Dunbar," she said, coming toward him unsmiling, her hand outstretched.

"Miss Marlowe," he answered, taking her hand. He was surprised at the strength in her fingers.

"I've looked forward to meeting you," she said. "I've heard a great deal about you."

He smiled, pleased. "I've heard a great deal about you, too."

She looked up and smiled for the first time. "I'll bet you have," she said without rancor. "That's why you're out here the first day you're in Hollywood. You probably wonder why in hell I should want to play in *Sunspots?*"

He was startled at her frank admission. "Why do you, Miss Marlowe? It seems to me you wouldn't want to rock the boat. You've got a pretty good thing going here."

She dropped into a chair. "Screw the boat," she said casually. "I'm supposed to be an actress. I want to find out just how much of an actress I am. And you're the one director who can make me find out."

He stared at her for a moment. "Have you read the script?"

She nodded.

"Do you remember the first lines the girl speaks when she wanders into the camp?"

"Yes."

"Read them for me," he said, giving her the script.

She took the script but didn't open it. " 'My name is Mary. Yes, that's it, I think my name is Mary.' "

"You're saying the lines, Miss Marlowe," he said, frowning at her, "but you're not thinking about them. You're not feeling the effort that goes into the girl's trying to remember her name.

"Think it through like this. I can't remember my name but if I could, it's a familiar one. It's a name I've been called all my life, and yet it's hard for me to remember it. Even though it's a name that is mentioned often in church and I have even said it in my prayers. It's coming back now. I think I've got it. 'My name is Mary. Yes, that's it. I think my name is Mary.' "

Rina stared back at him silently. Then she got up and walked over to the fireplace. She put her hands up on the mantelpiece, her back toward him. She tugged at the knot in her hair and it fell around her shoulders as she turned to face him.

Her face was suddenly gaunt and strained as she spoke. " 'My name is Mary,' " she whispered hoarsely. " 'Yes, that's it. I think my name is Mary.' "

He felt the tiny shivers of goose flesh rising on his arms as he looked at her. It was the same thing he always felt whenever something great in the theater got down inside him.

Bernie Norman came down to the set on the last day of shooting. He shook his head as he opened the door and walked onto the big shooting stage. He should have known better than ever to hire that *faigele* to direct the picture. Worse yet, he should have had his head examined before he ever let them talk him into buying such a story. Everything about it was crazy.

First, the shooting schedule had to be postponed for a month. The director wanted thirty days to rehearse Rina in the part. Norman had to give in when Rina insisted she wouldn't go on before Dunbar said she was ready. That cost a hundred and fifty thousand in stand-by salaries alone.

Then the director had insisted on doing everything like they had done it on stage. To hell with the budget. Another fifty thousand went there. And on top of everything, Dunbar insisted that the sound in each scene be perfect. No looping, no lip-synching. Every word perfect, as it was spoken on the stage. He didn't care how many takes were necessary. Why should he, the bastard? Norman thought. It wasn't his money.

Three months over the schedule the picture went. A million and a half thrown down the drain. He blinked his eyes as he came onto the brilliantly lighted section of the stage.

Thank God, this was the last scene. It was the one in front of the cabin when the girl opens the door in the morning and finds the two men dead, the younger man having killed the older, then himself, when he realized the depths to which the girl had led him. All she had to do was look at the two men and cry a little, then walk off into the desert. Simple. Nothing could go wrong with that. Ten minutes and it would be over.

"Places!"

The two actors stretched out in front of the cabin door. An assistant director and the script girl quickly checked their positions with photographs of the scene previously made and made a few corrections. The hand of one actor was in the wrong place; a smudge had appeared on the cheek of the other.

Norman saw Dunbar nod. "Roll 'em!" There was silence for a moment as the scene plate was shot, then Dunbar called quietly, "Action."

Norman smiled to himself. This was a cinch. There wasn't even any sound to louse this one up. Slowly the door of the cabin began to open. Rina stepped out and looked down at the two men.

Norman swore to himself. You'd think at least the *shmuck* would have enough sense to rip her dress a little. After all, it was supposed to be out on the desert. But no, the dress went right up to her neck like it was the middle of the winter. The finest pair of tits in the whole business Dunbar had to work with and he kept them hidden.

The big camera began to dolly in for a close-up. Rina raised her head slowly and looked into the camera. A moment passed. Another moment. "Cry, damn you!" Dunbar screamed. "Cry!"

Rina blinked her eyes. Nothing happened.

"Cut!" Dunbar yelled. He walked out on the set, stepping over one of the prostrate men to reach her. He looked at Rina for a moment. "In this scene, you're supposed to cry, remember?" he asked sarcastically.

She nodded silently.

He turned around and went back to his place beside the camera. Rina went back into the cabin, closing the door behind her. Again the assistant director and the script girl checked the positions, then walked off the set.

"Roll 'em!"

"Scene three seventeen, take two!" The plateman called and stepped away from in front of the camera quickly.

"Action!"

Everything happened exactly as before until the moment Rina looked into the camera. She stared into it for a moment. Unwinking. Dry eyes. Then, suddenly, she stepped aside.

"Cut!" Dunbar called. He started out onto the stage again.

"I'm sorry, Claude," Rina said. "I just can't. We'd better use make-up."

"Make-up!" the eager assistant director yelled. "Bring the tears!"

Norman nodded. There was no use wasting money. On screen, nobody could tell the difference. Besides, the phony tears photographed even better—they rolled down the cheeks like oiled ball bearings.

Dunbar turned. "No make-up!"

"No make-up!" his assistant echoed loudly. "Hold the tears!"

Dunbar looked at Rina. "This is the last scene of the picture," he said. "Two men are dead because of you and all I want is one lousy little tear. Not because you feel sorry for them or for yourself. It's just to let me know that somewhere inside you, you still have a soul. Not much, just enough to show you're a woman, not an animal. Understand?"

Rina nodded.

"O.K., then," he said quietly. "Let's take it from the top." He walked back to his place beside the camera. He bent slightly forward, peering intensely as Rina came out the door. She looked down at the men, then up as the camera began to dolly in close. "Now!" Dunbar's voice was almost a whisper. "Cry!"

Rina stared into the approaching camera. Nothing happened.

"Cut!" Dunbar yelled. He strode angrily into the scene. "What the fuck kind of a woman are you?" he screamed at her.

"Please, Claude," she begged.

He stared at her coldly. "For five months we were making this picture. I've worked day and night, for only one reason. You wanted to prove you were an actress. Well, I've done all I could. I'm not going to destroy the integrity of this picture in the last scene because of your inadequacy. You want to be an actress—well, prove it! Act!"

He turned his back on her and walked away. Norman covered his face with his hands. Ten thousand dollars a day this was costing him. He should have known better.

"Action!"

He opened his fingers and peered through them at the scene. This time, he could hear Dunbar speaking to Rina in a low voice.

"That's right, that's right, now you walk out. You look down and see them. First at Paul, then at Joseph. You see the gun in Joseph's hand and you know what has happened. Now you begin to look up. You're thinking, they're dead.

Maybe you didn't love them but you lived with them, you used them. Maybe for a moment one of them brings back a piece of your memory—the memory you lost and never recovered. But for a fraction of a second, the veil lifts. And it's your father, or your brother, or maybe the child you never had, lying there in the sand at your feet. The tears start up in your eyes."

Slowly Norman's hands slipped away from his face. He held his breath as he moved toward the side away from the camera, which blocked his view. Rina was crying. Real tears.

Dunbar was still whispering. "The tears have come but the veil has dropped again and you can't remember why you are crying. The tears stop and your eyes are dry. Now you turn and look out into the desert. Out there in the lonely sand someone is waiting, someone with your memory. You will find that person out there. Then you'll really know who you are. You begin to walk out into the desert . . . slowly . . . slowly . . . slowly."

Dunbar's voice faded as Rina began to walk away, even the proud, straight shape of her back calling for pity. Norman looked around him. The crew were staring at Rina. They had forgotten everything on the set except her. He felt a moisture in his eyes. The damn scene had even got to him.

"Cut!" Dunbar's voice was a hoarse, triumphant shout. "Print it!" He slumped back into his chair, exhausted.

The stage turned into bedlam, with everybody applauding. Even the hard-bitten veterans of the crew were grinning. Norman ran out onto the stage. He grabbed Rina's hand excitedly. "You were wonderful, baby!" he said. "Magnificent!"

Rina looked at him. For a moment, it seemed as if she were far away, then her eyes cleared. She looked toward Dunbar, seated in his chair, surrounded by the camera crew and his assistants, then back at Norman. "Do you really think so?"

"Would I say it if I didn't mean it, baby?" he replied, smiling. "You know me better than that. Now, you take a good couple of weeks' rest. I got *Scheherazade* all set to go."

She turned away from him and watched Dunbar, who was approaching them slowly, the lines of exhaustion showing clearly on his thin, forty-year-old face. "Thank you," she said, taking Dunbar's hand.

He smiled wearily. "You're a great actress, Miss Marlowe," he said, formal once again, now that their work was over. "It was a privilege working with you."

Rina stared at him for a moment, a new vitality flowing into her. "You're out on your feet," she said, concern in her voice.

"I'll be all right with some rest," he said quickly. "I don't think I've slept a night through since the picture began."

"We'll soon fix that," Rina said confidently. "Ilene."

From somewhere in the crowd, Ilene suddenly appeared. "Call James and have him prepare the guest room for Mr. Dunbar."

"But, Miss Marlowe," the director protested. "I can't put you to all that trouble!"

"Do you think I'd let you go back to that empty hotel room the way you're feeling?" Rina demanded.

"But I promised Mother I'd call her the moment the picture was finished."

"You can call her there." Rina laughed. "We do have telephones, really."

Norman clapped Dunbar on the shoulder. "You do like Rina says, Dunbar.

You can use the rest. You still got ten weeks of editing in front of you. But don't worry, you got a great picture here. I wouldn't be surprised if you both get Academy Awards!"

Norman didn't believe it when he said it, but that was exactly the way it turned out.

CHAPTER NINETEEN

NELIA DUNBAR, SIXTY-THREE YEARS OLD AND STRONG AS THE PROVERBIAL rock, crossed the room and looked down at her son. "That horrible creature," she said quietly.

She slipped into the seat beside her son and took his head on her shoulder. Absently she stroked his forehead. "I was wondering how long it would take you to see her in her true light," she said. "I told you not to marry her."

Claude didn't answer. There was no need to. There was a familiar safety in his mother's arms. There always had been. Even when he was a child and had come running home from school when the boys ganged up on him. His mother knew him. He didn't have to tell her when he was troubled. Instinctively she had moved out to California after his marriage to Rina.

He had never been very strong, always frail and thin, and the intense nervousness of his creative spurts left him drained and exhausted. At times like that, his mother would see to it that he took to his bed—for weeks on end, sometimes. She would serve him his meals, bring him the newspapers, read to him from the books they both loved.

Often he felt that these were the happiest moments of his life. Here in the gentle pastels of the room his mother had decorated for him, he felt warm and comfortable and at ease. Everything he wanted was at his fingertips. The dirtiness and petty meanness of the world were safely locked away outside the walls of that room.

His father had never been more than a vague nebulous shadow. He could scarcely remember him, for he had died when Claude was only five. His father's death had caused scarcely a noticeable ripple in the course of their lives, for they were left well off. They weren't wealthy but never was there want.

"You go back to the house and get what few things you need," his mother said. "You can spend the night here. In the morning, we'll see about a divorce."

He raised his head from his mother's shoulder and looked at her. "But, Mother, I wouldn't even know what to say to a lawyer."

"Don't worry," his mother said confidently. "I'll take care of everything."

He could feel a great weight lifting from his shoulders. Once again, his mother had spoken the magic words. But when he stood in the street in front of the house and saw Rina's car in the driveway, he was afraid to go in. There would only be another scene and he wasn't up to it. He had no more strength.

He looked at his wrist watch. It was almost eleven o'clock. She would be leaving soon because she had a luncheon date at the studio. He walked back down the hill to the cocktail lounge just off the corner of Sunset. He would have a drink while he waited. He would be able to see her car as it came down the hill.

The cocktail lounge was dark as he entered, the chairs still up on the tables. The bar was open, however, and there was already a customer seated with a glass of beer in front of him. Claude climbed up on a stool near the window, from which he could watch the street.

He shivered slightly. It had begun to drizzle as he came down the hill and was turning into one of those nasty, chilly afternoons peculiarly indigenous to sunny California. He shivered again. He hoped he wasn't catching cold. "Whisky and warm water," he said to the bartender, remembering the drink his mother always gave him at the first sign of a cold.

The bartender looked at him peculiarly. "Warm water?"

Claude nodded. "Yes, please." He looked up and noticed that the lone customer was also staring at him—a young man in a yellow lumber jacket. "And a slice of lemon, if you have it," he called after the bartender.

Claude picked up the small steaming mug. He sipped at it and felt its warmth creep down toward his stomach. He turned and looked out the window. It was really raining now. He picked up the mug again and to his surprise, it was empty. He decided to have another. There was time. He knew exactly what Rina was doing right now. He gestured to the bartender.

Right at this moment, she was seated in front of her dressing table, putting on her make-up, until it was precisely the way she wanted it. Then she would fuss with her hair, teasing it until it hung carelessly, but with every strand in its allotted place.

She had a fetish about not getting anywhere on time. She was always at least an hour late, most of the time even later. It used to drive him crazy having to wait for her, but it never seemed to disturb anyone else. They just took it for granted.

Claude looked down at the mug. It was empty again. He ordered another drink. He was beginning to feel better. Rina would be surprised when she came home and found his things gone. No more would she call him half a man. She'd find out just how much of a man he was when the lawyer served her with divorce papers. She'd know then that she couldn't push him around.

And she'd never look at him again the way she had the first night they were married—with pity and yet contempt, and worst of all, the knowledge in her eyes that she saw into him deeply, laying bare the very secrets of his soul, secrets that he kept even from himself.

He had come into the darkened bedroom, holding in his hand a tray on which stood an iced bottle of champagne and two glasses. "I have come bearing wine for my beloved."

They began to make love. Gently and beautifully, the way he had always known it would be, for he was a virgin. And there was comfort in the womanly curve of her body on the bed, lying there so passive and undemanding. He had even begun to compose a poem to her beauty when he felt her searching hand against his flesh.

For the tiniest fraction of a moment, he froze, startled by her alien fingers. Then he relaxed, for her touch was so light and gentle that he was scarcely aware of it. He felt a tremor shake her body, then another, and a sudden burst of heat seemed to rise from her.

Then a cry came from deep within her and she pulled him down toward her, her hands ripping off the bottom part of his pajamas. No longer was she suppliant and gentle, no longer did she care what he felt or needed, she was caught up in a frenzy of her own. Her fingers hurt him as she tried to guide him, to force him into her.

Suddenly, a wild terror began to run through him. A fear of the demanding sexuality of her body, which had lain dormant, waiting only for this moment to feed upon his manhood and devour him. In a near panic, he tore himself free and stood trembling near the bed.

He tried to pull the torn pajamas around him and heard the sound of her breathing become quieter. There was a rustle of the sheets and he looked down at her.

She had turned over on her side and was staring up at him, the sheet carelessly draped over her hips. Her breasts were heavy, the nipples still swollen with passion. Her eyes seemed to flame their way into him. "Are you the kind of man some people say you are?"

He felt the fire burning its way into his cheeks. He had not been unaware of the snide remarks made behind his back, but ordinary people did not understand his absorption in his work. "No!" he said quickly.

"Then what kind of man are you?"

He fell to his knees beside the bed and looked at her. "Please," he cried. "Please, you've got to understand. I married you because I love you but I'm not like the others. My mother says I'm more nervous and high strung."

She didn't answer and he saw the horrible combination of pity, contempt and knowledge come fleetingly into her eyes. "Don't look at me like that," he begged. "It will be better the next time. I won't be so nervous. I love you. I love you."

He felt her hand touch his head gently, then slowly stroke his temples. Gradually, his tears subsided and he seized her hands, kissing them gratefully. "It will be better, darling," he promised.

But it was never any better. There was something about the complete femaleness of her body, her terrifying sexuality, that frightened him into complete impotency.

"What did you say?" The words took him from the past into the present. He looked up. The other customer, the young man in the yellow jacket, was speaking to him. "I thought you said something to me. I'm sorry."

Claude felt foolish. There was no doubt that he had spoken. Very often he did while lost in thought. He began to feel embarrassed. "I did," he said, quickly trying to cover his embarrassment. "I said it turned into a rather nasty day, didn't it?"

The young man's eyes went past him to the window, then back. "Yes," he said politely. "It sure did."

Claude looked at him. He seemed like a nice enough young man. Handsome, too, in a rough sort of way. Probably an actor, down on his luck, who'd stopped in to nurse a beer until the rain stopped. He picked up his mug. It was empty again. "Let me buy you a drink," he said.

The boy nodded. "I'd like another beer. Thanks."

"Bartender, a beer for the young gentleman," Claude called. He tapped his mug. "And I'll have another of these."

It wasn't until three drinks later, when he saw Rina's car turn downtown onto Sunset, that he got the idea. After all, there were quite a few things he wanted to take with him and he couldn't carry all of them alone.

After he rang the bell the second time he remembered it was Thursday and all the servants were off. He took out his key. They went right up the staircase to his room. He opened the closet and took out a valise. "You empty those drawers," he said to the boy. "I'll get another suitcase."

He left the room for a moment and when he returned, his companion was holding a picture of Rina that had been standing on the bureau. "Who's this?"

"My wife," Claude answered tersely. Then he giggled. "Will she be surprised when she gets home and finds I'm gone."

"You Rina Marlowe's husband?"

Claude nodded. "But not for long now, thank God!"

The boy looked at him strangely. "What do you want to walk out on a dish like that for?" he asked.

Claude snatched the picture angrily from his hand and threw it against the wall. The glass shattered and fell into tiny bits on the carpet. He turned and walked into the bathroom. He took off his jacket and loosened his tie. He turned on the taps to wash his hands but the sound of the water rushing into the basin reminded him suddenly of the time he had walked into the solarium. He remembered the sound the water had made in the fountain as he became aware of Rina, lying nude on the table, being given a massage by Ilene.

Ilene was nude to the waist, her lower half enclosed in the tight-fitting black trousers she usually wore. He noticed the stringy muscles working along her back as her hands moved gently over Rina's body.

Rina had one arm thrown over her face to shield her eyes from the sun. Her body writhed sensuously under Ilene's touch. When they became aware of his presence, Rina lifted her arm. He felt a vague surprise at the straight flatness of Ilene's chest. "Don't stop, darling," Rina said huskily to Ilene.

Obediently Ilene began to massage again. The sensuous rhythm seemed to return to Rina's body as she lay there, her head turned to the side, watching him. After a moment, she put her arms up and drew Ilene's head down to her hips, "Kiss me, lover," she commanded, her eyes still watching Claude.

He turned suddenly and fled from the room, the sound of her mocking laughter, mixed with the sound of the water from the fountain, echoing in his ears.

Remembering, he lifted his hands to his face. It was bathed in perspiration. His clothing clung to him stickily. His skin began to feel crawly. He decided to take a shower.

The hot needle spray of the shower began to relax him. It seemed to bring the inner warmth of the whisky to the surface of his skin. Luxuriously he lathered himself with the delicately scented soap his mother ordered from London especially for him.

He stepped out of the shower, rubbing himself vigorously. He looked down with satisfaction at his pink, tingling skin. He liked being clean. He looked for his robe, but it wasn't on its usual hook. "Would you get the blue robe from the closet for me, please," he called automatically, without thinking.

He took the bottle of cologne down from the shelf and sprinkled it lavishly into his hand, then began to rub himself down. Some instinct caused him to look up into the mirror. The boy was standing in the open door, watching him. The robe was thrown over his arm. He had taken off his yellow jacket, revealing a dirty white T shirt.

Claude saw the thick black hair that sprouted wildly from the young man's arms, shoulders and chest. A feeling of distaste ran through him. "You can leave it on the chair," he said, covering himself partly with the towel.

Instead, the boy grinned knowingly at him and came into the bathroom, kicking the door shut behind him with his foot.

Claude turned around angrily. "Get out of here!"

The young man didn't move. His smile grew even broader. "Aw, come off it, old man," he said. "You didn't really bring me up here to help you with your packing, did you?"

"Get out or I'll call for help," Claude said, feeling a strangely exciting fear.

The boy laughed. "Who'll hear?" he asked. "I was wise to you the minute you told me the servants were off."

"You horrible thing!" Claude screamed. He felt a stunning blow on the side of his head and he fell sprawling. He pulled himself to his hands and knees. "Please go," he whispered, his voice breaking.

The young man raised his hand threateningly. Instinctively Claude shrank back but he wasn't quick enough. The open palm cracked smartly across the side of his face, knocking his head sideways against the toilet bowl. He stared up at the boy with frightened eyes.

"You don't really want me to go, do you?" the young man said, his hand tugging at the black leather belt around his waist. "You're the kind that likes to get roughed up a little first."

"I am not!"

"No?" The boy laughed derisively, raising the belt. "Don't crap me, I can see."

For a fraction of a moment, Claude did not know what he meant, then he looked down at himself. A crazy thought went racing through his mind. If Rina could only see him now, she would know he was a man.

The belt cut down across his back, sending a thin shiver of agony down his spine. "That's enough!" he whimpered. "Please don't hit me any more!"

He raised himself wearily from the floor and looked out into the bedroom. The boy was gone, taking with him all the money Claude had had with him. Slowly he got into the shower again and turned on the hot water.

He felt his strength returning as the water soaked into his skin. What a horrible thing to have happen, he thought, remembering all the indignities the young man had subjected him to. A warm feeling of satisfaction came to him. If he had been the stronger, he would have shown him. He felt the excitement begin to beat inside his chest as he thought how he would have torn the belt from the young man's hand and beaten him with it until he bled. He felt the sudden surge of power in his loins.

It was precisely at that moment that the truth came to him. "Oh, no!" He cried aloud in shock at the realization. What everyone had said about him was true. It was only he who had been blind to it until his own body betrayed him.

A dazed kind of anger came over him. Leaving the water running, he stepped from the shower stall. He opened the medicine cabinet and took down the old-fashioned straight razor that he had used ever since he began to shave—the razor that had stood proudly for him as a symbol of his manhood.

A wild, crazy kind of anger rolled blindly over him as he slashed viciously at himself. If he was not to be a man, at least he could turn himself into a woman.

Again and again, he slashed at himself. Until at last, his strength gone, he collapsed onto the floor.

"Damn you!" he cried. "Damn you, Mother!"

They were the last words he ever said.

CHAPTER TWENTY

DAVID WOOLF STOOD IN THE DOORWAY OF THE BATH-ROOM, NAUSEA RISing in the pit of his stomach. There was blood everywhere, on the white-and-blue tiles of the floor and walls, along the sides of the white bathtub, sink and toilet bowl.

It was hard to believe that it was only thirty minutes ago that the door of his office had burst open to reveal his uncle, his face flushed and purple, as it always was whenever he was upset. "Get right over to Rina Marlowe's house," Bernie Norman said. "One of the boys in publicity just got a tip from the Beverly Hills police station that Dunbar committed suicide."

David was already on his way to the door.

"Make sure she's protected!" the old man called after him. "Two million dollars in unreleased negatives we got on her!"

He picked up Harry Richards, chief of the studio guards, at the gate on the way out. Richards, a former police sergeant, was in good with all the cops. He took the short cut over the back roads through Coldwater Canyon to Sunset. He was at Rina's house in twenty minutes.

Now the two white-jacketed mortuary attendants were lifting Dunbar's somehow shrunken body into the small, basket-like stretcher and covering it with a white canvas sheet.

The attendants picked up the stretcher and David moved aside to let them pass. He lit a cigarette as they carried the body through the bedroom and out into the corridor. The first acrid taste of smoke settled his stomach. A faint screaming came from the downstairs foyer and he started hurriedly for the door, wondering if somehow Rina had got away from the doctor. But when he got to the head of the staircase, he saw that it wasn't Rina at all. It was Dunbar's mother.

She was struggling to free herself from the grasp of two red-faced policemen as the white-covered stretcher went by. "My baby!" she screamed. "Let me see my baby!"

The attendants moved impassively past her and out the door. David could see the crowd of reporters outside, pressing against the door as it opened and closed. He started down the staircase, hearing the old woman begin to scream again.

She had pulled herself partly free of one of the policemen and with one hand she held onto the railing of the staircase. "You murdered my son, you bitch!" The high-pitched voice seemed to fill the whole house. "You killed him because you found out he was coming back to me!" The old woman had her other hand free now. She seemed to be trying to pull herself up the stairs.

"Get that crazy old woman out of here!" David turned, startled at the harsh voice that came from the top of the stairway behind him.

Ilene stood there, a wild, angry look on her face. "Get her out!" she hissed harshly. "The doctor's having enough trouble with Rina as it is, without her having to listen to that crazy old bitch!"

David caught Richards' eye and nodded to him. Instantly, Richards walked over to one of the policemen and whispered to him. All pretense of politeness gone, the two policemen got a new grip on the old woman and, one of them covering her mouth with his hand, they half dragged, half carried her out of the room. A moment later, a side door slammed and there was silence.

David glanced back up the staircase but Ilene had already disappeared. He walked over to Richards. "I told the boys to take her over to Colton's Sanitarium," the ex-policeman whispered.

David nodded approvingly. Dr. Colton would know what to do. The studio sent many of their stars out there to dry out. He'd also make sure that she didn't speak to anyone until he had calmed her down.

"Call the studio and have them send a couple of your men out here. I don't want any reporters getting in when the police leave."

"I already did," Richards replied, taking his arm. "Come on into the living room. I want you to meet Lieutenant Stanley."

Lieutenant Stanley was seated at the small, kidney-shaped telephone desk, a notebook open in front of him. He got up and shook hands with David. He was a thin, gray-faced, gray-haired man, and David thought he looked more like an accountant than a detective.

"This is a pretty terrible thing, Lieutenant," David said. "Have you figured out what happened yet?"

The lieutenant nodded. "I think we've about got it put together. There's no doubt about it—he killed himself, all right. One thing bothers me, though."

"What's that?"

"We backtracked on Dunbar's movements like we usually do," the detective said. "And he picked up a young man in a cocktail lounge just before he came here. He flashed quite a roll of bills in the bar and we didn't find any money in his room. He's also got a couple of bruises on his head and back that the coroner can't explain. We got a pretty good description of him from the bartender. We'll pick him up."

David looked at him. "But what good will that do?" he asked. "You're sure that Dunbar killed himself; what more could he tell you?"

"Some guys think nothing of picking up a homo and beating him up a little for kicks, then rolling him for his dough."

"So?"

"So Dunbar isn't the only homo in our district," the lieutenant replied. "We got a list of them a yard long down at the station. Most of 'em mind their own business and they're entitled to some protection."

David glanced at Richards. The chief of the studio guards looked at him with impassive eyes. David turned back to the policeman. "Thank you very much for talking to me, Lieutenant," he said. "I'm very much impressed with the efficient manner in which you handled this."

He started out of the room, leaving Richards and the policeman alone. He could hear Richards' heavy whisper as he walked out the door.

"Look, Stan," the big ex-cop was saying. "If this hits the papers, there's goin' to be a mess an' the studio stands a chance of bein' hurt real bad an' it's bad enough just with the suicide."

David went through the door and crossed the foyer to the staircase. Bringing the old sergeant had been the smartest thing he could have done. He was sure now that there wouldn't be reference to any other man in the newspapers. He went up the stairs and into the small sitting room that led to Rina's bedroom. Ilene was slumped exhaustedly in a chair. She looked up as he entered. "How is she?"

"Out like a light," she answered in a tired voice. "The doctor gave her a shot big enough to knock out a horse."

"You could stand a drink." He walked over to the small liquor cabinet and opened it. "Me, too," he added. "Scotch all right?"

She didn't answer and he filled two glasses with Haig & Haig pinch bottle. He gave her one and sat down opposite her. A faint flush of color crept up into her face as the whisky hit her stomach. "It was terrible," she said.

He didn't answer.

She drank again from the glass. "Rina had a luncheon appointment so we got home from the studio about four o'clock. We came upstairs to dress about four thirty, and Rina said she thought she heard the water running in Claude's bathroom. The servants had the day off so she asked me to check. She must have sensed that something was wrong when I didn't come right back. She came into the bedroom while I was still phoning the police. I tried to keep her from seeing what had happened but she was already at the bathroom door when I turned around."

She put her glass down and hunted blindly for a cigarette. David lit one and handed it to her. She took it and placed it between her lips, the smoke curling up around her face. "She was standing there, staring down at him, staring down at that horrible mess of blood, and she was saying over and over to herself, 'I killed him, I killed him! I killed him like I killed everyone who ever loved me.' Then she began to scream." Ilene put her hands up over her ears.

David looked down at his glass. It was empty. Silently he got up and refilled it. Sitting down again, he looked into the amber liquid reflectively. "You know," he said, "what I can't understand is why she ever married him."

"That's just the trouble," she said angrily. "None of you ever tried to understand her. All she ever meant to any of you was a ticket at the box office, money in the bank. None of you cared what she was really like. I'll tell you why she married him. Because she was sorry for him, because she wanted to make a man of him. That's why she married him. And that's why she's lying there in her bedroom, crying even though she's asleep. She's crying because she failed."

The telephone rang. It rang again. David looked at her. "I'll get it," he said.

"Hello."

"Who is this?"

"David Woolf," he said automatically.

"Jonas Cord," the voice replied.

"Mr. Cord," David said. "I'm with Norman—"

"I know," Cord interrupted. "I remember you. You're the young man who does all the trouble-shooting for Bernie. I just heard over the radio about the accident. How's Rina?"

"She's asleep right now. The doctor knocked her out."

There was a long, empty silence on the line and David thought they might have been cut off. Then Cord's voice came back on the line. "Everything under control?"

"I think so," David said.

"Good. Keep it like that. If there's anything you need, let me know."

"I will."

"I won't forget what you're doing," Cord said.

There was a click and the line was dead. Slowly David put down the telephone. "That was Jonas Cord," he said.

Ilene didn't raise her face from her hands.

He turned and looked back at the telephone. It didn't make sense. From what he'd heard about Cord, he wasn't the kind of man who spent his time making sympathy calls. If anything, he was exactly the opposite.

Unconsciously he glanced at the closed door to Rina's bedroom. There had to be more to it than that, he thought.

It was four months before he saw Rina again. He looked up from the couch in his uncle's office as she swept into the room.

"Rina, darling!" Bernie Norman said, getting up from his desk and throwing his arms around her enthusiastically.

The producer stepped back and looked at her, walking around her as if she were a prize heifer in a cattle show. "Slimmer and more beautiful than ever."

Rina looked over. "Hello, David," she said quietly.

"Hello, Rina." He got to his feet. "How are you?"

"I'm fine," she answered. "Who wouldn't be after three months on a health farm?"

He laughed. "And your next picture will be another vacation," Norman interrupted.

Rina turned back to him, a faint smile coming over her face. "Go ahead, you old bastard," she said. "Con me into it."

Norman laughed happily. "For a minute, I was wondering if it was my old girl who was coming into the office, so nice she was!"

Rina laughed, too. "What's the vacation?" she asked.

"Africa!" Norman said triumphantly. "The greatest jungle script I read since *Trader Horn*."

"I knew it," Rina said, turning to David. "I knew the next thing he'd have me do would be a female Tarzan!"

After she was gone, David looked across the room at his uncle. "Rina seems quieter, more subdued, somehow."

Norman looked at him shrewdly. "So what?" he said. "Maybe she's growing up a *bissel* and settling down. It's about time." He got up from his desk and walked over to David. "Only six months we got to the stockholders' meeting next March."

"You still don't know who's selling us short?"

"No." Norman shook his head. "I tried everyplace. The brokers, the underwriters, the banks. They tried. Nobody knows. But every day, the stock goes down." He chewed on his unlit cigar. "I bought up every share I could but enough money I ain't got to stop it. All the cash I could beg or borrow is gone."

"Maybe the stock will go up when we announce Rina's new picture. Everyone knows she's a sure money-maker."

"I hope so," Norman said. "Everywhere we're losing money. Even the theaters." He walked back to his chair and slumped down into it. "That was the mistake I made. I should never have bought them. For them I had to float the stock, borrow all that money from the banks. Pictures I know; real estate, phooey! I should never have listened to those *chazairem* on Wall Street, ten years ago. Now I sold my company, the money I ain't got no more. And I don't even know who owns it!"

David got to his feet. "Well, there's no use in worrying about it. There's still six months till the meeting. And a lot can happen in six months."

"Yeah," Norman said discouragingly. "It can get worse!"

David closed the door of his office behind him. He sat down at his desk and ran down the list of enemies his uncle had made in the course of his life. It was a long list but there wasn't anyone who had the kind of money this operation required. Besides, most of them were in the picture business and they had done as much to his uncle as he had done to them. It was a kind of game among members of a club. They screamed and hollered a lot but none ever took it seriously enough to carry a grudge like this.

Suddenly, he remembered something—Rina. He glanced at the door, his hand going automatically to the telephone. He pulled his hand back sharply. There was no sense in making a fool of himself.

But he had a hunch. How right he was he wasn't to know until he had Ilene sign Rina into the hospital under a phony name six months later. She was just back from Africa after shooting *The Jungle Queen*, and suddenly took very sick. He hadn't wanted the press to find out until after the picture was released.

CHAPTER TWENTY-ONE

"JONAS CORD," NORMAN SAID BITTERLY. "JONAS CORD IT WAS THE whole time. Why didn't you tell me?"

David turned from the hotel window looking out over Central Park. "I didn't know. I was only guessing."

"Know, not know," the producer said, chewing on his dead cigar. "You should have told me, anyway."

"What good would it have done?" David asked. "I couldn't have proved it and even if I had, you didn't have the money to fight him."

Norman took the cigar out of his mouth and looked at it glumly. With an angry gesture, he threw it on the rug. "What did I ever do to him he should want to ruin me?" he asked angrily.

David didn't answer.

"Nothing! That's what I did. Only made money for him. More money that he should use to cut my throat with!" Bernie took a fresh cigar from his pocket and waved it in front of David's face. "That should be a lesson to you. Never do a favor for anybody, never make money for anybody, only your-self. Otherwise, you'll find a knife in your back made of your own silver!"

David looked at his uncle's angry purple face, remembering the scene that had taken place at the stockholders' meeting.

Norman had gone into it, feeling more confident than he had at any time during the past few months. The percentage of proxies that had been returned was about what they got every year. Only about twenty-five per cent of the stockholders ever bothered to send in their proxy forms. All they were interested in was when they'd begin receiving dividends again. But those proxies, plus the eight per cent of stock that Norman had in his own name, gave him a comfortable thirty-three per cent of the stock to vote.

The attendance at the meeting was the same as usual. A few retired businessmen and some women who wandered in off the street because they owned ten shares and it gave them something to do; those directors of the company who happened to be in town and the company officers from the New York office.

It was only after the formalities of the meeting were over and Norman was asking for nominations for the board of directors that he sensed there was something wrong. As he was speaking, Dan Pierce, the agent, and another man, whose face was familiar but whose name Norman couldn't remember, came into the room and sat down in the front row of the small auditorium.

A vice-president in charge of sales dutifully read off Norman's approved list of nominations for directorships. Another vice-president, in charge of theater operations, dutifully seconded the nominations. A third vice-president, in charge of foreign operations, then dutifully moved that the nominations be closed.

At that moment, Pierce got to his feet. "Mr. President," he said, "I have several more nominations to make for directors of the corporation."

"You got no right," Norman yelled from the podium.

"According to the bylaws of the company," Dan Pierce retorted, "any stockholder of record may nominate as many persons for directors as there are directors in the corporation!"

Norman turned to his vice-president and general counsel. "Is that true?"

The attorney nervously nodded. "You're fired, you dumb bastard, you!" Norman whispered.

He turned back to Pierce. "It's illegal!" he shouted. "A trick to upset the company."

The man seated alongside Pierce got to his feet. "Mr. Pierce's nominations are perfectly in order and I, personally, can attest to his legal right to make them."

It was then that Norman remembered the name—McAllister—Jonas Cord's attorney. He calmed down immediately. "I suppose you can prove you're stockholders?" he asked cannily.

McAllister smiled. "Of course."

"Let me see your proof. I got a right to demand that!"

"Of course you have," McAllister said. He walked up to the podium and handed up a stock certificate.

Norman looked down at it. It was a stock certificate for ten shares properly issued in the name of Daniel Pierce. "Is this all the stock you got?" he asked innocently.

McAllister smiled again. "It's all the proof I need," he said, evading the producer's attempt to find out just how much stock he represented. "May I proceed with the nominations?"

Norman nodded silently and Pierce got to his feet and presented six names for the nine-man board. Just enough to assure clear-cut control. Outside of his own and McAllister's, all the names were strange to Norman.

When the votes were ready to be counted, McAllister presented to the meeting proxies representing forty-one per cent of the company—twenty-six per cent in the name of Jonas Cord and fifteen held by various brokerage houses. All six of his nominees were elected.

Norman turned to his executives. He studied them silently for a moment, then withdrew six of his nominees, leaving only himself, David and the vice-president and treasurer on the board. The meeting over, he called for a directors' meeting at the company offices that afternoon, for the election of officers.

Silently he started out of the room, his usually ruddy face pale and white. Pierce stopped him at the door. "Bernie," Pierce said, "I'd like a minute with you before the directors' meeting."

Norman stared at him. "Traitors to their own kind I don't talk to," he said coldly. "Go talk to Hitler!" He stamped out of the room.

Dan Pierce turned to David. "David, make him listen to reason," he said. "Cord authorized me to offer three million bucks for the old man's shares. That's twice what they're worth. If he doesn't sell, Cord says he'll put the company in receivership and all the shares will be good for then is wallpaper."

"I'll see what I can do," David said, hurrying after his uncle.

Now Norman was yelling again, pacing up and down the room and threatening a proxy fight. He'd show that crazy Cord that Bernie Norman was no fool, that he hadn't built a business up from nothing with his bare hands without having something in his *kopf*.

"Wait a minute!" David said sharply. He had taken more than enough nonsense from his uncle. It was time somebody taught the old man the facts of life. "You're talking about a proxy fight?" he shouted. "With what are you going to fight him? Spitballs instead of money? And if you fight, do you honestly believe that anybody will go along with you? For the last four years, this company has been steadily losing money. The biggest picture we had during that time was *The Renegade*— Cord's picture, not ours. And the biggest picture on the market today is *Devils in the Sky*—Cord's picture, too. The one you wouldn't distribute for him because there wasn't enough *koom-shaw* in it for you! Do you think anybody in his right mind is going to pick you over Cord?"

The producer stared at him. "To think," he cried out, "that from my own flesh and blood should come such words!"

"Come off it, Uncle Bernie," David said. "Family's got nothing to do with it. I'm just looking at the facts."

"Facts?" Norman shouted. "Facts is it you want? Well, look at them. Who was it went out and bought *Sunspots*, a picture that won almost every award? Who? Nobody but me."

"It also lost a million dollars."

"That's my fault?" his uncle replied bitterly. "I didn't tell them before I did it? No, prestige they wanted, and prestige they got."

"That's over the dam, Uncle Bernie," David said. "It has nothing to do with today. Nobody cares about that any more."

"I care about it," Norman retorted. "It's my blood they're spilling. I'm the sacrifice they're making to the Golem. But not yet am I dead. When I tell them about the pictures I'm making with Rina Marlowe, I'll get all the proxies I want."

David stared at his uncle for a moment, then went to the telephone. "Long distance, please," he said. "I want to place a call to the Colton Hospital, Santa Monica, California, room three-o-nine, please."

He glanced at his uncle, who was looking out the window. "Ilene? This is David. How is she?"

"Not good," Ilene said, her voice so low he could scarcely hear her.

"What does the doctor say?"

David heard her begin to sob into the telephone. "Hold on," he said. "This is no time to start breaking down."

"He said—she's dying. That it's a miracle she's lasted this long. He doesn't know what's keeping her alive."

There was a click and the phone went dead in his hand. David turned to his uncle. "Rina won't make another picture for you or anybody else," he said. "She's dying."

The producer stared at him, his face going white. He sank back into a chair. "My God! Then what will happen to the company? She was the one chance we had to stay alive. Without her, the bottom will drop out of the stock, we're finished." He wiped at his face with a handkerchief. "Now even Cord won't bother with us."

David stared at his uncle. "What do you mean?"

"*Shmuck*!" Norman snapped. "Don't you see it yet? Do I got to draw for you diagrams?"

"See?" David asked, bewildered. "See what?"

"That Cord really don't give a damn about the company," the old man said. "That all he wants is the girl."

"The girl?"

"Sure," Norman said. "Rina Marlowe. Remember that meeting I had with him in the toilet at the Waldorf? Remember I told you what he said? How he wouldn't tell me the *courvehs*' names because I stole the Marlowe girl from under his nose?"

The light came on suddenly inside David's head. Why hadn't he thought of it? It tied up with the phone call from Cord the night Dunbar killed himself. He looked at his uncle with a new respect. "What are we going to do?"

"Do?" the old man said. "Do? We're going to keep our mouths shut and go down to that meeting. My heart may be breaking but if he offered three million for my stock, he'll go to five!"

The dream didn't slip away this time when Rina opened her eyes. If anything, it seemed more real than it had ever been. She lay very still for a moment, looking up at the clear plastic tent covering her head and chest. She turned her head slowly.

Ilene was sitting in the chair, watching her. She wished she could tell Ilene not to worry, there really wasn't anything to be afraid of. She had gone through this so many times before in the dream. "Ilene!" she whispered.

Ilene started and got up out of her chair. Rina smiled up at her. "It's really me, Ilene," she whispered. "I'm not out of my head."

"Rina!" She felt Ilene's hand take her own under the sheet. "Rina!"

"Don't cry, Ilene," she whispered. She turned her head to try and see the calendar on the wall but it was too far away. "What day is it?"

"It's Friday."

"The thirteenth?" Rina tried to smile. She saw the smile come to Ilene's face, despite the tears that were rolling down her cheeks. "Call Jonas," Rina said weakly. "I want to see him."

She closed her eyes for a moment and opened them when Ilene came back to the bed. "Did you get him?"

Ilene shook her head. "His office says he's in New York, but they don't know where to reach him."

"You get him, wherever he is!" Rina smiled. "You can't fool me any more," she said. "I've played this scene too many times. You call him. I won't die until he gets here." A faint, ironic smile came over her face. "Anyway, nobody dies out here on the weekend. The weekend columns have already gone to press."

JONAS – 1935
Book Five

CHAPTER ONE

I PULLED THE STICK BACK INTO MY BELLY WITH A LITTLE LEFT RUDDER. AT the same time, I opened the throttle and the CA-4 leaped upward into the sky in a half loop, like an arrow shot from a bow. I felt the G force hold me flat against my seat and bubble the blood racing in my arms. I leveled her off at the top of the loop and when I checked the panel, we were doing three hundred, racing out over the Atlantic with Long Island already far behind us.

I reached forward and tapped the shoulder of the Army flier seated in front of me. "How about that, Colonel?" I shouted over the roar of the twin engines and the shriek of the wind against the plastic bubble over our heads.

I saw him bob his head in answer to my question but he didn't turn around. I knew what he was doing. He was checking out the panel in front of him. Lieutenant Colonel Forrester was one of the real fly boys. He went all the way back to Eddie Rickenbacker and the old Hat in the Ring squadron. Not at all like the old General we'd left on the ground back at Roosevelt Field, that the Army had sent out to check over our plane.

The General flew an armchair back in Purchasing and Procurement in Washington. The closest he ever came to an airplane was when he sat on the trial board at Billy Mitchell's court-martial. But he was the guy who had the O.K. We were lucky that at least he had one Air Corps officer on his staff.

I had tabbed him the minute he came walking into the hangar, with Morrissey, talking up a storm, trotting beside him. There were two aides right behind him— a full colonel and a captain. None of them wore the Air Corps wings on their blouse.

He stood there in the entrance of the hangar, staring in at the CA-4. I could see the frown of disapproval come across his face. "It's ugly," he said. "It looks like a toad."

His voice carried clear across the hangar to where I was, in the cockpit, giving her a final check. I climbed out onto the wing and dropped to the hangar floor in my bare feet. I started toward him. What the hell did he know about streamline and design? His head probably was as square as the desk he sat behind.

"Mr. Cord!" I heard the hissed whisper behind me. I turned around. It was the mechanic. There was a peculiar grin on his face. He had heard the General's remark, too.

"What d'yuh want?"

"I was jus' gettin' ready to roll her out," he said quickly. "An' I didn't want to squash yer shoes."

I stared at him for a moment, then I grinned. "Thanks," I said, walking back and stepping into them. By the time I reached Morrissey and the General, I was cooled off.

Morrissey had a copy of the plans and specs in his hand and was going over them for the benefit of the General. "The Cord Aircraft Four is a revolutionary concept in a two-man fighter-bomber, which has a flight range of better than two thousand miles. It cruises at two forty, with a max of three sixty. It can carry ten machine guns, two cannon, and mounts one thousand pounds of bombs under its wings and in a special bay in its belly."

I looked back at the plane as Morrissey kept on talking. It sure as hell was a revolutionary design. It looked like a big black panther squatting there on the hangar floor with its long nose jutting out in front of the swept-back wings and the plastic bubble over the cockpit shining like a giant cat's eye in the dim light.

"Very interesting," I heard the General say. "Now, I have just one more question."

"What's that, sir?" Morrissey asked.

The General chuckled, looking at his aides. They permitted a faint smile to come to their lips. I could see the old fart was going to get off one of his favorite jokes. "We Army men look over about three hundred of these so-called revolutionary planes every year. Will it fly?"

I couldn't keep quiet any longer. The million bucks it had cost me to get this far with the CA-4 gave me a right to shoot off my mouth. "She'll fly the ass off anything you got in your Army, General," I said. "And any other plane in the world, including the new fighters that Willi Messerschmitt is building."

The General turned toward me, a surprised look on his face. I saw his eyes go down over my grease-spattered white coveralls.

Morrissey spoke up quickly. "General Gaddis, Jonas Cord."

Before the General could speak, a voice came from the doorway behind him. "How do you know what Willi Messerschmitt is building?"

I looked up as the speaker came into view. The General had evidently brought a third aide with him. The silver wings shone on his blouse, matching the silver oak leaves on his shoulders. He was about forty, slim and with a flier's mustache. He wore just two ribbons on his blouse—the *Croix de guerre* of France and the Distinguished Flying Cross.

"He told me," I said curtly.

There was a curious look on the lieutenant colonel's face. "How is Willi?"

The General's voice cut in before I could answer. "We came out here to look over an airplane," he said in a clipped voice, "not to exchange information about mutual friends."

It was my turn to be surprised. I flashed a quick look at the lieutenant colonel but a curtain had dropped over his face. I could see, though, that there was no love lost between the two.

"Yes, sir," he said quickly. He turned and looked at the plane.

"How do you think she looks, Forrester?"

Forrester cleared his throat. "Interesting, sir," he said. He turned toward me. "Variable-pitch propellers?"

I nodded. He had good eyes to see that in this dim light. "Unusual concept," he said, "setting the wings where they are and sweeping them back. Should give her about four times the usual lift area."

"They do," I said. Thank God for at least one man who knew what it was all about.

"I asked how you thought she looks, Forrester?" the General repeated testily.

The curtain dropped down over Forrester's face again as he turned. "Very unusual, sir. Different."

The General nodded. "That's what I thought. Ugly. Like a toad sitting there."

I'd had about enough of his bullshit. "Does the General judge planes the same way he'd judge dames in a beauty contest?"

"Of course not!" the General snapped. "But there are certain conventions of design that are recognized as standard. For example, the new Curtiss fighter we looked at the other day. There's a plane that looks like a plane, not like a bomb with wings attached."

"That baby over there carries twice as much armor, plus a thousand pounds of bombs, seven hundred and fifty miles farther, five thousand feet higher and eighty miles an hour faster than the Curtiss fighter you're talking about!" I retorted.

"Curtiss builds good planes," the General said stiffly.

I stared at him. There wasn't any use in arguing. It was like talking to a stone wall. "I'm not saying they don't, General," I said. "Curtiss has been building good airplanes for many years. But I'm saying this one is better than anything around."

General Gaddis turned to Morrissey. "We're ready to see a demonstration of your plane," he said stiffly. "That is, if your pilot is through arguing."

Morrissey shot a nervous look at me. Apparently the General hadn't even caught my name. I nodded at him and turned back to the hangar.

"Roll her out!" I called to the mechanics, who were standing there waiting.

Morrissey, General Gaddis and his aides walked out. When I got outside I saw that Morrissey and the others had formed a group around the General but Forrester stood a little to one side, talking to a young woman. I shot a quick look at her. She was stuff, all right—wild eyes and sensuous mouth.

I followed the plane out onto the runway. Hearing footsteps behind me, I turned around. It was Morrissey. "You shouldn't have teed off on the General like that."

I grinned at him. "Probably did the old bastard good. He's got enough yes men around him to be a movie producer."

"All the same, it's tough selling him as it is. I found out Curtiss is bidding their planes in at a hundred and fifty thousand each and you know the best we can do is two twenty-five."

"So what?" I said. "It's the difference between chicken shit and chicken salad.

You can't buy a Cadillac for the same price as a Ford."

He stared at me for a moment, then he shrugged his shoulders. "It's your money, Jonas."

I watched him walk back to the General. He might be a great aeronautical engineer, but he was too anxious ever to become a good salesman. I turned to the mechanic. "Ready?"

"Ready when you are, Mr. Cord."

"O.K.," I said, starting to climb up to the cockpit. I felt a hand tugging at my leg. I looked down.

"Mind if I come along for the ride?" It was the lieutenant colonel.

"Not at all," I said. "Hop in."

"Thanks. By the way, I didn't get your name."

"Jonas Cord," I said.

"Roger Forrester," he answered, holding out his hand.

I should have guessed it the minute I heard his name, but I didn't tie it up until now. Roger Forrester—one of the original aces of the Lafayette Escadrille. Twenty-two German planes to his credit. He'd been one of my heroes when I was a kid.

"I've heard about you," I said.

His smile changed into a grin. "I've heard quite a bit about you."

We both laughed and I felt better. I pulled on his hand and he came up on the wing beside me. He looked into the cockpit, then back at me.

"No parachute?"

"Never use 'em," I said. "Make me nervous. Psychological. Indicates a lack of confidence."

He laughed.

"I can get one for you if you like."

He laughed again. "To hell with it."

About thirty miles out over the ocean, I put her through all the tricks in the book and then some only the CA-4 could do, and he didn't bat an eyelash.

For a clincher, I took her all the way up in a vertical climb until, at fourteen thousand feet, she hung in the sky like a fly dancing on the tip of a needle. Then I let her fall off on a dead stick into a tailspin that whipped the air-speed indicator up close to the five hundred mark. When we got down to about fifteen hundred feet, I took both hands off the stick and tapped him on the shoulder.

His head whipped around so fast it almost fell off his neck. I laughed. "She's all yours, Colonel!" I shouted.

We were down to twelve hundred feet by the time he turned around; eight hundred feet by the time he had the spin under control; six hundred feet before he had her in a straight dive; and four hundred feet before he could pull back on the stick.

I felt her shudder and tremble under me and a shrill scream came from her wings, like a dame getting her cherry copped. The G pinned me back in my seat, choking the air back into my throat and forcing the big bubbles right up into my eyes. Suddenly, the pressure lifted. We were less than twenty-five feet off the water when we started to climb.

Forrester looked back at me. "I haven't been this scared since I soloed back in fifteen," he yelled, grinning. "How did you know she wouldn't lose her wings in a dive like that?"

"Who knew?" I retorted. "But this was as good a time as any to find out!"

He laughed. I saw his hand reach forward and knock on the instrument panel. "What a plane. Like you said, she sure does fly!"

"Don't tell me. Tell that old coot back there."

A shadow fell across his face. "I'll try. But I don't know if I can do much good. It's all yours," he said, raising his hands. "You take her back in now."

I could see Morrissey and the soldiers standing on the field, watching us through field glasses as we came in. I put her into a wide turn and tapped Forrester on the shoulder. He looked back at me. "Ten bucks says I can take the General's hat off on the first pass."

He hesitated a moment, then grinned. "You're on!"

I came down at the field from about a thousand feet and leveled off about fifteen feet over the runway. I could see the startled expression on their faces as we rushed toward them, then I pulled back the stick. We went over their heads, into an almost vertical climb, catching them full blast in the prop wash.

I looked back just in time to see the captain running after the General's hat. I tapped Forrester's shoulder again. He turned to look back. He was laughing so hard there were tears in his eyes.

She set down as lightly as a pigeon coming home to its roost. I slid back the plastic canopy and we climbed down. I glanced at Forrester's face as we walked over to the group. All the laughter was gone from it now and the wary mask was back on.

The General had his hat on his head again. "Well, Forrester," he said stiffly. "What do you think?"

Forrester looked into his commanding officer's face. "Without a doubt, sir, this is the best fighter in the air today," he said in a flat, emotionless voice. "I'd suggest, sir, that you have a test group make an immediate check to substantiate my opinion."

"Hmm," the General said coldly. "You would, eh?"

"I would, sir," Forrester said quietly.

"There are other factors to be considered, Forrester. Do you have any idea of what these planes might cost?"

"No, sir," Forrester answered. "My only responsibility is to evaluate the performance of the plane itself."

"My responsibilities go much further than that," the General said. "You must remember that we're operating under a strict budget."

"Yes, sir."

"Please bear it in mind," General Gaddis said testily. "If I went off half-cocked over every idea you Air Corps men had, there wouldn't be money enough left to keep the Army running for a month."

Forrester's face flushed. "Yes, sir."

I glanced at him, wondering why he stood there and took it. It didn't make sense. Not with the reputation he had. He could step out of the Army and knock down twenty times what he was making with any airline in the country. He had a name as good as Rickenbacker's any day.

The General turned to Morrissey. "Now, Mr. Morrissey," he said in an almost jovial voice. "Whom do we talk to about getting a few facts and figures on the cost of this airplane?"

"You can talk with Mr. Cord, sir."

"Fine!" boomed the General. "Let's go into the office and call him."

"You don't have to do that, General," I said quickly. "We can talk right here."

The General stared at me, then his lips broke into what he thought was an expansive smile. "No offense intended, son. I didn't connect the names."

"That's all right, General."

"Your father and I are old friends," he said. "Back during the last war, I bought a lot of the hard stuff from him and if it's all right with you, I'd like to talk this over with him. Purely for old times' sake, you understand. Besides, this can turn out to be a mighty big deal and I'm sure your daddy would like to get in on it himself."

I felt my face go white. I had all I could do to control myself. How long did you have to live in a man's shadow? My voice sounded flat and strained even to my own ears. "I'm sure he would, General. But I'm afraid you'll have to talk to me; you can't talk to him."

"Why not?" The voice was suddenly cold.

"My father's been dead for ten years," I said, turning my back on him and walking toward the hangar.

CHAPTER TWO

I WALKED THROUGH TO THE SMALL ROOM IN THE BACK THAT MORRISSEY used as an office. I shut the door behind me and crossing to his desk, took out the bottle of bourbon that was always there for me. Pouring a shot into a paper cup, I tossed the whisky down my throat. It burned like hell. I looked down at my hands. They were trembling.

There are some people who won't stay dead. It doesn't make any difference what you do to them. You can bury them in the ground, dump them into the ocean or cremate them. But the memory of them will still turn your guts into mush just as if they were still alive.

I remembered what my father said to me one morning down at the corral in back of the house. It was a little while after his marriage to Rina and I'd come down one morning to watch Nevada break a new bronc. It was along about five o'clock and the first morning sun was just raising its head over the desert.

The bronc was a mean one, a wiry, nasty little black bastard that, every time it threw Nevada, went after him with slashing hoofs and teeth. The last time it threw him, it even tried to roll on him. Nevada scrambled out of the way and just did make it over the fence.

He stood there leaning against the fence and breathing heavily while the Mex boys chased the bronc. Their shrill whoops and yells split the morning air. "He's a crazy one," Nevada said.

"What're you going to do with him?" I asked curiously. It wasn't often I saw Nevada take three falls in a row.

The Mexicans had the horse now and Nevada watched them lead it back. "Try him once more," he answered thoughtfully. "An' if that doesn't work, turn him loose."

My father's voice came from behind us. "That's just what he wants you to do."

Nevada and I turned. My father was already dressed as if he was going straight to the plant. He was wearing his black suit and the tie was neatly centered in the thickly starched white collar of his shirt. "Why don't you put a clamp on his muzzle so he can't snap at you?"

Nevada looked at him. "Ain't nobody can git near enough to that hoss without losin' an arm."

"Nonsense!" my father said tersely. He took a short lariat from the pegs on the fence and ducking between the bars, stepped out into the corral. I could see his hands working the rope into a small halter as he walked toward the horse.

The bronc stood there pawing the ground, its eyes watching my father balefully. The Mexicans tightened their grip on the lariats around the horse's neck. The bronc reared back as my father brought the loop up to catch it around the muzzle. At the same time, it lashed out with its forefeet. Father just got out of the way in time.

He stood there for a moment, staring into the horse's eyes, then reached up again. The bronc shook its head wildly and slashed savagely at my father's arm. Again the hoofs lashed out, just missing Father.

The bronc was really wild now, twisting and turning as if there were a rider on it. The Mexicans leaned on their lariats to hold it still. After a moment, it was quiet and Father walked back to it.

"You ornery son of a bitch," my father said quietly. The bronc bared its teeth and snapped at him. Father seemed to move his arm just a fraction of an inch and the bronc's head flashed by his arm. "Let him go," my father yelled to the Mexicans.

The two boys looked at each other for a moment, then shrugging in that almost imperceptible manner they had to absolve themselves of responsibility, let up on their lariats.

Free of restraint, the bronc was motionless for a fraction of a second, bewildered. My father stood there in front of him, tall and broad in his black suit. Their eyes were about on a level. Then slowly my father started to bring his hand up again and the bronc exploded, its eyes flashing, its teeth bared, as it reared back and struck out with its hoofs. This time, my father stepped back and then darted as the bronc came down.

I saw my father's clenched fist hanging high in the air over his head for a flashing second. The bronc's four hoofs struck the ground and Father's fist came down like a hammer, just over the bronc's eyes. The thud of the blow echoed back against the side of the house like a small explosion. The bronc stood there for a moment, then sagged slowly to its knees, its front legs crumpling as if they had suddenly turned to rubber.

Quickly my father walked around to the side and slapped his open palm against the bronc's neck. The horse toppled over on its side. For a moment, it lay there, its sides heaving, then it raised its head and looked up at my father. The four of us—the Mexicans, Nevada and I—were silent as we stood there watching them.

The bronc's raised head threw a long morning shadow in the corral dirt that was dwarfed only by the shadow of my father as they stared into each other's eyes. Then the bronc seemed to heave a giant sigh and dropped its head back on the ground.

My father looked down at the bronc for a moment, then bent over and taking the reins near the bronc's mouth, pulled the horse to its feet. The bronc stood there, its legs trembling, its head hanging dejectedly. It didn't even raise its head as my father crossed in front of it and came back through the fence to us.

"You won't have any trouble with him now." My father hung the lariat back on the peg and started for the house. "Coming in for breakfast, Jonas?" he called without turning his head or breaking his stride.

Nevada was already back in the corral, walking toward the bronc. "Yes, sir," I said, starting after my father. I caught up to him on the back porch. We turned and watched Nevada mount the horse. The bronc bucked and sawed but it was easy to see his heart wasn't in it.

My father turned to me, unsmiling. "Some horses are like people. The only language they understand is a clout on the head."

"I didn't think you cared that much about the horses," I said. "You never come down to the corral."

"I don't," he said quickly. "It's you I care about. You've still got a lot to learn."

I laughed. "Fat lot I learned from your hitting a bronc on its head."

"You learned that Nevada couldn't ride that horse until I made it possible."

"So?"

My father turned. He was a big man, over six feet, but I was taller. "So," he said slowly, "no matter how big you get, you won't be big enough to wear my shoes until I let you."

I followed my father into the dining room. Rina's back was to me and her hair shone like silver as she raised her cheek for his morning kiss. There was a quiet triumph in my father's eyes as he straightened up afterward and looked at me. He didn't speak as he sat down in his chair. He didn't have to. I knew what he was thinking. He didn't have to hit me over the head.

"Joining us for breakfast, Jonas?" Rina asked politely.

I stared at her for a moment, then at my father. I could feel the sick knot tying up my guts. "No, thanks. I'm not hungry."

I turned and walked hurriedly back through the dining-room door, almost colliding with Robair, who was just entering with a tray. By the time I got back to the corral, Nevada was walking the bronc up and down, breaking him to the meaning of the reins. Father had been right. The horse wasn't giving Nevada any trouble.

And here it was twelve years later and I could still hear his voice as it had echoed quietly on the back porch that morning.

"Let go, old man, let go!" I said angrily, my fist smashing down on the empty desk. The pain ran crazily up my arm into my shoulder.

"Mr. Cord!" I looked up in surprise. Morrissey was standing in the open doorway, his mouth partly open. It took an effort for me to bring myself back to the present.

"Don't stand there," I snapped. "Come in." He entered the office hesitantly, and a moment later, Forrester appeared in the doorway behind him. Silently they came into the office.

"Sit down and have a drink," I said, pushing the bottle of bourbon toward them.

"Don't mind if I do," Forrester said, picking up the bottle and a paper cup. He sloshed himself a good one. "Mud in your eye."

"Up the General's," I said. "By the way, where is the old boy?"

"On his way back to the city. He has a date with a toilet-paper manufacturer."

I laughed. "At least, that's one thing he can test for himself."

Forrester laughed but Morrissey sat there glumly. I pushed the bottle toward him. "You on the wagon?"

He shook his head. "What are we going to do now?" he asked.

I stared at him for a moment, then picked up the bottle and refilled my paper cup. "I was just thinking about declaring war on the United States. That's one way we could show him how good our plane is."

Morrissey still didn't crack a smile. "The CA-4 is the best plane I ever designed."

"So what?" I asked. "What the hell, it didn't cost you anything. It was my dough. Besides, how much did you ever make out of building planes? It doesn't amount to one-twentieth of your annual royalties on that trick brassiere you designed for Rina Marlowe."

It was true. But it had been McAllister who'd seen the commercial potential in the damn thing and applied for a patent in the name of Cord Aircraft. Morrissey had a standard employment contract, which provided that all his inventions and designs belonged to the company, but McAllister had been a sport about it. He'd given Morrissey a ten-per-cent interest in the royalties as a bonus and last year, Morrissey's share was in excess of a hundred thousand dollars. The market was getting bigger all the time. Tits weren't going out of fashion for a long time.

Morrissey didn't answer. But then, I hadn't expected him to. He was one of those guys who don't give a damn about money. All he lived for was his work.

I finished my drink and lit a cigarette. Silently I cursed myself. I should have known better than to let a chance remark about my father bug me like that. I could afford it but nobody likes to throw a million dollars down the drain.

"Maybe I can do something," Forrester said.

A ray of hope came into Morrissey's eyes. "Do you think you could?"

Forrester shrugged. "I don't know," he said slowly. "I said maybe."

I stared at him. "What do you mean?"

"It's the best plane I've seen," he said. "I wouldn't like to see us lose it because of the old man's stupidity."

"Thanks," I said. "We'd be grateful for anything you could do."

Forrester smiled. "You don't owe me anything. I'm one of those old-fashioned guys who wouldn't like to see us caught short if things suddenly started popping."

I nodded. "They'll start soon enough. Just as soon as Hitler thinks he's ready."

"When do you think that will be?"

"Three, maybe four years," I said. "When they have enough trained pilots and planes."

"Where'll he get them from? He hasn't got them now."

"He'll get them," I said. "The glider schools are turning out ten thousand pilots a month and before the summer is over, Messerschmitt will have his ME-109's on the production line."

"The general staff thinks he won't do much when he comes up against the Maginot line."

"He won't come up against it," I said. "He'll fly over it."

Forrester nodded. "All the more reason for me to try to get them to check out your plane." He looked at me quizzically. "You talk like you know."

"I know," I answered. "I was there less than nine months ago."

"Oh, yes," he said, "I remember. I saw something about it in the papers. There was some kind of a stink about it, wasn't there?"

I laughed. "There was. Certain people accused me of being a Nazi sympathizer."

"Because of the million dollars you turned over to the Reichsbank?"

I shot a quick glance at him. Forrester wasn't as simple as he pretended to be. "I guess so," I answered. "You see, I transferred the money just the day before Roosevelt slapped on his restriction."

"You knew the restriction was about to be placed, didn't you? You could have saved yourself the money by just waiting one day."

"I couldn't afford to wait," I said. "The money had to be in Germany, that was all there was to it."

"Why? Why did you send them the money when obviously you realize they're our potential enemy?"

"It was ransom for a Jew," I said.

"Some of my best friends are Jews," Forrester answered. "But I can't imagine shelling out a million dollars for one of them."

I stared at him for a moment, then refilled my paper cup. "This one was worth it."

His name was Otto Strassmer and he started out in life as a quality-control engineer in one of the many Bavarian china works. From ceramics he had turned to plastics and it was he who had invented the high-speed injection mold I'd bought and sold to a combine of American manufacturers. Our original deal had been on a royalty basis but after it had been in effect for several years Strassmer wanted to change it. That was in 1933, shortly after Hitler came to power.

He'd come into my hotel room in Berlin, where I'd been on my annual visit to Europe, and explained what he wanted. He was willing to relinquish all future share in royalties for a flat payment of one million dollars, to be held in escrow for him in the United States. This was agreeable to me, of course. His share of the royalties would amount to much more than that over the licensing period. But I didn't understand why. So I asked him.

He got up out of his chair and walked over to the window. "You ask me why, Herr Cord?" he asked in his peculiarly accented English. His hand pointed out the window. "That's why."

I walked over to the window and looked down. There in the street in front of the Adlon, a group of brown-shirted young men, scarcely more than boys, were tormenting an old frock-coated man. Twice while we were watching, they knocked the old man into the gutter. We could see him lying on the edge of the sidewalk, his head in the gutter, blood streaming from his nose. The boys stood there for a moment watching him, then walked away after kicking him several times contemptuously.

I turned to Strassmer questioningly.

"That was a Jew, Herr Cord," he said quietly.

"So what? Why didn't he call the police?"

Strassmer pointed across the street. Two policemen stood on the opposite corner. "They saw everything that happened."

"Why didn't they stop them?"

"They are under instructions not to," he answered. "Hitler claims that Jews have no right under German law."

"What has this got to do with you?"

"I am a Jew," he said simply.

I was silent for a moment. I took out a cigarette and lit it. "What do you want me to do with the money?"

"Keep it until you hear from me." He smiled. "My wife and daughter are already in America. I would be grateful if you'd let them know I'm all right."

"Why don't you join them?" I asked.

"Perhaps I will—in time. But I am German," he said. "And I still hope this madness will one day pass."

But Herr Strassmer's hopes were not to be realized. This I found out less than a year later, as I sat in the office of the Reichsmarschall. "The Jews of the world are doomed, as are the Jews of Germany," he said in his polite voice. "We of the New Order recognize this and welcome our friends and allies from across the sea who wish to join our crusade."

I was silent, waiting for him to speak again.

"We men of the air understand each other," he said.

I nodded. "Yes, Excellency."

"Good," he said, smiling. "Then we do not have to waste time." He threw some papers on the desk. "Under the new laws, the Reich has confiscated the properties of a certain Otto Strassmer. We understand there are certain monies due him which you are hereby instructed to pay over into the Reichsbank."

I didn't like the word "instructed." "I have been trying to get in touch with Herr Strassmer," I said.

Göring smiled again. "Strassmer had a severe breakdown and is presently confined to a hospital."

"I see," I said. I got to my feet.

"The Third Reich will not forget its friends," the Reichsmarschall said. He pressed a button on his desk.

A young German lieutenant appeared in the doorway. "Heil Hitler!" he said, his arm upraised in the Nazi salute.

"Heil Hitler!" Göring replied negligently. He turned to me. "Lieutenant Mueller will escort you to the Messerschmitt plant. I look forward to seeing you again at dinner, Herr Cord."

The Messerschmitt plant opened my eyes. There was nothing like it building airplanes in the United States. The only things comparable were the automobile production lines in Detroit. And when I saw some of the sketches of the ME-109 that adorned Messerschmitt's office, I didn't have to look twice. It was all over but the shouting unless we got up off our collective asses.

That night at dinner, the Reichsmarschall got me in a corner. "What did you think of our factory?"

"I'm impressed," I said.

He nodded, pleased. "It is modeled after your own plant in California," he said. "But much larger, of course."

"Of course," I agreed, wondering how they got in there. Then I realized it was no secret. Up to now, we'd never got any government work; all we'd built were commercial airlines.

He laughed pleasantly, then turned to move away. A moment later, he came back to me. "By the way," he whispered. "The Führer was very pleased about your co-operation. When may I inform him that we will receive the money?"

I stared at him. "On the day Herr Strassmer walks into my office in New York."

He stared back in surprise. "The Führer won't like this," he said. "I told him you were our friend."

"I'm also Herr Strassmer's friend."

He stared at me for another moment, "Now I don't know what to tell the Führer. He will be very disappointed when he learns we shall not receive the money."

"In that case," I said, "why disappoint him? One Jew more or less can't matter to Germany."

He nodded slowly. "Perhaps that is the best way."

Exactly a month later, the little German engineer walked into my office in New York.

"What are you going to do now ?" I asked.

"First, I'm going to join my family in Colorado and rest for a while," he said. "Then I must look for work. I'm no longer a rich man."

I smiled at him. "Come to work for me. I'll consider the million dollars an advance against your royalties."

When he left the office, I gave Morrissey the O.K. to go ahead on the CA-4. If my hunch was right, there wasn't enough time left for any of us. But it was another story to make the U.S. Army believe that.

I looked across the desk at Forrester.

"I'll get back to town and make a few calls to Washington. I still have a few friends down there," he said. "I'll stop by and talk to the General. Maybe I can persuade him to listen."

"Good," I said. I looked at my watch. It was almost twelve thirty. The stockholders' meeting ought to be over by now. McAllister and Pierce should be back in the hotel with Norman tucked safely away in their back pockets.

"I have a one-o'clock appointment at the Waldorf," I said. "Can I drop you off?"

"Thanks," Forrester said gratefully. "I have a luncheon date that I'd hate to miss."

He came into the Waldorf with me and cut off toward Peacock Alley as I walked over to the elevators. As I stood there waiting, I saw a woman rise to meet him. It was the same one I had seen him with out at the field. I wondered vaguely why she hadn't waited for him out there.

Idly I watched Rico, the maître d', lead them around the corner to a hidden table. I walked over to the entrance and stood there until he came back.

"Ah, Monsieur Cord." He smiled. "Dining alone?"

"Not dining, Rico," I said, pressing a bill into his ever ready hand. "A question. The lady with Colonel Forrester—who is she?"

Rico smiled knowingly. He kissed his fingers. "Ah, most *charmante*," he said. "She is Madame Gaddis, the wife of the General."

I looked around the lobby as I walked back to the elevators. The General should be somewhere around. From what I had seen of his attitude toward Forrester, I figured there had to be more than just Army and airplanes between them.

I spotted him as he crossed the lobby to the men's room next to the nearest bank of elevators. He was scowling and his face was flushed. He looked like a man who needed more relief than he could find where he was going.

I waited until the door swung shut behind him before I walked over to the elevators. For the first time since I'd landed the CA-4 at Roosevelt Field, I began to feel better. Everything was falling into place now.

I wasn't worried any more. The only problem that remained was how many planes the Army would buy.

CHAPTER THREE

WHAT I WANTED MOST WAS TO GRAB A SHOWER AND TAKE A NAP. I hadn't got to sleep until five o'clock that morning. I dropped my clothes on a chair and walked into the stall shower, turning on the needle spray. I could feel the tightness leave my muscles under the soothing warmth. The telephone rang several times while I was in the shower. I let it ring.

When I came out, I picked up the phone and told the operator I didn't want any calls put through until four o'clock.

"But Mr. McAllister told me to call him the moment you come in," she wailed. "He said it was very important."

"You can get him for me at four o'clock," I said. I put down the phone, dropped on the bed and went to sleep like a baby.

The ring of the telephone woke me. I looked at my wrist watch as I reached for the receiver. It was exactly four o'clock.

It was Mac. "I've been trying to get you all afternoon," he said. "Where the hell have you been?"

"Sleeping."

"Sleeping!" he shouted. "We have a board meeting over at the Norman offices. We're due there right now."

"You never told me."

"How in hell could I, when you wouldn't answer your phone?"

"Get General Gaddis for me," I told the operator. "I think he's registered here."

I lit a cigarette while I waited. The receiver crackled in my ear. "General Gaddis speaking."

"General, Jonas Cord here," I said. "I'm in my apartment. Thirty-one fifteen in the Towers. I'd like to talk with you."

The General's voice was cold. "We have nothing to discuss. You're an unconscionably rude young man—"

"It's not my manners I want to discuss, General," I interrupted. "It's your wife."

I heard him sputter through the telephone. "My wife? What's she got to do with our business?"

"A great deal, I believe, General," I said. "We both know whom she met in Peacock Alley today at one o'clock. I can't believe that the War Department would look favorably at a personal animosity being the basis for rejecting the CA-4."

There was a silence over the telephone.

"By the way, General," I asked, "what do you drink?"

"Scotch," he answered automatically.

"Good, I'll have a bottle here, waiting for you. Shall we say in about fifteen minutes?"

I hung up before he could answer and called room service. While I was waiting for an answer, a knock came at the outer door. "Come in," I yelled.

From the bed, I saw Mac and Dan Pierce enter. When they came into the bedroom, Mac's face wore its usual worried look but Dan's was wreathed in smiles. He was on the verge of getting everything he ever wanted.

Room service finally came on. In the background, I could hear the clatter of dishes and suddenly I was hungry. I hadn't eaten since breakfast. I ordered three steak sandwiches, a bottle of milk, a pot of black coffee, a bottle of Scotch, two bottles of bourbon and a double order of French fries. I put down the telephone and looked up at them. "Well, how'd it go?"

"Bernie squealed like a stuck pig." Pierce grinned. "But we had him by the short hairs and he knew it."

"What about his stock?"

"I don't know, Jonas," Mac said. "He wouldn't talk to Dan."

"I spoke to Dave Woolf, though," Dan said quickly. "I told him to get the old man in a selling mood or we'd throw the company into bankruptcy."

"You got the Section Seven Twenty-two ready?" I asked Mac. He knew what I was talking about—a petition to appoint a receiver in bankruptcy.

"In my brief case. Before the meeting this morning, I had a brief discussion with our attorneys here. They feel they could swing a favorable appointment as receiver."

I stared at him. "You don't sound happy about it."

"I'm not," he said. "Norman's a crafty old man. I don't think you'll bluff him that easily. He knows you stand to lose as much as anyone if you bankrupt the company."

"He's a real greedy old bastard, too. And he won't take the chance of losing what he's got just for the satisfaction of keeping me company."

"I hope you're right."

"We'll find out soon enough." I turned to Dan. "Have you been able to reach Rina yet?"

He shook his head. "I've tried all over. No luck. There's no answer at her home. The studio doesn't know where she is. I even had a contact try Louella but she doesn't know."

"Keep trying," I said. "We've got to find her. I want her to read that script."

"I do, too," Dan said. "She's the only thing holding us up, now I've got the De Mille thing squared away with Paramount."

"Paramount O.K. it?"

"This morning," he said. "I've got the wire from Zukor in my pocket."

"Good," I said. This would be the biggest picture ever made and right up De Mille's alley. We were going to shoot it in a new process called Technicolor and it would cost over six million bucks. It was the story of Mary Magdalene and we were going to call it *The Sinner*.

"Aren't you getting a little ahead of yourselves?" McAllister asked. "What if she doesn't want to do it?"

"She'll do it," I said. "What the hell do you think I want the Norman company for? Their contract with her is the only asset they've got."

"But her contract gives her script approval."

"She'll approve it," I said. She had to. I had the damn thing written especially for her.

When room service came, I swung my feet over the side of the bed and had the waiter set the table right up in front of me. I hadn't realized how hungry I was. I'd already eaten one of the steak sandwiches and drunk half the bottle of milk before the waiter got out the door.

I was in the middle of my second sandwich when the General showed. Dan brought him into the bedroom and I introduced them, then asked them to excuse us.

"Sit down, General," I said when the door closed. "And pour yourself a drink. The bottle of Scotch is on the table."

"No, thanks," the General said tightly, still standing.

I shrugged my shoulders and picked up the third sandwich. I came right to the point. "What's it worth to you if I get Forrester to leave the Army?"

"What makes you think I want that?"

I swallowed a mouthful of sandwich. "Let's not horse around, General. I'm a big boy now and I got eyes. All I want is a fair test for the CA-4. From there on out, it's up to you. There are no other strings attached."

"What makes you think I won't give your plane a fair test now?"

I smiled at him. "And build Forrester up even more in your wife's eyes?"

I could see the tightness leave him. For a moment, I almost felt sorry for him. The brigadier's star on his shoulder meant nothing. He was just another old man trying to hold a young dame. I felt like telling him to stop knocking himself out. If it wasn't Forrester, it would be some other guy.

"I think I'll take that drink now."

"Help yourself," I said.

He opened the bottle and poured himself a straight shot. He drank it and sank into the chair opposite me. "My wife's not a bad girl, Mr. Cord," he said half apologetically. "It's just that she's young—and impressionable."

He wasn't fooling me. I wondered whether he was fooling himself. "I understand, General," I said.

"You know how it is with young girls," he continued. "They see only the glamour, the excitement in a uniform. A man like Forrester—well, it's easy enough to understand. The silver wings on his blouse, the D.F.C. and *Croix de guerre.*"

I nodded silently as I poured myself a cup of black coffee.

"I suppose that was the kind of soldier she thought I was when we were married," he said reflectively. "But it wasn't long before she found out I was nothing but a kind of glorified purchasing agent."

He refilled his glass and looked at me. "Today's Army is a complex machine, Mr. Cord. For every man in the front line, there have to be five or six men behind the lines just to keep him supplied. I always took pride in myself because I took care to see that that man got the best."

"I'm sure of that, General," I said, putting down my coffee cup.

He got to his feet and looked down at me. Maybe it was my imagination, but as he spoke, he seemed to grow taller and straighter. "That was why I came up to talk with you, Mr. Cord," he said with quiet dignity. "Not because you chose to bring my wife into an extraneous matter but to tell you that a test group will be at Roosevelt Field tomorrow morning to check out your airplane. I requested it this morning as soon as I got back into the city. I phoned your Mr. Morrissey but I guess he couldn't reach you."

I looked up at him with surprise. A feeling of shame began to run through me. I should have had brains enough to call Morrissey on my own before I shot off my big mouth.

A faint smile flitted across the General's face. "So you see, Mr. Cord," he said, "you don't have to make any deals with Forrester on my account. If your plane checks out, the Army will buy it."

The door closed behind him and I reached for a cigarette. I leaned back against the headboard of the bed and dragged the smoke deep into my lungs.

The telephone operator at the Chatham found Forrester in the bar. "Jonas Cord," I said. "I'm in the Waldorf Towers down the street. I'd like to talk with you."

"I'd like to talk with you, too," he said. "They're testing your plane in the morning."

"I know. That's what I want to talk to you about."

He was in my apartment in less than ten minutes. His face was flushed and he looked as if he'd spent the whole afternoon wrapping himself around a bottle. "Looks like the old man saw the light," he said.

"That what you really think?" I asked, as he poured himself a drink.

"You can say what you like about him, but Gaddis is a good soldier. He does his job."

"Pour a drink for me," I said.

He picked up another glass and held it toward me. I took it. "I think it's about time you quit playing soldier."

He stared at me. "What have you got in mind?"

"I think that Cord Aircraft is going to be doing a lot of business with the Army from now on," I said. "And I need someone who knows the ropes—the men, what they want in a plane. Make friends for us, contacts. You know what I mean."

"I know what you mean," he said. "Like not seeing Virginia Gaddis any more because it wouldn't look good for the company."

"Something like that," I said quietly.

He threw his drink down his throat. "I don't know whether I'd be any good at it. I've been in the Air Corps ever since I was a kid."

"You never know until you try it," I said. "Besides, you'll do the Air Corps more good out of it than in. There'll be nobody to stop you if you want to try out some of your ideas."

He looked at me. "Speaking of ideas," he asked, "whose was this—yours or Gaddis's?"

"Mine," I said. "I had my mind made up this morning after our little talk in Morrissey's office. And it had nothing to do with whether or not they took the CA-4."

He grinned suddenly. "My mind was made up this morning, too," he said. "I was going to take the job if you offered it to me."

"Where would you like to start?" I asked.

"At the top," he said promptly. "The Army respects nothing but the top man."

"Good enough," I said. It made sense. "You're the new president of Cord Aircraft. How much do you want?"

"You let me pick the job," he said. "I'll let you name the salary."

"Twenty-five thousand a year and expenses."

He whistled. "You don't have to go that high. That's four times what I'm getting now."

"Just remember that when you come asking for a raise," I said.

We both laughed and drank to it. "There's a few changes on the plane I wanted to talk to you about before the test tomorrow," he said.

Just then, McAllister came into the bedroom. "It's almost six o'clock, Jonas," he said. "How long do you think we can keep them waiting? Dan just spoke to David Woolf. He says Norman is threatening to walk out."

"I'll be with you as soon as I get my pants on." The telephone rang while I was buttoning my shirt. "Get it for me, will you?"

"What about the changes?" Forrester asked, while Mac was picking up the phone.

"Get out to the field and work them out with Morrissey."

"It's Los Angeles," McAllister said, covering the mouthpiece with his hand. "We haven't much time."

I looked at him for a moment. "Tell them I just left for a meeting. That they can reach me at the Norman offices in about two hours."

CHAPTER FOUR

IT WAS JUST STARTING TO TURN COOL AND THE GIRLS WERE COMING OUT OF their apartments along Park Avenue, dressed in their summer clothes, their fur stoles draped casually over their shoulders.

Over on Sixth Avenue, the girls were coming out, too. But these girls weren't getting into cabs; they were hurrying toward the subways and disappearing into those gaping maws, glad to be done with their day's work.

New York had a curious twisted form of vitality that belied the general air of depression that hung over the country. Building was going on here despite the moans and groans of Wall Street—office buildings and expensive apartments. If all the money was supposed to be gone, how come so many expensive whores were still living in the best places? It wasn't gone. It had just gone into hiding, burrowing into the ground like a mole, only to emerge when risks were less and profits greater.

On Sixth Avenue, the signs hung dejectedly in front of the employment agencies. The blackboards with their white chalk job listings were already beginning to look tired, and the two-dollar chippies were already beginning their dark sky patrol.

One of them, standing on the fringe of the crowd, turned to look at me as I came by. Her eyes were large and tired and weary and wise. I caught her whisper from almost motionless lips. "You'll be the first today, honey. How about starting the day right?"

I grinned at her and she took it for a sign of encouragement. She came toward me. "Just a deuce," she whispered quickly, "and I'll teach you things you never learned in school."

I stopped, still smiling. "I'll bet you would."

Mac and Dan had walked a few steps farther on. Mac turned back to me, an annoyed look on his face. The woman flashed a quick glance at them, then back at me. "Tell your friends I'll make a special price for all of you. Five bucks."

I dug into my pocket and came up with a dollar, which I pressed into her hand. "Some other time. But I don't think my teachers would approve."

She looked down at the dollar. A glint of humor came into her dark, tired eyes. "It's guys like you spoil a girl and make it tough for her to go to work."

She ducked into a cafeteria across the street as we turned into the lobby of the new RCA Building in Rockefeller Center.

I was still smiling when we walked into the board room. Norman sat at the head of the long table, David Woolf on his right and a man whom I had met at the studio—Ernest Hawley, the treasurer—on his left. Down the table sat our nominees, the two brokerage men, a banker and an accountant.

Dan and Mac took seats on opposite sides of the table, leaving the seat at the end open for me. I started to sit down.

Bernie got to his feet. "Just a minute, Cord," he said. "This meeting is for directors only." He glowered at me. "Before I'd sit at the same table with you, I'd leave myself."

I pulled a package of cigarettes from my pocket and lit one. "Then leave," I said quietly. "You won't have anything to do around here after this meeting anyway."

"Gentlemen, gentlemen," McAllister said quickly. "This is no way to conduct an important meeting. We have many grave problems concerning the future of this company to consider. We'll settle none of them in an atmosphere of distrust."

"Distrust!" Bernie yelled. "You expect me to trust him? After the way he stole my company from me behind my own back!"

"The stock was for sale on the open market and I bought it."

"At what price?" he shouted. "First he forces down the market, then he buys up the stock. Below value he gets it. He don't care how bad he makes the company look while he's doing it. Then he comes to me and expects me to sell my stock at the same depressed price he paid the others."

I smiled to myself. The trading was on. The old man figured the best way to get what he wanted was by attacking me. Already, the propriety of my presence at the meeting had been forgotten. "The price I offered was twice what I paid on the open market."

"You made the market."

"I wasn't running the company," I retorted. "You were—and for the last six years, running it at a loss."

He strode around the table. "And you could do better?"

"If I didn't think so, I wouldn't be putting up better than seven million dollars."

His eyes stared into mine angrily for a moment, then he walked back to his chair and sat down. He picked up a pencil and tapped it on the table in front of him. "The regular meeting of the board of directors of the Norman Picture Company, Incorporated, is hereby called to order," he said in a quieter tone of voice. He looked over at his nephew. "David, you will act as secretary until we appoint a new one."

The old man continued. "A quorum is present, and also present by invitation is Mr. Jonas Cord. Make a note of that, David. Mr. Cord is present by invitation of certain of the directors but over the objection of the President."

He stared at me, waiting for me to react to his statement. I sat there impassively.

"We will now proceed to the first order of business, which is the election of officers of the company for the coming year."

I nodded to McAllister. "Mr. President," he said, "may I suggest that we postpone the election of officers until after you and Mr. Cord have completed discussions regarding the sale of your stock?"

"What makes you think I'm interested in selling my stock?" Bernie asked. "My faith in the future of this company remains as strong as ever. I've made plans to insure the successful operation of this company and if you fellows think you can stop me, I'll throw you into a proxy fight like you never saw before."

Even McAllister had to smile at that. What would he fight with? We were voting forty-one per cent of the stock already. "If the President's concern for the future of this company were as sincere as ours," McAllister said politely, "surely he would see the damage that could be done by starting a proxy fight he couldn't possibly win."

A look of cunning came over Bernie's face. "I'm not such a fool as you think," he said. "I've been busy all afternoon. I got pledges from enough stockholders to give me control if I fight. I should live so long as to give up my own company— the company that I built with the sweat of my brow—to Cord so he can donate more money to his friends the Nazis." He slammed his fist dramatically down on the table. "No, not even if he gave me seven million dollars for my stock alone."

I got to my feet, tight-lipped and angry. "I'd like to ask Mr. Norman what he would do with the seven million dollars if I did give it to him. Would he donate it to the Jewish Relief Fund?"

"It's no business of Mr. Cord's what I do with my money," he shouted down the table at me. "I'm not a rich man like he is. All I got is a few shares of my own company."

I smiled. "Mr. Norman, would you like me to read to the board a list of your liquid assets and holdings, both in your name and your wife's?"

Bernie looked confused. "List?" he asked. "What list?"

I looked at McAllister. He handed me a sheet of paper from his brief case. I began to read from it. "Deposits in the name of May Norman: Security National Bank, Boston—one million, four hundred thousand; Bank of Manhattan Company, New York—two million, one hundred thousand; Pioneer National Trust Company, Los Angeles—seven hundred thousand; Lehman Brothers, New York—three million, one hundred and fifty thousand; plus other minor accounts throughout the country amounting to six or seven hundred thousand more. In addition to that, Mrs. Norman owns one thousand acres of prime real estate in Westwood, near Beverly Hills, conservatively valued at two thousand dollars an acre."

Bernie stared at me. "Where did you get that list?"

"Never mind where I got it."

The old man turned to his nephew. "See, David," he said in a loud voice, "see what a good wife can save from her house money."

If he wasn't such a thief, I'd have laughed. But a look at his nephew's face showed that the boy hadn't known about those particular assets. Something told me David was in for further disillusionment.

The old man turned back to me. "So my wife put away a few dollars. That gives you the right to rob me?"

"During the past six years, while your company was losing about eleven million dollars, it seems strange to me that your wife should be depositing about a million dollars a year in her various accounts."

Bernie's face was flushed. "My wife is very clever with her investments," he said. "I don't spend my time looking over her shoulder."

"Maybe you should," I said. "You'd find out she has deals with practically every major supplier of equipment and services to the Norman Company. You can't tell me you're not aware that she takes a salesman's commission of from five to fifteen per cent on the gross purchases made by this company."

He sank back into his chair. "So what's wrong with that? It's perfectly normal business practice. She's our salesman on such sales, so why shouldn't she collect a commission?"

I'd had enough of his crap. "All right, Mr. Norman," I said. "Let's stop fooling around. I offered you a better than fair price for your stock. Do you want to sell it or don't you?"

"Not for three and a half million dollars, no. Five and I might listen."

"You're in no position to bargain, Mr. Norman," I said. "If you don't accept my offer, I'll put this company into receivership. Then we'll see if a Federal referee finds anything criminal in your wife's so-called legitimate transactions. You seem to have forgotten that what you do with the company is a Federal matter, since you sold stock on the open market. It's a little different than when you owned it all yourself. You might even wind up in jail."

"You wouldn't dare."

"No?" I said. I held out my hand. McAllister gave me the Section 722 papers. I threw them over to Bernie. "It's up to you. If you don't sell, these papers will be in court tomorrow morning."

He looked down at the papers, then back at me. There was a cold hatred in his eyes. "Why do you do this to me?" he cried. "Is it because you hate Jews so much, when all I tried to do was help you?"

That did it. I went around the table, pulled him out of his chair and backed him up against the wall. "Look, you little Jew bastard," I shouted. "I've had enough of your bullshit. Every time you offered to help me, you picked my pocket. What's bugging you now is I won't let you do it again."

"Nazi!" he spat at me.

Slowly I let him down and turned to McAllister. "File the papers," I said. "And also bring a criminal suit against Norman and his wife for stealing from the company."

I started for the door.

"Just a minute!" Bernie's voice stopped me. There was a peculiar smile on his face. "There's no need for you to go away mad just because I got a little excited."

I stared at him.

"Come back," he said, sitting down at the table again. "We can settle this whole matter between us in a few minutes. Like gentlemen."

❖ ❖ ❖

I stood near the window, watching Bernie sign the stock transfers. There was something incongruous about the way he sat there, the pen scratching across the paper as he signed away his life's work. You don't have to like a guy to feel sorry for him. And in a way that was just how I felt.

He was a selfish, despicable old man. He had no sense of decency, no honor or ethics, he'd sacrifice anyone on the altar of his power, but as the pen moved across each certificate, I had the feeling his life's blood was running out of the golden nib along with the ink.

I turned and looked out the window, thirty stories down into the street. Down there the people were tiny, they had little dreams, minute plans. The next day was Saturday. Their day off. Maybe they'd go to the beach, or the park. If they had the money, perhaps they'd take a drive out into the country. They'd sit on the grass next to their wives and watch the kids having themselves a time feeling the fresh, cool earth under their feet. They were lucky.

They didn't live in a jungle that measured their worth by their ability to live with the wolves. They weren't born to a father who couldn't love his son unless he was cast in his own image. They weren't surrounded by people whose only thought was to align themselves with the source of wealth. When they loved, it was because of how they felt, not because of how much they might benefit.

I felt a sour taste come up into my mouth. That was the way it might be down there but I really didn't know. And I wasn't particularly anxious to find out. I liked it up here.

It was like being in the sky with no one around to tell you what you could do or couldn't do. In my world, you made up your own rules. And everybody had to live by them whether they liked it or not. As long as you were on top. I meant to stay on top a long time. Long enough so that when people spoke my name, they knew whose name they spoke. Mine, not my father's.

I turned from the window and walked back to the table. I picked up the certificates and looked at them. They were signed correctly. Bernard B. Norman.

Bernie looked up at me. He attempted a smile. It wasn't very successful. "Years ago, when Bernie Normanovitz opened his first nickelodeon on Fourth Street on the East Side, nobody thought he'd someday sell his company for three and a half million dollars."

Suddenly, I didn't care any more. I no longer felt sorry for him. He had raped and looted a company of more than fifteen million dollars and his only excuse was that he had happened to start it.

"I imagine you'll want this, too," he said, reaching into his inside jacket pocket and taking out a folded sheet of paper.

I took it from him and opened it. It was his letter of resignation as president and chairman of the board. I looked at him in surprise.

"Now, is there anything else I can do for you?"

"No," I said.

"You're wrong, Mr. Cord," he said softly. He crossed to the telephone on the table in the corner. "Operator, this is Mr. Norman. You can put that call for Mr. Cord through now."

He held the phone toward me. "For you," he said expressionlessly. I took the telephone and heard the operator's voice. "I have Mr. Cord on the line now, Los Angeles."

There was a click, then another, as the call went through on the other end. I saw Bernie look at me shrewdly, then walk toward the door. He turned and looked at his nephew. "Coming, David?"

Woolf started to get out of his chair.

"You," I said, covering the mouthpiece with my hand. "Stay."

David looked at Bernie, then shook his head slightly and sank back into his chair. The old man shrugged his shoulders. "Why should I expect any more from my own flesh and blood?" he said. The door closed behind him.

A woman's voice came on in my ear. There was something vaguely familiar about it. "Jonas Cord?"

"Speaking. Who's this?"

"Ilene Gaillard. I've been trying to locate you all afternoon. Rina—Rina—" Her voice broke.

I felt an ominous chill tighten around my heart. "Yes, Miss Gaillard," I asked, "what about Rina?"

"She's dying, Mr. Cord," she sobbed into the telephone. "And she wants to see you."

"Dying?" I repeated. I couldn't believe it. Not Rina. She was indestructible.

"Yes, Mr. Cord. Encephalitis. And you'd better hurry. The doctors don't know how long she can last. She's at the Colton Sanitarium in Santa Monica. Can I tell her you're coming?"

"Tell her I'm on my way!" I said, putting down the phone.

I turned to look at David Woolf. He was watching me with a strange expression on his face. "You knew," I said.

He nodded, getting to his feet. "I knew."

"Why didn't you tell me?"

"How could I?" he asked. "My uncle was afraid if you found out, you wouldn't want his stock."

A strange silence came into the room as I picked up the telephone again. I gave the operator Morrissey's number at Roosevelt Field.

"Do you want me to leave now?" Woolf asked.

I shook my head. I had been neatly suckered into buying a worthless company, shorn like a baby lamb, but I had no right to complain. I'd known all the rules.

But now even that didn't matter. Nothing mattered. The only thing that did was Rina. I swore impatiently, waiting for Morrissey to pick up the phone.

The only chance I had of getting to Rina in time was to fly out there in the CA-4.

CHAPTER FIVE

T HE BRIGHTLY LIT HANGAR WAS A FRENZY OF ACTIVITY. THE WELDERS were up on the wings, their masks down, their torches burning with a hot blue flame as they fused the reserve fuel tanks to the wings. The pile of junk beside the plane was growing as the mechanics stripped her of everything that added weight and yet was not absolutely essential to flight.

I checked my watch as Morrissey came toward me. It was almost twelve o'clock. That made it near nine in California. "How long now?" I asked.

"Not too long." He looked down at the sheet of paper in his hand. "With everything stripped off her, we're still fourteen hundred pounds over lift capacity."

The Midwest was completely locked in by storms, according to our weather checks. If I wanted to get through, I'd have to fly south around them. Morrissey had figured we'd need forty-three per cent more fuel just for the flight itself and at least seven per cent more for a safety margin.

"Why don't you hold off until morning?" Morrissey asked. "Maybe the weather will lift and you can go straight through."

"No."

"For Christ's sake," he snapped. "You'll never even get her off the ground. If you're that anxious to get yourself killed, why don't you use a gun!"

I turned and looked over at the pile of junk beside the plane. "How much does the radio weigh?"

"Five hundred and ten pounds," he answered quickly. Then he stared at me. "You can't dump that! How the hell will you know where you are or what the weather is like up ahead?"

"Same way I did before they put radios in planes. Dump it!"

He started to walk back to the plane, shaking his head. I had another idea. "The oxygen-pressure system for the cockpit?"

"Six hundred and seventy pounds, including the tanks."

"Dump that, too," I said. "I'll fly low."

"You'll need oxygen to get over the Rockies."

"Put a portable tank in the cockpit next to me."

I went into the office and called Buzz Dalton at the Inter-Continental office in Los Angeles. He'd already left so they transferred the call to his home. "Buzz, this is Jonas."

"I was wondering when I'd hear from you."

"I want you to do me a favor."

"Sure," he said quickly. "What?"

"I'm flying out to the Coast tonight," I said. "And I want you to have weather signals up for me at every ICA hangar across the country."

"What's the matter with your radio?"

"I'm taking the CA-4 out nonstop. And I can't drag the weight."

He whistled. "You'll never make it, buddy boy."

"I'll make it," I said. "Use the searchlight blinkers at night, paint the rooftops during the day."

"Will do," he said. "What's your flight pattern?"

"I haven't decided the pattern yet. Just have all the fields covered."

"Will do," he said. "Good luck."

I put down the telephone. That's what I liked about Buzz. He was dependable. He didn't waste time with foolish questions like why, when or where. He did as he was told. The only thing he cared about was the airline. That was why ICA was rapidly becoming the largest commercial airline in the country.

I took the bottle of bourbon out of the desk and took a long pull off it. Then I went over to the couch and stretched out. My legs hung over the edge but I didn't care. I could grab a little rest while the mechanics were finishing up. I closed my eyes.

I sensed Morrissey standing near me and opened my eyes. "Ready?" I asked, looking up at him.

He nodded.

I swung my feet down from the couch and sat up. I looked out at the hangar. It was empty. "Where is she?"

"Outside," he said. "I'm having her warmed up."

"Good," I said. I looked at my watch. It was a few minutes past three. He followed me into the john. "You're tired," he said, watching while I splashed cold water on my face. "Do you really think you should go?"

"I have to."

"I put six roast-beef sandwiches and two quart Thermos bottles of black coffee in the plane for you."

"Thanks," I said, starting out.

His hand stopped me. He held out a small white bottle. "I called my doctor," he said, "and he brought these out for you."

"What are they?"

"A new pill. Benzedrine. Take one if you get sleepy. It'll wake you up. But be careful with them. Don't take too many or you'll go through the roof."

We started out for the plane. "Don't open your reserve fuel tanks until you're down to a quarter tank. The gravity feed won't pull if she registers more than that and it might even lock."

"How will I know if the reserve tanks are working?" I asked.

He looked at me. "You won't until you run out of gas. And if she locks, the air pressure will keep your gauge at a quarter even if the tank is dry."

I shot a quick look at him but didn't speak. We kept on walking. I climbed up on the wing and turned toward the cockpit. A hand pulled at my trouser leg. I turned around.

Forrester was looking up at me with a shocked look on his face. "What are you doing with the plane?"

"Going to California."

"But what about the tests tomorrow?" he shouted. "I even got Steve Randall out here tonight to look at her."

"Sorry," I said. "Call it off."

"But the General," he yelled. "How'll I explain to him? He'll blow his stack!"

I climbed into the cockpit and looked down at him. "That's not my headache any more, it's yours."

"But what if something happens to the plane?"

I grinned suddenly. I'd been right in my hunch about him. He'd make a first-rate executive. There wasn't an ounce of concern about me, only for the plane. "Then build another one," I shouted. "You're president of the company."

I waved my hand, and releasing the brakes, began to taxi slowly out on the runway. I turned her into the wind and held her there while I revved up the motor. I pulled the canopy shut and when the tachometer reached twenty-eight, I let go of the brakes.

We raced down the runway. I didn't even try to lift her until my ground speed reached a hundred and forty. We were almost out of runway before she began to chew off a piece of sky. After that, she lifted easily.

I leveled off at four thousand feet and headed due south. I looked over my shoulder. The North Star was right in the middle of my back, flickering brightly in the clear, dark sky. It was hard to believe that less than a thousand miles from here the skies were locked in.

I was over Pittsburgh when I remembered something Nevada had taught me when I was a kid. We were trailing a big cat and he pointed up at the North Star. "The Indians have a saying that when the North Star flickers like that," he said, "a storm is moving south."

I looked up again. The North Star was flickering exactly as it had that night. I remembered another Indian saying that Nevada taught me. The quickest way west is into the wind.

My mind was made up. If the Indians were right, by the time I hit the Midwest, the storm would be south of me. I banked the plane into the wind and when I looked up from the compass, the North Star was dancing brightly off my right shoulder.

My back ached, everything ached—my shoulders, my arms and legs—and my eyelids weighed a ton. I felt them begin to close and reached for the coffee Thermos. It was empty. I looked at my watch. Twelve hours since I had left Roosevelt Field. I stuck my hand into my pocket and took out the box of pills Morrissey had given me. I put one in my mouth and swallowed it.

For a few minutes, I felt nothing, then I began to feel better. I took a deep breath and scanned the horizon. The way I figured, I shouldn't be too far from the Rockies. Twenty-five minutes later, they came into view.

I checked the fuel gauge. It held steady on one quarter. I had opened the reserve tanks. The fringe of the storm I'd passed through in the Midwest had cost me more than an hour's supply of gasoline and I'd need a break from the wind to get through.

I turned the throttle and listened to the engines. Their roar sounded full and heavy as the richer mixture poured into their veins. I leaned back on the stick and began to climb toward the mountains. I still felt a little tired so I popped another pill into my mouth.

At twelve thousand feet, I began to feel chilly. I slipped the huaraches back on my feet and reached for the oxygen tube. Almost immediately, I felt as if the plane had just jumped three thousand feet. I looked at the altimeter. It read only twelve four hundred.

I sucked again on the tube. A burst of power came roaring through my body and I placed my hands on the dashboard. To hell with the gasoline! I could lift this baby over the Rockies with my bare hands. It was only a question of will power. Like the fakirs in India said when they confounded you with their tricks of levitation—it was only a question of mind over matter. It was all in the mind.

Rina! I almost shouted aloud. I stared at the altimeter. The needle had dropped to ninety-five hundred feet and was still dropping. I stared over the plane at the mountain creeping up at me. I put my hand on the stick and pulled back. It seemed like forever until the mountain began to fall beneath me again.

I lifted my hands to wipe the sweat from my brow. My cheeks were wet with tears. The strange feeling of power was gone now and my head began to ache. Morrissey had warned me about the pills and the oxygen had helped a little, too. I touched the throttle and carefully regulated the mixture as it went into the motors.

I still had almost four hundred miles to go and I didn't want to run out of gas.

CHAPTER SIX

I PUT DOWN AT BURBANK AT TWO O'CLOCK. I HAD BEEN IN THE AIR ALMOST fifteen hours. I taxied over to the Cord Aircraft hangars, cut the engines and began to climb down. The engines were still roaring in my ears.

I stepped to the ground and a mob surrounded me. I recognized some of them, reporters. "I'm sorry, men," I said, pushing my way through them toward the hangar. "I'm still motor deaf. I can't hear what you're saying."

Buzz was there, too, a big grin on his face. He grabbed my hand and pumped it. His lips were moving but I missed the first part of what he said, then suddenly my hearing was back.

". . . set a new east-to-west coast-to-coast record."

Right now that didn't matter. "Do you have a car waiting for me?"

"Over at the front gate," Buzz said.

One of the reporters pushed forward. "Mr. Cord," he shouted at me. "Is it true you made this flight to see Rina Marlowe before she dies?"

He needed a bath after the look I gave him. I didn't answer.

"Is it true that you bought out Norman Pictures just to get control of her contract?"

I made it into the limousine but they were still popping questions at me. The car began to roll. A motorcycle cop cut in front of us and opened up his siren. We picked up speed as the traffic in front of us melted away.

"I'm sorry about Rina, Jonas," Buzz said. "I didn't know she was your father's wife."

I looked at him. "Where'd you find out?"

"It's in the papers," he said. "The Norman studio had it in their press release, together with the story about your flying out here to see her."

I shut my lips tight. That was the picture business for you. They were like ghouls hovering around a grave.

"I've got a container of coffee and a sandwich here if you want it."

I reached for the coffee. The black stuff was hot and I could feel it reach down inside me. I turned and looked out the window. My back began to throb and ache again.

I wondered if I could wait until we got to the hospital before I went to the bathroom.

The Colton Sanitarium is more like a hotel than a hospital. It's set back high in the Pacific Palisades, overlooking the ocean. In order to reach it, you come off the Coast Highway onto a narrow winding road and there's a guard standing at the iron gate. You get past him only after showing the proper credentials.

Dr. Colton is no California quack. He's just a shrewd man who's recognized the need for a truly private hospital. Movie stars go there for everything from having a baby to taking the cure, plastic surgery to nervous breakdowns. And once inside the iron gate, they can breathe safely and relax, for no reporter has ever been known to get inside. They can feel certain that no matter what they've gone there for, the only word that will ever reach the outside world will be theirs.

The gateman was expecting us, for he began to open the gate the minute he spotted the motorcycle cop. Reporters shouted at us and photographers tried to take pictures. One of them even clung to the running board until we got inside the gate. Then a second guard suddenly appeared and lifted the man off bodily.

I turned to Buzz. "They never give up, do they?"

Buzz's face was serious. "From now on, you'd better get used to it, Jonas. Everything you do will be news."

I stared at him. "Nuts," I said. "That's only for today. Tomorrow it'll be somebody else."

Buzz shook his head. "You haven't seen the papers or listened to the radio today. You're a national figure. Something about what you were doing caught the public imagination. Radio stations gave your flight progress every half hour. Tomorrow the *Examiner* begins running your life story. Nothing like you has swept the country since Lindbergh."

"What makes you say that?"

He smiled. "Today's *Examiner* trucks. They've got billboards with your picture. '*Read the life story of Hollywood's man of mystery*—Jonas Cord. By Adela Rogers St. Johns.'"

I stared at him. I guess I would have to get used to it. St. Johns was Hearst's top syndicated sob sister. That meant the old man up at San Simeon had put the finger of approval on me. From now on, I would be living in a fish bowl.

The car stopped and a doorman appeared. "If you'll kindly step this way, Mr. Cord," he said respectfully.

I followed him up the steps into the hospital. The white-uniformed nurse behind the desk smiled at me. She indicated a black, leather-bound register. "If you please, Mr. Cord," she said. "It's a rule of the hospital that all visitors have to sign in."

I signed the register quickly as she pressed a button underneath the counter. A moment later, another nurse appeared at the desk. "If you'll come with me, Mr. Cord," she said politely, "I'll take you to Miss Marlowe's suite."

I followed her to a small bank of elevators at the rear of the lobby. She pressed the button and looked up at the indicator. A frown of annoyance crossed her face. "I'm sorry to inconvenience you, Mr. Cord, but we'll have to wait a few minutes. Both elevators are up at the operating room."

A hospital was a hospital no matter how hard you tried to make it look like a hotel. I looked around the lobby until I located what I was looking for. It was a door marked discreetly GENTLEMEN.

I pulled a cigarette from my pocket as the elevator doors closed behind us. Inside, it smelled like every other hospital. Alcohol, disinfectant, formaldehyde. Sickness and death. I struck a match and held it to my cigarette, hoping the nurse wouldn't notice my suddenly trembling fingers.

The elevator stopped and the door rolled open. We stepped out into a clean hospital corridor. I dragged deeply on the cigarette as I followed the nurse. She stopped in front of a door. "I'm afraid you'll have to put out that cigarette, Mr. Cord."

I looked up at a small orange sign:

NO SMOKING ALLOWED
OXYGEN IN USE INSIDE!

I took another drag and put it out in a receptacle next to the door. I stood there, suddenly afraid to go inside. The nurse reached around me and opened the door. "You may go in now, Mr. Cord."

The door swung open, revealing a small anteroom. Another nurse was seated in an armchair, reading a magazine. She looked up at me. "Come in, Mr. Cord," she said in a falsely cheerful tone. "We've been expecting you."

I crossed the threshold slowly. I heard the door close behind me and the footsteps of my escort disappearing. There was another door opposite the entrance. The nurse crossed to it. "Miss Marlowe's in here," she said.

I stood in the doorway. At first, I couldn't see her. Ilene Gaillard, a doctor and another nurse were standing next to the bed, their backs toward me. Then, as if activated by some signal, they all turned at once. I walked toward the bed. The nurse moved away and Ilene and the doctor separated slightly to make room for me. Then I saw her.

A clear plastic tent was suspended over her head and shoulders and she seemed to be sleeping. All but her face was completely covered with a heavy white bandage, which hid all her shining white-blond hair. Her eyes were closed and I could see a faint blue tinge under the flesh of the lids. The skin was drawn tightly across her high cheekbones, leaving a hollow around her sunken cheeks, so that you had the feeling that the flesh beneath had disappeared. Her wide mouth, usually so warm and vivid, was pale and drawn back slightly from her even white teeth.

I stood there silently for a moment. I couldn't see her breathe. I looked at the doctor. He shook his head. "She's alive, Mr. Cord," he whispered, "but just barely."

"May I speak to her?"

"You can try, Mr. Cord. But don't be disappointed if she doesn't answer. She's been like this for the last ten hours. And if she should answer, Mr. Cord, she may not recognize you."

I turned back to her. "Rina," I said quietly. "It's me, Jonas."

She lay there quietly, not moving. I put my hand under the plastic tent and found hers. I pressed it. It felt cool and soft. Suddenly everything came to a wild stop inside me. Her hand was cool. She was already dead. She was dead.

I sank to my knees beside the bed. I pushed the plastic aside and leaned over her. "Please, Rina!" I begged wildly. "It's me, Jonas. Please, don't die!"

I felt a slight pressure from her hand. I looked down at her, the tears streaming down my cheeks. The movement of her hand grew a little stronger. Then her eyes opened slowly and she was looking up into my face.

At first, her eyes were vague and far away. Then they cleared and her lips curved into a semblance of a smile. "Jonas," she whispered. "I knew you'd come."

"All you ever had to do was whistle."

Her lips pursed but no sound came out. "I never could learn to whistle," she whispered.

The doctor's voice came from behind me. "You'd better get some rest now, Miss Marlowe."

Rina's eyes went past my shoulder to him. "No," she whispered. "Please. I haven't much time left. Let me speak to Jonas."

I turned to look at the doctor. "All right," he said. "But just for a moment."

I heard the door click behind me, then I looked down at Rina. Her hand lifted slightly and stroked my cheek. I caught her fingers and pressed them to my lips.

"I had to see you, Jonas."

"Why did you wait so long, Rina?"

"That's why I had to see you," she whispered. "To explain."

"What good are explanations now?"

"Please try to understand, Jonas. I loved you from the moment I first saw you. But I was afraid. I've been a jinx to everyone who ever loved me. My mother and my brother died because they loved me. My father died of a broken heart in prison."

"That wasn't your fault."

"I pushed Margaret down the stairs and killed her. I killed my baby even before it was born, stole Nevada's career from him, and Claude committed suicide because of what I was doing to him."

"Those things just happened. You weren't to blame."

"I was!" she insisted hoarsely. "Look what I did to you, to your marriage. I should never have come to your hotel that night."

"That was my fault. I made you."

"Nobody made me," she whispered. "I came because I wanted to. When she came, I knew how wrong I was."

"Why?" I asked bitterly. "Just because she had a belly way out to here? It wasn't even my child."

"What difference does that make? What if she did sleep with someone else before she met you? You must have known it when you married her. If it didn't matter then, why should it have mattered just because she was going to have his child?"

"It did matter," I insisted. "All she was interested in was my money. What about the half-million-dollar settlement she got when the marriage was annulled?"

"That's not true," she whispered. "She loved you. I could tell from the hurt I saw in her eyes. And if the money was so important to her, why did she give it all to her father?"

"I didn't know that."

"There's a lot you don't know," Rina whispered. "But I haven't time to tell you. Only this. I ruined your marriage. It's my fault that poor child is growing up without your name. And I want to make it up to her somehow."

She closed her eyes for a moment. "There may not be much left in my estate," she whispered. "I've never been much good with money, but I've left it all to her and appointed you my executor. Promise me you'll see that she gets it."

I looked down at her. "I promise."

She smiled slowly. "Thank you, Jonas. I always could count on you."

"Now try to rest a little."

"What for?" she whispered. "So I can live another few days in the mad, crazy world that's running around in my head? No, Jonas. It hurts too much. I want to die. But don't let me die here, locked up in this plastic tent. Take me out on the terrace. Let me look at the sky once more."

I stared at her. "The doctor—"

"Please, Jonas."

I looked down at her and she smiled. I smiled back and pushed the oxygen tent aside. I scooped her up in my arms and she was as light as a feather.

"It feels good to be in your arms again, Jonas," she whispered.

I kissed her on the forehead and stepped out into the sun-light. "I'd almost forgotten how green a tree can be," she whispered. "Back in Boston, there's the greenest oak tree you ever saw in your life. Please take me back there, Jonas."

"I will."

"And don't let them make a circus out of it," she whispered. "They can do that in this business."

"I know," I said.

"There's room for me, Jonas," she whispered. "Next to my father."

Her hand fell from my chest and a new kind of weight came into her body. I looked down at her. Her face was hidden against my shoulder. I turned and looked out at the tree that had reminded her of home. But I couldn't see it for my tears.

When I turned around, Ilene and the doctor were in the room. Silently I carried Rina back to the bed and gently laid her down on it. I straightened up and looked at them.

I tried to speak but for a moment, I couldn't. And when I could, my voice was hoarse with my grief. "She wanted to die in the sunlight," I said.

CHAPTER SEVEN

I LOOKED AT THE MINISTER, WHOSE LIPS WERE MOVING SILENTLY AS HE READ from the tiny black-bound Bible in his hands. He looked up for a moment, then closed the Bible and started slowly down the walk. A moment later, the others began to follow him and soon Ilene and I were the only ones left at the grave.

She stood there opposite me, skinny and silent, in her black dress and hat, the tiny veil hiding her eyes. "It's over," she said in a tired voice.

I nodded and looked down at the grave marker. Rina Marlowe. Now it was nothing but a name. "I hope everything was the way she wanted it."

"I'm sure it was."

We fell silent then with the awkwardness of two people at a cemetery whose only link now lay in a grave. I took a deep breath. It was time to go. "Can I give you a lift back to the hotel?"

She shook her head. "I'd like to stay here a little while longer, Mr. Cord."

"Will you be all right?"

I caught a glimpse of her eyes beneath the veil. "I'll be all right, Mr. Cord," she said. "Nothing more can happen to me."

"I'll see that a car waits for you. Good-by, Miss Gaillard."

"Good-by, Mr. Cord," she answered formally. "And—and thank you."

I turned and walked down the path to the cemetery road. The morbid and curious were still there behind the police lines, on the far side of the street. A faint sound rose up from them as I came out the cemetery gate. I'd done the best I could but somehow there are always crowds of people.

The chauffeur opened the door of the limousine and I got in. He closed it and ran around to the driver's seat. The car began to move. "Where to, Mr. Cord?" he asked cheerfully. "Back to the hotel?"

I turned and looked out the rear window. We were atop a small rise and I could see Ilene inside the cemetery. She sat beside the grave, a pitiful, shrunken figure in black, with her face hidden by her two hands. Then we went around a bend and she was gone from my sight.

"Back to the hotel, Mr. Cord?" the chauffeur repeated.

I straightened up and reached for a cigarette. "No," I said, lighting it. "To the airport."

I drew the smoke deep inside my lungs and let it burn there. Suddenly, all I wanted to do was get away. Boston and death, Rina and dreams. I had too many memories as it was.

* * *

The roaring filled my ears and I began to climb up the long black ladder out of the darkness over my head. The higher I climbed, the louder the noise got. I opened my eyes.

Outside the window, the Third Avenue El rattled by. I could see the people pressed together inside and on the narrow open platforms. Then the train had passed and a strange silence came into the room. I let my eyes wander.

It was a small, dark room, its white paper already beginning to turn brown on its walls. Near the window was a small table, on the wall over it a crucifix. I was in an old brass bed. Slowly I swung my feet to the floor and sat up. My head felt as if it were going to fall off.

"So, you're awake now, are you?"

I started to turn my head but the woman came around in front of me. There was something vaguely familiar about her face but I couldn't remember where I'd seen her before. I put my hand up and rubbed my cheek. My beard was as rough as sandpaper.

"How long have I been here?" I asked.

She laughed shortly. "Almost a week," she answered. "I was beginnin' to think there was no end to your thirst."

"I was drinking?"

"That you were," she said.

I followed her eyes to the floor. There were three cartons filled with empty whisky bottles. I rubbed the back of my neck. No wonder my head hurt. "How did I happen to get here?" I asked.

"You don't remember?"

I shook my head.

"You came up to me in front of the store on Sixth Avenue and took me by the arm, sayin' you was ready for the lesson now. You were already loaded then. Then we went into the White Rose Bar for a couple of drinks and it was there you got into a fight with the barkeep. So I brought you home for safe-keepin'."

I rubbed my eyes. I was beginning to remember now. I had come from the airport and was walking up Sixth Avenue toward the Norman offices when I felt I needed a drink. After that, it was fuzzy. I remembered vaguely searching in front of a radio store for some whore who had promised to teach me some things I had never learned in school.

"Were you the one?" I asked.

She laughed. "No, I wasn't. But in the condition you were in, I didn't think it would make any difference. It wasn't a woman you were looking for, it was a sorrow you were drownin'."

I got to my feet. I was in my shorts. I looked up at her questioningly. "I took your clothes downstairs to the cleaner when you quit drinkin' yesterday. I'll go down now and get them while you're cleanin' up."

"The bathroom?"

She pointed to a door. "There isn't a shower but there's enough hot water for a tub. And there's a razor on the shelf over the sink."

The clothes were waiting for me when I came out of the bathroom. "Your money is on the dresser," she said, as I finished buttoning my shirt and put on my jacket. I walked over to the dresser and picked it up.

"You'll find it all there except what I took for the whisky."

Holding the bills in my hand, I looked at her. "Why did you bring me here?"

She shrugged her shoulders. "The Irish make lousy whores," she said. "We get sentimental over drunkards."

I looked down at the roll of bills in my hand. There was about two hundred dollars there. I took a five-dollar bill and stuck it in my pocket; the rest I put back on the bureau.

She took the money silently and followed me to the door.

"She's dead, you know," she said. "And all the whisky in the world won't be bringin' her back to life."

We stared at each other for a moment, then she closed the door and I went down the dark staircase and out into the street. I walked into a drugstore on the corner of Third Avenue and Eighty-second Street and called McAllister.

"Where in hell have you been?" he asked.

"Drunk," I said. "Did you get the copy of Rina's will?"

"Yes, I got it. We've been searching the whole town for you. Do you realize what's happening over at the picture company? They're running around there like chickens with their heads cut off."

"Where is the will?"

"On the foyer table of your apartment, where you told me to leave it. If we don't have a meeting about the picture company pretty soon, you won't have to worry about your investment. There won't be any."

"O.K., set one up," I said, hanging up before he had a chance to answer.

I got out, paid the cabby and began to walk along the sidewalk in front of the houses. Children were playing on the grass and curious eyes followed me. Most of the doors were open, so I couldn't read the house numbers.

"Who you lookin' for, mister?" one of the kids called.

"Winthrop," I said. "Monica Winthrop."

"She's got a little girl?" the kid asked. "About five?"

"I think so," I said.

"Fourth house down."

I thanked the kid and started down the street. At the entrance of the fourth house, I looked at the name plate under the bell. Winthrop. There was no answer. I pressed the bell again.

"She's not home from work yet," a man called over to me from the next house. "She stops at the nursery school to pick up the kid first."

"About when does she get home?"

"Any minute now," he said.

I looked at my watch. It was a quarter to seven. The sun was starting to go down and with it went some of the heat of the day. I sat down on the steps and lit a cigarette. My mouth tasted awful and I could feel the beginnings of a headache.

The cigarette was almost finished when Monica turned the corner and started up the walk, a little girl skipping along in front of her.

I got to my feet as the child stopped and looked up at me. Her nose crinkled and her dark eyes squinted. "Mommy," she piped in a high-pitched voice, "there's a man standing on our steps."

I looked at Monica. For a moment, we just stood there staring at one another. She looked the same and yet changed somehow. Maybe it was the way she wore her hair. Or the simple business suit. But most of all, it was her eyes. There was a calm self-assurance in them that hadn't been there before. Her hand reached out and she drew the child to her. "It's all right, Jo-Ann," she said, picking the child up. "He's a friend of Mommy's."

The child smiled. "Hello, man."

"Hello," I said. I looked at Monica. "Hello, Monica."

"Hello, Jonas," she said stiffly. "How are you?"

"O.K. I want to see you."

"About what?" she asked. "I thought everything was settled."

"It's not about us," I said quickly. "It's about the kid."

She held the child closely to her in a sudden gesture. Something like fright came into her eyes. "What about Jo-Ann?"

"There's nothing to worry about," I said.

"Maybe we'd better go inside."

I stepped aside while she opened the door, and followed her into a small living room. She put the child down. "Go into your room and play with your dolls, Jo-Ann."

The child laughed happily and ran off. Monica turned back to me. "You look tired," she said. "Were you waiting long?"

I shook my head. "Not long."

"Sit down," she said quietly. "I'll make some coffee."

"Don't bother. I won't keep you long."

"That's all right," she said quickly. "I don't mind. It isn't often we have visitors."

She went into the kitchen and I sank into a chair. I looked around the room. Somehow, I couldn't get used to the idea that this was where she lived. It looked as if it was furnished from Gimbels basement. Not that it wasn't good. It was just that everything was neat and practical and cheap. And Monica used to be more the Grosfeld House type.

She came back into the room, carrying a steaming cup of black coffee, and put it down on the table next to me. "Two sugars, right?"

"Right."

Quickly she put two lumps of sugar into the coffee and stirred it. I sipped it and began to feel better. "That's good coffee," I said.

"It's G. Washington."

"What's that?"

"The working girl's friend," she said. "Instant coffee. It's really not too bad when you get used to it."

"What will they think of next?"

"Can I get you a couple of aspirins?" she asked. "You look as if you have a headache."

"How do you know?"

She smiled. "We were married for a while once, remember? You get a kind of wrinkle on your forehead when you have a headache."

"Two, then, please," I said. "Thanks."

She sat down opposite me after I'd taken them. Her eyes watched me steadily. "Surprised to see me in a place like this?"

"A little," I said. "I didn't know until just a little while ago that you hadn't kept any of the money I gave you. Why?"

"I didn't want it," she said simply. "And my father did. So I gave it to him. He wanted it for his business."

"What did you want?"

She hesitated a moment before she answered. "What I have now. Jo-Ann. And to be left alone. I kept just enough money to come East and have the baby. Then when she was old enough, I went out and got a job." She smiled. "I know it won't seem like much to you but I'm an executive secretary and I make seventy dollars a week."

I was silent for a moment while I finished the rest of the coffee. "How's Amos?" I asked.

She shrugged her shoulders. "I don't know. I haven't heard from him in four years. How did you find out where I was living?"

"From Rina," I said.

She didn't say anything for a moment. Then she took a deep breath. "I'm sorry, Jonas." I could see sympathy deep in her eyes. "You may not believe me but I'm truly sorry. I read about it in the papers. It was a terrible thing. To have so much and go like that."

"Rina had no surviving relatives," I said. "That's why I'm here."

A puzzled look came over her face. "I don't understand."

"She left her entire estate in trust for your daughter," I said quickly. "I don't know exactly how much, maybe thirty, forty thousand after taxes and debts. She appointed me executor and made me promise to see that the child got it."

She was suddenly pale and the tears came into her eyes. "Why did she do it? She didn't owe me anything."

"She said she blamed herself for what happened to us."

"What happened to us was your fault and mine," she said vehemently. She stopped suddenly and looked at me. "It's foolish to get excited about it at this late date. It's over and done with."

I looked at her for a moment, then got to my feet. "That's right, Monica," I said. "It's over and done with." I started for the door. "If you'll get in touch with McAllister, he'll have all the papers ready for you."

She looked up into my face. "Why don't you stay and let me fix you supper," she said politely. "You look tired."

There was no point in telling her that what she saw was the beginning of a hangover. "No, thanks," I said, equally polite. "I have to get back. I have some business appointments."

A wry, almost bitter look came over her face. "Oh, I almost forgot," she said. "Your business."

"That's right," I said.

"I suppose I should be thankful you took the time to come out." Before I could answer, she turned and called to the child. "Jo-Ann, come out here and say good-by to the nice man."

The little girl came into the room, clutching a small doll. She smiled up at me. "This is my dolly."

I smiled down at her. "It's a nice dolly."

"Say good-by, Jo-Ann."

Jo-Ann held out her hand to me. "Good-by, man," she said seriously. "Come an' see us again. Sometime. Soon."

I took her hand. "I will, Jo-Ann," I said. "Good-by."

Jo-Ann smiled and pulled her hand back quickly, then ran out of the room again.

I straightened up. "Good-by, Monica," I said. "If there's anything you need, give me a call."

"I'll be all right, Jonas," she said, holding out her hand. I took it. She smiled tentatively. "Thank you, Jonas," she said. "And I'm sure if Jo-Ann could understand, she'd thank you, too."

I smiled back. "She's a nice little girl."

"Good-by, Jonas." She took her hand from mine and stood in the open doorway while I went down the walk.

"Jonas," she called after me.

I turned. "Yes, Monica?"

She hesitated a moment, then laughed. "Nothing, Jonas," she said. "Don't work too hard."

I laughed. "I'll try not to."

She closed the door quickly and I continued on down the sidewalk. Forest Hills, Queens, a hell of a place to live. I had to walk six blocks before I could get a cab.

"But what are we going to do about the company?" Woolf asked.

I looked across the table at him, then picked up the bottle of bourbon and refilled my glass. I went to the window and looked out over New York.

"What about *The Sinner?*" Dan asked. "We'll have to decide what to do about that. I'm already talking to Metro about getting Jean Harlow."

I turned on him savagely. "I don't want Harlow," I snapped. "That was Rina's picture."

"But my God, Jonas," Dan exclaimed. "You can't junk that script. It'll cost you half a million by the time you get through paying off De Mille."

"I don't care what it costs!" I snarled. "I'm junking it!"

A silence came over the room and I turned back to the window. Over to my left, the lights of Broadway climbed up into the sky; on my right, I could see the East River. On the other side of that river was Forest Hills. I grimaced and swallowed my drink quickly. Monica had been right about one thing. I was working too hard.

I had too many people on my back, too many businesses. Cord Explosives; Cord Plastics; Cord Aircraft; Inter-Continental Airlines. And now I owned a motion-picture company I didn't even want.

"Well, Jonas," McAllister said quietly. "What are you going to do?"

I walked back to the table and refilled my glass. My mind was made up. I knew just what I was going to do from now on. Only what I wanted to. Let them earn their keep and show me how good they really were.

I stared at Dan Pierce. "You're always talking about how you could make better pictures than anyone in the business," I said. "O.K. You're in charge of production."

Before he had a chance to answer, I turned to Woolf. "You're worried about what's going to happen to the company. Now you can really worry about it. You're in charge of everything else—sales, theaters, administration."

I turned and walked back to the window.

"That's fine, Jonas," McAllister said. "But you haven't told us who the officers will be."

"You're chairman of the board, Mac," I said. "Dan, president. David, executive vice-president." I took a swallow from my glass. "Any more questions?"

They looked at each other, then Mac turned back to me. "While you were away, David had a study made. The company needs about three million dollars of revolving credit to get through this year if we're to maintain the current level of production."

"You'll get a million dollars," I said. "You'll have to make do with that."

"But, Jonas," Dan protested. "How do you expect me to make the kind of pictures I want to make if you won't let us have the money?"

"If you can't do it," I snarled, "then get the hell out and I'll get someone who can."

I could see Dan's face whiten. He closed his lips grimly and didn't answer. I looked from him to the others. "The same thing goes for all of you. From now on, I'm through playing wet nurse to the world. Any man that doesn't deliver can get out. From now on, nobody bothers me about anything. If I want you, I'll get in touch with you. If you have anything to report, put it in writing and send it to my office. That's all, gentlemen. Good night."

As the door closed behind them, I could feel the hard, angry knot tightening in my gut. I looked out the window. Forest Hills. I wondered what kind of schools they had out there that a kid like Jo-Ann could go to.

I swallowed the rest of my drink. It didn't untie the knot; it only pulled it tighter. Suddenly I wanted a woman.

I picked up the phone and called Jose, the headwaiter down at the Rio Club. "Yes, Mr. Cord."

"Jose," I said. "That singer with the rumba band. The one with the big—"

"Eyes," he interrupted, laughing quietly. "Yes, Mr. Cord. I know. She'll be at your place in half an hour."

I put down the telephone and walked back to the table. I took the bottle to the window with me while I filled my glass. I'd learned something tonight.

People would pay any price for what they really wanted. Monica would live in Queens so she could keep her daughter. Dan would swallow my insults so he could make pictures. Woolf would do anything to prove he could run the company better than his uncle Bernie. And Mac kept on paying the price for the security I'd given him.

When you got down to it, people all had their price. The currency might differ. It could be money, power, glory, sex. Anything. All you needed to know was what they wanted.

A knock came on the door. "Come in," I called.

She came into the room, her dark eyes bright, her long black hair falling down her back almost to her hips, the black gown cut way down in front showing white almost to her navel. She smiled at me. "Hello, Mr. Cord," she said, without the accent she used in the cafe. "How nice of you to ask me up."

"Take off your dress and have a drink," I said.

"I'm not that kind of girl," she snapped, turning and starting for the door.

"I've got five hundred dollars that says you are."

She turned back to me, a smile on her lips, her fingers already busy with the zipper at the back of her dress. I turned and looked out the window while she undressed.

There weren't as many lights in Queens as there were in Manhattan. And what few lights there were weren't as bright. Suddenly, I was angry and I yanked the cord releasing the Venetian blind. It came down the window with a crash and shut out the city. I turned back to the girl.

She was staring at me with wide eyes. All she had on was a pair of skin-tight black sheer panties, and her hands were crossed over her bosom, hiding only the nipples of her large breasts. "What did you do that for?" she said. "No one out there can see in here."

"I'm tired of looking at Queens," I said and started across the room toward her.

THE STORY OF DAVID WOOLF
Book Six

CHAPTER ONE

DAVID WOOLF WALKED INTO THE HOTEL ROOM AND THREW HIMSELF down on the bed fully clothed, staring up at the dark ceiling. The night felt as if it were a thousand years old, even though he knew it was only a little past one o'clock. He was tired and yet he wasn't tired; he was elated and yet, somehow, depressed; triumphant and yet there was the faint bitter taste of intangible defeat stirring within him.

This was the beginning of opportunity, the first faint dawn of his secret ambitions, hopes and dreams. Then why this baffling mixture of emotions? It had never been like this before. He'd always known exactly what he wanted. It had been very simple. A straight line reaching from himself to the ultimate.

It must be Cord, he thought. It had to be Cord. There could be no other reason. He wondered if Cord affected the others in the same way. He still felt the shock that had gone through him when he entered the suite and saw him for the first time since the night Cord had left the board meeting to fly to the Coast.

Fifteen days had passed, two weeks during which panic had set in and the company had begun to disintegrate before his eyes. The whispering of the employees in the New York office still echoed in his ears, the furtive, frightened, worried glances cast as he passed them in the corridor. And there had been nothing he could do about it, nothing he could tell them. It was as if the corporation lay suspended in shock, awaiting the transfusion that would send new vitality coursing through its veins.

And now, at last, Cord sat there, a half-empty bottle of bourbon in front of him, a tortured, hollow shell of the man they had seen just a few short weeks ago. He was thinner and exhaustion had etched its weary lines deeply into his cheeks. But it was only when you looked into his eyes that you realized it wasn't a physical change that had taken place. The man himself had changed.

At first, David couldn't put his finger on it. Then, for a brief moment, the veil lifted and suddenly he understood. He sensed the man's unique aloneness. It was as if he were a visitor from another world. The rest of them had become alien to him, almost like children, whose simple desires he had long ago outgrown. He would tolerate them so long as he found a use for them, but once that purpose was served he would withdraw again into that world in which he existed alone.

The three of them had been silent as they came down in the elevator after leaving Cord's suite. It wasn't until they stepped out into the lobby and mingled with the crowd that was coming in for the midnight show on the Starlight Roof that McAllister spoke. "I think we'd better find a quiet spot and have a little talk."

"The Men's Bar downstairs. If it's still open," Pierce suggested.

It was and when the waiter brought their drinks, McAllister lifted his glass. "Good luck," they echoed, then drank and placed their glasses back on the table.

McAllister looked from one to the other before he spoke. "Well, from here on in, it's up to us. I wish I could be more direct in my contribution," he said in his somewhat stilted, formal manner. "But I'm an attorney and know almost nothing about motion pictures. What I can do, though, is to explain the reorganization plan for the company that Jonas approved before the deal was actually consummated."

It wasn't until then that David had got any idea of how farseeing Jonas had been—retiring the old common stock in exchange for new shares, the issuance of preferred stock to meet certain outstanding debts of the corporation and debentures constituting a mortgage lien on all the real properties of the company, including the studio and theaters, in exchange for his putting up a million dollars' working capital.

The next item McAllister covered was their compensation. David and Dan Pierce would be offered seven-year employment contracts with a salary starting at sixty-five thousand dollars and increasing thirteen thousand dollars each year until the expiration of the agreement. In addition, each would be reimbursed completely for his expenses and bonuses, if there were profits, to the amount of two and one half per cent, which could be taken either in stock or in cash.

"That's about it," McAllister said. "Any questions?"

"It sounds good," Dan Pierce said. "But what guarantee have we got that Jonas will keep us in business once the million dollars is gone? None at all. But he's completely covered by his stock and debentures."

"You're right," McAllister agreed. "You have no guarantee, but then, neither has he any guarantee about what his stock will be worth if your operation of the company should prove unsuccessful. As I see it, it's up to you two to make it work."

"But if the study David made is correct," Dan continued, "we won't be halfway through our first picture before we'll be unable to meet our weekly payroll. I don't know what got into Jonas. You can't make million-dollar pictures without money."

"Who says we have to make million-dollar pictures?" David asked quietly.

Suddenly, the whole pattern was very clear. Now he was beginning to understand what Jonas had done. At first, he had felt a disappointment at not being put in charge of the studio. He would have liked the title of President on his door. But Cord had cut through the whole business like a knife through butter. In reality, the studio was only a factory turning out the product of the company. Administration, sales and theaters were under his control and that was where the money came from. Money always dictated studio policy and he controlled the money.

"For a million bucks, we can turn out ten pictures. And be taking in revenue from the first before the fifth goes into production."

"Not me," Dan said quickly. "I haven't come this far in the business just to make quickies. That's for Republic or Monogram."

"Columbia, Warners and RKO aren't too proud," David said, a new hardness coming into his voice.

"Let them if they want to," Dan snapped. "I've got a reputation to maintain."

"Don't give me that crap," David exploded. "The only thing this business respects is success. And they don't care how you get it so long as it adds up at the box office. The whole industry knows you maneuvered Cord into buying the company so you could become a producer. You won't have any reputation left if you walk out."

"Who said anything about walking out?"

David relaxed in his chair. A new feeling of power came over him. Now he understood why his Uncle Bernie had found it so difficult to let go. He shrugged his shoulders. "You heard what Cord said. If you won't do it, somebody else will."

Pierce stared at him for a moment, then looked at McAllister. The attorney's face was impassive. "That's all very well for you to say," Pierce grumbled. "But while I'm out there getting my brains kicked in, what're you going to be doing?"

"Seeing to it that we survive long enough for you to get your production program working," David answered.

"How?" McAllister asked, an interested look coming over his face.

"Tomorrow I'm laying off forty per cent of personnel throughout the company."

"That's pretty drastic," McAllister said. "Will you be able to function under those conditions?"

David watched the attorney's face. This was another kind of test. "We'll be able to function," he said quietly.

"That's no way to make friends," Pierce injected.

"I couldn't care less," David replied caustically. "I'm not trying to win a popularity contest. And that will be only the beginning. I don't care who gets hurt— the company is going to survive."

For a moment, the attorney stared at him. Then David saw a frosty glimmer of a smile lurking deep in his eyes. McAllister turned to Dan. "What do you think?"

Dan was smiling. "I think we'll make it. Why do you think Jonas wanted him to stick around?"

McAllister reached into his brief case. "There's your contract," he said to David. "Jonas wants you to sign it tonight."

David stared at the lawyer. "What about Dan?"

McAllister smiled. "Dan signed his the day of the board meeting."

For a moment, David felt anger climbing up inside him. The whole thing had been an act. They had put him through the wringer just to see what would happen. Then he drew in his breath. What difference did it make? He reached for the fountain pen the attorney held out toward him.

This was only the beginning. They were still outsiders and it would be a long time before they knew as much about the company as he did. And by that time, it wouldn't matter any more.

Once he signed the contract, he was in charge.

The connecting door between his room and his uncle's opened and light spilled through into the darkness. "Are you in there, David?"

He sat up on the bed and swung his feet to the floor. He reached out and turned on the lamp next to the bed. "Yes, Uncle Bernie."

Norman came into the room. "*Nu?*" he said. "You saw him?"

David nodded, reaching for a cigarette. "I saw him." He lit the cigarette. "He looks terrible. Rina's death must have hit him pretty hard."

The old man laughed. "Sorry for him I can't feel," he said bitterly. "Not after what he's done to me." He took a cigar from his pocket and stuck it into his mouth unlit. "He offered you a job, no?"

David nodded.

"What job?"

"Executive vice-president."

His uncle raised his eyebrows. "That so?" he asked interestedly. "Who's president?"

"Dan Pierce. He's going to make the pictures. I'm to run everything else—administration, sales and theaters."

The cigar bobbed up and down excitedly in the old man's mouth. A broad smile came over his face. "My boy, I'm proud of you." He clapped his hand on David's shoulder. "I always said someday you'd amount to something."

David looked at his uncle in surprise. This wasn't the reaction he had expected. An accusation of betrayal would have been more like it. "You are?"

"Of course I am," Bernie said enthusiastically. "What else did I expect of my own sister's son?"

David stared up at him. "I thought—"

"Thought?" the old man said, still smiling. "What difference does it make what you thought? Bygones is bygones. Now we can really put our heads together. I'll show you ways to make money you never dreamed about."

"Make money?".

"Sure," Bernie replied, lowering his voice to a confidential tone. "A *goyishe kopf* is always a *goyishe kopf*. With you in charge, who will know what's going on? Tomorrow, I'll let all the suppliers know the old deal is still on. Only now you get twenty-five per cent of the kickback."

"Twenty-five per cent?"

"What's the matter?" Bernie asked shrewdly. "Twenty-five per cent isn't enough for you?"

David didn't answer.

"So your Uncle Bernie ain't a *chazer*. All right. Fifty, then."

David ground out his cigarette in the ash tray. He got to his feet and walked silently to the window. He looked down into the park across the street.

"What's the matter?" his uncle said behind him. "Fifty-fifty ain't fair? You owe me something. If it wasn't for me, you'd never have got this job."

David felt his bitterness rise up into his throat. He turned and looked at the old man. "I owe you something?" he said angrily. "Something for all those years you kept me hustling my tail off for a lousy three fifty a week? Every time I asked you for more money you cried about how much the company was losing. And all the time, you were siphoning off a million bucks a year into your own pocket."

"That was different," the old man said. "You don't understand."

David laughed. "I understand all right, Uncle Bernie. What I understand is that you've got fifteen million dollars free and clear. If you live to be a thousand, you couldn't spend all you've got. And still you want more."

"So what's wrong with that?" Bernie demanded. "I worked for it. I'm entitled to it. You want I should let go everything just because some *shlemiel* screwed me out of my own business?"

"Yes."

"You take the side of that—that Nazi against your own flesh and blood?" the old man shrieked at him, his face flushing angrily.

David stared at the old man. "I don't have to take sides, Uncle Bernie," he said quietly. "You yourself have admitted it's not your company any more."

"But you're running the company."

"That's right." David nodded. "I'm running the company. Not you."

"Then you're keeping everything for yourself?" the old man said accusingly.

David turned his back on his uncle, without speaking. For a moment, there was silence, then his uncle's voice. "You're even worse than him," Bernie said bitterly. "At least, he wasn't stealing from his own flesh and blood."

"Leave me alone, Uncle Bernie," David said without turning around. "I'm tired. I want to get some sleep."

He heard the old man's footsteps cross the room and the door slam angrily behind him. He leaned his head wearily against the side of the window. So that was why the old man hadn't gone back to California right after the meeting. He felt a lump come into his throat. He didn't know why but suddenly he felt like crying.

The faint sound of a clanging bell came floating up to him from the street. He moved his head slightly, looking out of the window. The clanging grew louder as an ambulance turned west on to Fifty-ninth from Fifth Avenue. He turned and walked slowly from the window back into the room, the clanging growing fainter in his ears. All his life it had been like that, somehow.

When he rode up front on the junk wagon, with his father sitting next to him on the hard wooden seat, it had seemed that was the only sound he'd ever heard. The clanging of a bell.

CHAPTER TWO

THE COWBELLS SUSPENDED ACROSS THE WAGON BEHIND HIM CLANGED LA-zily as the weary horse inched along through the pushcarts that lined both sides of Rivington Street. The oppressive summer heat beat down on his head. He let the reins lay idle in his fingers. There wasn't much you could do to guide the horse. It would pick its own way through the crowded street, moving automatically each time a space opened up.

"Aiyee caash clothes!" His father's singsong call penetrated the sounds of the market street, lifting its message high to the windows of the tenements, naked, blind eyes staring out unseeing into the hungry world.

"Aiyee caash clothes!"

He looked down from the wagon to where his father was striding along the crowded sidewalk, his beard waving wildly as his eyes searched the windows for signs of business. There was a certain dignity about the old man—the broad-brimmed black beaver hat that had come from the old country; the long black coat that flapped around his ankles; the shirt with its heavily starched but slightly wilted wing collar; and the tie with the big knot resting just below his prominent Adam's apple. The face was pale and cool, not even a faint sign of perspiration dampened the brow, while David's was dripping with sweat. It seemed almost as if the heavy black clothing provided insulation against the heat.

"Hey, Mister Junkman!"

His father moved out into the gutter to get a better look. But it was David who saw her first—an old woman waving from the fifth-floor window. "It's Mrs. Saperstein, Pop."

"You think I can't see?" his father asked, grumbling. "Yoo-hoo, Mrs. Saperstein!"

"Is that you, Mr. Woolf?" the woman called down.

"Yes," the old man shouted. "What you got?"

"Come up, I'll show to you."

"I don't want winter clothes," the old man shouted. "Who's to buy?"

"Who said about winter clothes? Come up, you'll see!"

"Tie the horse over there," his father said, pointing to an open space between two pushcarts. "Then come to carry down the stuff."

David nodded as his father crossed the street and disappeared into the entrance of a house. He nudged the horse over and tied it to a fire hydrant. Then he slipped a feed bag over its weary muzzle and started after his father.

He felt his way up through the dark, unlit hallway and staircase and stopped outside the door. He knocked. The door opened immediately. Mrs. Saperstein stood there, her long gray hair folded in coils on top of her head. "Come in, come in."

David came into the kitchen and saw his father sitting at the table. In front of him was a plate filled with cookies. "A *gluz tay*, David?" the old woman asked, going to the stove.

"No, thanks, Mrs. Saperstein," he answered politely.

She took a small red can from the shelf over the stove, then carefully measured two teaspoonfuls of tea into the boiling water. The tea leaves immediately burst open and spun around madly on the surface. When she finally poured the tea into a glass through a strainer and set it in front of his father, it was almost as black as coffee.

His father picked up a lump of sugar from the bowl and placed it between his lips, then sipped the tea. After he swallowed the first scalding mouthful, he opened his mouth and said, "Ah!"

"Good, isn't it?" Mrs. Saperstein was smiling. "That's real tea. Swee-Touch-Nee. Like in the old country. Not like the *chazerai* they try to sell you here."

His father nodded and lifted the glass again. When he put it back on the table, it was empty and the polite formalities were over. Now it was time to attend to business. "*Nu*, Mrs. Saperstein?"

But Mrs. Saperstein wasn't quite ready to talk business yet. She looked over at David. "Such a nice boy, your David," she said conversationally. "He reminds me of my Howard at his age." She picked up the plate of cookies and held it toward him. "Take one," she urged. "I baked myself."

David took a cooky and put it in his mouth. It was hard and dry and crumbled into little pieces. "Take another," she urged. "You look thin, you should eat."

David shook his head.

"Mrs. Saperstein," his father said. "I'm a busy man, it's late. You got something for me?"

The old woman nodded. "*Kim shayn.*"

They followed her through the narrow railroad flat. Inside one room, on the bed, were a number of men's suits, some dresses, shirts, one overcoat and, in paper bags, several pairs of shoes.

David's father walked over and picked up some of the clothing. "Winter clothing," he said accusingly. "For this I came up four flights of stairs?"

"Like new, Mr. Woolf," the old woman said. "My son Howard and his wife. Only one season. They were going to give to the Salvation Army but I made them send to me."

David's father didn't answer. He was sorting out the clothing rapidly.

"My son Howard lives in the Bronx," she said proudly. "In a new house on Grand Concourse. A doctor."

"Two dollars for the *ganse gesheft*," his father announced.

"Mr. Woolf," she exclaimed. "At least twenty dollars this is worth."

He shrugged. "The only reason I'm buying is to give to HIAS. Better the Salvation Army don't get."

David listened to their bargaining with only half a mind. HIAS was the abbreviation that stood for Hebrew Immigrant Aid Society. His father's statement didn't impress him one bit. He knew the clothing would never find its way there. Instead, after it was carefully brushed and cleaned by his mother, it would turn up in the windows of the secondhand clothing stores along the lower Bowery and East Broadway.

"Ten dollars," Mrs. Saperstein was saying. The pretense was gone now; she was bargaining in earnest. "Less I wouldn't take. Otherwise, it wouldn't pay my son Howard to bring it down. It costs him gas from the Bronx."

"Five dollars. Not one penny more."

"Six," the old woman said, looking at him shrewdly. "At least, the gasoline money he should get."

"The subways are still running," David's father said. "I should pay because your son is a big shot with an automobile?"

"Five fifty," the old woman said.

David's father looked at her. Then he shrugged his shoulders and reached under his long black coat. He took out a purse, tied to his belt by a long black shoestring, and opened it. "Five fifty," he sighed. "But as heaven is watching, I'm losing money."

He gestured to David and began counting the money out into the old woman's hand. David rolled all the clothing into the overcoat and tied it by the sleeves. He hefted the clothing onto his shoulder and started down the stairs. He tossed the bundle of clothing up into the cart and moved around to the front of the wagon. He lifted the feed bag from the horse, and untying the reins from the hydrant, climbed on the wagon.

"Hey, Davy!"

He looked down at the sidewalk. A tall boy stood there looking up at him and smiling. "I been lookin' for yuh all day."

"We been in Brooklyn," David answered. "My father will be here in a minute."

"I'll make it quick, then. Shocky'll cut yuh in for ten bucks if yuh bring the horse an' wagon tonight. We got to move a load uptown."

"But it's Friday night."

"That's why. The streets down here will be empty. There won't be nobody to wonder what we're doin' out at night. An' the cops won't bother us when they see the junky's license on the wagon."

"I'll try," David said. "What time, Needlenose?"

"Nine o'clock back of Shocky's garage. Here comes your ol' man. See yuh later."

"Who were you talking to?" his father asked.

"One of the fellers, Pop."

"Isidore Schwartz?"

"Yeah, it was Needlenose."

"Keep away from him, David," his father said harshly. "Him we don't need. A bum. A nogoodnik. Like all those other bums that hang around Shocky's garage. They steal everything they can get their hands on."

David nodded.

"Take the horse to the stable. I'm going to the *shul*. Tell Mama by seven o'clock she should have supper ready."

Esther Woolf stood in front of the *Shabbas nacht lichten*, the prayer shawl covering her head. The candles flickered into yellow flame as she held the long wooden match to them. Carefully she blew out the match and put it down in a plate on the small buffet table. She waited until the flame ripened into a bright white glow, then began to pray.

First, she prayed for her son, her *shaine Duvidele*, who came so late in life, almost when she and her husband, Chaim, had given up hope of being blessed. Then she prayed that Jehovah would give her husband, Chaim, a greater will to succeed, at the same time begging the Lord's forgiveness because it was the Lord's work at the *shul* that kept her husband from his own. Then, as always, she took upon herself the sin for having turned Chaim away from his chosen work.

He had been a Talmudical student when they'd first met in the old country. She remembered him as he was then, young and thin and pale, with the first soft curl of his dark beard shining with a red-gold glint. His eyes had been dark and luminous as he sat at the table in her father's house, dipping the small piece of cake into the wine, more than holding his own with the old rabbi and the elders.

But when they'd been married, Chaim had gone to work in her father's business. Then the pogroms began and the faces of Jews became thin and haunted. They left their homes only under the cover of night, hurrying about like little animals of the forest. Or they sat huddled in the cellars of their houses, the doors and windows barred and locked, like chickens trying to hide in the pen when they sense the approach of the *shochet*.

Until that night when she could stand it no longer. She rose screaming from the pallet at her husband's side, the letter from her brother Bernard, in America, still fresh in her mind. "Are we to live like rabbits in a trap, waiting for the Cossacks to come?" she cried. "Is it into this dark world that my husband expects I should bring forth a child? Even Jehovah could not plant his seed in a cellar."

"Hush!" Chaim's voice was a harsh whisper. "The name of the Lord shall not be taken in vain. Pray that He does not turn His face from us."

She laughed bitterly. "Already He has forsaken us. He, too, is fleeing before the Cossacks."

"Quiet, woman!" Chaim's voice was an outraged roar.

She looked at the other pallets in the damp cellar. In the dim light, she could barely see the pale, frightened faces of her parents. Just then there was a thunder of horse's hoofs outside the house and the sound of a gun butt against the locked door.

Quickly, her father was on his feet. "Quick, *kinder*," he whispered. "The storm cellar door at the back of the house. Through the fields, they won't see you leaving that way."

Chaim reached for Esther's hand and pulled her to the storm door. Suddenly, he stopped, aware that her parents were not following them. "Come," he whispered. "Hurry! There is no time."

Her father stood quietly in the dark, his arm around his wife's shoulder. "We are not going," he said. "Better someone be here for them to find or they will begin searching the fields."

The din over their heads grew louder as the gun butts began to break through the door. Chaim walked back to her father. "Then we all stay and face them," he said calmly, picking a heavy stave up from the floor. "They will learn a Jew does not die so easily."

"Go," her father said quietly. "We gave our daughter in marriage. It is her safety that should be your first concern, not ours. Your bravery is nothing but stupidity. How else have Jews survived these thousand years except by running?"

"But—" Chaim protested.

"Go," the old man hissed. "Go quickly. We are old, our lives are finished. You are young, your children should have their chance."

A few months later, they were in America. But it was to be almost twenty years before the Lord God Jehovah relented and let her have a child.

Last, she prayed for her brother Bernard, who was a *macher* now and had a business in a faraway place called California, where it was summer all year round. She prayed that he was safe and well and that he wasn't troubled by the Indians, like she saw in the movies when she used the pass he'd sent her.

Her prayers finished, she went back into the kitchen. The soup was bubbling on the stove, its rich, heavy chicken aroma almost visible in the air. She picked up a spoon and bent over the pot. Carefully she skimmed the heavy fat globules from the surface and put them in a jar. Later, when the fat was cold and had congealed, it could be spread on bread or mixed with chopped dry meats to give them flavor. While she was bent like this over the stove, she heard the front door open.

From the footsteps, she knew who it was. "That you, Duvidele?"

"Yes, Mama."

Her task finished, she put down the spoon and turned around slowly. As always, her heart leaped with pride as she saw her son, so straight and tall, standing there.

"Papa went to *shul*," David said. "He'll be home at seven o'clock."

She smiled at him. "Good," she said. "So wash your hands and clean up. Supper is ready."

CHAPTER THREE

W HEN DAVID TURNED THE HORSE INTO THE LITTLE ALLEY THAT LED to the back of Shocky's garage, Needlenose came hurrying up. "Is that you, David?"

"Who did yuh think it would be?" David retorted sarcastically.

"Geez, we didn't know whether you'd show up or not. It's almost ten o'clock."

"I couldn't sneak out until my old man went to sleep," David said, stopping the wagon at the side of the garage.

A moment later, Shocky came out, his bald head shining in the dim light. He was of medium height, with a heavy barrel chest and long tapering arms that reached almost to his knees. "You took long enough gettin' here," he grumbled.

"I'm here, ain't I?"

Shocky didn't answer. He turned to Needlenose. "Start loading the cans," he said. "He can help you."

David climbed down from the wagon and followed Shocky into the garage. The long row of metal cans gleamed dully in the light from the single electric bulb hanging high in the ceiling. David stopped and whistled. "There must be forty cans there."

"So he can count," Shocky said.

"That's four hundred pounds. I don't think Old Bessie can haul that much."

Shocky looked at him. "You hauled that much last time."

"No, I didn't," David said. "It was only thirty cans. And even then, there were times I thought Old Bessie was goin' to croak on me. Suppose she did? There I'd be with a dead horse and two hundred gallons of alky in the wagon. It's bad enough if my old man ever finds out."

"Just this once," Shocky said. "I promised Gennuario."

"Why don't you use one of your trucks?"

"I can't do that," Shocky replied. "That's just what the Feds are lookin' for. They won't be lookin' for a junk wagon."

"The most I'll take is twenty-five cans."

Shocky stared at him. "I'll make it twenty bucks this one time," he said. "You got me in a bind."

David was silent. Twenty dollars was more than his father netted in a whole week, sometimes. And that was going out with the wagon six days a week. Rain or shine, summer heat or bitter winter cold, every day except Saturday, which his father spent in *shul*.

"Twenty-five bucks," Shocky said.

"O.K. I'll take a chance."

"Start loadin', then." Shocky picked up a can with each of his long arms.

David sat alone on the wagon seat as Old Bessie slowly plodded her way uptown. He pulled up at a corner to let a truck go by. A policeman slowly sauntered over. "What're ye doin' out tonight, Davy?"

Furtively David cast a look at the back of the wagon. The cans of alcohol lay hidden under the tarpaulin, covered with rags. "I heard they're payin' a good price for rag over at the mill," he answered. "I thought I'd clean out the wagon."

"Where's your father?"

"It's Friday night."

"Oh," the policeman answered. He looked up at David shrewdly. "Does he know ye're out?"

David shook his head silently.

The policeman laughed. "You kids are all alike."

"I better get goin' before the old man misses me," David said. He clucked to the horse and Old Bessie began to move. The policeman called after him and David stopped and looked back.

"Tell your father to keep an eye peeled for some clothes for a nine-year-old boy," he called. "My Michael is outgrowin' the last already."

"I will, Mr. Doyle," David said and flicked the reins lightly. Shocky and Needlenose were already there when David pulled up against the loading platform. Gennuario stood on the platform watching as they began to unload.

The detectives appeared suddenly out of the darkness with drawn guns. "O.K., hold it!"

David froze, a can of alcohol still in his arms. For a moment, he thought of dropping the can and running, but Old Bessie and the wagon were still there. How would he explain that to his father?

"Put the can down, boy," one of the detectives said.

Slowly David put down the can and turned to face them. "O.K., against the wall."

"Yuh shouldn't 'a' tried it, Joe," a detective said to Gennuario when he arrived.

Gennuario smiled. David looked at him. He didn't seem in the least disturbed by what had happened. "Come inside, Lieutenant," he said easily. "We can straighten this out, I'm sure."

The lieutenant followed Gennuario into the building and it seemed to David that they were gone forever. But ten minutes later, they came out, both smiling.

"All right, you guys," the lieutenant said. "It seems we made a big mistake. Mr. Gennuario explained everything. Let's go." As quickly as they had come, the detectives disappeared. David stood staring after them with an open mouth.

Needlenose sat silently on the wagon beside David as they turned into the stable. "I tol' yuh everything was fixed," he said when they came out in the street.

David looked at him. Fixed or not, this was as close as he wanted. Even the twenty-five dollars in his pocket wasn't worth it. "I'm through," he said to Needlenose. "No more."

Needlenose laughed. "Yuh scared?"

"Damn right I'm scared. There must be an easier way to make a living."

"If yuh find one," Needlenose said, "let me know." He laughed. "Shocky's got a couple of Chinee girls over at his flat. He says we can screw 'em tonight if we want."

David didn't answer.

"Sing Loo will be there," Needlenose said. "You know, the pretty little one, the dancer who shaves her pussy."

David hesitated feeling the quick surge of excitement leap through him.

It was one o'clock by the big clock in the window of Goldfarb's Delicatessen when he turned the corner of his street. A police car was parked in front of the door. There was a group of people surging around, peering curiously into the hallway.

A sudden fear ran through David. Something had gone wrong. The police had come to arrest him. For a moment, he felt like running in the opposite direction. But a compulsion drew him toward the house. "What happened?" he asked a man standing on the edge of the crowd.

"I dunno," the man answered. He peered at him curiously. "I heard one of the cops say somebody was dying up there."

Suddenly, frantically, David pushed his way through the crowd into the house. As he ran up the staircase toward the apartment on the third floor, he heard the scream.

His mother was standing in the doorway, struggling in the arms of two policemen. "Chaim, Chaim!"

David felt his heart constrict. "Mama," he called. "What happened?"

His mother looked at him with unseeing eyes. "A doctor I call for, policemen I get," she said, then turned her face down the hallway toward the toilets. "Chaim, Chaim!" She screamed again.

David turned and followed her gaze. The door to one of the toilets stood open. His father sat there on the seat, leaning crazily against the wall, his eyes and mouth open, moisture trickling down into his gray beard.

"Chaim!" his mother screamed accusingly. "It was gas you told me you got. You didn't tell me you were coming out here to die."

CHAPTER FOUR

"So it's my fault his father dies before he can finish school?" Uncle Bernie said angrily. "Let him get a job and go nights if he wants to go so bad."

David sat on the edge of his chair and looked at his mother. He didn't speak. "It's not charity I'm asking, Bernie," she said. "David wants a job. That's all I'm asking you for."

Norman turned and looked down at his nephew suspiciously. "Maybe a job you'd like in my company as a vice-president, hah?"

David got to his feet angrily. "I'm going out, Ma," he said. "Everything they said about him is true."

"Say about me?" his uncle shouted. "What do they say about me?"

David looked at him. "Down at the *shul* when I went to say *Yiskor* for Papa, they told me about you. They said you didn't come to the funeral because you were afraid somebody might ask you for a few pennies."

"From California I should come in one day?" Norman shouted. "Wings I ain't got."

He started for the door. "Wait a minute, David," his mother said quietly. She turned to her brother. "When you needed five hundred dollars before the war for your business, who did you get it from?"

She waited a moment before answering herself. "From your poor *schnorrer* of a brother-in-law, Chaim, the junkman. He gave you the money and you gave him a piece of paper. The piece of paper I still got but did we ever see the money?"

"Paper?" Bernie said. "What paper?"

"I still got it," she said. "In the box Chaim put it in that night, the night he gave you the money."

"Let me see." Bernie's eyes followed her as she left the room. He was beginning to remember now. It was a certificate promising his brother-in-law five per cent of the Norman Company stock when he bought out the old Diamond Film Company. He had forgotten all about it. But a smart lawyer could make it worth a lot of money.

His sister came back into the room and handed him a sheet of paper. It was faded and yellow but the date on it was still bright and clear. September 7, 1912. That was fourteen years ago. How time had flown.

He looked at his sister. "It's against my policy to hire relatives," he said. "It looks bad for the business."

"So who's to know he's your nephew?" Esther said. "Besides, who will do more for you than your own flesh and blood?"

He stared at her for a moment, then got to his feet. "All right, I'll do it. It's against my better judgment but maybe you're right. Blood is thicker than water.

Over on Forty-third Street, near the river, we got a warehouse. They'll put him to work."

"Thank you, Uncle Bernie," David said gratefully.

"Mind you, not one word about being my nephew. One word I hear and you're finished."

"I won't say anything, Uncle Bernie."

Norman started for the door. But before he went out, he turned, the paper in his hand. He folded it and put it into his pocket. "This I'm taking with me," he said to his sister. "When I get back to my office, they'll send you a check for the five hundred dollars with interest for the fourteen years. At three per cent."

A worried look came over his sister's face. "Are you sure you can afford it, Bernie?" she asked quickly. "There is no hurry. We'll manage if David is working."

"Afford it, shmafford it," Norman said magnanimously. "Let nobody say that Bernie Norman doesn't keep his word."

It was a dirty gray factory building down near the Hudson River, which had fallen into disuse and been converted into lofts. There were two large freight elevators in the back and three small passenger elevators near the front entrance, scarcely large enough to handle the crowd of workers that surged in at eight o'clock each morning and out at six o'clock each night.

The building was shared by five tenants. The ground floor housed an automobile-parts company; the second, a commercial cosmetic manufacturer; the third, the pressing plant for a small record company; the fourth, the factory of the Henri France Company, the world's largest manufacturer of popular-priced contraceptives and prophylactics. The fifth and sixth floors belonged to Norman Pictures.

David arrived early. He got off the elevator on the sixth floor and walked slowly down the wide aisle between rows of steel and wooden shelves. At the end, near the back windows, were several desks, placed back to back.

"Hello," David called. "Anybody here?" His voice echoed eerily through the cavernous empty floor. There was a clock over one of the desks. It said seven thirty.

The freight-elevator door clanged open and a white-haired man stuck his head out and peered down the aisle at David. "I thought I heard somebody calling," he said.

David walked up to him. "I'm supposed to see the foreman about a job."

"Oh, are you the one?"

David was confused. "What d'yuh mean?"

"The new boy," the elevator operator replied. "Old man Norman's nephew."

David didn't answer. He was too surprised. The elevator operator got ready to swing shut the doors. "Nobody's here yet. They don't get in till eight o'clock."

The steel doors closed and the elevator moved creakingly down out of sight. David turned from the elevator thoughtfully. Uncle Bernie had told him not to say anything. He hadn't. But they already knew. He wondered if his uncle knew that they knew. He started back toward the desks.

He stopped suddenly in front of a large poster. The lettering was in bright red—*Vilma Banky and Rod LaRocque*. The picture portrayed Miss Banky lying on a sofa, her dress well up above her knees. Behind her stood Mr. LaRoque, darkly handsome in the current Valentino fashion, staring down at her with a look of smoldering passion.

David studied the poster. A final touch had been added by someone in the warehouse. A milky-white condom hung by a thumbtack from the front of the male star's trousers. Next to it, in neat black lettering, were the words: *Compliments of Henri France*.

David grinned and began to walk up the aisle. He looked into the steel bins. Posters, lobby cards, displays were stacked there, each representing a different motion picture. David looked them over. It was amazing how much each looked like the next one. Apparently, the only thing the artist did was to change the names of the players and the title of the picture.

He heard the passenger elevator stop, then the sound of footsteps echoed down the aisle. He turned and waited.

A tall, thin man with sandy-red hair and a worried look on his face turned the corner near the packing tables. He stopped and looked at David silently.

"I'm David Woolf. I'm supposed to see the foreman about a job here."

"I'm the foreman," the man said. He turned away and walked over to one of the desks. "My name is Wagner. Jack Wagner."

David held out his hand. "I'm pleased to meet you, Mr. Wagner."

The man looked at the outstretched hand. His handshake was soft and indecisive. "You're Norman's nephew," he said accusingly.

Suddenly, David realized the man was nervous, more nervous even than he was himself. He wondered why. It didn't make sense that the man should be upset because of his relationship to Uncle Bernie. But he wasn't going to talk about it, even though it seemed everyone knew.

"Nobody is supposed to know that but me," Wagner said. "Sit down here." He pointed to a chair near the desk, then took out a sheet of paper and pushed it over to David. "Fill out this personnel application. Where it asks for the name of any relatives working for the company, leave that one blank."

"Yes, sir."

Wagner got up from behind the desk and walked away. David began to fill out the form. Behind him, he heard the passenger-elevator doors open and close. Several men walked by. They glanced at him furtively as they walked over to their packing tables and began to get out equipment. David turned back to the form.

At eight o'clock, a bell rang and a faint hum of activity began to permeate the building. The day had begun.

When Wagner came back, David held out the application. Wagner looked it over carelessly. "Good," he said vaguely, and dropping it back on his desk, walked away again.

David watched him as he talked to the man at the first packing table. They turned their backs and David was sure they were discussing him. He began to feel nervous and lit a cigarette. Wagner looked over at him and the worried look on his face deepened.

"You can't smoke in here," he called to David. "Can't you read the signs?"

"Oh, I'm sorry," David answered, looking around for an ash tray. There wasn't any. Suddenly, he was aware that work had stopped and everyone was looking at him. He felt the nervous perspiration breaking out on his forehead.

"You can smoke in the can," Wagner called, pointing to the back of the warehouse. David walked down the aisle to the back, until he found the men's room. Suddenly he felt a need to relieve himself and stepped up to a urinal.

The door behind him opened and he sensed a man standing beside him. "*Khop tsech tu,*" he said.

David stared at him. The man grinned back, exposing a mouth filled with gold teeth. "You're Chaim Woolf's boy," he said in Yiddish.

David nodded.

"I'm the Sheriff. Yitzchak Margolis. From the Prushnitzer Society, the same as your father."

No wonder the word had got around so quickly. "You work here?" David asked curiously.

"Of course. You think I come this far uptown just to piss?" He lowered his voice to a confidential whisper. "I think it's very smart of your uncle to put you in here."

"Smart?"

The Sheriff nodded his bald head. "Smart," he repeated in the same stage whisper. "Now they got something to worry about. Too long they been getting way with murder. All you got to do is look at the tickets."

"Tickets?" David asked.

"Yeah, the shipping tickets. I pack three times in a day what it takes any of them a week. Me, I don't have to worry. But the loafers, let them worry about their jobs."

For the first time, David began to understand. The men were afraid of him, afraid for their jobs. "But they don't have to worry," he burst out. "I'm not going to take their jobs."

"You're not?" Margolis asked, a puzzled look in his eyes.

"No. I'm here because I need the job myself."

A disappointed look came over the Sheriff's face. Suddenly a shrewd look came into his eyes. "Smart," he said. "A smart boy. Of course you won't take away anybody's job. I'll tell 'em."

He started out. At the door, he stopped and looked back at David. "You remind me of your uncle," he said. "The old fart never lets his left hand know what his right hand is doing."

The door closed behind him and David flipped his cigarette into the urinal. He was half way down the aisle when he met Wagner.

"You know how to work a fork lift?"

"The kind they use to lift bales?"

The foreman nodded. "That's the kind I mean."

"Sure," David answered.

The anxious look left Wagner's eyes for a moment. "Good," he said. "There's a shipment of five hundred thousand heralds downstairs on the platform. Bring it up."

CHAPTER FIVE

T HE ELEVATOR JARRED TO A STOP AT THE GROUND FLOOR AND THE HEAVY doors opened on the busy loading platform. Several trucks were backed up to the platform and men were scurrying back and forth, loading and unloading. Along the back wall of the platform were stacks of cartons and materials.

David turned to the elevator operator. "Which is the stuff I'm supposed to bring up?"

The man shrugged his shoulders. "Ask the platform boss. I jus' run the elevator."

"Which is the platform boss?"

The elevator operator pointed at a heavy-set man in an undershirt. Thick black hair spilled out from his chest and sprouted furiously from his forearms. His features were coarse and heavy and his skin had the red flush of a heavy drinker. David walked over to him.

"What d'yuh want?" he asked.

"Mr. Wagner sent me to pick up the heralds."

The platform boss squinted at him. "Wagner, huh? Where's Sam?"

David stared at him. "Sam?"

"Sam the receiving clerk, yuh dope."

"How the hell do I know?" David asked. He was beginning to get angry.

The platform boss looked over his head at the elevator operator. "They didn't can Sam to give this jerk a job, did they?" he yelled.

"Naw. I seen him workin' upstairs at one of the packing tables."

The platform boss turned back to David. "Over there." He pointed. "Against the wall."

The heralds were stacked on wooden racks in bundles of a thousand. There were four racks, one hundred and twenty-five bundles on each. David rolled the fork lift over to one and set the two prongs under it. He threw his weight back against the handles, but his one hundred and thirty pounds wasn't enough to raise the rack off the floor.

David turned around. The platform boss was grinning. "Can't you give me a lift with this?"

The man laughed. "I got my own work to do," he said derisively. "Tell ol' man Norman he hired a boy to do a man's job."

David was suddenly aware of the silence that had come over the platform. He looked around. The elevator operator had a peculiar smirk on his face; even the truck drivers were grinning. Angrily he felt the red flush creep up into his face. They were all in on it. They were waiting for the boss's nephew to fall flat on his face. He pulled a cigarette absently from his pocket and started to light it.

"No smoking on the platform," the boss said. "Down in the street if yuh want to smoke."

David looked at him a moment, then silently walked down the ramp to the street. He heard a burst of laughter behind him. The platform boss's voice carried. "I guess we showed the little Jew bastard where to get off!"

He walked around the side of the building and lit his cigarette. He wondered if they were all in on it. Even the foreman upstairs, Wagner, hadn't been exactly happy to see him. He must have given him the job knowing he didn't have the weight to swing a fork lift.

He looked across the street. There was a garage directly opposite and it gave him an idea.

Fifty cents to the mechanic and he came back, pushing the big hydraulic jack the garage used for trucks. Silence came over the platform again as he jockeyed the jack under the wooden rack. Quickly he pumped the handle and the rack lifted into the air.

In less than five minutes, David had the four racks loaded on the elevator. "O.K.," he said to the operator. "Let's take her up." He was smiling as the doors clanged shut on the scowling face of the platform boss.

The men looked up from their packing tables as the elevator door swung open. "Wait a minute," he said to the elevator operator. "I'll go ask Wagner where he wants these."

He walked down the aisle to the foreman's empty desk. He turned and saw the men watching from their tables. "Where's Wagner?"

They looked at each other awkwardly for a moment. Finally, the Sheriff answered him. "He's in the can, sneaking a smoke."

David thanked him and walked down the back aisle to the washroom. The foreman was talking to another man, a cigarette in his hand. David came up behind him. "Mr. Wagner?"

Wagner jumped. He turned around, a strange expression on his face. "What's the matter, David?" he asked angrily. "Can't you get those heralds up?"

David stared at him. The foreman was in on it, all right. They were all in on it. He laughed bitterly to himself. And Uncle Bernie had said it was going to be a secret.

"Well," the foreman said irritably, "if you can't do it, let me know."

"They're up here now. I just want to know where to put them."

"You got them up here already?" Wagner said. His voice lost the faint note of sureness it had contained a moment before.

"Yes, sir."

Wagner threw his cigarette in the urinal. "Good," he said, a faintly puzzled look on his face. "They go over on Aisle Five. I'll show you which bins."

It was almost ten thirty by the time David had the racks empty and the bins filled. He pushed the last package of heralds into place and straightened up. He felt the sweat streaming through his shirt and looked down at himself. The clean white shirt that his mother had made him wear was grimy with dust. He wiped his forehead on his sleeve and walked down to the foreman's desk. "What do you want me to do next?"

"Were there five hundred bundles?" the foreman asked.

David nodded.

The foreman pushed a sheet of paper toward him. "Initial the receipt slip, then."

David looked over the paper as he picked up a pencil. It was the bill for the heralds: "500 M Heralds @ $1.00 per M—$500.00." Expensive paper, he thought, as he scribbled his initials across the bottom.

The telephone on the desk rang and the foreman picked it up. "Warehouse."

David could hear a voice crackling at the other end, though he could not distinguish the words. Wagner was nodding his head. "Yes, Mr. Bond. They just came in."

Wagner looked over at David. "Get me a sample of one of those heralds," he said, shielding the phone with his hand.

David nodded and ran down the aisle. He pulled a herald from one of the bundles and brought it back to the foreman. Wagner snatched it from his hand and looked at it. "No, Mr. Bond. It's only one color."

The voice on the other end of the telephone rose to a shriek. Wagner began to look uncomfortable, and shortly afterward, put the receiver down slowly. "That was Mr. Bond in purchasing."

David nodded. He didn't speak.

Wagner cleared his throat uncomfortably. "Those heralds we just got. It was supposed to be a two-color job."

David looked down at the black-and-white handbill. He couldn't see what they were so excited about. After all, they were only throw-aways. What difference did it make whether it was one color or two?

"Mr. Bond says to junk 'em."

David looked at him in surprise. "Junk 'em?"

Wagner nodded and got to his feet. "Get them out of the bins and downstairs again," he said. "We'll need the space. The new ones will be here this afternoon."

David shrugged. This was a screwy business, when something could be junked even before it was paid for. But it was none of his concern. "I'll get right on it."

It was twelve thirty when he came out on the loading platform, pushing the first rack of heralds. The platform boss yelled. "Hey, where yuh goin' with that?"

"It's junk."

The platform boss walked over and looked into the elevator. "Junk, eh?" he asked. "All of it?"

David nodded. "Where shall I put it?"

"You ain't puttin' it no place," the boss said. "Beat it right back upstairs an' tell Wagner to shell out five bucks if he expects me to get rid of his junk."

Again David could feel his anger rising slowly.

Wagner was at his desk when David got back upstairs. "The platform boss wants five bucks to get rid of that junk."

"Oh, sure," Wagner said. "I forgot." He took a tin box out of his desk and opened it. He held out a five-dollar bill.

David stared down at it. "You mean you really got to give to him?" he asked in disbelief.

Wagner nodded.

"But that's good newspaper stock," David said. "My father would haul that away all day long. It's worth a dime a hundredweight. That batch would bring fifty bucks at any junk yard."

"We haven't the time to bother with it. Here, give him the five bucks and forget about it."

David stared at him. Nothing in this business made any sense to him. They junked five hundred dollars' worth of paper before they'd paid for it, then didn't even want to salvage fifty bucks out of it. They'd rather pay five bucks more just to get rid of it.

His uncle couldn't be as smart as they said he was if he ran his business like this. He must be lucky. If it wasn't luck, then his father would have been a millionaire. He took a deep breath. "Do I get an hour for lunch, Mr. Wagner?"

The foreman nodded. "Sure. We all do."

"Is it all right if I start my lunch hour now?"

"You can start right after you take care of the heralds."

"If it's all right with you," David said, "I'll get rid of them on my lunch hour."

"It's O.K. with me, but you don't have to. You get a full hour off for lunch."

David looked at the telephone. "May I make a call?"

Wagner nodded and David called Needlenose at Shocky's garage. "How quick can you get here with a truck?" he asked, quickly explaining the deal.

"Twenty minutes, Davy," Needlenose said. There was a moment's silence, then Needlenose came on again. "Shocky says he'll only blast yuh ten bucks for the truck."

"Tell him it's a deal," David said quickly. "And bring along a pair of dusters. We might have a little trouble."

"Gotcha, Davy," Needlenose said.

"O.K., I'll be out in front."

Wagner looked at him anxiously as he put down the telephone. "I don't want any trouble," he said nervously.

David stared at him. If they were all so afraid of him they wouldn't let him do his job, he might as well give them something to be afraid of. "You'll know what trouble is, Mr. Wagner, if Uncle Bernie ever finds out you've been spending five dollars to lose fifty."

The foreman's face suddenly went pale. A faint beading of perspiration came out on his forehead. "I don't make the rules," he said quickly. "I just do what purchasing tells me."

"Then you've got nothing to worry about."

Wagner put the five-dollar bill back in the tin box, then put the box back in his desk and locked the drawer. He got to his feet. "I think I'll go to lunch," he said.

David sat down in the foreman's chair and lit a cigarette, ignoring the no-smoking sign. The men at the packing tables were watching him. He stared back at them silently. After a few minutes, they began to leave, one or two at a time, apparently on their way to lunch. Soon the only one left was the Sheriff.

The old man looked up from the package he was tying. "You take my word for it," he said. "It ain't worth you getting killed over. That Tony downstairs, he's a Cossack. You tell your uncle to give you a different job."

"How can I do that, pop?" David asked. "It was tough enough talking him into this one. If I come cryin' to him now, I might as well quit."

The old man walked over toward him. "You know where they went?" he asked in a shrill voice. "All of them? They didn't go to lunch. They're downstairs in the street. They're waiting to see Tony kill you."

David dragged on his cigarette thoughtfully.

"How come five bucks is that important?"

"From every tenant in the building he gets a little payoff. He can't afford to let you off the hook. Then he loses everybody."

"Then he's a *shmuck*," David said, suddenly angry. "All I wanted to do was my job. Nothing would have happened; he could still have gone on collecting his little graft."

David got to his feet and threw the cigarette on the floor. He ground it out under his heel. There was a bitter taste in his mouth. The whole thing was stupid. And he was no smarter than the rest; he let himself fall right into the trap they'd prepared for him. He couldn't back down now even if he wanted to. Neither could he afford to lose the fight downstairs. If he did, his uncle sure as hell would hear about it. And that would be the end of the job.

Needlenose was waiting for him downstairs.

"Where's the truck?" David asked.

"Across the street. I brought the dusters. Which ones do you want—plain or spiked?"

"Spiked."

Needlenose's hand came out of his pocket and David took the heavy set of brass knuckles. He looked down at them. The round, pointed spikes shone wickedly in the light. He slipped them into his pocket.

"How do we handle the guy?" Needlenose asked. "Chinee style?"

It was a common trick in Chinatown. A man in front, a man behind. The victim went for the man in front of him and got clipped from the rear. Nine times out of ten, he never knew what hit him. David shook his head. "No," he said. "I gotta take care of this one myself if it's going to do any good."

"The guy'll kill yuh," Needlenose said. "He's got fifty pounds on yuh."

"If I get into trouble, you come and get me out."

"If you get into trouble," Needlenose said dryly, "it'll be too late to do anything except bury yuh."

David looked at him, then grinned. "In that case, send the bill to my Uncle Bernie. It was all his idea. Let's go."

CHAPTER SIX

THEY WERE WAITING, ALL RIGHT. THE SHERIFF HAD BEEN RIGHT. THE whole building knew what was going to happen. Even some girls from the cosmetic company and Henri France.

It was hot and David felt the perspiration coming through his clothing. The platform had been a clatter of sound—people talking, pretending to eat their sandwiches or packed lunches. Now the pretense was gone, conversations and lunches forgotten.

The wave of silence rolled over him and he felt their curious, almost detached stares. Casually he looked over the crowd. He recognized several of the men from the packing tables upstairs. They averted their eyes when he passed by.

Suddenly, he was sick inside. This was madness. He was no hero. What purpose would it serve? What was so big about this lousy job that he had to get himself killed over it? Then he saw the platform boss and he forgot it all. There was no turning back.

It was the jungle all over again—the streets down on the East Side, the junk yards along the river, and now a warehouse on Forty-third Street. Each had its little king who had to be ever ready to fight to keep his little kingdom—because someone was always waiting to take it away from him.

A great realization came to David and with it a surge of strength and power. The world was like this; even his uncle, sitting way up on top there, was a king in his own way. He wondered how many nights Uncle Bernie stayed awake worrying about the threats to his empire.

Kings had to live with fear—more than other people. They had more to lose. And the knowledge was always there, buried deep inside them, that one day it would be over. For kings were human, after all, and their strength would lessen and their minds would not think as quickly. And kings must die and their heirs inherit. It would be that way with the platform boss and it would be that way with his Uncle Bernie. Someday, all this would be his, for he was young.

"Get the truck," he said, out of the corner of his mouth.

Needlenose walked down the ramp and across the street to where the truck was parked. David turned and pushed the big jack over to the nearest wooden rack. He pumped the handle and the rack lifted off the floor. He came to the edge of the loading platform just as Needlenose backed the truck to a stop.

Needlenose came down from behind the wheel. "Want a hand, Davy?"

"I'll manage," David said. He pushed the loaded jack onto the open platform of the truck and pulled the release. The wooden platform sank to the truck floor. He sneaked a look at the platform boss as he went back for the next rack of heralds. The man hadn't moved.

A faint hope began to stir inside David. Maybe he'd been wrong, maybe they'd all been wrong. He rolled the last rack onto the truck and pulled the release. There wasn't going to be a fight after all.

He heard a faint sigh come from the people on the platform as he turned the jack around to wheel it off the truck. He looked up. The platform boss was standing there, blocking the end of the truck. Stolidly David pushed the jack toward him. As he neared the platform boss, he put his foot on the front of the jack and stared at David silently. David looked down at his foot. The thick-soled, heavy-toed work boot rested squarely on the front of the jack.

David looked up at the man and tried to push the jack up onto the loading platform. The platform boss's foot moved quickly. The handle of the jack was torn from David's grasp and the jack itself skidded to the side, the front half completely off the truck. Its wheels spun in the narrow space between the loading platform and the truck. The nervous sigh came again from the crowd.

The platform boss spoke in a flat voice. "It'll cost yuh five bucks to get off that truck, Jew boy," he said. "If yuh ain't got it, jus' stay there!"

David slipped his hand into his pocket. The metal was icy cold against his fingers as he slipped the brass knuckles over his hand. "I got something for you," he said quietly, as he walked toward the man, his hand still in his pocket.

"Now you're getting smart, Jew boy," the boss said, his eyes turning away from David toward the crowd. It was at that moment David hit him. He felt the shock of pain run up his arm as the duster tore into the man's face. A half scream of pain came from his throat as the metal spikes tore his cheek open like an overripe melon.

He turned, swinging wildly at David, the blow catching him on the side of the head, slamming him back against the side of the truck. David could feel his forehead beginning to swell. It had to be a quick fight or the man would kill him. He shook his head to clear it and looked up to see the platform boss coming at him again. He braced his feet against the side of the truck and using the added leverage this gave him, lashed out at the man's face.

The blow never reached its target. The platform boss caught it on his raised arm but it spun him backward toward the edge of the platform. Again David lashed out at him. He sidestepped the blow but stumbled and fell from the platform to the ground.

David leaned over the big hydraulic jack and looked down at him. He was getting to his hands and knees. He turned his face up to David, the blood running down his cheeks, his lips drawn savagely back across his teeth. "I'll kill yuh for this, yuh Jew bastard!"

David stared down at him. The man was up on one knee. "You wanted it like this, mister," David said as he reached for the handle of the jack.

The platform boss screamed once as the heavy jack came down on him. Then he lay quietly, face on the ground, the jack straddling his back like a primeval monster.

Slowly David straightened up, his chest heaving. He stared at the crowd. Already they were beginning to melt away, their faces white and frightened. Needlenose climbed up on the truck. He looked down at the platform boss. "Yuh think yuh croaked him?"

David shrugged. He slipped the brass knuckles into his friend's pocket. "You better get the truck out of here."

Needlenose nodded and climbed behind the wheel as David stepped across onto the loading platform. The truck pulled out into the street just as Wagner came up with a policeman. The policeman looked at David. "What happened?"

"There's been an accident," David answered.

The policeman looked down at the platform boss. "Call an ambulance," he said quickly. "Somebody help me get this thing off him."

David turned and went up in the freight elevator. He heard the clanging of the ambulance while he was in the bathroom, washing up. The door behind him opened and he turned around.

The Sheriff was standing there, a towel in his hand. "I thought you could use this."

"Thanks." David took the towel and soaked it in hot water, then held it to his face. The heat felt soothing. He closed his eyes. The sound of the ambulance grew fainter. "You all right?" the old man asked.

"I'm O.K.," David answered.

He heard the old man's footsteps. The door closed behind him and David took the towel from his face. He stared at himself in the mirror. Except for a slight lump on his temple, he looked all right. He rinsed his face with cold water and dried it. Leaving the towel hanging over the edge of the sink, he walked out.

A girl was standing near the staircase, wearing the blue smock with Henri France lettered on the pocket. He stopped and looked at her. She looked vaguely familiar. She must have been one of the girls he had seen downstairs.

She smiled at him boldly, revealing not too pretty teeth. "Is it true you're old man Norman's nephew?"

He nodded.

"Freddie Jones, who runs your still lab, says I ought to be in pictures. He had me pose for him."

"Yeah?"

"I got them here," she said. "Want to see 'em?"

"Sure."

She smiled and took some photographs out of her pocket. He took the pictures and looked at them. This Freddie, whoever he was, knew how to take pictures. She looked much better without a smile. And without her clothes.

"Like 'em?"

"Yeah."

"You can keep 'em," she said.

"Thanks."

"If you get a chance, show 'em to your uncle sometime," she said quickly. "Lots of girls get started in pictures that way."

He nodded.

"I seen what happened downstairs. It was sure time that Tony got his lumps."

"You didn't like him?"

"Nobody liked him," she said. "But they were all afraid of him. The cop asked me what happened. I told him it was an accident. The jack fell on him."

He looked into her eyes. They were hard and shining.

"You're nice," she said. "I like you." She took something out of her pocket and gave it to him. It looked like a small tin of aspirin but the lettering read: *Henri France De Luxe*.

"You don't have to worry about those," she said. "They're the best we make. You can read a newspaper through 'em. I inspected and rolled them myself."

"Thanks."

"Got to get back to work," she said. She walked back to the stairway. "See yuh."

"See yuh." He looked down at the small tin in his hand and opened it. She was right. You could read right through them. There was a slip of paper in the bottom. Written on it in black pencil was the name Betty and a telephone number.

Wagner was sitting at his desk when David walked by. "You were pretty lucky," he said. "The doctor said that all Tony has is a concussion and a couple of broken ribs. He'll need twelve stitches in his cheek, though."

"He was lucky," David said. "It was an accident."

The supervisor's gaze fell before his. "The garage across the street wants ten bucks to fix the jack."

"I'll give it to them tomorrow."

"You don't have to," Wagner said quickly. "I already did."

"Thanks."

The foreman looked up from his desk. His eyes met David's squarely. "I wish we could pretend this morning never happened," he said in a low voice. "I'd like to start all over again."

David stared at him for a moment. Then he smiled and held out his hand. "My name is David Woolf," he said. "I'm supposed to see the foreman about a job."

The foreman looked at David's hand and got to his feet. "I'm Jack Wagner, the foreman," he said, and his grip was firm. "Let me introduce you to the boys."

When David turned toward the packaging tables, all the men were grinning at him. Suddenly, they weren't strangers any more. They were friends.

CHAPTER SEVEN

BERNARD NORMAN WALKED INTO HIS NEW YORK OFFICE. IT WAS TEN o'clock in the morning and his eyes were bright and shining, his cheeks pink from the winter air, after his brisk walk down from the hotel.

"Good morning, Mr. Norman," his secretary said. "Have a nice trip?"

He smiled back at her as he walked on into his private office and opened the window. He stood there breathing in the cold fresh air. Ah, this was *geshmach*. Not like the day-in, day-out sameness of California.

Norman went over to his desk and took a large cigar from the humidor. He lit it slowly, relishing the heavy aromatic Havana fragrance. Even the cigars tasted better in New York. Maybe, if he had time, he'd run down to Ratner's on Delancey Street and have blintzes for lunch.

He sat down and began to go over the reports lying on his desk. He nodded to himself with satisfaction. The billings from the exchanges were up over last year. He turned to the New Yorker theater reports. The Norman Theater, his premiere house on Broadway, had picked up since they started having stage shows along with the picture. It was holding its own with Loew's State and the Palace. He leafed through the next few reports, then stopped and studied the report from the Park Theater. An average gross of forty-two hundred dollars a week over the past two months. It must be a mistake. The Park had never grossed more than three thousand tops. It was nothing but a third-run house on the wrong side of Fourteenth Street.

Norman looked further down the report and his eyes came to rest on an item labeled Employee Bonuses. They were averaging three hundred a week. He reached for the telephone. Somebody must be crazy. He'd never O.K.'d bonuses like that. The whole report must be wrong.

"Yes, Mr. Norman?" his secretary's voice came through.

"Tell Ernie to get his ass in here," Norman said. "Right away." He put down the telephone. Ernie Hawley was his treasurer. He'd be able to straighten this out.

Hawley came in, his eyes shadowed by his thick glasses. "How are you, Bernie?" he asked. "Have a good trip?"

Norman tapped the report on his desk. "What's with this on the Park Theater?" he said. "Can't you bastards get anything right?"

Hawley looked confused. "The Park? Let's see it."

Norman gave him the report, then leaned back in his chair, savagely puffing at his cigar. Hawley looked up. "I can't see anything wrong with this."

"You can't?" Norman said sarcastically. "You think I don't know the Park never grossed more than three thousand a week since it was built? I'm not a dope altogether."

"The gross on the report is correct, Bernie. Our auditors check it every week."

Bernie scowled at him. "What about those employee bonuses? Twenty-four hundred dollars in the last two months! You think I'm crazy? I never O.K.'d anything like that."

"Sure you did, Bernie," Hawley replied. "That's the twenty-five-per cent manager's bonus we set up to help us over the slump after Christmas."

"But we set the top gross for the theaters as a quota," Norman snapped. "We figured out it would cost us next to nothing. What figure did we use for the Park?"

"Three thousand."

Bernie looked down at the report. "It's a trick," he said. "Taubman's been stealing us blind. If he wasn't, how come all of a sudden he's grossing forty-two hundred?"

"Taubman isn't managing the theater now. He's been out with appendicitis since right after Christmas."

"His signature's on the report."

"That's just a rubber stamp. All the managers have them."

"So who's managing the theater?" Norman asked. "Who's the wise guy beating us out of three hundred a week?"

Hawley looked uncomfortable. "We were in a spot, Bernie. Taubman caught us at a bad time; we didn't have anybody else to send in."

"So stop beating around the bush and tell me already," Norman snapped.

"Your nephew, David Woolf," the treasurer said reluctantly.

Norman clapped his hand to his head dramatically. "Oy! I might have known."

"There wasn't anything else we could do." Hawley reached for a cigarette nervously. "But the kid did a good job, Bernie. He made tie-ins with all the neighborhood stores, pulled in some give-aways and he swamps the neighborhood with heralds twice a week. He even started what he calls family night, for Monday and Tuesday, the slow nights. A whole family gets in for seventy-five cents. And it's working. His candy and popcorn sales are four times what they were."

"So what's the extra business costing us?"

Again the treasurer looked uncomfortable. "It added a little to operating expenses but we figure it's worth it."

"So?" Norman said. "Exactly how much?"

Hawley picked up the report. He cleared his throat. "Somewhere between eight and eight fifty a week."

"Somewhere between eight and eight fifty a week," Bernie repeated sarcastically. He got to his feet and glared at the treasurer. "A bunch of *shmucks* I got working for me," he shouted suddenly. "The whole increase does nothing for us. But for him it's fine. Three hundred a week extra he puts in his pocket."

He turned and stormed over to the window and looked out. The cold air came in through the open frame. Angrily he slammed down the window. The weather was miserable here, not warm and sunny like it was in California.

"I wouldn't say that," Hawley said. "When you figure the over-all, including the concession sales, we're netting a hundred and fifty a week more."

Norman turned around. "Nine hundred a week of our money he spends to make himself three hundred. We should maybe give him a vote of thanks that he lets us keep the hundred and fifty?" His voice rose to a shrill shriek. "Or maybe it's because he ain't yet figured out a way to beat us out of that!"

He stamped back to his desk angrily. "I don't know what it is, but every time I come to New York, I got to find *tsoris!*" He threw the cigar into the wastebasket and took a new one from the humidor. He put it between his lips and began to chew it.

"A year and a half ago, I come to New York and what do I find? He's working by the warehouse a little over a year and already he's making more on it than we do. A thousand a year he's making selling junked heralds, two thousand selling dirty pictures he's printing by the hundreds on our photo paper in our own still laboratory. A concession he's developed in all our offices around the country selling condoms wholesale. It's a lucky thing I stopped him, or we all would have wound up in jail."

"But you got to admit, Bernie, the warehouse never ran more smoothly," Hawley said. "That rotating perpetual inventory saved us a fortune in reorders."

"Hah," Norman exclaimed. "You think he thought about us when he did it? Don't be a fool! Seventeen dollars a week his salary was and every day he drives to work in a twenty-three-hundred-dollar Buick."

Bernie struck a match and held it to his cigar, puffing rapidly until it was lit. Then he blew out a gust of smoke and threw the match into the ash tray. "So I put him into the Norman as an assistant manager. Everything will be quiet now, I think. I can sleep in peace, I think. What trouble can he make for me in a big house like that?

"Trouble, hah!" He laughed bitterly. "Six months later, when I come back, I find he's turned the theater into a whorehouse and bookie joint! All the vaudeville acts in the country suddenly want to play the Norman. And why shouldn't they? Does Loew's State or the Palace have the prettiest usherettes on Broadway, ready to hump from ten o'clock in the morning until one o'clock at night? Does Loew's or the Palace have an assistant manager who'll take your bet on any track in the country, you shouldn't ever have to leave your dressing room?"

"But Gallagher and Shean, Weber and Fields, and all the other big acts played the house, didn't they?" Hawley asked. "And they're still playing it. It made the theater for us."

"It's a lucky thing I got him out of there and sent him to the Hopkins in Brooklyn before the vice squad got wise," Norman said. "Now I don't have a worry, I think. He can stay there as assistant manager the rest of his life. What can he do to us in Brooklyn, I think. I go back to the Coast, my mind at ease. I can forget about him."

Suddenly, he got to his feet again. "So six months later, I come back and what do I find? He's making a monkey out of the whole company. He's taking home more money than a vice-president."

Hawley looked at him. "Maybe that's what you ought to do."

"What?"

"Make him a vice-president," Hawley said.

"But—but he's only a kid," Norman said.

"He was twenty-one last month. He's the type boy I'd like on our side."

"No," Norman said, sinking back into his chair. He looked at the treasurer thoughtfully. "How much is he getting now?"

"Thirty-five a week," Hawley answered quickly.

Norman nodded. "Take him out of there, transfer him to the publicity department at the studio," he said. "He won't get into any trouble out there. I'll keep an eye on him myself."

Hawley nodded and got to his feet. "I'll take care of it right away, Bernie."

Bernie watched the treasurer leave the office, then reached for the telephone.

He would call his sister and tell her not to worry. He would pay their moving expenses to California. Then he remembered. She had no telephone and they'd have to call her from the candy store downstairs. He put the telephone back on the desk. He'd take a run up to see her after he got through with his blintzes and sour cream at lunch. She never went anywhere. She was always home.

He felt a strange pride. That nephew of his was a bright boy, even if he had crazy ideas. With a little guidance from himself, something the boy never got from his own father, who could know what might happen? The boy might go far.

He smiled to himself as he picked up the report. His sister had been right. Blood was thicker than water.

CHAPTER EIGHT

Harry Richards, chief of the studio police, was in the booth when Nevada drove into the main gate of the studio. He came out of the booth, his hand outstretched. "Mr. Smith. It's great to see you again."

Nevada returned his smile, pleased by the man's obvious warmth. He shook his hand. "Good to see you again, Harry."

"It's been a long time," Richards said.

"Yeah." Nevada smiled. "Seven years." The last time he'd been at the studio was just after *The Renegade* had been released, in 1930. "I've got an appointment with Dan Pierce."

"He's expecting you," Richards said. "He's in Norman's old office."

Nevada nodded. He shifted into gear and Richards stepped back from the car. "I hope everything works out, Mr. Smith. It would be like old times having you back."

Nevada smiled and turned the car down the road to the executive building. One thing, at least, hadn't changed around the studio. There were no secrets. Everybody knew what was going on. They obviously knew more than he did. All he knew was what he'd read in Dan's telegram.

He'd come in from the range and found it lying on the table in the entrance-way. He picked it up and ripped it open quickly.

HAVE IMPORTANT PICTURE DEAL FOR YOU. WOULD APPRECIATE YOU CONTACT ME RIGHT AWAY.

DAN PIERCE.

Martha came into the hall while he was reading it. She had an apron on over her dress, having just come from the kitchen. "Lunch is about ready," she said.

He handed her the telegram. "Dan Pierce has a picture deal for me."

"They must be in trouble," she said quietly. "Why else would they call you after all these years?"

He shrugged his shoulders, pretending a casualness he didn't feel. "It doesn't have to be that," he said. "Jonas ain't like Bernie Norman. Maybe things have changed since he took over the studio."

"I hope so," she said. Her voice took on a little spirit. "I just don't want them using you again." She turned and went back into the kitchen.

He stared after her for a moment. That was what he liked about her. She was solid and dependable. She was for him and nobody else, not even herself. Somehow, he had known it would be like that when they were married two years ago. Charlie Dobbs's widow was the kind of woman he should have married a long time ago.

He followed her into the kitchen. "I've got to go up to Los Angeles, to see the bank about the thousand acres I'm buying from Murchison," he said. "It wouldn't do any harm to drop by and see what Dan has on his mind."

"No, it wouldn't," she said, putting the coffeepot on the table.

He straddled a chair and filled his cup. "Tell yuh what," he said suddenly. "We'll drive up there. We'll stay at the Ambassador an' have ourselves a high old time."

She turned to look at him. There was a sparkling excitement hidden deep in his eyes. It was then she knew he'd go back if there was anything for him. It wasn't that they needed the money. Nevada was a rich man now by any standards. Everything was paying off—the Wild-West show, which still used his name; the dude ranch in Reno in which he and her late husband had been partners; and the cattle ranch here in Texas, where they were living.

No, it wasn't the money. He'd turned down an offer of a million dollars' down payment against royalties for the mineral rights to the north quarter. Oil had been found on the land adjoining it. But he wanted to keep the range the way it was, didn't want oil derricks lousing up his land.

It was the excitement, the recognition that came when he walked down the street. The kids clamoring and shouting after him. But they had other heroes now. That was what he missed. That—and Jonas.

In the end, it was probably Jonas. Jonas was the son he'd never had. Everything else was a substitute—even herself. For a moment, she felt sorry for him.

"How about it?" he asked, looking up at her.

A feeling of tenderness welled up inside her. It had always been like that. Even years ago, when they'd been very young and he'd come up from Texas to the ranch in Reno where she and Charlie had settled. Weary and beaten and hiding from the law, he'd had a haunted, lonely look in his eyes. Even then she'd felt the essential goodness in him.

She smiled. "I think that would be real nice," she said, almost shyly.

"It's a rat race," Dan said. "We don't make pictures any more. We're a factory. We have to grind out a quota of film each month."

Nevada slid back in his chair and smiled. "It seems to agree with you, Dan. You don't look none the worse for it."

"The responsibilities are killin' me. But it's a job."

Nevada looked at him shrewdly. Pierce had put on weight. "But it beats the hell out of workin' for a livin', don't it?"

Dan held up his hands. "I knew there'd be no point in looking for sympathy from you, Nevada." They both laughed and Dan looked down at his desk. When he looked up again, his face was serious. "I suppose you're wondering why I sent you that telegram?"

Nevada nodded. "That's why I'm here."

"I appreciate your coming," Pierce said. "When this deal came up, you were the first one I thought about."

"Thanks," Nevada said dryly. "What's the hitch?"

Dan's eyes grew round and large and pretended hurt. "Nevada, baby," he protested. "Is that the way to talk to an old friend? I used to be your agent. Who got you your first job in pictures?"

Nevada smiled. "Who sold my show down the river when he found he could get more money for the Buffalo Bill show?"

Pierce dismissed it with a wave of his hand. "That was a long time ago, Nevada. I'm surprised you even brought it up."

"Only to keep the record straight, Dan," Nevada said. "Now, what's on your mind?"

"You know how pictures are being sold nowadays?" Pierce asked, then went on without waiting for Nevada to answer. "We sell a whole year in advance. So many A pictures, so many B's, so many action-adventures, so many mystery-horrors and so many Westerns. Maybe ten per cent of the program is filmed when the sale's made, the rest as we go along. That's what I meant by rat race. We're lucky if we can keep ahead of our contracts."

"Why don't you accumulate a backlog for release?" Nevada asked. "That ought to solve your problem."

Dan smiled. "It would but we haven't the cash reserve. We're always waiting for the buck to come in from the current release so we can produce the next one. It's a vicious cycle."

"I still haven't heard your proposition," Nevada said.

"I'm going to lay it right on the line. I feel I can speak frankly to you."

Nevada nodded.

"Jonas has us on a short budget," Dan said. "I'm not complaining; maybe Jonas is right. At least, we didn't lose any money last year and it's the first time in almost five years we broke even. Now, this year, the sales department thinks they can sell fourteen Westerns."

"Sounds fine," Nevada said.

"We haven't got the money to make them. But the bank will lend us the money if you'll star in them."

"You know?" Nevada asked.

Pierce nodded. "I spoke to Moroni myself. He thought it was a great idea."

"How much will they advance you?" Nevada asked.

"Forty thousand a picture."

Nevada laughed. "For the entire negative cost?"

Dan nodded.

Nevada got to his feet. "Thanks, pal."

"Hold on a minute, Nevada," Dan said. "Wait until I finish. You didn't think I'd get you up here unless I thought you could make a buck, did you?"

Nevada sank back into his seat silently.

"I know how you feel about quickies," Dan said. "But believe me, these will be different. We still have the sets we used for *The Renegade*, out on the back lot. Dress them up a little and they'll be good as new. I'll use my top production staff. You can have your choice of any director and cameraman on the lot. That goes for writers and producers, too. I think too much of you, baby, to louse you up."

"That's fine," Nevada said. "But what am I supposed to work for? Spit and tobacco?"

"I think I've got a good deal for you. I had our accountants look into it and figure out a way you can keep some money instead of paying it all out in these damn taxes Roosevelt is slapping on us."

Nevada stared at him. "This better be good."

"We'll salary you ten grand a picture," Dan said. "That breaks down to five grand a week, because each picture will only take two weeks to shoot. You defer your salary until first profits and we'll give you the picture outright after seven years. You'll own the entire thing—negative and prints—lock, stock and barrel. Then, if you want, we'll buy it back from you. That'll give you a capital gain."

Nevada's face was impassive. "You sound just like Bernie Norman," he said. "It must be the office."

Pierce smiled. "The difference is that Norman was out to screw you. I'm not. I just want to keep this factory running."

"What would we use for stories?"

"I didn't want to look into that until after I'd talked to you," Dan said quickly. "You know I always had a high regard for your story sense."

Nevada smiled. He knew from Pierce's answer that he hadn't even thought about stories yet. "The important thing would be to hang the series on a character people can believe in."

"Exactly how I felt about it," Dan exclaimed. "I was thinking maybe we'd have you playing yourself. Each time, you'd get into another adventure. You know, full of the old stunts, tricks and shoot-outs."

Nevada shook his head. "Uh-uh. I can't buy that. It always seems phony. Gene Autry and Roy Rogers do that at Republic. Besides, I don't think anybody else would believe it. Not with this white hair of mine."

Pierce looked at him. "We could always dye it black."

Nevada smiled. "No, thanks," he said. "I kinda got used to it."

"We'll come up with it," Dan said. "Even if we have to pick up something from Zane Grey or Clarence Mulford. Just you say the word and we're off."

Nevada got to his feet. "Let me think about it a little," he said. "I'll talk it over with Martha and let you know."

"I heard you got married again," Dan said. "My belated congratulations."

Nevada started for the door. Halfway there, he paused and looked back. "By the way," he asked, "how's Jonas?"

For the first time since they had met, Pierce seemed to hesitate. "All right, I guess."

"You guess?" Nevada asked. "Why? Haven't you seen him?"

"Not since New York, about two years ago," Pierce answered. "When we took over the company."

"And you haven't seen him since?" Nevada asked incredulously. "Doesn't he ever come to the studio?"

Dan looked down at his desk. He seemed almost embarrassed. "Nobody sees him much any more. Once in a while, if we're lucky, he'll talk to us on the telephone. Sometimes he comes here. But it's always late at night, when there's nobody around. We know he's been here by the messages he leaves."

"But what if something important comes up?"

"We call McAllister, who lets Jonas know we want to talk to him. Sometimes he calls us back. Most of the time, he just tells Mac how he wants it handled."

Suddenly, Nevada had the feeling that Jonas needed him. He looked across the room at Dan. "Well, I can't make up my mind about this until I talk to Jonas."

"But I just got through telling you, nobody sees him."

"You want me to do the pictures?" Nevada asked.

Pierce stared at him. "He may not even be in this country. We might not hear from him for a month."

Nevada opened the door. "I can wait," he said.

CHAPTER NINE

"ARE YOU STAYING FOR SUPPER, DUVIDELE?"

"I can't, Mama," David said. "I just came by to see how you were."

"How am I? I'm the way I always am. My arthritis is bothering me. Not too much, not too little. Like always."

"You should get out in the sun more often. For all the sun you get, you might as well be living back in New York."

"A son I got," Mrs. Woolf said, "even if I never see him. Even if he stays in a hotel. Once every three months, maybe, he comes. I suppose I should be glad he comes at all."

"Cut it out, Mama. You know how busy I am."

"Your Uncle Bernie found time to come home every night," his mother said.

"Times were different then, Mama," he said lamely. He couldn't tell her that her brother had been known all over Hollywood as the matinee man. Besides, Aunt May would have killed him if he stayed out. She kept a closer guard on him than the government kept on Fort Knox.

"One week you're here already and this is only the second time you've been to see me. And not even once for supper!"

"I'll make it for supper soon, Mama. I promise."

She fixed him with a piercing glance. "Thursday night," she said suddenly.

He looked at her in surprise. "Thursday night? Why Thursday night, all of a sudden?"

A mysterious smile came over her face. "I got someone I want you should meet," she said. "Someone very nice."

"Aw, Mama," he groaned. "Not another girl?"

"So what's wrong with meeting a nice girl?" his mother asked in hurt innocence. "She's a very nice girl, David, believe me. Money her family's got. A college girl, too."

"But, Mama, I don't want to meet any girls. I haven't the time."

"Time you haven't got?" his mother demanded. "Already thirty years old. It's time you should get married. To a nice girl. From a nice family. Not to spend your whole life running around in night clubs with those *shiksas*."

"That's business, Mama. I have to go out with them."

"Everything he wants to do he tells me is business," she said rhetorically. "When he doesn't want to do, that's business, too. So tell me, are you coming to dinner or not?"

He stared at his mother for a moment, then shrugged his shoulders resignedly. "All right, Mama. I'll come. But don't forget, I'll have to leave early. I've got a lot of work to do."

She smiled in satisfaction. "Good," she said. "So don't be late. By seven o'clock. Sharp."

There was a message to call Dan Pierce waiting for him when he got back to the hotel. "What is it, Dan?" he asked, when he got him on the telephone.

"Do you know where Jonas is?"

David laughed. "That name sounds familiar."

"Quit kidding," Dan said. "This is serious. The only way we'll get Nevada to make those Westerns is if Jonas talks to him."

"You really mean he'll go for the deal?" David asked. He hadn't really believed that Nevada would. He didn't need the money and everybody knew how he felt about quickies.

"He'll go," Dan said, "after he talks to Jonas."

"I'd like to talk to him myself," David said. "The government is starting that antitrust business again."

"I know," Dan said. "I got the unions on my neck. I don't know how long I can keep them in line. You can't cry poverty to them; they saw the last annual reports. They know we're breaking even now and should show a profit next year."

"I think we better talk to Mac. We'll lay it on the line. I think two years without a meeting is long enough."

But McAllister didn't know where Jonas was, either. As David put down the telephone, a faint feeling of frustration ran through him. It was like working in a vacuum. Everywhere you turned, there was nothing. All you did was try and make deals. Deals. Piled one on top of the other like a pyramid that had no end. You traded with Fox, Loew's, RKO, Paramount, Warner. You played their theaters, they played yours. All you could do was stand on one foot, then on the other.

He wondered why Jonas took that attitude toward them. He wasn't like that with his other interests. Cord Aircraft was rapidly becoming one of the giants of the industry. Inter-Continental Airlines was already the largest commercial line in the country. And Cord Explosives and Cord Plastics were successfully competing against Du Pont.

But when it came to the picture company, they were just keeping alive. Sooner or later, Jonas would have to face up to it. Either he wanted to stay in this business or he'd have to get out. You had to keep pushing forward. That was the dynamics of action in the picture business. If you stopped pushing, you were dead.

And David had done all the pushing he could on his own. He'd proved that the company could be kept alive. But if they were ever going to make it for real, they'd have to come up with something really big. Deals or pictures—he didn't care which.

Actually, he preferred deals. They were safer and much less risky than big-budget pictures. Disney, Goldwyn and Bonner were all looking for new distribution outlets. And they all came up with big pictures, which grossed big and, best of all, were completely financed by themselves. He was still waiting for replies to the feelers he'd put out to Goldwyn and Disney. He'd already had one meeting with Maurice Bonner. But the approval for any such deal had to come from Jonas. It could come from no one else.

Bonner wanted the same kind of setup that Hal Wallis had at Warner's, or Zanuck had over at Twentieth Century-Fox—over-all executive supervision of the program, personal production of his own four major projects each year, stock and options in the company.

It was a stiff price to pay but that was what you paid if you wanted the best. Skouras hadn't hesitated when he wanted Zanuck. One man like that could add twenty million to your gross. It was the difference between existing and reaching for the brass ring.

But meanwhile, where was Jonas? Jonas held the one key that could unlock the golden door.

"There's a Mr. Irving Schwartz calling," his secretary said on the intercom.

David frowned. "What does he want? I don't know any Irving Schwartz."

"He says he knows you, Mr. Woolf. He told me to say Needlenose."

"Needlenose!" David exclaimed. He laughed. "Why didn't he say so the first time? Put him on."

The switch clicked as the girl transferred the call. "Needlenose!" David said. "How the hell are you?"

Needlenose laughed softly. "O.K. And you, Davy?"

"Fine. I've been working like a dog, though."

"I know," Needlenose said. "I been hearin' lots of good things about you. Makes a guy feel good when he sees one of his friends from the old neighborhood make it big."

"Not so big. It's still nothing but a job." This was beginning to sound like a touch. He figured rapidly how much old friends were worth. Fifty or a hundred?

"It's an important job, though."

"Enough about me," David said, eager to change the subject. "What about you? What are you doing out here?"

"I'm doin' O.K. I'm livin' out here now. I got a house up in Coldwater Canyon."

David almost whistled. His old friend was doing all right. Houses up there started at seventy-five grand. At least it wasn't a touch. "That's great," he said. "But it's a hell of a long way from Rivington Street."

"It sure is. I'd like to see you, Davy boy."

"I'd like to see you, too," David said. "But I'm so goddamned tied up here."

Needlenose's voice was still quiet, but insistent. "I know you are, Davy," he said. "If I didn't think it was important, I wouldn't bother you."

David thought for a moment. Now that it wasn't a touch, what could it be that was so important? "Tell you what," he said. "Why don't you come out to the studio? We can have lunch here, then I'll show you around."

"That's no good, Davy. We got to meet someplace where nobody'd see us."

"What about your house, then?"

"No good," Needlenose replied. "I don't trust the servants. No restaurants, either. Someone might snoop us out."

"Can't we talk on the telephone?"

Needlenose laughed. "I don't trust telephones much, either."

"Wait a minute," David said, remembering suddenly. "I'm having dinner at my mother's tonight. Come and eat with us. She's at the Park Apartments in West-wood."

"That sounds O.K. She still make those *knaidlach* in soup swimming with chicken fat?"

David laughed. "Sure. The matzo balls hit your stomach like a ton of bricks. You'll think you never left home."

"O.K.," Needlenose said. "What time?"

"Seven o'clock."

"I'll be there."

David put down the telephone, still curious about what Needlenose wanted. He didn't have long to wonder, for Dan came into his office, his face flushed and excited, his heavy jowls glistening with sweat. "You just get a call from a guy named Schwartz?"

"Yeah," David said, surprised.

"You going to see him?"

"Tonight."

"Thank God!" Dan said, sinking into a chair in front of the desk. He took out a handkerchief and mopped at his face.

David looked at him curiously. "What's so important about my seeing a guy I grew up with?"

Dan stared at him. "Don't you know who he is?"

"Sure," David said. "He lived in the house next to me on Rivington Street. We went to school together."

Dan laughed shortly. "Your friend from the East Side has come a long way. They sent him out here six months ago when Bioff and Brown got into trouble. He's union officially, but he's also top man for the Syndicate on the West Coast."

David stared at him, speechless.

"I hope you can get to him," Dan added. "Because, God knows, I tried and I couldn't. If you don't, well be out of business in a week. We're going to have the biggest, goddamnedest strike you ever saw. They'll close down everything. Studio, theaters, the whole works."

CHAPTER TEN

DAVID LOOKED AT THE DINING-ROOM TABLE AS HE FOLLOWED HIS mother into the kitchen. Places were set for five people. "You didn't tell me you were having a lot of company for dinner."

His mother, who was peering into a pot on the stove, didn't turn around. "A nice girl should come to supper for the first time with a young man without her parents?"

David suppressed a groan. It was going to be even worse than he'd suspected. "By the way, Mama," he said. "You better set another place at the table. I invited an old friend to have dinner with us."

His mother fixed him with a piercing glance. "Tonight, you invited?"

"I had to, Mama," he said. "Business."

The doorbell rang. He looked at his watch. It was seven o'clock. "I'll get it, Mama," he said quickly. It was probably Needlenose.

He opened the door on a short, worried-looking man in his early sixties with iron-gray hair. A woman of about the same age and a young girl were standing beside him. The worried look disappeared when the man smiled. He held out his hand. "You must be David. I'm Otto Strassmer."

David shook his hand. "How do you do, Mr. Strassmer."

"My wife, Frieda, and my daughter, Rosa," Mr. Strassmer said.

David smiled at them. Mrs. Strassmer nodded nervously and said something in German, which was followed by the girl's pleasant, "How do you do?"

There was something in her voice that made David suddenly look at her. She was not tall, perhaps five four, and from what he could see, she was slim. Her dark hair, cropped in close ringlets to her head, framed a broad brow over deep-set gray eyes that were almost hidden behind long lashes. There was a faint defiance in the curve of her mouth and the set of her chin. An instant realization came to David. The girl no more cared for this meeting than he did.

"Who is it, David?" His mother called from the kitchen.

"I beg your pardon," he said quickly. "Won't you come in?" He stepped aside to let them enter. "It's the Strassmers, Mama."

"Take them into the living room," his mother called. "There's schnapps on the table."

David closed the door behind him. "May I take your coat?" he asked the girl.

She nodded and slipped it off. She was wearing a simple man-tailored blouse and a skirt that was gathered at her tiny waist by a wide leather belt. He was surprised. He was experienced enough to know that the pert thrust of her breasts against the silk of the blouse was not fashioned by any brassière.

Her mother said something in German. Rosa looked at him. "Mother says you and Papa go in and have your drink," she said. "We'll go into the kitchen and see if we can help."

David looked at her. Again that voice. An accent and yet not an accent. At least, it wasn't an accent like her father's. The women turned and started toward the kitchen. He looked at Mr. Strassmer. The little man smiled and followed him into the living room.

David found a bottle of whisky on the coffee table, surrounded by shot glasses. A pint bottle of Old Overholt. David suppressed a grimace. It was the traditional whisky that appeared at all ceremonies—births, *bar mizvahs*, weddings, deaths. A strong blend of straight rye whiskies that burned your throat on the way down and flooded your nose unpleasantly with the smell of alcohol. He should have had enough brains to bring a bottle of Scotch. He was sure it was Old Overholt that had kept the Jews from ever acquiring a taste for whisky.

It was apparent that Mr. Strassmer didn't share his feelings. He picked up the bottle and looked at it. He turned to David, smiling. "Ah, *Gut* schnapps."

David smiled and took the bottle from his hand. "Straight or with water?" he asked, breaking the seal. That was another thing that was traditional. The bottle was always sealed. Once it was opened and not finished, it was never brought out for company again. He wondered what happened to all the open, half-empty bottles. They must be languishing in some dark closet awaiting the day of liberation.

"Straight," Mr. Strassmer said, a faintly horrified note in his voice.

David filled a shot glass and handed it to him. "I'll have to get a little water," he apologized.

Just then Rosa came in, carrying a pitcher of water and some tumblers. "I thought you might need this." She smiled, setting them on the coffee table.

"Thank you."

She smiled and went out again as David mixed himself a drink, liberally diluting it with water. He turned to Mr. Strassmer. The little German held up his glass. "*L'chaim.*"

"*L'chaim,*" David repeated.

Mr. Strassmer swallowed his drink in one head-tilted-back gesture. He coughed politely and turned to David, his eyes watering. "*Ach, gut.*"

David nodded and sipped at his own. It tasted terrible, even with water. "Another?" he asked politely.

Otto Strassmer smiled. David refilled his glass and the little man turned and sat down on the couch. "So you're David," he said. "I've heard a great deal about you."

David smiled back and nodded. This was the kind of evening it would be. By the time it was over, his face would ache from all this polite smiling.

"Yes," Mr. Strassmer continued. "I have heard a great deal about you. For a long time, I've wanted to meet you. We both work for the same man, you know."

"The same man?"

"Yes." Mr. Strassmer nodded. "Jonas Cord. You work for him in the movie business. I work for him in the plastics business. We met your mother at *shul* last year when we went there for the High Holy Day services." Mr. Strassmer smiled. "We got to talking and found that my wife, Frieda, was a second cousin to your father. Both families came originally from Silesia."

He swallowed the whisky in *his* glass. Again he coughed, and looked up at David through teary eyes. "A small world, isn't it?"

"A small world," David agreed.

His mother's voice came from behind him. "So, *nu*, it's time to sit down to supper already and where's this friend?"

"He should be here any minute, Mama."

"Seven o'clock you told him?" his mother asked suspiciously.

David nodded.

"So why isn't he here? Don't he know when it's time to eat, you should eat or everything gets spoiled?"

Just then the doorbell rang and David heaved a sigh of relief. "Here he is now, Mama," he said, starting for the door.

The tall, good-looking young man who stood in the doorway was nothing like the thin, intense, dark-eyed boy he remembered. In place of the sharp, beaklike proboscis that had earned him his nickname was a fine, almost aquiline nose that contrasted handsomely with his wide mouth and lantern-like jaw. He smiled when he saw David's startled expression. "I went to a face factory and had it fixed. It wouldn't look good I should walk around Beverly Hills with an East Side nose." He held out his hand. "It's good to see you, Davy."

David took his hand. The grip was firm and warm. "Come on in," he said. "Mama's ready to bust. Dinner's ready."

They went into the living room. Mr. Strassmer got to his feet and his mother looked at Needlenose suspiciously. David glanced around quickly. Rosa was not in the room. "Mama," he said. "You remember Irving Schwartz?"

"Hello, Mrs. Woolf."

"Yitzchak Schwartz," she said. "Sure I remember. What happened to your nose?"

"Mama," David protested.

Needlenose smiled. "That's all right, David. I had it fixed, Mrs. Woolf."

"A *mishegass*. With such a small nose, it's a wonder you can breathe. You got a job, Yitzchak?" she demanded belligerently. "Or are you still hanging around with the bums by Shocky's garage?"

"Mama!" David said quickly. "Irving lives out here now."

"So it's Irving now." His mother's voice was angry. "Fixing his nose is not enough. His name, too, he's got to fix. What's wrong with the name your parents gave you—Isidore—hah?"

Needlenose began to laugh. He looked at David. "I see what you mean," he said. "Nothing's changed. Nothing's wrong with it, Mrs. Woolf. Irving's easier to spell."

"You'd finish school like my son, David," she retorted, "It shouldn't be so hard to spell."

"Come on, Mrs. Woolf. David promised me *knaidlach*. I couldn't wait; all day I was so hungry thinking about it."

Mrs. Woolf stared at him suspiciously. "You be a good boy, now," she said, somewhat mollified, "and every Friday you come for *knaidlach*."

"I will, Mrs. Woolf."

"All right," she said. "So now I'll go see if the soup is hot."

Rosa came into the room just as David was about to introduce Needlenose to the Strassmers. She stopped in the doorway, a look of surprise on her face. Then she smiled and came into the room. "Why, Mr. Schwartz," she said. "How nice to see you."

Irving looked up. He held out his hand. "Hey, Doc," he said. "I didn't know you knew my friend David."

She took his hand. "We just met this evening."

Irving looked at David. "Doc Strassmer did my nose retread. She's really great, David. Did you know she did that job on Linda Davis last year?"

David looked at Rosa curiously. No one had ever said anything about her being a doctor. And the Linda Davis operation had been a big one. The actress's face had been cut to ribbons in an automobile accident, yet when she went before the cameras a year later, there wasn't the slightest visible trace of disfigurement.

He was suddenly aware that Mr. and Mrs. Strassmer were staring at him nervously. He smiled at Rosa. "Doctor, you're just the one I wanted to talk to. What do you think I ought to do about the terribly empty feeling I suddenly got in my stomach?"

She looked at him gratefully. The nervousness was gone from her eyes now and they glinted mischievously. "I think a few of your mother's *knaidlach* might fix that."

"*Knaidlach?* Who said something about my *knaidlach?*" his mother said from the doorway. She bustled into the room importantly. "So everybody sit down," she said. "The soup's on the table and already it's getting cold."

CHAPTER ELEVEN

WHEN THEY HAD FINISHED DINNER, ROSA LOOKED AT HER WATCH. "You'll have to excuse me for a little while," she said. "I have to run over to the hospital to see a patient."

David looked at her. "I'll drive you over, if you like."

She smiled. "You don't have to do that. I have my own car."

"It's no bother," David said politely. "At least, let me keep you company."

Irving got to his feet. "I have to be going, too," he said. He turned to Mrs. Woolf. "Thank you for a delicious dinner. It made me homesick."

David's mother smiled. "So be a good boy, Yitzchak," she said, "and you can come again."

Rosa smiled at David's mother. "We won't be long."

"Go," Mrs. Woolf said. "Don't you children rush." She glanced beamingly at Rosa's parents. "We older ones have a lot to talk about."

"I'm sorry, Irving," David said as they came out of the apartment house. "We didn't have much of a chance to talk. Maybe we can make it tomorrow?"

"We can talk right now," Irving said quietly. "I'm sure we can trust Rosa. Can't we, Doc?"

Rosa made a gesture. "I can wait in the car," she said quickly.

David stopped her. "No, that's all right." He turned back to Irving. "I must have seemed stupid when you called yesterday. But Dan Pierce mostly handles our labor relations."

"That's O.K., Davy," Irving said. "I figured something like that."

"Dan tells me we're looking down the throat of a strike. I suppose you know we can't afford one. It'll bust us."

"I know," Irving answered. "And I'm trying to help. But I'm in a spot unless we can work out some kind of a deal."

"What kind of a spot can you be in? Nobody's pressing you to go out on strike. Your members are just getting over the effects of the depression layoffs."

"Yeah." Irving nodded. "They don't want to strike but the commies are moving in. And they're stirring up a lot of trouble about how the picture companies are keeping all the gravy for themselves. A lot of people are listening. They hear about the high salaries stars and executives get and it looks good to them. Why shouldn't they get a little of it? And the commies keep them stirred up."

"What about Bioff and Brown?"

"They were pigs," Irving said contemptuously. "One side wasn't enough for them. They were trying to take it from both. That's why we dumped them."

"You dumped them?" David asked skeptically. "I thought they got caught."

Irving stared at him. "Where do you think the government got its documentation to build a case? They didn't find it layin' around in the street."

"It seems to me you're trying to use us to put out a fire your own people started," David said. "You're using the commies as an excuse."

Irving smiled. "Maybe we are, a little. But the communists are very active in the guilds. And the entire industry just signed new agreements with the Screen Directors Guild and Screen Writers Guild calling for the biggest increase they ever got. The commies are taking all the credit. Now they're starting to move in on the craft unions. And you know how the crafts are. They'll figure that if the commies can do it for the guilds, they can do it for them. The craft-union elections are coming up soon. The commies are putting up a big fight and if we don't. come up with something soon, we're going to be on the outside looking in. If that happens, you'll find they're a lot harder to deal with than we were."

David looked at him. "What you're suggesting, then, is for us to decide who we want to deal with—you or the communists. How do the members feel about it? Haven't they got anything to say?"

Irving's voice was matter-of-fact. "Most of them are jerks," he said contemptuously. "All they care about is their pay envelope and who promises them the most." He took out a package of cigarettes. "Right now, the commies are beginning to look real good to them."

David was silent while his friend lit a cigarette. The gold lighter glowed briefly, then went back into Irving's pocket. His jacket opened slightly and David saw the black butt of a gun in a shoulder holster.

Gold lighters and guns. And two kids from the East Side of New York standing in a warm spring night under the California stars talking about money and power and communism. He wondered what Irving got out of it but he knew better than to ask. There were some things that were none of his business.

"What do you want me to do?" he asked.

Irving flicked the cigarette into the gutter. "The commies are asking an increase of twenty-five cents an hour and a thirty-five-hour week. We'll settle for five cents an hour now, another nickel next year and a thirty-seven-and-a-half-hour work week." He looked into David's eyes. "Dan Pierce says he hasn't the authority to do anything about it. He says he can't get to Cord. I been waiting three months. I can't wait any longer. You sit on your can, the strike is on. You lose and we lose. Only you lose more. Your whole company goes down the drain. We'll still get lots of action other places. The only real winners are the commies."

David hesitated. He had no more authority than Dan to make this kind of deal. Still, there wasn't time to wait for Jonas. Whether Jonas liked it or not, he'd have to back him up.

He drew in his breath. "It's a deal."

Irving's white teeth flashed in a grin. He punched David lightly on the shoulder. "Good boy," he said. "I didn't think I'd have any trouble making you see the light. The negotiating committee has a meeting with Pierce tomorrow morning. We'll let them make the announcement."

He turned to Rosa. "Sorry to bust in on your party like this, Doc," he said. "But it was good seeing you again."

"That's all right, Mr. Schwartz."

They watched Irving walk over to the curb and get into his car, a Cadillac convertible. He started the motor and looked up at them. "Hey, you two. Yuh know what?"

"What?" David asked.

Irving grinned. "Like your Mama would say, you make a nice-looking couple."

They watched him turn the corner, then David looked at Rosa. It seemed to him that her face was slightly flushed. He took her arm. "My car is across the street."

She was silent almost the whole way to the hospital. "Something bothering you, Doc?" he asked.

"Now you're doing it," she said. "Everybody calls me Doc. I liked it better when you called me Rosa."

He smiled. "What's on your mind, Rosa?"

She looked down at the dashboard of the car. "We came all the way to America to get away from them."

"Them?" David asked.

"The same as in Germany," she said tersely. "The Nazis. The gangsters. They're the same, really. They both say the same things. Take us or you'll get the communists. And we'll be easier to get along with, you can deal with us." She looked up at him. "But what do you say when you find they've taken everything away from you? That was the gimmick they used to take over Germany. To save it from the communists."

"You're intimating my friend Irving Schwartz is a Nazi?"

She stared at him. "No, your friend is not a Nazi," she said seriously. "But the same insanity for power motivates him. Your friend is a very dangerous man. He carries a gun, did you know that?"

David nodded. "I saw it."

"I wonder what he would have done if you'd refused him," she said softly.

"Nothing. Needlenose wouldn't harm me."

Again her gray eyes flashed at him. "No, not with a gun," she said quickly. "Against you, he has other weapons. Economic weapons that could bankrupt your business. But a man does not carry a gun if he does not intend to use it, sooner or later."

David stopped the car in front of the hospital. "What do you think I should have done? Refuse to make a deal with Irving and let everything I've worked for all these years go to pot? Ruin every lousy investor who has put his faith and money in the company? Put our employees out on the streets looking for jobs? Is that what I should have done? Is it my fault that my employees haven't brains enough to choose decent representatives and see to it that they have an honest union?" Without realizing it, his voice had risen in anger.

Suddenly, she leaned over and put her hand on his where it rested on the wheel. Her hand was warm and firm. "No, of course it's not your fault," she said quickly. "You did what you thought was right."

A doorman came down the long steps and opened the car door. "Good evening, Dr. Strassmer."

"Good evening, Porter," she said. She straightened up and looked at David. "Would you like to come in and see where I work?"

"I don't want to get in your way. I don't mind waiting here if you'd rather."

She smiled and pressed his hand suddenly. "Please come," she said. "It would make me feel happier. Then, at least, I'd know you weren't angry at me for putting my—how do you say it—two cents into your business."

330 ❖ HAROLD ROBBINS

He laughed, and still holding his hand, she got out of the car and led him up the steps to the hospital.

He stood in the doorway and watched as she gently lifted the bandage from the child's face. She held out her hand silently and the nurse took a swab from a bottle and handed it to her. "This may hurt a little, Mary," she said. "But you won't move or talk, will you?"

The girl shook her head.

"All right, then," Rosa said. "Now we'll be still, very still." Her voice murmured, low and soothing, as her hand quickly traced the edge of the girl's lips with the swab. David saw the child's eyes fill with sudden tears. For a moment, he thought she was going to move her head but she didn't.

"That's fine," Rosa said softly as the nurse took the swab from her hand. "You're a brave girl." The nurse efficiently replaced the bandage across the girl's mouth. "Tomorrow morning, we'll take off the bandage and you'll be able to go home."

The girl reached for a pad and pencil on the table next to her bed. She scribbled quickly for a moment, then handed it to Rosa. She looked down at the paper and smiled. "Tomorrow morning, after the bandage comes off."

David saw the sudden smile that leaped into the child's eyes. Rosa turned to him as they walked down the corridor. "We can go back to your mother's now."

"That was a pretty little girl," he said as they waited for the elevator.

"Yes."

"What was the matter with her?"

She looked at him. "Harelip," she said. "The child was born with it." A note of quiet pride came into her voice. "Now she'll be just like anyone else. No one will stare at her or laugh when she talks."

The door opened and they stepped into the elevator. David pressed the button and the door closed. He noticed the note the girl had given Rosa still in her hand. He took it from her. It was in a childish scrawl. "When will I be able to talk?"

He looked at Rosa. "It must make you feel good."

She nodded. "Plastic surgery isn't all nose jobs, or double-chin corrections for movie stars. The important part is helping people so they can live normal lives. Like Mary up there. You've no idea how a deformity like that can affect a child's life."

A new respect for her grew in him as they crossed the lobby toward the front door. The doorman touched his cap. "I'll get your car, sir."

As he ran down the steps and crossed over to the parking lot, a big limousine came to a stop in front of them. David glanced at it casually, then turned toward Rosa. He pulled a package of cigarettes from his pocket. "Cigarette, Rosa?"

He heard the limousine door open behind him as Rosa took the cigarette. He put one in his own mouth and held a light for her. "You wanted to see me, David?"

David spun around, almost dropping his lighter. He saw the white blur of a shirt, then a head and shoulders appeared in the open doorway of the limousine. It was Jonas Cord. David stared at him silently.

Involuntarily David glanced at Rosa. There was a strange look in her eyes. He thought she might be frightened and his hand reached out for her.

Jonas' voice was a quiet chuckle behind him. "It's all right, David," he said. "You can bring Rosa with you."

CHAPTER TWELVE

ROSA SANK BACK ONTO THE SEAT IN THE CORNER OF THE LIMOUSINE. SHE glanced at David sitting next to her, then at Jonas. It was dark inside the car and occasionally the light from an overhead street lamp would flicker across Jonas' face as he sat facing them on the jump seat, his long legs stretched across the tonneau.

"How is your father, Rosa?"

"He is fine, Mr. Cord. He speaks of you often."

She sensed rather than saw his smile. "Give him my best when you see him."

"I will do that, Mr. Cord," she said.

The big automobile picked up speed as they came out on the Coast Highway. Rosa glanced out of the window. They were going north toward Santa Barbara, away from Los Angeles.

"McAllister said you wanted to see me, David."

She felt David stir on the seat beside her. He leaned forward. "We've gone about as far as we can on our own, Jonas. If we're to go any further, we'll need your O.K."

Jonas' voice was emotionless. "Why go any further?" he asked. "I'm satisfied with the way things are. You've eliminated your operating losses and from now on, you should be in the black."

"We won't stay in the black for long. The unions are demanding increases or they'll strike. That will absorb any profits."

"Let them," Jonas said, his voice still emotionless. "You don't have to give it to them."

"I already did," David answered.

Rosa could almost hear the moment's silence. She looked from one to the other, though she couldn't see their faces.

"You did?" Jonas said quietly, but an undercurrent of coldness had come into his voice. "I thought union negotiations were Dan's province."

David's voice was steady. There was a cautious note in it but it was the caution used by a man seeking his way through unknown territory, not that of fear. "It was, until tonight," he said. "Until it affected the welfare of the company. Then it became my business."

"Why couldn't Dan settle it?"

"Because you never replied to his messages," David said quietly. "He felt he couldn't make a deal without your approval."

"And you felt differently?"

"Yes."

Jonas' voice grew colder. "What makes you think you don't need my approval any more than he does?"

She heard a click as David flicked his lighter and held the flame to his cigarette. Light danced across his face for a moment, then went out. The cigarette glowed in the dark. "Because I assumed that if you'd wanted me to bankrupt the company, you'd have told me so two years ago."

Jonas ignored the answer. "What else did you want to see me about?"

"The government's starting that antitrust business again," David said. "They want us to separate the theaters from the studio. I sent you all the pertinent data some time ago. We'll have to give them an answer."

Jonas sounded uninterested. "I've already told Mac what to do about that. We'll be able to stall until after the war, when we ought to get a good price for the theaters. There's always an inflation in real estate after a war."

"What if we don't have a war?"

"We'll have a war," Jonas said flatly. "Sometime within the next few years, Hitler is going to find himself in a bind. He'll have to expand or bust the whole phony prosperity he's brought to Germany."

Rosa felt a knot in her stomach. It was one thing to feel that it was inevitable because you always kept hoping you were wrong. But to put it as simply and concisely as Jonas . . . Sans emotion; one plus one equals two. War. And then there would be no place left to go. Germany would rule the world. Even her father said that the Fatherland was so far ahead of the rest of the world that it would take them a century to catch up.

She stared at David. How could Americans know so little? Did they honestly believe that they could escape this war unscathed? How could he sit there talking business as if nothing were going to happen? He was a Jew. Didn't he, too, feel the shadow of Hitler falling across him?

She heard David chuckle. "Then we're in the same boat," he said. She stared at him in shocked surprise as he went on talking. "What we've done by virtue of enforced economies is to build a false economy for ourselves. One in which we count as profit the savings produced by eliminating the waste from our own body. But we haven't created any new sources of real profit."

"And that's why you've been talking to Bonner?"

She felt David start in surprise. For the first time that evening, his voice wasn't assured. "Yes," he answered.

"I suppose you felt it was quite within your authority to initiate such discussions without prior consultations with me?" Jonas' voice was still quiet.

"As far back as a year ago, I sent you a note asking your permission to talk to Zanuck. I never received a reply and Zanuck signed with Fox."

"If I'd wanted you to talk to him, I'd have let you know," Jonas said sharply. "What makes you think Dan can't do what Bonner can?"

David hesitated. He ground his cigarette out in the ash tray on the arm rest beside him. "Two things," he said cautiously. "I'm not knocking Dan. He's proved himself an extremely able administrator and studio executive. He has developed a program that keeps the factory working at maximum efficiency, but one of the things he lacks is the creative conceit of men like Bonner and Zanuck. The ability to seize an idea and personally turn it into a great motion picture."

He stared at Jonas in the dark. They passed a street lamp, which revealed Jonas for a moment, his eyes hooded, his face impassive. "Lack of creative conceit is the difference between a real producer and a studio executive, which Dan really is. The creative conceit to make him believe he can make pictures better than anyone else and the ability to make others believe it, too. To my mind, you showed more of it in the two pictures you made than Dan has in the fifty-odd pictures he's produced in the last two years."

"And what's the second?" Jonas asked, ignoring the implied flattery of David's words. Rosa smiled to herself as she realized that he'd accepted the remark as fact.

"The second is money," David replied. "Assuming Dan could develop this quality, it would take money to find out. Five million dollars, to make two or three big pictures. Money which you don't want to invest. Bonner brings his own financing. He'll make four pictures a year, and our own investment is minimal, only the overhead on each. Between distribution fees and profit-sharing, we can't get hurt, no matter what happens. And his supervision of the rest of the program can do nothing but help us."

"You've thought about what this would do to Dan?" Jonas asked.

David took a deep breath. "Dan is your responsibility, not mine. My responsibility is to the company." He hesitated a moment. "There'd still be a lot Dan could do."

"Not the way you want it," Jonas said flatly. "No business can run with two heads."

David was silent.

Jonas' words cut sharply through the dark like a knife. "All right, make your deal with Bonner," he said. "But it'll be up to you to get rid of Dan."

He turned in the jump seat. "You can take us back to Mr. Woolf's car now, Robair."

"Yes, Mr. Cord."

Jonas turned back to them. "I saw Nevada earlier," he said. "He'll make that series for us."

"Good. We'll begin checking story properties right away."

"You don't have to," Jonas said. "We settled that already. I suggested to him we pick up the character Max Sand from *The Renegade* and take it from there."

"How can we? At the end of the picture, he rode off into the hills to die."

Jonas smiled. "We'll presume he didn't. Suppose he lived, took another name and got religion. And that he spends the rest of his life helping people who have no one else to turn to. He uses his gun only as a last resort. Nevada liked it."

David stared at Jonas. Why shouldn't Nevada like it? It captured the imagination immediately. There wasn't a Western star in the business who wouldn't jump at the chance of making a series like that. That was what he'd meant by creative conceit. Jonas really had it.

The car came to a stop in front of the hospital. Jonas leaned over and opened the door. "You get off here," he said quietly.

The meeting was over.

They stood in front of his car and watched the big black limousine disappear down the driveway. David opened the door and Rosa looked up at him. "It's been a big night, hasn't it?" she asked softly.

He nodded. "A very big night."

"You don't have to take me back. I can get a cab here. I'll understand."

He looked down at her, his face serious, then he smiled. "What do you say we go someplace for a drink?"

She hesitated a moment. "I have a cottage at Malibu," she said. "It's not far from here. We could go there if you'd like."

They were at the cottage in fifteen minutes. "Don't be upset at how the place looks," she said, putting the key into the lock. "I haven't had time lately to straighten up."

She flicked on the light and he followed her into a large living room that was very sparsely furnished. A couch, several occasional chairs, two small tables with lamps. At one end was a fireplace, at the other a solid glass wall facing the ocean. In front of it was an easel holding a half-finished oil painting. A smock and palette lay on the floor.

"What do you drink?" she asked.

"Scotch, if you have it."

"I have it. Sit down while I get ice and glasses."

He waited until she went into another room, then crossed to the easel. He looked at the painting. It was a sunset over the Pacific, with wild red, yellow and orange hues over the almost black water. He heard ice clink in a glass behind him and turned. She held out a drink to him.

"Yours?" he asked, taking the glass from her.

She nodded. "I'm not really good at it. I play the piano the same way. But it's my way of relaxing, of working off my frustrations over my incapabilities. It's my way of compensating for not being a genius."

"Not many people are," he said. "But from what I've heard, you're a pretty good doctor."

She looked at him. "I suppose I am. But I'm not good enough. What you said tonight was very revealing. And very true."

"What was that?"

"About creative conceit, the ability to do what no other man can do. A great doctor or surgeon must have it, too." She shrugged her shoulders. "I'm a very good workman. Nothing more."

"You might be judging yourself unfairly."

"No, I'm not," she replied quickly. "I've studied under doctors who were geniuses and I've seen enough others to know what I'm talking about. My father, in his own way, is a genius. He can do things with plastics and ceramics that no other man in the world can. Sigmund Freud, who is a friend of my father's, Picasso, whom I met in France, George Bernard Shaw, who lectured at my college in England—they are all geniuses. And they all have that one quality in common. The creative conceit that enables them to do things that no other man before them could do." She shook her head. "No, I know better. I'm no genius."

He looked at her. "I'm not, either."

David turned toward the ocean as she came and stood beside him. "I've known some geniuses, too," he said. "Uncle Bernie, who started Norman Pictures, was a genius. He did everything it now takes ten men to do. And Jonas Cord is a genius, too, in a way. But I'm not sure yet in what area. There are so many things he can do, it's a pity."

"I know what you mean. My father said almost the same thing about him."

He looked down at her. "It's sad, isn't it?" he said. "Two ordinary nongeniuses, standing here looking out at the Pacific Ocean."

A glint of laughter came into her eyes. "And such a big ocean, too."

"The biggest," he said solemnly. "Or so some genius said. The biggest in the world." He held up his glass. "Let's drink to that."

They drank and he turned again to the ocean. "It's warm, almost warm enough to swim."

"I don't think the ocean would object if two just ordinary people went for a swim."

He looked at her and smiled slowly. "Could we?"

She laughed. "Of course. You'll find swimming trunks in the locker in the utility room."

David came out of the water and collapsed on the blanket. He rolled over on his side and watched her running up the beach toward him. He held his breath. She was so much a woman that he had almost forgotten she was also a doctor.

She dropped beside him and reaching for a towel, threw it across her shoulders. "I didn't think the water would be so cold."

He laughed. "It's wonderful." He reached for a cigarette. "When I was a kid, we used to go swimming off the docks in the East River. It was never like this." He lit the cigarette and passed it to her.

"Feel better now?" she asked.

He nodded. "It's just what the doctor ordered." He laughed. "All the knots came untied."

"Good," she said. She dragged on the cigarette and passed it back to him.

"You know, Rosa," he said, almost shyly, "when my mother asked me to dinner to meet you, I didn't want to come."

"I know," she said. "I felt the same way. I was sure you'd be a real slob."

She came down into his arms, her mouth tasting of ocean salt. His hand found her breast inside her bathing suit. He felt a shiver run through her as the nipple grew into his palm, then her fingers were on his thigh, capturing his manhood.

Slowly he reached up and slipped the suit from her shoulders and drew it down over her body. He could hear her breath whistling in her chest as he pressed his face against her breasts. Her arms locked around his head, closing out the night. Suddenly, her fingers were frantic, leading him to her, her voice harsh and insistent. "Don't be so gentle, David. I'm a woman!"

CHAPTER THIRTEEN

ROSA CAME INTO THE COTTAGE AND WENT DIRECTLY INTO THE BEDROOM. She glanced at the clock on the night table. It was time for the six-o'clock news. She turned on the radio and the announcer's voice filled the room as she began to undress:

Today the pride of the German army, Rommel, the "Desert Fox," got his first real taste of what it felt like to eat desert sand as, in the midst of a whirling, blinding sandstorm, Montgomery began to push him back toward Tobruk. Obviously inadequately prepared for the massive onslaught, the Italians, supporting Rommel's flanks, were surrendering en masse. With his flanks thus exposed, Rommel had no choice but to begin to fall back to the sea. In London today, Prime Minister Winston Churchill said—

She flicked off the radio. War news. Nothing but war news. Today she didn't want to hear it. She turned and looked at her naked body in the mirror over the dresser.

She pressed her hand to her stomach. It felt strong and somehow full to her. She turned sideways and studied herself. She was still flat and straight. But in a little while, she would begin to get round and full. She smiled to herself as she remembered the surprise she had heard in Dr. Mayer's voice. "Why, Doctor, you're pregnant!" There had been a look of amazement in his eyes.

She had laughed. "That's what I thought, Doctor."

"Well," he sputtered. "Well!"

"Don't be so shocked, Doctor," she said, almost dryly. "These things are known to happen to many women."

Then she was surprised by the sudden feeling of pride and happiness that swept through her. She had never thought she would feel like this. The thought of having a child had always frightened her. Not a physical kind of fear but rather that pregnancy might keep her from her work, interfere with her life.

But it turned out to be not like that at all. She was proud and happy and excited. This was something only she could do. There had never been a man, in all medical history, who had given birth to a child.

She threw a robe around her shoulders and went into the bathroom, turning on the tub water. Almost languidly she sprinkled the bath salts into it. The fragrance came up and tickled her nostrils. She sneezed. *"Gesundheit!"* she said aloud to herself and pressed her hands to her stomach.

She laughed aloud. The baby wasn't even shaped inside her yet and already she was talking to it. She looked at her face in the bathroom mirror. Her skin was clear and pink and her eyes were sparkling. She smiled again. For the first time in her life, she was glad she was a woman.

Carefully she stepped into the tub and sank into the warm water. She would not soak too long. She wanted to be at the telephone at seven o'clock when David called from New York. She wanted to hear the happiness in his voice when she told him.

David looked down at the blue, leather-bound book of accounts. Six million dollars' profit this year. Almost two million last year. If nothing else, the figures proved how right had been the deal he made with Bonner three years ago.

True, Bonner made almost as much for himself. But he had a right to it. Almost all that profit had come from his own big pictures, those he had produced and financed himself. If only David had been able to persuade Jonas to come up with the financing when Bonner offered it to them. If he had, the profit this year would have been ten million dollars.

Only one thing troubled David. During the past year, Cord had been gradually liquidating part of his stock as the market rose. He'd already recovered his original investment and the twenty-three per cent of the stock he still owned was free and clear. Ordinarily, in a company this size, that meant control. But someone was buying. It was the story of Uncle Bernie all over again. Only this time, Jonas was on the wrong side of the fence.

One day, a broker named Sheffield had come to see David. He was rumored to be the head of a powerful syndicate and their holdings in the company were considerable. David had looked at him questioningly, as he sat down.

"For almost a year now, we've been trying to arrange a meeting with Mr. Cord to discuss our mutual problems," Sheffield said. "But no one seems to know where he is or how he can be reached. We've never even received an answer to our letters."

"Mr. Cord is a busy man."

"I know," Sheffield said quickly. "I've had dealings with him before. The least I can say is that he's erratic." He drew a gold cigarette case from his pocket and opened it. Carefully he took out a cigarette and placed it between his lips. He lit the cigarette and as carefully put the case back in his pocket. He blew a cloud of smoke toward David. "Our patience is at an end," he said. "We have a considerable investment in this company, an investment that will tolerate neither a dilettante operation nor an obvious neglect of profit opportunities."

"It seems to me the investors have very little to complain about," David said. "Especially in view of the profits this year."

"I commend your loyalty, Mr. Woolf," Sheffield said. He smiled. "But we both know better. My group of investors was willing to advance the financing needed for certain pictures which might have doubled our profit. Mr. Cord was not. We are willing to work out an equitable stock and profit-sharing plan for certain key executives. Mr. Cord is not. And definitely we are not interested in burdening the company with certain expenses, like those at the Boulevard Park Hotel."

David had been wondering how long it would take him to get around to that. It was an open secret in the industry. Cord's harem, they called it.

It had begun two years ago, when Jonas tried to get a suite in the hotel for a girl and was refused. Using the picture company as a subterfuge, he then rented several floors of the staid establishment on the fringe of Beverly Hills. On the day the lease was signed, he had the studio move in all the girls on the contract-players' list.

There had almost been a riot as thirty girls swarmed into as many apartments under the shocked eyes of the hotel management. The newspapers had a field day, pointing out that none of the girls made as much in a year as each apartment would have ordinarily cost in a month.

That had been two years ago but the lease ran for fifteen years. Admittedly, it cost the company a great deal of money. The hotel would have been only too willing to cancel the lease but Jonas would have no part of it. Gradually most of the girls moved out. Now most of the apartments were empty, except when Jonas came across a girl he thought had possibilities.

David leaned back in his chair. "I don't have to point out, of course, that Mr. Cord receives no remuneration or expenses from the company."

Sheffield smiled. "We would have no objections if Mr. Cord rendered any service to the company. But the truth is that he is not at all active. He has not attended a single board meeting since his association with the company began."

"Mr. Cord bought the controlling interest in the company," David pointed out. "Therefore, his association with it is not in the ordinary category of employees."

"I'm quite aware of that," Sheffield said. "But are you quite sure control of the company still remains in his hands? We now have as much and perhaps more stock than he has. We feel we're entitled to a voice in management."

"I'll be glad to relay your suggestion to Mr. Cord."

"That won't be necessary," Sheffield said. "We are certain, because of his refusal to reply to our requests for a meeting, that he is not interested."

"In that case, why did you come to me?" David asked. Now the preliminaries were over; they were getting down to the heart of things.

Sheffield leaned forward. "We feel that the success of this company is directly attributed to you and your policies. We have the highest regard for your ability and would like to see you take your proper place in the company as chief executive officer." He ground out his cigarette in the ash tray before him. "With proper authority and compensation, of course."

David stared at him. The world on a silver platter. "That's very gratifying," he said cautiously. "What if I were to ask you to leave things as they are? What if I were to persuade Mr. Cord to adopt some of your suggestions? Would that be satisfactory to you?"

Sheffield shook his head. "With all due respect to your sincerity—no. You see, we're firmly convinced that Cord is detrimental to the progress of this company."

"Then you'd launch a proxy fight if I didn't go along with you?"

"I doubt that it would be necessary," Sheffield said. "I have already mentioned that we own a considerable amount of the stock outstanding. Certain brokers have pledged us an additional five per cent." He took a paper from his pocket and handed it to David. "And here is a commitment from Mr. Bonner to sell us all of the stock in his possession on December fifteenth, the day of the annual meeting, next week. Mr. Bonner's ten per cent of the stock brings our total to thirty-eight per cent. With or without the five per cent you own, we have more than sufficient stock to take control of the company. Even with proxies, Mr. Cord would not be able to vote more than thirty per cent of the stock."

David picked up the sheet of paper and looked at it. It was a firm commitment, all right. And it was Bonner's signature. He pushed the paper back to Sheffield silently. Suddenly, he remembered the old Norman warehouse, where he had first gone to work. The king must die. But now it was no mere platform boss, it was Jonas. Until this moment, he had never let himself think about it. Jonas had seemed invulnerable.

But all that had changed. Jonas was slipping. And what Sheffield was saying in effect was, string along with us and we'll make you king. David took a deep breath. Why shouldn't it be he? It was something he had felt ever since that first day in the warehouse.

Rosa put the newspaper down on the bed and reached for a cigarette. She looked at the clock. It was after eight. That made it after eleven o'clock in New York. David should have called by now. Usually, if he expected to be out late, he would let her know.

Could something have happened to him? Could he be lying hurt in the streets of New York, three thousand miles away, and she'd never know until it was too late?

She picked up the telephone and called him at his hotel in New York. She heard the rapid relay of the telephone across the country, then the phone ringing in his suite. It rang for a long time.

"Hello," he said. His voice was low and cautious.

"David, are you all right?"

"I'm fine," he said.

"I was worried. Why didn't you call?"

"I'm in the middle of a meeting."

"Oh. Are you alone? Are you in the bedroom?"

"Yes," he answered, in the same low, cautious voice. "I'm in the bedroom."

"Are you sitting on the bed?"

"Yes."

"I'm lying on the bed." She waited for him to ask the usual question. This time he didn't, so she told him, anyway. "I have nothing on," she whispered. A sudden warmth rose up in her. "Oh, David, I miss you so. I wish you were here beside me."

She heard the faint sound of a striking match. "I'll be out there by the end of the week."

"I can't wait, David. Can you?"

"No," he said, still cautiously.

"Stretch out on the bed for a moment, David," she whispered. "I want you to feel me as I feel you."

"Rosa—"

"Oh, David," she whispered, interrupting. "I can see you now. Hard and strong. I can feel you pouring life into me." She closed her eyes against the flush of heat spreading upward from her loins. She could hear his breathing in the telephone. "David," she whispered. "I cannot wait."

"Rosa!" His voice was harsh. "I—"

Her voice was warm and languid. "Freud would have a wonderful time with me," she whispered. "Are you angry with me, David, for being so greedy?"

"No," he said.

She took a deep breath. "I'm glad," she said. "I have wonderful news to tell you, darling."

"Can it wait until tomorrow, Rosa?" he said quickly. "I'm in the middle of an important meeting."

She hesitated in stunned silence.

He took it for acquiescence. "That's a good girl, darling," he said. "Bye now."

There was a click and he was off the line before she could answer. She stared at the telephone in bewilderment for a moment, then put it down slowly.

She reached for the cigarette still smoldering in the ash tray. The acrid smoke burned in her throat. Angrily she ground it out. She turned her face into the pillow and lay there silently.

I shouldn't have called him, she thought. He said he was busy. She got up from the bed and went into the bathroom. She looked at herself in the mirror.

You ought to be able to understand, she told herself. There have been times you've been too busy to come to the telephone when he called. You, of all people.

Almost surprised, she saw the tears well up into her eyes and begin to run down her cheeks. Then they overwhelmed her and she sank to her knees, her face against the cold porcelain bathtub. She covered her face with her hands.

Was this what it meant to be a woman?

CHAPTER FOURTEEN

MAURICE BONNER SAT UP IN THE BED AND WATCHED THE GIRL WALK over to a chair and sit down. He studied her appreciatively. The girl was naked. And beautiful. The strong, full breasts resting on the finely boned rib cage. The flat, hard stomach swelling abruptly into the surprising rise of her pubis, then tapering gently into the thighs of her long, slim legs.

He watched the muscles of her back suddenly come into play as she turned to pick up a pack of cigarettes from the table. He nodded to himself. She was beautiful, all right. Perhaps not in the ordinary sense of the word but beautiful as a whore had any right to be. And never was.

"Christ, you're ugly," the girl said, looking at him.

He grinned, exposing the crooked, uneven teeth in his long horse face. What she said was nothing new. He was not unaware of it himself; he could see it in his mirror. He threw back the sheet and got out of bed.

"Here, cover yourself," the girl said, flinging a towel at him. "You look like an ape with your cock hanging down like that." He caught the towel deftly and wrapped it around his waist. "Was it any good?" he asked curiously, taking a cigarette from the package.

She didn't answer.

"Was it worth it?"

"I guess it was," she said unemotionally.

He went back to the bed and sat down on the edge. "Is that all it is to you?" he asked. "Just another John?"

She stared at him. "You're supposed to be a pretty hep guy. You want the truth?"

He smiled again. "The truth, of course."

"You're all the same to me," she said, meeting his gaze steadily. "You might as well be goosing me with a Coca-Cola bottle for all the difference it makes."

"Don't you feel anything, ever?"

"Sure," she answered. "I'm human. But not with the customers. I can't afford it. They pay for perfection." She ground out the cigarette in the tray. "When I feel I got to get my kicks, I take a week off and go out to one of those dude ranches that cater to married women on holiday. There's always some cowpoke out there who thinks he's making it big for me. And he is, because I don't have to give him the best. But the Johns pay. You're entitled."

"But aren't you cheating the Johns?"

She smiled at him. "Do you feel cheated?"

"No," he said. Then he added quickly, "I don't know. I didn't know you were acting."

"I wasn't acting," she said, taking another cigarette. "I was working. That's my job."

He didn't speak.

She lit the cigarette and gestured toward him. "Look," she said. "You eat a good dinner. Afterwards, you say to your friends, that was a great steak. The greatest. You don't mind talking about it. You even tell your friends where you had it so they can get themselves one. Right?"

He nodded.

"It's like that with me," she said. "You got a friend. This time it's Irv Schwartz. You're playing gin and he looks at you and says, 'I had a great piece last night. The greatest. Jennie Denton. Give her a blast.' So you come over and put your money on the table. You climb up, you climb down. You get filled with air like a balloon and float around the world. I'll bet it's a long time since you popped three times in as many hours. Do you still feel cheated?"

He laughed, suddenly feeling young and strong. She was right. He hadn't felt like this in a long time, maybe twenty years. He felt the warmth return to his loins. He got up, letting the towel fall to the floor.

She laughed. "You're younger than I thought. Look, it's midnight."

"So?" He stared at her.

"The deal was two bills till midnight," she said. "You're all paid up. It's three bills from here till morning. But that includes breakfast."

He laughed. "You're worse than MCA. O.K., it's a deal."

She smiled and got to her feet. "Come on."

He followed her into a large bathroom with a giant square marble tub sunken into the floor. There was a rubbing table against the wall under the window. She gestured to it. "Get up there."

He sat on the edge of the table and watched her open the medicine cabinet. She took down a safety razor, a tube of shaving cream and a brush. She filled a tumbler with water and soaked a washcloth under the tap. These she placed on the edge of the sink near the table. "Lie down," she said, dipping the brush into the tumbler and working up a lather with the cream.

"What are you going to do?"

"What does it look like?" she asked. "I'm going to shave you."

"I shaved this evening."

She laughed. "Not your face, stupid." She reached out a hand and pressed him back onto the table. "I want to see what you look like underneath all that fur."

"But—"

"Lie still," she said fiercely, already beginning to brush the lather on his chest. "I won't cut you. I used to do this all the time when I worked in the hospital."

The lather was oddly soothing. "You worked in a hospital?"

She nodded. "I graduated from nursing school when I was twenty," she said. "Cum laude, too."

"Why'd you leave it?"

He scarcely felt the razor moving over his body. She turned to rinse it under the tap. "Sixty-five a month, eighteen hours a day," she said, turning back to him. She began to lather the other side of his chest. "And too many jokers thinking it was free."

He laughed as the razor glided across his stomach. "That tickles."

She rinsed the razor again. "Turn over," she said. "I want to do your back and shoulders."

He rolled over on his stomach and rested his face on his arms. The faint menthol smell of the lather came up into his nostrils. He felt the razor moving quickly over him. He closed his eyes.

She tapped him on the shoulders and he opened his eyes. She reached into the cabinet and took out a bar of soap. Breaking off the wrapping, she handed it to him. "Now take a hot shower and scrub yourself clean."

The water shot down at him in a needle spray, filling the stall with steam and the scent of jasmine from the soap. He could feel his skin beginning to tingle and glow. When he came out, his face was ruddy and smiling.

She held a large bath sheet toward him. "Dry yourself and get back on the table."

He toweled himself quickly and stretched out. She took a small hand vibrator from the cabinet and plugged it into the socket. She began to massage him slowly. The buzzing sound of the vibrator seemed to stretch and loosen the muscles in his body. "This is better than a Turkish bath," he said.

"This is a Turkish bath," she said dryly, then switched off the vibrator and threw the towel over him. "Now, you just lie there for a few minutes."

He watched as she leaned over the marble tub and turned on the water. She tested it carefully until it was just the temperature she wanted, then let it run. When the water had risen about four inches up the side of the tub, she turned it off. "O.K.," she said. "Get up."

He sat up, the towel falling behind him. "You know," she said, "you don't look half bad with all that hair off." She kicked the bathroom door closed, revealing a full-length mirror on the back.

He looked into the mirror and a smile broke over his lips. She was right. Suddenly, he looked twenty years younger. His body was clean and white under all that hair. He even felt slimmer.

She smiled at him in the mirror. "Enough narcissism," she said. "Get into the tub."

He sat down in the water. It was just slightly warmer than body temperature. "Stretch out. I'll be right back."

He leaned back in the tub and in a moment, she came back into the bathroom. In one hand she carried a magnum bottle of champagne, in the other a small vial. She put the champagne on the floor, opened the vial and let a few drops from it fall into the water. The heavy scent of jasmine immediately filled the room. She put the vial back on the basin and picked up the champagne bottle.

Expertly she ripped the foil and sprung the wire from around the cork. The cork popped and the champagne flowed over her fingers. "You forgot the glasses," he said, watching her.

"Don't be silly. Only fools drink this stuff. This is for the tub. It's better than bubble bath." She began to empty the bottle into the water around him.

The wine fizzed and tickled his skin with a refreshing sensation. She put the empty bottle on the floor and took a cigarette box from the cabinet. Opening it, she took out a cigarette and lit it. He smelled the dull, acrid pungency of marijuana.

She dragged once on the cigarette and held it toward him. "Here," she said. "Two puffs. No more."

He shook his head. "No, thanks. I don't go for that stuff."

"Don't give me a hard time," she said. "I only want to slow you down a little."

He took the cigarette from her hand and gingerly put it between his lips. He drew on it. The smoke went down deep inside him. There was no need for him to blow it out. His body had soaked it up like a sponge.

He looked down at himself in wonder. Suddenly he felt so buoyant. His body was so clean and strong. He looked up at her as she stepped into the tub. He dragged on the cigarette again. He could feel himself floating lightly in the water.

"That's enough." She took the cigarette from his lips and tossed it into the bowl.

"This is crazy," he said, smiling, as she stretched out in the water beside him.

"It had better be," she said, lowering her head to his chest, where he lay covered with a shallow layer of water. He gave a start of surprise as he felt her teeth scrape lightly across his breast. She raised her head, smiling as she looked at him. "It had better be," she repeated. "That bottle of champagne cost me twenty bucks."

He never knew exactly when the idea came to him. It was probably while he was asleep. But it didn't matter. It was there when he came down to breakfast that morning. And he had the confidence that came with the success of many such ideas in the past.

She looked up from the dining-room table when she heard the sound of his feet on the staircase. "Good morning, Mr. Bonner. Hungry?"

He returned her smile with appreciation. "Starved," he said, surprising himself. It had been a long time since he'd felt like eating a good breakfast. Juice and coffee was his usual routine.

He saw her foot move as she pressed a button on the floor under the table. A chime echoed from the kitchen in the back of the house. "Drink your juice," she said. "Your breakfast will be out in a minute."

He sat down opposite her and lifted the large glass of tomato juice out of the ice in which it had been resting. "Cheers."

He looked at her with approval. In the clear light of morning, there wasn't a trace of a line on her face. Her eyes were clear and dark and there was only a light touch of color on her lips. Her pale-brown hair was secured neatly behind her head in a pony tail. Her arms were tan against her white, short-sleeved sport blouse, which was tucked neatly, almost primly, into a casually tailored, gored skirt.

The door behind her opened and a heavy-set Mexican woman waddled in carrying a large tray, the contents of which she transferred to the huge Lazy Susan in the center of the table. Then she deftly removed the empty glass from in front of him and replaced it with a large dinner plate. "*Café, un momento*," she said quickly and vanished.

"Help yourself, Mr. Bonner," Jennie said. "You'll find ham, bacon, steak, kippers and kidneys on the plates with the green covers. There are fried eggs, scrambled eggs and French fries under the yellow covers."

He spun the Lazy Susan until he found the ham and served himself. As he filled his plate, the Mexican woman came back with a pot of coffee and hot rolls and toast. He looked down at his plate. The ham was just the way he liked it.

Jennie was helping herself to a generous portion of steak. "You set a hell of a fine table," he said as the Mexican woman filled his coffee cup.

Jennie smiled at him. "There's nothing cheap in this house."

The Mexican servant walked over and filled Jennie's cup, then waddled back into the kitchen. "You look like you're playing tennis this morning," he said.

She nodded. "That's exactly what I'm doing. I play for two hours every morning."

"Where do you play?"

"Bel Air. I have a standing date with Frankie Gardner."

He raised an eyebrow. Frankie Gardner was one of the top tennis pros in the country. He was expensive—at least twenty-five dollars an hour. "Is he one of your customers?" he asked curiously.

"I don't play with my customers. It's bad for business. I buy his time like anybody else."

"Why?"

"I like the exercise," she said. "It helps me keep in shape. You know by now that sometimes I put in some pretty long hours."

"I see what you mean. Have you ever thought about doing anything else?"

"What do you mean?" she asked. "I told you I studied nursing."

"I don't mean that. How come you never tried the movies?"

She laughed merrily. "I'm a native Californian, Mr. Bonner. I've seen what happens to the kids that come out here. Better-looking than I ever was. They wind up as car hops, hustling hamburgers, or five-dollar whores working the Strip. I know better."

"I mean it," he said earnestly. "Do you know who I am?"

"Of course, Mr. Bonner. I read the papers. You're one of the biggest producers in Hollywood."

"So maybe I know what I'm talking about, eh?"

"Maybe you do." She smiled. "But I know myself and I'm no actress."

"That wasn't what you said last night."

"That's something else," she said. "That's my business. Besides, you see the way I live. It would be a long time before I could earn a grand a week in pictures."

"How do you know? We've had a script around for five years that we haven't been able to find a lead for. It was written for Rina Marlowe. I think you could do it."

"You're crazy!" She laughed. "Rina Marlowe was one of the most beautiful women on the screen. I couldn't hold a candle to her."

He was suddenly serious. "There are things about you that remind me of her."

"Could be," she said. "I hear she was pretty wild."

"That, too," he said, leaning toward her. "But that isn't what I'm talking about. Come down to the studio tomorrow and I'll set up a screen test. If it doesn't work, we forget about it. If it does—well, there's just one man's approval I need and you're good for two grand a week."

"Two grand?" She stared at him. "You're joking."

He shook his head. "I don't joke about money."

"Neither do I," she said seriously. "Who is this man whose approval you'd need?"

"Jonas Cord."

"We might as well forget about it," she said. "From all I heard around town from some of the girls, he's a real nut."

CHAPTER FIFTEEN

IRVING FOLLOWED DAVID INTO THE LIVING ROOM AS ROSA BEGAN TO CLEAR the dishes. "I never saw her looking so good," he said, stretching out in a chair in front of the fire.

David nodded absently. "Yeah."

Irving looked at him. "You got something on your mind, Davy?"

"The usual things," David said evasively.

"That ain't the way I hear it."

Something in his voice made David tense. "What do you hear?"

"The word is out they're giving your boy the squeeze," Irving said in a low voice.

"What else do you hear?"

"The new crowd wants to make you top dog if you throw in with them," Irving said. "They're also saying that Bonner has sold out to them already."

David was silent. He couldn't believe that Jonas didn't know about what was happening. But it was possible.

"You ain't talking, Davy," Irving said quietly. "You didn't bring me out here for nothing."

"How did you find out?"

Irving shrugged his shoulders. "We got stock," he said casually. "Some of the boys called up and told me that their brokers were contacted. They want to know what we should do."

"How much stock?"

"Oh, eighty, ninety thousand shares around the country. We figured it would be a good deal the way you were running things."

"Have you—" David corrected himself. "Have the boys made up their minds yet which way they're going?" That stock could be important. It was over three per cent of the two and a half million shares outstanding.

"No, we're pretty conservative," Irving said. "We like to go where the money is. And they been making it sound real pretty. Complete financing, doubling the profits, maybe even splitting the stock in a couple of years."

David nodded. He reached for a cigarette thoughtfully. It hung in his lips unlit. Why hadn't Jonas replied to his messages? Three times he'd tried to locate him and each time there had been no reply. Surely he must know by now. The last place he checked had sent word that Jonas was out of the country. If that was true, the whole thing would be a *fait accompli* by the time he returned.

"What are you going to do, Davy?" Irving asked softly.

"I don't know," he said. "I don't know what to do."

"You can't ride the fence much longer, chum," Irving said. "There's no way on earth to live with the loser."

"I know." David nodded. He finally struck a match and held it to his cigarette. "But it's like this. I know Cord doesn't pay much attention to us, maybe sometimes he even holds us back a little. But I also know he can make a picture, he's got a real feel for this business. That's why he bought in. It's not just all cold ass like it is with Sheffield and the others. Plain banker-and-broker arithmetic and to hell with everything except the profit-and-loss statement and balance sheet."

"But the bankers and brokers hold all the cards," Irving said. "Only a fool bucks the house."

"Yeah," David said almost savagely, grinding out his cigarette.

Irving was silent for a moment, then he smiled. "Tell you what, Davy. I'll get all our proxies together and deliver 'em to you. When you decide what's best, vote 'em for us."

David stared at him. "You'd do that?"

Irving laughed. "The way I see it, I got no choice. Didn't you haul that alky for us from Shocky's garage?"

"Here comes the coffee," Rosa announced, carrying in a tray. "Jesus!" Irving exclaimed. "Lookit that choc'late layer cake."

Rosa laughed in a pleased voice. "I baked it myself."

Irving leaned back against the couch. "Oh, Doctor!" he said, looking at Rosa and rolling his eyes.

"Another piece?"

"I had three already. Another and you'll have to do a plastic job on my stomach to get me back in shape."

"Better have some more coffee, then," she said, refilling his cup. She began to gather up the cake plates.

"I meant to ask you, Davy," Irving said. "You ever hear of a broad named Jennie Denton?"

"Jennie Denton?" David shook his head. "No."

"I forgot," Irving said, glancing up at Rosa. "You been out of circulation."

"What about her?" Rosa asked. "I knew a Jennie Denton."

"You did? Where did you know her, Doc?"

"At the hospital. Four years ago there was a nurse there by that name."

"About five six, dark eyes, long, light-brown hair, good figure and an interesting way of walking?"

Rosa laughed. "Sexy, you mean?"

Irving nodded. "Yeah, that's what I mean."

"Sounds like the same girl," Rosa said.

"What about her?" David asked.

"Well, Jennie is probably the most expensive hooker in L.A. She has her own six-room house in the hills and you want to see her, it's by appointment only and you go there. She won't walk into a hotel room. She's got a real exclusive list and you want a date, you got to wait maybe two, three weeks. She only works a five-day week."

"If you're recommending her to my husband," Rosa interrupted, smiling, "you'd better stop right there."

Irving smiled. "Well, it seems one night, earlier this week, Maurice Bonner went there and she gave him the full treatment. So, nothing will do the next day but he has Jennie down to the studio for a screen test. He shoots her in color, some scenes from some old script he's got laying around. While he's at it, he decides to make it real good. He dresses her in a white silk sheet. It's supposed to be a baptism scene and when she comes up out of the water in the big tank on Stage Twelve, you can see everything she's got. In two days, that test becomes the biggest picture on the home circuit. Bonner's got more requests for it than Selznick's got for *Gone With the Wind!*"

There was only one script David remembered that had a baptism scene. "You wouldn't remember the name of the script?" he asked. "Was it *The Sinner*?"

"Could be."

"If it was, that's the script Cord had written especially for Rina Marlowe before she died."

"I don't care who it was written for." Irving smiled. "You gotta see that test. You'll flip. I sat through it twice. And so did everybody else in the projection room."

"I'll look at it tomorrow," David said.

"I'd like to see it, too."

David looked at Rosa. He smiled. It was the first time she'd ever expressed any interest in a picture. "Come down to the studio at ten o'clock," he said. "We'll both look at it."

"If I didn't have an important meeting," Irving said, "I'd be down there myself."

David tied the sash of his pajamas and sat down in the chair near the window, looking out at the ocean.

He could hear the water running in the bathroom basin and the faint sound of Rosa's voice, humming as she rinsed her face. He sighed. At least, she could be happy in her work. A doctor didn't have to survive a war of nerves in order to practice medicine.

The door clicked open behind him and he turned around. She looked at him, a musing expression on her face, as she stood in the doorway.

"You had something to tell me?" He smiled. "Go ahead."

"No, David," she replied, her eyes warm. "It's a wife's duty to listen when her lord and master speaks."

"I don't feel much like a lord and master."

"Is anything wrong, David?"

"I don't know," he said and began to tell her the story, beginning with his meeting with Sheffield the night she had called. She walked over to him and put her arms around his head, drawing him to her bosom. "Poor David," she whispered sympathetically. "So many problems."

He turned his face up to her. "I'll have to make a decision soon," he said. "What do you think I ought to do?"

She looked down at him, her gray eyes glowing. She felt strong and capable, as if her roots were deep into the earth. "Whatever decision you make, David," she said, "I feel sure will be the right one for us."

"For us?"

She smiled slowly. This new-found strength, too, was what it meant to be a' woman. Her voice was low and happy.

"We're going to have a baby," she said.

CHAPTER SIXTEEN

THE BRIGHT SUNLIGHT HURT THEIR EYES AFTER THE DARK OF THE SCREEN-ing room. They walked along silently toward David's office, in one of the executive cottages.

"What are you thinking, David?" she asked quietly. "That test make you sorry you're married?"

He looked at her and laughed. He opened the door to his cottage and they went past his secretary into his private office. David walked around behind his desk and sat down.

She seated herself in a leather chair in front of his desk. The thoughtful expression was still on his face. She took out a cigarette and lit it.

"What did you think of the test?" he asked.

She smiled. "Now I understand why she's driving all the men crazy," she answered. "The way that sheet clung to her when she came out of the water was the most suggestive thing I ever saw."

"Forget that scene. If it weren't in the test, what would you think of her?"

She dragged on the cigarette and the smile left her face. "I thought she was wonderful. She almost tore my heart out in that scene where all you saw was Jesus' feet walking, the bottom of the Cross dragging along as she crawled in the dirt after Him, trying to kiss His feet. I found myself crying with her." She was silent for a moment. "Were those real tears or make-up?"

David stared at her. "They were real tears," he said. "They don't use make-up tears in tests."

He felt his excitement begin to hammer inside him. In her own way, Rosa had given him the answer. He hadn't felt like this since he'd first seen Rina Marlowe on the screen. They'd all been too blinded by the baptismal scene to see it.

He pulled a buck slip from the holder on his desk and began to write on it. Rosa watched him for a moment, then walked around the desk and looked down curiously over his shoulder. He had already finished his scribbling and was reaching for the telephone.

JONAS—

I THINK IT'S ABOUT TIME WE GOT BACK INTO THE PICTURE BUSINESS. LET ME HEAR FROM YOU.

DAVID

"Get me McAllister, in Reno," David said into the telephone. He looked up at Rosa and smiled. She smiled back and returned to her chair.

"Hello, Mac," David said, his voice firm and forceful. "Two questions you can answer for me."

A feeling of pride began to run through her. She was glad she'd come down to the studio. This was a facet of her husband she had never known before.

"First," David said into the telephone, "can I sign an actress to a contract with Cord Explosives? I have specific reasons for not wanting to sign her with us. Important reasons." David relaxed slightly.

"Good. Next question. I have some film I want Jonas to see right away. Can you get it to him?"

He waited a moment. "Can't ask for anything more than that. I'll have the film at your L.A. office in two hours. Thanks, Mac. Good-by."

He pressed down the bar on the telephone and raised it again. "Miss Wilson, get me Jess Lee in printing and developing, then come right in here."

He held onto the telephone and reached for a cigarette. He put it in his mouth. She leaned across the desk with a match. He drew in on the cigarette and smiled at her.

"Jess," he said, as the door opened and his secretary came in. "I'm shooting down a buck slip to you. I want you to photograph it on the title card and splice it onto the end of the Jennie Denton test, right away."

David covered the mouthpiece with his hand. "Take that buck slip down to Jess Lee yourself," he said to the secretary, indicating the paper on his desk. She picked it up silently and walked out.

"I know it's a wild test, Jess," he said into the phone. "Make up one print with my buck slip and shoot it right over to Mr. McAllister's secretary at Cord Aircraft. It's got to be there by noon."

"You've made up your mind?"

He nodded. "I'm playing a long shot," he said. "If I'm wrong, it won't matter which of them wins. I lose."

Rosa smiled. "There comes a time like that in every operation. You're the surgeon, you hold the knife and the patient is open before you. According to the book, there are many things you can do, many ways you can go. But you have only one way to go—the right way. So you make the decision. Your way. No matter what the pressures are, no matter what the books say. You have to go your own way." She looked at him, still smiling. "Is that what you're doing, David?" she asked gently. "Going your own way?"

He looked at her, marveling at her insight and knowledge. "Yes," he said unhesitantly. "I'm going my own way."

He had never thought of it quite like that. She was right, though. He was on his own now.

Jennie was sitting at her desk in the living room, writing checks for the monthly bills, when the door chime rang. She heard the Mexican woman waddle past her on the way to answer it. She frowned, looking down at the desk.

She'd been a fool, she thought bitterly, letting herself be talked into that screen test. She should have known the John was only shooting his mouth off. Now they were laughing their heads off all over Hollywood. At least four other Johns had called her up, sarcastically congratulating her on her screen test. They'd all seen it.

She had known she wasn't an actress. Why the hell had she fallen for the gag?

Just like every stage-struck kid that came out here. But she thought she was too wise. She'd never fall into a trap like that. Then she'd gone for it, just like all the others.

She should have known the moment she stood in front of the cameras that it wasn't for her. But she'd read the script. Mary Magdalene. At first, she'd almost died laughing. No wonder Bonner had thought of her. It was type-casting of a high order.

Then something of the story had got to her. She'd felt moved and shaken. She'd lost herself in the part and there were times when she cried while the cameras were on her. And that was something she hadn't done since she was a little girl. No wonder they were laughing. She'd have laughed herself if it had been anyone else. The whore crying for the whore. She never should have listened. The week had gone by and there hadn't been even a word from Bonner.

The heavy footsteps of the Mexican woman sounded behind her. She looked around. The servant's beady eyes were inscrutable. "*Señor Woolf está aquí.*"

Woolf. She knew no one by that name. Maybe he was the new man from the cops. They'd told her a new man was coming around to pick up the pay-off.

"*De las películas,*" the servant added quickly.

"Oh." She nodded. "*Tráigale aquí.*" She turned back to her desk as the servant moved away. Quickly Jennie made a neat pile of the bills and put them in a drawer. She turned in her chair just as the Mexican returned with a young man.

She looked coldly at him, rising from her chair. "Bonner sent you?"

"No," he said. "As a matter of fact, Bonner doesn't even know I'm here."

"Oh." She knew now why he had come. "You saw the test?"

He nodded.

Her voice grew even colder. "Then you might as well go," she said. "I see no one except by appointment."

A faint smile tugged at his lips. She grew even angrier. "And you can tell Bonner for me that he'd better stop showing that test around town or he'll regret it."

He laughed, then his face grew serious. "I've already done that, Miss Denton."

"You have?" She felt her anger dissipating. "A thing, like that could ruin my business."

"I think you're out of that business," he said quietly.

She stared at him, her eyes large. "What do you mean?"

"I'm afraid you don't understand," he said, taking a card from his pocket and handing it to her. She looked down at it. It was an expensive engraved card. David Woolf, it read simply, and down in one corner, the words: Executive Vice-President. Below that was the name of the motion-picture company Bonner was connected with. Now she remembered who he was. She'd read about him in the papers. The bright young man. Cord's boy wonder. She looked up at him.

The faint smile was playing around his lips again. "Would you like to play Mary Magdalene?"

Suddenly, she was nervous. "I don't know," she said hesitantly. "I thought—it was all a kind of joke to Bonner."

"Perhaps it was," David Woolf said quickly. "I don't know what he thought. But it's no joke to me. I think you can be a great star." He was silent for a moment. "And my wife does, too."

She looked at him questioningly.

"Rosa Strassmer. She knew you at the hospital four years ago."

A light came into her eyes. "You mean Dr. Strassmer? The one who performed the skin graft on Linda Davis' face?"

He nodded again, smiling. "I was chief nurse in surgery that day," she said. "She was great."

"Thank you. Now, would you like to play Mary Magdalene?"

Suddenly, she wanted to more than anything else in the world. "Yes."

"I hoped that would be your answer," he said, taking a folded sheet of paper from his inside pocket. "How much did Bonner say he would pay you?"

"Two thousand a week."

He already had the pen in his hand and was writing on the sheet of paper. "Wait a minute, Mr. Woolf," she said quickly. "I know Bonner only meant it as a gag. You don't have to pay me that much."

"Perhaps he did. But I don't. He said two thousand, that's what you'll get." He finished writing and handed the contract to her. "You'd better read that carefully."

She looked down at the printed form. The only thing written on it was her name and the salary figure. "Do I have to?"

David nodded. "I think you should," he said. "Contracts are easy to sign but not that easy to get out of."

Jennie sank back into the chair and began to read the contract. "I notice it's with Cord Explosives."

"That's standard practice with us. Cord owns the company."

"Oh." She finished reading and reached for a pen. Quickly she signed her name and handed the contract back to him. "Now what do we do?" she asked, smiling.

He put the contract into his pocket. "The first thing we do is change your name."

"What's the matter with it?"

"Too many people will recognize it," he said. "It might prove embarrassing later."

Jennie thought for a moment, then laughed. "I don't give a damn," she said. "Do you?"

David shook his head. "Not if you don't."

She laughed again. Let the Johns eat their hearts out over what they were missing.

He looked around the room. "Do you own or rent this?" he asked.

"Rent."

"Good," he said. "Close down and go away for a while. Out on the desert. Palm Springs, maybe. Don't let anyone know where you are except me."

"O.K.," she said. "What do I do then?"

"You wait," he said. "You wait until we discover you!"

CHAPTER SEVENTEEN

"SORRY, DAVID, PIERCE SAID, GETTING TO HIS FEET. HE WAS SMILING but his eyes were cold. "I can't help you out."

"Why not?"

"Because I sold the stock a year ago."

"To Sheffield?" David asked.

The agent nodded.

"Why didn't you get in touch with Jonas?"

"Because I didn't want to," Pierce snapped. "He's used me enough. I was good enough for him during the rough years. To do the dirty work and keep the factory going. But the minute things were good enough to make the big ones, he brings in Bonner."

"You used him, too. He went into the hole for millions because you wanted a studio to play with. You're a rich man because of him. And you knew by the time Bonner came that you were an agent, not a producer. The whole industry knew it."

"Only because he never gave me a chance." Dan grinned mirthlessly. "Now it's his turn to sweat a little. I'm waiting to see how he likes it." He walked angrily to the door but by the time he turned back to David, his anger seemed to have disappeared. "Keep in touch, David. There's an outside chance I could spring Tracy and Gable from Metro on loan if you came up with the right property."

David nodded as the agent walked out. He looked down at his desk. Business as usual, he thought bitterly. Pierce would think nothing of setting up a deal like that and handing the company a million-dollar profit. That was his business. It had nothing to do with Jonas Cord personally. But the sale of his stock in the company was another matter.

He picked up the telephone on his desk wearily. "Yes, Mr. Woolf."

"Call Bonner's office and find out if I can see him right away."

"In your office or his?" his secretary asked.

He smiled at himself. Ordinarily, protocol dictated that Bonner come to him. But it was amazing how sensitive the studio grapevine was. By now, everyone was aware that something was up, and even his secretary wasn't completely sure of his position. This was her way of probing.

"My office, of course," he said testily, putting down the telephone.

Bonner came into his office about three-quarters of an hour later. It wasn't too bad, considering their relative importance. Not too long to appear rude, not too quickly to appear subservient. He crossed the room to David's desk and sat down. "Sorry to disturb you, Maurice," David said politely.

"That's quite all right, David," Bonner answered, equally polite. "I managed to finish the morning production meeting."

"Good. Then you have a little time?"

Bonner looked at his watch. "I do have a story conference due about now."

David smiled. "Writers are used to waiting."

Bonner looked at David curiously. Unconsciously, his hand crept inside his jacket and he scratched his shirt. David noticed and grinned. "Got a rash?"

"You heard the story?" Bonner asked.

David nodded.

Bonner grinned, scratching himself overtly now. "It's driving me nuts. It was worth it, though. You got to try Jennie sometime. That girl can make your old fiddle twang like a Stradivarius."

"I'll bet. I saw the test."

Bonner looked at him. "I meant to ask you. Why did you pull all the prints?"

"I had to," David said. *The Sinner* isn't our property. It belongs to Cord personally. And you know how he is. I wasn't looking for any trouble."

Bonner stared at him silently. There wasn't any point in beating around the bush, David decided. "Sheffield showed me your commitment to sell him your stock."

Bonner nodded. He wasn't scratching now. "I figured he would."

"Why?" David asked. "If you wanted to sell, why didn't you talk to Cord?"

Bonner was silent for a moment. "What would be the point? I never even met the man. If he wasn't polite enough to look me up just once in the three years I've been working for him, I see no reason to start running after him now. Besides, my contract is up next month and nobody has come around to talk about renewing it. I didn't even hear from McAllister." He began scratching again.

David lit a cigarette. "Why didn't you come to me?" he asked softly. "I brought you over here."

Bonner didn't meet his gaze. "Sure, David, I should have. But everybody knows you can't do anything without Cord's O.K. By the time you could have got to him, my contract would have run out. I'd have looked like a damn fool to the whole industry."

David dragged the smoke deep into his lungs. They were all alike—so shrewd, so ruthless, so capable in many ways, and still, so like children with all their foolish pride.

Bonner took his silence as resignation. "Sheffield told me he'd take care of us," he said quickly. "He wants us both, David. You know that. He said he'll set up a new deal the minute he takes over. He'll finance the pictures, give us a new profit-sharing plan and some real stock options."

"Do you have that in writing?"

Bonner shook his head. "Of course not," he said. "He can't sign me to a contract before he's taken over. But his word is good. He's a big man. He's not a goof ball like Cord who runs hot and cold."

"Did Cord ever break his word to you?"

Bonner shook his head. "No. He never had a chance to. I had a contract. And now that it's almost over, I'm not going to give him a chance."

"You're like my uncle." David sighed. "He listened to men like Sheffield and ended up in stocks and bonds instead of pictures. So he lost his company. Now you're doing the same thing. He can't give you a contract because he doesn't control the company, yet you give him a signed agreement making it possible for him to take over." David got to his feet, his voice angry. "Well, what are you going to do, you damn fool, when he tells you, after he's got control, that he can't keep his promise?"

"But he needs us to run the business. Who's going to make the pictures for him if I don't?"

"That's what my Uncle Bernie thought, too," David said sarcastically. "But the business ran without him. And it will run without us. Sheffield can always get someone to run the studio for him. Schary at MGM is waiting for a job like this to open up. Matty Fox at Universal would take to it like a duck takes to water. It wouldn't be half as tough for him here as it is over there."

David sat down abruptly. "Do you still think he can't run the company without us?"

Bonner stared at him, his face white. "But what can I do, David? I signed the agreement. Sheffield can sue the ass off me if I renege."

David put out his cigarette slowly. "If I remember your agreement," he said, "you agreed to sell him all the stock you owned on December fifteenth?"

"That's right."

"What if you only happened to own one share of stock on that day?" David asked softly. "If you sell him that one share, you've kept your word."

"But that's next week. Who could you get to buy the stock before then?"

"Jonas Cord."

"But what if you can't reach him in time? Then I'm out four million dollars. If I sell that stock on the open market, it'll knock the price way down."

"I'll see to it you get your money." David leaned across his desk. "And, Maurice," he added softly. "You can start writing your own contract, right now."

"Four million bucks!" Irving screamed. "Where the hell do you think I can lay my hands on that kind of money?"

David stared at his friend. "Come on, Needlenose. This is *tuchlas*."

"And what if Cord says he don't want the stock?" Irving asked in a quieter voice. "What do I do with it then? Use it for toilet paper?" He chewed on his cigar. "You're supposed to be my friend. I go wrong on a deal like this, I'm nobody's friend. The late Yitzchak Schwartz, they'll call me."

"It isn't as bad as that."

"Don't tell me how bad it is," Irving said angrily. "From jobs like mine you don't get fired."

David looked at him for a moment. "I'm sorry, Irving. I have no right to ask you to take a chance like this." He turned and started for the door.

His friend's voice stopped him. "Hey, wait a minute! Where d'you think you're going?"

David stared at him.

"Did I say I definitely wouldn't do it for you?" Irving said.

Aunt May's ample bosom quivered indignantly. "Like a father your Uncle Bernie was to you," she said in her shrill, rasping voice. "Were you like a son to him? Did you appreciate what he done for you? No. Not once did you say to your Uncle Bernie, while he was alive, even a thank you." She took a handkerchief from the front of her dress and began to dab at her eyes, the twelve-carat diamond on her pinkie ring flashing iridescently like a spotlight. "It's by the grace of God your poor *tante* isn't spending the rest of her days in the poorhouse."

David leaned back in the stiff chair uncomfortably. He felt the chill of the night in the big, barren room of the large house. He shivered slightly. But he didn't know whether it was the cold or the way this house always affected him. "Do you want me to start a fire for you, *Tante*?"

"You're cold, Duvidele?" his Aunt May asked.

He shrugged his shoulders. "I thought you might be chilly."

"Chilly?" she repeated. "Your poor old *tante* is used to being chilly. It's only by watching my pennies I can afford to live in this house."

He looked at his watch. "It's getting late, *Tante*. And I have to get going. Are you going to give me the proxies?"

The old woman looked at him. "Why should I?" she asked. "I should give proxies to help that *momser*, that no-good, who stole his company from your uncle?"

"Nobody stole the company. Uncle Bernie would have lost it anyway. He was lucky to find a man like Cord to let him off so easy."

"Lucky he was?" Her voice was shrill again. "Out of all the shares he had, only twenty-five thousand I got left. What happened to the rest of them? Tell me. What happened, hah?"

"Uncle Bernie got three and a half million dollars for them."

"So what?" she demanded. "They were worth three times that."

"They were worth *bupkas*," he said, losing his temper. "Uncle Bernie was stealing the company blind and you know it. The stock wasn't worth the paper it was printed on."

"Now you're calling your uncle a thief." She rose to her feet majestically. "Out!" she screamed, pointing at the door. "Out from my house!"

He stared at her for a moment, then started for the door. Suddenly he stopped, remembering. Once his uncle had chased him out of his office, using almost the same words. But he'd got what he wanted. And his aunt was greedier than Bernie had ever been. He turned around.

"True, it's only twenty-five thousand shares," he said. "Only a lousy one per cent of the stock. But now it's worth something. At least, you got somebody in the family looking out for your interests. But give your proxies to Sheffield and see what happens. He's the kind that got Uncle Bernie into Wall Street in the first place. If you do, I won't be there to watch your interests. Your stock won't be worth *bupkas* again."

She stared at him for a moment. "Is that true?"

He could see the calculating machine in her head spinning. "Every last word of it."

She took a deep breath. "So come," she said. "I'll sign for you the proxies." She turned and waddled to a cabinet. "Your uncle, *olev a'sholem*, always said I should listen to you when I wanted advice. That David, he said, has a good head on his shoulders."

He watched her take some papers from the cabinet. She walked over to a desk, picked up a pen and signed them. He took them and put them in his jacket pocket. "Thanks, Aunt May."

She smiled up at him. He was surprised when she reached out her hand and patted his arm almost timidly. "Your uncle and me, we were never blessed with children," she said in a tremulous voice. "He really thought of you like his own son." She blinked her eyes rapidly. "You don't know how proud he was, even after he retired from the company, when he read about you in the trade papers."

He felt a knot of pity for the lonely old woman gather in his throat. "I know, Aunt May."

She tried to smile. "And such a pretty wife you got," she said. "Don't be a stranger. Why don't you sometime bring her here to have tea with me?"

He put his arms around the old woman suddenly and kissed her cheek. "I will, Aunt May," he said. "Soon."

Rosa was waiting in his office when he got back to the studio. "When Miss Wilson called and told me you'd be late, I thought it would be nice if I came down and we had dinner out."

"Good," he said, kissing her cheek.

"Well?"

He sat down heavily behind his desk. "Aunt May gave me her proxies."

"That means you've got nineteen per cent to vote."

He looked at her. "It won't do much good if Jonas doesn't back me up. Irving told me he'd have to sell the stock to Sheffield if Cord wouldn't pick it up."

She got to her feet. "Well, you've done all you could," she said in a practical voice. "Now let's go to dinner."

His secretary came in just as David got to his feet. "There's a cablegram from London, Mr. Woolf."

He took the envelope and opened it.

SET PRODUCTION DATE SINNER MARCH I.
CORD.

Just as he was about to hand it to Rosa, the door opened and his secretary came in again. "Another cablegram, Mr. Woolf."

Quickly he ripped it open. His eyes skimmed through it and he felt a sudden relief surge through him.

MCALLISTER READY WHATEVER CASH NEEDED SPIKE SHEFFIELD. GIVE IT TO HIM GOOD.

Like the first cablegram, it was signed CORD. He passed them both to Rosa. She read them and looked up at him with shining eyes. "We did it!" he said excitedly. He had started to pick her up in his arms when the door opened again.

"Yes, Miss Wilson?" he said in an annoyed voice.

The girl stood hesitantly in the doorway. "I'm sorry to disturb you, Mr. Woolf," she said, "but another cablegram just arrived."

"Well, don't stand there. Give it to me." He looked at Rosa. "This one is for both of us," he said, handing it to her. "You open it."

She looked down at the envelope, then back at David. A smile came over her face.

He looked down at the cable in her hand.

MAZEL TOV! HOPE IT WILL BE TWINS!

This one was signed JONAS.

JONAS – 1940
Book Seven

CHAPTER ONE

"THIS IS DAMN STUPID!" FORRESTER MUTTERED AS HE LIFTED THE CAB-200 into the air behind the formation of Spitfires.

"What's stupid?" I asked, looking down behind me from the co-pilot's seat, to see London dropping back into the early-morning haze. There were several fires still burning from last night's raid. "They didn't buy our plane but they'll buy all the B-17's we can turn out. What the hell, we both know they have to standardize."

"I'm not talking about that," Roger grumbled.

"Engines one and two, check," Morrissey called from behind us. "Engines three and four, check. You can cut the fuel now."

"Check." Roger turned down the mixture. "That's what I'm talking about," he said, motioning toward Morrissey, who was acting as flight engineer. "It's stupid—all of us on the same plane. What if it went down? Who'd be left to run the company?"

I grinned at him. "You worry too much."

He returned my smile without humor. "That's what you pay me for. The president of the company has to worry. Especially the way we're growing. We grossed over thirty-five million last year; this year we'll go over a hundred million with war orders. We'll have to start bringing up personnel who can take over in case something happens to us."

I reached for a cigarette. "What's going to happen to us?" I asked, lighting it. I looked at him through the cloud of smoke. "Unless you got a little jealous of the R.A.F. back there and are thinking about going back into the service."

He reached out and took the cigarette from my mouth and put it between his lips. "You know better than that, Jonas. I couldn't keep up with those kids. They'd fly rings around me. If I have to be an armchair pilot, I'd rather do it here, where at least I'm on your general staff."

There was something in what he said. The war was pushing us into an expansion that neither of us had ever dreamed of. And we weren't even in it yet.

"We'll have to get someone to run the Canadian plant."

I nodded silently. He'd been right—it was a hell of a wise move. We'd fabricate the parts in our plants in the States and ship them to Canada, where they'd go on the production line. As they rolled off, the R.C.A.F. would fly them to England. If it worked, we could knock about three weeks off the production time for each plane.

The idea also had some fiscal advantages. The British and Canadian governments were willing to finance the building of the plant and we'd save two ways. The factory would cost less because we would have no interest charges and the tax on net income could be taken in Canada, where the depreciation allowance was four times that allowed by Uncle Sam. And His Majesty's boys were happy, too, because living in the sterling bloc, they'd have fewer American dollars to pay out.

"O.K., I agree. But none of the boys working for us has the experience to take on a big job like that except Morrissey. And we can't spare him. You got anybody in mind?"

"Sure," he said, shooting a curious look at me. "But you aren't going to like it."

I stared at him. "Try me and see."

"Amos Winthrop."

"No!"

"He's the only man around who can handle it," he said. "And he won't be available for long. The way things are going, somebody's going to snap him up."

"Let them! He's a prick and a lush. Besides, he's bombed out on everything he ever did."

"He knows aircraft production," Forrester said stubbornly. He glanced at me again. "I heard what happened between you two but that's got nothing to do with this."

I didn't answer. Up ahead of us, I saw the Spitfire formation leader waggle his wings. It was the signal to break radio silence. Forrester leaned forward and flipped the switch. "Yes, Captain?"

"This is where we leave you, old boy."

I looked down. The gray waters of the Atlantic stared back at me. We were a hundred miles off the coast of the British Isles.

"O.K., Captain," Forrester said. "Thank you."

"Safe home, chaps. And don't forget to send us the big ones. We'll be needing them next summer to pay Jerry back a little."

Forrester laughed in his mike. The British had just taken the shellacking of their lives and here they were worried about getting their licks in. "You'll have them, Captain."

"Righto. Radio out."

He waggled the wings of his Spitfire again and the formation peeled away in a wide, sweeping circle back toward their coast. Then there was silence and we were alone over the Atlantic on our way home.

I pulled out of my safety belt and stood up. "If it's O.K. with you, I'm going back and grab a little snooze."

Roger nodded. I opened the compartment door. "You just think about what I said," he called after me.

"If you're talking about Amos Winthrop, forget it."

Morrissey was sitting dejectedly in the engineer's bucket seat. He looked up when I came in. "I don't understand it," he said sadly.

I sat down on the edge of the bunk. "It's easy enough to figure out. The B-17 flies with a five-man crew against our nine. That means they can put almost twice as many planes in the air. Round trip to Germany at the most is two thousand miles, so they don't need a five-thousand-mile range. Besides, the operational costs are just a little more than half ours."

"But this plane can go ten thousand feet higher and two hundred miles an hour faster," Morrissey said. "And it carries almost twice the pay load of bombs."

"The trouble with you, Morrissey, is you're ahead of the times. They're not ready for planes like this one yet."

I saw the stricken look come over his face. For a moment, I felt sorry for him. And what I'd said was true. For my money, he was the greatest aircraft engineer in the world. "Forget it. Don't worry, they'll catch up to you yet. Someday, they'll be flying planes like this by the thousands."

"Not in this war," he said resignedly. He picked up a Thermos from a cardboard carton. "I think I'll take some coffee up to Roger."

He went forward into the pilot's compartment and I stretched out on the bunk. The drone of the four big engines buzzed in my ears. I closed my eyes. Three weeks in England and I don't think I had a good night's rest the whole time. Between the bombs and the girls. The bombs and the girls. The bombs. The girls. I slept.

The shrill shriek of the falling bomb rose to its orgiastic climax as it fell nearby. All conversation at the dinner table hung suspended for a moment.

"I'm worried about my daughter, Mr. Cord," the slim, gray-haired woman on my right said.

I looked at her, then glanced at Morrissey, seated opposite me. His face was white and strained. I turned back to the woman. The bomb had landed practically next door and she was worried about her daughter, safe in America. Maybe she should be. She was Monica's mother.

"I haven't seen Monica since she was nine years old," Mrs. Holme continued nervously. "That was almost twenty years ago. I think of her often."

You didn't think of her often enough, I thought to myself. I used to think it was different with mothers. But they were no different than fathers. They thought of themselves first. At least that was one thing I'd had in common with Monica. Our parents never gave a damn about us. My mother died and hers had run away with another man.

She looked up at me from the deep violet eyes under the long black lashes and I could see the beauty she'd passed on to her daughter. "Do you think you might see her when you return to the States, Mr. Cord?"

"I doubt it, Mrs. Holme," I said. "Monica lives in New York now. I live in Nevada."

She was silent for a moment, then again came the piercing look from her eyes. "You don't like me very much, do you, Mr. Cord?"

"I hadn't really thought about it, Mrs. Holme," I said quickly. "I'm sorry if I give that impression."

She smiled. "It wasn't anything you said. It was just that I could sense a shrinking in you when I told you who I was." She played nervously with her spoon. "I expect Amos told you all about me—about how I ran off with someone else, leaving him with a child to raise alone?"

"Winthrop and I were never that close. We never discussed you."

"You must believe me, Mr. Cord," she whispered, a sudden intensity in her voice. "I didn't abandon my daughter. I want her to know that, to understand it."

Nothing ever changed. It was still more important for parents to be understood than to understand.

"Amos Winthrop was a woman-chaser and a cheat," she said quietly, without bitterness. "The ten years of our marriage were a hell. On our honeymoon, I discovered him with other women. And finally, when I fell in love with a decent, honest man, he blackmailed me into giving up my daughter under the threat of exposure and the ruination of that man's career in His Majesty's service."

I looked at her. That made sense. Amos was a cute one with tricks like that. I knew. "Did you ever write Monica and tell her that?"

"How does one write something like that to one's own daughter?"

I didn't answer.

"About ten years ago, I heard from Amos that he was sending her over to stay with me. I thought then that when she got to know me, I'd explain and she'd understand." She nodded slightly. "I read in the papers of your marriage and she never came."

The butler came and took away the empty plates. Another servant placed demitasse cups before us. When he went away, I spoke. "Just what is it you would like me to do, Mrs. Holme?"

Her eyes studied my face for a moment. I saw the slight hint of moisture in them. Her voice was steady, though. "If you should happen to speak with her, Mr. Cord," she said, "let her know that I asked for her, that I think of her and that I'd appreciate hearing from her."

I nodded slowly. "I'll do that, Mrs. Holme."

The butler began to pour coffee as the dull thud of bombs rolled into the heavily draped room like a muffled sound of thunder in peacetime London.

The roar of the four big motors came back into my ears as I opened my eyes. Morrissey was in the bucket seat, his head tilted uncomfortably to one side as he dozed. He opened his eyes as I sat up. "How long was I sleeping?" I asked.

"About four hours."

"I better give Roger some relief," I said, getting to my feet.

Forrester looked up as I came into the compartment. "You must have been tired. For a while, you were snoring so loud back there I was beginning to think we had five motors instead of four."

I sank into the copilot's seat. "I thought I'd give you a little relief. Where are we?"

"About here," he said, his finger pointing to the map on the holder between us. I looked down. We were about a thousand miles out over the ocean.

"We're slow."

He nodded. "We ran into heavy head winds."

I reached for the wheel and pulled it back to me until it locked in. "O.K.," I said. "I got her."

He released his wheel, got to his feet and stretched. "I think I'll try to get a nap."

"Fine," I said, looking out through the windshield. It was beginning to rain.

"Sure you can keep your eyes open for a few hours?"

"I'll manage."

He laughed. "Either you're a better man than I am, Gunga Din, or I'm getting old. For a while, back there, I thought you were going to fuck every woman in England."

I looked up at him, grinning. "With the way those bombs were coming down, I thought I better make the most of it."

He laughed again and left the compartment. I turned back to the controls. Apparently, I wasn't the only one who felt that way. The girls must have felt it, too. There'd been something desperate in the way they insisted you accept their favors.

It was beginning to snow now, heavy, swirling flakes against the windshield. I switched the de-icers on and watched the snowflakes turn to water against the Plexiglas. The air speed was two hundred and slowing. That meant the head winds were picking up speed. I decided to see if we could climb up over it.

I moved the wheel back and the big plane began to lift slowly. We came through the clouds at thirteen thousand feet into bright sunlight. I locked in the gyrocompensator and felt the plane level off.

It was a clear and smooth flight all the rest of the way home.

CHAPTER TWO

ROBAIR WAS STANDING IN THE OPEN DOORWAY WHEN I CAME OUT OF THE elevator. Though it was four o'clock in the morning, he looked as fresh and wide-eyed as if he'd just awakened. His dark face gleamed in a welcoming smile over his white shirt and faultlessly tailored butler's jacket. "Good morning, Mr. Cord. Have a good flight?"

"Fine, thank you, Robair."

He closed the door behind him. "Mr. McAllister's in the living room. Been waiting since eight o'clock last night."

"I'll talk to him," I said, starting through the foyer.

"I'll fix some steak sandwiches and coffee, Mr. Cord."

I stopped and looked back at the tall Negro. He never seemed to age. His hair was still black and thick, his frame giant-sized and powerful. "Hey, Robair, you know something? I missed you."

He smiled again. There was nothing subservient or false about his smile. It was the smile of a friend. "I missed you, too, Mr. Cord."

I turned and walked into the living room. Robair was more than just a friend. In a way, he was my guardian angel. I don't know how I would have held together after Rina died if it hadn't been for Robair.

By the time I'd got back to Reno from New York, I was a wreck. There was nothing I wanted to do. Just drink and forget. I'd had enough of people.

My father rode my shoulders like a desert Indian on a pony. It had been his woman I had wanted. It had been his woman who had died. Why did I cry? Why was I so empty?

Then one morning, I awakened in the dirt of the yard, back of Nevada's room in the bunkhouse, to find Robair bending over me. I vaguely remembered having leaned my back against the wall of the bunkhouse while I finished a bottle of bourbon. That had been last night. I turned my head slowly. The empty bottle lay beside me.

I placed my hands in the dirt and braced myself. My head hurt and my mouth was dry and when I tried to get to my feet, I found I didn't have the strength.

I felt Robair's arm slip around behind me and lift me to my feet. We started to walk across the hard-packed earth. "Thank you," I said, leaning against him gratefully. "I'll be all right once I get a drink."

His voice had been so soft that at first I thought I hadn't heard him. "No more whisky, Mr. Cord."

I stared up into his face. "What did you say?"

His large eyes were impassive. "No more whisky, Mr. Cord," he repeated. "I reckon it's time you stopped."

The anger pulled up in me and gave me strength. I shoved myself away from him. "Just who in hell do you think you are?" I shouted. "If I want a drink, I'll take a drink!"

He shook his head. "No more whisky. You're not a little boy no more. You can't run an' hide your head in the whisky bottle ever' time a little bad comes your way."

I stared at him, speechless for a moment, as the shock and anger ran through me in ice-cold waves. Then I found my voice. "You're fired!" I screamed. "No black son of a bitch is going to own me!"

I turned and started for the house. I felt his hand on my shoulder and turned. There was a look of sadness on his face. "I'm sorry, Mr. Cord," he said.

"There's no use in apologizing, Robair."

"I'm not apologizing for what I said, Mr. Cord," he replied in a low voice. Then I saw his giant, hamlike fist racing toward me. I tried to move away but nothing in my body seemed to work the way it should and I plunged into the dark again.

This time when I woke up, I was in bed, covered with clean sheets. There was a fire going in the fireplace and I felt very weak. I turned my head. Robair was sitting in a chair next to the bed. There was a small tureen of hot soup on the table next to him. "I got some hot soup here for you," he said, his eyes meeting mine levelly.

"Why'd you bring me up here?"

"The mountain air'll do you good."

"I won't stay," I said, pushing myself up. I'd had enough of this cabin when I was here the last time. On my honey-moon.

Robair's big hand pushed me back against the pillow. "You'll stay," he said quietly. He picked up the tureen and dipped a spoon into it, then held the spoon of soup out to me. "Eat."

There was such a note of authority in his quiet voice that involuntarily I opened my mouth before I thought. The hot soup scalded its way down. Then I pushed his hand away. "I don't want any."

I stared into his dark eyes for a moment, then I felt rise up inside me a hurt and a loneliness that I had never felt before. Suddenly, I began to cry.

He put down the tureen. "Go ahead an' weep, Mr. Cord. Cry yourself out. But you'll find tears won't drown you any more than whisky."

He was sitting on the porch in the late-afternoon sun when I finally came out. It was green all around, bushes and trees all the way down the side of the mountain, until it ran into the red and yellow sands of the desert. He got to his feet when I opened the door.

I walked over to the railing and looked down. We were a long way from people. I turned and looked back at him. "What's for dinner, Robair?" I asked.

He shrugged his shoulders. "To tell the truth, Mr. Cord, I was kind of waitin' on how you felt."

"There's a brook near here that has the biggest trout you ever saw."

He smiled. "A mess o' trout sounds fine, Mr. Cord."

It was almost two years before we came down from the mountain. Game was plentiful and once a week, Robair would drive down for supplies. I grew lean and dark from the sun and the bloat of the cities disappeared as the muscles tightened and hardened in my body.

We developed a routine and it was amazing how well the business got along without me. It merely proved the old axiom: once you reached a certain size, it was pretty difficult to stop growing. All the companies were doing fine except the picture company. It was undercapitalized but it didn't matter that much to me any more.

Three times a week, I spoke to McAllister on the telephone. That was generally sufficient to take care of most problems. Once a month, Mac would come driving up the winding road to the cabin, his brief case filled with papers for me to sign or reports for me to study.

Mac was a remarkably thorough man. There was very little that escaped his observant eye. In some mysterious way, everything of importance that was going on in any of the companies found its way into his reports. There were many things I knew I should attend to personally but somehow, everything seemed a long way off and very unimportant.

We'd been there almost a year and a half when we had our first outside visitor. I'd been out hunting and was coming back up the trail, with a brace of quail swinging from my hand, when I saw a strange car parked in front of the cabin. It was a Chevy with California license plates.

I walked around and looked at the registration on the steering column: Rosa Strassmer, M.D., 1104 Coast Highway, Malibu, Cal. I turned and walked into the cabin. There was a young woman seated on the couch, smoking a cigarette. She had dark hair, gray eyes and a determined jaw.

When she stood up, I saw she was wearing a faded pair of Levi's that somehow accentuated the slim, feminine curve of her hips. "Mr. Cord?" she asked, holding her hand out to me, a curious, faint accent in her voice. "I'm Rosa Strassmer, Otto Strassmer's daughter."

I took her hand, staring at her for a moment. Her grip was firm. I tried to keep the faint tinge of annoyance from showing in my voice. "How did you know where to find me?"

She took out an envelope and gave it to me. "Mr. McAllister asked me to drop this off when he heard I was driving through here on my vacation."

I opened the envelope and looked at the paper inside. It was nothing that couldn't have waited until his next visit. I dropped it on the table. Robair came into the room just then. He looked at me curiously as he took the brace of quail and my gun and went back into the kitchen.

"I hope I haven't disturbed you, Mr. Cord," she said quickly.

I looked at her. Whatever it was I felt, it wasn't her fault. It was Mac's not too subtle reminder that I couldn't stay on the mountain forever. "No," I answered. "You must forgive my surprise. We don't get many visitors up here."

She smiled suddenly. When she smiled, her face took on a strange bright beauty. "And I can understand why you don't ask people to come, Mr. Cord," she said. "More than two people would crowd a paradise like this."

I didn't answer.

She hesitated a moment, then started for the door. "I must be going now," she said awkwardly. "I'm glad to have met you. I've heard so much about you from my father."

"Dr. Strassmer!"

She turned toward me in surprise. "Yes, Mr. Cord?"

"I'll have to ask you to forgive me again," I said quickly. "Living up here as I have, I seem to have forgotten my manners. How is your father?"

"He's well and happy, Mr. Cord, thanks to you. He never gets tired of telling me how you blackmailed Goring into letting him out of Germany. He thinks you're a very brave man."

I smiled. "It's your father who is brave, doctor. What I did was very little."

"To Mother and me, it was a great deal," she said. She hesitated again. "Now I really must be going."

"Stay for dinner," I said. "Robair has a way of stuffing quail with wild rice that I think you'd enjoy."

Her eyes searched mine for a moment. "I will," she answered. "Under one condition—that you call me Rosa, not doctor."

"Agreed. Now sit down again and I'll get Robair to bring you something to drink."

But Robair was already in the doorway with a pitcher of Martinis. It was too late for her to leave when we were through with dinner, so Robair fixed up the tiny guest room for her. She went to bed and I sat in the living room for a while and then went to my room.

For the first time in a long while, I could not fall asleep. I stared up at the shadows dancing on the ceiling. There was a sound at the door and I sat up in the bed.

She stood there silently in the doorway for a moment, then came into the room. She stopped at the side of my bed and looked down at me. "Don't be frightened, lonely man," she whispered in a soft voice. "I want nothing more from you than this night."

"But, Rosa—"

She pressed a silencing finger to my lips and came down into the bed, all warmth and all woman, all compassion and all understanding. She cradled my head against her breast almost as a mother would a child. "Now I understand why McAllister sent me here."

I cupped my hands beneath her firm young breasts. "Rosa, you're beautiful," I whispered.

I heard her laugh softly. "I know I'm not beautiful, but I am happy that you should say so."

She lay her head back against the pillow and looked up at me, her eyes soft and warm. "*Kommen sie, liebchen*," she said gently, reaching for me with her arms. "You brought my father back to his world, let me try to bring you back to yours."

In the morning, after breakfast, when she had gone, I walked back into the living room thoughtfully. Robair looked at me from the table, where he was clearing away the dishes. We didn't speak. We didn't have to. In that moment, we both understood that it was only a matter of time before we would leave the mountain.

The world was not that far away any more.

McAllister was asleep on the couch when I entered the living room. I walked over to him and touched his shoulder. He opened his eyes and looked up at me. "Hello, Jonas," he said, sitting up and rubbing his eyes. He took a cigarette and lit it. A moment later, the sleep was gone from his eyes. "I waited for you because Sheffield is pressing for a meeting," he said.

I dropped into the chair opposite him. "Did David pick up the stock?"

"Yes."

"Does Sheffield know it yet?"

"I don't think so," he said. "From the way he's talking, my guess is he still thinks he's got it in the bag." He ground the cigarette out in the ash tray. "Sheffield said that if you'd meet with him before the meeting, he'd be inclined to give you some consideration for your stock."

I laughed. "That's very kind of him, isn't it?" I kicked off my shoes. "Tell him to go to hell."

"Just a minute, Jonas," Mac said quickly. "I think you'd better meet with him, anyway. He can make a lot of trouble. After all, he'll be voting about thirty per cent of the stock."

"Let him," I snapped. "If he wants a fight, I'll curl his hair."

"Meet him, anyway," Mac urged. "You've got too many things coming up to get involved in a fight right now."

He was right, as usual. I couldn't be in six places at one time. Besides, if I wanted to make *The Sinner*, I didn't want a stupid minority-stockholder's suit holding up production.

"O.K. Call him and tell him to come over right now."

"Right now?" Mac asked. "My God! It's four o'clock in the morning."

"So what? He's the one who wanted a meeting."

Mac went over to the telephone.

"And when you get through talking to him," I said, "call Moroni on the Coast and find out if the bank will let me have the money to buy in Sheffield's stock if I give them a first mortgage on the theaters."

There was no sense in using any more of my own money than I had to.

CHAPTER THREE

I WATCHED SHEFFIELD LIFT THE COFFEE CUP TO HIS LIPS. HIS HAIR WAS A little grayer, a little thinner, but the rimless eyeglasses still shone rapaciously over his long, thin nose. Still, he accepted defeat much more graciously than I would have, if the shoe had been on the other foot.

"Where did I go wrong, Jonas?" he asked casually, his voice as detached as that of a doctor with a clinic patient. "I certainly was willing to pay enough."

I slumped down in my chair. "You had the right idea. The thing was that you were using the wrong currency."

"I don't understand."

"Movie people are different. Sure, they like money just like everybody else. But there's something they want even more."

"Power?"

I shook my head. "Only partly. What they want more than anything else is to make pictures. Not just movies but pictures that will gain them recognition. They want to regard themselves as artists. Well insulated by money, of course, but artists, just the same."

"Then because you've made motion pictures, they accepted your promises rather than mine?"

"I guess that's about it." I smiled. "When I produce a picture, they feel I'm sharing the same risks they are. I'm not risking money. Everything I am goes on the line. My reputation, my ability, my creative conceit."

"Creative conceit?"

"It's a term I got from David Woolf. He used it to rate certain producers. Those who had it made great pictures. Those who didn't, made pictures. In short, they preferred me because I was willing to be judged on their own terms."

"I see," Sheffield said thoughtfully. "I won't make the same mistake again."

"I'm sure you won't." I felt a suspicion growing in me. This was too easy. He was being too nice about it. He was a fighter. And fighters die hard.

Besides, his whole approach had been inconsistent with his usual way of doing business. Sheffield was a financial man. He dealt with business people about finances. Yet, in this case, he'd gone directly to the picture people. Ordinarily, he'd have contacted me right off the bat and we'd have battled it out. We'd each have compromised a little and been satisfied.

There could be only one answer. Something that had happened in England when I was there began suddenly to make sense. I'd come out of the projection room of our office in London, where I had gone to see the Jennie Denton test, with our British sales manager.

The telephone had rung when we walked into his office. He picked it up and spoke into it a few minutes, then put it down. He looked up at me.

"That was the circuit-buyer for the Engel theater chain," he said. "They are frantic for product now. Their studios were lost completely in the first raid and they had never made a deal for American product, as have the other companies."

"What are they going to do?" I asked, still thinking about the test. For the first time since Rina had died, I began to feel the excitement that came only from making a motion picture again. I only half listened to his answer.

"I don't know," he replied. "They have four hundred theaters and if they can't get additional product in six months, they'll have to close half of them."

"Too bad," I said. I couldn't care less. Engel, like Korda, had come to England from Middle Europe and gone into the picture business. But while Korda had concentrated on production, Engel had gone in for theaters. He came into production only as an answer to his problem of supply. Rank, British Lion, Gaumont and Associated among them managed to control all the product, both British and American. Still, there was no reason to mourn for him. I had heard that his investments in the States were worth in excess of twenty million dollars.

I'd forgotten about the conversation until now. It all fitted together neatly. It would have been a very neat trick if Engel could have stolen the company right out from under my nose. And it was just the kind of deal his Middle-European mind would have dreamed up.

I looked at Sheffield. "What does Engel plan to do with the stock now?" I asked casually.

"I don't know." Then he looked at me. "No wonder," he said softly. "Now I know why we couldn't get anywhere. You knew all along."

I didn't answer. I could see the look of surprise on Mac's face behind him but I pretended I hadn't.

"And I was beginning to believe that stuff you were handing me about picture people standing together," Sheffield said.

I smiled. "Now that the deal fell through, I suppose Engel has no choice but to close those theaters. He can't get product anywhere else."

Sheffield was silent, his eyes wary. "All right, Jonas," he said. "What's on your mind?"

"How would Mr. Engel like to buy the Norman Film Distributors of England, Ltd.? That would assure him access to our product and he might not have to close those theaters."

"How much would it cost him?" Sheffield asked.

"How many shares of stock does he own?"

"About six hundred thousand."

"That's what it would cost him," I said.

"That's five million dollars! British Norman only nets about three hundred thousand a year. At that rate, it would take him almost twenty years to get his money back."

"It all depends on your point of view. Closing two hundred theaters would mean a loss to him of over a million pounds a year."

He stared at me for a moment and then got to his feet. "May I use your phone for a call to London? In spite of the time difference, I just might still catch Mr. Engel before he leaves the office."

"Help yourself," I said. As he walked to the telephone, I looked down at my watch. It was nine o'clock and I knew I had him. Because no one, not even Georges Engel, left his office at two o'clock in the afternoon. Not in merry old England, where the offices were open until six o'clock and the clerks still sat at their old-fashioned desks on their high stools. Engel was probably waiting at the telephone right now for Sheffield's call.

By noon it was all arranged. Mr. Engel and his attorneys would be in New York the next week to sign the agreement. There was only one thing wrong with it: I would have to remain in New York. I reached for the telephone.

"Who're you calling?" Mac asked.

"David Woolf. He's the executive officer of the company. He might as well be here to sign the papers."

"Put down the telephone," Mac said wearily. "He's in New York. I brought him along with me."

"Oh," I said. I walked over to the window and looked down. New York in midmorning. I could sense the tension in the traffic coming up Park Avenue. I was beginning to feel restless already.

I turned back to McAllister. "Well, get him up here. I'm starting a big picture in two months. I'd like to know what's being done about it."

"David brought Bonner along to go over the production details with you."

I stared at him. They'd thought of everything. I threw myself into a chair. The doorbell rang and Robair went to open it. Forrester and Morrissey came in. I looked up at them as they crossed the room.

"I thought you were supposed to leave for California this morning, Morrissey," I said coldly. "How the hell are we ever going to get that new production line started?"

"I don't know if we can, Jonas," he said quickly.

"What the hell do you mean?" I shouted. "You said we could do it. You were there when we signed that contract."

"Take it easy, Jonas," Forrester said quietly. "We have a problem."

"What kind of problem?"

"The U.S. Army just ordered five CA–200's. They want the first delivery by June and we're in a bind. We can't make them B–17's on the same production line. You're going to have to decide which comes first."

I stared at him. "You make the decision. You're president of the company."

"You own the goddamn company," he shouted back. "Which contract do you want to honor?"

"Both of them. We're not in the business of turning away money."

"Then we'll have to get the Canadian plant in operation right away. We could handle prefabrication if the B–17's were put together up there."

"Then do it," I said.

"O.K. Get me Amos Winthrop to run it."

"I told you before—no Winthrop."

"No Winthrop, no Canadian plant. I'm not going to send a lot of men to their death in planes put together by amateurs just because you're too damn stubborn to listen to reason."

"Still the fly-boy hero?" I sneered. "What's it to you who puts the planes together? You're not flying them."

He crossed the room and stood over my chair, looking down at me. I could see his fists clench. "While you were out whoring around London, trying to screw everything in sight, I was out at the airfields watching those poor bastards come in weary and beat from trying to keep the Jerry bombs off your fucking back. Right then and there, I made up my mind that if we were lucky enough to get that contract, I'd personally see to it that every plane we shipped over was the kind of plane I wouldn't be afraid to take up myself."

"Hear, hear!" I said sarcastically.

"When did you decide you'd be satisfied to put your name on a plane that was second best? When the money got big enough?"

I stared at him for a moment. He was right. My father said the same thing in another way once. We'd been walking through the plant back in Nevada and Jake Platt, the plant supervisor, came up to him with a report on a poor batch of powder. He suggested blending it in with a large order so the loss would be absorbed.

My father towered over him in rage. "And who would absorb the loss of my reputation?" he shouted. "It's my name that's on every can of that powder. Burn it!"

"All right, Roger," I said slowly. "You get Winthrop."

He looked into my eyes for a moment. When he spoke, his voice was quieter. "You'll have to find him for us. I'm sending Morrissey up to Canada to get the new plant started. I'll go out to the Coast and start production."

"Where is he?"

"I don't know," he answered. "Last I heard, he was in New York, but when I checked around this morning, nobody seemed to know where he is. He seems to have dropped out of sight."

CHAPTER FOUR

I SLUMPED BACK INTO A CORNER OF THE BIG LIMOUSINE AS WE CAME OFF the Queensboro Bridge. Already, I regretted my decision to come out here. There was something about Queens that depressed me. I looked out the window while Robair expertly threaded the big car through the traffic. Suddenly, I was annoyed with Monica for living out here.

I recognized the group of houses as the car rolled to a stop. They hadn't changed, except that the lawn was dull and brown with winter now, where it had been bright summer-green the last time.

"Wait here," I said to Robair. I went up the three steps and pressed the doorbell. A chill wind whistled between the buildings and I pulled my light top-coat around me. I shifted the package uncomfortably under my arm.

The door opened and a small girl stood there, looking up at me. Her eyes were dark violet and serious. "Jo-Ann?" I asked tentatively.

She nodded silently.

I stared at her for a moment. Leave it to children to remind you of the passing of time. They have a way of growing that ticks off your years more accurately than a clock. The last time I had seen her, she was little more than a baby. "I'm Jonas Cord," I said. "Is your mother home?"

"Come in," she said in a small, clear voice. I followed her into the living room. She turned to face me. "Sit down. Mummy's dressing. She said she wouldn't be long."

I sat down and she sat in a chair opposite me. She stared at me with wide, serious eyes but didn't speak. I began to feel uncomfortable under her candid scrutiny and lit a cigarette. Her eyes followed my hand as I searched for an ash tray for my match. "It's over there," she said, pointing to a table on my right.

"Thanks."

"You're welcome," she said politely. Then she was silent again, her eyes watching my face. I dragged on the cigarette and after a moment's silence, spoke to her. "Do you remember me, Jo-Ann?"

Her eyes dropped and she was suddenly shy, her hands smoothing the hem of her dress across her knees in a typically feminine gesture. "Yes."

I smiled. "The last time I saw you, you were just so big," I said, holding my hand out just about level with my knee.

"I know," she whispered, not looking at me. "You were standing on the steps waiting for us to come home."

I took the package out from under my arm. "I brought you a present," I said. "A doll."

She took the package from me and sat down on the floor to open it. Her eyes were smiling now. She lifted out the doll and looked at me. "It's very pretty."

"I hoped you'd like it," I said.

"I do. Very much." Her eyes grew solemn again. "Thank you," she said.

A moment later, Monica came into the room. Jo-Ann leaped to her feet and ran to her. "Mummy! Look what Mr. Cord brought me!"

"It was very thoughtful of you, Jonas," Monica said.

I struggled to my feet. We stood looking at each other. There was an almost regal quality of self-possession about her. Her dark hair fell almost to her bare shoulders over a black cocktail dress.

Then the doorbell rang. It was the baby sitter and Jo-Ann was so busy showing her the new doll, she didn't even have time to say good-by when we left.

Robair was standing at the car door when we came out. "Robair!" Monica put out her hand. "It's nice to see you again."

"It's nice to see you again, Miss Monica," he said as he bowed over her hand.

I looked out at the cruddy Queens scenery as the car rolled back to Manhattan. "What do you want to live out here for?" I asked.

She reached for a cigarette and waited while I held the match for her. "Jo-Ann can play outside when the weather is good and I don't have to worry about her being hurt in the city streets. And I can afford it. It's much more reasonable than the city."

"From what I hear, you're doing all right. If you want to live in the suburbs, why don't you move up to Westchester? It's nicer up there."

"It's still too expensive," she said. "I don't make that kind of money. I'm only the office manager at the magazine. I'm not an editor yet."

"You look like an editor."

She smiled. "I don't know whether you mean that as a compliment or not. But at *Style*, we try to look the way our readers think we should."

I stared at her for a moment. *Style* was one of the most successful new fashion magazines aimed at the young matron. "How come you're not an editor yet?"

She laughed. "I'm one step away. Mr. Hardin's an old-fashioned businessman. He believes that every editor should put in some time on the practical side. That way, they learn something about the business problems involved in getting out a magazine. He's already hinted that the next editorial opening is mine."

I knew old Hardin. He was a magazine publisher from way back. He paid off in promises, not in dollars. "How long has he been promising?"

"Three years," she said. "But I think it will happen soon. He's planning a new movie magazine. A slick. Something on the order of the old *Photoplay*. We'd have been on the presses, only the finances are holding it up."

"What would you do on it?"

"Feature editor," she said. "You know, arrange stories about the stars, that sort of thing."

I glanced at her. "Wouldn't you have to be out in Hollywood for that?"

She nodded. "I suppose so. But Hardin hasn't got the money yet so I'll cross that bridge when I come to it."

Monica put her coffee cup down and smiled at me. "It's been a perfectly lovely dinner, Jonas, and you've been a charming host. Now tell me why."

"Does there have to be a reason?"

She shook her head. "There doesn't have to be," she said. "But I know you. When you're charming, you want something."

I waited until the waiter finished holding a match for her cigarette. "I just got back from England," I said quietly. "I ran into your mother over there."

A kind of veil dropped over her eyes. "You did?"

I nodded. "She seems very nice."

"I imagine she would be, from what I can remember of her," Monica said, a slight edge of bitterness in her voice.

"You must have a very good memory. Weren't you about Jo-Ann's age?"

The violet eyes were hard. "Some things you don't forget," she said. "Like your mother telling you how much she loves you, then disappearing one day and never coming back."

"Maybe she couldn't help it. Maybe she had a good reason."

"What reason?" she asked scornfully. "I couldn't leave Jo-Ann like that."

"Perhaps if you wrote to your mother, she could tell you."

"What could she tell me?" she said coldly. "That she fell in love with another man and ran away with him? I can understand that. What I can't understand is why she didn't take me with her. The only reason I can see is that I didn't matter."

"You may not know your mother, but you do know your father. You know how he can hate when he feels someone has crossed him."

Her eyes looked into mine. "Someone like you?"

I nodded. "Someone like me," I said. "That night, when you both came up to the hotel in Los Angeles—was he thinking about you or was he thinking about how much he wanted to get even with me?"

She was silent for a moment, then her eyes softened. "Was it like that with my mother, too?"

I nodded again. "Something like that," I said quietly.

She looked down at the tablecloth silently. When she looked up at me, her eyes were clear once more. "Thank you for telling me, Jonas. Somehow, I feel better now."

"Good." The waiter came by and refilled our coffee cups. "By the way," I said, "seen anything of your father lately?"

She shook her head with a wry smile. "About two years ago, he came out to dinner and borrowed a thousand dollars. That's the last I saw of him."

"Do you have any idea where he might be?"

"Why?"

"I've got a good job for him up in Canada, but he seems to have dropped out of sight."

A strange look came into her eyes. "You mean you'd give him a job after what he did to you?"

"I haven't much choice," I said reluctantly. "I don't especially like the idea but there's a war on. I need a man like him."

"I had a letter from him about a year ago. He said something about taking over as manager of the Teterboro Airport."

"Thanks," I said. "I'll look out there."

Her hand suddenly came across the table and pressed mine. I looked at her in surprise. She smiled. "You know, Jonas, I have the strangest feeling you're going to make a much better friend than husband."

CHAPTER FIVE

MCALLISTER WAS WAITING FOR ME IN THE HOTEL WHEN I GOT BACK the next afternoon. "You find him?" he asked.

I shook my head. "He only stayed out there long enough to pass a bum check for five hundred bucks on some poor jerk."

"That's pretty far down the ladder for him. Any idea where he went next?"

"No," I said. I threw my topcoat across a chair and sat down. "For all I know, he's in jail in some hick town we never heard of. Bum check—Jesus!"

"What do you want me to do?" Mac asked.

"Nothing," I said. "But I promised Roger I'd try to find him. We better put an agency on the job. If they can't turn him up, at least Roger will know I tried. You call Hardin?"

Mac looked at me curiously. "Yes. He'll be here any minute now. Why do you want to see him?"

"We might go into the publishing business."

"What for?" Mac asked. "You don't even read the papers."

I laughed. "I hear he's thinking of putting out a movie magazine. I'm making a picture. The best way I know to grab space is to own a magazine. I figure if I help him out with the movie magazine, he'll give us a plug in his others. That adds up to twelve million copies a month."

Mac didn't say anything. The doorbell rang and Robair went to open it. It was S. J. Hardin, right on time. He came into the room, his hand outstretched. "Jonas, my boy," he wheezed in his perennially hoarse voice. "It's good to see you."

We shook hands. "You know my attorney, Mr. McAllister?" I said.

S. J. gave him the glad eye. "It's a real pleasure, sir," he said, pumping Mac's hand enthusiastically. He turned back to me. "I was surprised to get your message. What's on your mind, boy?"

I looked at him. "I hear you're thinking about putting out a movie magazine."

"I have been thinking about it," he admitted.

"I also hear that you're a little short of cash to get it started."

He spread his hands expressively. "You know the publishing business, boy," he said. "We're always short of cash."

I smiled. To hear him, one would think he didn't have a pot to piss in. But S. J. had plenty, no matter how much he cried. The way he raided his own company made old Bernie Norman look like a Boy Scout.

"I'm about to make my first movie in eight years."

"Congratulations, Jonas," he boomed. "That's the best news I've heard in years. The movies can use a man like you. Remind me to tell my broker to pick up some Norman stock."

"I will, S. J."

"And you can be sure my magazines will give you a big play," he continued. "We know what makes good copy."

"That's what I wanted to talk to you about, S. J. I think it's a shame your chain has no movie magazine in it."

He fixed me with a shrewd glance. "I feel the same way, Jonas."

"How much would it take to get one on the stands?" I asked.

"Oh, two, maybe three hundred thousand. You've got to make sure of a year's run. It takes that long for a magazine to catch on."

"A magazine like that depends on the kind of editor you have, doesn't it? The right kind of editor and you got it made."

"That's entirely correct, boy," he said heartily. "And I have the finest group of editors in the business. I see you know the publishing business, Jonas. I'm always interested in a fresh point of view. That's what makes the news."

"Who's going to be your feature editor?"

"Why, Jonas," he said in wide-eyed innocence. "I thought you knew. The little lady you had dinner with last night, of course."

I started to laugh. I couldn't help it. The old bastard was smarter than I figured. He even had spies planted in "21."

After he left, I turned to McAllister. "I don't really have to stay here to sign those Engel papers, do I?"

He looked at me sharply. "I don't suppose so. Why?"

"I want to go to the Coast," I said. "Here I'm about to make a picture. What am I doing in New York, getting nothing done?"

"David and Bonner are here. They've been waiting for a call from you."

"Get David on the phone for me." A moment later, he handed me the telephone. "Hello, David. How's Rosa?"

"She's fine, Jonas, and very happy."

"Good," I said. "I just wanted to tell you what a great job I thought you did on that stock bit. Look, I don't feel right hanging around New York while I'm trying to get *The Sinner* ready. I'm going to shove off for the Coast."

"But, Jonas. I brought Bonner into New York."

"That's fine," I said. "But you get him back to the studio and tell him I'll see him there. That's the only place to handle a picture."

"O.K., Jonas," he said, a faint disappointment in his voice. "You flying out?"

"Yeah. I think I can make the ICA two-o'clock flight. That way, I'll be in California tomorrow morning."

"Give Rosa a call, will you, Jonas? She'd be pleased to hear from you."

"I will, David," I said. "By the way, how do I get in touch with that Jennie

Denton? I think I ought at least to meet the girl who's going to play the lead in *The Sinner*."

"She's in Palm Springs, at the Tropical Flower Hotel, registered under the name of Judy Belden."

"Thanks, David," I said. "Good-by."

"Have a safe trip, Jonas."

It was 11:30 A.M., California time, the next day, when I parked my convertible in the driveway of the Tropical Flower Hotel in Palm Springs. I checked at the desk and walked down to Cottage No. 5. When I knocked on the door, there was no answer. But the door was unlocked, so I walked in. "Miss Denton?" I called.

There was no answer. Then I heard the shower running in the bathroom. I walked through and opened the bathroom door. I could see the outline of her body against the opaque shower curtain. She was singing in a low, husky voice.

I closed the bathroom door behind me and sat down on the can. I lit a cigarette while I watched her through the shower curtain. I didn't have to wait long.

She turned off the water and I could hear her sniff at the cigarette smoke. Her voice, from behind the curtain, was calm. "If that's one of the bellboys waiting out there, he'd better go before I come out," she said, "or I report him to the desk."

I didn't answer.

She stuck her head through the shower curtain, groping for a towel. I reached over and put one in her hand. Through the curtain, I could see her wrap it around herself, then the curtain slid back and she stared at me. Her eyes were dark gray and unafraid. "The bellboys in this hotel are the worst," she said. "They walk in on you at the oddest times."

"You could try locking your door."

She stepped out of the tub. "What for? They all have pass-keys."

I got to my feet. "Jennie Denton?"

"It's Judy Belden on the register." A questioning look came over her face. "You the law?"

I shook my head. "No. I'm Jonas Cord."

She looked up at me, a slow smile spreading over her face. "Well, hey! I've been waiting to meet you."

I smiled back at her. "What for?"

She came very close to me and reached up to put her arms around my neck. She drew my face down and the towel slipped from her body to the floor as she stretched up to her tiptoes and kissed me. Then she leaned her head back and looked up at me with mischievous, laughing eyes.

"Boss," she whispered, "ain't it about time you signed my contract?"

CHAPTER SIX

I T WAS THE SAME BUNGALOW OFFICE I'D USED TEN YEARS AGO, WHEN WE were making *The Renegade*. Nothing had changed except the secretaries. "Good morning, Mr. Cord," they trilled in unison as I came in.

I said good morning and walked through to my office. Bonner was pacing up and down nervously. Dan Pierce was seated on the long couch underneath the window. I looked at him for a moment, then without speaking, walked behind my desk and sat down.

"I asked Pierce to come over and help convince you," Bonner said. "You can't make a picture costing this much without a name."

"Dan couldn't convince me to go to the can if I had the runs."

"Wait a minute, Jonas," Dan said quickly. "I know how you feel. But believe me, I'm only looking out for your good."

I turned to him. "Like you did when you sold your stock to Sheffield without checking with me?"

"The stock was mine," he said hotly. "I didn't have to check with anybody. Besides, who could get in touch with you? Everybody knew that you didn't give a damn about the company, that you were unloading part of your own stock."

I reached for a cigarette. After a moment, I nodded. "You're right, Dan," I said. "The stock was yours; you didn't owe me anything. You did your job and I paid you for it—in full, for the five years your contract still had to run." I leaned back in the chair and dragged on the cigarette. "I just made a mistake. You were a good agent when I met you. I should have left well enough alone."

"I'm trying to keep you from making another mistake, Jonas. When the script of *The Sinner* was written, it was a vehicle for a big star—Rina Marlowe. She was the biggest there was. You can't just take a girl with no experience, and who nobody's heard of, and put her in a picture without stars to support her. They'll laugh you out of the theater."

I looked up quizzically. "What do you think I ought to do, then?"

I could see the quick look of confidence come into his eyes. "Get a couple of big names," he said. "Use the girl if you want but back her up. Bogart. Tracy. Colman. Gable. Flynn. Any one of them insures it for you."

"I suppose you can get them for me?"

He missed the sarcasm. "I think I could help," he said cautiously.

"Well, bless your little bleeding, ten-per-centing heart. That's very kind of you." I got to my feet. "Get out, Dan. Get out before I throw you out. And don't ever come back on this lot while I'm on it."

He stared at me, his face turning white. "You can't talk to me like that," he blustered. "I'm not one of your flunkies who you can buy and sell."

"I bought you and I sold you," I said coldly. "You're the same guy you were when you tried to dump Nevada's show for Buffalo Bill's. You'd sell your own mother if there was anything in it for you. But you're not selling me any more. I'm not buying."

I pressed the buzzer on my desk and one of the secretaries came in. "Yes, Mr. Cord?" she asked from the open doorway.

"Mr. Pierce was just leaving—"

Dan's face was livid with rage. "You'll regret this, Jonas."

The door slammed behind him and I turned to Bonner. "I'm sorry, Jonas," he stammered. "I—didn't know—"

"That's O.K.," I said easily. "You didn't know."

"But the way the picture is shaping up now, it's going over three million dollars. I'd feel better if we had some stars in it."

I shook my head. "Stars are great, I'm not fighting them. But not this time. We're doing a story based on the Bible. When somebody looks up at that screen at John or Peter, I want them to see John or Peter, not Gable, Tracy or Bogart. Besides, the girl is the important thing."

"But nobody ever heard of the girl."

"So what?" I asked. "What have we got a publicity department for? By the time this picture comes out, there won't be a man, woman or child in the world who won't know her name. You thought enough of her to make the test, didn't you? And all you knew about her was that she was a girl you met at a party."

A curiously embarrassed look came over Bonner's face. "That was different. It was almost a gag. I never thought anybody would take it seriously."

"David saw the test and took it seriously. So did I."

"But a test isn't a whole picture. Maybe she can't sustain—"

I cut him short. "She'll sustain," I said. "And you know it. You knew it when you asked her to make the test."

He looked at me with his ugly horse face. Nervously his hand scratched at himself. "She—she told you about the party?" he asked hesitantly.

I nodded. "She told me how you'd watched her all evening, how you came over and asked her to take the test." I laughed. "You guys beat me. You find a Lana Turner at a soda fountain. You find Jennie at a dinner party. How do you do it?"

A puzzled look came into his eyes. He started to say something but the telephone on my desk rang. I picked it up. It was one of the secretaries. "Miss Denton is finished in Hairdressing. Do you want her to come down?"

"Yes." I put down the phone and turned back to Bonner. "I sent Jennie up to Hairdressing. I had an idea I wanted to try out."

The door opened and Jennie came in. She moved slowly, almost hesitantly, to the center of the office. She stopped in front of my desk. She spun slowly, her long hair no longer a pale brown but a sparkling champagne. It swirled down around her neck and shoulders, spilling a translucent radiance around her tanned face.

Bonner's voice was an eerie whisper. "My God!"

I looked at him. There was a strange look on his face. His lips moved silently, his eyes were fixed on her. "It's as if—as if she was standing here."

"That's right," I said slowly. I looked back up at Jennie. I began to feel a pressure in my heart. Rina.

"I want Ilene Gaillard to dress her," I said softly to Bonner.

"I don't know," he said. "She's retired. She's moved back East. Boston, I think."

I remembered the forlorn, white-haired figure kneeling by Rina's grave. "Send her a picture of Jennie. She'll come."

Bonner walked over to the desk and stood next to Jennie, looking down at me. "By the way, I heard from Austin Gilbert. He likes the script. He's coming over to see the test this afternoon. If he likes the girl, he'll do the picture."

"Good," I said. That was the way it was with big directors. The two hundred grand you paid them meant nothing; they could get that on any picture. The important thing was the script. And the players.

Bonner walked to the door and stood there a moment, looking back at Jennie. "So long," he said finally.

"Good-by, Mr. Bonner," Jennie said politely.

I nodded as he went out the door.

"Can I sit down now?" Jennie asked.

"Help yourself."

She sat down and watched silently as I ran through the papers on my desk. The preliminary budget. Set-construction estimates. Bonner was right—this was going to cost money.

"Do I have to look like her?" Jennie asked softly.

I glanced up. "What?"

"Do I have to look like her?"

"Why do you ask?"

She shook her head. "I don't know. I just feel funny, that's all. Like it's not me, any more. Like I'm a ghost."

I didn't answer.

"Is that all you saw in the test—Rina Marlowe?"

"She was the biggest thing ever to hit the screen."

"I know," she said slowly. "But I'm not her. I could never be."

I stared at her. "For two thousand dollars a week," I said, "you'll be whatever I tell you to be."

She didn't answer. Just looked at me. Her eyes were masked and somber and I couldn't tell what she was thinking. "You remember that," I said quietly. "A thousand girls like you come to Hollywood every year. I could take my pick of any of them. If you don't like it, go back to what you were doing before Bonner saw you at that party."

A kind of caution came into her eyes. It wouldn't hurt to have her a little afraid of me. She was entirely too cocky. "Bonner told you about me?"

"Not a word. He didn't have to. You told me all I needed to know. Girls like you are always looking for a producer to impress. Well, you were lucky—you got one. Don't louse it up."

She let her breath out slowly. The cautious look had gone out of her eyes. Suddenly, she smiled. "O.K., massa, anything you say."

I walked around the desk, and pulled her up into my arms. Her mouth was soft and warm and when I looked down, her eyes were closed. And then the damn telephone rang. I reached around behind her and picked it up. It was McAllister, calling from New York.

"That agency located Winthrop for you," he said.

"Good. Get in touch with him and tell him to get his ass out here."

"Their man says he won't come."

"Then call Monica and have her talk to him. He'll listen to her."

"I did," Mac said quickly. "But she's already left for California, on the

Twentieth Century, this noon. If you want him, you'd better do it yourself."

"I'm too busy to come running back to New York."

"You don't have to. Amos is in Chicago. The agency office out there will tell you how to locate him."

"Chicago? Well, I guess I'll have to go after him." I put down the telephone and looked at Jennie. "The weekend's coming up," she said softly. "I'm not doing anything. Chicago's a great town."

"You'll come?" I asked.

She nodded. "We'll fly, won't we?"

"All the way," I said.

CHAPTER   SEVEN

JENNIE LOOKED AT ME. "THIS IS THE WAY TO TRAVEL, SHE SAID. "A WHOLE plane to ourselves."

I looked around the empty cabin of the ICA that Buzz had put on special flight for me when I had called. I checked my watch. It was almost nine o'clock. I moved it forward two hours to Chicago time. I felt the slight change of pressure in my ears. We were starting to come down.

"It must be great to own an airline," Jennie said, smiling.

"It comes in handy when you have to get someplace in a hurry."

"I don't get you."

"What don't you get, girl?"

"You," Jennie said. "You baffle me. Most guys I understand. They got their eye on the ball and they're always for making points. But you, you're different. You already got everything."

"Not everything."

She nodded at the lights of Chicago below us. "By that, I suppose you mean you don't own what's down there."

"That's right. I don't want much though, I'm satisfied just owning what's in here."

Her eyes grew cloudy. "What happens if we go boom?"

I snapped my fingers. "What the hell! Easy come, easy go."

"Just like that?"

"Just like that."

She glanced out of the window for a moment, then turned back to me. "I guess you do own me in a kind of way."

"I wasn't talking about you," I said. "I was talking about this plane."

"I know, but all the same, it's true. You do own everybody who works for you, even if you don't feel you do. Money does that."

"Money does lots of things for me," I said.

"Why don't you let it buy you a pair of shoes?"

I looked down at my stockinged feet. "Don't worry," I said. "I got shoes. They're somewhere on this plane."

She laughed, then became serious again. "Money can buy you time. It also lets you make people over, into what you want them to be."

I raised an eyebrow. "I didn't know you were a philosopher as well as an actress."

"You don't know that I'm an actress—yet."

"You better be," I said. "Otherwise, I'm going to look awful foolish."

Again, her eyes were serious. "You wouldn't like that, would you?"

"Nobody likes it," I said. "I'm no different than anybody else."

"Then why do you do it, Jonas? You don't need to. You don't need the money. What do you want to make pictures for?"

I leaned my head back against the seat. "Maybe because I want them to remember me for something else besides gunpowder, airplanes and plastic dishes."

"They'll remember you longer for that than a movie."

"Will they?" I turned my head to look at her. "How do you remember a man? Because of the thrill he gave you? Or because he built the tallest building in the world?"

"You remember all those things," she said softly. "If those were the things he did."

"You *are* a philosopher. I didn't think you understood men so well."

She laughed. "I've been a woman all my life. And men are the first thing a girl tries to understand."

I felt the wheels touch and we were on the ground. Unconsciously I felt myself leaning forward against the wheel to keep her from bucking. Then I relaxed. Habit was a funny thing. You landed every plane, whether you were at the controls or not.

Jennie shivered and pulled her thin coat around her as the first cold blast of air came through the open door. There was snow on the ground as we walked across the landing strip to the terminal.

A chauffeur stopped me, his hand touching his cap respectfully. "Your car's right outside, Mr. Cord."

Jennie was still shivering as we got into the car. "I forgot how cold winter can be," she said.

In forty-five minutes, we were at the Drake Hotel. The assistant manager greeted us at the door. "Good to see you again, Mr. Cord. Your apartment is all ready. Your office called from the Coast." He snapped his fingers and an elevator appeared by magic. We sped up with him in solitary splendor.

"I took the liberty of ordering a hot supper for you, Mr. Cord."

"Thank you, Carter," I said. "That was thoughtful of you."

Carter held open the apartment door. A small table was set up in the dining alcove and there were fresh, gleaming bottles on the bar.

"If you'll just call down when you're ready, Mr. Cord, we'll send it right up."

"Give us a few minutes to wash up, Carter," I said.

"Very good, sir."

I glanced at Jennie, who was still shivering from the cold. "Carter!"

"Yes, Mr. Cord?"

"Miss Denton obviously wasn't prepared for the cold. Do you think we could manage to get her a warm coat?"

Carter allowed himself a brief glance at Jennie. "I believe it could be arranged, sir. Mink, of course?"

"Of course," I said.

"Very good, sir. I'll have a selection up here shortly for mademoiselle."

"Thank you, Carter."

He bowed and the door closed behind him. Jennie turned to me, her eyes wide. "That does it! I thought nothing could impress me any more but that does. Do you know what time it is?"

I looked at my watch. "Ten after twelve."

"Nobody, but nobody, can go shopping for mink coats after midnight."

"We're not going shopping. They're being sent up here."

She stared at me for a moment, then nodded. "Oh, I see," she said. "That makes a difference?"

"Of course."

"Tell me. What makes you so big around here?"

"I pay my rent."

"You mean you keep this apartment all the time?"

"Of course," I said. "I never know when I might be in Chicago."

"When were you here last?"

I rubbed my cheek. "About a year and a half ago."

The telephone rang. I picked it up, then held it out to Jennie.

A look of surprise came over her face. "For me?" she said. "But nobody knows I'm here."

I went into the bathroom and closed the door. When I came out, a few minutes later, she was sitting on the side of the bed, a dazed look on her face. "It was the furrier," she said. "He wanted to know which I preferred—light or dark mink. Also, what size."

"What size did you tell him?"

"Ten."

I shook my head. "I would have thought you took a twelve. Nobody ever buys a mink coat size ten. It hardly pays."

"Like I said, you're crazy," she said. Then she threw herself into my arms and hugged me. "But you're crazy nice."

I laughed aloud. Mink will do it every time.

CHAPTER EIGHT

THE MAN FROM THE DETECTIVE AGENCY ARRIVED WHILE WE WERE EATING supper. His name was Sam Vitale and if he thought it was odd that Jennie was eating in a full, almost black mink coat, his weary, wise eyes evinced no surprise.

"It's cold in Chicago," Jennie explained.

"Yes, ma'am," he answered politely.

"Did you have any trouble finding him?" I asked.

"Not too much. All we had to do was check the credit agencies. He left a trail of bad checks. It was just a matter of time. When we narrowed it down to around

Chicago, we checked Social Security. They may change their names but they generally don't fool with their Social Security. He's going under the name of Amos Jordan."

"Where is he working?" I asked curiously.

"In a Cicero garage, as a mechanic. He makes enough to keep him in booze. He's hitting the bottle pretty hard."

"Where does he live?"

"In a rooming house, but he only goes there to sleep. He spends most of his spare time in a clip joint called La Paree. You know the kind of joint. Continuous entertainment. There's always a stripper working on the stage, while the other girls take turns hustling the suckers for drinks."

Amos hadn't changed, I thought. He still went where the girls were. I pushed back my coffee cup. "O.K., let's go get him."

"I'm ready," Jennie said.

Vitale looked at her. "Maybe you'd better stay here, ma'am. It's a pretty rough place."

"What?" Jennie said quickly. "And miss the chance of breaking in my new mink coat?"

La Paree was one of about twenty similar clubs on a street that looked like every other Strip Street clear across the country. Its windows were covered with posters of half-naked girls—Maybellene, Charlene, Darlene and the inevitable Rosie Tookus. All were dancing tonight.

The doorman wore an ear-to-ear grin as the big limousine rolled to a stop. He opened the door with a flourish. "Welcome, folks. They come from all over the world to La Paree."

They certainly did. The doorman rushed into the club, where a small man in a dark suit materialized before us. A hat-check girl, in a pair of tights, took our coats. Jennie shook her head and kept her coat on as we followed him down the dark, narrow smoke-filled room to a tiny table right in front of the stage.

A stripper was working just over our heads. The drums were taking a slow beat and she was grinding away, almost down to the bare essentials.

"Two bottles of your best champagne," I said. This wasn't the place to order whisky. Not unless you had a zinc-lined stomach.

At the word champagne, the stripper paused in her routine, right in the middle of a bump, and looked down. I saw her appraising eyes flick over me as she put on her most seductive smile.

Then Jennie let her coat fall back on the seat and took off her turban. Her long blond hair caught all the flashes of light from the spot as it tumbled down around her shoulders. As quickly as it had appeared, the stripper's smile vanished.

I looked at Jennie. She smiled back at me. "You gotta fight fire with fire," she said.

I laughed. A white-shirted waiter came up with two bottles of champagne in a bucket. Quickly he put three glasses down on the table and opened the first bottle. The cork popped and the champagne spilled down over the sides of the bottle. He filled all three glasses without waiting for me to taste the wine and hurried off.

It was still warm but it was a good champagne. I looked at the bottle.

Heidsieck, 1937. Even if the label was a phony, it wasn't half bad. Then I noticed a white chit beside me on the table. Eighty dollars.

"If you'd come in a cab," Vitale said, "it only would have cost you twenty bucks a bottle."

"How much if we'd walked?"

He grinned. "Fifteen."

"Cheers," I said, lifting my glass.

No sooner had we put down our glasses than the waiter was refilling them. He moved quickly, slopping some over the edge of the glasses, then started to upend the bottle into the ice bucket.

I stopped him with my hand. "Not so fast, friend. If I don't squawk at the tariff, the least you can do is let us finish the bottle."

He stared at me, then nodded. He put the bottle into the bucket right side up and disappeared. There was a roll of drums and the stripper went off, to a desultory clatter of half-hearted applause.

"He's over there, down at the end of the bar," Vitale said.

I turned to look. There still wasn't much light. All I could see was a figure hunched over the bar, a glass cupped in his hands.

"I might as well go get him."

"Think you'll need any help?" Vitale asked.

"No. You stay here with Miss Denton."

The lights went down again and another stripper came on. As I walked toward the bar, a girl brushed against me in the dark. "Looking for someone, big boy?" she whispered. It was the stripper who had just come down off the stage.

I ignored her and walked down the bar to Amos. He didn't look up as I climbed onto the empty stool alongside him. "A bottle of Budweiser," I said to the bartender. The bottle was in front of me and my dollar gone before I was fully settled on the stool.

I turned to look at Amos, who was watching the stage, and a feeling of shock ran through me. He was old. Incredibly old and gray. His hair was thin and his skin hung around his cheeks and jowls the way a skinny old man's flesh hangs.

He lifted his drink to his lips. I could see his hand shaking and the grayish-red blotches on the back of it. I tried to think. He couldn't be that old. The most he could be was his middle fifties. Then I saw his eyes and I knew the answer.

He was beat and there was nothing left for him but yesterdays. The dreams were gone because he'd failed all the challenges and the dry rot of time had set in. There was nowhere left for him to go but down. And down and down, until he was dead.

"Hello, Amos," I said quietly.

He put his drink down and turned his head slowly. He looked at me through bloodshot, watery eyes. "Go away," he whispered in a hoarse, whisky-soaked voice. "That's my girl dancing up there."

I glanced up at the stage. She was a redhead who'd seen better years. They were a good combination, the two of them. They'd both fought the good fight—badly—and lost.

I waited until the music crashed to its finale before I spoke again. "I got a proposition for you, Amos."

He turned toward me. "I told your messenger I wasn't interested."

For a moment, I was ready to get down off that stool and walk off. Out into the fresh, cold night and away from the stench of stale beer and sickness and decay. But I didn't. It wasn't only the promise I'd made Forrester. It was also that he'd been Monica's father.

The bartender came up and I ordered us both a round. He picked up the five and left.

"I told Monica about the job. She was very happy about it."

He turned and looked at me again. "Monica always was a damn fool," he said hoarsely, and laughed. "You know, she didn't want to divorce you. She was crazy mad, but afterward she didn't want to divorce you. She said she loved you."

I didn't answer and he laughed again. "But I straightened her out," he continued. "I told her you were just like me, that neither of us could ever resist the smell of cunt."

"That's over and done with," I said. "A long time ago."

He slammed the glass down on the bar with a trembling hand. "It's not over!" he shouted. "You think I can forget how you screwed me out of my own company? You think I can forget how you beat me out of every contract, wouldn't let me get started again?" He laughed craftily. "I'm no fool. You think I didn't know you had men following me all over the country?"

I stared at him. He was sick. Much sicker than I had thought.

"And now you come with a phony proposition, huh?" He smiled slyly. "Think I'm not wise to you? Think I don't know you're tryin' to get me out of the way because you know if they ever get a look at my plans, you're through?"

He slid off the stool and came at me with wildly surging fists. "Through, Jonas!" he screamed. "Through! Do you hear me?"

I swung around on the stool and caught at his hands. His wrists were thin and all fragile old bone. I held his arms and suddenly he slumped against me, his head on my chest.

I looked down at him and saw that his eyes were filled with weak old tears of rage at his helplessness. "I'm so tired, Jonas," he whispered. "Please don't chase me any more. I'm sorry. I'm so tired I can't run any—"

Then he slipped from my grasp and slid down to the floor. The redhead, who had come up behind him, screamed and the music stopped, suddenly. There was a press of people around us as I started to get down from the stool. I felt myself pushed back against the bar violently and I stared into the face of a big man in a black suit. "What's goin' on here?"

"Let him go, Joe." Vitale's voice came from behind and the bouncer turned his head around. "Oh, it's you, Sam." The pressure against my chest relaxed.

I looked down at Amos. Jennie was already kneeling beside him, loosening his shirt collar and slipping down his tie. I bent over. "He pass out?"

Jennie looked up at me. "I think it's more than that," she said. "He feels like he's burning up with fever. I think we'd better get him home."

"O.K.," I said. I took out a roll and threw a hundred-dollar bill down on the bar. "That's for my table." I looked up and saw the redhead staring at me, a mascara track of tears streaming down her cheeks. I peeled off another hundred and pressed it into her hand. "Go dry your tears."

Then I bent down and picking Amos up in my arms, started for the door. I was surprised at how light he was. Vitale got our coats from the hat-check girl and followed me outside.

"He lives just a couple of blocks away," he said as I put Amos into the car.

It was a dirty gray rooming house and two cats stood on open garbage cans in front of the door, glaring at us with their baleful yellow night eyes. I looked up at the building from the car window. This was no place for a man to be sick in.

The chauffeur jumped out and ran around to open the back door. I reached out and pulled the door shut. "Go back to the Drake, driver," I said.

I turned and looked down at Amos, stretched out on the back seat. Just because he was sick didn't make me feel any different about him. But I couldn't get over the feeling that if things had turned out a little differently, it might have been my own father lying there.

CHAPTER NINE

THE DOCTOR CAME OUT, SHAKING HIS HEAD. JENNIE WAS RIGHT BEHIND him. "He'll be all right when he wakes up in the morning. Somebody fed him a slug of sodium amytal."

"What?"

"Knockout drops," Jennie said. "A Mickey."

I smiled. My hunch was right. Vitale had left nothing to chance. I wanted Amos, he saw to it that I got him.

"He's very run down," the doctor added. "Too much whisky and too little food. He has some fever but he'll be all right with a little care."

"Thank you, doctor," I said, getting up.

"You're welcome, Mr. Cord. I'll stop by in the morning to have another look at him. Meanwhile, Miss Denton, give him one of those pills every hour."

"I'll do that, doctor."

The doctor nodded and left.

I looked at Jennie. "Wait a minute. You don't have to sit up all night taking care of that slob."

"I don't mind," she said. "It won't be the first time I sat up with a patient."

"A patient?"

"Of course." She looked at me quizzically. "Didn't I ever tell you I graduated from nursing school?"

I shook my head.

"St. Mary's College of Nursing, in San Francisco," she said. "Nineteen thirty-five. I worked as a nurse for a year. Then I quit."

"Why'd you quit?"

"I got tired of it," she said, her eyes masking over.

I knew better than to push. It was her own business, anyway. "Want a drink?" I asked, going over to the bar.

She shook her head. "No, thanks. Look, there's no sense in both of us staying up all night. Why don't you go to bed and get some rest?"

I looked at her questioningly.

"I'll be O.K. I can catch up on my sleep in the morning." She came over and kissed me on the cheek. "Good night, Jonas. And thank you. I think you're a very nice man."

I laughed. "You didn't think I'd let you walk around Chicago in a light coat like that?"

"For the coat, too. But not only for the coat," she said quickly. "I heard what he said about you. And still you brought him here."

"What else could I do? I couldn't just leave him lying there."

"No, of course not," she said, her eyes wide. "Now go to bed."

I turned and walked into the bedroom. It was a dark and crazy night. In my dreams, Amos and my father were chasing me around a room, each trying to make me do what he was shouting at me. But I couldn't understand them—they were speaking a kind of gibberish. Then Jennie, or maybe Rina, came into the room dressed in a white uniform and the two of them began running after her. I tried to stop them and finally, I managed to get her out of the room and shut the door. I turned and took her in my arms but it turned out to be Monica and she was crying. Then somebody slammed me back against the wall and I stared into the face of the bouncer at La Paree. He began to shine a flashlight in my eyes and the light grew brighter and brighter and brighter.

I opened my eyes and blinked them. The sunlight was pouring in the window and it was eight o'clock in the morning.

Jennie was sitting in the living room with a pot of coffee and some toast in front of her. "Good morning. Have some coffee?"

I nodded, then walked over to Amos' room and looked in. He was lying on his back, sleeping like a baby. I closed his door, walked over to the couch and sat down beside her. "You must be tired," I said, picking up my coffee cup.

"A little. But after a while, you don't feel it any more. You just keep on going." She looked at me. "He talked quite a bit about you."

"Yeah? Nothing good, I hope?"

"He blames himself for breaking up your marriage."

"All of us had a little to do with it," I said. "It was no more his fault than it was mine—or hers."

"Or Rina Marlowe's?"

"Most of all, not Rina's," I said quickly. I reached for a cigarette. "Mainly, it was because Monica and I were too young. We never should have got married in the first place."

She picked up her coffee cup and yawned. "Maybe you better get some rest now," I said.

"I thought I'd stay up until the doctor came."

"Go on to bed. I'll wake you when he comes."

"O.K.," she said. She got up and started for the bedroom. Then she turned and walked back, picking up her mink coat from the chair.

"You won't need it," I said. "I left the bed nice and warm."

She nuzzled her face against the fur. "Sounds nice."

She went inside, closing the door behind her. I filled my coffee cup again and picked up the telephone. Suddenly, I was hungry. I told room service to send up a double order of ham and eggs and a fresh pot of coffee.

Amos came out while I was eating breakfast. He had a blanket wrapped around him like a toga. He shuffled over to the table and looked down at me. "Who stole my clothes?"

In the daylight, he didn't look as bad as he had the night before. "I threw them out," I said. "Sit down and have some breakfast."

He remained standing. He didn't speak. After a moment, he looked around the apartment. "Where's the girl?"

"Sleeping," I said. "She was up all night, taking care of you."

He thought about that. "I passed out?" It was more a statement than a question. I didn't answer.

"I thought so," he said, nodding. Then he groaned. He raised his hand to his forehead, almost losing his blanket. "Somebody slipped me a Mickey," he said accusingly.

"Try some food. It's supposed to have vitamins."

"I need a drink," he said.

"Help yourself. The bar's over there."

He shuffled over to the bar and poured himself a shot. He drank it swiftly, throwing it down his throat. "Ah," he said. He took another quick one. Some color flooded back into his gray face.

He shuffled back to the table, the bottle of whisky still in his hand, and slumped into the chair opposite me. "How'd you find me?"

"It was easy. All we had to do was follow the trail of rubber checks."

"Oh," he said. He poured another drink but left this one standing on the table in front of him. Suddenly, his eyes filled with tears. "It wouldn't be so bad if it was anyone but you."

I didn't answer; just kept on eating.

"You don't know what it is to get old. You lose your touch."

"You didn't lose it," I said. "You threw it away."

He picked up the whisky glass.

"If you're not interested in my proposition," I said, "just go ahead and drink that drink."

He stared at me silently for a moment. Then he looked at the small, amber-filled glass in his hand. His hand trembled slightly and some of the whisky spilled on the tablecloth. "What makes you such a do-gooder all of a sudden?"

"I'm not," I said. I reached for my coffee cup and smiled at him. "I haven't changed at all. I still think you're the world's champion prick. If it was up to me, I wouldn't touch you with a ten-foot pole. But Forrester wants you to run our Canadian factory. The damn fool doesn't know you like I do. He still thinks you're the greatest."

"Roger Forrester, huh?" he asked. Slowly the whisky glass came down to the table. "He tested the Liberty Five I designed right after the war. He said it was the greatest plane he ever flew."

I stared at him silently. That was more than twenty years ago and there had been many great planes since then. But Amos remembered the Liberty Five. It was the plane that set him up in business.

A hint of the Amos Winthrop I had known came into his face. "What's my end of the deal?" he asked shrewdly.

I shrugged my shoulders. "That's between you and Roger," I said.

"Good." A kind of dignity came over him as he got to his feet. "If I had to deal with you, I wouldn't be interested, at any price."

He stalked back to his bedroom door. He turned and glared at me. "What do I do about clothes?"

"There's a men's shop downstairs. Call them and have them send up what you want."

The door closed behind him and I reached for a cigarette. I could hear the faint murmur of his voice on the telephone. Leaning back in the chair, I let the smoke drift idly out through my nose.

When the clothing arrived, I had them leave it in his bedroom. Then the buzzer sounded again and I cursed to myself as I went to the door. I was beginning to feel like a bloody butler. I opened the door. "Hello, Mr. Cord."

It was a child's voice. I looked down in surprise. Jo-Ann was standing next to Monica, clutching the doll I had given her in one hand and her mother's coat in the other.

"McAllister sent me a telegram, on the train," Monica explained. "He said you'd probably be here. Did you find Amos?"

I stared at her dumbly. Mac must be losing his marbles. He must have known there was a three-hour layover in Chicago and that Monica would show up here. What if I didn't want to see her?

"Did you find Amos?" Monica repeated.

"Yes, I found him."

"Oh, goody," Jo-Ann suddenly exclaimed, spotting the breakfast table. "I'm hungry." She ran past me and climbing up on a chair, picked up a piece of toast. I stared after her in surprise.

Monica looked up at me apologetically. "I'm sorry, Jonas," she said. "You know how children are."

"You said we'd have breakfast with Mr. Cord, Mommy."

Monica blushed. "Jo-Ann!"

"It's all right," I said. "Won't you come in?"

She came into the room and I closed the door. "I'll order some breakfast for you," I said, going to the telephone.

Monica smiled. "Just coffee for me," she said, taking off her coat.

"Is the doctor here yet, Jonas?"

Monica stared.

I stared.

Jennie stood in the open doorway, her long blond hair spilling down over the dark mink coat, which she held wrapped around her like a robe. Her bare neck and legs made it obvious she wore nothing beneath it.

The smile had gone from Monica's face. Her eyes were cold as she turned to me. "I beg your pardon, Jonas," she said stiffly. "I should have known from experience to call before I came up."

She crossed the room and took the child's hand. "Come on, Jo-Ann."

They were almost to the door before I found my voice. "Wait a minute, Monica," I said harshly.

Amos' voice cut me off. "Ah, just in time, child," he said calmly. "We can leave together."

I turned to look at him. The sick, dirty old man we had found in the bar last night had disappeared. It was the Amos of old who stood there, dressed neatly in a gray, pin-striped, double-breasted suit, with a dark chesterfield thrown casually over his arm. He was every inch the senior executive, the man in charge.

There was a faintly malicious smile on his lips as he crossed the room and turned, his hand on the door. "My children and I do not wish to impose—" He paused and bowed slightly in the direction of Jennie. Angrily I started toward the door. I opened it and heard the elevator doors open and close, then there was silence in the hall.

"I'm sorry, Jonas," Jennie said. "I didn't mean to louse things up for you."

I looked at her. Her eyes were large with sympathy. "You didn't do anything," I said. "Things were loused up a long time ago."

I went to the bar and poured myself a drink. All the good feeling had gone. This was the last time I'd ever play the good Samaritan. I swallowed the drink and turned back to Jennie. "Did you ever get laid in a mink coat?" I asked angrily.

There was sadness and understanding on her face. "No."

I poured myself another drink and swallowed it. We stood there, looking at each other silently across the room for a moment. Finally, I spoke. "Well?"

Her eyes still on mine, she nodded slowly. Then she raised her arms and held them out toward me, the coat falling open, away from her naked body. When she spoke, there was a note in her voice as if she'd always known that this was the way it was going to be. "Come to mother, baby," she whispered gently.

THE STORY OF JENNIE DENTON
Book Eight

CHAPTER ONE

JENNIE WALKED THROUGH THE CURTAINED DOORWAY INTO THE CAMERA and the director shouted, "Cut! Wrap it up!" And it was over.

She stood there for a moment, dazed, blinking her eyes for a moment as the powerful kliegs dimmed. Then the oppressive August heat came down on her and she felt faint. She reached out a hand to steady herself. As if from a distance, she heard the giant sound stage turn into bedlam. It seemed that everybody was laughing and talking at once.

Someone pressed a glass of water into her hands. She drank it quickly, gratefully. Suddenly, she began to shiver, feeling a chill, and the dresser quickly threw a robe over her shoulders, covering the diaphanous costume. "Thank you," she whispered.

"You're welcome, Miss Denton," the dresser said. He looked at her peculiarly for a moment. "You feeling all right?"

"I'm fine," Jennie said. She felt cold perspiration breaking out on her forehead. The dresser gestured and the make-up man hurried up. He swabbed at her face quickly with a moist sponge. The faint aroma of witch hazel came up in her nostrils and she began to feel better.

"Miss Denton," the make-up man said, "you'd better lie down for a while. You're exhausted."

Docilely she let him lead her back to the small portable dressing room. She looked back over her shoulder as she went in. The bottles were out and the whisky flowing. Everyone was gathered around the director, shouting congratulations, supplying him with the adoration they felt necessary to insure their employment on his next picture. Already, they seemed to have forgotten her.

She closed the door behind her and stretched out on the cot. She closed her eyes wearily. The three months the picture was supposed to take had stretched out into five. Five months of day-and-night shooting, of exhaustion, of getting up at five o'clock in the morning and falling into bed like a stone at midnight, and sometimes later. Five months, until all the meaning that had been in the script was lost in a maze of retakes, rewrites and plain confusion.

She began to shiver again and pulled the light wool blanket up over her and lay there trembling. She closed her eyes. She turned on her side, drawing her knees up and hugging herself. Slowly the heat from her body condensed around her and she began to feel better.

When she opened her eyes, Ilene Gaillard was seated on a chair opposite. She hadn't even heard her come into the small room. "Hello," Jennie said, sitting up. "Was I asleep long?"

Ilene smiled. "About an hour. You needed it."

"I feel so silly," Jennie said. "I usually don't go off like that. But I felt so weak."

"You've been under a terrible strain. But you have nothing to worry about. When this picture comes out, you're going to be a big star—one of the biggest."

"I hope so," Jennie said humbly. She looked at Ilene. "When I think of all those people, how hard they worked and how much they put into the picture. I couldn't bear it if I turned out to be a disappointment to them."

"You won't. From what I saw of the rushes, you were great." Ilene got to her feet and looked down at Jennie. "I think you could use a hot drink."

Jennie smiled when she saw Ilene take down the can of cocoa. "Chocolate?"

"Why not?" Ilene said. "It will give you more energy than tea. Besides, you don't have to worry about your diet any more. The picture is finished."

"Thank God for that," Jennie said, standing up. "One more lunch of cottage cheese and I was ready to throw up." She crossed the tiny room to the closet. "I might as well get out of this."

Ilene nodded. She watched as Jennie slipped out of the costume—the sheer, flowing silk harem pantaloons, the diaphanous gauze blouse and gold-beaded blue velvet jacket that had been her costume in the last scene. She scanned the girl's figure appreciatively, her designer's eyes pleased with what she saw.

She was glad now that Jonas had sent for her. She had not felt that way at first. She hadn't wanted to come back to Hollywood, back to the gossip, the jockeying for importance, the petty jealousies. But most of all, she hadn't wanted to come back to the memories.

But as she'd studied the photograph, something about the girl had drawn her back. She could understand what Jonas had seen in her. There was something of Rina about her but she also had a quality that was peculiarly her own.

It wasn't until she'd studied the photograph a long while that she realized what it was. It was the strangely ascetic translucence that shone from the photograph despite its purely sensuous appeal. The eyes in the picture looked out at you with the clear innocence of a child, behind their worldly knowledge. It was the face of a girl who had kept her soul untouched, no matter what she had experienced.

Jennie fastened her brassière and pulled the thick black sweater down until it met the top of her baggy slacks. She sat down and took the cup of steaming chocolate from Ilene. "Suddenly, I'm empty," she said, sipping at it. "I'm all used up."

Ilene smiled and tasted her own cup of chocolate. "Everyone feels like that when a picture is finished."

"I feel that I could never make another movie," Jennie continued thoughtfully. "That another part wouldn't make any sense to me at all. Somehow, it's like all of me went into this picture and I've nothing left at all."

Ilene smiled again. "That will disappear the moment they put the next script into your hands."

"Do you think so?" Jennie asked. "Is that what happens?"

Ilene nodded. "Every time."

A blast of noise came through the thin walls. Jennie smiled. "They're having themselves a ball out there."

"Cord ordered a table of food sent down from the commissary. He's got two men tending bar." Ilene finished her chocolate and put the cup down. She got to her feet and looked down at the girl. "I really came in to say good-by."

Jennie looked up at her questioningly. "You're leaving?"

Ilene nodded. "I'm going back East on the train tonight."

"Oh," Jennie said. She put down her cup and stood up. She held her hand out to Ilene. "Thank you for everything you've done. I've learned a great deal from you."

Ilene took her hand. "I didn't want to come back but I'm glad now that I did."

They shook hands formally. "I hope we'll work together again," Jennie said.

Ilene started for the door. She looked back at Jennie. "I'm sure that we will," she said. "If you want me, write. I'd be glad to come."

In a moment, the door opened again and Al Petrocelli, the publicity manager, stuck his head in. A blast of music came from behind him. "Come on," he said. "The party's going great guns. Cord sent over an orchestra."

She put down her cigarette. "Just a minute," she said, turning to the mirror and straightening her hair.

He stared at her. "You're not coming like that?" he asked incredulously.

"Why not? The picture's finished."

He came into the room and closed the door behind him. "But, Jennie baby, try to understand. *Life* magazine is covering the party. How would it look to their readers if the star of the biggest picture we've made in ten years was wearing a loose black sweater and pants? We've got to give 'em more to look at than that."

"I'm not getting into that costume again," Jennie said stubbornly.

"Please, baby. I promised them some cheesecake."

"If that's what they want, give them the photo file."

"Now is no time to make with the temperament," Al said. "Look, you've been a good girl up to now. Just this once, please."

"It's O.K., Al." Bonner's voice came from behind him. "If Jennie doesn't want to change, she doesn't have to." He smiled his pleasantly ugly smile as he came into the tiny dressing room. "As a matter of fact," he said, "I think it might be a welcome change for *Life's* readers."

Al looked at him. "O.K. if you say so, Mr. Bonner," he said.

Bonner turned to her, smiling. "Well, you did it."

She didn't answer, just looked at him.

"I've been thinking about you," he said, his eyes on her face. "You're going to be a big star."

She didn't say anything.

"*The Sinner* is going to be a tough picture to follow."

"I hadn't thought about it," she said.

"Of course. You haven't and neither has Jonas." Bonner laughed. "But why should you? That's not your job. It's mine. All Jonas does is what he feels like doing. If he wants to make a picture, he makes a picture. But it might be another eight years before he feels like it again."

"So?" she said, meeting his eyes levelly.

He shrugged his shoulders. "It's up to me to keep you working. If you go that long between pictures, they'll forget all about you." He reached into his jacket for a package of cigarettes. "Is that Mexican woman still working for you?"

"Yes."

"Still living in the same place?"

"Of course."

"I thought I might drop by one evening next week," he said. "I've got some scripts we might go over."

She was silent.

"Jonas is going away," he said. "To Canada, on a business trip." He smiled. "You know, I think it's fortunate he hasn't heard any of the stories about you, don't you?"

She let her breath out slowly. "Yes."

"I thought maybe Wednesday night."

"You'd better call first," she said through stiff lips.

"Of course, I forgot. Nothing has changed, has it?"

She looked up at him. "No," she said dully. Then she walked past him to the door. A great weariness came into her. Nothing had changed. Things turned out the way they always did for her. Nothing ever changed but the currency.

CHAPTER TWO

S HE AWOKE TO THE SIGHT OF WHITE LINEN FLOATING IN THE WIND ON THE clothesline outside the window. The rich aroma of corned beef and cabbage, wafting into her room on the heavy summer breeze from the kitchen next door, told her it was Sunday. It was always like that on Sundays, only when you were a little girl it had been more fun.

On Sundays, when she'd returned from church with her mother, her father would be awake and smiling, his mustache neatly trimmed and waxed, his face smooth and smelling of bay rum. He tossed her into the air and caught her as she came down, hugging her close to him and growling, "How is my little Jennie Bear this morning? Is she sweet and filled with God's holiness fresh from the fount in the back of the church?"

He laughed and she laughed and sometimes even her mother laughed, saying, "Now, Thomas Denton, is that the proper way for a father to talk to his own daughter, sowing in her the seeds of his own disobedience to God's will?"

Her father and mother were both young and filled with laughter and happiness and God's own good sunshine that shone down on San Francisco Bay. And after the big dinner, he dressed himself carefully in his good blue suit and took her by the hand and they went out of the house to seek adventure.

They first met adventure on the cable car that ran past their door. Holding her in his arms, her father leaped aboard the moving car, and waving his blue-and-white conductor's pass, which entitled him to ride free on any of the company's cars, pushed forward to the front of the car, next to the motorman. There he held her face up to the rushing wind until the breath caught in her throat and she thought she'd burst with the joy of the fresh, sweet wind in her lungs.

"This is my daughter, my Jennie Bear," he shouted to all who would listen, holding her proudly so that all who cared to look could see.

And the passengers, who up to now had been engrossed in their own private thoughts, smiled at her, sharing somehow in the joy that glowed like a beacon in her round and shining face.

Then they went to the park, or sometimes to the wharf, where they ate hot shrimp or crabs, swimming in garlic, and her father drank beer, great foaming glasses of it, bought from the bootlegger who operated quite openly near the stands. But only to wash away the smell of the garlic, of course. Or sometimes, they went out to the zoo and he bought her a bag of peanuts to feed the elephant or the monkeys in their cages. And they returned in the evening, and she was tired and sometimes asleep in her father's arms. And the next day was Monday and she couldn't wait until it would be Sunday again.

No, nothing passed as quickly as the Sundays of your childhood. And then she went to school, frightened at first of the sisters, who were stern and forbidding in their black habits. Her small round face was serious above her white middy blouse and navy-blue guimpe. But they taught you the catechism and you made your confirmation and lost your fear as bit by bit you accepted them as your teachers, leading you into a richer Christian life, and the happy Sundays of your childhood fled deeper and deeper into the dim recesses of your mind, until you hardly remembered them any more.

Jennie lay quietly on her sixteen-year-old bed, her ears sharpening to the sounds of the Sunday morning. For a moment, there was only silence, then she heard her mother's shrill voice. "Mr. Denton, for the last time, it's time to get up and go to Mass."

Her father's voice was husky, the words indistinguishable. She could see him in her mind's eyes, lying unshaven and bloated with Saturday-night beer in his long woolen underwear, on the soft, wide bed, burying his face in the big pillow. She heard her mother again. "But I promised Father Hadley ye'd come this Sunday for sure. If ye have no concern for your own soul, at least have some for your wife's and daughter's."

She heard no reply, then the door slammed as her mother retreated to the kitchen. Jennie swung her bare feet onto the floor, searching for her slippers. She found them and stood up, the long white cotton nightgown trailing down to her ankles as she crossed the room.

She came out into the kitchen on her way to the bathroom and her mother turned from the stove. "Ye can wear the new blue bonnet I made for ye to Mass, Jennie darlin'."

"Yes, Mother," she said.

She brushed her teeth carefully, remembering what Sister Philomena had told the class in Hygiene. Circular strokes with the brush, reaching up onto the gums, then down, would remove all the food particles that might cause decay. She examined her teeth carefully in the mirror. She had nice teeth. Clean and white and even.

She liked being clean. Not like many of the girls at Mercy High School, who came from the same poor neighborhood and bathed only once a week, on Saturdays. She took a bath every night—even if she had to heat the water in the kitchen of the old tenement in which they lived.

She looked at her face out of her clear gray eyes and tried to imagine herself in the white cap and uniform of a nurse. She'd have to make up her mind soon. Graduation was next month and it wasn't every student who could get a scholarship to St. Mary's College of Nursing.

The sisters liked her and she'd always received high marks throughout her attendance at Mercy. Besides, Father Hadley had written Mother M. Ernest, commending her for her devout attendance and service to the church, not like so many of the young ladies today, who spent more time in front of a mirror over their make-up than on their knees in church in front of their God. Father Hadley had expressed the hope that the Good Mother would find a way to reward this poor deserving child for her devotion.

The scholarship to St. Mary's was given each year to the one student whose record for religious and scholastic achievements was deemed the most worthy by a committee headed by the Archbishop. This year, it was to be hers, if she decided to become a nurse. This morning, after church, she'd have to present herself to Mother M. Ernest, at the Sister House, to give her answer.

"It is God's mercy you'll be dispensing," Sister Cyril had said, after informing her of the committee's choice. "But you will have to make the decision. It may be that attending the sick and helpless is not your true vocation."

Sister Cyril had looked up at the girl standing quietly in front of her desk. Already, Jennie was tall and slim, with the full body of a woman, and yet there was a quiet innocence in the calm gray eyes that looked back at her. Jennie did not speak. Sister Cyril smiled at her. "You have a week to make up your mind," she said gently. "Go to the Sister House next Sunday after Mass. Mother Mary Ernest will be there to receive your answer."

Her father had cursed angrily when he heard of the scholarship. "What kind of life is that for a child? Cleaning out the bedpans of dirty old men? The next thing you know, they'll talk her into becoming a nun."

He turned violently to her mother. "It's all your doing," he shouted. "You and those priests you listen to. What's so holy about taking a child with the juices of life just beginning to bubble inside of her and locking her away behind the walls of a convent?"

Her mother's face was white. "It's blasphemy you're speaking, Thomas Denton," she said coldly. "If only once you'd come and speak to the good Father Hadley, ye'd learn how wrong ye are. And if our daughter should become a religious, it's the proudest mother in Christendom I'd be. What is wrong in giving your only child as a bride to Christ?"

"Aye," her father said heavily. "But who'll be to blame when the child grows up and finds you've stolen from her the pleasures of being a woman?"

He turned to Jennie and looked down at her. "Jennie Bear," he said softly, "it's not that I object to your becoming a nurse if you want to. It's that I want you to do and be whatever you want to be. Your mother and I, we don't matter. Even what the church wants doesn't matter. It's what you want that does." He sighed. "Do you understand, child?"

Jennie nodded. "I understand, Papa."

"Ye'll not be satisfied till ye see your daughter a whore," her mother suddenly screamed at him.

He turned swiftly. "I'd rather see her a whore of her own free choice," he snapped, "than driven to sainthood."

He looked down at Jennie, his voice soft again. "Do you want to become a nurse, Jennie Bear?"

She looked up at him with her clear gray eyes. "I think so, Papa."

"If it's what you want, Jennie Bear," he said quietly, "then I'll be content with it."

Her mother looked at him, a quiet triumph in her eyes. "When will ye learn ye cannot fight the Lord, Thomas Denton?"

He started to answer, then shut his lips tightly and strode from the apartment.

Sister Cyril knocked at the heavy oaken door of the study. "Come in," called a strong, clear voice. She opened the door and gestured to Jennie.

Jennie walked into the room hesitantly, Sister Cyril behind her. "This is Jennie Denton, Reverend Mother."

The middle-aged woman in the black garb of the Sisterhood looked up from her desk. There was a half-finished cup of tea by her hand. She studied the girl with curiously bright, questioning eyes. After a moment, she smiled, revealing white, even teeth. "So you're Jennie Denton," she said, holding out her hand.

Jennie curtsied quickly and kissed the ring on the finger of the Reverend Mother. "Yes, Reverend Mother." She straightened up and stood in front of the desk stiffly.

Mother M. Ernest smiled again, a hint of merriment coming into her eyes. "You can relax, child," she said. "I'm not going to eat you."

Jennie smiled awkwardly.

The Reverend Mother raised a questioning eyebrow. "Perhaps you'd like a cup of tea?" she asked. "A cup of tea always makes me feel better."

"That would be very nice," Jennie said stiffly.

The Reverend Mother looked up and nodded at Sister Cyril. "I'll get it, Reverend Mother," the nun said quickly.

"And another cup for me, please?" Mother M. Ernest turned back to Jennie. "I do love a good cup of tea." She smiled. "And they do have that here. None of those weak tea balls they use in the hospitals; real tea, brewed in a pot the way tea should be. Won't you sit down, child?"

The last came so fast that Jennie wasn't quite sure she'd heard it. "What, ma'am?" she stammered.

"Won't you sit down, child? You don't have to be nervous with me. I want to be your friend."

"Yes, ma'am," Jennie said and sat down, even more nervous than before.

The Reverend Mother looked at her for a few moments. "So you've decided to become a nurse, have you?"

"Yes, Reverend Mother."

Now the Reverend Mother's curiously bright eyes were upon her. "Why?" she asked suddenly.

"Why?" Jennie was surprised at the question. Her eyes fell before the Reverend Mother's gaze. "Why?" She looked up again, her eyes meeting the Reverend Mother's. "I don't know. I guess I never really thought about it."

"How old are you, child?" the Reverend Mother asked.

"I'll be seventeen next month, the week before graduation."

"It was always your ambition to be a nurse and help the sick, ever since you were a little child, wasn't it?"

Jennie shook her head. "No," she answered candidly. "I never thought about it much until now."

"Becoming a nurse is very hard work. You'll have very little time to yourself at St. Mary's. You'll work and study all day; at night, you'll live at the school. You'll have only one day off each month to visit your family." The Reverend Mother turned the handle of her cup delicately so that it pointed away from her. "Your boy friend might not like that."

"But I haven't got a boy friend," Jennie said.

"But you came to the junior and senior proms with Michael Halloran," the Reverend Mother said. "And you play tennis with him every Saturday. Isn't he your boy friend?"

Jennie laughed. "No, Reverend Mother. He's not my boy friend, not that way." She laughed again, this time to herself, as she thought of the lanky, gangling youth whose only romantic thoughts were about his backhand. "He's just the best tennis player around, that's all." Then she added, "And someday I'm going to beat him."

"You were captain of the girl's tennis team last year?"

Jennie nodded.

"You won't have time to play tennis at St. Mary's," the Reverend Mother said.

Jennie didn't answer.

"Is there anything you'd rather be than a nurse?"

Jennie thought for a moment. Then she looked up at the Reverend Mother. "I'd like to beat Helen Wills for the U.S. tennis championship."

The Reverend Mother began to laugh. She was still laughing when Sister Cyril came in with the tea. She looked across the desk at the girl. "You'll do," she said. "And I have a feeling you'll make a very good nurse, too."

CHAPTER THREE

TOM DENTON KNEW THERE WAS SOMETHING WRONG THE MOMENT HE came up to the window for his pay envelope. Usually, the paymaster was ready with a wisecrack, like did he want him to hold the envelope for his wife so that the Saturday-night beer parlors wouldn't get it? But there was no wisecrack this time, no friendly raillery, which had been a part of their weekly meeting for almost fifteen years. Instead, the paymaster pushed the envelope under the slotted steel bars quickly, his eyes averted and downcast.

Tom stared at him for a moment. He glanced quickly at some of the faces on the line behind him. They knew, too. He could see it from the way they were looking at him. An odd feeling of shame came over him. This couldn't be happening to him. Not after fifteen years. His eyes fell and he walked away from the window, the envelope in his hand.

Nobody had to tell him times were bad. This was 1931 and the evidence was all around him. The families on relief, the bread lines, the endless gray, tired faces of the men who boarded his car every morning.

He was almost out of the barn now. Suddenly, he couldn't wait any longer and he ducked into a dark corner to open the pay envelope. He tore at it with trembling fingers. The first thing that came to his hand was the dreaded green slip.

He stared at it unbelievingly. It must be a mistake. They couldn't mean him. He wasn't a one-year or two-year man, not even a five-year man. He had seniority. Fifteen years. They weren't laying off fifteen-year men. Not yet.

But they were. He squinted at the paper in the dim light. Laid off. What a bitter irony. That was the reason given for all the pay cuts—to prevent layoffs. Even the union had told them that.

He shoved the envelope into his pocket, trying to fight the sudden sick feeling of fear that crawled around in his stomach. What was he to do now? All he knew was the cars. He'd forgotten all about everything else he'd ever done. The only other thing he remembered was working as a hodcarrier when he was young.

He came out of the dark barn, blinking his eyes at the daylight. A group of men were standing there on the sidewalk, their worn blue uniforms purplish in the light. One of them called to him. "You got it, too, Denton?"

Tom looked at him. He nodded. "Yes."

"We did, too," another said. "They're letting out the senior men because we're getting a higher rate. All the new men are being kept on."

"Have you been to the union yet?" Tom asked.

"We've been there and back. The hall is closed. The watchman there says come back on Monday."

"Anybody call Riordan?"

"His phone home don't answer."

"Somebody must know where Riordan is," Tom said. "Let's go to the hall and make the watchman let us in. After all, what do we pay dues for if we can't meet there?"

"That's a good idea, Tom. We can't just let them replace us with fifty-five-centers, no matter what they say."

They began to walk to the union hall, about two blocks from the car barn. Tom strode along silently. In a way, he still couldn't believe it. Ten cents an hour couldn't mean that much to the company. Why, he'd have taken even another cut if they'd asked him. It wasn't right, the way they were doing it. They had to find Riordan. He'd know the answers. He was the union man.

The union hall was dark when they got there and they banged on the door until the old night watchman opened it. "I tol' you fellers Riordan ain't here," he said in an aged, irritated voice.

"Where is Riordan?"

"I don't know," the watchman answered, starting to close the door. "You fellers go home."

Tom put his foot in the door and pushed. The old man went flying backward, stumbling, almost falling. The men surged into the building behind Tom.

"You fellers stay outa here," the old man cried in his querulous voice.

They ignored him and pushed their way into the meeting hall, which was a large room at the end of the corridor. By now, the crowd had swelled to close to thirty men. Once they were in, they stood there uncertainly, not knowing what to do next. They milled around, looking at each other. "Let's go into Riordan's office," Tom suggested. "Maybe we can find out where he is in there."

Riordan's office was a glass-enclosed partition at the end of the meeting hall. They pushed down there but only a few of them were able to squeeze into the tiny cubbyhole. Tom looked down at the organizer's desk. There was a calendar, a green blotter and some pencils on it. He pulled open a drawer, then, one after another, all of them. The only thing he could find were more pencils, and dues blanks and receipts.

The watchman appeared at the back of the hall. "If you fellers don't get outa here," he shouted, "I'm gonna call the cops."

"Go take a shit, old man," a blue-coated conductor shouted back at him.

"Yeah," shouted another. "This is our union. We pay the dues and the rent. We can stay here if we want."

The watchman disappeared back into the corridor. Some of the men looked at Tom. "What do we do now?"

"Maybe we better come back Monday," one of them suggested. "We'll see what Riordan has to say then."

"No," Tom said sharply. "By Monday, nobody will be able to do nothing. We got to get this settled today."

"How?" the man asked.

Tom stood there for a moment, thinking. "The union's the only chance we got. We got to make the union do something for us."

"How can we if Riordan ain't here?"

"Riordan isn't the union," Tom said. "We are. If we can't find him, we got to do it without him." He turned to one of the men. "Patrick, you're on the executive board. What does Riordan usually do in a case like this?"

Patrick took off his cap and scratched at his gray hair. "I dunno," he said thoughtfully. "But I reckon the first thing he'd do would be to call a meetin'."

"O.K." Tom nodded. "You take a bunch of the men back to the barns and tell the day shift to come down here to a meeting right away."

The men moved around excitedly and after a few minutes, several of them left to go back to the car barns. The others stood around, waiting. "If we're to have a meetin'," someone said, "we gotta have an agenda. They don't have no meetin's without they have an agenda."

"The agenda is, can the company lay us off like this," Tom said.

They nodded agreement. "We got rights."

"This meetin' business is givin' me a awful thirst," another man said. "All this talkin' has dried out me throat somethin' terrible."

"Let's send out for a barrel of beer," a voice yelled from the back.

There was real enthusiasm in the shout of agreement and a collection was quickly taken up. Two men were dispatched on the errand and when they returned, the keg was mounted on a table at the back of the room.

"Now," said one of them, waving his beer glass in front of him, "now we can get down to business!"

❖ ❖ ❖

The meeting hall was a bedlam of noise and confusion as more than a hundred men milled around, talking and shouting. The first keg of beer had run out long ago. Two new ones rested on the table, pouring forth their refreshment.

Tom pounded on the table with the gavel he'd found in Riordan's desk. "The meeting will now come to order!" he shouted, for the fifth time in as many minutes. He kept pounding on the table until he caught the attention of a few men down at the front.

"Quiet!" one of them bellowed. "Le's hear what good ol' Tom has to say."

The noise subsided to a murmur, then all the men were watching him. Tom waited until it was as quiet as he thought it would get, then he cleared his throat nervously. "We called this meetin' because today the company laid off fifty men an' we couldn't find Riordan to tell us why." He fumbled with the gavel for a moment. "The union, which is supposed to give us protection on our jobs, has now got to act, even if we don't know where Riordan is. The men that were laid off today had seniority an' there's no reason why the company shouldn't take them back."

A roar burst from the crowd.

"While you fellers was drinkin' beer," Tom said, "I looked up the rules in the bylaws printed in my union book, an' it says that a meetin' is entitled to call for a strike vote if more than twenty-five members is present. There's more than twenty-five members here an' I say we should vote a strike by Monday, unless the company takes us back right away."

"Strike! Strike!"

"We've all been faithful employees of the company for many years an' always gave them an honest count an' they got no right to kick us out like that."

"Y-aay!"

"Don't let the nickels stick to your fingers, Tom," a man in the back shouted. "There may be a spotter in the crowd."

There was laughter.

"If there is a spotter," Tom said grimly, "let him go back to the company an' tell 'em what we're doin' here. We'll show 'em they can't push us around."

There was a burst of applause.

Tom waved his hand. "Now we'll vote on a strike," he said. "All in favor say aye."

The men were suddenly quiet. They looked at each other nervously. The door at the back of the hall had opened and Riordan was standing in it. "What's all this loose talk about a strike, men?"

They turned in surprise and stared at him. The ruddy-faced, heavy-set union organizer started down through the meeting hall. A buzz came up as they saw him. It was almost a sigh of relief. Riordan was here. He'd tell them what to do. He'd straighten everything out.

"Hello, Tom," Riordan said, walking around the table. He held out his hand. Tom shook hands with him. It was the first time he'd done so.

"We came down here because we thought the union should be doin' somethin' for us."

Riordan gave him a shrewd look. "Of course, Tom," he said soothingly. "And it's the right thing ye did, too."

Tom sighed in relief. For a moment, he had thought Riordan would be angry at the way they'd come in and taken over the hall. He watched as Riordan turned toward the men and held up his hand. A silence came over the hall.

"Men," Riordan said in his deep voice, "the reason you couldn't find me was I beat it up to the company office the minute I learned about the layoffs. There was no time to call a meeting but I want you to know that the union was right on the job."

A cheer went up from the men. They looked at each other embarrassedly.

"And I want to express my appreciation to Brother Tom Denton here for his prompt action in bringing you all down here to the union hall. It shows that Tom Denton, like every one of you, knows that the union is his friend."

Tom blushed as the men cheered again. Riordan turned back to the crowd. "I've been working all afternoon, fighting with the management, and finally I got them to back down a little."

A loud cheer shook the ceiling.

Riordan raised his hand, smiling. "Don't cheer yet, boys. Like I say, I only got them to back down a little bit, but it's a start. They promised to have more meetings with me next month."

"Are they takin' us back?" Tom asked.

Riordan looked at him, then turned back to the men. "The management agreed to take back ten of the men who were laid off this week. They also agreed to take back ten more men next month."

A strange silence came over the room. The men eyed each other nervously. "But more than fifty of us were laid off," Tom said loudly. "What's ten men out of that many?"

"It's a start, Tom," he said. "You can't do it all at once."

"Why not?" Tom demanded hotly. "They laid us all off at once."

"That's different," Riordan said. "The company has the right to lay off if business is bad."

"We know that. What we're sore about is the way they did it. They paid no attention to the seniority they agreed to in the union agreement. They laid off all the sixty-five cent men and kept the fifty-five-centers."

"I know," Riordan said. A harsh edge had come into his voice. "But their taking back ten men is a start. It's better than having all fifty of ye out on the street." He turned back to the men. "Ten of you will go back to work. Maybe next month, ten more will go back. That's better than nothing. The company doesn't care if you go on strike. They claim they'll save money by not running."

"I say we take it," one of the men shouted. "Ten of us workin' is better than none workin', like Riordan says."

"No," Tom said angrily, getting to his feet. "The company should take us all back. Each of us has as much right to work as the next one. If all us sixty-five-cent men would accept a cut to fifty-five cents, the company could keep us all on."

Riordan laughed hoarsely. "You hear that, men?" he shouted. "Would you like to take another pay cut?"

There was a murmur from the crowd. They shifted uneasily. "I'd rather take a pay cut than have us all laid off," Tom said.

Riordan glared at him. There was no friendliness in his eyes now. He had been angry ever since he got a call from the company personnel manager, advising him he'd better get down to the union hall. The call had caught him at a very embarrassing time. He got out of bed, cursing as he struggled into his clothing. "What is it, honey?"

"Some jerky conductor has taken over the hall and is talking strike to the boys."

"But he can't do that," his paramour answered in a shocked voice. "You promised the company they'd have no trouble."

"They won't," he said harshly. "Nobody can make Riordan break his word!"

By the time he'd driven down to the union hall, he'd simmered down. But now he was getting angry again. He had a hard enough job explaining to his wife where he was spending his Saturday nights, without having it loused up by a bunch of stupid trolley men.

He turned back to the crowd. "I propose we settle this here and now," he shouted. "You have a choice. Ten men go back to work or you strike."

"Wait a minute," Tom protested.

"The men already turned your proposal down," Riordan snapped. He raised his right hand. "All in favor of returning to work raise your right hand."

About ninety men raised their hands.

"Nays?"

There were only a few raised hands besides Tom's.

"The ayes have it. Now you men go home to your wives. I'll let you know on Monday which of you go back to work."

Slowly the men began to file out of the room. Tom looked at Riordan but the man didn't meet his eyes. Instead, he went back into his little glass cubbyhole and picked up the telephone.

Tom walked wearily toward the door. Some of the men looked at him, then quickly hurried by, as if they were ashamed to meet his gaze. At the doorway, he turned and looked back. Riordan was still using the telephone.

The night was clear and bright and a warm breeze came in from the bay. He walked along thoughtfully. He wasn't going to be one of the lucky ten who were going to be taken back. He was sure of that. He'd seen the anger in Riordan's eyes. He turned the corner and walked to the car stop on the next block. Idly he wondered if his pass was still good now that he was laid off.

Two men came past him on the darkened street. One of them stopped. "Got a match?"

"Sure," Tom said. He fumbled in his pocket. He might not have a job but matches he still had. He struck the match. The sudden hardening in the man's eyes and the sound of footsteps behind him were a warning that came too late. There was a sharp blow to the back of his head and he stumbled to his knees.

He reached out, grabbing the man in front of him around the legs. The man swore under his breath and kicked upward with his knee, catching Tom in the groin.

Tom grunted from the pain as he went over backward, his head striking the sidewalk. As if from a long way off, he felt the men kicking at him as he lay there. He rolled over toward the edge of the sidewalk and into the gutter.

He felt a hand reach into his pocket and take out his pay envelope. Feebly he tried to grab the hand. "No," he pleaded. "Please, no, that's my pay, it's all I got!"

The man laughed harshly. He aimed a final kick at the side of Tom's head.

Tom saw the heavy boot coming but he couldn't duck away from it. Then the lights exploded in his face and he rolled over, face down, in a puddle of water in the gutter. He came to slowly, painfully, to the sound of water against his face.

He moved his head wearily. A gentle rain had begun to fall.

His body ached as he pushed himself up on his hands and slowly got to his feet. He swayed dizzily for a moment and reached out to the street lamp to steady himself. The lamp flickered and then went out. It was almost morning. The sick gray light of the day spilled down around him.

He saw his blue conductor's cap lying in the gutter, not far from where he stood. Slowly he knelt and picked it up. He brushed it off against his coat and walked toward the corner. There was a mirror in the corner of the drugstore window. He paused in front of it and looked at himself.

His uniform was torn and shredded, his tie askew, the shirt buttons ripped away. He put his hand up to his face in touching wonder. His nose was puffed and swollen, and one eye had already turned purple. With the tip of his tongue, he could feel the jagged edges of broken teeth.

He stared for a moment, numb with shock, then he began to understand what had happened to him. Riordan had done it. He was sure of that. That's why Riordan had been on the telephone when he'd left the union hall.

Suddenly, he realized he'd never be able to go back to work for the cable-car company. Riordan would see to that, too. He stood there looking at himself and the tears began to run down his cheeks. Everything had gone wrong. Everything. Now he had no job and no money. And worst of all, he'd have to tell Ellen.

She'd never believe he hadn't been out on a drunk, and the ironic thing was that he hadn't so much as taken one glass of beer.

CHAPTER FOUR

"ARE YE GOIN' TO BE SITTIN' THERE ALL DAY READING THE NEWSPApers, studyin' what kind of a job would suit your highness best?" Ellen Denton asked caustically.

Her face was grim as she wrapped Jennie's lunch in a piece of wax paper. Tom didn't speak, looking down at the paper again as Jennie came into the room. "Good morning, Mom," she said brightly. "Morning, Daddy."

"Good morning, Jennie Bear," he said, smiling at her. "How's my Winnie Winkle this morning?"

"Just fine, Daddy." It was a private joke between them. He'd called her that when she got a job as a typist in the insurance company last month. It had been just five weeks after he'd lost his job on the cable cars and two weeks after she graduated from Mercy High School.

"You're the Winnie Winkle," he'd said. "But I'll get something in a few weeks. Then you'll be able to go to St. Mary's, like you planned."

"Ye have too much lipstick on, Jennie," her mother said. "Best take some of it off."

Tom looked at his daughter. She didn't have that much lipstick on. It was much less than most of the girls wore whom he used to see every morning on the cable car.

"Oh, Mother." Jennie protested. "I'm working in an office now, not going to school. I have to look decent."

"Decent ye should look, not painted."

"Aw, Ellen, leave the girl alone," Tom said slowly.

Ellen glared angrily at him. "When you're bringin' home some of the money to feed your family, then ye can talk."

Tom stared at her, his face setting grimly. He could feel the color draining from it. Jennie smiled sympathetically at him and that made it even worse. He never expected Jennie to be pitying him. He tightened his lips against a flood of angry words.

"Golly, I'm going to be late," Jennie said, jumping to her feet. She snatched at the paper bag on the table and started for the door. " 'By, Mom," she said over her shoulder. " 'By, Daddy. Good luck today."

Tom could hear her footsteps running down the stairs. He looked down at the paper again. "Could I have another cup of coffee?"

"No, one cup is all ye get. How much coffee d'ye think we can afford on the child's eleven dollars a week?"

"But you have the coffee right there. It's already made."

"It's for warming again tomorrow mornin'," she said.

He folded the paper carefully, got up and walked into the bathroom. He turned on the tap and let the water run as he took down his shaving brush and razor. He held his hand under the tap. The water was still cold. "Ellen, there's no hot water for my shave."

"Use the cold, then," she called. "Unless ye have a quarter for the gas meter. I'm savin' the gas we have left for the child's bath."

He looked at himself in the mirror. His face had healed from the beating, but his nose was a little crooked now and there were broken edges on his two front teeth. He put down the brush and walked into the kitchen.

Ellen's back was still toward him. He put his hands on her shoulders and turned her around. "Ellen, Ellen," he said gently. "What's happened to us?"

She stared up into his face for a moment, then reached up and pushed his hands from her shoulders. "Don't touch me, Thomas Denton. Don't touch me."

His voice was resigned. "Why, Ellen, why? It's not my fault what happened. It was God's will."

"God's will?" She laughed shrilly. "You're the one to be talkin' of God's will. Him that hasn't been in the church for more years than I can remember. If ye thought more of your Saviour than you did of your Saturday-night beer, He'd have shown ye some of His mercy."

He took a deep breath and let it out slowly. Then he turned, went back into the bathroom and began to shave with the cold water. She hadn't always been like this—sharp-tongued and acid-touched. And fanatical about the church and the priests. Once, she'd been Ellen Fitzgerald, with laughing eyes and dancing feet, and he remembered her at the Irish Ballroom on Day Street the time he first met her.

She was the prettiest girl on the floor that night, with her dark-brown hair and blue eyes and tiny feet. That was in 1912 and they were married the next year. A year after that, Jennie had been born.

He was a motorman with the car line even then, and when he came back from the war, they moved into this apartment. A year later, a son was born.

Poor tiny little Tommy. The world was not long for him and when he was two years old, they laid him to rest in Calvary Cemetery. Jennie was eight then and barely understood what had happened to her brother, but Ellen found her solace in the quiet of the church, and every day she took her daughter there with her. At first, he didn't pay much attention. Ellen's overattachment to her church was only natural; it would wear off soon enough.

But it didn't. He found that out one night, when he reached for her in the bed and found her cold and unresponsive. He felt for her breast inside the heavy cotton nightgown but she turned her back to him. "You've not made your confession in months. I'll not have ye planting another child in me."

He tried to make a joke of it. "Who wants to make a baby? All I want is a bit of lovin'."

"That's even worse, then," she said, her voice muffled by the pillow. "It's sinful and I'll share no part of that sin."

"Is that what the priests have been dunning into your ears? To deny your husband?"

She didn't answer. He gripped her shoulder and forced her to turn toward him. "Is that it?" he asked fiercely.

"The priests have told me nothing. What I do is of me own doing. I know the Book enough to know right from wrong. And stop your shouting. You'll be waking Jennie in the next room."

"I'll stop shouting," he said angrily, as the heat of her shoulder came warm into his hands and the fever rose up in him and he took her by force. The spasm shook him and he subsided into a heavy-breathing quiet atop her, his eyes staring into hers.

She looked up at him quietly, not moving, passive as she had been all through his assault upon her. A last shiver drained his vitals. Then she spoke. Her voice was calm and distant and detached, as if he weren't there at all. "Are ye all through spending your filth in me?"

He felt a cold sickness rising in his stomach. He stared at her for a moment more, then rolled off her onto his side of the bed. "I'm all through," he said tonelessly.

She got out of the bed and knelt beside the tiny crèche she had placed beneath the crucifix. He could sense her face turning toward him in the darkness. "I shall pray to the Virgin Mother that your seed has found no home in me," she whispered harshly.

He closed his eyes and turned his back. This was what they'd done to her, spoiled everything between them. A bitterness began to gall him.

He never set foot in a church again.

CHAPTER FIVE

I T WAS QUIET HERE IN THE NAVE OF THE CHURCH. ELLEN DENTON, ON HER knees before the holy statuary, her head bowed and her beads threaded through her clasped fingers, was at peace. There was no prayer on her lips, no disturbing thoughts in her mind—only a calm, delicious emptiness. It per-meated her whole being and closed off the world, beyond the comforting walls.

The sins of omission, which plagued her hours while she was outside these walls, were but faint distant echoes. Little Tommy lay quiet in his grave, no reproach on his tiny rosebud lips, for her neglect during his illness. No memories rose to torture her of her white, naked body, writhing in passion and pleasure, while her son lay dying in the same room.

It had seemed just a tiny cold, a cold such as children have so often and awaken free from in the morning. How was she to know that while she lay there, whis-pering her delight into her husband's ear, a minute piece of phlegm had lodged in her son's throat, shutting off the air from his lungs? So that, when she got up to adjust his covers, as she usually did before she closed her eyes for the night, she found him strangely cold and already blue. How was she to know that this was to be her punishment for her own sins?

Father Hadley had tried to comfort her in her grief. "Do not blame yourself, my child. The Lord giveth, the Lord taketh away. His will be done."

But she'd known better. The memory of her joy in her sin was still too strong within her, though she sought to free her soul of its burden by a thousand visits to the confessional. But all the soothing words of the priests brought no solace to her soul. Her guilt was her own and only she, herself, could expunge it. But here, in the quiet peace of the nave, beneath the silent, sorrowing Virgin, there was calmness and emptiness and oblivion.

Johnny Burke was bored. He took a last drag on the butt and spun it out into the gutter. The pimply-faced boy next to him said, "Let's go over and see if Tessie is busy."

"Tessie is always busy. Besides, I hear she give a feller a dose. I ain't takin' any chances." Johnny took out another cigarette and lit it, his eyes nervously looking up the street. "Just for once, I'd like to get me a dame that nobody else has banged."

"How yuh goin' do that, Johnny?"

"There are ways, Andy," Johnny said mysteriously. "There are ways."

Andy looked at him interestedly. "You talk like yuh know."

Johnny nodded. He tapped his pocket. "I got a little somethin' in here that'll make any girl put out."

"Yeah, Johnny?" Andy asked quickly. "What?"

Johnny lowered his voice carefully. "Mosca cantharides."

"What's that?"

"Spanish fly, yuh dope," Johnny said. "I stole some when Doc asked me to watch the store while he went upstairs."

"Gee," Andy said, impressed. "Will it work on any girl?"

Johnny nodded. "Sure. If yuh can slip it into her drink. Just a little an' she's as hot as a biscuit right out of the oven."

The druggist stuck his head out of the doorway. "Johnny, watch the store for me, will you? I want to run upstairs a minute."

"O.K., Doc."

They watched him turn into the entrance next door, then went into the drugstore. Johnny walked behind the counter and leaned carelessly against the cash register.

"How about a Coke, Johnny?"

"Uh-uh," Johnny said. "No handouts while I'm watchin' the store for Doc." Idly Johnny opened and closed some drawers under the counter. "Hey, Andy," he called. "Want to see where Doc keeps all the rubbers?"

"Sure," Andy said. He walked around behind the counter.

"May I have a Coke, please?"

The girl's voice came from the soda fountain. Both boys looked up guiltily. Quickly Johnny snapped the drawer shut. "Sure, Jennie."

"Where's Doc?"

"He went upstairs for a minute."

"She saw us," Andy whispered. "She knows what we were lookin' at."

Johnny looked at Jennie as he walked over to the soda fountain. Maybe she did. There was a peculiar smile on her face. He pressed the plunger on the Coke-sirup pump and watched the dark fluid squirt into the glass. "Yuh hear from the Champ yet, Jennie?"

She shook her head. "We were supposed to go to the movies tonight but he didn't get back from Berkeley. I hope nothing went wrong with his scholarship."

Johnny smiled. "What could go wrong with it?" he said. "He already took the state finals."

Andy came up behind him. "Will it work on her?" he whispered. Johnny knew what he meant. He looked up suddenly. All at once it seemed to him that he'd never really seen Jennie. She was one of the cherries and usually he paid no attention to them. She had left her Coke and was over looking at the magazines. He liked the way the thin summer dress clung to her. He never knew she had such big ones. No wonder Mike Halloran kept her on the leash. Suddenly, he put his hand in his pocket and took out the little piece of paper and emptied the pinch of powder into her glass.

Jennie took a magazine from the rack and went back to the fountain. Johnny looked down at her glass. Some traces of powder were still floating on top. He took it and put in another squirt of sirup, then held the glass under the soda spigot while he stirred vigorously. He put the drink down in front of her and looked up at the clock. "Kind of late for you to be out, isn't it?"

"It's Saturday night," Jennie answered. "It was so hot in the apartment, I thought I'd come down for some air." She put a nickel on the counter and took a straw from the glass container.

Johnny anxiously watched her sip the drink. "Is it all right?"

"A little sweet, maybe."

"I'll put a little more soda in it," Johnny said quickly. "How's that?"

She sipped at it. "Fine now. Thanks."

He picked up the nickel, went back to the cash register and rang it up. "I saw what you did," Andy whispered.

"Shut up."

Jennie was turning the pages of the magazine slowly as she sipped her drink. Her glass was half empty when the druggist came back into the store. "Everything O.K., Johnny?"

"O.K., Doc."

"Thanks, Johnny. Want a Coke?"

"No, thanks, Doc. See you tomorrow."

"What did you go an' do that for?" Andy asked, when they came out onto the street. "Now we won't never know if it worked."

"We'll know," Johnny said, turning to look through the window.

Jennie had finished her drink and was climbing down from the stool. She put the magazine back on the rack and started for the door. Johnny moved over to intercept her.

"Going home, Jennie?"

She stopped and smiled at him. "I thought I'd go down to the park. Maybe there's a cool breeze coming in from the bay."

"Mind if we come along?" Johnny asked. "We're not doin' anything."

She wondered what made Johnny ask to walk with her all of a sudden. He'd never seemed interested in her before.

It was almost ten o'clock when Tom Denton came out of the saloon across from the car barn. He was drunk. Sad, weeping, unhappy drunk. He stared across the street at the car barn. Old Two-twelve was in there. His old car. But she wasn't his car any more. She'd never be his car any more. She was somebody else's car now.

The tears began to roll down his cheeks. He was a failure. No car, no job, not even a wife to come home to. Right now she was probably sitting in a corner of the church, praying.

Didn't she understand a man had to have more than a prayer when he got into bed? If he had a couple of dollars in his pocket, he knew where he'd go. The girls at Maggie's knew how to treat a man. He fished in his pocket for some coins. Carefully he counted them. Thirty-five cents. He thought about going back into the saloon. He had enough for one more drink. But then he'd have to ask Ellen for pocket money on Monday.

He felt the effects of the liquor beginning to wear off. Angrily he put the change back in his pocket. Drinking wasn't any fun when you had to worry about every nickel you spent. Almost sober now, he began to walk home slowly.

He was sitting at the kitchen table in the dark when Ellen came home half an hour later. He looked up wearily as she turned on the light. "I didn't expect ye home so early," she said. "What happened? Did they run out of whisky?"

He didn't answer.

She walked out of the kitchen into the narrow hallway. He heard her open Jennie's door, then close it. A moment later, she came back into the kitchen. "Where's Jennie?"

"I don't know. She's probably out with Mike."

"Mike is still in Berkeley. Jennie was here when I left for church. She said she was going to bed early."

"It's warm," he said. "She probably went out for a breath of air."

"I don't like her being out alone like that."

"Now, don't start on her, Ellen," he said. "She's a big girl now."

She took a kettle down from the shelf and filled it with water. She placed it on the stove and lit the gas under it. "Would ye like a cup of tea?"

He looked up in surprise. It had been a long time since Ellen asked him to share an evening cup of tea. He nodded gratefully.

She took the cups from the cupboard and placed them on the table. Then she sat down opposite him to wait for the water to boil. There was a worried expression on her face.

"Don't worry," he said, suddenly feeling sorry for her. "Jennie'll be home any minute now."

She looked up, and in a rare moment of insight, saw what she was doing to him and to herself. She felt the tears coming into her eyes and placed her hand over his. "I'm sorry, Tom. I don't know what's the matter with me. Half the time, I imagine things that never happen."

"I know, Ellen," he said gently. "I know."

It was then that the policeman came to the door and told them that Jennie had been found in the park, raped and beaten. And from the look on Ellen's face, Tom knew that they were lost forever.

CHAPTER SIX

THE THREE OF THEM CAME OUT OF THE CHURCH INTO THE BRIGHT SUN-light. They felt almost immediately the curious watching eyes. Tom felt the sudden shrinking in his daughter and noticed the flush of shame creeping up into her face, still puffed from the beating of almost two weeks ago. Her eyes looked down at the steps as they began to walk down toward the sidewalk.

"Hold your head up, Jennie Bear," he whispered. "It's their sons should bear the shame, not you."

Jennie lifted her head and smiled at him gratefully. "And you, too, Ellen Denton," he added. "Stop lookin' down at the ground."

In a way, Ellen felt a sort of triumph. Her husband had finally returned to the church. She thought of how it had been early that morning. She'd been all dressed and ready to leave for church when she called Jennie. She opened the door of Jennie's room. Her daughter was sitting in a chair, staring out the window. "You're not dressed yet, Jennie," she said in a shocked voice. "It's time we were leaving for Mass."

"I'm not going, Mama," Jennie said tonelessly.

"But you've not been to church since ye came home from the hospital. You've scarcely been out of the house."

"I've been out, Mama." She turned toward her mother and the dark circles under her eyes looked even darker in the light. "And everybody stared at me and whispered as I went by. I can't stand it. I won't go to church and be a freak for everybody to stare at."

"You're denying the Savior!" Ellen said heatedly. "How do ye expect forgiveness for your sins if ye don't attend church?"

"What sins does the child need forgiveness for?" Her husband's voice came from behind her. She whirled around, her temper immediately rising. "It's enough we have one traitor to the church in this house," she said. "We don't need another." She turned to Jennie. "Get dressed. You're coming with me if I have to drag ye."

THE CARPETBAGGERS ❖ 413

"I'm not going, Mama," Jennie said. "I can't."

Ellen took a threatening step toward her daughter. She raised her hand. Suddenly, she felt her wrist caught in a grip of steel and she turned to look up into the face of her husband. His usually soft blue eyes were cold and hard. "Leave the child be! Have you gone completely mad?"

She looked up at him for a moment and then the flashing anger dissolved within her, leaving her spent and weak. The tears started in her eyes. "Father Hadley asked me to bring her. He said he'd offer up a prayer for her comfort."

He felt the release of her anger and let go of her wrist. Her arm fell limply at her side. He turned to his daughter. "Is that the reason you won't go to church, Jennie Bear?" he asked gently. "Because they stare at you?"

She nodded silently.

"Would you go if I were to come with you?" he asked suddenly.

Jennie looked into his eyes and saw the love there. After a moment, she nodded. "Yes, Daddy."

"All right, then. Get dressed. I'll be shaved in a minute." He turned and left the room quickly. Ellen stared after him, almost too surprised to realize what had happened.

There had been a buzz of surprise as they walked down the aisle to their pew. Tom could see heads twisting as they gaped, and a shudder ran through him at all the cruelty that was inherent in all human beings. His hand tightened on his daughter's and he smiled as he knelt toward the altar and crossed himself before taking his seat.

But as bad as it had been when they came in, it was that much worse when they came out. The curious had had time to gather on the steps in the bright morning sunshine. It was like running a gantlet of idiots.

"It's over now," he said softly as they turned the corner.

They crossed the street, walking toward the drugstore on the next corner. A group of boys were lounging about the store window, dressed in their Sunday best. The boys fell silent as they approached, staring at them with their wise, street-corner eyes. Tom stared back angrily at them and their eyes fell before his. They walked by and turned the corner to their house.

From around the corner behind him, Tom could hear the sudden explosion of their whispered conversation. Then one boy snickered and another boy laughed and the merriment had a sick, dirty sound to it that tore at his heart. Abruptly he let go of Jennie's arm and walked back around the corner. They looked at him in surprise, the laughter frozen on their lips.

"What's the joke, boys?" he asked, his anger making his face white and cold. "Tell it to me so I may laugh with you."

They stared at him silently, shamefaced. They looked down at their feet, they shuffled awkwardly, glancing at each other with secret looks filled with a meaning that Tom remembered from his own youth. It was as if they'd been surprised looking at dirty pictures.

A shame for what he'd been at their age came over him and a sick weariness replaced the anger. "Get off this corner," he said softly. "And if ever I hear of any of you laughing or making any remarks about me or any member of my family, I'll come down here and tear the lot of you apart with my bare hands!"

The tallest of the boys took a step toward him. His eyes were sly and insolent. He was slightly taller than Tom and he looked down at him with a faint, contemptuous smile. "It's a free country. We can stand here if we like."

The resentment in Tom suddenly exploded. He seized the boy by his jacket lapels and forced him to his knees. "Free, is it?" he shouted, his veins purple on his forehead. "Free for you to stand here and choose who you'll rape tonight?" He raised an open hand to slap the boy across the face.

The boy cringed, the insolence gone from his face. "What yuh pickin' on us for, Mr. Denton? We aren't the ones fucked Jennie."

The words seemed to freeze the blood in Tom's veins. He stood there, his hand still upraised, staring down at the boy. Fucked Jennie. They could say that about his own daughter and there was nothing he could do that could change the fact of it. Slowly he let his hand fall to his side, then with a violent gesture, he flung the boy away from him.

Tom glared at them, looking from one to another. They were only boys, he told himself. He couldn't hate all boys because of what two had done. The boy was right. They weren't the guilty ones.

A sense of failure came over him. If anyone was guilty, he was the guiltiest of all. If he'd been a man and kept his job, all this might never have happened. "Get off this corner," he said. "If any of you ever see me coming this way again, you'd better be on the other side of the street."

They looked at him and then at each other and it almost seemed now as if they were pitying him. Suddenly, as if a secret message had been passed mysteriously between them, they began to disperse in ones and twos.

A moment later, he was alone on the corner. He stood there for a moment to quiet the sudden trembling that came over him, then he, too, turned and walked around the corner to where his wife and daughter were waiting for him. "It's over now," he said for the second time that morning, as he took Jennie's arm and started for the house again. But this time, he knew, even as he said it, that it wasn't over—that it would never be over as long as he was alive to remember.

The cool September breeze held the first hint of autumn. Jennie looked out the cable-car window toward her stop. Her father was standing there under the street lamp, waiting for her as he did each night now. The car stopped and she stepped down.

"Hello, Daddy."

"Hi, Jennie Bear."

She fell into step beside him as they turned the corner toward home. "Any luck today?"

He shook his head. "I don't understand it. There just are no jobs."

"Maybe there'll be one tomorrow."

"I hope so," he said. "Maybe after the election, things will look up. Roosevelt says the government has to take the lead in providing work, that big business has fallen down on its responsibilities. He makes more sense for the working man than Hoover and the Republicans." He looked at her. "How did it go today?"

"All right," she said. But there still was an uncomfortable feeling in the office. Many of the company agents had taken to stopping at her desk on their way in and out of the office. Sometimes they just chatted, but some of them had tried to date her. Maybe if things had been different, she'd have gone out with them. But when she looked up from her desk into their eyes, she knew what they were thinking. She'd refuse politely and some of them would stammer or even blush, for they knew somehow that she knew.

"You don't have to meet me every night, Daddy," she said suddenly. "I'm not afraid to come home alone."

"I know you're not. I've known it from that first day I came to meet you. But I want to do it. It's the one time of the whole day that I feel I've really got something to do."

Jennie didn't answer and they walked along silently for a moment. "Do you want me to stop?"

"Not if you want to meet me, Daddy."

They were at the steps of the house now and she started up. Her father placed a hand on her arm. "Let's not go up just yet, Jennie Bear. Let's sit here and talk a minute."

She looked down at him. His face was serious. "What is it, Daddy?"

"I didn't tell your mother. I went to see Father Hadley today."

"Yes?"

"He won't come down to court to testify to your character. He told me it's against the rules of the church. And the same goes for the sisters at the school."

"Oh," she said. The sick feeling came up inside her again. The lawyer had been right. He'd come to see them a month ago, a little man with the eyes of a weasel.

He'd sat down in the kitchen and looked across the table at them. "Mr. Burke and Mr. Tanner asked me to see you," he said. "I think you know how much they regret this, er—" He had glanced at her quickly and then away. "—this incident and they would like to make amends if they can."

Her father's face had flushed angrily. "In the first place, Mr. O'Connor," he had said quickly. "That incident you are referring to was not an incident. Those two boys ra—"

The lawyer held up his hand interrupting. "We know what they did," he said. "But surely, Mr. Denton, what purpose would their trial serve except to call even greater attention to your daughter and remind her of what already must be a painful experience. And what if the boys should be adjudged not guilty?"

Her father laughed. "Not guilty? I was at the station when the police brought them in. I heard them sniveling and crying then how sorry they were that they did it."

"What they said then, Mr. Denton," the attorney had said, "is unimportant. It's what they say in court that counts. And they will say that your daughter led them on, that she asked them to go to the park with her."

"They will have to prove that," Tom said grimly.

"It will be harder for you to disprove it," the lawyer said. "There's two of them and only the word of your daughter. And they will have as many character witnesses for them as you will have to have for your daughter."

"It's beginning to sound as if my daughter were on trial, not them!" Tom burst out.

"Exactly," the lawyer nodded. "That is the way it is in these cases. The accuser stands to lose more than the accused."

"My daughter's reputation speaks for itself," Tom said. "Father Hadley of St. Paul's and the sisters at Mercy High School will tell you of my Jennie."

The lawyer had smiled mysteriously. "I doubt it, Mr. Denton," he said quietly. "I doubt it very much." He glanced at Jennie again, then back at Tom. "I am authorized by my clients to offer you a thousand dollars if your daughter will drop the charges against the boys."

"I think you might as well go, Mr. O'Connor," her father had said, getting to his feet. "You cannot buy what's already been stolen."

The attorney rose also. He took a card from his pocket and placed it on the table and walked to the door. "You can reach me at my office any time before the trial begins if you should change your mind."

"What do we do now, Daddy?" she asked, back in the present again.

"Father Hadley said they'd told your mother the same thing three weeks ago."

She stared at her father. "Then she knew all along and never told us?"

He nodded. A chill ran through her. There was something wrong with a God who would let a mother expose her own child to shame and ridicule just to save her own conscience.

"Father Hadley also said the scholarship to St. Mary's is still open if you want it, Jennie."

Suddenly, she began to laugh. They refused to give her a good name, yet were willing to give her charity. She couldn't reconcile the two attitudes. Was one merely to compensate for the other?

Tom looked up at her in surprise. "What are you laughing at, Jennie?"

Her laughter died and she looked at him, unsmiling. "Nothing, Daddy," she said. "I think you might as well give that lawyer a call."

"Then you'll take the thousand dollars?"

She nodded. "And the scholarship to St. Mary's, too. That way, you'll be able to live while I'm away."

"I won't accept your money."

"Yes, you will, Daddy," she said softly. "At least, until you find a job and get back on your feet again."

He felt the tears rush into his eyes and suddenly he pulled her to him. "Do you love me, Jennie Bear? Do you love your poor miserable failure of a father?"

"You know I do, Daddy," she said quickly, her head against his chest. And they clung to each other, crying, there on the steps in the quiet, cool autumn twilight.

CHAPTER SEVEN

THE ONLY SOUND FOR A MOMENT WAS THE SLIGHT HISSING THAT CAME from the fluorescent lamps over the surgical area. Dr. Grant's hands were quick and sure as he deftly lifted the perfectly normal appendix from the heavy-set, wealthy woman lying on the operating table. His deep, masculine voice rumbled in the silence. "That will do it," he said, sighing in satisfaction. "You can close her up now, Dr. Lobb."

He turned away from the table and one of the nurses quickly wiped the perspiration from his face as the surgical resident began to clamp the edges of the incision together.

Jennie glanced up at Sister M. Christopher. If the senior nurse was aware that the appendix had not been infected, her dark eyes, visible over the face mask, gave no indication.

"Suture," Dr. Lobb grunted, holding out his hand. Automatically Jennie gave it to him. Then she didn't have time to look up for a few minutes. She was too busy. But she was aware that Sister Christopher was watching her. It didn't make her nervous, as it had at first. But that was almost three years ago. Next month was graduation.

Sister Christopher watched Jennie with approbation. This girl was one of the bright spots in her class. Perhaps one girl in a hundred had a vocation for surgery the way Jennie had. There were so many things needed and Jennie had them all. The sight of blood didn't upset her, not even the first time she'd experienced it. And Jennie was deft and sure in her actions. Quickly she'd developed an affinity between herself and the instruments, then between herself and the surgeons. Without the affinity, which permitted an unspoken form of communication between the doctor and the nurse, surgery could be dangerously delayed while instruments were fumbled back and forth.

The final important factor was strength. No one ever quite realized how important it was for a surgical nurse to be strong. To be able to stand for hours beside the quiet white table, even though your feet hurt and your thighs and back ached from that peculiar, slightly-leaning-forward position. To be able to feed the doctor that strength and reassure him with it, so that the chain of healing formed one unbroken line. And the strength to be stoic when the chain was broken and the now forever silent patient was wheeled away; to stand there quietly and begin to scrub up again, sure that the chain would rebuild itself when a new patient was wheeled in.

Dr. Lobb looked up and nodded. "Dressing." He held his white-gloved hand out over the neatly stitched incision.

Jennie was ready with the gauze packing as he lifted his hand. Immediately, she covered the incision, while with her other hand, she lifted the strips of adhesive tape from the clip board at the side of the table. She pressed the tape down firmly with her fingers, checking the bandage for smoothness and support, then lifted both hands to signify she had finished.

Sister Christopher nodded and the patient was quickly wrapped and transferred to another table by the assistants. There was a click as the fluorescents went out. The morning operating-room schedule at St. Mary's had been completed.

"That's the fourth good appendix he's taken out this month," Jennie whispered above the gush of water into the basin. "Why does he do it?"

The young resident laughed. "At two hundred and fifty dollars a crack, you don't fight the patients."

"But he doesn't have to," she whispered. "He's a great surgeon. He has scarcely enough time for all he has to do."

"Sure," Dr. Lobb whispered back. "But even great surgeons have to eat. Most of the trick cases are either for free or tough collections. So who's to blame if once in a while, he lifts a harmless appendix from some rich old hypochondriac?

There's no risk in it. The doctor can pay his bills and the patient can brag about his operation."

He straightened up, reaching for a towel. "Oh-oh," he said warningly. "Here comes the great man himself."

Jennie took a towel from the rack and began to dry her hands. The doctor's voice came from behind her. "Miss Denton?"

She turned around, looking at him. "Yes, Dr. Grant?"

"I understand you're graduating next month."

"I hope so."

"I don't think you have anything to worry about," he said. "I was just talking to Sister Christopher. She thinks a great deal of you. And so do I."

"Thank you."

"Have you made any plans yet for after graduation?"

"Not really," Jennie answered. "I'm going to take the state exam and get my name on the lists for one of the big hospitals."

"All hospitals are pretty well staffed."

Jennie knew what he really meant. They weren't well staffed, at all. Actually, they were all understaffed because there was no money to pay for the staff they needed. Especially those in the operating room. They were the best paid of all. "I know," she said.

He hesitated a moment. "Are you doing anything right now?"

"I was just going down to the cafeteria for lunch."

"I'd like to talk to you. Sister Christopher said it would be all right if you left the hospital for lunch. How about the Steak 'n' Sauce?"

"That sounds fine," Jennie said.

"Good." He smiled. "I'll meet you down at my car. It's the black Packard."

"I know," she said quickly. All the nurses knew the car. It was always parked just opposite their dormitory. Outside of Dr. Gedeon's black Cadillac, it was the most expensive car at the hospital.

"See you in fifteen minutes, then."

Jennie walked out into the corridor and pressed the button for the elevator. The door opened and she stepped in. Dr. Lobb rushed in right after her.

"The Steak 'n' Sauce!"

"I wonder what he wants?" Jennie asked.

His grin grew broader. "I know what he wants," he said lewdly. "But I didn't have any luck getting it at the Greasy Spoon."

She returned his grin. "His luck won't be any better at the Steak 'n' Sauce."

"I don't know." He laughed. "One of these days, you're goin' to give it up to somebody. There's no sense feeding it to the worms."

"That will never happen," she said. Too late for that, she thought. But it didn't matter now. It was forgotten and no one here had heard about it. "I still wonder what he wants?"

"Maybe he wants you to work for him. Ever think of that?"

"I thought about it," she admitted. "But it doesn't make sense. Why me? He can have his pick of the best around."

Dr. Lobb grinned but his eyes were serious. "You are the best around, honey. It's about time you realized that."

The elevator door opened and they stepped out into the basement corridor, where the employees' cafeteria was. Jennie looked down at her white uniform. "I'd better get out of this and into a dress."

"I'd be just as happy if you just got out of that." He laughed. "You don't have to put on a dress for me."

She looked up at him, smiling. Someday, this young man was going to be one of the really good ones. "Maybe I'll surprise you sometime."

"Surprise me by bringing back a steak sandwich," he called after her. "I've about given up on the other."

Doctor Grant held a package of cigarettes out toward her. She took one and he held a match. His eyes met hers over the flickering flame. "I suppose you're wondering why I asked you to lunch?"

She nodded. "I was curious, to say the least."

He smiled. "I'm sorry if I provoked your curiosity. But I really meant it when I said I like to forget about my practice during lunch. But I guess now it's time to get down to business."

She didn't answer.

"During the past year, Miss Denton, I've had an excellent opportunity to observe your work in surgery. From the very first, I was aware of your aptitude and I have always appreciated, as a surgeon, the extremely competent manner in which you render assistance."

"Thank you, Dr. Grant."

"As you may know, Miss Denton, I have a rather extensive and busy practice. There are many physicians who refer their patients to me for surgery. Much of this practice is of a minor nature and under proper conditions, can be attended to in my office. It relieves the patient of a considerable part of the economic burden."

Jennie nodded silently.

"This morning, I learned from Miss Janney, who's been associated with me for many years, that she's getting married and plans to move to Southern California." He drew on his cigarette. "When I came to the hospital today, I took the liberty of speaking to Sister Christopher about you. She agrees that you'd make an excellent replacement for Miss Janney."

"You mean you want me to work for you?"

He smiled. "In my roundabout manner, that is what I was about to ask. Are you interested?"

"Of course. What girl wouldn't be?"

"It's not an easy job, you know," he said. "I have a few beds in my clinic and very often, we'll have to work late. Occasionally, I even keep a patient overnight. At such times, you'd have to remain on duty."

"Dr. Grant," Jennie said, smiling, "I've put in two eight-hour shifts a day with only four hours' sleep between, for the last week. Working for you will seem like a picnic."

He smiled and reaching across the table, patted her hand reassuringly. Jennie smiled back at him. He wasn't so bad, after all, even if he did take out a few perfectly healthy appendixes. He was only the surgeon. He couldn't be responsible for the faulty diagnosis of every physician who sent him a patient.

But that was before she went to work for him and found out that healthy appendixes weren't the only things he removed. He also had a very busy practice in unborn babies up to ten weeks after conception. As a matter of fact, he was probably the busiest abortionist in California.

But by the time she was aware of that, it didn't matter, because she was in love with him. Nor did it matter that he was already married and had three children.

CHAPTER EIGHT

THE TELEPHONE RANG JUST AS SHE WAS ABOUT TO LEAVE THE TINY TWO-room apartment over the clinic. She went back and picked it up. "Dr. Grant's office," she said. It was an extension of the telephone in the office downstairs.

"Jennie?" came the whisper.

"Yes."

"Will you be there for a while?"

"I was just leaving to see my folks. I haven't seen them for three weeks. This is the third Sunday in a row—"

His voice interrupted her. "I'll see to it you have time off during the week. Please, Jennie, I've got to see you."

She hesitated a moment and he sensed her faltering over the telephone. "Please, Jennie! I'll go crazy if I don't see you."

She looked across at the clock. It was already after seven o'clock. By the time she got across town, it would almost be time for her father to go to bed. He had a WPA job and had to be at work very early.

"Oh, all right," she said quietly.

Some of the tension left his voice. "Good, Jennie. I'll be there in twenty minutes. I love you."

"I love you," she said and heard the click as he put down the phone. She replaced the receiver and slowly took off her coat. Carefully she put it back in the closet, walked over to the couch and sat down. She lit a cigarette thoughtfully.

Who would have thought when she came to work here, three months ago, that he'd fall in love with her? And she with him. But then, how could she help herself? Especially when she knew what it was like for him at home. Married to a spoiled rich young woman who constantly threw up to him that it was her money that had enabled him to open his office, that it was her father's influence that had established him in the community. Married to a woman who bore him three children not out of love for him but out of an insane desire to keep him forever bound to her.

No wonder he'd found refuge in his work and spent almost every waking moment at his practice. Now she understood what drove him. And those girls and young women who came for his surgery? And he'd explained why he did it, she understood that, too.

She saw the inner kindness in his sensitive face as he spoke. "What am I to do, Jennie?" he'd asked. "Turn them away and let them ruin their lives because of one foolish mistake? Or let them fall into the hands of some quack who'll make them sick forever or perhaps even kill them, all because of some outworn religious code? Religious laws like that have hung on until gradually they've become dogma, just like the Jewish nonsense about kosher meat. Even our civil laws permit abortion under certain circumstances. Someday, it will be open and aboveboard, as it is in many countries throughout the world—Cuba, Denmark, Sweden, many others."

He'd turned his deep-set brown eyes toward her. "I took an oath when I became a doctor, that I would strive to do my best for my patients, to help them in every way I could, physically and psychologically. That oath is more important than anything else to me. When some poor, frightened child comes to me for help, I can't play God and refuse her."

It made sense to her. There were many things about the church she did not understand. She knew how they'd acted in her own case and the bitterness still rankled deep within her. If her goodness had been so important, why wouldn't they come forward to support her good name? All they really sought was power over her, not responsibility for her.

So, gradually she'd come to recognize the women who came to him for help and feel a compassion for them. The young matron who couldn't afford to leave her job because already she and her husband had more children than they could support; the frightened young girls, some still in school or just out; the middle-aged women just approaching the change of life, with their families already grown; even the call girls, who lived casually from day to day, yet came into the office with a haunting fear buried deep beneath their bright, brittle laughter. She had the capacity to feel sorry for them, even as he had. And from there, it was only one step to falling in love with him.

It happened after she'd been there about a month. She was upstairs in the apartment and heard a noise in the office below. It was about eight o'clock at night. At first, she was confused, thinking that this was an office night. But then she realized it was Tuesday, and the doctor had office hours only on Monday, Wednesday and Friday evenings. She turned down the flame under the coffeepot and reaching for her robe, went down to investigate.

When she opened the door to his private office and looked in, he was seated behind his desk, his face gray and tired looking. "I beg your pardon, Doctor. I didn't know it was you. I heard a noise—"

He smiled wearily. "That's all right, Miss Denton."

"Good night, Doctor," she said, starting to close the door.

"Just a minute, Miss Denton," he said suddenly.

She opened the door and looked at him. "Yes, Doctor?"

He smiled again. "We've been so busy, I haven't had time to ask. Are you happy here?"

She nodded. "Yes, Doctor. Very."

"I'm glad."

"You ought to be getting home, Doctor. You look exhausted."

"Home?" he asked, a wry smile coming to his lips. "This is my home, Miss Denton. I just sleep in that other place."

"I—I don't understand, Doctor."

"Of course you don't," he said gently. "I wouldn't expect you to. You're much too young and beautiful to worry about the likes of me." He got to his feet. "Go back upstairs now, Miss Denton. I'll try to be very quiet and not disturb you."

The light from the lamp on his desk shining up onto his face made him look even more handsome than usual. She stood in the doorway, staring at him. She felt her heart pumping strangely within her. "But I do worry about you, Doctor. You work too hard."

"I'll be all right," he said in a toneless voice. He turned to look at her and their eyes locked and held. It seemed as if she were spinning into a swirling vortex deep in his gentle brown eyes. She felt a trembling in her legs and placed her hand on the doorjamb quickly, to support herself. No words came to her lips; she stared at him, speechless.

"Is anything wrong, Miss Denton?"

It took a desperate effort for her to shake her head. "No," she whispered, forcing her eyes to turn away. "No." Suddenly, she turned and ran toward the stairway.

She wasn't even aware that he had come after her until he caught her in the doorway of her apartment. The warmth of his hand touching her shoulder came through the thin robe. "Are you afraid of me, Jennie?" he asked harshly.

She looked up into his face and saw the anguish in his eyes. A curious weakness came over her and she would have fallen if he had not been holding her. "No," she whispered.

"Then what is it?"

She looked down, not speaking, the warmth from his hand beginning to radiate into a fire inside her. "Tell me!" he urged, shaking her.

She looked up at him, the tears coming into her eyes. "I can't."

"You can, Jennie, you can," he said insistently. "I know what you feel. You feel the same things I feel. I can't sleep without dreaming of you, without feeling you close to me."

"No. Please! It's not right."

His strong surgeon's hand held her chin. "I love you, Jennie," he said. "I love you."

She stared up into his eyes, seeing his face coming closer and closer, then his mouth pressed down on hers. She closed her eyes for a moment, feeling the fire envelop her. Abruptly she tore her face away. She backed into the apartment. He stepped in after her, kicking the door shut with his foot. "You love me," he said. "Say it!"

Her eyes were wide as she stared up at him. "No," she whispered.

He stepped forward again, his strong fingers digging deep into her shoulders. "Say it!" he commanded harshly.

She felt the weakness as his touch flowed through her again. She couldn't turn her face from his eyes. "I love you," she said.

He pressed his mouth to hers again and kissed her. She felt his hands inside her robe, his fingers on her back unfastening her brassière, her breasts rising from their restraint, the nipples leaping joyfully into his hands. A shiver of ecstasy raced through her and she almost fell. "Please don't," she whispered, her lips moving under his. "It's wrong."

He picked her up in his arms and carried her across the room to the bed. He placed her on it gently and knelt beside her. "When a man and a woman are in love," he whispered, "nothing they do in the privacy of their own home is ever wrong. And this is our home."

He pressed his lips down on her mouth again.

❖ ❖ ❖

Tom looked across the table at the kitchen clock. It was a few minutes past ten. He folded his newspaper. "I guess she won't be coming now," he said, "so I might as well be turning in." He got to his feet. "The boys down at the Alliance tell me I'll be making supervisor any day now, so I better get my sleep. It won't do for me to be showing up late to work."

Ellen sniffed contemptuously. "If ye keep listenin' to them communists down at the Workers' Alliance, you'll be lucky even to hold your job with the WPA."

"They're in pretty good, you can't deny that. It was them that got me onto full time instead of half time and you know it. It's them that's for the working man."

"Communists are heathens," she said. "Father Hadley told me they're against the church because they don't believe in God. He says they're only playing up to the workin' man until they get in power, like in Russia. Then they'll close the churches and make slaves out of us all."

"What if they are?" he asked. "I don't see Father Hadley getting me a job or paying our bills. No, it was the Alliance that put me to work and saw to it I earned enough to pay rent and buy food. I don't care what Father Hadley calls them, as long as they do good for me."

She smiled bitterly. "A fine family I have. A husband who's a communist and a daughter who never has the time to come home."

"Maybe she's busy," Tom said lamely. "You know it's a responsible position she's got. Didn't the sister at St. Mary's say, when she graduated, that she was very lucky to be working for such an important doctor?"

"Yes, but she still should come home once in a while. I'm willin' to bet she hasn't been to Mass since she left St. Mary's."

"How do you know?" Tom asked angrily. "St. Paul's ain't the only church in San Francisco."

"I know," she said. "I feel it. She doesn't want to come see us. She's makin' so much money now, she's ashamed of us.

"And what has she got to be proud of? With you preaching religion at her all the time and the boys on the street still sniggering and laughing behind her back when she walks by? Do you think that's something to make a young girl want to come home?"

Ellen ignored him. "It's not right that a girl should stay away like this," she said stubbornly. "We both know what goes on up there on the hill, with everybody sleepin' with each other's wives and the drink. I read the papers, too, ye know."

"Jennie's a good girl. She wouldn't do a thing like that."

"I'm not too sure. Sometimes a taste of temptation is like a spoonful of honey. Just enough to sweeten your tongue but not enough to fill your whole mouth. And we both know she's tasted temptation."

"You still don't believe her, do you?" he asked bitterly. "You'd rather take the word of those two hoodlums than your own daughter."

"Then why didn't she go into court? If there wasn't just a little truth in what they said, she wouldn't have been afraid. But no, she takes the thousand dollars and lets herself be labeled a whore."

"You know as well as I why she didn't," Tom answered. "And you can thank your church for it. They'd not even come into court to say she was a good girl.

No, they were afraid the boys' parents might not like it and cut off their weekly contributions."

"The church sent her to college. And they found her this job. They did their duty."

"Then what are you complaining about?"

She sat there quietly for a moment, listening to him drop his shoes angrily to the floor as he undressed in the bedroom. Then she got out of the chair and felt the hot-water heater. A hot bath would soothe her aches and pains a little; all this damp fall weather was bringing out her arthritis. She took a match and kneeled down beside the heater. Striking the match, she turned the pet cock. The flame caught for a moment, then died out in a tiny yellow circle. She looked up at the meter. They were out of gas. The red flag was up. She got to her feet and walked over to her pocketbook. She opened the small change purse and searched through it. She had no quarters, only nickels and dimes. For a moment, she thought of asking Tom for a quarter, then shrugged her shoulders. She'd had enough of his blasphemous tongue. She'd do without her bath. She could take it in the morning, when she came back from Mass. She went into the bathroom and used the last of the hot water to wash her face. Tom was standing in the kitchen when she came out, his chest bare above his trousers. She swept by him silently and closed the bedroom door behind her.

Tom went into the bathroom and washed up noisily. Suddenly, the water went cold. He swore and dried himself quickly, then fished in his pocket for a quarter. He reached up and put the quarter into the meter, then watched the red on the dial disappear. He nodded, satisfied.

In the morning, he'd turn on the heater and in a few minutes, he'd have enough hot water for his shave. He went into the bedroom, leaving the door open behind him, unaware of the slight hiss coming from under the heater.

He draped his pants on the chair and sat down on the bed. After a moment, he stretched out with a sigh. His shoulder touched Ellen and he felt her turn away.

Ah, the hell with her, he thought, turning on his side, his back to her. Maybe the commies were right with their ideas of free love. At least a man wouldn't have to put up with a woman like her.

His eyes began to feel heavy. He could hear the soft, even sounds of her breath. She was asleep already. He smiled to himself in the dark. With free love, he'd have his pick of women. She'd act different then, all right. His eyelids drooped and closed and he joined his wife in slumber. And death.

Jennie sat up in the bed, clutching the sheet to her naked body and staring with wide, frightened eyes at the woman who stood in the doorway. On the other side of the bed, Bob was already hurriedly buttoning his shirt.

"Did you think he'd leave me for you?" she screamed at Jennie. "Did you think you were the first? Hasn't he told you how many times I've caught him like this?" Her voice grew contemptuous. "Or do you think he's really in love with you?"

Jennie didn't answer.

"Tell her, Robert," his wife said angrily. "Tell her you wanted to make love to me tonight and when I refused, you came running over here. Tell her."

Jennie stared at him. His face was white and he didn't look in her direction. He grabbed his coat from the chair and walked over to his wife. "You're all upset. Let me take you home."

Home. Jennie felt a sick feeling in her stomach. This was home—his and hers. He had said so. It was here they had loved, here they had been together. But he was talking about someplace else. Another place.

"I'm always upset, aren't I, Robert? Every time you promise it will never happen again. But I know better, don't I? All right," she said suddenly, her voice hard and cold. "We'll go. But not until you tell her."

"Please, dear," he said quickly. "Another time. Not now."

"Now, Robert," she said coldly. "Now—or the whole world will know about Dr. Grant, the quack, the abortionist, the great lover."

He turned and looked back at Jennie on the bed. "You'll have to leave, Miss Denton," he said huskily. "You see, I don't love you," he said in a strained voice. "I love my wife."

And almost at the same moment that the door closed behind him, there was an explosion in an old tenement on the other side of the city. After the firemen pulled the charred bodies from the fire, they gave their verdict. The victims had been fortunate. They were already dead before the fire started.

CHAPTER NINE

CHARLES STANDHURST WAS EIGHTY-ONE YEARS OLD WHEN HE MET JENNIE Denton. It was eight o'clock of a spring morning in 1936 and he was in the operating room of the Colton Sanitarium at Santa Monica. He was the patient just being placed on the operating table and she was acting as Chief Nurse in Surgery.

He felt them place his legs over the stirrups and quickly arrange a sheet so that even if he moved his head, he could not see his lower half. When they had finished, he saw her come from somewhere behind him and walk down to the foot of the table. She lifted up the sheet.

He felt a moment's embarrassment at the impersonal manner in which she scrutinized his private parts. After five wives, countless mistresses and more than forty children that he was sure about, only eight of whom were the result of his marriages, it seemed strange to him that anyone could look at him in such a detached manner. So much life had sprung from that fountain.

She let the covering fall around him again and looked up. A glint of humor flickered in her intelligent gray eyes and he knew that she understood.

She came around to the side of the table and reached for his pulse. He looked up at her as she studied her watch. "Where's Dr. Colton?"

"He'll be along in a minute. He's washing up."

She let go of his wrist and said something to someone behind him. He rolled his eyes back and caught a glimpse of another nurse. Feeling the prick of a needle in his arm, he turned his head back quickly. Already, she was taking the small hypodermic out of his arm. "Hey, you're fast," he said.

"That's my job."

"I am, too."

Again that smile in her gray eyes. "I know. I read the papers."

Just then, Dr. Colton came in. "Hello, Mr. Standhurst," he said in his jovial manner. "Did we pass any water today?"

"Maybe you did, Doc, but you know damn well I didn't," Standhurst said dryly. "Or they'd never have got me back in this slaughterhouse."

Dr. Colton laughed. "Well, you've got nothing to worry about. We'll have those kidney stones out in a jiffy."

"All the same, Doc, I'm glad we've got a specialist doing it. If I left it up to you, God knows what you'd cut out."

His sarcasm didn't disturb Dr. Colton. They'd known each other for too long. It was Charles Standhurst who'd advanced him most of the money to start this hospital. He laughed again.

The surgeon came in and stood beside Dr. Colton. "Ready, Mr. Standhurst?"

"Ready as I'll ever be. Just leave something for the girls, eh, Doc?"

The surgeon nodded and Standhurst felt a prick in his other arm. He turned his head and saw Jennie standing there. "Gray eyes," he said to her. His second wife had had gray eyes. Or was it his third? He didn't remember. "I suppose you wouldn't take your mask off so that I could see the rest of your face?"

Again he saw the glint of humor. "I don't think the doctors would approve," she said. "But after the operation, I'll come visit you. Will that do?"

"Fine. I've got a feeling you're beautiful."

He didn't see the anesthetist behind him nod. Jennie leaned over his face. "Now, Mr. Standhurst," she said, "count down from ten with me. Ten, nine, eight—"

"Seven, six, four, five, two, nine." His lips were moving slowly and everything seemed so comfortable and far away. "Ten, eight, one, three . . . six . . . four . . . one . . . two." His voice faded away.

The anesthetist looked up at the surgeon. "He's under," he said.

They all saw it at the same time, looking down into the cavity the surgeon had cut into his body—the mass of brackish gray covering almost the entire side of one kidney and threading its way in thin, radiating lines across the other. Without raising his head, the surgeon dropped the two pieces of matter he'd snipped away onto the slides that Jennie held under his hand. She gave the slides to a nurse standing behind her without turning around. "Pathology," she whispered.

The nurse left quickly and Jennie, with the same deft motion, picked up two hemostats. The assisting surgeon took them from her hand and tied off two veins as the surgeon's knife exposed them.

"Aren't you going to wait for the biopsy?" Dr. Colton asked from his position next to the surgeon. The surgeon didn't look up. His fingers were busy probing at the mass. "Not unless you want me to, Doctor." He held out his hand and

Jennie placed a fine curette in it. He was working quickly now, preparing to remove the infected kidney.

Colton hesitated. "Charles Standhurst isn't just an ordinary man." Everyone around the operating table knew that. At one time or another, the old man quietly lying there could have been almost anything he'd wanted. Governor, senator, anything. With more than twenty major newspapers stretched across the nation and a fortune founded from oil and gold, he'd never really wanted anything more than to be himself. He was second only to Hearst in the state's pride for its home-grown tycoons.

The surgeon, a comparatively young man who'd rapidly become one of the foremost GU men in the world and had been flown out from New York especially for this job, began to lift out the kidney. The nurse behind Jennie tapped her on the shoulder. Jennie took the slip of paper from her and held it out for him to see. She could see the typed words plainly.

Carcinoma. Metastasis. Malignant.

The surgeon sighed softly, and glanced up at Dr. Colton. "Well, he's an ordinary enough man now."

Mr. Standhurst was awake the next morning when the surgeon came into his hospital room. If he paid any attention to the teletype clicking away in the corner, it wasn't apparent. He walked over to the side of the bed and looked down. "I came in to say good-by, Mr. Standhurst. I'm leaving for New York this morning."

The old man looked up and grinned. "Hey, Doc," he said. "Anybody ever tell you that your old man was a tailor?"

"My father was a tailor, Mr. Standhurst."

"I know," Standhurst said quickly. "He still has the store on Stanton Street. I know many things about you. You were president of the Save Sacco-Vanzetti Society at City College when you graduated in twenty-seven, a registered member of the Young Socialists during your first year at P. and S., and the first surgeon ever to become an F.A.C.S. in his first year of practice. You're still a registered Socialist in New York and you'll probably vote for Norman Thomas for President."

The surgeon smiled. "You know a great deal about me."

"Of course I do. You don't think I'd let just anybody cut me up, do you?"

"I should think you'd have worried just a little knowing what you do about me," the doctor said. "You know what we Socialists think of you."

The old man started to laugh, then grimaced in pain. "Hell! The way I figure it, you're a doctor first and a Socialist second." He looked up shrewdly. "You know, Doc, if you voted the straight Republican ticket, I could make you a millionaire in less than three years."

The doctor laughed and shook his head. "No, thanks. I'd worry too much."

"How come you don't ask me how I feel, Doc? Colton's been in here four times already and each time he asked me."

The doctor shrugged his shoulders. "Why should I? I know how you feel. You hurt."

"I hurt like hell, Doc," Standhurst said. "Colton said those stones you took out of me were big as baseballs."

"They were pretty big, all right."

"He also said I'd be wearing this bag you hooked into me until the kidney healed and took over again."

"You'll be wearing it quite a while."

The old man stared at him. "You know, you're both full of shit," he said calmly. "I'll wear this in my grave. And that isn't too far off, either."

"I wouldn't say that."

"I know you wouldn't," Standhurst said. "That's why I'm saying it. Look, Doc, I'm eighty-one years old. And at eighty-one, if a man lives that long, he gets to be a good smeller of death—for anyone, including himself. You learn to see it, in the face or eyes. So don't bullshit me. How long have I got?"

The doctor looked into the old man's eyes and saw that he wasn't afraid. If anything, there was a look of lively curiosity reflected there. He made up his mind quickly. Colton was all wrong in the way he was handling it. This was a man. He deserved the truth. "Three months, if you're lucky, Mr. Standhurst. Six, if you're not."

The old man didn't blink an eyelash. "Cancer?"

The surgeon nodded. "Malignant and metastatic," he answered. "I removed one complete kidney and almost half of the other. That's why you have that waste bag."

"Will it be painful?"

"Very. But we can control it with morphine."

"To hell with that," the old man said. "Dying is about the only thing in life I haven't experienced. It's something I don't want to miss."

The teletype began to clatter suddenly and the old man glanced over at it, then back at the doctor. "How will I know when it's close, Doc?"

"Watch the urine in that bag," the doctor said. "The redder it gets, the nearer it is. That means the kidney is passing clear blood instead of urine, because the cancer will have choked off the kidney completely."

The look in the old man's eyes was bright and intelligent. "That means I'll probably die of uremic poisoning."

"Possibly. If nothing else goes wrong."

Standhurst laughed. "Hell, Doc," he said, "I could have done that twenty years ago if I'd just kept on drinking."

The surgeon laughed. "But look at all the fun you'd have missed."

The old man smiled up at him. "You Socialists will probably declare a national holiday."

"I don't know, Mr. Standhurst." The doctor returned his smile. "Who would we have to complain about then?"

"I'm not worried," the old man said. "Hearst and Patterson will still be around."

The doctor held out his hand. "Well, I've got to be going, Mr. Standhurst."

Standhurst took his hand. "Good-by, Doc. And thanks."

The surgeon's dark eyes were serious. "Good-by, Mr. Standhurst," he said. "I'm sorry." He started for the door. The old man's voice turned him around.

"Will you do me a favor, Doc?"

"Anything I can, Mr. Standhurst."

"That nurse up in the operating room," Standhurst said. "The one with the gray eyes and the tits."

The surgeon knew whom he meant. "Miss Denton?"

"If that's her name," the old man said.

The surgeon nodded.

"She said if I wanted to see her without her mask, she'd come down. Would you leave word with Colton on your way out that I'd like her to join me for lunch?"

The surgeon laughed. "Will do, Mr. Standhurst."

CHAPTER TEN

JENNIE PICKED UP THE BOTTLE OF CHAMPAGNE AND POURED IT INTO THE tall glass filled with ice cubes. The wine bubbled up with a fine frothy head, then settled back slowly as she filled it to the brim. She put the glass straw into the glass and handed it to Standhurst. "Here's your ginger ale, Charlie."

He grinned at her mischievously. "If you're looking for something to bring up the gas," he said, "champagne beats ginger ale any time." He sipped at it appreciatively. "Ah," he said and burped. "Have some, maybe it will make you feel sexy."

"What good would it do you if I did?" Jennie retorted.

"I'd feel good just remembering what I'd have done if it were twenty years ago."

"Better make it forty, to be safe."

"No." He shook his head. "Twenty was the best. Maybe it's because I appreciated it more then, knowing it wasn't going to last very long."

The teletype in the corner of the library began to chatter. Jennie got up out of the chair and walked over to it. When it stopped, she tore the message off and came back to him. "They just nominated Roosevelt for a second term." She handed him the yellow sheet.

"I expected that," he said. "Now they'll never get the son of a bitch out of there. But why should I worry? I won't be around."

The telephone began to ring almost as he finished speaking. It was the direct wire from his Los Angeles paper. She picked it up off the desk and brought it over to him. "Standhurst," he said into it.

She could hear a faint buzz on the other end of the wire. His face was expressionless as he listened. "Hell, no! There's time enough to editorialize after he's made his acceptance speech. At least, then we'll have an idea of what promises he's going to break. No editorials until tomorrow. That goes for all the papers. Put it on the teletype."

He put down the telephone and looked at her. Immediately, the teletype began to clatter again. She walked over and looked down at it. Green letters began to appear on the yellow paper.

FROM CHARLES STANDHURST TO ALL PAPERS: IMPORTANT. ABSOLUTELY NO EDITORIALS RE NOMINATION ROOSEVELT UNTIL ACCEPTANCE SPEECH IS MADE AND EVALUATED. REPEAT. ABSOLUTELY NO EDITORIALS RE NOMINATION ROOSE—

She walked away from the teletype while it was still chattering. "That's your orders, boss."

"Good. Now turn the damn thing off so we can talk."

She went over and flipped the switch, then came back and sat down opposite him. She took a cigarette and lit it as he sipped the champagne through the straw reflectively. "What are your plans when this job is over?"

"I haven't thought much about it."

"You better start," he said. "It won't be long now."

She smiled at him. "Anxious to get rid of me?"

"Don't be silly," he said. "The only reason I've stayed alive this long is because I didn't want to leave you."

Something in his voice made her look searchingly at him. "You know, Charlie, I believe you really mean that."

"Of course I do," he snapped.

Suddenly touched, she came over to the side of his chair and kissed his cheek. "Hey, Nurse Denton," he said. "I think you're breaking down. I'll get you in the sack yet."

"You got me a long time ago, Charlie. The only trouble is, we didn't meet soon enough."

When she thought about it, that was true. The very first time she'd come down to have lunch with him in the hospital, the day after the operation, she'd liked him. She knew he was dying and after a moment, she knew that he knew it. But it didn't stop him from playing the gallant. None of that bland, tasteless hospital food for him, even if he couldn't eat.

Instead, the food was rushed by motorcar from Romanoff's with a police escort out in front and the siren blaring all the way. And along with the food came a maître d' and two waiters to serve it.

He sat up in his bed, sipping champagne and watching her eat. He liked the way she ate. Picky eaters were usually selfish lovers. They gave you nothing, demanding the same sort of unattainable satisfaction in bed that they demanded from the table. He made up his mind instantly, as he always did. "I'm going to be sick for a while," he said. "I'm going to need a nurse. How would you like the job?"

She'd looked up from her coffee, her gray eyes quizzical. "There are nurses who specialize in home care, Mr. Standhurst. They'd probably be better at it than I am."

"I asked you."

"I have a job at Los Angeles General," she said. "A good job. Then sometimes I get special calls to help out here, like this one. It's the kind of work I'm good at."

"How much do you make?"

"Eighty-five a month, room and board."

"I'll pay you a thousand a week, room and board," he said.

"But that's ridiculous!"

"Is it?" he asked, watching her steadily. "I can afford it. When the doctor left here this morning, he told me I've only got three months to go. I always expect to pay a little bit more when I can't offer a steady job."

She looked down as the waiter refilled her coffee cup. "You'll be here for about three weeks," she said. "That will give me time to give notice. When do you want me to start?"

"Right now. And don't worry about the notice. I already told Colton and Los Angeles General that you were coming to work for me."

She stared at him for a moment, then put down her cup and got to her feet. She gestured to the maître d' and immediately the waiters began to wheel the table out. "Hey, what's the idea?" Standhurst asked.

Jennie didn't answer as she walked to the foot of the table and picked up the chart. She studied it for a moment and then came over and took the glass of champagne out of his hand. "If I'm working for you now," she said, "it's time you got some rest."

Time never passes as quickly as when it's running out, he thought. Somehow, everything seems sharper, clearer to the mind, even decisions are arrived at more easily. Perhaps it was because the responsibility for them couldn't come home to roost. No one can win an argument with a grave.

He felt the pain race through him like a knife. He didn't flinch but from her face, he knew that she knew. A strange kind of communication had grown between them. Words weren't necessary. There were times he thought she felt the pain, too.

"Maybe you'd better go to bed," she said.

"Not just yet. I want to talk to you."

"O.K.," she said. "Go ahead."

"You're not going back to the hospital, are you?"

"I don't know. I haven't really thought about it."

"You'll never be happy in a job like that again. I've spoiled you. There's nothing like a lot of money."

She laughed. "You're so right, Charlie. I've been thinking about that. Nothing's going to seem right ever again."

He studied her thoughtfully. "I could leave you something in my will, or even marry you. But my children would probably make a federal case out of it and say you influenced me. All you'd get is a lot of grief."

She met his gaze. "Thanks for thinking about it, anyway, Charlie."

"You need to make a lot of money," he said. "Why did you decide to be a nurse? You always wanted to be one?"

"No." She shrugged her shoulders. "What I really wanted to be was another Helen Wills. But I got a scholarship to St. Mary's, so I went."

"Even being a tennis bum takes money."

"I know. Anyway, it's too late now. I'd be satisfied if I could just make enough to hire the best pro around and play two hours every day."

"See!" he said triumphantly. "That's a hundred bucks a day, right there."

"Yeah. I'll probably end up back at the hospital."

"You don't have to."

"What do you mean?" she asked, looking at him. "That's all I ever trained for."

"You started training for something else long before you studied nursing. Becoming a woman."

"Well, I couldn't have trained so well, then," she said wryly. "The first time I ever acted like a woman, I got my head knocked off."

"You mean Dr. Grant in Frisco?"

"How do you know about that?"

"Mostly a guess," he said. "But the paper automatically checks up on everyone who comes near me. Grant's got that reputation and the fact that you worked for him and left in such a hurry led me to that surmise. What happened? His wife catch you?"

She nodded slowly. "It was horrible."

"It always is when you're emotionally involved," he said. "It's happened to me more than once." He refilled his glass with champagne. "The trick is not to become emotionally involved."

"How do you do that?"

"By making it pay," he said.

"What you're saying, then, in effect, is that I should become a whore?" she said in a shocked voice.

He smiled. "That's only the Catholic in you that's talking. In the back of your mind, even you have to admit that it makes sense."

"But a whore?" she said, her voice still shocked.

"Not a whore, a courtesan or its modern equivalent, the call girl. In ancient civilizations, being a courtesan was a highly respected profession. Statesmen and philosophers alike sought their favors. And it isn't only the money that made it attractive. It's a way of life that's most complete. Luxurious and satisfying."

She began to laugh. "You're nothing but a dirty old man, Charlie. When do you bring out the French postcards?"

He laughed with her. "Why shouldn't I be? I was a dirty young man, too. But I was never stupid. You have all the equipment necessary to become a great courtesan. The body, the mind—even your nurse's training won't be wasted. True sex demands a greater intellectualism than simple animal rutting."

"Now I know it's time for you to go to bed." She laughed. "Next thing I know, you'll be suggesting I go to a school to learn all about it."

"That's an idea." He chuckled. "They're always after me to endow one college or another. Why didn't I think of it? The Standhurst College of Sex. Otherwise known as the Old Fucking School." He began to laugh heartily, then suddenly he grimaced in pain. His face whitened and beads of perspiration broke out on his forehead. He hunched over in his wheel chair.

In a moment, she was at his side, pushing up the sleeve of his robe, exposing his arm. Quickly she shot the syrette of morphine into his vein. His bony fingers gripped her arm, trying to push it away, as he stared at her with agony-laden eyes.

"For Christ's sake, Charlie," she said angrily. "Give yourself a break. Stop fighting it!" His grip relaxed for a moment and she emptied another syrette into him. She looked into his eyes and saw him fighting the comfort the drug would bring him. She took his fragile, thin hand and raised it swiftly to her lips.

He smiled as the drug began to cloud his eyes. "Poor little Jennie," he said softly. "Any other time and I'd have made you my queen!" His fingers brushed her cheek gently. "But I won't forget what we were talking about. I'm not going to let you go to waste just because I'm not going to be around to enjoy it!"

CHAPTER ELEVEN

THREE DAYS LATER THEY WERE HAVING LUNCH ON THE TERRACE WHEN she saw the gray Rolls-Royce come to a stop in the driveway. A smartly dressed chauffeur opened the door and a woman stepped out. A few minutes later, the butler appeared on the terrace. "A Mrs. Schwartz to see you, Mr. Standhurst."

Standhurst smiled. "Set another place, Judson, and ask Mrs. Schwartz if she'll join us."

The butler bowed. "Yes, Mr. Standhurst."

A moment later, a woman came through the doorway. "Charlie!" she said, unmistakable pleasure in her voice. She held her hands out toward him as she walked. "How good to see you."

"Aida." Standhurst kissed her hand. "Forgive my not getting up." He looked into her face. "You're as beautiful as ever."

"You haven't changed a bit, Charlie. You can still keep a straight face and lie like hell."

Standhurst laughed. "Aida, this is Jennie Denton."

"How do you do?" Jennie said. She saw a woman, perhaps in her middle or late fifties, quietly and expensively dressed. The woman turned, her smile warm and friendly, but Jennie suddenly had the feeling that there was little about her that the woman didn't take in.

She turned back to Standhurst. "Is this the girl you spoke to me about on the phone?"

Standhurst nodded.

The woman turned back to Jennie. This time, her eyes were openly appraising. She smiled suddenly. "You may have lost your balls, Charlie," she said in a conversational tone of voice, "but you certainly haven't lost your taste."

Jennie's mouth hung open as she stared at them. Standhurst began to laugh and the butler reappeared at the doorway, carrying a chair. He held it for Mrs. Schwartz as she sat down at the table.

"A sherry flip for Mrs. Schwartz, Judson." The butler bowed and disappeared. Standhurst turned to Jennie. "I suppose you're wondering what this is all about?"

Jennie nodded, still unable to speak.

"Twenty-five years ago, Aida Schwartz ran the best cat house west of the Everleigh sisters in Chicago."

Mrs. Schwartz reached over and patted his hand. "Charlie remembers everything," she said to Jennie. "He even remembered that I never drink anything but a sherry flip." She looked down at his glass on the table. "And I suppose you still drink champagne in a tall glass over ice?"

He nodded. "Old habits, like old friends, Aida, are hard to give up."

The butler placed a drink in front of her. She raised the glass daintily to her lips and sipped. She looked at the butler and smiled. "Thank you."

"Thank you, madam."

She raised her eyebrows in good-humored surprise. "This is very good," she said. "You don't know how hard it is to get a decent cocktail, even in the most expensive restaurants. It seems that ladies drink nothing but Martinis nowadays." She shuddered politely. "Horrible. In my time, no lady would dream of even tasting anything like that."

Standhurst looked at Jennie. "Aida would never let any of her girls drink anything but sherry."

"Whisky befuddles the brain," Aida said primly. "And my girls weren't being paid for drinking."

The old man chuckled reminiscently. "They certainly weren't. Aida, do you remember before the war when I used to come down to your house for a prostate massage?"

"I do, indeed." She smiled.

He looked across the table at Jennie. "I'd developed a bit of trouble and the doctor recommended prostate massage three times a month. The first time I went to his office. After that, I made up my mind that if I had to have massage, I'd at least enjoy it. So, three evenings a week, I showed up at Aida's for my treatment."

"What he didn't tell you," Aida added, "was that the treatments got him terribly aroused. And my girls were trained never to disappoint a guest. When Charlie went back to see the doctor two weeks later and explained, the doctor was horribly upset."

Standhurst was still laughing. "The doctor said he'd bring Aida up before the authorities on charges of practicing medicine without a license."

Mrs. Schwartz reached over and patted Standhurst's hand fondly. "And do you remember Ed Barry?"

"I certainly do." He chuckled and looked at Jennie. "Ed Barry was one of those hard-shelled Southern Baptists who look down the end of their nose at everything and immediately label it sin. Well, this was election eve and Ed was running for governor on a reform ticket. I managed to get him drinking in the excitement of it all and by midnight, he was weeping drunk. So without telling him where I was taking him, we went down to Aida's. He never forgot it."

Standhurst laughed, wiping the tears from his eyes. "Poor old Ed, he never knew what hit him. He lost the election but he never seemed to mind it. On the day Aida closed down her place, after we got into the war, he was downstairs in the bar, weeping as if the world had come to an end."

"Those were the good old days," Aida said. "We'll never see them again."

"Why did you close down?" Jennie asked curiously.

"There were several reasons," Aida said seriously, turning to Jennie. "After and during the war, there was too much free competition. It seemed as if every girl was determined to give it away. And it simply became too difficult to find girls who were interested and dedicated enough in their work to measure up to the high standards I wanted to maintain. All they were interested in was being whores. Since I didn't need the money, I closed up."

"Aida's a very wealthy woman. She put all her money into real estate and apartment houses, here and in most of the big cities around the country." Standhurst looked over at her. "Just about what are you worth right now, Aida?"

She shrugged her shoulders. "About six million dollars, give or take a little," she said casually. "Thanks to you and a few good friends like you."

Standhurst grinned. "Now are you still determined to go back to the hospital?"

Jennie didn't answer.

"Well, Jennie?" he asked.

Jennie stared at him, then at Aida. They were watching her intently. She started to speak but no words came to her lips.

Mrs. Schwartz reached over suddenly and patted her hand reassuringly. "Give her a little time to think it over, Charlie," she said gently. "It's a decision a girl has to make for herself."

There was a curiously fond look in Standhurst's eyes as he smiled at Jennie. "She'll have to make up her mind pretty soon," he said softly. "There isn't that much time left."

He didn't know it then, but there were exactly two days.

He turned his head to watch her as she came into his room two mornings later. "I think I'll stay in bed today, Jennie," he said in a low voice. Drawing the drapes back from the windows, she looked at him in the light that spilled across the bed. His face was white and the skin parchment-thin over the bones. He kept his eyes partly closed, as if the light hurt them.

She crossed to the side of the bed and looked down. "Do you want me to call the doctor, Charlie?"

"What could he do?" he asked, a faint line of perspiration appearing on his forehead. She picked up a small towel from the bedside table and wiped his face. Then she pulled down the blanket and lifted his old-fashioned nightshirt. Quickly she replaced the waste pouch and saw his eyes dart to the pouch as she covered him. She picked up the waste bag and went into the bathroom.

"Pretty bad?" he asked, his eyes on her face, when she returned.

"Pretty bad."

"I know," he whispered. "I looked before you came in. It was as black as the hubs of hell."

She slipped an arm behind him and held him up as she straightened his pillow. She let him sink back gently. "I don't know. Some mornings I've seen it worse."

"Don't kid me." He closed his eyes for a moment, then opened them. "I got a hunch today's the day," he whispered, his eyes on her face.

"You'll feel better after I get some orange juice into you."

"The hell with that," he whispered vehemently. "Who ever heard of going to hell on orange juice? Get me some champagne!"

Silently she put down the orange juice and picked up a tall glass. She filled it with cubes from the Thermos bucket and poured the champagne over it. Putting the glass straw into the glass, she held it for him.

"I can still hold my own drink," he said.

The teletype in the corner of the room began to chatter. She walked over to look at it. "What is it?"

"Some speech Landon made at a Republican dinner last night."

"Turn it off," he said testily.

He held out the glass to her and she took it and put it back on the table. The telephone began to ring. She picked it up. "It's the feature editor in L.A.," she said. "He's returning the call you made to him yesterday."

"Tell him I want Dick Tracy for the paper out here." She nodded and repeated the message into the telephone and hung up. She turned back and saw his face was covered with perspiration again.

"Your son Charles made me promise to call him if I thought it was necessary."

"Don't," he snapped. "Who needs him here to gloat over me? The son of a bitch has been waiting around for years for me to kick off. He wants to get his hands on the papers." He chuckled soundlessly. "I'll bet the damn fool has the papers come out for Roosevelt the day after the funeral."

A spasm of pain shot through him and he sat up suddenly, almost bolt upright, in the bed. "Oh, Jesus!" he said, clutching at his belly. Instantly, her arm was around his shoulders, supporting him, while with her other hand, she reached for a syrette of morphine. "Not yet, Jennie, please."

She looked at him for a moment, then put the syrette back on the table. "All right," she said. "Tell me when."

He sank back against the pillow and she wiped his face again. He closed his eyes and lay quietly for a moment. Then he opened them and there was a look of terror in them she had never seen before. "I feel like I'm choking!" he said, sitting up, his hand over his mouth.

Quickly, without turning around, she reached for the drain pan on the table behind her and held it under his mouth. He coughed and heaved and brought up a black brackish bile. She put down the pan and wiped his mouth and chin and let him sink to the pillow again.

He looked up at her through tear-filled eyes, trying to smile. "Christ," he whispered hoarsely. "That tasted like my own piss!"

She didn't answer and he closed his eyes wearily. She could see him shiver under the onslaught of the pain. After a few minutes, he spoke without opening his eyes. "You know, Jennie," he whispered, "I thought the sweetest agony I'd ever know was coming. But going's got it beat a million miles."

He opened his eyes and looked at her. The terror was gone from them and a deep, wise calm had taken its place. He smiled slowly. "All right, Jennie," he whispered, looking into her eyes. "Now!"

Her eyes still fastened to his, she reached behind her for a syrette. Automatically she found the sunken vein and squeezed the syrette dry. She picked up another. He smiled again as he saw it in her hand. "Thanks, Jennie," he whispered.

She bent forward and kissed the pale, damp forehead. "Good-by, Charlie."

He leaned back against the pillow and closed his eyes as she plunged the second syrette into his arm. Soon there were six empty syrettes lying on the cover of the bed beside him. She sat there very quietly, her fingers on his pulse, as the beat grew fainter and fainter. At last, it stopped completely. She stared down at him for a moment, then pressed down the lids over his eyes and drew the cover over his face.

She got to her feet, putting the syrettes into her uniform pocket as she wearily crossed the room and picked up the telephone.

The butler met her in the hallway as she was going to her room. He had an envelope in his hand. "Mr. Standhurst asked me to give this to you, Miss Denton. He gave it to me before you came on duty this morning."

"Thank you, Judson." She closed the door behind her and tore open the envelope as she crossed the room. Enclosed were five thousand-dollar bills and a small note in his scratchy handwriting.

DEAR JENNIE,

By now you must understand the reason I wanted you to stay with me. One thing I could never understand is that false mercy so many proclaim while prolonging the agony of approaching death.

Enclosed find your severance pay. You may use it as you will—to provide for a rainy day while you continue to waste your life in the generally unrewarding care of others; or, if you've half the intelligence I give you credit for and are half the woman I think, you'll use it as tuition to Aida's school, which for the sake of a better name I shall call Standhurst College, and go on from there to a more luxurious manner of living.

With gratitude and affection, I remain,

Sincerely,
C. STANDHURST

Still holding the note in her hand, she went to the closet and took down her valise. She placed it on the bed and slowly began to pack. Less than an hour later, she left the cab and hurried up the steps into the church, adjusting the scarf she wore around her throat over her head. She genuflected at the back of the church and hurried down the aisle to the altar, turning left toward the statue of the Virgin.

She knelt and clasped her hands as she bowed her head for a moment. Then she turned and took a candle from the rack and held a burning taper to it before placing it among the other candles beneath the statue. Again she bowed her head and knelt for a moment, then turned and hurried back up the aisle. At the door, she dipped her fingers into the Holy Fount and blessed herself, then opened her purse and pressed a bill into the slot of the collection box.

That night, the rector had a very pleasant surprise. There, in the collection box, amidst all the silver and copper coins, was a neatly folded thousand-dollar bill.

The gray Rolls-Royce was parked in the driveway of the old house on Dalehurst Avenue in Westwood as Jennie pulled up in a cab. She got out and paid the driver, then went to the door and put her valise down as she pressed the bell.

From somewhere in the house, a chime sounded. A moment later, the door opened and a maid said, "This way, please, miss."

Aida was seated on the couch, a tray of tea and cookies on the table before her. "You can put the valise with the others, Mary."

"Yes'm," the maid said.

Jennie turned and saw the maid put her valise next to some others standing by the door. She turned back to Aida. A newspaper was open on the couch beside her, the big, black headlines staring up.

STANDHURST DEAD!

Aida got up and took her hand, gently pulling her down to the couch. "Sit down, my dear," she said softly. "I've been expecting you. We have plenty of time for a cup of tea before we go to the train."

"To the train?" "Of course, my dear," Aida said. "We're going to Chicago. It's the only place in the United States for a girl to start her career."

CHAPTER TWELVE

THE BIG TWENTY-FOUR SHEET FROM THE BILLBOARD HUNG OVER THE makeshift stage at the Army camp. It was an enlargement of the famous color photograph from the cover of *Life* magazine. Looking up at it, Jennie remembered the photographer perching precariously on the top rung of the ladder near the ceiling, aiming his camera down toward her on the bed.

From that angle, her legs had been too long and had gone out of the frame, so he'd turned her around and placed her feet up on the white satin tufted headboard. Then the flash bulb had gone off, blinding her for a moment as they always did, and history had been made.

She'd been wearing a decorously cut black lace nightgown, which covered her completely from throat to ankles. Yet it had clung so revealingly, the soft tones of her flesh glowing in contrast to the black lace, that it left nothing to the imagination—the swollen nipples, irritated by the material across her jutting breasts, the soft curve of her stomach, and the sharply rising pubis, which couldn't be hidden because of the position of her legs. Her long blond hair spilled downward over the edge of the bed and the blinding light of the flash bulb had thrown a sensual invitation into her eyes as she smiled at the invisible onlooker, upside down, from the lower-left-hand corner.

Life had published the photograph with but one word emblazoned in white block letters beneath it:

DENTON

That had been almost a year ago, in October of 1941, about the time *The Sinner* was having its world première in New York. She remembered the surprise she'd felt, walking through the lobby of the Waldorf, with Jonas at her side, coming onto rows of photographs of herself hanging across the newsstand magazine racks.

"Look," she'd said, stopping in wonder. Jonas smiled at her in that particular way which, she knew by now, meant he was particularly pleased with something. He'd crossed to the newsstand and throwing a coin down picked up the magazine from the rack. He handed it to her as they went into the elevator.

She opened the magazine on the way up. The headline loomed over the text: *Spirituality in Sex.*

Jonas Cord, a wealthy young man, who makes airplanes, explosives, plastics and money (see *Life*, Oct. '39) and, when the spirit moves him, occasionally makes a motion picture (*The Renegade*, 1930, *Devils in the Sky*, 1932), has come up with a highly personalized version, in the De Mille tradition, of the story of Mary Magdalene. He calls it, with his customary frankness, *The Sinner.*

Without a doubt, the single most important factor contributing to the impact of this motion picture is the impressive performance of the young woman Mr. Cord selected to play the title role, Jennie Denton.

Miss Denton, without prior experience in motion pictures or at acting, has a most newsworthy effect upon audiences. With all the overtly sexual awareness that the motions of her body (37-21-36) seem to suggest, the viewer is at the same time aware of the deeply spiritual quality that always emanates from her. Perhaps this stems from her eyes, which are wide-set and gray and deep with a knowledge and wisdom of pain and love and death, far beyond her years. In some strange manner, she appears to project the paradoxical contrasts of our times—the self-seeking aggressions of man's search for physical satisfaction and his desire for spiritual values greater than himself.

The elevator door opened and she felt Jonas' hand on her arm. She closed the magazine and they walked out of the elevator. "My God, do they really believe that?"

He smiled. "I guess they do. That's one magazine you can't buy for advertising. I told you you were going to be a star," he said as they walked into his apartment.

She was to leave for the Coast immediately after the premiere to begin another picture. She saw the script lying on the table in front of the couch. Jonas walked over and picked it up, and riffled the pages. "I don't like it."

"I don't like it, either. But Maurice says it will make a mint."

"I don't care," he said. "I just don't like the idea of you being in it." He crossed to the telephone. "Get me Mr. Bonner at the Sherry-Netherland."

"Maurice, this is Jonas," he said curtly, a moment later. "Cancel *Stareyes*. I don't want Denton in it."

She heard Bonner's excited protest all the way across the room. "I don't care," Jonas said. "Get someone else to play it. . . . Who? . . . Hayworth, Sheridan. Anyone you want. And from now on, Denton isn't to be scheduled for any picture until I approve the script."

He put down the telephone and turned to her. He was smiling. "You hear that?"

She smiled back at him. "Yes, boss."

The photograph had been an instant success. Everywhere you went, it stared out at you—from walls, from display counters, from calendars and from posters. And she, too, had gone on to fame. She was a star and when she returned to the Coast, she found that Jonas had approved a new contract for her.

But a year had gone by, including the bombs at Pearl Harbor, and still she had made no other picture. Not that it mattered. *The Sinner* was in its second year at the big Norman Theater in New York and was still playing limited-first-run engagements wherever it opened. It was proving to be the biggest-grossing picture the company had ever made.

Her routine became rigid and unvarying. Between publicity appearances at each première, as the picture opened across the country, she remained on the Coast. Each morning, she'd go to the studio. There her day would be filled— dramatic lessons in the morning; luncheon, generally with some interviewer; voice, singing and dancing lessons in the afternoon. Her evenings were generally spent alone, unless Jonas happened to be in town. Then she was with him every night.

Occasionally, she'd have dinner with David and Rosa Woolf. She liked Rosa and their happy little baby, who just now was learning how to walk and bore the impressive name of Henry Bernard, after David's father and uncle. But most of the time she spent alone in her small house with the Mexican woman. The word was out. She was Jonas' girl. And Jonas' girl she remained.

It was only when she was with him that she did not feel the loneliness and lack of purpose that was looming larger and larger inside. She began to grow restless. It was time for her to go to work. She read scripts avidly and several times, when she thought she'd found one she might like to do, she got in touch with Jonas. As always, he'd promise to read it and then call her several days later to say he didn't think it was right for her. There was always a reason.

Once, in exasperation, she'd asked him why he kept her on the payroll if he had nothing for her to do. For a moment, he'd been silent. When he spoke, his voice was cold and final. "You're not an actress," he said. "You're a star. And stars can only shine when everything else is right."

A few days later, Al Petrocelli, the publicity man, came to her dressing room at the studio. "Bob Hope's doing a show for the boys at Camp Pendleton. He wants you on it."

She turned on the couch on which she was sitting and put down the script she'd been reading. "I can do it?" she asked, looking at him.

They both knew what she meant. "Bonner talked to Cord. They both agreed the exposure would be good for you. Di Santis will be in charge of whipping up an act for you."

"Good," she said, getting to her feet. "It will be great having something to do again."

And now, after six weeks of extensive rehearsal of a small introductory speech and one song, which had been carefully polished, phrased and orchestrated to show her low, husky voice to its greatest advantage, she stood in the wings of the makeshift stage, waiting to go on. She shivered in the cool night air despite the mink coat wrapped around her.

She peeked out from behind the wings at the audience. A roar of laughter rolled toward her from the rows upon rows of soldiers, stretching into the night as far as the eye could see. Hope had just delivered one of his famous off-color, serviceman-only kind of jokes that could never have got on the air during his coast-to-coast broadcasts. She pulled her head back, still shivering. "Nervous, eh?" Al asked. "Never worked before an audience before? Don't worry, it'll soon pass."

A sudden memory of Aida and the routine she'd made her perform before a small but select group of wealthy men in New Orleans flashed through her mind. "Oh, I've worked in front of an audience before." Then when she saw the look of surprise on his face, "When I was in college," she added dryly. She turned back to watch Bob Hope. Somehow, the memory made her feel better.

Al turned to the soldier standing next to him. "Now, you know what you got to do, Sergeant?"

"I got it down perfect, Mr. Petrocelli."

"Good," Al said. He glanced out at the stage. Hope was nearing the end of his routine. Al turned back to the soldier, a twenty-dollar bill appearing magically in his hand. "She'll be going on any minute," he said. "Now, you get down there in the front near the stage. And don't forget. Speak up loud and clear."

"Yes, Mr. Petrocelli," the soldier said, the twenty disappearing into his pocket.

"There'll be another after the show if everything goes right."

"For another twenty, Mr. Petrocelli," the soldier said, "you don't have to worry. They'll hear me clear to Alaska."

Al nodded worriedly and turned toward the stage as the soldier went out and around the wings. Hope was just beginning Jennie's introduction. "And now, men," he said into the microphone, "for the high spot of the evening—" He paused for a moment, holding up his hands to still the starting applause. "The reason we're all here. Even the entire officer's club." He waited until the laughter died away. "Girl-watching!"

"Now, men," he continued, "when I first told the War Department who was coming here tonight, they said, "Oh, no, Mr. Hope. We just haven't enough seat belts for that many chairs." But I reassured them. I told them you soldiers knew how to handle any situation." There was laughter again but this time, there was an expectancy in its sound. Hope held up his hands. "And so, fellers, I give you—"

The lights suddenly dimmed and a baby spot picked up Jennie's head as she peeked out past the curtain. "Fasten your seat belts, men!" Hope shouted. "Jennie Denton!"

And the stage went to black except for the spotlight on Jennie. A roar burst from the audience as she cautiously and tentatively, in the manner in which she had thoroughly rehearsed, walked out on the stage, covered completely by the full mink coat.

The noise washed over her and she felt its vibrations in the wooden floor beneath her feet as she came to a stop in front of the microphone. She stood there quietly, looking at them, her blond page-boy haircut catching and reflecting the gleaming light. The soldiers whistled and screamed and stomped.

After a few minutes had passed, during which the noise showed no signs of abatement, she leaned toward the microphone. "If you men will give me just a minute," she said in a low voice, letting her coat slip from one shoulder, "I'll take my coat off."

If possible, the noise grew even louder as she slowly and deliberately took off the coat. She let it fall to the stage behind her and stood there, revealed in a white, diamond-sequined, skin-tight evening gown. She leaned toward the microphone again and one shoulder strap slipped from her shoulder. Quickly she caught at it. "This is most embarrassing. I've never been with so many men before."

They roared enthusiastically.

"Now I don't know what to do," she said in a soft voice.

"Don't do nothin', baby," came a stentorian roar from down front, near the stage, "Jus' stand there!"

Again, pandemonium broke loose as she smiled and peered in the direction of the voice. She waited until the sound died down slightly. "I have a little song I'd like to sing for you," she said. "Would you like that?"

"Yes!" The sound came back from a thousand throats.

"O.K.," she said and moved closer to the microphone, clutching again at her falling strap. "Now, if you'll just pretend you're at home, listening to the radio, if you'll close your eyes—"

"Close our eyes?" the stentorian voice roared again. "Baby, we may be in the Army but we're not crazy!"

She smiled helplessly at the roar of laughter as the music slowly came up.

Slowly the spot narrowed to just her face as silence came down on the audience. The music was the studio arranger at his best. An old torch song but done in beguine rhythm with the piano, the winds and the violins playing the melody against the rhythm of the drums and the big bass.

She came in right on cue, her eyes half closed against the spotlight, her lower lip shining. "I wanna be loved by you," she sang huskily. "And nobody else but you.

"I wanna be loved by you.

"A-low-oh-ohne."

The roar that came rolling out from the audience all but drowned out her voice and for a moment she was frightened by all the repressed sexuality she heard in it.

CHAPTER THIRTEEN

M AURICE BONNER WALKED INTO THE HOLLYWOOD BROWN DERBY, THE thick blue-paper-bound script under his arm. The headwaiter bowed. "Good afternoon, Mr. Bonner. Mr. Pierce is already here."

They walked down to a booth in the rear of the restaurant. Dan looked up from a copy of the *Hollywood Reporter*. He put down the paper next to his drink. "Hello, Maurice."

Bonner dropped into the seat opposite him. "Hello," he said. He looked over at the trade paper. "See the write-up our girl got?"

Dan nodded.

"That wasn't the half of it," Bonner said. "Al Petrocelli told me he never saw anything like it. They wouldn't let her get off the stage and then when it was over, they almost tore her clothes off while she was getting to the car. Hope called me first thing this morning and said he wants her any time she's available."

"More proof that I'm right," Pierce said. "I think she's bigger now than Marlowe ever was." He shot a shrewd glance at Bonner. "Still going up there one night a week?"

Bonner smiled. There were no secrets in this town. "No. After *The Sinner* opened in New York, Cord tore up her old contract and gave her a new one."

"I don't get it."

"It's simple," Bonner said. "The morning she got the contract, she came into my office. She borrowed my pen and signed it, then looked up at me and said, "Now I don't have to fuck for nobody. Even you!" And she picks up the contract and walks out."

Pierce laughed. "I don't believe her. Once a cunt, always a cunt. She's got an angle."

"She has. Jonas Cord. I got a hunch she's going to marry him."

"That would serve the son of a bitch right," Pierce said harshly. "He still doesn't know she was a whore?"

"He doesn't know."

"Just shows you. No matter how smart you think you are, there's always some bint that's smarter." Pierce laughed. "How's Jonas doing?"

"Making nothing but money," Bonner said. "But you know Jonas. He still isn't happy."

"Why not?"

"He tried to get into the Air Corps and they wouldn't take him. They refused to give him a commission, saying he was too important to the war effort. So he leaves Washington in a huff and flies to New York and enlists as a private, the *schmuck*."

"But he still ain't in the Army," Pierce said.

"Of course not. He flunked the physical—perforated eardrums or something stupid like that. So they classify him 4-F and the next week, they take Roger Forrester back as a brigadier general."

"I hear David's going up for his physical soon," Pierce said.

"Any day now, the jerk. He could easily get a deferment. Married, with a baby; especially now the industry's got an essential rating. But he won't ask for it." He looked across the table at Pierce. "Even Nevada's taking his Wild-West show out on the road to work for free on the War Bond drives."

"It just proves that there are still some people around who think the world is flat," Dan said. He signaled the waiter for another round of drinks. "All those guys. I practically started them in the business. Today they all got it made and where am I? Still trying to make a deal."

Bonner looked at him. He didn't feel sorry for Pierce. Dan was still one of the most successful agents in Hollywood. "Yeah," he said sarcastically. "My heart bleeds for you. I already heard the story of your life, Dan. That isn't why I came to lunch."

Dan was a sharp enough agent to know he was in danger of losing his audience. He turned off the complaints and lowered his voice to a confidential tone. "You read the script?"

Bonner picked the script up from the seat beside him and placed it on the table. "I read it."

"Great, isn't it?" Pierce asked, the selling enthusiasm beginning to creep into his voice.

"It's good." Bonner nodded his head pedantically. "Needs a lot of work, though."

"What script doesn't?" Pierce asked with a smile. He leaned forward. "Now, the way I see it, this script needs a strong producer like you. Wanger, over at Universal, is nuts about it. So is Zimbalist, over at Metro. But I can't see it for them. They just ain't got the feel and showmanship you got."

"Let's skip the bullshit, Dan. We both know the script is good only if we can get a certain girl to play in it. And we both know who that is."

"Denton," Pierce said quickly. "That's my thinking, too. That's why I brought it to you. She's under contract to your studio."

"But Jonas has the final say on what pictures she makes. And he's turned thumbs down on some pretty good ones."

"What's he trying to do?" Pierce asked. "Hide her away in a closet and keep her for himself? You can't do that to a star. Sooner or later, she busts out."

Bonner shrugged. "You know Jonas. Nobody asks why."

"Maybe he'll like the script."

"Even if he did," Bonner said, "once he sees you're the agent, the whole deal goes out the window."

"What if the girl puts the pressure on and says she's got to do it?"

Bonner shrugged. "Your guess is as good as mine. But I'm not going to give it to her. I'm not getting into trouble over any script. No matter how good it is, there's always another."

Pierce stared at him, his fleshy lips tightening grimly. "I got an idea we can make her see it our way," he said. "I got my hands on—"

Bonner stopped him. "Don't tell me. If it happens, let it come as a pleasant surprise. I don't want to know anything about it."

Pierce stared at him for a moment, then relaxed back into his seat. He picked up the menu. "O.K., Maurice," he said, smiling. "What you going to eat?"

The mail was on the small desk in the living room when Jennie got back from the studio. She walked over to the desk and sat down. "We'll have dinner about eight thirty," she said. "I want to take a bath and rest up first."

"*Sí, señorita,*" Maria answered and waddled away.

Jennie looked at the mail. There were two envelopes, one large manila one, which from experience she guessed contained a script, and a letter. She opened the letter first. The letterhead across the top read: *St. Mary's College of Nursing.* Her eyes flicked down the page. It was in Sister M. Christopher's precise script.

DEAR JENNIE,

This is just a short note to express the appreciation of the students and the staff of St. Mary's College for the special screening of your picture which you were kind enough to arrange for us.

The Reverend Mother and the sisters, including myself, were all most impressed by the moving expression of the faith and love for our Saviour, Jesus Christ, that you brought to your interpretation of what must have been a most exacting and difficult portrayal. It is unfortunate indeed that the makers of the motion picture thought it necessary to include certain scenes which we felt could very easily have been omitted without impairment to the story of the Magdalen. But on the whole, we were extremely pleased that in these troubled times, so noble a demonstration of the Redeeming Grace to be found in the Love of Our Lord is available for all to see.

Now I must close for I am soon due in Surgery. Since the war, all of us in the school, and in the hospital, are working double shifts due to the shortages of help. But with Our Lord's Grace, we shall redouble our poor efforts to extend His Mercy.

The Reverend Mother extends to you Her Most Gracious blessing and prays that you may continue to find success and happiness in your new career.

Sincerely yours in J. C.,
SISTER M. CHRISTOPHER

A vision of the sister's austere, observant face flashed through her mind, together with a twinge of nostalgia for the years she had spent at the college. Somehow, it seemed such a long time ago. It was as if she were a completely different person from the wide-eyed, nervous girl who first appeared in the Reverend Mother's office.

She remembered the quiet hours of study and the long hours of training and the exhausting hours of sheer drudgery in the hospital. There had been times when she'd cry out of sheer frustration at her inability to learn all that was taught her. It was during those moments that the mask of austerity would disappear from the sister's face and she would place her hand comfortingly on the girl's shoulder. "Work hard and pray hard, Jennie," she'd say gently, "and you will learn. You have the true gift of healing within you."

And she would feel comforted and her strength would be renewed as she saw how unsparingly the sister gave of herself to all, both patients and students. It seemed that no matter what hour of the day or night Jennie was on duty, Sister Christopher was always nearby.

Jennie reached for a cigarette. All of them must be working terribly hard if the sister mentioned it in a letter. Sister Christopher was never given to make much of her own efforts. A feeling of uselessness swept through Jennie as she thought of the comparatively easy life she led. She looked down at her strong, lean hands. She did so little with them now. The knowledge that was in them seemed to tingle in her fingertips. There must be something she could do to help the sisters.

There was. She reached for the telephone at the same time she had the idea and dialed quickly. "Rosa? This is Jennie."

"How are you, Jennie? David told me how you almost broke up the United States Army with the Hope show."

Jennie laughed. "The poor kids have been away from women too long."

"Don't hand me that. The trade papers said you were great."

"Don't tell me David's got you reading them?"

"Sure thing," Rosa said. "Isn't that what every wife in the business does? It's the only way they can keep track of what their husbands are doing."

"How's little Bernie?"

"Why don't you come over for dinner one night and see for yourself? It's been a long time."

"I will. Soon."

"Do you want to talk to David?"

"If he's there," Jennie said politely.

"Good-by, dear," Rosa said, "and dinner real soon? Here's David."

"How's the pride and joy of the Norman lot?"

"Fine. I'm sorry to disturb you at home, David, but I had a little problem I thought you could advise me on."

His voice became serious. "Shoot."

She cleared her throat. "I went to St. Mary's College of Nursing on a scholarship and I was wondering if I could arrange with the studio to take something out of my pay check each week and send it to them the way they do with the Motion Picture Relief Fund. It would be sort of paying them back a little for all they did for me."

"That's easy." David laughed, a kind of relief in his voice. "Just send a note to my office tomorrow morning telling me how much you want taken off and we'll do the rest. Anything else?"

"No, that's all."

"Good. Now, you come to dinner like Rosa said."

"I will, David. Good-by."

She put down the telephone and looked at the letter again. She began to feel better. At least, even if she couldn't be there herself to help, her money would do some good. She put down the letter and picking up the manila envelope, ripped it open. She had been right. It was a script, a long one.

Curiously she read the title on the blue cover. *Aphrodite; a screenplay based on a novel by Pierre Louys.* She opened the script to the first page and a note fell out. It was brief and to the point.

DEAR MISS DENTON:

It has been a long time since you made a motion picture and I believe you were wise to wait for the proper script with which to follow up your tremendous success in *The Sinner.*

Aphrodite, I believe, is that script. It is the one property I have seen that has the scope and the quality to add luster to your career. I shall be most interested in your reaction.

Sincerely,
DAN PIERCE

She folded the letter and put it back in the script. That Dan Pierce was a cutie. He knew better than to submit the script to the studio in the usual manner. She picked up the script and started upstairs to her room. She would read it in bed after dinner.

CHAPTER FOURTEEN

DEAR MR. PIERCE:

Thank you for sending me the enclosed script of *Aphrodite*, which I am returning. It is a most interesting screenplay. However, it is not one that I should particularly care to do.

JENNIE DENTON

S HE WONDERED WHETHER SHE HAD BEEN RIGHT IN SO SUMMARILY DIS-missing the script. She had mixed feelings about it. At night, in bed, reading it for the first time, she could not put it down. There was a fascination about the story that brought to her mind Standhurst's description of the courtesan who helped rule the world. The screenplay seemed to capture the sensual imagery and poetry of the original work and yet bring it all within the limitations and confines of the Motion Picture Code. Yet, the more she read, the less enthusiastic she became.

There was not one single line or scene that could be found objectionable. On the surface. Yet, beneath the surface, there was an acute awareness of the erotic byplay that would subtly work on an audience's subconscious. By the time she reached the end of the screenplay, she felt this was the writer's only purpose.

She fell asleep, oddly disturbed, and awoke still disturbed. At the studio, the next morning, she'd sent to the library for a copy of the original novel, then spent all of that day and part of the next reading it. After that, she again read the screenplay. It was not until then that she realized how boldly the beauty and purpose of the story had been distorted.

Still, there was no doubt in her mind that it could be made into a great motion picture. And even less doubt that the actress who played Aphrodite would become the most talked about and important actress of that season. The Aphrodite of the script was truly the goddess and woman who was all things to all men.

But that was not enough. For, nowhere in the screenplay could she find the soul of Aphrodite, the one moment of spiritual love and contemplation that would lift her out of herself and make her one truly with the gods. She was beautiful and warm and clever and loving and even moral, according to her own concept. But she was a whore, no better than any since time immemorial, no better than any Jennie had known, no better than Jennie herself had been. And something inside Jennie was appalled by what she had read. For, in another time and another place, she saw herself—what she had been and what she still remained.

She put the envelope on the dressing table and pressed the button for a messenger just as the telephone rang. She picked it up. It was not until she heard his voice that she knew how much she'd missed him. "Jonas! Where are you? When did you get in?"

"I'm at the plant in Burbank. I want to see you."

"Oh, Jonas, I want to see you, too. It will seem like such a long day."

"Why wait until tonight? Can't you come over here for lunch?"

"You know I can."

"One o'clock?"

"I'll be there," she said, putting down the telephone.

"You can leave it here, John," Jonas said. "Well help ourselves."

"Yes, Mr. Cord." The porter looked at Jennie, then back at Jonas. "Would it," he began hesitantly, "would it be all right if I troubled Miss Denton for her autograph?"

Jonas laughed. "Ask her."

The porter looked inquiringly at Jennie: She smiled and nodded. He took a pencil and paper from his pocket and quickly she scrawled her name on it. "Thank you, Miss Denton."

Jennie laughed as the door closed behind him. "Signing my autograph always makes me feel like a queen." She looked around the office. "This is nice."

"It's not mine," Jonas said, pouring coffee into two cups. "It's Forrester's. I'm just using it while he's away."

"Oh," she said curiously. "Where is yours?"

"I don't have any, except the one that used to be my father's in the old plant in Nevada. I'm never in any one place long enough to really need one." He pulled a chair around near her and sat down. He drank his coffee and looked at her quietly.

She could feel an embarrassed blush creeping over her face. "Do I look all right? Is my make-up smeared or something?"

He shook his head and smiled. "No. You look fine."

She sipped at her coffee and an awkward silence came between them. "What have you been doing?" she asked.

"Thinking, mostly. About us," he answered, looking at her steadily. "You. Me. This last time I was away from you, for the first time in my life I was lonely. Nothing was right. I wanted to see no other girls. Only you."

Her heart seemed to swell, choking her. She felt, somehow, that if she tried to move, she would faint. Jonas put his hand in his pocket and came out with a small box, which he handed to her. She stared down at it dumbly. The small gold letters stared up at her. *Van Cleef & Arpels.*

Her fingers trembled as she opened it. The beautifully cut heart-shaped diamond suddenly released its radiance. "I want to marry you," he said softly.

She felt the hot, grateful tears push their way into her eyes as she looked at him. Her lips trembled but she could not speak.

It was the headline and lead story in Louella's column the next day. The telephone had been ringing in her dressing room all morning, until finally she'd asked the switchboard to screen all her calls. The operator's voice had a new respect in it. As Jennie started to put the telephone down the operator said, "Miss Denton?"

"Yes."

"The girls on the switchboard all wish you the best of luck."

Jennie felt a sudden happy rush of warmth go through her. "Why, thank you."

Later in the afternoon, Rosa called. "I'm so happy for both of you."

"I'm in a daze," Jennie laughed, looking down at the diamond sparkling on her finger.

"You know that dinner invitation?"

"Yes."

"David and I were just thinking. How would you like to make it an engagement party? At Romanoff's with all the trimmings."

"I don't know." Jennie hesitated. "I'd better check with Jonas."

Rosa laughed. "Jonas? Who's he? Only the groom. Nobody ever asks the groom what he wants. It doesn't have to be a big party, if you don't want one."

"All right." Jennie laughed. "You've twisted my arm."

"And you'll have a chance to show off your engagement ring. I hear it's a real smasher."

Jennie held out her hand and the diamond winked at her. "It's very nice," she said.

"Bernie is yelling for his dinner. I'll call you at home tonight and we'll make the arrangements."

"Thanks, Rosa. "By."

There was a strange car parked in the driveway when she got home from the studio that night. She drove into the garage and entered the house through the back door. If it was another reporter, she didn't want to see him. The Mexican woman was in the kitchen. "A Señor Pierce is in the living room, señorita."

What could he want, she wondered. Perhaps he hadn't received the script yet and had dropped by for it. Pierce was seated in a deep chair, a copy of the script open on his lap. He got to his feet and nodded. "Miss Denton."

"Mr. Pierce. Did you get the script? I sent it out several days ago."

He smiled. "I got it. But I thought perhaps we might discuss it further. I'm hoping I can talk you into changing your mind."

She shook her head. "I don't think so."

"Before we talk about it," he said quickly, "may I offer my congratulations on your engagement?"

"Thank you. But now I must ask you to excuse me. I do have an appointment."

"I'll only take a few minutes of your time." He bent over and picked up a small carrying case that had been lying on the floor behind the chair.

"But, really, Mr. Pierce—"

"I'll only be a few minutes." There was a peculiar sureness in his voice. It was as if he knew she would not dare to refuse him. He pressed a button and the top of the carrying case popped open. "Do you know what this is, Miss Denton?" he asked.

She didn't answer. She was beginning to get angry. If this was his idea of a joke, she wasn't going to like it. "It's an eight-millimeter projector," he said in a conversational tone, as he snapped on a lens. "The kind ordinarily used for the showing of home movies."

"Very interesting. But I hardly see what it has to do with me.

"You will," he promised, looking up. His eyes were cold. He turned, looking for an electrical outlet. He found one against the wall behind the chair and swiftly plugged the cord from the projector into it.

"I think that white wall across from you will do very well for a screen, don't you?" He turned the projector toward it and flicked a switch. "I took the liberty of putting on the reel of film before I came here."

The whir of film sounded and Jennie turned to watch the picture being thrown against the wall. The scene showed two naked girls on a couch, their arms around each other, their faces hidden. A warning bell echoed in her mind. There was something curiously familiar about the scene.

"I got this film from a friend of mine in New Orleans." Pierce's voice came casually from behind her as a man walked into the scene. He, too, was nude and one of the girls turned toward him, facing directly into the camera.

Unconsciously Jennie let out a gasp. The girl was herself. Then she remembered. It had been that time in New Orleans. She turned to stare at Dan Pierce, her face white.

"You were photogenic even then. You should have made sure there was no camera."

"There wasn't any," she gasped. "Aida would never have permitted it." She stared at him silently, her mouth and throat suddenly dry.

He pressed a switch and as the film stopped, the light faded. "I can see you're not very interested in home movies."

"What do you want?" she asked.

"You." He began to close up the machine. "But not in the usual sense," he added quickly. "I want you to play Aphrodite."

"And if I don't choose to?"

"You're lovely, you're a star, you're engaged," he said casually. "You might not be any of the three if this film should happen to fall into the wrong hands. Together with a summary of your professional activities." His cold eyes flashed at her. "No man, even one as crazy as Jonas Cord, wants to marry the town whore."

"I'm under contract to Norman. My contract doesn't allow me to make any outside pictures."

"I know," Dan said calmly. "But I'm sure Cord would authorize the purchase of this script if you asked him. Bonner will make the picture."

"What if he won't? Jonas has pretty definite ideas about pictures."

A faint smile came to his lips. "Then, make him change them."

She drew in her breath slowly. "And if I do?"

"Why, then you get the film, of course."

"The negative, too?"

He nodded.

"How do I know that there are no dupes?"

His eyebrows went up approvingly. "I see you've learned," he said. "I paid five thousand dollars for that little can of film. And I wouldn't have done that if I hadn't been sure there were no other copies. Besides, why kill the goose? We may want to do business together again sometime."

He packed up the projector. "I'll leave the script with you."

She didn't answer.

He turned, his hand on the door, and looked back. "I told you I'd only be a few minutes," he said.

CHAPTER FIFTEEN

DAN PIERCE GOT TO HIS FEET, RAPPING HIS CUP WITH A TINY SPOON. HE surveyed the table owlishly. He was drunk, happy drunk, as much on success as on the Scotch whisky he had so generously imbibed.

He nodded his head as they all looked up at him. "Dan Pierce doesn't forget who his friends are. He does things righ'. I brought the engaged couple each a presen'." He turned, snapping his fingers.

"Yes, Mr. Pierce," the maître d' said quickly. He gestured and a waiter came up with two packages, looked down at the tag on each and deposited the large gold-wrapped box in front of Jonas, the smaller silver-wrapped package by Jennie.

"Thank you, Dan," Jonas said.

"Open it up, Jonas," Dan said drunkenly. "I wan' ev'ybody to see the presents."

Jennie felt a strange foreboding. "We'll open them later, Dan."

"No," he said insistently. "Now."

She looked around the table. They were all watching curiously. She looked at Jonas. He shrugged his shoulders and smiled at her. She started to open her gift. It was wrapped so tight, she reached for a knife to cut it just as Jonas finished taking the wrapping from his. "Hey," Jonas said, laughing, as he held it up for all to see. "A magnum of champagne!"

Her present was in a small but beautifully inlaid mahogany case. She opened it and stared down, feeling the color drain from her face. Jonas took the case

from her hands and held it up for everyone to see. "It's a set of English razors."
he said and grinned at Dan. "The waiter must have got the labels mixed. Thanks
again, Dan."

Abruptly Pierce sat down. He was smiling.

Jennie felt them all watching her. She raised her head and looked around the
table. It was as if she knew what they were thinking. Of the twelve other couples
seated around the large table, she had known five of the men before she'd made
the test. Irving Schwartz, Bonner, three others, who were top-ranking executives
with other companies. The other seven men all knew. Some of their wives, too.
She could see it in their eyes. In only two of the men could she see any sympathy.
David and Nevada Smith.

David she could understand. But she did not understand why Nevada should
feel sorry for her. He scarcely knew her. He had always seemed so quiet, even
shy, when they met at the studio. But now there was a wild sort of anger deep
in his black Indian eyes as he looked from her to Dan Pierce.

Thirteen men, she thought, and all but one of them knew her for what she'd
been. And the thirteenth was the unlucky one. He was going to marry her. She
felt a light touch on her arm. Rosa's voice broke the silence that threatened to
engulf her. "I think it's about time we went to the little girl's room."

Jennie nodded dumbly and followed her from the table silently. She could feel
the eyes of other diners following her. Without even returning their glances, she
recognized several other men she had known and saw their wise, knowing smiles.
She began to feel sick. Rosa drew the curtain in front of the small alcove in the
corner as Jennie sank silently onto the couch. Rosa lit a cigarette and handed it
to her.

Jennie looked up at her, the cigarette in her fingers already forgotten. The
tears started to come into her eyes. "Why?" she asked in a hurt, bewildered voice.
"I don't understand. What did I ever do to him?"

She began to cry silently as Rosa sat down beside her and drew her head down
to her shoulder.

Dan Pierce chuckled to himself as he threaded his way to his car through the
dark and deserted parking lot. Wait until he told the story in the locker room at
Hillcrest tomorrow morning. The men would laugh their heads off. None of them
really liked Jonas, anyway.

True, they tolerated him. But they didn't accept him. There was a difference.
They all respected Jonas' success but they wouldn't lift a finger to help him. Not
like they would for Dan Pierce if he needed their help, which he didn't. He was
one of them, he'd grown up in the business with them. They had their rules.
They stuck together.

Wait until he told them how the broad looked. Like she was ready to sink
through the floor, while all the time, Jonas stood there like a *shmuck*, smiling
and thinking how nice everybody was. It would break them up.

A dark figure suddenly appeared out of the shadows in front of him. He peered
anxiously through the darkness as it silently came closer. "Oh, it's you, Nevada.
I didn' know who it was."

Nevada stood there silently.

Dan laughed aloud as he remembered. "Wasn' that a bitch, though?" He chortled, reaching out a hand toward Nevada to steady himself. "I thought she'd bust when she opened the case and saw the razors. An' Jonas, the jerk, he don' even know what he's gettin' into—"

Dan's voice suddenly choked off in a grunt of pain as Nevada sank his fist into his belly. He fell back against a car, clutching at it to hold himself up. He stared at Nevada. "Wha' you go an' do that for?" he asked in a hurt voice. "We're ol' buddies."

He saw Nevada's hand coming toward his face and tried to duck. He wasn't quick enough and felt the pain explode in his eyes. Again the hammer tore into his belly. He bent over, retching, and another blow on the side of his face sent him sprawling into his own vomit. He looked up at Nevada with frightened eyes.

It was not until then that Nevada spoke, and an icy fear came up and clutched at Dan's heart. "I should've done this a long time ago," Nevada said, looking down at him. "I oughta kill you. But you ain't worth goin' to the gas chamber for."

He turned his back contemptuously and walked away. Dan waited until the sound of the high-heeled boots faded away. Then he put his face down on his hands against the cold concrete. "It was only a joke," he cried drunkenly. "It was only a joke."

Jonas followed Jennie into the darkened house. "You're tired," he said gently, looking down at her white face. "It's been a big night. Go on up to bed. I'll see you tomorrow."

"No," she said flatly. She knew what she had to do. She turned and walked into the living room, switching on the light. He followed her curiously.

She turned, slipping the ring from her finger, and held it out to him. He looked at it, then at her. "Why?" he asked. "Is it because of anything I did tonight?"

She shook her head. "No," she said quickly. "It has nothing to do with you at all. Just take the ring, please."

"I'm entitled to know why, Jennie."

"I don't love you," she said. "Is that reason enough?"

"Not now it isn't."

"Then I have a better reason," she said tightly. "Before I made that screen test, I was the highest-priced whore in Hollywood."

He stared at her for a moment. "I don't believe you," he said slowly. "You couldn't have fooled me."

"You're a fool," she said sharply. "If you don't believe me, ask Bonner or any of the other four men at the table who laid me. Or any of a dozen other men I saw in the restaurant tonight."

"I still don't believe you," he said in a low voice.

She laughed. "Then ask Bonner why Pierce gave me that present. There wasn't any mix-up, he meant the razors for me. The story was all over Hollywood, the morning after Bonner left here. How I shaved all the hair off his body, then blew him in a bathtub filled with champagne."

He began to look sick.

"And why do you think I asked you to let me do *Aphrodite?*" she continued. "Not because I thought it was any good. It was to pay Pierce off for this." She walked quickly to the desk and took out two small reels of film. She spun one out at him, the film unwinding from the reel like a roll of confetti. "My first starring role," she said sarcastically. "A pornographic picture."

She took a cigarette from the box on the desk and lit it. She turned back to him. Her voice was quieter now. "Or maybe you're the kind of man who enjoys being married to that kind of woman, so that every time you meet another man, you can wonder. Did he or didn't he? When, where and how?"

He took a step toward her. "That's over now. It doesn't matter."

"It doesn't? Just because I was a fool for a moment, you don't have to be. How much of tonight do you think you'd have been able to take if you'd known what you know now?"

"But I love you!"

"You even kid yourself about that. You don't love me. You never have. You're in love with a memory. The memory of a girl who preferred your father to you. The first chance you had, you tried to make me over in her image. Even in bed— the things you wanted me to do. Did you really think I was so naïve I didn't know those were the things she did to you?"

The ring was still in her hand. She put it on the table in front of him. "Here," she said.

He stared down at the ring. The diamond seemed to shoot angry sparks at him. He looked up at her, his face lined and drawn. "Keep it," he said curtly and walked out.

She stood there until she heard his car pull out of the driveway. Then she turned out the light and walked upstairs, leaving the ring on the table and the film, like confetti after a party, on the floor.

She lay wide-eyed on her bed staring up into the night. If she could only cry she would feel better. But she was empty inside, eaten away by her sins. There was nothing left for her to give anyone. She had used up her ration of love.

Once, long ago, she had loved and been loved. But Tom Denton was dead, lost forever, beyond recall.

She cried out into the darkness, "Daddy, help me! Please! I don't know what to do."

If she could only go back and begin again. Back to the familiar Sunday smell of corned beef and cabbage, to the gentle sound of a whispered morning Mass in her ears, to the sisters and the hospital, to the inner satisfaction of being a part of God's work.

Then her father's voice came whispering to her out of the gray light of the morning, "Do you really want to go, Jennie Bear?"

She lay very still for a moment thinking, remembering. Was that time forever gone? If she were to withhold from confession that part of her life which no longer seemed to belong to her it need not be. They would not know. It was her one real transgression. The rest of her life they already knew about.

To do so would be a sin. A sin of omission. It would invalidate any future confession that she might make. But she had so much to give and without giving it she was denying not only herself but others who would have need of her help. Which was the greater sin? For a moment she was frightened, then decided that this was a matter between her and her Maker. The decision was hers, and she alone could be held responsible, both now and at any future time.

Suddenly she made her mind up and she was no longer afraid.

"Yes, Daddy," she whispered.

His soft voice came echoing back on the wind. "Then get dressed, Jennie, and I'll go with you."

CHAPTER SIXTEEN

I T WAS ALMOST TWO YEARS FROM THE NIGHT OF THE PARTY BEFORE ROSA heard from Jennie again. It was almost six months from the time she received the dreaded impersonal message from the War Department that David had been killed at the Anzio beachhead in May of 1944.

No more dreams, no more big deals, no more struggles and plans to build a giant monument of incorporation that would span the earth, linked by thin and gossamer strands of celluloid. They had come to a final stop for him, just as they had for a thousand others, in the crashing, thundering fire of an early Italian morning.

The dreams had stopped for her, too. The whisper of love in the night, the creaking of the floor beneath the footsteps on the other side of the bed, the excitement and warmth of shared confidences and plans for tomorrow.

For once, Rosa was grateful for her work. It used her mind and taxed her energy and consumed her with the day-to-day responsibilities. In time, the hurt was pushed back into the corner recesses of her mind, to be felt only when she was alone.

Then, bit by bit, the understanding came to her, as it always must to the survivors, that only a part of the dreams had been buried with him. His son was growing and one day, as she saw him running across the green lawn in the front of their home, she heard the birds begin to sing again. She looked up at the blue sky, at the white sun above her head, and knew that once again she was a living, breathing human being with the full, rich blood of life in her body. And the guilt that had been in her, because she had remained while he had gone, disappeared.

It all happened that day after she read Jennie's letter. It was addressed to her in a small, feminine script that she did not recognize. At first, she thought it another solicitation when she saw the imprimatur on the letterhead.

†

Sisters of Mercy
Burlingame, California

October 10, 1944

DEAR ROSA,

It is with some trepidation and yet with the knowledge that you will respect my confidence that I take my pen in hand to write. I do not seek to reopen wounds which by this time have already partly healed but it is only a few days ago that I learned of your loss and wanted to extend to you and little Bernie my sympathy and prayers.

David was a fine man and a genuinely kind human being. All of us who knew him will miss him. I mention him in my prayers each day and I am comforted by the words of Our Lord and Saviour: "I am the resurrection and the life; he who believes in me, even if he die, shall live; and whoever lives and believes in me shall never die."

Sincerely yours in J. C.
SISTER M. THOMAS
(JENNIE DENTON)

It was then, when Rosa went outside to call her son in from his play, that she heard the birds singing. The next weekend, she drove to Burlingame to visit Jennie.

There were tiny white puffballs of clouds in the blue sky as Rosa turned her car into the wide driveway that led to the Mother House. It was a Saturday afternoon and there were many automobiles parked there already. She pulled into an open space some distance from the sprawling building.

She sat in the car and lit a cigarette. She felt a doubt creeping through her. Perhaps she shouldn't have come. Jennie might not want to see her, wouldn't want to be reminded of that world she'd left behind. It was pure impulse that she had followed in driving here and she couldn't blame Jennie if she refused to see her.

She remembered the morning after the engagement party. When Jennie hadn't shown up at the studio, no one had thought very much about it. And David, who been trying to reach Jonas at the plant in Burbank, told her that he couldn't locate him, either.

When the next day and the day after that had passed and there was still no word from Jennie, the studio really began to worry. Jonas had finally been located in Canada at the new factory and David called him there. His voice had been very curt over the telephone as he told David that the last time he'd seen Jennie was when he left her home the night of the party.

David immediately called Rosa and suggested she run out to Jennie's house. When she got there, the Mexican servant came to the door. "Is Miss Denton in?"

"Señorita, she not in."

"Do you know where she is?" Rosa asked. "It's very important that I get in touch with her."

The servant shook her head. "The señorita go away. She not say where."

Deliberately Rosa walked past her into the house. There were packed boxes all along the hallway. On the side of one was stenciled *Bekins, Moving & Storage*. The servant saw the surprise on her face. "The señorita tell me to close the house and go away, too."

Rosa didn't wait until she got home, but called David from the first pay telephone she came to. He said he'd try to speak to Jonas again.

"Did you reach Jonas?" she asked, as soon as he came in the door that evening.

"Yes. He told me to close down *Aphrodite* and have Pierce thrown off the lot. When I said we might wind up with a lawsuit, he told me to tell Dan that if he wanted to start anything, Jonas would spend his last dollar to break him."

"But what about Jennie?"

"If she doesn't show up by the end of the week, Jonas told me to have her put on the suspended list and stop her salary."

"And their engagement?"

"Jonas didn't say, but I guess that's over, too. When I asked him if we should prepare a statement for the press, he told me to tell them nothing and hung up."

"Poor Jennie. I wonder where she is?"

Now Rosa knew. She got out of the car and started to walk slowly toward the Mother House.

Sister M. Thomas sat quietly in her small room, reading her Bible. A soft knock came at the door. She got to her feet, the Bible still in her hand, and opened it. The light from the window in the hall outside her room turned her white novice's veil a soft silver. "Yes, sister?"

"There's a visitor to see you, sister. A Mrs. David Woolf. She's in the visitors' room downstairs."

Sister Thomas hesitated a moment, then spoke. Her voice was calm and quiet. "Thank you, sister. Please tell Mrs. Woolf that I shall be down in a few minutes."

The nun bowed her head and started down the corridor as Sister Thomas closed the door. For a moment, she leaned her back against it, weak and breathless. She had not expected Rosa to come. She drew herself up and crossed the small room to kneel before the crucifix on the bare wall near her bed. She clasped her hands in prayer. It was as if it were only yesterday that she had come here, that she was still the frightened girl who had spent all her life trying to hide from herself her love for God.

She remembered the kind voice of the Mother Superior as she had knelt before her, weeping, her head in the soft material across the Mother Superior's lap. She felt once again the gentle touch of the stroking fingers on her head.

"Do not weep, my child. And do not fear. The path that leads to Our Lord may be most grievous and difficult but Jesus Christ, Our Saviour, refuses none who truly seeks Him."

"But, Reverend Mother, I have sinned."

"Who among us is without sin?" the Reverend Mother said softly. "If you take your sins to Him who takes all sins to Himself to share, and convince Him with your penitence, He will grant you His holy forgiveness and you will be welcome in His house."

She looked up at the Reverend Mother through her tears. "Then, I may stay?"

The Mother Superior smiled down at her. "Of course you may stay, my child."

Rosa rose from the chair as Sister Thomas came into the visitors' room. "Jennie?" she said tentatively. "Sister Thomas, I mean."

"Rosa, how good it is to see you."

Rosa looked at her. The wide-set gray eyes and lovely face belonged to Jennie, but the calm serenity that glowed beneath the novice's white veil came from Sister Thomas. Suddenly, she knew that the face she was looking at was the same face she had once seen on the screen, enlarged a thousand times and filled with the same love as when the Magdalen had stretched forth her hand to touch the hem of her Saviour's gown.

"Jennie!" she said, smiling. "Suddenly, I'm so happy that I just want to hug you."

Sister Thomas held out her arms.

Later, they strolled the quiet paths around the grounds in the afternoon sunlight and when they came to the top of a hill, they paused there, looking down into the green valley below them.

"His beauty is everywhere," Sister Thomas said softly, turning to her friend, "I have found my place in His house."

Rosa looked at her. "How long do you remain in the novitiate?"

"Two years. Until next May."

"And what do you do then?" Rosa questioned.

"If I prove worthy of His grace, I take the black veil and go forth in the path of the Founding Mother, to bring His mercy to all who may need it."

She looked into Rosa's eyes and once again Rosa saw the deep-lying pool of serenity within them. "And I am more fortunate than most," Sister Thomas added humbly. "He has already trained me in His work. My years in the hospital will help me wherever I may be sent, for it is in this area I can best serve."

JONAS – 1945
Book Nine

CHAPTER ONE

Outside the white-hot mid-July sun beat down on the Nevada air strip, but here in the General's office, the overworked air-conditioner whirred and kept the temperature down to an even eighty degrees. I looked at Morrissey, then across the table to the General and his staff.

"That's the story, gentlemen," I said. "The CA-JET X.P. should reach six hundred easier than the British De Havilland-Rolls jet did the five-o-six point five they're bragging about." I smiled at them and got to my feet. "And now, if you'll step outside, gentlemen, I'll show you."

"I have no doubt about that, Mr. Cord," the General said smoothly. "If there'd been any doubts in our minds, you never would have got the contract."

"Then what are we waiting for? Let's go."

"Just a moment, Mr. Cord," the General said quickly. "We can't allow you to demonstrate the jet."

I stared at him. "Why not?"

"You haven't been cleared for jet aircraft," he said. He looked down at a sheet of paper on his desk. "Your medical report indicates a fractional lag in your reflexes. Perfectly normal, of course, considering your age, but you'll understand why we can't let you fly her."

"That's a lot of crap, General. Who the hell do you think flew her down here to deliver her to you?"

"You had a perfect right to—then," the General replied. "It was your plane. But the moment she touched that field outside, according to the contract, she became the property of the Army. And we can't afford the risk of allowing you to take her up."

I slammed my fist into my hand angrily. Rules, nothing but rules. That was the trouble with these damn contracts. Yesterday, I could have flown her up to Alaska and back and they couldn't have stopped me. Or for that matter, even catch me. The CA-JET X.P. was two hundred odd miles an hour faster than any of the conventional aircraft the Army had in the air. Someday, I'd have to take the time to read those contracts.

The General smiled and came around the table toward me. "I know just how you feel, Mr. Cord," he said. "When the medics told me I was too old for combat flying and put me behind a desk, I wasn't any older than you are right now. And I didn't like it any more than you do. Nobody likes being told he is growing older."

What the hell was he talking about? I was only forty-one. That isn't old. I could still fly rings around most of those damp-eared kids walking around on the field outside with gold and silver bars and oak leaves on their shoulders. I looked at the General.

He must have read the surprise in my eyes, for he smiled again. "That was only a year ago. I'm forty-three now." He offered me a cigarette and I took it silently. "Lieutenant Colonel Shaw will take her up. He's on the field right now, waiting for us."

Again, he read the question in my eyes. "Don't worry about it," he said quickly. "Shaw's completely familiar with the plane. He spent the last three weeks at your plant in Burbank checking her out."

I glanced at Morrissey but he was carefully looking somewhere else at the time. He'd been in on it, too. I'd make him sweat for that one. I turned back to the General. "O.K., General. Let's go outside and watch that baby fly."

Baby was the right word and not only for the plane. Lieutenant Colonel Shaw couldn't have been more than twenty years old. I watched him take her up but somehow I couldn't stand there squinting up at the sky, watching him put her through her paces. It was like going to a lot of trouble to set yourself up with a virgin and then when you had everything warmed up and ready, you opened the bedroom door and found another guy copping the cherry right under your nose.

"Is there anywhere around here I could get a cup of coffee?"

"There's a commissary down near the main gate," one of the soldiers said.

"Thanks."

"You're welcome," he said automatically, never taking his eyes from the plane in the sky, while I walked away.

The commissary wasn't air-conditioned but they kept it dark and it wasn't too bad, even if the ice cubes in the iced coffee had melted before I got the glass back to my seat. I stared morosely out of the window in front of my table. Too young or too old. That was the story of my life. I was fourteen when the last one ended, in 1918, and almost over the age limit when we got into this one. Some people never had any luck. I always thought that war came to every generation but I was neither one nor the other. I had the bad fortune to be born in between.

A medium-size Army bus pulled up in front of the commissary. Men started to pile out and I watched them because there was nothing else to look at. They weren't soldiers; they were civilians, and not young ones, either. Most of them carried their jacket over their arm and a brief case in their free hand and there were some with gray in their hair and many with no hair at all. One thing about them caught my eye. None of them were smiling, not even when they spoke to one another in the small groups they immediately formed on the sidewalk in front of the bus.

Why should they smile, I asked myself bitterly. They had nothing to smile about. They were all dodoes like me. I took out a cigarette and struck a match. The breeze from the circulating fan blew it out. I struck another, turning away from the fan and shielding the cigarette in my cupped hands.

"Herr Cord! This is indeed a surprise! What are you doing here?"

I looked up at Herr Strassmer. "I just delivered a new plane," I said, holding out my hand. "But what are you doing out here? I thought you were in New York."

He shook my hand in that peculiarly European way of his. The smile left his eyes. "We, too, made a delivery. And now we go back."

"You were with that group outside?"

He nodded. He looked out through the window at them and a troubled look came into his eyes. "Yes," he said slowly. "We all came together in one plane but we are going back on separate flights. Three years we worked together but now the job is finished. Soon I go back to California."

"I hope so," I laughed. "We sure could use you in the plant but I'm afraid it'll be some time yet. The war in Europe may be over but if Tarawa and Okinawa are any indication, we're good for at least six months to a year before Japan quits."

He didn't answer.

I looked up and suddenly I remembered. These Europeans were very touchy about manners. "Excuse me, Herr Strassmer," I said quickly. "Won't you join me in some coffee?"

"I have not the time." There was a curiously hesitant look in his eyes. "Do you have an office here as you do everywhere else?"

"Sure," I said, looking up at him. I'd passed the door marked *Men* on my way over. "It's in the back of this building."

"I will meet you there in five minutes," he said and hurried out.

Through the window, I watched him join one of the groups and begin to talk with them. I wondered if the old boy was going crackers. You couldn't tell, but maybe he had been working too hard and thought he was back in Nazi Germany. There certainly wasn't any reason for him to be so secretive about being seen talking to me. After all, we were on the same side.

I ground my cigarette into an ash tray and sauntered out. He never even glanced up as I walked past his group on my way to the john. He came into the room a moment after I had got there. His eyes darted nervously toward the booths. "Are we alone?"

"I think so," I said, looking at him. I wondered what you did to get a doctor around here if there were any signs of his cracking up.

He walked over to the booths, opened the doors and looked. Satisfied, he turned back to me. His face was tense and pale and there were small beads of perspiration across his forehead. I thought I'd begun to recognize the symptoms. Too much of this Nevada sun is murder if you're not used to it. His first words convinced me I was right.

"Herr Cord," he whispered hoarsely. "The war will not be over in six months."

"Of course not," I said soothingly. From what I had heard, the first thing to do was agree with them, try to calm them down. I wished I could remember the second thing. I turned to the sink. "Here, let me get you a glass of—"

"It will be over next month!"

What I thought must have been written on my face, for my mouth hung open in surprise. "No, I'm not crazy, Herr Cord," Strassmer said quickly. "To no one else but you would I say this. It is the only way I can repay you for saving my life. I know how important this could be to your business."

"But—but how—"

"I cannot tell you more," he interrupted. "Just believe me. By next month, Japan will be *verfallen!*" He turned and almost ran out the door.

I stared after him for a moment, then went over to the sink and washed my face in cold water. I felt I must be even crazier than he was, because I was beginning to believe him. But why? It just didn't make any sense. Sure, we were pushing the Nips back, but they still held Malaya, Hong Kong and the Dutch East Indies, and with their kamikaze philosophy, it would take a miracle to end the war in a month.

I was still thinking about it when Morrissey and I got on the train. "You know who I ran into back there?" I asked. I didn't give him a chance to answer. "Otto Strassmer."

There seemed to be a kind of relief in his smile. I guess he'd been expecting to catch hell for not telling me about that Air Corps test pilot. "He's a nice little guy," Morrissey said. "How is he?"

"Seemed all right to me," I said. "He was on his way back to New York." I looked out the window at the flat Nevada desert. "By the way, did you ever hear exactly what it was he was working on?"

"Not exactly."

I looked at him. "What was it you did hear?"

"I didn't hear it from him," Morrissey said. "I got it from a friend of mine down at the Engineers' Club, who worked on it for a little while. But he didn't know very much about it, either. All he knew was that it was called the Manhattan Project and that it had something to do with Professor Einstein."

I could feel my brows knit in puzzlement. "What could Strassmer do for a man like Einstein?"

He smiled again. "After all, Strassmer did invent a plastic beer can that was stronger than metal."

"So?" I asked.

"So maybe the Professor got Otto to invent a plastic container to store his atoms in," Morrissey said, laughing.

I felt a wild excitement racing inside me. A container for atoms, energy in a bottle, ready to explode when you popped the cork. The little man hadn't been crazy. He knew what he was talking about. I'd been the crazy one.

It would take a miracle, I'd thought. Well, Strassmer and his friends had come into the desert and made one and now they were going home, their job done. What it was or how they did it I couldn't guess and didn't care.

But deep inside me, I was sure that it had happened.

The miracle that would end the war.

CHAPTER TWO

I GOT OFF THE TRAIN AT RENO, WHILE MORRISSEY WENT ON TO LOS ANGE-les. There was no time to call Robair at the ranch, so I took a taxi to the factory. We barreled through the steel-wire gate, under the big sign that read **CORD EXPLOSIVES**, now more than a mile from the main plant.

The factory had expanded tremendously since the war. For that matter, so had all our companies. It seemed that no matter what we did, there never was enough space.

I got out and paid the cabby and as he pulled away, I looked up at the familiar old building. It was worn now, and looked dingy and obsolete compared with the new additions, but its roof was gleaming white and shining in the sun. Somehow, I could never bring myself to move out of it when the other executives had moved their offices into the new administration building. I dropped my cigarette on the walk and ground it into dust beneath my heel, then went into the building.

The smell was the same as it always was and the whispers that rose from the lips of the men and women working there were the same as I always heard when I passed by *"El hijo."* The son. It had been twenty years and most of them hadn't even been there when my father died and still they called me that. Even the young ones, some of them less than half my age.

The office was the same, too. The heavy, oversized desk and leather-covered furniture now showed the cracks and wear of time. There was no secretary in the outer office and I was not surprised. There was no reason for one to be there. They hadn't expected me.

I walked around behind the desk and pressed the switch down on the squawk box that put me right through to McAllister's office in the new building, a quarter of a mile away. The surprise echoed in his voice as it came through the box. "Jonas! Where did you come from?"

"The Air Corps," I said. "We just delivered the CA-JET X.P."

"Good. Did they like it?"

"I guess they did," I answered. "They wouldn't trust me to take it up." I leaned over and opened the door of the cabinet below the telephone table, taking out the bottle of bourbon that was there. I put the bottle on the desk in front of me. "How do we stand on war-contract cancellations in case the war ends tomorrow?"

"For the explosive company?" Mac asked.

"For all the companies," I said. I knew he kept copies of every contract we ever made down here because he considered this his home office.

"It'll take a little time. I'll put someone on it right away."

"Like about an hour?"

He hesitated. When he spoke, a curious note came into his voice. "All right, if it's that important."

"It's that important."

"Do you know something?"

"No," I said truthfully. I really didn't know. I was only guessing. "I just want it."

There was silence for a moment, then he spoke again. "I just got the blueprints from Engineering on converting the radar and small-parts division of Aircraft to the proposed electronics company. Shall I bring them over?"

"Do that," I said, flipping up the switch. Taking a glass from the tray next to the Thermos jug, I filled it half full with bourbon. I looked across the room to the wall where the portrait of my father looked down on me. I held the glass up to him.

"It's been a long time, Pop," I said and poured the whisky down my throat.

I took my hands from the blueprints on the desk and snapped and rolled them up tight, like a coil spring. I looked at McAllister. "They look all right to me, Mac."

He nodded. "I'll mark them approved and shoot them on to Purchasing to have them requisition the materials on standby orders, to be delivered when the war ends." He looked at the bottle of bourbon on the desk. "You're not very hospitable. How about a drink?"

I looked at him in surprise. Mac wasn't much for drinking. Especially during working hours. I pushed the bottle and a glass toward him. "Help yourself."

He poured a small shot and swallowed it neat. He cleared his throat. I looked at him. "There's one other postwar plan I wanted to talk to you about," he said awkwardly.

"Go ahead."

"Myself," he said hesitantly. "I'm not a young man any more. I want to retire."

"Retire?" I couldn't believe my ears. "What for? What in hell would you do?"

Mac flushed embarrassedly. "I've worked pretty hard all my life," he said. "I've got two sons and a daughter and five grandchildren, three of whom I've never seen. The wife and I would like to spend a little time with them, get to know them before it's too late."

I laughed. "You sound like you expect to kick off any minute. You're a young man yet."

"I'm sixty-three. I've been with you twenty years."

I stared at him. Twenty years. Where had they gone? The Army doctors had been right. I wasn't a kid any more, either. "We'll miss you around here," I said sincerely. "I don't know how well manage without you." I meant it, too. Mac was the one man I felt I could always depend on, whenever I had need for him.

"You'll manage all right. We've got over forty attorneys working for us now and each is a specialist in his own field. You're not just one man any more, you're a big company. You have to have a big legal machine to take care of you."

"So what?" I said. "You can't call up a machine in the middle of the night when you're in trouble."

"This machine you can. It's equipped for all emergencies."

"But what will you do? You can't tell me you'll be happy just lying around playing grandpa. You'll have to have something to occupy your mind."

"I've thought about that," he said, a serious look coming over his face. "I've been playing around so long with corporate and tax laws that I've almost forgotten about the most important part of all. The laws that have to do with human beings." He reached for the bottle again and poured himself another small drink. It wasn't easy for him to sit there and tell me what he was thinking.

"I thought I'd hang my shingle outside my house in some small town. Just putter around with whatever happened to come in the door. I'm tired of always talking in terms of millions of dollars. For once, I'd like to help some poor bastard who really needs it."

I stared at him. Work with a man for twenty years and still you don't know him. This was a side to McAllister that I'd never even suspected existed.

"Of course, we'll abrogate all of the contracts and agreements between us," he said.

I looked at him. I knew he didn't need the money. But then, neither did I. "Why in hell should we? Just show up at the board of directors' meeting every few months so at least I can see you once in a while."

"Then you—you agree?"

I nodded. "Sure, let's give it a spin when the war is over."

The sheets of white paper grew into a stack as he skimmed through the summary of each of the contracts. At last, Mac was finished and he looked up at me. "We have ample protective-cancellation clauses in all the contracts except one," he said. "That one is based on delivery before the end of the war."

"Which one is that?"

"That flying boat we're building for the Navy in San Diego."

I knew what he was talking about. *The Centurion*. It was to be the biggest airplane ever built, designed to carry a full company of one hundred and fifty men, in addition to the twelve-man crew, two light amphibious tanks and enough mortar, light artillery, weapons, ammunition and supplies for an entire company. It had been my idea that a plane like that would prove useful in landing raiding parties behind the lines out in the small Pacific islands.

"How come we made a contract like that?"

"You wanted it," he said. "Remember?"

I remembered. The Navy had been skeptical that the big plane could even get into the air, so I'd pressured them into making a deal predicated on a fully tested plane before the war ended. That was over seven months ago.

Almost immediately, we'd run into trouble. Stress tests proved that conventional metals would make the plane too heavy for the engines to lift into the air. We lost two months there, until the engineers came up with a Fiberglas compound that was less than one tenth the weight of metal and four times as strong. Then we had to construct special machinery to work the new material. I even brought Amos Winthrop down from Canada to sit in on the project. The old bastard had done a fantastic job up there and had a way of bulling a job through when no one else was able to.

The old leopard hadn't changed any of his spots, either. He had me by the shorts and he knew it. He held me up for a vice-presidency in Cord Aircraft before he'd come down.

"How much are we in for up to now?" I asked.

Mac looked down at the sheet. "Sixteen million, eight hundred seventy-six thousand, five hundred ninety-four dollars and thirty-one cents, as of June thirtieth."

"We're in trouble," I said, reaching for the telephone. The operator came on. "Get me Amos Winthrop in San Diego. And while I'm waiting to talk to him, call Mr. Dalton at the Inter-Continental Airlines office in Los Angeles and ask him to send down a special charter for me."

"What's the trouble?" Mac asked, watching me.

"Seventeen million dollars. We're going to blow it if we don't get that plane into the air right away."

Then Amos came on the phone. "How soon do you expect to get *The Centurion* into the sky?" I asked.

"We're coming along pretty good now. Just the finishing touches. I figure we ought to be able to lift her sometime in September or early October."

"What's missing?"

"The usual stuff. Mountings, fittings, polishing, tightening. You know."

I knew. The small but important part that took longer than anything else. But nothing really essential, nothing that would keep the plane from flying. "Get her ready," I said. "I'm taking her up tomorrow."

"Are you crazy? We've never even had gasoline in her tanks."

"Then fill her up."

"But the hull hasn't been water-tested yet," he shouted. "How do you know she won't go right to the bottom of San Diego Bay when you send her down the runway?"

"Then test it. You've got twenty-four hours to make sure she floats. I'll be up there tonight, if you need a hand."

This was no cost-plus, money-guaranteed project, where the government picked up the tab, win, lose or draw. This was my money and I didn't like the idea of losing it.

For seventeen million dollars, *The Centurion* would fly if I had to lift her out of the water with my bare hands.

CHAPTER THREE

I HAD ROBAIR TAKE ME OUT TO THE RANCH, WHERE I TOOK A HOT SHOWER and changed my clothes before I got on the plane to San Diego. I was just leaving the house when the telephone rang.

"It's for you, Mr. Jonas," Robair said. "Mr. McAllister."

I took the phone from his hand. "Yes, Mac?"

"Sorry to bother you, Jonas, but this is important."

"Shoot."

"Bonner just called from the studio," he said. "He's leaving at the end of the month to go over to Paramount. He's got a deal with them to make nothing but blockbusters."

"Offer him more money."

"I did. He doesn't want it. He wants out."

"What does his contract say?"

"It's over the end of this month," he said. "We can't hold him if he wants to go."

"To hell with him, then. If he wants to go, let him."

"We're in a hole," Mac said seriously. "We'll have to find someone to run the studio. You can't operate a motion-picture company without someone to make pictures."

That was nothing I didn't know. It was too bad that David Woolf wasn't coming back. I could depend on him. He felt the same way about movies that I did about airplanes. But he'd caught it at Anzio.

"I want to make San Diego tonight," I said. "Let me think about it and we'll kick it around in your office in L.A. the day after tomorrow." I had bigger worries on my mind just now. One *Centurion* cost almost as much as a whole year's production at the studio.

We landed at the San Diego Airport about one o'clock in the morning. I took a taxi right from there to the little shipyard we had rented near the Naval base. I could see the lights blazing from it ten blocks away. I smiled to myself. Leave it to Amos to get things done. He had a night crew working like mad, even if he had to break the blackout regulations to get it done.

I walked around the big old boat shed that we were using for a hangar just in time to hear someone yell, "Clear the runway!"

And then *The Centurion* came out of the hangar, tail first, looking for all the world like an ugly giant condor flying backward. Like a greased pig, it shot down the runway toward the water. A great roar came from the hangar and I was almost knocked over by a gang of men, who came running out after the plane. Before I knew it, they'd passed me and were down at the water's edge. I saw Amos in the crowd and he was yelling as much as any of them.

There was a great splash as *The Centurion* hit the water, a moment's groaning silence as the tail dipped backward, almost covering the three big rudders, and then a triumphant yell as she straightened herself out and floated easily on the bay. She began to turn, drifting away from the dock, and I heard the whir of the big winches as they spun the tie lines, drawing her back in.

The men were still yelling when I got to Amos. "What the hell do you think you're doing?" I shouted, trying to make myself heard over the noise.

"What you told me to do—water-test her."

"You damn fool! You might've sunk her. Why didn't you get a pressure tank?"

"There wasn't time. The earliest I could've got one was three days. You said you were taking her up tomorrow."

The winches had hauled the plane partly back on the runway, with her prow out of the water. "Wait here a minute," Amos said, "I gotta get the men to work. They're all on triple time."

He went down the dock to where a workman had already placed a ladder against the side of the giant plane. Scrambling up like a man half his age, Amos opened the door just behind the cabin and disappeared into the plane. A moment later, I heard the whir of a motor from somewhere inside her and the giant boarding flap came down, opening a gaping maw in her prow that was big enough to drive a truck through. Amos appeared at the top of the ramp inside the plane. "O.K., men. You know what we gotta do. Shake the lead out. We ain't paying triple time for conversation."

He came back up the dock toward me and we walked back into his office. There was a bottle of whisky on his desk. He took two paper cups from the wall container and began to pour whisky into them. "You mean it about taking her up tomorrow?"

I nodded.

He shook his head. "I wouldn't," he said. "Just because she floats don't mean she'll fly. There's still too many things we're not sure of. Even if she does get up, there's no guarantee she'll stay up. She might even fall apart in the sky."

"That'll be rough," I said. "But, I'm taking her up, anyway."

He shrugged his shoulders. "You're the boss," he said, handing me one of the paper cups. He raised his to his lips. "Here's luck."

By two o'clock the next afternoon, we still weren't ready. The number-two starboard engine spit oil like a gusher every time we started it up and we couldn't find the leak. I stood on the dock, staring up at her. "We'll have to pull her off," Amos said, "and get her up to the shop."

I looked at him. "How long will that take?"

"Two, three hours. If we're lucky and find what's wrong right away. Maybe we better put off taking her up until tomorrow."

I looked at my watch. "What for? We'll still have three and a half hours of daylight at five o'clock." I started back toward his office. "I'm going back to your office and grab a snooze on the couch. Call me as soon as she's ready."

But I might as well have tried to sleep in a boiler factory, for all the shouting and cursing and hammering and riveting. Then the telephone rang and I got up to answer it. "Hello, Dad?" It was Monica's voice.

"No, this is Jonas. I'll get him for you."

"Thanks."

Laying the telephone down on the desk, I went to the door and called Amos. I went back to the couch and stretched out as he picked up the phone. He shot a peculiar look at me when he heard her voice. "Yes, I'm a little busy." He was silent for a little while, listening to her. When he spoke again, he was smiling. "That's wonderful. When are you leaving? . . . Then I'll fly to New York when this job is finished. We'll have a celebration. Give my love to Jo-Ann."

He put down the telephone and came over to me. "That was Monica," he said, looking down at me.

"I know."

"She's leaving for New York this afternoon. S. J. Hardin just made her managing editor of *Style* and wants her back there right away."

"That's nice," I said.

"She's taking Jo-Ann back with her. You haven't seen the kid for a long time now, have you?"

"Not since the time you walked the two of them out of my apartment at the Drake in Chicago, five years ago."

"You oughta see her. The kid's turning into a real beauty."

I stared up at him. Now I'd seen everything—Amos Winthrop playing proud grandpa. "Man, you've really changed, haven't you?"

"Sooner or later, a man has to wise up," Amos said, flushing embarrassedly. "You find out you did a lot of fool things to hurt the people you love and if you're not a prick altogether, you try to make up for them."

"I heard about that, too," I said sarcastically. I wasn't in the mood for any lectures from the old bastard, no matter how much he'd reformed. "They tell me that generally happens when you can't get it up any more."

A trace of the old Amos came into his face. He was angry, I could see it. "I got a mind to tell you a couple of things."

"Like what, Amos?"

"Ready to remount the engine, Mr. Winthrop," a man called from the doorway.

"I'll be there in a minute." Amos turned back to me. "You remind me of this after we get back from the test flight."

I grinned, watching him walk out the door. At least, he hadn't gone so holy-holy that I couldn't get his goat. I sat up and started looking under the couch for my shoes.

When I got outside, the engine was turning over, sweet and smooth. "She seems O.K. to me now," Amos said, turning to me.

I looked at my watch. It was four thirty. "Then, let's go. What're we waiting for?"

He put a hand on my arm. "Sure I can't make you change your mind?"

I shook my head. Seventeen million dollars was a lot of argument. He raised his hands to his mouth, making a megaphone of them. "Everybody off the ship except the flight crew."

Almost immediately, there was a silence in the yard as the engine shut off. A few minutes later, the last of them came down the boarding flap. A man stuck his head out of the small window in the pilot's cabin. "Everybody off except the crew, Mr. Winthrop."

Amos and I walked up the flap into the plane, then up the small ladder from the cargo deck to the passenger cabin and on forward into the flight cabin. Three young men were there. They looked at me curiously. They were still wearing the hard hats from the shipyard.

"This is your crew, Mr. Cord," Amos said formally. "On the right, Joe Cates, radioman. In the middle, Steve Jablonski, flight engineer starboard engines, one, three and five. On the left, Barry Gold, flight engineer port engines, two, four and six. You don't have to worry about them. They're all Navy veterans and know their work."

We shook hands all around and I turned back to Amos. "Where's the copilot and navigator?"

"Right here," Amos said.

"Where?"

"Me."

"What the hell—"

He grinned at me. "You got anybody knows this baby better? Besides, I been sleeping every night with her for more than half a year. Who's got a better right to get a piece of her first ride?"

I stared at him for a moment. Then I gave in. I knew exactly how he felt. I felt the same way myself yesterday, when they wouldn't let me fly the jet.

I climbed up into the pilot's seat. "Take your stations, men."

"Aye, aye, sir."

I grinned to myself. They were Navy men, all right. I picked up the check list on the clip board. "Boarding ramp up," I said, reading.

A motor began to whine beneath me. A moment later, a red light flashed on the panel in front of me and the motor cut off. "Boarding ramp up, sir."

"Start engines one and two," I said, reaching forward and flicking down the switches that would let the flight engineers turn them over. The big engines coughed and belched black smoke. The propellers began to turn sluggishly, then the engines caught and the propellers settled into a smooth whine.

"Starboard engine one turning over, sir."

"Port engine two turning over, sir."

The next one on the check list was a new one for me. I smiled to myself. This wasn't an airplane, it was really a Navy ship with wings. "Cast off," I said.

From the seat to my right, Amos reached up and tripped the lever that released the tow lines. Another red light flashed on the panel before me and I could feel *The Centurion* slide back into the water. There was a slight backward dip as she settled in with a slight rocking motion. The faint sound of water slapping against her hull came up from beneath us. I leaned forward and turned the wheel. Slowly the big plane came about and started to move out toward the open bay. I looked over at Amos. He grinned at me.

I grinned back. So far, so good. At least we were seaborne.

CHAPTER FOUR

A WAVE BROKE ACROSS THE PROW OF THE PLANE, THROWING SALT SPRAY UP on the window in front of me, as I came to the last item on the check list. There had been almost a hundred of them and it seemed like hours since we'd started. I looked down at my watch. It was only sixteen minutes since we'd left the dock. I looked out the windows. The six big engines were turning over smoothly, the propellers flashing with sun and spray. I felt a touch on my shoulder and looked back.

The radioman stood behind me, an inflatable Mae West in one hand and a parachute pack hanging from the other. "Emergency dress, sir."

I looked at him. He was already wearing his; so were the other two men. "Put it behind my seat."

I looked across at Amos. He already had the vest on and was tightening the cross belt of the parachute. He sank back into his seat with an uncomfortable grunt. He looked at me. "You ought to put it on."

"I've got a superstition about 'em," I said. "If you don't wear 'em, you'll never need 'em." He didn't answer, shrugging his shoulders as the radioman went back to his seat and fastened his seat belt. I looked around the cabin. "Secure in flight stations?"

They all answered at once. "Aye, aye, sir!"

I reached forward and flipped the switch on the panel and all the lights turned from red to green. From now on, they'd only go back to red if we were in trouble. I turned the plane toward the open sea. "O.K., men. Here we go!"

I opened the throttle slowly. The big plane lurched, its prow digging into the waves then slowly lifting as the six propellers started to chew up the air. Now we started to ride high, like a speedboat in the summer races. I looked at the panel. The air-speed indicator stood at ninety.

Amos' voice came over to me. "Calculated lift velocity, this flight, one ten."

I nodded without looking at him and kept opening the throttle. The needle went to one hundred, then one ten. The waves were beating against the bottom of the hull like a riveting hammer. I brought the needle up to one fifteen, then I started to ease back on the stick.

For a moment, nothing happened and I increased our speed to one twenty. Suddenly, *The Centurion* seemed to tremble, then jump from the water. Free of the restraining drag, she seemed to leap into the air. The needle jumped to one sixty and the controls moved easily in my hands. I looked out the window. The water was two hundred feet beneath us. We were airborne.

"Hot damn!" one of the men behind me muttered.

Amos squirmed around in his seat. "O.K., fellers," he said, sticking out his hand. "Pay me!" He looked over at me and grinned. "Each of these guys bet me a buck we'd never get off the water."

I flashed a grin at him and kept the ship in a slow climb until we reached six thousand feet. Then I turned her west and aimed her right at the setting sun.

"She handles like a baby carriage." Amos chortled gleefully from his seat.

I looked up at him from behind the radioman, where I had been standing as he explained the new automatic signaling recorder. All you had to do was give your message once, then turn on the automatic and the wire recorder would repeat it over and over again until the power gave out.

The sun had turned Amos' white hair back to the flaming red of his youth. I looked down at my watch. It was six fifteen and we were about two hundred miles out over the Pacific. "Better turn her around and take her back, Amos," I said. "I don't want it to be dark the first time we put her down."

"The term in the Navy, captain, is 'Put her about'." The radioman grinned at me.

"O.K., sailor," I said. I turned to Amos. "Put her about."

"Aye, aye, sir."

We went into a gentle banking turn as I bent over the radioman's shoulder again. Suddenly, the plane lurched and I almost fell over him. I grabbed at his shoulder as the starboard engineer yelled, "Number five's gone bad again."

I pushed myself toward my seat as I looked out the window. The engine was shooting oil like a geyser. "Kill it!" I shouted, strapping myself into my seat.

The cords on Amos' neck stood out like steel wire as he fought the wheel on the suddenly bucking plane. I grabbed at my wheel and together we held her steady. Slowly she eased off in our grip.

"Number five dead, sir," the engineer called.

I glanced out at it. The propeller turned slowly with the wind force but the oil had stopped pouring from the engine. I looked at Amos. His face was white and perspiration was dripping from it, but he managed a smile. "We can make it back on five engines without any trouble."

"Yeah." We could make it back on three engines, according to the figures. But I wouldn't like to try it. I looked at the panel. The red light was on for the number-five engine. While I was watching, a red light began to flicker on and off at number four. "What the hell?"

It began to sputter and cough even as I turned to look at it. "Check number four!" I yelled. I turned back to the panel. The red light was on for the number-four fuel line.

"Number-four fuel line clogged!"

"Blow it out with the vacuum!"

"Aye, aye, sir!" I heard the click as he turned on the vacuum pump. Another red light jumped on in front of me. "Vacuum pump out of commission, sir!"

"Kill number four!" I said. There was no percentage in leaving the line open in the hopes that it would clear itself. Clogged fuel lines have a tendency to turn into fires. And we still had four engines left.

"Number four dead, sir!"

I heaved a sigh of relief after ten minutes had gone by and there was nothing new to worry about. "I think we'll be O.K. now," I said.

I should have kept my big fat mouth shut. No sooner had I spoken than the number-one engine started to choke and sputter and the instrument panel in front of me began to light up like a Christmas tree. The number-six engine began to choke.

"Main fuel pump out!"

I threw a glance at the altimeter. We were at five thousand and dropping. "Radio emergency and prepare to abandon ship!" I shouted.

I heard the radioman's voice. "Mayday! Mayday! Cord Aircraft Experimental. Going down Pacific. Position approx one two five miles due west San Diego. I repeat, position approx one two five miles due west San Diego. Mayday! Mayday!"

I heard a loud click and the message began over again. I felt a hand on my shoulder. I looked around quickly. It was the radioman. There was a faint surprise in the back of my mind until I remembered the recorder was now broadcasting the call for help. "We'll stay if you want us, sir," he said tensely.

"This isn't for God and country, sailor! This is for money. Get goin'!"

I looked over at Amos, who was still in his seat. "You, too, Amos!"

He didn't answer. Just pulled off his safety belt and got out of his seat. I heard the cabin door behind me open as they went through to the emergency door in the passenger compartment.

The altimeter read thirty-eight hundred and I killed the one and six engines. Maybe I could set her down on the water if the two remaining engines could hold out on the fuel that would be diverted from the others. We were at thirty-four hundred when the red light for the emergency door flashed on as it opened. I cast a quick look back out the window. Three parachutes opened, one after the other, in rapid succession. I looked at the board. Twenty-eight hundred.

I heard a noise behind me and looked around. It was Amos, getting back into his seat. "I told you to get out!" I yelled.

He reached for the wheel. "The kids are off and safe. I figure between the two of us, we got a chance to put her down on top of the water."

"Suppose we don't?" I yelled angrily.

"We won't be missing much. We ain't got as much time to lose as they have. Besides, this baby cost a lot of dough!"

"So what?" I yelled. "It's not your money!"

There was a curiously disapproving look on his face. "Money isn't the only thing put into this plane. I built her!"

We were at nine hundred feet when number three began to conk out. We threw our weight against the wheel to compensate for the starboard drag. At two hundred feet, the number-three engine went out and we heeled over to the starboard. "Cut the engines!" Amos yelled. "We're going to crash!"

I flipped the switch just as the starboard wing bit into the water. It snapped off clean as a matchstick and the plane slammed into the water like a pile driver. I felt the seat belt tear into my guts until I almost screamed with the pressure, then suddenly it eased off. My eyes cleared and I looked out. We were drifting on top of the water uneasily, one wing pointing to the sky. Water was already trickling into the cabin under our feet.

"Let's get the hell out of here," Amos yelled, moving toward the cabin door, which had snapped shut. He turned the knob and pushed. Then he threw himself against it. The door didn't move. "It's jammed!" he yelled, turning to me.

I stared at him and then jumped for the pilot's emergency hatch over our heads. I pulled the hatch lock with one hand and pushed at the hatch with the other. Nothing happened. I looked up and saw why. The frame had buckled, locking it in. Nothing short of dynamite would open it.

Amos didn't wait for me to tell him. He pulled a wrench from the emergency tool kit and smashed at the glass until there was only a jagged frame left in the big port. He dropped the wrench, picked up the Mae West and threw it at me. I slipped into it quickly, making sure the automatic valve was set so it would work the minute I hit the water.

"O.K.," he said. "Out you go!"

I grinned at him. "Traditions of the sea, Amos. Captain's last off the ship. After you, Alphonse."

"You crazy, man?" he shouted. "I couldn't get out that port if they cut me in half."

"You ain't that big," I said. "We're going to give it a try."

Suddenly, he smiled. I should have known better than to trust Amos when he smiled like that. That peculiarly wolfish smile came over him only when he was going to do you dirty. "All right, Gaston. You're the captain."

"That's better," I said, bracing myself and making a sling step with my hands to boost him up to the port. "I knew you'd learn someday who's boss."

But he never did. And I never even saw what he hit me with. I sailed into Dream Street with a full load on. I was out but I wasn't all the way out. I knew what was going on but there was nothing I could do about it. My arms and legs and head, even my body—they all belonged to someone else.

I felt Amos push me toward the port, then there was a burning sensation, like a cat raking her claws across your face. But I was through the narrow port and falling. Falling about a thousand miles and a thousand hours and I was still looking for the rip cord on my parachute when I crashed in a heap on the wing.

I pulled myself to my feet and tried to climb back the cabin wall to the port. "Come on out of there, you no-good, dirty son of a bitch!" I yelled. I was crying. "Come on outa there and I'll kill you!"

Then the plane lurched and a broken piece of something came flying up from the wing and hit me in the side, knocking me clear out into the water. I heard the soft hiss of compressed air as the Mae West began to wrap her legs around me. I put my head down on those big soft pillows she had and went to sleep.

CHAPTER FIVE

I N NEVADA, WHERE I WAS BORN AND RAISED, THERE IS MOSTLY SAND AND rocks and a few small mountains. But there are no oceans. There are streams and lakes, and swimming pools at every country club and hotel, but they're all filled with fresh, sweet water that bubbles in your mouth like wine, if you should happen to drink it instead of bathe in it.

I've been in a couple of oceans in my time. In the Atlantic, off Miami Beach and Atlantic City, in the Pacific, off Malibu, and in the blue waters of the Mediterranean, off the Riviera. I've even been in the warm waters of the Gulf Stream, off the white, sandy beach of Bermuda, chasing a naked girl whose only ambition was to do it like a fish. I never did get to find out the secret of how the porpoises made it, because somehow, in the salt water, everything eluded me. I never did like salt water. It clings too heavily to your skin, burns your nose, irritates your eyes. And if you happen to get a mouthful, it tastes like yesterday's leftover mouthwash.

So what was I doing here?

Hot damn, little man, all the stars are out and laughing at you. This'll teach you some respect for the oceans. You don't like salt water, eh? Well, how do you like a million, billion, trillion gallons of it? A gazillion gallons?

"Aah, the hell with you," I said and went back to sleep.

I came trotting around the corner of the bunkhouse as fast as my eight-year-old legs could carry me, dragging the heavy cartridge belt and holstered gun in the sand behind me.

I heard my father's voice. "Hey, boy! What have you got there?"

I turned to face him, trying to hide the belt and gun behind me. "Nothin'," I said, not looking up at him.

"Nothing?" my father repeated after me. "Then, let me see."

He reached around behind me and tugged the belt out of my grip. As he raised it, the gun and a folded piece of paper fell from the holster. He bent down and picked them up. "Where'd you get this?"

"From the wall in the bunkhouse near Nevada's bed," I said. "I had to climb up."

My father put the gun back in the holster. It was a black gun, a smooth, black gun with the initials M. S. on its black butt. Even I was old enough to know that somebody had made a mistake on Nevada's initials.

My father started to put the folded piece of paper back into the holster but he dropped it and it fluttered open. I could see it was a picture of Nevada, with some numbers above it and printing below. My father stared at it for a moment, then refolded the paper and shoved it into the holster.

"You put this back where you got it," he said angrily. I could tell he was mad. "Don't you ever let me catch you taking what doesn't belong to you again or I'll whomp you good."

"Ain't no need to whomp 'im, Mr. Cord." Nevada's voice came from behind us. "It's my fault for leavin' it out where the boy could get to it." We turned around. He was standing there, his Indian face dark and expressionless, holding out his hand. "If you'll jus' give it to me, I'll put it back."

Silently my father handed him the gun and they stood there looking at each other. Neither of them spoke a word. I stared up at them, bewildered. Both seemed to be searching each other's eyes. At last, Nevada spoke. "I'll draw my time if you want, Mr. Cord."

I knew what that meant. Nevada was going away. Immediately, I set up a howl. "No," I screamed. "I won't do it again. I promise."

My father looked down at me for a moment, then back at Nevada. A faint smile came into his eyes. "Children and animals, they really know what they want, what's best for them."

"They do say that."

"You better put that away where nobody'll ever find it."

The faint smile was in Nevada's eyes now. "Yes, Mr. Cord. I sure will.'"

My father looked down at me and his smile vanished. "You hear me, boy? Touch what isn't yours and you'll get whomped good."

"Yes, Father," I answered, loud and strong. "I hear you."

I got a mouthful of salt water and I coughed and choked and sputtered and spit it out. I opened my eyes. The stars were still blinking at me but over in the east, the sky was starting to turn pale. I thought I heard the sound of a motor in the distance but it was probably only an echo ringing in my ears.

There was a pain in my side and down my leg, like I'd gone to sleep on it. When I moved, it shot up to my head and made me dizzy. The stars began to spin around and I got tired just watching them, so I went back to sleep.

The sun on the desert is big and strong and rides the sky so close to your head that sometimes you feel like if you reached up to touch it, you'd burn your fingers. And when it's hot like that, you pick your way carefully around the rocks, because under them, in the shade, sleeping away the heat of the day, are the rattlers, coiled and sluggish, with the unhappy heat in their chilled blood. They're quick to anger, quick to attack, with their vicious spittle, if by accident you threaten their peace. People are like that, too.

Each of us has his own particular secret rock, under which we hide, and woe to you if you should happen to stumble across it. Because then we're like the rattlers on the desert, lashing out blindly at whoever happens to come by.

"But I love you," I said and even as I said them, I knew the hollowness of my words.

And she must have known, too, for in her scathing self-denunciation, she was accusing me with the sins of all the men she'd known. And not unjustly, for they were also my sins.

"But I love you," I repeated and as I said it, I knew she recognized the weakness in my words. They turned empty and hollow in my mouth. If I had been honest, even unto my secret self, this is what I would have said: "I want you. I want you to be what I want you to be. A reflection of the image of my dreams, the mirror of my secret desires, the face that I desire to show the world, the brocade with which I embroider my glory. If you are all these things, I will grace you with my presence and my house. But these are not for what you are, but for me and what I want you to be."

And I did little but stand there, mumbling empty platitudes, while the words that spilled from her mouth were merely my own poison, which she turned into herself. For unknowing, she had stumbled across my secret rock.

I stood there in the unaccustomed heat and blazing brightness of the sun, secretly ashamed of the cool chill of the blood that ran through my veins and set me apart from the others of this earth. And unprotesting, I let her use my venom to destroy herself.

And when the poison had done its work, leaving her with nothing but the small, frightened, unshriven soul of her beginnings, I turned away.

With the lack of mercy peculiar to my kind, I turned my back. I ran from her fears, from her need of comfort and reassurance, from her unspoken pleading for mercy and love and understanding. I fled the hot sun, back to the safety of my secret rock.

But now there was no longer comfort in its secret shade, for the light continued to seep through, and there was no longer comfort in the cool detached flowing of my blood. And the rock seemed to be growing smaller and smaller while the sun was growing larger and larger. I tried to make myself tinier, to find shelter beneath the rock's shrinking surface, but there was no escape. Soon there would be no secret rock for me. The sun was growing brighter and brighter. Brighter and brighter.

I opened my eyes.

There was a tiny pinpoint of light shining straight into them. I blinked and the penetrating pinpoint moved to one side. I could see beyond it now. I was lying on a table in a white room and beside me was a man in a white gown and a white skullcap. The light came from the reflection in a small, round mirror that he wore over his eye as he looked down at me. I could see on his face the tiny black hairs that the razor had missed. His lips were grim and tight.

"My God!" The voice came from behind him. "His face is a mess. There must be a hundred pieces of glass in it."

My eyes flickered up and saw the second man as the first turned toward him. "Shut up, you fool! Can't you see he's awake?"

I began to raise my head but a light, quick hand was on my shoulder, pressing me back, and then her face was there. Her face, looking down at me with a mercy and compassion that mine had never shown.

"Jennie!"

Her hand pressed against my shoulder. She looked up at someone over my head. "Call Dr. Rosa Strassmer at Los Angeles General or the Colton Sanitarium in Santa Monica. Tell her Jonas Cord has been in a bad accident and to come right away."

"Yes, Sister Thomas." It was a young girl's voice and it was, came from behind me. I heard footsteps moving away.

The pain was coming back into my side and leg again and I gritted my teeth.

I could feel it forcing the tears into my eyes. I closed them for a moment, then opened them and looked up at her. "Jennie!" I whispered. "Jennie, I'm sorry!"

"It's all right, Jonas," she whispered back. Her hands went under the sheet that covered me. I felt a sharp sting in my arm. "Don't talk. Everything's all right now."

I smiled gratefully and went back to sleep, wondering vaguely why Jennie was wearing that funny white veil over her beautiful hair.

CHAPTER SIX

FROM OUTSIDE MY WINDOWS, FROM THE STREETS, BRIGHT NOW WITH THE morning sun, still came the sounds of celebration. Even this usually staid and quiet part of Hillcrest Drive skirting Mercy Hospital was filled with happy noises and throngs of people. From the Naval Station across the city of San Diego came the occasional triumphant blast of a ship's horn. It had been like this all through the night, starting early the evening before, when the news came. Japan had surrendered. The war was over.

I knew now what Otto Strassmer had been trying to tell me. I knew now of the miracle in the desert. From the newspapers and from the radio beside my bed. They had all told the story of the tiny container of atoms that had brought mankind to the gates of heaven. Or hell. I shifted in my bed to find another position of comfort, as the pulleys that suspended my leg in traction squeaked, adding their mouselike sound to the others.

I had been lucky, one of the nurses told me. Lucky. My right leg had been broken in three places, my right hip in another, and several ribs had been crushed. Yet I still looked out at the world, from behind the layer of thick bandages which covered all of my face, except the slits for my eyes, nose and mouth. But I'd been lucky. At least I was still alive.

Not like Amos, who still sat in the cabin of *The Centurion* as it rested on the edge of a shelf of sand, some four hundred odd feet beneath the surface of the Pacific Ocean. Poor Amos. The three crewmen had been found unscathed and I was still alive, by the grace of God and the poor fishermen who found me floating in the water and brought me to shore, while Amos sat silent in his watery tomb, still at the controls of the plane he had built and would not let me fly alone.

I remembered the accountant's voice over the telephone from Los Angeles as he spoke consolingly. "Don't worry, Mr. Cord. We can write it all off against taxes on profits. When you apply the gross amount to the normal tax of forty per cent and the excess-profits tax of ninety per cent, the net loss to us comes to under two million—"

I had slammed down the phone, cutting him off. It was all well and good. But how do you charge off on a balance sheet the life of a man who was killed by your greed? Is there an allowable deduction for death on the income-tax returns? It was I who had killed Amos and no matter how many expenses I deducted from my own soul, I could not bring him back.

The door opened and I looked up. Rosa came into the room, followed by an intern and a nurse wheeling a small cart. She came over to the left side of my bed and stood there, smiling down at me. "Hello, Jonas."

"Hello, Rosa," I mumbled through the bandages. "Is it time to change them again? I didn't expect you until the day after tomorrow."

"The war is over."

"Yes," I said. "I know."

"And when I got up this morning, it was such a beautiful morning, I decided to fly down here and take off your bandages.

I peered up at her. "I see," I said. "I always wondered where doctors got their logic."

"That isn't doctor's logic, that's woman's logic. I have the advantage of having been a woman long before I became a doctor."

I laughed. "I'm grateful for the logic, whichever one of you it belongs to. It will be nice to have the bandages off, even for a little while."

She was still smiling, though her eyes were serious. "This time, they're coming off for good, Jonas."

I stared at her as she picked up a scissors from the cart. I reached up and stayed her hand. Suddenly, I was afraid to have her remove the bandages. I felt safe having them wrapped about my face like a cocoon, shielding me from the prying eyes of the world. "Is it soon enough? Will it be all right?"

She sensed my feeling. "Your face will be sore for a while yet," she said, snipping away at the cocoon. "It will be even sorer as the flesh and muscles take up their work again. But that will pass. We can't spend forever hiding behind a mask, can we?"

That was the doctor talking, not the woman. I looked up at her face as she snipped and unwound, snipped and uncovered, until all the bandage was gone and I felt as naked as a newborn baby, with a strange coolness on my cheeks. I tried to see myself reflected in her eyes but they were calm and expressionless, impersonal and professionally detached. I felt her fingers press against my cheek, the flesh under my chin, smooth the hair back from my temples. "Close your eyes."

I closed them. I felt her fingers touch the lids lightly. "Open."

I opened them. Her face was still quiet and unrevealing. "Smile," she said. "Like this." She made with a wide, humorless grin that was a slapstick parody of her usual warm smile.

I grinned. I grinned until the tiny pains that came to my cheeks began to burn like hell. And still I grinned.

"O.K.," she said, suddenly smiling now. Really smiling. "You can stop now."

I stopped and stared up at her. "How is it, Doc?" I tried to keep it light. "Pretty horrible?"

"It's not bad," she said noncommittally. "You were never a raving beauty, you know." She picked up a mirror from the cart. "Here. See for yourself."

I didn't look at the mirror. I didn't want to see myself just yet. "Can I have a cigarette first, Doc?"

Silently she put the mirror back on the cart and took a package of cigarettes from her coat pocket. She sat down on the edge of my bed, put one in her mouth, lit it, then passed it to me. I could taste the faint sweetness of her lipstick as I drew the smoke into me.

"You were cut pretty badly when Winthrop pushed you through that port. But fortunately—"

"You knew about that?" I asked, interrupting. "About Amos, I mean. How did you find out?"

"From you. While you were under the anesthetic. We kept getting the story in fragments, along with the fragments of glass we were picking out of your face. Fortunately, none of your important facial muscles were severely damaged. It was largely a matter of surface lesions. We were able to make the necessary skin grafts quickly. And successfully, I might add."

I held out my hand. "I'll take the mirror now, Doc."

She took my cigarette and handed me the mirror. I raised it and when I looked into it, I felt a chill go through me.

"Doc," I said hoarsely. "I look exactly like my father!"

She took the mirror from my hand and I looked up at her. She was smiling. "Do you, Jonas? But that's the way you've always looked."

Later that morning, Robair brought me the papers. They were filled with the story of Japan's capitulation. I glanced at them carelessly and tossed them aside. "Can I get you something else to read, Mr. Jonas?"

"No," I said. "No, thanks. I just don't feel much like reading."

"All right, Mr. Jonas. Maybe you'd like to sleep some." He moved toward the door.

"Robair."

"Yes, Mr. Jonas?"

"Did I—" I hesitated, my fingers automatically touching my cheek. "Did I always look like this?"

His white teeth flashed in a smile. "Yes, Mr. Jonas."

"Like my father?"

"Like his spittin' image."

I was silent. Strange how all your life you tried not to be like someone, only to learn that you'd been stamped indelibly by the blood that ran in your veins.

"Is there anything else, Mr. Jonas?"

I looked up at Robair and shook my head. "I'll try to sleep now."

I leaned back against the pillow and closed my eyes. I heard the door close and gradually the noise from the street faded to the periphery of my consciousness. I slept. It seemed to me I'd been sleeping a great deal lately. As if I was trying to catch up on all the sleep I'd denied myself for the past few hundred years. But I could not have slept long before I became aware that someone was in the room.

I opened my eyes. Jennie was standing next to my bed, looking down at me. When she saw my eyes open, she smiled. "Hello, Jonas."

"I was sleeping," I said, like a child just waking from a nap. "I was dreaming something foolish. I was dreaming I was hundreds of years old."

"It was a happy dream, then. I'm glad. Happy dreams will help you get well faster."

I raised myself up on one elbow and the pulleys squeaked as I reached for the cigarettes on the table next to the bed. Quickly she fluffed the pillows and moved them in behind me to support my back. I dragged on the cigarette. The smoke drove the sleep from my brain.

"In another few weeks, they'll have the cast off your leg and you can go home."

"I hope so, Jennie," I said.

Suddenly, I realized she wasn't wearing her hospital white. "This is the first time I've seen you in a black veil, Jennie. Is it something special?"

"No, Jonas. This is what I always wear, except when I'm on duty in the hospital."

"Then this is your day off?"

"There are no days off in the service of Our Saviour," she said simply. "No, Jonas, I've come to say good-by."

"Good-by? But I don't understand. You said it would be a few weeks before I—"

"I'm going away, Jonas."

I stared up at her stupidly. "Going away?"

"Yes, Jonas," she said quietly. "I've only been here at Mercy Hospital until I could get transportation to the Philippines. We're rebuilding a hospital there that was destroyed in the war. Now I am free to leave, by plane."

"But you can't, Jennie," I said. "You can't leave the people you know, the language you speak. You'll be a stranger there, you'll be alone."

Her fingers touched the crucifix hanging from the black leather cincture beneath her garment. A quiet look of calm deepened in her gray eyes. "I am never alone," she said simply. "He is always with me."

"You don't have to, Jennie," I said. I took the pamphlet that I'd found on the table by my bed and opened it. "You've only made a temporary profession. You can resign any time you want. There's still a three-year probationary period before you take your final vows. You don't belong here, Jennie. It's only because you were hurt and angry. You're much too young and beautiful to hide your life away behind a black veil."

She still did not answer.

"Don't you understand what I'm saying, Jennie? I want you to come back where you belong."

She closed her eyes slowly and when she opened them, they were misted with tears. But when she spoke, her voice was steady with the sureness of her knowledge and faith. "It's you who don't understand, Jonas," she said. "I have no place to which I desire to return, for it is here, in His house, that I belong."

I started to speak but she raised her hand gently. "You think I came to Him out of hurt and anger? You're wrong," she said quietly. "One does not run from life to God, one runs to God for life. All my years I sought Him, without knowing what I was seeking. The love I found out there was a mere mockery of what I knew love could be; the charity I gave was but the smallest fraction of the charity in me to give; the mercy I showed was nothing compared with His mercy within me. Here, in His house and in His work, I have found a greater love than any I have ever known. Through His love, I have found security and contentment and happiness, in accordance with His divine will."

She paused for a moment, looking down at the crucifix in her fingers. When she looked up again, her eyes were clear and untroubled. "Is there anything in this world, Jonas, that can offer more than God?"

I didn't answer.

Slowly she held out her left hand toward me. I looked down and saw the heavy silver ring on her third finger. "He has invited me into His house," she said softly, "and I have taken His ring to wear so that I may dwell in His glory forever."

I took her hand and pressed my lips to the ring. I felt her fingers brush my hair lightly, then she moved to the foot of my bed, where she turned to look at me. "I shall think of you often, my friend," she said gently. "And I shall pray for you."

I was silent as I ground my cigarette out. There was a beauty in Jennie's eyes that had never been there before. "Thank you, Sister," I said quietly.

Without another word, she turned and went out the door. I stared down at the foot of the bed where she had stood, but now even the ghost of her was gone.

I turned my face into the pillow and cried.

CHAPTER SEVEN

I LEFT THE HOPITAL EARLY IN SEPTEMBER. I WAS SITTING IN THE WHEEL chair, watching Robair pack the last of my things into the valise, when the door opened. "Hi, Junior."

"Nevada! What are you doing way down here?"

"Came to carry you home."

I laughed. Funny how you can go along for years hardly thinking about someone, then all of a sudden be so glad to see him. "You didn't have to do that," I said. "Robair could have managed all right."

"I asked him to come up, Mr. Jonas. I figured it would be like old times. It gets mighty lonely out there at the ranch with nothing to do."

"An' I figured I could use a vacation," Nevada said. "The war's over an' the show's closed down for the winter. And there's nothin' Martha likes better than to do a little invalidin'. She's down there now, gittin' things ready for us."

I looked at the two of them and grinned. "It's a put-up job, huh?"

"That's right," Nevada said. He came over behind the wheel chair. "Ready?"

Robair closed the valise and snapped it shut. "All set, Mr. Nevada."

"Let's go, then," Nevada said, and started the wheel chair through the door.

"We have to stop off at Burbank," I said, looking back at him. "Mac has a flock of papers for me to sign." I might be laid up, but business went on.

Buzz Dalton had an ICA charter waiting for us at the San Diego airport. We were at Burbank by two o'clock that afternoon. McAllister got up and came around his desk when they wheeled me into his office. "You know, this is the first time I can remember seeing you sit down."

I laughed. "Make the most of it. The doctors say I'll be moving around as good as new in a couple of weeks."

"Well, meanwhile, I'm going to take advantage of it. Push him around behind the desk, fellows. I've got the pen ready."

It was almost four o'clock when I'd signed the last of a stack of documents. I looked up wearily. "So what else is new?"

Mac looked at me. He walked over to a table against the wall. "This is," he said, and took the cover off something that looked like a radio with a window in it.

"What is it?"

"It's the first product of the Cord Electronics Company," he said proudly. "We knocked it out in the converted radar division. It's a television set."

"Television?" I asked.

"Pictures broadcast through the air like radio," he said. "It's picked up on that screen, like home movies."

"Oh, that's the thing that Dumont was kicking around before the war. It doesn't work."

"Does now," Mac said. "It's the next big thing. All the radio and electronics companies are going into it. RCA, Columbia, Emerson, IT&T, GE, Philco. All of them. Want to see how it works?"

"Sure."

He walked over and picked up the phone. "Get me the lab." He covered the mouthpiece. "I'll have them put something on," he said.

A moment later, he went over to the set and turned a knob. A light flashed behind the window, then settled into a series of circles and lines. Gradually, letters came into view.

CORD ELECTRONICS PRESENTS—

Suddenly, the card was replaced by a picture, a Western scene with a man riding a horse toward the camera. The camera dollied in real close on the face and I saw it was Nevada. I recognized the scene, too. It was the chase scene from *The Renegade*. For five minutes, we watched the scene in silence.

"Well, I'll be damned," Nevada said, when it was over.

I looked across at Robair. There was an expression of rapt wonder on his face. He looked at me. "There's what I call a miracle, Mr. Jonas," he said softly. "Now I can watch a movie in my own home without goin' to sit in no nigger heaven."

"So that's why they all want to buy my old pictures," Nevada said.

I looked up at him. "What do you mean?"

"You know those ninety-odd pictures we made and I own now?"

I nodded.

"People been after me to sell 'em. Offered me good money for 'em, too. Five thousand dollars each."

I stared at him. "One thing I learned in the picture business," I said. "Never sell outright what you can get a percentage on."

"You mean rent it to 'em like I do to a theater?"

"That's right," I said. "I know those broadcasting companies. If they'll buy it for five, they plan to make fifty out of it."

"I'm no good at big deals like that," Nevada said. "Would you be willin' to handle it for me, Mac?"

"I don't know, Nevada. I'm no agent."

"Go ahead and do it, Mac," I said. "Remember what you told me about making a point where it counts?"

He smiled suddenly. "O.K., Nevada."

Suddenly, I was tired. I slumped back in my chair. Robair was at my side instantly. "You all right, Mr. Jonas?"

"I'm just tired," I said.

"Maybe you better stay at the apartment tonight. We can go on out to the ranch in the morning."

I looked at Robair. The idea of getting into a bed was very appealing. My ass was sore from the wheel chair.

"I'll order a car," Mac said, picking up the phone. "You can drop me at the studio on your way into town. I've got some work to finish up there."

My mind kept working all the time we rode toward the studio. When the car stopped, at the gates, suddenly everything was clear to me.

"We'll have to do something about a replacement for Bonner," Mac said, getting out. "It isn't good business having a lawyer run a studio. I don't know anything about motion pictures."

I stared at him thoughtfully. He was right, of course. But then, who did? Only David, and he was gone. I didn't care any more. There were no pictures left in me, no one I wanted to place up there on the screen for all the world to see. And back in the office I'd just left, there was a little box with a picture window and soon it would be in every home. Rich or poor. That little box was really going to chew up film, like the theaters had never been able to. But I still didn't care.

Even when I was a kid, when I was through with a toy, I was through with it. And I'd never go back to it. "Sell the theaters," I whispered to Mac.

"What?" he shouted, as if he couldn't believe his ears. "They're the only end of this business that's making any money."

"Sell the theaters," I repeated. "In ten years, no one will want to come to them, anyway. At least, not the way they have up to now. Not when they can see movies right in their own home."

Mac stared at me. "And what do you want me to do about the studio?" he asked, a tinge of sarcasm coming into his voice. "Sell that, too?"

"Yes," I said quietly. "But not now. Ten years from now, maybe. When the people who are making pictures for that little box are squeezed and hungry for space. Sell it then."

"What will we do with it in the meantime? Let it rot while we pay taxes on it?"

"No," I said. "Turn it into a rental studio like the old Goldwyn lot. If we break even or lose a little, I won't complain."

He stared at me. "You really mean it?"

"I mean it," I said, looking away from him up at the roof over the stages. For the first time, I really saw it. It was black and ugly with tar. "Mac, see that roof?"

He turned and looked, squinting against the setting sun.

"Before you do anything else," I said softly, "have them paint it white."

I pulled my head back into the car. Nevada looked at me strangely. His voice was almost sad. "Nothing's changed, has it, Junior?"

"No," I said wearily. "Nothing's changed."

CHAPTER EIGHT

I SAT ON THE PORCH, SQUINTING OUT INTO THE AFTERNOON SUN. NEVADA came out of the house behind me and dropped into a chair. He pulled a plug out of his pocket and biting off a hunk, put the plug back. Then from his other pocket, he took a piece of wood and a penknife and began to whittle.

I looked at him. He was wearing a pair of faded blue levis. A sweat-stained old buckskin shirt, that had seen better days, clung to his deep chest and broad shoulders and be had a red-and-white kerchief tied around his neck to catch the perspiration. Except for his white hair, he looked as I always remembered him when I was a boy, his hands quick and brown and strong.

He looked up at me out of his light eyes. "Two lost arts," he said.

"What?"

"Chewin' an' whittlin'," he said.

I didn't answer.

He looked down at the piece of wood in his hands. "Many's the evenin' I spent on the porch with your pa, chewin' an' whittlin'."

"Yeah?"

He turned and let fly a stream of tobacco juice over the porch rail into the dust below. He turned back to me. "I recall one night," he said. "Your pa an' me, we were settin' here, just like now. It'd been a real bitcheroo of a day. One of them scorchers that make your balls feel like they're drownin' in their own sweat. Suddenly, he looks up at me an' says, 'Nevada, anything should happen to me, you look after my boy, hear? Jonas is a good boy. Sometimes his ass gets too much for his britches but he's a good boy an' he's got the makin's in him to be a better man than his daddy, someday. I love that boy, Nevada. He's all I got.'"

"He never told me that," I said, looking at Nevada. "Not ever. Not once!"

Nevada's eyes flashed up at me. "Men like your daddy ain't given much to talkin' about things like that."

I laughed. "He not only didn't talk it," I said. "He never showed it. He was always chewing on my ass for one thing or another."

Nevada's eyes bore straight into mine. "He was always there whenever you were in trouble. He might have hollered but he never turned you down."

"He married my girl away from me," I said bitterly.

"Maybe it was for your own good. Maybe it was because he knew she never really was for you."

I let that one go. "Why are you telling me this now?" I asked.

I couldn't read those Indian eyes of his. "Because your father asked me once to look after you. I made one mistake already. I seen how smart you was in business, I figured you to be growed up. But you wasn't. An' I wouldn' like to fail a man like your father twice."

We sat there in silence for a few minutes, then Martha came out with my tea.

She told Nevada to spit out the chaw and stop dirtying up the porch. He looked at me almost shyly, got up and went down to get rid of the chaw behind the bushes.

We heard a car turn up our road as he came back to the porch. "I wonder who that is?" Martha asked.

"Maybe it's the doctor," I said. Old Doc Hanley was supposed to come out and check me over once a week.

By that time, the car was in the driveway and I knew who it was. I got to my feet, leaning on my cane, as Monica and Jo-Ann approached us. "Hello," I called.

They'd come back to California to close up their apartment, Monica explained, and since she wanted to talk to me about Amos, they'd stopped off in Reno on their way back to New York. Their train wasn't due to leave until seven o'clock.

I saw Martha glance meaningfully at Nevada when she heard that. Nevada got to his feet and looked at Jo-Ann. "I've got a gentle bay horse out in the corral that's just dyin' for some young lady like you to ride her."

Jo-Ann looked up at him worshipfully. You could tell she'd been to the movies from the way she looked at him. He was a real live hero. "I don't know," she said doubtfully. "I've never really ridden a horse before."

"I can teach you. It's easy, easier than fallin' off a log."

"But she's not dressed for riding," Monica said.

She wasn't. Not in that pretty flowered dress that made her look so much like her mother. Martha spoke up quickly. "I got a pair of dungarees that shrunk down to half my size. They'll fit her."

I don't know whose dungarees they were but one thing was for sure. They'd never been Martha's. Not the way they clung to Jo-Ann's fourteen-year-old hips, tight and flat with just the suggestion of the curves to come. Jo-Ann's dark hair was pulled back straight from her head in a pony tail and there was something curiously familiar about the way she looked. I couldn't quite figure out what it was.

I watched her run out the door after Nevada and turned to Monica. She was smiling at me. I returned her smile. "She's growing up," I said. "She's going to be a pretty girl."

"One day they're children, the next they're young ladies. They grow up too fast."

I nodded. We were alone now and an awkward silence came down between us. I reached for a cigarette and looked at her. "I want to tell you about Amos."

It was near six o'clock when I finished telling her about what happened. There were no tears in her eyes, though her face was sad and thoughtful. "I can't cry for him, Jonas," she said, looking at me. "Because I've already cried too many times because of him. Do you understand?"

I nodded.

"He did so many things that were wrong all his life. I'm glad that at last he did one thing right."

"He did a very brave thing. I always thought he hated me."

"He did," she said quickly. "He saw in you everything that he wasn't. Quick, successful, rich. He hated your guts. I guess at the end he realized how foolish that was and how much harm he'd already done you, so he tried to make it right."

I looked at her. "What wrong did he do me? There was nothing but business between us."

She gave me a peculiar look. "You can't see it yet?"

"No."

"Then I guess you never will," she said and walked out onto the porch.

We could hear Jo-Ann's shout of laughter as she rode the big bay around the corral. She was doing pretty good for a beginner. I looked down at Monica. "She takes to it like she was born to the saddle."

"Why shouldn't she?" Monica replied. "They say such things are inherited."

"I didn't know you rode."

She looked up at me, her eyes hurt and angry. "I'm not her only parent," she snapped coldly.

I stared at her. This was the only time she'd ever mentioned anything about Jo-Ann's father to me. It was sort of late to be angry about it now.

I heard the chug of Doc Hanley's old car turning into the driveway. He stopped near the corral and getting out of the car, walked over to the fence. He never could drive past a horse.

"That's Doc Hanley. He's supposed to check me out."

"Then I won't keep you," Monica said coolly. "I'll say good-by here."

She went down the steps and started walking toward the corral. I stared after her bewilderedly. I never could figure her out when she got into those crazy moods. "I'll have Robair drive you to the station," I called after her.

"Thanks!" She flung it back over her shoulder without turning around. I saw her stop and talk to the doctor, then I turned and walked back into the house. I went into the room that my father used as his study and sank down on the couch. Monica always did have a quick temper. You'd think by now she'd have learned to control it. I started to smile, thinking of how straight her back was and how sassy she'd looked walking away from me, her nose in the air. She still looked pretty good for a woman her age. I was forty-one, which meant she was thirty-four. And nothing on her jiggled that shouldn't.

The trouble with Doc Hanley is that he's a talker. He talks you deaf, dumb and blind but you don't have much choice. Since the war started, it's been him or nothing. All the young docs were in the service.

It was six thirty by the time he'd finished his examination and begun to close up his instrument case. "You're doin' all right," he said. "But I don't hold with them newfangled notions of getting you out as soon as you kin move. If it'd been up to me, now, I'd have kept you in the hospital another month."

Nevada leaned against the study wall, smiling as I climbed into my britches. I looked at him and shrugged. I turned to the doctor. "How long now before I can really begin to do some walking?"

Doc Hanley peered at me over the edges of his bifocals. "You kin start walkin' right now."

"But I thought you didn't agree with those city doctors," I said. "I thought you wanted me to rest some more."

"I don't agree with them," he said. "But since you're out, an' there ain't nothin' that can be done about that, you might as well git to movin' about. There ain't no sense in you jist layin' aroun'."

He snapped his case shut, straightened up and walked to the door. He turned and looked back at me. "That's a right pert gal you got there, your daughter."

I stared at him. "My daughter?"

"That's right," he said. "With her hair tied back like that, I never seen a gal who took so after her father. Why she's the spittin' image of you when you was a boy."

I couldn't speak, only stare. Had the idiot gone off his rocker? Everybody knew Jo-Ann wasn't my daughter.

Doc laughed suddenly and slapped his hand on his thigh. "I'll never forget the time her mother came down to my office," he said. "She was your wife then, of course. I never seen such a big belly. I figured, no wonder you got married so sudden like. You'd been doin' your plantin' early."

He looked up at me, still smiling. "That was before I examined her, you understand," he said quickly. "You could have knocked me over with a feather when the examination showed her only six weeks gone. It was just one of those peculiar things where she carried real high. She was so nervous an' upset just about then that she blew up with gas like a balloon. I even went back to the papers an' checked your weddin' date just to make sure. An' dang my britches if it weren't a fact you'd knocked her up at most two weeks after you were married. But there's one thing I got to say for yuh, boy." He turned back at the door. "When you ram 'em, you ram 'em good. Right up the ol' gazizzis, where it sticks!" And still laughing lewdly, he walked out.

I felt the tight, sick knot ball up inside me. I sat down on the couch. All these years. All these years and I had been wrong. Suddenly, I knew what Amos had been going to tell me after we returned from the flight. He'd seen how crazy I'd been that night and turned my own hate against me. And there was little Monica could have done about it.

What a combination, Amos and me. But at least, he'd seen the light by himself. No one had to hit him over the head with it. And he'd tried to make up for it. But I—I never even turned my head to seek the truth. I'd been content to go along blaming the world for my own stupidity. And I was the one who'd been at war with my father because I thought he didn't love me. That was the biggest joke of all.

Now I could even face the truth in that. It never had been his love that I'd doubted. It had been my own. For deep inside of me, I'd always known that I could never love him as much as he loved me. I looked up at Nevada. He was still leaning against the wall, but he wasn't smiling now. "You saw it, too?"

"Sure." He nodded. "Everybody saw it—but you."

I closed my eyes. Now I could see it. It was like that morning in the hospital when I looked into the mirror and saw my father's face. That was what I'd seen in Jo-Ann when I thought she looked so familiar this afternoon. Her father's face. My own.

"What shall I do, Nevada?" I groaned.

"What do yuh want to do, son?"

"I want them back."

"Sure that's what you want?"

I nodded.

"Then get 'em back," he said. He looked at his watch. "There's still fifteen minutes before the train pulls out."

"But how? We'd never get there in time"

He gestured to the desk. "There's the phone."

I looked at him wildly, then hobbled to the phone. I called the stationmaster's office at Reno and had them page her. While I was waiting for her to come on, I looked at Nevada. Suddenly, I was frightened, and when I'd been little, I'd always turned to Nevada when I was frightened. "What if she won't come back?"

"She'll come back," he said confidently. He smiled. "She's still in love with you. That's something else everybody knew but you."

Then she was on the phone, her voice worried and anxious. "Jonas, are you all right? Is there anything wrong?"

For a moment, I couldn't speak, then I found my voice. "Monica," I said. "Don't go!"

"But I have to, Jonas. I have to be on the job by the end of the week."

"Screw the job, I need you!"

The line was silent, and for a moment, I thought she'd hung up. "Monica, are you there?"

I heard her breathe in the receiver. "I'm still here, Jonas."

"I've been wrong all the time. I didn't know about Jo-Ann. Believe me." Again the silence.

"Please, Monica!"

Now she was crying. I could hear her whispered voice in my ear. "Oh, Jonas, I've never stopped loving you."

I looked up at Nevada. He smiled and went out, closing the door behind him.

I heard her sniffle, then her voice suddenly cleared and filled with the warm sound of love. "When Jo-Ann was a little girl she always wanted a baby brother."

"Hurry home," I said, "I'll do my best."

She laughed and there was a click as the line went dead in my hands. I didn't put the phone down because I felt that as long as I held it, she was close to me. I looked down at the photograph of my father on the desk.

"Well, old man," I said, asking his approval for the first time in my life, "did I do right?"

79 PARK AVENUE

AND *they began to go out one by one, beginning with the eldest, till Jesus was left alone with the woman, still standing in full view. Then Jesus looked up and asked her, Woman, where are thy accusers? Has no one condemned thee? No one, Lord, she said. And Jesus said to her, I will not condemn thee either.*

THE GOSPEL According to St. John, CHAPTER 8

CONTENTS

The State vs.
Maryann Flood

I PULLED THE CAR INTO THE PARKING-LOT ACROSS THE STREET FROM CRIM-
inal Courts. Before I had a chance to cut the engine, the attendant was
holding the door for me. I eased out slowly, picking up my briefcase from
the seat beside me. I had never rated this kind of service before.

"Nice day, Mr. Keyes," he said, falling into step with me as I walked toward
the exit.

I looked up at the sky. It was—if you liked gray December days. I nodded.
"Yes, Jerry."

I stopped and looked at him. There was a grin on his face. He didn't have to
tell me that he already knew. I could see it. That was why I rated today.

"Thanks," I said and cut across the street to the courthouse. It had been only
twenty minutes since I myself found out. Eight miles and twenty minutes ago,
in a hospital room in the Harkness Pavilion. Yet they knew it down here already.

The Old Man's face had been gray with pain against his pillow. I was standing
at the foot of his bed. "You're gonna have to take it, Mike," he whispered.

I shook my head. "No, John. I can't."

"Why?" His whisper had an almost eerie quality.

"You know why," I answered. I hesitated a moment. "Give it to one of the
others. You have enough assistants. Why pick on me?"

His whisper exploded into a sharp sound. "Because they're all political hacks,
that's why. You're the only one I can trust, you're the only one I hired for myself.
All the others were shoved down my throat, and you know it!"

I didn't answer even though I knew he wasn't speaking the truth. Ever since Tom Dewey had been D.A., the office had been free of political persuasion. The only thing political about the office was John DeWitt Jackson's ambitions.

His eyes were fixed on mine. I couldn't turn away from them now. "Remember when you first came to me? You were a cop then, and the soles of your shoes were almost an inch thick. You had your law diploma in your hand. You even called yourself by your fancy real name, Millard Keyes. There were marbles in your mouth when you asked me for a job. I asked you: 'Why my office?' Do you remember your answer?"

I remembered, all right. That was the only time I didn't use the name people called me by, Mike. I didn't speak.

"I'll tell you what you said." He raised his head on the pillow. "You said, 'I'm a cop, Mr. Jackson, and there's only one side to the law for me.'

"I gave you the job because I believed what you told me." His head sank back against the pillow wearily and his voice returned to a whisper again. "Now you want to run out on me."

"I'm not running out on you, John," I said quickly. "I just can't take this case. It's not fair to me, and I'm afraid I wouldn't be fair to you. I told you that when it first started."

"I wasn't worried about you then and I'm not worried now," he whispered vehemently. He turned his face away for a second. "Damn this appendix! Why couldn't it keep another few weeks?"

In spite of myself, I smiled. The Old Man didn't miss a trick. He pulled out all the stops. "You know what the doctor said. This was one time he couldn't freeze it for you," I answered with a proper show of sympathy.

He nodded sorrowfully. "That's doctors for you. On the eve of the most important trial of my career."

I knew what he meant. A few months from now the boys would be sitting down in the back rooms all over the state. By the time they got around to opening the windows to air out the smoke and whisky fumes, the next Governor would have been picked out.

The Old Man had timed it very cleverly. Not so early they would forget, not so late they would have decided. But now he was scared. What would serve for him would serve for the others. And he didn't want to take any chances.

He looked down the bed at me. His eyes filled with an inexpressible sorrow. "Mike," he whispered, "you've never been like the others. You've been almost—well, almost like a son to me. You were my one hope, the only thing in the whole damn office that I was proud of. You were my boy.

"I'm not a young man any more. I've made my plans, and if they miss, I accept it. It's God's will." He shrugged his shoulders almost imperceptibly in the white cotton hospital nightshirt. He was silent a moment; then his voice grew hard. "But I don't want any slimy, son-of-a-bitchin' opportunists climbing up my ladder!"

We stared at each other silently for a few moments, and then he spoke again. "Go into court for me, Mike," he pleaded. "You got a free hand. You're the boss. You can do anything you like. You can even ask the court to dismiss the charge on the grounds that we haven't been able to make a case. You can make a monkey out of me if you like. I don't care. Just don't let any of the others climb on my body."

I took a deep breath. I was licked and I knew it. I didn't believe he meant a word of what he had said, but it made no difference. He was mean and crafty and gave away ice in the winter, but there were tears in my eyes and I loved every lying bone in his body.

He knew it, too, for he began to smile. "You'll do it, Mike?"

I nodded. "Yes, John."

He reached under the pillow and pulled out some typewritten notes. "About the jurors," he said, his voice stronger now. "Look out for number three—"

I interrupted him. "I know about the jurors. I've been reading the minutes." I headed for the door. I opened it and looked back at him. "Besides, you promised me a free hand—remember?"

The reporters hit me almost before I set foot on the courthouse steps. I smiled grimly to myself as I tried to push my way through them. The Old Man must have been on the phone the minute I left the room.

"We hear you're taking over for the D.A., Mr. Keyes. Is that true?"

He wouldn't have gotten an answer even if I had been so minded. I hated people who made it sound like *keys*. The name was Keyes, rhyming with *eyes*. I kept walking.

They followed me with a barrage of questions.

I stopped on the steps and held up my hands. "Give me a break, fellers," I pleaded. "You know I just came back from my vacation this morning."

"Is it true that the D.A. sent you a telegram before he went into the hospital the day before yesterday? That the adjournment was only to give you time to return?"

I pushed my way through the revolving doors, turned right, and headed past the press room for the elevators. A couple of flashbulbs exploded, sending crazy purple spots flashing across my eyes. At the elevator door I turned and faced them.

"We'll have a statement for you at the noon recess, gentlemen. From then on I'll try to answer every question I can. All I want now is a few minutes alone before I have to be in court."

I ducked through the door, and the operator shut it in their faces. I got out on the seventh floor and went to my office at the end of the hall.

Joel Rader was waiting there for me. He came toward me, his hand outstretched. "Good luck, Mike."

I took his hand. "Thanks, Joel," I said. "I'll need it." Joel was one of the men the Old Man meant. He was bright, tough, and ambitious, just a few years older than I.

"How's the Old Man?" he asked.

"You know him," I said, grinning. "Bitchin'." I walked toward my desk.

"Man, you should've heard him the other day when the doctor gave him the sad news," he said, following me. "Practically tore the doctor's head off."

"I can imagine," I said, tossing my hat and coat on the small wooden bench opposite my desk. I sat down and looked up at him. "I didn't mean to cut in on your deal, Joel," I said.

He smiled insincerely. "You're not cutting in, Mike," he answered quickly. "After all, you worked with the Old Man on the investigation. I understand."

I understood, too. He was clearing himself in advance in case anything went wrong. That didn't mean he wouldn't have wanted it for himself. He was headline-happy, but he wasn't taking any chances. "Is Alec around?" I asked. Alec Carter was the other attorney who assisted the Old Man in court with Joel.

"You know Alec." Joel deadpanned. "But he left the Old Man's notes on your desk for you."

I knew Alec. He had nervous kidneys and spent most of his time in the can before going into court. He was all right once he was in the courtroom. I looked down at the desk. The neatly typed notes were in front of me.

I turned back to Joel. He beat me to the punch. He was five years my senior in the office and wasn't going to give me a chance to dismiss him.

"I'll be in my office if you need anything, Mike," he said.

"Thanks, Joel," I answered, watching the door close behind him. I fished a pack of butts out of my pocket and lit one before I looked down at the papers on my desk.

The indictment was right on the top of the pile. I picked it up and stared at it. I turned my chair so that the light from the window behind me would fall directly on the paper. The heavy black type flashed up at me.

People of the State of New York against

Maryann Flood, Defendant

I could feel a sudden pain clutching at my heart. This was it. Everything that had gone before was like nothing. Now I have to live with it. I closed my eyes. I shouldn't have let the Old Man con me into it. The roots went too deep.

I took a deep breath and tried to clear the pain from my chest. I wondered if I would ever be free of her. I remembered the first time I had seen her. It seemed a thousand years ago. But it wasn't that far back. It was the summer of 1935.

Remember what it was like that season of anxiety? Men out of work, the summer heat resting heavily on their already overburdened shoulders. My father was like the others. Two years of being a house superintendent had made a prematurely aged man of him.

I had a job of a sort. At the corner newsstands at 86th Street and Lexington Avenue. Saturday nights and Sunday mornings. Putting the multiple-sectioned papers together. I came on at nine o'clock at night and worked through until ten-thirty in the morning. I was sixteen then and Mother insisted I shouldn't miss Mass. So I made the eleven o'clock Mass at St. Augustine's on my way home.

This Sunday had been no different. I got into church at the last minute, crept into an almost deserted rear pew, and promptly fell asleep. Almost before I had shut my eyes, I felt a nudge in my side.

Automatically I moved in to allow the newcomers to enter the pew. Again the nudge. This time I opened my eyes. It took almost a minute before what I saw registered. Then I drew in my breath and let them pass.

I gave the older woman no more than a glance. The faded gray-blond hair and weary face didn't interest me. She passed me muttering something under her breath which I took for an apology. It was the girl, her daughter, who hit me where I lived.

The ash-blond Polack hair that fell like shimmering gold around her face, the wild wide mouth slashed sensually with scarlet, the slightly parted lips and white teeth just showing beneath their shadows. The thin, almost classical nose with nostrils that flared suddenly below highly set cheekbones, the brown penciled line that delineated her eyes.

Her eyes were a book in themselves. They were wide-set and lazy brown, flecked with hell's own green around the edge of the irises. They were warm and bright and intelligent and hinted at a passion I was yet to understand. They touched you and drew you, yet chased you in a subtle manner. I tried to look beneath their surface, but couldn't get through the invisible guard. There was something about brown eyes I could never fathom. You couldn't look into them and read them the way you could blue eyes.

She looked away from me as she passed in front of me, and a million tiny electric shocks ran through my body. Her mother, who was twice her size, had passed without touching me. But not she.

"Excuse me," she whispered, a hidden laughter in her voice.

I stammered an unintelligible answer that was lost in a rustle of clothing as the congregation knelt in their pews. I looked at her as I got down on my knees.

She was already kneeling, her hands folded demurely on the rail before her, her eyes down. Beyond her, her mother rested her head heavily on her clasped hands, praying indistinctly in some foreign tongue. My eyes came back to the girl.

Her body swelled against the light summer cotton dress. A warm muskiness came from her, and I could see the faint patch of perspiration spreading slowly on the dress under her arm.

I closed my eyes and tried to concentrate on my prayer. A few seconds passed and I began to feel better. It wasn't so bad if I kept my eyes shut. I felt the girl shift slightly next to me. Her thigh pressed lightly against mine.

I opened my eyes and looked at her. She seemed to be unaware of the pressure, her eyes shut in prayer. I moved slightly away from her and held my breath. Her eyes still shut, she moved with me. I was at the edge of the pew now and could move no farther without falling into the aisle.

I stayed there as best I could and tried to concentrate on God's Word. But it was no use. The devil was at my side.

At last the prayer was over and the congregation got achingly to their feet. It was not until then that I dared open my eyes and look at her.

She didn't look at me; her eyes were focused carefully forward. I started to step out of the pew, but she was already passing me. I stepped back in the pew, and she stopped and stepped back with me.

I was startled, but she smiled politely and let her mother cross in front of her. She leaned back against me as her mother passed out into the aisle. Then she slowly turned completely around.

I stared into her eyes. There was a teasing laughter in them that I had never seen in any eyes before. A wild, dangerous fire that crept into my soul. Her lips parted in a smile and suddenly I heard words from her, though I could swear her lips never moved. "Havin' a ball, Mike?" she breathed.

It wasn't until a moment later when she had been lost in the crowds of people pushing up the aisle that I realized she knew my name.

Slowly I moved up the aisle, wondering who she was. Maybe it would have been a better life if I had never found out.

* * *

I drew the blinds down on memory. The papers were still in my hand. They still had to be read. In another forty minutes I would be in court. Slowly, in order to concentrate, I began to read the indictment word by word.

We entered the courtroom through the side door. A hush fell over the crowd of people as we made our way to our seats at the table to the right of the court. I didn't raise my eyes to look at the spectators. I didn't want them to see the anger I felt at their insatiable curiosity.

I sat down in a chair, my back to them, and began to spread my papers out on the table. I could feel the tension growing inside me. In a way, a trial was like a prize fight. I wet my lips slightly and hoped the knot in my stomach would loosen.

For the sake of hearing my own voice, I spoke to Joel. "What time is it?"

He glanced at the big clock on the wall. "Almost ten."

"Good." It wouldn't be long before the court would convene. I stole a glance at the defendant's table. It was still vacant.

Joel caught my glance. "Vito always stalls to the last minute. Gives him a chance to make an impressive entrance."

I nodded. Vito knew his business. He was one of the most successful criminal lawyers in New York. A tall, good-looking man with a shock of gray hair framing piercing blue eyes. He lost very few cases He worked at his job. Every one of us in the office had a healthy respect for him.

A sudden murmur of excitement rippled through the courtroom behind us. Several splashes of light came down the room from the flashbulbs. I didn't have to turn around to know they were coming down the aisle. The sound of whispers plotted that better than radar.

I raised my head and turned toward them just as they were at the railing. Vito had already swung the gate and was standing, his back toward me, allowing his client to precede him. Her eyes caught mine as she looked up to thank him.

Her eyes widened slightly and I began to see inside them. It had been so long. So long ago. Our glance lasted only a moment; then she turned away and hurried to her seat.

I watched her walk. She had that free stride I always remembered, her ankles thin and twinkling in their sheer nylons. She wore a dark, man-tailored suit, and a blue poodle-cloth coat hung from her shoulders. Her hair was a burnished copper-gold, cut short in small ringlets piled high on her head. She sat down circumspectly and adjusted her skirt around her knees. Vito sat down next to her and they began to talk.

Joel's whisper was in my ear. "A real woman."

At the tone of admiration in his voice, I nodded my head without speaking.

"There isn't a guy in this court who would turn down a piece of that." He was still whispering.

I had all I could do to keep my anger from showing. That was the trouble. That had always been the trouble. She was the kind of woman whose sex fit her like a halo. No man could ever miss it.

"It's almost a shame to put a woman on the rack for doing what's she's made for," he kept on, with a little laugh. "And from what I hear, there's nothing she likes better."

This time I couldn't keep my anger from bursting out. "Can it, Joel," I said coldly. "This is a courtroom, not a poolroom."

He started to speak, then caught a glimpse of my eyes. The words froze on his lips and he turned back to the papers on the table before him. I picked up a pencil and began to doodle on a scratch pad. Alec nudged me and I looked up.

Henry Vito was walking toward our table. I watched him stroll assuredly until he was opposite me. He looked down at me, smiling confidently. "How's the Old Man, Mike?" he asked.

"Coming along, Hank," I said, smiling back at him.

His voice was just low enough to carry to the press rows. "Mighty lucky appendix he suddenly came up with."

I stretched my voice so they could hear my answer. "All the luck coming out of that appendix landed on your side of the court."

He didn't change expression. "If he ever becomes Governor, Mike, he'll owe you a big vote of thanks."

I got to my feet slowly. Vito was a tall man, but I'm taller. I stand six foot two in my stocking feet, and I'm broad-shouldered and with my broken nose look ugly enough to make him seem frail. He looked up into my face and I smiled. "Thanks for them kind words, Hank. I know after the trial you'll agree I deserved them."

The smile was still on his face, but he didn't speak. I blocked him off from his audience, so there wasn't any reason for him to continue. He turned back to his table with a jaunty wave of his hand. I watched him walk across the court before I returned to my seat.

Joel was whispering in my ear, "Don't let him get your goat, Mike."

I smiled coldly. "I won't."

"I thought you were going to slug him when he got up," Alec whispered from the other side.

My smile turned into a grin. "I thought about it."

"I could see that look on your face—" Alec's whisper was interrupted by the tapping of the gavel.

There was a quick rustle of clothing as we got to our feet. The judge was coming into the court. Peter Amelie was a short, stocky man and as he went to the bench he looked like a little kewpie doll with his cherubic face and bald head rising from the black cloth of his official robes. He sat down and with a quick motion tapped the bench before him with a gavel.

The clerk's voice boomed out. "Hear ye, hear ye. The Court of General Sessions, Part Three, is now in session. The Honorable Justice Peter Amelie presiding."

This was it. There was no turning back now. The fight was on, the referee in the ring. Suddenly all the tension left me. From now on nothing would bother me, no memories torture me. I would have no time for them. I had a job to do.

A few moments later, at a nod from the judge, I got to my feet. I walked slowly across the court to the jury box. She didn't look up as I passed the defendant's table, yet I knew she was watching every motion I made in that crazy way she had of seeing out of the corners of her eyes. I stopped in front of the jury and gave them a chance to look me over.

After a few seconds I began to speak. I started slowly. "Ladies and gentlemen of the jury, I feel pretty much like a pinch hitter being sent in to bat for Di Maggio. For who—" I paused a moment to let a ripple of warm laughter die down in the courtroom. "For who can follow Di Maggio?" I continued, and answered my own question "Nobody."

I let the faint, friendly smile fade from my lips. "But the people of the State of New York are entitled to the representation and protection of their elected officers. And the people of the State of New York through their Grand Jury found grounds to present to this court an indictment against a certain person for violating its laws and its decencies. So I humbly beg your indulgence while I, in my poor fashion and manner, represent the people of the State of New York against the crimes of Maryann Flood."

Vito came in on schedule with his objection. As I expected, the court upheld it. But I had made my point. I turned back to the jury.

"I would like to read from the indictment currently before this court. It is charged in this indictment that the defendant, Maryann Flood, has committed and engaged in the following activities, which we will prove beyond a reasonable doubt.

"Maryann Flood, hiding behind the façade of a respectable model agency, Park Avenue Models, Inc., procured for profit young girls and women for illicit and immoral purposes and led them to lead lives of prostitution.

"Maryann Flood in several instances paid off or bribed certain public officials, in order to protect her illicit activities.

"Maryann Flood, by virtue of her contacts in this nefarious trade, was able to extort varying sums of money from her clients by threatening them with exposure."

I let the indictment drop to my side and looked at the jury. I could sense their interest.

"Procurement for purposes of prostitution.

"Bribery of public officials.

"Extortion and blackmail.

"Not a pretty picture for the people of the State of New York to contemplate. Each year thousands of young girls come to New York with their eyes on the stars. Broadway, TV, modeling. Each with their connotations of glamour and success.

"And lying in wait for these poor innocents is someone like Maryann Flood. Secure in the knowledge that her bribery and extortion will protect her from harm and molestation by such prosaic and mundane things as the laws of the people of the State of New York."

For the first time I turned to face the defendant's table. She was looking down at the table, a pencil tightly clutched in her fingers. Vito had a thin smile on his lips.

"Maryann Flood!" I called out.

Automatically she raised her head, and her eyes fixed on mine. There was something hurt in them I had never seen before. I let mine go hard and blank as I turned back to the jury and spoke as if I hadn't called to her.

"Maryann Flood," I repeated, "sits before her court of judgment, before a jury of her peers, charged with violating the laws of her society.

"And we, the people of the State of New York, the people for whom she had so much contempt, will prove these charges we make against her so that there will never be in any mind a vestige of doubt as to her guilt. We will follow, step by step, each and every action of her illicit and illegal career. We will establish in detail each action. And when the whole of the story is revealed, you, the jury, will be called upon to render such a verdict as to discourage and restrain any person who feels he has a right to flaunt and evade the responsibilities and laws of the people."

I gave the jury time to chew on what I had said while I went back to my table and exchanged the indictment for some other papers. Then slowly I walked back to the jury box.

"Ladies and gentlemen of the jury, I would like to trace for you the manner in which the State became acquainted with the activities of Maryann Flood." The jurors leaned forward, a look of interest on their faces. "One afternoon last May a young woman was admitted to Roosevelt Hospital. She was hemorrhaging internally. The result of an illegal operation. Despite all efforts, she began to sink rapidly.

"As is usual in matters of this kind, our office was notified. The girl was too weak to answer many questions, but this much we were able to learn from her. She was a model registered with Park Avenue Models, Inc. She also asked that Miss Flood be notified. She seemed sure that Miss Flood would be able to help her.

"A first routine telephone call to Park Avenue Models, Inc., brought forth the reply that they had never heard of a model by that name. About an hour later Miss Flood called our office, saying that there had been a mistake on the part of one of her employees. That this young woman had been registered with her agency. In particular she seemed concerned about what the girl had said, and as an afterthought offered her assistance.

"Both the telephone call and the offer of assistance came too late. The young woman had died shortly before.

"A check of the young woman's acquaintances revealed that she had come to New York approximately a year before. For six months she had been barely able to make ends meet. Suddenly she blossomed forth in a complete new wardrobe and furs. To her friends she explained her newfound prosperity by saying that she had made a connection with Park Avenue Models. She began to go out frequently, and her friends saw less and less of her. She explained this to them by saying she was constantly on call. That her work kept her busy all hours of the day and night.

"Yet when these statements were checked with the employment record maintained by the agency, there was a great discrepancy. The agency had listed only two or three jobs for her during that six-month period. Her total earnings during that period, after commissions were deducted, came to about one hundred and twenty-five dollars."

I shuffled some papers in my hand and pretended to look at them while I rested. After a moment I looked up at the jury. They were ready for me to continue.

"While this routine investigation was taking place, a report came to the Vice Squad of wild parties being held at the East Side apartment of a prominent manufacturer of ladies' undergarments. It was also brought to the attention of the police that the man had made statements in various quarters that he had contacts with a certain model agency that enabled him to have a supply of girls at any hour of the day or night and that his friends just had to call on him for the favor.

"On the last day of May the police interrupted a party going on in his apartment. Four men and six women were found in varying stages of undress and in certain—shall we say for the sake of being delicate?—compromising attitudes.

"Each of the girls gave her occupation as model. One admitted she was registered at Park Avenue Models, Inc. Several of the other girls whispered something to her. Immediately the girl retracted her statement. A check proved that each of the girls was registered there.

"It was at that point that the police and the District Attorney's office realized they had come across a vicious example of organized vice. An investigation of the agency immediately ensued."

I switched papers in my hand and began reading from one of them. "Park Avenue Models, Inc. Incorporated June 1948. Licensed to represent models for art, photography, fashion shows, etc. President, Maryann Flood."

I turned the page. The next sheet was a police report on Marja. I scanned it quickly as I walked silently toward the jury. *Maryann Flood, born November 16, 1919, New York City. Unmarried. Record of first arrest, April 1936. Charge— assault with a deadly weapon against stepfather. Before Magistrate Ross, Juvenile Court. Committed to Rose Geyer Home for Wayward Girls, May 1936. Discharged November 1937 upon reaching age of eighteen. Arrested February 1938. Charge—loitering for the purpose of and committing an act of prostitution. Pleaded guilty. Received thirty days in the workhouse. Arrested April 1943. Charge—grand larceny after committing an act of prostitution. Pleaded not guilty. Case dismissed for lack of evidence. No further record of arrests. Was known as associate of persons with criminal records. Held as material witness in slaying of Ross Drego, prominent gambler and racketeer, in Los Angeles, California, in September 1950.*

I put the papers carefully together in my hand and pointed them at the jury. "From this beginning the State began to assemble a story of vice and corruption that made even its most callous and hardened officers sick to their stomachs. A story of innocent young girls being forced into a life of prostitution and perversion, of extortion, blackmail, and corruption that reached high into the business, social, and official life of our city. And behind all this sorry mess the evidence points to the machinations and planning of just one person."

I turned and pointed the papers dramatically at the defendant's table. "Maryann Flood!"

Without looking back at the jury I crossed the room to my table. I sat down amid the rising murmur of voices in the courtroom behind me. I stared down at the table. My eyes were burning. I blinked them wearily.

"Good boy!" I heard them whisper.

"You sure pasted her!" Alec's voice came from the other side.

I didn't look up. I didn't want to have to see her. It seemed as if a thousand years had passed since I had got up to address the jury.

I heard the sound of the judge's gavel on his desk. Then his heavy voice: "The court will adjourn until two o'clock."

Automatically I got to my feet as he left the court. Then without speaking I made for the private entrance to the District Attorney's offices.

We ducked the reporters by going out to lunch through the Tombs. I went into the Old Mill restaurant and was given a table in the far corner. I sat down with my back to the room, facing Joel and Alec. The waitress came up to us.

"I need a drink," I said and ordered a gin over rocks, with a twist of lemon peel. "How about you fellows?"

They shook their heads and ordered their food. There was a murmur in the room behind us. I didn't have to turn around to know who had come in. I looked questioningly at Joel.

He nodded. "They're here."

I smiled thinly. "It's a free country." Suddenly I couldn't wait for the drink. I wished the damn waitress would hurry back. "Where's my drink?" I growled irritably.

"The waitress stopped to pick up their order on the way back," Alec said quickly.

A moment later she put the drink down in front of me. There was a peculiar expression on her face which I understood the moment I lifted my glass. There was writing on the doily under the glass.

I didn't have to look at the signature to recognize the writing. She still had the same childish scrawl.

"Welcome to the big time, Counselor," it read. "Good luck!" It was signed "Marja."

I crumpled the doily with my fingers so that the others could not see it had been written on, and sipped my drink. That was one thing I had always liked about her. She was afraid of nothing.

She wished me luck knowing full well that if I were lucky she could spend the next ten years of her life in jail. She was like that even when she was a kid.

I remembered once when I tried to stop her from crossing against a light into traffic that was moving wildly. Angrily she shook me off.

"That's the trouble with you, Mike," she had said. "Afraid to take chances. Even on a little thing like this!"

"But, Marja," I had protested, "you could get hurt, or maybe even killed."

She had looked at me, the wild light blazing in her eyes. "So what, Mike?" she said, stepping into the gutter. "It's my body, not yours."

That, in its essence, was the difference between us. That philosophy and a lot of other things. Like the way we had been brought up. She had an amazingly paradoxical capacity for both affection and cruelty.

I sipped again at my drink. The cold sweetish taste of the gin burned its way down my throat. I think my mother put her finger on it one night when I came home dejected from waiting for Marja to return from a date.

I was too big to cry, but the tears hovered beneath my eyes. Mom knew it the moment I came in the door. She moved quickly toward me. I turned away to go to my room, but her hand caught mine and held me.

"She's not for you, Mike," she said softly.

I didn't answer, just stared at her.

"I'm not telling you who to like, son," she added. "It's just that she's not for you. She's been brought up without love and has no understanding of it."

I had pulled my hand away and went to my room, but what she had said stayed in mind. Without love.

Now I could understand at last what Mother had meant.

That in all its simplicity was the story of Marja's life.

Without love.

Book One
MARJA

CHAPTER ONE

S HE PUSHED OPEN THE DOOR OF THE CANDY STORE AND STOOD THERE A moment while her eyes adjusted to the dimness. The bright sun behind her framed her face in the shimmering gold of her hair. The violent scarlet slash that was her mouth drew back over white, even teeth in a tentative smile. She walked toward the counter.

There was no one in the store. Impatiently she tapped a coin on the marble top.

There was an immediate answer from the rear of the shop, where Mr. Rannis had his rooms. "Just a minute, just a minute. I'm coming."

"That's all right, Mr. Rannis," she called. "It's only me. I'll wait."

The old man appeared in the doorway of his rear room. His hands were still busy adjusting his clothing. "Marja!" he exclaimed, a pleased tone coming into his voice. He moved stiffly behind the counter toward her. "What can I do for you?"

She smiled at him. "Gimme five Twenty Grands."

Automatically he turned to the shelf behind him, then hesitated. He glanced back at her over his shoulder questioningly.

"It's okay, Mr. Rannis," she said quickly. "I got a nickel."

He picked up an open package and shook five cigarettes out carefully and placed them on the counter before her, his hand covering them.

She pushed a nickel toward him. He lifted his hand from the cigarettes and covered the coin. He slid it back along the counter toward himself and it dropped into the cash drawer just beneath the counter.

The white-papered cigarettes were bright against the dirty gray marble. Slowly she picked one up and stuck it in her mouth. She reached toward the open box of wooden matches on the counter.

Before she could strike a match he had one flaming in front of her. She dipped the cigarette into it and dragged deeply. She could feel the harsh, acrid smoke filter back into her lungs. She exhaled, the smoke rushing from her lips and nostrils. "Man, that's good," she said. She looked at the old man. "I thought I'd never get out of school. I wanted that smoke all day and nobody would even give me a drag."

The old man looked at her, his lips drawing back over his partially toothless gums in a smile. "Where have you been, Marja?" he asked. "I haven't seen you all week."

She stared at him. "I been broke," she answered bluntly. "An' I owe yuh enough."

He rested his elbows on the counter and looked at her in what he thought was a winning way. "Why'd you do that, Marja?" he asked reproachfully. "I never asked you for money, did I?"

She took another puff at the cigarette and didn't answer.

His hand reached across the counter and took her free hand and squeezed it. "You know I'm always glad to see you, Marja."

She looked down at her hand, but made no effort to withdraw it. She flashed her eyes up at him. "You're glad to see any of the girls," she said flatly. "You like all of them."

"None of them like you, Marja," he said earnestly. "I'd rather see you than anybody. You were always my favorite, even when you were a little baby."

"I bet," she said skeptically.

"I mean it," he protested. "You're the only one I give credit to. I wouldn't let nobody else owe three dollars and twenty-five cents and not bother them."

She slipped her hand from his slowly, watching his eyes as she moved. She smiled slightly as she saw a film come over them. "What about Francie Keegan? She said you let her owe yuh."

He ran his tongue over suddenly dry lips. "I made her pay me, though, didn't I?" he demanded. "I never asked you, though."

She stepped back from the counter without speaking and looked around the store questioningly. "Something seems different here."

He smiled proudly. "I had the back rooms painted."

She raised a studied eyebrow. "Oh."

"A nice light green," he added. "I'm thinking of doing the store, too, if I can get the money together."

"Don' gimme that, Mr. Rannis," she laughed. "You got more money than God."

A hurt expression came over his face. "All you kids say that. I don't know why. You see the kind of business I do."

"That's just it," she said. "I do see." She turned suddenly and leaned over the candy counter against the glass.

The old man caught his breath. The full young lines of her body were revealed against the glass. Her strong young breasts pressed against the thin white blouse. "Want some candy?" he asked.

She looked at him over the counter top, her eyes speculative. "I haven't any more money," she said carefully.

"I didn't ask you for any, did I?" he asked, quickly bending down behind the counter and opening the door. He stared up at her through the glass. "What would you like?"

Her eyes were laughing as they met his. "Anything. A Milky Way."

Without taking his eyes from her, he reached for a candy bar. His hands were trembling. The bright light from the street behind her framed her body through the flimsy skirt. He had long ago found this vantage point of observation. It was one of the main reasons he kept the store lights dim. The other was the high cost of electricity.

She looked down at him, wondering how long he would stay there. It was a standing joke among the girls in the neighborhood. She knew what he was looking at. The Rannis display case worked both ways, but she didn't care. He was a horny old goat and it served him right if you could get something out of him. Especially for nothing.

In a few seconds she became bored with her little game and moved back to the other counter. Almost immediately he got to his feet, the, candy bar in his hand.

His face was flushed with the exertion of kneeling. He pushed the candy across the counter to her with one hand and grabbed hers with the other as she reached for it. She let her hand remain still as he spoke.

"You're the prettiest girl in the neighborhood, Marja," he said.

She sniffed disdainfully.

"I mean it, Marja," he said, squeezing her hand earnestly. He turned her hand over in his and opened it. "You got pretty hands, too, for a kid."

"I'm no kid," she said quickly. "I'm goin' on sixteen."

"You are?" he asked in a surprised voice. Time went so quickly in this neighborhood. They grew up in a hurry. Before you could turn around, they were married and gone.

"Sure," she said confidently. "In the fall."

"I bet the boys in school are all wild for you," he said.

She shrugged her shoulders noncommittally.

He looked down at her hands. "I bet they're always trying to get you in corners."

She purposely made a puzzled expression. "What do yuh mean, Mr. Rannis?" she asked innocently.

"You know what I mean," he said.

"No, I don't, Mr. Rannis," she insisted, a glimmer of laughter lurking in her eyes. "You tell me."

He withdrew his hand with the candy bar, released hers, and walked down behind the counter to the back of the store. At the end of the counter, where the display concealed him from the front of the store, he called to her. "Come back here, Marja," he said, "and I'll tell you."

Slowly she walked to the back of the store. There was a half-smile on her lips. She stepped partly behind the display stand and looked up into his face.

His face was flushed and there were beads of moisture on his upper lip. His mouth worked tensely, but no words came out.

Her smile grew broader. "What, Mr. Rannis?"

His hand reached toward her. She stood very still. "Don't they ever want to touch you?" he asked in a hoarse voice.

She looked down at his hand a few inches from her and then up at his face. "Where?" she asked.

He brushed his fingertips against the front of her blouse lightly. The firm flesh sent a flame up his fingers. "Here?" he asked tensely, watching her face for signs of fear.

There were none. She didn't even make a move to get away from him. Instead she smiled. "Oh," she answered. "Yes, Mr. Rannis. All the time."

Her answer took him by surprise. He almost forgot that he was holding her. "You let them?"

Her eyes were still frankly fixed on his. "Sometimes I do. Sometimes I don't. It depends on how I feel. If I like it." She turned slightly, moving away from him. "My candy, Mr. Rannis," she said, holding out her hand.

Without thinking, he gave it to her. He stared at her, the memory of her breasts in his fingers still flooding his mind. "You want to see the paint job in the back room?" he asked.

She didn't answer, just looked at him as she unwrapped the bar and bit it slowly.

"If you come in the back," he said anxiously. "Maybe if you're real nice, I'll forget about the three and a quarter you owe me."

She swallowed a piece of the candy and looked at him reflectively. Then, without answering, she turned and started for the door.

"Marja!" he called after her in a pleading voice. "I'll even give you some money!"

She paused at the marble-topped counter and picked up her cigarettes and a few matches, then continued on to the door. She started to open it.

"Marja!" the old man pleaded. "I'll give you anything you want!"

She stood there a moment, her hand on the door before answering. When she did speak, he realized that she had been thinking over her reply.

"No, Mr. Rannis," she said politely in her husky voice. "I ain't ready for yuh. Not just yet."

The door closed behind her and the store seemed dull and empty without the bright, flashing gold of her hair. Wearily, as if he had been in battle, he turned and went into the back room.

CHAPTER TWO

T HE EARLY JUNE SUN HAD BAKED THE CITY STREETS TO A SOFT SPONGE-like asphalt surface that clung maliciously to the feet and made every step an effort. It bounced wildly off the flat concrete walls of the tenements and beat against the face like the licking flame of an open fire.

She hesitated a moment in the doorway of the store before stepping into the inferno of the street. Slowly she ate the last of the candy bar while her eyes scanned the street for signs of life.

It was almost deserted except for a few children who were playing down near the corner of Second Avenue. One lone woman came out of Hochmeyer's Pork Store carrying a shopping-bag and made her way up the block. A taxi roared down the street, leaving bluish tracks in the pavement

The candy was finished, and carefully she wiped her fingers on the wrapper and threw the paper into the gutter. She slipped the cigarettes into a small purse and stepped down onto the sidewalk. The heat and the sun hit her face and she blinked her eyes rapidly. She could feel the perspiration spring out like a flood all over her body. For a moment she regretted not having stayed in the candy store and played the old man along for a little while. At least it was almost cool in there.

She headed up the street toward her house reluctantly. The clock in one of the store windows told her it was near three. She hesitated. If it weren't so warm she wouldn't be going home, but only a fool would stay out on the street on a day like this. She wished she had the money to go to the show. The RKO 86th Street Theatre had a cooling-system. Fans blowing over big cakes of ice. For a dime you could stay in there all day and beat the heat.

"Marja!" A girl's voice behind her called.

She turned and looked back. It was her friend Francie Keegan. She waited for the girl to come up to her. "Hi, Francie."

Francie was out of breath from hurrying up the block. She was a big girl, heavy-set, with full, ripe breasts and hips. She was a year older than Marja and had thick black hair and dark-blue eyes. "Where yuh goin', Marj?" she asked, still breathing harshly.

"Home," Marja answered succinctly. "It's too damn hot to stay out."

A look of disappointment crossed Francie's face. "I thought we might go to a show."

"Got money?" Marja asked.

"No."

"Neither have I," Marja said and turned back up the block.

Her friend fell into step with her. "Christ!" she exclaimed "Everybody in the whole world is broke!"

A half-smile crossed Marja's face. She looked at her friend out of the corners of her eyes. "Now she tells me."

They walked another few steps silently; then Francie put her hand on Marja's arm. "I got an idea."

Marja looked at her.

"Old Man Rannis," Francie explained. "Maybe we can promote some change outta him."

Marja shook her head. "Uh-huh. I just been there."

"An'?" Francie asked curiously.

"Nothin'," Marja said. "I got a candy bar after lettin' him use his X ray on me."

"So?"

"That's all," Marja continued. "Then he wanted me to go in the back with him an' see the new paint job, but no money. I owe him three and a quarter already. I even gave him a feel, but all he wanted was to go in the back."

Francie thought over her friend's statement. At last she spoke. "Akey's on the candy bar." Marja smiled.

"Too late." She rubbed her stomach meaningly. "I already ate it."

"Damn!" Francie swore. "I got no luck today at all." She began to walk again.

"I guess we might as well go home." She wiped her face on the short cotton sleeve of her dress. "Damn! It's hot."

Marja didn't speak. They walked silently. They were almost halfway up the block before they exchanged another word.

"Who's home?" Francie asked.

"Everybody, I guess," Marja answered. "My mother doesn't go to work until five o'clock." Her mother was a cleaning woman in an office downtown and worked until two in the morning.

"Your stepfather, too?"

A cold look came into Marja's eyes, making them almost black. "Especially him," she said contemptuously. "He wouldn't leave his three cans of beer for all the money in the world."

"Doesn't he work at all? Ever?" Francie asked

Marja laughed. "Why should he? He never had it so good. Three squares an' all the beer he can drink. He's no dope. Jus' sits aroun' all day an' burps."

A strange look came into Francie's eyes. "He stopped me in the hall the other day."

Marja turned to her. "What'd he want?"

"He asked some questions about you."

"Like what?"

"Like about what you did outside. With boys. That kind uh thing."

"Oh." Marja thought for a moment. "He's always asking me, too. What'd you tell him?"

"Nothin'," Francie answered. "I'm no dope."

A mild sigh of relief escaped Marja's lips. "He'd just love to get somethin' on me. He hates me."

"I know," Francie said. "Sometimes I can hear him hollerin' upstairs." Francie lived in the apartment over Marja.

"He's always hollerin'," Marja answered.

They were almost at the house now. The tenements were all alike on this block. The same faceless brown stone that once had known better days, black and dirty windows staring blindly into the street.

They stopped at the stoop There was an uncovered garbage can near the entrance. While they stood there, a gray alley cat jumped up onto it, chasing the swarm of flies, and began to rummage through it. They watched him silently.

Marja wrinkled up her nose. "You'd think the super would have the brains to cover the can in this weather." She sniffed the air. "It stinks."

Francie didn't speak. They started up the steps. A wolf whistle came from across the street. They both turned around.

Three boys had just come from the pool parlor opposite their house and were looking at them. One of them called out: "Hey, Francie, who's yer blond friend?"

The girls exchanged looks quickly and a tight smile came to their lips. "Why'n't yuh come over an' find out?" Francie called back.

The three boys whispered something to each other in the doorway while Marja tried to recognize them. The one who had called to Francie she had seen several times before. He lived down the block. She couldn't remember his name. The other two she had never seen.

The two strangers were both tall. One was fair-haired—brown, almost blond— with an open face and gentle blue eyes; the other, almost the opposite. Dark, good-looking, with handsome Grecian features and a full, sensual mouth. After a moment the blond one walked away from the others with a wave of his hand and the remaining boys sauntered slowly across the street.

"Hullo, Jimmy," Francie said as they drew near.

Jimmy was a thin boy, his eyes slightly protruding, his face covered with the remains of a vanishing acne. He smiled, showing white buck teeth. "Where yuh been keepin' yerself, Francie?" he asked.

"Aroun'," she answered. "You?"

He looked down at the sidewalk a moment before he answered. "Around." He looked at his friend quickly. "What're yuh doin'?"

"Nothin'," Francie answered. "We were jus' goin' up to get outta this heat."

"Ross an' me were jus' goin' fer a swim," Jimmy said quickly. "Wanna come?"

Francie looked at Marja, who had been silent up to now. There was a glimmer of interest in Marja's eyes. "If we go upstairs to get our bathing-suits," she explained, "we couldn't come back."

The other boy laughed. His laugh was surprisingly deep. "We can get suits where we're going," he said.

"Ross's got a car," Jimmy said. "We were goin' out tuh Coney Island."

Marja spoke for the first time. "Then what're we standin' here talkin' for?"

The other boy reached for Marja's arm. His grip was firm and sure, and she came down off the stoop toward him. The laughter was still deep in his throat. "That's it, baby," he said, his eyes challenging her. "I like a girl what knows her mind."

She fell into step beside him and looked up at him, her own eyes meeting his challenge. "It ain't my mind I know," she laughed. "It's my body. And it's hot."

"Can't be too hot for me," he said.

The others fell into step behind them. She looked over her shoulder at Francie. Jimmy was whispering something to her and Francie was smiling and nodding. She looked up at the boy next to her. "Where yuh parked?"

"Just around the corner," he said. "My name's Ross Drego, what's yours?"

"Marja," she answered.

"Your whole name, I mean," he insisted.

She looked into his eyes. "Marja Anna Flood."

"Flood's an English name," he said in a puzzled voice.

"I'm Polish," she said quickly. "It was changed from Fluudjincki."

"I can see why." His smile took the edge off his phrase.

They were around the corner now, and he steered her to a Buick roadster with the top down. He opened the door with a flourish. "Your chariot, girls."

Marja stopped and looked at the car, then at him.

"What are you waiting for?" he asked. "Get in."

She shook her head. "Uh-uh. This looks like the wrong kind uh hot to me."

A puzzled expression came into Ross's eyes. "What do you mean?"

"I ain't goin' for no joy ride in a stolen car," she said. "I can get into enough trouble on my own."

Ross began to laugh. "The car isn't stolen," he said. "It's mine."

She looked at him doubtfully. "Oh, yeah? Where do you come to a job like this? That's probably why your friend didn't want to go with yuh."

Ross grinned. "You mean Mike Keyes? He had to go back to work. He helps his old man around the house. He's the super."

She was still skeptical. "I don't buy it," she insisted stubbornly.

Jimmy's voice came over her shoulder. "Go ahead, get in. It's his car, all right. His old man gave it to him."

She stepped back from the car. "Prove it first," she said.

The laughter had left Ross's eyes. "You don't believe me?" His voice was flat and cold.

"I believe yuh," she said, looking right at him. "But I ain't takin' any chances. I know a girl on the block who also believed a guy and she's up in Bedford now."

A flush of anger surged into his dark face. "Then blow," he said tensely. "I can get a thousand cheap chips like you to come with me."

She turned and began to walk back up the street. She was almost to the corner when his voice stopped her. She waited for him to catch up to her.

"Wait a minute, Marja," he said, his hand fishing in his pocket. "It's my car. I'll show you."

He took out a wallet and handed it to her. She looked down at it. There was more green folding money in there than she had ever seen in her life. She looked at him questioningly.

She opened the wallet. On one side was a driver's license, on the other was an owner's registration. Both were made out to Ross Drego, 987 Park Avenue, N.Y.C. She glanced at his age quickly. He was eighteen. Silently she closed it and gave it back to him.

"Now will you come?" he asked.

"Why couldn't you do that in the first place?" she countered.

"I was sore," he said quickly. A smile came to his lips. "I'm sorry. Forgive me?"

She stared at him for a moment. He was a strange guy. She had never met anyone like him. He spoke so well, and yet there was a wildness and meanness in him that she could feel. But it disappeared when he smiled. An answering smile parted her lips.

She reached out and took his arm "C'mon, hurry," she said. "It's so damn hot, I can't wait to get into the water."

CHAPTER THREE

"WHAT PART OF CONEY ISLAND IS THIS?" MARJA ASKED AS ROSS stopped the car at a gate and tooted the horn.

He looked at her, a smile in his eyes. "Sea Gate. We have a house here."

"What d'yuh mean, house? A locker?" she said.

The smile slipped to his lips. "No. A regular house. This is a private section."

A gateman peered through the grating at them.

"Open up, Joe," Ross called.

"Oh, it's you, Mr. Drego," the gateman said. Slowly the big iron gate began to swing open.

"It's a summer house," Ross explained as he drove through the entrance. "We stay here when Dad is too busy to get away from the office."

Marja looked around. On either side of the road were beautiful houses set on rolling lawns and shaded by towering trees. "Christ!" she exclaimed. "It's like livin' in a park."

Ross didn't answer. She turned around to Francie in the back seat. "Ain't it, Francie?" she asked.

Francie and Jimmy were impressed, too. Both of them were goggling at the homes along the road. Francie nodded. "I bet ony millionaires live here," she said.

Marja turned back to Ross. "Did yuh hear that?" she asked.

Ross nodded without speaking, his eyes watching the road.

"Is that true?" she asked.

Ross shook his head. "No."

"Your old man must be rich," she said.

He turned the car into a driveway and stopped. He reached forward and cut the ignition. Then he looked at her, his eyes bleak and cold. "Does it make any difference to you what my father is?" he asked. "I brought you here."

Marja stared at him, wondering what she had said to make him angry. After a moment she answered: "No."

Quickly as it had appeared, the coldness left his eyes and he smiled. "Then, come on in and get a suit. The water looks great from here."

She followed his pointing finger past the house. The beach and the rolling ocean were right behind it. He jumped out of the car and held the door for her. She got out and looked at the house.

It was a big house. Two stories. Wood and shingles, painted a cool dark green. She didn't care what Ross said, his old man had to have plenty of cabbage to keep a joint like this.

He led them up the front porch and, taking out a key, opened the door. "Follow me," he said, starting up a flight of stairs.

She caught a glimpse of an elaborately furnished parlor and dining-room as she went up. She looked down at the steps. Her shoes didn't make a sound on the thick carpeting. She had never known people could live like this except in the movies.

He stopped in front of a door and opened it. "This is my sister's room," he said. "Come inside and we'll find a bathing suit that'll fit you."

Marja followed him into the room. Behind her, she could hear Francie's gasp. Without turning, Marja knew what she meant. Never in her life had she seen a room like this.

It was all pink and blue satin. The drapes, the bedspread, even the long, funny chair near the bed. The carpet was a warm rose color and the furniture a rich cherry tinted wood.

Ross opened a closet. "The suits are here," he announced. He pointed to another door. "That's the bathroom." He moved back toward the doorway in which Jimmy stood. "We'll give you ten minutes to get ready."

Jimmy snickered. "Maybe the girls can use some help."

Francie giggled.

He came into the room. Ross's voice stopped him. "Come on, Jimmy. We'll get our suits."

Obediently Jimmy went back through the door, and it closed behind them. The two girls looked at each other.

"I don't care what Ross says," Francie whispered. "His old man must be a millionaire."

Marja's voice dropped to a whisper. "Either that or he's a racketeer."

Francie's eyes grew big and round. "What d'yuh think?"

Marja smiled. "I think we better get dressed before they come back." She walked over to the closet. "My God, Francie!" she exclaimed. "Look here."

Francie peered through the open door. "Jeez!" she said in speechless wonder.

There were about twenty bathing-suits hanging there. Gently Francie reached out and touched one. "Marja, feel it. Real wool!" She turned to her friend.

Marja had already slipped out of her blouse and skirt and was busy unfastening her brassiere.

She came racing out of the water, laughing breathlessly, Ross at her heels. "Don't, Ross, don't!" she cried. "I'll get my head full of sand."

"It can be washed," he laughed, trying to grab her ankle. She turned away from him and he stumbled to his knees.

She looked over her shoulder. Ross picked himself up and lunged at her. His hand caught her flying ankle and she tumbled into the sand. He fell down beside her.

They lay there quietly, trying to catch their breath. She could hear the wind whistling deep in his chest. At last her breath came back to her and she rolled over on her back. The sun was warm on her face. She closed her eyes. It was like living in paradise.

She could hear the breath still in him, and now he was lying there quietly. Slowly she opened her eyes.

He was resting on one elbow, looking at her. "Having a good time?" he said, smiling.

She smiled back at him. "I'm havin', a ball," she answered.

"I'm glad," he said. He rolled over and sat up. "Francie and Jimmy are still in the water."

She liked the way he said "water." *Wahter*—quick like. She looked down the beach. "I don't blame them," she answered. "It's real great."

He turned to her. "Then why did you come out?"

"I had enough," she said. "I'm not greedy. Besides, too much of a good thing'll spoil me. An' I can't afford it."

His face came down very close to hers. "I'd like to spoil you," he said in a low voice. "And I can afford it."

Her eyes stared directly into his. After a moment his lids began to feel heavy. No one had ever looked at him like this. So straight and unwinking, as if her eyes looked into the very depths and crevices of his mind.

"How d'yuh know?" she asked huskily. "Maybe I'm too rich for yuh blood."

"I know," he answered, putting his hand on her shoulder. Her lips were parted and waiting for him. Her tongue traced the corners of his mouth, leaving tiny flames in its wake. A pulse began to pound in his temple.

He pressed her head back into the beach, his arm beneath her neck. Her hands pressed lightly against the back of his head. He closed his eyes. No one had ever kissed him like this.

Her eyes were still open, and she watched him. A pleasant warmth was flowing through her. It was funny when they kissed her how they all looked alike. When their faces were so close that their two eyes blurred almost into one before they closed. At least in this he was no different from anyone else.

She felt his searching hand. She liked his touch. It was warm and somehow gentle. Not like others who had hurt her. She let the suit strap slip so that she could feel his hand on her naked skin. His breath began to come hard into her mouth.

She let her fingers drift lightly across his wet bathing-suit from his stomach to his thigh. He was strong, too. All ridged muscles etched sharply on him. She closed her hand gently on him. She took her face from him and pressed his head down to her breast.

She felt his teeth hard behind his lips. He tried to turn his face, but she held him tight. She looked down at him, half smiling to herself. This was what was so wonderful. What they would do for her, what she could make them do. This was what she liked about being a woman. Because, in the end, she was always the stronger.

"Ross," she whispered. She could see the flaming agony in his eyes.

He almost cried aloud. She felt him shudder, then the heat of his body came through his wet bathing-suit. An echoing warmth ran through her and she caught her breath. For a moment she clung to him tightly, then it was gone and they were still.

He rolled away from her and lay face downward on the sand. He was breathing deeply.

She turned toward him and stroked his hair gently. "Ross, baby," she whispered. "You're sweet."

Slowly he turned his face to her. There was a curious shame in his eyes. "Why did you do that, Marja?" he asked harshly.

Her eyes were wide, the smile on her lips held the knowledge of all women. "Because I like you, honey," she replied easily. "And I wanted you to be happy."

The corners of his mouth worked as he tried to keep his lips from trembling. For a moment he felt on the verge of tears. He knew he was older than she, but right now he felt like a child next to her. He tore his eyes from her gaze. "Don't do it again. Ever." His voice was cracked and rough.

"Don't you like it, honey?" she asked softly.

He didn't look at her. He spat out his answer. "No."

"Then I won't, honey," she said.

He felt her move in the sand beside him and turned to look at her. She was sitting up, running her hand through the sparkling gold of her hair. An animal vitality seemed to flow from her.

She looked down at him and smiled. "I told yuh the sand would get in my hair." She got to her feet. "I'm goin' in to wash it out. Come in with me." She held out her hands toward him.

He didn't move from his place in the sand. He looked up at her over his shoulder. "Go ahead in," he said. "I'll be along in a minute."

He watched her run into the water and tumble into a breaker before he got to his feet and ran down the beach after her.

CHAPTER FOUR

THE FIRST DUSKY PURPLE OF EVENING CLOUDED THE SKY. IN THE WEST the sun still fought back the night, a flaming red ball reaching back desperately to all its yesterdays. The warmth began to leave the air.

Marja sat up on the blanket Ross had spread for them. "I wonder what time it is," she said.

He opened his eyes and squinted at the sky. "About a quarter after six," he answered.

"How can you tell?"

He grinned at her. "I was a Boy Scout once."

"I never knew a Boy Scout before," she laughed, dropping her hand to his knee.

Instinctively he tensed. She felt his movement and took her hand away quickly. "I'm sorry, I forgot."

"Don't be sorry," he said.

"But you don't like me to touch you," she said.

He shook his head. "It's not that, really. I'm just not used to it, I guess."

"Then you do like me?" she asked.

"I liked you from the moment I saw you through the dirty windows of the poolroom."

"Honest?" She was smiling now.

"Honest," he answered, his eyes serious. "I saw you walking down the block with Francie and I couldn't keep my eyes off you. You ruined my game. Mike took me to the cleaners."

"Mike?" she said questioningly. "That's the blond boy who didn't want to come with us?"

He nodded. "He didn't even look up from the table when I told him about you."

She was piqued. "What did you say?"

He grinned. " 'Mama,' I said, 'buy me some of that!' "

She punched his side playfully. "Fresh!"

"It's a good thing Jimmy was around. Otherwise, I might never have met you," he said.

"Yeah," she said sarcastically. "Your other friend wouldn't have been no help."

"Mike is all right," he protested. "It's just that he's too serious. He never bothers with girls. Studies all the time. He's going to be a lawyer."

"Is he as old as you?" she asked.

He shook his head. "A year younger. But we're in the same class at school."

Her vanity was hurt. It was a matter of pride that all boys must like her. "I bet he's not as nice as you are."

"Thanks," he said dryly. "You're the first girl I know that thinks so. Usually when they see him, I'm a gone pigeon."

"He must be terribly conceited," she said flatly. "I can't stand conceited fellas."

"He's really very nice," Ross said. "I don't think he even knows that they like him."

She shivered slightly as the cool of twilight hit her shoulders. "I don't care about him, anyway," she said indifferently. She looked down the beach. "Where's Francie?"

"They went up to the house about an hour ago while you were dozing," he answered. "Francie said it was getting too cold for her."

She got to her feet and stretched. "I guess we'd better go, too. I'm beginnin' to feel it."

He stared up at her. Idly he wondered how old she was. About seventeen, he guessed. He had never known a girl to be so much a woman at her age, though. Her clear, fair skin and high cheekbones, the wide, sensual, almost sullen mouth, the firm cast of her chin. She stretched again, holding her arms high over her head. He could see the tiny blond tufts in her armpits trailing down to the curve of her young full breasts, which molded down to a tiny, solid waist and then flared out into generous hips and rounded high flanks. She stood squarely on long, straight, yet feminine legs.

She was aware of his inventory. She smiled down at him. She liked him to look at her.

The question came involuntarily to his lips. "How old are you, Marja?"

"Guess," she answered, still smiling.

"Seventeen," he ventured.

She felt proud that he thought her older. "Almost," she said with just the right degree of hesitation.

He put his arms around her legs and toppled her toward him. She fell, laughing, her face very close to his. He made a fierce scowl. "Ready for a kiss, me fair young beauty?" he said in his best villainous voice.

Her eyes didn't change expression. "Always ready," she said huskily.

He put his mouth to her lips. He was vaguely surprised to find that she was right. Again her lips worked against his mouth, making a place for her tongue. This time he was going to be ready for her. She wasn't going to take him by surprise. He fought the surge of passion in him. He held her close but cautiously. He felt her fingers trailing lightly on his cheek and the flame leaped high inside him and he knew that he had lost.

Desperately, almost angrily, he pulled his mouth from her. "I think we'd better get going," he said sullenly.

"Okay," she said quietly. She got to her feet and waited for him.

Avoiding her gaze, he began to gather up the blanket. When it was folded, he slipped his arm through it and rose to his feet, holding it in front of him. He started back to the house without looking at her.

She fell in step beside him. Her hand reached out and touched the blanket. He looked at her. She was smiling. "Hiding something, honey?" she asked.

His face flamed scarlet. An angry retort was on his lips, but they were already at the house. Instead of speaking, he silently held the door open for her.

They entered the house through the beach entrance. It was the rear section of the cellar, made over into a sort of bath house. She stepped into the room and then stood very still. She reached a hand behind her and gestured a finger to her lips to silence him.

"Look," she whispered, a teasing smile on her lips. "The lovers."

He stared Francie and Jimmy were fast asleep on the couch in each other's arms. Both were completely nude. His first impulse was one of shock, but it quickly gave way to laughter. It was funny. Jimmy was so skinny and Francie was a big girl. He put his hand over his mouth to still his laughter.

"Shall we wake them?" he whispered.

She shook her head. "No. They look so tired, the poor darlings."

Quietly they tiptoed past them and into the hall. She looked at him. "How do I get back to the bedroom?" she asked. "I want to get dressed."

He gestured and she followed him up the stairs. He opened the door of her room. She turned to look at him. "Can I take a shower?" she asked.

"If you won't mind the cold water," he answered. "The hot-water heater hasn't been turned on yet."

"I don't mind," she said. She picked up her clothing from the chair and went into the bathroom. She closed and locked the bathroom door, then waited, listening. She heard the bedroom door click behind him as he left. Then, smiling to herself, she stepped into the tub, pulled the shower curtain around her, and turned on the water.

Even cold, it was wonderful. She loved showers. At home all they had was a tub, and that was in the kitchen. The toilet was out in the hall. This was the way to live. She began to sing in a clear, unmusical voice. She had been there almost ten minutes when she reluctantly turned off the water.

She pulled aside the shower curtain and had one foot out of the tub before she looked up. Her hand flew to her mouth in surprise "Oh!"

Ross was standing there smiling, a big bath towel in his outstretched hands. "I thought you could use this," he said.

She didn't move. "How did you get in?" she asked.

"My door." He gestured behind him. "It's on the other side." He stared down at her. "Better take this," he said, holding the towel toward her. "I hear real blondes are very susceptible to colds."

She took the towel and wrapped it around her. "Thank you," she said coldly.

"Wait a minute," he said. "You're not angry, are you?"

She shook her head. "I don't like people sneaking up on me, that's all."

He pulled her toward him. "It was just a joke, Marja." He tried to kiss her.

She turned a cheek toward him. "It's not funny," she said. "Now leave me alone. I wanna get dressed."

He could feel the warmth of her through the thick towel. An excitement began to run through him. In his mind he could see the couple downstairs on the couch as they had tiptoed through the room. He held her tightly to him. "You're not going to leave me like this," he said in a strained voice, his heart hammering inside him.

She stared up into his eyes. Her eyes were the coldest he had ever seen. She didn't speak.

Anger ran through him violently. He tried to force his lips to her mouth. Silently she squirmed and twisted away from him. He couldn't hold her still. He leaned his weight against her and pushed her back against the wall. Now she couldn't move away from him.

He stared into her eyes, breathing heavily. She looked back at him without fear. "Cut the teasing, Marja," he said harshly. "What do you think I brought you out here for?"

She didn't answer. Just kept watching him.

He tried to rip the towel from her, but she held it tightly. He felt his temper run away with him. There was a wild joy in his violence. He slapped her across the face with the back of his hand. "Come on, you bitch!" he snapped. "Put out! Francie said you would!"

He felt her freeze and straighten up against the wall. He looked at her. The marks of his fingers were white against her sun-flushed cheek. A half-smile came to her lips, her eyelids drooped. "Ross, baby," she whispered gently.

A confident smile came to his lips. These cheap little tramps were all alike. Sometimes they needed a little handling to show them who was boss. He moved toward her surely.

He didn't see the vicious upward sweep of her knee until the pain exploded in his groin. He stood there unbelieving for a moment, swaying in front of her. "Marja!" he said in a shocked voice, through rapidly whitening lips. "My God! Marja?" Then the second climax of pain tumbled him to the floor in front of her.

He could see her watching him coldly through his pain-blurred eyes as he lay doubled up before her. He writhed as the waves of agony ripped through him.

He felt rather than saw her step over him and pick up her clothing from the chair. He felt a draft on his cheek as she opened the door. He strained, trying to look up at her.

She was in the doorway looking back at him. Her voice fell coldly on his ears. "If that was what you wanted, why didn't you pick Francie?"

The pain was receding now. He could breathe again, but didn't dare move for fear it would return. He forced himself to speak. "Because it was you I wanted, Marja," he mumbled through numb lips.

Her voice was not quite so cold now. "There's some things I do, some things I don't," she said patiently, as if explaining to a child. "What kind uh girl do you think I am, Ross?"

The door closed behind her and he was alone on the floor of the room. He pressed his burning cheek to the cool tile and closed his eyes. A vision of her as she stepped from the shower flashed before him, and the pain returned. He caught his breath.

"Marja," he whispered to the cold tile floor. "What kind of a girl are you?"

CHAPTER FIVE

WEARILY HE OPENED HIS EYES. THE ROOM WAS DARK, THE NIGHT OUT-side the windows still. He rolled over, the soft bed giving beneath him; the blanket caught his arms and held them. Vaguely he wondered how he had got here. An ache came back to him and he began to remember. He had stumbled from the bathroom and tumbled into bed. He remembered sinking into its welcoming softness, but that was all. He didn't remember covering himself.

"Feeling better, Ross?"

He turned his head toward Marja's voice. A cigarette glowed from a chair in the corner of the room. He sat up. Now he remembered everything. She had come into the room and covered him while he was dozing. He had been shivering as if with a chill.

"Yes," he answered sullenly.

The cigarette made an upward sweep, glowed bright, and then dimmed. "Want a drag?" she asked.

"Please."

He heard her move in the darkness, then her silhouette crossed the window. He felt the bed sink beneath her weight. The cigarette was in front of him. He took it gratefully and put it between his lips. The acrid smoke filtered deep into his lungs. He began to feel better.

"What time is it?" he asked.

"About nine," she answered.

He puffed again at the cigarette and let the smoke drift slowly out his nostrils. It seemed to help him waken. "Where are the others?" he asked, trying unsuccessfully to see her in the glow of the cigarette. "Still downstairs?"

"No," she answered shortly. "Francie was scared when we came upstairs and found you on the bed. She wanted to go home. Jimmy went with her."

He thought silently, bitterly: Fine friends, run out when you need them. But it was just what he could expect from Jimmy. Mike would never have done that. A thought ran through his mind. "Did you tell them what happened?"

"No," she replied. "Why should I? That was between us."

"Then what did they think?" he asked.

"I tol' 'em you were sick," she answered. The bed shook slightly as if she was laughing, but he couldn't tell. "Yuh sure acted like it. Shiverin' away."

A resentment came up in him. If they thought he was really sick, that made their actions even more cowardly. He might have really needed them. He tried to see her, but it was too dark. He leaned over and turned on a light near the bed. For a moment the light hurt his eyes and he blinked; then he turned toward her. "Why didn't you go with them?" he asked bitterly.

She didn't answer.

"You knew what happened, you didn't have to stay," he added. "I could have managed."

Her eyes were luminous in the light from the lamp. Her hair, almost white in its glow, was pulled straight back across her head and tied behind with a tiny ribbon. Her mouth was scarlet with lipstick, and full and shining. She sat motionlessly opposite him, still not speaking.

"Well?" he asked nastily. "Lost your tongue?"

"I came with you," she said quietly. "I was going back with you."

A perverseness prompted his tongue. "Did you think I was going to take you back after what happened? That I would want to?"

She watched him silently, the pupils of her eyes growing large and black so that the irises almost seemed to disappear. That was the strangest thing about her. Her eyes always seemed to be speaking, yet he could never understand what they were saying.

"Did you?" he asked again.

She took a deep breath and silently got to her feet. She walked back to the chair in the corner, picked up her tiny purse, and started for the door. She didn't look at him.

He waited until she had her hand on the door before he spoke. "Marja!"

She stopped and looked down at him silently.

"Where are you going?" he asked unnecessarily.

"Home," she answered in a flat, expressionless voice. "You're okay now."

"Do you have carfare?"

"I can manage," she said in the same flat voice.

His hand moved swiftly, snatching the tiny purse from her grasp. "Where did you get money?" he asked coldly. "Francie said neither of you had a cent with you."

She didn't answer. The expression on her face didn't change. "I said I could manage," she repeated expressionlessly.

He opened the purse and looked into it. It was empty except for a lipstick, two slightly beaten cigarettes, a comb, and some wooden matches.

"Your wallet is under your pillow," she said quietly. "I put it there."

Instinctively he reached for it and flipped it open. The bills were still there. He began to feel ashamed of his suspicion.

"Now kin I have my bag back?" she asked. "I wanna get goin'. It's late."

He looked up at her, then down at her empty purse. He took a ten-dollar bill from his wallet and stuffed it into her purse. "Take a cab," he said, handing the purse back to her.

The ten-dollar bill fluttered back onto the bed. "No, thanks," she said dryly. "I don't want nothin' from you." The door closed behind her.

He sat there for a moment in surprise, then jumped to his feet. At the last second he realized that they had stripped the wet bathing-suit from him. Pulling the bedspread around him to hide his nakedness, he ran into the hall after her. "Marja!" he called. "Marja! Wait a minute!" He stumbled over the trailing bedspread and grabbed at the railing to keep from falling down the staircase.

She was already at the bottom of the steps when she turned to look back at him. She stared for a moment, then a smile spread across her face and she began to roar with laughter.

Her laughter floated mockingly up to him. He began to get angry. "What the hell are you laughing at?" he yelled.

She couldn't stop. "Look at yerself, Ross," she gasped, pointing. "You look like a pitcher of a ghost!"

He turned to the full-length mirror on the wall near him. His pale face and wild hair over the white bedspread did make him look like a ghost. He began to smile and then, laughing, turned back to her. "Give me time to get dressed, Marja," he said, "and I'll take you home."

"Better stop the car and let me out here," she said as they came to her corner. "My stepfather might be sittin' at the window."

Silently he pulled the car to the curb. He got out of the car and walked stiffly around it and opened her door. He held her hand as she stepped out.

They stood there awkwardly on the sidewalk for a moment, then she put out her hand. "Thanks for a nice time, Ross," she said politely.

He searched her eyes for a trace of sarcasm, but there was none. He took her hand. "Will I see you again, Marja?" he asked.

Her hand was quiet in his. "If you want," she answered.

He put his foot on the running-board. The movement made him wince. "I want to," he said.

She noticed the flash of pain on his face. "I didn't mean to hurt you so bad, Ross," she said quietly.

He looked into her eyes. "I deserved it," he said simply. "I should have known better."

A few seconds passed and then she withdrew her hand. "I better go," she said. "The ol' man'll be wild."

"What's your number?" he asked quickly. He saw a puzzled expression on her face. "So I can call you," he added.

"Oh," she replied, suddenly understanding. "We haven't got a phone."

"Then how will I get in touch with you?" he asked. It was his turn to be puzzled. He had always thought everyone had a telephone.

She looked up at him. "I'm generally at Rannis's candy store at three o'clock. It's up the block, across the street from the poolroom."

"I'll call you there tomorrow," he said.

"Okay." She hesitated a moment. "Good night, Ross."

He smiled. "Good night, Marja."

He watched her walk up the block, her half-high heels clicking on the pavement. He liked the way she walked, her head high, her step sure, her body swaying slightly as if she owned the earth. There was a natural pride in her.

He waited until he saw her walk up the steps and into her house before he got back into the car. He turned up the block after her. The lights were on in the poolroom as he passed by. On an impulse he stopped the car and got out.

He had been right. Jimmy was in there, leaning over a table cue in hand, in the midst of a group of boys.

He heard Jimmy's voice as he approached. It was low, but with the confidential penetration of lewdness. "—like a mink," he was saying. "Ross was layin' on the bed there like he had his ears screwed off. Stoned. My girl says we better get out before the cops come. Th' blonde says somebody gotta stay wit' him. So we blows an' leaves him there wit' th' blonde—"

A sixth sense made him look up. He forced a smile to his face. "Ross," he said, the tone of his voice changing. "Hi yuh feelin', pal? Man, did we have a ball or didn't we?"

Ross's face was cold, his eyes bleak. His lips scarcely moved, but the words spilled out like vitriol. "Chicken-livered bastard! What did you run away for?"

"Francie got scared, Ross." The words tumbled from his lips in his eagerness to explain. "Somebody had to take her home. Besides, Marja was stayin' wit' yuh. She said she would."

Ross walked around the pool table toward him deliberately. The boys fell away from him as he came closer to Jimmy. "What if I was really sick, Jimmy?" he asked, his voice suddenly deceptively soft. "If I really needed help? And only a girl there to do it?"

The smile was still on Jimmy's lips, but a terror was growing in his eyes. "And that girl sure could do it, couldn't she, Ross?" he said quickly. "I bet she sure knew how."

Ross's fist caught him on the mouth, and he tumbled backward against a table. He braced himself against it for a moment, then, reversing the cue stick in his hand, lunged at Ross's face.

Ross deflected the stick with his arm and stepped in close to Jimmy. His fists moved so quickly they were a blur in the yellow light. The cue stick fell from Jimmy's fingers. A moment later Ross stepped back.

There was a wild throbbing pain in his temples as he watched Jimmy sink slowly to the floor, bleeding from his nose and mouth. Pain was the only way to get even. Jimmy had to know what it was like.

Jimmy was sitting on his haunches, his eyes glazed and bewildered. His lips moved, but no sound came out. Slowly he rolled over on his side on the floor.

Ross picked up the cue stick from the floor and reversed it in his hand. His eyes were like frosty blue icicles as he stood over the prostrate figure. Deliberately he pressed the blunt edge down against Jimmy's trousers. He twisted it in his hand, leaning his weight against it. "Yellow son of a bitch!" he said.

There was an involuntary scream from Jimmy's lips before the others could pull Ross from him. The cue stick broke sharply in Ross's hands.

"Stop it, Ross!" one of them yelled. "Yuh want tuh kill 'im?"

Ross looked at the sharp jagged edge of the broken cue in his hand. The flames were leaping all around him. As if in the distance, he heard a door slam. "That's an idea!" he yelled, breaking from their grip and lunging at Jimmy's face with the stick.

Before he could reach Jimmy, he felt two arms around him, pinning his arms to his waist. He struggled wildly. "Let me go! Let me go!" he screamed. "I'll kill him!"

But the two arms only grew tighter and dragged him back. "Take it easy, Ross," a familiar voice said in his ear. "We don't want no more trouble."

The deep, gentle voice was like a spray of cool water. Ross felt the wild trembling inside him leave and sanity return. He stood very still, his breath rattling deep inside him. At last his control came back and he could speak. "Okay, Mike," he said, without turning around. "You can let me go. I'm all right now."

The strong arms released him. Ross didn't look up. He turned and walked toward the door. At the cashier's desk he stopped and dropped a bill on the counter. "That will pay for the mess I made," he said.

The white-faced old man sitting there didn't speak. Ross went out the door. He got into his car and sat there waiting.

A few seconds later he heard footsteps coming toward the car. They stopped outside the door. "Drive me home, will you please, Mike?" he asked without looking up. "I'm very tired."

The footsteps went around the car. The door on the opposite side opened and his friend got in. A match flared, and a second later he felt a cigarette shoved into his hand. He dragged on it deeply, leaning his head back against the cushion and closing his eyes.

"Good thing I came by just then," he heard his friend's voice say. "I had a hunch I'd better go lookin' for yuh."

A faint smile traced Ross's lips. "Still running interference for me, Mike?" he asked. When they played football together, Mike did the blocking while he carried the ball.

There was a chuckle in Mike's voice. "Why th' hell not? We're buddies, ain't we?" He leaned forward and started the motor. He raced it a moment. "What happened, anyway? Yuh would've killed him if I didn't grab yuh."

"There was this girl—" Ross started to explain.

"That blonde you were creamin' over this afternoon?" Mike interrupted.

"Yes," Ross answered. "She—"

Again Mike's voice cut in. There was a chiding tone in it. "I gave yuh credit for more sense 'n that, Ross."

Ross turned his head. "What do you mean?"

Mike struck a match and held it to his cigarette. The flame flared golden in his eyes. "I don't understand you at all, Ross. No girl's worth gettin' in trouble over."

Ross stared at his friend. Mike was right about one thing—he didn't understand. He closed his eyes and leaned back against the seat. He felt the car start as Mike put it into gear.

Mike didn't understand. It wasn't Marja at all. A faint doubt came into him. Or was it? He turned and looked at Mike.

Mike was driving carefully, concentrating on the street ahead. But, then, Mike did everything carefully. He allowed no margin for error. That was the trouble with Mike. That was why he ran interference instead of carrying the ball. He didn't like to take chances. It wasn't that he was afraid, it was just the way he was.

Mike didn't understand. How could he? He didn't know Marja.

CHAPTER SIX

SHE COULD HEAR THE THIN WAIL OF THE BABY AS SHE ENTERED THE downstairs hall and began to climb the stairs. It grew louder as she neared her door. A light came from beneath it. She hesitated a moment before opening it.

She blinked as the ugly white light hit her eyes. The baby's cries tore at her ears. She stepped into the room quickly and closed the door behind her. Footsteps came from the hallway on her left. She turned toward them.

Her stepfather was standing there, his trousers hanging loosely over his wide hips. He wore no shirt; the white tops of his B.V.D.'s hung on the mat of coarse black hair that framed his barrel chest. He didn't speak, but his coal-black eyes stared meanly at her.

"What's he cryin' for?" she asked, gesturing toward the bedroom.

"Where yuh been?" he asked in a heavy voice, ignoring her question.

She began moving toward the bedroom. "Swimmin'," she answered succinctly.

"Till ten thirty at night?" he asked, looking at the kitchen clock.

"It's a long way back from Coney Island," she answered, opening the bedroom door.

His hand caught her arm and spun her around. She stared at him, her eyes cold and bleak. "Why didn't you stop an' tell yer mother?" he shot at her angrily. "She was worried about you. An' you know she ain't feelin' too good."

"She'd be a lot better if you got a job so's she wouldn't have to work nights," she replied nastily.

He raised his hands as if to strike her.

"Go ahead, I dare you!" she taunted, her lips bared over her teeth.

He swore at her in Polish. "*Coorva*! Whore!"

A contempt came into her eyes. "Beer-guzzlin' bum!" she snapped. "Yuh wouldn't dare. Yuh know my mother would throw yuh out if yuh did!"

Slowly his hand fell to his side. "If I wasn't such a good friend of your father's when he was alive, I would have no care for you," he muttered.

"Leave him out of this!" she said quickly. "At least he was a man. He took care of his family. He didn't lay aroun' drinkin' beer all day."

He was on the defensive now. She could sense it, and a triumph rose in her. "Your mother doesn't want me to work the buildings any more," he said uncertainly. "She made me promise when we got married. She said losing one man to them was enough."

"You saw him fall," she said coldly. "Was it your promise or your fear that keeps you home?"

The baby's cries grew louder and more urgent. He stood there a moment breathing heavily, then turned away from her. "Go see what Peter wants," he said.

The bedroom door closed behind her. He lumbered over to the icebox and took out a can of beer. Expertly he punctured the top and tilted it over his lips. Some of the beer ran down his cheeks, spilling onto his under shirt. He drank long and thirstily and threw the empty can into a paper bag on the sink.

He looked at the closed bedroom door. The baby's cries had stopped. He stared at the door. She was a bitch, there was no other word for her. He wiped his mouth with the side of his arm. Nobody could do anything with her. It had been like that since the time her mother told her they were to be married.

He closed his eyes with the effort of remembering. It was only three years ago. A month after her father had stepped from a steel girder twenty-three stories in the skies.

He could still see the look of surprise on Henry's face when he realized the scaffold that should have been there, wasn't. It was a moment of paralysis of action. His lips started to form the word "Peter!" His hand reached anxiously for his friend.

Then he spun suddenly toward the earth. Looking down, Peter could see Henry's cap sailing gently away from him, his friend's blond hair sparkling iridescently in the sun as he tumbled over and over.

The beer came up in him at the remembered nausea. He held his breath a moment, then belched. The nausea went away. He could see his friend every time he looked at Marja. The same white-blond hair, high Polack cheekbones, and sensual mouth. And the way she walked, too, reminded him of her father. They both had the same sure-footed, catlike step.

He had first noticed it the night he came to propose to Katti. A month after Marja's father had died. He had put on his best suit, the one he wore to church on Sundays, and bought a two-dollar box of candy at the drugstore. The druggist had assured him it was the best he had, and fresh, too. He had climbed the stairs to the apartment and stood outside in the hall, sweating from the exertion and nervousness. He hesitated a moment, then knocked cautiously at the door.

A moment later he heard her mother's voice. "Who is it?" Katti asked.

"Me, Peter," he answered.

A mumbled hurrying sound came from behind the closed door, then it opened. Marja stood there, looking up at him. Her eyes were wide. "Hello, Uncle Peter," she said.

He smiled down at her, his eyes searching the room for her mother. She was nowhere in sight. The kitchen table was covered with pins and pieces of white material. "Hello, Marja," he answered foolishly. "Is your mother in?"

Marja nodded. "She's putting on a dress." She stepped back from the door. "Come in, Uncle Peter."

He shuffled into the room clumsily and held the box of candy toward her. "I brought candy."

She took it gravely. "Thank you," she said, putting it on the kitchen table. "Mama says for me to take you into the parlor."

He took his hat off and stood there awkwardly. "You don't have to bother," he said formally. "I can stay in the kitchen."

She shook her head commandingly. "Mama says I should take you into the parlor."

Without looking back, she led him into the long, narrow hallway that led to the front room. She was a white shadow dancing in front of him. He stumbled in the sudden dimness. He felt her hand touch his.

"Take my hand, Uncle Peter," she said quietly. "I know the hall. You'll trip in the dark."

Her hand was warm in his big fist. She stopped suddenly and he stumbled into her. "I'm sorry," he said, aware of his clumsiness.

"It's okay," she said, taking her hand away. "I'll turn on the light."

He heard her walk away in the dark, then a click, and light flooded the room. She was standing in front of the lamp, and the light poured through her white dress. He stared at her. She seemed to have nothing underneath it.

She saw him looking, and a slight smile came to her lips. "Like my new graduation dress, Uncle Peter?" she asked archly. "Mama just finished it before you came."

He nodded, his eyes still on the shadow of her. "Very pretty."

She didn't move away from the lamp. "I'm graduating this term, you know."

"I know," he answered. "Your father told me. He was very proud."

A shadow came into her eyes. For a moment he thought she was about to cry, but it vanished quickly. She came away from the lamp. "Next term I'll be going to high school," she said.

"So soon?" he asked in simulated surprise. "I still think of you as a baby."

She was standing in front of him now. She looked up at him. "I'm going on thirteen," she said. "I'm not a baby any more."

He didn't argue with her. He had seen that much.

"But I'm not too old to kiss you for the nice candy you brought us, Uncle Peter," she said, smiling.

He felt an embarrassed flush creep into his face. He shifted awkwardly, not speaking.

"Bend down, Uncle Peter," she said imperiously. "I can't reach you."

He bent forward, holding his cheek toward her. Her action took him by surprise. She put her arms around his neck and kissed him on the lips. It was not the kiss of a child, but the kiss of a woman who had been born for kissing. He felt her young body pressing against his jacket.

Clumsily he put out his hands to push her away, but accidentally they touched her breasts. He dropped his hands to his sides as if they had been in a flaming oven.

She stepped back and looked up at him, a smile in her eyes. "Thanks for the candy, Uncle Peter."

"You're welcome," he answered.

"Sit down," she said, walking past him to the hallway. She paused in the entrance and looked back at him. "I'm not such a baby any more, am I, Uncle Peter?"

"No, you're not," he admitted.

She smiled at him proudly, then turned and ran down the hall. "Mama!" she called out. "Uncle Peter brought us a box of candy!"

He sank into a chair, remembering what her father had said to him a few days before the accident. "Another year, Peter," he had said, "and the boys will be after her like dogs after a bitch in heat."

He shook his head, his fingers still tingling where they had touched her, a strange excitement in him. Henry must have been blind. Surely the boys were after her already.

He heard Katti's footsteps in the hall and got to his feet. He was standing there, his face flushed, when she came into the room.

She held out her hand, and they shook hands, man fashion. "Peter," she said, "you're too good to us. You shouldn't have brought the candy. It's so expensive."

He still held her hand. "I want to be good to you, Katti," he said huskily.

She withdrew her hand. "Sit down, Peter," she said, seating herself in a chair opposite him.

He studied her. She was a good-looking woman. Big and generously proportioned. An Old Country woman, not like these American women who dieted themselves into matchsticks. And a wonderful cook, too. He remembered the envy he had felt every time Henry opened his lunchbox. The delicious sandwiches she had made for him. All Peter's landlady ever packed was dried-out *wurst*.

He had always told Henry the reason he never married was that there weren't any more women around like Katti. Henry had laughed at him. Said he was too set in his ways to try to please any woman.

But it wasn't so. It was just that any woman wouldn't please him. Katti was the kind of woman that could make him happy.

"I'm making some fresh coffee for you," she said.

"You shouldn't bother," he said awkwardly. "I don't want you should trouble for me."

"It's no bother," she answered.

They sat there silently for a few minutes, then she slipped into Polish. "You like Marja's new dress?"

He nodded, unconsciously answering her in the same tongue. "She's a big girl now."

Katti agreed. "Yes. She graduates on Friday."

"I know," he said quickly. "Henry had told me."

Tears sprang into her eyes, and she averted her face.

"I'm sorry," he said apologetically. "I didn't mean—"

She waved her hand. "I know." The tears continued to run down her cheeks. "Things get too much for me sometimes, and I can't get used to it. I don't know what to do. Henry always knew."

He was on his feet looking down at her. That was what he meant by an Old Country woman. They knew their place, and that it was a man's place to make decisions. A thought came to him. "Yes," he said solemnly. "He always used to say to me: 'Peter, if anything happens, look after Katti and the baby for me.' "

The tears stopped as quickly as they had come. Katti looked at him with wide eyes. "He did?" she breathed in a voice filled with wonder.

He nodded silently.

"Is that why you come to see us twice a week?" she asked.

"At first it was, Katti," he said, a sudden daring in him. "But not now."

She dropped her eyes to the floor. "Now why do you come?" she asked in a hushed voice.

"To see you, Katti," he said, feeling bolder than he ever had in his life. "I want to make a home for you and Marja."

A long moment passed before she spoke. Then her hand sought his. "Peter, you're so good to us."

Later, when the coffee was ready, they went into the kitchen. The pins and material had been cleared from the table, and Marja, who had changed her dress, was seated there doing her homework. The open box of candy was in front of her, and chocolate was smeared on her mouth.

She smiled at him. "The candy is delicious, Uncle Peter."

"I'm glad you like it, child," he said.

Katti had gone over to the stove. "Marja," she said over her shoulder as she poured the coffee, "how would you like Uncle Peter as a father?"

Peter saw the child's eyes widen. There was an expression there he couldn't fathom. "What do you mean, Mama?" she asked in a suddenly hurt voice.

Katti was smiling as she brought the coffee to the table. "I mean your Uncle Peter and me," she said. "We're going to get married."

"Oh, no!" Marja's voice was an anguished cry.

They both stared at her in surprise. She was standing, and the box of candy spilled to the floor in front of her.

Katti's voice grew stern. "Marja," she snapped, "you don't understand now, but you will when you grow up. It's not good for a woman to be alone without a man to take care of her and the children."

Marja was crying. "But, Mama! We were getting along. The two of us. We don't need nobody." She wiped at her eyes with her hands. "Nobody can take Papa's place."

Katti's voice was still gentle. "Nobody will, my child. It's just that Uncle Peter wants to be good to us. He loves us and wants to take care of us."

Marja turned to him savagely. "I don't believe it!" she screamed. "He's a funny, dirty, little black man, not like Papa at all!"

Katti's voice grew stern. "Marja," she snapped, "you mustn't talk like that to your new father."

"He's not my father!" Marja shouted. "And he never will be!" She turned and ran into her room just off the kitchen and slammed the door.

They stared at each other helplessly after she left. Silently Peter sat down at the table. She's wild, he was thinking. Henry had been right when he said Marja had a temper. She would need some handling. He would take care of her after they were married. A few red marks on that pretty little behind and she would be all right.

Katti came around the table and put her hand on his shoulder. "Don't feel bad, Peter," she said. "She's all upset. Just yesterday she started bleeding. You know how young girls are at that time."

CHAPTER SEVEN

THE DULL GRAY LIGHT OF MORNING, FILTERED THROUGH THE TINY courtyard, crept through the window as Katti opened the door. She stood a moment in the doorway looking at her daughter.

She wondered at the sight of Marja sleeping. Awake, she was almost a woman; now she was like a child. Her features were relaxed and soft, her breath so gentle it barely moved the light cover across her chest. This was the Marja she knew, her quiet, lovely little baby.

She moved into the room and turned to the crib. Quickly she touched the baby. A miracle. He was still dry. He made a small sound at her touch. She turned quickly to look at her daughter.

Marja's eyes were open. She was looking at her mother, all the sleep gone from her eyes. "Mornin', Mama."

Katti didn't answer. She remembered how she had worried yesterday when Marja didn't come home from school. Peter had said that she had gone swimming. She hadn't come home until almost eleven o'clock.

Marja sat up in bed, the cover falling to her waist, revealing her nude body. She yawned and stretched, the flesh of her breasts startlingly white against the red flush where the sun had burned her.

"Marja! Cover yourself!" Katti exclaimed in a shocked voice. "How many times have I told you you must not go to sleep without your pajamas? It's not nice."

"But, Mama, it was so hot." Marja reached for the pajama top and slipped into it as she spoke. "Besides, nobody's going to see me."

"I don't care!" Katti insisted. "It's not decent to sleep like that. Only animals do it."

Marja kicked back the covers and got out of bed, the pajama top falling to her thighs. She walked over to her mother and kissed her cheek. "Don't be mad, Mama," she said.

In spite of herself, Katti smiled. She pushed her daughter away. "Don't try to make up to me," she said. "I know all your tricks."

Marja smiled back at her mother. "I went swimming yesterday," she said quickly, anticipating her mother's next question. "See my sunburn?"

"I saw," Katti answered dryly. "How could I miss?"

"Francie's friend has a place in Coney Island," Marja explained. "It's a house in Sea Gate."

Katti was impressed. "Sea Gate?" she breathed. "That's very expensive. Her family must be very rich."

"They are," Marja said. She didn't correct her mother's assumption that Francie's friend was a girl. "They live on Park Avenue."

The baby began to cry suddenly. Katti bent over the crib and picked him up. The baby stopped crying and gurgled at her. "Still, you should have come home to tell me," Katti said over the baby's head to Marja. "I was worried about you."

"There wasn't time, Mama," Marja answered. "We went right after school."

"But you didn't come home until after ten thirty," Katti said, placing the baby on Marja's bed. Deftly she began to remove his diaper.

Marja took a fresh diaper from the top of the old dresser and handed it to her mother. "She wanted me to eat with her, Mama," she answered, "so I did."

Katti glanced at her quickly out of the corners of her eyes. "Don't do it again," she said quietly. "Your father was worried."

A cold look came into Marja's eyes. "Why?" she queried sarcastically. "He run out of beer?"

"Marja!" Katti spoke sharply. "That's no way to talk about your father."

Marja went to the closet and took out a worn bathrobe, which she slipped into. "He's not my father," she said stubbornly.

Katti sighed. "Why do you keep saying that, Marja?" she asked in a hurt voice. "He loves you and wants you to love him. He can't help it if you don't try to like him."

Marja didn't answer. She picked up her toothbrush from a glass tumbler on the dresser and walked to the door. She stopped there and looked back at her mother. "I'll make Peter's bottle," she said.

In the kitchen, she put the baby's bottle in a pan of water on the stove. She turned on the flame beneath it and went to the sink. Quickly, efficiently, she washed herself, then picked up the bottle and went back into her room.

"Give Peter the bottle," Katti said, getting up from the bed. "I'll go make your breakfast. I don't want you to be late for school."

Marja bent over the baby, holding the bottle in her hand. She laughed at him. "Want yuh breakfast, Peter?"

Peter's dark little eyes smiled at her. His tiny hands reached for the bottle, a smile splitting his toothless mouth.

"Yuh're so pretty," she said, putting the bottle to his mouth.

He gurgled happily, his lips closing over the long rubber nipple. A tiny trickle of milk ran down from the corner of his mouth.

"Slob," Marja laughed, wiping him with the towel she still held in her hand. She looked down at him. "Think you can keep from falling off the bed while Marja gets dressed?" she asked.

Peter sucked happily at the bottle.

She straightened up, the baby's dark eyes following her. "I guess you can manage," she said, smiling. She went over to the dresser and took out some clothing.

She threw off the bathrobe and slipped out of the pajama top. Deftly, in almost the same motion, she stepped into her panties and reached for the brassiere on the dresser. A flash of light caught her eye, and she looked into the mirror over the dresser.

The door behind her was open and she could see into the kitchen. Her stepfather was seated at the table, watching her. A look of contempt came into her face. He dropped his eyes.

Still watching him, she slipped the brassiere straps over her arms and fastened it. Then she turned and walked to the door. He looked up again. She stood there silently a moment, then closed the door quickly and finished dressing.

Peter had finished his bottle. She picked him up gaily and went out into the kitchen. Her stepfather was no longer there.

Katti put a bowl of cereal on the table and held out her arms for the baby. "He finish the bottle?" she asked.

Marja nodded. She handed Peter to her mother and sat down. "Oatmeal again?" she asked, staring into the bowl.

"Oatmeal is good for you," Katti said. "Eat it."

Marja made no move toward the food. She wanted a cigarette. She looked at her mother speculatively, wondering if she dared light one before breakfast. She decided against the idea. "I'm not hungry," she said.

Her stepfather had come back into the kitchen. "Isn't oatmeal good enough for your rich tastes?" he asked clumsily. "Maybe you'd prefer ham and eggs?"

Marja stared up at him coldly. "To tell the truth," she said, "I would."

"Isn't that too bad?" he queried sarcastically. He turned to Katti. "I think she's ashamed because we're too poor to afford it."

Marja's eyes were wide. "We wouldn't be if you could tear yourself away from the beer long enough to go to work," she said blandly.

Peter held out his hands hopelessly toward his wife. "Respect for her parents she ain't got," he said. "Only insults. That what she learns bumming around to all hours of the night?"

"Respect for my parents I have," Marja said swiftly. "Not for you."

"Marja! Stop!" her mother spoke sharply.

"Tell him to stop pickin' on me," she answered sullenly, picking up her spoon. She tasted the oatmeal. It was dull and flat.

"Your father is right," Katti continued. "You should speak to him nicer. He's only thinking of you—"

"Crap!" Marja exploded, throwing down her spoon. "The only one he ever thinks about is himself!" She got to her feet. "If he was half a man, he wouldn't let you be out working all night while he sat around the house in his B.V.D.'s He's nothin' but a leech!"

Katti moved quickly, her hand a blur against the gray-white walls. The slap echoed resoundingly in the suddenly quiet kitchen.

Marja's hand was against her cheek, the red flush spreading quickly around the white fingermarks. There was a strange look of wonder in her eyes. "You hit me," she said to her mother, a tone of horror in her voice.

Katti looked at her. She could feel a lump coming into her throat. She realized that this was the first time she had ever slapped her daughter. "To teach you respect for your parents," she said in a suddenly shaking voice.

Marja's eyes seemed to fill, and for a moment Katti thought that her daughter was about to cry. But no tears fell. Instead, a coldness came into them, an icy, chilling calm that told her Marja had grown up and gone away from her.

"Marja!" she said in an appealing voice and took a step toward her.

Marja stepped back. "I'm sorry, Mother," she said softly. It was almost as if she were apologizing for striking her mother. "I'm terribly sorry."

She turned and went quietly out the kitchen door.

Katti turned to Peter. She could hear Marja's steps hurrying down the stairway. She began to cry. "What have I done, Peter? What have I done to my baby?"

He didn't move toward her. There was a distant echo of triumph in his voice. "What you should have done long ago, Katti. You did right."

She looked at him. "You really think so, Peter?" she asked, lapsing into Polish.

He nodded his head, a satisfaction deep in his eyes. "Yes."

She stared at him. The baby in her arms began to cry. Automatically she began to soothe him. She wanted to believe her husband. She wanted to feel she had been right. But no matter how much she wanted to believe, somewhere deep inside her lurked a preying doubt.

CHAPTER EIGHT

THE TELEPHONE BEGAN TO RING JUST AS MARJA CAME IN THE DOOR. "I'LL get it, Mr. Rannis," she called. "It's for me."

She pulled the door of the booth closed and picked up the receiver. "Hello."

"Marja?" Ross's voice was thin through the receiver.

"Yeah," she answered.

"Ross," he said.

"I know," she answered.

"What are you doin'?" he asked.

"Nothin'," she answered. "It's too hot."

"Want to go for a ride?" he asked. "We'll go up Riverside Drive. It's cool there."

"Okay," she said.

"I'll pick you right up," he said quickly. "Wait there for me."

"No—" She hesitated. "I gotta go home first an' change. My dress is soakin'. I'll meet yuh someplace."

"At the garage," he said. "Eighty-third between Park an' Lex. Will you be long?"

"Half-hour," she said. "So long."

"So long," he answered.

She heard the click of his phone before she replaced the receiver. She came out of the booth.

Mr. Rannis was standing there. He looked at her suspiciously. "Who was that?"

"A friend," she answered noncommittally. She started toward the door.

He put out a hand and stopped her. "How about a Milky Way?"

She shook her head. "No, thanks." She started to move again, but his hand tightened on her arm.

"I'm not askin' for money," he said.

She smiled. "Wouldn't do you no good. I'm flat." She pulled her arm free. "Besides, I gotta go. My mother is expectin' me."

Reluctantly he watched her go to the door. "Don't forget, Marja," he called. "'f you want anything, all you gotta do is ask me."

"Thanks, Mr. Rannis," she said as she went out the door. "I'll keep it in mind."

Katti was coming out the door as Marja reached the steps to her house. She stood there watching the sun glint in her daughter's hair. She waited until Marja was halfway up the stoop before she spoke. "Hello, Marja."

Marja's voice was quiet. "Hello, Mama."

"Everything go all right in school today?" Katti asked.

Marja glanced quickly at her mother. "Yeah," she answered. "Why shouldn't it?"

Katti felt herself thrown on the defensive. "I was just asking," she answered. She wanted to say she was sorry for what had happened that morning, but she couldn't make the words come from her lips.

"Where yuh goin'?" Marja asked.

"Shopping," Katti answered. She was lying. But she didn't want her daughter to know she was going to the clinic for an examination. "What are you doing this afternoon?"

"I'm goin' over to a friend's house to study," Marja answered. "I just came home to get out of these things. I'm all sweated up."

"Be quiet," Katti said. "The baby's sleeping. I don't want you to wake him."

"I will," Marja answered.

She went upstairs and opened the door softly. The apartment was still. She went into the kitchen and stood in the center of the room listening. There was no sound. Quietly she walked up the hall to the front room and peeked in.

Her stepfather was fast asleep in a chair near the open window, his head lolling to one side, the newspaper across his knees. She tiptoed carefully back through the hall and kitchen to her room.

The baby was sleeping in his crib. Gently she opened the closet door and took out a clean blouse and skirt. She placed them on the bed and, next to them, fresh underclothes. Quickly she slipped out of her blouse and skirt and went back into the kitchen.

She opened the water faucet to a gentle trickle. She didn't want any noise to disturb her stepfather. She shrugged off her brassiere and hung it over the back of a kitchen chair. It took her only a moment to cover the upper half of her body with soap. Another moment to remove the soap with the aid of a wash rag. She then washed her face. Her eyes shut tightly against the soap, she reached for a towel. The rack nearest her was empty. She groped for the next rack.

She pulled the towel down and rubbed her face vigorously, then under her arms and across her body. She put the towel back on the rack and reached behind her for the brassiere. It wasn't on the chair.

She turned, automatically looking at the floor, thinking it might have fallen. Her stepfather's voice startled her.

"It did fall, Marja," he said, holding it toward her. "But I picked it up for you."

She stared at him for a moment, surprise showing in her eyes. Then she reached out her hand, taking it from him. "Gee, thanks," she said sarcastically, holding it in front of her. "It made so much noise falling that it woke you."

He smiled slowly, ignoring her tone of voice. "Your mother used to look like that back in the Old Country when we were young."

"How would you know?" she asked snidely. "She never even knew you were alive then." She started to walk around him, but he stepped in front of her.

He reached out his hand and caught her arm. "Marja, why do you act so mean to me?"

She stared up into his face, her eyes blank. "I don't mean to, Uncle Peter," she said. "It's just that I can't stand seeing you around the house."

He misunderstood her sarcasm completely. "If I got a job?" he asked almost pleadingly. "Then, would you be nice to me?"

A calculating glint came into her eyes. "I might," she said.

"Then we could be friends again?" He pulled her toward him and clumsily tried to kiss her.

She turned her face so that his kiss landed awkwardly on her cheek, and she slipped out of his grasp. At her door she turned and looked at him. "Maybe," she said.

The door closed behind her. He could feel the pulses throbbing in his temples. The little bitch. Someday he would show her what she could do with her teasing. He turned to the icebox for another can of beer.

Katti sat on the row of benches between two other women and stoically waited her turn for examination. It wouldn't take long now. There was only one other woman before her.

In the corner of the room the young nurse at the reception desk stared down at the cards in front of her. After a while all the strange-sounding names came off your tongue as easily as Smith and Jones. When that happened, you knew you were a veteran.

An intern stopped at the desk and whispered to her. She nodded and picked up the next two cards. "Mrs. Martino, booth four, please. Mrs. Ritchik, booth five."

Katti and the woman next to her got up at the same time. They smiled at each other in sudden kinship. Katti followed her to the desk.

The woman took the card the nurse gave her, went into a booth, and pulled the curtain closed behind her.

Katti spoke to the nurse. "Mrs. Ritchik," she said.

The nurse looked at her without curiosity and handed her a card. "First visit?" she asked.

Katti shook her head. "No. I was here before. When my Peter was born."

The nurse shook her head impatiently. These people were so dumb. "I mean this time."

Katti hesitated. "Yes."

The nurse reached under the desk and found a short, wide-lipped bottle. "Make a sample," she said, "and give it to the doctor when he comes in to see you."

Katti took the bottle and walked down the aisle past the crowded benches and went into the booth with the number 5 over the door. She pulled the curtain shut.

Methodically she undressed and prepared herself for the doctor. At last everything was ready and she took the cotton sheet from the hook and draped it around her. She sat down on the little stool in the corner and waited for him to arrive.

A few minutes later there was a light tap on the outside of the booth and a student nurse came in. She was carrying a pad. "Mrs. Peter Ritchik?"

Katti nodded.

Then followed the list of questions without which the clinic couldn't operate. It took the nurse only about five minutes because Katti had all the answers ready for her. She remembered the form from the last time she had been here.

The nurse tore the top sheet from her pad and put it in a clip hung just inside the door. She left the booth and a moment later was back with another sheet of paper, which she affixed to the clip. Then she smiled at Katti. "The doctor will be with you in a minute."

"Thank you," Katti said. She sat down stoically to wait. It generally was at least fifteen minutes before the doctor came.

This time it was closer to a half-hour before the curtain lifted and the doctor came in, followed by his retinue of two interns. He took the chart down from the wall and looked at it briefly, then at her. "Mrs. Ritchik?"

She nodded. "Yes, Doctor."

"I'm Dr. Block," he said. "How long have you been pregnant?"

She shrugged her shoulders. "A month, maybe two."

He repressed an expression of distaste. These people were so careless in their habits. "Get up on the table and we'll see," he said curtly.

Silently she climbed onto the small examination table and put her feet in the stirrups. The small yellow bulb in the ceiling over her head shone into her eyes. She blinked.

His voice seemed to float over her. "Take a deep breath."

She filled her lungs with air and held perfectly still against the searching intrusion of his fingers. His touch was light and efficient and was gone in a moment. She started to sit up, but his hand against her shoulder stopped her. She lay quietly waiting.

He lifted the cotton sheet until it shielded her eyes from the light. His voice came quietly through it. He was talking to the interns.

"Caesarian section on last childbirth. Constricted Fallopian tubes. Will need again."

The sheet dropped and she sat up. She looked at the doctor questioningly.

"Why did you become pregnant, Mrs. Ritchik?" he asked. "According to the chart, you were told to be careful, that you would endanger your life if you had another child."

She shrugged her shoulders. These men never understood. To them everything was simple.

The doctor turned away from her and began to wash his hands in a clean basin of water just left there for him by the student nurse. He spoke to her over his shoulder. The words were routine to him. He knew that they would be ignored.

"Get plenty of sunshine and fresh air and rest. Refrain from cohabitation for at least two months. Eat plenty of nourishing foods, milk, orange juice." He scribbled a prescription and handed it to her. "Take this, and come in next month."

She looked at him. "When will the baby come, Doctor?"

His eyes were bleak. "Your baby won't come," he said cruelly. "We'll have to take it from you."

She kept her face impassive. She had known that before he did. "When, Doctor?" she persisted gently.

"November or December," he answered. "We can't let you carry the full nine months."

"Thank you, Doctor," she said quietly.

The doctor turned and went out, the two interns following him silently. The curtain fell rustling behind them.

Slowly Katti got off the table and reached for her clothes. It wasn't so bad. She would be able to work right up to October. The curtain rustled and she held her dress up in front of her.

It was one of the interns. He smiled at her apologetically. "Excuse me, Mrs. Ritchik," he said, "but I forgot this." He reached up and took the urine sample from the shelf.

"It's okay," she said.

He glanced at her quickly, then smiled again, a shy smile. "Don't worry, Mrs. Ritchik," he said. "Everything will be all right."

She smiled back at him. "Thank you, Doctor."

The curtain fell and he was gone. Quietly she finished dressing and went outside and paid the nurse the fifty-cent clinic fee. Then she went down the hall to the dispensary and gave them the prescription.

While she was waiting for the prescription to be filled, she wondered how she would tell Marja. Marja wouldn't understand. She would only take it as another rebuff and be hurt.

They called her name and she picked up the prescription. Tablets. She had to take them three times a day. She put them in her pocketbook and went out into the street. Down the block she could see the spires of St. Augustine.

She decided to stop there and talk to Father Janowicz. He was a very smart man. He would tell her what to do.

CHAPTER NINE

MARJA SAT UP IN THE GRASS AND HUGGED HER KNEES, LOOKING ACROSS the Hudson River. It was dusk, and lights were coming on like fireflies on the Jersey shore. A slight warm breeze rustled her hair. "I gotta get a job for the summer," she said suddenly.

Ross rolled over on his side and looked up at her. "Why?" he asked, smiling.

"We need the dough," she answered simply. "My old man loves the beer too much to go to work. My mother works nights. There ain't enough to go round."

"What can you do?" he asked curiously. "What kind of a job do you want?"

"I dunno," she answered honestly. "I never thought about it before. Maybe clerk in the five-and-ten."

He laughed.

"What's so funny?" she asked.

"You don't get much for that," he said. "Maybe eight bucks a week."

"Eight bucks is eight bucks," she retorted. "It's a lot better'n nothin'."

He looked at her quizzically. His sister often spoke about going to work, but somehow never got around to it. "You mean it?"

She nodded.

He pulled a blade of grass from the ground and chewed it reflectively. In some ways she reminded him of Mike. They were both so serious about money. He had an idea. "Do you dance?" he asked.

She glanced at him curiously. "Sure," she said.

"I mean, good?" he persisted.

She nodded. "Pretty good."

He got to his feet and brushed off his trousers. He reached out a hand toward her and pulled her to her feet. "C'mon," he said, starting toward his car. "We'll see."

The faint discordant bleat of a dance band trickled down the narrow hallway to them. The walls were covered with pictures of girls, all with the same inviting smile on their lips. Under the pictures was a long white painted sign.

COME AND DANCE WITH ME. ONLY 10 CENTS.

The music grew louder as she followed him up the stairway. At the head of the stairs was a small booth. Ross stopped in front of it.

"Two," he said, pushing a dollar bill through the small grill.

Silently the man shoved two tickets at him. Ross picked them up and led her through the door. Another man took the tickets and put them in a chopper.

The ballroom was long and narrow, painted a dingy blue. The electric lights were dim. The band at the far end had just finished a number. A few couples, left stranded on the floor, started walking toward the sides of the room. Some girls were seated at tables near the door. They had looked up quickly when Ross came in, smiles coming to their lips automatically, and as automatically fading when they saw he wasn't alone.

On their right were a long, narrow bar and several rows of uncovered tables. Ross led her to one and they sat down. A waiter stood over them immediately.

"Beer," Ross said without looking up. He looked at her questioningly.

"Coke," she answered.

The waiter went away and the band began to play again. It was a soft fox trot.

"Ready?" Ross asked.

That strange smile came to her lips. "Always ready," she answered.

"Let's dance," he said.

His face was warm and flushed when he led her back to the table. There was no doubt in his mind about her dancing. She followed him as if she were part of him. Her rhythm was good, and though other girls danced closer and held him tighter, there was none who could make it seem as if the music flowed through them and held them together.

She smiled as he lifted his beer and drank it. "Well?" she asked.

"You can dance," he said grudgingly, lowering his glass "Where did you learn?"

"I never took a lesson in my life," she said, still smiling.

They were silent a moment. She was waiting for him to speak.

"The girls here make between twenty and fifty bucks a week," he said.

The smile was still on her lips. "Just from dancing?" There was an echo of skepticism in her voice.

He hesitated. "Mostly."

"The dancing averages about twenty," she guessed.

He nodded, watching her carefully.

She lifted her Coke and sipped it. "Yuh don't have to go?" she asked. "Only dance?"

He nodded again without speaking.

"That's a lot of dough," she said.

Suddenly he was disgusted with himself. He threw a bill on the table and rose to his feet. "Come on," he said, "let's go."

She got to her feet silently. A man's voice boomed over her shoulder. "Hey, Ross, long time no see. Where yuh been?"

She turned, startled. A tall man with gray-black hair and dark, shadowed eyes was standing behind her. He was smiling.

The man looked at her and spoke again before Ross had time to answer. "So don't explain," he boomed. "No wonder my girls ain't good enough for yuh."

Marja smiled and looked at Ross. His lips smiled, but his eyes were cold. "Hello, Joker." He hesitated a moment. "Joker Martin, Marja Flood."

"C'mon over the bar," Martin said. "I'll buy yuh a drink."

Ross shook his head. "No, thanks, Joker. We gotta be going."

Martin put his arm on Ross's elbow. "I ain't seen this guy in four months, young lady," he said to Marja in his loud, harsh voice, "'an now he's in a hurry. Tell him it's okay fer us to have a quick one."

Marja smiled. It was flattering to think that this man thought she could tell Ross what to do. It was almost as if he thought she was Ross's girl.

Ross's voice cut into her thoughts. "Okay, Joker. A quick one."

The men had beers and Marja ordered another Coke. Martin turned to Marja. "I oughtta be mad at you, girl," he said. "Ross here was one of our real good customers. Now we never see him, but when I look at you I don't blame him."

"Joker runs this place, Marja," Ross explained. "He's always thinkin' about money."

Marja's eyes looked up at the gray-haired man. "Who isn't?" she asked.

Joker grinned. His hand clapped her shoulder. "Bright girl," he said. "We can't all be rich like our young friend here." For the first time Marja noticed his eyes. They were shrewd and observant. "Lookin' for a job, girl?" he asked.

Before she could answer, Ross spoke up. "No," he said sharply. "She's still in school."

Wisely, Marja kept silent and sipped her Coke. Joker turned back to Ross. "I'm glad yuh dropped in, Ross," he said. "We got some things squared away here."

Ross looked interested. "How come?"

"Made a connection," Joker replied. "Reg'lar thing now. Stud an' dice in the room behind my office. Lots of action."

Ross's voice was guarded, but a yellow light gleamed for a moment in his eyes. "Maybe I'll come by an' take a look some night."

"Do that," Joker boomed. "An' bring the little lady with yuh fer luck." He looked at Marja. "She's always welcome."

"Thank you, Mr. Martin." She smiled up at him.

They finished their drinks and Joker walked them to the door. His voice echoed flatly against the narrow hallway. "Good seein' yuh again, Ross. Don't be a stranger."

The music started again as they walked down the stairs. It followed them out into the street until it was lost in the sounds of traffic.

"Where to now?" Ross asked as he nosed the car out into the street.

"I don't know," she said. "You're drivin'."

He glanced at her quickly out of the corner of his eyes. She was staring straight ahead. He wished he knew what she was thinking.

"How about coming up to my place and getting a bite to eat?" he asked.

"Your folks won't mind?" she asked.

He shook his head. "They went away for the week-end."

"Okay," she said.

"Evening, Mr. Drego," the doorman said.

"Evening, Mr. Drego," the elevator-operator said as he took them up.

They made small talk until the car stopped and they got off. The door closed behind them and Ross fished in his pocket for a key. The apartment door was opposite the elevator.

He held the door for Marja and she stepped into the apartment. He closed the door behind them and reached for a foyer light.

She put out a hand and stopped him. "I been with yuh all afternoon an' yuh haven't kissed me."

He looked down at her in the semi-darkness, trying to read the expression in her face. He didn't speak.

"What're yuh mad about, honey?" she asked. "Did I do somethin' wrong? Say somethin'?"

He shook his head silently. He couldn't tell her that he was angry with himself for having taken her to the Golden Glow Ballroom. She wouldn't stand a chance with a bunch like that. They would make a whore of her in a week. He never should have thought of it, no matter how much she needed the money.

She stood very close to him and brushed her lips against his cheek. "Don't be mad at me, honey," she whispered.

His hand came away from the light switch and caught her shoulder. He leaned back against the door, pulling her toward him. She came willingly, her weight resting against him. He kissed her.

She made sandwiches and a pot of coffee. He carried them into the living-room, and they ate sitting on the couch with the radio going and a small lamp shining from the corner of the room.

When they were finished, she stretched back against the couch cushions and heaved a sigh of contentment. "I was hungry," she said.

He smiled and lit a cigarette.

"Gimme," she said, her hand outstretched.

He handed it to her. She placed it between her lips and took a deep drag, then closed her eyes and let the smoke idle from her lips. "You don't know how lucky you are," she said.

He was surprised. "Why?"

She opened her eyes and looked at him. "You should see my place," she said. "Then you'd know what I mean. Things are so quiet here. No noise comes up from the street—you're too high. No smells from the courtyard. No noise from the neighbors."

He didn't answer, he didn't know what to answer. He picked up the sandwich tray and carried it into the kitchen. When he came back to the living-room she was lying quietly on the couch, her eyes closed again.

"Marja," he whispered.

She didn't answer. Her chest rose and fell with her quiet breathing.

He sat down on the couch beside her. Her eyes flew open. "I was dozing," she said.

"I know." He smiled.

"What time is it?" she asked.

"Almost ten o'clock."

She sat up suddenly. "I better get goin'," she said quickly.

He gripped her shoulders. "Marja," he said, "you know I'm crazy for you."

She met his gaze evenly for a moment, then nodded.

"Do you like me?" he asked.

She got to her feet and looked at him. His face was white and pleading. "You're the sweetest guy I know," she said. "Of course I like you."

He rose angrily. "I don't mean that!" He pulled her toward him violently and kissed her. "I want you," he said harshly. "You know it, you can feel it. Do you want me the same way?"

She stood quietly in his arms for a moment, her eyes looking into his. When she spoke, her voice was gentle. "Even if I do, Ross, there's nothing I can do about it. I'm a girl, an' if I give in, I wind up in trouble. An' that's no good."

"But there are things—"

She interrupted him. "They don't always work." She pressed her cheek to his face and whispered in his ear: "I'll do anything you want to make you happy, Ross, but I can't do that."

He stared at her. "Anything?"

"Anything," she answered.

He pulled her to him and they sank back on the couch. He closed his eyes. There was the rustle of their clothing in his ears, then her breast, warm and strong, was in his hand. The pain inside him was intense and agonizing. He pressed her head against his chest. "Help me, Marja," he cried. "Please help me."

He looked down at her. Her white-blond hair shimmered against him. Her whisper came softly to his ears. "I'll help you, Ross, baby. Lie still."

CHAPTER TEN

"SNAP INTO IT, MIKE! THE *TIMESES* ARE COMIN' UP!" RIORDAN'S VOICE was harsh from years of hawking papers.

Mike jumped off the small bench and moved toward the sidewalk. The *Times* truck was just pulling to the curb. Automatically Mike looked at the clock in the store window opposite. Ten thirty. Just time enough to get the papers made up for the crowd that would spill out of the 86th Street Theatre a little after eleven.

The helper clambered over a pile of papers. "'s a bitch tonight. Twelve sections," he grumbled.

Mike didn't answer. He didn't care. Each week the papers grew larger. He hefted a bundle to his shoulder, carried it behind the stand, and dropped it. It thudded dully on the sidewalk. He went back to the truck.

By the time he came back with the second bundle, Riordan's wife, a thin, scrawny woman, was already cutting the baling-wire around the first bundle with a pair of pliers. "Yuh better hurry, Mike," she said nervously, looking around the newsstand at her husband. "We ain't got much time."

The sweat was starting to come through his shirt, so he took it off and hung it on a nail. The muscles in his frame glistened damply in the yellow electric light. The sections were spread out now. Rapidly he began to flip them together and stack them in a neat pile.

Other newspapers began to come up, and the night began to race by. It was after one o'clock before he was able to grab a few minutes' rest. He clambered up onto a bale of papers and lit a cigarette. He closed his eyes gratefully. He was tired.

He had worked the elevator in the house all afternoon. The day man had been sick, and chances were that he would have to do the same thing tomorrow. He hoped the night would be over quickly.

"Hey, Mike."

He opened his eyes. Ross was standing in front of him, smiling. He grinned slowly. "I thought you went outta town with your folks," he said.

Ross shook his head. "Uh-uh. I had things to do."

"Like what?" Mike asked skeptically.

Ross gestured at his car. "Like that little blonde there."

Mike peered at the car, but the girl's face was in the shadows and he couldn't see her. He looked back at Ross. "I mighta known it was some twist."

Ross's face flushed. "That's no way to talk, Mike," he chided gently. "You don't even know the kid."

Mike looked at him in some surprise. Ross must be hit hard. He had never known him to act like this. He tried again to see the girl, but the light was too dim.

Ross spoke again. "Come over to the car. I'll introduce you."

A curious perverseness came into Mike. He shook his head. "What for?" he asked in an unnecessarily loud voice. "A broad is a broad. Seen one an' you seen 'em all." He flipped his cigarette butt toward the curb. It spattered sparks in front of the car. He climbed off the bale. "Want your papers, Ross?" he asked.

Ross nodded, not speaking.

Mike bent and pulled out a group of them. He held them toward Ross. Ross dropped a few coins into his hand and took the papers.

Riordan's voice came around the newsstand. "Bring up some *Americans*, Mike. We're runnin' short."

Automatically Mike bent to pick up a stack of papers. When he straightened up, Ross was halfway back to his car. He looked after him. Some guys had it soft. They had nothing to worry about. He hefted the papers to his shoulder and started around the stand.

Ross climbed into the car and leaned forward to touch the starter button. The motor whirred and caught, and he turned out into the street.

"Your friend don't like me," Marja's voice said.

He looked at her. "How could that be?" he asked defensively. "He doesn't even know you."

"I heard what he said," she replied.

"He's just tired," Ross explained. "Usually he's not like that."

They rode a block silently. Then Marja spoke again "Is that Mike? The one who wouldn't come out to the island with us?"

"Yeah," he answered.

She thought about the way Mike had stood there in back of the stand. The sweat had formed an oily sheen on his arms, and the muscles were like wire cords in his back and arms. "Thinks he's pretty great, doesn't he?" she asked sarcastically. "Too good for the rest of us?"

Wisely, Ross didn't answer. He knew better than to get into a foolish argument. Besides, he didn't care what they thought of each other.

Her voice was speculative. "Maybe someday I'll show him a little bit."

He glanced at her in surprise. There was a hurt expression in her eyes. Suddenly he understood. She was still brooding over what Mike had said.

Katti had started for the front pews of the church as usual, but Marja grabbed her arm.

"There's no room down there, Mama," she whispered, "Let's get in here."

Katti turned into the pew that Marja steered her to. She wasn't thinking about anything except what Father Janowicz had said the other day. To tell Marja as soon as she could. That was the only way to stop worrying about it.

There was a young man in the pew. Katti mumbled an apology and she pushed past him. She settled down heavily on the bench and bent her head forward as the Mass began.

She closed her eyes and prayed hard to God to make everything right. For Marja to understand. For Peter to get a job. She prayed for everyone except herself. When the Mass was over, she felt better. She glanced at Marja.

There was a faint flush on the girl's face, a touch of contentment in the echo of a smile in the corners of her mouth. She was glad she had been able to take Marja to Mass with her.

The congregation was filing out, and Katti pushed past Marja toward the aisle. She glanced at the young man's face as she crossed in front of him. There were beads of sweat on his forehead. It was warm in the church today.

Marja was a few steps behind her, and she turned, waiting for her to catch up. Marja's eyes were laughing as she took her mother's arm.

For a long moment Katti looked at her daughter. It had been long since she had seen Marja look so happy. She was beautiful when she smiled. Katti decided not to say anything about the baby until the evening.

She didn't want to do anything to take the smile of happiness from Marja's face.

CHAPTER ELEVEN

H E PUT THE LOCK ON THE ELEVATOR DOOR AND SAT DOWN ON THE small bench in the hall. He picked up his math book and turned to his place. He wasn't as tired this afternoon as he had expected. He had slept from ten o'clock, when he had come home from church, until almost four, when his mother had awakened him.

He turned the page slowly. He didn't mind Sunday afternoons on the elevator. The house was fairly quiet and he could catch up on his studies.

He heard footsteps come down the hall and go past him into the elevator. He didn't look up. He wanted to finish the last part of his problem.

A soft voice came out of the elevator. It was vaguely familiar. "Today, Mike?"

He dropped the book, startled.

She was standing in the elevator, smiling at him. Her white-blond hair was almost gold in the light. "Any time you're ready," she said.

He got to his feet clumsily, aware of a sudden jumping inside him. He stepped into the elevator and sprang the lock. The door began to close. He looked at her. "How do you know my name?" he asked.

She didn't answer. Her eyes looked right into him. Her lips were parted in a kind of smile, showing even white teeth.

Unable to meet the challenge in her glance, he turned away from her. He could feel the flush creeping red into his cheeks. "Floor, please?" he asked sullenly, pressing down the lever and starting the car.

"Twelve," she answered.

Then he understood. He turned to look at her. "You're Ross's girl." It was more a statement than a question.

Her face was expressionless, she didn't speak.

He stopped the car between floors and turned away from the board. "You are Ross's girl?" he repeated.

"Am I?" she asked challengingly. "You ought to know. You're an expert on broads. Seen one an' you seen 'em all."

His face flushed. She had heard him the other night. No wonder she had acted the way she had. It was her only way to get even. He looked down at the floor. "I'm sorry," he said.

She didn't answer.

He looked up at her. "I said, I'm sorry."

Her gaze was still cold and level. "I heard you."

He began to feel angry. "You might at least say something."

She smiled. "Hooray." Her eyes stared into his. "What're you lookin' for—applause?"

He leaned against the wall of the car. He knew how to treat dames like this. He surveyed her carefully from head to toe. This always made them uncomfortable. No babe liked to be stared at as he was doing.

She didn't speak, and when his eyes came back to her face he saw no trace of embarrassment.

"Ross was right," he said cuttingly. "You're built for it."

There was confidence in her eyes. "Thanks," she said dryly. "I needed you to tell me. I was beginning to worry."

A smile came to his lips. He was sure of himself now. She was nothing but a cheap little teasing floosie. He reached out his hand and pulled her toward him.

She smiled and came toward him willingly. He looked down into her face. Her eyes were sparkling. He bent to kiss her.

He felt her hand move behind his back, and suddenly the elevator floor dropped out sickeningly from beneath him. For a bewildered second he stood paralyzed. Then with a muttered curse he turned and grabbed the lever.

He snapped into stop-and-lock and hoped that it would take. She had thrown it into fast drop. He heard the power whine, and the car stopped.

He turned back to her. "You crazy bitch!" he snarled. "We could've been killed!"

There was a wild excitement in her face that he had never seen on anyone. There was no trace of fear in her. "Really?" she asked, politely sarcastic. "That would have been too bad."

He turned back to the lever and started the car upward again. "Okay," he said. The car rose slowly. He stopped at Ross's floor and opened the door.

She stepped out of the car. "Thank you, Mike," she said politely, smiling at him.

"You're welcome," he said in an equally formal tone. He kept the door open as she walked down the corridor. He watched her in the small mirror in the corner of the elevator. She had a good walk, and she knew it.

He saw her stop in front of Ross's door and press the buzzer. The door opened almost immediately. He could see the smile on Ross's face and hear his voice.

"Come in, Marja, I was waitin' for you."

The door closed behind them. He stood there a moment, then closed the elevator door and dropped the car back to the lobby. He put the lock on the door and sat down on the bench, picking up his math book again.

He stared down at the pages with unseeing eyes. She was standing there in front of him. He snapped the book angrily shut. It was no use. He couldn't stop thinking about her.

He could see her walking down the corridor away from him. He could see Ross's smile and hear his greeting. He got to his feet and went back into the elevator.

It wasn't until he stopped the car on Ross's floor that it came to him. For the first time in his life he was jealous over a girl.

A buzz came from inside the elevator. He got to his feet and looked at the board. The red letters blinked at him: 12. He snapped the door shut and pulled the lever.

He waited until she came into the car before he spoke. "Marja, I'm sorry. I had yuh pegged wrong."

She looked at him skeptically.

"I mean it, Marja," he said earnestly. "I didn't mean to act nasty."

The doubt began to fade from her eyes. For the first time he realized how deep and dark her eyes were. "Things ain't easy for me like they are for Ross," he continued. "Ross is bright and fast. I don't get nothin' unless I sweat it out."

She smiled at him. It was a real smile, warm and genuine. "I wasn't so nice either," she admitted. "We'll call it square."

He stuck out his hand. "Deal?"

She took it, smiling. "Deal."

He looked down at her hand, small in his palm. "Are yuh really Ross's girl?"

"Ross is nice to me," she said. "Real nice. Not like most fellas, if yuh know what I mean."

He nodded. "Ross is a nice guy." He looked up at her face, still holding her hand. "Yuh think, sometime, maybe, we can take in a show?"

She nodded silently, her eyes on his face. Something was happening to her. It came from his hand to her, something that had never happened before. She knew a lot of boys, and they never bothered her like this. She was always sure of how she felt about them. But this was different. It was another kind of feeling. A kind of weakness inside.

He stepped toward her. She raised her mouth to his lips. Even the kiss was different. It was warm and sweet and gentle and hungry and possessive. She closed her eyes. It was floating in warm, lazy water. She could feel a heat running through her. Instinctively she knew what it was. This wasn't the game that it had been with others. This was her very own. The way she felt. The beginning of desire.

She pushed him away. Her face was flushed. "Take me down," she said in a small, embarrassed voice.

"Marja," Mike said huskily.

She didn't look at him. "Take me down, please," she repeated, wondering what could be wrong with her. She felt warm and happy, and yet she felt like crying.

He turned and started the car. They didn't speak again until the car stopped at the lobby. He opened the door and turned to her.

"I'll see yuh again?" he asked.

She looked at him for a moment. "If you want to." Then she turned and fled from the elevator and out of the house.

She climbed the stairs slowly to her landing. She didn't understand herself. Boys were all alike. They were a game she played. Something impersonal, like the jacks she used to tumble on the stoop, or hopscotch. It was fun to her, a curious sense of power, of strength, of superiority. But this had been different. Mike had been different. And she didn't know why.

A retching sound came from the toilet in the hall. She glanced toward the closed door, wondering who was sick now. That was one of the things she resented. You couldn't be sick in private when the toilets were in the hallway.

The toilet door opened and her stepfather came out. He saw her standing at the kitchen door. "Get a glass of water," he called. "Your mother is sick!"

Quickly she filled a tumbler at the sink and ran back into the hallway. The toilet door was open now. She could see her mother leaning weakly against the wall, her stepfather's arm under her shoulders.

He took the glass from her hand and held it to Katti's lips. Katti rinsed her mouth quickly and spat into the bowl, then drank the rest of the water thirstily.

It was not until then that Marja spoke. "What's the matter, Mama?"

Katti shook her head weakly. "It's nothing. I just felt nauseous."

"But—" Marja was bewildered. Her mother was never sick to her stomach. Only the last time—when Peter was born. A sudden fear came into her. She looked at her mother questioningly. It couldn't be that again. The doctor had said she shouldn't. "Mama, are you all right?"

Katti nodded her head. She started to speak, but her husband took the words from her mouth.

"Of course she's all right," he said coarsely. "It's nothing to throw up when you're pregnant."

Marja stared at her mother, unbelieving. "No, Mama, you can't be," she said in a hurt, protesting voice. "The doctor said it was too dangerous."

Katti tried to smile. "You can't always believe them. They're always trying to scare you."

Peter threw out his chest boastfully. "It will be another boy," he said proudly. "I got it all figured out."

Marja stared at him coldly. "You got everything figured out, haven't you?"

He nodded, grinning. "Yah."

"While you're at it, figure out how we're gonna eat when Mama has to stop working," she snapped.

He stared at her in bewilderment.

"And figure out who's gonna keep yuh in beer, 'cause it ain't gonna be me." She turned and ran down the stairs.

"Marja!" Katti called. But it was too late. Marja was already out of sight. Katti could hear her footsteps on the flight below.

She looked at her husband for a moment, then turned and walked back into the apartment. A pain ran through her for a moment, and she felt weak. She wanted to lie down for a while. Maybe she would feel better then. Maybe this depression she felt would disappear. Father Janowicz was right.

She should have had the courage to tell Marja herself. It was her own fault. Maybe then she could have made Marja understand.

CHAPTER TWELVE

"JOKER'S RUNNING A GAME IN THE BACK ROOM," ROSS SAID. Mike looked up. That familiar expression was in his friend's eyes—a yellow glow of excitement. "So what?" Mike asked.

"I'd like to get in on it," Ross said.

Mike got to his feet and looked down at Ross. "Yuh know what your old man said. Get into trouble an' he packs you off to the country for the summer."

"I won't get into trouble," Ross insisted. "Just feel like a little charge, that's all."

Mike shrugged his shoulders. "That's what you said the last time. Your father yelled bloody murder when he had to get you out of the can."

"He'll never know," Ross answered, remembering the time he had been grabbed with a gang shooting craps behind a garage. "Joker says he's got protection."

"Go ahead," Mike said, turning away. "It's your funeral."

"I wanted you to come with me," Ross said.

Mike looked at him. "What for? I got no dough."

"I'm takin' Marja with me," Ross answered, "an' I don't want those wolves makin' passes when my back is turned."

Mike was interested. "Then leave her home."

"No. I got a hunch she's lucky for me." Ross smiled apologetically. He had a real gambler's apologia for his superstitions. "I think I can make it real big with her around."

"Nuts," Mike said.

Ross looked at him. "Got something better to do?"

Mike shook his head. He was thinking about Marja. It had been more than a week since he had met her in the elevator. He still hadn't been able to get up the courage to try to see her.

"Come on, then," Ross urged. "Live a little. What're you going to do? Spend the rest of your life with your nose in those books?"

"Okay," Mike said.

Marja was waiting in the car. Her eyes widened in surprise as she saw Mike approaching. Ross reached the car first and opened the door.

"I been waiting a long time to get the two of you together," he said. "Marja, my friend Mike. Mike, this is my girl."

A flush crept into Marja's face. A smile came to her lips as she held out her hand. "I heard a lot about you," she said almost formally.

Mike was a little embarrassed. He played along with her. "Me, too," he mumbled, taking her hand. It was warm and electric in his grip. He dropped it quickly.

"Shove over," Ross said to her as he climbed into the car. "Mike is coming with us."

Neither Marja nor Mike spoke until they reached the dance hall. Ross kept a steady flow of comment. If he noticed that they weren't speaking, he said nothing about it. They got a table near the floor. It was almost nine o'clock and the floor was fairly crowded.

Ross ordered beer for Mike and himself and a Coke for Marja. He looked out over the floor, his eyes sparkling. "I gotta check Joker an' see what time the game starts."

"It'll start soon enough," Mike grunted. He looked at Marja, and a slight sarcasm came into his voice. "Why don't you dance with your girl first?"

Ross shook his head peremptorily. "No," he answered. "You two go ahead. I'll check up on things."

Marja got to her feet and Mike stared at her in surprise. She smiled. "Well?"

He got out of his chair and led her to the floor. The orchestra was playing a fast fox trot. He felt himself tighten as she came into the circle of his arms. He stumbled almost immediately, stepping on her foot.

"Oh, I'm sorry," he muttered, his face turning red.

She smiled up at him. "Relax," she said. "I won't eat you."

They danced for a moment in silence, then she spoke again. "I thought you were going to see me."

"I've been busy," he answered. He took a few steps. "Besides, you're Ross's girl."

"I didn't say that," she said.

"But he did," Mike countered. "And you didn't stop him."

"I can't keep him from talkin'," she answered. "Besides, you never told him you knew me."

"You didn't say anything either." He looked down into her face. "I kind uh got the idea you didn't want to."

The music stopped and she broke away from him. She started from the floor and he followed her back to the table. She stopped in front of Ross. "I want a beer," she said.

Ross didn't look at her. "Sure, baby, sure," he answered. He was watching a small door across the floor.

Mike stood behind her chair and she sat down. He pushed his glass toward her. "Drink this," he said. "I'll get another."

She picked it up and drank some. He looked at her, wondering what he had said that had made her angry. She didn't speak.

"Well?" Mike asked Ross.

"I'm waiting," Ross answered. "The waiter said he'd check an' let me know."

Marja was bewildered. "Let you know what?" she asked. "I thought we came to dance."

Ross looked at her. It was almost as if she were a stranger. He didn't seem to see her at all. "Explain it, Mike," he said, waving his hand.

Mike felt an anger inside him. Same old Ross. Leave the dirty work for others. "Explain it yourself," he said.

Ross looked at them, his eyes suddenly clearing. "What's the matter with you two?" he asked.

They didn't answer.

He looked at Marja. "I came to get into the game that Joker spoke to me about, that's all."

Marja got to her feet. "Then what the hell did you ask me to go dancing for?" she asked. "Why didn't you say so in the first place?" She turned away.

Ross grabbed her arm. "I wanted you with me for luck," he said with a smile. "I got a hunch you're good for me."

She looked down at him. "What about Mike?" she questioned shrewdly. "Yuh bring him along to watch out for me?"

"Sure," Ross said, still smiling. "Think I'm gonna take any chances with all these wolves around? At least Mike's my friend. I know I can depend on him."

Mike looked at her, then across the table at him. A slow smile came over his lips. "I wouldn't be too sure of that, Ross," he said.

Ross's eyes grew cold. "What d'yuh mean?"

Mike didn't take his eyes from Marja's face. "Like yuh said, Ross. She's terrific."

A slow smile came to Marja's face and she sat down. "Okay, boys," she said, laughter deep in her voice, "fight over me."

They all burst into a raucous, happy laugh.

❖ ❖ ❖

The slight beads of perspiration stood out clearly on Ross's forehead as he reached for the dice. He turned to Marja and held them toward her. "Blow on 'em for luck, baby."

Marja pursed her lips and blew into his cupped palm. "Get hot," she said, looking down at the shrinking pile of money in front of Ross. He hadn't been doing well. She figured he must have lost almost forty dollars.

"Blow harder," he said in a tight, tense voice, pushing his clenched palms closer to her lips.

She took a deep breath and blew into his hands. She could see his fingers working smoothly over the dice. They opened for a second and her breath caught in her throat. She looked into his face, her eyes wide.

For a fraction of a second his eyes were cold, then he smiled. He knew that she had seen. "Thanks, baby," he said, turning back to the table.

She stood very still, her eyes going around the table. It seemed improbable that nobody else had seen. Then she understood. Ross had been clever. The others had been watching her.

Ross's voice was harsh. "C'mon dice, now!" The cubes spun twinkling over the green cloth and bounced off the backboard. They tumbled over and over and came to a stop. A natural. Ross pulled the money toward him and scooped the dice with his other hand. He began to shake the cubes.

He looked down the table. "I'm hot," he chortled. "Get your dough down before the fever goes."

He began to cover the bets as she stepped back from the table toward Mike, who was leaning against the wall, watching them. He smiled as she came up. "You did good that time."

Her face was expressionless. He hadn't seen Ross switch dice either. "I've had enough. I want to go," she said.

His voice was surprised. "But Ross isn't finished yet."

"I don't care," she insisted. "I want to go."

"I'll tell Ross," he said.

Her hand stopped him. "No," she said. "Leave him be." She looked at the table. Ross had just thrown another seven. There was an excited, happy look on his face. "He got what he came here for."

Mike stared into her face. "What's wrong?"

"Nothin'," she repeated. "I just wanna go."

"Okay." He took her arm. "We're goin', Ross," he called.

Ross waved his hand at them. It was doubtful that he even understood what Mike had said. He was shaking the dice again.

The orchestra was playing as they walked through the dance hall. "Dance?" Mike asked.

She shook her head and kept walking. A man blocked the exit in front of her. "Hello, baby."

Without looking up, she started around him. He stepped in front of her. "Runnin' out on your boy friend?" he asked.

She looked up into Joker Martin's face. Her eyes were cold. "I'm tired an' I'm leavin'," she said.

The smile disappeared from Martin's lips. He looked at Mike. Mike shrugged his shoulders. Martin stepped out of the doorway. She started past him, but he stuck out a hand and stopped her.

She looked at him.

There was a strange glint in his eyes as he looked down at her. "I don't know what's eatin' yuh, kid," he said. "But when yuh get over it, I got a job waitin' here at the Golden Glow for yuh."

For the first time her expression changed. "Thanks, Mr. Martin," she said. "I might come back an' take you up on it." She turned and started down the stairway.

CHAPTER THIRTEEN

SHE STOPPED IN FRONT OF HER HOME AND TURNED TO MIKE. "THANKS for bringin' me home," she said.

Mike smiled. "My pleasure."

"I didn't mean to break up your evening," she said.

He didn't answer.

She started up the stoop. His voice stopped her. "When 'm I going to see you again?"

"I don't know," she said, hesitating.

He came up to the step below her. "Why?" he asked. "Because you're Ross's girl?"

Her eyes met his. "I'm not Ross's girl," she said. "I told you that before."

"Then when will I see you?" he repeated.

She shook her head. "I really don't know. School will be over next week an' I gotta get a job. It's hard to say."

A twinge of jealousy irked him. "But you'll make time to see Ross," he said sarcastically. "He's got a buck to spend."

Her temper flared. "I'm not gonna see him either. He can take his dough an' shove it. An' you can tell him I said so."

He was surprised. It showed in his voice. "Why me? You can tell him yourself."

Her eyes stared coldly down at him. "You know damn well why. You both took me there, you both knew what Ross was goin' to do."

"You knew it, too," he said angrily. "You knew he was going to shoot craps, not play tiddlywinks. So what're yuh sore about?"

"Yeah," she answered sarcastically. "I knew he was goin' to gamble after he told me, but I didn't think he was goin' to switch dice. I don't go for that."

"Switch dice?" he asked, puzzled.

"Yeah," she answered. "When I blew on 'em. He knew they'd be watchin' me. I don't like bein' made the patsy."

He let out a breath. Now he knew why she had suddenly decided to leave. "Yuh may not believe it, but I didn't know about that either."

She stared at him skeptically.

"I don't play like that," he said.

She was still for a moment. "I don't know," she said, hesitating. "I could understand it if you played like that. You could use the dough. But Ross? He don't need nothin'."

He reached for her hand. "I didn't know about it, Marja," he said earnestly.

She looked down at his hand, then up into his face. "Okay," she answered finally. "I'll buy." She pulled her hand from his grasp. "Good night."

"Good night, Marja." He watched her go inside the house before he turned toward home.

He turned between the house into the alleyway that led to his family's apartment in the basement of the large apartment building.

Ross stepped out of the darkness toward him. "Mike," he called.

Mike stopped. "Yeah?"

"Where the hell did you disappear to?" Ross asked. "I won almost a hundred and twenty dollars."

"Marja wanted to go home," Mike answered.

Ross ignored his statement. He took a roll of money from his pocket. "I wanted to give you your cut," he said, peeling off some bills. "Here's twenty."

Mike looked down at Ross's outstretched hand, but made no motion to take the money.

"What's the matter with you?" Ross demanded. "Take it."

Mike looked at him. "No, thanks. I want no part of it. It's all yours."

Ross peered into his face. "Don't be a jerk. Take the dough. Is it poison or something?"

"Keep it, Ross," Mike said. "It's all yours. You earned it."

A sudden light came into Ross's eyes. "Oh! Marja's been talkin'."

Mike didn't answer.

Ross grinned suddenly. "It was easy. Like takin' candy from a baby. They were so busy watching Marja when she bent forward that it was a cinch."

Mike still didn't speak.

Ross clapped him on the shoulder. "Here, boy," he said patronizingly, "take the money. It'll all look better in the morning."

"I don't want it!" Mike's hand made a flashing motion, and the money fluttered out of Ross's grip.

Ross stared at him. "What's got into you?"

"Nothin'," Mike answered angrily. "I just don't like it, that's all. You played the kid for a sucker. If you got caught, we'd all have to pay off. Her, too. That wouldn't uh been so pretty, would it?"

"But we didn't get caught," Ross protested. "So why the beef?"

Mike didn't answer.

Ross knelt to pick up the money. "I don't know what the hell got into you," he muttered. He looked up at Mike, his eyes suddenly growing suspicious. "Where did you take her?" he asked, clambering back to his feet.

"Home, I tol' yuh," Mike answered.

"You took long enough," Ross said. "I've been waitin' here over an hour for you."

"We walked," Mike said succinctly. "My old man never gave me a Buick."

"You didn't stop off in the park for a little?" Ross asked. "Maybe you stopped in some dark corner an' she gave you a hand job. The little whore likes that."

Mike could feel the pulse in his temples explode. His arm flashed up and pinned Ross against the brick wall. "Don't talk like that about her," he snarled.

There was a wild excitement in Ross's eyes. "I was right," he said triumphantly. "She did get to you." A grin came to his lips. "She's the greatest action there is, boy, but don't let it fool you. It's there for everybody."

Mike's hand was a blur in the night. Ross's head snapped back and he slowly slid toward the ground, blood coming from a corner of his mouth. Mike stepped back and looked down at him. "Next time you'll keep your mouth shut," he said.

Ross sat dully on the ground for a moment. Then he raised his hand slowly and held it to his mouth. The blood seeped into his fingers. He looked up at Mike, his eyes growing cold behind their mask of pain.

"I'll pay you back for this, Mike," he mumbled through aching lips. "Pay you back double."

"Try it any time you want," Mike taunted.

Ross still sat on the ground, looking up. "The time will come," he said slowly. "Don't worry."

"I ain't worryin'," Mike said. He went on down the alley toward his apartment.

CHAPTER FOURTEEN

ROSS BOUGHT A FISTFUL OF TICKETS AT THE DOOR. HE STOPPED A MO-ment as he entered the dance hall to let his eyes get used to the light. He looked around.

She was there. Sitting with the girls in the corner. Even in one of the cheap gowns that Martin supplied to his girls, there was something about her that made her stand out from the others. There was an excitement about her. A man-and-woman kind of excitement that few women ever had.

He walked down the steps and stopped in front of her. "Hello, Marja," he said.

She looked up at him. "Hello, Ross." Her eyes were masked. He couldn't read any expression in them.

"Want to dance?" he asked awkwardly.

"Got tickets?" she replied.

He held out his hand silently.

She got to her feet. "We'll dance," she said, leading him to the floor.

She slipped into his arms, but it was as if he were holding a total stranger. Automatically they picked up the rhythm of the orchestra.

"It's been two weeks since school closed, Marja," he said. "Three weeks since I saw you."

"Time flies, doesn't it?" she said without smiling.

"You've been ducking me," he accused.

"I've been busy," she said politely. "I gotta work for a living."

"You haven't given me a chance to explain," he said.

"You don't owe me no explanation," she retorted swiftly. "You're a big boy. You run your own life."

"Then why don't you want to see me?" he asked.

She looked up into his eyes. There was something about him that reminded her of an animal. Wild and uncontrollable. Completely selfish. "I don't like bein' used," she said.

The music stopped and she started for the tables. His hand stopped her. There was another ticket in it. She took the ticket and stood waiting until the music started again before she came back into his arms.

"I thought you liked me, Marja," he said.

"I did," she answered. "But you didn't level with me."

"I'm sorry." He smiled. "But everything worked out. Nobody got hurt."

A sad look came into her eyes. "I did," she said. "I thought you were goin' to be different."

"But it was for laughs, Marja," he said, trying to pull her closer to him. He could feel the warmth of her through his jacket. All the excitement was still there. "A guy's gotta get some kicks."

She shook her head. "It wasn't like you needed the dough. I could understand that."

"Marja," he said. They were standing in a dark corner now. He tried to kiss her.

She turned her face. "Cut it, Ross," she said sharply. "I need the job here."

"But, Marja," he pleaded. "I'm goin' away the day after tomorrow and I won't be back for five months. I gotta see you before I go."

She shook her head. "Can't."

"Why?" he demanded.

The music stopped again, and she slipped out of his arms and turned toward the tables. His arm spun her back to him violently.

"Here," he said savagely. "Here's all the damn tickets. Don't be runnin' off every time the music stops."

Silently she took the rack of tickets and stuffed them into a small purse. The music started and she came back into his arms.

"Why can't you see me?" he asked.

She met his eyes. "Yuh really want to know?"

He nodded. "Tell me."

She took a deep breath. "One, I don't want to," she said. "Two, I haven't the time. My mother's sick in bed. She lost her job an' I gotta take care of her an' my baby brother during the day. That enough reasons?"

"No," he said roughly. He backed her into the dark corner again and tried to kiss her. She turned her face. He couldn't see her signaling with her purse. In a moment a rough hand spun him around.

The big apelike bouncer was behind him. Joker Martin was standing next to him, smiling. "Listen, bud," the bouncer said, "you behave yourself or you'll get t'run outta here."

Ross could feel the color leaving his face. He glanced at Marja. Her face was expressionless. He took a deep breath. "Okay, Marja," he said. "If that's the way you want it." He turned and walked off the floor.

Joker Martin fell into step with her as she started back to the tables. "Your friend seemed pretty mad," he said.

"He's no friend," she said.

He assumed a surprised expression. "But you were so chummy the last time you were here."

"Yeah," she said flatly. "It was different then. But I didn't like somethin' he did."

Martin looked down at her. "What'd he do?"

She shrugged her shoulders noncommittally. "I just didn't like it, that's all."

"Was it somethin' like switchin' dice?" Martin asked in a conversational voice. The surprise was written on her face.

He smiled. "Yuh think we're stupid, kid? We're pro's. We spotted that right off." He lit a cigarette. "I figured that was why you blew so quick. Did yuh know what he was gonna do?"

"No," she said.

"I figured that, too," he said.

"If you knew, why didn't you do somethin'?" she asked.

He smiled gently. "His old man's gotta lot of pull. Someday he'll come back an' we'll take the dough back with interest. Until then we can wait. We're patient. They always come back."

She hung the evening dress carefully in her locker. After a quick check of her face in the mirror, she darted out the door. It was a few minutes after twelve. The job wasn't so bad during the week—she was on her feet for only six hours. But Fridays and Saturdays were tough. On those days she worked from five o'clock in the evening until two in the morning.

She stepped out into the noisy street and saw him lounging against a car, waiting for her. He had been there every night since she had begun working.

A smile came to her lips. "Hello, Mike."

He grinned at her. "Hi, baby."

They fell in step. "You don't have to wait for me every night, Mike," she said. "I can get home okay."

"I want to," he said.

"But you must be dead. You work that newsstand for twelve hours a day."

He grinned. "Don't take all the fun outta life, baby," he said gently. "How about some coffee?"

She nodded. "Okay, but it's my turn to buy, don't forget."

"Why d'yuh think I asked yuh?" he laughed.

They turned into a drugstore and climbed onto two counter stools. "Two java," Mike ordered. He looked at her. "Split a jelly doughnut with me?"

She nodded.

He called the order to the counter man and turned back to her. "How's your mother feeling?" he asked.

"Better today, thanks," she said. "The bleeding stopped, and the doctor says if it stays like that she can get out of bed tomorrow."

"Good," he said.

She was quiet for a moment while she thought about her mother. Katti had been in bed almost a week. Had come home early from work when she began to bleed. At first the doctor thought it was a miss, but everything had turned out all right. She couldn't go back to work, though. Those heavy pails and mops were too much for her.

Marja remembered how upset her mother had been when she told her about the job. But the twenty a week had been a life-saver. Without it they all would have starved. Peter was no good for anything.

The counter man put the coffee and a jelly doughnut down in front of her. Quickly she divided it and gave Mike the larger piece.

"How'd it go today?" Mike asked.

"Okay." She smiled. "I was pretty busy."

He grinned. "Good dancer, huh?"

She grinned back. "The best." The smile vanished suddenly. "Ross came in to see me tonight."

Mike stared into his coffee. "What'd he want?"

"He said he was going away for a while. He wanted me to go out with him."

Mike still didn't look at her. "What'd you say?"

"I told him no dice. He got fresh and Mr. Martin came over, so he walked out."

Mike was silent for a moment. "His father's sending him to Europe."

She drew in her breath. "Man," she whispered, "it must be great to have dough like that."

Mike looked down into his coffee again. "You still like him, don't yuh?"

She looked over at Mike. "I don't really know," she said honestly. "He's different than all the other boys I know. He speaks different. He acts different."

"He's got money," Mike said bitterly.

"That's not it," she said quickly.

"What is it, then?" Mike asked.

She looked at him. He could see she was thinking carefully. "It's the way he is. He acts all the time like I want to some of the time. Like he's on top of the world and everybody is gonna play up to him. It must be good to be the guy on top."

She put her hand on his arm. "Y'know," she said, lowering her voice to a confidential whisper, "Mr. Martin knew he switched dice on them that time."

Mike was surprised. "Then why didn't he stop him?"

"On accounta Ross's father," she said. "Mr. Martin said the old man's got a lot of pull." Her voice sounded impressed.

He looked at her. "Is that what you like?"

She put a cigarette in her mouth and lit it. She dragged deeply on it. "Maybe," she answered. "I would like a little of the de luxe. Who wouldn't? It's a hell of a lot better'n livin' the way I am now."

CHAPTER FIFTEEN

KATTI PUT DOWN HER SEWING AND LOOKED AT THE CLOCK. IT WAS nearly eleven. She got out of her chair and went to the window. The August night was heavy and humid. Wearily she wiped the perspiration from her face with a towel that hung around her neck.

There was a sharp twinge of pain in her back, and she swayed dizzily. She reached quickly for a table and held on to it until the dizziness passed. The doctor had warned her about such spells. He had told her to spend most of her time in bed, to do no work. There was something about her pregnancy that placed too great a strain on her heart.

The dizzy spell passed and she went back into the kitchen and put away her sewing. She would lie down for a while and try to rest.

The house was very still, and in the dark of her room she found herself listening for every sound. Often she could not go to sleep until Marja came home, but tonight was even worse than usual. Peter had gone out after supper and had not as yet returned. She knew what that meant.

He would be nasty and irritated and drunk with beer when he came in. She would have to keep him away from Marja or there would be an argument.

After a few minutes she began to feel better, but still she could not sleep. It was too hot in the room, and her bed was warm with the heat of her body. She got out of her bed and went into Marja's room. In the crib, the baby was sleeping restlessly, his tiny body pink with a faint summer rash. As she looked at him, he suddenly awoke and began to cry.

She picked him up and whispered soothingly, but he continued to cry. She carried him into the kitchen and gave him a bottle of cool water. He sucked at it happily and she placed him back in his crib.

There was a sound at the kitchen door and she turned toward it. It must be Peter, it was too early for Marja to come home. One look at his flushed face and she knew where he had been.

He closed the door and looked at her. His eyes were bloodshot and puffed. "Still up?" he asked.

"You see," she said, walking past him toward the bedroom. "Come to bed."

"It's too hot," he said. He crossed the room to the icebox and opened it. "I want a beer."

"Haven't you had enough?" she asked expressionlessly.

He didn't answer as he punctured a can and held it to his lips. Some of it trickled down his chin and slopped onto his shirt. He put the can down and stared at her. "Mind your own business," he snarled.

She stared back at him for a moment, then turned and went into the parlor. She leaned out the window and looked up the street anxiously. It was almost time for Marja to be home.

"What are you doing?" he asked pugnaciously.

She didn't answer. He knew what she was doing. She began to walk past him.

His hand on her arm stopped her. "Looking for your daughter?" he asked nastily.

"Yes," she answered, lapsing into Polish. "Is there anything wrong in it?"

He answered in the same language. "You don't have to worry about her. She's probably making a few extra bucks in some hallway on the way home with that fellow who walks her home every night."

"Go to bed," she said coldly. "You're drunk."

His grip tightened on her arm. "You think I don't know what I'm saying?" he asked shrewdly.

"I know you don't," she said, pulling her arm from his grip and turning back to the window. She looked out. Marja and Mike were walking down the block toward the house.

A moment's pleasure ran through her. This Mike was such a nice boy. They looked so good walking together. Maybe someday—but that was too far off.

Sometimes she had to force herself to realize that Marja was still a child. This wasn't the Old Country. She turned away from the window, the trace of her pleasure still in the corners of her mouth.

"I'm going to bed," she said. "You'd better come, too."

He didn't move. "No. It's too hot. I'm going to have another beer."

She went into the bedroom and began to undress. She could hear him stumbling in the kitchen—the icebox door and the sharp sound when the beer can was opened. She threw a light kimona over her nightgown and went into the kitchen to wash.

He was sitting at the table, the half-empty can in his hand, staring at the door.

"What are you waiting for?" she asked. "Come to bed."

He shook his head stubbornly. "I'll show you who knows what they're talking about. Wait'll she comes in."

She tried to smile. "Don't be a fool, Peter," she said. "Leave the girl alone and come to bed."

"A whore she is," he muttered.

Her stinging slap left a white imprint on his face. He stared up at her in surprise.

Katti's face was white with anger. He had never seen her like this. "Shut up!" she said angrily. "The girl has more brains than you. If it weren't for her, we'd be starving!" She walked toward the bedroom. At the hallway she turned and looked back at him. "You forget it was Marja who got a job when we needed money, not you." Her voice was contemptuous. "She's like her father. You're not half the man he was. I only hope your children are like him, not like you. Else, God help them!"

He got to his feet quickly and moved toward the kitchen door. "I'll show you who's a man!" he shouted, opening it. "No girl in my house is going to be a whore!"

She caught his arm and tried to pull him back into the apartment. "Leave her alone, you drunken bum!" she shouted. "She's my daughter, not yours!"

He pushed her away roughly and she stumbled back against the kitchen table. A wave of pain ran through her body. She looked at him, her eyes blurring.

He was pulling his belt from around his waist. He shook it at her. "Hold your tongue, woman!" he said hoarsely. "Or you'll get more of this than she will. When I get through with her, you'll see what she is." He went out into the hall.

Katti took a deep breath and ran after him. The man was crazy. Marja had been right all the time. If only she had listened to her! A wave of dizziness grabbed at her temples, but she fought it off. He was at the stairway now. She grabbed both his arms.

"Leave her alone!" she whispered, trying to hold him back. With an almost superhuman strength she forced him around. Her eyes stared wildly into his. "If you touch her, you'll never come into this house again!"

The words spilled into his brain like a spray of cold water. A sudden sanity returned to his eyes. He shook her hands violently from his arms. She grabbed at the banister to hold herself erect.

He walked past her to the kitchen door, where he turned and looked back at her. "It's your daughter," he said coldly. "May her sins be on your own head!"

The dizziness reached up to her temples, and his face blurred before her. She let go of the railing and took a hesitant step toward the apartment, but the pain in her temples spread a mantle of darkness over her mind.

"Marja!" she screamed into the suddenly aching void. Then time came rushing up to meet her in the shape of a flight of stairs.

They heard the sound, and almost before Mike could move, Marja was halfway up the first flight of steps. He ran after her, his heart pounding in fright at the piercing scream. He got to the third landing a step behind her.

"Mama!" Marja's voice in his ears was like a frightened child's. He saw her sink to her knees beside the crumpled woman. He stood there dumbly.

"Mama!" Marja's voice was the sound of tears in the cradle. Her blond hair shimmered as she pressed her lips to the still face.

"Katti!"

Mike looked up. The man's face was ashen as he stood on the stairway above their heads and stared at them. "Marja, what happened?"

Marja shook her head dumbly. She turned and looked at Mike. Her eyes were hurt beyond understanding and dull with shock.

He reached down and touched her shoulder. He could feel the trembling in her body. "Is there a phone somewhere in the house?" he asked.

She didn't answer. Somehow he knew she hadn't heard him. He looked up the steps. The man was coming down slowly, both hands gripping the railing tightly as if he was afraid he might fall.

A door beside him opened and a man's face looked out. "There's been an accident," Mike said quickly. "Have you a phone I could use?"

The man nodded and came out into the hall. Behind him Mike could see a woman clutching a wrapper around her.

Mike stepped into the apartment. The woman pointed silently to the telephone. Mike picked it up and was about to speak when the faint whispering sound came to his ears.

It was the only time in his life he was ever to hear Marja cry.

CHAPTER SIXTEEN

IT WAS A WEEK BEFORE MARJA WENT BACK TO WORK AT THE GOLDEN GLOW. Her face was thin and there were deep hollows under her eyes. First had come Katti's funeral.

The Mass at St. Augustine's had been simple. Father Janowicz had been kind and thoughtful. He spoke graciously of her mother's great courage and devotion to Catholic principles, and prayed fervently that her children would guide themselves by her example.

She sat beside Peter in silence as the lone car followed the hearse to the cemetery. The burial was done quickly and inexpensively, and they returned home.

Welfare was waiting for them. Francie's mother, who had been minding the baby while they were out, went upstairs and left them. The young man and older woman who represented Welfare were concerned with their ability to take proper care of the child.

Marja persuaded them that all would be well. She was home during the day and Peter would be home in the evening while she was at work. They agreed to let things stand as they were until fall, when Marja would have to return to school.

She stood in the entrance of the dance hall for a moment. It seemed strange to her that while so much had changed, the dance hall was still the same. The cheap, tinselly decorations, the dim blue lights, the tired music with its false rhythms—everything was the same.

The bouncer came toward her. His apelike, dull face was without expression. "Mr. Martin wants to see yuh," he said, jerking his thumb in the direction of the office.

Without answering him, she cut across the dance floor. She knocked at the door.

Martin's voice came through it. "Come in."

She opened the door. He was seated at his desk, some papers spread out before him. She hesitated until he looked up. Then she came into the room, closed the door behind her, and stood in front of his desk.

"You wanted to see me?" she asked in a dull voice.

He nodded. "Sit down. I'll be with yuh soon's I finish this."

She slipped into a chair beside the desk and watched him. His face was harsh and lined, and his gray-black hair gave his blue eyes an even colder look. His chin was firm and square, but his lips, though thin, had an almost strange gentility about them.

At last he looked up. "I'm sorry about your mother, Marja," he said gently.

She looked down at her hands. "Thanks," she said, her throat tight and constricted. It was still difficult for her to talk about it.

He was silent for a moment. "An investigator was here from the Welfare Department. They were checking up on your job."

Her face held a sudden fear. She looked at him questioningly.

He smiled reassuringly. "Don't be frightened. I told him you were a cashier."

She looked down at her hands again. Her voice was perilously close to breaking. "I don't know how to thank you, Mr. Martin."

He looked down at the papers on his desk. "Why didn't you tell me how old you are, Marja?" he asked suddenly.

"Would you have given me a job if I had?" she countered.

He hesitated. "I guess not."

"That's why," she answered. "Besides, you never asked me."

His eyes searched her face. "I never thought about it. You look old enough."

A faint smile came to her lips. "I am old enough."

He got to his feet and came around the desk to her. His hand reached out and touched her shoulder. He nodded thoughtfully. He remembered his own youth. He had come from a neighborhood very much like Marja's. "I guess you are," he said.

She looked up at him questioningly. "It's okay if I go back to work, then, Mr. Martin?"

"Yes," he answered. "But keep your eyes open. If there's any trouble or anything, get out in a hurry. We can't have you caught here or our license is gone."

"I'll be careful, Mr. Martin," she said, getting to her feet. "I promise."

He opened the door for her and she stood there a moment, a grateful smile on her lips. "Thanks very much, Mr. Martin," she said in a low, husky voice. "I won't forget how nice you've been."

He stood in the doorway watching her make her way to the dressing-room. He shook his head wonderingly. Even now that he knew, it was still hard to believe. Not even sixteen. Still, some of these Polacks came to it early. He grinned to himself as he closed the door and walked back to his desk.

The calendar would never mean very much to her. She had now all the wisdom she would ever need. She had man sense. It was the sixth sense that most women spent all their lives without ever finding.

She opened the door and stepped into the kitchen. Her stepfather was reading a paper spread on the table. He looked up at her.

"How is the baby?" she asked.

"Okay," he answered stiffly. "He was sleeping quiet all night."

She went into her room and glanced into the crib. Peter was sleeping peacefully, his thumb stuck into the corner of his mouth. Gently she removed it. Suddenly she was aware of her stepfather's gaze. She turned swiftly.

He was standing in the doorway of her room, watching her. His face flushed suddenly.

"What do you want?" she asked.

He cleared his throat. "Nothin'," he answered. He went back into the kitchen.

She slipped out of her dress and slip. Throwing on a robe, she went into the kitchen and turned on the water in the sink.

Peter looked up at her from his chair. "That feller Mike," he asked cautiously. "He come home with you?"

"Yeah," she answered, scrubbing her face vigorously with soap and water.

"He like you, eh?"

"I suppose so," she replied, still busy with her face.

"You spend lots of time with him downstairs?" A leering sound had crept into his voice. "Before you come up?"

She turned on him coldly. "What are you trying to find out?"

He couldn't meet her gaze. He looked down at the table. "Nothing."

"Then mind your own business," she said, crossing the room and going out into the hall.

He was waiting at the door when she came back into the kitchen. His hand caught her arm. She stared up into his face, her eyes narrowing slightly. She didn't speak.

"You're very pretty girl, Marja." His voice had a pleading sound in it.

She still didn't speak.

"Sometime, maybe, you be nice to me like you are to him," he said awkwardly. "Then everybody happy, eh?"

She shook his hand from her arm. She was too weary to be very angry. Her voice was dull and flat. "Peter," she said—it was the first time she had ever called him by his given name without the prefix "Uncle"—"don't be a jerk. I'm stayin' here because that's the way Mama would have wanted it. But that's all. No more."

He followed her to the bedroom door. He sucked in his breath and dared another question. "But, Marja, you know how I always feel about you?"

"I know," she said coldly. "But you're not my type. If you need a woman that bad, go out and get yourself one."

She slammed the door swiftly in his face and turned the key loudly so he could hear it. She waited there a moment until she could hear his footsteps walking away. Then she quickly finished undressing and climbed into her bed.

She stretched her arms behind her head and let the faint breeze from the window drift over her body. There was a dull, lonely ache inside her. She closed her eyes, and her mother's face jumped before her in the darkness.

"Be a good girl, Marja," Katti seemed to be saying.

"I will. Mama," she promised in a half-whisper, turning on her side. She heard the faint click of the icebox door as she drifted off to sleep.

CHAPTER SEVENTEEN

JOKER MARTIN LOOKED UP AT HER. SHE WAS STANDING IN FRONT OF HIS desk. "I got it fixed," he said. "Welfare agreed it was okay for you to take an afternoon session at school and continue workin' here."

Her hands made a simple expressive gesture. "I don't know how to thank you," she said. "It seems like you're always doin' somethin' nice for me."

He smiled, embarrassed. "Maybe it's because I like yuh."

She didn't speak.

"You're steady, Marja," he said. "You show up every night, yuh never give me no trouble like the other girls. Maybe that's why."

"I still don't know how I can ever pay you back," she said.

He started to speak, but the telephone on his desk began to ring. He picked it up. "Martin speaking."

The voice spoke for a few seconds and Joker looked up at her. She turned and started to leave, but a gesture of his hand bade her stay. "Hold on a minute," he said into the phone.

He covered the mouthpiece with his hand while he spoke to her. "Here is a way you can pay me back," he said. "I got a very important guy on the phone. He's short a dame on a party tonight. There's five bucks in it for yuh if yuh want to go."

She hesitated. "I—I don't think so, Mr. Martin. I'd be outta place there."

He knew what she meant. "Go on," he said. "This guy's okay. There won't be no rough stuff. All yuh gotta do is dance a little with 'em an' have a few laughs. Yuh'll be outta there by three thirty."

She still hesitated. "You sure?"

He nodded. "Sure."

"But I haven't got the kind of clothes to wear." She shook her head. "I'd better not."

"You can take your gown," he said. "You can bring it back tomorrow night. Besides, you'll be doin' me a big favor."

She drew in her breath. She didn't see how she could refuse to go. He had been so good to her. "Okay."

He smiled. "Good girl." He waved his hand at her. "Go get your bag an' come back here. I'll give you the address."

He waited until the door had closed behind her before he spoke into the phone again. Then he spoke quickly, cautiously. "I'm sendin' over a green kid, Jack, so take it easy. I don't want her scared off."

He was silent while the voice on the other end of the telephone crackled in his ear. The sound stopped and he spoke again, a laughing sound in his voice. "Look, it's the most gorgeous thing you ever saw. But don't let that fool yuh. It's under age, and trouble if anything goes wrong. Play it straight an' give it a little time. It'll come around." He put the telephone down as she came back into the office.

She got out of the cab in front of the large apartment building. The doorman held the door for her while she paid the driver and got out of the cab. "Mr. Ostere's apartment."

There was a knowing look in his eyes. "Penthouse D, seventeenth floor."

The elevator-operator had the same look in his eyes as he took her up. "To your left," he said, holding the door for her.

She heard the elevator door close behind her as she pressed the buzzer. The door opened. A man in full evening dress looked out at her.

"Mr. Ostere?" she asked. "I'm Marja Flood."

The man's face was cold. "Come in," he said formally. "I'll tell Mr. Ostere you're here."

She waited in the foyer. The man disappeared and returned in a moment, followed by a shorter man. This man wore a dark business suit.

He came up to her, his hand outstretched. "I'm Jack Ostere," he said, smiling.

"Marja Flood," she answered, taking his hand.

He stepped back and looked at her. "My God!" he exclaimed dramatically. "Joker was right for once in his life. You are beautiful."

A pleased smile crossed her lips. "Thank you, Mr. Ostere," she said.

"Make it Jack," he answered quickly. "Come inside and let me fix you a drink before the others get here." He took her arm and steered her into the largest living-room she had ever seen.

He paused before a small portable bar on wheels. "What will it be? Manhattan? Martini?"

"Coke?" she questioned hesitantly.

He wrinkled his brow quizzically, then smiled. "As you wish." He turned and pulled a cord near the wall.

The butler appeared almost immediately. "Yes, sir?"

"Jordan, a Coke for Miss Flood," Ostere said.

The butler's face was impassive. "Yes, sir," he said, turning away.

"With lots of ice," Marja said.

The butler looked at her. "With lots of ice, ma'am." He left the room.

Marja turned to her host. "I hope I wasn't too early. Joker told me to come right over."

Ostere had poured some whisky over ice. He held the glass toward her. "No one as pretty as you could ever be too early, Marja."

A chime sounded in the apartment. "Please excuse me," Ostere apologized. "Some of my guests are arriving and I must greet them."

The butler brought Marja her Coke, and she looked around the room quickly. It must have been forty feet long, and at one end were high French windows that opened onto a terrace.

Her host came bustling back into the room with the new arrivals. Marja's eyes widened.

One of the girls was a movie star whom she had seen many times on the screen at the RKO 86th Street Theatre. And one of the men was a newspaper columnist whose column she often read in the morning paper.

Before Ostere had finished the introductions, the chime rang again and he hurried off to welcome other guests. Marja's eyes were wide. Even though she did not recognize all the names, they had the familiar ring of the daily paper.

She was quiet and shy most of the time, for she did not know what to say to people like these. From the conversation she gathered that Ostere was a rich man who often dabbled in backing plays.

He was a kind host, however, for though he circulated freely throughout the room talking to his guests, every few minutes he would appear at her side to see that she was happy and comfortable. She liked him. He was such a nice, busy little man.

Once the columnist got her in a corner and asked her what she did for a living. At first she didn't know what to say to him. Then it came to her.

"I'm a dancer," she answered. It was near enough to the truth.

Ostere appeared suddenly beside them and smiled approvingly at her reply.

"Where do you work?" the columnist persisted. "I'll give you a plug in the column."

"I'm not ready for that yet," she said, smiling. "But I'll count on you remembering that when I am."

The columnist had already had a few drinks and was slightly loaded. He knew what kind of girls Ostere usually had around him on evenings like this. He wanted to make her uncomfortable. "Let's see you dance," he said nastily. "I don't believe you."

A silence fell around the room at his words. They looked at Marja curiously, waiting for her reaction. Ostere's girls were no secret.

Marja kept her eyes wide as she answered. "I'd love to," she said. "But unfortunately I can't right now. You see, I suffer from a dancer's occupational hazard at the moment."

"What occupational hazard?" the columnist spoke loudly, almost triumphantly. "I never heard of any."

"You don't know very much, do you?" Marja asked sweetly. "Didn't you ever hear of sore feet?"

The gust of laughter that swept the room eased the tension, and Ostere patted her shoulder and whispered: "Good girl."

The guests began to leave about two thirty, and by three o'clock Marja and Ostere were alone again. He sank into a chair and looked up at her. "My God!" he exclaimed. "I'm glad that's over for this week."

She was puzzled. "If you don't like it, why do you do it?"

He smiled. "I must, my dear. It's business. Besides, they would be disappointed if I didn't. It's become a weekly custom."

"You mean this happens every week?" she asked.

He nodded. "New York wouldn't be the same without Tuesday midnight at Jack Ostere's." His voice held a note of pride.

She shook her head. It was beyond her. She didn't see what difference it made whether anybody came or not. "It's time I was going, Mr. Ostere," she said, suddenly reverting to formality.

He looked up with what he thought was an appealing expression. "Must you go?" he asked archly. "I've got lots of room here."

Her eyes were cold. "I have to, Mr. Ostere. My father's waiting up for me."

He jumped to his feet. "Of course," he said. "I should have realized." He reached into his pocket for a bill, which he pressed into her hand.

She didn't look at it. "Thank you very much, Mr. Ostere," she said, holding out her hand. "I had a very good time."

He pressed her hand. "I enjoyed having you here, my dear. I hope you'll come again. Next week, maybe."

She hesitated. "I can't say. I'd have to check with Mr. Martin."

He smiled as he walked her to the door. "Don't worry about Joker. I'll talk to him."

"Good night, Mr. Ostere."

"Good night, Marja."

The elevator door opened and she stepped into the car. She waved at Ostere, still standing in his doorway, and the elevator door closed on his answering smile. It wasn't until then that she peeked at the bill tightly clutched in her left hand.

A gasp of surprise parted her lips. It was twenty dollars—as much as she made in a whole week's work. She slipped it into her purse quickly, wondering whether he had made a mistake.

The doorman's face held an expression of surprise when she came out of the building. "Cab, ma'am?" he asked.

She stared at him for a moment. Then she shrugged her shoulders. Why not? She was loaded.

CHAPTER EIGHTEEN

IT WAS THREE THIRTY WHEN THE CAB STOPPED IN FRONT OF HER DOOR. She got out and started up the steps.

"Marja!" A figure stepped from the shadows near the doorway.

"Mike! What are you doing here?"

His voice was unhappy. "I was waiting for yuh. I was worried. Are you all right?"

She lit a cigarette. The match flared, illuminating her face briefly. "I'm okay."

"I waited down at the Golden Glow until half past twelve," he said, his voice growing unhappier. "Then I asked an' they told me you left early. I came here thinking you weren't feeling well, but your father said you hadn't come home yet."

"You didn't have to wait," she said quickly. "I went to a party."

"Where?"

"Jack Ostere's," she answered without thinking. "You don't know him," she added.

"How come?" he asked.

"Joker asked me to go."

His voice was low. "I don't like it."

"Why not?" She was annoyed and her voice betrayed it.

"I just don't like you doing it, that's all," he said. "He's got no right sending you out on things like that."

She was angry now. "Nobody asked you what you thought," she flared.

His voice was stubborn. "You shouldn' 've gone."

"If you didn't hang aroun' spyin' on me," she said angrily, "you never would've known."

"I'm not spying on you, Marja," he said in a hurt, low voice. "I was scared something might have happened to you."

Her voice was cold. "Now that you see I'm okay, you can go home. Yuh're beginnin' to bother me!" She ran up the steps into the hall, leaving him standing in the street looking after her.

He stood there a moment. Then, a strange sadness in him, he turned and began to walk home. There were times when he felt that he didn't know her at all.

Peter was sitting at the table, the inevitable can of beer in front of him. He looked at her with bloodshot eyes. "Where you been?" he asked.

"Workin'," she answered briefly.

His eyes took in her dress. "Your boy frien', he says you left early. You didn't come home."

She didn't answer, but started through the kitchen to her room. He was out of his chair quickly, blocking her path. "Where you been in that dress?"

She stared into his eyes levelly. "Workin', I said."

His hands gripped her shoulders. "Like that? With your tits hangin' out?"

"This is my working clothes," she answered. "I was too tired to change, so I came home in them." She tried to shake off his grip. "Lay off. I gotta return it tomorrow. It ain't mine."

His hand fell from her shoulder swiftly. Before she could stop him, he had opened her purse and spilled its contents on the table. The twenty-dollar bill lay on top of the pile. He picked it up and turned it over in his hand. "Where'd you get this?"

She stared at him. "It was a tip."

"They don't give tips like this for just dancing," he said.

She didn't answer.

His hand lashed out. "Slut!"

She spun half around and stumbled against the wall, a white blotch on her face. The snap of her shoulder strap opened and her dress began to fall. She clutched it to her breast.

His voice was harsh. "I told your mother what you were, but she didn't believe me. It's a good thing she's not here to see this."

Her voice was expressionless. "Good for you, you mean."

His hand began to pull the belt from around his waist. He moved toward her menacingly.

She ducked around him and pulled a sharp meat knife from the table drawer. She held it, its gleaming edge pointing viciously at his face. Her teeth drew back over her lips in a snarl. "Come on!" she taunted. "Try somethin'!"

He stared at the knife, then at her. Her eyes were flaming with hate. He stepped back. "Marja! You don't know what you're doin'!"

She grinned. "Wanna bet?"

He took a deep breath. The girl was mad. Cautiously he backed away from her. "Okay, okay," he said anxiously.

"The money." Her eyes were still on his face.

He tossed the twenty-dollar bill on the table. She shoveled it quickly into her bag along with the other things.

Her face was still grim. "If yuh ever come near me," she said in a low, deadly voice, "or try to touch me, so help me God, I'll kill yuh."

He didn't answer. He had no doubt that she meant every word she said. Her door closed behind her, and he turned to the icebox with a suddenly trembling hand.

Marja leaned her back against the closed door and shut her eyes. It was as if a thousand years had passed since her mother had died, yet it was only a little more than a month. She opened her eyes and looked down at the knife she held in her hand.

A cold chill ran through her and she shuddered convulsively. She dropped the knife on the bed and began to undress. She didn't notice it again until she was about to get into bed. Then, thoughtfully she slipped it under the corner of her mattress. She never went to bed after that without checking first to see that it was there.

CHAPTER NINETEEN

FROM THAT TIME ON, SHE WENT WHERE JOKER SENT HER. GRADUALLY she came to trust him. She never had trouble with any of the men she met. They were more respectful to her than the boys in school.

The boys were always ganging up on her and grabbing at her. She didn't mind them. She felt superior in many ways to the children in school around her. What did they know of what was going on in the world?

She began to see Mike less and less as the winter wore on. Several times she made dates with him and then had to break them because Joker had a job for her. Since the night he had waited at her house, he had stopped waiting for her at the dance hall. Then one evening she was called to the phone at the dance hall.

"Hello," she said into the speaker.

"Marja?" the familiar voice spoke in her ear. "It's Mike."

A sudden warmth came into her. She hadn't realized until this minute how much she had missed him. She smiled into the phone. "How are yuh, Mike?"

"Fine," he answered. "And you?"

"Okay," she answered.

"I wanted to talk to you," he said, "but I've been busy up at school."

"I'm glad you called, Mike," she said softly. "I missed you."

His voice was suddenly light and happy. "You did?"

"Honest, Mike."

"Meet me when you get through work?" he asked.

"Sure," she answered quickly.

"Downstairs. Same place. First car off the corner," he said quickly.

"Okay."

"Marja?" He hesitated.

"What, Mike?"

"You won't stand me up this time?" he pleaded.

"I'll be there, Mike," she said as she put down the telephone.

He was leaning against a car when she came out. He straightened up as she walked toward him. She looked up into his face. He seemed tired and thin. "Hi," she said.

A crooked smile split his face. "Hi."

They stood there staring at each other for a moment. Marja broke the silence. "Aren't you gonna ask me for a cup of coffee?"

"Sure," he said. "You took the words outta my mouth."

She started toward the drugstore, but he took her arm and steered her to a restaurant near by. They entered and sat down at a table.

She looked down at the white tablecloth. "Boy, we're livin'."

He grinned. "Nothin' but the best."

But she noticed he was careful in ordering. "What you been doin'?" she asked.

"Nothin' much," he answered. "School. Studying. Working."

"You lost weight," she said.

He shrugged his shoulders. "I was getting too heavy, anyway."

The waiter put the coffee and buns in front of them. She took a sip of coffee and waited for him to speak.

"How is little Peter?" he asked.

"Fine." She smiled. "He's walking and beginning to talk. He calls me 'Ja-Ja.' " She noticed he didn't ask about her stepfather.

"How's the job going?" he asked.

"Okay," she answered.

He was silent as he watched her drink the coffee, but he didn't touch the cup in front of him. "You're not drinkin' your coffee," she said.

"I'm not hungry," he answered. He got to his feet abruptly, throwing a bill on the table. "C'mon, let's go."

She followed him out into the street. "What's wrong, Mike?"

He looked into her face. "I got a message for yuh," he said expressionlessly.

She was puzzled. "For me?"

He nodded. "From Ross. He said to tell yuh he'd be home next month."

Her hand fell from his arm. "Is that why you called me? To give me a message?"

He didn't answer. His face was grim.

"What am I supposed to do?" she asked sarcastically. "Do somersaults?"

He was still quiet.

She stopped. He took two steps before he realized she wasn't with him. "What?" he asked in a puzzled tone.

"Okay, so I got the message," she said in a cold voice. "Thanks."

"He still thinks you're his girl," he said.

Her eyes were wide in the night. "What do *you* think?"

He stood there miserably. "I don't know what to think. He seems so sure of himself."

She backed into a dark doorway. "Mike," she said.

"Yes?"

"C'mere, Mike."

He followed her into the doorway. She put her arms around his shoulders and pulled his face down to her. She kissed him. At first he stood frozen, then his arms tightened and pulled her close to him. They stood there for moments while rockets exploded in his brain.

Finally she drew back. All her body was tingling from the tightness of his embrace. "*Now* what do you think, Mike?"

"But you never said anything," he said confusedly. "You didn't act like you wanted to see me. Like the last time you stood me up. I waited over an hour for you to show up, but you didn't."

Her eyes were green in the night and glowed like a cat's. "I gotta work, Mike. I need the dough. You know that."

"There's just so much you can do for money," he said.

She shook her head. "I don't do anything wrong. I just want enough so I don't have to live like my mother did. I saw what happened to her."

"But you never—"

"Shut up," she said softly. pressing her fingers to his lips. "Yuh talk too much. You never tried to kiss me. I was wonderin' if there was somethin' the matter with you."

He smiled. It was as if his whole face lit up. He bent his face to her. "Maybe it's just as well," he said. "I got that much more to make up for."

The street was quiet when they reached her house. The last winds of March were beating faintly at them as they stepped into the vestibule. She closed the door quietly and looked up into his face.

He stared down at her. His eyes were serious, and he spoke in a whisper. "I love yuh, Marja. Yuh know that, don't you?"

She nodded.

"I loved yuh since that day in the elevator, but I never thought you could see me. Ross has so much. I got nothin'."

"I never asked for anything," she said.

"I know," he answered. "But you can get anything you want. Every guy you meet is crazy for yuh."

She smiled slowly. "I know," she said contentedly. "But I don't care about them. They're all jerks. They all think they can get something out of me, but I ain't givin'."

He grinned teasingly. "I'm a jerk, too?"

"You're the biggest of them all," she taunted gently. "Except me. I go for you."

He pulled her toward him. She came willingly into his arms. Her lips and mouth were warm and open. Her tongue flashed fires into his mouth. He caught his breath sharply, then closed his eyes, slipping into the vortex of heat.

She drew back suddenly, a puzzled look in her eyes. "Mike, yuh make me crazy."

"Good," he said.

She shook her head. "I don't understand it. Nobody ever made me feel like that."

He pulled her to him again. "That'll teach yuh not to mess around with me, gal," he laughed. He kissed her throat. "Now you really got a feller."

CHAPTER TWENTY

PETER SAT AT THE WINDOW IN THE DARKNESS. HE LOOKED OUT INTO THE street. Marja should have been home an hour ago. She wasn't working late tonight. He knew that.

He craned his neck out the window. There were two people walking slowly up the block. They passed a street light.

One was Marja.

That boy was with her. Mike. They were walking with their arms around each other's waists. A twinge of jealousy ran through him. Marja was a woman now. The last few months had made many changes in her. She was sure of herself. It was that job.

He had heard many stories about the girls who worked in dance halls. They were a wild lot. He remembered some that he had known before he married. They were no better than whores, most of them.

Erotic thoughts crowded into his mind. He felt warm. It wasn't right. He had seen Marja before any of them. She had no right to treat him the way she did. Walking around the house that way. Half undressed. She knew that got him excited.

He felt the beads of sweat break out on his forehead. He reeled drunkenly into the dark kitchen and opened the icebox. There was no more beer. He stood there cursing silently. Then he remembered the bottle of slivovitz in the closet.

He took the bottle down and pulled out the cork. He held the bottle to his mouth, feeling the fiery liquor burn its way down his throat and hit his stomach. Its heat radiated through him. He felt strong and capable now.

Holding the bottle carefully, he walked back into the parlor and looked out the window. They weren't in sight. He listened carefully for Marja's footsteps on the stairs. There was no sound.

He waited almost ten minutes. He took another drink from the bottle. She wasn't fooling him. He knew what she was doing downstairs. His thoughts infuriated him. The teasing little bitch. Everybody got their share except him. She laughed at him.

He had a brilliant idea. Softly he walked back through the apartment and out the kitchen door. He crept down the stairway silently to the first landing and peered through the banister to the ground floor.

He could see them standing in the corner of the hall. Marja's arms were around the boy's neck, and they were kissing. The boy's back hid Marja from Peter's gaze, but he knew what they were doing. He could tell from the way they were standing.

A sound of muffled laughter came to his ears, and Marja stepped back from the boy. He could see her face now. Her lips seemed puffed and swollen in the dim yellow light. She was smiling.

"Tomorrow?" he heard Mike ask.

Marja laughed happily. "Tomorrow, for sure." She turned toward the stairway.

Peter scrambled quickly up the stairs to the apartment. He waited at the kitchen door until he could hear her footsteps. Then he hurried through the dark apartment to the parlor.

He sat down in the chair in the corner from which he could watch the kitchen in the mirror on the wall. A wild anger was bursting inside him. There was a tightness in his belly. He held the bottle to his lips. Some of the liquor ran down his chin.

The kitchen door opened, and light from the hall showed Marja standing there. He heard her voice.

"Peter?"

He didn't answer.

"Peter, are you asleep?"

Cautiously he held his breath. Let the bitch think he was asleep. He didn't have to tell her what he was doing.

She came into the kitchen and walked through the darkness to the door of her room. A moment later the soft light from the lamp on her dresser came from the room.

He watched carefully. She thought he was asleep, for she didn't close her door. He saw her cross the room and begin to take off her dress. A faint sound of her humming came to his ears. The little whore sounded actually happy for a change.

She was in her underwear now. She looked up. He held his breath, wondering whether she suspected he was watching her. But apparently that wasn't what was on her mind. She came out of the bedroom and crossed the kitchen to the sink, out of his sight. The sound of pans being lifted from the washtub came to his ears, then the noise of water running softly.

She came back into sight, still humming softly. She unfastened her brassiere as she went into her room. He could see her rubbing her back where the red welt from the straps marked her flesh. She went into a corner of the room near her closet and he couldn't see her.

He lifted the bottle to his lips and took another swift, cautious drink, then wiped his mouth on the back of his hand. He could feel the sudden pounding of his heart. At the sound of footsteps, he looked up again.

She was coming through the doorway, a kimona hanging loosely around her. It flashed open as she moved; she was naked beneath it. She crossed to the washtub, and he heard her fiddling with the faucet. Suddenly he understood. She was going to take a bath.

Usually she waited until he had gone out, but she must believe he was asleep. He grinned to himself. She wasn't so smart. He was much smarter than she.

She crossed the room and went out into the hall, leaving the door half open behind her. He got out of his chair swiftly and moved into the kitchen on silent feet. He listened carefully at the door for a moment. He heard the hall toilet noise and looked around swiftly. There wasn't time for him to get back to the parlor. He ducked into her room and hid behind the open door.

She sat back in the wash basin that served for a tub and let the warm water press against her skin. Someday she would have a real bathtub in a real bathroom.

She was tired of bathing in the kitchen and going out into the hall to the toilet. But right now the water felt good. Luxuriously she spread the soap lather all over her.

She closed her eyes and thought of Mike. He was wonderful. It was funny how things worked out. The way he made her feel when he kissed her—it was like the way it happened in books. Warm and exciting inside. There was such a new longing that for a moment when they kissed she could hardly stand, her legs felt so weak.

The water began to cool and she opened her eyes. It was late, time she got to bed. She rinsed off the soap and climbed out of the basin. She pulled the towel from the back of the chair and rubbed herself dry. She could feel her skin glowing and warm. She wrapped the towel around her and went back into her room.

She went right to her closet and hung up her kimona. She pulled her nightgown from her hanger and started to cross to the bed, dropping her towel on the back of a chair. She had begun to raise the gown over her head when an instinct made her look up.

Her heart constricted in her bosom and the sudden pain of fear knifed through her body. Peter was standing in the corner. Her arms dropped and she held the gown in front of her.

He took a step toward her, grinning foolishly. "Marja," he said, his hand reaching for her.

She dodged away from him behind the crib. The fear congealed into an icy anger. "Get out!" she snarled.

He stood there weaving slightly. The sweat stood out on his forehead, his eyes were glazed. His tongue ran over his lips.

"Get out!" she yelled. "Yuh no-good drunken bum!"

"Marja," he mumbled, "why are you all the time mad at me? I like you." He stepped around the crib toward her.

She moved away from him cautiously. "Yuh stink," she said. "Get out!"

The baby woke and suddenly began to cry. Instinctively her eyes turned to the crib. Peter moved swiftly and caught her hand before she was aware of it. He pulled her to him and tried to kiss her.

She twisted in his grasp, turning her face away from him. Her nails slashed at his face. "Lemme go! Yuh son of a bitch!"

His hand was caught in the gown she held before her. Her hands were raking at his face. With a cry of pain he pulled back, the tearing sound of the gown coming to his ears. He still held her by one wildly waving hand. With his other hand, he reached up to his face. It came away sticky with blood. He stared at it stupidly.

She looked up at him, her chest heaving. "Now will yuh get out?" she gasped.

He shook his head to clear it. "You bitch!" he yelled. "You not goin' to tease me no more! I'll show yuh!"

He raised his hand and hit her across the face. She spun away from him, half falling to the floor. He followed her slowly, his eyes fixed on her face.

There was no fear in her eyes, only an all-consuming hatred. She pulled her legs up under her. Suddenly she sprang, diving past him for the bed, her hand reaching for the knife under the mattress.

He caught her by the hair, snapping her head back so that she lay in a half-arc on the edge of the bed. She saw his hand coming toward her face. She tried to twist away from the blow. A sharp light exploded in her brain and she fell forward, trying to keep tears of pain from coming to her eyes.

She felt his hand turn her over. Quick tiny flashes of pain ran all over her body as his hand became a blur in the dim light. Her body felt heavy, as if there was a great weight upon it. Then the last, most exquisite pain of all burst in her groin and she began to slide almost gratefully into the night that was closing fast around her bed. The last thing she knew was the sound of the baby crying in his crib.

She came awake slowly. Sensation returned to her body and, with it, pain. Her body felt as if a thousand tiny needles were sticking into her. She turned her head cautiously.

The light was still on in the room and she was alone. Gradually memory came back to her. She sat up in the bed, a cry of pain escaping her lips.

She saw Peter's clothing lying on the floor near the bed. Nausea swept through her, and she ran into the kitchen. The pain hit her stomach in wave after wave as she retched into the sink. At last it was gone and a cold chill came over her.

Quickly she turned the hot water on in the basin and climbed into it. Desperately she scrubbed at her skin with the soap, but the grime she felt wasn't on the surface. It was deep inside her where she could never get it out.

But the warm water stilled some of the pain, and at last she got out of the basin. She walked dripping into her room and took a towel from the closet. Slowly she dried herself, then carefully began to dress.

In front of the mirror she carefully applied lipstick and combed back her hair. Her face stared back at her, dull and impassive. Only her eyes were still alive. They were green and filled with hate.

She went to her bed and straightened it. The pillowcase was bloodstained; she found a fresh one. She pulled the blanket tight and tucked it in.

A faint sound came from the crib. She looked into it. The baby was wet. Quickly she changed his diaper, and filling a small bottle with water, placed it near his lips. Then she walked back to the bed and took the knife from under the mattress.

Dully she walked through the apartment to Peter's room. She opened the door silently and looked in. He lay in a hulking shadow across his bed. She pulled the light chain over her head. Light flooded into the room. Peter didn't move.

He lay on his back, breathing heavily, the blanket clutched around him.

She placed the knife close to his face. "Peter, wake up," she said quietly.

He lay silent. A snore escaped his mouth.

Her hand swiped viciously across his face. "Wake up!" Her lips drew back over her teeth in a snarl.

His eyes opened almost immediately. For a moment he lay absolutely still. Then he saw the knife, and terror sprang into his eyes. His voice caught in his throat. "What are you doing, Marja?"

"I've come to keep my promise, Peter." Her voice was very tight and very low. "Remember what I said?"

He stared up at her, afraid to move. "You're crazy!" he gasped.

"No crazier than you." She smiled. The knife swiped viciously across his face.

The flesh parted like a ripe melon bursting in the sun. A pool of blood rushed in to fill the wound from his cheek to his jawbone. He screamed agonizedly and leaped from the bed toward the door, the blanket trailing on the floor behind him.

He ran through the apartment into the hallway, still screaming. Through the open door he could see her walking slowly after him. He began to run down the stairs. He tripped in the blanket and fell the few steps to the next landing.

She stood at the head of the stairway, looking down at him. He was still screaming. She closed her eyes. It was not long since her mother had been lying there. She turned and went back into the apartment.

She closed the door behind her and walked over to the sink. She turned on the water and washed the knife carefully. Then she placed it on the table and sat down in a chair facing the door. It was the same chair that her mother had always sat in while waiting for her to come home.

Her eyes were burning. She was tired, very tired. Her eyelids closed.

There was a heavy knock at the door. She opened her eyes. There was a hint of tears in them. "Come in," she said quietly.

That was how she was when the police came into the room.

CHAPTER TWENTY-ONE

"BUT THERE MUST HAVE BEEN A REASON FOR YOU TO DO SUCH A thing, Maria," the woman insisted.

Marja looked at the Welfare worker. She shook her head stubbornly. She didn't speak.

"You don't want to be sent to a reform school, do you?" the woman persisted.

Marja shrugged her shoulders. "No matter what I say, I won't be let loose. They're gonna put me away, no matter what."

"But there's a big difference between a correctional institution and a state home," the woman explained.

Marja's eyes were wide. "Not to me. One is as bad as the other."

The woman heaved a sigh. "Don't you want to be with your little brother any more?"

Marja looked at her swiftly. "Would they let me stay with him if I talk? I can work and keep him."

The woman shook her head regretfully. "No, they couldn't do that. You're too young. But—"

"Then it doesn't make any difference, does it?" Marja asked.

The woman didn't answer.

Marja got to her feet. "Come on," she said. "Let's get it over with."

The courtroom was almost empty. Only a few spectators sat in the rows near the railing. She glanced idly at them as she passed. They looked up at her curiously but impersonally. She meant nothing to them.

A hand reached out and brushed her arm as she walked by. "Hello, Marja." She looked up, startled.

It was Mike. There was a friendly, reassuring smile on his lips. "I tried to see yuh," he whispered quickly, "but they wouldn't let me."

Her face settled into a dull, impassive mask. There was no use telling him she had given orders that she didn't want to see anyone. She continued walking.

The Welfare woman was just behind her. "That's a nice looking boy," she said in a friendly voice. "Your boy friend?"

Marja's eyes were blank. "I don't know who he is. I never saw him before in my life."

The judge was a tired, bored-looking old man. He peered down at Marja. "You are charged with attacking your stepfather with a knife, young woman."

She didn't answer.

"Is Mr. Ritchik here?" he asked, turning to the clerk.

The clerk called: "Mr. Ritchik."

Peter came forward from the back of the court. His face was still covered with a big white bandage. Marja looked at him. It was as if he were a stranger. The five weeks since she had seen him had been a lifetime.

"Mr. Ritchik," the judge asked, "will you tell us what happened?"

Peter cleared his throat nervously. "She's no good, Your Honor. A tramp. She wouldn't listen to nobody. She worked at the dance hall and never came home nights. When she did, it was late. That night I spoke to her about coming in decent hours like other girls. When I went to sleep, she sneaked into my room and cut me."

Marja had to smile. If it weren't for her mother's memory she would tell them what had really happened. But Katti was entitled to that much peace.

It was over in a little while. She stood in front of the desk while the judge looked down over his spectacles at her.

"Marja," he said, "we are sending you to the Rose Geyer Correctional Home for Girls until you are eighteen. It is my hope that you will put your time there to good use and learn a trade and a Christian way of life."

She looked up at him blankly.

"Any questions?" he asked.

She shook her head.

He rapped his gavel on the desk and got to his feet. Everybody in the court stood as he walked pompously from the bench. The door closed behind him, and the Welfare woman turned to her.

"Come with me, Marja," she said.

Dumbly, Marja followed her. Mike was standing behind the rail. He tried to speak, but she looked right through him. A hurt expression came over his face. It wasn't until she was through the door that she realized he was crying.

The Rose Geyer Home was in the far end of the Bronx. She looked at it curiously as she got out of the car with the policeman and the Welfare matron. It was almost like the country up here. The Home was surrounded by open fields.

An hour later she was escorted to the doctor's office by one of the girls, who looked at her questioningly, but spoke not a word as they walked down the long gray corridor.

She held the door open for Marja. "In here, honey," she said in a not unpleasant voice. She followed Marja into the office. A thin, gray-haired man looked up. "I got a new fish for you, Doc," the girl said.

The doctor shrugged his shoulders wearily. "In there." He pointed to a small room. "Take off all your clothes."

His examination was brief and efficient. Twenty minutes after she had come into his office she was dressed and back in the entrance room.

The doctor handed her a prescription. "Get this filled at the dispensary and take it all during your pregnancy," he said.

Marja was startled. She cast a quick glance behind her. The girl who had brought her was sitting against the wall. She turned back to the doctor. "Who, me?" she asked incredulously.

The girl's voice came from behind her. It was flat but not without humor. "He don't mean me, honey. I been here without a guy for two years now, damn it!"

Marja looked at the doctor, then at the paper in her hand. Suddenly she realized what it meant. She sank into a chair beside the desk and began to laugh.

The doctor stared at her. "What's so funny?" he asked.

She looked up at him, the tears running down her cheeks. That was the hell of it. He would never know. Nobody would.

The State vs.
Maryann Flood

I WAITED WHILE THE CLERK ADMINISTERED THE OATH TO THE STATE'S FIRST witness. She was a tall, dark girl with a dramatic·part in the middle of her long jet-black hair. She seemed quite calm and uninterested in the people in the court. Her eyes were dark and unreadable.

"Your name, please?" the clerk asked.

"Raye Marnay," she answered. The voice was surprisingly light and thin in such a tall girl.

The clerk nodded to me and I walked forward slowly. I stopped in front of her and looked up. "How old are you, Miss Marnay?" I asked.

The answer came promptly. "Twenty-three."

"Where were you born?"

"Chillicothe, Ohio."

"When did you come to New York?" I asked.

"About two years ago."

I was beginning to get used to the strange, thin sound of her voice. "What did you do in Chillicothe?"

"I lived there," she said.

I could hear the faint sound of laughter in the courtroom. I waited for it to subside before I spoke again. "I meant, what did you work at for a living in Chillicothe, Miss Marnay?"

"Oh," she said. "I didn't know that was what you meant. I was a schoolteacher."

I looked at her. The hell of it was that she really had been a schoolteacher. "What grade did you teach?"

"Kindergarten," she answered promptly. "I love children."

I couldn't help smiling at the way she said it. "I don't doubt that, Miss Marnay," I said. I let the smile leave my face. "What made you decide to come to New York?"

"I wanted to be an actress," she said. "Professor Berg, he was the dramatic teacher at the senior school, wrote a play which we put on in the little theater. It was called *Lark in the Valley*, and I played the leading part in it. He said I had so much talent that it was a shame that I had to waste it in a small town like Chillicothe. He said I was another Mary Astor. So I decided to come to New York."

"And what happened after you arrived in New York?" I asked.

"Nothing," she said. "I walked around for weeks and nobody would even see me. Even with the letters that Professor Berg gave me."

"Then why didn't you go back to Chillicothe?"

"I couldn't," she answered in her small voice. There was a note of hurt in it. "Everybody would know then that I was a failure."

"I see," I said. "Then, what did you do for a living?"

"I got a job in a restaurant on Broadway as a waitress. It was a place where a lot of show people came in. I had heard that many girls who worked there found jobs on the stage."

"How long did you work there?" I asked.

"About three weeks," she said.

"What happened then?"

"I was fired," she answered in an even tinier voice, if that was possible. "The manager said he ran a restaurant, not a dramatic school."

Another ripple of laughter ran through the courtroom. I waited for it to pass. "Then what did you do?"

"I looked for another job, but I didn't find any. One day I was talking to another girl in the rooming-house where I lived. She said with my face and figure I ought to become a model. I thought that was a good idea. Many models become actresses, you know. I asked her how I could become a model. She sent me up to Park Avenue Models."

I nodded. "Was this the first time you had ever thought of modeling?"

"Yes," she answered.

"What did you do then?" I asked.

"I went up to Park Avenue Models and applied for work."

"Who did you speak to when you went up there?"

"Mrs. Morris."

"What did she tell you?"

"She said I would have to get some pictures taken and then she would put them in her file. She gave me a card with the names of about four photographers on it. Until I had them, she said, she couldn't do anything for me. I explained to her that I didn't have the money for it. She said she was sorry but she couldn't do anything for me until then. I was just about to leave when Miss Flood came out of her office and saw me."

"You mean the Miss Flood who is here in this courtroom?" I asked.

She nodded. "Yes."

"What happened then?"

"When Miss Flood saw me, she snapped her fingers and said I was the girl. She sent me to the 14th Street Fur Shop. That was the first time I ever modeled.

I wore one of their fur coats and walked up and down in their windows so people could see it." There was a note of pride in her voice. "I was their favorite model. You see, I'm very tall, and people can see me a long way off. I worked there at least three days a week ever since."

"What other modeling did you do?" I asked.

She hesitated a moment. "That was the only place I ever worked."

I nodded. "How much did they pay you?"

"Ten dollars a day," she answered.

"That came to about thirty dollars a week," I said. "Was that enough for you to live on?"

She shook her head. "No. My dramatic lessons cost more than that each week."

"How did you make extra money?"

"I used to date a lot," she said.

"Date?" I asked.

She nodded. "That's what we called it."

"Who do you mean by 'we'?" I asked.

"The girls I knew," she said.

"How did you go about this—er—dating, as you call it?"

"It began after I had been working a few weeks as a model. I asked Miss Flood for some extra work and she called me into her office. She said that a model's life was often very difficult and sometimes took a long time in paying off. She told me that sometimes clients called her up and asked her to recommend some girls to go out with them. She said these men were very generous and always tipped the girls well for just spending time with them. She asked if I was interested."

"What did you say?" I asked.

"I was interested," she replied.

Another ripple of laughter ran through the courtroom. I didn't blame them. "What did you do then?"

"Miss Flood arranged a date for me that night. He was a nice gentleman. He took me to dinner, then we went up to his apartment for a few drinks. He was very amusing. He gave me ten dollars when I left. He said that was for being so nice and for me to tell Miss Flood that he was very pleased."

"Is that all you did?" I asked. "Have a few drinks?"

Her face changed color slightly. She seemed to be blushing. "We had two parties," she almost whispered.

"Parties?" I questioned, looking at the jury. "What do you mean by parties?"

"Intercourse." She was still speaking in that low, hard-to-hear voice.

"You mean you had intercourse twice with this man?" I asked.

She nodded. "Yes. That's what I mean."

"Weren't you surprised that the man wanted that? That he took it for granted?"

She shook her head. "No. The men were no different back in Chillicothe. They all look for the same thing."

Laughter scaled the courtroom walls. The judge rapped his gavel. The noise subsided.

"What did you do next?" I asked.

"I went home to sleep. I was tired," she said.

The roar almost blew the courtroom apart. Even I had to work to keep a straight face. Finally I could speak. "I mean when you went back to Park Avenue Models the next time."

"That was the next day. I went back to thank Miss Flood for being so nice to me. She asked me if I had a good time and if I was willing to go on any more dates. I said I would if all the gentlemen were as nice as this one. She assured me that she knew nothing but nice gentlemen, then she asked me how many parties we had. I told her and she took some money out of her desk and gave it to me. I didn't want to take it, I told her that the gentleman had given me ten dollars. She laughed and said that was my tip, and made me take the money."

"How much was it?" I asked.

"Fifty dollars," she said.

"Did you realize what this meant?" I asked. "That you were committing an act of prostitution?"

"I didn't look at it like that," she protested. "If I didn't like the gentleman, I didn't have to do anything. I wouldn't."

"Did you ever meet any gentleman you didn't like?" I asked sarcastically.

She shook her head. "No. Miss Flood was right. She only knew the finest-type gentlemen."

Laughter again echoed through the court. I waited until it had subsided. "Before you knew Miss Flood, did you ever have intercourse for money?"

She shook her head. "No."

"Did you ever have intercourse for money after you met Miss Flood that she did not arrange?"

"No, sir," she said. "I'm not a whore."

"That's all, thank you," I said, walking away from her. I paused in front of Vito's table. Marja looked up at me. Her eyes, wide and dark and proud, stared right into me. I had the strangest feeling that the pride in them was for me. I kept my eyes carefully guarded and turned to Vito.

"Your witness," I said and continued on to my table. I sat down and watched Vito get slowly to his feet.

There was no doubt about it, he was a real pro. Even the way he walked toward the witness indicated his sureness and his ability. His voice was warm and rich.

"Miss Marnay," he called.

She looked up at him. "Yes, sir."

I nodded to myself in reluctant grudging admiration. In just the way he spoke her name he had asserted his dominance over her.

"You mentioned that you appeared in a play in Chillicothe. *Lark in the Valley*, I believe you called it."

She nodded. "Yes, sir."

"It was written by a Professor Berg, you stated, a professor of dramatics in the senior school?"

"Yes, sir."

"You said that you came to New York after that at the suggestion of the professor, who said you had too much talent to waste it in a small town like Chillicothe?"

"Yes, sir." "I assume he meant dramatic talent. That was what he meant, wasn't it?"

The girl hesitated.

Vito's voice was impatient. "Come, Miss Marnay. That was what he meant, wasn't it?"

Her voice was even smaller than before. "I think so."

"You can be more positive than that, Miss Marnay," he said sarcastically.

"That was what he meant," she said. "Yes, sir."

"What?" he asked.

"Dramatic talent," she said.

"You said that the play was presented at a little theater in Chillicothe. What theater was it?"

Her brows knotted together. She cast a worried glance at me. I tried to look confident, but I didn't know what the hell he was getting at. "It—it wasn't exactly a theater," she stammered.

"If it wasn't a theater, what was it?" Vito asked.

"It was at the Antelope Club," she said. "It was a special show the professor wrote for their annual affair."

"The Antelope Club," Vito said. He looked at the jury. "I see." He turned back to her. "That wouldn't be a stag affair, would it?"

She looked down at her feet. "I believe it was."

"Were you the only female in the cast?" he asked.

She nodded. "I was."

"What part did you play?"

Her voice hardly carried to my table. "I was the farm girl."

"What was theme of the play? Did you have many lines to speak?" His voice was harsh.

"It was about this girl and the three men that worked on the farm. The farmer, his son, and the hired hand, and what they did on that one particular night. I didn't have any lines to speak. It was all in pantomime. The professor was a great believer in the Stanislavsky method of drama."

"Stanislavsky, hmm . . ." Vito scratched his head. "Wasn't that the Russian who believed in action instead of speech?"

"That's right," she said.

"And the professor's play was all action?" he added.

She nodded. "Yes."

His voice turned very heavy and sarcastic. "So much so that the play was raided by the police and all of you were charged with giving an indecent performance. As a result of that, you and the professor were dismissed from your posts in school. Isn't that true?"

She didn't answer. She bit her lower lip to keep it from trembling.

Vito was shouting now. "Come now, Miss Marnay, answer my question."

Her face had lost all its color; the rouge stood out in dark blotches on her cheeks. She looked down at the floor. Her voice had vanished into a tiny whisper. "Yes."

"That's all, Miss Marnay." Vito looked at the jury as if to say: *How can you believe anything a girl like that might say?* He half shrugged, and turned back to his table.

Joel and Alec leaned toward me as I called the next witness. Their whispers were hoarse in my ear.

"He sure kicked hell out of her," Joel said.

"Yeah," Alec answered, his glance following the girl as she took her seat. "He really ripped her."

I drew in my breath. "One thing you guys are forgetting. He ripped her, not the story she told about Flood. Notice he stayed away from that?"

Joel nodded. "He's no dope. He's trying to destroy her credibility."

"It won't do him any good," I answered. "The payoff will still come on facts pertinent to the case. And he knows it."

"All the same, I'd be careful, Mike," Alec whispered. "He's got a bagful of tricks."

The clerk was administering the oath to another girl, the second witness for the State. I began to get to my feet. "He'll still have to find something better than the truth if he expects to get anywhere with this one," I said as the court clerk nodded to me. I moved around the table and walked toward the witness stand.

The hospital room was dark and quiet as I came in. I could hear the sounds of the Old Man's breathing. It was slow and easy.

A nurse held her finger to her lips. "He's sleeping."

I nodded and started to back out of the room.

"Who's sleeping?" The Old Man's voice was loud and strong in the quiet. "That you, Mike?"

I stepped forward again. "Yes, sir."

"Come over here and speak up," he said irascibly. "I can't hear you."

I walked over to the head of the bed. His bright, dark eyes looked up at me. A half-smile was on his lips. "How did it go today, Counselor?"

"All right," I said. "We got through the first four witnesses. Vito couldn't do very much with their stories. All he did was bang at the people themselves. I think we did pretty good, on the whole."

"I know," the Old Man said. "I heard."

I glanced at the telephone next to the hospital bed. He must have been burning up the wire all day.

"There's one thing that bothers me, though," he said. "I can't figure Vito's strategy at all. Right now it looks like he's feeding the girl to the wolves."

I didn't speak. There was a curious sinking feeling in my heart. I could have put up a much better argument than Vito had that day. "It's almost as if he didn't care what happens with our case," I said. "He's letting me get away with everything in the book."

"Did you see Flood?" the Old Man asked. "How'd she look?" His eyes were watching me very carefully.

"I saw her," I said. "She seems okay."

"Mike," he said, "it's me you're talkin' to."

"She looks fine," I said. "Real fine."

"Still got the same feeling toward her? Even now?"

"I—I don't know, John," I said "I only know that when I look at her I choke up inside."

He nodded slowly. "I know what you mean, Mike. I spoke to her a couple of times. She's got great strength and real courage, son. She might have been a great lady if she had gone in another direction."

"Maybe she never had a chance, sir," I said.

The shrewd look came back into his eyes. "She had her chance, Mike. No matter what you say or what anyone did, she had the final say. She herself threw it away."

I didn't answer. I was remembering a time long ago. That time she left me standing in the road when I went to pick her up. The day she got out of the Geyer Home.

Something had happened to her up there. I knew it the moment I saw her walking down the path. She was different. It wasn't until I could see her eyes that I knew what it was. She was older. Far older then than I would ever be. I could see her getting into the cab and leaving me standing there on the sidewalk.

I went back to my car, the one I had borrowed to bring her home in, and slowly drove downtown. I walked into the apartment.

Mom and Pop were sitting at the kitchen table. Pop was wearing his Sunday suit and a tie. My feet were like lead as I dragged them into the kitchen. I could see them looking at the doorway behind me.

"She didn't come, Ma," I said slowly.

My mother got to her feet, her eyes soft and calm. "Maybe it's for the best, son," she said gently.

I shook my head violently. So hard that I could feel the tears rolling inside my eyes. "No, Ma," I cried. "It's not for the best. She needs me. I know she needs me. But there's something that's holding her back and I don't know what it is."

My father got to his feet. "I'll put your things back in your room, Mike," he said. He walked slowly out of the kitchen.

I looked after him. Poor Pop. He just didn't understand at all. I turned back to my mother. "What should I do now, Ma?" I asked.

She stared at me for a moment, then spoke softly. "Forget her, son. She's not for you."

"That's easy to say, Mom," I said. "But I'm not a kid any more. I'm almost twenty-one. And I still love her."

"Love her?" My mother's voice was filled with scorn. "What do you know about love? You're still a baby yet. All you can do is hurt and cry." Suddenly her voice broke and she turned away from me.

I went to her quickly and caught at her arms. Her eyes were filled with unshed tears. "Stop it, Ma," I said. "Stop it. It's bad enough the way it is."

There was a look in my mother's eyes I had never seen before. "Stop it?" she cried. "I hate her! May the Good Lord forgive me, but I hate her soul to hell for what she's done to my baby."

"Maybe she can't help it, Ma," I said.

My mother looked up at me. "She can help it, son," she said slowly. "Never forget that. She can always decide what she wants to do."

That had been many years ago, and now it was strange to hear the Old Man say almost the same things. I wondered if I would ever understand their point of view. I had long since given up hoping they would understand mine.

"Who are you calling tomorrow?" the Chief asked.

I told him.

He calculated carefully. "At this rate you should be ready for summation in less than two weeks."

I nodded.

"I'll be out of here by then. Maybe I can give you a hand," he said.

"We made a bargain, John," I said. "It's my show. You promised."

"Oh," he said innocently, "I wouldn't tell you what to do. I would just make a little suggestion and try to be of help."

I grinned. I knew his way of helping—he took over. "No, thanks," I said dryly. "Okay, okay," he said testily.

I went right to bed when I got home. Somehow I was glad I was alone in the apartment. It was better that way. I had persuaded Ma to stay up in the country. I think the only reason she agreed was that she knew I didn't want her around while the trial was on.

I stretched out on the bed and closed my eyes. Marja's face jumped in front of me. The look on her face was the one I had seen in court that day. I still didn't get it.

Why should she be proud of me? I was trying to send her to jail. A guilt began to run through me. Could it be that she expected me to look out for her? Was it that she was counting on how I felt about her? But she didn't know how I felt now. For all she knew, I could have changed. There could be someone else.

But as soon as I thought it, I knew that she knew. We had that between us. A sense of recognition that no one ever shared.

I rolled over, trying to put her from my mind. But it didn't work. No matter what I did, she kept creeping back. I wondered about her. There were so many things I didn't know, so many things had happened to her that I hadn't shared.

I remembered thinking about her up at the hospital. Strange that it should have come to me there because of what the Old Man had said.

But there was one period that I knew nothing about—the four months between the time she left the Home and the time her name first appeared on the police blotter. She must have gone through hell then. I tried to remember what I was doing during that time. My own memories were too vague, my mind kept turning back to her. What did she do? Where did she go? I didn't know.

I could only sense that she had needed me then more than at any other time in her life.

And I could only feel that I had failed her.

Book Two
MARY

CHAPTER ONE

SHE WAS STANDING IN THE OPEN DOORWAY, THE SUNLIGHT SPARKLING iridescently in her white-gold hair. She hesitated a moment; then, transferring her small valise from her right hand to her left, she held out her hand to the woman who stood slightly behind her. "Good-by, Mrs. Foster," she said huskily.

The woman took her hand with an almost masculine grip. "Good-by, Mary," she answered. "Take care of yourself."

A half-smile crossed Mary's lips. "I will, Mrs. Foster," she promised. "I learned a lot in the year an' a half I been here."

There was no humor in the woman's voice. "I hope so, Mary. I wouldn't want to see you in trouble again."

The faint smile disappeared from Mary's mouth. "You won't," she said quietly. She dropped the woman's hand and quickly went out the door. The bright sunlight hit her eyes, and she paused at the head of the steps and blinked.

She heard the door swing shut behind her with the heavy clinking sound of metal. A sudden sense of freedom ran through her, as exhilarating as old wine. She turned and looked back at the closed door.

"Yuh won't see me again," she half-whispered to it. "I learned too much. Yuh taught me too good."

The door stared at her, its two small windows like empty eyes of a stranger. She shivered suddenly as a chill chased the sense of freedom from her. She began to walk toward the street.

She was tall and slim in the thin dark coat authorities had given her. The late

November wind pressed it close to her body, outlining her deep breasts, narrow waist, and gently flaring hips. She walked easily on strong, straight legs.

The old man who sat in the little house near the gate came out as he saw her approaching. He smiled at her through rheumy eyes. "Goin' home, Marja?"

She smiled at him. "Got no home, Pop," she said. "Changed everything. My name, too. It's Mary now, remember?"

The old man smiled at her with sudden wisdom. "I remember. But it won't do yuh no good. Yuh still look like Marja to me. The hot Polack blood is still runnin' around inside yuh, and yuh can't change that."

She looked at him, the smile still on her lips. "I'll change lots o' things before I'm through."

"But not yourself," he said quickly. He began to turn the crank that opened the gate. "Where yuh goin'?" he asked.

"I don't know," she said. "But first I'm gonna check into a hotel and sit in a bathtub for two hours without anybody draggin' me out. Then I'm goin' to buy me some clothes I feel good in, not these rags. Then I'm gonna treat myself to a big dinner an' go to the movies, maybe Radio City. Then I'm gonna have me two ice-cream sodas an' go to the hotel an' sleep till two tomorrow afternoon."

"After that, what're you goin' to do?" he asked.

"I'm goin' to find me a job an' go to work," she answered.

"Do that first," he said wisely. "You may need your money." The iron gate was open. He gestured toward it. "Your world waits, Marja. I hope it's kind to you."

She took a half-step toward it, then turned back to the old man. Quickly she kissed him on the cheek. "Good-by, Pop."

"Good-by, Marja," he said, an unexpected sadness in his voice.

Caught by the sound, she looked into the old man's eyes. "You're the only thing about this place I'll miss, Pop."

"Yeah," he said, gruffly embarrassed. "I bet you tell that to all the boys."

A mischievous smile came to her lips. "No, Pop. Only to you. Want a quick feel for old times' sake?"

A curious dignity came into the old man. "No, Marja."

"No?" she echoed, a note of surprise in her voice. "Why?"

"It's only for my girls," he said quietly. "Not for me. It makes 'em feel good to know that someone's botherin' 'em. Even an old man like me. It's bad enough in there. All women, an' not feelin' wanted by nobody. Their families. Nobody. So I bother them an' they laugh an' feel good."

Impulsively she kissed his cheek again. "Thank you, Pop." She turned and started through the gate.

"Be good, Marja," he called after her.

She looked back at him. "I'll try, Pop," she laughed. The gate clanged shut behind her and she walked out into the street. She stepped off the sidewalk into the gutter. Looking down at her feet, she kicked her heel into the pavement.

It made no sound beneath her, and there was a curious softness to its feel. Asphalt, not cement. Cement gave off a funny sound beneath your feet and had no give to it. Cement was beneath your feet everywhere back there. In the halls and on the walks outside. You could hear yourself everywhere you went. But this was quiet. Happily she walked along in the gutter. Free. Really free.

A strong hand closed over hers, the one that gripped the valise. A familiar voice spoke in her ear. "Yuh can get killed walkin' in the street like that. Forget about automobiles?"

She knew who it was without looking up. She had been expecting him from the moment she stepped through the gate. She looked up slowly, still holding onto her valise. Her voice was as expressionless as her eyes. "Yuh forget about a lot of things in a year an' a half, Mike."

There was a nervous smile on Mike's face. "I came to take yuh home, Marja."

She didn't speak.

"I been waiting here all morning," he said.

She drew a deep breath and shook her head. "No," she said. "No."

She could see the hurt creep into his eyes. "But, Marja, I—"

She pulled the valise from his grip. "Yuh got the wrong girl, Mike. Everything's changed. Even the name."

"I don't care what's changed, Marja. I don't care what's happened. I know yuh never answered my letters, but I came to take yuh home."

She stepped up onto the sidewalk and looked into his eyes. "Who sent for you?" she asked coldly.

His eyes stared back into hers. "I love you, Marja. You said you loved me."

"We were kids then," she said quickly. "We didn't know any better."

"Kids!" he said angrily. "How much older are you now? Two years make that much difference?"

"Yes, Mike," she said slowly. "Two years can make a thousand years' difference. I grew up in a hurry."

"I grew up, too," he said almost boyishly, "but I still feel the same about you. I'll always feel the same."

"I don't," she said.

"What have they done to you, Marja?" There was anguish deep in his voice.

She shook her head wearily. "Nothing," she answered. "I did it all myself. It's over, Mike. We can't go back. We'll never be kids again."

She began to turn away from him, but his strong hands on her shoulders spun her back. "Why, Marja? What happened?"

She didn't answer.

His eyes burned into her face. "Yuh owe me that much for what we were. Tell me!"

He would never forget the mask that dropped over her eyes at that moment. It was as if they were suddenly so deep that nothing was reflected in them, not even the sunlight of the morning. "Tell me, Marja!"

"I had a baby, Mike. While I was in there I had a baby, and I don't even know whether it was a boy or a girl. I signed it away before it was born." Her voice was flat and expressionless. "Yuh still want to know what happened, Mike?"

There was a look of disbelief on his face. His grip on her shoulders had slackened. "Whose was it? Ross's?" he asked hoarsely.

She shook her head. "It couldn't be. He was away. Remember?"

His hands slipped from her shoulders. Lines of pain had formed around his mouth. "You mean there were others?"

She didn't answer.

His eyes were a deep, hurt blue, and there were tears in them. "How could you, Marja? You loved me."

Her voice was still cold, still calm. "There were other things too, Mike. There was a girl back in there. She liked me. She taught me games to help pass the time. Yuh want to hear about them, Mike? It was fun."

"I don't want to hear," he said in a shaking voice. "You're telling me that Ross was right all the time. He said you were a cheap—" He couldn't bring himself to say the word.

She said it for him. "Whore."

His hands gripped her shoulders tightly. He stared down into her face. "Were you, Marja? Were you what he said?"

She didn't answer.

"Why did you lie to me, Marja? Why?" he asked fiercely. "I would have done anything for you. Why did you lie to me?"

Her eyes met his gaze without flinching. "Nothing matters now, Mike," she said slowly. "The truth is something you believe, not what someone tells you."

A taxi came down the block. She signaled, and it pulled in to the curb. "Let me go, Mike. The cab's waiting."

His hands dropped from her shoulders. She entered the cab swiftly and shut the door. As it pulled away from the curb, she looked out the window. Mike was standing there, looking after her. She felt a sudden rush of tears to her eyes. Desperately she fought them back until her eyes were burning. Freedom was so many things she had almost forgotten. It was people you loved and people you hurt. "I love you, Mike," she whispered to herself.

"Where to, lady?"

The cab-driver's voice turned her from the window.

"Hotel Astor on Broadway," she said in a shaking voice.

When she turned back to the window, Mike was gone. Suddenly she could hold the tears back no longer. She could never be right for him. Too many things had happened to her. She was tainted with an ugly scar, and she would have it in her all her life.

He deserved something better. Someone clean and new and fresh. Someone who shone like he did. Not someone like her, who would cheat him of what he deserved.

CHAPTER TWO

S HE LOOKED DOWN AT THE REGISTRATION PAD THE DESK CLERK PUSHED toward her. She hesitated a moment. Three and a half dollars a day was a lot of money. Even for a de-luxe room with private bath and shower. Her money wouldn't go too far at this rate. She had only a little more than a hundred dollars.

But she had waited too long for that fact to stop her. She had promised herself this treat ever since she had gone up there. Quickly she began to scrawl:

Mary Flood . . . Yorkville, N. Y. . . . Nov. 20, 1937

She pushed the pad back to the clerk. He looked at it, then punched a bell on the desk. He smiled at her. "Just down from school, Miss Flood?"

She nodded. He didn't know how right he was.

A bellboy came up and picked up her valise. The desk clerk pushed the key to him. "Show Miss Flood to room twelve-oh-four."

She waited until the door closed behind the bellboy and then threw herself on the bed. She felt herself sinking deliciously into it. It was like resting on a cloud. This was a bed, a real bed. Not one of those imitations they had up there. She rolled completely over and off the other side, and opened the door to the bathroom.

Its shining white porcelain and tiles gleamed at her. She gazed admiringly at the tub. It was the new kind, sunk into the floor. Tentatively she touched its sides. Smooth, not scratchy like the old iron tubs. She let her hand rest on it lightly while she looked around the room.

Turkish towels were on the rack. She moved quickly and picked one up. It was light and soft and fluffy. She buried her face in it. It wasn't coarse like the cotton towels. She took a deep breath. This was living.

She looked at her watch. It was almost noon. She had some shopping to do before she would take that lazy bath she had promised herself. Almost reluctantly she put the towel back on the rack and left the bathroom.

She picked up her handbag and opened it. Once again she counted her money. One hundred and eighteen dollars. That was what she had left of the pay they had given her for working in the laundry. She shook her head for a moment as if to clear it of the steam and the acrid smell of harsh soap and sodium-hypochlorite solution that had hung around her for so long. Resolutely she snapped the bag shut and went to the door.

She stood on the steps of the hotel and looked down at Broadway. It was lunch hour and the streets were even more crowded than usual. Everybody was going somewhere. People had intent, serious faces and never once stopped to look around. She marveled at them. They took so much for granted, so much that she would never take for granted again.

She looked down the street. The Paramount was playing the new Bing Crosby picture, the one with Kitty Carlisle. The Rialto had two horror pictures, and the New Yorker was showing two westerns. The Nedick's on the corner across the street was busy, the customers standing there deep around the counter. The Chinese restaurant between 42nd and 43rd still advertised a thirty-five-cent lunch. Hector's cafeteria opposite the hotel still boasted the biggest selection of pastry in town, and the faint sound of music from the dance hall on 45th mingled with the discordant blare of traffic.

With a feeling of contentment she started down the steps to begin her shopping. There were some stores here where she knew she could buy clothes fairly cheap. Plymouth for underwear and blouses, Marker's for skirts and dresses, Kitty Kelly's for shoes. She found herself humming as she crossed the street. She had been wrong in what she had told Pop that morning.

She was home.

* * *

She leaned back in the tub lazily, a delicious languor seeping through her. The water was covered with sparkling, exploding bubbles, and their perfume hung heavily in the air. Slowly she stirred, running her hands down over her body. She could feel the sting of the cheap soap they had used in the Home. Somehow she had never felt clean after using it. It seemed to leave a coarse layer over her skin. But this was different. She could feel her flesh soften in the water.

She pulled a towel from the rack beside the tub and wadded it into a small pillow. Carefully she placed it on the edge of the tub and leaned back on it. It would keep her hair from getting wet, and it made it easier for her to rest. She closed her eyes. It was so good. So good. She was warm and comfortable and safe. No one could bother her now. No one could call her. No one could tell her what to do. She began to doze lightly. It wasn't like the time in the Home.

Not at all like the time when the baby was born.

The pains had been intense through most of the morning. At last the nurse had taken her down to the infirmary. The doctor examined her quickly. He nodded to the nurse. "Get her ready. It won't be long now."

She stretched out, gasping, on a hard white bed. The nurse began to prepare for delivery. Between the waves of pain she was conscious of a sense of shock when the nurse shaved her pubis. Finished at last, the nurse covered her with a white sheet and left the room.

She closed her eyes, breathing heavily. She was glad it was almost over. It had seemed so long to carry a sense of shame and violation inside her. There was a rustling sound at the side of the bed and she turned toward it.

The superintendent was standing there, her gray-black hair frosty over her glasses. She held a sheet of paper in her hand. "How are you, Mary?"

She nodded. "Okay, Mrs. Foster."

"You haven't told me yet about the baby, Mary."

She managed a wan smile. There was nothing to tell. In a little while it would be here. She didn't answer.

"The father, Mary," Mrs. Foster insisted. "He should be made to pay for the child's care."

A pain wrenched through her and she closed her eyes against it. A moment later she turned to the woman. "It doesn't matter," she said in a shaking voice. "It never mattered."

Mrs. Foster shrugged her shoulders and looked down at the sheet of paper. "Okay, Mary. According to this, you want the child placed for adoption."

Mary nodded.

"You know what it means," Mrs. Foster said in a cold voice. "You give up all rights to the child. You may never see it or even know who has it. It will be as if it had never been born, as far as you are concerned."

The girl was silent.

"Did you hear me, Mary?" Mrs. Foster asked.

She nodded.

"You won't know anything about the child," the woman said implacably.

Pain turned into anger in Mary's voice. "I heard you!" she screamed. "I heard you the first time! What do you think I could do about it? Could I take care of it here? Would you let me keep it here?"

"If we knew the father," Mrs. Foster said stolidly, "we could make him contribute to its care. Then we could keep it in a home for you until you are in a position to claim it."

"And when will that be?" Mary's voice was trembling.

"When you have proved that you can support it morally and financially," the woman answered.

"Who decides that?"

"The courts," Mrs. Foster replied.

"Then I can't have it until they say okay. It stays in an orphanage. Right?" Mary asked quietly.

Mrs. Foster nodded.

"But this way it gets adopted? It gets a home right away?"

Mrs. Foster's voice was low. "Yes."

Mary took a deep breath. "That's the way I want it." There was a tone of finality in her voice.

"But—" Mrs. Foster's voice was shaking now.

Pain tore through the girl. It forced her into a half-sitting position on the bed. "That's the way I want it!" she screamed. "Don't you see that's the only chance I can give it?"

The woman turned and left the room and Mary didn't see her again until three hours later. It was all over then. Mrs. Foster stood near the bed again and looked down at her.

Mary's face was white and drawn and there were faint beads of perspiration on her upper lip. Her eyes were shut tight.

"Mary," Mrs. Foster whispered.

She didn't move.

"Mary," the woman said again. "Marja."

Mary's eyes opened slowly and the woman could see she hadn't been asleep.

"You're all right, Marja," Mrs. Foster whispered. "And the baby is fine—"

"Don't tell me!" The girl's voice was a fierce, harsh sound. "I don't want to know!"

"But—" The woman hesitated.

Mary's voice was suddenly weary. She turned her face into the pillow. "Let it go," she whispered. "It's bad enough the way it is."

Mrs. Foster didn't speak. The common bondage of their sex brought them together. Her hand sought the girl's hand beneath the thin cover.

Mary turned her face to the woman, her eyes all pupil, deep and black. A faint sense of shock came to the woman. It was as if she were gazing into the bottomless wells of time. She felt the slight pressure of the girls fingers as she began to speak.

"It hurt me," Mary whispered, an echo of pain in her voice. "It hurt me coming out."

"I know, child," the woman said gently. "It always hurts."

"Do yuh, Mrs. Foster?" Mary asked in a wondering voice. And with her next words the woman realized that she didn't know at all. "It didn't hurt the way its father hurt me when he tore me apart to put it there, but the way it hurts you to gain something you know you can't keep."

Suddenly the woman understood. The memory of why the girl had come here came into her mind. Her eyes deepened with sympathy behind her glasses. Now she could see all the pain behind the shadows in the girl's eyes.

They looked deep into each other for a moment, then Mary spoke again. Her voice was very gentle. "Let it go."

Almost without realization the woman nodded her acceptance. "Yes, Mary."

Silently the tears sprang full born to the girls eyes and began to roll down her cheeks. She made no sound of crying. There were only the tears chasing each other inexorably to the pillow beneath.

CHAPTER THREE

THE DETECTIVE WAS A SLIM, POLITE MAN. HE HELD THE CHAIR FOR HER as she sat down opposite his desk. He studied her for a moment before he walked around the desk to his own seat. This one was born for trouble. There was something about her.

It wasn't the way she looked. There was no coarseness in her. Even the white-blond hair, which cheapened so many of them because of its artificiality, became her. Probably because it was her own. But her face, her body, the way she walked—everything told you this was a woman. The kind that was made for man.

He glanced at the card before him. *Mary Flood*. His eyes widened. Now he understood. He looked up at her. "Where are you staying, Miss Flood?"

"Hotel Astor." Her voice was husky. She took out a cigarette.

Quickly he struck a match and held it for her. He thought he saw a glint of a smile in her dark-brown eyes as she looked over the flame at him. But he could have been wrong. No kid could be that sure of herself on the first visit to the police. It was probably the reflection of the light. "Pretty expensive," he said.

She drew deeply on the cigarette. "It's a treat I promised myself," she answered, as if that explained everything.

He looked down at the card. "Got a job?" he asked.

She shook her head. "I've only been out two days. I haven't even looked yet."

"Don't you think you should?" he asked gently. "They're pretty hard to find."

"I will," she said.

"You can't have much money left," he continued. "I see you bought yourself some new clothes."

For the first time a note of challenge crept into her voice. "It's my dough. There's no law against my doin' what I want with it, is there?"

He shook his head. "No, Miss Flood. We just want to be sure you don't get into trouble, that's all. People get into trouble quicker when they're broke."

"I'm not broke yet," she said quickly.

He didn't answer. He sat there quietly studying her while he lit a cigarette. This girl would have no trouble getting money; her trouble would come from finding too many men willing to give it to her. He waited for her to speak. The one thing they couldn't stand was the silent treatment.

This one was different. She just sat there watching him, her eyes fixed on his face. After a while he began to feel uncomfortable. It was as if he were the probationer and she the reporting officer. He cleared his throat.

"You know the regulations, Miss Flood," he said. "They were explained to you up there."

She nodded.

He repeated them anyway. "You're to report here once each month. You're not to consort or associate with anyone with a criminal record. You're to inform me of any change in your address. You're to let me know where you're working when you get a job. You're not to leave the state unless we give you permission. You're not allowed to possess firearms or other dangerous weapons—" He stopped in surprise. She was smiling. "Why the amusement, Miss Flood?" he asked.

She got to her feet, a half-smile on her lips, and let the coat fall from her shoulders back onto the chair. It seemed to him as if she had disrobed. "Do you think I need any?" she asked.

He felt his face flush. The laws were damned foolish sometimes. But there was nothing you could do about the weapons you were born with. "I'm just reiterating them for your benefit, Miss Flood," he said testily.

"Thank you, lieutenant," she said, sitting down again.

"What kind of a job are you looking for, Miss Flood?" he asked. "Maybe we can help you find one."

She stared at him quizzically. "Do you know of any?"

He nodded. "Waitress or clerk in some of the larger chain stores."

"What do they pay?"

"Twelve to fifteen a week."

"No, thanks," she said dryly.

"What's the matter with them?" he asked, his annoyance showing plainly in his voice.

She smiled suddenly. "It won't even pay my rent. I need a job that pays me a lot of money."

"Not everybody has to live at the Astor," he said sarcastically.

"I like it," she said, still smiling. "I spent enough of my life livin' in dumps. No more."

"Where you going to get that kind of money?" he asked.

She didn't answer.

"Whoring?" His voice was flat and cold.

Her eyes were wide on his. The smile disappeared from her lips. "Does it pay that well, lieutenant?"

His voice became threatening again. "You'll get into trouble. Real trouble, not kid stuff. Woman's prison is a lot different than the Home. You'll find out."

"Don't be too sure, lieutenant," she said quietly. "I haven't done anything—yet."

He got to his feet. "Just make sure you don't do anything you'll be sorry for." He pushed the card across the desk toward her and handed her his fountain pen. "Sign the card."

She signed it and he picked it up and looked at her signature. "Okay," he said. "You can go now. But remember what I told you."

She got to her feet, slipped into her coat, and went to the door. When she had opened it, she looked back at him. There was a teasing smile on her lips. "Thanks for the encouragement, lieutenant."

He looked at her coldly. "For your information, I'm not a lieutenant. Just keep in touch with us, that's all."

"I will," she said, still smiling. She looked around the small room slowly, then at him. "Maybe some afternoon when things are dull around here, lieutenant, you'll feel like killing a little time. Drop in on me. We can talk it up awhile."

His mouth dropped open, but he couldn't find any words. His face began to flush.

Her smile grew broader. "You know where I live, lieutenant. Room twelve-oh-four. Just ask the desk clerk to send you on up."

The door closed behind her before he could find an answer. He stared at the closed door thoughtfully. After a minute he picked up his pencil and made a few notes on her card, then reached for the telephone.

"Get Joker Martin for me," he said to the answering voice.

A few seconds later the receiver crackled. "Joker?"

The earphone buzzed.

"This is Egan at the 54th Street station. That girl you were lookin' for just checked in. . . . Yeh. . . . She calls herself Mary now, not Marja. . . . Yeah, same girl. . . . Blonde and built. . . . But real poison, she's not afraid of anything on God's earth. . . . Thanks, Joker. . . . Glad to do you the favor."

CHAPTER FOUR

JOKER MARTIN LEANED BACK IN HIS CHAIR AND HELD A MATCH TO HIS CI-gar. There was a quiet satisfaction in him. The breaks had been right. He had been smart. He had known a year and a half ago that syndication had to come someday. There had been too many killings.

He remembered the time Mike Rafferty had come back to the clubhouse fuming. "Who does that punk think he is?" Iron Mike had growled.

"What punk?" Joker asked.

"Kane. Frank Kane. He calls a meeting up in the hotel. We're all there. He says from now on we all got territories and nobody jumps the line."

Martin turned the name over in his mind. He looked up at Mike. "You mean Fenelli's boy? Where does Silk fit in? Top dog?"

Rafferty shook his head. "No. Kane took over. That's when I walked out. No punk is goin' to tell me what to do."

"How about the others?" Joker asked. "They stay?"

"The chicken-livered bastards!" Iron Mike swore. "They stayed."

Joker hesitated. "Maybe you should've stayed too, Mike."

"I'll burn in hell first!" Rafferty swore. "I always run me own business. Nobody's movin' in on me."

"Okay, Mike," Joker answered.

"I'm goin' home fer dinner," Mike said. "I'll see yuh afterwards. We'll figger out what to do next." He turned and stamped out of the room.

Joker waited until the door had closed behind him, then reached for the phone. Just as the operator spoke, he heard what sounded like the muffled explosion of a backfiring automobile. He put the telephone down quickly and ran to the window.

A crowd was gathering in the street in front of the clubhouse. He couldn't see who was lying on the sidewalk because of the people, but he could see the trail of blood running toward the gutter.

Slowly he walked back to the telephone and picked it up. Iron Mike had been right. He would burn in hell first. Joker wondered whether he liked it. He whispered a number to the operator. A voice answered.

"Mr. Kane," he said in a low, unhurried voice, "this is Joker Martin. No, Iron Mike hasn't changed his mind. It's too late. But I just want yuh to know I'm with yuh. A thousand per cent. . . ."

The breaks had been right and he had prospered. It was a long haul from the dance hall and backroom gambling that Iron Mike had first allotted him. And now Kane had given him this territory and no one could move in on him. He was home now, for Kane kept the peace.

But things were going big and he needed help. Not hood help, but brains help, class help. Along with the new division of territory he had picked up Park Avenue all the way up to 81st Street. That was when he had first thought of Ross Drego.

The kid was young and wild, but he was bright. He had gambling sense. Good thing his father had cut him off after the last piece of trouble he had been in. It was six months now since Ross had come to Joker, but the kid was worth all the dough he got. He knew all the Park Avenue and big business trade by their first names. He had grown up with them.

The one thing Joker had to watch was the kid's ambition. There were times when it ran away with him. He was in too much of a hurry, he wanted a piece of everything. Joker smiled thoughtfully as he drew on his cigar. He could control Ross, especially now with that new deal that Kane had brought up to the syndicate. It would give Ross something to shoot at and would keep him content until it happened.

He picked up the telephone. His secretary answered. "Is Ross here yet?" he asked.

"He's on his way in now, Mr. Martin," she answered.

He put down the phone as the door opened and Ross came in. He looked down for a moment at the sheet of paper on the desk, then back at Ross. "Got the dough?" he asked.

Ross nodded. He threw a package on the desk. "Ten grand, Joker. Everything I got."

Joker opened a desk drawer and dropped the package into it. He took out a stock certificate from the drawer and pushed it back to Ross.

Ross picked it up and looked at it. Angrily he threw it back on the desk. "What the hell are you pulling, Joker? This is only one share. I thought it was a big deal."

Joker smiled. "It is."

"Crap!" Ross exploded. "What the hell is this Blue Sky Development Corporation? I never heard of it!"

"That's Las Vegas," Joker answered.

"Las Vegas? Where the hell is that?"

"Nevada," Joker answered. "It's goin' to be the biggest money town in the country. Hotels, gambling, night clubs. And everything legit."

"Give me back my dough," Ross snapped. "If you want me to buy somethin', sell me a piece of Miami or Reno or—"

"Don't be a shmuck," Joker said. "Miami's wrapped up by the Chicago mobs and the stink is climbing up to the heavens. How long do you think that'll last? They gotta wrap up. Reno's a heartbreak city. People won't go there for a ball. Dandy Phil and Big Frank have locked up New Orleans and that'll have to close in time. Sun Valley, Palm Springs, n.g. for gambling."

"So what?" Ross asked. "I know what I'm gettin' there. Real dough."

"Yuh're doin' better here," Joker said. "Yuh're in on the ground floor. We're buyin' the town. Real estate an' all. We'll make the laws. There'll be no stink. Everything'll be legal."

Ross's voice was calmer now. "When is all this goin' to happen?"

"It takes time for a deal like this," Joker answered thoughtfully. "Kane says between five and ten years. Depends on the breaks."

"I'll be an old man by then," Ross snapped.

Joker smiled broadly. "You'll be the richest old man of thirty in the country."

"I don't know." Ross hesitated. "I could use the dough now."

Joker leaned across the desk, his voice lowered to a confidential tone. "Who can't? I got ten shares like yours. Think I wouldn't rather keep a hundred G's kickin' aroun' in my pocket any day? Sure, but not when it'll bring back a million. All legal that nobody can rap you for."

"You got a hundred grand in this?" Ross asked incredulously.

Joker nodded.

"How many shares are there out?" Ross continued.

"One thousand shares." Joker's voice was flat.

"Ten million bucks!" There was a note of awe in the boy's voice.

"An' the only reason I'm lettin' you in on it," Joker said quickly, "is because I got big plans for you."

Ross looked at him through suddenly narrowed eyes. "What plans?"

Joker leaned back in his chair. He took another cigar from his pocket and lit it. "This is a legit operation, see? No hood is goin' to be able to go out there. It has to be real clean. I'm buildin' you up to Kane to be the guy to handle the whole operation for us."

"Do you think it will work?" Ross asked.

"It'll work," Joker said confidently.

Ross picked up the stock certificate and looked at it. "You know, it's beginning to look better to me already."

Joker smiled. "It smells like money, you mean."

Ross laughed as he put the certificate in his pocket. "One of the three smells I can't resist. New money, new cars, and new dames."

Joker grinned. "That reminds me. I just got a line on an old girl of yours, if you're interested."

"Old girls don't interest me," Ross said quickly. "I told you, new dames."

"This one might," Joker said smiling. "That blonde Polack kid—"

"Marja?" Ross's voice had a strange tone. It sounded as if it was almost painful to him to speak the name.

"Yeah." Joker spoke carefully. "I was thinkin' of linin' it up for myself, but first I wanted to check if you still had any ideas"

Ross looked down at his fingers. He had stepped into Joker's trap neatly. There was nothing he could do or say now. He looked up at Joker. The older man was looking at him as an indulgent father would at a child. He kept his voice low. "I got no ideas, Joker. She's all yours."

CHAPTER FIVE

SHE SAT IN THE ROOM AND WAITED FOR THE TELEPHONE TO RING. A PILE of cigarettes mounted in the tray. It was Friday morning. She had been here four days, and there was just enough money in her pocketbook for the rent. But Evelyn had said that she would call Friday morning. They had worked out everything between them.

It had started in the laundry about six months before she came out. The slim, dark-haired girl who stood at the ironing board opposite hers looked up suddenly.

"What're you gonna do when you get out, Mary?"

Mary finished a pillowcase and began to fold it neatly. She thought for a moment. "I don't know. Get a job, I guess. I never thought about it."

"What kind of job?"

She began to press a sheet. "I don't know. Any kind I can."

Evelyn laughed. "You'll starve. Your ass'll be out before you know it."

Mary looked at her curiously. "What're you doing?"

"I got plans," Evelyn said mysteriously. "Big plans."

"Like what?"

Evelyn started to answer, but saw a matron coming down the aisle toward them. She spoke quickly out of the corner of her mouth. "See me when the lights are out tonight an' I'll tell yuh. I think we can do somethin' together."

It was almost ten o'clock when Mary stood at the side of Evelyn's bed and looked down at her. "Are yuh up?" she whispered.

The dark-haired girl sat upright. "Yeah."

Mary sat down on the edge of the bed. "What're you goin' to do?"

"I'm gonna make me some real money. I'm goin' into show business. My boy friend is fixin' up a place for me when I get out."

"When is that?" Mary asked.

"Three days after you," Evelyn said. "He tol' me to find a partner and start workin' up an act. That's why I spoke to you. I think we'd make a good team, with you blonde and me dark. That's what they like. Contrast."

Mary hesitated, a growing suspicion in her mind. "What kind of act?" she whispered. "I don't know any routines."

Evelyn laughed silently. "I can show you all the routines in one night."

"Oh," Mary said. "That?"

Evelyn shook her head. "It's better'n beatin' your head in for ten bucks a week."

"I don't know," Mary said. "I never thought about it."

"Pipe down!" a voice called from one of the beds. "We're tryin' to get some sleep."

Evelyn threw back the cover. "Get in here with me," she said quickly. "We can talk without them longears hearin' us."

"I think I better go back to bed," Mary said.

Evelyn's white teeth gleamed. "Chicken?"

Mary didn't answer. She moved over on the bed and Evelyn pulled the cover over them. They lay there quietly for a moment. Mary could feel the warmth coming from the girl's body. "What's real money?" she asked.

"Twenty to thirty bucks a day, each," Evelyn whispered. "And it's easy."

Mary was still. Money was the only important thing. Without it you were a bum. Besides, there was nothing more for her. No decent guy would have her if he found out what had happened. "What's the routine?" she asked.

The girl didn't answer. Her hands moved swiftly, and Mary caught her breath. She twisted away. "Cut it!" she snapped.

"You asked me what the routine was," the girl said.

"Yeah," Mary whispered fiercely, "but I didn't think you were a dike."

"I'm not," Evelyn whispered. "That's the routine."

Mary didn't answer. The girls hands were on her again. She stiffened involuntarily.

"Relax, relax," her friend whispered. "I won't hurt yuh. A little sport will do yuh some good. It makes the time pass easier."

The day before Mary left, Evelyn helped her pack her valise. "Remember what I told you," she said. "Wait in your room Friday morning until I call."

"I'll remember," Mary answered. . . .

She looked at her watch again. It was almost noon. She put out her cigarette and placed her valise on the bed. Slowly she began to pack. There would be no call, and she had to get out anyway while she still had enough money to pay the bill.

The phone rang. She picked it up quickly. "Evelyn?"

A man's voice answered. "This is Joe. Evelyn's boy friend. She's outside in the car. You ready?"

"I'm almost packed." she said.

"Good," he said. "I'll come up and get you."

She had finished packing by the time he knocked at the door. She opened it. A big florid man stood there. She smiled at him. "Joe?"

He nodded and came into the room, holding out his hand. She took it. "You're as pretty as Evelyn said you would be," he said in a false hearty voice.

She dropped his hand quickly. "Thank you." She said. "I'm ready to go now." She moved toward the phone. "I'll call a boy."

He shook his head. "Don't." He said. "I'll take the bag out the side door for you. You go out the front door as if you're stepping out. No bill that way."

She looked at him steadily. "I pay my bills, thanks."

He shrugged his shoulders. "It's your money."

She picked up the phone and called the desk.

Evelyn was sitting in the car. She smiled as they approached it. "I was wondering if you'd still be there, honey."

"I'd about given you up," Mary confessed as she climbed up beside her.

Evelyn grinned. "Joe was anxious, so we stopped off for a minute while he picked up his bags."

Mary looked quickly at her friend. Evelyn's face was faintly flushed. "He picked up his bags?" she questioned.

"Yeah," Joe grunted as he put the car into gear and they moved out into traffic. "Yuh don't expect a guy to go away without his clothes."

"Go away?" Mary echoed. "Where are we goin'?"

"Florida," Joe said. "Miami. I got a great little apartment out in North Beach. The pickin's will be great there this season."

The tall gray-haired man stepped up to the desk. "Mary Flood, please. Room twelve-oh-four."

The desk clerk looked up at him. "You just missed her, sir. She checked out five minutes ago."

Joker Martin stared at him. "Checked out?" A suspicion leaped into his mind. "Was there anyone with her?"

The desk clerk nodded. "There was a gentleman, sir."

"What did he look like?" Joker demanded.

"He was a big man, sir. About your height. Red face."

"Oh." Joker turned away from the desk.

"Is there anything wrong, sir?" the desk clerk asked.

Joker looked back at him. "No, nothing wrong." He walked through the lobby to the street. At least it wasn't Ross. At first he had thought it might have been, but Ross was dark and not as tall as he.

He pushed through the revolving door into the street. It served him right for waiting. He should have come right over when he heard about her. He might have known that a girl like her wouldn't take long in making a connection. He pushed a cigar into his mouth and chewed on it without lighting it. Maybe it was just as well for the while. He had too many things on his mind. He could wait.

She would turn up again. Sooner or later they all turned up again.

CHAPTER SIX

FOR THE THIRD CONSECUTIVE MORNING HE WATCHED HER COMING OUT of the water. She came from the sea like a goddess. She was wearing a white bathing-suit that hung on her figure as if it were her skin. Her high, full breasts, tiny waist, slim yet generous hips seemed carved out of white marble. Slowly she pulled off the white bathing-cap. A mass of sparkling white-gold hair tumbled down around her sun-darkened face.

Slowly she walked up the beach to her blanket. She bent and picked up a towel and rubbed herself vigorously. He could almost feel the animal tingling of the towel against his skin. He had never seen anyone enjoy herself as much as this girl coming out of the water.

He knew what she would do next. She would stretch out on the blanket, loosen the shoulder straps of her suit, and lie in the sun. Not once would she glance up at the crest of the small hill where his house looked over the ocean. After she had been in the sun for an hour she would get up and neatly pack all her things in a small beach bag. Then she would slip a robe over her shoulders, walk down to the edge of the beach, climb into a small convertible, and drive off.

That was the routine she followed every morning. He could almost set his clock by her. He would see her from his bedroom window every morning walking up the beach at eleven o'clock. This had happened regularly since he had come down to Florida toward the end of January, almost three weeks ago. He had first seen her the night after the Senator's party.

He had awakened with a terrible hangover and had yelled for his man to bring him some tomato juice. But Tom was half deaf and either couldn't or wouldn't hear him. Angrily he tumbled out of bed and crossed to the bellpull near the window. He leaned on it heavily, looking out the window.

She was coming out of the water then. At first he shook his head, thinking he was seeing things. In the hazy morning light he thought she was nude. When his head cleared, he could see her white suit. He turned away thinking himself a fool. But the next morning he found himself at the window hoping she would appear.

"Jerk!" he told himself. "You're Gordon Paynter. You're supposed to be the catch of the season. Every mother in Florida has set her daughter's cap for you, and you're mooning after some dame on the beach. You don't even know who she is. She's probably some cracker without a thought in her head except for the sun and the sand."

Suddenly he was aware of his man standing next to him. He turned quickly. Tom was staring down at the beach. "That's a right purty gal, Mr. Gordon," Tom said.

Gordon smiled. "Is that why I can't get you in the mornings? You've been watching her, too?"

Tom looked up at him. He spoke with a familiarity that came from long association. "I may be old, Mr. Gordon, but I got eyes."

"Do you know who she is?" Gordon asked.

"Uh-uh," the old man answered. "I never see'd her nowhere but here."

"Do you think she would have lunch up here?"

The old man looked at him with suddenly wise eyes. "Y' cain't tell unless you ax her."

Gordon turned and looked down at the beach. Stretched out on her blanket, she almost blended with the sand. He grinned. "Go ahead, Tom. Ask her to lunch with me."

She lay quietly in the sand, her head resting on her arms. The warm sun burned into her back. It was a good, clean heat. It wasn't a dirty heat like the white lights that had shone down on her at last night's show. She thought of the men whose stares hung heavy on her body almost like something you could feel. What were men like that they could find their kicks in second-hand exhibitions?

The worst part of the whole thing was making them understand, after the show was over, that that was all. She had nothing more for them. She and Evelyn would dress and they would wait outside in the car while Joe picked up the other half of their money. Then they would drive off.

Usually Evelyn and Joe would go out somewhere, but she went right home and climbed into the tub. A hot bath cleaned out a lot of the poisons. Then she would go to bed, read awhile, and then fall asleep. Sometimes she would awaken when Joe and Evelyn came home. There would be sounds in the night, and she would be very still until there was silence again.

In the morning she would be up while they were still asleep, put on her bathing-suit, go out to the car, and drive down to the beach. They would be up when she got back from the beach, and usually she would make breakfast. Then Joe and Evelyn would dress and go to the race track. They would come back in the late afternoon. Occasionally they blew all their money and had to borrow from her for the next day. They never repaid her, but she knew better than to ask them for it.

On the whole, it wasn't too bad. She had managed to save about five hundred dollars, which she kept in a savings bank in Miami. Once a week she would go into town and catch a picture, have lunch, and stop at the bank. The routines, as Evelyn called them, had long since stopped bothering her. She was able to regard them impersonally. After all, they were a kind of performance. You didn't have to feel anything to put on an act.

It was almost time for her to turn over. Her back was warm and toasted. As she began to roll over, she became aware of someone standing near her. She sat up quickly, her hands holding the bathing-suit straps in front of her.

A wizened, gray-haired colored man was standing there. He smiled at her. "Ma'am," he said in a gentle, hesitating voice.

"Yes?" she answered coldly.

"Mistuh Gordon Payntuh's compliments to you, ma'am," the old man said formally, "an' would like you to jine him for lunch up in his house."

Her eyes followed the half-wave of his hand to the house on the crest. She had noticed the house before. It was a rich man's place, with an iron fence running all around it and right down to the beach. She turned back to the colored man. "Tell Mr. Paynter that I appreciate his invitation, but if he wants to ask me to lunch, he can damn well come down here and ask me himself."

A smile twinkled deep in the old man's eyes. "Yes, ma'am," he said gravely. "I'll sho' tell him." He bowed slightly and turned back toward the house.

Mary watched him walk away and begin the climb toward the house. Then she stretched out on the sand and closed her eyes. A strange way to pick up a girl—send a servant after her. She wondered what Mr. Paynter was like. Probably some old geezer with one foot in the grave. Probably she had put him in his place. She dozed a few minutes, then prepared to leave.

She had already packed her bag and was starting toward the car when she heard the sound of footsteps in the sand. She turned back.

A young man was running toward her. He was wearing white duck pants and a white knit shirt. His hair was light brown and curly in the ocean wind. "Miss!" he called. "Miss!"

She waited for him to come up. He was tall, and his eyes were light blue. His face was a little heavy and there were slight lines of dissipation around his mouth and eyes.

"I thought you would leave before I got here." His voice rasped heavily after his unaccustomed exercise. "But I had to get some clothes on."

She didn't speak.

He smiled suddenly. "Man, am I out of condition! I can't catch my breath. I'm Gordon Paynter."

He watched her closely. She made no sign of recognizing the name. She still didn't speak.

"I've seen you swimming several times. People generally don't come this far up the beach. It's too lonely here." He was breathing easier now.

Her voice was low. "That's why I like it. I don't want to be bothered by people."

"Oh, I'm sorry," he said. "I didn't mean to intrude. I just thought it would be nice if—"

"Thanks, Mr. Paynter," she said quickly. "It was nice of you. Maybe some other time." She turned away.

"Let me walk to your car with you," he said. "I've seen you somewhere, I'm sure. Was it at the Senator's party?"

She looked at him swiftly. His face was open and free of guile. He didn't look like the type who attended those stags. He was just fishing. She smiled slowly. "I don't think we've met, Mr. Paynter."

"You're sure, Miss, er—Miss—?"

She didn't answer. When they reached the car, she threw her bag into the back seat and climbed in.

"You're from New York," he said, looking at the license plate. "I am, too. Maybe we met up—"

"No, Mr. Paynter." She turned on the ignition. "We've never met, I'm sure."

"Look, Miss—Miss—" He gave up waiting for her to supply her name. "I hope you won't let me drive you away from the beach."

"You won't," she said quickly. "I like it here."

"Maybe you'll come to lunch tomorrow then?" he asked, encouraged.

The motor roared as it caught. "Maybe," she laughed. "Why don't you ask me tomorrow, Mr. Paynter?" The car moved away.

He stood at the edge of the road looking after it. He scratched his head. Strange girl. She didn't sound as if she had ever heard of him. He wondered if she was putting on an act. He shook his head as he turned back to the house. Maybe he would find out tomorrow.

CHAPTER SEVEN

WHEN SHE GOT TO THE BEACH THE NEXT MORNING, SHE BLINKED HER eyes in amazement. A table stood on the sand, an umbrella over it. It was completely set with food, and Gordon Paynter stood next to it. He grinned. "You're ten minutes late."

"I—uh—" She couldn't speak.

"I wasn't taking any chances. I had Tom set us up down here," he explained.

"It seems to me that you're goin' to a lot of trouble for nothing, Mr. Paynter," she said.

"I don't think so, Miss No-name," he said.

"What'd you call me?" she asked.

"Miss No-name," he answered quickly. "I kind of like it. Makes you very mysterious."

She smiled slowly. "I don't think I'm very mysterious."

"Any girl without a name is mysterious in Miami." He turned to the table. "I hope you like shrimp. Tom makes the meanest shrimp salad."

"I love shrimp," she said.

"Good," he said, sitting down. "Let's eat."

She dropped her robe on the beach. "I'd like to swim first."

"Okay," he said. He stood up and took off his shirt. He dropped his trousers into the sand beside her robe. He was wearing a bright yellow pair of shorts. "Let's go."

He followed her down to the water. She dove into a breaker and came up sputtering. "The water's cold," she shouted back to him, her teeth chattering.

He grinned. "I'll speak to Tom about it. I'll see if we can run some hot-water pipes down here for you."

"Crazy man," she laughed, her back to the breakers. A big wave broke behind her and tumbled her to her knees. She felt his hands grab her under the shoulders and lift her to her feet. She stood there staring into his face.

His eyes were serious. "Now that I've saved your life, miss, do you think you can tell me your name?"

She caught her breath. There was something about his eyes that reminded her of Mike. They had the same decency about them, the same gentleness in the way they looked at her. She smiled slowly. "I guess it's only polite," she said.

He nodded, still holding her. "It's only polite."

"Flood," she said, "Mary Flood."

"Pleased to meet you, Miss Flood," he said. He kissed her cheek quickly and let her go. "Very pleased to meet you, Miss Flood."

"I never ate so much in my life, Gordon," she said, pushing her plate away from her.

He smiled. "Tom will be happy. He likes people to enjoy his food."

"You can tell him for me that it's the greatest," she said, grinning.

"More coffee?" he asked.

She shook her head. "No, thanks. I've had it." She looked at her watch. "Golly! It's after one. I've gotta run!"

"What about tonight, Mary?" he asked. "Have we got a date?"

"Uh-uh," she said. "I'd like to, but I can't."

"Why?" he asked.

"I've gotta work," she said.

"Tomorrow night, then?"

She shook her head. "No nights. That's when I work."

"What do you do?" he asked curiously.

"My girl friend and I have a routine," she said carefully. "We work a different club every night."

"Where are you working tonight?" he asked. "I'll come and see you."

"I don't know," she said quickly. "We're a fill-in. We wait at the agent's place until we get a call. When some act doesn't show up, then we rush over and go on."

"Oh," he said. "Maybe some time when you know in advance you'll tell me."

She nodded. "I will, Gordon." She picked up the bag from the sand beside her. "Thanks for the lunch."

"Let me carry it to the car for you," he said, taking the bag from her.

"Okay."

They walked slowly to the car. "I'll see you tomorrow," he said.

She looked down at her feet in the sand. She had already made up her mind. She wasn't coming back to this beach. Ever. She would have to find another place to swim. "Sure," she said.

They were at the car now. He opened the door for her, and she got inside. He put the bag on the seat beside her. "Thanks for everything, Gordon," she said.

"Thank you, Mary."

She held out her hand. He took her by surprise. Instead of shaking it, he held it to his lips. "Until tomorrow," he said.

He let go of her hand and she turned on the ignition. The motor roared. "Good-by, Gordon," she said. "You've been real sweet. Thanks again."

She came into the apartment humming. Joe and Evelyn were sitting at the table having coffee. Joe looked up at her. "What do you feel so good about?"

"I just feel good, that's all," she said. "Some guy bought me lunch."

Joe laughed harshly. "He'd better be good for more than lunch. I just got the word from my contact. We're shut down for a couple of weeks."

Mary looked at him. "What do yuh mean?"

"We gotta lay low. The cops are gettin' hot."

"Oh." Mary sat down at the table. She looked at her fingernails carefully. "What're we gonna do?" she asked.

Joe shot a quick glance at Evelyn. Without speaking, he got up and went into the bedroom.

Mary looked over at her. "What's with him?"

Evelyn shrugged her shoulders. "You know Joe," she said. "He's such a sensitive guy about some things."

Mary laughed. Evelyn's words were even funnier to her because of the seriousness with which they were spoken. "The only thing he's sensitive about," she said, "is his wallet."

Evelyn didn't see the humor. "Yeah, that's it," she agreed. "He's ashamed to ask you for the dough to pick us up outta here an' go to New Orleans."

Mary's eyes opened wide. "What happened to his dough? He gets half of everything we make."

Evelyn didn't meet her gaze. "It's gone. The track. Other reasons." She smiled at Mary. "I told him not to worry. That if you had any dough you'd be glad to put it up for us."

Mary's face was straight. "I got about twenty-two bucks in my bag. He can have that, if it'll help."

A look of disappointment came into Evelyn's eyes. "That all? What about the rest of the dough? You must have a couple of hundred dollars around. You never blew any of it."

Mary smiled. "I spent it on clothes. It wasn't much when yuh go shoppin'."

Joe's voice came angrily from the bedroom door. "I tol' yuh, Evelyn, she ain't goin' to give us nothin'. We been treatin' her too good. There's only one way to make a broad like that understand who's boss." He came threateningly toward Mary.

Calmly she reached into her pocketbook and took out the switch knife she had bought on her first shopping-trip. She looked up into his eyes steadily as she pressed the button, flipping out the blade. Its sharp, shining edge reflected all the light in the room. "Did Evelyn ever tell yuh how come I got sent up to that school?" she asked in a quiet voice.

Joe stopped short, his face flushed. He looked at his girl questioningly.

Evelyn's face was white. "She cut up her stepfather pretty bad."

He looked down at Mary. Idly she began to clean her nails with the blade. He turned back to Evelyn. "Fine class of friends you pick," he said in a disgusted voice. "I thought you said she was a high-class dame."

CHAPTER EIGHT

SHE WENT TO HER ROOM EARLY AND READ AWHILE BEFORE GOING TO sleep. The low hum of conversation came to her through the closed door. She smiled to herself. Joe had taken the twenty-two dollars without a murmur. She wondered what they were going to do next. At last she turned off the light and went to sleep. Time enough to worry tomorrow.

Bright sunlight was tumbling through the open window when she awakened. She rolled over on the bed and stretched. It was great going to bed at a decent hour. She had almost forgotten what it was like. She climbed out of bed and picked up her housecoat from the chair. There were no closets in this small room, only in the big room which Joe and Evelyn shared.

Slipping into it, she walked into the other room. Her brows knitted in puzzlement. The bed was empty. It hadn't been slept in. She walked over to the window and looked out. The car was gone too.

She went to the sink and filled the coffeepot, still thinking. They must have gone out last night and not yet returned. She turned on the burner under the coffee and walked to the closet.

It was empty. All the clothing was gone. Quickly she opened the dresser drawers. Everything was gone. She swore to herself silently. The only clothing in the whole apartment was what she had on at the moment. A nightgown, a cheap housecoat, and a pair of mules. They had taken all her clothes, even the bathing-suit.

The coffee was bubbling. She poured herself a cup and sat down to think. Idly she reached for the package of cigarettes that was always on the table. Even that was gone. She went into the bedroom and took the package from her purse.

A knock came at the door. She opened it. The landlord was standing there. "Yes?" she asked.

A short, thick-set man, he looked at her from under bushy eyebrows. "Your friends are gone," he said.

She stood in the doorway. "Yeah," she said.

He made a move to come into the apartment. She blocked his way. "They said you'd square the rent," he said, trying to look over her shoulder and see what was left in the apartment.

"How much do they owe yuh?" she asked.

"Three weeks," he said, his eyes not meeting her gaze. "Ninety bucks."

She couldn't tell whether he was lying. If he was telling the truth, Joe had been pocketing her share of the rent. "He told me he had paid you up to last week," she said.

His eyes turned shrewd. "Got the receipts?"

"They must be here somewhere," she said.

He knew she didn't have them. When he had heard the motor start in the middle of the night, he had come out of his room in a hurry. He always slept with one ear tuned in on the tenants. You had to be like that in the furnished apartment business or you'd soon be without your shirt. Someone was always trying to con you out of your rent money.

The man and the girl were putting their bags in the car. "Hey!" he said, tying his bathrobe around him. "Where're you goin'?"

The man turned to him. "We're checkin' out." "What about my rent?" he asked.

"Your rent is okay," the man said. "The blonde is still there. She ain't comin' with us."

"How do I know she's got the dough?" he demanded.

The man looked over at his girl friend quickly, then took the landlord's arm and led him behind the car where she couldn't hear them. "She's got dough," he whispered. "You can sock her for a couple of weeks, not only this one."

Unconsciously the landlord lowered his voice. "But you got the receipts."

The man chuckled and took a few slips of paper from his pocket. "Now you got 'em back."

The landlord looked down at his hand. They were the printed rent receipts for the last few weeks.

The man chuckled again. "I gotta get out. You know how dames are. My girl is jealous, an' the blonde won't leave me alone." He looked at the landlord as if he had a sudden idea. "You might even—"

The landlord felt his mouth go dry. He had seen her go down to the car in her bathing-suit. "D'ya think?" he asked.

The man nodded. "Easy," he said.

The landlord stood there indecisively. Actually, the rent was only two days behind. "How do I know?" he asked.

The man put his hand confidentially on his shoulder. "Y' can't miss," he said. "The kid's got round heels. A real nympho, can't do without it. All you gotta do is show it to her."

The landlord took a deep breath. "Okay," he said, stepping back. "I'll take a chance."

He watched the car drive off into the night and then went back into his room. Even if the man were wrong, the worst that could happen was that he would pick up an extra few bucks. . . . .

He put his foot in the jamb of the door. "Look," he said positively, "the rent wasn't paid. I want my dough."

Mary looked down at his foot, then up at his face. "Yuh can't get it," she said. "Not until I go down to the bank and take it out."

He shook his head. "I've had those gags pulled before. You'll disappear an' I'll be out in the cold. I want it now."

"I haven't got it here," she said.

"You got it," he said, letting his gaze travel meaningly down her housecoat. "All you need."

She let a smile come to her lips. Understanding came to her in a hurry. "Okay," she said. "But I'll need a little time to get ready. I gotta bathe an'—"

He reached a hand toward her. He felt the firm swell of her breast under the housecoat, then adroitly she slipped away from him.

She was still smiling. "Not now," she said.

He looked at her. The guy was right. "Okay," he said magnanimously. "I'll give you an hour."

"Thanks," she said dryly.

"But don't fool around," he said. "The cops down here are hell on rent-beaters. Especially when they're tourists."

She closed the door behind him and listened to his footsteps go down the corridor. For a moment she stood there, then went back to the table. She picked up her cup and tasted the coffee. It was cold.

Lighting another cigarette, she carried the coffee back to the stove and stood there, thoughtfully looking down at the pot while it was heating. Deep inside her she had always known what would happen. Sooner or later she would have to make up her mind.

When the coffee was hot, she carried it back to the table and sat down. If only she had some clothes in the place, she could get out. But even if she did, the landlord would call the cops. Joe had said the cops were getting hot. Maybe they would recognize her as part of the act. Then things would be even worse.

She sipped at the coffee and lit one cigarette from the end of the other. She smiled grimly to herself. It wasn't as if she had anything to lose. She was no virgin who had to protect this invisible barrier. Her stepfather had seen to that. And she knew how to take care of herself, too. That business would never happen again. That was another thing she had learned up at the school. There was nothing to worry about. Still, something had always held her back.

She closed her eyes almost wearily. They were always after that. Men were all the same. She knew it. She used to laugh at it. It had been a game to her then to see how far she could go with them and still get away. If only there were something inside her that could match their desires. Then maybe she could feel differently about it. Only when she was near Mike had she felt something stirring.

Strange that she should think of him now. It seemed as if he belonged to a completely different world. She wondered if it was the love she felt for him that had made it different. It must have been. She had never felt like that with anyone else.

She finished her second cup of coffee and looked at the clock. Fifteen minutes to go. She got up and rinsed out the cup and saucer. Slowly she dried them and put them neatly back on the shelf. She sat down again and looked at the clock. Ten minutes.

She lit another cigarette and waited, staring up at the clock. She wished she could feel something inside her. Anything. Even fear. But she didn't even feel that. Only the cold certainty that this had been bound to happen, that it had only been a question of time.

She was still staring up at the clock when the knock came at the door. She got to her feet. "Come in," she called.

The door opened and the landlord stood there. He hesitated a moment, then entered the room and shut the door quickly behind him. His face glistened with excitement. "Well?" he asked.

Her eyes looked at him levelly. Automatically she noted that he had shaved and put on a clean shirt. She half smiled to herself. "Well?" she answered.

"Ready?" he asked, walking toward her.

"Always ready," she answered automatically, her eyes still on his face.

His hands reached out for her and pulled her to him roughly. He kissed her. She could feel his teeth hard behind his lips. She didn't move. His hands moved swiftly and the sound of her clothing tearing came almost distantly to her. It was then that she pushed him away.

Regretfully she looked at the torn housecoat on the floor, then at herself. Now she had no clothes at all. She looked at him.

He was staring at her, his eyes white all around the edges. "My God," he was muttering. "My God!" He moved toward her.

She spun him toward the bedroom. Now it was all clear to her. It had taken a long time, but now she understood. It was for this life that she had been born. Some girls were born to be wives, some secretaries, some clerks, some actresses. But she had been born to be a whore. That was why things had always gone as they had for her. That was what everyone else could see in her.

"In there," she said calmly, gesturing toward the door.

He came toward her again.

She shook her head slightly. "What's your hurry?" she asked. "I'm not runnin' away."

He hesitated, then turned and walked into the bedroom, stripping off his shirt as he went. She picked up her torn housecoat and followed him into the room. She could see the faint matting of hair that covered his chest and shoulders.

She remembered Evelyn's line from the routine. It was always good for a wave of excitement from the audience. If she had been born to be a whore, she was going to be the best there was. The words came to her lips as if she had been saying them all her life.

"How d'yuh want it? Straight or special?"

CHAPTER NINE

S HE WALKED INTO THE HOTEL LOBBY AND CHOSE A SEAT IN A DISCREET out-of-the-way corner. Opening a copy of *Vogue* that she had carried with her, she glanced through it idly. Anyone looking at her would think her an attractive girl, young, sun-tanned, healthy, waiting for her boy friend. Which was just what she was doing—in a way.

A few minutes passed. Then a bellboy stopped in front of her. "Room three-eleven," he said in a low voice.

"Three-eleven," she repeated, a smile on her lips.

He nodded. "Right. He's waiting there now."

"Thank you." She smiled, holding out her hand.

"You're welcome, miss," the bellboy answered, taking the two bills from her. He walked away quickly.

Slowly she closed the magazine, glancing around the lobby as she stood up. It was normal. The house dick was looking the other way, the desk clerks were busy with check-ins, the other people in the lobby were all guests. Satisfied with her quick check, she sauntered toward the elevators. She had nothing to worry about. Everyone was taken care of. Mac, the landlord of the rooming-house, had put her wise to that.

"Pick a place to operate from," he had said knowingly. "Then before you do anything, make sure that everybody who might be interested is paid off. They'll leave you alone then, even help you."

She nodded. "That makes sense."

He looked at her intently. "Just be careful you don't bring nobody here. I'm runnin' a straight joint. I'm not lookin' for no trouble."

"I'll get out, then, if you want," she said.

He thought for a minute. "No, wait. I got an idea. A friend of mine is bell captain at the Osiris. I'll talk to him. Maybe he can set you in right."

The Osiris was one of the new hotels on the beach. The bell captain had been more than willing to co-operate. There was always a call for new girls. In little more than a month she had made more money than she had ever seen in her life, but by the time she was through paying off she kept only a small part of it.

She averaged four visits a day, as she called them. They were spread out among all the hotels that the bell captain had contacts in, so that she wouldn't become too conspicuous. At ten dollars a visit, it came to forty dollars a day. Thirty dollars went into the payoff.

She pressed the button and waited for the elevator. While she waited she took out another bill. The elevator-operator had to be tipped, too. A hand fell on her shoulder.

Involuntarily she jumped as she turned.

Gordon Paynter grinned at her. "I didn't mean to startle you, Miss Flood."

She held her breath. "Mr. Paynter!"

"I was wondering what had happened to you," he said quickly. "You never came back to the beach."

"The act broke up that day," she said. "I was busy looking for somethin' else."

"Come into the bar and have a drink with me," he said. "We'll bring each other up to date."

The elevator doors opened and the operator stuck his head out. "Up, please."

She looked up at Gordon. "I can't," she said. "I have an appointment."

"It can keep a few minutes," he said. "I've been looking all over town for you."

She smiled to herself. She was easy enough to find if you knew the right people. All he had to do was to check into the hotel and order a young blonde. "No, really," she said, "I got to see this man. It's about a job."

"I'll wait," Gordon said. "Will you be long?"

She thought for a moment. "Not long. Half-hour to an hour."

"I'll be in the bar," he said. "You'll be able to recognize me easy. I'll be draped over a martini."

"All right, Mr. Paynter," she said.

"You had already got around to Gordon," he said, smiling.

"Okay, Gordon," she said, going into the elevator. "I'll try not to be too long."

The door closed and the operator turned toward her. "Friend or customer?" he asked in a curious voice.

"Fourth floor, nosey," she said, holding the dollar out to him.

He took it, grinning. "Don't you give anybody discounts, Mary?"

She smiled at him as the elevator stopped. "Can't afford to. Operating-expenses are too high." The doors opened and she walked out.

"Maybe on your night off," he called after her.

"Save your money, bub," she flung back over her shoulder. "I got no nights off."

She heard the door close as she walked down the corridor. At the door of room 311 she stopped and knocked gently.

A man's voice came muffled through the door. "Who is it?"

She spoke softly but strongly enough to be heard through the door. "Room service."

She looked at her watch as she came into the bar. Three quarters of an hour. She paused, waiting for her eyes to get used to the dimness. He was sitting in a booth at the back. He waved to her and got up as she walked toward him.

"Get the job?" he asked as he made room for her.

"In a way," she answered, sitting down.

A waiter came to the table. "Another martini for me," Gordon said. "What about you?"

She looked at him. "Cassis and soda."

"Vermouth cassis and soda," the waiter repeated.

"No vermouth," she corrected. "Just cassis and soda."

As the waiter walked away, Gordon said: "That's a strange drink."

She met his gaze. "That's the way I like it."

"You're a strange girl," he said, finishing the remainder of the drink before him.

She looked at him sharply. Maybe one of the bellboys had put him wise. She didn't speak.

"You never came back, never called. Nothing," he said. "If I hadn't happened to run into you, I might never have seen you again."

"Maybe you would have been better off," she said solemnly.

His eyes narrowed. "What do you mean?"

She looked straight at him. "I'm no bargain. I'm not the kind of a girl you ordinarily run around with."

His lips parted in a smile. So she had heard about him. "What kind of girls are they?" he asked.

"Society an' stuff," she said. "You know what I mean."

"And because you're a working girl I can't bother with you?" he said.

She didn't answer.

The smile left his lips. "You're the real snob," he said. "It's not my fault I don't have to work. It could have happened to you. Nobody picks his parents."

She smiled suddenly. "It should have," she agreed. "I could think of worse things."

His hand reached for her hand across the table. "So could I." He smiled with her.

The waiter placed their drinks on the table. Gordon picked up his martini and held it toward her. "A toast," he said.

She picked up her drink. "To what?"

"To us," he said. "And to our dinner tonight. Tom's been waiting a long time to roast a duck for you."

She hesitated.

"I won't take any refusal," he said quickly. "I'm taking you right out to the beach after this drink."

She took a deep breath. A feeling of disappointment ran through her. He was no different from the others. He wanted the same thing. "Okay," she said.

He still held his drink toward her. "And to no more mysteries. I want to see a lot of you."

She nodded slowly.

"Tom and I think that you're the prettiest girl in Miami Beach," he said. "I think we're both in love with you."

Slowly she put her glass down on the table. "Don't say that," she said. "Don't say it even if you're joking. You don't have to."

CHAPTER TEN

"COFFEE AND BRANDY OUT ON THE TERRACE, TOM," GORDON SAID, pushing his chair back from the table.

Tom held Mary's chair while she got up. "It was great, Tom." She smiled. "I never ate so much in my life."

The old man grinned at her. "You sho' got a powerful appetite, miss. You eats like a puhson oughter."

"Thanks to you, Tom. Nobody can resist that food."

"Thank you, ma'am." He bowed, grinning.

Gordon held the door for her. She stepped out into the night. The sky was clear, and a soft, cooling breeze blew in from the ocean.

She took a deep breath. "This is like heaven," she said.

He smiled. "It's not simple, but it's home."

She turned to him quickly. "You invite everybody to your home like this, Gordon?"

He was puzzled. "What do you mean?"

"I mean, without knowing them? Really? For all you know, I might be on the make for yuh. It could be nothing but trouble." Her face was serious.

He grinned. "That kind of trouble I like. Make me."

"I'm serious, Gordon," she insisted. "You're a rich man and well known. Somebody could take advantage of you."

"I wish they would," he said, still laughing. "It would save me the trouble of trying to take advantage of them."

She walked to the railing. The moonlight sparkled on the water below. "There's no use talking to you," she said.

He put his arms on her shoulders and turned her around. His lips were smiling, but his eyes were serious. "Keep talking, baby. It's nice having someone to worry about me for a change. Usually everybody's after me for something."

She stared into his eyes. "You're a nice guy. I don't want nothin' from you."

"I know you don't," he said. "If you did, you would have been back."

She didn't answer.

"You're the first person in a long time who doesn't give a damn that I'm Gordon Paynter," he said.

"I like you," she said. "You're decent."

His hands dropped to his sides. "Famous last words. Just when I was trying to set you up, you take the wind out of my sails."

She smiled at him. "Don't get discouraged There's a fresh wind coming in from the ocean."

She put down her coffee cup. "You drink an awful lot," she said. "What for?"

He put down his fourth brandy and looked at her. "I like it," he said. He was beginning to feel the liquor. The words weren't coming just right. "Besides, there's nothing else to do."

"Nothing?" she asked in a wondering voice.

"Nothing," he answered heavily. "I keep away from business because every time I try something I lose money. Finally I gave it up. I get all I need without working."

She didn't speak.

He stared at her. "You think that's wrong, don't you?" he asked accusingly.

She shook her head.

He grabbed her arm. "You do, really, don't you? Everybody else does. They think it's terrible that I don't have to work while half the world is starving."

"I don't give a damn about the rest of the world," she said. "I only worry about me."

He let go of her arm. He felt incredibly sad and lonely. "Well, I do," he said. "I think it's terrible."

Her eyes glowed in the dark. "Then why don't you do something about it?"

"They won't let me," he said. He was near tears. "My lawyers won't let me. I can't even give my money away if I want to. They would stop me."

"Poor Gordon," she said, patting his hand.

"Yes, poor Gordon," he agreed.

"I wish I could feel sorry for you," she said.

His head snapped up. His eyes were suddenly clear. "What do you mean?"

She smiled at him. "Nobody ever had it so good."

He began to laugh. He threw his head back and the laughter rolled up from deep inside him. It roared against the house and down toward the surf.

She looked at him with wide eyes. "What're you laughin' at?"

He managed to control himself for a moment. He looked into her face. "Of all places to find an honest woman!" he gasped. "I'd never have believed it. Miami Beach!"

A puzzled look came into her eyes. "What's wrong with Miami Beach?" she asked. "I like it fine."

"I do, too," he said, still laughing. He went to the railing and looked down at the water, then turned back to her. "I have extra bathing-suits inside. How about a swim?" he asked.

She nodded silently.

They came back to the terrace wrapped in big Turkish towels. "Tom!" he yelled. "Some hot coffee. We're freezing!"

There was no answer.

He walked over to the doors and called: "Hey, Tom! Get us some coffee."

Tom's voice came back faintly. "Git it yo'self, boss. I gone to bed already."

Gordon came back from the door shaking his head. "I can't do a thing with him. He's been with me too long."

She smiled. "I can make coffee."

"Would you?" he asked.

"I insist," she said. "I'm cold, too. The water's great, but you gotta be used to it."

He led her into the kitchen. There was coffee on the stove. She lighted the burner under it. A few minutes later they were sitting on the big chaise sipping the coffee from steaming mugs.

"This is good," he said, putting down his cup.

She nodded.

He stretched out flat. "Did you ever notice how big the stars are down here at night?" he asked.

She glanced up at them for a moment, then back at him. "They look the same to me."

He turned toward her. "Woman, have you no romance in your soul?"

She smiled. "It's late. I better be getting dressed." She started to get up.

His hand caught her arm. "Mary Flood," he said.

She looked down at him. "That's my name."

"Don't go away now that I've found you," he said.

"Yuh don't know what you're sayin'," she said.

He pulled her down on the chaise. She looked into his eyes. He put his hands on her cheeks and drew her face to his. His mouth was warm and soft. It wasn't like all the others. A warmth ran through her. She closed her eyes.

She felt his hands on her breasts. She moved her shoulders and the straps slipped off. She heard his breath catch in his throat and she opened her eyes.

He was staring at her. "You're beautiful," he whispered. "Beautiful."

Her arms went around his neck, pulling his head down to her bosom. She could hardly hear his voice.

"Ever since you came out of the water the first morning I saw you," he was saying, "I knew you'd be like this."

She slipped her hands along his waist. She heard him gasp as her fingers touched him.

"I waited and waited," he whispered. "I waited so long."

"Shut up!" she said huskily, a strange fierceness in her. "You talk too much!"

Two days later he asked her to marry him.

CHAPTER ELEVEN

THE COFFEE WAS BUBBLING ON THE STOVE WHEN A KNOCK CAME AT THE door. "Who is it?" she called without turning around.

"Me," came the heavy, muffled voice. "Mac."

"The door's open," she called. "Come in." She filled two cups with coffee and carried them to the table.

He had the papers in his hands. "Yuh see these?" he asked.

She looked at him. "No," she answered. "I been too busy."

"That's what the paper says," he said quickly. "You're in all of them."

Her brows knitted in puzzlement. "Me?"

He nodded. "It says here you're goin' to marry Gordon Paynter."

She shrugged her shoulders. "What'd they print that for?" She sipped her coffee. "What's such a big deal? People get married all the time."

He stared at her. "You kiddin'? Not Gordon Paynter. He's one of the richest guys in the state."

She didn't answer, just reached for the papers and began to scan them. One of them had printed a picture of her leaving the license bureau with Gordon. She hadn't thought anything about it when the photographer snapped the picture. She remembered what Gordon had said before they went to the license bureau: "They'll make a big fuss. Don't pay any attention to them. Nothing they can do will change the way I feel about you."

She had looked up at him, her eyes somber. A sudden fear had begun to come into her. "Maybe we shouldn't do it, Gordon. Maybe we ought to wait a little. You don't know nothin' about me."

He had smiled reassuringly at her. "I know everything I want to know. I don't care what you did. I only know what you are to me. That's the only thing that matters in the end. . . ."

The landlord sipped his coffee. "Is it true, Mary? Are you really marryin' him?"

She lifted her eyes from the paper and nodded slowly. "Yes."

He whistled. "That's a real break. Does he—?"

She didn't let him finish his question. "He says it doesn't matter. That nothing matters," she said quickly, evading the truth.

"He must be real crazy about you." Mac put down his cup and got to his feet. "I guess this means that I lose a tenant."

She didn't answer, just looked at him. Something in his manner had changed. It was a subtle change, but it was there all the same. She sensed a subservience in him that had not been there before. She shook her head. "Not for a while, Mac," she said. "It's three days before we can marry."

He walked to the door and opened it, then stood there looking back at her. "If there's anything you want, Mary," he said in a low voice, "just yell. I'll come a-runnin'."

"Thanks, Mac," she said.

He hesitated a moment. "I jus' don't want yuh to forget I always been your friend."

"I won't forget, Mac," she said. The door closed behind him, and she picked up the cups and put them in the sink. Name and money changed a lot of things. Her lips tightened into a grim line. Her mind was made up. It had taken Mac to show her the way. She would have them both. Then let anybody try to step on her.

Gordon stepped from the shower, pulled a large towel from the rack, and began to rub himself briskly. He began to hum with satisfaction. Only one more day.

He looked in the mirror as he combed his hair. It was thinning a little in the front, but still seemed heavy and luxuriant enough. He wondered how much heredity had to do with it. His father had been bald before thirty. He grinned into the mirror, pleased with himself.

Slowly he began to dress. His physique was still good. The frame was not spare, but neither was he soft. He remembered what Mary had said. Less drinking. She was right about that. He had always known, but it hadn't mattered. There had been nothing else to do.

He walked into the bedroom and picked up his shirt from the pillow where Tom had placed it. A faint scent came from the pillow—the perfume she wore. A stirring of excitement echoed in him. She was like a tiger in her passion. Wild and clawing and demanding. There had never been anyone like her for him, so perfect they were together.

He could hear her muted voice echoing harshly in his ear: "Fill me, lover, drown me." His flesh tingled as if he could still feel her fingers tearing into his skin. He had never felt so much a man.

"Mr. Gordon." Tom's voice floated up from downstairs.

He tore himself from his memories. "Yes, Tom?"

"They's a gen'mun here to see you."

"Who is it?" Gordon was annoyed. He had told him many times to get names.

"He won' say," Tom answered. "He says it's privut an' confidential. About Miss Flood."

Gordon's brow knitted. He wondered what the man wanted. It was probably a reporter, they always acted mysteriously. "Ask him to wait," he called. "I'll be down in a minute."

A few seconds later he walked into the living-room. A heavyset, florid man got out of a chair and stood up.

"Mr. Paynter?" he asked.

Gordon nodded, waiting for the man to introduce himself.

"My name is Joe," the man said nervously. "Last name doesn't matter. I'm only here to do you a favor. What d'yuh know about this girl Mary Flood?"

Gordon felt an instinctive anger begin to rise in him. "Get out!" he snapped, jerking his finger at the door.

The man didn't move. "Yuh should know somethin' about her if yuh're goin' to marry her," he said.

"I know all I need to know," Gordon answered, moving threateningly toward the man. "Get out!"

The man shifted nervously. His hand reached into a pocket and came out with a few pieces of paper. "Before yuh lose your temper," he said quickly, "maybe yuh better look at these." He thrust them into Gordon's hand.

Automatically Gordon glanced at them. They were photographs. Two girls. Nude. He could feel a chill running in his blood. One of them was Mary. He looked up at the man. His voice was shaking. "Where did you get these?"

The man didn't answer his question. "Her real name is Marja Fluudjincki. She was released from a reform school in New York less than a year ago. I know where I can get the negatives of these pictures if yuh want them."

Gordon's lips tightened. Blackmail. He walked across the room and picked up the telephone. "Police headquarters," he said to the operator.

The man stared at him. "That won't do yuh no good," he said. "I'm givin' yuh the pictures as a favor. All it will do is get into the papers an' everybody will have a laugh on yuh."

Slowly Gordon put down the phone and sank into a chair. She should have told him. It wasn't right. He looked up at the man. "How do I know they're not fakes?" he asked, a faint hope inside him.

"I'll show yuh," the man said. He went to the door and opened it. "Evelyn!" he called. "Come in here!"

A moment later he came back into the room with a girl. She had short dark hair. Gordon looked down at the pictures. She was the other girl with Mary.

"Tell him the story," the man said.

The girl looked at him nervously. "But, Joe—"

The man's voice was harsh. "Tell him. We didn't drive all night from New Orleans for nothin'. Tell him!"

The girl looked down at Gordon. "I met Marja in the Geyer Home for Girls. We worked up an act and came down here. We worked stags and private clubs and parties. When the cops got hot, Joe an' me left town. Mary stayed here. We heard that—"

Gordon got out of his chair and crossed the room quickly. Her voice faded out as she looked at him, startled. He opened the rolling bar and took out a bottle of whisky. He poured himself a glass and turned back to them. There was a heavy aching pain inside him. "How about a drink?" he asked.

The man answered first. "Don't mind if we do," he said with a forced laugh. "Do we, Evelyn?"

CHAPTER TWELVE

THE JITNEY DROPPED HER AT THE HOUSE, AND SHE WENT UP THE WALK to the door and rang the bell. Gordon opened it.

The whisky on his breath hit her as she entered. She turned toward him. "You've been drinking" she said reproachfully. "And you promised you wouldn't."

He laughed nervously. "Jus' celebratin', honey. It isn't every day that old friends stop in for a visit."

"Old friends?" she questioned.

He nodded and led the way into the living-room. She stopped in the doorway, frozen with shock. Evelyn was sprawled on the couch, clad only in a brassiere and panties. Her clothing was strewn all over the room. She waved drunkenly at Mary.

Joe lumbered toward her. "My ol' girl Mary," he cried. "Got a kiss for ol' Joe?" Abruptly he began to sing. *"Here comes the bride—here comes the bride."*

"What're you doin' here?" she asked angrily.

Joe laughed. "We came to help our girl celebrate the weddin', that's all, honey." She turned to Gordon. "When did they get here?"

"Thish—thish afternoon." He tried to concentrate his gaze on her, but there was too much pain in his head. He needed another drink. He picked up the bottle and held it toward her. "Drink?"

She shook her head.

He drank from the bottle. The whisky felt good in his throat. It was warm and reassuring. He lowered the bottle and looked at her. "I needed that," he said. "Sure you won't have one?"

"No, thanks," she said dryly. She took out a cigarette and lit it. The smoke curled slowly from her lips.

Joe stood in front of her. "C'mon, have a drink," he urged. "It'll put yuh in the mood for the show."

Her voice was cold. "What show?"

Evelyn staggered from the couch. "We was tellin' your boy frien' about our act. Joe thought it would be fun to put it on for him."

She turned to Gordon, ignoring the girl. "They told you." It was more statement than question.

He nodded.

Her voice was calm. "You listened without giving me a chance to tell you?" This was more question than statement.

He held the photographs toward her. "The pictures did all the talking. I didn't have to hear anything."

She glanced at them briefly, then silently handed them back to him. He threw them on the table and turned away from her, unable to meet her gaze. "You should have told me," he muttered.

"You wouldn't let me," she answered. "Every time I wanted to, you said you didn't care what I had been. You said you knew enough about me."

He didn't answer.

She turned to Joe, her voice cutting. "Same old Joe. Anything to grab a buck. Hope you made out real good this time."

"Don't be sore, honey," he said, coming toward her. "The heat's off. We can put on the ol' act again." He tried to take her arm.

Her hand moved so swiftly that his eye couldn't follow. There was just the sharp shock, then the red-and-white stain on his face where her open palm had struck.

"Why, you bitch!" he exclaimed, taking an angry step toward her. "I'll learn yuh!"

A taunting smile came to her lips. "Learn me," she said softly.

He stopped, his eyes focused on her hand. The blade gleamed in the light. He stepped back quickly.

Gordon stared at them. "Mary!" he cried.

She turned to him. There was a hurt, angry sound in her voice. "Yuh're just as bad as they are. Yuh wouldn't listen to me, but yuh'd listen to anyone who came to yuh with a story. Did they tell yuh how they ran out an' stuck me without money an' clothes in an apartment? I bet yuh got a big yak outta that, too!"

He didn't speak, but his eyes stared into hers.

"They didn't tell yuh all of it, they didn't know," she continued angrily. "After they left, I hit the turf. I had to. To pay off the rent an' live. I did real good. Forty bucks a day. That's what I was doin' the day yuh picked me up!"

"No, Mary," he groaned.

"But it wasn't enough that I left yuh alone," she said. "You had to come after me. You had to make it a big thing." Her voice broke suddenly and became very small. "I was the sucker, not you. I thought this was the McCoy, the genuine article. I thought that for once there was somethin' in this world for me. I was wrong." She turned and started for the door.

Gordon caught her arm. There was a curious guilt in him. "Mary."

She looked up into his face, a faint flicker of hope coming into her eyes. "Yuh stopping me, Gordon?" she asked.

He didn't answer. He saw the light fade suddenly from her eyes.

She shook his hand from her arm, and the door closed quickly behind her. He stood there staring at it for a moment, then turned to the others.

Joe forced a laugh to his lips. "Yuh're better off without her, buddy."

Gordon didn't answer for a moment. When he spoke, he didn't recognize his own voice. It was harsh and filled with hatred. "Get out!" he said. "Get out, the two of you, before I kill you both!"

She staggered blindly down the walk. Tears filled her eyes and silently spilled down her cheeks.

A gentle voice spoke next to her. "Kin I git you a jitney, Miss Mary?"

She looked up. The old colored man was standing there, a world of understanding in his eyes. She shook her head. "No, thank you, Tom." Her voice was cracked and husky. "I—I think I'll walk a bit."

"I'll walk a ways with you if you allows me, Miss Mary," he said in his gentle, polite voice. "It's lonely out this way at night."

"I'll be all right," she said. "I'm not afraid."

He nodded slowly. "You sho' ain't, Miss Mary. You the mos' woman I seen in a long time."

She stared at him without speaking. Suddenly she understood. "You knew all the time," she said in a wondering voice.

He nodded.

"Yet you never told him. Why?"

His eyes looked right into hers. "Because what I said. You a real woman. But Mr. Gordon, he's nothin' but a boy. I was hopin' you would be his makin'. Not no more. Not ever."

She took a deep breath. "Thank you, Tom." She began to walk away.

He hurried after her. "I got some money, Miss Mary," he said quickly, "in case you is a little short."

For the first time that evening a real warmth seeped through her. Instinctively she took the old man's hand. "I can manage, Tom."

The old man dropped his eyes. "I'm sorry, pow'ful sorry, Miss Mary."

She looked at him for a moment, and a warm, friendly look came into her face. "I've changed my mind, Tom. There is something you can do for me."

He looked up quickly. "Yes, Miss Mary?"

"I'm goin' to ride home. Get me a jitney," she said.

"Yes, Miss Mary."

She watched him hurry down the street toward the main avenue, where cars would be running. She took out another cigarette and lit it. She dragged deeply on the cigarette and looked up at the sky.

The stars were bright and shining and the moon hung heavy in the sky. The faint roar of the surf came to her ears and a warm, soft breeze came from the ocean. Suddenly she snapped the cigarette out into the gutter. Her mind was made up.

She had enough of Florida. She was going back to New York. The stars were too bright down here.

CHAPTER THIRTEEN

MIKE LIFTED HIS EYES FROM THE BOOK IN FRONT OF HIM AND RUBBED them wearily. They felt red and raw and burning. He looked out the window. It was still snowing. In the next room the telephone began to ring. He could hear his mother's voice answering it.

Slowly he closed the books. It was almost time for him to go to work. He had the night beat this month. He got out of the chair and went into the bathroom. His shaving-gear was already spread out on the sink.

He was working the lather into his face when his mother came to the door behind him. "I'm gettin' your breakfast ready, son," she said.

"Thanks, Mom," he answered, taking the razor and beginning to shave.

She stood there watching him. After a few moments he became conscious of her gaze. "What is it, Mom?" he asked.

She shook her head and began to turn away, then turned back to him. "You didn't sleep much," she said. "I heard you up around three o'clock."

"I wasn't tired," he answered. "Besides, I had those books to read. The police examinations come up in a couple of months. You wouldn't want me to be a rookie all my life, would you?"

"No," she answered. "But I would like it better if you were more like other lads. It would do you good to go out once in a while instead of all the time burying your nose in them books. Now there's that Gallagher girl, the druggist's daughter. I see her on the street every day, and every time she asks about you—"

"Ma, I told yuh a dozen times I ain't got no time for girls," he said impatiently. "There'll be time enough for that later. Right now I got too much to do."

She met his eyes steadily in the mirror. "If it was that Marja, you would have time."

He could feel his face flush. "Forget her, Mom. I told yuh that was over."

His mother's eyes were suddenly gentle. "I can forget her, son," she said, turning away. "But can you?"

He listened to her footsteps go down the hall, then looked at his face in the mirror. Absently he took a stroke with the razor. A tingling, burning sensation caught his cheek. "Damn!" he said aloud, lowering the razor. He reached for the styptic pencil to stanch the blood.

Quickly he held the white pencil to the cut in his cheek. Its caustic edge burned deeply. Marja, he thought. Marja. He wondered if his mother was right. He dried his face and walked over to the window. It was still snowing.

He wondered what Marja was doing.

The big clock in the lobby said eight o'clock when Mary came out of the hotel. The snow had covered the streets with a white blanket and muffled all the traffic noises. She turned up 49th Street toward Sixth Avenue. There would be more action around Rockefeller Center.

Altogether, there was a better class of trade. The tourists and the white-collar workers from that area had more to spend. Broadway and Seventh and Eighth Avenues were nothing but two-dollar tricks. A girl had a chance for a five- or ten-dollar trick on Sixth Avenue.

She looked up at the sky. It was still snowing heavily. There wouldn't be much doing tonight, but she couldn't afford to stay in. She had no money left, and rent was due in a few days. She walked along slowly, her face turned away from the street toward the store windows as if she were interested in what they had to offer.

Actually, she was looking at the windows as if they were mirrors. Each man who came by was carefully scrutinized and, by instinct alone, appraised. She turned left on Sixth and walked to the corner of 50th. Almost no one was out. She went into the cafeteria on the corner and ordered a cup of coffee.

She took it to a seat near the window, where she could watch the entrance to the Music Hall across the street. There would be a show break in about twenty minutes. Crowds would pour out then, and very often there was some action in them. The yokel sports made the early show so they could have the night free.

Her cup was almost empty when the theater began to empty. Quickly she finished the coffee and walked across the street. She stood in a corner of the lobby as if waiting for an appointment.

An usher walked by. She glanced at her watch impatiently as if tired of waiting. People pushed by, but they were nothing but faces. The crowd was thinning now. A few minutes more and she would go out into the snow again. It looked as if there was nothing here tonight.

She was about to leave when an instinct made her look up. A man standing across the lobby was watching her. Quickly she looked at his shoes. They were brown. Automatically that made him safe. Cops wore black shoes. Slowly she looked up into his face again, her eyes carefully blank, then turned and sauntered out into the street.

She waited on the corner for the traffic light. Without turning around, she knew that the man had followed her. When the light changed she crossed the street and entered the RCA building. She went down a small flight of stairs into the arcade and stopped in front of a window.

In its reflection she could see the man pass behind her.

He stopped at a window a few doors away. She walked slowly past him, through the revolving door, and up the steps. She went past the post office and stopped in front of a restaurant that had the lower half of its windows painted black so that you could not see into it. Here she opened her pocketbook and took out a cigarette. She was about to light it when a flame sprang up next to her. The man's hand was trembling slightly as she looked up at him. He had a round, smooth face and dark eyes. He seemed okay. "Thank you," she said, lighting her cigarette.

He smiled. "Can I buy you a drink?" His voice was guttural and heavy.

She raised an inquiring eyebrow. Her voice was friendly and devoid of insult. "Is that all you want?"

The man seemed flustered. "No-no," he stammered. "But—"

"Then why add to the overhead?" she smiled. "You don't have to spend money on me."

He cleared his throat, drawing himself up as if hoping to appear a man of the world. "Er—ah, how much?"

"Ten dollars," she said quickly, watching him carefully, ready to come down in price if he seemed to balk.

"Okay," he said.

She smiled and took his arm. Together they walked up the stairs and out into the street. She led him toward the hotel. "There's nothing like snow in the winter," she said.

"Yeah," he answered.

"But it's no good in the city. Everything gets all slopped up. You can't do anything."

He ventured a joke. "I'm doin' okay."

She laughed and held his arm tighter. He wasn't so dumb. They were near the hotel now. She took her hand from his arm. "I'm goin' in here," she said. "Give me five minutes, then come up to room 209, second floor. Room 209. Got it?"

He nodded. "Two-oh-nine. Five minutes."

She was wearing a kimona when the knock came at the door. Quickly she crossed the room and opened it. The man stood there hesitantly. "Come in," she said.

He entered slowly and stood in the middle of the room as she closed and locked the door. She turned toward him. "Your coat," she said.

"Oh, yes." He shrugged off his coat and handed it to her. She put it on a hanger and hung it on the door. When she turned back, he already had his jacket off and was loosening his tie.

She smiled and sat on the edge of the bed, her legs swinging. He watched her as he took off his shirt. Muscles rippled in his shoulders. "What's your name?" he asked.

"Mary," she answered.

"How come you're doin' this, Mary?" he asked. "You seem like too nice a girl—"

A bored look crossed her face. They all had the same question. Sometimes she thought they came more for the story than for anything else. She shrugged her shoulders. "A girl's gotta eat," she said.

He started to loosen his belt.

"Haven't you forgot something?" she asked.

He looked startled. Then understanding came to him. "Yeah," he said, putting his hand in his pocket. He held a bill toward her.

She put it in her pocketbook on the dresser. Then she threw off the kimona and went back to the bed. Completely nude, she stretched out and looked at him.

He was standing there, his trousers still on, staring at her.

"Come on," she said. "What're yuh waitin' for?"

He ran his tongue over his lips. Slowly his hand went into his pocket again and came out with a small black leather wallet. He flipped it open. The sparkling silver of a badge gleamed at her. He turned his face away. "Detective Millersen, Vice Squad," he said. "You're under arrest. Get dressed."

She sat up quickly, her heart pounding inside her. It had to happen sometime. She had always known it. But not so soon.

She forced a smile to her lips. "My mistake, officer," she said. "This one'll be on the house."

He shook his head. "Get dressed." He wouldn't meet her eyes.

"You're pretty good-lookin' for a cop," she said, coming near him.

He walked away and planted himself in front of the door. He was already putting on his shirt. "No use tryin', sister," he said stolidly. "Might as well get your clothes on."

Slowly she began to dress. "What's the rap for this?" she asked.

"This the first offense?"

She nodded, trying to fasten the hook in the back of her dress. Her fingers were trembling so that she couldn't make it. "Be a good felluh, will yuh?" she asked. "See if yuh could forget that badge long enough to hook this for me?"

He came around behind her and hooked the dress. "Thirty days," he said.

"Thirty days for what?" she said, for she had already forgotten her question.

"Thirty days for a first offense," he said, going back to the door.

"Oh," she exclaimed. "What day is this?"

"February 27," he answered.

She opened the closet and took out her coat. "There goes the month of March." She turned to him. "Have I got a few minutes to pack my things? You know these flea bags. Thirty days from now I'll never get my clothes back."

He nodded. "Okay, but snap it up."

He watched as she took a valise from the closet. There wasn't very much to pack. It all fitted into the valise. She snapped the lid down and turned to him. "I'm ready now. Thanks."

He opened the door and followed her out of the room. She looked up into his face as she crossed the threshold. "There must be an easier way to make a living," she said.

His eyes widened with a sudden respect. The girl had guts. He nodded somberly. "There must be."

She took his arm as if they were old friends going for a stroll. Her voice was low and husky. "For both of us, I mean."

The State vs. Maryann Flood

I WALKED SLOWLY PAST THE JURORS. THEIR EYES FOLLOWED ME WITH IN-
terest as I went up to the judge to answer Vito's motion for dismissal before
he presented his case. I hoped they could hear me despite the fact that I
spoke in a low voice.

"There are two things to remember in any court of justice. They are moral
guilt and legal guilt. We can punish only for that we find legally guilty. But it is
seldom in any court of justice that we find both moral and legal guilt so close
together.

"We have carefully presented to the court and jury the accusations against the
defendant. We have carefully documented them with facts and evidence and
witness. We have presented the State's case without dramatics, without flimflam,
and with a deep sense of responsibility to all the parties concerned. We have
done our duty without fear or favor, and in so doing have created a structure of
guilt that encompasses and incriminates the defendant.

"The people of the State of New York look to you for justice. Justice, for now,
will be served by denying the motion of the defendant!"

I walked slowly away from the bench and stopped midway across the court. I
heard the judge's voice over my shoulder:

"Motion denied."

Instantly pandemonium broke loose. Behind me reporters were running up
the aisles to get the news to their papers. The judge banged his gavel. At last he
could make himself heard over the uproar.

"The court will adjourn until ten o'clock tomorrow morning."

❖ ❖ ❖

I was soaking wet when I walked into my office and sank into a chair.

Joel and Alec were right behind me. "You need a drink, man," Joel said, studying me.

I nodded and closed my eyes. I needed more than that. I didn't know how I would get through the next two weeks of the trial while Vito presented his case. I felt as if I had no strength left in me.

"Here," Joel said.

I opened my eyes, took the glass from him, and threw the liquor down my throat. It burned all the way down to my gut. I coughed.

"Hundred-proof bourbon," he said.

I looked up at him. "Thank God that's over," I said fervently.

Alec grinned. "You were good. Real good."

"Thanks," I said, "but you don't have to say it. I know just how bad I was."

"You weren't bad at all" a new voice said.

We turned to the doorway in surprise. I scrambled to my feet. "Chief!"

He was smiling as he came into the room. "Pretty good, I would say."

Alec and Joel exchanged glances. These were the highest words of praise they had ever heard from the Old Man.

"Thank you, sir," I said.

He held up his hand. "Don't thank me," he said. "It isn't over yet. Vito still has his chance. It's never over until the jury comes back."

I pulled a chair out for the Old Man. He sat down carefully. It was the first time he had come to the office since the operation.

"You're looking very well, sir," Joel said. I glanced at him quickly. He was right back in the groove. Politics as usual.

The Old Man took it in his stride. "I feel pretty good," he said. He took out a package of cigarettes and put one in his mouth. Alec almost broke a finger beating Joel with the light.

I smiled to myself. Normalcy had returned in a hurry. I was beginning to feel better. Maybe it was the whisky warming my stomach.

The Old Man turned to me. "What do you think Vito will do?"

I shook my head. "I don't know, sir."

"I don't like the way he looks," the Old Man said. "He's sitting too easy."

"Vito always looks like that, whether he's got something or not," Joel broke in quickly.

The Old Man shot him a withering glance. "I've known Hank Vito for almost twenty years. I can tell when he's acting. He's not acting this time. He's got something up his sleeve." He took a puff on his cigarette. "I'd give another appendix to know what he's sitting on."

We sat around silently for a moment, each trying to think of some possibility that we had overlooked.

At last the Old Man got to his feet. "Well," he said heavily, "I don't think we'll have long to wait. He'll probably hit us with it first thing in the morning."

"What makes you think that, sir?" Joel asked.

The Old Man walked to the door and looked back at us. "He didn't subpoena any witnesses for tomorrow. Not a solitary one."

The rest of us looked at one another in amazement. It was Alec who drew the first breath. The Old Man's statement had caught us flatfooted.

He looked shrewdly at the three of us. "If any of you guys had been on your toes, you would have checked before you left the courtroom." He disappeared into the corridor.

It was Joel who gave voice to our grudging admiration. "Leave it to the old bastard," he said affectionately. "He may be old, but he hasn't lost any of his marbles."

I stayed at the office until after eleven o'clock that night going over the case. I did everything. Checked the data we had on his witnesses. Matched the questions he had asked the State's witnesses. Nowhere in any of the information I had could I find a pattern that indicated his course of action. At last I closed my desk and took my hat and coat from the clothes tree.

I was tired, but I wasn't sleepy. It was raw cold out, but I decided to walk a bit, hoping the fresh air would clear my head. I headed up Broadway.

Down here Broadway was a dark and deserted street. Far uptown I could see the haze of lights that Times Square threw vividly upward. But here the office buildings loomed large and black with night. Only occasional lights where cleaning women were working flickered sporadically.

I turned up my coat collar to stave off the wind and began to walk briskly. I had gone almost four blocks when I noticed an automobile idling slowly along the street beside me. I glanced at it curiously, but couldn't see into it. It was too dark.

I kept walking, busy with my thoughts. When I reached the next corner the car cut in front of me. I jumped back onto the curb, swearing.

A low burst of laughter reached my ears. It was a familiar laugh. I put my hand on the front door of the car and opened it.

She was seated behind the wheel. In the dim light of the dash I could see the white reflection of her teeth. "Hello, Mike," she said in a husky voice.

"Marja!" I couldn't keep the surprise from my voice. I stood frozen to the curb.

"Get in," she said. "I'll give you a lift."

I hesitated a moment, then got into the car. She put it into gear immediately and the car moved off. I kept staring at her.

At the next corner a traffic signal brought the big car to a stop. She turned and looked at me. "You work pretty late," she said. "I've been parked outside your office since six o'clock."

"Why didn't you let me know?" I said sarcastically. "I wouldn't have kept you waiting."

"Uh-oh," she said, starting the car again. "The man is mad."

I took a cigarette and lit it. In the light from the match her hair was almost white. There was a quiet smile on her lips. She drove silently with casual carelessness.

After a while she spoke. "You were very good today, Mike." It was almost as if she were not on trial.

"Thanks," I said.

She turned the car into a side street, pulled over to the curb, and cut the ignition. From somewhere she pulled a cigarette. I held a match for her.

Her eyes searched mine over the flame. "It's been a long time, Mike." ·

I nodded. "I've heard those words before—I think."

The match flickered out, but not before I saw a strange hurt leap into her eyes. There was a gladness in me. I hadn't believed anyone had the power to hurt her.

She put her hand on mine. "Let's not fight, Mike." Her voice was gentle.

"What do you think we've been doing ever since this trial began?" I asked angrily. "This isn't a game we're playing."

Her eyes stared into mine over the glow of the cigarettes. "That's something else, Mike. It's got nothing to do with us personally."

I could feel the drag in those eyes. I began to swim dizzily in their depths. Things hadn't changed a bit. I leaned forward and kissed her.

Her mouth was soft and warm. I could feel the pressure of her teeth behind her lips. I felt an instant passion surging in me. I pulled my mouth away from her. This was crazy.

Her eyes were still closed. "Mike," she whispered. Her hand sought mine and held it tightly. "Why did this have to happen to us?"

I dragged on my cigarette. "I don't know," I said harshly. "I've wondered many times myself."

Her eyes opened slowly. Never had they seemed so gentle as now. They looked straight into mine. "Thanks, Mike," she said softly. "I was afraid you had changed."

I didn't answer.

After a minute she spoke again. "How're your folks?"

I didn't look at her. "Pa died two years ago. Heart attack."

"I'm sorry, Mike," she whispered. "I didn't know." She dragged on her cigarette. "And your mother?"

I looked at her quickly, wondering if she was aware of how my mother felt about her. I looked away again. Of course not. How could she be? "Ma's okay. She's in the country right now. I expect her home in a couple of weeks."

We fell silent again. Our cigarettes burned down and I tossed mine out the window. We seemed to have run out of conversation. "I hear you have a daughter," I said.

A smile came to her lips. "Yes."

"She must be very pretty," I said. "Any child of yours would have to be."

A strange look came into her eyes. Her voice was very quiet. "She is."

Again silence descended upon us. There were a million things to say to her, a thousand questions I wanted to ask, but my tongue was frozen with time and circumstance. I cleared my throat.

"Yes, Mike?" she asked.

I looked at her. "I didn't say anything," I said awkwardly.

"Oh," she said.

A police car came down the block and flashed its lights into our car. I fought an impulse to raise my hand and cover my face, but it kept on going.

I turned to her. "This was a crazy thing to do," I said.

She smiled. "I like crazy things."

"I don't," I said. "That was always one of the differences between us."

"Don't preach, Mike," she said quietly. "I've heard enough of that the last few weeks."

I stared at her. "Why, Marja? Why?"

Her eyes met mine levelly. She shrugged her shoulders. "It happened."

"But why couldn't it be two other people, Marja? Why did it have to be us?" She didn't answer.

I reached forward and turned the ignition key angrily. "Let's go," I said.

Obediently she started the car. We moved out into the street. "Where to?" she asked.

"You can drop me on Broadway and Canal," I said. "I can get a cab there."

"Okay."

A few minutes later we were there and she pulled to the curb. I opened the door and was halfway out of the car before she spoke. I stopped and looked back at her. There was a reflection from the light in the window of the store on the corner. It threw wild highlights on her face—the high cheekbones, wide mouth, and delicately flaring nostrils.

"I wish it had been two other people, Mike," she said.

There was an ache inside me. "It's too late now."

She took a deep breath. "Not for one thing, Mike."

I stared at her. "What?"

She leaned forward swiftly and her lips brushed my cheek. "I love you, Mike," she whispered. "It's always been you. No matter what happened. I just didn't know any better."

Then the car was off in a roar of the motor and I was standing on the corner looking after it. Its taillight vanished around a corner and I began to walk toward the cab stand.

I could still feel the light pressure of her lips, and the perfume she used clung to my nostrils. I didn't understand. I would never understand. The more I knew her, the less I knew her.

That time during the war, for instance. There had been a wonderful week-end. She was for me then—I knew it, I could feel it. But she had gone away with Ross. I rubbed the broken bridge of my nose reflectively. I didn't need a greater reminder. Ross had done that.

I got into a cab and gave the driver my address, then settled back in the seat. So many years. So many things had changed. Ross was dead. Nothing was the same any more.

I took a deep breath. Nothing—except the way I felt about her.

Book Three
MARYANN

CHAPTER ONE

THE SHOESHINE BOY WAS WAITING WHEN HENRY VITO GOT TO HIS OFFICE. He came in briskly, threw his coat on the small leather sofa, and sat down behind his desk. He put his foot on the shine box. "Good morning, Tony," he said, reaching for the stack of papers on his desk.

"*Bon giorno*, Signor Vito," the boy replied, already rubbing the shoe with a polishing-cloth.

Vito looked quickly at the newspaper which was on the top of the pile. The front-page headlines were the same as yesterday's. The Germans were falling back in North Africa, or the Germans were advancing—they had been the same all that spring of 1943. He tossed the paper into the wastebasket and began to skim through the morning mail. Nothing important. Restlessly he changed feet on the box at the boy's tap and looked out the window.

Across the street was a park and beyond it the gray stone of Criminal Courts He felt like a gladiator looking out at the arena. It had been always like that, ever since he had been a boy in Little Italy downtown. The challenge of the symbol of authority. To flout the law was too easy; to make it ridiculous by its own standards was the fun. It was the profit too. Freeing the guilty conscience of its legal bonds was a lucrative profession.

He felt a tap on his foot signifying that the shine was finished. He spun a quarter toward the boy and turned back to his desk. The telephone buzzed as the boy left. He picked it up.

"There's a Maryann Flood here to see you," the receptionist's voice said in his ear.

The name wasn't familiar. "What does she want?" he asked.

"Client," the girl's reply came laconically. "She says you were recommended to her."

"By who?" he asked.

"She said she would tell you when she saw you. She also said she pays cash in advance."

Vito grinned to himself. Whoever the woman was, she knew her business. "Send her in," he said.

A moment later the door opened and his secretary appeared, followed by a young woman. Vito struggled to his feet. "Mr. Vito, Miss Flood," his secretary introduced.

The young woman came toward him, her hand outstretched. Vito took her hand. Her grip was firm and casual like a man's, yet there was an electric warmth in it that made you know she was a woman. "Thank you for seeing me," she said. Her voice was low and well modulated.

"You're quite welcome." Vito gestured toward the chair opposite his desk. "Please sit down."

His secretary retrieved his coat from the sofa where he had thrown it, and went out. Vito sat down and looked at the young woman.

She wore a light tweed suit and matching topcoat, and a white silk blouse showed beneath the jacket. Her hands were well shaped. She wore no jewelry, and no make-up other than a gentle shading of lipstick. Her eyes, set wide apart, were large, dark brown, almost black. Faint strands of blond hair peered out from beneath her soft cream-colored beret.

Vito prided himself on his ability to appraise a client. This girl had breeding. It was evident from everything about her. She had come to see him about her brother or some relative who had got himself into trouble. This was the sort of case that he liked. It meant money. He smiled at her. "How can I help you, Miss Flood?" he asked.

The young woman didn't answer immediately. She took out a cigarette and waited for him to light it. He did so, even more sure now of his analysis. Only girls of fine background had that imperious manner of waiting to have their cigarettes lighted. He watched her draw the smoke gently into her mouth.

"I hear you're a good lawyer, Mr. Vito," the young woman said softly. "The best in New York."

He preened inwardly. "That's very flattering, Miss Flood." he said modestly "but not quite true. I do my best, that's all."

"I'm sure that's more than anyone else can do," the girl said. There was a hint of a smile in her eyes.

He noticed it and went on the defensive immediately. He wasn't going to have a society broad mocking him. "I try very hard Miss Flood," he said, his voice chilling.

The girl looked straight into his eyes. "That's why I came to you, Mr. Vito. I need a lawyer, and I want the best." There was no laughter in her eyes now.

"Why?" he asked.

"I received a call this morning from a friend of mine. A warrant has been issued for my arrest and I'm to be picked up this afternoon." Her voice was flat and emotionless.

A sense of shock ran through him. "You're to be arrested? On what charge?"

She still looked into his eyes. "Grand larceny after committing an act of prostitution."

For a moment his voice failed him. "What?" he managed after his voice came back.

She smiled, genuine amusement in her eyes, and repeated the charge. "That's why I'm here," she added.

He had never been so wrong in his judgment of a client. He took out a fresh cigar, bit off the end, and applied a flaming wooden match until its tip glowed a cherry red. Then he put the match down. By this time he had control of himself. "Tell me what happened," he said unemotionally.

"I was in the bar at the Sherry last night about eleven having a nightcap when this man came up. He was drunk, and insisted on buying me a drink. He told me he was very rich, and waved a fat roll of bills to emphasize it. We had a few drinks there. Then he came up to my place and we continued drinking." Her voice was as flat and unexpressive as if she were reciting a story about someone else. "He left about four thirty. He gave me twenty dollars, and I kissed him good night."

"Then what happened?" he asked.

"I went to bed," she said. "This morning my phone rang. A friend was calling me from headquarters. He said this man had appeared this morning and sworn out a warrant for me."

"Did you take his money?" Vito asked.

"No," the young woman answered. "He put the roll back in his pocket after he gave me the twenty."

"Who recommended me?" he asked.

"Detective Lieutenant Millersen, 54th Street station," she answered. "I've known him for about five years now. He knows I would never do such a thing."

He knew Millersen. A good cop. He wouldn't slip him a bad deal. But the cop could be wrong, too. He shot a shrewd glance at the girl. "Sure you didn't take the money?" he asked. "You can tell me. I don't care whether you did or not. I'll handle the case anyway. I just want to know for myself."

The girl looked at him, her eyes wide and unblinking. Slowly she reached up and took off her beret. She shook her head and her hair tumbled down around her face in a sparkling golden shower. "Mr. Vito," she said in a low husky voice, "I'm a whore, not a thief."

CHAPTER TWO

"MR. BELL, HOW MANY DRINKS DID YOU HAVE BEFORE YOU MET Miss Flood that evening?" Vito's voice was clear and unemotional. The heavy-set man in the witness chair looked uncomfortably at the judge. The judge stared straight in front of him. "I don't know," Bell answered, his voice strained. "I been drinkin' quite a lot."

"Ten drinks? Twelve? Twenty?" Vito's voice was curious.

"Maybe ten," the man admitted.

"Maybe ten." Vito turned back to his client. She nodded slowly. He faced the man again. "And how many drinks did you have with her in the bar?"

"Four?" the man replied in a questioning voice.

"I'm sure I don't know, Mr. Bell," Vito said sarcastically. "You were there, not I."

"But I'm not sure," the man said.

"You're not sure," Vito repeated. He walked a few steps away from the witness chair. "You're not sure how many drinks you had before you met my client, you're not sure how many drinks you had at the bar with her. Is it possible you know how many drinks you had in her apartment?"

"I—I don't know," the man said. "I can't be sure. I had a lot to drink that night."

Vito smiled. "That's something we all are sure of, Mr. Bell." He turned to let the ripple of laughter run through the almost empty courtroom. He turned back to the man in the witness chair. "Apparently you're not sure of anything that happened that night, Mr. Bell, are you?"

Bell flushed. "I had fifteen hundred dollars in my pocket when I started that night," he said angrily. "I didn't have it the next morning."

"When did you first miss the money, Mr. Bell?" Vito asked.

"When I woke up," the man said. "I looked on the dresser. When I saw the money wasn't there, I went through my pockets. It was gone."

"Where was that, and what time, Mr. Bell?"

"In my room at the hotel about nine thirty in the morning."

"And you immediately called the police and reported the theft?" Vito continued.

"No," Bell answered. "I got dressed and called downstairs to the desk to find out if anyone had reported finding the money."

"*Then* you called the police?" Vito's voice was gentle.

"No, I called the cab company to find out if any of their drivers had turned in the money."

"Was that all the money you had on you, Mr. Bell?" Vito asked casually.

Mr. Bell nodded. "Yes, I never keep change in my pockets. It's too much bother. I never take any. I always tell 'em to keep the change."

"That's all Mr. Bell. Thank you." Vito walked away abruptly.

The man looked around him embarrassedly, then awkwardly got down from the chair and went back to a seat. Vito waited a moment, then called out a name. A short, thin man got to his feet and went to the witness chair. The clerk administered the oath and the man sat down.

Vito came toward the man. "What is your occupation, Mr. Russo?"

"I'm a cab-driver, sir," the man said in a guttural voice.

"Who do you work for?" Vito asked.

"The Shaggy Dog Cab Company," the witness answered. "I work nights."

"Do you recognize anyone in this court?" Vito asked.

"Yes, sir," Russo answered. He looked around quickly. "Him," he said, pointing at Bell.

"Did you know him by name before you came into this court?" Vito asked.

"No," Russo replied. "I recanized him because I rode him one night."

"When was that?" Vito asked.

Russo took out a sheet of paper. "I got my ride sheet for that night. It was Tuesday night a week ago."

Vito took the sheet of paper from him. "What is this?"

"That's my ride sheet. It tells where I pick up a fare and where I left him off an' how much the clock reads. That's so the boss can tell how much mileage is on the clock an' how much is cruising. It also tells the time of each call."

Vito looked at it. "Would you have Mr. Bell's ride on this sheet?"

The hack man nodded. "Yeah, it's there. Four forty a.m."

"Four forty a.m.," Vito read. "72 Street and C.P.W. to the Sherry Hotel." He looked at the witness. "Is that the ride?"

"Yeah," the cab-driver answered.

"Sixty cents," Vito read from the sheet.

"That's what was on the clock," the cab-driver said quickly.

Vito looked at him. "How did he pay you?"

"He pulled a dollar bill off his roll an' tol' me to keep the change," the cab-driver said.

Vito looked up at the judge, his face innocent of expression. "One more question, Mr. Russo. What was the condition of your fare? Was he intoxicated?"

"He was drunk as a lord," the cab-driver said quickly.

"That's all, Mr. Russo. Thank you." Vito still looked up at the judge. He waited until the witness left the chair and then a faint smile came to his lips.

A twinkle of answering amusement sparkled in the judge's eye. He nodded slightly toward Vito.

Vito was smiling broadly now. "I move that the case against my client be dismissed on the grounds that no evidence of any crime on her part is shown."

"Motion granted. Case dismissed," the judge said.

"Thank you, Your Honor." Vito turned toward Maryann as the judge adjourned the court.

She held out her hand, smiling. "Thank you, Hank."

He grinned at her. "You said I was the best. I dared not do less."

She stood up and he helped her on with her coat. From the corners of his eyes he could see a man handing Bell a paper. He chuckled to himself as they started to walk out.

Bell pushed up to him as they passed. "Mr. Vito," he said angrily, waving the paper, "what is the meaning of this?"

Vito answered calmly: "What?"

"This suit for false arrest. Slander—damages to your client's reputation. Two hundred and fifty thousand dollars!" Bell's voice was trembling with rage.

Vito pushed Maryann down the aisle before him as he answered the man. "Next time you accuse a poor innocent, Mr. Bell, we trust you will remember there are also laws for her protection."

Maryann was laughing when they got out of the courtroom. "You had the paper all ready for him. What if we had lost?"

Vito was smiling. "We couldn't lose."

"We couldn't?" she asked doubtfully.

He didn't answer her question. "We have a date for dinner?" he asked instead. She nodded.

"What time?"

"Pick me up at my place. Seven thirty," she answered.

"Good," he said. "I got to get back to my office. I'll get you a cab." He signaled and a cab pulled to a stop. He opened the door for her.

She stepped in and looked at him. "What do you mean we couldn't lose? If you hadn't found that cab-driver, we'd have had a hard time."

"Who found the cab-driver?" he asked innocently.

"You mean you—" She broke off, a growing knowledge in her eyes.

He grinned at her. "Who was to say no? Bell was so drunk he didn't remember which driver he had. It was simple enough to get a man from the same company who could remember more than Bell could. Especially a man who works nights and was willing to pick up a few bucks for an easy afternoon's work."

"You are the best," she said, smiling.

He closed the door. "Seven thirty sharp," he said and walked off whistling.

He looked at his wristwatch. It was almost six o'clock. He picked up the telephone, and when his secretary answered, he said: "Call the barber and tell him to wait for me. I'll be down for a shave in a few minutes."

"Right, Mr. Vito," the girl said. He started to put down the receiver, but her voice continued. "I have Mr. Drego on the telephone."

"I didn't call him," Vito said.

"He called just as you picked up the phone," the girl explained.

Vito punched the connecting button. "Yes, Ross?"

"I gotta see you tonight, Hank." Ross's voice was earnest.

"Can't it keep, kid?" Vito said. "I talked the ol' woman into giving me a night off and I got a beautiful babe lined up. Any other time."

"It's got to be tonight, Hank," Ross answered. "They want me to go out west next week. There's some things we have to straighten out first."

"Christ! I got no luck at all," Vito said.

Ross laughed into the phone. "I won't keep you long."

"Yeah," Vito said.

Ross laughed again. "This babe must be somethin' I never heard you sweat over a dame before."

"I don't think there's another like her in the world," Vito said. "She was born to be a woman."

"This I gotta see," Ross said. "Bring her along if she can keep her mouth shut."

"Okay," Vito said. "We'll be at your place at eight."

"No," Ross answered, "better make it the Shelton Club at eight thirty. I'll bring a dame, too. That way, if anyone sees us we'll be out on a ball."

"Right," Vito agreed. He put down the telephone. Ross was a bright boy. Sometimes too bright. He picked up the telephone again and dialed a number.

A voice answered. "Get Joker to the phone," he said. Joker was right. Many years ago he had said the kid would need a lot of handling.

CHAPTER THREE

T HE CAB DROPPED HIM AT A BROWNSTONE HOUSE ON WEST 73RD Street. He paid the driver and walked up the steps. The light in the hall was dim, and he had to strike a match to find her name. *Maryann Flood*. He pressed the bell.

Almost immediately there was an answering buzz at the door. He pushed it open and came into an old-fashioned hallway. Her door, marked by a gold letter C, was at the top of a flight of stairs. He was about to knock when she opened it.

"Come in," she said, smiling, and stepped back to let him enter.

He came into the room, taking off his hat. At first glance he was surprised It was neatly and simply furnished, and still there was a sense of the exotic in the apartment It was in the thick, rich pile of the rug, the bizarre wall fixtures, a sword, an ancient gun, a cat-o'-nine-tails The light was soft on the deep-maroon paint of the walls and ceiling Under the windows were bookshelves filled with books and knickknacks.

"Your coat?" she asked, still smiling.

"Oh—sure." He slipped it off.

She took it from him. "There's ice and whisky on the side table," she said. "I'll be ready in a few minutes."

He walked over to the side table. The ice bucket was sterling silver. The glasses were good Steuben tumblers. The Scotch was Johnnie Walker Black Label, the rye Canadian, the bourbon Old Grand-dad, the gin House of Lords. "You live pretty good," he said.

Her quilted housecoat of green velvet swirled as she turned to look at him. "I should," she said, unsmiling. "That's the only reward of my profession. And there's no guarantee that it will continue, so I make the most of the moment."

He filled a glass and walked over to the bookshelves. They contained current fiction, some good, some bad. "Did you read all these?" he asked curiously.

She nodded. "I generally have the whole day to kill."

He tasted his whisky. "Can I fix you a drink?" he asked.

"No, thanks," she said. "I'll get one." She poured some creme de cassis into a tumbler, added a few ice cubes and then soda. She raised the glass. "To the smartest lawyer in New York."

He grinned. "Thank you." He held up his own glass. "To the most fascinating client an attorney ever had the good fortune to serve."

"Thank you." She put down her drink and walked toward the bedroom. "How shall I dress? Where are we going?"

He followed her to the bedroom door and stood looking at her. "Dress it up," he said. "We're going to the Shelton Club. I have to meet a client."

She raised her eyebrows. "The Shelton Club—we're really livin'."

"Nothing but the best," he said, grinning.

She slipped out of her housecoat and sat down in front of a vanity table. He caught his breath, she had done it so casually. She wore nothing but a strapless brassiere, panties, and long silk stockings that were secured to, a tiny garter belt around her waist. She glanced at him mischievously. "Excuse the working clothes."

He held his hands in front of his eyes. "I'll be all right in a minute," he said. "It's just that I'm not used to women."

She laughed as she began to put on make-up. "You're nice, Hank. I like you." "Thanks," he said.

She turned to him. "I mean it. There are very few men I do like. They're mostly animals."

His face was suddenly serious. She ought to know better than most. "I hope we can be friends," he said.

Her eyes were wise. "I hope so," she said candidly, "but I doubt it."

He was surprised. "Why?"

She got to her feet and turned toward him. An indefinable change had come over her. He felt a pulse beating in his temple. In the soft light of the room she seemed suddenly to have turned into an erotic statue; her breasts were full and thrusting, the curve of her belly warm and inviting, her legs like long-stemmed flowers. His mouth was suddenly dry. He held his glass to his mouth, but did not drink from it. He just wanted the cold moistness against his lips. "You're beautiful," he whispered.

A half-smile came to her lips. "Am I?" she asked. "Not really. My legs are too long, my bust too full, my shoulders too broad, my eyes too big, my chin too square, my cheekbones too high, my mouth too wide. Everything's wrong, according to the fashion. Yet you say I'm beautiful."

"You are," he said.

Her eyes stared through him. "You mean something else, not beauty. You mean I'm good for something else, don't you?"

"What else is the measure of beauty?" he asked.

The smile disappeared from her lips. "That's what I mean. That's why I doubt we can be friends. It always comes to that."

He smiled at her. "I know you," he said softly. "You don't want it any other way. It's your only weapon. It's your only way to be equal."

She stared at him a moment, then sat down again at the vanity table. She picked up a powder puff and offered it to him. "Powder my back," she said. "Maybe you'll be different from all the others. You're smarter."

He stared at the powder puff for a moment, then turned away. "If we're goin' to be friends," he said, "powder your own back. I'm only human."

When she came out of the bedroom he got to his feet and whistled. She wore a simple off-the-shoulder dress of gold lamé that clung lightly to her figure and fell to her calf. Sheer silk stockings and gold shoes. In her ears she wore tiny heart-shaped gold earrings, and around her throat a single large topaz-like stone hung on a gold-mesh chain. Her hair was white-blond and shimmering against the yellow gold of her costume.

She smiled at him. "You like?"

He nodded. "Fabulous!"

She brought his coat from the closet and draped a light-colored mink scarf around her shoulders.

"Ready?" he asked, smiling. Ross's eyes would pop out.

"Always ready," she replied.

As they started for the door, the telephone began to ring. He stopped and looked at her. "Don't you want to answer it?" he asked.

Her eyes met his. "My answering-service will get it. It's probably a client who doesn't know I'm taking a night off."

They sat back in the cab and he gave the driver the destination. She put her hand through his arm. The light scent of her perfume came to him.

"What do you want out of life, Maryann?" he asked.

The darkness hid her eyes from him as she spoke. "Everybody asks the same question. Do you want the stock answer or the truth?"

"The truth, if we're to be friends," he said.

"The same thing that everyone else wants," she said. "Love. A home. Family. Security. Marriage. I'm no different from any other girl."

He hesitated. "But—" he started to say.

She interrupted him. "I'm a whore, you were going to say."

It was as if she picked the thought from his mind. He coughed embarrassedly.

"That doesn't make me a second-class citizen," she said quietly "I feel everything that any other girl feels. I bleed as much when I'm cut, I cry as much when I'm hurt I work just as hard at my profession as any other girl works at hers It's more difficult to be a competent whore than it is to be a competent secretary or clerk."

"Then how come you never tried anything else?"

"How do you know what I tried?" she asked quietly. "Why are you a lawyer instead of a doctor? Because this is what you're best at. Well, this is what I'm best at."

"I'm a lawyer also because it's what I want, what I was born for," he said quickly.

"As one professional to another"—she smiled—"all my life I fought it. Ever since I was a kid and the boys were ganging up after me, I fought it. Someone once told me that this was what I was born for. I didn't believe him, but he was right. I know it now."

He took her hand and patted it gently. Suddenly he realized he liked this girl very much. She had a curious form of honesty. "I hope someday you'll get what you want."

At the restaurant she waited while Vito checked his hat and coat. Ross's back was to them as they approached. He was busy talking to a dark-haired girl seated next to him.

Vito stood behind him, his hand on Maryann's arm. "Ross," he said.

Ross turned around quickly and looked up, smiling, his dark eyes bright. "Hank!"

"Ross, I'd like you to meet Maryann Flood," Hank said. "Maryann, this is Ross Dre—" His voice suddenly vanished.

Ross's face had gone white. For a moment Hank thought the man had become ill, there was such agony in his expression. Only Ross's eyes were alive—alive and bright with a hunger in them that Vito had never seen before. Finally Ross spoke. His voice trembled. "Mar—Marja!"

Vito looked at Maryann. Beneath her make-up her face was pale, but she was more composed than Ross. She held out her hand to him.

"Ross!" she said in a husky voice. "It's been a long time."

"Seven years, Marja," Ross said. He struggled to his feet. "Sit down, Hank."

They seated themselves. "We grew up together, Hank," Ross explained, his eyes on Maryann. "Remember what you said over the phone, Hank? This is the only girl in the world I would believe that about!"

Vito looked from one to the other. The same angry vitality was in each. They were so alike in their differences that they might have come from the same mold, with only a different finish to each. He put his hand on the table and leaned forward. "Tell me about it," he said.

CHAPTER FOUR

THE DARK-HAIRED GIRL WHO HAD COME WITH ROSS WAS ANNOYED. FOR all the attention she had been getting throughout dinner, she might as well not have been there. It made no difference to her what Ross and Maryann had done when they were kids.

But it did to Hank Vito. It explained to him a lot of things about Ross and about Maryann. Things that had puzzled him. Silently he filed away their reminiscences. He was a collector of odd bits of information about people. In his business, such information not infrequently came in handy.

One thing he saw at once: he would have to wait his turn with Maryann. If ever there had been unfinished business between two people, here it was between these two. He looked at the dark-haired girl and smiled. "What do you say we buzz off and leave these two to their old-times reunion, honey?"

The girl returned his smile gratefully. "I'd like nothing better, Mr. Vito. Other people's memories are so dull."

Hank didn't agree with her, but he got to his feet. "Let's go," he said.

Ross looked up at him. "But we haven't got around to our business yet," he protested.

Hank smiled. "Make it at my office first thing in the morning." He held out a hand to Maryann. "Good night, friend."

Her smile was bright and warm. "Good night, counselor."

Ross watched them leave, then turned to Maryann. "Sit next to me."

Silently she moved into the place the other girl had vacated. Ross covered her hand with his own.

"Another drink?" he asked.

She shook her head. "No thanks."

"I'll have one." He gestured and the waiter brought him another Scotch. "How did you meet Hank Vito?" he asked.

She looked into his eyes. "I was in trouble and needed a lawyer. I went to him."

"You went to the best," Ross said. "He's expensive, but there aren't any better."

"Sometimes the most expensive is the cheapest in the long run," she answered.

"He's my lawyer, too," Ross said.

She raised her eyebrows questioningly.

"I work for the syndicate," Ross said. "You know what that is?"

She nodded.

"I'm clean, though," he said quickly. "I handle the legit operations. Right now they want me to move out to L.A. to set up a construction company. That's why I wanted to see Hank tonight."

She didn't speak.

"Remember Joker Martin?" Ross asked.

She nodded.

"He's one of the wheels now. I used to be with him, but now I'm independent. I convinced them that I'm better off working alone." Ross offered her a cigarette and held a light to it. "He was the only one who would give me a job when the old man kicked me out."

She looked into his eyes. "You're doin' pretty good."

He nodded with satisfaction. "There's a lot of dough around, baby, and I'm in line for it."

"If the Army don't get you," she said.

He laughed. "They won't get me."

"You seem sure."

"It's easy to beat the draft if you know the right medics," he said.

"They can't help once you're down at Grand Central," she said. "All the notes in the world don't hold up there."

He tugged his ear lobe. "I've got draft insurance. A twenty-five-hundred dollar hole in my eardrum."

She shook her head. "You haven't changed a bit, Ross. Still got an angle for everything." Suddenly she was tired. Ross reminded her of times long past and of things she didn't want to remember. She reached for her scarf. "It's getting late, Ross. I think I'll go home."

"I'll take you," he said quickly. "My car's outside."

"Got gas?" she asked.

"Sure," he laughed. "This is Ross you're talkin' to, remember, honey?"

She had never got used to the dimout in the city and the way it made everything seem hushed and quiet. She gave him her address and leaned back in the car as it sped through the night. She closed her eyes, feeling far away from the people and places she knew.

It seemed she had been riding a long time when the car stopped. She opened her eyes. She wasn't home. "Ross" she said sharply.

"Look, baby." He gestured toward the car window. "It's been a long time."

She turned and looked at the river, sparkling in the occasional flickers of light.

Riverside Drive—where they had been together so many times.

She felt his arm move along the seat behind her, and turned to him. "Cut it, Ross. It *has* been a long time, an' yuh can't go back. Take me home."

She saw his mouth set in the petulant look she remembered as he started the car again. A few silent minutes later they were at her door.

Ross looked at her. "You could invite me in for a drink," he said. "Just for old times' sake."

"Okay," she said reluctantly. "Just one."

He followed her into the apartment. "There's liquor on the side table," she said.

She put his coat on a chair and went into the bedroom. A few minutes later she returned wearing a green velvet housecoat.

He looked up at her and smiled. "You're still the greatest."

"Thanks," she said dryly.

He wrinkled his brow quizzically "What's eatin' you, baby? Still mad over what happened between us so long ago?"

She shook her head "Not any more Ross. Too much has happened to me I can't be angry over that"

He reached for her arm, but she stepped out of reach. "Then what is it? I still got that big yen for you I always had."

She smiled slowly. "I know. The same yen you have for all the girls."

His voice lowered. "It's different with you, baby. It's always been different."

"Yeah, Ross, yeah." Her voice was sarcastic.

He put down his drink and moved quickly. Catching her shoulders in his big hands, he held her still. Her eyes looked at him without fear. "Still the same little tease, ain't you, baby?"

"Still the same rough-action boy, ain't you, Ross?" she replied.

"I'm older now," he said. "You can't get rid of me as easily as you did the first time." He pulled her to him. Her arms went around his neck. He smiled. "That's better, baby." He bent his head to kiss her.

A sudden blinding pain seared through his temples. With a curse, he slipped to the floor and looked up at her. The pain was gone as soon as he let her go, but there was a dull ache in his neck. "You bitch!" he snarled. "What did you do?"

She smiled down at him. "A friend of mine in the service taught me. It's called pressure points. Judo."

He got to his feet and reached for his drink. "You haven't changed a bit, have you?"

Without answering, she turned to the sideboard and mixed herself a drink. He watched her. "What's that?" he asked.

"Cassis and soda," she said.

He made a face. "That's like medicine."

"I like it," she said.

He looked around the apartment. "Nice place you got here."

"Thanks," she said.

"You must be doin' pretty good yourself."

"I make out."

"What line are you in?" he asked curiously.

She stared at him for a moment. Just then the telephone began to ring. She walked over to it and picked it up. Covering the mouthpiece with her hand, she looked right into his eyes. "I'm a whore," she said.

His breath seemed imprisoned in his chest. As if from a distance he heard her speak into the phone. "No, honey, not right now. I'm busy. Try tomorrow, will yuh?"

She put down the telephone and walked across the room and picked up his coat. She held it toward him. "Now, will yuh go, Ross? I'm tired."

He didn't move from where he stood. His eyes were still on her face. His hand went into his pocket and came out with a roll of bills. He snapped his fingers and the bills shot toward her and cascaded down around her. "I just bought the rest of the night," he said.

They lay quietly in the bed. The faint night sounds of the city seeped into the room through the closed windows. He turned toward her. The glow of her cigarette flickered, throwing a soft red glow on her face.

Something inside him ached. He reached toward her. Her hand was soft and cool. He remembered her touch and the wild excitement that it brought to him. "Marja," he whispered.

He felt the soft answering pressure of her fingers. "Marja," he whispered softly, "didn't you feel anything? Anything at all?"

Her voice was low and husky. "Sure, honey. You're quite a man."

"Marja, I don't mean that!" His sound was an agonized whisper Suddenly something burst inside him and he began to cry. So much had been lost. Deep, racking sobs tore through him.

Her arms went around him, drawing his head down to her breast. "There, baby, there," she whispered soothingly.

CHAPTER FIVE

THE ODOR OF FRYING BACON HIT HIM AS HE CAME OUT OF THE BATHROOM, still warm from the shower. He finished rubbing himself briskly, then strode into the kitchen, the towel draped around his waist.

Maryann, wearing a simple housedress, was breaking some eggs into a pan on the small stove. She looked up briefly. "Get dressed," she said. "Breakfast'll be ready in a minute."

He stared at her. Her eyes were clear and she showed no trace of the long and angry night. She wore no make-up, and yet her skin glowed with the same healthy animal quality it had always had. "What for?" he asked. "I'm not goin' anywhere."

"Yes, you are," she said, gesturing to a small clock on the stove. "It's almost noon. That's checkout time in this hotel."

His face flushed. It was almost as if he felt the shame she should have felt. "You're checkin' out with me," he said.

"Don't be a fool," she replied quietly. "You can't afford it."

He walked over to her and took her hand. "Marja," he almost pleaded, "is that all I am to you? Just another Joe?"

Her eyes met his steadily. "The name is Maryann. Marja's gone a long time, and all guys are Joe to Maryann."

His gaze fell before hers. "I want to go back, Marja. I want us to do it over. You and me. I'm grown up now. We can have a lot of things together."

"What?" she asked sarcastically. "Marriage?"

He flushed again.

She didn't give him time to answer. "Uh-uh. I'm satisfied the ways things are. I don't have to tie up with anybody." She began to shake the eggs onto a plate. "Better hurry," she said, "or the eggs'll get cold."

He could feel a futile anger rising in him. "If it was Mike, I bet you wouldn't act like that!" She flinched suddenly and he knew that he had scored. "What has that dope got for you, anyway? He'll never be anything but a jerk cop again once he gets out of the Army!"

Her voice was low. "Mike's in the Army?"

"Yeah," he said. "He enlisted the day after Pearl Harbor. Just a week after he got on the regular force, too."

"Oh," she said. "Is he overseas?"

"How the hell should I know?" he snarled. "I have better things to do than to keep tabs on him!" He turned back to the bedroom. "Maybe you would like me to look him up for you," he flung back nastily over his shoulder. "I'll tell him you have special rates for servicemen!"

Joker Martin entered the restaurant and came over to Vito's table. Vito looked up and signaled the waiter as he sat down. "You look worried, Joker," he said.

"I am worried," Joker answered. "I can't get Ross to stay out west. He keeps comin' in every other month. I just had another wire from him. He's on his way in now."

Vito ordered two drinks. "How about another boy?" he asked.

Joker stared down at the table. "I thought about that, too, but who could I use? The crowd out there likes Ross. His family background is a great cover. Besides, there's no one else smart enough, an' if they are, I can't trust 'em."

Vito scratched on the tablecloth idly with a pencil. "This has been goin' on for about five months now?"

Joker nodded.

Vito threw the pencil down. "It's that dame," he said.

Joker looked at him shrewdly. "What dame?"

"Maryann," Vito said. "She told me that Ross was after her to go out west with him, but she doesn't want to."

"Maryann?" Joker was puzzled. "Who is she? Ross want to marry her?"

Vito shook his head. "No, he doesn't want to marry her. At least, she never said he did. He just flipped his lid over her, that's all." He laughed. "I can't blame him for that, though. I almost did myself."

"Ross never mentioned no dame to me," Joker said. "What kind of a broad is she?"

Vito looked at him. "She's a special kind of broad. Made for it. A whore with a code of ethics."

"No hustler's got ethics," Joker said. "The only language they understand is dough."

"You don't know Maryann," Vito said. "You can buy her time, but you can't buy her."

"Maryann," Joker said softly. "That's a queer name for a whore."

"Maryann Flood," Vito said.

Joker's face was suddenly red and excited. "A blonde girl with wide brown eyes that stare right through you?"

"Yeah," Vito answered curiously. "You know her?"

Joker didn't answer. He pounded the table softly with his fist. "The son of a bitch!" he swore. "The no-good bastard!"

"What's got into you?" Vito asked. "What're you sore about?"

Joker picked up his drink and swallowed it. "I should've guessed. Marja Flood."

"That's what Ross calls her," Vito said in a surprised voice. "Then you do know her?"

Joker nodded. "I know her, all right. She worked for me at the Golden Glow when she was a kid. I damn near lost my license for givin' her a job. She was under age then."

"Oh," Vito said.

"She was sent up for cuttin' her stepfather with a kitchen knife. I heard about her when she got out, but lost track after that," Joker said. He signaled for another drink. "Ross always had a yen for that dame, but she couldn't see him. There was another guy, Ross's pal. He was her boy."

"What happened?" Vito asked.

"She got sent up, I tol' yuh," Joker said. "After that I don't know what happened. First I hear in five years is from you."

Vito's legal mind didn't like loose ends. "I mean about this friend of Ross's. What happened to him?"

"He became a cop an' then went into the Army. Ross mentioned it once before he went up for his operation." Joker sipped his drink reflectively. "She was quite a broad even when she was a kid. She had man sense even then. She still the same?"

Vito laughed.

Joker held up his hand. "Don't tell me, I know." He lit a cigarette, and Vito noticed that his fingers were trembling. "I had big plans for that kid myself," Joker said.

The muffled sound of the telephone bell penetrated her sleep. She rolled over on the bed and put her face in the pillow. It kept ringing, and reluctantly she woke up. Only in an emergency did the answering-service let the telephone ring. She picked up the phone. "Hello," she said into it.

"Maryann?" a cautious voice asked. "Frank."

She was wide awake now. It was Frank Millersen. Detective Lieutenant Millersen. "Trouble again, Frank?" she asked, looking at the clock. It was almost ten in the morning. He hadn't called since the time she had been charged with that larceny rap.

"No," the cautious voice laughed softly. "You're okay."

An almost inaudible sigh of relief escaped her lips. It had been a long time since Millersen had first picked her up. A green kid she was then. She had spent thirty days in the can, but she had made friends with him. "What is it, then?" she asked, her voice growing husky. "Want to see me?"

The voice laughed again. "No, thanks, Maryann. I can't afford it on a cop's pay."

"You know it ain't the dough with you, Frank," she said "I like you."

"Don't con me, Maryann," he laughed "We both know better. I just called to tell you I located that ex-cop you asked me about a few months ago. The one that went into the Army. Mike Keyes, your girl friend's brother"

An excitement ran through her. She had called him as soon as Ross had left that first time, and told him the first story that came to her mind. "Yeah?" she said, controlling her voice carefully. "Where is he?"

"St. Albans Veterans Hospital," he said. "Been there three weeks. He was wounded in North Africa."

Despite herself, a note of concern crept into her voice. "He was wounded?"

"Yeah. But not too bad, from what I hear. He's gettin' out on a week-end pass tomorrow mornin'. If your girl friend wants to catch him, she better get out there before eight o'clock. Otherwise, it'll be too late. You know how soldiers are." Millersen chuckled again. "The last thing they go lookin' for is their sisters."

"Thanks very much, Frank," she said, putting down the telephone. She reached for a cigarette and lit it thoughtfully. She could see Mike's face in the blue smoke before her. The hurt in his eyes the last time she had seen him.

She wondered what he would do on his week-end pass. His father and mother were in California, where the old man had a defense job. That was what she had been told when she called the house where Mike had lived.

She wondered if he had a girl friend he was going to see. Something inside her ached at that thought. He probably never thought about her any more. Slowly she ground out the cigarette in an ash tray. She was sorry she had ever given in to the impulse to ask Frank to locate Mike for her.

CHAPTER SIX

SHE PARKED THE CAR ACROSS THE STREET FROM THE GATE TO THE HOS-pital and waited. The big A.W.V.S. bus was at the corner, waiting to take the soldiers into the city. She looked at her watch. It was seven thirty. She shivered slightly and lit a cigarette. It had been a long time since she had been up so early in the morning.

After a while she began to feel a little silly. It was stupid to get up in the middle of the night and drive all the way out here just to look at him. Not to talk to him, not to touch him. Just to see him walk a few feet and get into a bus. He would never even know she was here.

She was on her third cigarette when the gate opened and the first group of soldiers came out. A sudden fear came into her. They all looked so much alike in their uniforms. She wondered whether she would recognize him. He might have changed.

A small Red Cross Mobile Canteen was set up in front of the gate, and women were busy handing out doughnuts and cups of hot coffee to the boys. Two more buses came up and pulled in behind the first one.

Eagerly she scanned the soldiers' faces. The first bus was full now, and its motors caught with a roar. It pulled off, and the second bus moved up to take its place. The raucous sounds of the men's laughter came to her.

The second bus drove off and the last bus moved up. She looked at her watch nervously. It was a quarter past eight. Millersen had been wrong. Mike wasn't coming out. There were fewer soldiers now. The rush was over.

She scanned each face quickly. Maybe she had missed him in the crowd which had got on the earlier buses. Now there were only a few soldiers coming down the path. The Mobile Canteen was shutting its flaps. She heard the woman who seemed to be in charge telling the other that it was time to go. The Canteen drove off.

She ground out her cigarette in the dashboard tray and turned on the ignition. Either she had missed him in the crowd or he wasn't coming out. She pressed the starter, and the motor caught. The last bus started out into the road before her.

She put the car into gear and started to move. A last impulse made her look across the road. He was just turning through the gate. Her foot hit the brake automatically and she stared.

He was thin, terribly thin; his cheekbones stuck out, and his eyes were blue hollows above them. He walked with a slight limp, as if favoring his right leg. As he saw the bus disappearing around the corner, he stopped and she saw him snap his fingers in a familiar gesture of disappointment. She could almost hear the "Damn!" his lips framed.

Slowly he shifted his small canvas bag from his right hand to his left hand. He struck a match and lit a cigarette, then flipped the match into the gutter, and began to walk down the street.

She sat as if paralyzed, looking after him. He seemed strange in a uniform, and yet it was as if he had always worn it. Everything about him was wholly familiar. As she stepped from the car, she felt almost as if a magnet were drawing her. She found herself running after him.

Her hand reached out and covered his own on the handle of the bag. There was such a pounding in her ears that she could hardly hear her own voice. "Carry your bag, soldier?"

He turned slowly. Her vision blurred and she couldn't see his face clearly. Was he annoyed? Frightened, she spoke again. "Carry your bag, soldier?"

The cigarette hanging from his lips began to fall. It tumbled crazily across his lapel and dropped to the sidewalk between them. She stood trembling, waiting for him to speak.

His lips moved, but no sound came out. His face began to whiten and he seemed to sway. She put out a hand to steady him. Then it was as if there were a fire between them, for she was in his arms and kissing his mouth and the salt of someone's tears was on their lips.

❖   ❖   ❖

She turned the key in the lock and pushed open the door, looking up at him in the shadows of the hallway. "We're home, Mike," she said.

He walked into the room and turned to face her. Her explanations had already been made. She had told him about the friend who had found him for her.

She closed the door behind her, and a sudden shyness came over her. "Sit down and rest," she said. "I'll fix you a drink." She walked over to the sideboard. "What'll it be?"

"Gin over rocks," he said, his eyes following her.

Quickly she poured the drink and handed it to him. She took the cap from his head and studied his face. "You've changed, Mike."

He smiled slowly. "I'm a man now, Marja. I couldn't stay a boy forever. You told me that, remember?"

Her eyes were on his. She nodded.

He raised his drink to her. "To the children we were," he said.

"Mike!" There was the echo of pain in her voice. "Let's not remember. Let's pretend we are just meeting, with all our yesterdays forgotten and nothing but bright tomorrows before us."

The corners of his mouth twisted. "It's pretty hard to pretend, Marja. Too many things are happening all around us."

"For just these few days, then, Mike. Please!"

He put his drink down and held out his arms toward her. She came into them quickly and he placed her head against his chest. She could hear his voice rumbling deep inside him. "I don't have to pretend anything, Marja. Being with you is all I ever wanted."

The telephone began to ring, and he released her.

She shook her head. "I don't want to answer it."

"It may be important," he said.

"The only thing important this week-end is us," she answered.

When the phone stopped ringing, she dialed a number. "This is Miss Flood. I'm going away for the week-end. Will you take all the messages, please, and tell everyone who asks for immediate service."

He watched her put down the telephone. "You must have a pretty good job to be able to afford this place."

She smiled. "I've been lucky."

A kind of pride came into his eyes. "Smart, too. Yuh don't get all these things without being smart."

Suddenly cautious, she studied his face for hidden meanings. Then she drew a deep breath. "I don't want to talk shop," she said. "I get enough of that all week. This weekend is for me."

It was near midnight when they came in from dinner, still laughing at something he had said in the cab. But his face, she realized, was drawn and tired. She was immediately contrite.

"I been havin' such a ball," she said, "I forgot you were just out of the hospital."

"I'm fine," he said.

"No, you're not," she insisted, crossing the bedroom. "I'll make the bed and draw your bath. You're goin' right to sleep."

"Marja," he protested. "You make me feel like a baby."

"For this week-end," she said, smiling at him, "that's just what you are. My baby."

Quickly she turned down the covers of the bed and went into the bathroom and turned on the hot water. When she came out into the bedroom, he was standing in the doorway looking at her.

"You don't have to give up your bed for me," he said. "I can sleep on the couch."

She could feel a flame creeping up in her face. She crossed the room and put her arms around his neck. "Mike," she whispered, "you're such a fool." She kissed him.

He stood very still for a moment, then his arms tightened around her until she could hardly breathe. There were lights spinning before her eyes and the room was turning over and over. She could feel his muscles tighten strongly against her. She closed her eyes. It had never been like this. Never. This was for her. This was her feeling, her emotion, her life force. It was her beginning and her ending. The world and the stars were exploding inside her.

"Mike!" she cried. "I love you, Mike!"

CHAPTER SEVEN

S HE LAY QUIETLY IN THE BED WATCHING HIM SLEEP. THE GRAY LIGHT OF the morning filtered through the drawn blinds. A stray shaft of sunlight fell across his mouth. He seemed to be smiling. She rested her head on the pillow, scarcely daring to breathe for fear it would disturb him. The weekend had so quickly become yesterday. She closed her eyes to better remember.

"We could be married before I check in." His voice was low.

Startled, she opened her eyes. "I thought you were sleeping," she said.

"We have time. I don't have to report until noon." He was looking right into her eyes.

She didn't answer.

His hand sought her fingers. "What's wrong, Marja?"

She shook her head. "Nothing."

"Something is," he said. "I feel it. Ever since I first asked you yesterday. Don't you want to marry me?"

She turned her face to him. "You know better than that."

"Then what is it?" he asked. "From here I go to officer candidate school. Lieutenants get pretty good pay. We can manage on that. At least we could be together until I go overseas again."

"Mike," she whispered, "please stop. Don't ask me any more."

"But I love you, baby," he said. "I want you with me always. Is it your job? The money you get?"

She shook her head.

"When I get out of service, I'm goin' to law school," he said. "Lawyers make out pretty good."

"No, Mike, no."

He pulled her to him and kissed her. "If there's something you're afraid of, baby, tell me. I don't care what it is. Nothing you can do or have done can keep us apart. I love you too much."

She looked up into his eyes. "Yuh mean that, don't you?" she whispered.

He nodded.

"Someone else said that to me once, but he didn't mean it."

"He didn't love you like I do," he said. "Nobody ever has or will."

She took a deep breath. "I wish I could believe it. Maybe someday—"

"Marry me and see," he said, smiling.

The doorbell rang sharply. He looked at her. "Expecting someone?"

She shook her head as the bell rang again. "It's probably the milkman. He'll go away."

But the bell didn't stop ringing. "Maybe you better go see who it is," he said.

"Oh, all right," she said, reaching for her robe. She slipped into it and went into the other room, closing the bedroom door behind her.

She opened the hall door. "Yes?" she asked.

"I knew you were home," Ross said, "even though you didn't answer the phone all week-end."

She placed her foot behind the door. "You can't come in," she whispered. "I told you never to come unless we spoke first."

He stared at her balefully. "How's anybody goin' to talk to you when you don't answer the phone?"

"Come back this afternoon," she said, starting to close the door on him.

He pushed it back and she fell back with it. He came into the apartment. She could smell liquor on his breath. "I'm not comin' back this afternoon," he said. "I'm goin' to the coast to stay, an' you're comin' with me!"

"Ross, you're nuts!" she said angrily. "I'm not goin' anywhere with you!"

He grabbed her arm "You're comin'!" he shouted.

The bedroom door opened and Mike stood there. He didn't recognize Ross at first. "Need any help, Marja?" he asked.

Ross knew him at once. "Mike!" he yelled. Then he began to laugh.

Mike was bewildered. "What's the matter with him?"

"He's drunk," she said.

Ross staggered over to Mike. "My ol' buddy," he said. "Will you tell this crazy broad that she's better off comin' to California with me than stayin' on the turf here?"

Mike's voice was cold. "Cut it, Ross. That's no way to talk in front of Marja."

Ross stopped. He looked first at one, then the other. A look of shrewd understanding crept over his face. He seemed to sober suddenly. "That's why you didn't answer the phone all week-end," he said to her.

She didn't answer.

"You were shacked up with him."

Still she said nothing.

He turned to Mike. "I hope she gave you a better rate than I got. A hundred bucks a night is a lot of dough for a soldier. Even if she does throw in bacon and eggs for breakfast."

Mike stared at her. Her face was white.

Ross saw the question in Mike's eyes. "You mean to say she didn't tell you?" he said sarcastically. He turned to her. "That's not fair, baby. Waitin' till the last minute to hand him the tab. He might not have that much dough." He took a roll from his pocket and peeled several bills from it. "Here, Marja. This one's on me."

She didn't move, but stared at Ross as one might gaze in fascination on the face of death.

Ross turned back to Mike. "Here, soldier, take the dough. I just bought you a week-end with the best whore in New York. I always wanted to do something for the Army, anyway."

Mike was staring at her. "It's not true," he said in a husky voice. "Tell me it's not true."

Marja didn't speak, but Ross's voice cut in. "Don't be a schmuck, Mike. I don't have to lie."

"You said you loved me," Mike said.

Still she was silent.

Ross's voice was heavy and sarcastic. "And when she held you, did she tell you how handsome you were? And when you kissed her, did she ask you to feed on her? And when you were flying, did she put—"

A low animal growl sounded in Mike's throat as he sprang at Ross. Too late he saw something flashing in Ross's hand. There was a sharp pain across his head, and he tumbled to the floor. He tried to push himself to his feet, but another pain exploded behind his ear and he sank into a welcome darkness.

Ross stood over him, panting heavily. His eyes were glazed with hatred, the small billy still swinging in his hand. He slashed Mike viciously across the face. "I've owed you that for a long time," he said. Then a fever took hold of him and he began to swing wildly.

"Stop, Ross, stop!" she screamed, clawing at him. "You'll kill him!"

"That's just what I want to do," he said crazily. "For a long time now!" He raised his arm again.

"I'll go with you if you stop!" she cried.

His hand was suspended in mid-air. He shook his head as if to clear it. "What'd you say?"

"I'll go with you if you stop." Her voice was clearer now.

Slowly his hand came down. He looked at the billy in it as if surprised that it was there. Slowly he dropped it into his pocket. His eyes were clear, and his voice was as calm as if nothing had happened. "Get your things," he said softly.

She didn't move. She was looking down at Mike.

He followed her gaze to the floor. "Christ! He's a mess!" A note of wonder was in his voice. He bent over and slipped his arms under Mike's shoulders. "I'll get him into bed and clean him up a little while you're packing."

It was almost dark when Mike opened his eyes. There was a dull, throbbing pain across the bridge of his nose. He stifled a groan. "Marja!" he called.

There was no answer.

Reluctantly, memory came to him. Stiffly he got out of the bed. A wave of dizziness rolled over him. He held on to a chair until he fought it off, then made his way to the bathroom. In the dark he turned on the cold water. He put his mouth to the faucet and drank thirstily. At last the dryness in his throat was gone.

He straightened up and turned on the light. A strange face stared at him from the mirror over the sink. The cheekbones were bruised and sore, the nose crushed and flattened, and the lips cut and split. Most of all, the eyes had changed. They were hollow and deep with pain that was not a physical thing. He closed them slowly, then opened them quickly to see if the look would vanish. It didn't. It was still there.

It would always be there. Just as it was now. A look of pain that no amount of tears could ever wash away.

CHAPTER EIGHT

THE BRIGHT CALIFORNIA SUNSHINE WAS BEGINNING TO SLIDE BEHIND THE blue-black shadows of the hills as the tall gray-haired man walked up the steps of the house and pressed the doorbell. From deep within the house came the slight echo of chimes. He looked along the side of the house.

The shimmering aqua blue of the swimming-pool threw off sparkling diamonds of light as the spray reached up into the sun. He could hear the faint sound of a child's laughter coming from the water and the gently admonishing tones of the colored nurse who was patrolling the walk around the pool vigilantly. He was nodding with pleased satisfaction as the door opened.

An old colored man looked out at him. A polite smile of recognition appeared on his face. "Come in, Mr. Martin," he said in a deep, rich voice. "I'll tell Miz Drego you're here."

Joker followed the old man into the large living-room and went over to the big picture window looking out on the pool. He watched the little girl climb out of the water, her white-gold hair shining. Quickly the nurse threw a big Turkish towel around the child and began to dry her.

The child was just like her mother, he thought. There was nothing of Ross in her. Strange that a man as strong as Ross could make no mark on his child. A faint smile came to his lips. But was Michelle really Ross's child? Only Marja could answer that, and he knew better than to ask her. He thought that Ross did too. Joker was sure that if Ross ever asked, Marja would tell him the truth, even if the truth was not to his liking.

The sound of footsteps behind him made Joker turn around. As always when he saw her, he could feel the faint stirrings inside him. Time had not taken anything from her; if anything it had added. There was something about her so rich and basic and vital that you could almost feel it reaching out and touching you. The smile disappeared from his lips. He held out his hand. "Maryann," he said.

She took it. Her hand was warm and strong. Her even white teeth gleamed quickly. "Joker," she said. "It's been a long time."

He nodded. "Four years." He gestured toward the window. "Michelle was only two years old then. She's a big girl now."

Maryann smiled. "Six."

"She's just like her mother. She's going to be a heartbreaker," Joker laughed.

A strange expression flitted across Maryann's face. "Oh, God, I hope not!" she said fervently.

Joker reached for his cigarettes. "You haven't done so bad."

A shadow came into her eyes. "Depends on what you look for, Joker. We all look for different things."

"True," he said.

She pulled the bell cord next to the window. "Can I get you a drink while you're waiting, Joker? Ross won't be home for another hour yet."

"Thanks," he said. "I can use one."

She glanced at him sharply. "Anything wrong?"

His eyes were shrewd. "Depends on what you look for, Maryann." He held a match to his cigarette. "I didn't come to see Ross this time. I came to see you."

Her face was inscrutable. "Yes?" Her voice had just the right amount of polite curiosity.

The old servant came into the room. "Yes, Miz Drego?"

Maryann turned to him. "Bring Mr. Martin some Scotch."

The old man turned and disappeared. Joker looked after him. "Still have the same man, I see."

She nodded. "I don't know how I'd get along without Tom. He's a real friend."

"He worked for that millionaire that got killed in the plane crash, didn't he? What was his name?"

"Gordon Paynter," she answered. "When I read about it, I went and looked Tom up. I was very lucky that he was willing to come to me. Gordon had left him well taken care of."

"You knew Paynter, then?" His voice was polite.

"I knew him," she answered in a flat voice. "We were almost married."

Tom came into the room bringing Scotch, glasses, and ice. "Shall I fix the drinks, ma'am?" he asked.

Maryann nodded. They were silent until Tom had given Joker his drink and left the room. Then Joker held up his glass. "Your good health."

"Thank you," she said politely. She sat down in a chair opposite the fireplace and looked at him expectantly. There was that about her which reminded him of a cat. Maybe it was the tawny color of her eyes, or the way she sat there, sensitive and alert.

"Have you noticed any changes in Ross lately?" he asked suddenly.

The expression in her eyes changed only slightly. There was a wariness in them that had not been there a moment before. "What do you mean?" she parried.

His voice was harsh. "You know what I mean."

She didn't answer.

"Ross is getting to be a big man," he said. "Some people can't take it."

"He's very nervous," she said. "He works hard."

"So do I," Joker said flatly. "So do a lot of people, but they don't act like Ross."

"You know Ross," she said. "He's a kid in some ways."

"I know Ross," he said. "That's why I'm out here."

Her eyes looked at him levelly. "What do you expect me to do?" she asked.

He turned to the sideboard and made himself another drink before he spoke. He looked out the window. The child and the nurse were coming toward the house. They disappeared around the corner. "Do you love Ross?" he asked.

There was a faintly admonishing tone in her voice. "Joker, isn't that a silly question?"

He turned from the window and looked at her. "I don't know. You tell me. Is it silly?"

She didn't answer.

"You've been livin' with him for seven years now. You must feel somethin' for him or you wouldn't still be here." He sipped his drink. "All I want to know is whether it is love or not."

Her eyes gazed directly into his. "I like Ross, if that's what you want to know."

He shook his head. "That's not what I want to know. I want to know if you love him."

A shadow came into her eyes. "No, I don't love him."

He let a deep breath escape his lips. He had been counting on just this answer. It would make things easier. He sat down in the chair opposite her. "Ross has an incurable disease," he said slowly. "Ambition. It's going to kill him."

He could see her face whiten under the tan. "It is really incurable or do some people just think it is?"

He shook his head. "It's too far gone, there's no way to cure it now. Nobody has faith in the patient."

"Is it that last hotel? The Shan Du?" she asked.

"That and other things. That was the last straw. He should have known better than to use our money for himself."

"But he paid it all back," she said.

"The money, yes," he said. "But he shared nothing else. We didn't put him out here to be an independent operator. We took too many chances."

"If I spoke to him?" she asked.

"It wouldn't help now," he said. "They've already made up their minds."

"You mean you've made up your mind," she snapped.

He shook his head slowly. "No. The only reason I came out was to see that you're all right."

CHAPTER NINE

"YOU'RE GETTING TOO WELL KNOWN, ROSS," JOKER SAID AS HE reached for another roll. "You're goin' to have to cut back a little bit. Too many eyes are on you. The columns report every move you make."

Ross shoved another slice of steak into his mouth. "What difference does it make?" he asked surlily. "I'm gettin' things done."

"We can't afford the publicity," Joker repeated.

Ross threw his fork down angrily. "What's eatin' you guys back east anyway? The only way to get things done out here is to make a big noise. Then everybody knows you an' runs to help."

"Along with the cops and Internal Revenue and the F.B.I.," Joker added, smiling.

"Nobody's been able to tie anything on me yet, have they?" Ross asked.

"Depends on who you're talkin' about," Joker answered. "And what."

Ross looked at him quickly. He pushed his plate away with a decisive gesture. "You didn't fly out here to give me a lecture on behavior," he snapped. "What's eatin' you?"

Maryann chose that moment to get up. "I'm going up to see that the baby's in bed," she said.

Ross didn't look up. He was staring at Joker as she left the room. "Well?" he asked.

"The Shan Du, for one thing," Joker said softly.

"What about it?" Ross demanded. "It's mine."

Joker shook his head. "You don't understand, kid. That's what's wrong. We got enough opposition without it being from inside."

"There's room in Vegas for twenty more hotels," Ross said.

"Right," Joker answered. "That's why we went into this so long ago. We want as many of them as possible to be ours."

Ross got to his feet. "You mean I can't have anything for myself?"

Joker held up his hands. "Don't get me wrong, Ross. You can have anything you want. I just don't think it's wise."

"I made a lot of dough for you guys," Ross said.

Joker got to his feet and stared at him. "You got your share out of it," he said harshly. "More than just a percentage. Your trouble is that you grab too much. You been like that ever since you were a kid. Always tryin' to grab more than you should. This time you tried too hard." He turned to leave the room.

Ross grabbed at his arm. "What do you mean?"

Joker's eyes were cold and gray. "Remember that time you came to the crap game in the back room of the dance hall? The first time you brought Marja?"

Ross nodded. "What's that got to do with it?"

"You thought you were smart, switchin' dice on us. You weren't so smart. I covered for you then because I thought you'd learn. I can't cover any more." He pulled his arm from Ross's grip and walked out of the room.

Maryann was just coming down the stairs. "Going so soon?" she asked.

He looked at her. "Yeah," he said, "I can't wait. I got some people to see."

"There's no other way?" she asked.

He shook his head almost imperceptibly. He hesitated a moment, then spoke in a very low voice. "I'd take the kid and go for a little trip if I were you."

She stood very still. "It's that bad?"

"It's that bad," he said. "You'll go away?"

She shook her head. "No. I can't leave him now. I'll send the baby away in the morning, though."

A look of admiration crossed his face. "Okay, but be careful. Stay away from the open windows." He walked to the door and opened it. He looked back at her. "I'll call yuh some time."

She watched the door close behind him, then walked into the living-room. Ross was pouring himself a drink. "What did Joker want?" she asked.

"Nothing," he answered.

"Nothing?" she asked. "That's not like him. He didn't come all the way out here for nothing."

He drained the glass quickly. "I said nothing, and that's what I mean." He slammed the glass down on the sideboard. "Leave me alone," he said angrily. "I gotta think."

She stared at him for a moment, then turned and left the room.

When she had gone, he went to the telephone and dialed quickly. A voice answered. "Pete," he said, "I want you to get two boys out here right away. Joker just left."

The receiver crackled. Ross laughed tensely. "It had to come some time," he said. "We couldn't pay off to them forever. . . . No—I'm not worried. They won't dare try anything. They know everybody's watchin' me. I'm just being careful."

He put down the telephone and mixed another drink. He sank into a chair and sipped it. How much did Marja know? he wondered. He could never figure her out. You could only get so far with her and then you ran into a stone wall. He remembered the time she had told him she was pregnant. It had been a long time ago. They had been out here only two months.

He had come into the apartment they had rented temporarily while he was looking for a house. It was a lavish apartment in one of the big hotels. He walked into the bedroom, looking for her.

A valise was on the bed and she was folding her clothing into it. He crossed the room quickly. "Where do you think you're goin'?" he asked.

Her eyes met his gaze calmly. "Away." Her voice was flat and emotionless.

"What for?" he asked. "I'm treatin' you good."

She nodded. "I'm not complaining."

"Then why are you goin'?"

Her eyes looked right into him. "I'm goin' to have a baby," she said.

"Oh, that," he said, a curious relief running through him. "We can get it fixed. I know a doc that'll—"

She shook her head. "Uh-uh. I want this baby."

A proud smile came over his face. "Then have it. We'll get married and—"

"I don't want to marry you," she said.

He was puzzled. "But you said you wanted the baby."

She nodded. "I do." She snapped the valise shut, brought another valise from the closet, and put it on the bed.

He watched her begin to pack the second valise. "Then, why not get married?" he asked. "After all, if I'm going to be a father, everything might as well be right."

Again her eyes met his across the bed. "That's just it. It's not your child."

He stood very still. He could feel the blood running from his face, leaving it white and pallid. "Whose is it?" he asked, his throat suddenly harsh and hurting.

She shrugged her shoulders casually. "What difference does it make, as long as it isn't yours?"

His hand grabbed her arm across the bed and pulled her toward him roughly. She fell across the bed and looked up at him. There was pain in her eyes, but no fear. He spat the word out: "Mike's?"

She didn't answer.

His free hand flew up and slashed viciously across her face. He could see the white marks of his fingers, then the sudden rush of blood to fill the marks. There was a pounding in his temple. "It was Mike, wasn't it?" he snarled.

A painful, taunting smile came to her lips. "What difference does it make? There's been a lot of guys."

He hit her again. Her head spun to one side and a soft moan escaped her lips. Blood trickled from the corner of her mouth.

"Whore!"

Slowly she raised her eyes to his face. "I never said you could call me by my first name."

He whipped his hand back across her face. She slid across the bed and off onto the floor, where she lay huddled in a small heap. He walked around the bed and looked down at her. She didn't move.

He reached out with his foot and roughly pushed her over. She sprawled out on the rug, her eyes staring up at him without emotion. That was the worst thing of all to him. No expression at all. Not even hatred.

"You're not goin' anywhere," he said, "until I get damn good and ready to kick you out."

"It's Mike's baby," she said dully.

"I don't care," he said heavily. "I don't care whose it is. You're mine. That's all I care about."

CHAPTER TEN

SHE WAS HAVING COFFEE WHEN HE CAME DOWN FOR BREAKFAST. HIS EYES felt heavy and burning. He hadn't slept all night. Silently he sat down at the table. "Morning," he growled.

She smiled. "Good morning." She got up and went into the kitchen. A few seconds later she reappeared with a tray of toast and a fresh pot of coffee.

He looked up in surprise. "Where's Bunny?" Bunny was the maid.

"I sent her away with Michelle," she answered. "I thought it'd be better if they went up to Arrowhead for a while. The baby looked peaked."

He glanced up at her in surprise. Her face was blank. She knew. He could tell that. "Good idea," he said. "Tom go with them, too?"

"No," she said. "He didn't want to."

She poured some coffee into his cup. He sipped it quickly. He needed something to straighten him out. He was tired from tossing and turning all night. Slowly he bit into the toast. It had no taste. He chewed anyway.

"Your watchdogs are waiting in a car outside," she said.

Again surprise ran through him. There was very little she missed. A feeling of bravado ran through his veins. "Joker's not going to get away with this," he said.

She didn't speak.

"You heard me," he said almost hysterically. "Joker can't do anything."

"I heard you," she said softly. "But did Joker?"

He stood up angrily. "I've gone too far to let them push me around."

She didn't speak.

He stared at her for a moment, then left the room. A few minutes later he came back with a gun in his hand. It was an automatic. Quickly he checked the clip, and dropped it in his jacket pocket. He sat down at the table again and picked up his coffee cup. His hands were trembling, and the coffee spilled.

"Give me the gun, Ross," she said quietly.

He frowned at her. "What for?"

"You don't know anything about them," she said. "And you're so jumpy, you might hurt somebody who's got nothing to do with you."

The gun slid across the table, and she dropped it into a drawer. "I feel better this way," she said.

"Maybe you ought to go up to Arrowhead, too," he said.

"Not me." She smiled. "It's lousy for my sinuses. I told you that a thousand times."

"You might get hurt," he said.

"I can fall down the stairs, too," she answered.

He didn't speak, nor did he look at her. He would never understand her. He put down his cup. "Gotta get goin'."

She got to her feet. "I'll be waitin' for you, Ross."

He looked up at her gratefully. "Thanks, Marja," he said almost humbly.

He climbed into the car and sat between the two men. "What's the latest word?" he asked as the car moved out into the street.

"I spoke to Pete a half-hour ago," one of them said.

"Martin hasn't budged out of his hotel room since one this morning."

"Good," he said in a satisfied voice. "Let's go get him."

A tall heavy-bearded man came toward the car as Ross got up. "He's still up there," the man whispered. "I been here all night."

"Thanks, Pete."

"Got the pass key and bribed the freight-elevator boy to go get some coffee," the man continued.

Ross looked at him. "You think of everything."

The tall man's face was impassive. "I do what I'm paid for."

Ross nodded to the two men in the car. Silently they got out and went into the building. Ross could feel his heart pounding inside him. This was it. The big one. He couldn't afford to miss this time. If he did, he was finished.

They walked down a long gray-painted cement-block corridor in the basement of the hotel. Before a door they stopped and Pete pressed a button. The door opened, revealing an elevator. Quickly the men stepped into it.

Pete pressed a button and the door closed. The elevator began to rise. Silently they watched the indicator flash the numbers of the floors. At five the car stopped and the door opened.

"You stay here and hold the car," Pete said to one of the men.

The man nodded and the others walked down the hall Pete studied the doors. At last he nodded. Quickly Ross looked up and down the corridor. It was empty.

Pete slipped a police positive out of his pocket. With his left hand he quickly screwed a silencer on the muzzle. He handed the key to Ross.

Ross looked down at it. It shone brightly in his palm. He took a deep breath. He could feel the sweat trickling down his face and knew that Pete was watching him closely. "Ready?" he whispered hoarsely.

Pete nodded.

Ross put the key in the lock. It seemed to make a loud ratcheting sound as it turned. Quickly he pushed the door open and Pete leaped into the room. Ross followed, half pushed through the door by the man behind him.

Pete cursed softly and ran through to another room. Ross ran after him, only to hear Pete break into a loud string of curses. "What is it?" Ross called as he reached the other door.

He knew the answer as soon as he stepped into the other room. The sweat began to run down his face again. He stared stupidly at Pete. "What the hell went wrong?" he asked.

Pete shook his head. "I dunno."

Ross stared around the room again. It was clean. The room was empty. Joker had gone.

The drone of the engines made Joker drowsy. They always made him drowsy. He could never decide whether it was the sound of the engines or the dramamine he took to keep from being plane-sick that did it, but he usually spent his trips sleeping. He closed his eyes.

Her face jumped in front of his lids, and he stirred uncomfortably. He wasn't like that with dames. He remembered how she had looked at him a long time ago when she was a kid. She had been too young then. Or had he been a fool? She had never been too young!

Then there was the time she got out of the correctional school. He had missed her by only a few minutes. He took a deep breath. It would not be long now. His turn was coming.

Her kid bothered him, though. If it wasn't Ross's kid, that meant there was someone else. He wondered who it could be. She was no dope. Before he got on the plane he had heard that she'd sent the kid up to Arrowhead at five in the morning.

A half-smile came to his lips. That was one of the things he liked about her She was smart. If Ross had had only half her brains he wouldn't be in the mess he was in.

CHAPTER ELEVEN

ALMOST A MONTH HAD PASSED SINCE JOKER HAD GONE, AND ROSS WAS beginning to feel reassured. He felt he had been right: they couldn't do anything to him, he was too much in the public eye. Sooner or later they would have to call him and agree to go along on his basis.

He came into the house, a whistle on his lips. Maryann, waiting in the foyer, looked surprised. It was so complete a change from his nervousness of the past few weeks. She looked at the open doorway behind him. There was no one there.

"Where are your watchdogs?" she asked.

He smiled at her. "I sent 'em away. I got tired of them hanging around."

Her eyes widened slightly. "Yuh think it's wise?"

He walked into the living-room and poured himself a drink. "Joker knows when he's licked. They don't dare do anything."

She watched him silently.

He threw the drink down his throat. The whisky burned slightly and warmed him. The evenings were getting chilly. "Tomorrow we'll go up to Arrowhead, pick up the baby, and go down to Vegas for a little vacation," he said.

She shook her head. "I think we ought to wait a little longer."

"I'm tired of hangin' around," he said. "I don't have to be afraid. We're going tomorrow."

"I'll go see if Tom's got dinner ready," she said, leaving the room.

He watched her go, then poured himself another drink. He would never understand her. If she was afraid, why did she stay with him? There was nothing to keep her here. They weren't married. He wouldn't have blamed her if she had gone away. He sipped his drink slowly. Maybe someday he would know. Maybe someday he would cross the barrier of understanding that lay between them.

She came back into the room. "Dinner's ready," she said.

He stood there for a moment. Suddenly he felt an understanding come into him. He crossed the room and took her hand. "Marja," he said gently, "let's get married tomorrow. We'll make it a real honeymoon."

She looked up into his eyes. For some reason she could feel an ache steal inside her. "Is it what you really want, Ross?"

He nodded. "I know that now. I need you. It's not like it used to be."

She looked down at her hand. His strong brown fingers gripped it tightly. She knew what he meant. Something about him had changed. It was as if the Ross whom she had always known had suddenly grown up. She looked into his eyes, and for the first time she found nakedness and loneliness there. She felt the muscles in her throat tighten. "Okay, Ross," she whispered. "We'll be married tomorrow."

He pulled her close to him and kissed her. "You won't be sorry," he promised.

At dinner he was gay and filled with plans, and told Tom to open a bottle of champagne. His excitement and happiness reached out to her and she began to respond to it.

"We'll build a house," he said.

She laughed. "What's the matter with this one?"

"I want one for ourselves. With our ideas," he said. "Besides, we can't buy this one. The owner won't sell. He'll only rent."

"We can wait a little while," she said.

He shook his head. "Uh-uh. We'll do it now. I got my eye on some property in the hills. An acre and a half. I want everything to be right."

She assumed a demure expression. "You're the boss."

He put down his coffee cup, got to his feet, and came around to where she sat. "I want you to be happy. That's the only thing that is important now."

She took his hand. "I will be, Ross."

The clock chimed ten as they walked into the living-room. He sprawled on the couch and took out a cigarette. "I feel good," he said. "I feel that everything is goin' to be great."

She struck a match and held it for him. "It will be great, Ross. All we gotta do is try and make it so."

"We will," he said. He pulled her down on the couch beside him and kissed her cheek. "I never told you how great I think you are, did I, baby?" he whispered.

She shook her head.

He pulled her head against his chest. "I love you. You know that, don't you? I guess I always loved you, but I never really knew it. I thought it would make me less to admit it."

She didn't answer.

"I remember how I used to feel when I looked at you," he said. "I could almost have bust."

She grinned. "You don't have to be so nice, Ross," she teased. "I already said yes."

He looked down at her, a smile on his lips. "I mean it," he said, his voice serious. "There are so many things I wanted to tell you and never did, it would take me a whole lifetime to remember them all."

A gentle expression came into her eyes. Impulsively she placed her lips against his cheek. "Thank you, Ross," she whispered.

He cleared his throat with embarrassment. He wasn't used to having her say thank you to him. He sat up. "How about some television?" he asked. "We might as well practice up on our marital behavior."

She smiled. "Okay."

He crossed the room, turned on the set, and adjusted the dials. "How's the picture?" he called over his shoulder.

"Pretty good," she said, watching the wavering figures on the screen.

"Can't do any better," he said, coming back to the couch. "It's a kine."

"I'm not complainin'," she said.

He sat down beside her and took her hand. Silently they watched the comedian on the screen. He wasn't very funny, but he worked very hard. Two weeks ago this show had been done live in New York; the coast re-broadcast was on film. On film it lacked spontaneity.

She studied Ross as he looked at the screen. His black hair fell across his forehead. His eyes were no longer the hard, metallic blue of old; they were soft and somehow warmer. She smiled to herself. He had been a long time in growing up.

The telephone began to ring deep within the house. He paid no attention to it. Abruptly it stopped ringing and she heard Tom's soft voice, but couldn't understand his words. She turned her attention back to the screen.

"Miz Drego," Tom's voice came from the foyer entrance.

She looked up. "Yes?"

"They's a call for you, ma'am," the old man said.

She got to her feet. Ross looked up at her. "Hurry back, baby," he said, smiling.

Impulsively she kissed his forehead. "I will, honey."

She crossed the foyer into the small library and picked up the telephone. "Hello," she said into the mouthpiece.

There was no answer. Just a faint hollow sound on the wire.

An icy chill suddenly ran through her. "Hello, hello," she said.

A whisper with an echo of a familiar sound came through the receiver. "Marja?"

"Yes," she said. "Who is this?"

"Marja?" the voice repeated as if she hadn't spoken.

Her fingers turned white under the pressure of her grip on the phone. She knew the voice. She knew why she had been called to the phone.

"Ross!" she screamed suddenly, her voice bursting in her ears. "Ross!"

The sound of a few faint coughs came from the living-room and was lost in a tinkling of glass. The telephone fell from her nerveless fingers and she ran back to the living-room.

Ross was still sitting on the couch. He leaned back against the armrest, his face white and eyes filled with hurt and surprise, his hands clasped tight across his chest. "Marja!" he whispered hoarsely.

She could see blood seeping between his fingers. She glanced at the big picture window opposite the couch. Half of it had shattered and fallen into the room.

She ran to Ross. "Tom!" she screamed. "Call a doctor!"

Ross began to fall toward her. She caught him and held his head against her breast.

"Baby, baby, baby," she cried.

She could feel him shudder with pain. Slowly he turned his face toward her. "I was wrong, Marja," he whispered.

"No, baby," she said.

He spoke slowly, as if each word had to travel a great distance before it could leave his lips. "I was wrong, Marja, but I tried so hard."

"I know, Ross." Tears were running down her cheeks. She kissed his black hair. It was shiny and soaking with perspiration.

He looked up at her. "Marja."

"Yes, Ross?"

"I'm glad the phone rang, Marja. I love you very much." His voice was a hollow echo of pain.

"I love you too, Ross," she said, weeping.

A faint note of surprise was in his voice. "You do, Marja?"

She nodded violently. "Why did you think I stayed?"

He closed his eyes wearily. "You did stay." He was silent for a moment. When he opened his eyes again, there was a curious contentment in them. "I'm glad you stayed, Marja," he whispered. "I would have been afraid if you hadn't."

"I'll always stay, baby," she cried, turning his head to her breasts.

He coughed and a tiny thread of blood sprayed from his lips across her blouse. His head fell forward. She looked down at him. His eyes were blank and unseeing.

She looked down at her white blouse. The small stain of blood was growing wider and wider. The television blasted at her ears with the roar of audience laughter. Gently she lowered his head to the couch.

She got to her feet.

Tom was standing in the doorway, his dark face an ashen gray. "I called the doctor, Miz Maryann."

"Thank you, Tom," she said wearily and crossed the room to turn off the television set.

CHAPTER TWELVE

MIKE CAME INTO THE OFFICE AND TOOK OFF HIS HAT. HE SCALED IT onto a chair opposite his desk, his forehead glistening with sweat. He went to his desk and sat down heavily.

Joel looked up from the other desk. "Warm," he said.

Mike smiled. "Very warm for May. From the looks of it, it's goin' to be a bitch of a summer."

Joel leaned back in his chair wearily. "I'm beat. I had a hell of a week-end. I can't take this heat any more. You'd think the Old Man would okay air-conditioners for the offices."

Mike grinned. "He has an idea that good lawyers are distilled from their own sweat."

"I don't think he's ever sweat in his life, he hasn't enough blood," Joel complained. He picked up a paper from his desk and held it toward Mike. "This has been waitin' for you."

Mike took it from him and glanced at it. "Damn!" he swore.

Joel grinned. "What's the matter, baby?"

Mike looked at him and got to his feet slowly. He picked up his hat from the chair. "Don't crap me. You read it."

"What're you complaining about?" Joel laughed. "You're goin' for a nice automobile ride uptown an' spend a couple of hours in a nice, cool, clean-smelling hospital. You're lucky not to have to stay in this stuffy old office."

Mike was already at the door. "Balls," he said and went out, followed into the corridor by Joel's raucous laughter. He pressed the elevator button and looked again at the paper in his hand.

Suspected abortion.

The elevator doors opened and he stepped into the car. He continued to read as the car descended.

Florence Reese. Admitted Roosevelt Hospital, 7:10 a.m., May 10, '54. Internal hemorrhages due to abortion. Condition critical.

The doors opened and he walked out. He crossed the corridor and opened a door. As he entered, a few men looked up from their newspapers and then looked down again. He went through the room to another door whose frosted glass bore the name *Captain F. Millersen.* He opened the door and went in.

The dark-haired man at the desk looked up. "Hello, Mike," he said in a deep voice.

Mike smiled. "Hi, Frank. I need a man to go up to Roosevelt Hospital with me. Suspected abortion." He tossed the slip of paper onto the detective's desk.

Captain Millersen looked at it briefly. "One of those, eh?"

Mike nodded.

The detective got to his feet. "I think I'll go with yuh on this one, Mike."

Mike's eyes widened. Millersen never went out on a case unless it was a big one. Upstairs they said that he had an uncanny instinct for the big ones, that he smelled them coming. "You're comin' with me, Frank?" he asked in tones of disbelief.

The detective nodded. "Yeah, I'm gettin' a little tired of sittin' behind this desk keepin' my fanny warm."

Mike watched him pick up his hat. "You know somethin' about this that I don't?" he asked skeptically.

Millersen put a cigar in his mouth. "I don't know nothin'. Only that I'm tired of sittin'. Let's go."

The smell of disinfectant was all around them as they strode down the green-walled corridor. They followed the nurse into a ward. At its far end, curtains had been drawn around one of the beds.

"She's in here," the nurse said, holding aside the curtains.

"Is she in condition to talk?" Mike asked the nurse.

"She's very weak," the nurse answered. "Be careful."

He stepped through the curtains, followed by Millersen, and stood beside the bed. For a moment they looked silently down at the young girl lying there.

She seemed to be sleeping. Her eyes were closed and her face was white, a pallid bluish-white color, as if there were no blood beneath the skin. Her mouth was open and her lips were only slightly darker than her cheeks.

Mike looked at the detective. Millersen nodded. He spoke softly to the girl: "Miss Reese."

The girl didn't move. He spoke her name again. This time she stirred slightly. Slowly she opened her eyes. They were so filled with agony that Mike couldn't tell their color. Her lips moved, but no sound came out.

Mike moved closer to the bed. "Can you hear me, Miss Reese?"

The girl nodded faintly.

"I'm Mike Keyes and this is Captain Millersen. We're from the District Attorney's office."

The beginnings of fear began to fleck the girl's eyes. Mike spoke quickly to reassure her. "You're perfectly all right, Miss Reese. You're in no trouble. We just have some routine questions to ask so that we may be able to help you."

Slowly the fear began to vanish. Mike waited for a moment. His words echoed mockingly in his ear. No trouble. Of course she was in trouble. She was only dying.

He smiled slowly and reassuringly. "Have you any relatives we can notify for you?"

The girl shook her head.

"In the city, or out?"

"No!" The girl's voice was a whisper.

"Where do you live, Miss Reese?"

"Hotel Allingham," she answered.

Mike nodded. It was one of the less expensive women's hotels on the west side. "You have a job, Miss Reese?"

The girl shook her head.

"What do you do?"

The girl's voice was faint. "Model."

He exchanged a knowing look with the detective. Half the unemployed girls in New York were models, the other half were actresses. "Free lance or agency?" he asked.

"Agency," the girl replied.

"Which agency?"

"Park Avenue Models," the girl answered. For the first time since Mike had spoken to her, her expression changed. "Let—let Maryann know—"

It seemed to Mike that the girl had an expression of hope on her face. "We will," he said. "Maryann who—where?"

The girl seemed to be gathering her strength for an effort to speak. "Maryann at—at the agency. She knows what to do. She is—" Her voice trailed away and her head slipped to one side.

The nurse stepped quickly to the head of the bed. She felt for the girl's pulse. "She's sleeping," she announced. "You'll have to finish your questions later."

Mike turned to Millersen. The detective's face was white, almost as white as the girl's had been. Mike instantly changed his opinion about the man. He had heard that Millersen was as hard as nails.

Millersen nodded and stepped outside the curtain. Mike followed him. "What d'you think, Frank?"

"We're not going to find anything," Millersen said.

Mike was surprised. "What makes you say that?"

Millersen smiled mirthlessly. "I seen too many of these. They lead to no-wheres."

"But the girl is dying!" Mike said. "We got to do something to find out who did it. The butcher is liable to go to work on another—"

The detective reached out a quieting hand. "Take it easy, Mike. We'll look. But we won't find. Unless the girl tells us."

"I'm gettin' on the phone to that agency. Maybe they'll have some dope for us." Mike started down the aisle between the beds.

Millersen's hand caught his arm. "I'll get on the phone, Mike," he said quickly. "You wait here an' talk to her when she comes to. She's used to you already."

Mike nodded "Good idea." He watched Millersen walk out of the ward, then turned back to the curtains,

The nurse was just coming out. She raised an eyebrow when she saw him.

"I'll wait until she can talk to me again," Mike explained.

The nurse looked up at him. "You can wait at my desk out in the corridor," she said. "It'll be a little while before she can speak again—if ever."

CHAPTER THIRTEEN

TOM OPENED THE DOOR GENTLY, BALANCING THE TRAY WITH HIS FREE hand. "You up, Miz Maryann?" he asked softly.

There was no answer from the large double bed.

He stepped quietly into the room and put the tray down on a small table. Without looking at the bed, he went to the window and drew back the drapes. Bright sunlight spilled into the room. He stood there for a moment looking out the window.

Far below he could see the East River as it wound its way toward the Hudson. The flashing green of Gracie Square Park contrasted with the gray of the buildings surrounding it. He watched a long black automobile turn up the driveway to Gracie Mansion. He looked down at his watch. Eight o'clock. The mayor of this town went to work early. He turned back into the room.

She was already awake, her large brown eyes watching him lazily from the pillow. Slowly she stretched, her arms and shoulders brown and strong.

"Good mornin', Miz Maryann," he said, walking back toward the bed.

She smiled. "Good morning, Tom. What time is it?"

"Eight o'clock," he answered, placing the tray across the bed in front of her. "Time to get up."

She grimaced and sat up. He picked up a silk bed jacket from a chair near the bed and held it while she slipped it over her shoulders. "What's for breakfast, Tom?"

"This diet day, Miz Maryann. Juice an' coffee," he answered.

"But I'm hungry," she protested.

"You very pretty today, Miz Maryann," he said. "You want to stay that way?"

She grinned. "Tom, you're an old butter-spreader."

He grinned back at her. "Go on and eat. Mr. Martin say he goin' come by at ten to take you down to the office."

She picked up the glass of orange juice and sipped it slowly. "Before long you're goin' to be running my whole life, Tom."

"Not me," he said, shaking his gray-flecked kinky black hair. "But I would sho' like to see the man who could."

She laughed and finished her juice. "Any mail?"

"I'll go down and see, Miz Maryann." He turned and left the room, closing the door behind him.

Idly she picked up the paper on the tray and glanced at it. The usual news: rape, arson, murder, and war. She turned to the comic strips as she sipped her coffee. She looked up as Tom came back into the room, carrying a letter.

She took it from him and ripped it open quickly. "It's from Michelle," she said happily.

"Yes'm," he said, even though he had already known. He loved to see her happy. To him, she seemed the saddest and most beautiful woman in the world.

"She passed her midterm exams with the second-highest marks in the class," she said excitedly. "And she can't wait until June and we get out there for her vacation."

A strange look crossed Tom's face. "Kin we go for sure?" he asked.

"I'd like to see anyone try to stop us."

"But Mr. Martin say you might be very busy this summer," he said.

"Mr. Martin can go to hell," she said strongly. "He kept me from going last summer, but he won't this time."

He was waiting in the living-room as she came down the steps of the duplex apartment. He smiled at her. "Good morning, Maryann."

"Morning, Joker. Hope I didn't keep you waiting."

His smile turned into a grin. "I've been waiting a long time now, Maryann. A few minutes won't bother me."

Her eyes met his gaze levelly. "We made a deal."

He nodded.

"A deal's a deal," she said.

"Sometimes I think you're cold as ice."

"Not cold, Joker," she said. "Just bored with it. Enough not to bother any more."

"Even for me?" he asked.

"Even for you," she said. "Remember what we agreed?"

He nodded again. He remembered. Too well.

He had come to the house and Tom had shown him into the living-room. The big picture window had new glass, and through it he could see the edge of the pool. Only this time no child was splashing in its water. He turned when he heard her footsteps.

She stood in the entrance, wearing a simple black dress. Her blond hair shimmered in the fading daylight as she walked toward him. Her face was impassive. "Hello, Joker," she said. She did not extend her hand.

"Maryann," he said.

She didn't take her eyes from his face. "Thanks for the telephone call."

"What call?" he asked.

"Don't pretend, Joker," she said calmly. "I recognize your voice even when you whisper."

He walked over to the couch. "What are you goin' to do now?" he asked.

She shrugged her shoulders. "I don't know. Go to work, if I can find a job."

A look of surprise crossed his face. "I thought Ross left you pretty well fixed."

"He left me nothing," she said without bitterness.

"But you're his widow," he said. "You're even wearing black for him."

"I may be his widow, but I was never his wife," she said. "And that's what they pay off on." A faint smile came to her lips. "Besides, I'm not wearing black for him. It happens to be a good color for me."

He smiled. "It certainly is."

As usual, but still to his surprise, she came directly to the point. "You didn't come here just to tell me how good I look. What did you come for?"

"The boys are worried about you," he said.

Her eyes went blank. "What have they got to worry about? I went through the whole inquest and didn't tell anything."

"They're still worried," he said. "They're afraid someday you might be in trouble and just decide to talk a little bit."

"I know better than that," she said.

"Yeah," he said, "but they're not convinced."

"What do I have to do to convince them?" she asked.

"Come back east with me. They've got a job for you," he answered.

"What kind of job?" she asked suspiciously.

"Running a model agency," he said. "They'll feel better if you're where they can keep an eye on you."

"A model agency?" she asked. "What do I know about that business?"

A smile crossed his lips. "Don't be naïve, Marja."

She stared at him. "And what if I don't come back?"

He took a package of cigarettes from his pocket and held them toward her. She shook her head. He lit one, put the package back in his pocket, and brought out a small photograph. He flicked it over to her.

She looked at it. It was a photograph of a small blonde girl playing on a lawn with her nurse. "It's Michelle," she said, a hollow note of fear in her voice.

He nodded. "Don't worry. She's all right. We just thought you might like to have this picture of her. It was taken up at Arrowhead last week."

She stood there quietly for a moment, then turned and walked to the window. Her voice as it came back to him over her shoulder was empty and resigned. "Nothing else would satisfy them?"

"Nothing else."

"If I do that, there'll be no other ties?" she asked.

"What do you mean?" he asked.

She turned and looked at him with knowing eyes. "Now you're being naïve," she said.

He could feel his face flush. "There'll be no other ties," he said. "But you can't keep a guy from hoping."

She drew in her breath. "Okay," she said.

"Then it's a deal?" he asked.

She nodded.

"I'm glad, Maryann," he said. "I was hoping you wouldn't be stubborn."

"Don't call me Maryann," she said. "Call me madame."

CHAPTER FOURTEEN

"YOU CAN DROP ME AT THE CORNER OF PARK AND 38TH," SHE SAID. "I'll walk from there."

"Okay," he answered, pulling the car over to the curb. He leaned across the seat and opened the door for her. "Dinner tonight?"

She nodded.

"Pick you up at eight at your place," he said.

"Okay," she answered, closing the door.

He watched her walk into the crowd at the corner and cross in front of him. He liked the way she walked. It was the same young stride she had always had. He smiled to himself as he noticed the involuntary second glances that men threw after her. He didn't blame them. A horn honked behind him and he looked up to see that the light had changed. He put the car into gear.

The house was set back in a row of old-fashioned brownstones that had long since become uneconomical to use as dwellings in New York, and had been converted for use as offices. They were filled with small advertising-agencies and con men who labeled themselves *Enterprises*, and anyone else who wanted to pay a little bit more for a little less space but still have a Park Avenue address.

The polished brass plate at the side of the door gleamed at her. 79 Park Avenue. Below it on smaller brass plates were the names of tenants. The plate cost five dollars a month extra. She opened the large outside door and stepped into a long, old-fashioned corridor. A door on her right was labeled *Park Avenue Models, Inc.*, and along the wall beyond it a flight of stairs led up to the other offices.

She walked past the staircase to another door behind it. There was no name on this one. She unlocked it and stepped directly into a comfortable office. She shrugged off her light coat and sat down behind the desk. The shades had been drawn. She switched on a lamp, and the room sprang suddenly into life. On the walls were two very good paintings, and several color photographs of girls. A basket on the desk contained more pictures, and beside it lay a copy of the models' directory.

She pressed a buzzer. A moment later a middle-aged woman came in, obviously excited. "Miss Flood," she said, "I'm so glad you're here. A man called from the police department!"

Maryann looked up sharply. "What?"

"From the police, Miss Flood," the woman repeated.

"About what, Mrs. Morris?"

"Florence Reese. She's in a hospital. An abortion." Mrs. Morris was out of breath. "They wanted to know if she worked for us."

"What did you tell them?"

Mrs. Morris drew herself up. "I told them she didn't work here, of course. That kind of publicity would ruin us. We have a hard time getting work for legitimate girls as it is."

Maryann looked thoughtful. "You shouldn't have lied, Mrs. Morris. Maybe the poor kid is in real trouble and needs our help."

Mrs. Morris looked down at her indignantly. "You know how I feel about girls like that, Miss Flood. You shouldn't even waste a minute with them. They don't appreciate it, and all they do is disgrace themselves and everybody they come in contact with."

Maryann looked down at her desk. That was what made Mrs. Morris such a wonderful front—her honest indignation at the abuses to the profession. She would bust a gut if she knew what went on over the two private phones on Maryann's desk. But Maryann had no time now for Mrs. Morris's indignation. She would have to call Hank Vito and find out the right thing to do. "Okay, Mrs. Morris, thank you. Were there any other calls?"

"Two, Miss Flood. One from Mr. Gellard. He needs three special girls this afternoon. Some buyers are in town and he wants to run a show for them. I suggested some girls to him, but he insisted that he talk to you first. The other is from the 14th Street Fur Shop. They needed a window girl. I sent them Raye Marnay."

"Good," Maryann said, reaching for the telephone. "I'll call Mr. Gellard back."

She waited until the woman had closed the door behind her before beginning to dial. She stared at the closed door thoughtfully while the phone at the other end of the wire rang.

Poor Flo. She had told her just last week not to try the abortion. That she had waited too long. She was almost three months gone. It would have been much smarter to have the baby and place it for adoption. That way was cleaner all around, and, besides, Hank would have seen that Flo got a few bucks out of it. But the panic must have set in and she had probably wound up in the hands of a butcher. Maryann could feel an anger rise up inside her. What kind of doctor could the man be if he would take a chance like that with a kid's life? She was a whore, but she was a human being, too.

A man's voice answered the telephone.

"Maryann," she said.

"Oh." The man's voice sounded relieved. "I was afraid I wouldn't hear from you before lunch. I got these three Texans in, and they're howling for something out of this world. They're up in the hotel now. I promised it to them at lunchtime."

"It's pretty short notice, John," Maryann said.

"I can't help it, honey," the man said. "I didn't know myself until I got to the office this morning."

"Full treatment?" she said. "Act and party?"

"Yeah," he answered.

"It'll be a lot of dough," she said.

"How much?"

"A grand," she answered.

He whistled. "Take it easy, honey," he said. "An expense account can only go so far."

"I can't help it," she said. "The Jelke trial has made good performers hard to get."

"Okay," he said after a moment's hesitation. "Tell yuh where to send them."

She made a few notes with her pencil and hung up the telephone. She waited a moment, then dialed again. A woman's voice answered this time.

She spoke quickly. "Luncheon date, Cissie. Get Esther and Millie. Full booking. It's a charge account."

The woman's voice spoke rapidly. "I got another date."

"I'll switch it," Maryann said. "Here's where you go." When she had finished, she lit a cigarette and reached for the telephone again. Before, she could touch it, it rang. She picked it up. "Yes?"

"Maryann?"

The man's voice was familiar. "Yes," she answered.

"Frank," he said.

"Anything wrong?"

"Girl at Roosevelt Hospital," he said. "Florence Reese. Your office said she didn't work for you. She says she did. Conflicting stories mean trouble. Your woman there is stupid. If she hadn't denied it, I could have stopped it right there, but now too many people are curious."

"What should I do?" she asked.

"I don't know," he said.

"How's Florence?"

"She's dying," he said flatly.

"The poor kid," she said. "I told her not to."

"Stop worrying about her," he said. "It's too late now. You have to think of something."

"Okay, Frank. I'll call Vito. He'll know what to do." She dragged on her cigarette.

"He'd better," Frank said. "I came out on this with one of the D.A.'s white-haired boys. He's boiling over it."

"Who is he?" she asked absently.

"Keyes. Mike Keyes," he answered.

Her throat tightened. "Mike Keyes?" she repeated.

He hesitated. "Yes. I knew there was something about him I was trying to remember. He used to be a cop. Wasn't he the guy you were trying to locate for a dame during the war?"

"I—I don't remember," she stammered. "It was so long ago." Slowly she put down the telephone, staring at the door.

It had been so long ago, it might almost have been another world.

CHAPTER FIFTEEN

IT WAS NEAR FOUR IN THE AFTERNOON WHEN THE NURSE CAME OUT OF THE ward and walked over to his seat near her desk. He looked up at her expectantly.

"You might as well go back to your office, Mr. Keyes. She's gone," she said unemotionally.

Mike got to his feet slowly. "Just like that," he said in a tired voice.

She nodded. "She never had a chance. She was all torn apart." For the first time he heard a sound of feeling in her voice. "The son-of-a-bitch must have used crocheting needles!"

He picked up his hat from the desk. "Hold the body for a p.m. I'll be in touch with the hospital for the results."

His feet felt like lead as he dragged them down the corridor. Florence Reese. He wondered what it had been like for her. It couldn't have been too good. She seemed just a kid. He reached the steps just as Captain Millersen was coming in.

"Learn anything, Mike?" Millersen asked.

He shook his head. "She never spoke again. You?"

Millersen's face settled into an unreadable mask. "I spoke to the bookkeeper at the model agency this morning. She didn't know anything about her. I checked the hotel. The kid got here from some hick town in Pennsylvania about a year ago. She had it pretty tough until about six months ago. Then she seemed to settle down and do all right."

"Her folks alive?" Mike asked as he followed Millersen down to his car.

Millersen nodded. "I spoke to them about an hour ago. They're on their way here now." He laughed. "They thought their daughter had New York by the balls."

"They didn't know how right they were," Mike said grimly.

He came into the office and scaled his hat onto the chair. Joel Rader looked up from his desk. "Had a call for you about an hour ago."

Mike looked at him wearily. "Who was it?"

"Some dame from that agency. Park Avenue Models. The one you had Frank check. It seems the kid had done some work for them, and the dame wanted to know if there was anything she could do."

Mike took his pen and began to fill in the report. "Nothin' nobody could do now. She's dead."

"Too bad," Joel said. "Was she pretty?"

Mike shrugged his shoulders. "Hard to tell when I saw her. Guess so. Anyway, she was young." He finished the report, signed it, and got to his feet. "I guess I'll knock off. I'm beat."

Joel grinned. "Better not let the Old Man see yuh. He's on the warpath. Chewed Alec out somethin' mean."

"Poor Alec," Mike said, smiling. "He always gets it." He tossed the report onto Joel's desk. "Turn that in for me, will yuh?"

"Sure thing."

Joel spun his chair away from his desk and turned to Mike. "Whatever came of that check you ran on that girl? The abortion case last week?"

Mike shrugged his shoulders. "Nothing. The girl died. Why do you ask?"

Joel handed him a sheet of paper. "Look at that."

It was an arrest-and-release report. Several girls had been arrested in a Vice Squad raid on a party. One of them had first said she was a model working for Park Avenue Models, Inc. Later she had changed her story. All the girls had been released the next morning on bail. They had been represented in court by an attorney from Henry Vito's office. The party had been at the apartment of John Gellard, a manufacturer. The raid had been on the basis of complaints against Mr. Gellard by people and parties unspecified. In their complaints they had said that he had openly bragged of his connections with certain unspecified vice rings. A wiretap set that afternoon had revealed that the party to take place that night would be wide open. Mr. Gellard had also been admitted to bail. He had been represented in court by Henry Vito himself.

Joe waited until Mike had finished reading it. "Wasn't Park Avenue Models the same agency that girl mentioned?"

Mike nodded silently. He read the report again.

"What do you think?" Joel asked.

"Too close for coincidence," Mike answered. He got to his feet. "I'm goin' down to see Frank Millersen with this. Maybe he knows something about it."

"Let me know what happens," Joel said, turning back to his desk.

Frank Millersen looked up as Mike walked into his office. "Hello, Mike, what can I do for you?"

"Look at this, Frank." Mike threw the report down on the desk.

Frank picked it up and scanned it quickly. His face was impassive when he looked up again at Mike. "What about it?"

"You know anything about it I don't?" Mike asked.

Millersen put a pipe in his mouth. "Nothing much," he said, lighting it. "Just a routine Vice Squad action." He laughed shortly. "I spoke to one of the boys.

It must have been quite a brawl. He told me when they got there the girls were all—"

"I don't mean that," Mike interrupted. "One of the girls mentioned Park Avenue Models. That's the same one that Florence Reese said she had worked for."

"I don't think that means much," Frank said through a cloud of smoke. "A lot of girls would probably know the name."

"Maybe," Mike admitted. "But why would she later deny it? That's what seems strange to me. Another thing that bothers me is how they could afford Vito's office. He doesn't work for buttons. The ordinary floosie can't get anywhere near him."

"Gellard had him, according to the report," Frank said. "He probably paid for the girls, too. A matter of self-defense."

Mike shook his head. "I don't know. It just doesn't hit me right."

Frank smiled at him. "Forget it, Mike. When you're in the office long enough, you'll see so many of these coincidences that you'll stop bothering about it."

"I can't," Mike said. "I keep remembering that poor kid in the hospital. The way she looked. That wasn't what she came to this town for."

Frank nodded. "She didn't come for that. But if a kid's straight, she never gets into that kind of trouble. I spoke to her old man when he came for the body. She was always a wild one."

"There's a difference between wild ones and bad ones," Mike said. He picked up the report and scanned it again. "I wish I could forget it."

"What are you goin' to do?" Frank asked.

Mike looked up from the report. There was a strange expression in the detective's eyes. An unaccustomed wariness guided Mike's tongue. "I don't know," he answered. "I'll sleep on it first. If there's anything more, I'll call you in the morning."

Frank got to his feet, smiling. "That's smart. Maybe a good night's rest will make a big difference. I'll still be here tomorrow if you decide to go further."

"Thanks, Frank." Mike left the office, but as he crossed the corridor toward the elevator he noticed that he had picked up another paper in addition to the report. He turned back.

He walked through the outer office and opened Frank's door. "Frank—" he said, before he noticed that the detective was on the telephone.

"Hold on a minute, Mary," Frank said, quickly covering the mouthpiece with his hand.

Mike looked at him curiously. Millersen's face, usually florid, seemed to blanch suddenly. "I'm sorry, Frank," he apologized automatically. "I didn't know you were on the phone. I picked this up by mistake." He put the paper down on the desk.

A strained smile came to Frank's lips. "That's okay, Mike. I was just talkin' to the little woman. Thanks."

Mike nodded and left the office, closing the door carefully behind him. Not until he began to walk away from the door did he hear the hum of Frank's voice on the telephone. He went back to his own office, sat down heavily, and stared at the report.

"Well?" Joel asked.

Mike frowned. "Millersen thinks it's nothing."

"Frank ought to know," Joel said. "He's the expert."

Mike studied the report again. After a moment he turned to Joel. "Do you happen to know the name of Frank's wife?"

Joel grinned. "Sure. Mrs. Millersen."

"Not funny," Mike said. "Do yuh know?"

"Why?" Joel asked.

"Just curious," Mike answered. "He was talkin' on the phone to her when I came in."

"Elizabeth," Joel said. "I had a few drinks with them one night. He calls her Betty."

Mike lit a cigarette. He turned his chair and stared out the window. Down in the street men were already walking about in shirt sleeves. Summer was racing to New York with all the promising fires of hell. Betty. Why would Millersen lie to him?

He turned back to his desk and picked up the report. Park Avenue Models. What kind of outfit was that? He had never heard of it, and now twice within a few weeks its name had come up. He reached for the telephone on his desk.

"Get Alec Temple for me," he said into it. Alec had just been transferred to the Rackets office.

Alec's voice came on the wire. "Yes, Mike?"

"Do me a favor," Mike said. "I want a q.t. check on an outfit, Park Avenue Models, Inc., 79 Park Avenue, City."

"What d'yuh want to know?" Alec asked.

"Everything you can find out about it," Mike answered. "But it's very important that no word goes downstairs about it. I don't want Millersen's office to hear about it. This is one time I think we can show 'em something."

"Okay, Mike," Alec laughed. There was always a void between the attorneys and the police who were assigned to the office. "I understand."

"As quick as you can, Alec," Mike said.

"Tomorrow morning quick enough?" Alec asked.

"That will be fine. Thanks." Mike put down the phone. He ground out his cigarette just as the phone rang.

He picked it up. "Keyes."

"Mike, Frank Millersen here." Millersen's voice was heavy over the wire.

"Yes, Frank," Mike said.

"I was just thinkin' maybe we ought to look into that model agency if you want." Millersen sounded slightly apologetic.

"Forget it, Frank," Mike said. "You're probably right about it. Just coincidence. Sorry to have bothered you."

"Okay, Mike." Millersen's voice was hesitant. "If you're sure."

"I'm sure, Frank. Thanks anyway," Mike said.

"You're quite welcome, Mike." He rang off, leaving Mike wondering whether that had been a note of relief he had heard in the man's voice.

CHAPTER SIXTEEN

THE DISTRICT ATTORNEY PEERED SHREWDLY AT MIKE FROM BEHIND WIDE horn-rimmed glasses. He gently tapped the papers on the desk before him with a gold pencil. "So you want to resign?" he asked quietly.

Mike nodded. "Yes, sir."

"Why?"

"Personal reasons, sir," Mike answered stiffly.

The Old Man swung away from him and looked out the window. "Unhappy in your work here, Mike?"

"No, sir."

The Old Man fell silent, and for a long time the only sound in the office was his stertorous breathing. At last he spoke. "I never figured you for chicken, Mike."

Mike didn't answer.

"This job you did on Park Avenue Models is a big one. One of the most important ever to come through this office. Yet, just because it reaches into influential places, you want to quit."

Still Mike didn't speak.

The Old Man turned to face him. "How do you think I feel," he asked suddenly, "when I find my own chief detective involved? Don't you think I want to quit?" He didn't wait for Mike to answer. "But I can't. I took an oath. You took the same oath when I hired you. We can't quit."

"That has nothing to do with it, sir," Mike said.

"Balls!" The Old Man exploded. "So what if a dozen stinking politicians and rich businessmen are involved? Afraid they'll wreck your career?"

Mike didn't reply.

"You'll have no career for them to wreck if you run out now. Everybody will know you're yellow," the Old Man said.

Mike took a deep breath. "I'm sorry, sir. Is that all?"

The Old Man leaned forward over the desk, breathing heavily. "You don't understand, Mike. This is the opportunity of your lifetime. Look where Tom Dewey went with one case like this. After this is over, you can call your shots, you can go anywhere you want. Don't throw your life away, boy."

"May I leave now, sir?" Mike answered.

Contempt crept into the Old Man's voice. "It's seldom I guess wrong on a man, but I guessed wrong when I took you on. It proves that there's more to guts than the ability to stand in front of bullets."

Mike's face flushed. He bit his lips to keep from answering.

"It's bad enough to have to swallow what I must about Millersen, but the thing that does it is to find you're a coward." The tone of his voice changed abruptly. "I'm an old man, Mike. I've spent a good part of my life in this office. All I ever wanted was to do a good job, an honest job, to protect the people who placed their faith in me. This is the first time I ever felt I failed them."

"You didn't fail them, sir," Mike said. "All the information is right there on your desk."

"I am responsible for every man in my office," the Old Man said. "I will pay for Millersen, I will pay for you. Being District Attorney is more than just going before a Grand Jury and getting indictments, it's more than getting a conviction in criminal court. It's pride. Pride in doing your job without fear, without favor. When you quit, it's just as if I quit. The whole world will know it."

Mike didn't speak.

"All right," the Old Man said. "Quit if you want to, but at least have the decency to tell me why. I know you're not a coward."

Mike took a deep breath. Suddenly he realized his hands were trembling.

"Tell me, Mike," the Old Man said gently. "You were a good cop and you were a good assistant. Why are you quitting?"

Mike met the Old Man's eyes. "She was my girl, sir." His voice was dull.

"She?" The Old Man's voice was puzzled. "Who?"

"Marja," Mike said. "Maryann Flood, I mean."

"*This* Maryann Flood?"

Mike nodded.

"But how—what?" The Old Man was confused.

"I didn't know she was in it when I called Alec for the check on Park Avenue Models three weeks ago, sir." Mike paused to light a cigarette. "If I had known, I might not have begun."

The District Attorney looked up at him. There was a new understanding in his eyes. "I was right," he half whispered. "I was right about you."

Mike went on as if he hadn't heard the Old Man. "Then when I got the report, I had to continue. I sent up and got permission to continue. We got a wiretap and began to check. Everything began to fall into place—things we hadn't even thought about. How so many of our raids missed. Lots of things. Especially when we checked back on her first arrest and found that Frank Millersen was the arresting officer. It was even more convincing when we found out that he had banked close to twenty thousand a year. Isn't a cop in the world that can do that on his pay. From there to the businessmen who kept her in business, to the politicians she paid off, to the cops and detectives the girls took care of. Then, as suddenly as it had begun, the investigation was over. Everything was ready to go before the Grand Jury for an indictment. It was then I knew I couldn't do it. I asked Joel Rader to take it for me."

The Old Man looked up at him. "You called in sick."

Mike nodded. "I was sick. Sick inside."

"But you've come up here while Joel is still in the courtroom."

"Yes," Mike answered. "I want to get out before I know how much damage I've done to her."

"You can't run away from that, Mike," the Old Man said gently.

Mike dragged deeply on the cigarette. "I can try, John."

"You're still in love with her." It was more statement than question.

Mike looked down at him. He didn't speak.

The door behind him opened, and Joel Rader came in, an excited expression on his face.

"You've done it, Mike!" he cried. "We've got an indictment against every one of them. Flood, Millersen. It'll be the biggest thing ever to hit this town!" He turned to the District Attorney, still seated behind the desk. "I've got warrants with me for their arrest. We're going downstairs to pick up Millersen now."

The D.A. got to his feet. "I'll go with you." He looked at Mike. "Coming, copper?"

Frank Millersen stuck a pipe in his mouth and lit it carefully. When it was burning easily, he began to skim through the papers on his desk. Nothing special. He could look forward to a relaxing week-end with Betty and the kids. It would be the first in a long while.

There was a knock at the door. "Come in," he called.

The shuffle of several men's footsteps made him look up. The D.A. was standing in front of his desk, and behind him were Keyes and Rader. Beyond the door he could see the blue uniform of a patrolman. He felt an unaccustomed tightness in his chest, but he forced a smile to his lips and got to his feet, holding out his hand. "It's been a long time since you've been down here, Chief," he said.

His hand hung in space between them. The District Attorney made no move to take it. Awkwardly Millersen raised his hand to remove the pipe from between his lips, trying to make it seem one unbroken gesture.

The D.A.'s voice was low. "We have a warrant for your arrest, Frank."

He could feel his face whiten. "What are the charges, sir?" he asked. But he could read them in Mike's face.

"Do I have to tell you, Frank?" the Old Man asked gently.

Millersen's shoulders drooped, and he slumped into his chair. He was suddenly an old man. He looked down at his desk. Aimlessly his hand shuffled the papers on it. He shook his head. "No."

Without looking up, he knew that the District Attorney had turned and walked out of the office. Rader's voice beat down at his head. "You better come with us, Frank."

He looked up, agony in his eyes. "Give me a minute to get myself together," he said heavily. "I'll be right out."

Joel looked at Mike, who nodded. "Okay," Joel said. "We'll wait for you."

They started out the door. Millersen's voice stopped them. "Mike."

Mike turned to face him.

Millersen forced a smile to his lips. "I should have remembered you were a damn good cop before you joined the D.A. I couldn't have done better myself."

Mike's lips were stiff. "I'm sorry, Frank."

"It was your job, Mike," Frank said quietly.

Mike nodded and followed Joel through the door. Millersen watched it close behind them. He picked up the pipe and stuck it in his mouth and drew on it. He could feel the heavy smoke deep in his lungs.

There was no regret for himself when he opened his desk drawer and took out the blue-gray revolver. There was only a vast sorrow in him for Betty and the kids as he substituted the cold metal of the revolver's muzzle for the warm bit of the pipe in his mouth.

CHAPTER SEVENTEEN

A S HE WEARILY OPENED THE DOOR, HE COULD HEAR HIS MOTHER TALKING to someone in the kitchen. He walked through the parlor to his room slowly. He could not remember ever having been so tired, so completely exhausted.

His mother's voice called from the kitchen. "That you, Mike?"

It was an effort for him to raise his voice. "Yes, Ma." He went into his room and closed the door. He took off his jacket and sank into the easy chair near the window. He lit a cigarette and stared out with unseeing eyes.

The door opened behind him. He didn't turn. "Are you all right, son?"

"I'm okay, Ma," he answered.

She came around his chair and looked down at him. "You're home early. Is there anything wrong?"

He looked up at her. Concern was written on her face. "There's nothing wrong, Ma."

"You look poorly," she said. "I'll make you some tea."

A note of annoyance crept into his voice. "Leave me alone, Ma," he said sharply. "I'm okay."

He saw the hurt creeping into her eyes, and he reached for her hand. "I'm sorry, Ma," he said. "I didn't mean to be harsh."

"That's all right, son," she said. "I understand."

"No, Ma," he said. No one could really understand. Only he knew how he felt.

His mother stood there hesitantly. "I know the look on your face, son."

"What look, Ma?" he asked absently, looking out the window again.

"That girl," his mother said. "She's back. I can tell by your eyes."

He looked up quickly. He didn't speak.

"It's the same look you had that time you went up to the Bronx to bring her home and she didn't come with you." His mother's voice was tinged with pain for him. "You can't get her out of your mind, can you, son?"

He dropped her hand. "I tried, Ma. I don't know what it is. It's like she's a part of me."

"You saw her?" his mother asked.

He shook his head. "No, Ma."

"What is it, then?"

"The police are on their way to arrest her now. I prepared a case against her that will send her to jail."

His mother didn't speak for a moment. "It's your job, son."

"Don't you tell me that, Ma," he said with a flash of anger. Millersen had said that too. Now Millersen was dead. "You know better!"

"I told you a long time ago that she's no good for you," she said, starting for the door. "Maybe you'll believe me now."

"But what do you do when you know there's no one else for you?" he said in an agonized voice.

Maryann looked up from the desk. Tom was standing in front of her. He was smiling. "I got the cab waiting, Miz Maryann," he said. "We got just an hour to get to the airport."

She smiled back at him. "I'll be just a few minutes, Tom."

"I'll wait outside," he said. "I just cain't wait to see my li'l blonde baby."

"I can't wait either," she said.

Tom went out of the office and the door closed behind him. She looked for a moment at the photograph of Michelle on the desk, then picked up a few papers and scanned them quickly: bills that could wait until she returned in two weeks. She put them in a folder and placed it in the basket on the desk. She locked the desk drawer and got to her feet.

Picking up her coat from a chair, she cast a last glance around the room. The telephone began to ring. She hesitated and then, making a face, started toward the door. If it was Joker, let him find out tomorrow that she had gone. To hell with him! She would be back soon enough. This time she was going to keep her promise to Michelle.

As she reached for the doorknob, the door opened and a tall man confronted her. Automatically her eyes dropped to his feet. She felt the hair on the base of her neck begin to rise. Copper!

"Did you ever hear of knocking before you enter a room?" she asked coldly.

He came into the office, and she saw that there were several men behind him. The first man smiled. "Going someplace, baby?" he asked.

"None of your business," she snapped.

A short, dark man pushed his way through the group. "Cut the comedy, George," he said sharply. He turned to her. "Are you Maryann Flood?"

She nodded.

"I'm Joel Rader of the District Attorney's office. These men are police. We would like you to come with us," he said.

She stepped back against her desk. "Is this an arrest?"

"It sure is, baby," the tall man said coarsely.

She ignored him and spoke to the short, dark man. "What am I charged with, Mr. Rader?" she asked.

"This warrant will spell it out, Miss Flood," Rader said, handing her a folded sheet of paper.

She took it from him and scanned it quickly. When she looked up, her face was impassive. "May I call my attorney?" she asked calmly.

Joel nodded. He watched her admiringly as she walked behind the desk and picked up the telephone. She dialed quickly. No wonder the woman could do what she did. She had nerves of ice.

He could hear a man's voice answer the phone. "Hank," she said quietly, "I've just been arrested . . . . No, I'm still at the office . . . . Yes . . . . I'll see you down there."

She put down the telephone and looked at Joel. "I'm ready now," she said.

He stepped aside to let her pass. She walked through the door to the outer office. The old colored man stood there, his face grayish. She stopped to speak to him. "Don't worry, Tom," she said. "Go home and fix dinner. And wire the baby that we were held up on business."

Tom looked across Vito's office at Joker with a worried expression. "Is Miz Maryann in big trouble?"

Joker looked at Hank Vito, then turned back to Tom. "She's in big trouble."

"All on 'count of that there lawyer? That one they mention in the papers who done prepared the case? That Mr. Keyes? That one that gone on a vacation while Miz Maryann is in all that trouble?" Tom's voice was indignant.

"That's the boy." Joker's voice was quiet.

"He's a mean man, Mr. Joker," Tom said seriously, "to do that to Miz Maryann jus' because she won' marry up with him."

"What?" Joker leaned forward. "What do you mean?" A vague, torturing memory began to bother him. That friend of Ross's, the boy who used to pick her up after work at the dance hall. His name had been Mike. He stared at Tom. "What do you mean?" he repeated.

"He Michelle's father," Tom said.

"How do you know?" Vito asked. "Did she tell you?"

Tom shook his head. "She never do that."

"Then how do you know?" Vito asked. "If we could prove that, I could get her off easy. No jury in the world would believe it was anything but a frame-up."

"She keep Michelle's birth certificate in the dresser at home. It says his name next to *Father*. I see it many times when I clean," Tom said.

Vito got to his feet excitedly. "You go right home and get it. Then bring it right down here. Don't give it to anybody but me. Understand?"

Tom was already on his way to the door. He looked back at them with a happy grin. "Yes suh, Mr. Hank. I understand."

The door closed behind him and Vito turned to Joker. "Well, what do you make of that?" he asked.

"I'll be damned!" Joker said in wonder. "And all the time she never said a thing to us."

"You think she still goes for the guy?" Vito asked.

Joker shrugged. "I've stopped trying to figure her a long time ago."

"I won't spring it until the trial," Vito said. "I wouldn't want the D.A. to bring it out before we do." He paused, interrupted by a thought. "You think Keyes knows?"

Joker shook his head. "Uh-uh. I don't think she ever told anyone. Except maybe Ross. And he can't tell nobody."

Vito walked behind his desk. "I don't understand that woman," he said in a puzzled voice. "I saw her in jail this morning. It's her third day there, and she never said a word to me. I wonder if she knows that this could spring her."

"Even if she does, I doubt she would say anything." Joker smiled. "Remember what you said to me a long time ago, Hank? When you first told me about her?"

Vito shook his head. "No."

"She's a special kind of broad," Joker quoted. "A whore with a code of ethics."

The State vs.
Maryann Flood

JOEL LOOKED UP FROM HIS DESK AS I WALKED INTO THE OFFICE. THERE was a worried expression on his face. "The Old Man has been yelling like hell for yuh," he said. "You better jump upstairs on the double."

"What's he want?" I asked, throwing my hat and coat onto a chair.

"I don't know," Joel said. "I heard Vito was with him. I don't like it."

"Vito?" I questioned.

Joel nodded. "You better snap it up."

The Old Man's secretary waved me right into his office. The Old Man was seated behind his desk, his eyes cold. Vito sat in a chair opposite him. He turned around when I came in.

I walked past him to the desk. "You sent for me, sir?"

The Old Man nodded, his eyes still cold. "You didn't tell me everything about yourself and Miss Flood." His voice was as cold as his eyes.

I felt anger creeping up in me. This was one thing I hadn't bargained for. I had told the Old Man everything that was pertinent. It was he who had asked me to stay on when I wanted to quit. I made my voice as cold as his. "I'm afraid I don't understand you."

"One Frank Millersen is enough for any man in one lifetime!" the Old Man shouted, his fist pounding the desk.

I kept my voice calm, though my temper was going through the roof. I had been through enough hell without having this old bastard yell at me. "I still don't know what you're talking about."

"Maybe you don't know about this?" the Old Man asked sarcastically, pushing a piece of paper at me.

I picked it up and looked at it. It was a birth certificate. *Michelle Keyes*. I read farther, feeling the blood leave my face. *Mother—Maryann Flood. Father—Michael Keyes*. I looked at the date. I could feel my heart pounding. It had to be right. It matched the time we had been together.

Now I understood a lot of things. That strange look she had given me last night when I asked about her daughter. I hadn't suspected that the child was mine.

The Old Man's voice rasped at my ears. "Why didn't you tell me about it?"

I looked up at him and kept my voice as steady as I could. "How could I?" I asked. "This is the first I ever knew of it."

The Old Man snorted. "You don't expect me to believe that, do you?"

My temper finally blew the roof. "I don't give a damn what you believe!" I shouted.

"You know what this will do to our case?" the Old Man asked. "It will kick it into a cocked hat!"

I glared at him. He was the guy who said the only way to win was to go with the truth. "Why should it?" I asked coldly. "Vito hasn't been able to disprove any of the charges."

For the first time since I had come into the room, he spoke. "Why should I bother?" he asked. "What jury is going to believe your charges when they see this? It'll make everything seem like a frame. A personal vendetta."

I looked down at him and sneered. "I heard you were a good lawyer, Vito. One of the best. I didn't know you included blackmail in your arsenal."

Vito started out of his chair toward me. I pushed him back with one hand. He sat there glaring at me.

The intercom on the Old Man's desk buzzed. He flipped the switch. "Yes?" he barked into it.

"Miss Flood is here," his secretary's voice said.

"Send her in," the Old Man said.

The door opened and Marja came in. Her gold hair was brushed loosely. She wore the same blue poodle-cloth coat she had worn all through the trial. She came into the office with the same sure walk that had always distinguished her from other women.

She ignored me and looked down at Vito. "What's up?" Her voice was husky.

His smile was tight under his elegant mustache. "I think the D.A.'s about to make us a deal."

She looked up at me. A glow came into her eyes. "Mike, are you—?"

Vito's voice was sharp. "I said the D.A., not your boy friend."

The glow faded from her eyes as quickly as it had appeared. She looked at him again. "How come?" she asked.

Silently I handed her the birth certificate. She looked at it quickly, then up at me. A naked pain had come into her eyes. "Where did you get this?" she asked, her voice trembling.

I nodded at Vito.

She looked down at him. "How'd you get this, Vito?" Her voice had gone cold as ice.

He smiled up at her. "Tom brought it to me."

"Why didn't you tell me about it?" she asked.

"And have you louse up your own case because you wanted to protect your boy friend?" he retorted. "I'm your lawyer. I'm supposed to defend you. Even against yourself."

She took a deep breath. "Who cares about him? If I wanted him to know, I would have told him a long time ago. It's Michelle I care about. She's happy now. She thinks her father was killed in the war. How do you think she would feel if she found out how she was born?"

"You think she'd like it better to know that her mother is in the can?" Vito asked.

"It's a lot better than finding out she's a bastard!" Marja snapped.

Vito got to his feet. "You'll do as I say," he said. "There's too much at stake for you to back out now." He turned to the D.A. "Well, John, what do you say?"

The Old Man looked at him silently.

"Have we got a deal?" Vito persisted.

The D.A. spoke softly, his eyes on me. "Keyes is trying the case. I make it a point never to interfere with my assistants. Ask him."

Vito looked at me questioningly.

"There'll be no deal," I said.

"You won't like it, Mike," he said. "I'm goin' to put you on the stand, and when I get through with you, you'll have no place to go. You'll be all washed up here."

"I'll take the chance," I said grimly.

Vito turned back to the Old Man. "That ends your crack at the Governor's chair."

The Old Man's eyes were inscrutable. "I'll go with Mike," he said.

Vito turned toward the door, his face red and angry. "Come on, Maryann."

She started after him.

"Marja," I called.

She stopped and looked back at me. I walked over to her and took her hand. "Why didn't you tell me?" I asked gently.

She didn't answer. Her eyes were shining with a strange brilliance. I wondered if there were tears behind those lids.

"Why, Marja?" I persisted.

Her eyes stared into mine, wide and unblinking. "I lost one baby because they didn't think I could take care of it, Mike," she half whispered. "I didn't want to lose this one."

"Coming, Maryann?" Vito's voice sounded harshly from the doorway.

"I'm sorry, Mike," she whispered, pulling her hand from mine and going out the door.

I walked slowly back to the Old Man. "Well, I really snafued that one for you."

He smiled. "I apologize for not trusting you, Mike."

"Forget it, John," I said. "It's not important now."

He got to his feet heavily. "Court will be open in a few minutes. We better get down there."

I felt as the ancient Roman gladiators must have felt as they marched into the arena. "*Morituri te salutamus,*" I said.

He was busy with his own thoughts. "What's that?" he asked sharply.

I grinned at him. He was proud of his knowledge of Latin. It wasn't often one had the chance to rub him, even if it was through inattention on his part. "We who are about to die salute you," I translated, grinning.

❖ ❖ ❖

There was an atmosphere of repressed excitement in the courtroom. It was as if some mysterious sense had communicated to everyone there that something was about to break. Even the normally blasé court clerks were fidgeting restlessly.

The judge arrived twenty minutes late. We rose as he ascended the bench. A moment later the court was in session.

Vito rose to his feet and walked toward the bench. His voice rang through the courtroom. "The defense would like to call as its first witness Mr. Michael Keyes of the District Attorney's staff!"

Even the judge was visibly startled. He glanced toward us while a roar went up in the courtroom. I could hear the footsteps of several reporters racing up the aisles to the doors. He banged his gavel for order. A moment later it was quiet.

"That's a most extraordinary request, counselor," he said. "I presume you have sufficient reason for your action."

"I have, Your Honor," Vito answered. "I believe it most important in the interest of securing justice for my client that Mr. Keyes be asked to take the stand."

The judge looked at me and I began to stroll across the court. Vito watched me, his face impassive.

She looked up at me as I walked past her table. Her face was white and drawn. Then she was behind me and the witness chair in front of me. I climbed the step and turned to face the court clerk who was about to administer the oath. A dozen flashbulbs went off, blinding me for a moment.

I heard her voice while I was blinking my eyes. It was strong and clear. "Your Honor, may I have a moment to talk to my attorney? I want to change my plea to guilty!"

Another roar broke out in the courtroom, even greater than the one that had preceded it. More flashbulbs went off, and by the time I could see, Vito had gone back to her table.

They argued visibly for a moment, then Vito looked up at the judge. "May I ask for a ten-minute recess, Your Honor? I need a moment with my client in private."

The judge's gavel banged. "The court will recess for ten minutes." He left the bench and I stepped down from the witness stand and crossed to my table.

Marja and Vito had already vanished into the conference room. I looked around the court. The people standing in the back of the court were packed like sardines. I felt a hand tugging at my sleeve. I looked down.

It was the Chief. "You were right," he whispered in an admiring voice. "The girl's sheer guts. All the way!"

The conference door opened and Vito came out alone. He looked at the crowd, seeming to search for someone. I tried to follow his gaze, but he was too quick for me. He made a motion with his head that seemed almost like a nod and went back into the conference room.

I was still watching the crowd. A moment later a man got to his feet. His steel-white hair shone in the overhead lamps. He began to walk up the aisle toward the door. I recognized him immediately: Joker Martin. I wondered what he had been doing here, but the conference door opened and I forgot all about it.

Marja came into the court first; her face was set and calm. Vito followed her. They went to their table and sat down.

A moment later the court was in session again. Vito got to his feet and faced the judge. His face was white, but his voice was steady. "My client wishes to enter a plea of guilty to all the charges."

The judge looked down at her: "Is that your wish, Miss Flood?"

She got to her feet slowly. "It is, Your Honor."

We fought our way through the crowd to the elevators. My back ached from all the pounding I had taken from well-wishers. At last I was alone in the elevator with the Chief.

"You'll have my resignation on your desk in the morning, sir," I said.

He didn't look at me.

"I'm sorry about all the mess, sir," I said.

He didn't speak.

The elevator stopped at my floor and I got off, leaving him alone in the car. I walked down the hall to my office. Joel and Alec were still downstairs. I sat down at my desk and pulled out a sheet of paper. I wrote the resignation quickly, put it in an envelope, and sent it up to the Chief.

The phone on my desk rang. I picked it up. "Keyes," I said. I wouldn't be doing this for long.

"Mike, this is Marja."

"Yes, Marja," I said wearily.

"I'm in the Boyd Cocktail Lounge over on Broadway. Can you meet me right away?"

They had certainly worked fast. Her bail had been set at fifty thousand dollars, and here she was in a bar almost before I had time to get upstairs. I hesitated.

"Please, Mike," she said. "It's very important."

"Okay," I said. "I'll be right over." I reached for my coat. I'd come back tomorrow to clean out my desk.

It had begun to snow when I pushed my way through the door into the dimly lit interior. She was seated at a table in the corner. I sat down beside her. A waiter came up.

"What'll it be?" I asked her.

"Cassis and soda," she said.

"Gin over rocks for me," I said to him. He went away, and I turned to her. "You're still drinking that crazy stuff."

"I like it," she said.

The waiter came back and put the drinks before us.

I lifted my drink. "Here's to crime."

Her eyes were steady on me. "I won't drink to that."

I made a face.

"Ross always used to say that," she said. "I'm superstitious about it."

"Got something better?" I asked.

She nodded.

"What?" I asked.

Her eyes looked into mine. "Here's to us," she said steadily.

I could feel the warmth of her reaching out to me. "Good enough," I said, sipping my drink. I put the glass down and looked at her. "What was it you wanted to see me about?"

A man came into the restaurant. She glanced at him briefly, then back at me. "About us, Mike," she said. Her hand moved along the table and rested on mine. "I think it's about time."

I could feel the electricity shooting up my arm from her fingers. I tried to keep my voice calm. "Is it?"

She nodded slowly. "Nobody else will do for me."

I took a deep breath. "It took a long time for you to come to that conclusion."

"I'm sorry, Mike," she said. "I couldn't help it. I didn't know any better. I told you that last night. In the car."

I needed time to think. The pulses in my temples were pounding. I changed the subject. "Who went your bail?" I asked.

The door opened and another man came through. Automatically she looked at him briefly, appraisingly, then back at me. "Joker Martin," she said.

So that was what he had been doing in the courtroom. Vito had probably come out to get an okay from him on the plea. I had heard that he had almost all the rackets in town sewed up. I didn't speak.

She leaned toward me. I could smell the warm perfume of her. "It won't be long, Mike," she said. "I'll be out in a couple of years with good behavior. Then we can go off someplace and start clean. Nobody will know anything about us."

Another man came through the door and her eyes flicked over him, then back to me. Her voice was low and husky. "Are we goin' to make it, Mike?"

I took a deep breath. Slowly I began to disengage our fingers. She looked down at my hands, then up at me. Her eyes were suddenly veiled "What is it, Mike? The jail sentence?"

I shook my head. I still didn't trust myself to speak.

Her voice was a shade sharper now. "What is it, then? I got a right to know, Mike."

"What's my daughter like, Marja?" My voice seemed to be coming from someone else, not from me.

A sudden flash of understanding came into her eyes. "So that's it," she said.

I nodded. "That's it." I looked down at my hands. I could see the veins on the backs of them pulsing slowly. "I could never keep your child from you the way you did mine from me."

"What else could I do, Mike?" she asked. "We were worlds apart then."

"What makes you think we're any closer now?" I said brutally. I looked right into her eyes. "I spent my life waiting for you. I thought there was nothing you could do that I could not condone or find excuses for. But I was wrong. The one thing you never should have done was cheat me of my child."

"She's my child, too, Mike, don't forget that," she said quickly. "She's the only thing in this world that's mine, really mine. She's more mine than yours."

"That's what I mean, Marja," I said, a weariness creeping into me. "She could have been *our* child. But you were only thinking of yourself. Not of her, not of me. Only that you wanted her."

"It's not too late, Mike. We can still do it over."

"No, Marja." I shook my head. "You can't turn back the clock. You told me that once yourself. Remember?"

Her eyes were wide and dark. So much about them was familiar, and yet they seemed almost like the eyes of a stranger. A moment passed. Then her face settled into an inscrutable mask and she slowly got to her feet. Without a word, she walked out into the street.

Through the glass door I could see her standing in the street, the snow falling like velvet around her. A long black limousine stopped in front of her. A man got out. He took off his dark homburg as he held the door for her. I could see his white hair. It matched the falling snow. He was Joker Martin. He followed her into the car and it moved off slowly.

I threw the rest of my drink down my throat and got to my feet. I tossed a few bills on the table and started for the door.

I walked into the court for my last official act. To hear Marja's sentence.

I could see her face as she faced the bench. She was pale, but her eyes were calm and unafraid as the judge's voice rolled down on her.

"On the first count—procurement for the purposes of prostitution—you hereby are sentenced to imprisonment for an indeterminate term of three to five years and fined five thousand dollars.

"On the second count—bribing certain public officials—you hereby are sentenced to imprisonment for one year and fined five thousand dollars.

"On the third count—extortion by oral threats—you hereby are sentenced to imprisonment for one year and fined five hundred dollars."

The rustle and hum of conversation rose behind us as the judge finished pronouncing sentence. He rapped his gavel for order. The courtroom became quiet.

His voice was very low, but it carried to the back of the courtroom. "It has been brought to the attention of this court by the District Attorney that the defendant by her action has indicated a desire to rehabilitate herself in the eyes of society. Therefore, it is the decision of this court to allow the defendant to serve her various terms of imprisonment concurrently."

A louder buzz ran through the courtroom. This was a real break. It meant that she wouldn't have to serve more than two years, with time off for good behavior. I turned to Alec. "Did you know the Old Man was going to do this?" I asked.

He shook his head. I looked at Joel. He, too, looked blank. I looked across the room at Marja. She was watching me, her eyes steady and somehow grateful. I wanted to tell her that it was the Chief, not I, who had arranged it, but there was no way to speak to her.

Joel fell into step beside me as we left the court. "The Old Man is gettin' soft," he said. "How about a drink?"

I shook my head and left him at the elevator. As I reached the door to my office, it opened suddenly and the Old Man stood there. In his hand he held an envelope which he waved at me excitedly. "You don't think I'd accept this, do you?" he yelled.

I saw that it was my resignation. "Yes, sir," I said. "I think it's only right."

"Then you're even more stupid than I thought, Keyes," he shouted. With a flourishing gesture he tore the letter into shreds and threw them on the floor. He stamped off angrily.

For a moment I stared down at the floor. The tiny bits of paper were startlingly white on the dusty gray flooring. Then I took off after him. I caught his arm and he turned around. "Thanks, Chief," I said.

He nodded testily. "It's okay, Mike. You didn't think I would give up a good assistant that easily, did you?"

I smiled slowly. "Not for me, sir. For Marja."

He looked into my eyes and his gaze grew gentle. "Don't ever forget, Mike," he said softly, "that the scales of justice must always be tempered with mercy."

I stood there silently for a moment. Mercy. It was a big word. The biggest. I wondered if I would ever be man enough to show it.

Before I could speak, he clapped me on the shoulder. "Go back to your office, lad. There's someone waiting there to see you."

He stomped off down the hall and I turned back to my office. I opened the door slowly. There was no one there. The Old Man must be cracking up. I went in and sat down behind my desk. I heard a rustle of clothing from the small couch against the wall behind the door. I looked up.

A small girl was walking toward me. Her hair was the whitest gold I had ever seen. Her eyes were big and round and blue, and looking into them was like looking into a mirror. They were my eyes. I could feel a tightening in my chest. I couldn't breathe.

She stopped in front of my desk and looked at me solemnly. Her eyes were wide and unwinking. "I'm Michelle," she said. Her voice was young and clear.

I nodded, unable to speak.

"Mother said I was to stay with you for a while," she said.

I nodded again. I wanted to speak, but I couldn't.

"She said you would look after me." The faintest hint of tears began to creep into those beautiful blue eyes.

A pain began to echo in me and my eyes blurred. I moved slowly around the desk and knelt beside her. I took both her hands in mine. "I'll look after you, Michelle."

A STONE FOR DANNY FISHER

What man is there of you,
whom if his son ask bread,
will he give him a stone?
—MATTHEW vii, 9

CONTENTS

PREFACE

A Stone for Danny Fisher is one of the three novels that compose what I have come to think of as *The Depression in New York Trilogy*, the other novels being *Never Love a Stranger* and *79 Park Avenue*. While each novel has story and characters peculiar to itself, they are novels of passion and struggle and survival in that time between the two World Wars.

Each of these novels was conceived and written primarily as an entertainment and it was only after a time that I began to realize that I had written stories about the world in which I grew up, the world to which I had been born and that any of these stories could have been and were, in part, my own. I lived in all the streets and neighborhoods, I was, and I knew, all the characters that peopled these novels.

With these novels my shape as a novelist was formed. Falling, as they did, broadly into the picaresque genre, they reflected my concerns with the individual's search for his own identity, the concerns for the social problems and sexual mores of the times that could raise him to heights and plunge him to the depths of human behavior. These concerns were equally true of the novels that were to follow. The times would change, the moralities would change, the scenes would broaden from the streets of New York to Los Angeles, to Europe, South America, Asia. But the principal subject of each novel was people.

If there is nothing else evident in my work, for myself there is only one thing that stands out. I am a people writer. Because people, with all their hopes and dreams, greed and ambitions, strength and weakness, love and hate, are all that interest me.

And in *A Stone for Danny Fisher* you will find a part of how it all began. And where I come from.

Harold Robbins

New York
April, 1979

A Stone for Danny Fisher

CHAPTER ONE

T HERE *are many ways to get to Mount Zion Cemetery. You can go by
automobile, through the many beautiful parkways of Long Island, or by
subway, bus or trolley. There are many ways to get to Mount Zion Cemetery, but during this week there is no way that is not crushed and crowded with
people.*

*"Why should this be so?" you ask, for in the full flush of life there is something
frightening about going to a cemetery—except at certain times. But this week,
the week before the High Holy Days, is one of these times. For this is the week
that Lord God Jehovah calls His angels about Him and opens before them the
Book of Life. And your name is inscribed on one of these pages. Written on that
page will be your fate for the coming year.*

*For these six days the book will remain open and you will have the opportunity
to prove that you are deserving of His kindness. During these six days you devote
yourself to acts of charity and devotion. One of these acts is the annual visit to
the dead.*

*And to make sure that your visit to the departed will be noted and the proper
credit given, you will pick up a small stone from the earth beneath your feet and
place it on the monument so that the Recording Angel will see it when he comes
through the cemetery each night.*

* * *

You meet at the time appointed under an archway of white stone. The words MOUNT ZION CEMETERY *are etched into the stone over your head. There are six of you. You look awkwardly at one another and words come stiffly to your lips. You are all here. As if by secret agreement, without a word, you all begin to move at once and pass beneath the archway.*

On your right is the caretaker's building; on your left, the record office. In this office, listed by plot number and burial society, are the present addresses of many people who have walked this earth with you and many who have walked this earth before your time. You do not stop to think of this, for to you, all except me belong to yesterday.

You walk up a long road searching for a certain path. At last you see its white numbers on a black disk. You turn up the path, your eyes reading the names of the burial societies over each plot section. The name you have been looking for is now visible to you, polished black lettering on gray stone. You enter the plot.

A small old man with a white tobacco-stained mustache and beard hurries forward to meet you. He smiles tentatively, while his fingers toy with a small badge on his lapel. It is the prayer-reader for the burial society. He will say your prayers in Hebrew for you, for such has been the custom for many years.

You murmur a name. He nods his head in birdlike acquiescence; he knows the grave you seek. He turns, and you follow him, stepping carefully over other graves, for space is at a premium here. He stops and points an old, shaking hand. You nod your head, it is the grave you seek, and he steps back.

An airplane drones overhead, going to a landing at a nearby airport, but you do not look up. You are reading the words on the monument Peace and quiet come over you. The tensions of the day fall from your body. You raise your eyes and nod slightly to the prayer-reader.

He steps forward again and stands in front of you. He asks your names, so that he may include them in his prayer. One by one you answer him.

My mother.

My father.

My sister.

My sister's husband.

My wife.

My son.

His prayer is a singsong, unintelligible gibberish of words that echoes monotonously among the graves. But you are not listening to him You are-filled with memories of me, and to each of you I am a different person.

At last the prayer is done, the prayer-reader paid and gone to seek his duty elsewhere. You look around on the ground beneath you for some small stone. Carefully you hold it in your hand and, like the others, one at a time, step forward toward the monument.

Though the cold and snow of winter and the sun and rain of summer have been close to me since last you were here together, your thoughts are again as they were then. I am strong in each of your memories, except one.

To my mother I am a frightened child, huddling close to her bosom, seeking safety in her arms.

To my father I am a difficult son, whose love was hard to meet, yet strong as mine for him.

To my sister I am the bright young brother, whose daring was a cause of love and fear.

To my sister's husband I am the friend who shared the common hope of glory.

To my wife I am the lover, who, beside her in the night, worshiped with her at the shrine of passion and joined her in a child.

To my son—to my son I know not what I am, for he knew me not.

There are five stones lying on my grave and still, my son, you stand there wondering. To all the others I am real, but not to you. Then why must you stand here and mourn someone you never knew?

In your heart there is the tiny hard core of a child's resentment. For I have failed you. You have never made those boasts that children are wont to make: "My daddy is the strongest," or the smartest, or the kindest, or the most loving. You have listened in bitter silence, with a growing frustration, while others have said these things to you.

Do not resent nor condemn me, my son. Withhold your judgment, if you can, and hear the story of your father. I was human, hence fallible and weak. And though in my lifetime I made many mistakes and failed many people, I would not willingly fail you. Listen to me then, I beg you, listen to me, O my son, and learn of your father.

Come back with me to the beginning, to the very beginning. For we who have been of one flesh, of one blood, and of one heart are now come together in one memory.

Moving Day

JUNE 1, 1925

I GO BACK TO THE BEGINNING OF MEMORY, AND IT IS MY EIGHTH BIRTHDAY. I am sitting in the cab of a moving-van, scanning the street-corner signs anxiously. As the big van neared one corner, it slowed down. "Is this the block?" the driver asked the colored man sitting next to me.

The big Negro turned to me. "Is this the block, boy?" he asked, his teeth, large and white, showing in his face.

I was so excited I could hardly speak. "This is it," I squeaked I squirmed to look at the street. This was it. I recognized the houses, each looking like the others, with a slim young tree in front of each. It looked just as it did the day I went with Mamma and Papa, the day they bought the house for me, for my birthday.

Everybody had been smiling then, even the real-estate man who sold Papa the house. But Papa hadn't been fooling. He meant it. He told the real-estate man that the house had to be ready by June 1 because that was my birthday, and it was my birthday present.

And it was ready on the first just like Papa had wanted, because here it was June 1 and it was my eighth birthday and we were moving in.

Slowly the truck turned up the block. I could hear the soft biting of the tires into the gravel on the street as the van left the pavement. My new street wasn't even paved yet. It was covered with grayish-white gravel. Stones rattled as the tires picked them up and threw them against the mudguards.

I jumped up in the cab of the truck. "There it is!" I shouted, pointing. "That's my house! The last one on the block! The only one that stands by itself!"

The truck began to roll to a stop in front of the house. I could see our car standing in the driveway. Mamma and my sister, Miriam, who was two years older than I, had gone on before us to take the loaf of bread and box of salt into the house and to have things ready. Mamma had wanted me to come with her, but I had wanted to ride on the truck, and the head driver had said I might.

I tried to open the door of the cab before the truck had stopped, but the colored man kept his hand on it. "Wait a minute, boy," he said, smiling. "You'll be here a long time."

When the truck stopped, he released the door. Clambering down from the cab, I slipped on the running board in my hurry and sprawled in the street. I heard a muttered curse behind me and then, felt strong hands pick me up and put me on my feet.

The Negro's deep voice asked in my ear: "Are you hurt, boy?"

I shook my head. I don't suppose I could have spoken even if I'd wanted to; I was too busy looking at my house.

It was brown-red brick halfway up and then brown shingles up to the edge of the roof. The roof was covered with black shingles, and there was a little porch, sort of, in front of the house, like a stoop. It was the most beautiful house I had ever seen. I drew a deep proud breath and looked down the street to see if anybody was watching. There was no one there. We were the first people on the whole block to move in.

The colored man was standing beside me. "Sho is a pretty house," he said. "You a mighty lucky boy to own a fine house like that."

I smiled at him gratefully because when I had told him how Papa had given it to me for my birthday, he had scoffed like everyone else. Then I was running up the steps and knocking at the door. "Mamma, Mamma!" I hollered. "It's me. I'm here!"

The door opened and Mamma was standing there, a rag tied around her head I pushed past her into the house and came to a stop in the middle of the room. Everything in the house smelled new. The paint on the walls, the wood on the stairs, everything was new.

I heard Mamma ask the driver what took him so long. I missed his reply because I was looking up the staircase, but Mamma came back into the room saying something about their stretching the job because they get paid by the hour.

I grabbed at her arm. "Mamma, which room is mine?" I asked. For the first time I was going to have a room of my own. Before this we had lived in an apartment and I had shared a room with my sister. Then one morning just before Papa decided to buy me a house, Mamma came into our room as I was sitting up in bed watching Mimi get dressed. Mamma looked at me and later that day at breakfast told us that we were going to get a house and from now on I would have a room of my own.

Now she shook her hand free of mine. "It's the first one at the side of the stairs, Danny," she answered excitedly. "And keep out of the way. I have a lot to do!"

I bolted up the stairs, the heels of my shoes making loud clumping sounds. At the top of the stairs I hesitated a moment while I look around. Mamma and Papa had the big room in front, then came Miriam's room, then mine. I opened the door to my room and walked in softly.

It was a small room about ten feet wide and fourteen feet long. It had two windows in it and through them I could see the two windows of the house across the driveway from us. I turned and closed the door behind me. I crossed the room and put my face against the windowpane and tried to look out, but I couldn't see very far, so I opened the window.

I looked out on the driveway that ran between the houses. Right underneath me was the top of the new Paige, the car Papa had just bought, and up the driveway behind the house was a garage. Behind the garage was nothing but fields. This was a new section in Flatbush. All these lots had once been dumps, but the city had filled them in. Around the corner from us they were building more houses that looked like ours, and I could see them when I hung out the window far enough.

I came back into the middle of the room. Slowly I turned in a circle, studying each wall. "My room, this is my room," I kept saying to myself over and over.

I could feel a lump come into my throat, a funny sort of feeling. Like the time I stood next to Grandpa's coffin, holding Papa's hand and looking down at the still white face with the little black yamalka on the head, so startling against the plain white sheet. Papa's voice had been very soft. "Look at him, Danny," he said to me, but it was more as if he were speaking to himself. "This is the end to which all men come, this is the last time we can look at his face." Then Papa bent and kissed the still face in the coffin and I did too. Grandpa's lips were icy cold and they didn't move when mine touched them. Some of the chill of them ran through me.

A man was standing beside the coffin with a pair of scissors. Papa opened his jacket, and the man snipped off a piece of his tie. The man looked at me questioningly. Papa nodded his head and spoke in Yiddish. "He is of his blood," he said. The man snipped off a piece of my tie and I could feel a lump rise in my throat. It was a new tie and this was the first time I had ever worn it. Now I would never be able to wear it again. I looked up at Papa. He was looking back at the coffin and his lips were moving. I strained my ears to hear what he was saying but I couldn't. He let my hand fall from his and I ran to Mamma with the lump still in my throat.

That was the way I felt now.

Suddenly I threw myself on the floor and pressed my cheek against it. The floor felt cool to my face, and the smell of the new shellac came up through my nose and made my eyes smart. I closed my eyes and lay there a few minutes. Then I turned and pressed my lips to the cool floor. "I love you, house," I whispered. "You're the most beautiful house in the whole world, and you're mine and I love you."

"Danny, what are you doing there on the floor?"

I scrambled to my feet quickly and faced the door. It was Miriam. She had a handkerchief tied around her head like Mamma. "Nothin'," I answered awkwardly.

She looked at me queerly. I could see she hadn't been able to figure out what I had been doing. "Mamma says for you to come downstairs and get out of the way," she said bossily. "The men are ready to bring the furniture upstairs."

I followed her down the staircase. Already the newness of the house was beginning to wear off. I could see places on the steps where our feet had rubbed off the paint. The furniture was already in the living-room, and the rug, which had been rolled up on a bamboo stick, was standing in the corner ready to be put down when the men were through.

Mamma was standing in the middle of the room. There were smudges of dirt on her face. "Is there anything you want me to do, Mamma?" I asked.

I heard Mimi's derisive snort behind me. She didn't like boys and didn't think they were good for anything. It made me mad. "Is there, Mamma?" I repeated.

Mamma smiled at me. When she smiled at me her face softened. I liked her to smile at me. She put her hand on my head and playfully tugged at my hair. "No, Blondie," she answered. "Why don't you run outside and play for a while? I'll call you when I need you."

I smiled back at her. I knew she was feeling good when she called me Blondie. I also knew it made Mimi mad. I was the only one in the whole family with blond hair; all the others were dark. Papa used to tease Mamma about it sometimes and it always made her angry, I don't know why.

I made a face at Mimi and went outside. The men had unloaded the truck and there was a lot of furniture on the street. I stood there watching them for a while. It was a warm day and the Negro had taken off his shirt and I could see the muscles rippling under his black skin. The sweat was pouring down his face because he was doing most of the work while the other man was always talking and telling him what to do.

After a while I got tired of watching them and looked up the block toward the corner, wondering what the neighborhood was like. The open fields on the next block in back of my house, which I had seen from my window, made me curious. In the old neighborhood there had never been an empty lot, only the big ugly apartment houses.

Through the open door of my house I saw that Mamma was busy, and when I called to ask her if I could walk up the block, she didn't answer. I stepped off the stoop and headed for the corner, feeling pleased and proud, I had such a nice house and it was such a nice day. I hoped all my birthdays would be as nice.

I could hear a dog's frightened yips almost as soon as I had turned the corner. I looked in the direction of the sound, but couldn't tell where it came from. I walked toward it.

The neighborhood was just being developed—Hyde Park they called it, in the East Flatbush section of Brooklyn. I walked down the street of half-finished houses, their naked white wooden frames gleaming in the bright midafternoon sun. I crossed the next street and the buildings fell behind me. Here was nothing but open fields. The dog's frightened barks were slightly louder now, but I still couldn't tell where they came from. It was strange how far sounds could carry out here in the open. Where we used to live before, down by Papa's drugstore, you couldn't hear a noise even if it was just around the corner. The field in the next block hadn't been filled in yet and was nothing but a deep empty pit running from corner to corner. As soon as they filled in these pits, I guessed, they would start building here too.

Now I could tell where the dog's yips were coming from: the block after next. I could see two boys standing at the edge of the pit there, looking down. The dog must have fallen into the hole. I quickened my step and in a few moments was standing beside the boys. A little brown dog was yelping as he tried to scramble up the sides of the pit. He could manage to get only part way; then he would slip and fall back to the bottom. That was when he would yip the loudest, as he rolled over and over on his way down Then the two boys would laugh. I don't know why. I didn't think it was funny.

"Is he your dog?" I asked.

They both turned and looked at me. They didn't answer.

I repeated the question.

The bigger of the two boys asked: "Who wants to know?" Something in the tone of his voice frightened me. He wasn't friendly at all.

"I'm only asking," I said.

He came toward me, swaggering a little. He was bigger than I. "And I said: 'Who wants to know?' " His voice was even rougher now.

I took a step backward. I wished I hadn't left the new house. Mamma had only told me to keep out of the way until the moving-men had finished bringing the furniture, into the house. "Is he your dog?" I asked, trying to smile and wishing my voice wouldn't quaver.

The big boy put his face very close to mine. I looked him steadily in the eye. "No," he answered.

"Oh," I said. and turned to look at the little dog again. He was still trying to scramble up the side of the pit.

The boy's voice was in my ear. "Where you from?" he asked. "I never seen you before."

I turned back to him. "East Forty-eighth Street. We just moved in today. In the new houses. We're the first people on the whole block."

His face was dark and glowering. "What's your name?" he asked.

"Danny Fisher," I replied. "What's yours?"

"Paul," he said. "And this is my brother, Eddie."

We fell silent for a minute watching the dog. He made it about halfway up before he fell back.

Paul laughed. "That's funny," he said. "That dopey mutt ain't got enough sense to get outta there."

"I don't think it's so funny," I said. "Maybe the poor dog'll never get out."

"So what?" Paul snorted. "It serves him right for goin' down there in the first place."

I didn't say anything. We stood there on the edge of the pit looking down at the dog. I heard a movement on the other side of me and turned. It was Eddie. He was smaller than me. I smiled at him, and he smiled back.

Paul walked around me and stood next to him. There was something in his manner that made both of us stop smiling. Eddie looked sort of ashamed. I wonder why.

"What school yuh goin' to?" Paul asked.

"I don't know," I answered. "That one over near Utica on Avenue D, I guess."

"What class you in?"

"Four A."

"How old are yuh?"

"Eight," I answered proudly. "Today's my birthday. That's why we moved. Papa bought me the house for a birthday present."

Paul sniffed scornfully. I could see that I hadn't impressed him. "You're a smart kid, huh? You're in my class an' I'm nine."

"Well, I skipped 3 B," I explained half-apologetically.

His eyes became cold and wary. "You gonna go to Sacred Heart?"

I was puzzled. "What's that?" I asked.

"Sacred Heart Church," he answered. "Near Troy."

"No," I said, shaking my head.

"Holy Cross?" he asked. "The big church that owns the cemetery?"

"What cemetery?" I asked. I was beginning to feel strange. I didn't want to answer his question. I wondered what was so important about it that he should keep asking.

He pointed across Clarendon Road. About a block past it I could see the black iron picket fence of the cemetery. I turned back to him "No," I said.

He was silent for a moment while he thought it over. "Don't you believe in God?" he finally asked.

"Sure I do," I replied, "But I don't go to church."

He looked at me skeptically. "If you don't go to church, then you don't believe in God," he said emphatically.

"I do so," I insisted. I could feel angry tears start coming to my eyes. He had no right to say that. I stood up as straight as I could. "I'm a Jew," I said, my voice shrill, "and I go to shul."

The two brothers looked at each other, a sudden knowing look in their eyes. Their faces settled into dull unfriendly masks. Paul took a threatening step toward me. Instinctively I stepped back. My heart was pounding. I wondered what I had said to make them mad.

Paul stuck his face in mine. "Why did you kill Christ?" he snarled at me.

I was really scared at the savagery in his voice. "I didn't kill Him," I quavered, "I never even knew Him."

"You did!" Eddie's voice was higher than his brother's but it was just as savage. "My father told us! He said the Jews killed Him, they nailed Him to the cross. He told us the kikes would move into all the new houses in the neighborhood."

I tried to pacify them. "Maybe some Jews I don't know killed Him," I said placatingly, "but my mother always said that He was a king of the Jews."

"They killed Him just the same," Paul insisted.

I thought for a second. The dog started to yelp again, but I was afraid to turn and look. I tried to change the subject. "We oughtta try to get that dog outta there."

They didn't answer. I could see they were still mad. I tried to think of something that would satisfy them. "Maybe they killed Him because He was a bad king," I suggested.

Their faces grew white. I got frightened and turned to run away, but I wasn't fast enough. Paul caught me and held my arms pinned to my side. I tried to wriggle loose but couldn't. I began to cry.

Paul's face suddenly broke into a contemptuous smile. He let go of my arms and stepped back. "So you wanna get the dog outta there?" he asked.

I tried to stifle my sobs. With one hand I wiped at my eye. "Y-yes," I said.

He took a deep breath, still smiling. "Okay, Jew-baby, go get him!" He rushed at me suddenly, his arms straight out in front of him.

In a panic I tried to get out of his way, but his hands hit my chest, and all the wind went out of me. And then I was falling, rolling over and over, down the sides of the pit. I tried to grab at something to keep myself from slipping, but there wasn't anything. I hit the bottom and for a minute lay there trying to catch my breath.

I heard a whining happy sound and felt a warm tongue licking my face. I sat up. The little brown dog, which was only a puppy, was licking my face, his little tail wagging, and happy little noises deep in his throat.

I got to my feet and looked up. I felt ashamed now because I had cried, but somehow the dog seemed so happy to see me that I wasn't afraid any more.

Paul and Eddie were looking down at me. I shook my fist at them. "You dirty bastards!" I shouted. It was the worst name I knew.

I saw them bend down and pick something up from the ground. A second later a shower of stones and pebbles came pouring down on us. The dog yelped as one hit him. I covered my head with my arms until the shower stopped, but none hit me. Then I looked up again.

"I'll get you for this," I shouted.

They laughed derisively. "Jew son of a bitch," Paul shouted.

I picked up a stone and threw it up at them, but it fell short and another shower of rocks and pebbles came down on me. This time I didn't cover my face quickly enough and one stone cut my cheek. I tossed another at them but it, too, fell short. They bent down to pick up more stones.

I turned and ran out into the center of the pit, where their rocks couldn't reach me. The dog ran beside me. In the middle of the pit I sat down on a big rock. The dog came over to me and I scratched his head. I wiped my face on my sleeve and looked up at the two brothers again.

They were shouting and waving their fists at me, but I couldn't hear what they were saying. The dog was sitting on my foot, wagging his tail and looking into my face. I bent down and put my cheek against his face. "It's all right, doggy," I whispered. "When they go away, we'll get outta here."

Then I straightened up and thumbed my nose at them. They got sore and began to throw more rocks at me, but I only laughed at them. They couldn't touch me from where they were.

The sun had started to go down in the west when they finally went away. I sat there on the rock and waited awhile. I waited almost half an hour before I made up my mind that they had really gone. By that time it was almost dark.

I walked back to the side of the pit and looked up. It was pretty high and steep, but I didn't think I'd have much trouble getting to the top. There were plenty of rocks and bushes I could hold on to. I grabbed hold of a big rock and started up slowly, climbing on my hands and knees to keep from slipping back. I had got maybe five feet up when I heard a whining sound below me. I looked back.

The little dog was sitting in the pit watching me with bright shining eyes. When he saw I had turned to look at him, he gave a sharp, happy yip. "Well, come on," I said to him. "What are you waiting for?" He leaped against the side of the pit and began crawling up toward me. He, too, was moving on his belly. Almost a foot from me, he began to slide back. I grabbed at him, caught him by the scruff of the neck, and pulled him next to me. His tail was wagging happily. "Come on," I said. "We gotta get outta here."

I started upward again and moved a few feet, but when I looked to see how the dog was doing, he wasn't there. He was crouching where I had left him, his eyes on me, his tail drooping. I called him. His tail started wagging, but he didn't move. "What's the matter?" I asked. "You afraid?" He just wagged his tail. He wasn't going to move, so I started to climb again.

I had gone another few feet when he began to cry in highpitched whining sounds. I stopped and looked down. Immediately his whining ceased and his tail started wagging. "All right," I said, "I'll come down and help you."

Carefully I slid back to where he was and grabbed him again by the scruff of the neck. Holding onto him with one hand, I started inching up again. It took almost fifteen minutes to get halfway up, pulling him up to me after every step. There I stopped to catch my breath. My hands and face were covered with dirt and my shirt and trousers were scuffed and torn. The dog and I clung there to the side of the pit, afraid to move for fear of slipping back.

After a few minutes we started up again. We were almost at the top when a stone gave way under my foot and I slipped. Frantically I let go of the dog and clutched at the dirt to keep myself from sliding down. I had lost only a few feet when I could feel my fingers catch and take hold in the earth. The dog began to yip. When I turned to see, he was gone.

I looked back into the pit. He was just picking himself up. He looked up at me and gave a short bark, but when I turned away from him and started on, he began to whine again. I tried not to listen to his soft, piteous little cries, coming from deep in his throat. He was running back and forth, stopping almost every second to cry up at me, and he seemed to be limping. I called to him. He stopped and looked up at me, his head cocked to one side.

"Come on, boy," I called.

He sprang to the side of the pit and tried to scramble toward me, but fell back. I called again, and again he tried and fell. Finally he sat down and held one paw toward me and barked.

I sat down and slid back to the bottom. He ran into my arms wagging his tail. His paw made a bloody imprint on my shirt as I picked him up to look at it. Its soft puppy pads had been cut and scraped on the rocks.

"All right, doggy," I said softly, "we'll get out of here together. I won't leave you."

He seemed to understand my words, for his tail wagged in happy circles as his soft moist tongue washed my face. I put him down and walked toward the other side of the pit to find an easier place to climb out. He ran along beside me, his eyes looking up at my face. I hoped Mamma would let me keep him.

It was almost dark now. We started climbing again, but it was no good. Less than halfway up I slipped and went to the bottom. once more. I was very tired, and hungry too. We couldn't make it. Until the moon came up, there was no use trying any more.

I sat down on a rock in the middle of the pit and tried to figure out what to do now. Mamma would be angry because I hadn't come home in time for supper. It had turned cool. I began to shiver and tried to button the collar of my shirt, but the button had been torn off.

A gray-black shape ran past me in the darkness. The dog let out a growl and snapped after it. Suddenly I was afraid; there were rats in this pit. I put my arms around the dog and began to cry. We would never get out of here. Another rat ran past us in the dark. With a frightened scream I ran to the side of the pit and tried to scramble up. Again and again I tried to climb out, but each time I fell back.

At last I lay on the ground, too exhausted to move. I was wet and uncomfortable. I caught my breath and began to yell. "Mamma! Mamma!" My voice echoed hollowly back across the pit to me. I kept shouting until my voice was hoarse and a mere squeak in my throat. There was no answer.

The moon had come up now and its white light threw a deep shadow from every rock. The night was alive with strange sounds and peculiar movements. As I began to get to my feet, a rat came hurtling through the air against my chest. I fell back screaming in terror. The dog jumped after the rat and caught it in midair. With an angry toss of his head, he broke the rat's neck and flung it away from him.

I stood up and placed my back against the wall of the pit, too cold and frightened to do anything but stare out into it. The dog stood in front of me, the hackles standing out sharply as he barked. The echoes sounded as if a hundred dogs were waking up the night.

I don't know how long we stood there like that. My eyes kept closing and I tried to keep them open, but I couldn't. At last I sank wearily to the ground.

Now I didn't know whether Mamma would be angry with me. It wasn't my fault. If I hadn't been a Jew, Paul and Eddie wouldn't have pushed me into the pit. When I got out I would ask Mamma if we please couldn't be something else. Then, maybe, they wouldn't be mad at me any more. But deep inside me I somehow knew even that wouldn't do any good. Even if Mamma was willing, Papa wouldn't change. I knew that about him. Once his mind was made up, he never changed. That must be why he had remained a Jew all these years. No, it wouldn't do any good.

Mamma would be very angry with me. Too bad, I remembered thinking as I began to doze, too bad this had to happen after the nice way the day had started out.

The dog's barks were louder now, and somewhere mixed up in their harsh echo I could hear someone calling my name. I tried to open my eyes but couldn't, I was so tired.

The voice grew louder, more insistent. "Danny! Danny Fisher!"

My eyes were open now and the eerie white light of the moon threw crazy shadows in the pit. A man's voice called my name again. I struggled to my feet and tried to answer, but my voice was gone It was only a weak, husky whisper. The dog began to bark furiously again. I heard voices at the top of the pit, and the dog's barks became more shrill and excited.

The gleam of a flashlight came pouring into the pit and moved around searching for me. I knew they couldn't hear me calling, so I ran after the ray of light, trying to show myself in it. The dog ran at my heels, still barking.

Then the light was on me and I stood still. I put my hands over my eyes; the light was hurting them. A man's voice shouted: "There he is!"

Another voice came from the darkness above me: "Danny! Danny!" It was Papa's voice. "Are you all right?"

Then I heard a scrambling, sliding sound of a man coming down the side of the pit toward me. I ran to him, crying, and felt myself caught up in his arms. He was shaking. I could feel his kisses on my face. "Danny, are you all right?" he was asking.

I pressed my face against him. My face was sore and scratched, but the feel of the rough wool of his suit was good. "I'm all right, Papa," I said between sobs, "but Mamma will be sore. I peed in my pants."

Something that sounded like a laugh came from his throat. "Mamma won't be angry," he reassured me. Raising his face toward the top of the pit, he shouted: "He's okay. Throw down a rope and we'll get him out."

"Don't forget the dog, Papa," I said. "We got to take him out too."

Papa bent and scratched the dog's head. "Sure, we'll take him out," he told me. "If it wasn't for his barking, we wouldn't have known where you were." He turned suddenly and looked at me. "Is he the reason you're down here?"

I shook my head. "No," I answered. "Paul and Eddie threw me down here because I'm a Jew."

Papa stared at me strangely. The rope fell at our feet and he bent to pick it up. I could hardly hear the words he was muttering under his breath: "The neighborhood is new, but the people are the same."

I didn't know what he meant. He fastened the rope around his middle and picked me up under one arm and the dog under the other. The rope tightened and we began to move up the side of the pit.

"You're not mad, are you, Papa?"

"No, Danny, I'm not mad."

I was silent for a moment as we inched further up the side. "Then is it okay if I keep the dog, Papa?" I asked. "He's such a nice little dog." The dog must have known I was talking about him; his tail thumped against my father's side. "We'll call him Rexie Fisher," I added.

Papa looked down at the little pup and then at me. He began to laugh. "You mean you'll call *her* Rexie Fisher. It isn't a him, it's a her."

The room was dark, but I was warm and cozy from my bath as I lay in my bed. There were new sounds in the night, new sounds coming in the window from a new neighborhood. New sounds to live with.

My eyes were wide with the wonder of them, but I wasn't afraid. There was nothing to be afraid of. I was in my own house, in my own room. Suddenly my eyes began to close. I half turned in my bed, and my hand brushed against the wall. It was rough from the freshly stippled paint.

"I love you, house," I murmured, already half asleep.

Under my bed the dog moved, and I put my hand down alongside it. I felt her cold nose in the palm of my hand. My fingers scratched the top of her head. Her fur was damp and cool to my touch. Mamma had made Papa give Rexie a bath before she would let me take her up to my room. Her tongue was licking my fingers. "I love you too, Rexie," I whispered.

A sense of warmth and comfort and belonging began to steal through me. Slowly I could feel the last trace of tautness, slip from my body, and the nothing that is sleep came over me.

I was home. And the first day of my life that I remembered faded into yesterday, and all the days of my life became tomorrow.

All the Days of My Life

THE FIRST BOOK

CHAPTER ONE

THE SUN PRESSED WARMLY AGAINST MY CLOSED LIDS. VAGUELY ANNOYED, I threw an arm over my eyes and moved restlessly on the pillow. For a few minutes I was comfortable; then the light seemed to creep under my arm and search me out. I stopped trying to hide from it and sat up in bed, rubbing my eyes. I was awake.

I stretched. I yawned. I pushed my hair back from my eyes and looked sleepily toward the window. It was a bright, clear morning. I wished I could have gone on sleeping, but my windows faced east and the first morning sun always hit me in the face.

I looked lazily around the room. My clothes lay rumpled on a chair. The half-strung tennis racket I never got around to fix was leaning against the side of the dresser. The old alarm clock on the dresser, next to my comb and brush showed it was a quarter past seven. My purple and white Erasmus Hall High School pennant hung drooping across the mirror.

I looked down at the side of the bed for my slippers. They weren't there. I grinned to myself. I knew where they were. Rexie usually pulled them under the bed and made a pillow out of them for her head. I reached down and gave her a scratch. She lifted her head and lazily wagged her tail. I gave her another scratch and took the slippers away from her. Then I got out of bed and stepped into them. Rexie had closed her eyes and gone back to sleep.

I could hear a faint sound coming from my parents' room as I walked over to the open window. That reminded me. Today was the big day: my Bar Mitzvah day. I began to feel an excited nervousness in me. I hoped I wouldn't forget any of the elaborate Hebrew ritual I had specially learned for the occasion.

I stood by the open window and breathed deeply. Slowly I counted to myself: "In—two—three—four; out—two—three—four." After a few moments of this I began to feel the nervousness go away. I would be all right, I wouldn't forget anything. Still facing the window, I pulled my pajama top over my head and threw it on the bed behind me. Bar Mitzvah day or not, I had to get my setting-up exercises in or I would never weigh enough to go out for the football team in the fall.

I stretched out on the floor and did ten push-ups, then I stood up and began to do knee-bends. I looked down at myself. The thin stringy muscles on my body stood out sharply. I could count my ribs I scanned my chest carefully to see if any real hairs had come out in the night, but it was still the same small golden fuzz. Sometimes I wished that my hair was black like Paul's instead of blond. Then they would show up more plainly.

I finished the knee-bends and picked up the pair of Indian clubs from the corner of the room. Back in front of the window I began to swing them. I heard the click of a light-switch through the open window and a flood of light poured into the windows of the room across the driveway from mine. Almost instantly I dropped to my knees and cautiously peered over the windowsill.

That was Marjorie Ann Conlon's room. She was Mimi's closest girl friend. Sometimes her shade was up and I could get a good look. I was glad her house faced west, for that made it necessary for her to turn the light on every morning.

Carefully I peeked over the windowsill and held my breath. The shades were up. That was the third time this week she had forgotten to pull them down. The last time I had watched her I thought she had known I was looking, so I had to be extra careful. She was a funny kind of a girl, always teasing me and staring at me when I spoke to her. In the last few weeks we'd had several hot arguments about almost nothing and I didn't want to invite her to my Bar Mitzvah party, but Mimi insisted on it.

I saw the closet door in her room move slightly and she came out from behind it. All she had on was her panties. She stopped in the middle of the room for a moment, looking for something. Finally she found it and leaned toward the window to pick it up. I felt a damp sweat break out on my forehead. I could see her real good.

Paul said she had the nicest figure in the neighborhood. I didn't agree with him. Mimi's was much nicer. Besides, Mimi wasn't all out of proportion around the breasts the way Marjorie Ann was.

Paul had suggested that we get the girls down cellar and find out. I got mad at that and grabbed him by the collar and told him I'd beat hell out of him if he ever did that. Paul only laughed and pushed my hand away. The only reason I didn't have the nerve, he said, was that I was afraid Mimi would snitch on us.

Marjorie Ann was facing the window now, seeming to be looking out at me. I lowered my head even more. She was smiling to herself as she hooked on her brassiere, and I began to feel uncomfortable. It was a very knowing smile. I wondered if she knew I was watching. There seemed to be a peculiar awareness in the way she moved around the room.

She had the brassiere half on when a frown crossed her face. She shrugged her shoulders and it slipped down on her arms. She cupped her breasts in her hands for a moment and moved nearer to the window, seeming to be examining them in the light.

My heart began to hammer excitedly. Paul was right. She really had them. She looked up again, the proud smile back on her face, and went back into the room. Carefully she slipped into the brassiere and hooked it behind her.

Outside in the hall there was a noise. I could hear Mimi's voice. Quickly I turned and dove back into bed. I didn't want Mimi to catch me peeking. I stole a quick glance out the window and saw the light go out in Marjorie Ann's room. I sighed. That proved it. I had been right: she knew I was watching her. I heard footsteps coming toward my door, and I closed my eyes and pretended I was asleep.

Mimi's voice came from the doorway. "Danny, are you up?"

"I am now," I answered, sitting up in bed and rubbing my eyes. "What do yuh want?"

Her eyes swept across my bare chest and shoulders. A suspicious light came into them. "Where's your pajama top?" she asked. Then her eyes fell on it lying at the foot of the bed. "You were out of bed already?"

I stared at her. "Yeah."

"What were you doing?" she asked suspiciously. Her eyes wandered over to Marjorie Ann's windows across the driveway.

I made my eyes big and innocent. "My exercises," I said. "Then I hopped back in bed for a snooze."

I could see my answer didn't satisfy her, but she didn't say anything. She bent over the foot of the bed and picked up my pajama top from where it lay, half on the floor. Her breasts were pushed hard against the thin rayon pajamas she wore. I couldn't keep my eyes from them.

Mimi noticed where I was looking and her face flushed. Angrily she threw the pajama top back on my bed and walked toward the door. "Mamma told me to wake you up and remind you to shower," she flung back over her shoulder. "She doesn't want you to be dirty for your Bar Mitzvah."

I jumped out of bed as soon as the door closed behind her, and dropped my pajama pants. I felt warm and tingling, as I always felt after I had watched Marjorie Ann. I looked down at myself. I was in good shape all right. I was five foot four and weighed close to one hundred and fourteen pounds. Six more pounds and I'd be okay for the football team. I knew how to handle the tingling too, I wasn't worried about that. "Cold showers," the P.T. teacher in school had said. "Cold showers, boys." And a cold shower was just what I was going to have.

I slipped into my bathrobe and looked out into the hall. It was empty. The bathroom door was open, so I started toward it. Mimi's door was open too, and she was standing there making her bed. I thumbed my nose at her as I passed, and my robe slipped open. I snatched it close around me. Damn! Now she would know how I felt when she came into my room. Maybe I'd better make peace with her or she might snitch. You could never figure her out. I went back to her door still holding the robe around me.

"Mimi."

She looked at me. "What do you want?" Her voice was cold.

I looked down at my slippers. "Yuh want to use the toilet first?"

"Why?" she asked suspiciously.

I could hear Mamma and Papa talking downstairs. I kept my voice as low as possible. "I'm—uh—goin' to shower an' maybe you're in a hurry."

"I'm in no hurry," she answered, her voice still cold and formal.

I could see she was sore. "Mimi," I said again.

"What?" She was staring at me.

My eyes fell from her gaze. "Nothin'," I answered. I started to turn and then looked up at her suddenly.

She had been watching my hands where they clutched the robe. This time she lowered her eyes. "You boys are disgusting," she muttered. "You're getting more like your friend Paul every day. He's always looking."

"I wasn't looking," I said defensively.

"You were too," she said accusingly. "I bet you were spying on Marjorie Ann too."

My face flushed. "I was not!" I said, waving my hands emphatically. The robe fell open again. I saw Mimi's eyes fall and I hurriedly snatched it close. "I notice you don't mind lookin', Miss Hoity Toity!"

She paid no attention to me. "I'm going to tell Mamma what you were doing," she said.

I crossed the room to her quickly and grabbed her hands. "You will not!"

"You're hurting me!" Her eyes fell from my face. She was staring at me.

"You will not!" I repeated harshly, gripping her wrists tighter.

She looked up into my face, her brown eyes wide and frightened, yet with a curiosity deep within them. She drew a deep breath. "Okay," she said, "I won't tell Mamma, but I'm going to tell Marge she was right. She said you were peeping on her. I'm going to tell her to keep her shades down!"

I let go of her wrists. A vague triumph coursed through me. I had been right, Marge had known all along that I was watching. "If Marge leaves her shades up," I said, contempt creeping into my voice, "she knows what she's doing."

I left Mimi standing beside the bed and went into the bathroom. Papa's shaving brush was still on the sink drying out. I put it back in the medicine chest and closed the door. Then I threw my bathrobe on the toilet seat and got under the shower.

The water was ice-cold, but I gritted my teeth. After a while my teeth began to chatter, but I still stood there. It was good for me. I knew what I was doing. When I finally came out of the shower and looked in the mirror, my lips were blue with cold.

CHAPTER TWO

I FINISHED BUTTONING MY SHIRT AND LOOKED IN THE MIRROR. I PICKED UP the comb and ran it through my hair again. Mamma would be pleased. My skin was clean and shining, even my hair seemed lighter in color.

I bent down and looked under the bed. "Wake up, Rexie," I told her. "Time to go out." She jumped to her feet, wagging her tail. I bent over and scratched her head. She licked my hand. "How are you this morning, girl?" I asked, giving her a quick hug. Her tail began to go around in circles and she rubbed against my trousers.

I walked out of the room and down the stairs. I could hear Mamma's voice coming from the kitchen. She sounded all excited over something. She was saying: "You know your sister-in-law, Bessie. She'll be looking for something to talk about. She thinks she's the only one that could ever make a Bar Mitzvah. Her Joel—"

Papa interrupted her. "Now, Mary," he said soothingly, "keep calm. Everything'll go all right. After all, you were the one that decided to have the reception at home."

I heaved a sigh of relief. At least they weren't talking about me. Mimi hadn't said anything. This argument had been going on for six months—ever since the subject of my Bar Mitzvah had come up.

Papa had wanted to hire a small hall for the reception, but Mama would have none of it. "We can't spare the money," she had said. "You know how bad business is, and you're having a hard enough time meeting the payments on your loan as it is. And the Corn Exchange Bank won't wait for its three thousand dollars." Papa had given in to her. He had to; he had no other choice. Business hadn't got any better. If anything, judging from what he had let drop around the house, it had got worse. In the past few months he had become very nervous and irritable.

I pushed open the door and walked into the kitchen, Rexie close on my heels "Good morning," I said to both of them. "What do you want at the store?" I asked Mamma.

She scarcely looked at me. "The usual, Danny," she replied.

"Can I get some jelly doughnuts, Ma?"

She smiled at me. "All right, Danny." She took a dollar from a glass tumbler on the shelf over the sink and gave it to me. "After all, it's your Bar Mitzvah day."

I took the dollar and started out the kitchen door. I heard Mamma's voice behind me: "Don't forget to count your change, Danny."

"I won't, Ma," I called back over my shoulder, opening the door to let Rexie out. The dog loped down the driveway ahead of me, running for the gutter.

I heard voices on the Conlon stoop as I came out of the driveway. Out of the corner of my eye I saw Mimi and Marjorie Ann, their heads very close together. I walked past them as if I hadn't seen them, but I had to stop for Rexie in front of the stoop. Marge was looking at me and began to giggle. I could feel my face turn red.

"I'll be at your party this afternoon," she called.

I was angry with myself for blushing. "Don't do me any favors," I told her insultingly. "You don't have to come for my sake."

Her laugh was taunting. "Why, Danny, how you talk!" she said sarcastically. "You know you wouldn't feel right if you didn't see me! Besides, you'll be a man when you come back from your Bar Mitzvah. It'll be fun to see how you act then!"

Rexie began to run happily down the street. I followed her without answering.

The light in the synagogue was dim and gray as it came through the small windows high on the walls. I looked around nervously. I was standing on the small platform looking down on the room in front of the Torah. The three old men on the platform with me all wore little black yamalkas. Mine was of white silk.

The faces below the platform looked up at me expectantly. I recognized most of them. They were my relatives. At the back of the synagogue there was a small table covered with cakes and bottles of whisky and wine, gleaming in the dimness.

Rev Herzog, my teacher, took down the Torah and opened it. He motioned me toward the edge of the railing, then turned toward the congregation and spoke in Yiddish.

"In these troubled days," he said, in a thin and wavering voice, "it is good for a man to find a boy who is not ashamed to be a Jew. It is also good for a man to teach such a boy. It is an honor for a man to prepare such a boy for Bar Mitzvah and to welcome him into the state of Jewish manhood." He turned to me solemnly. "I have with me such a boy." He turned back to the congregation and continued to speak.

I tried to keep a straight face. The old hypocrite! He used to yell at me all the time he was giving me the lessons. I was no good, would never be any good; I would never make my Bar Mitzvah because I was too stupid.

I caught a glimpse of my sister's face watching him. There was a rapt, intent look on her face. She smiled up at me swiftly, a gleam of pride in her eyes, and I smiled back at her.

Rev Herzog's voice was fading away and he turned toward me. Slowly I moved to the center of the platform and placed my hands on the Torah. Nervously I cleared my throat. I could see Mamma and Papa smiling up at me expectantly. For a moment my mind went blank and a panic went through me. I had forgotten the elaborate ritual I had spent so many months memorizing.

I heard Rev Herzog's hoarse whisper in my ear: *"Borochu ess—"*

Gratefully I picked up the cue. *"Borochu ess Adonai. . . . "* I was all right now and the rest of the words came easily. Mamma was smiling proudly at the people around her.

I began to feel the solemnity of the prayer. I wished I had paid more attention to what the words I was reciting so glibly in Hebrew meant. Vaguely I remembered that I was asking God's assistance to become an honorable man and to help me lead a good Jewish life. A deep sense of responsibility came over me. One day you were a boy, the next a man. In this ritual I accepted that responsibility. I swore before a group of relatives and friends that I would always discharge my obligations as a good Jew.

I had never thought much about that before. Deep inside me I knew I had never wanted to be a Jew. I remembered the first time I had thought about it: the time Paul and his kid brother, Eddie, had pushed me into the pit at Clarendon and Troy, the day I found Rexie. The pit was filled in now and there were houses on the spot, but I could never pass the place without remembering. I remembered asking Mamma the next day if we couldn't be something other than Jews. Whatever her answer had been, it wasn't important now. I was consecrating myself to be a Jew.

The last phrases of the prayer passed my lips and, looking down at the congregation, I had a feeling of triumph. Mamma was crying, and Papa was blowing his nose into a large white handkerchief. I smiled at them.

Rev Herzog was draping the tallith on my shoulders, the white silk tallith with the blue star of David emblazoned on it that Mamma had bought for me. He spoke a few words and it was over.

I ran down the steps. Mamma threw her arms around me and kissed me, saying my name over and over. I began to feel embarrassed, I wished she would let me go. I was supposed to be a man now, but she was acting as if I was still a kid.

Papa clapped me on the shoulder. "Good boy, Danny." He was smiling. He turned to Rev Herzog, who had come down the steps behind me. "He was good, Rev, wasn't he?" he asked.

Rev Herzog nodded his head briefly without answering and pushed past Papa, heading for the refreshment table. The other men on the platform followed him quickly.

Papa caught at my arm and led me toward the table. He was pleased, I could see. Ceremoniously he poured a little whisky into a paper cup and offered it to me.

"Harry!" Mamma's voice was protesting.

He smiled happily at her. "Come now, Mary," he said jovially, "the boy's a man now!"

I nodded my head. Papa was right. I took the cup from him.

"*L'chaim!*" Papa said.

"*L'chaim,*" I replied.

Papa tipped his head back and threw the whisky down his throat. I did the same thing. It burned like fire on the way down to my stomach. I began to choke and cough.

"See what you've done, Harry," Mamma said reproachfully.

I looked at Papa through the tears in my eyes. He was laughing. Another paroxysm of coughing overtook me, and Mamma pulled my head close to her bosom.

CHAPTER THREE

THE HOUSE WAS OVERFLOWING WITH PEOPLE. I HAD TO PUT REXIE UP IN my bedroom and close the door. Crowds always made her nervous. I pushed my way through the living-room on my way to the cellar stairs. Mamma had fixed up a play-room for the kids down there.

My Uncle David called me. He was standing in a corner of the room, talking to Papa. I walked over to him, and he held out his hand. "*Mazeltov*, Danny!"

"Thanks, Uncle David." I smiled automatically.

Taking my hand, he turned to Papa. "It seems like only yesterday I was at his B'riss, Harry," he said.

Papa nodded his head in agreement.

I flushed impatiently. I knew just what he was going to say, I had heard the same thing twenty times already today. And he didn't disappoint me.

"Time flies, doesn't it?" Uncle David's head was nodding too. "And now you're a big boy." He reached into his pocket and took out a coin. "Here, Danny, for you."

I turned the gold coin over in my fingers—a ten-dollar gold piece. "Thanks, Uncle David," I said.

He grinned at me. "A big boy," he said. He turned to Papa. "Soon he'll be able to give you a hand in the store like my Joel does for me."

Papa shook his head in disagreement. "No store for my Danny," he answered firmly. "My Danny's going to be a professional man. He's going to be a lawyer or a doctor maybe, and if things are right I'll open a fine office for him some day."

I looked at Papa in surprise. This was the first time I had heard about it. I never thought very much about what I was going to be. I never cared very much.

A knowing look came into Uncle David's face. "Of course, Harry, of course," he said soothingly. "But you know how times are. Not good. And you're having enough of a struggle as it is. Now, if your Danny came into the store for the summer like my Joel does for me, what harm can it do? None at all. And you save five dollars a week for a boy. Five dollars is five dollars." He looked at me. "And Danny's a fine boy. I'm sure he would want to help out like my Joel does. Wouldn't you, Danny?"

I nodded my head. Nobody was going to say that my cousin, Joel, was better than I. "Sure, Uncle David," I said quickly.

Papa looked at me. There was a troubled shadow in his eyes. His lips trembled slightly. "There's time enough to talk about that, Danny," he said slowly. "Vacation time's a month away yet. Meanwhile, you run downstairs. The children must be looking for you."

I headed for the stairway, slipping the coin into my pocket. Behind me I could hear Uncle David's voice repeating that it was a good idea and would do me no harm.

On the stairway I stopped and looked into the playroom. Mamma had hung streamers on the walls and ceiling and it looked very gay and partylike, but the kids were very quiet. Upstairs the grownups were all talking loudly, each trying to outshout the others, all talking at once as if they would never have the chance to talk to one another again, and their voices echoed hollowly down here. All the boys were on one side of the room, the girls on the other. Their voices were muted and self-conscious. It wasn't like upstairs at all.

As I walked over to the boys' side of the room, my cousin, Joel, came forward to meet me. He was about a year and half older than me and his face was covered with pimples. I'd heard stories about that. I hoped I wouldn't get them.

"Hello, Joel," I said awkwardly. "Having a good time?"

He nodded politely, his eyes on the girl across the room. "Sure," he answered quickly—too quickly.

I followed his gaze. He was looking at Marjorie Ann. She saw me looking at her and whispered something to my sister, who began to giggle. I walked over to her, Joel at my side.

"What's funny?" I asked belligerently. I had the idea they were laughing at me.

Mimi shook her head silently and giggled again. Marge smiled tauntingly. "We were waiting for you to come down and liven up the party," she said.

I forced a smile on my face and looked around. All the kids were looking at me solemnly. She was right, the party was dying. The grownups were having a good time, but the kids didn't know what to do.

"Hey, what are we so quiet about?" I yelled, holding up my hands. "Let's play games."

"What games?" Mimi's voice was challenging.

I looked at her dumbly. I hadn't thought about that. I looked around the room helplessly.

"How about starting with post office?" Marge suggested.

I made a wry face. That was just the kind of game I didn't want to play. Sissy stuff.

"What do you want to play?" she snapped sarcastically, seeing my expression. "Touch tackle?"

I started to speak, but Joel cut me off. "That's okay," he said eagerly, "I'm willing."

I turned to him with a look of disgust on my face. I knew why he had pimples all right: girls. I would have given him an argument, but all the other kids went for the suggestion big.

When we were sitting in the semicircle on the floor. I looked sullenly down at my crossed legs, wishing I had been able to think of another game. Joel had called Marge into the small furnace room that acted as the post office and I was sure that she would send for me when it was her turn.

I was right. The furnace-room door opened and Joel was standing in front of me. He made a jerking motion with his thumb at the closed door behind him. I could feel my face flush as I got to my feet. "What a gal!" he whispered as I passed him.

I looked down at Mimi. She was watching me with a speculative look on her face. I could feel my cheeks burning.

I hesitated a moment before the furnace-room door, then opened it and stepped inside. I leaned against the closed door behind me, trying to see through the dimness in the room. Its only light came from a tiny window in the corner.

"I'm over here, Danny." Marge's voice came from the other side of the furnace.

I was still holding the doorknob. I could feel a pulse begin to race in my temples. "What—what do you want?" I stammered hoarsely. I was suddenly afraid of her. "What did you call me for?"

She was whispering. "What do you think I called you for?" There was a taunting quality in her voice. "I wanted to see if you really were a man."

I couldn't see her. She was standing behind the furnace. "Why don't you leave me alone?" I asked bitterly, not moving from the door.

Her voice was flat. "If you want to get this over with, you'd better come here." I could hear her almost silent laugh. "I won't hurt you, Danny boy."

I walked around the furnace. She was leaning against it, smiling. Her teeth shone brightly in the dim light. Her hands were behind her. I didn't speak.

Her eyes were laughing. "You were watching me through the window this morning," she shot at me suddenly.

I stood there stiffly. "I was not!"

"You were too!" she snapped. "I saw you, and Mimi said you were."

I stared at her. I'd get even with Mimi for this. "If you were so sure," I said angrily, "then why didn't you pull down the shades?"

She took a step toward me. "Maybe I didn't want to," she said teasingly.

I looked down into her face. I didn't understand it. "But—"

Her fingers on my lips silenced me. There was a strained, tense expression on her face. "Maybe I wanted you to look." She paused for a second, watching my face. "Didn't you like what you saw?"

I didn't know what to say.

She began to laugh softly. "You did," she whispered. "I could see you did. Your cousin, Joel, thinks I'm terrific, and he hasn't even seen half as much of me as you."

She was standing very close to me. She put her arms around my neck and pulled me toward her. I moved woodenly. I felt her breath against my mouth, then her lips. I closed my eyes. This was like no kiss I had ever known before. Not like my mother's, not like my sister's, nor like anyone's I ever kissed.

She pulled her face away from mine. I could feel the rush of her breath still against my mouth. "Give me your hand," she demanded quickly.

Stupidly I held out my hand. My head was reeling and the room seemed vague and distant. Suddenly a shock seemed to run through my fingers like an electric current. She had put my hand down the front of her dress and I could feel her breast, her nipple hard. Frightened, I jerked my hand away.

She began to laugh softly, her eyes shining up at me. "I like you, Danny," she whispered. She went to the door and turned back to look at me. The mockery was back on her face again. "Who shall I send in now, Danny?" she asked. "Your sister?"

CHAPTER FOUR

I WALKED THROUGH THE PARLOR, REXIE AT MY HEELS. "DANNY, COME HERE a minute." Papa's voice came from the couch where he was sitting next to Mamma.

Mamma looked tired. She had just finished cleaning up after everyone had gone. The house seemed curiously quiet now.

"Yes, Papa." I stood in front of them.

"You had a good Bar Mitzvah, Danny?" Papa said, half questioningly.

"Very good, Papa," I answered. "Thanks."

He waved his hand slightly. "Don't thank me," he said. "Thank your Mamma. She did all the work."

I smiled at her.

She smiled wearily up at me, and her hand patted the cushion beside her. I sat down. Her hand reached up and rumpled my hair. "My little Blondele," she said wistfully. "All grown up now. Soon you'll be getting married."

Papa began to laugh. "Not so soon yet, Mary. He's still young."

Mamma looked at him. "Soon enough," she said. "Look how quick the thirteen years went."

Papa chuckled. He took a cigar out of his pocket and lit it, a thoughtful expression settling on his face. "David made the suggestion that Danny come to work in the store this summer."

Mamma started forward in her seat. "But, Harry, he's still a baby yet!"

Papa laughed aloud. "Today he's getting married, but this summer he's too young to work." He turned toward me. "How do you feel about it, Danny?"

I looked at him. "I'll do anything you want, Papa," I answered.

He shook his head. "That's not what I meant. I asked what do you want to do. What do you want to be?"

I hesitated a moment. "I really don't know," I confessed. "I never thought about it."

"Time you should start thinking about it, Danny," he said seriously. "You're a smart boy. A year in high school already and you're just thirteen. But all that smartness is no good unless you know where you're going. Like a ship without a rudder."

"I'll come into the store this summer, Papa," I said quickly. "After all, if it will help you, that's what I want. I know business is not so hot these days."

"It's bad enough, but not so bad that I want you to do something you don't want," he said, looking at his cigar. "Your mamma and me, we have great hopes for you. That you would be a doctor or a lawyer and go to college. Maybe if you come into the store you won't go to college. That's what happened to me. I never finished school. I don't want it to happen to you."

I looked at him, then at Mamma. She was watching me, sadness in her eyes. They were afraid that what had happened to him would happen to me. Still, business was bad and Papa needed my help. I smiled at them. "Going to work in the store for the summer doesn't mean anything, Papa," I said. "In the fall I go back to school again."

He turned to Mamma. For a long moment they looked at each other. Then Mamma nodded her head slightly and he turned back to me. "All right, Danny," he said heavily. "Let it be that way for a while. We'll see."

The boys were shouting as the volley ball shuttled back and forth across the net. There were four games going in the school gymnasium. Out of the corner of my eye I could see Mr. Gottkin walking toward us. I pulled my eyes back to the ball. I wanted to look good for him. He coached the football team.

The ball was coming toward me, high over my head, but I leapt and stabbed at it. It caught the top of the net, rolled over the other side, and fell to the floor. I looked around proudly, feeling pretty good. That made the eighth point I had scored out of the fourteen for my side. Mr. Gottkin couldn't help noticing that.

He wasn't even looking my way. He was talking to a boy on the next court. The ball came back into play again. I missed what seemed like a couple of easy shots, but each time they were recovered. When the play seemed to be going over to the other side of the court, I stole another glance at the teacher.

From behind me I could hear Paul's sudden shout: "Danny! Your ball!"

I spun around quickly. The ball was floating easily across the net toward me. I set myself for it and jumped. A dark figure on the other side of the net flashed up before me and hit the ball toward the floor. Automatically my hands went up to cover my face, but I wasn't fast enough. I went A.O.E. on the floor.

I scrambled to my feet angrily, one side of my face red and stinging where the ball had hit me. The dark boy on the other side of the net was grinning at me.

"Yuh fouled it!" I shot at him.

The smile left his face. "What's the matter, Danny?" he sneered. "You the only hero allowed in the game?"

I started under the net for him, but a hand gripped my shoulder firmly and stopped me.

"Get on with the game, Fisher," Mr. Gottkin said quietly. "No roughhousing."

I ducked back under the net to my side. I was angrier now than before. All Gottkin would remember was that I had got sore. "I'll get hunk," I whispered to the boy.

His lips formed a soundless raspberry accompanied by a gesture of derision.

My chance came on the very next play. The ball floated over my head and the boy shot up for it. I beat him to it and hit it savagely downward with both hands. It struck him squarely in the mouth and he rolled over on the floor. I hooted loudly at him.

He came off the floor and, charging under the net, tackled me around the legs. We rolled over and over on the floor pummeling each other. His voice was hot and angry in my ear: "Yuh son of a bitch!"

Gottkin pulled us apart. "I tol'yuh, no roughhousing."

I looked down at the floor sullenly and didn't answer.

"Who started this?" Gottkin's voice was harsh.

I looked at the other boy and he glowered at me, but neither of us answered.

The P.T. teacher didn't wait for an answer. "Get on with the game," he said in a disgusted voice. "And no roughhousing." He turned away from us.

Automatically we started for each other as his back turned. I caught the dark boy around the middle and we were on the floor again before Mr. Gottkin pulled us apart.

His arms held us at each side of him. There was a weary, speculative look on his face. "You guys insist on fightin'?" he stated rather than asked.

Neither of us answered.

"Well," he continued, "if you're gonna fight, you'll fight my way." Still holding us, he called over his shoulder to the substitute teacher who was his assistant: "Get out the gloves."

The sub came up with the gloves, and Gottkin gave a pair to each of us. "Put 'em on," he said almost genially. He turned to the boys in the gym who had started to crowd around. "Better lock the doors, boys," he said. "We can't have anyone walking in on us."

They laughed excitedly while I fumbled with the unfamiliar gloves. I knew what they were laughing at. If the principal came in, there would be hell to pay.

The boxing gloves felt clumsy on my hands. I'd never had a pair on before. Paul silently began to tie the laces for me. I looked over at the other boy. The first flush of anger had died away in me. I didn't have anything against this kid. I didn't even know his name. The only class we were in together was this one. He looked like he was beginning to feel the same way. I walked up to him. "This is stupid," I said.

Mr. Gottkin replied before the boy could open his mouth. "Goin' yella, Fisher?" he sneered. There was a peculiar excitement in his eyes.

I could feel the heat flaming in my cheeks. "No, but—"

Gottkin cut me off. "Then get back there an' do what I tell yuh. Come out fightin'. When one of you is knocked down, the other will not hit him until I give the okay. Understand?"

I nodded. The boy wet his lips and also nodded his head.

I could see Gottkin felt good again. "All right, boys," he said, "go to it."

I felt someone shoving me forward. The dark boy was coming toward me. I raised my hands and tried to hold them the way I had seen some fighters in the movies do. Warily I circled around the boy. He was just as cautious as I was, watching me carefully. For almost a minute we didn't come within two feet of each other.

"I thought you guys wanted to fight," Gottkin said. I stole a glance at him. His eyes were still burning with excitement.

A light exploded in my own eyes. I could hear the boys begin to yell. Another light flashed. Then a sharp stinging pain in my right ear, then on my mouth. I could feel myself falling. There was a grinding buzzing sound in my head. I shook it angrily to clear it and opened my eyes. I was on my hands and knees. I looked up.

The boy was dancing in front of me. He was laughing.

The louse had hit me when I wasn't looking. I got to my feet, anger surging in me. I saw Gottkin tap him on the shoulder, then he was all over me. Desperately I pushed in close and grabbed at his arms and held on.

My throat was raw, I could feel my breath burning in it. I shook my head. I couldn't think with that buzzing around in there. I shook my head again. Suddenly the noise stopped and the breath was easier in my throat.

I felt Gottkin pull us apart. His voice was husky in my ears. "Break it up, boys."

My legs were steady now. I held my hands up and waited for the other boy to come after me.

He came charging in, arms flailing. I moved aside and he surged past me. I almost smiled to myself. This was easy: you just had to keep your head on your shoulders.

He turned around and came after me again. This time I waited for him. I could see his fists were high. I drove my right hand into his belly. His hands came down and he doubled up. His knees began to buckle and I stepped back. I looked questioningly at Mr. Gottkin.

He pushed me back toward the boy roughly. I hit the boy twice and he straightened up, a dazed look on his face.

I was standing flatfooted now. I could feel a surge of power flowing through my body into my arms. I brought my right up almost from the floor, and it caught him flush on the chin. The shock of the punch ran through my arm. He spun around once and then fell forward, flat on his face.

I stepped back and looked at Mr. Gottkin. He was standing there with a flushed look, staring down at the boy. His tongue was running nervously over his lips, his hands were clenched, and the back of his shirt was covered with sweat as if he had done the fighting.

A sudden silence fell over the gymnasium. I turned back to the boy, who lay there quietly, not even moving. Slowly Mr. Gottkin knelt beside him.

He rolled the boy over on his back and slapped at his face. The teacher was pale now. He looked up at the sub. "Get me the smelling-salts!" he cried hoarsely.

His hands were trembling violently as he waved the bottle back and forth under the boy's nose. "Come on, kid." He seemed to be pleading. "Snap out of it." There were beads of sweat on his face.

I stared down at them. Why didn't the kid get up? I shouldn't have let them bulldoze me into a fight.

"Maybe we better get a doctor," the sub whispered anxiously to Mr. Gottkin.

Gottkin's voice was low, but I could hear him as I bent down. "Not if yuh like this job!"

"But what if the kid dies?"

The sub's query went unanswered as color began to flood back into the boy's face. He tried to sit up, but Gottkin held him back on the floor.

"Take it easy, kid," Gottkin said almost gently. "You'll be okay in a minute."

He picked the boy up in his arms and looked around. "You fellas keep your mouths shut about this. Understand?" His voice was menacing. Silently they gave their assent. His eyes swept past them and came to me. "You, Fisher," he said harshly, "come with me. The rest of you get back to your games."

He strode into his office, still carrying the boy, and I followed. He put the kid down on a leather-covered dressing-table as I closed the door behind us. "Get me that water pitcher over there," he called over his shoulder.

Silently I handed it to him and he upended it over the boy's face. The boy sat up sputtering.

"How're yuh feeling, kid?" Gottkin asked.

The boy forced a grin to his face. He looked at me shyly. "As if a mule kicked me," he replied.

Gottkin began to laugh in relief. Then his glance fell on me and the smile disappeared. "Why didn't yuh tell me yuh knew how to fight, Fisher?" he snarled. "I got a mind to—"

"I never fought with gloves before, Mr. Gottkin," I said quickly. "Honest."

He looked at me dubiously, but he must have believed me, for he turned back to the boy. "Okay if we forget the whole thing?" he asked him.

The boy looked at me and smiled again. He nodded his head. "I don't even want to remember it," he said earnestly.

Gottkin looked back at me for a second, a speculative look in his eyes. "Then, shake hands, you two, an' get outta here."

We shook hands and started out the door. As I closed it I could see Mr. Gottkin opening a drawer in his desk and taking something out of it. He began to raise it toward his mouth.

Just then the sub pushed past me on his way into the office. "Give me some of that," he said as the door shut. "I never want to go through another minute like that again."

Gottkin's voice boomed through the closed door. "That Fisher kid's a natural fighter. Did you see—?"

I looked up self-consciously. My former opponent was waiting for me. Awkwardly I took his arm and together we walked back to the volley-ball game.

CHAPTER FIVE

I STOOD IMPATIENTLY ON THE CORNER OF BEDFORD AND CHURCH AVENUES behind the school waiting for Paul. The clock in the drugstore window across the street showed a quarter after three. I'd give him five more minutes, then I'd start for home without him.

I was still tingling with a new excitement. The news of my fight in the gym had run through the school like wildfire. All the boys were treating me with a new respect and the girls were looking at me with a curiously restrained awareness. Several times I had overheard groups of people talking about me.

A Ford roadster pulled to the curb in front of me and honked its horn. I looked up at it.

"Hey, Fisher, come over here." Mr. Gottkin was leaning out of the car.

Slowly I walked toward him. What did he want now?

He opened the door. "Hop in," he invited. "I'll drive yuh home."

I looked at the clock quickly and made up my mind. Paul would have to walk home alone. I got into the car silently.

"Which way do you go?" Mr. Gottkin asked in a friendly voice as he pulled the car away from the curb.

"Over to Clarendon."

We rode a few blocks in silence. I watched him out of the corner of my eye. He must have had a reason for picking me up. I wondered when he was going to talk. Suddenly he slowed the car and pulled toward the curb.

A young woman was walking there. Gottkin leaned out of the car and shouted after her. "Hey, Ceil!"

She stopped to look back at us and I recognized her: Miss Schindler, the art teacher. Her class was one of the most popular in school. The girls couldn't understand why all the boys suddenly signed for art in the third term, but I could. Next term I would be in her class.

She had dark brown hair, dark eyes, and a soft tan skin. She had been to Paris to study. and the boys said she never wore a brassiere. I had heard them talking about how she looked when she bent over their desks.

"Oh, it's you, Sam," she said, smiling and walking back toward the car.

"Hop in, Ceil," he urged her, "I'll take you home." He turned to me. "Shove over, kid," he told me. "Make room for her."

I moved closer to him, and Miss Schindler sat down beside me and closed the door. There was just room enough for the three of us on the seat. I could feel the press of her thigh against me. I stole a look at her out of the corner of my eyes. The boys were right. I shifted uncomfortably.

Gottkin's voice was louder than usual. "Where you been keepin' yourself, baby?"

Her voice was low. "Around, Sam," she answered evasively, looking at me.

Gottkin caught her look. "You know Miss Schindler, Fisher?" he asked.

I shook my head. "No."

"This is Danny Fisher," he said to her.

She turned to me, curiosity in her eyes. "You're the boy who had the fight in school today?" she said half-questioningly.

"You know about it?" Gottkin sounded surprised.

"It's all over the school, Sam," she replied in a peculiar tone of voice. "Your boy here is the most famous man in the place today."

I fought back an impulse to smile proudly.

"You can't keep anything quiet in that place," Gottkin grumbled. "If the old man gets wind of it, I'm sunk."

Miss Schindler looked at him. "That's what I always told you, Sam," she said in the same peculiar tone of voice. "Teachers can't lead their own lives."

I looked up at her quickly, puzzled.

She caught my glance and her face flushed. "I heard it was quite a fight," she said.

I didn't answer. I had the idea she wasn't really interested in the fight.

Gottkin answered for me. "It was. Fisher got off the floor and knocked the other kid for a loop. Yuh never seen nothin' like it."

There was a shadow in her dark eyes. "You can't forget what you were once," she said bitterly, "can you, Sam?"

He didn't answer.

She spoke again, her voice unchanged. "You can let me out here, Sam. This is my corner."

Silently he stopped the car. She got out and leaned over the running board to us. "Nice to meet you, Danny"—she smiled pleasantly—"and try not to get in any more fights. So long, Sam." She turned and walked away. She had a nice walk too.

I turned back to the P.T. teacher. He was staring after her thoughtfully, his lips tight across his teeth. He put the car into gear. "If you got a few minutes to spare, kid," he said, "I'd like you to come over to my place. I got somethin' I want to show you."

"Okay, Mr. Gottkin," I replied, my curiosity returning in full force.

I followed him through the basement entrance of a small two-family house. Gottkin pointed at a door. "Go in there, kid," he told me. "I'll be with yuh in a minute."

I watched him run up the steps to the upper floor, then turned and went into the room he had indicated. I could hear faint voices upstairs as I opened the door. I stopped in the doorway and gaped at the room. It was fixed up as a small but complete gym—parallel bars, punching bag, horse, chinning bar, weights. On a small leather couch against the wall were several pairs of boxing gloves. Photographs were scattered all around the walls of the room. I went over to look at them. They were pictures of Mr. Gottkin, but he looked different. He wore trunks and boxing gloves and on his face a menacing scowl. I hadn't known he was a fighter.

A telephone on a small table near the couch began to ring. I looked at it hesitantly. It rang again. I didn't know whether to answer it or not. When it rang once more, I picked up the receiver. As I was just about to speak, I heard Mr. Gottkin's voice answer. There must have been an extension upstairs.

I listened. I had never used an extension before and I was afraid to hang up for fear I'd disconnect the call. A woman's voice was talking now. "Sam," she was saying, "you're a damn fool for picking me up with that kid in the car."

I recognized that voice too. I kept on listening.

Gottkin's voice had a pleading sound in it. "But, baby," he said, "I couldn't stand it any more. I gotta see yuh. I'm goin' crazy, I tell yuh."

Miss Schindler's voice was hard. "I said we were through and I meant it. I was crazy to start up with you anyway. If Jeff ever found out, we'd all be washed up."

"Baby, he'd never find out. He's too busy with his classes. He don't even know what day it is. I don't know how you ever came to marry that lunkhead anyway."

"He's not as crazy as you are, Sam. Jeff Rosen will be principal some day. He'll get further than you," she said defensively. "You'll wind up getting thrown out."

Gottkin sounded more sure of himself now. "But, baby, he pays you no mind. With night school an' all, he's got no time to keep a real woman like you happy."

"Sam!" she said, protesting weakly.

His voice was strong on the phone. "Remember what you said the last time, Ceil? How it was with us? There was never anything like it. Remember, you said so yourself? I remember. I get hard just rememberin'. Come on over, baby, I want you."

"I can't, Sam," Her voice was pleading now. "I said—"

"I don't care what you said, Ceil," he interrupted. "Come on over. I'll leave the downstairs open and you can duck right in."

There was a moment's pause, then her voice came heavily through the receiver: "Do you love me, Sam?"

"Like mad, baby." Gottkin's voice was roughly tender. "Like mad. Yuh comin' over?"

I could almost hear her hesitation, then her voice came through softly. "I'll be there in half an hour, Sam."

"I'll be waitin', baby." Gottkin sounded like he was smiling.

"I love you, Sam," I heard her say, and then the phone clicked dead in my hand. They had hung up. I put the receiver back on the hook. Outside on the stairs I heard footsteps and turned back to the pictures on the wall.

The door opened behind me and I turned around. "Mr. Gottkin," I said, "I didn't know you were a fighter."

His face was flushed. He glanced at the telephone quickly, then back at me. "Yeah," he answered. "I wanted to show yuh my stuff, an' if yuh was interested, I'd give yuh some lessons. I think yuh got the makin's of a great fighter, kid."

"Gee, Mr. Gottkin, I'd like that," I said quickly. "You want to start now?"

"I'd like to, kid"—he sounded embarrassed—"but some unexpected business just came up an' I can't. I'll let you know in class tomorrow when we can start."

"Aw, gee, Mr. Gottkin," I said disappointedly.

He put his hand on my shoulder and steered me toward the door. "I'm sorry, kid, but it's business. You understand?"

I smiled at him from the doorway. "Sure, Mr. Gottkin, I understand. Tomorrow'll be okay."

"Yeah, kid. Tomorrow." Mr. Gottkin quickly closed the door.

I ducked quickly across the street and up a driveway. I sat down where I could watch his door and waited. About fifteen minutes passed before she came walking down the street.

She was walking quickly, not looking around until she reached his door. Then she glanced up and down the street and ducked into the door, closing it behind her.

I sat there another few minutes before I got up. Mr. Gottkin would be surprised if he knew just how much I understood. What a day this had been! First the fight in school, now this. And Miss Schindler was married to Mr. Rosen in the math department, too. There was a new feeling of power in me. One word from me and they were all through.

There was a fire hydrant in my path. I leapfrogged over it easily. Boy, was I glad Paul had been late!

CHAPTER SIX

MY ARMS WERE TIRED. THE SWEAT WAS RUNNING DOWN MY FOREHEAD into my eyes, which were beginning to burn. I brushed at them with the back of my boxing glove and turned, facing the teacher.

His voice was harsh and he, too, was covered with sweat. "Keep your left up, Danny. And snap it. Sharp! Don't swing it like a ballet dancer. Snap, from the shoulders Fast! See, like this." He turned toward the punching bag and snapped his left at it. His hand moved so quickly it seemed like a blur. The bag rocked crazily against the board. He turned back to me. "Now, snap it at me—fast!"

I put my hands up again and moved warily around him. This had been going on for two weeks now and I had learned enough to be careful with him. He was a rough teacher and if I made a mistake I usually paid for it—with a poke in the jaw.

He circled with me, his gloves moving slightly I feinted with my right hand. For a split second I noticed his eyes following it, and I snapped my left into his face just as I had been told.

His head jerked back with the punch, and when it came forward again there was a red bruise marking his cheekbone. He straightened up and dropped his hands.

"Okay, kid," he said ruefully, "that's enough for the day. You learn fast."

I let my breath out gratefully. I was tired. I pulled at the laces on the gloves with my teeth.

"School's over next week, Danny." Mr. Gottkin was looking at me thoughtfully.

I managed to get one glove off. "I know," I answered.

"Goin' to camp for the summer?" he asked.

I shook my head. "Nope. I'm gonna help my dad out in the store."

"I got a job for the summer as a sports director at a hotel in the Catskills," he said. "I can get you a busboy's job if you want. I'd like to keep these lessons up."

"Me too, Mr. Gottkin"—I looked down at the gloves hesitantly—"but I don't know whether Pop'll let me."

He sat down on the couch. His eyes swept over me. "How old are yuh, Danny?"

"Thirteen," I answered. "Made my Bar Mitzvah this month."

He looked surprised. "That all?" he said in a disappointed voice. "I thought you were older. You look older. You're bigger than most fifteen-year-old kids."

"I'll ask Papa though," I said quickly. "Maybe he'll let me go with you."

Gottkin smiled. "Yeah, kid. Do that. Maybe he will."

I slipped Rexie a scrap of meat under the table and looked over at Papa. He seemed in a good mood. He had just belched and opened his belt. He was stirring sugar into his glass of tea.

"Papa," I said hesitantly.

He looked at me. "Yes?"

"My gym teacher's got a job in the country at a hotel," I said hurriedly, "and he says he can get me on as a busboy if I want to go."

Papa continued to stir his tea while I watched him. "You told Mamma about this yet?" he asked.

Mamma came in from the kitchen just then. She looked at me. "Told me what?"

I repeated what I had told Papa.

"And what did you tell him?" she asked me.

"I told him I was going to help Papa out in the store, but he said to ask anyway."

She looked at Papa for a moment, then turned back to me. "You can't go," she said with finality. She picked up some dishes and started back to the kitchen.

I was disappointed even though she had answered what I had expected. I looked down at the table.

Papa called her back. "Mary," he said softly, "such a bad idea, it's not."

She turned to him. "It was decided already that he's going into the store this summer and that's where he is going. I'm not going to let him go away for the whole summer by himself. He's still a baby yet."

Papa sipped at his tea slowly. "Such a baby he can't be if he's coming into the store. You know the neighborhood. Besides, a summer in the country will do him good." He turned back to me. "Is it a good hotel?"

"I don't know, Papa," I said hopefully. "I didn't ask him."

"Get for me all the facts, Danny," he said, "and then your Mamma and me, we'll decide."

I was sitting on the stoop when they came out of the house. Papa stopped in front of me.

"We're going to the Utica to the movies with Mr. and Mrs. Conlon," he said. "Now, remember to go to bed by nine o'clock."

"I will, Papa," I promised. I didn't want to do anything that might queer my chances of going to the country with Mr. Gottkin.

Papa walked across the driveway and rang the Conlons' bell. Mimi came out on the stoop with her coat on.

I looked at her questioningly. "You going too?" I asked. I really didn't care much. We hadn't been on such good terms since the Bar Mitzvah party. She had wanted me to tell her what Marge and I did in the furnace room and I had told her to find out from her friend if she wanted to know so much.

"Marge and I are going," she said importantly. "Papa said I could." She walked down the steps haughtily.

The Conlons came out on their stoop. Marge wasn't with them.

Mimi asked: "Isn't Marjorie Ann coming, Mrs. Conlon?"

"No, Mimi," Mrs. Conlon answered. "She was tired, so she's going to bed early."

"Maybe you better stay home too, Mimi," Mamma said doubtfully.

"But you said I could go." Mimi's voice was pleading.

"Let her come, Mary," Papa said. "We promised her. We'll be home by eleven."

I watched them all get into Papa's Paige. The car pulled away. I looked into the living-room at the clock on the fireplace. It was a quarter to eight. I felt like a cigarette. I got up and went to a hall closet, where I found a crumpled pack of Luckies in one of Papa's jackets. Then I went back out on the stoop and sat down and lit the cigarette.

The street was quiet. I could hear the breeze rustling the leaves on the young trees. I leaned my head against the cool bricks and closed my eyes. I liked the feel of them against my cheek I liked everything about my house.

"Is that you, Danny?" It was Marge's voice.

I opened my eyes. She was standing on her stoop. "Yeah," I answered.

"You're smoking!" she said incredulously.

"So?" I dragged on the cigarette defiantly. "I thought your mother said you went to bed."

She came over to my stoop and stood at the bottom of the steps. Her face shone white in the light of the street lamps. "I didn't feel like going," she said.

I took a last drag on the butt and threw it away, stood up and stretched. "I guess I'll turn in," I said.

"Do you have to?" she asked.

I looked down at her. There was an intent expression on her face. "Nope," I said shortly, "but I might as well. There's nothin' doin' around here."

"We can sit out and talk," she said quickly.

The way she said that made me curious. "About what?" I asked.

"Things," she answered vaguely. "There's lots of things we can talk about."

A peculiar excitement began to fill me. I sat down on the steps again. "Okay," I said, deliberately casual. "So we'll talk."

She sat down on the steps beneath me. She was wearing a smock that tied on the side. As she turned to look up at me, it parted slightly and I could see the shadow fall between her breasts. She smiled.

"What are you smiling at?" I asked, instantly defiant.

She tossed her head. "You know why I stayed home?" she countered.

"No."

"Because I knew Mimi was going."

"I thought you liked Mimi," I said with surprise.

"I do," she said earnestly, "but I knew if Mimi went you'd be home, so I didn't go." She looked up at me mysteriously.

The excitement was surging in me again. I didn't know what to say, so I kept quiet. I felt her hand touch my knee and I jumped. "Don't do that!" I snapped, pulling my leg away.

Her eyes were round and innocent. "Don't you like it?" she asked.

"No," answered. "It gives me the shivers."

She laughed softly. "Then you do like it. That's what it's supposed to do." Her next question took me by surprise. "Then why do you always watch me through your window?"

I could feel my face flush in the darkness. "I told you before, I wasn't!"

She laughed again, excitedly. "I watch you," she said almost in a whisper. "Almost every morning. When you do your exercises. And you haven't any clothes on. That's why I leave my shades up—so you could see me."

I lit another cigarette. My fingers were trembling. In the glow of the match I could see her laughing at me. I threw it away. "So I looked," I said defiantly. "What're you gonna do about it?"

"Nothing," she said, still smiling. "I like you to look at me."

I didn't like the way she stared at me. "I'm going in now," I said, getting to my feet.

She stood up, laughing. "You're afraid to stay out here with me!" she challenged.

"I am not," I retorted hotly. "I promised my father I would go to bed early."

Her hand made a quick movement and caught mine. I pulled away from her. "Cut it!" I snapped.

"Now I know you're afraid!" she taunted. "Otherwise you'd stay out yet. It's still early."

I couldn't go now, so I sat down again. "Okay," I said, "I'll stay out until nine."

"You're funny, Danny," she said in a puzzled voice. "You're not like the other boys."

I dragged at the cigarette. "How?" I asked.

"You never try to feel me or anything."

I looked down at the butt in my hand. "Why should I?"

"All the other boys do," she said matter-of-factly, "even my brother, Fred." She began to laugh. "You know what?" she asked.

I shook my head silently. I didn't trust my voice any more.

"He even tried to do more, but I wouldn't let him. I told him I'd tell Pa. Pa would kill him if he knew."

I didn't speak. I dragged on the cigarette. The smoke burned into my lungs. I coughed and threw it away. It would raise hell with my condition. I glanced up at her. She was staring at me. "What're you lookin' at?" I asked.

She didn't answer.

"I'm going to get a drink of water," I said quickly. I hurried into the house and through the darkened rooms into the kitchen. I turned on the water, filled a tumbler, and drank it thirstily.

"Aren't you going to give me any?" she said over my shoulder.

I turned around. She was standing behind me. I hadn't heard her follow me. "Sure," I said. I filled the glass again.

She held it in her hands for a moment, then put it back on the sink, untouched. She put her hands on my face. They were cold from the tumbler.

I stood there woodenly, my body stiff and unmoving. Then her mouth was against mine. She was bending me back, across the sink. I tried to push her away, but I was off balance.

I gripped her shoulders tightly and heard her gasp in pain. I squeezed harder and she cried out again. I straightened up. She was standing in front of me, her eyes swimming in pain. I laughed. I was stronger than, she. I squeezed her shoulders again.

She grimaced and her hands caught wildly at mine. Her lips were against my ear. "Don't fight with me, Danny. I like you. And I can tell you like me!"

I pushed her away violently. She half stumbled back a few steps, then stood looking at me. Her eyes were glowing, almost luminously, like a cat's eyes in the dark, and her chest was heaving from exertion. I knew it then as I watched her: she was right.

The noise of a car turning up the block came to our ears. My voice was a frightened sound in the night. "They're coming back! You better get out of here!"

She laughed and took a step toward me. Alarmed by a fear I didn't understand, I bolted for the stairway and stood nervously on the steps, listening to her voice float up to me out of the dark.

She was so sure, so wise. She knew so much more than I that as I answered her I knew it would do no good. Nothing could stop what was happening to me.

Then she was gone, the house was quiet, and I climbed slowly up the stairs to my room.

CHAPTER SEVEN

I LAY THERE ON THE BED, STARING OUT INTO THE DARK. I COULDN'T SLEEP. The sound of her laughter, sure and knowing, still echoed in my ears. I felt soiled and dirty. I would never be able to look at anybody now, everyone was sure to know what had happened.

"Never again," I had said to her.

She had laughed that funny knowing laugh of hers. "That's what you say, Danny. But you'll never stop now."

"Not me." But I knew I was lying. "Not me. I feel too dirty."

Her laughter followed me up the stairs. She sounded sure of herself. "You can't stop, Danny. You're a man now and you'll never stop."

I had stood at the head of the stairs, wanting to shout down to her that she was wrong; but there was no use. She was already gone. I went into my room and undressed and threw myself on the bed in the dark.

My body was weak and there was an aching in my legs. I tried to close my eyes, but sleep escaped me. I felt drained and empty.

I could hear the light click on in her room. Automatically I glanced toward it. She was there, looking toward my windows and smiling. She took off her smock slowly and her naked body glistened in the electric light. Her voice was a husky half-whisper as it came through the open window. "Danny, are you awake?"

I shut my eyes and turned away from the window. I wouldn't look. I wouldn't answer.

"Don't try to fool me, Danny. I know you're up." Her voice had grown harsh, with a tone of command. "Look at me, Danny!"

I couldn't stand the sound of her voice hammering at me any longer. Angrily I went to the window and leaned against the windowsill, my body trembling. "Leave me alone," I begged her. "Please leave me alone. I told you never again."

She laughed at me. "Look at me, Danny," she said softly. "Don't you like to look at me?" She arched herself proudly, her hands stretching high, her head bending all the way back.

I stood there staring at her speechlessly. I didn't want to look at her, but I couldn't turn away.

She straightened up and laughed. "Danny!"

"What?" I asked in an agonized voice.

"Turn on your light, Danny. I want to see you!"

For a moment I didn't understand her; then her words sank into the depths of my mind. My breath caught sharply in my throat and I was suddenly aware of myself. I had been betrayed. My own body betrayed me.

"No!" I cried out. Shame and fear tore through me. I moved away from the window. "Leave me alone, I tell you, leave me alone!"

"Turn on the light, Danny." Her voice was soft and persuading. "For me, Danny, please."

"No!" I screamed at her in a blazing moment of rebellion.

I hesitated a moment, my hand half reaching for the lightswitch. She was right, I would never escape her. I was lost.

"No!" I screamed at her in a blazing moment of rebellion. I hated everything that was happening to me—all the things I would become, my growing manhood and its manner of expression.

"I won't!" I shouted, and ran out, slamming the door on my room and all that I could see from it.

I ran down to the bathroom and stripped off my pajamas. I stared down at my traitorous body. Angrily I slapped at myself. Pain brought with it some sense of satisfaction. This was right. I would make it pay for what it did to me. I hit myself again. The pain tore through me and I bent over.

I held onto the sink with one hand and turned the water on in the shower. The sound of the water drumming against the bottom of the tub was soothing. For a moment I stood there, then stepped under the spray.

The cold water striking my heated body sent a rapid chill through me. I braced myself against the needle spray. Then suddenly I slumped to the floor of the tub and began to cry.

In the morning when I woke up it was as if nothing had happened. As if last night had been part of a dream, a nightmare, that sleep had washed away.

I brushed my teeth and combed my hair, and while I dressed I hummed a song. In surprise I looked at myself in the mirror. With a sense of wonder I realized there was nothing wrong with me. Everything they had told me would happen to me was a lie. My eyes were blue and clear, my skin was shining and smooth, the soreness had gone from my lips.

I left the room smiling. No one would know what had happened. Mimi was in the hall, going to the bathroom. "Good morning," I sang out.

She looked at me and smiled. "Good morning," she replied. "You were sleeping so soundly last night you didn't even hear us come in."

"I know." I grinned at her. I guessed our private war was over. Rexie followed me down the stairs.

"Morning, Ma," I called, going into the kitchen. "Rolls today?"

Mamma smiled tolerantly at me. "Don't ask foolish questions, Danny."

"Okay, Ma." I took the money from the tumbler at the sink and started for the door. "C'mon, Rexie."

Wagging her tail, she followed me out of the house. She ran past me in the alleyway and out into the street, where she squatted down in the gutter. I looked at her smiling. It was a beautiful morning, it would be a wonderful day. The sun was shining and the air was fresh and crisp.

Rexie started off down the block and I followed her. Last night was a bad dream, that's what it was, it never really happened. I took a deep breath. I could feel my chest bursting against my shirt as my lungs filled.

"Danny!"

Her soft, quiet voice stopped me in my tracks. Slowly I turned and looked up at her stoop. She was standing there, her eyes wise and smiling. "Why did you run away last night?" she asked, almost reproachfully.

A bitter taste rose into my mouth. It was true. It wasn't a dream, then; I couldn't escape. I began to hate her. I spat on the sidewalk. "You bitch!"

She was still smiling as she came off the stoop toward me. Her body reflected the sureness she felt. Her walk reminded me of the way she'd looked last night in front of her window. She was close to me, her lips smiling up into my face. "You like me, Danny, so don't fight," she said cajolingly. "I like you."

I stared at her coldly. "I hate your guts," I said.

She stared back at me. The smile left her face, and an expression of excitement came into it. "You think you mean it, but you don't," she said, lifting her hands and making a curious gesture. "You'll get over it. You'll come back for more of this."

I stared at her fingers as she slid her forefinger around in the palm of her other hand. I looked up at her face again and she was smiling. I knew what she meant. She was right. I would come back.

I turned quickly and ran down the block, calling Rexie. But I wasn't really running after the dog; I was running away from her. And I knew I could never run fast enough to keep from growing up.

CHAPTER EIGHT

I COULDN'T WAIT FOR THE LAST CLASS TO END. MR. GOTTKIN HAD GIVEN ME all the information that Papa had asked for, and I had decided to run down to the store and tell him. Papa would like that; he always was glad when I came down there. I remember when I was smaller Papa used to send me into the stores of all the other merchants on the block in order to show me off. I used to get a kick out of it too, they all made such a fuss over me.

I caught the trolley at Church and Flatbush, went downtown, and transferred to the crosstown trolley that ran out along Sands Street near the Navy Yard. The trolley let me off two blocks from the store.

I hoped Papa would let me go to the country with Mr. Gottkin. I wanted to go more than ever now. It was the only way I could get away from Marjorie Ann. I was afraid of her, of how she made me feel. I would be okay if I could stay away the whole summer.

The sound of a bugle came to my ear. I looked across the street to the Navy Yard. It was four o'clock and they were changing the guard. I decided to watch them—a few minutes more wouldn't make any difference.

I WASN'T THERE WHEN—

Papa lifted the lid of the cash register and looked in. The dial showed nine dollars and forty cents. He shook his head and looked at the big clock on the wall. Four o'clock already. In normal times the register would show ten times as much. He didn't know how he could keep up his loan payments if things continued like this.

He heard the sound of a truck pulling to a stop in front of the store and looked out. It was the Towns & James truck. They were jobbers he had dealt with for as many years as he had been in business. The truckman came into the store with a small package under his arm.

"Hello, Tom," Papa said smiling.

"Hi ya, doc," the man answered. "Got a package for yuh. Twelve 0 six."

Papa took a pencil out of his pocket. "All right," he said, "I'll sign for it."

The truckman shook his head. "Sorry, doc. C.O.D."

"C.O.D.?" Papa asked, a sudden hurt coming into his eyes. "But I've done business with them for almost twenty years and I always paid my bills."

The driver shrugged his shoulders sympathetically. "I know, doc," he said gently, "but I can't help it. Them's orders. It's stamped on the bill."

Papa rang up no sale on the register and counted out the money slowly on the counter. The driver picked it up and left the package on the counter. Papa was ashamed to look at him. His credit had always been a great source of pride.

A woman came into the store and Papa put a smile on his face. "Yes, ma'am?"

She put a dime down on the counter. "Kin I have two nickels, doc? I wanna use the phone."

Silently he picked up the dime and pushed two nickels toward her. He watched her go into the phone booth. The package was still on the counter where the truckman had left it. Papa didn't feel like unpacking it yet. He didn't want to touch it.

I turned the corner in front of the speakeasy and looked across the street. The blue and gray lettering on the store windows reached out to me:

FISHER'S PHARMACY
FARMICIA ITALIANA NORSK APOTHEKE
EX-LAX

I ran past the open door of the speakeasy. From inside, the sound of loud angry voices came to me, but I didn't stop. There were always arguments going on in there.

I stood in the doorway of the store. Papa was behind the counter, a small dark man in a light tan store jacket. He seemed to be studying a package on the counter in front of him. I walked in.

"Hello, Papa." My words seemed to echo in the empty store. The musty familiar smell of drugs came to my nose. I would always remember that smell whenever I saw a drugstore. When I was little I used to smell it on the clothes Papa wore home from work.

"Danny!" Papa's voice sounded pleased. He came around the counter. "What are you doing down here?"

"I got that information on the country hotel from Mr. Gottkin," I explained, looking into his face.

Papa smiled wearily. He seemed very tired. "I should have known you'd have a reason," he said ruefully.

"I was comin' down anyway," I said quickly.

Papa looked at me knowingly. I wasn't fooling him. He pushed his hand fondly across my head. "Okay," he said gently. "Come into the back room and we'll talk it over."

I started to follow him to the back of the store. I had just passed the counter when a scream came from the doorway. I spun around, startled.

"Doc!" the man screamed again.

I felt Papa's hands on my shoulders and he pushed me behind him. Papa's face was white.

The man in the doorway was covered with blood. There was a long, ragged gash on the side of his face running down to his neck. The flesh hung open and the white of the jawbone showed beneath the welling blood. He took several hesitant steps into the store, the blood spattering at his feet. His hands found the counter and he gripped it desperately, turning a pain-ridden face toward us. "They cut me, doc."

His grip weakened and he began to slide to the floor. He sank to his knees in front of the counter, still gripping the edge over his head, his face still turned toward us. He looked like a man at prayer. "Help me, doc." His voice was a weak, husky whisper. "Don't let me die."

· Then his grip broke and he sprawled out on the floor at our feet. I could see the slow welling of blood in the wound. I looked up at Papa. His face was white and his lips were moving silently. He looked sick. There were cold beads of sweat on his forehead.

"Papa!" I cried.

He stared down at me with empty, anguished eyes.

"Papa, aren't you going to help him?" I couldn't believe that he would let the man die there.

Papa's lips tightened grimly. He dropped to one knee at the man's side. The man had fainted, his mouth hung open loosely. Papa looked up at me. "Go to the phone, Danny," he said calmly, "and call for an ambulance."

I ran to the telephone. When I came back the store was filled with people crowded around the man on the floor, and I had to push my way through them.

Papa was pleading with them: "Stand back. Give him air."

They paid no attention, but another voice took up his plea—a cop's voice. "You hoid the doc," it rasped with accustomed authority. "Now do what he sez!"

The ambulance came too late. The man was already dead. He had died there on the floor because he and another man had quarreled over a glass of beer. I didn't know a glass of beer could be that important, but this one was. It was worth a man's life.

I finished wiping the last trace of blood from the counter. Papa was watching me from the back of the store. This was exciting. I turned to him. "Gee, Papa," I said, filled with admiration, "you were brave, helping the man like that. I couldn't do it. I would have got sick."

Papa looked at me curiously. "I was sick, Danny," he said quietly, "but there was nothing else I could do."

I smiled at him. "I changed my mind, Papa," I said. "I don't want to go away this summer after all. Do things like this happen often?"

"No," Papa said. He took a pack of cigarettes from the counter behind him, took one out, and lit it. "You're going away," he said.

"But, Papa—" There was real disappointment in my voice.

"You heard me, Danny," he said firmly. "You're going away."

I straightened up slowly. Something was wrong, something seemed to be missing. "Did you take the package on the counter, Papa?" I asked.

Papa looked curiously at the counter. A shadow came into his eyes then went away quickly. He took a deep breath, and his lips twisted into a wry grin. "I didn't take it," he said.

I was puzzled. "You think somebody clipped it, Papa?"

The weary lines etched themselves into his face as he answered. "It doesn't matter really, Danny. It wasn't anything important. I didn't want it anyway."

CHAPTER NINE

I SAT QUIETLY ON THE STOOP, MY HAND IDLY SCRATCHING REXIE'S HEAD. IT was my last night at home. Tomorrow morning Mr. Gottkin would pick me up in his Ford and we would go off to the country. I felt sad. It would be the first time I had been away from home for any length of time.

The night hung quietly around us. The house was dark. Only the kitchen was lit up, where Mamma and Papa were still talking. I leaned over the dog. "Now you be a good girl while I'm away," I whispered to her. She wagged her tail slowly. She understood everything I said to her, she was the smartest dog I ever saw.

"The summer isn't very long anyway," I said. "Before you know it, it'll be fall an' I'll be back."

She nuzzled her cold nose into my hand, and I rubbed her under her chin. She liked that.

I heard the Conlons' door open and looked up. Marjorie Ann came out on the stoop. I got to my feet quickly, called Rexie, and started down the block. I didn't want to talk to her.

"Danny!" I could hear Marjorie Ann's footsteps running after me. I turned back. She caught up to me all out of breath.

"You're going away tomorrow?"

"Yeah." I nodded my head.

"Mind if I walk a little way with you?" she asked in a small, humble voice.

I looked at her in surprise. This didn't seem like her at all. "It's a free country," I said, starting off again.

She fell into step alongside me. "Pass everything, Danny?" she asked sociably.

"Uh-huh," I said proudly. "Eighty-five average."

"That's good," she said flatteringly. "I almost flunked math."

"Math is easy," I said.

"Not for me," she replied brightly.

We turned the corner silently, our footsteps echoing hollowly on the sidewalk. We walked another block before she spoke again.

"Still mad at me, Danny?"

I looked at her out of the corner of my eye. There was a hurt expression on her face. I didn't answer.

We walked almost another block. Then I heard her sniff. I stopped and turned to her. If there was anything I hated it was a girl bawling. "Now what?" I asked harshly.

Her eyes shone with tears. "I didn't want you to go away mad, Danny," she sniffed. "I like you."

I snorted derisively. "You have a funny way of showing it. Always teasing me and making me do things I don't want to."

She was really bawling now. "I—I was only trying to do what you'd like, Danny."

I started on again. "Well, I don't like it," I said shortly. "It makes me nervous."

"If I promise to stop, Danny, will you still be mad at me?" Her hand caught at mine.

I looked down at her. "Not if you really promise to stop," I said.

"Then I promise," she said quickly, a smile breaking through her tears.

I returned her smile. "Then I'm not mad any more," I said. Suddenly I realized I had never really been mad at her. It was myself that I had been angry with. I had liked what she had done to me.

We walked along, her hand still holding mine. Rexie ran into some open lots, and we waited for her to come out.

Marjorie Ann looked up into my face. "Can I be your girl, Danny?"

"Holy cow!" The exclamation burst from me involuntarily.

Instantly the tears spilled over into her eyes again. She turned and began to run away from me, sobbing.

I stood there for a moment gawking after her. Then I ran and caught her by the arm. "Marjorie Ann!"

She turned to face me, her body still shaking with her tears.

"Stop bawlin'," I said. "You can be my girl if you want."

"Oh, Danny!" She threw her arms around my neck and tried to kiss me.

I dodged her. "Aw, cut it, Marge. You promised."

"Just a kiss, Danny," she said quickly. "That's all right if I'm your girl."

I stared at her. There was no arguing with her logic. Besides, I wanted to kiss her. "Okay," I said grudgingly, "but that's all!"

She pulled my face down to her and kissed me. I could feel her warm lips moving under mine. I pulled her closer to me and she hid her face against my shoulder. I could hardly hear her voice. "I'll do anything you want, now I'm your girl, Danny!" She pressed my hand against her breast. "Anything you want," she repeated. "I won't tease you any more."

Her eyes were shining earnestly. She didn't seem like the same girl I had known all this time. There was a warmth in her that I had never seen before.

I kissed her again, slowly. I could feel her pressing closely against me, and a fever rising in my blood. A pulse began to pound in my temples. Quickly I pushed her away.

"Then let's go home, Marjorie Ann," I said gravely. "This is all I want."

Papa called me as I started up the stairs. I came back to him. "Yes, Papa?"

There was an embarrassed look on his face. He looked at Mamma, but she was reading the evening paper and didn't even look up. He fixed his eyes somewhere on the floor and cleared his throat. "You're going away for the first time, Danny," he said awkwardly.

"Yes, Papa."

He was looking up at the ceiling now, carefully avoiding my eyes. "You're a big boy, Danny, and there's certain things your mother and I feel we ought to tell you."

I grinned. "About girls, Papa?" I asked.

He looked down at me in surprise. Mamma had put down her paper and was watching me.

I smiled at them. "You're a little late, Papa. They teach those things in school nowadays."

"They do?" he asked incredulously.

I nodded my head, still grinning. "If there's anything you want to know, Papa, don't be shy. Just ask me."

A smile of relief came to his lips. "See, Mary," he said, "I told you we didn't have to say anything to him."

Mamma looked at me doubtfully.

I smiled at her reassuringly. "You don't have to worry, Mamma," I reassured her. "I can take care of myself."

I went up the stairs still smiling. They just didn't know who they were talking to. I was an expert on girls. Hadn't I just proved that this evening?

CHAPTER TEN

"**D**OES SHE LAY, DANNY?" I GLANCED AT THE BOY DISGUSTEDLY. HIS face was flushed as his eyes followed the girl onto the porch.

I reached down and locked the concession counter before I answered him. If I had heard the question once, I had heard it a thousand times since I'd come up here. This was my third summer at the Mont-Fern Hotel and Country Club.

"They all do," I replied casually. "What the hell do you think they come up here for, fresh air and sunshine?"

The other boys around the counter all joined in the laughter, but he was still watching her. "Man," he said in an awed voice, "there's something about some dames in slacks!"

"Who looked at the slacks?" I asked carelessly. "I'm strictly a blouse man myself." I started to lock up the concession while they were still laughing. These waiters and busboys never spent a dime. They were up here for the few bucks and the tail. They weren't even good at their work, but the hotel didn't care. All they wanted them for was to keep the guests happy, and the guests were mostly dames, so everybody was happy with the arrangement.

The boys drifted out on the porch and I watched them go. Most of them were older than me, but I thought of them as kids. I felt old. Maybe it was my size—

I was five eleven—or maybe it was just because I was a veteran of three summers. I picked up the daily receipts report and began to make it out. Sam liked to have his reports in order.

I remembered my first summer up here. I was real green then. That was right after my Bar Mitzvah. I was just a punk kid sucking after Gottkin, hoping it would get me on the football team in the fall. What a lot of crap that was!

Gottkin never came back to school. The first night up here he cleaned out the concessionaire in a crap game. The next day he was in business. Before the first week had passed, he knew he wasn't going back. "This is for me," I remember him saying. "Let some other shmoe wet-nurse a bunch of kids."

I helped him instead of working for the hotel, and he did all right. Hit the Miami Beach route in the winter, and the next summer he took over the concession at the next hotel along the road as well as this one. This summer he had five working. A couple of boys in each place and all he did was come around once a day and pick up the dough. No more Ford for him, he drove a Pierce roadster with the top down now.

But that first summer had been rough. I guess the green stuck out of my ears. I was the butt of every joke the boys could think of, and all the girls teased hell out of me. Sam finally had to tell them to lay off. He was afraid I would lose my temper and belt one of them.

I didn't want to go back the next summer, but when Sam came over to the house and told me that he had picked up the second spot and I would run this one, I had gone with him. We needed the money. Papa's business was really up the creek. I picked up five hundred dollars for my end of the summer.

I remember Mamma's face when I put the dough on the kitchen table and told her to keep it. There were tears in her eyes; she turned to Papa, trying to hide them from me. Her lips were quivering, but I could hear what she said: "My Blondie." That's all.

Papa came close to tears himself. Each day in the store had become more frustrating than the one before. The money would go a long way. But his lips had tightened with stubborn pride. "Put it in the bank, Danny," he had said. "You'll need the money to go to college."

I had smiled. He wasn't kidding me, I knew better. "We can use the dough now," I had said with undeniable logic. "I got two more years before college stares me in the face. We can worry about it then."

Papa had looked at me for what seemed like a very long time. Then he reached out a trembling hand and picked up the money. "All right, Danny," he had said, "but we'll remember it. When things get better, you'll get it back."

But even as he spoke we all knew the money was gone. Business wasn't getting any better, it was getting worse. It went the same way everything else did, down the drain.

But that was last summer and I had already kissed the dough good-by. This summer Sam had promised me an extra hundred if I beat last year's take. I finished the report and summed up the season's business thus far. All I needed was a break during these last few weeks of the season and I was set. I looked at my watch. There was just time enough for me to grab a swim before lunch.

I finished locking up the concession and went out on the porch. The new broad and the boy with big eyes were playing table tennis. The girl had style all right, but her backhand could stand a little work.

I walked up behind her and took the racket out of her hand. "Loose, baby, loose," I said confidently. "Watch me. You're too stiff."

Big Eyes glared at me viciously and slammed the ball at me. Easily I returned it. He smashed it back at me. Again I returned it. I was good and I knew it. The next time I cut a little English onto the ball and it veered away sharply from his frantic stab.

I smiled at the girl. "See, baby, it's easy."

"The way you do it," she snowed me, smiling back, "but not for me."

"Sure it is," I said casually. "I'll show yuh."

I put the racket in her hand and stood behind her. I reached out and held her hands from the back. Slowly I brought her right arm across her left side almost shoulder high. She pressed back against me as our arms crossed together. She couldn't help it, I had her tied up. I could feel her breasts taut against my forearm. I smiled knowingly at Big Eyes. He was flaming with anger, but he didn't dare open his yap. I was too big for him.

I socked it into her and looked down smiling. "Isn't it easy?" I asked conversationally.

Her face was turning red. I could see the color coming up from her throat. Unobtrusively she tried to shake my grip. She could just as easy have tried to fly. She couldn't. I was too strong for her. She didn't dare say anything because all the fellows were watching us and she'd be marked lousy. "I—I guess so," she finally answered.

I grinned and let her go. That was one ping-pong lesson she wouldn't forget in a hurry. The fellows wouldn't forget it either. I saw them watching me, envy in their eyes. Dollars weren't the standard up here, dames were. None of them would ever suspect now that all I ever got out of my summers here was dough.

"Just keep practicin', baby," I said, and sauntered off the porch feeling pretty satisfied with myself.

I cut across the ballfield toward the casino. Sam and I shared a one-room bungalow behind it. The first year we had been up here we had slept in a room over the casino and had never been able to get any rest. This year Sam had taken the bungalow and we used it as a combination stock room and sleeping-quarters. Sam even had a telephone put in so he could keep in touch with the other concessions.

I unlocked the door of the bungalow, went in, and looked around me disgustedly. The place was a mess. Cartons and boxes were all over the room. It seemed I never could get time to straighten it out.

From a line over the bed I took a faded pair of gabardine swim trunks and slipped into them. Stepping carefully over the boxes, I made my way to the door and out. I promised myself I would straighten up the room this afternoon. I locked the door carefully and walked to the pool.

The pool was the way I liked it—deserted. I liked room to swim in. That's why I came down in the morning; the guests rarely showed up until after lunch. I looked at the old sign over the entrance to the pool as I walked under it. I got a kick out of that sign. It used to be a bright red color at the beginning of the summer, when it was newly painted, but now it was faded and only a gentle whisper.

BEWARE OF ATHLETE'S FOOT
ALL BATHERS MUST STEP IN
FOOT BATH BEFORE ENTERING
POOL—by ord. Bd. Health

I obeyed its order religiously. One thing I didn't want was athlete's foot. I stood there almost two minutes before I walked out on the rim of the pool, my feet leaving wet tracks on the cement walk.

I looked down at the porch to see if anyone was watching me. Big Eyes and the dame were still at the tennis table. Nobody was looking. I felt oddly disappointed.

I cut into the water smoothly and swam briskly down to the far end of the pool. The water was cold this morning and I'd have to keep on swimming if I didn't want to chill. Good enough. I could practice up on my crawl stroke while there was nobody around. Sometimes I would lose my count and inhale when I should exhale and I'd get a noseful of water. Then I'd come up sputtering and choking and feeling like a fool.

I settled into the stroke, counting grimly. I had been swimming for about fifteen minutes when I heard a man's voice calling me. Startled, I lost my count and got a mouthful of water. I looked up angrily.

It was one of the bellhops. "There's a dame down at the desk lookin' for your boss."

I swam over to the side of the pool and looked up at him. "You know he ain't here," I said heatedly, "so why bother me? Tell her to blow."

"I tol' her," the bellhop said quickly, " 'nen she asked for you."

Who could be asking for me? "She say who she is?" I asked.

The bellhop shrugged his shoulders. "How'n hell would I know? I didn't ask. I was too busy lookin' at this babe. I'd see 'er 'f I were you. She's really got it." He rolled his eyes expressively and smacked his lips.

I grinned and climbed out of the pool. The water ran down off me and formed small puddles around my feet. I reached for a towel and began to dry myself. "What are you waitin' for, then?" I asked. "Send her up here."

He looked at me lewdly. "Okay, Danny." He laughed as he turned away. "But 'f I were you I'd make sure muh jock is on good an' tight before she got here."

As I finished drying myself and sat down on a bench to slip into my sandals, a shadow fell across my feet. I looked up.

"Hello, Danny." Miss Schindler was standing there smiling at me.

I jumped to my feet, suddenly self-conscious. With surprise I realized I was a good head taller than she was. "Muh—Miss Schindler," I stammered.

She looked up into my face, still smiling. "You've grown, Danny. I wouldn't have recognized you."

I stared down at her. It was funny how she made me think of home. It was almost like another world up here. Suddenly I remembered that I had to answer Mamma's letter. It had been lying on the table back in the bungalow for almost a week.

CHAPTER ELEVEN

"SAM ISN'T HERE RIGHT NOW," I REPLIED IN ANSWER TO HER QUESTION. "He's checking the other concessions. He'll be back tonight."

A curious look of relief came over her face. "I was just in the neighborhood," she said quickly, "and I thought I'd drop by." She stood there awkwardly in the bright sunlight and squinted up into my face.

I kept it blank and unknowing. Close neighborhood. Ninety miles from the city. "Sure," I said. I had an idea. "Where are you staying? I can have him call you when he gets back."

"Oh, no, he can't do that!" she answered. Too quickly, I thought. Her husband must be around somewhere; she wouldn't want him to know. She must have guessed what was going through my mind. "You see, I'm traveling around and I don't know where I'll be stopping tonight."

"How about here?" I suggested brightly. "It's a nice place and I can get you a discount."

She shook her head.

"Sam will feel bad if I tell him you left without waiting," I said.

Her eyes were shrewd as she looked at me. "No," she said definitely. "I'd better not."

I was disappointed. Suddenly I realized that I wanted her to stay. In a way she was a touch of home and I was glad to see her. The telephone in the bungalow began to ring. I grabbed my towel and started to run toward it.

"Wait a minute," I called back over my shoulder. "That's probably Sam calling. I'll tell him you're here."

I pushed open the door and grabbed at the phone. "Hello. Sam?"

"Yeah." His voice was husky through the receiver. "How's it goin'?"

"Okay, Sam," I answered. Excitement crept into my voice. "Miss Schindler's up here to see you."

Sam's voice grew huskier. "What's she doin' up there?"

"She said she was just passing through an' she thought she'd drop in an' see you."

"Tell her I can't get back till late tonight," he said quickly. "Get her a good room an' keep her there till I get back."

"But, Sam," I protested, "I already asked her. She don't want to stay."

His voice grew confidential. "Listen, kid, I'm dependin' on you. If you ever had a yen for a babe like I got for her, you'd know what I mean. Get her anythin' she wants, but keep her there. I'll be back before one in the mornin'."

The phone went dead in my hand. I looked at it bewilderedly. What did he expect me to do? Kidnap her? Slowly I put the receiver down and turned to the door. Sam had spoken as if I knew what to do, as he would to another man, not a kid. I began to feel a glow of pride as I started for the door, but before I reached it she stood framed in the doorway.

She peered into the bungalow curiously. "May I come in?" she asked.

I stood still in the center of the room. "Sure, Miss Schindler." I pushed some boxes from the floor in front of her so she could pass. "I was supposed to straighten up, but I haven't had time," I explained.

She closed the door behind her and I straightened up to face her. My face was flushed.

"Was it Sam?" she asked.

My eyes met her gaze. I nodded silently.

"What did he say?"

"He said for me to get you a room an' anything you want an' to keep you here until he comes," I said boldly.

Her voice grew challenging and suspicious. "He seems pretty sure of himself, doesn't he?"

I could feel the flush grow deeper and my eyes fell away from her piercing look. I didn't answer.

She sounded angry now. I had been too wise. Somehow she realized that I knew. "What will you tell him if I don't stay?" she snapped.

I turned away from her and fiddled with a few of the boxes. I still didn't answer.

Her hand gripped my shoulder and turned me around. Her face was flushed now. "What will you tell him?" she repeated heatedly.

I looked deep into her eyes. To hell with her. There was nothing she could do to me. I wasn't in school now. "Nothing," I said mockingly. I took her hand from my shoulder.

She looked at my hand gripping her wrist, then slowly around the room. I could see she was making up her mind. Her eyes came back to me. "All right," she said suddenly, "I'll stay. Clean up this room for me."

I was startled. "But Sam said for me to get you a room—"

Her voice grew stubborn. "I said I'll stay here."

"But it's all messed up," I protested. "You'll be much more comfortable up in the hotel."

She turned toward the door and opened it. "Sam said you were to do anything I wanted if I stayed. I'm staying here." She stepped over the threshold and looked back at me. "I'm going down to get my car. You can clean up the room while I'm gone."

I watched her close the door. She had me and she knew it. I wondered why she was so angry. I couldn't have let on that much. I walked over to the window and looked out after her.

She disappeared below the swimming-pool. I could understand how Sam felt. She sold more with her walk than most of the broads up here did in a bathing suit.

I turned back from the window and looked disgustedly around the room. Mamma's last letter gleamed whitely at me from the table. I hadn't answered it yet, in more than a week. Now I wouldn't have time.

I WASN'T THERE WHEN—

Mamma tied the smock around her as she walked down the stairs. The air was still and quiet and she knew it would be another hot day. She was tired before the day began. She was always tired lately. She hadn't been sleeping well.

Papa had brought home a tonic for her. She had taken it every morning for a week, but it hadn't helped. Of course she had told him that it had helped her— it made him feel good. A man had to feel useful, and he felt bad enough over the way business was going.

She felt sorry for Papa. Last night in his sleep he had cried. His voice in the dark woke her up and she lay there quietly, listening to the soft, mumbled words coming from his heart. He seemed so bewildered that tears had come to her eyes.

She hadn't been able to fall asleep afterwards. The night seemed to last forever. Now she was tired again and nothing would help. The muggy heat of the morning didn't make it any easier. These last few weeks of August were generally the worst. She felt she could not take much more of this heat and wished the summer was over already.

She walked through the kitchen and opened the icebox door and looked in. It was almost empty. She had always taken great pride in keeping a well-stocked icebox. She had always said that she liked to keep enough in the house so that she didn't have to run out shopping every day. Now something about its bleakness was another ache in her body. The small piece of ice, shrunk from the day before; the almost empty carton of eggs; the half a quarter pound of butter. Even the milk bottle with the small drop of milk in it seemed to hurt her.

She closed the icebox door slowly. The three eggs would do for breakfast. Suddenly she was glad I wasn't home. She decided to look in the mailbox to see if my letter had arrived.

The sound of the milk wagon came to her. She began to feel better; she would be able to get eggs and butter from him as well as milk. And at least he would put in on the bill so she could use the few dollars she had in the tumbler over the sink for a soup chicken. She hurried to the front door to catch him before he went away.

The milkman was kneeling in front of the storage box when she opened the door. He slowly rose to his feet with a peculiarly guilty expression on his face. "Mornin', Missus Fisher," he said in a strained, embarrassed voice.

"Good morning, Borden, it's a good thing I caught you," Mamma replied. The words were spilling from her lips breathlessly from her slight exertion. "I need some eggs and butter this morning."

The milkman shifted awkwardly on his feet. "Gee, Missus Fisher, I'm sorry but—" His voice trailed off into nothingness.

Disappointment etched her face. "You mean you're all out?"

He shook his head silently. His hand gestured toward the storage box on the stoop in front of her.

Mamma was bewildered. "I—I don't understand," she said hesitantly, her eyes following his pointing fingers. Then she did understand. There was a yellow note in the box. Only the note, no milk.

She picked up the note slowly and began to read it. They were stopping her service. She owed them three weeks' bills. The eyes she raised to the milkman were filled with horror. Her face was white and sick-looking.

"I'm sorry, Misus Fisher," he murmured sympathetically.

A spray of water began to fall across the lawn in front of the house. She was suddenly aware of Mr. Conlon, who had been watering his garden. He was watching them.

He saw her glance. "Good morning, Mrs. Fisher," his voice boomed out.

"Good morning," she replied automatically. She would have to do something

She was sure that he had seen and heard everything. She looked down at the bill again: four dollars and eighty-two cents. There was just five dollars in the tumbler over the sink.

She forced her voice up into her throat and tried to smile. Her lips were almost white and the smile was more like a grimace on a stone statue. "I was just going to pay you," she said to the milkman in a purposely steady voice. "Wait a minute."

She closed the door quickly behind her. For a second she leaned against it weakly; the bill fluttered to the floor from her trembling fingers. She didn't try to pick it up; she was afraid she would faint if she did. Instead she hurried back into the kitchen and took the money from the tumbler over the sink.

She counted the bills slowly, reluctantly, as if with each recounting some miracle would make them double. There were only five dollars. She felt cold. A shiver ran nervously through her as she turned and went back to the door.

The milkman was standing on the stoop where she had left him, but now he had milk, butter, and eggs in a little wire basket on his arm She handed him the money silently, and he put it in his pocket and counted out the eighteen cents change into her hand.

"Here's your order, Missus Fisher," he said understandingly, not quite meeting her eyes.

She wanted to tell him to keep it, but didn't dare. Shame coursed inside her as she took the basket from his hands. She didn't speak.

He cleared his throat. "It's not my fault, Missus Fisher. It's the credit man down at the office. You understand?"

She nodded her head. She understood all right. He turned and ran down the steps as she watched him. Mr. Conlon's voice boomed out at her.

"It's gonna be a scorcher today, Mrs. Fisher." He was smiling.

She looked at him absently. Her mind was far away. "Yes, it is, Mr. Conlon," she replied gently, and, closing the door behind her, went back into the kitchen.

She put the milk, butter, and eggs into the icebox thoughtfully. The box still looked empty. She felt she should be crying, but her eyes were dry. There was a noise on the stairs. She closed the icebox door quickly. The family was coming down for breakfast.

A few minutes later the milk and butter and eggs were out on the table and they were eating. As she watched them, a slight warmth came into her body.

Mimi was excited. There had been an ad in the papers last night. A&S, one of the downtown Brooklyn department stores, wanted some part time girls to act as clerks and she was going down there. Papa ate his breakfast silently. His face was drawn and weary, showing the lines that appear when sleep is not restful.

Then the kitchen was empty and Mamma was alone. Slowly she finished washing the dishes. Then she noticed the milk and butter and eggs still on the table. She picked them up and balanced them on her arm. With her free hand she opened the icebox door and put them in. Nothing remained of the little piece of ice; it had melted. She closed the door.

She heard footsteps on the stoop. It must be the mailman, she thought. She ran to the front door and opened it. The mailman had already gone on to the next house. She opened the mailbox quickly, took out a few letters, and turned them over in her hand. Nothing from me. Only bills. She went back into the kitchen slowly, opening them as she walked. Gas, telephone, electricity—all overdue.

She dropped them on the table, holding one more unopened letter in her hand. She didn't recognize its marking. She opened it. It was a notice from the bank that the mortgage payment on the house was overdue.

Heavily she sank into a chair beside the table. Jarred by the vibration, the icebox door swung slowly open. She sat there staring into the open box. She ought to get up and close the door. Whatever cold was left in it would escape, but somehow it didn't matter. She didn't have the strength to get up and close the door. Nothing mattered any more. There wasn't even the strength in her to cry. Her body felt terribly weak. She stared into the almost empty icebox until it seemed to grow larger and larger and she was lost in its half-empty, half-cold world.

CHAPTER TWELVE

I WAS BUSY YAKKING WITH A BROAD JUST AFTER I HAD CLOSED THE CONCES-sion when I saw Miss Schindler come into the casino. I watched her out of the corner of my eye as she stood in the doorway looking around.

I had seen her only once before that evening, when I had run over to the bungalow to pick up a few cartons of cigarettes that I needed for the concession. It was one of those nights you feel you can almost reach out and touch the stars that hang so brightly over your head—one of those nights you never see in the city. She had been sitting on the front step of the cottage and the faintly off-beat sound of music came from the casino. She had looked at me and for a moment I thought she was going to speak, but evidently she changed her mind. She didn't say a word—just watched me in sulky silence as I picked up the cartons and left. I didn't speak to her.

I looked down at my watch. Eleven thirty. The night must have dragged back there in the bungalow. I had been wondering all evening whether she would come down.

Her gaze settled on me and she started to walk toward me. I shook the girl with me quickly. "The boss's wife is coming, baby," I lied. "I gotta report."

I left the girl with an angry expression on her face, but I didn't care. I met Miss Schindler before she got halfway across the room. "Hello," I said, smiling at her. "I been wonderin' how long you would take to get down here."

She smiled back at me. It was a real smile and I knew she had got over her mad. "Hello, Danny," she said. Her eyes met mine. "I'm sorry for the way I acted this afternoon."

I checked her eyes. She meant what she said. I relaxed suddenly and felt very warm and friendly toward her. "That's all right, Miss Schindler," I replied gently. "You were upset."

Her hand reached out toward mine. "I was lonely back there in the bungalow."

"I know how you feel," I said slowly, looking down at her hand where she touched my arm. "Sometimes I feel the same way up here. In the city you don't notice it, but up here in the country the sky is so big you feel kinda small."

We stood there in awkward silence for a moment, then I heard the band go into a rumba. I smiled at her. "D'ya wanna dance, Miss Schindler?"

She nodded her head and I led her to the dance floor. She came into my arms and we picked up the rhythm of the music. She was light on her feet and easy to dance with.

"You dance very well, Danny." She smiled up at me. "Do you do everything else as well?"

"I'm afraid not, Miss Schindler." I shook my head ruefully. I knew I was a good dancer, though; after three summers up here I had to be. "But Sam says I got a good sense of rhythm. He says that's why I'm a good boxer."

"You still want to be a fighter?" she asked curiously.

"I never wanted to be one," I replied, "but Sam says I'm naturally good at it an' that I can make a lotta dough when I'm old enough."

"And money is that important?"

I could feel the sure movement of her hip under my hand as I led her through an intricate dip. "You tell me, Miss Schindler," I parried. "Isn't it?"

She had no answer for that. Nobody had an answer when you talked money. She looked up at me. "We don't have to be so formal up here, Danny," she said with a smile. "My name is Ceil."

"I know," I said quietly.

Then we were dancing and I was humming the music half under my breath. Siboney—tum tum, ti tum-tum tum, ti tum—Siboney. There was something about rumba music. If you really like it, you can lose all sense of time when you're dancing. I liked it and I could tell that she did too. It was the way the music brought us close together. It was as if we had danced together many times before.

Abruptly the orchestra switched into *Auld Lang Syne* and we were mildly surprised. We stood awkwardly smiling at each other.

"That's all for the night, Ceil," I said. "It must be twelve o'clock."

She checked her watch. "Exactly."

"Thanks for the dance, Miss Schindler."

She laughed. I was surprised to hear her laugh. It was the first time since she came up here. "I told you—Ceil." She smiled.

I laughed too. "I enjoyed the dance, Ceil," I said quickly, "but now I gotta scrounge up a room for myself or I'll be sleeping on the porch."

Her voice was filled with dismay. "Did I put you out of your room?"

I smiled down at her. "It's okay, Ceil, you didn't know."

"I'm really sorry, Danny," she said contritely. "Will you be able to get a place?"

I grinned. "I won't have any trouble." I turned to leave her. "Good night, Ceil."

Her hand caught at my arm. "I'd like a drink, Danny," she said quickly. "Can you get me one?"

There was a nervous look on her face—like you get when you're waiting for someone and you don't know whether they're going to show. I felt sorry for her. "I got some cold three-point-two stashed away for Sam that I can let you have," I said. Three-point-two beer had just been legalized the spring before.

She shuddered delicately. "Not beer. Anything else?"

"Sam's got a bottle of Old Overholt in the cottage. I can get you some seltzer and some ice cubes."

She smiled. "That will be fine."

I unlocked the small refrigerator behind the concession counter, I took out a bottle of seltzer and a tray of ice cubes, and locked the refrigerator again.

The casino was almost empty when I came back to her. "Here you are," I smiled. "I'll carry it up to the bungalow for you and show you where the liquor is."

She followed me into the night. As we left the casino someone turned out the lights, and the grounds were plunged into darkness. I felt her hesitate beside me. "Hold onto my arm," I suggested. "I know my way around here."

I expected her to rest her hand on my arm, but instead she slipped her arm under mine and walked very close to me. I was so conscious of her that several times I almost stumbled. I could feel my face warm and flushed when I turned on the light just inside the cottage door.

I stood there looking at her. There was laughter deep in her eyes. She had me all mixed up. I didn't know what to say.

"I'm still thirsty, Danny," she said pointedly.

Turning to the bureau in hurried confusion, I pulled open a drawer and took out a bottle.

She was on her third or maybe fourth drink and we were sitting on the cottage steps when the telephone began to ring. She had been laughing at me, trying to tease me into taking a drink.

I jumped to my feet, went inside, and picked up the receiver. She followed me but not so quickly. By now the whisky had hit her and she was slightly rocky, but she was next to me at the telephone when I answered it.

Sam's voice crackled through the receiver and roared through the darkened room. "Danny?"

"Yeah, Sam."

"I can't get up there tonight like I said."

"But, Sam—" I started to protest.

The sound of a woman's laughter echoed in the phone. Ceil drew in her breath sharply beside me. Her face seemed very white in the darkness.

Sam seemed to be choosing his words very carefully. "Tell this guy that's waitin' for me that I got jammed up an' that I'll be up tomorrow after lunch to close the deal, y' unnerstan'?"

"Yeah, Sam." I understood all right. "But—"

"Okay then, kid," Sam shouted into the phone. "I'll see yuh tomorrow."

The phone went dead and I hung up. I turned to her. "Sam got jammed up on a deal," I said clumsily. "He can't get up here tonight."

She was staring at me, weaving a little. But she wasn't rocky enough not to know the score. "Don't lie to me, Danny!" Her voice was husky with rage. "I heard him!"

I looked at her. There was a hurt expression on her face. That was the second time that evening I'd felt sorry for her. I started for the door. "I guess I'd better be going, Ceil."

I felt her hand clutch at my arm and I turned in surprise. I saw her other hand swinging and I ducked. I wasn't fast enough. The side of my face was stinging from her slap and then she was swinging wildly at me with both hands.

In the dark I grabbed her wrists and held them. "What the hell are you trying to do?" I gasped.

She was trying to pull her hands free, but I was too strong for her. Her voice was husky and bitter as she spilled the words out over me. "You think it's funny, don't you?" she shouted. Her voice echoed out into the night.

I tried to hold her with one hand and cover her mouth with the other. Her teeth sank into my fingers and I pulled my hand away with a cry of pain.

She laughed wildly. "That hurt, didn't it? Now you know how I feel! Now maybe it won't be so funny!"

"Ceil!" I whispered urgently, my heart pounding. "Please be quiet. I'll get thrown out of here!" The night watchman didn't give a damn what went on up here as long as you didn't make any noise.

But I didn't have to worry, for now she was leaning against me weakly and sobbing. I stood there quietly, not daring to move for fear I'd start her off again.

Her voice was muffled against my chest between her sobs. "No good, no good. You're all alike. No good."

I smoothed her hair. It was soft under my fingers. "Poor Ceil," I said softly. I was really sorry for her.

She looked up at me. Her eyes couldn't seem to focus in the darkness. She weaved slightly as I held her. "Yes," she agreed with me. The rage had mixed with the liquor and had made her more rocky. "Poor Ceil. Only Danny knows how she feels."

Her eyes narrowed speculatively. "Danny knows why Ceil came here?"

I didn't answer. I didn't know what to say to her.

Her arms went around my neck, she turned her face up to me. "Danny feels sorry for Ceil," she whispered. "Kiss Ceil."

I stood there woodenly, afraid to move. I wasn't looking for any more trouble.

She tightened her arms around my neck and pulled my face down to her. I could feel her teeth sinking into my lower lip and I started in pain. Her voice whispered to me: "Danny knows why Ceil came here and he wouldn't let her go away without, would he?"

I stared down through the darkness at her face. Her eyes were closed and her lips were soft across her mouth. I began to laugh suddenly. This was for me.

My arms tightened around her and I kissed her. Again and again. The press of her teeth was strong against my lips. She seemed to wilt in my arms and go limp. I picked her up and carried her toward the bed. Her teeth were biting into my neck as I put her on it.

I stood there looking down at her, my fingers impatiently loosening my clothes. Then I leaned over her, my grip firm on her bodice. Her arms reached up to me in the darkness. I could hear the ripping, tearing sound of her dress as I sank toward her.

Her voice was a roaring whisper in my ear; and mine, a muted echo first, then rose slowly to meet her in a screaming crescendo.

"Danny!"

"Oh God, Miss Schindler! Ceil!"

The night was quiet and I was listening to her soft breath against my shoulder. I touched her eyes gently, they were closed; her cheeks, they were wet, she had been crying; her lips, they were bruised and slightly swollen and moved under my fingers. I leaned forward to kiss her.

Her face turned under mine, her lips moved. "No more, Danny. No more, please."

I smiled to myself and sat up in the bed. I stretched and felt my body tingling and warm. I left the bed and walked to the door and opened it. The night air was cool and soothing on me.

I went down the steps and onto the grass, flexing my toes into the ground and feeling the strength of earth seeping up into me. I raised my hands to the night sky, trying to touch the shining stars. I jumped high in the air after them and fell, rolling over and over on the ground, laughter bubbling deep in my throat.

This was the joy of discovery. This was what I had been created for, this was why I was here in this world. I scooped up a handful of earth and rubbed it in my palms. It trickled through my fingers to the ground. This was my earth, my world. I was part of it and it was part of me.

I turned and went back into the cottage and stretched out beside her naked body. In a moment I was sound asleep.

CHAPTER THIRTEEN

THE HAND SHOOK MY SHOULDER VIOLENTLY AND I SAT UP IN BED, RUB-bing my eyes sleepily. Sam's voice roared in my ears. "Where is she?"

My eyes flew open. The bed beside me was empty. The faint gray of morning had come into the bungalow. Sam's bloodshot eyes stared angrily at me. "Where is she?" he roared again.

I stared at him bewildered. I didn't know what to say. My heart began to pound frightenedly. The bungalow was empty except for us, but I was too scared to think of lying.

His arms gripped my shoulders and dragged me out of bed. "Don't try to lie to me, Danny!" he said fiercely, his clenched fist waving in my face. "I know she was here. The clerk told me she didn't take a room, she was staying down here. You been sleepin' with my girl!"

I opened my mouth to answer, but there was no need for me to speak. Ceil's voice came from the doorway.

"Who's your girl, Sam?"

We both turned and looked toward her in surprise. Frantically I grabbed at the bedsheet and wrapped it around me as Sam loosened his grip. She was in a bathing suit and dripping wet from the pool. Her feet made wet tracks across the floor as she walked toward us. She stopped in front of Sam and looked up into his face.

"Who's your girl, Sam?" she repeated quietly.

It was his turn to be bewildered. "You came up here lookin' for me," he said confusedly.

Her eyes widened. "That's what I thought, Sam," she said in the same low voice, "but I found out different." She took a step away from him and looked back. "But you don't know why I really came up here, do you, Sam?"

He shook his head and looked at me. I was already slipping into my trousers. He turned back to her.

Her voice was low and bitter and she didn't look at either of us. "I came up here to tell you that I believed all your promises. That I would divorce Jeff and go with you."

Sam took a step toward her. She held out her hand and pushed him back. She was looking up into his eyes.

"No, Sam," she said quickly. "That was yesterday. Today it's another story. I was standing right next to the phone when you spoke to Danny last night and heard everything you said." Her lips twisted in a bitter smile. "That was the first time anything made sense to me. About you. About myself. It wasn't that I wanted you, or that you wanted me. It was just that we were alike. We wanted. Period. Who it was didn't matter."

She picked up a cigarette from the table and lit it. "Now if you both will get the hell out of here, I want to get dressed."

I turned in the doorway. I didn't understand half of what she said, but somehow I felt grateful toward her. She didn't look at me, just dragged at her cigarette.

Sam and I walked in awkward silence toward the hotel, our shoes crunching in the crisp morning grass. His head was down and he seemed thoughtful.

"I'm sorry, Sam," I said.

He didn't look at me.

"I couldn't help it. She was wild," I continued.

"Shut up, Danny!" His voice was rough.

Our footsteps clumped on the wooden steps of the hotel porch and we walked over to the concession counter. I went around behind it and picked up the report sheet. "I'll leave as soon as I square the report for you," I said stiffly.

He was staring at me thoughtfully. "What for?" he asked.

I was surprised. "You know what for," I replied.

He smiled, and suddenly his hand reached out and rumpled my hair. "Take it easy, Champ. Nobody said nothin' about your leavin'."

"But, Sam—"

"But hell!" He laughed aloud. "I couldn't expect you to stay a kid forever. Besides, maybe you did me a favor at that!"

I went home the day after Labor Day with six hundred dollars. I put the money on the kitchen table, feeling almost like a stranger. The summer had changed all of us.

I had grown even more. I towered head and shoulders over Mamma and Papa. They seemed to have shrunk in some indefinable manner. Both were thinner than in the spring. Papa's usually round cheeks were hollow and his eyes had strange blue circles under them. Mamma's hair was almost all gray. This time they made no pretense about the money. The need was too urgent.

We spoke of many things at that first supper together, but some things were left unsaid. It was better so. No need to talk about what we already knew. It was visible in our faces, in the way we spoke and acted.

After supper I went out and sat on the stoop. Rexie came and stretched out beside me. I scratched her ear. "Yuh miss me, girl?" I asked softly. She wagged her tail and laid her head in my lap. She'd missed me all right. She was glad I was home.

I looked out at the street. It, too, had changed that summer. It had been paved and its asphalt gave the street a brighter, newer look.

Mimi came out and sat down on the step beside me. For a long while we sat there without speaking. Fat Freddie Conlon came out of his house and, seeing me, called a greeting. I waved my hand and watched him walk down the block.

At last Mimi spoke. "Marjorie Ann got engaged this summer." She was watching me closely.

"Yeah," I said casually. I felt nothing about her. She belonged to my kid days.

"To a cop," Mimi continued. "She's getting married when he graduates in January. He's much older than she is. He's in his thirties."

I turned to look at her. "Why bother me about it?" I asked directly.

Her face reddened. "I was just bringing you up to date on what went on around here this summer," she said defensively.

I looked away from her and down the street again. "So what?" I asked quietly. At least this hadn't changed much. I'd been back only a few hours and was fighting with Mimi already.

Her voice hardened and took on a nasty edge. "I thought you liked Marjorie Ann."

I almost smiled to myself. "What made you think that?"

She looked down at Rexie, lying between us and scratched the dog's head. "I thought you were always sweet on her. She told me—"

"What did she tell you?" I cut in.

Our eyes locked in silent battle. Hers fell before mine. I still watched her, my eyes wide and unblinking.

"She—she told me you did things with her," she stammered.

"What things?" I asked insistently.

"Things you shouldn't," she said, studying her nail polish. "After you went away last June she told me she was afraid she was going to have a baby."

I smiled suddenly. "She's crazy!" I exploded. "I never even touched her."

Relief flooded into Mimi's eyes. "Honest, Danny?"

I was still smiling. I remembered what had happened up in the country. Marjorie Ann was a nut. No girl ever got knocked up by a finger. I looked at her. "Honest, Mimi," I said quietly. "You know I wouldn't lie to you."

She was smiling back at me. "I never believed her really, Danny. She makes up so many stories." Her hand touched mine lightly. "I'm glad she's going to get married and go away now. I don't like her any more."

We looked silently down the street. It was growing dark and the street lamps came on with a sudden yellow radiance.

"The days are getting shorter again," I said.

She didn't answer and I turned to her. She looked like a kid sitting there in the glow of the street lamp, her black hair cascading down to her shoulder. Though she was two years older than I, I felt much older. Maybe it was the features of her face. Her bones were small and her mouth was unmarked. I wondered if she had ever been kissed. Really kissed, I mean. Then I put the thought quickly out of my mind. Not my sister, she wasn't that kind of a girl.

"Papa and Mamma look tired," I said, changing the subject. "It must have been hot down here in the city."

"It's not only that, Danny," she answered. "Things haven't been going too good. Business is bad and we're behind on all our bills. Just the week before last the milk company almost cut us off. It was a good thing I got some part time work at A&S; otherwise things might have been worse."

My eyes widened. I had known things were bad but I hadn't realized they were that bad. "I didn't know," I said. "Mamma never said anything in her letters."

She looked at me seriously. "You know Mamma. She wouldn't write anything like that."

I didn't know what to say. I reached into my pocket and took out a pack of butts. I put one in my mouth and was about to light it when she interrupted me.

"Me too, Danny," she said.

I held the pack toward her. "I didn't know you smoked," I said in surprise.

"I didn't know you did," she countered. She looked up at the house. "And we both better be careful Mamma don't see us or we'll both catch it."

We laughed together and held the cigarettes concealed in the cupped palms of our hands.

"I'm glad I'm graduating this summer," Mimi said. "Then maybe I'll be able to get a job and really help out."

"Things are really that rough, eh?" I said thoughtfully.

"Yes," she answered simply. "Mamma is even talking about having to give up the house. We can't keep up the mortgage payments."

"We can't do that!" I was really startled now. Not my house. I just couldn't believe that.

Mimi shrugged her shoulders expressively. "Whether we can or we can't's got nothing to do with it. We're running out of money."

I was quiet for a moment. I wasn't a kid any more and I never really believed that this was my house as Papa had once said, but I didn't want to move out of it. Somehow the thought of this house with other people living in it, another family eating in the kitchen, some other person sleeping in my room, bothered me. I liked it here, I didn't want to have to move away.

"Maybe I ought to quit school and get a job," I said carefully.

"Danny, you couldn't!" Her voice was protesting. "You gotta finish school. Mamma and Papa got their hearts set on it."

I didn't speak.

"Don't worry, Danny," she said consolingly, placing her hand on my shoulder. "Everything'll work out okay. I just know it will."

I looked at her hopefully. "You really think so?"

She smiled at me. "Sure I do." She got to her feet and threw her cigarette into the gutter. "I'd better get in and help with the dishes or Mamma'll be after me."

I hoped she was right. She had to be. We just couldn't move from here. There was no other place to live as far as I was concerned.

CHAPTER FOURTEEN

My name is Danny Fisher. I'm fifteen years and four months old. I'm in the sixth term at Erasmus Hall High School and I attend the morning session. It is one o'clock in the afternoon and school is over for the day. I am standing on the corner of Flatbush and Church Avenues watching the pupils stream by on their way home.

They say there are more than three thousand pupils in the school, and at this moment it seems as if all of them are walking past this corner. They are laughing. Some boys are kidding some girls. There is envy in my glance as I watch them. Nothing bothers them.

They have nothing on their minds until tomorrow when they must return to class. Not like me. I got a house I want to keep more than anything else in the world. So I have to go to work. I look at a clock in the window. It is already a few minutes past one. I hurry, for I have to be at work by half past the hour.

I walk down Flatbush Avenue. It is late October and the first chill of winter settles about me. I tighten my lumberjacket. I stop for a minute in front of a movie house and read the lobby cards. It looks like a good show, and as I stand there some of the kids from school go in to see it. I'd like to catch the show too, but I can't spare the time. I start walking again.

I am past the heavy shopping district. The stores here are smaller and seem to cater more to the neighborhood shopper than they did farther up the avenue near the school. My pace quickens. There isn't much here to catch my eye and slow me up.

I have been walking almost a half-hour when I get to the six corners, where Flatbush and Nostrand come together. It is the terminal station of the Flatbush division of the IRT subway.

There are many food stores on this corner: A&P; Bohack's; Roulston's; Daniel Reeves; Fair-Mart. It is this last that I enter. I walk through a long, narrow store.

A man behind the counter looks up and yells at me. "Snap it up, Danny. We got a flock of orders waiting."

I break into a run and go into the back of the store. I place my schoolbooks on a shelf, take down an apron, and wrap it around me while running back to the front of the store. The orders are on the floor near the door and I begin to carry them out to the hand wagon.

One of the clerks comes out and checks the bills with me. He gives me the exact change for the C.O.D.'s and I start off. The wagon and I weave in and out of the streets and traffic all afternoon until the sun sets and it is six o'clock. Then I take a heavy broom and begin to sweep down the store.

At seven o'clock I take off my apron and fold it neatly back on the shelf so that it will be ready for tomorrow. I pick up my schoolbooks and walk to the front of the store and the manager lets me out, locking the door carefully behind me. I hurry up Nostrand Avenue to Newkirk. A bus is waiting at the subway exit there and I board it. I stand, for the bus is crowded with people coming home from work.

I get off on my corner and walk up the block. My feet hurt and my neck and shoulder muscles are sore from lifting the heavy cartons, but I forget the pain when Rexie comes running down the street to greet me. She is wagging her tail happily in her excitement and I laugh and scratch her head. I go into my house still smiling, warm from the joy of her greeting.

I spill a handful of change on the kitchen table. Slowly I tot up the nickels and dimes. Eighty-five cents. Tips were good today. I put twenty-five cents in my pocket and spill the rest of the change into the tumbler over the sink.

Mamma has been watching me. Now she speaks. "Go upstairs and wash, Danny. Supper is waiting."

Papa has been sitting at the table. He reaches out a hand and sort of pats my shoulder as I walk by. He doesn't speak and neither do I. We both know how we feel. I am content.

For every day there is the little stream of change, and on Saturdays after I've worked a full day, from seven in the morning until eleven at night, the manager hands me my week's pay. Three and a half dollars. Good weeks it can come to as much as ten dollars altogether with the tips.

It is a good thing that school work comes easy to me, because most nights I fall asleep over my homework and have to finish it in a study period the next day. I sink into bed and sleep the sleep of the exhausted, but when I wake the next morning I am new and strong again. I have the indefatigability of youth on my side.

There are times when I watch the boys in the street playing touch tackle and I feel like joining their game. Sometimes I get my hands on a football that one of the boys has failed to catch. I pick it up and my fingers instinctively caress the soft, smooth pigskin. I remember how much I wanted to be on the team at school. Then I throw the ball back. I watch it spiral lazily in the air until it falls into the receiver's hands. Then I turn away.

I have no time for play. I am somber and thoughtful. I am engaged in a much greater game. I am working to keep my home secure.

But there are forces at work of which I know nothing. The cold unemotional mechanics of finance and credit, the machinery of business and economics, which hold a careful level on every life in every stratum of society and are only words in a textbook to me. And there are the people who watch this machine.

They are people very much like Papa and Mamma, Mimi and me. They are victims as well as administrators. They are as much subject to the rule of the level as the people to whom they apply it. When the level is far enough out of balance, they make a note on a slip of paper. This note is then given to other people. If these agree with the first watchers, other slips of paper are filled out and forwarded, and then all the rules of the level are taken away. For what they do disturbs the balance so much that it is impossible to get a straight ruling from the level ever again.

Then we become a statistic.

Statistics are very cold things. They are levels of another sort administered by actuaries. From them many things are determined. All sorts of reasons are drawn from them as the source of our failure to maintain an even level on our economics. But none of these things sum up my emotions, my feelings, upon learning of the failure. Either mine or that of my family. It is only the balance they are interested in, not the way we feel.

And surely not the way I felt that night shortly before the end of October when I came home from work and found Mamma crying.

CHAPTER FIFTEEN

I WASN'T THERE WHEN—

Mamma looked up at the clock. In a few minutes it would be time for lunch. She wondered where the morning had gone. She had awakened with such a strong presentiment of evil and bad luck hovering over her that she forced herself to keep busy every moment.

She had cleaned and dusted every corner of the house, had even gone down into the cellar and sifted through the ashes to save the half-burned lumps of coal that fell through when the grate was shaken out. But in spite of all her preoccupation the feeling hung about her. It was always there in the back of her mind.

She hurried into the kitchen and put some water into a pot on the stove and turned the light on underneath it. She heard a rustling on the floor. Rexie had got up from underneath the kitchen table and gone to the door, where she stood wagging her tail and looking back at Mamma.

"You want to go out?" Mamma said to the dog as she opened the kitchen door. The dog ran out barking happily and she turned back to the stove. She put an egg into the water, which was just beginning to boil.

After she had eaten she cleaned off the table and put the dishes into the sink. She was tired. She stood looking into the sink at them. She was too tired even to wash them.

Suddenly she could feel her heart pounding so heavily that it seemed to vibrate all through her body. She was frightened. She had heard many times how heart attacks come upon people without warning. She went into the parlor and sat down on the couch, leaning back against the pillows. The palms of her hands were wet with perspiration. She closed her eyes and rested.

Slowly the beating of her heart quieted. Her breathing was easier and her fear disappeared. "I'm just tired," she said aloud. The words echoed in the empty room. She would take a hot bath; it would relax her and do her good. It was all nerves anyway, she decided. She undressed in the bathroom while the tub was filling, folded her clothes neatly and hung them on the towel rack, and looked into the mirror.

Her hand reached up wonderingly and touched her hair. There was a great deal of gray in it, and the black seemed faded and dull. It seemed only yesterday that it had been alive and lustrous. And her face had tired little lines etched into it, the skin was not soft and smooth as she remembered it. It seemed almost as if someone else, not she, was looking at her from the mirror.

She unhooked her brassiere. Her breasts, free of the mechanical support, tumbled from it and sagged shapelessly against her chest. She studied herself in the mirror. She had always been proud of her breasts. She remembered how well shaped they had always been, how firm and strong and bursting with life while she had been nursing the children. Papa used to love to watch her. He would sit admiringly and after a while would say laughingly to the child: "Hey there, little monster, haven't you had enough? Can't you leave something for Papa?" She used to blush and laugh and tell him to go away and not be such a pig, but she was always proud. Now look at her. There was no joy in them for him any more. Who could be attracted to such things as these?

She turned away from the mirror toward the tub. It didn't make much difference now. Neither of them had any appetite left. The struggle of the past few years had taken it from them. The memory of pleasure was dim in her mind. It was best left for youth and those without care.

She sank into the tub carefully. Slowly the warmth of the water seeped through her. She felt light and buoyant. The gentle swishing of the water seemed to drive away her fears and once more she felt comfortable and secure. She leaned back against the tub, loving the feel of the water as it crept up to her shoulders. She rested her head against the tiles over the tub. She was drowsy and her eyelids felt heavy.

"I'm getting to be a silly old woman," she thought as she closed her eyes. She dozed.

Her heart was pounding again. She tried to move her arms, but they felt heavy and lifeless. She must get up, she thought desperately, she must. With an effort she raised her head and opened her eyes. She looked about her with a startled look.

The ringing of the telephone came to her ears. Suddenly she was wide awake. She remembered having come upstairs to take a bath. She must have been dozing for quite a while, she realized; the water was almost cold. The telephone downstairs was ringing with an urgency she could not ignore. She got out of the tub quickly, hurriedly dried her feet on the bathmat and, throwing a towel around her wet body, ran downstairs to answer it.

As soon as she picked up the phone and heard Papa's voice she knew something was wrong. Somehow she had been expecting it all day.

"Mary," he cried, his voice shaking, "the bank's got a judgment out against me and they're gonna serve it tomorrow!"

She tried to be calm. "Did you talk to them?" she asked, her voice reflecting his fears.

"I did everything," he answered resignedly. "I begged them, I pleaded with them to give me more time, but they told me they couldn't do any more."

"Did you talk to your brother, David?" Mamma asked. "Maybe he can spare you some money."

"I spoke to him too," he answered. He paused for a moment and a sound of finality came into his voice. "We're finished—through."

"Harry, what are we going to do?" A vision of the family walking through the street in rags flashed before her. She fought her hysteria.

"David is coming with his car tonight," Papa replied. "We're gonna try to empty the store as much as we can. We'll hide the stuff in his place until I can find a way to open up somewhere else."

"But if you're caught, you'll go to jail," she cried.

"So I'll go to jail," he answered, his voice flat and dull. "Things can't be much worse." Somehow in telling what had happened he had lost all capacity for emotion. "They attached the house too." He lapsed into Yiddish, as he didn't do very often. "*Alles iss forloren,*" he said, "everything is lost."

That was the night I came home and found Mamma crying at the kitchen table, and Mimi, with tears in her eyes too, holding her hand.

That was the night I left without supper and went down to Papa's store and helped move hastily packed cartons of merchandise out to Uncle David's car.

That was the night when I stood in the darkened street at two o'clock in the morning and my father, crying bitterly all the while, looked at the store windows and murmured: "Twenty-five years, twenty-five years."

That was the night I watched my mother and father fall sobbing into each other's arms and learned that they too had feelings they could not control. For the first time I saw fear and despair and hopelessness plainly in their faces.

I went quietly to my room and undressed, crept into bed and lay there looking up into the dark. The muted sounds of their voices came from downstairs. I could not fall asleep and watched the morning creep into my room, and there was nothing I could do. Nothing.

That was the night when for the first time I admitted to myself that it was not my house, that it really belonged to someone else, and there was no heart left in me for tears.

Moving Day

DECEMBER 1, 1932

I T WAS WRONG. EVERYTHING WAS WRONG, NOTHING WAS RIGHT. I KNEW IT the minute I went into the BMT subway station at Church Avenue instead of walking home. When I got up that morning, there was a dull choked feeling in my gut as if someone had poked me in the solar plexus and it had been getting worse all day. Now I could feel its ache spreading all through me. I was going home from school, but I wasn't going home any more.

There was an express in the station when I got down the steps and automatically I ran for it. I got aboard just as the door was closing. There weren't any seats, so I leaned against the door on the other side. This door opened only once on the way, at Atlantic Avenue, so at least I could stand there with as little disturbance as possible.

It was cold in the train and I pulled the collar of my sheepskin jacket up around my neck. It had snowed a few days before, but the streets were pretty well cleaned up by now. Some snow still lay on the tracks as the train pulled into Prospect Park. The tunnel closed around us, choking off the day. I took a deep breath trying to get rid of the sick feeling inside me. It didn't help. If anything, it only made it worse.

That morning the barrels and boxes around the already strange, empty-looking rooms had reminded me: today was moving day. I had left my room without a backward glance, Rexie close upon my heels. I wanted to forget all about it—forget I was ever kid enough to believe that it was really my house. I was old enough now to know that was the kind of a story you told to children.

Suddenly day swept back into the train. I looked out the window: we were on Manhattan Bridge. The next stop was mine, Canal Street. I had to change there for the Broadway Brooklyn train. The train went back into the tunnel and in a moment the doors were opening. I had to wait a few minutes for the other train, but it was only a quarter to four when I came up on the street at the corner of Essex and Delancey.

It was like a different world. The streets were crowded with people moving restlessly, talking in many languages. There were street peddlers with pushcarts, hawkers shouting, standing on the corner with their little stands, ready to collapse them and run when the cops told them to move on. It was cold, but many were without overcoats and hats, women with only shawls thrown around their shoulders. And all about me I could hear the low, muted voice of poverty. There was little laughter on the street except from children, and even they were restrained in their joy.

I walked down Delancey Street, past the cheap stores with their gaudy sales, past the movie house with its big sign still advertising the early-bird matinee, admission ten cents. I turned left at Clinton Street and walked the two blocks to Stanton with my head down. I didn't want to look around me, and all the time the tight feeling in the pit of my stomach seemed to grow larger until I could feel it choking in my throat.

I looked up suddenly. This was it: an old gray house with faded narrow windows reaching five stories into the sky. A small stoop led up to its entrance, and on each side of the stoop was a store. One was a tailor shop, its windows dark and covered with dust; the other was empty.

Slowly, reluctantly, I climbed the steps. At the top I stood and looked down into the street. This was where we were going to live. A woman came out of the house and pushed past me on her way down the steps. I could smell the garlic on her breath. I watched her cross the street to a pushcart, where she stopped and began to haggle with the man standing there.

I turned and went into the house. The hall was dark and I stumbled over something on the floor. With a muttered curse I bent to straighten it up. It was a paper bag filled with garbage. I dropped it quickly where I found it and began to climb the stairs.

Three flights up, and at every landing, I saw the small paper bags standing in front of the door, waiting for the superintendent to collect them. The heavy odor of cooking hung in the stale cold air of the hallways. I knew which apartment was ours by the barrels standing in the hall beside the door. I knocked.

Mamma opened the door. We stood there for a moment looking at each other and then, not speaking, I walked into the apartment. My father was sitting at the table. I could hear Mimi's voice coming from somewhere in the front.

I was standing in the kitchen and the walls were covered with a strangely colored flat white paint that fought unsuccessfully to hide the layers of dirt beneath it. The bright yellow curtains Mamma had already put on the small window beside the table gave the room a forced air of gaiety. She looked at me anxiously. I didn't know what to say. Just then Rexie came running to me from another room, wagging her tail, and I knelt to pet her.

"It's very nice," I said, not looking up.

There was silence for a moment, and from the corner of my eyes I could see Mamma and Papa looking at each other. Then my mother spoke. "It's not so bad, Danny. It will do for a little while until your father gets back on his feet. Come, I'll show you the rest of the apartment."

I followed her through the rooms. There wasn't much to see, I don't suppose there ever is in a small four-room apartment. My room was about half the size of my old room, and theirs wasn't much larger. Mimi was going to sleep on the couch in the parlor.

I didn't say anything as I looked at them. The rooms were all covered with the same discouraged-looking white paint. What could I say? The rent was cheap and that was the main thing: twenty-eight dollars a month with steam heat and hot water.

We went back into the kitchen, Rexie still following at my heels. My father hadn't said a word. He just sat there at the table smoking his cigarette, his eyes watching me.

I scratched the dog's ear. "Was Rexie any trouble?" I asked him.

He shook his head. "She was no bother," he said almost formally. His voice sounded different, not like his at all, as if he weren't sure of himself any more.

"You better take her out, Danny," my mother said. "She hasn't gone all day. I think she's a little upset."

I was glad to have something to do. I went to the door and called her.

"Take her leash, Danny, it's a strange neighborhood and she might get lost," my father said, holding it toward me.

"Yeah, that's right," I said. Rexie and I went out into the dark hallway and I started down the stairs.

About halfway down the first flight I realized she hadn't come with me. She was standing at the head of the stairs, looking down at me. I called: "Come on, girl." She didn't budge. I called again. She crouched down on the floor and looked at me, wagging her tail nervously. I went back up the stairs and snapped the leash onto her harness. "Come on, now," I said to her, "don't be such a baby."

When I started down the stairs again, she followed me cautiously. At each landing I had to urge her down the next flight. At last we were out on the stoop, where she stood looking out into the street. Suddenly she tried to dart back into the hallway. The leash pulled her up short and she crouched down. I knelt beside her and took her head in my hands. I could feel her body trembling. I picked her up and carried her down the stoop. In the street she didn't seem so afraid, but as we started off toward Clinton Street, she kept looking around apprehensively. The noise of the traffic seemed to frighten her.

Down the block there seemed to be less traffic, so I decided to walk her that way. In front of a candy store I waited for the light to change. A big truck came rattling past, and she began to pull anxiously on her leash. I could hear the rasping sounds in her chest as the leash tightened on her throat. Her tail was down between her legs. She was really frightened now. As I knelt down again to comfort her, I heard a raucous laugh behind me and looked back over my shoulder.

Three boys, somewhere around my age, were standing in front of the candy store. One of them was laughing at the dog's fright. They saw me looking at them.

"What's a matter, pal?" the boy who was laughing said sneeringly. "Your mutt yella?"

"No more than you, pal," I replied sarcastically, still trying to soothe her.

The other two boys fell quiet at my answer. They seemed to look at the boy I was talking to expectantly. He looked at them knowingly for a second and then swaggered over to me. I knew the setup too well. He would have to make good his words. I smiled grimly to myself. He had a surprise coming. I began to feel a little better; the opportunity for violence seemed to ease the pain in my belly.

He stood over me. From beside the dog, I looked up at him, my hands still busy with her. "Wat'cha say, pal?" he said very slowly.

I smiled thinly. "You heard me the first time, pal," I replied, mimicking his tone of voice. I started to get to my feet.

I saw his foot coming, but I couldn't move fast enough. His shoe caught me flush on the mouth and I spilled over backward in the gutter. The leash flew from my grasp. I rolled over desperately to grab it, but it sped out of my reach. I shook my head dizzily, trying to clear it; then I heard the scream.

I scrambled to my feet anxiously, the fight forgotten. Rexie was running out in the middle of the street among the traffic, darting back and forth crazily.

"Rexie!" I screamed at her.

She turned in her tracks and started back for me. I heard her high-pitched yip as she disappeared beneath the wheels of a small delivery truck, turning the corner, racing to make the light. I ran toward her. She cried once more, but more weakly. She was lying on her side in the gutter, her chest heaving, her beautiful brown fur covered with blood and dirt. I fell to my knees in the gutter beside her.

"Rexie!" I cried, my voice choked. As I picked her up, a soft moan escaped her, almost a sigh. Her eyes were soft and filled with pain. Her tongue crept out from between her lips and licked at my hands gently, leaving a smear of blood.

I was holding her against me now, her body trembling violently. Suddenly she gasped and was still. Her paws fell limply against my jacket. The light had gone from her eyes. "Rexie," I said pleadingly. I couldn't believe it. She had been so alive, so beautiful. "Rexie, girl."

A man pushed his way through the crowd of people that had gathered around. His face was pale. "Jesus, kid, I didn't even see her."

I stared at him for a moment without seeing him. All I could remember about him was that his face was pale—nothing else. I started toward the house still carrying Rexie. People moved away from in front of me silently. I couldn't cry. My eyes were burning, but I couldn't cry. I was at the stoop, now in the dark hallway on the strange stairway with the heavy odors, now in front of our door. I kicked it open.

Mamma rose from her chair with a half scream. "Danny! What happened?"

I looked at her dumbly. For a moment I couldn't speak. Papa and Mimi had come running into the room when they heard her. Now they were all facing me, staring at me.

"She's dead," I said at last. I didn't recognize my own voice. I was hoarse and gruff. "She got run over."

On the floor in front of me was an empty cardboard carton. I knelt and placed her in it gently. Slowly I closed the flaps down over her and stood up.

Mimi's eyes were filled with tears. "H-how did it happen?"

I envied her tears. I wished that I could cry; maybe I would feel better. The bitterness rose in my throat. "It happened," I said flatly. "What difference does it make now how?"

I washed the blood from my hands at the sink and dried them on a dish towel. Then I picked up the carton and started to open the door.

My father's voice stopped me. "Where are you going?"

"To bury her," I answered dully. "I can't keep her here."

His hand was on my shoulder, his eyes looking into mine. "I'm sorry, Danny," he said, his voice filled with sympathy. His eyes were dark with understanding, but it didn't matter—nothing mattered any more.

I wearily brushed his hand from my shoulder. "You should be," I said bitterly, accusingly. "It's all your fault. If we hadn't lost the house and had to move, this would never have happened."

I saw the flash of pain in his eyes as his hands fell to his side. I went out into the hall and shut the door behind me. It was his fault. He didn't have to lose the house.

I boarded the Utica-Reid trolley in the plaza beneath the bridge and held the carton on my lap all through the long ride over the bridge, through Williamsburg, and at last into Flatbush. I got off the trolley at Clarendon Road, and the box was heavy in my hands as I walked through the familiar streets. In my mind I could see her running after me. I could see the beautiful reddish-brown fur and feel its soft silkiness as I scratched behind her ears. I could feel her cool, moist tongue licking my ears when I knelt to greet her.

It was dark when I reached the house. I stood in the street looking into it. Its windows were wide and gaping and empty. We had only moved out that morning, but already it had assumed a forlorn, deserted look. I looked up and down the street to see if anyone had seen me. The street was empty.

Some lights were on in the Conlons' house as I quietly walked up the driveway, but no one heard me. I went into the back yard and put the carton down. It was only right. This was where she had lived, this was where she should rest. Where she had been happy.

I looked around me. I would need a shovel to scoop out the ground for her. I wondered if there was still one in the cellar, the one we used for the furnace. I started for the house. Then I stopped and went back for her. She never liked being left alone.

I still had my key in my pocket and I opened the door. I carried the box inside and put it on the kitchen steps. The house was dark but I didn't need any light. I knew every inch of it.

I went down into the cellar. The shovel was up against the coalbin just where it always had been. I picked it up and went back up the stairs. I was going to take her outside with me while I dug her grave, but I changed my mind and left her on the kitchen steps. She had always been shy of the shovel.

I dug as silently as I could; I didn't want anyone to hear me. The cold night air began to beat against my face, but I didn't care. I was sweating beneath my sheepskin jacket. When the hole was big enough for her, I went back into the house, picked up the box, and carried it outside. There I placed it gently in the ground. As I stood up and reached for the shovel, a thought came to me: what if she wasn't dead? What if she was still alive?

I knelt down and lifted the lid of the carton, placed my face close to the box, and listened. I heard nothing. I still didn't trust myself. I put my hand in the box and felt her muzzle. The warmth had already gone from her body. Slowly I closed the carton and got to my feet.

The tears came to my eyes as I spilled the dirt over her. Do you say prayers for dogs? I didn't know, but I said a prayer for her. It passed my lips soundlessly in the night and at last the earth lay evenly on her. I smoothed the ground with my feet. The moon had risen and its cold winter light cast eerie shadows in the yard. She liked the cold weather, it made her brisk and frisky and want to run. I hoped she would like the weather wherever she was.

I don't know how long I stood there, the shovel in my hand, but I was chilled through when I turned away. The tears were streaming silently down my cheeks, but I wasn't crying.

I went back into the house and without thinking went up to my room. I put the shovel against the wall and went over to where my bed used to be. By the bright moonlight that came in the window I could see the markings on the floor where Rexie used to sleep under my bed. I lay on the floor and cried. The bitter salt of my tears rolled into my mouth as my body responded to my grief. At last I was spent and rose to my feet dully. Without looking back I left the room and walked down the stairs and out of the house.

Fat Freddie Conlon was coming home as I walked out of the driveway. He looked at me in surprise. "Danny! What are you doing here?" he asked. "Did you leave something behind?"

I pushed past him without answering, leaving him standing in the street behind me. Yes, I had left something behind all right. More than I had expected.

The clock in the window of the jewelry store near the corner of Clinton and Delancey Streets read nine o'clock when I turned down the block. I was moving as if in a dream. People were pressing around me and there was noise and confusion, but I didn't see it or hear it. My body seemed to be throbbing with a dull aching pain and the side of my face was sore where I had been kicked.

I was on the steps of the house when suddenly I seemed to waken. I could hear the noises of the traffic, the voices of people. I looked around me as if I were seeing it for the first time. The light from the candy store on the corner seemed to beckon to me. A group of boys were still hanging out in front of it. I went down the steps again and started for the corner.

There I stopped and looked at the gang in front of the store. He wasn't there. After watching them quietly for a few minutes I was just about to turn away when I saw him. He was inside the store, sitting at the counter drinking an egg cream.

I walked slowly into the store. His back was toward the door and he didn't see me. I tapped him gently on the shoulder. He turned. A look of recognition spread quickly on his face.

"Outside." I gestured with my hand.

He looked at me, then at the other boys in the store. I didn't give him any time to think. My hand prodded at his shoulder again, this time roughly. "Outside," I said, my voice harsh and flat.

He pushed his drink away from him and stood up. "Save this for me, Moishe," he said to the counterman in a cocky voice, "I'll be back for it in a minute."

I picked up the glass and emptied it in the sink behind the counter. Its chocolate flowed into the dirty water. "Forget it, Moishe," I said in the same flat voice. "He won't be drinking this."

I turned my back on him and walked out into the street. His footsteps sounded behind me on the concrete floor. At the curb I stopped and turned. "Put up your hands," I said almost casually.

He looked at me for a moment, then stepped very close to me. His lips bared over his teeth in a half snarl. "Tough, eh? Think yer tough, huh?" he sneered.

That crazy feeling I'd had in my gut all day began to explode in me. "Yeah, tough enou—" I started to answer when I suddenly remembered.

I moved back quickly, but not quickly enough. His knee caught me in the groin and his fist lashed across my face. I fell forward on my hands and knees. I saw his shoe coming at my face and tried to roll away from it. The toe of his boot caught me behind the ear and I went flat on the ground.

The noise of the traffic seemed to be coming from far away, there was strange dizziness in my head. I shook myself and got to my knees again.

He was laughing at me. "Tough, huh?"

I grabbed a hydrant near me and pulled myself up. I shook my head again. It was clearing rapidly and I could taste the warm blood running down inside my mouth.

He was still laughing, still taunting. "Think yer tough now, Shmuk?"

I watched him cautiously, still clinging to the hydrant. Let him keep talking, he was doing me a favor. He was giving me time. I could feel the strength coming back into my legs.

He came toward me again, slowly, deliberately, taking his time. He was full of confidence.

Still stalling for time, I moved around the hydrant. All I needed was a few more seconds. For once I was glad Sam had taught me to gauge my strength and how to save it.

He stopped and sneered again. "Yella, too?" he taunted. "Jus' like yer dog!"

I let go of the hydrant. I was all right now. I stepped in front of it.

He came at me swinging, leading with his right. He didn't know it, but that was his second mistake, and par for the course. His first was in giving me time.

My left brushed aside his right lead, my right hand tore into his belly just below his belt. He started to bend forward, his hands going down to his crotch, and I caught him with a left uppercut on the side of the jaw. He half turned sideways and started to go down. I hit him eight times on the face and jaw before he hit the sidewalk.

There he sprawled at my feet. I bent over him. He must have been as strong as a horse, he was trying to get up. I kicked him in the side of his head and he went out flat.

For a few seconds I watched him; then I turned and started away. For the first time I became aware of the crowd of people that had gathered around us. I sensed rather than heard a sudden movement behind me.

Quickly I whirled. He was on his feet after me. Something shining in his upheld hand slashed down at me as I jumped aside. I could feel it ripping down my sleeve. Switch knife. He carried past me with the momentum of his swing and I rabbit punched the back of his head.

The crowd parted in front of him as he staggered against the side of the building. I followed him quickly. I couldn't give him a chance to turn around.

I gripped his knife hand and pulled it back toward me. He screamed. I pulled again and the knife fell clattering to the sidewalk. I kicked it away and turned him around. His face was contorted with pain and fear. His eyes bugged out in their sockets. Holding his head against the brick of the building, I began to pound his face with my free fist.

A wild violence was running through me, a savage joy. For the first time in my life I liked fighting. My first punch flattened his nose against his face. I could feel the bone crunching beneath my fist. He screamed again.

I laughed wildly and hit him in the mouth. When he gasped for breath I could see a hole where some teeth had been. I was happy. I had never been so happy before. Blood was running down the side of his face. I wanted to turn it all into blood, I didn't want him to have a face at all. A red haze settled over my eyes and I was laughing and hitting him and yelling for joy.

Then I felt hands tearing at me, pulling me away from him. I fought them to let me go. There was sudden sharp pain at the back of my head and I felt curiously weak. I let him go and he fell forward to the ground at my feet. Arms pinioned my hands to my sides. I looked up to see who was holding me. As the red haze began to lift, I saw the dark-blue uniforms of the cops.

They took me to the station house just off Williamsburg Bridge and threw me into a cell. A man came in to see me, a doctor, who put some adhesive tape on my arm where I had been cut. Then he left me.

I sat there almost four hours before anyone came near my cell again. I was tired, but I couldn't sleep. My eyes were heavy, but they wouldn't close. All I could do was think. All I could see in front of my eyes was a little reddish-brown puppy trying to scramble up the side of a pit after me.

The cell door clanked. A cop stood there. "Your father's come to get you, son," he said gently.

I stood and picked up my coat from the bunk behind me. It was almost as if I had done this many times before, but I was past all feeling. Slowly I followed him down the gray-painted corridor and up the stairs. He opened a door and motioned me through it. My father and a man were sitting there in the room.

Papa jumped to his feet. "I've come to take you home, Danny," he said.

I stared at him dully for a moment. Home? To that place? It would never be home to me.

The man beside my father stood up and looked at me. "Lucky for you, kid, we found out what happened. That boy you beat up will be in the hospital for weeks. But he's no good and maybe you did us a favor. Go along now and don't give us any more trouble."

I didn't answer him but started out the door. My father's voice behind me was thanking the man for what he had done. I walked through the station house and out into the street, where my father caught up to me and fell into step beside me. At Delancey Street we waited for the traffic light.

"Your mother and I were frightened, Danny. We didn't know what happened to you." His voice was husky, but he was trying to speak easily. His usually ruddy face was pale in the glow of the street lamp. It seemed to me that I had heard those words before. Another time, another place. I didn't answer.

The light changed and we crossed the street. On the other side he tried to speak again. "Why did you do it, Danny?" There was anguish on his face. Something had happened that he did not understand. "It's not like you to do something like that."

Maybe it wasn't before, but it was different now. I was in a different world and maybe I was a different Danny Fisher. I didn't know. Again I didn't answer.

He tried to speak once more and then fell silent. We walked two blocks and turned up our street. At the corner we hesitated for a moment and caught each other's eye and then looked quickly away.

Up the block the street was empty now and dirty and filled with garbage left by the day. Our footsteps clattered on the sidewalk.

It had begun to snow. I pulled the collar of my jacket up around my neck. From the corner of my eye I could see my father walking beside me. It was then I first caught a glimpse of what would be: my father and I were strangers as we walked silently through the night.

All the Days of My Life

THE SECOND BOOK

CHAPTER ONE

PAPA LOOKED AT HIS WATCH AS WE CAME OUT OF THE DARK HALLWAY into the street. He thrust it quickly back in his pocket and glanced at me awkwardly. "Quarter to three," he muttered. "I gotta hurry or I'll be late."

I looked at him without interest. Five months of living down here and it seemed as if years had separated us. Since the very first day we moved, nothing had gone right. Now Papa had a job, in a drugstore on Delancey Street. Twenty-three a week.

"Walking my way?" Papa asked.

I nodded silently. Might as well. I was going to meet the gang on the corner near the five and dime. My step quickened to match his as he hurried off.

The memory of those five months was fresh in our minds. The days I came home from school and found him sitting in the kitchen of the dingy apartment, staring at the walls, an expression of hopelessness and despair painted on his face. I had tried to feel sorry for him but I couldn't. He had brought it on himself. If only he had been a little smarter.

Still there was something about his expression the night he had come a few days ago and told us about the job he had just snagged. It reached out and caught me in the gut. Twenty-three bucks a week for a registered pharmacist with twenty-five years' experience. It wasn't right. It was barely eating-dough.

We turned the corner at Delancey and were in front of the store where Papa worked. He stopped and looked at me hesitantly. I could see he wanted to ask me what I was going to do the rest of the afternoon, but he was too proud. I didn't offer to tell him.

"Tell Mamma I'll be home by two thirty," he said at last.

I nodded.

He opened his mouth as if to say more, then closed it as if he had changed his mind. Instead he shook his head slightly and, squaring his shoulders, walked into the store. The clock in the window showed exactly three as he walked in.

I had some time to kill so I leaned against the store window and watched the people walking by. A voice from inside the store came to my ears and I turned and looked in.

A man was coming out from behind the drug counter, taking off his jacket. "Christ, Fisher," he was saying in that quiet kind of voice that carries twenty yards in front and not one inch behind, "am I glad to get out of here! The boss is got his tail up and he's been eatin' my ass off all day."

Papa took the jacket from him silently and looked up at the wall clock to check his time. An expression of relief crossed his face.

A small, pompous man with an irascible face came out of the back room. He peered up through the store, his thick glasses shining in the light. "That you, Fisher?" he queried in a thin, irritating voice. He didn't wait for an answer. "Snap it up," he continued, "I got a couple of Rx's waiting for you."

There was a sound of fear and meekness in Papa's voice. I had never heard it before. "Yes, Mr. Gold," Papa answered. He hurried toward the back of the store. His hat and jacket were already in his hand as he turned toward the little man with an apologetic look. "I didn't mean to keep you waiting, Mr. Gold."

The little man looked at him contemptuously. "You could get here early, you know. It wouldn't hurt."

"I'm sorry, Mr. Gold," Papa said abjectly.

"Well, don't stand there like a fool, Fisher," Mr. Gold said, thrusting two slips of paper into Papa's hand. "Put on your jacket and get to work!" He turned his back and walked away.

Papa stared after him for a moment, with no expression on his face at all. Then he looked at the prescriptions in his hand and walked slowly to the prescription counter. He put his hat and jacket on a chair and slipped into the store jacket quickly.

He placed the prescriptions on the counter, smoothed them with his hand, and studied them again for a moment. Then he took a bottle and a measure from the shelf. I could almost hear the thin rattling sound the bottle made against the glass measure as he poured some liquid into it with trembling hands.

Suddenly he looked up and saw me staring at him. Embarrassment came into his eyes and a quick shame crossed his face. I let my eyes go vague and blank as if I hadn't seen him and turned away casually.

The gang was already waiting when I got there. Quietly we moved away from the corner. We didn't want to drag any eyes. I didn't waste any time with them.

"You know what to do," I said in a low careful voice. "We drift in easylike. Two at a time. Quiet. When we're all in there, I'll give the signal an' Spit and Solly will start the fight in the back of the store. When everybody's lookin' that way, the rest of you get busy. An' remember these things. Don't grab no crap, only stuff we can sell. Don't hang around to see how the other guy made out. As soon as you made your snatch, blow. Don't wait for nothin'. Get out fast! You all know where we're meetin' afterwards. Kill an hour before you show up."

I looked around at them. Their faces were serious. "Understan'?" There weren't any replies. I grinned. "Okay then. I'm goin' in now. Keep an eye on me an' don't do nothin' till I give the signal."

The gang scattered and I walked away quickly. I turned the corner and went into the five and ten. It was crowded with people. Good, it would make things easier.

I pushed my way through the aisle along the soda fountain to the end of the counter. There I climbed up on a seat and waited for the girl to come up and serve me. In the mirror behind the counter I could see Spit and Solly walking past me.

The counter girl stood in front of me. "What'll you have?"

"What you got, baby?" I countered. I was stalling for time. Things weren't ready yet.

She looked at me tiredly, pushing some stray hairs back from her forehead. "It's all on the signs," she replied in a flat, bored voice. "You can read."

I pretended to read the signs pasted on the mirror behind her. Two of the other boys were coming in. "A double-dip chocolate ice-cream soda," I said. "The dime special."

The girl walked down the counter and tossed the soda together with a careless expert skill. So much syrup, so much carbonated water, then the ice cream—two scoops, with the top of the scoop toward the customer so that he couldn't see it was really half empty—then some more carbonated water. I looked around the store.

The boys were all set up and ready to go. I waited for the soda, wishing she would snap it up. All at once I wanted to get this over with. It had been a bright idea when we were talking about it, but now I was jumpy. She came back down the aisle and put the soda on the counter in front of me.

I pushed a dime toward her and she rang it on the register.

The boys were watching me from the corners of their eyes. I put the straws into the soda, stirred it, and began to suck on the straws. The taste of the soda was sweet in my mouth when the noise of the fight broke out behind me.

I was grinning to myself as I turned toward the sound. Solly was just falling into a display case filled with canned goods. The crash roared through the store and people began running toward it. The boys were working smoothly. The counter girl spoke and I jumped, startled. She was looking past me curiously.

"What's goin' on there?"

"I dunno. A fight, I guess."

"Looks like a setup to me," she said.

I felt my pulse quicken nervously. "What do you mean?" I asked.

"Those boys ain't hurtin' each other," she said flatly. "I bet they got friends cleanin' out the joint. It's an old gimmick." Her eyes were roving through the store. "Look over there, see?"

She had spotted one of the boys stuffing his pockets at the cosmetic counter. Just then the boy turned and looked at me. He began to smile, but I shook my head quickly and he started out the door.

I turned back to the counter. The girl was staring at me, her eyes wide. "You're in on it," she whispered.

I reached across the counter quickly and grabbed her arm, smiling coldly. "What're you gonna do about it?" I asked quietly.

She stared at me for a moment, then smiled back. "Nothin'," she answered. "It's none of my business. Barbara Hutton can afford it."

I let go of her hand and looked back at the store. All the boys had gone and Solly was just being pushed out of the door by a couple of men. Relief came over my face. Still smiling, I turned back to the soda and took a spoonful of ice cream. I could taste the chocolate melting there.

"You make a mean soda," I said.

She smiled again. She had thick black hair, and her eyes were a soft dark brown. Her lipstick was a startling red against her pale thin face. "You're pretty smooth, all right," she whispered.

I felt a glow spread through me. I could see I had scored with this kid. "What's your name, baby?" I asked.

"Nellie," she answered.

"Mine's Danny," I told her. "Live in the neighborhood?"

"Over on Eldridge Street."

"What time you get through?"

"Nine o'clock, when the store closes," she replied.

I stood up proudly. I was very sure of myself. "I'll pick you up on the corner," I said. "Maybe we'll get some chinks." I didn't wait for her answer but sauntered down to where the men were busy putting up the display that Solly had fallen into. I watched them for a few minutes, then walked back to the counter.

The girl was still watching me. I grinned at her. "See you at nine, Nellie."

She flashed me a quick smile. "I'll be on the corner, Danny."

I half waved my hand to her and walked toward the entrance. I could feel her eyes following me. As I passed the drug counter, I picked up a comb and idly ran it through my hair. Then I went out the door, dropping the comb into my shirt pocket.

CHAPTER TWO

THE PEDDLER LOOKED UP AT ME WISELY. "WHERE'D YOU GET THIS stuff?" he asked.

"Yuh wanna buy it," I countered sarcastically, "or yuh want its pedigree?"

He looked down at the small carton. His hand picked up a jar of Mum and he tossed it nervously from one hand to the other as he spoke. "I don't want the cops should bother me," he said.

I reached for the carton meaningfully. "Then somebody else will buy it."

He grabbed at my hand quickly. "Wait a minute. I didn't say I didn't want the stuff."

I let go of the carton. "Then don't ask so many questions. Fifteen dollars and it's all yours."

He parted his lips over yellowed teeth. "Ten."

"Fourteen," I said quickly. The ritual had begun. You bargained for everything on the East Side. It was expected.

"Eleven."

I shook my head.

"Twelve." He was studying my face.

"Nope," I replied.

He drew a sharp breath. "Twelve fifty," he almost whispered. "That's the top."

I looked at his face for a moment, then I put out my hand. "Pay me," I said.

He reached into his pocket, took out a dirty old change purse, and snapped it open, revealing a small roll of bills. Carefully he counted the money into my hand.

I counted it again, shoved the money into my pocket, and turned to walk away, but the peddler called me back.

"When you got some more stuff," he said greedily, "bring it to me. I'll treat you right."

I was looking at him, but I couldn't see him. I couldn't see the whole thing for dust. Twelve fifty cut seven ways was less than two bucks apiece. It wasn't worth the effort. "Sure," I answered, turning away. "I'll remember." But he wouldn't see me again. There was no percentage in it.

I looked at my watch as I crossed Rivington Street. It was almost six o'clock. I didn't have to pick up the gang at the candy store before seven. I decided to stop by the house and pick up Papa's supper. Every day Mamma sent his supper down to the store. It would save her a trip.

The halls smelled. Disgustedly I noticed the paper bags of garbage stuck in front of the doors. The lousy super had been drunk again and forgotten to collect the garbage that morning. Much as I had seen of it, I couldn't get used to it.

I stumbled on a loose stair and cursed under my breath. I hated it here. I wished we had enough dough to get out. Some day I would get enough dough together and we would buy our house back and leave this stinking neighborhood.

I opened our door and walked in. Mamma was bending over the stove. She looked up at me wearily.

"Papa said he would be home by two thirty," I told her.

She nodded her head.

"I thought I'd bring him his supper," I volunteered.

She looked at me in some surprise. It was the first time since he'd had the job that I'd offered. "You want your supper first?" she asked.

I shook my head. "I'm not hungry," I lied. "A guy treated me to a couple of hot dogs at Katz's."

"Some soup you'll have, maybe?" she persisted.

"No, Mamma," I answered. "I'm full." I could see from the pot there was barely enough to go around as it was.

She was too tired to argue and took down a white enamel dinner pail from the closet and began to fill it. When she had finished she carefully wrapped it in a paper bag and gave it to me. I started out the door.

"Come home early tonight, Danny," she called after me as the door closed.

"Sure, Ma," I called back as I started down the stairs.

I stopped in front of the store and looked in. There were a few customers inside and a clerk was waiting on them. Papa must be in the back room. I walked into the store and waited at the counter.

The high-pitched sound of a man's shouting came from the back room. Involuntarily I listened, remembering it from earlier in the day.

"You stupid ass," the thin nasty voice was shouting, "I don't know why I hired you anyway. That's the trouble with all you guys who been in business for yourselves. You think you know everything, you don't listen to anybody!"

The voice faded away and the low-pitched murmur of Papa's voice took its place. I couldn't make out the words, so I looked back through the glass partition separating the back room from the store. Papa was standing there talking to Mr. Gold. Mr. Gold was glaring up at him, his face ruddy with rage. He began to shout again even before Papa had finished speaking.

"I don't want no excuses, no alibis! I felt sorry for you when you came in here crying how you needed a job, but, Goddammit, you'll either do the work the way I want it done or out on your ass you'll go! You hear me, Fisher? My way or out! That's all!"

I could hear Papa distinctly now. "I'm sorry, Mr. Gold," he was saying. There was a beaten, servile quality in his voice that made me sick to my stomach. "It won't happen again, Mr. Gold. I promise."

A wild impulse was running through me. I could kill the little son of a bitch who spoke to my father like that, who made him crawl like he did. No man had the right to do that to another. Papa had turned to the little man. I saw his back through the glass partition, his shoulders drooping heavily, his head inclined respectfully.

The clerk's voice interrupted my thoughts. "Anything I can do for you, sir?"

I turned to him bewilderedly. The sickish feeling had replaced my rage. I shook my head and started for the door angrily. Then I remembered the dinner pail I had in my hand and went back to the counter and put it down. "This is Doc Fisher's supper," I told the clerk, and ran out the door, Mr. Gold's high-pitched voice following me out into the street.

"A buck and a half apiece?" Spit's voice was querulous.

I looked at him coldly. My voice was flat. "You kin do better, you fence it."

Saliva ran in tiny beads from the corner of Spit's mouth as it always did when he was excited. "Okay, Danny, okay," he said hastily. "I ain't arguin'."

I finished distributing the money, then looked up at them. I had held out two bucks on them, but that was my due. I had figured out the job.

"What we gonna do next, Danny?" Spit asked, looking at me expectantly.

"I dunno," I answered, taking out a cigarette. "But no more uh this. There ain't enough in it." I lit the cigarette. "Don't worry, I'll think of somethin'." I looked at my watch. It was almost seven o'clock. "I'm gonna take a shot at the crap game in the garage," I said. "Anybody wanna come with me?"

"Not for me," Spit drooled quickly. "I got a dame lined up. At least I'll get somethin' outta my dough that way."

The gang broke up and I walked alone around the corner. Spit had reminded me. I had a date at nine with that girl behind the soda fountain. She seemed like a bright kid. That was okay with me, I liked them bright. I couldn't stand the stupid ones. They only knew one thing when you wanted them to polish doorbells with their behinds. No. The bright ones could be talked into it—sometimes.

I was almost at the garage now. I felt better as I came near the entrance. The three and a half bucks I had in my pocket was as good as nothing. If I was lucky I could afford to buy the dame some chinks.

A thin-faced Italian kid was standing in the garage entrance acting as lookout. I walked past him. The kid put out a hand to stop me. "Where ya goin'?" he asked.

I brushed his hand off me without anger. "Easy, luksh," I smiled. "I'm just gonna try my luck."

The Italian boy smiled back at me in recognition. "Okay, Danny," he said, turning back to the entrance.

I walked through the darkened garage toward a light in the back. In a space hidden by the automobiles surrounding it, a group of men and boys were standing in a small semicircle. Their voices were low and quiet, punctuated only by the metallic clicking of the dice. Several of them looked at me as I came up, but their gaze returned quickly to the floor as they recognized me. Their attention was riveted on the dice as they rolled along the floor and bounced back from the wall.

I stood there quietly for a few minutes trying to get the feel of the game. I didn't believe in bucking the dice, I tried to nose out who was hot and then follow that player. There was a small swarthy guy who seemed to be doing all right. I watched him for a while. He had picked up two bets before I made up my mind. The next time he bet against the dice I went along with him. I threw a buck down on the floor. "Against," I said. The bookie covered it.

The shooter made the point and I lost my bet. I followed the swarthy man again. This time I won. Again I bet and won. I began to feel excitement stirring in me. I bet again and won. I had seven bucks now, I began to feel lucky.

The man who had been shooting looked up. "I'm through," he said disgustedly, standing up and dusting off his trousers.

The book looked around. "Who wants them?" he asked. There were no takers. Nobody wanted the dice. The book was used to that. There was something in the small gambler's lexicon that said pro dice were jinxed. Still, he had to keep the game going. He looked at me. "Take 'em, Danny," he gestured. "First buck for free."

I moved forward reluctantly and picked up the dice. I had no choice. I was last in the game and that was regulation. I couldn't refuse. I began to rattle the dice in my hand.

Suddenly a feeling of sureness came over me. I felt my heart begin to hammer excitedly. I couldn't miss. I was hot. I threw two bucks down on the floor. Another dollar floated down beside it, that was the book's stake. I blew hotly into the palms of my hands as more money floated down on the floor. I snapped the dice out. They bounced crazily against the wall and came to a stop.

A natural! I picked up the dice again and began to shake them. This time I talked the whole thing over with them. Dice talk no outsider could understand. I could feel them warm up in my hand and I knew that they understood me if nobody else did. I rode the six bucks.

Four was the point. I picked them up again and continued to whisper to them. When they were nice and cozy I spun them out and made my point.

I picked up nine bucks and let the rest ride. I could feel the perspiration breaking out on my face as the dice rattled in my hand. I had the fever.

It was almost a quarter to nine when I came to and looked at my watch. I turned in the dice and checked out of the game. I was better than twenty fish ahead. My shirt clung damply to my back as I walked out of the garage.

The kid at the door grinned at me. "Clean already, Danny?" he jeered.

I grinned back at him and tossed him a half a buck. "Buy yourself a shtickel fleish, luksh," I told him. "You'll find it more fun than your fist."

CHAPTER THREE

I STOOD ON THE CURB IN FRONT OF THE FIVE AND TEN AND WATCHED THE girls coming out. I lit a cigarette. It was ten after nine. She was certainly taking her time. Maybe she was giving me a stand-up. I'd give her five more minutes and then to hell with her.

"Hello, Danny," she said quietly. She was standing beside me. I had watched her come out the door, but hadn't recognized her, she looked so much younger in her own clothes than in her uniform.

"Hi, Nellie." My eyes widened. She was just a kid. At the most she was no older than me. "Yuh hungry?" I asked after a moment's hesitation.

She nodded quietly. She seemed a little embarrassed, not as sure of herself as she had been behind the counter of the store.

I took her arm and steered her toward the corner, looking at her from the corner of my eyes. Her hair was jet-black, and bluish tones seemed to flicker in it as the lights from the store windows struck it. Her eyes were wide and looked straight ahead as she walked. She wore lipstick but of a softer shade than she had worn during the day.

"You look younger," I exclaimed in a sort of surprise.

She turned her face toward me. "A lot of girls make up to look older in the store. Otherwise they might not hold their jobs." A shy warmth came into her eyes. "You look older than you did in the store."

I smiled back at her. That made me feel good. We were in front of the restaurant, its faded yellow and blue sign blinking at us:

CHOW MEIN 30¢ CHOP SUEY

"Let's eat," I said, opening the door and letting her walk in before me.

A tired-looking, wizened old Chinese showed us to a table. He dropped two menus on the table before us and shuffled slowly back to the door. The restaurant was almost empty; only two other tables were occupied. I glanced down at the menu perfunctorily, I already knew what I wanted. Then I looked across the the table at her.

She met my glance. "Chow mein for me." She smiled.

"And fried rice. We'll mix it," I added quickly. I didn't want her to get any wrong ideas. I wasn't made out of dough.

A young Chinese waiter, as tired-looking as the old man who had seated us, placed a pot of tea on the table and languidly waited for our order. I gave it to him quickly and he went away. Then I turned back to the girl. As my eyes caught her gaze, she lowered her glance. A faint flush began to creep into her face and a strained air suddenly came between us.

"What's the matter?" I asked.

She raised her eyes to meet mine. "I shouldn't be here," she replied nervously. "I don't even know who you are. My father—"

"Your old man wouldn't like it?" I interrupted, smiling confidently. I felt more sure of myself now. "How old are you anyway?"

Her eyes met mine levelly. "Sev—no, sixteen," she answered hesitantly.

"Been working there long?" I asked.

"Almost a year," she said. "They think I'm older."

"Your old man rough on you?" I asked. A sympathy I couldn't restrain had crept into my voice, and it seemed to lessen the strangeness between us.

"He's all right, I guess. You know those old-fashioned Italians. It's always in the old country this, the old country that." She looked into my eyes candidly. "I'm supposed to come right home after work. I'm old enough to lie about my age to get a job and bring home money, but I'm not old enough to go out with boys. If he knew I was out with you, he'd give me hell."

I looked at her speculatively, wondering why the long buildup. "Then why did you come?" I asked.

She smiled. "Maybe I'm getting tired of living in the old country. Maybe it's time he learned this is a new place. We do things differently here."

"Is that the only reason?" I asked, still watching her closely.

Her face began to blush under my scrutiny. "No, it isn't," she confessed, shaking her head slightly. "I wanted to come with you. I wanted to see what you were like."

"Do you like what you see?"

She nodded silently, her face still flushing. "Do you?" she asked in a shy little voice.

I reached across the table and took her hand. This was going to be a pushover. "I sure do, Nellie," I said confidently. "I sure do."

She stopped on the street corner under the light. "You better leave me here, Danny," she said, looking up at me. "My father might be waitin' on the steps for me."

"That's a good brush," I said coldly.

A shadow came into her eyes. "Danny, it's not." Her voice was earnest. "Really, it's not. You don't know my old man."

I couldn't help it, she sold me. "Sure," I said lightly, "I know it's an old gag, but I'm a sucker for it. I half believe yuh."

Her hand caught mine. "You must believe me, Danny," she said quickly. "I wouldn't fool you. Honest, I wouldn't."

I still held onto her hand tightly. "What'll yuh tell him you're comin' in so late for?"

"I'll tell him we got stuck in the store. He knows sometimes we have to stay."

"Will he be mad?"

"No," she replied. "He don't care if it's that. He don't care how late I work."

I let go of her hand and stepped back into the doorway of a store, away from the street lamp. "C'mere," I said.

She watched me for a second, then took a hesitant step toward me. Her voice was suddenly nervous. "What for?"

I looked at her steadily. "You know what for," I said quietly. "C'mere."

She took another half step and then stopped. A strange hurt came into her face. "No, Danny. I'm not that kind."

I made my voice bitter and cutting. "Then it is the brush." I took a cigarette from my pocket and put it between my lips. "Okay, baby. Beat it. You had your fun."

I struck a match and held it to my cigarette. When I looked up she was still watching me. There was a peculiar tenseness in the way she stood there, like a doe about to run. The street light behind her threw blue sparkling lights into her hair.

I blew a cloud of smoke toward her. "What're you waitin' for? Go on home. Your ol' man's waitin'."

She took another step toward me. "Danny, that ain't the way I want it. I don't want you to be mad at me."

I was getting sore. If I got the brush, I got the brush, that's all. I never expected to bat a thousand. But why was she making such a big deal out of the whole thing? My voice mimicked her: "Danny, that ain't the way I want it!" I laughed bitterly. "What the hell d'yuh think I took you out for?" I snapped harshly. "To get the brush on the corner? I can get plenty of dames. I didn't have to bother with you."

There were tears in her eyes. "I thought you liked me, Danny," she said in a small voice. "I liked you."

I reached out quickly and grabbed her arm and pulled her toward me in the dimly lit doorway. I dropped the cigarette to the ground and put my arms around her.

I could feel the stiffness in her body as she looked up at me, her eyes wide and frightened. But she stood still, very still. "Danny!"

I kissed her swiftly, feeling her lips crush beneath mine, her hard teeth behind them. Her lips were cold. I kissed her again. They were a little warmer now and parted slightly. I felt them move and kissed her again. They were warm now and pressed back against me.

I looked down at her, smiling slightly. "Is that so bad, Nellie?"

She hid her face against my shoulder. "You'll think I'm no good," she cried.

I was puzzled. This wasn't what I had expected at all. My confusion spilled over into my voice. "What you play up to me this afternoon for? Yuh should know the score by now. You been aroun' long enough."

She looked up at me and in the dark her eyes were soft and wide but no longer afraid. "I liked you, Danny, that's why. That's why I didn't go home when you told me."

I looked at her for a moment; then I sought her lips again. I could feel the tension seep from her body and she loosened up as she kissed me back. This kiss was for real. I held her close to me. "But yuh acted so wise," I whispered. "About the fight an' all that. You knew that Spit and Solly were fakin'. How'd yuh know somethin' like that if yuh never been aroun'?"

"My oldest brother, Giuseppe, was a pug," she answered, not stirring in my arms. "He taught me to tell when they were fakin' it."

Our eyes met in the dark and held. "You're not givin' me the business?" The last remaining trace of skepticism was in my voice.

"No, Danny." Her voice was level.

I kissed her again. It was different this time. There was a new looseness, a comfortable understanding in the kiss. The fierce urgency had gone.

"I like you," I said, laughing suddenly. "You're funny but you're nice."

She smiled up at me. "Not mad any more?"

I shook my head. "No, baby."

This time she held her face up to me and waited for my lips. I looked down at her, not moving. Her eyes were closed. "Danny," she whispered shyly, "kiss me, Danny."

I felt the change in her lips. They were suddenly open to me and she was pressing desperately against me. My arms tightened around her. I dropped my hand along her spine, molding her to me.

Her eyes were still closed. We were drifting in a hazy cloud. The corner was gone, the street lamp was gone, the doorway was gone. Everything had vanished except the pressure of our lips. I closed my eyes as my hands sought the warmth of her body.

Her whisper was almost a scream in my ears. "Danny! Danny, stop!" Her hands were grabbing excitedly at mine, pushing them away from her.

I caught her wrists and held them. Her body was trembling frightenedly. "Easy, baby, easy," I said gently. "I ain't gonna hurt you."

The panic left her as suddenly as it had come and she hid her face against my shoulder. "Oh, Danny, I never felt like this before."

I put my hand under her chin and lifted her face toward me. Tears were standing in her eyes. "Me neither," I said earnestly. And I meant it too.

Her eyes grew large and round with wonder. "Danny, do you—" her voice hesitated. "Do you think maybe we're in love?"

I was puzzled. I didn't know. I tried to smile. "Maybe we are, Nellie. Maybe we are."

Almost as I spoke, an embarrassment seemed to spring up between us and we moved apart. She looked down and began to rearrange her clothing. By the time she had finished I was smoking a cigarette. Her hand reached toward me and I took it. We stood there silently, hand in hand, until the cigarette burned down.

Then I threw it away and it fell into the gutter, spilling small sparks, and we turned and looked at each other. I smiled. "Hi, Nellie."

"Hello, Danny," she whispered back shyly.

We stared at each other for a moment and then began to laugh. With our laughter, the embarrassment seemed to fall away. I bent and kissed her quickly, our handclasp tightening and loosening as our lips met and quit.

"Hope your father won't be mad," I said.

"He won't be," she smiled. "I'll tell him I was working."

We walked out of the doorway to the corner under the street light. Her face was flushed and bright, her eyes shining with a brand-new warmth, and her teeth were white and sparkling under her red lips as she smiled at me.

"Did I tell you you were pretty?" I asked jestingly.

"No," she answered.

"I guess I didn't have time," I grinned, "so I'll tell you now. You're very pretty. Like a movie star."

"Oh, Danny!" Her hand clung to mine very tightly.

"I guess yuh gotta go," I said seriously.

She nodded.

"Well—good night then," I said, letting go of her hand.

"Will I see you again, Danny?" Her voice was very small.

"Sure thing." I grinned quickly. "I'll drop around to the store tomorrow."

Her face brightened. "I'll make you a special soda. Three full scoops of ice cream!"

"Three scoops!" I exclaimed. "You couldn't keep me away then!"

She was smiling again. "Good night, Danny."

"Good night, baby."

She started across the street, then turned back to me. There was an anxious look on her face. "You won't bring your friends, will you? They might get caught."

"Yuh worried about them, Nellie?" I laughed.

"I don't give a damn about them," she said fiercely. "It's you I'm worried about."

I felt a glow kiting through me. She was a good kid. "I won't bring them."

The serious look was still on her face. "Do you have to run around with them and do things like that, Danny? You might get caught. Can't you get a job?"

"No," I answered stiffly. "My folks won't let me quit school."

Her hand reached for mine and squeezed it understandingly. There was deep concern in her eyes. "Be careful, Danny," she said softly.

I smiled down at her. "I will," I promised.

She stepped up on the curb and kissed me quickly. "Good night, Danny."

"Night, baby."

I watched her run across the street and turn into a doorway. She stopped there for a moment and waved at me. I waved back. Then she disappeared into the hallway.

I turned and started down the street. I felt good. I felt so good I almost forgot how much I hated living down here until I crossed Delancey Street in front of Papa's store and saw Mr. Gold again.

CHAPTER FOUR

HE WAS STANDING IN FRONT OF THE STORE STUFFING A SMALL CANVAS and leather pouch into his pocket. I knew what it was right away. It was a pouch used to make a night deposit in the bank.

Automatically I ducked into a doorway and watched him. A glance at my watch told me it was a few minutes to twelve. He glanced once more in the store window, then started down Delancey Street toward Essex. I followed him slowly, lagging half a block behind.

At first I didn't know why I did it, but as I moved along behind him, the reason came to me. He turned up Essex and began to walk quickly. I crossed to the opposite side of the street and kept pace with him, the idea taking quick shape in my mind.

He walked to the bank on the corner of Avenue A and First Street. There he took the little pouch from his pocket and dropped it in the night depository. Then he turned and started up Avenue A.

I lingered behind on the corner, watching him go. I had no further interest in where he was going. I lit a cigarette and began to think.

When I had first moved down here, it had seemed like another world. And it was. It was a different world from any I had ever known. Down here there was only one rule: you either fought or went hungry. And there were no holds barred.

The kids knew that even better than the adults. There were brought up to scrounge for themselves as early as they could. They were tough, bitter, and cynical beyond anything I had ever imagined. There was only one thing that kept me from being killed. I could fight better than they could and in many ways think faster.

It had taken a little time, though. For a while they looked at me crosseyed. They couldn't figure me. After the fight I had the day Rexie was run over they had shown a certain respect for me. It wasn't until I had taken to hanging out in the candy store on the corner that I began to know them.

From that point on, it became my show. The boy I had beaten up was the leader of the gang. Now they shifted around without purpose. Spit and Solly had tried to take over, but they couldn't command respect from the others. The only language they could understand was physical superiority.

Then one day Spit came over to me while I was having an egg cream. Covering me with a fine spray of saliva, he invited me to join the gang. I listened to him cautiously, but after a while I came in with them. I was too lonely down here, I had to identify myself with somebody. It might as well be with the Stanton Street Boys.

But the main concern remained dough. Lack of money was the miasma that hung over the lower East Side like a plague. You could see it everywhere you turned, in the dirty streets, in the placarded store windows, in the ill-kept tenements. You could hear it everywhere, in the crying hawk of the street peddlers on Rivington, in the careful haggling over pennies in the shops.

If you had a buck in your pocket you were a king; if you didn't, you looked for someone who did and would pay your freight. But kings did not live on the East Side any more unless they were the kind who could drag enough pennies from the general poverty to make life comfortable for themselves.

There were plenty of those—bookies, shylocks, and petty criminals. They were the smart ones, the heroes. They were the envied, the strong who managed to survive. They were our examples, our men of distinction.

They were the people we wanted to be. Not shnooks like our fathers, who had fallen by the wayside because of an inability to cope with the times. Our fathers were the people of the lower East Side. And there were enough of them as it was. We weren't going to be like them if we could help it. We were smarter than they were. We were going to be kings. And when I was king I would buy back my house in Brooklyn and move away from this rotten place.

I strolled back toward my house. Spit had asked me what we were going to do next. I hadn't known then. All I knew was that the five-and-dime job wasn't worth the effort. But I knew now. I could knock over two birds with this caper. I decided to drop in at the candy store before I went upstairs to talk it over with Spit and Solly.

I stirred restlessly in the bed. I was too steamed up to fall asleep. A horn honked loudly in the street outside my window. I got out of bed silently and sat down near the window. I lit a cigarette and stared out.

A D.S. truck was parked down there. The faint metallic sounds of the garbage cans clanging against its sides as the men emptied them came up to me. I remembered the expression on Spit's face when I first explained the job to the boys.

He had been afraid. But Solly was hot for it, and that won him over. Just the three of us could handle it. But first Gold's routine would have to be checked; that was important.

One of us would have to follow him for several nights in a row as he left the store and make sure of all his stops and habits. Then on the right night we'd jump him.

There was a couple of hundred bucks in it, I had told them. All we had to do was coldcock the geezer and snatch the dough. It was a cinch. I hadn't told them anything about my father working in the store. It was none of their business.

The sound of a girl's voice coming in the open window made me think of Nellie. She was a strange kid for a luksh. Usually they were loud and tough and you could tell they were Italian as soon as they opened their mouths, but she was different. She was soft-spoken and gentle and nice.

She had liked me, too. I knew that. It was funny how things happened. You took out a dame for one reason and suddenly you find out that things weren't what they seemed. That the dame was level and that you really liked her. Then you didn't want to do anything that might make her dislike you.

That was a strange thing. I had never felt like that about any dame before. I remembered what she had said: "Maybe we're in love." Maybe we were. I couldn't explain any other way how I felt. There had never been any other dame I was content just to hold and talk to and be near. Maybe she was right in what she said.

The girl's voice floated in the window again. I craned my neck into the street in order to see her. The street was empty. Again I heard the girl's voice. There was something familiar about it, I knew that voice, but it sounded strange coming in my window.

The girl was talking again. This time I traced the sound to the roof over my head. I looked up. I could see the glow of a cigarette over the parapet. Then I recognized the voice. It was Mimi's. I wondered what she was doing up on the roof at this hour. It was after one o'clock. Then I remembered she had said something about a date with that guy in her office she had a crush on—a George somebody. I had twitted her about going out with a jerk who worked in an office and she had been angry. "He's better than those candy-store bums you hang out with," she had retorted.

I decided to go up there and see what Miss High-and-Mighty was doing. All I knew was that if you went up on the roof down in this neighborhood at night, you weren't going to look at the stars. I slipped into my trousers and silently left my room.

The roof door was open and I quietly stepped outside. I hid in the shadow of the door and looked toward the front of the roof. She was there all right. So was the guy. They were in a hell of a clinch. I watched them.

They separated and in the moonlight I could see Mimi's face. I caught my breath sharply. She didn't look like no goody-goody now. The guy was talking, his voice low. I couldn't make out his words, but he seemed to be pleading. Mimi shook her head and he went off again in another torrent of words.

She shook her head again and began to speak. "No, George, forget about marriage. I like you very much but I'm tired of worrying about money and we'll only have the same thing. I don't want that."

I grinned to myself. Mimi was no dope. A buck was a buck. Still, it seemed funny to think about her getting married. It made me realize that she was all grown up now, she wasn't a kid any more.

The fellow pulled her to him again. He said something to her and kissed her. I watched them, still grinning. For all her high-and-mighty ways, she knew the score when it came to necking. It didn't look like this was the first time she had been up on a roof. I turned silently and went back down the stairs to my room.

About fifteen minutes later I heard the door open and I went out into the hall. She was closing the door silently and she jumped when she turned around and saw me.

"What are you doing up, Danny?" she asked in surprise.

I didn't answer, just stood there grinning at her.

She stared at me angrily. "What are you grinning at?"

"Your lipstick is smeared," I told her, my grin becoming broader and more knowing.

Her hand flew to her mouth. "You stayed up to spy on me!"

"Uh-uh." I shook my head. "You and your boy friend were making so much noise up on the roof over my head I couldn't sleep."

"You got a dirty mind!" she flung at me.

"Have I?" I asked, still smiling. I pointed at her dress.

She looked down, her eyes widening in surprise. The whole front of her dress was covered with lipstick stains. She looked up at me, her face reddening.

"Take some advice from your kid brother, baby," I said. "Next time you go in for any heavy lovin', wipe your lipstick off first. It don't clean out an' it saves wear an' tear on your clothes."

She bit her lip furiously. She was too angry to think of a retort.

I grinned again and went back to my room. "Good night, Mimi," I said over my shoulder. "Remember what I said."

CHAPTER FIVE

PAPA CAME IN FOR BREAKFAST JUST AS WE WERE BEGINNING TO EAT. I looked up at him. There were lines on his face that hadn't come from weariness alone. Lines of pain and discouragement that came from eating humble pie were etched sharply into his once round cheeks.

A twinge of sympathy for him ran through me. The fierce pride I had in my being was hurt by the slow disintegration of his own. I stood up. "Here, Papa," I said quickly, "sit here by the window." It was the comfortable place in the kitchen.

Slowly he slumped into the chair. He looked over at me gratefully. "Thanks for bringing me over my supper, Danny," he said wearily. "I was busy and I didn't see you come in."

I nodded my head. "The clerk told me," I said, sparing his feelings. I knew he wouldn't want me to admit I had heard Gold hollering at him.

Mamma came over to the table and put a bowl of cereal in front of him. "Why didn't you sleep later, Harry?" she asked concernedly.

He looked up at her. "Who can sleep when the daylight comes? I can't get used to it."

"You should rest, though," Mamma said. "You work hard."

He picked up the spoon and began to eat without answering, but he had no appetite and soon he pushed the plate away from him. "Just give me coffee, Mary," he said in a tired voice.

Mamma put a cup of coffee in front of him. "Were you busy yesterday?" she asked.

"Mr. Gold kept me busy," he said without looking up. Then he looked at me, realizing what he had said. I could see he was wondering what I knew.

I kept my face impassive. As far as he was concerned, I knew nothing, had seen nothing, and had heard nothing. "What kind of a guy is this Gold like?" I asked, looking down at my plate.

I could feel Papa's gaze on me. "Why do you ask?"

I didn't look up. "Just curious, I guess," I answered. I couldn't tell him the real reason.

Papa thought for a moment. When he spoke, his words were very carefully chosen. He surprised me with his understatement. "He's all right, only very nervous. Got a lot of things to do, a lot of things on his mind."

I put another spoonful of cereal in my mouth. "Yuh like workin' for him, Papa?" I asked as casually as I could manage.

Our eyes met and his fell to his coffee cup. "It's a job," he answered evasively.

"How come he's manager?" I asked.

"The man before him got sick and had to quit. He had my job as the only other registered man, so naturally he was promoted."

I looked at him interestedly. That was an angle. "If he quit would you get the job, Pop?"

Papa laughed self-consciously. "I don't know, but I guess I might. The supervisor likes me."

"Who's that?"

"He's the boss of a group of stores. He comes from the main office."

"He's boss over Mr. Gold too?" I continued.

Papa nodded. "Over everybody." He looked at me with a curious smile. "So many questions, Danny," he chided. "You thinking of going to work in a drugstore for the summer?"

"Maybe," I said evasively.

"You're not going to work for Mr. Gottkin in the country?" he asked.

"I don't know," I said, shrugging my shoulders. "I haven't heard from him yet." I was disappointed about that too. I had expected that Sam would drop me a line by now, but I guess that business last year with Miss Schindler had burned him more than he let me know.

"Why don't you write him?" Mamma asked.

I turned to her. "Where? I don't even know where he is. He's always traveling. For all I know, he may have given up the business entirely." I couldn't tell them the reason why I wouldn't write him.

Just then Mimi came rushing in. "I've just got time for coffee, Mamma," she said. "I'll be late for work."

Mamma shook her head. "I don't know what's the matter with you, staying up so late you can't get up in the morning."

"I do," I said grinning, remembering last night. "Mimi's got a feller."

Papa looked at her with interest. "A nice boy, Miriam?" he asked.

I answered before she had a chance. "A schmoe," I said quickly. "A jerk from her office."

"He is not!" she retorted angrily. "He's really a very nice boy, Papa. He goes to college at night."

"Yeah," I teased her, "Tin Beach U."

She turned on me furiously. "Keep your mouth shut!" she snapped. "At least he's got more sense than to hang around a candy store all day and night like you do. He's going to make something out of himself, not be a street-corner bum."

Mamma put out a placating hand. "Don't say things like that to your brother. It's not nice."

Mimi turned angrily to her. Rage was shaking her voice. "Why not?" she queried, almost shouting. "Who is he? God? Who does he think he is that everybody has to be afraid to tell him what they think? Ever since we moved here, it's been Danny this and Danny that. When he changed school it was terrible, but I changed school in the last term and nobody said anything. Does he try to get a job after school or do some work? He knows how bad we need money but he doesn't lift a finger to help and nobody says nothing to him. Everybody's afraid to hurt his feelings. All he does is hang out in a candy store all day and night with a bunch of bums and comes home to eat and sleep like a king. He's a bum, nothing but a bum, and it's about time somebody told it to him!"

"Mimi, shut up!" Papa was on his feet, his face pale. He looked at me guiltily.

She was staring at him, her eyes filled with angry tears; then she turned toward me. I stared at her coldly. For a moment she looked at me, then turned and ran, crying, from the kitchen.

Papa sat down heavily and looked at me. Mamma was watching me too. They were waiting for me to speak, but I had nothing to say. At last Papa spoke in a heavy voice. "Altogether wrong she's not, Danny," he said gently.

I didn't answer. My lips were grimly shut.

"Those fellers down at the candy store, they're no good," he continued.

I pushed my plate away from me and stood up. "I didn't pick this neighborhood. It wasn't my fault we moved down here. What d'ya want me to do, become a hermit because Mimi doesn't approve of my friends?"

Papa shook his head. "No, but other friends you can't find?"

I stared at him. It was no use. He would never understand. There was nothing to say. The estrangement I had felt between us the first day we moved down here grew stronger. And it was too late to go back. "There are no other friends to find," I said flatly.

"Then there's something you can do," he persisted. "There must be."

I shook my head with finality. "It's not anything I can do, Papa," I told him coldly. "Only you can do it."

"What's that?" he asked.

Mamma came toward me. "Yes, what's that?" she echoed.

"Get back my house," I said slowly. "You lost it. You get it back. Then maybe we can start all over."

I watched the pain grow and grow in their eyes until I couldn't stand it any longer. Then I walked out of the apartment.

❖   ❖   ❖

She spotted me instantly, almost as soon as I came through the door. I sauntered down the counter to where she stood. I could see her look hurriedly in the mirror behind her and pat her hair. I climbed up on a stool and she turned around smiling.

"Hello, Danny," she whispered shyly. I could see a blush running up her neck into her face.

I smiled back at her. She was a nice kid. "Hi, Nellie," I whispered quietly. "Was your father mad?"

She shook her head. "He believed me," she whispered. She looked up suddenly. In the mirror I could see the manager walking toward us. "A chocolate soda," she said quickly in a businesslike tone. "Yes, sir."

She turned and took a glass from the shelf behind her. I smiled at her in the mirror. The manager passed us without a glance. She sighed in relief and went about making the soda.

She came back down the counter and placed the soda in front of me. "Your hair is so blond it's almost white," she whispered. "I dreamed about you last night."

I looked at her quizzically. The kid had it bad. But I felt flattered. "A good dream?" I asked, slipping the straws into the soda.

She nodded, excitement lurking in her eyes. "Did you think about me?"

"A little," I admitted.

"I want you to think about me," she said quickly.

I stared at her. Her face was warm and attractive. She had less makeup on today than yesterday. Today she looked younger. She began to blush under my gaze.

"Will you meet me tonight?" she asked eagerly.

I nodded. "Same place."

I could see the manager coming back toward us again. "That will be ten cents, please," she said in her business voice.

My dime rang on the counter and she picked it up. She pressed down the register keys and the bell rang as the drawer opened. She dropped in the dime and closed it. The manager had gone again. She came back to me. "Nine o'clock," she whispered.

I nodded my head again and she turned away in answer to another customer. I finished my soda quickly and left the store.

The three of us walked down Delancey Street. Solly slouched along listening to Spit and me.

I pulled them to a stop in front of the drugstore. "This is the place," I said.

Spit's voice was surprised. "This is the joint where your old man works," he said.

It was my turn to be surprised. I didn't think he knew. But I should have known better, there were no secrets down here. "So?" I asked belligerently.

"What if he gets wise?" Spit asked excitedly.

"What's he got to get wise to?" I retorted. "They'll never think of me."

"But this is the McCoy," Spit said; "this ain't no penny-ante rap. If the cops getcha, yuh go in the can an' they throw away the key."

"Yuh like workin' the five and dime for peanuts," I asked sarcastically, "or yuh lookin' for some real dough?"

Solly finally spoke. "Danny's right. To hell with the cheap seats. This looks okay to me."

I gave him a grateful glance. We walked on to the corner before we stopped again. There I turned to face Spit. "Quit crappin' around. Yuh in or out?" I asked flatly.

Spit looked from one to another. We watched him steadily. His face flushed. "Okay," he said quickly, "I'm in."

I could feel my face relax into a smile. I slapped Spit on the shoulder heartily. "Good boy," I said softly. "I knew I could count on yuh. Now listen again, this is the way we'll work it."

We stood on the corner and figured the job. Around us swirled the hungry lower East Side. A cop stood a few feet away, but he paid no attention to us. Nor us to him. He had no reason to bother us. Kids always stood on street corners down here and always would. He couldn't go around chasing all of them. If he did, he wouldn't have time to do anything else.

CHAPTER SIX

IT WAS DRIZZLING AND WE HUDDLED TOGETHER IN THE DOORWAY ACROSS the street from Nellie's house. Somehow we began to think of it as if we owned it, and whenever someone else came near it we would resent them as if they were trespassers. My lips were sweet with the taste of her, but now we stood quietly, my arms around her, looking out into the wet, dark streets. Her voice seemed to float in the night. "Next week will be June, Danny."

I nodded my head and looked down at her. "Yeah," I said.

Her eyes were almost shy as she looked up at me. "I know you almost three weeks now, but it seems like I knew you all my life."

I smiled at her. I felt the same way. I felt good when she was around. It was like being home again. "Like me, Nellie?" I fished.

Her eyes were shining now. "Like you?" she whispered softly. "I'm crazy about you. I love you, Danny. I love you so much I'm afraid."

I pressed my lips to her. "I love you too," I whispered back.

She gave a soft cry deep in her throat and her arms pulled me close to her. "Oh, Danny," she cried, "I wish we were old enough to get married!"

I couldn't help it, at first it seemed so funny. My lips began to twitch with a smile.

She pulled her face away from me. "You're laughing at me!"

I shook my head, smothering the smile. "I'm not, doll. Really. I was just think-ing what your old man would say if he knew."

She pulled my face down to her again. "Who gives a damn what he would say, once we got married!" she whispered wildly.

I kissed her again and held her tight. I could feel her shiver in my grasp.

"Hold me, Danny," she cried breathlessly. "Hold me. I love you to hold me. I love the feel of your hands on me. I don't care if they say it is a sin!"

I looked at her in surprise. "A sin?" I questioned. "Who says so?"

Her hands held mine against her bosom as her wide dark eyes looked up at me. "I really don't care, Danny," she said earnestly. "Even if Father Kelly says so. I'll do whatever penance I have to just so long as you don't stop loving me."

I was puzzled. "What's Father Kelly got to do with it?" It was the first time I had thought about the difference in our religions.

She looked at me trustingly. "I'm not supposed to say it, but each week after confession he gives me a lecture about you."

"You tell him about us?" I asked curiously. "What does he say?"

She rested her head against my shoulder. "He says that it's wrong and I should stop," she answered in a low voice, "and that it's even worse with you."

"Why with me?" I asked, beginning to get a little angry.

"Because you're not even Catholic. He says we'll never be able to get married. No church would accept us. He says I shouldn't bother with you, that I should find some nice Catholic boy."

"The bastard!" I said bitterly. I looked across the street toward her house. What difference did it make to him what she did? I looked back at her. "What if he tells your father?" I asked worriedly.

She looked surprised at my question. "He would never do that!" she replied quickly in a shocked voice. "A priest would never tell. What you tell him is for God's ears alone. He is just the communicant for your confession. I thought you knew that."

"I didn't know," I admitted. I was still curious about her relationship with the priest. "What does he make you do when you tell him about us?"

"I have to say prayers and do penance before the Virgin Mother. After that I'm all right."

"He doesn't punish you?" I asked.

She seemed bewildered. "You don't understand, Danny," she replied. "He just tries to make you realize that you've done wrong and feel sorry for it. When you feel sorry for it, then you're punished enough."

I began to smile. This was nothing. "Are you sorry?" I asked.

She looked up at me guiltily. "No, I'm not sorry at all," she said in a wondering voice. "Maybe that's what seems so wrong about the whole thing. I guess I'll never be forgiven then."

I pulled her to me laughing. "Don't worry about it then, baby," I reassured her. "Nothing can be wrong as long as we love each other." I was just about to kiss her when I heard footsteps coming toward us in the street. We separated hastily. A man walked by without a sideward glance.

I looked at my watch. "Jesus! It's after eleven! You better get goin' or your old man will raise the roof!"

She smiled at me. "I don't want to go, Danny. I want to stay here with you forever!"

I grinned back at her. I didn't want her to go either, but tonight I had something else to do. We had finally decided that tonight we'd pull that job. Spit and Solly would be waiting for me at the store at half past eleven. "Go on," I said with a forced lightness. "I got to get home even if you don't."

She leaned toward me. "All right, Danny." She kissed me. "Tomorrow night?"
I grinned at her. "Tomorrow night."

She walked across the street. I watched her get to her house and stop in the doorway to wave at me. I waved back and she disappeared inside.

I looked at my watch again. It was twenty-five after eleven. I would have to snap it up if I wanted to get there in time. I broke into a half run and then slowed down suddenly. Too many people notice a guy running through the streets at this time of night.

Solly was standing on the corner across the street from the store. "Where's Spit?" I asked, a little out of breath.

Solly gestured with his hand. "Over there." Spit was standing on the other corner, grinning at me.

Across the street Mr. Gold was standing in the middle of the store talking to Papa. Papa was listening to him with a downcast expression on his face. The son of a bitch was probably giving the old man hell again, I thought bitterly. I turned back to Solly. "I hope the old man don't go with him again tonight or we'll have to put it off until next week."

That was what had held us back this long. Some nights Papa used to walk Mr. Gold as far as the bank. Twice before we had been primed to do the job, but each time we'd had to call it off.

Solly's eyes were blank. "We'll see," he replied succinctly.

I looked at him. Solly was okay, he didn't talk very much but I could depend on him. I turned back to the store and we quietly took up our wait.

Mr. Gold was still talking to my father. Gold's hands were flying as he talked. They were always moving, first pointing one way, then another. He seemed generally disgusted. Papa stood there patiently listening, an attitude of resignation in the droop of his shoulders. He was getting it, all right. I could tell. My lips tightened bitterly. Mr. Gold wouldn't feel much like talking after we got through with him tonight.

Solly's hand touched my arm. "He's gettin' ready to go!"

I craned my neck to see what Gold was doing. He had walked away from Papa and was looking at the register. He pointed at the register, his lips moving rapidly. Slowly Papa walked over and looked in, nodding his head. Gold came out in front of the counter and started for the door, leaving Papa at the register, a tired look on his face.

I turned quickly to Solly. "Yuh remember what I tol' yuh, now?" There was just the slightest trace of excitement in my voice.

Solly nodded. "I remember."

"Okay," I said hurriedly. "Gimme the sap." I held out my hand and Solly swiftly passed it to me. I slipped it into my pocket and started across the street.

"Let's get goin', boy," I said as I picked Spit up on the other corner. We turned up the street, walking in an opposite direction to Gold's path, reached the next corner, and turned to look back.

Mr. Gold was just turning up Essex Street. Solly, right behind him, seemed to be coming home from a late movie. I knew that he saw us watching him because he made a tiny gesture with his hand: thumb and index finger circled. Okay.

I sent it back to him and in a moment we were moving quickly up Ludlow

Street which runs parallel to Essex. We were walking rapidly, our breath coming hard with excitement.

I looked at Spit. "Got everything straight?"

"Yeah, Danny. I got it." Spit's face was wet clear down to his chin. He wiped it on his sleeve as we continued to move along.

I nodded my head and we hurried on. There was no time to lose. We covered three blocks before we came to the open lot just before Houston Street. I looked at Spit. This was it. The lot went clear through to Essex. I was beginning to feel frightened. Vaguely I wished I had never started this thing. Then I remembered how Mr. Gold had spoken to my father.

"This is for me," I said. My voice seemed to ring loudly in my ears.

Spit grinned. "Good luck."

I gave Spit a shove with my hand and tried to smile. I don't know how it came off, but he turned and continued on toward the corner. I watched him fade around it, then ducked into the shadows of the lot.

I was standing in the dark, my back against a building. My heart was beating so loudly it could be heard half a block away. I held my breath trying to quiet its noise. That only seemed to make it worse. I reached into my pocket, took out the sap, and slapped it softly in my hand to get the feel of it. It made a shallow dull thump. My hands felt wet and I wiped them on my trousers to dry them.

I was beginning to worry. What if something went wrong? Why weren't they there? I wished I dared to stick my head out from beside the building to see if they were coming but I couldn't take any chances. I drew a deep breath. Stop worrying, I told myself angrily. Nothing could go wrong. I had the whole thing too well worked out.

It was simple. Too easy to go wrong. Solly would be walking up the street behind Mr. Gold. He could see anyone coming toward them. Spit would be walking down the street, facing them. He would be able to see anyone coming up behind them. If there was the slightest chance of anyone spotting us, they would start whistling and I would let Mr. Gold walk by. It was that simple. Nothing could go wrong. I leaned back against the building, watching the far corner for the first sign from Spit that was to tip me off that they were coming.

The seconds seemed to drag by. I was beginning to get nervous again. I wished I could light a cigarette. I strained my eyes through the dark. There were footsteps coming down the sidewalk toward me.

It was Spit, shuffling along in that funny walk he had. Suddenly my nervousness was gone and calm settled down over me. There was no backing out now. I let the sap hang loosely in my hand and waited, poised on the balls of my feet, ready to move at the signal.

I began to count slowly to myself, like I was trying to set up a rhythm for the punching bag. "One—two—three—four—one two—"

Spit lifted his hand to his cheek. I began to move swiftly toward the edge of the building. Mr. Gold came into view just across the building line and I slipped out silently behind him.

In the dark the falling sap was a swift blur. There was a dull, sickening sound and then Solly caught the falling man and was hauling him into the shadows of the lot.

Mr. Gold lay silently on the ground and we looked down at him. Spit's voice was frightened; his words made a fine spray over my face. "Maybe yuh croaked him!"

I could feel my heart leap in sudden fright. I dropped to one knee and slipped a hand inside Mr. Gold's vest. With a sense of relief I felt his heart beating. I took my hand from beneath his vest and ran my fingers lightly over his head. No dent, no blood. I was in luck. No concussion or broken head.

Solly's voice snapped from over my head. "Quit the crappin'!" he said flatly. "Get the dough. We ain't got all night!"

His words dispelled my fear. Solly was right. We hadn't done this so I could play doctor. I ran my fingers through his pockets quickly and found the money pouch just as Spit dropped to one knee beside me. Spit was fumbling with Mr. Gold's wrist.

"What're yuh doin'?" I barked.

"Grabbin' his watch. It's a beaut!"

I slapped his hand away. I was myself again. I could think now that I was no longer afraid. "Jerk! Leave it! Yuh want the cops should finger you the first time yuh show with it?"

Spit got to his feet grumbling. Again I slipped my hand inside Gold's vest. His heart was beating stronger now. I withdrew my hand and started to my feet. "Okay," I whispered, "let's blow!"

Before I could start moving, a hand suddenly gripped at my ankle. Mr. Gold's voice rang out like a clarion in the quiet lot. "Help! Police!"

Spit and Solly started running. I looked down wildly. Mr. Gold was holding my ankle with both hands, yelling at the top of his lungs, his eyes tightly shut.

I looked around frantically. Spit and Solly were almost out of sight across Essex Street. My heart was really banging now. I tried to move but couldn't. Fear had paralyzed my legs. I looked across the empty lot. Someone had come out of Katz's delicatessen and was running toward us.

I had to get out of here. I kicked violently at Gold's hand and felt the toe of my shoe strike his arm. Something seemed to snap under my foot and the man groaned, then screamed in pain and I was free and running.

The street behind me was suddenly alive with noise, but by that time I was around the corner on Stanton Street. An instinct made me stop running and I stood on the corner, hesitating a second. Quickly I made up my mind. I had to find out whether he had seen me. I cut up the block. There was a crowd in the lot now.

I pushed my way through them. The cops were there already, yelling for everybody to stand back. Mr. Gold was sitting up on the ground, holding his arm and rocking to and fro in pain.

"What happened?" I asked one of the spectators.

The man answered without turning his head to me. He was too busy watching Mr. Gold. "That guy there got mugged."

I pushed my way closer to Mr. Gold. A cop was kneeling beside him. I could see his lips move but I couldn't hear what he was saying. I was almost on top of them now and I could hear Mr. Gold's voice. His words chased the fear in me.

"How could I see who it was?" Mr. Gold was yelling, his voice shrill with pain. "I was unconscious, I told you." He moaned again. "Oy, get me a doctor. The son of a bitch broke my arm!"

Slowly I let myself drift back through the crowd. When I was near its fringe the cops began to chase us. "Go on, now," they were saying, "break it up."

The crowd began to disperse and I went with them. I took them at their word and headed for home. I slipped into the house quietly and it wasn't until I took my trousers off that I remembered I still had the money pouch with me.

I ducked into the bathroom and locked the door. Then I opened the pouch by cutting through it with my penknife and counted the dough. A fortune! One hundred and thirty-five bucks!

I shoved the money into my pocket and looked around the room. I had to get rid of the pouch. There was a small window over the toilet that opened on an airshaft that was never cleaned. I climbed up on the toilet seat and dropped the pouch out the window. I heard it clink against the sides of the building as it went down, and I went back to my room and got into bed.

I closed my eyes and tried to fall asleep, but thoughts kept chasing crazily through my mind. What if the cops were only playing dumb? What if Mr. Gold remembered once his pain had gone? He had plenty of time to get a good look at me. My pajamas were becoming clammy with perspiration and clinging to my skin. I squeezed my eyes tightly shut in the dark and desperately tried to fall asleep. There was no use. My nerves were jumping at every little sound in the night. A door slammed and I bolted upright in the bed. They were coming after me.

I jumped out of bed quickly and into my trousers and went to the door, straining my ears to hear the voices just beyond it. It was only my mother and father. Papa had just come home.

I slipped out of my trousers and got back into bed again. I sank back against the pillow with a sigh of relief. I was being a fool. Nobody could suspect me. Slowly my nervousness began to leave me, but still I couldn't sleep.

The night seemed a thousand hours long. At last I turned on my side and stuffed the corner of the pillow into my mouth to keep from screaming. I began to pray silently. I had never consciously prayed before. I begged God not to let them catch me. I swore I would never do it again.

But the gray light of morning had come into the room before my eyes closed in sheer exhaustion. And then I didn't really sleep. For echoing in my mind was the sickening sound of the snapping bone as I had kicked and Mr. Gold's sharp piercing scream was ringing in my ears.

CHAPTER SEVEN

SOMEONE WAS SHAKING ME. I TRIED TO MOVE AWAY FROM THE HANDS that were holding me. I put up my arms to fend them off. Why couldn't they leave me alone? I was so tired.

A voice was yelling in my ear. It repeated the same words over and over: "Wake up, Danny! Wake up!"

I rolled over on my side. "I'm tired," I mumbled, burying my face in the pillow. "Go away."

I heard footsteps leave the room and I dozed tensely. I was waiting for the signal. There it was, Spit's hand was going up to his face. I was moving quickly now. Mr. Gold had just come past the edge of the building. My hand went up.

The weight of the sap was heavy in it. It started falling. Just then Mr. Gold turned around.

His white frightened face was staring at me. "I know you!" he screamed. "You're Danny Fisher!" Just then the sap came down and hit him on the side of the head and he was falling.

"No!" I groaned. "Never again!" I tried to claw my way into the pillow. A hand fell on my shoulder and I jumped around in bed, my eyes open and staring.

"Danny!" Mamma's voice was startled.

I sat up in bed quickly, my eyes adjusting to the realities of the room. I was breathing heavily, as if I had been running.

Mamma was staring at my face. It felt white and clammy with sweat. "Danny, what's the matter? Don't you feel good?"

I looked at her for a moment; then I slowly sank back against the pillow. I was very tired. It was only a dream, but it had seemed so real. "I'm all right, Ma," I said slowly.

A look of concern crossed her face. She placed a cool hand on my hot forehead and pressed me back against the pillow. "Go back to sleep, Danny," she said gently. "You were crying in your sleep all night."

The sun was bright in the street outside when I opened my eyes again. I stretched lazily, pushing my feet all the way down against the foot of the bed.

"Feeling better, Blondie?"

My head snapped round. Mamma was sitting next to the bed. I sat up. "Yeah," I said shamefacedly. "I wonder what was the matter with me."

I was glad Mamma didn't insist on an answer to my question. All she did was hold a glass of tea toward me. "Here," she said quietly. "Drink this tea."

I looked at the kitchen clock as I walked into the room. It was after two o'clock. "Where's Papa?" I asked.

"He had to go down to the store early," Mamma answered without turning from the stove. "Something happened to Mr. Gold."

"Yeah," I said noncommittally, crossing to the door. I opened it.

The sound made her turn around. "Where are you going?" she asked anxiously. "You're not going out feeling like you do?"

"I gotta," I answered. "I promised some fellas I would meet them." Spit and Solly would be wondering about me.

"So you'll meet them some other time. It's not so important. Go back to bed and lie down."

"I can't, Mamma," I said quickly. "Besides, a little fresh air will do me good!" I slammed the door quickly and ran down the stairs.

I caught Solly's eye as I walked past the candy store, gave him the come-on, and continued down the block. A few doors away I ducked into a building and waited in the hallway. I didn't have to wait long. The money was in my hand when they came in. "Here y'are," I said, shoving it at them.

Solly put the money quickly into his pocket without counting it, but Spit thumbed through the bills. He looked up at me suspiciously.

"Only thirty bucks?" he asked.

I met his gaze. "Yer lucky to get that," I snapped. "I oughtta give you crap the way you powdered."

Spit's eyes fell. "I thought it would be more'n that."

I clenched my fist. "Why didn't yuh stay an' count it?" I half snarled at him.

His eyes came up suddenly and he looked at me through half-closed lids. I could see he didn't believe me, but he was afraid to say anything. I stared back at him and his eyes fell again. "Okay, Danny," he said, placating me with a fine spray. "I ain't beefin'." He turned and slipped silently out the doorway.

I turned to Solly. He had been watching us. "Anything on your mind?" I asked nastily.

Solly's lips spread in a slow smile. "No, Danny. I ain't got no complaints."

I smiled back at him and placed my hand on his shoulder, gently pushing him toward the doorway. "Go on, then, beat it," I said gently. "I don't want to stay in here all day."

We got off the trolley car and Nellie took my arm. She looked up at my face. "Where we going?" she asked curiously.

"You'll see." I smiled, not wanting to tell her yet.

It had been like that all night. I had picked her up at the store after closing. "C'mon," I had told her. "I wanna show you something."

Willingly she had come down into the plaza with me and we had boarded the Utica-Reid trolley. All through the ride we had been silent, looking out the window, our hands clasped tightly together. I had wanted to tell her where we were going but I was afraid to. I was afraid she might laugh at, me. But now I could tell her because we were there. We were standing on a dark empty corner, almost ten o'clock at night, in a neighborhood of Brooklyn she had never even known about. I raised my hand and pointed across the street. "See it?" I asked.

She peered across the street, then turned back to me, a bewildered expression on her face. "See what?" she asked. "There's nothing there but an empty house."

I smiled at her. "That's it." I nodded happily. "Beautiful, isn't it?"

She turned back to look at it. "There's nobody living in it," she said in a disappointed voice.

I turned back to the house. "That's what we came out to see," I said to her. For a moment I had almost forgotten she was there. I stared at the house intently. I didn't imagine there would be much trouble in getting the house back when Papa got Mr. Gold's job.

Her voice interrupted my thoughts. "Is that what we came out to see in the middle of the night, Danny?" she asked. "An empty house?"

"It's not an empty house," I told her. "It's my house. I used to live there Maybe soon we'll be able to move back."

A sudden light came into her eyes. She glanced quickly at the house, then back at me. Her mouth softened gently. "It is a beautiful house, Danny," she said in an understanding voice.

My hand tightened on her arm. "Papa gave it to me for my birthday when I was eight years old," I explained to her. "On the very first day we moved in I fell into a pit and found a little dog and they had to get the cops out to find me." I took a deep breath. The air was sweet and fresh out here. "She died when we moved. She was run over on Stanton Street. I brought her back here and buried her. This was the only home we had ever known an' I loved that little dog more'n anything. That's why I brought her back. It's the only place she—we could be happy."

Her eyes were shining and tender in the night. "And now you will move back here," she whispered softly, pressing her face against my shoulder. "Oh, Danny, I'm so happy for you!"

I looked down at her. A warm feeling came into me. I knew she would understand, once she knew about it. I raised her fingers and pressed them to my lips. "Okay, Nellie. Now we can go back." Somehow I didn't mind going back now. I knew it wouldn't be for long.

I stood in the doorway, my eyes blinking in the bright kitchen light. Mamma and Papa were staring at me as I stepped into the room. "You're home early," I said to my father, smiling. Maybe he had the good news already.

Papa's face was tense and angry. "But you're late," he snapped. "Where were you?"

I closed the door behind me and looked at him. He wasn't acting the way I had expected. Maybe something had gone wrong; maybe Gold had recognized me. "Around," I said cautiously. Better to say nothing yet.

Papa's anger raged through his self-control. "Around?" he shouted suddenly. "What kind of an answer is that? Your mother has been worrying herself sick over you all night. You don't come home, you don't say nothing, you're just 'around!' Where were you? Answer me!"

I tightened my lips stubbornly. Something had gone wrong. "I told Mamma I was all right, she didn't have to worry."

"Why didn't you come home for supper, then?" Papa screamed. "Your mother didn't know what happened to you. You could have dropped dead in the street and we wouldn't have known about it. She got herself sick worrying over you!"

"I'm sorry," I said sullenly. "I didn't think she would worry."

"Don't be sorry!" Papa shouted at me. "Just answer me! Where were you?"

I looked at him for a moment. There was no use in saying anything to him now. He was purple with rage. I turned and started from the room without a word.

Suddenly Papa's hand was on my shoulder, spinning me back toward him. My eyes widened in surprise. Papa was holding his leather belt in his hand and waving it threateningly at me.

"Don't go without answering me!" he shouted. "I got enough of your high-and-mighty ways! Ever since we moved down here, you think you can come and go as you please with nobody to answer to. Well, I've had enough of it! You'll come down to earth if I have to beat you down to it! Answer me!"

I pressed my lips firmly together. Papa had never hit me in anger in his life. I couldn't believe he would do it now. Not when I was bigger than he was and stood there looking silently down at him.

He shook me roughly. "Where were you?"

I didn't answer.

The belt came whistling through the air. It caught me on the side of the face. Lights flashed in front of my eyes and I could hear my mother screaming. I shook my head and opened my eyes.

Mamma was grabbing at his arm, begging him to stop. He pushed her away, shouting: "I've had enough, I tell you, enough! A man can only take so much, but from his own son he'll get the proper respect!" He spun toward me and the belt came flying through the air.

I threw up my arms to ward it off, but the belt tore its way past them to my face. The buckle caught me on the forehead and I felt myself slipping dizzily to the floor.

I looked up at my father through a sea of pain. I didn't have to let him hit me. I could take the belt away from him any time I wanted. Yet I didn't. I didn't even make a move to escape the next blow. The belt came down again and I gritted my teeth against the pain.

Mamma threw her arms around his sides. "Stop, Harry! You'll kill him!" she screamed.

He shook his arm and she fell back helplessly into a chair. His eyes, staring down at me, were rimmed with red and puffed as if he had been crying. The belt rose and fell, rose and fell until it seemed as if I had lived forever in this curious world of pain. I closed my eyes.

His voice came floating down to me. "Now will you answer me?"

I looked up at him. Papa seemed to have three heads and they were all going around in circles, first past and then through each other. I shook my head trying to clear it. Papa was raising three hands. There were three belts flying down at me. I shut my eyes quickly against them.

"I was out at the house!"

The blow I expected didn't come and I opened my eyes. The three belts hung suspended in the air over my head. Papa's voice was coming from a long way off: "What house?"

It was then I first realized that I had answered him. I let out a slow sigh. My voice was barely a squeak, I didn't know it at all. "Our house," I answered. "I went out to see if anyone was living there yet. I thought with Mr. Gold out, Papa would be managing the store and we would be able to move back there!"

There was a silence in the room that seemed to drag interminably. The only sound was the rasping of my breath in my ears and then Mamma was on the floor beside me, cradling my head against her bosom.

I opened my eyes again and looked at Papa. He had sunk exhaustedly into a chair and was staring at me with wide, frightened eyes. He seemed to grow old and shrunken before me. His lips moved, almost silently. I could hardly hear him.

"Where did you get that idea?" he was saying. "Last night Gold told me they were closing the store at the end of the month. They were losing money and I'll be out of a job on the 1st."

I couldn't believe it. I just couldn't. The tears began to run silently from my eyes and down my cheeks. Then gradually I began to understand. That's what Gold had been doing, when he called Papa over to the cash register last night. That's why Papa had looked so beaten.

Everything was clear to me now. Papa's anger, Mamma's worried look this morning, her preoccupation at the stove. For a moment I was very young again and I turned my head back to the comfort of her bosom.

It was for nothing. The whole damn thing was for nothing.

How long could I go on living a kid's life, dreaming a kid's dream? It was about time I stopped. There was no way on God's earth for me to get the house back.

CHAPTER EIGHT

I ROLLED EASILY AWAY FROM A TIRED RIGHT-HAND PUNCH AND SHOT BACK sharply with my left. I felt it tear through the boy's guard and I knew I had him. I cocked my right just as the bell rang ending the round.

I let my hands drop to my sides quickly and swaggered back to my corner. I dropped down on the stool and grinned at the man who clambered into the ring with the towel and pail of water. I opened my mouth and let some of the water trickle into it from the sponge on my face.

"How you feelin'?" he asked anxiously.

I grinned again. "Okay, Gi'sep," I said confidently. "I'll take him in this round. He shot his load."

Giuseppe Petito shushed me. "Save yer breat', Danny." He ran the sponge across my neck and shoulders. "Be careful," he warned me. "The guy's still got a wicked right. Don't take no chances. I promised Nellie I wouldn' let yuh get hoit. She'd have me head if I did."

I brushed my glove fondly across Giuseppe's head. I liked this guy. "I guess you're safe this time," I grinned.

Giuseppe smiled back at me. "Make sure I am," he retorted. "She may be your girl but she's my sister an' you don' know her like I do. I still catch hell from her for gettin' you into this."

I was just about to answer when the bell sounded. I bounced to my feet as Giuseppe slipped out of the ring. I walked quickly to the center of the ring and touched gloves with my opponent. The referee struck up the gloves and I side-stepped a sudden left jab.

I held my hands high and loose in front of me, circling the boy carefully, waiting for an opportunity to start punching. I dropped my left slightly, trying to feint him into a right-hand lead. The kid didn't bite and I dropped back.

I started circling him again. The crowd began to boo and stamp their feet in unison. I could feel the vibration in the taut canvas floor of the ring. What did they want us to do for a ten-dollar gold watch? Kill each other? I looked anxiously back to my corner.

A sixth sense made me duck. From the corner of my eye I had caught a glimpse of a right hand coming toward my chin. I sailed over my shoulder and I came up inside the kid's guard.

I brought my right hand up in an uppercut carried by the momentum of my body. It landed flush on the boy's chin. His eyes glazed suddenly and he stumbled toward me, trying to grope his way into a clinch.

The crowd was roaring now. I stepped away from him quickly and shot my left. It tore into the kid's unprotected face and he stumbled forward and fell flat on his face. I turned and walked confidently back to my corner. Nobody had to tell me the fight was over.

Giuseppe was already in the ring, throwing a towel around my shoulders. "Cripes!" he grinned. "I wish you was eighteen already!"

I laughed and went back to the center of the ring. The referee came toward me and held up my hand. He whispered out of the side of his mouth: "Yer gettin' too good for this racket, Fisher."

I laughed again and swaggered back to my corner.

Giuseppe stuck his head into the dressing-room. "Yuh dressed yet, kid?" he asked.

"Tyin' my shoes, Zep," I called back.

"Snap it up, Danny," Zep said. "The house boss wants to see yuh in hid office."

I straightened up and followed him out into the corridor. The noise of the crowd came faintly to our ears. "What's he want, Zep?" I asked. Generally when Skopas wanted to see one of the simon-pures it meant no good. Everybody knew Skopas fronted for the fight mob even though he was officially the arena manager.

Zep shrugged his shoulders. "I dunno. Maybe he wants to give yuh a medal or somethin'." But I could tell from his tone of voice that he was worried.

I looked at him quizzically. My voice was light and caustic, I didn't want him to think I was worried too. "I don't care what he gives me so long as I can hock it for ten bucks."

We stopped in front of a door marked: *"Private."* Giuseppe opened it. "In yuh go, kid," he said.

I entered the room curiously. I had never been in here before. This was only for the big-time boys, the boys who worked for dough, not us punks who fought for watches. I was disappointed to find it only a small room with dirty gray painted walls and photographs of fighters hanging on them. I had expected something grander.

There were several men in the room and they were all smoking cigars and talking. When I came in they stopped talking and turned to look at me. Their eyes were shrewd and appraising.

I glanced at them briefly and then, ignoring their gaze, looked at the man sitting behind the small littered desk. "You sent for me, Mr. Skopas?"

He looked up at me. His eyes were gray and expressionless and his bald head gleamed in the light of the single overhead bulb. "You Danny Fisher?" His voice was just as expressionless as his eyes.

I nodded.

Skopas smiled mirthlessly at me, showing irregular yellowed teeth. "My boys been tellin' me you got the makin's. I hear you got a big collection of watches."

I smiled back at him. He didn't sound as if he was going to make trouble. "I would have," I said, "if I could afford to keep them."

Giuseppe nudged me nervously. "He means he gives 'em all to his ol' man, Mr. Skopas," he injected quickly. His eyes flashed warnings at me about the other men in the room. I knew what he meant right away. One of them might be an A.A. inspector.

Skopas turned to Giuseppe. "Who are you?" he asked, fish-eyed.

It was my turn to butt in. "He's my manager, Mr. Skopas. He used to fight under the name of Peppy Petito."

Skopas's eyes widened slightly. "I remember. A fancy boy with a glass jaw." His voice took on a chill. "So that's what you do now—work the punks."

Giuseppe shifted uncomfortably. "No, Mr. Skopas, I—"

Skopas's voice cut in on him. "Blow, Petito," he said coldly. "I got business with your friend."

Giuseppe looked down at hind and then at me. His face was pale under his swarthy complexion. He hesitated a moment and then, with a miserable look in his eyes, started for the door.

I put my hand on his arm and stopped him. "Hold it, Zep." I turned back to Skopas. "Yuh got Zep wrong, Mr. Skopas," I said quickly. "Zep's my girl's brother. He's only lookin' out for me because I asked him. If he goes, I'm goin' with him."

The expression on Skopas's face changed swiftly. He smiled. "Why didn't yuh say so in the first place? That makes it different." He took a cigar from his pocket and proffered it to Giuseppe. "Here, Petito, have a cigar, an' no hard feelin's."

Zep took the cigar and put it in his pocket. The sick look had gone from his eyes and he was smiling.

I stared down at Skopas. "Yuh sent for me," I said flatly. "What about?"

Skopas's face went blank. "You been doin' pretty good aroun' this club, so I wanted you should know it."

"Gee, thanks," I snapped sarcastically. "What about this 'business' I heard yuh mention a minute ago?"

For a second a light blazed in his eyes and then it was gone and they were cold and empty as before. He continued speaking as if I hadn't interrupted him. "The boys uptown are always on the lookout for promisin' new talent so I tol' them about you. I wanted you to know they was watchin' your last few fights an' they liked what they saw." He paused importantly, put a fresh cigar in his mouth, and chewed on it for a moment before he began speaking again. "We think you're too good for this racket, kid, an' from now on we're takin' you over. You're through fightin' for watches." He struck a match and held it up to his cigar.

I waited until the match burned down before I spoke. "What do I fight for now?" I asked impassively. There was no use in asking for who. I already knew that.

"Glory, kid," Skopas replied, "glory. We decided you're goin' into the Gloves to build yourself a rep."

"Great!" I exploded. "And what do I do for dough? At least I get ten bucks for the watch."

Skopas's smile was as cold as his eyes. He blew a cloud of smoke toward me. "We ain't pikers, kid. Yuh get a hunnert a month until yer old enough to turn pro, then we split outta yer earnin's."

"I knock down more'n ten watches a month on this beat," I retorted heatedly. I felt Giuseppe's hand restrainingly on my arm. Angrily I shook it off. This wasn't what I was looking for. "What if I don't buy this deal?" I asked.

"Then yuh get nothin'," Skopas said flatly. "But you look like a bright kid. You know better'n to buck the boys. We even got a guy down here who's goin' to manage yuh when yuh move over to the pros."

I sneered. "You're too sure of yourselves. What makes you guys think I want to be a fighter anyway?"

Skopas's eyes were wise. "You need the dough, kid," he said surely. "That's why you'll be a fighter. That's why you took up the gold-watch beat."

He was right about that. I did need the dough. Papa was still out of work and this was the only buck I could be sure of outside of knocking somebody over the head. And my experience with Mr. Gold had taught me that I didn't have the stomach for that business. But now I'd had enough of this. It was okay to pick up a few bucks here and there, but I didn't buy it for a living. I'd seen too many guys walking around with their punches showing. That wasn't for me.

I turned to Zep. "Come on, let's go," I said succinctly. I looked back at the desk. "So long, Mr. Skopas. Thanks for nothing. It's been nice knowing you."

I flung the door open and stalked out. A man standing in the doorway put out a hand to stop me. I pushed his hand away without looking up and started to step around him. A familiar voice beat at my ears: "Hey, Danny Fisher, ain't yuh gonna stop an' say hello to your new manager?"

I looked up suddenly, a grin leaping to my face. My hand flew out, grabbing the man's arm. "Sam!" I ejaculated. "Sam Gottkin! I should've known!"

Skopas's voice came over my shoulder. It had a slightly apologetic note in it. "The kid ain't buyin', Mr. Gottkin."

Sam's eyes were looking questioningly at me. I made up my mind quickly. I turned to Skopas, a smile on my face. "If it's okay with you, Mr. Skopas," I said, "you can tell your friends uptown they got themselves a new boy!"

CHAPTER NINE

"C'MON, DANNY," SAM SAID A FEW MINUTES LATER. "I'LL GET YOU somethin' to eat."

I grinned at him. "Sure, Sam," I said. "Just a minute." I walked over to Skopas's desk and looked down at him. The tension had gone from the room; even Skopas was smiling. The other men were watching me carefully. They knew if I had been tapped by boys uptown I was a real comer.

"Mr. Skopas," I said with a smile, "I'm sorry I blew up. Thanks for what you did."

He smiled at me. "It's okay, kid."

I held out my hand. "But don't forget my watch."

He laughed loudly and turned to the men in the room. "The kid's okay," he announced. "He'll go far. If I had five grand I would have gone for him myself."

The surprise showed on my face, for the men laughed aloud. I looked at Sam and he nodded his head. I turned back to Skopas, wondering. Sam must be doing all right if he could afford to shell out five grand for me.

Skopas fished two bills from his pocket and placed them in my hand. "I ain't got any watches on me, kid, so this time we'll cut out the middleman."

I put the money in my pocket. "Okay, Mr. Skopas," aid. walked back to Sam with a new respect. "Let's go."

I looked down at my plate regretfully. One thing about Gluckstern's special Rumanian broilings. If you could eat all of it you were a hero. I put down my fork. "I'm bustin'," I admitted. I turned to Giuseppe. "How you doin'?"

Giuseppe grinned with a mouthful of steak. "Okay, Danny."

I looked across the table at Sam. He had quit too. He was watching me, a curious look on his face. "I see you couldn't make it either," I said.

"Too much," he said. "I gotta watch my weight now."

He was right about that. He had put on a little weight since I saw him last. "How come yuh never answered the letter I sent yuh last year?" he asked suddenly.

I looked at him in surprise. "I never got it," I said simply.

"I was lookin' for yuh," he said. "I even went out to your old house to see yuh, but nobody had your address." He lit a cigarette. "I had a job for yuh."

"Last summer?" I asked.

He nodded.

I fished a cigarette out of the pack Sam had left on the table. "I could'a used one too," I said. "Things were pretty rough."

"Did yuh graduate school yet?"

I shook my head. "This June," I replied. I looked at Sam curiously. "How'd you happen to find me?" I asked. "Last I heard you had gone to Florida."

"I did go," Sam answered. "Did good too. But I didn't forget about you. I always said some day I'd make a champ outta you, so I put out the word to some friends to keep an eye peeled for yuh. I figured sooner or later you'd turn up. A guy who fights as good as you don't stay out altogether." He reached across the table and plucked the cigarette from my mouth with a smile. "you ain't usin' these any more if you're workin' for me."

"I like working for you," I said, watching him squash out the butt. "But I don't know if I like the idea of being a fighter."

"Then what were you doin' in those penny-ante clubs fightin' for watches?" he asked pointedly.

I nodded toward Giuseppe. "I needed the dough and he knew where I could pick up maybe three, four watches a week for three-round amateurs. It looked like easy dough, so I did it. But I never meant to turn pro—it was only till I got out of school."

"Then what were you gonna do?" Sam asked. "Set the world on fire? Get a job for ten bucks a week? If you're lucky, that is?"

I flushed. "I didn't think about that," I admitted.

Sam smiled. "I thought so," he said confidently. "But from now on, I'm gonna do your thinkin'."

Zep left us on the corner. He started off but I called him back. "Wait a minute, Zep, you forgot somethin'." I held a bill toward him. "Tell Nellie it's for the account."

Zep put the dough in his pocket. "I'll tell her, Danny."

"Tell her I'll pick her up at the store tomorrow night," I called after him as he walked away. I turned back to Sam. "Nice guy," I said.

Sam looked at me. "A luksh?" he said questioningly.

I stared back at him coldly. "So what?"

Sam raised his hands protestingly. "It don't mean nothin' to me, kid," he said quickly, "but what do your folks say to your goin' with an Italian girl?"

I watched him steadily. "They don't like it, but hell, her folks don't like the idea of me either. They say 'kike' like we say 'wop.' It's nobody's business but Nellie's and mine anyway."

"Sure, kid," Sam said placatingly. "Don't get sore."

"I'm not sore," I said quietly. But I was. This went on all the time at home.

Sam took my arm. "Come on over to the car an' I'll give yuh the lowdown on this business."

I studied him as he leaned his back against the car. He was doing okay, I could see that. His face was round and he had developed a little pot. Good living did that.

He took but a cigar and bit the end off it, stuck it in his mouth, and chewed on it reflectively. "Now," he said in a low voice, "I want yuh to listen carefully to me an' remember what I say. Because from now on until you turn pro we can't bed seein' too much of each other. But I'll be in touch with you, unnerstan'?"

I nodded. I understood. The rules covering amateur fighters were pretty strict.

Sam held a match to his cigar. It flickered briefly, giving his face a round moon-shape quality. "Tomorrow you go down to the East Side Boys Club. Ask for Moe Spritzer, and when you see him, tell him your name an' that I sent you. He'll know what to do. He has an entry in the Gloves already made out in your name, all you gotta do is sign it. From now on until you move over, he'll be your trainer. You'll do everything he says, unnerstan'?"

"I understand." In spite of myself I was impressed. Sam had thought of everything.

"Each month you keep in line, Moe'll give you a hundred bucks. If you kick off, you're through. Behave yourself, kid, and you got the world by the tail. I'll drop into the club every now and then to see how you work out. When I do, pay no attention to me. If I want to talk to you, I'll arrange it."

He opened the door of his car and got behind the wheel. "Yuh got any questions, Danny?"

I shook my head and then changed my mind. I had one question: "What if I don't show up good in the Gloves, Sam? What then?"

Sam looked at me for a moment before he answered. His voice was calm and low. "Then I'm out the five grand I shelled out to get yuh, kid. The boys were just about to move in on yuh when I bought 'em off." His eyes were suddenly bright and hard in the glowing light of the cigar. "Yuh're gonna be what I couldn't, Danny. I put a lot of hard-earned dough on you an' I don't expect to lose it."

He turned on the ignition key and started the motor. His voice rose slightly above its hum. "You're not a kid any more, Danny. You're in a rough business. I won't expect you to ever do what you can't, but don't cross me once you start. I won't like it."

The car started smoothly from the curb and I could feel my heart pounding in excitement. Sam wasn't fooling, he meant what he said. A hand fell on my shoulder and I turned around startled. Zep was standing next to me.

"You heard him?" I asked. I had known he wouldn't go too far away.

Zep nodded.

"What do you think?"

His dark eyes met mine, and his lips parted in a smile. "He's riding a lot of dough on you, but he ain't taking any chances an' he knows it. You're gonna be champ some day, kid, I know it already. The fix is in even now."

I turned and looked after the car. Its rear light was just turning the corner. I was still doubtful. "You think I ought to take it, Gi'sep?" I asked.

His voice. rang in my ear with excitement. "Would yuh turn down a million bucks, Danny?"

CHAPTER TEN

I LOOKED AT MY FACE IN THE MIRROR. OUTSIDE OF THE SMALL BRUISE HIGH on my cheekbone I didn't show any signs of the fight last night. I grinned at my reflection. I was lucky.

I finished combing my hair and left the bathroom. As I approached the kitchen, I could hear Papas voice. I went into the room smiling. "Good morning," I said.

Papa's voice stopped in the middle of what he had been saying, his face turned toward me. He didn't answer.

"Sit down, Danny," Mamma said quickly, "and eat your breakfast."

I slipped easily into the chair. Papa had been watching me. Each day had brought more lines to his face, lines of worry and hopelessness. His eyes seemed veiled with a curtain of despair that vanished only in the heat of his temper and anger. It seemed to me that Papa's temper was displayed more and more frequently as time went on, as if he found some sort of relief from his worries in giving way to it.

I put my hand in my pocket, took out a ten-dollar bill, and tossed it on the table. "I made a few bucks last night," I said casually.

Papa looked at the money, then up at me. His eyes began to glitter. I knew the look: it was a sign he was working up his temper. I bent my head over my plate and began to shovel the oatmeal into my mouth rapidly. I wanted to avoid the scene I knew would follow.

For a moment Papa was quiet, then his voice, strangely husky, rasped at my ears: "Where'd you get it? Fighting?"

I nodded without looking up from the plate. I continued to spoon the cereal quickly into my mouth.

"Danny, you didn't?" Mamma's voice was anxious, and her face had set in worried lines.

"I had to, Ma," I said quickly. "We need the dough. Where else we gonna get it?"

Mamma looked at my father. There was a faint white pallor showing beneath his skin. It gave him a sick, unhealthy look. She turned back to me. "But we told you we didn't want you to do it," she protested weakly. "You might get hurt. We'd manage to get along somehow."

My eyes were on her face. "How?" I asked matter-of-factly. "There are no jobs anywhere. We'd have to go on relief."

Mamma's face was set. "That might be better than you taking chances of getting yourself killed."

"But, Ma," I said, "I'm not taking any chances. I've gone through thirty of these things already and the worst that happened was that I got a scratch over my eye that healed in a day. I'm careful and the dough is handy."

She turned hopelessly to Papa. There was no use arguing with me. I had all the logic on my side.

Papa's face was completely white now, his fingers trembled against the coffee cup in his hand. He was staring at me but he didn't talk directly to me, he spoke to Mamma. "It's his girl," he said in a flat nasty voice, "that shiksa. She gets him to do it. She doesn't care if he gets himself killed as long as he has a buck to take her out and show her a good time."

"It is not!" I flared hotly. Somewhere in the back of my mind I had known this was coming the moment I saw him this morning. "She doesn't want it any more than you do! I'm doin' it because it's the only way to make a buck that I know!"

Papa ignored me. His bright feverish eyes were the only thing in his face that seemed alive. His voice was freezing with contempt. "A shiksocha whore!" he continued, his eyes fixed on me. "How much do you have to give her for the nights you spend with her in hallways and on street corners? A Jewish girl is not good enough for you? No, a Jewish girl won't do the things she does. A Jewish girl won't let a boy fight to get money for her, let a son become a stranger to his own parents. How much do you pay her, Danny, for the things she gives to her own kind for nothing?"

I felt a chill hatred replace the heat of anger in me. I rose slowly to my feet and looked down at him. My voice was shaking. "Don't talk like that, Papa, don't ever say things like that about her again. Not where I can hear them."

I could see Nellie's white frightened face dancing in front of my eyes, the way she had looked when I first told her I was going to pick up some dough fighting. "She's a good girl," I went on, barely able to speak, "as good as any of our own and better than most. Don't let out on her your own failures. It's your fault we are where we are, not hers."

I leaned over the table glaring into his eyes. For a moment he stared back at me, then his gaze dropped and he raised the coffee cup to his lips.

Mamma put her hand on my arm. "Sit down and finish your breakfast. It's getting cold."

Slowly I dropped back into my chair. I wasn't hungry any more. I was tired and my eyes burned. Chill and drained of feeling, I reached for my coffee and drank it quickly, its hotness running through me, warming my body.

Mamma sat down next to me. For a while there was a smoldering tense silence in the kitchen. Her voice cracked into it. "Don't be angry with your father, Danny," she said softly, "he only talks for your own good. He's worried about you."

There was a curious hurt in me as I looked at her. "But she's a good girl, Mamma," I said, bitterness in my voice. "He shouldn't talk like that."

"But, Danny, she's still a shiksa." Mamma was trying to show understanding.

I didn't answer. What good would it do? They would never understand. I knew a lot of Jewish girls who were nothing but tramps. What made them any better than Nellie?

"Maybe Papa will get a job and you can stop this fighting," Mamma added hopefully.

Suddenly I felt old, very old. Those words were lollipops for children, I had heard them before. They might as well know it now. "It's too late, Mamma," I said wearily. "I can't stop."

"What—what do you mean?" Her voice was trembling.

I got to my feet. "I'm through fighting in the dumps. The boys uptown think I'm good. I made a deal with them." I stared at my father. "I'm going into the Gloves and start building a rep. They're gonna give me a hundred a month, and when I'm old enough I turn pro."

Mamma looked at me with a stricken face. "But—"

I felt sorry for her but there was nothing I could do about it; we had to eat. "No buts, Mamma," I interrupted her. "I made the deal and it's too late to back out now. A hundred a month is as much as Papa would get on a job. We can live on that."

The tears sprang into her eyes and she turned helplessly to Papa. "Harry, what are we going to do now?" she cried. "He's only a baby. What if he gets hurt?"

Papa was staring at me, a muscle in his cheek twitching. He drew a deep breath. "Let him," he answered without taking his eyes from my face. "I hope he does get hurt, it would serve him right!"

"Harry!" Mamma was shocked. "He's our son!"

His eyes narrowed slightly, still burning into mine. "More like the son of the devil, he is," he said in a low, bitter voice, "than a son of ours."

CHAPTER ELEVEN

I CAME OUT OF THE DARK HALLWAY, MY EYES BLINKING AT THE BRIGHT SUN-light, and stood for a moment letting the warm spring air roll over me. The house still hadn't shaken the chill and damp of winter, and before you knew it, it would turn into a smoldering oven.

I felt good. Four months had passed since I had thrown in with Sam. Good months, too. I'd come through the Gloves eliminations and now had only one more fight to go and I would be ready for the finals in the Garden—if I won. But I had no doubts about winning.

I filled my lungs with the fresh air. My collar cut into my neck and I opened it. Spritzer was a bug for conditioning. Sam was, too. They made me toe the mark, but they were right. Condition was half the fight.

If Papa would only realize that it was just another way to make a living, every-thing would be perfect. But he didn't, he kept harping on me, blaming the whole thing on Nellie and saying only bums were fighters. Now we hardly spoke to each other any more. He wouldn't give an inch. He was too stubborn, like just now when I left the house.

Papa had been reading a paper spread across the kitchen table as I walked through the room. He didn't look up.

"I'll be a little late tonight, Ma," I had said.

She had asked anxiously: "Another fight?"

I nodded. "The semifinal, Ma. Out at the Grove in Brooklyn." My voice was proud. "And after this the finals at the Garden and then no more till next year."

"You'll be careful, Danny?" she asked doubtfully.

I had smiled confidently. "Don't worry, Ma, I'll be all right."

Papa had raised his head from the newspaper at my words and spoken to Mamma as if I weren't in the room at all. "Don't worry, Mary, he'll be all right. Listen to what the paper has to say about him." He began to read from the paper in a low sarcastic voice:

"Danny Fisher, the sensational East Side flash with dynamite in each fist, is expected to take another step toward the championship in his division when he meets Joey Passo in the Gloves semifinals at the Grove tonight. Fisher, called by many 'the Stanton Street Spoiler,' because of his record of fourteen straight kayos, is being closely watched by the whole fighting world. There is a strong rumor that he is set to turn pro as soon as he is of age.

"A slim, quiet speaking blond boy, Fisher, in the ring, turns into a cold merciless killer, going to work on his opponent without feeling or compassion, like a machine. This writer believes without a doubt that Fisher is the most ruthlessly promising amateur he has ever seen. If you fight fans will show up at the Grove tonight, we can safely promise you won't be disappointed. You will see blood, gore, and sudden death, for when Fisher goes to work with either hand, friend, it's nothing short of 'murder'!"

Papa let the paper rattle back to the table in front of him and looked up at Mamma. "Good words to read about your own son—'killer, murder, sudden death.' Words to make a man proud of his child."

Mamma looked at me hesitantly. I could see she was upset. "Danny, is it true what the man said?"

I tried to reassure her. I felt embarrassed. "Naw, Ma, you know how it is. After all, his paper sponsors the Gloves an' they try to build it up so's to sell more tickets."

She wasn't convinced. "You'll be careful anyway, Danny," she insisted.

Papa laughed shortly. "Don't worry, Mary," he said sarcastically. "Nothing will happen to him. He won't get hurt. The devil looks after his own." He turned to me. "Go on, Killer," he taunted. "For a dollar you can murder all your friends."

Those were his first direct words to me in weeks. I had taken enough side insults from him and kept my mouth shut; now I was through taking them. "I'll kill 'em for the dollar, Pop," I said through tight lips, "so you can sit here in the kitchen on your fat ass an' live off it!"

I had slammed out of the house and down the stairs, but now in the sunlight and warm air I began to feel better. I checked my watch. I had promised Spritzer I would be at the gym by four o'clock. There was just twenty minutes left to make it. I scaled down the steps and headed for the corner.

As I turned the corner, a voice called to me. Spit was standing in a doorway, waving. "Hey, Danny, c'mere a minute."

"I can't, Spit, I'm late," I called back, hurrying on.

Spit came running after me and grabbed at my arm excitedly. "Danny, my boss wants to meet'cha."

I looked at him. "Who, Fields?"

"Yeah, yeah, Mr. Fields." Spit's head bobbed up and down. "I tol'him I knew yuh an' he says get him."

The doorway from which Spit had come was a store entrance. On the plate glass of the window were the words: FIELDS CHECK CASHING SERVICE. "Okay," I said. You don't slough off a guy like Maxie Fields down here. Not if you like being happy. Fields was the big man in the neighborhood. Politics, gambling, shylocking—the works. He was top dog.

I remembered how envious some of the gang had been when Spit had told us that his uncle, who was a numbers runner, had talked Fields into giving him a job as an errand boy. He had shown us his working papers proudly and bragged that he wouldn't have to go to school any more; that some day he, like Fields, would be a big man in the neighborhood while the rest of us would be knocking our brains out trying to make a living. I didn't see much of him after he got the job, but when I did, I couldn't see where he was doing so great. Like now, he was still wearing the same sloppy clothes he always wore, the saliva-stained shirt, shiny trousers, and dirty scuffed shoes.

I followed Spit into the store and through a small room with cages in it like a bank. A man behind a cage looked at us without curiosity as we walked through a door in the back. We passed through a horse room, where a few men were standing, idly studying the big blackboard. They paid no attention to us as we went through another doorway, behind which was a stairway. I followed Spit up to the first landing, where he stopped in front of a door and knocked softly.

"Come in," a voice roared.

Spit opened the door and walked in. I stopped dead in my tracks, blinking my eyes. I had heard about this but I'd never really believed it. This room was out of the moving pictures, it didn't belong in a partly condemned old dump like this.

A big man with a red face, a fat stomach, and the largest shoes I ever saw came toward us. Nobody had to tell me: this was Maxie Fields. He didn't look at me. "I thought I told yuh not to bother me, Spit," he roared angrily.

"But, Mr. Fields," Spit stammered, "yuh tol' me to bring Danny Fisher here as soon as I saw him." He turned to me. "This is him."

Field's rage disappeared as quickly as it had come. "You Danny Fisher?"

I nodded.

"I'm Maxie Fields," he said, holding out his hand.

He had a good warm grip—too warm. I didn't like him.

He turned to Spit. "Okay, kid, beat it."

Spit's smile disappeared. "Yes, Mr. Fields," he said hurriedly, and the door closed behind him.

"I wanted to meet yuh," Fields said, walking back to the center of the room. "I heard a lot about yuh." He sat down heavily in a chair. "Care for a drink?" he asked casually.

"No, thanks," I replied. Maybe this guy wasn't so bad after all. At least he wasn't treating me like a punk. "I got a fight tonight," I added quickly.

Fields's eyes sparkled. "I seen yuh last week. Yer good. Sam's a lucky guy."

I was surprised. "You know him?"

"I know everybody an' everything," he replied, smiling. "Nothin' goes on down here that I don't know about. There ain't no secrets kept from Maxie Fields."

I had heard that. Now I believed it.

He waved his hand at me. "Sit down, Danny. I want to talk to you."

I stayed on my feet. "I gotta run, Mr. Fields. I'm late at the gym."

"I said sit down." His voice was friendly, but an undertone of command had come into it.

I sat down.

After watching me for a moment, he turned his head and yelled into the next room: "Ronnie! Bring me a drink!" he turned back to me. "Sure you won't have any?"

I shook my head and smiled. No use getting him sore at me. Just then a young woman came into the room carrying a drink. I blinked my eyes again. This dame was out of place down here too. Like the apartment, she belonged uptown.

She walked over to Fields's chair. "Here, Maxie." She looked at me curiously.

He almost drained the glass with one draught, then he put it down and wiped his mouth on his shirtsleeve. "Christ, I was thirsty," he announced.

I said nothing, I was watching the girl standing next to his chair. He laughed. His hand went out and he patted the girl on the behind. "Beat it, Ronnie," he said jovially. "Yer distractin' my friend here an' I wanna talk to him."

She turned silently and left the room. I could feel my face flush, but I couldn't take my eyes off her until the door had closed behind her. Then I looked at Fields.

He was smiling. "Yuh got good taste, kid," he said heartily, "but yuh gotta be able to afford it. That kind of stuff sets you back twenty bucks an hour."

My eyes widened. I didn't know chippies could come that high. "Even when she's serving drinks?" I asked.

His laughter roared in the room. When he stopped laughing he said: "Yer okay, Danny. I like yuh."

"Thanks, Mr. Fields."

He took another swallow of his drink. "Yuh gonna win tonight, kid?" he asked.

"I think so, Mr. Fields," I answered, wondering what he wanted.

"I think yer gonna win, too," he said. "An' so do a lot of people. Yuh know a lot of people down here think yer gonna take the championship."

I smiled. Maybe my father didn't think I was much, but a lot of other people did. "I hope they're not wrong," I said modestly.

"I don't think they will be. The boys downstairs tell me they took about four grand in bets on you from the neighborhood. That's a lot of dough even for me to shell out, but you look like a right guy an' I don't mind it now that I met you." It was a long speech for him and he finished out of breath. He picked up his glass and emptied it.

"I didn't think you bet the simon-pures," I said.

"We bet anything. That's our business. Nothing too big, nothing too small, Fields takes 'em all." He finished in a semi-chant, laughing.

I began to feel bewildered. What did he want me up here for? I wondered what he was getting at. I sat there silently.

Fields's laughter stopped suddenly. He leaned forward and slapped my knee. "Yer okay, kid, an' I like yuh." He turned his head. "Ronnie!" he shouted. "Bring me another drink."

The girl came back into the room carrying the drink. I watched her. She put the drink down and started from the room.

"Don't go, baby." Fields called her back.

She turned around in the center of the room and looked at us.

Fields's face leered at me. "Yuh like that, huh, kid?"

I could feel my face flame.

He grinned. "Well, I like yuh, kid, an' tell yuh what. You win tonight 'n' then come back here. It'll be waitin' for yuh an' the treat's on me. How yuh like that?"

I gulped. I tried to speak, but the words couldn't get past the lump in my throat. There was nothing wrong with it that I could see, but somehow I knew it wasn't for me. Nellie had changed a lot of things.

Fields was watching me closely. "Don't be bashful, kid," he grinned. "She ain't."

I found my voice. "No, thanks, Mr. Fields," I stammered. "I got a girl. Besides I'm in training."

His voice was persuasive. "Don't be a fool, kid. It won't kill yuh." He turned to the girl. "Take yer dress off, Ronnie. Show the kid what he's passin' up."

"But, Max!" the girl protested.

His voice went cold and harsh. "You heard me!"

The girl shrugged her shoulders. She reached behind her and unfastened a button, and the dress slipped to the floor. Fields got out of his chair and walked over to her. His hand reached out and settled on her breast. He made a sudden motion and her brassiere came off in his hand.

He turned back to me. "Take a good look at that, kid. The sweetest meat in town. What d'yuh say?"

I was on my feet, edging toward the door. Something about this guy scared me. "No thanks, Mr. Fields." My hand found the doorknob behind me. "I gotta be goin'. I'm late down at the gym."

Fields grinned at me. "Okay, kid, if that's the way yuh want it. But remember, the offer holds any time."

"Thanks, Mr. Fields." I looked at the girl. She was standing there, her face a mask. Suddenly I was sorry for her. Twenty bucks an hour was a lot of dough, but it couldn't buy you pride. It was still spelled the same way, cheap or expensive. I smiled awkwardly at her. "Good-by, miss."

Her face flushed suddenly and she turned away from me. I stepped outside the door and began to close it. "Good-by, Mr. Fields," I said.

He didn't answer.

I shut the door quickly and ran down the steps. The man was a gopher. He was real gone. I was glad to get out in the street. Even the dirty streets seemed clean after being inside that room with him. But I had the feeling as I headed toward the gym that I hadn't seen the last of him yet.

CHAPTER TWELVE

I CAME BACK TO MY CORNER MOVING STIFFLY, MY BACK AND SIDES A RED welted sheet of pain. Slowly I slumped back on the stool. I leaned forward, my mouth open, taking great gulps of air.

Zep was on his knees in front of me, pressing a damp towel to my forehead. Mr. Spritzer was massaging my side, his hands moving in a slow circular motion. Zep peered into my face. "Yuh all right, Danny?"

I nodded painfully. I didn't want to speak, I had to save my breath. Something had gone wrong. This was supposed to be a cinch for me. I couldn't understand it. According to the papers, I should have taken him by the second round, but here it was going into the third and I hadn't been able to land one solid punch.

"He okay, Mr. Spritzer?" Zep's voice was anxious.

Spritzer's voice was dry. It cut through the fog that was beginning to gather in my head. "He's okay. He's been reading the papers too much, that's all."

My head snapped up. I knew what he meant. He was right, too; I had been too sure of myself. I had begun to believe everything I had read about myself. Across the ring, Passo was sitting in his corner, breathing easily and confidently, the lights shining brightly on his ebony skin.

The bell sounded and I sprang to my feet, moving toward the center of the ring. Passo was coming toward me confidently, a sort of smile on his face. I knew the look. I had worn it many times when I knew I had the fight won. Seething anger began to surge through me. The wrong face was wearing that look tonight. I shot my right viciously.

A fountain of pain geysered through my side. I had missed and Passo caught me with a left to the kidneys. I dropped my hands to cover my side. A flashbulb exploded in my face.

I shook my head to clear it. There was blackness in front of my eyes as if I had just come from staring at the sun. A hollow sound came floating toward me. "Five!" I turned my head and looked in the direction of the sound.

The referee's arm was going up again, his mouth shaping another word. I looked down and a dull surprise came through me. What was I doing on my hands and knees? I hadn't fallen. I stared at the gleaming white canvas.

"Six!" A shock tore through me. He was counting me out! He couldn't do that. I scrambled to my feet awkwardly.

The referee seized my hands and wiped my gloves off on his shirt. I could hear the crowd roaring as he stepped back. It sounded different, somehow. To-night they weren't yelling for me, they were yelling for Passo. There were yelling for him to finish me off.

I fell into a clinch. Passo's body was wet with perspiration. I gasped gratefully for the moment's respite. The referee pushed us apart.

Again a pain shot through my side, then on the other side. Passo's dark face was dancing in front of my eyes. He was smiling. He was coming toward me.

His gloves were flashing at me, tearing at me. I had to get away from them, they were cutting me to ribbons. I looked desperately toward my corner.

Zep's eyes, wide and frightened, stared at me. I turned my head quickly back to Passo. He was swinging. The punch was coming at me, the kayo punch. I could see it. It was coming with a tantalizing slowness. A crazy fear tore through me. I had to stop it. I swung wildly, desperately at his uncovered jaw.

Suddenly Passo was falling. I stumbled toward him. The referee turned me around and pushed me toward my corner. Tears of pain were streaming down my face. I had to get out of there, I couldn't stand any more.

Zep was coming through the ropes, grinning. I looked bewilderedly at him. What was he grinning about? It was over and I had lost. Relief came over me, I was glad it was finished. Nothing else mattered.

I lay on the dressing table, my head cradled in my arms, feeling Spritzer's hands moving soothingly on my back. I could feel the pain subsiding slowly and a sense of comfort coming over me. I was tired. I closed my eyes.

I heard Zep put down the bottle of rubbing alcohol, and his voice drifted toward me. "He gonna be all right, Mr. Spritzer?"

Spritzer's hands were still kneading my back. "He'll be okay. He's tough an' young an' he's got guts."

I didn't move. At least he wasn't sore because I'd lost. There was a knock on the door and Zep opened it. I heard a heavy footstep in the room.

"Is he okay, Moe?" Sam's voice was worried.

The trainer's voice was flat. "He's okay, Sam. Nothing to worry about."

"So what the hell happened then?" Sam's voice was harsh with anger. "He looked lousy out there tonight. He took a hell of a beating."

Spritzer's voice was patient. "Take it easy, Sam. The kid was just beginning to believe his own clippings, that's all. He went out there thinkin' all he had to do was look at Passo an' it was all over."

"But you're supposed to keep him on edge." Sam's voice was still harsh.

"There's some things even I can't do," Spritzer answered. "I been expectin' this before, but from now on he'll be all right. He learned his lesson."

I heard Sam's footsteps coming over to me and felt his hand rest lightly on my head. He ruffled my hair gently. I kept my eyes closed. I began to feel good; he wasn't angry with me.

The last trace of harshness disappeared from his voice; there was a note of pride in it now. "You see that last wallop he hit the nigger, Moe? It was murder!"

"It almost was," Spritzer replied soberly. "That boy's jaw is broke in two places."

I spun around on the table and sat up. They were all staring at me. "That true?" I asked.

Zep nodded his head. "I just got the word a few minutes ago, Danny."

"Then I—I won?" I still couldn't believe it.

Sam smiled. "Yeah, kid, you won."

I sank slowly back on the table, but there was no triumph in me. All I could think about was what my father said: "Go on, Killer, for a dollar you can murder all your friends."

❖ ❖ ❖

We stood on the corner of Delancey and Clinton Streets. It was a few minutes after midnight. The lights still shone brightly: in the store windows and people still thronged the sidewalks.

"Kin yuh get home okay, Danny?" Zep asked.

"Sure I can," I laughed. Most of the pain had gone, leaving just an aching soreness in my back and sides. "Don't be an old woman."

Spritzer looked at me closely. "Sure, kid?"

I turned to him. "I wouldn't be sayin' I could, Mr. Spritzer, if I couldn't. I'm okay now."

"Okay if you say so," he said quickly, "but do what I tell you. Get a good night's rest and stay in bed as much of tomorrow as you can. Don't bother comin' down to the gym until the day after."

"I'll do it, Mr. Spritzer," I promised. I turned back to Zep. "Tell Nellie I'll come over tomorrow night."

"Okay, Danny, I'll tell her."

I left them on the corner and walked down Clinton Street heading for home. I took a deep breath. It had been a close one. Mr. Spritzer had been right, though. I had been reading the papers too much. I wouldn't after this. I turned my corner and walked toward home.

A figure came out of the shadows next to my door. "Danny!" Spit was standing there.

"What d'yuh want?" I asked impatiently. I wanted to get to bed.

"Mr. Fields wants to see yuh," he answered.

"Tell him I'm bushed," I said quickly, pushing past him. "I'll see him some other time."

Spit's hand caught my arm. "Yuh better come, Danny," he said. "Fields is no guy to give the brush. He might take a notion to make it tough for yuh." Spit's eyes were blinking rapidly, as they always did when he was excited. "You'd better come," he repeated.

I thought for a moment. Spit was right. You don't screw around when Maxie Fields sends for you. I had to go, but I would only spend a few minutes and then get out. "Okay," I said gruffly.

I followed Spit back around the corner. At the doorway next to Fields's store Spit took a key out of his pocket and opened the door. I followed him into the hallway.

He turned to me and held out the key. "Go on upstairs," he said. "You know the door."

I looked at the key, then at him. "Ain't yuh comin' along?"

He shook his head. "No. He said he wanted to see yuh alone. Don't ring, the key'll let yuh in." He pressed the key quickly into my hand and vanished out into the street.

I stared after him and then looked down at the key in my hand. It twinkled brightly in the hall light. I took a deep breath and slowly began to climb the stairs.

CHAPTER THIRTEEN

THE KEY WORKED SMOOTHLY IN THE LOCK AND THE DOOR SWUNG OPEN with hardly a sound. I stood in the doorway looking into the room. It was empty. For a second I hesitated. Something seemed to be wrong and suddenly I knew what it was: the lights were on.

I was used to turning off the lights when I walked out of a room—Edison had enough money. But all the lights in this room were on though nobody was there.

I stepped in, leaving the door open behind me. "Mr. Fields!" I called. "I'm here, Danny Fisher. You wanted to see me?"

The door on the other side of the room opened and the girl I had seen earlier in the day came out. "Close the door, Danny," she said quietly. "You'll wake the neighbors."

Automatically I shut the door. "Where's Mr. Fields?" I asked. "Spit said he wanted to see me."

There was a doubting look in her eyes. "Is that why you came?" she asked, her disbelief echoing in her voice.

I stared back at her. Then my face flushed as I remembered Fields's invitation. "That's why," I answered gruffly. "Where is he? I want to see him and get home to bed. I'm dead tired."

A quick smile came over her face. "You sound like you mean it."

"Of course I mean it," I said coldly. "Now take me to him. I want to get this over with."

"All right," she said. "Follow me."

She led me through a small kitchen, past an open bathroom door, and into a bedroom. She flicked on a light and gestured toward a bed. "There he is—the great Maxie Fields in all his glory. The son of a bitch!" There was a raw grating hatred in her voice.

I stared down at the bed. Fields was stretched across it, fast asleep. His shirt was open to the waist, exposing the heavy mass of black hair on his chest to the light. He was breathing heavily, one arm thrown across his face. There was a strong reek of liquor in the room.

I looked at the girl. "He's out?" I asked questioningly.

"He's out," she confirmed bitterly. "The fat pig!"

I stepped back out of the bedroom and held the key toward her. "Give him this and tell him I couldn't wait. I'll see him some other time."

As I started back through the apartment, she called me. "Wait a minute," she said quickly. "Don't go. He said for me to keep you here until he wakes up."

"Christ!" I exploded. "He's out for the night! I can't wait."

She nodded. "I know, but wait a little while anyway to make it look good. If you go right now, he'll know I didn't keep you and he'll be angry."

"How'll he know?" I asked. "He's dead to the world."

"He'll know," she said quietly. She walked over to a window and lifted a slat of the venetian blind. "C'mere, look."

I looked out the window but I didn't see anything. "What?" I asked.

"Over there in the doorway of the store across the street."

There was a faint shadow there and a cigarette was glowing. Just then an automobile turned the corner, its headlights piercing the darkness of the doorway, and I saw Spit standing there.

I dropped the blind and turned to her. "So he's watchin'," I said. "So what?"

"He'll tell Fields how long you stayed."

"What if he does?" I asked impatiently. "He's out anyway. I can't stay until he wakes up." I started for the door again.

She caught my arm, a sudden fear painted on her face. "Kid, give me a break," she pleaded, a note of desperation in her voice. "Stick around a little while. Make it look good. You don't know that guy inside. He'll make it rough for me if he finds out I didn't keep you at least for a little while."

Her eyes were wide and frightened and her hand was trembling on my arm. I remembered how sorry I had been for her when I had seen her last. "Okay," I said, "I'll stay."

Her hand dropped quickly from my arm. "Thanks, Danny," she said with relief.

I sat down on the couch and leaned back against the cushions wearily. A throbbing ache came back into my body. "Christ, I'm tired," I said.

She came to the couch and looked down at me sympathetically. "I know, Danny," she said softly. "I saw the fight. Maybe I could get you some coffee?"

I looked up at her curiously "No, thanks," I said. "You saw it?"

She nodded "Maxie took me out there."

There was a twinge of pain in my back and I shifted uncomfortably. "What's his angle?" I asked wearily.

She didn't answer my question. "You're tired," she said. "Why don't you stretch out and make yourself comfortable?"

It was a good idea. My body sank into the soft down cushions and I closed my eyes for a moment. This was even softer than my bed. Living was good when you had the dough. I heard the light-switch click and opened my eyes. She had turned off the ceiling light; now only a corner lamp was glowing. She was just sitting down in a chair opposite me, holding a drink in her hand.

"You didn't answer my question," I said.

She lifted her glass and drank. "I can't," she replied. "I don't know."

"He must have said something," I insisted. I raised myself on one elbow. My back suddenly twinged and a groan escaped my lips.

She was on her knees beside the couch, her arm around my shoulder. "You poor kid," she said softly. "You're hurt."

I sat up, moving away from her arm. "My back is sore," I admitted, trying to smile. "I caught a lot of punches."

Her hand slipped down to my back, rubbing it gently. She looked at her watch. "Lie down again," she said gently. "It's half past twelve; another half-hour and you can go. I'll rub your back."

I stretched out, feeling her hands moving on me. Their touch was light and soothing. "Thanks," I said. "That feels good."

She was still on her knees, her face close to mine. She smiled suddenly. "I'm glad," she answered. She leaned forward quickly and kissed me.

I was surprised, and stiffened awkwardly. She withdrew her lips at once.

"That's my way of saying thanks," she explained. "You're a good kid, Danny."

I stared at her. I was all mixed up. "Yuh shouldn' a done that," I said. "I got a girl. Besides, it's what he wants me to do an' I don't like doin' anythin' unless I want to."

"You don't want to?"

"I didn't say that," I said stubbornly. "I only said it's what he wants and I don't know the angle."

Her eyes were wide. "What if I say this is between us? That he'll never know."

I searched her eyes. "I wouldn't believe yuh."

Her voice was level. "Would you believe me if I told you I hated his guts?"

"He's payin' for your time," I said flatly. "For that kind of dough I don't believe nothin'."

She was silent for a moment, then she looked at the floor. "Would you believe me if I told you what he wants from you?"

I didn't answer. I watched her face impassively, waiting for her to speak.

"He wants you to throw the next fight. He stands to lose a lot of money if you win." Her voice was low.

I nodded my head. I had guessed something like that. "He ought to know better," I said.

Her hand caught at my arm. "You don't know him," she whispered bitterly. "He's bad and he's mean. He won't stop at anything. You should have seen him at the fight while you were taking a beating. He was laughing and happy as could be. It was a lot of fun for him until you knocked that boy out. If you had lost, he wouldn't have bothered getting you up here tonight."

I laughed shortly. "I won, an' now there's nothin' he can do."

Her fingers were gripping tightly into my arm. "You're just a kid, Danny, and you don't know him. He'll stop at nothing. If he can't buy you one way or another he'll have his boys take care of you. Then you won't be able to fight."

I stared at her, my lips tightening. "Where do you fit in?" I asked.

She didn't answer, she didn't have to. She was no different from anyone else. Nobody had a chance against the guy with the buck. It was the old story, I thought bitterly. Now I had all the answers. To go along with Sam and become a fighter was my only way out, the only chance to escape being a nebuch like everybody else, a nobody, one of the many who walked the streets of the city anonymously, who are never missed. It was my only chance to make a buck.

Slowly I sat up. She slipped into the seat beside me, her eyes alive with sympathy. She knew what I was thinking. "Now do you believe me?" she asked. "We're both in the same boat."

I got to my feet, nodding silently, and went to the window. I raised the blind and peeked out. Spit was still in the doorway, his cigarette glowing.

"Is he still there?"

"Yeah," I said in a dull voice.

She looked at her watch. "Another fifteen minutes and you can go. You might as well sit down until then."

I slumped into a chair, facing her, and felt the tiredness all through me.

"What are you going to do, Danny?" she asked.

"Nothin'." I shrugged my shoulders. "What can I do?"

She came over to me and sat down on the arm of my chair. Her hand stroked my forehead. I closed my eyes wearily.

"Poor Danny," she said gently. "There's nothing you can do, nothing anybody can do." Her voice grew suddenly bitter. "He's got you like he's got me, like he's got everybody around him. Like a blood-sucking monster that lives off everything around it." There were tears running from her open eyes.

"You're crying," I said in surprise.

"So I'm crying." She stared back at me defiantly. "You know a law that stops a whore from crying, or don't you think he'd like that either?"

"I'm sorry," I said quickly. It wasn't her fault. We were both lost, neither of us could escape. There was no use in kidding ourselves. We couldn't win.

I put my hand on her shoulder and pulled her down to me. I kissed her. Her lips were soft and I could feel her teeth behind them. Now she lay across my lap, looking up at me. Her eyes were wide and wondering. "Danny," she said softly, "you said you had a girl."

"I have." I laughed grimly. "But you're here." I kissed her again. "What's your name?" I asked suddenly.

"Ronnie," she answered. "But that's not my real name. My name is Sarah, Sarah Dorfman. I want you to know it."

"What difference does it make?" I laughed bitterly. "Maybe my name is not my own. Nothing else belongs to me. The only thing important is that if I have to do what he says, I might as well take everything he's willing to give me."

Her arms went up around my neck and pulled me down to her. I felt her lips moving against my ear. "What I have to give you, Danny, is something he could never buy—no matter how much he is willing to pay."

Her lips were against mine. I dropped my hands to her body, and her flesh was warm for me. I could hear her crying softly.

Then the tension had gone, dissolved in a caldron of heat, and we were silent, our breath rushing in each other's ears. She was staring at me. I could see she understood.

"You're going to take his money?" she asked, a sound of disappointment in her voice.

I stared back at her. "I don't know," I said bitterly. "I don't know what I'm gonna do."

CHAPTER FOURTEEN

I CLOSED THE DOOR BEHIND ME AND STEPPED OUT ON THE SIDEWALK. THE night air was cool on my face. It was fresh and sweet and for a few short hours would stay that way—until the street started waking up. Then it would grow heavy and dirty again so that you couldn't stand the taste of it in your lungs.

The glow of a cigarette in a doorway across the street caught my eye. I crossed the street quickly, anger swelling inside me. Spit was still in the doorway, a pile of cigarette butts scattered around him. His startled face stared at me.

"Gimme a butt, will yuh, Spit?" My voice was cold and echoed flatly in the empty street.

"Sure, Danny," Spit's voice was nervous, but his hand held a cigarette toward me.

I put it in my mouth. "Light."

"Sure, Danny." Spit's hand held a trembling match. It flickered and burst into flame, casting a dancing shadow over his face.

I drew the smoke deep into my lungs. It felt good, it had been such a long time. Mr. Spritzer insisted on it, but it didn't make any difference now.

"Did yuh see him, Danny?" Spit's voice was anxious.

I stared at him. There was a wise and knowing look on his face. Even he had known what Fields wanted. I could feel the anger growing stronger inside me. The whole world knew what Fields wanted. It also knew what I would do. Nobody expected anything different. I was just another shnook. I didn't stand a chance.

"No," I answered, a sudden tension in my voice. "He was out cold. Drunk."

"You were up there wit' the dame alla time?" Spit's voice was curious, yet knowing.

I nodded silently. She hated Fields too, but there was nothing she could do about it. We were all caught just as she said. We couldn't escape him. He held all the cards.

Spit's leering voice grated in my ear. "Did yuh lay 'er, Danny?"

My eyes jumped to his face. The saliva was running crazily from the corner of his mouth, giving him a wickedly obscene expression. It was almost as if in the shadows behind him I could see Maxie Fields hanging over his shoulder. I grabbed his shirt and pulled him toward me. "What if I did?" I asked harshly, remembering what she had said: "What I have to give you, Danny, is something he could never buy—no matter how much he was willing to pay."

"What if I did?" I repeated angrily. It was none of his affair.

Spit struggled in my grasp. "Nothin', Danny, nothin'." His frightened eyes stared up at me. "Le'me go!"

I stared at him coldly. "What for?" I asked, my grip still tight in his shirt.

"I'm yer friend, Danny," Spit gasped, his collar suddenly tight around his neck and choking him where I held it. "Didn' I bring yuh to Fields? Put yuh in a way to make some dough?"

I laughed. That was rich. My friend? I laughed again and let go of his shirt.

He stepped back, staring at me nervously. "Jeeze, Danny," he wheezed hoarsely. "Fer a minute I t'ought yuh was gonna slug me."

I laughed again. About that he was right. My fist sank into his soft belly clear up to my wrist. He doubled over and began to sink to his knees. I looked down at him contemptuously. "I was," I said.

He stared up at me, his eyes blurred with stupid confusion. His voice was hoarse. "What's wrong wit' yuh, Danny? I was on'y doin' you a favor."

I slapped him across the face with my open hand, knocking him on his side. "I don't want any favors," I snapped harshly.

He sprawled flat at my feet for a moment; then his hand reached for the doorknob and he began to pull himself to his feet. The expression in his eyes had changed to raw hatred. His free hand fumbled beneath his shirt.

I waited until the switch knife was free in his hand, then I hit him again, low in the groin, and the knife clattered to the sidewalk. He fell forward, retching violently.

I watched the pool of vomit spread around his face. There was cold satisfaction coursing in me. Maybe I had no chance against Maxie Fields, but there was somewhere along the line I could level.

His face turned up to me. "I'll get yuh for this, Danny," he swore in a low, husky voice. "God help me, I'll get yuh for this!"

I laughed again. "I wouldn't try that, Spit," I said, bending over him and pushing him back into his vomit. "Your boss might not like it."

I turned my back and left him lying in the mess in the doorway.

I paused in my hallway and looked at my watch. It was almost two thirty. I began to climb the stairs. A light was coming from under our kitchen door when I reached the landing. I hoped Papa wasn't up. I'd had enough for one night.

I put my key in the door and opened it. Mamma's face looked out at me. I smiled at her. "You didn't have to wait up for me, Ma," I said, closing the door behind me.

She got out of her chair and came toward me, her eyes searching my face. "Are you all right, Danny?" she asked anxiously.

"Sure, he's all right." Papa's voice came from the other doorway. "That's Dynamite Danny Fisher. Nothing can hurt him. It says so here in the morning paper." His hand waved the paper at us. "A new name they got for him," he continued sarcastically, "in honor of breaking a boy's jaw in two places with one punch in tonight's fight."

I stared at him in surprise. "It's in the paper already?"

Papa waved the paper again. "What did you think? It would be a secret? What were you doing all night, celebrating with your shiksa?"

I didn't answer him. There was no use in talking to him any more. He could never understand that it was an accident.

Mamma's hand was on my shoulder. Her face was lined and worried. "It said in the paper you took a terrible beating in the first two rounds."

I squeezed her hand gently. "It wasn't so bad, Mamma. I'm okay now."

"But that boy's not!" Papa burst out. "Now you'll stop maybe? Or you'll go on until you kill somebody?"

"Don't be a fool, Papa," I snapped. "It was an accident. Those things happen sometimes. I didn't mean it!"

"Accident, hah!" Papa shouted disbelievingly. "How can it be an accident when the main purpose is to beat up the other boy? Baloney!" He turned to Mamma. "Some day we'll have in our house a murderer, and then he'll tell us that's an accident, too!"

The harsh monotony of his continual shouting ripped apart my nerves. "Leave me alone!" I shouted hysterically. "Leave me alone, I tell yuh!" I sank into a chair and covered my face with my hands.

I felt Mamma's hands grip my shoulders. Her voice came from over my head, filled with quiet strength. "Harry, go in to bed," she told him.

"You're doing wrong, coddling him," he warned ominously. "Some day he'll kill somebody and you'll be to blame as much as him!"

"So I'll be to blame," she answered quietly without hesitation. "He's our son and whatever he is or will be, we'll have to take the blame."

"You will, not me," Papa retorted angrily. "I made up my mind. He gives up this fighting or I'm through. One more fight and he don't have to come home.

I won't have any murderers sleeping under my roof!"

His footsteps stamped down the hall to the bedroom. There was a moment's silence, then Mamma spoke gently to me. "Danny, I got some fresh-made chicken soup. I'll warm it up for you." Her hands were stroking my hair.

I raised my head and looked at her. Her eyes were filled with a sorrowing sympathy. "I'm not hungry." I felt dull and numb.

"Take some," she insisted. "It'll do you good." She turned the light on under the pot.

Maybe Papa was right, but if we hadn't been so hard up for dough, it might never have happened. There was nothing else to do now.

Mamma put the plate of soup in front of me. "Eat," she said, slipping into the chair next to me.

I tasted the soup. It was good and I could feel it warm away the numbness in me. I smiled gratefully at her, and she smiled back.

The warm soup was making me drowsy. I could feel the weariness creeping through me, the ache returning to my back and sides. I picked up the paper idly from the table where Papa had dropped it and began to turn the pages to the sports section. Some pieces of white notepaper fell from it. I looked at them curiously. There were figures scrawled in pencil all over them.

"What's this?" I asked, holding them toward Mamma.

She took them from me. "Nothing," she said. "Your father was just trying to figure out something."

"What?"

"A friend of his has a store he wants Papa to buy, and Papa was trying to figure out where he could get the money for it." She looked at the sheets of paper in her hand. "But there's no use," she continued, a note of hopelessness creeping into her voice. "He can't get the money. He's got enough stock that he put away at Uncle David's the night he closed up the other store, but he can't raise enough cash for a down payment. We might as well forget it."

I was awake again. Maybe if I could get the money he wouldn't think I was so bad. "How much does he need?" I asked.

Mamma got to her feet and took the empty plate from in front of me. She went to the sink and began to wash it. "Five hundred dollars," she said tonelessly over her shoulder, "but it might as well be five million. We can't get it."

I stared at her back. Her shoulders were drooping tiredly. There was an air of futility and resignation about her. The fight had gone, the only thing left was the concern of existing from day to day.

Five hundred dollars. Fields should be good for that—easy. He had told me himself that he had booked over four grand on the fight. I looked up suddenly. Mamma was speaking.

It was almost as if she were speaking to herself, though she had turned around and her eyes were on my face. "It was nice even to think about, Blondie. Then maybe things would be again like they were. But it's no use."

I got to my feet. My mind was made up. "I'm tired, Ma. I'm going to bed."

She came toward me and took my hand. "You'll listen to your father, Danny," she said gently, her eyes pleading with me. "You'll give up this fighting business. He means what he said. He swore it all night."

I wanted to tell her what had happened, but I couldn't. She wouldn't understand. There was only one answer I could give her now. "I can't, Mamma."

"For my sake, then, Blondie," she begged. "Please. In June you'll graduate school, then you'll get a job and everything will work out."

I shook my head. I looked down at the sheets of notepaper with the figures on them that Mamma had left on the table. That wasn't the answer. We both knew it. "I can't quit now, Mamma. I gotta do it."

As I started from the room, her hand caught at my arm and pulled me toward her. She pressed her hands to the side of my face and looked into my eyes. Fear was mirrored in her face. "But you might be hurt, Danny. Like that boy tonight."

I smiled reassuringly at her and caught her head to my chest. "Don't worry, Mamma," I said, pressing my lips to her head. "I'll be all right. Nothing will happen to me."

CHAPTER FIFTEEN

I PAUSED IN FRONT OF THE STORE FOR A MOMENT, PEERING THROUGH THE window. My reflection peered back at me, my hair gleaming with a bluish tinge from the glass that made it almost white. The store was empty, only one man behind the small cages. I walked in.

The man looked up at me. "What d'yuh want, kid?" he asked in a surly voice.

"I want to see Mr. Fields," I replied.

"Beat it, kid," the man snapped. "Fields ain't got no time for punks."

I stared at him coldly. "He'll see me," I said levelly. "I'm Danny Fisher."

I could see his eyes widen slightly. "The fighter?" he asked, a note of respect coming into his voice.

I nodded. The man picked up a phone and spoke into it quickly. People were beginning to recognize my name. I liked that. It meant I wasn't a nobody any more. But it wouldn't last. After the next fight I'd be just another name again, another guy who tried and didn't make it. I'd be forgotten.

He put down the phone and gestured at the door in the back. "Fields said for you to go right up."

I turned silently and went through the door. The horse room was empty. It was still morning, too early for the players to be out. I went through it and up the stairway, stopped in front of Fields's door, and knocked. The door swung open and Ronnie stood there. Her eyes widened and she stepped back.

"Come in," she said.

I brushed past her into the room. It was empty and I turned back to her. "Where is he, Ronnie?" I asked.

"Shaving. He'll be out in a minute." She came toward me quickly. "Spit was up here this morning," she whispered, her face close to mine. "He told Maxie what you did. Maxie was boiling."

I smiled. "He'll get over it, Ronnie."

Her hand caught at mine. "Last night you called me Sarah. I thought you weren't coming back."

"That was last night," I said in a low voice. "I changed my mind."

Her eyes dipped into mine. "Danny," she asked breathlessly, "did you come back on account of me?"

I closed my memory. "Yeah, Ronnie," I said flatly, shaking off her hand. "For you—and money."

"You'll get both," Fields's voice boomed from the doorway. I turned toward him as he came into the room. "I said you were a smart boy, Danny. I knew you'd be back."

He was wearing a lounge robe of pure red silk. It was tied around his big middle with a contrasting blue cord, and yellow pajama trousers stuck out beneath it. His blue jowls were shiny from the soap, and a big cigar was already clenched between his teeth. He looked as I always thought Maxie Fields would look.

"I hear you pay good, Mr. Fields," I said quietly. "I came back to see if what I heard was true."

He dropped into a chair in front of me and looked up into my face. He was smiling, but his eyes hadn't changed; they remained crafty. "You did a job on Spit," he said softly, ignoring my statement. "I don't like my boys handled that way."

I kept my face impassive. "Spit used to be my friend," I said slowly. "We did a couple of jobs together. But he broke the contract when he spied on me. I don't like that from a friend."

"He was doing what I told him," Fields said gently.

"That's okay with me—now," I said, my voice as gentle as his. "But not before, when he was supposed to be my friend."

The room was silent except for the sound of Fields sucking on his cigar. I stared into his eyes, wondering what was going on behind them. He was no fool, I knew that. I knew he had understood what I had said. But I didn't know whether he would buy it.

At last he took a match from his pocket, struck it, and held it to his cigar. "Ronnie, get me some orange juice," he said between puffs.

Slowly she started from the room. "And get some for Danny too," he called after her. "That won't break his training."

When the door closed behind her, he turned to me, chuckling. "She treat you right?" he asked.

I allowed myself the flicker of a smile to hide the surge of relief coursing through me. "Good enough."

Fields laughed aloud. "I told her I'd beat hell outta her if she didn't. She knows her business."

I dropped into the chair opposite him. I had kissed her in this chair last night. And she had kissed me and told me things. I had believed her, too. Suddenly I wanted to get it over with. "How much?" I asked.

Fields put on a look of pretended innocence. "How much for what?"

"For throwin' the fight," I said bluntly.

Fields chuckled again. "Bright boy," he rasped. "You catch on quick."

"Sure," I said caustically, growing more sure of myself. "Mr. Fields don't waste time unless there's a buck in it for him. I can do worse than follow him. What's in it for me?"

Ronnie came back into the room with a glass of orange juice in each hand. Silently she handed one to each of us. I tasted it. It was good. It had the taste that only freshly squeezed oranges could have. It had been a long time since I'd had orange juice. Oranges were pretty expensive. I drained my glass.

Fields was sipping his juice slowly, his eyes watching me appraisingly. Finally he spoke. "What do yuh say to five C's?"

I shook my head. I was on home grounds. I knew a bargain when I saw one. "You'll have to do better than that."

He finished his juice and leaned forward in his seat. "What do you think it's worth?"

"A grand," I said swiftly. That would leave him with a clean three according to his own words.

He waved his cigar at me. "Seven fifty. And the doll here."

"Talk money," I smiled. "I already had the doll. She's too rich for my blood."

"Seven fifty's a lot of dough," Fields grumbled.

"Not enough," I told him. "It's gotta look good. That means I gotta take a helluva beating to make three grand for you."

He got to his feet suddenly, came over to my chair, and looked down at me. His hand clapped down on my shoulder heavily. "Okay, Danny," he boomed. "A grand it is. You get the dough right after the fight."

I shook my head. "Uh-uh. Half before an' half after."

He laughed aloud and turned to Ronnie. "I told yuh the kid was sharp." He turned back to me. "Deal. Pick it up the afternoon before the fight. You can come aroun' the day after for the rest."

I rose to my feet slowly, keeping my eyes veiled and cautious. I didn't want him to know how good I felt. "You got yourself a boy, Mr. Fields," I said, starting for the door. "I'll be seein' yuh."

"Danny." Ronnie's voice turned me around. "You'll be coming back?"

My gaze swung from her to Fields and then back to her. "Sure, I'll be coming back," I said carefully. "For the dough!"

Fields's laughter boomed in the room. "The kid also makes with the fast answer."

Her face flushed angrily and she took a quick threatening step toward me, her hand raised to slap me. I caught her arm in midair and held it tight. For a second we stood staring into each other's eyes.

My voice was low, it carried only to her ears. "Let it go, Sarah," I said. "We can't afford dreams."

I released my grip and her arm fell slowly to her side. There was something in her eyes that almost seemed like tears, but I wasn't sure, for she turned her back on me and walked over to Fields. "You're right, Max," she said, her back to me. "He is a bright kid. Too bright."

I closed the door behind me and started down the stairway. Someone was coming up and I stood aside to let him pass. It was Spit.

His eyes were startled as he recognized me. Instinctively his hand shot to his pocket and came out with a switch knife.

I smiled slowly, watching carefully. "I'd stash the shiv if I were you, Spit," I said softly. "The boss might not like it."

He glanced quickly up at Fields's door, then back at me. Indecision showed on his face. I didn't take my eyes from him. Suddenly Fields's voice bellowed out into the hallway: "Goddammit! Spit, where the hell are you?"

Quickly the knife disappeared back into Spit's pocket. "Comin', boss," he called out, and hurried up the stairs.

I watched him enter Fields's apartment before I continued down the stairway.

It was a bright, clear day and I decided to run over to Nellie's house. It was early and there might be just enough time for me to see her before she left for work.

And the way I felt, seeing her could do me nothing but good.

CHAPTER SIXTEEN

I AWOKE THAT MORNING TO THE DRONE OF MY FATHER'S VOICE. I LAY SLEEPily on the bed, vaguely trying to puzzle out his words. Suddenly I was wide awake. Today was the day. Tomorrow it would be over and I would go back to normal. Back to being a nobody.

I swung my feet over the side of the bed, found my slippers, and stood up, stretching. Maybe it was better so. The old man should be happy then. He would have his dough and I would be through fighting. Then maybe things would be quiet around here. This last week between fights had been hell; Papa had picked on me all the time.

I tied my bathrobe around me and went into the bathroom. I looked in the mirror and fingered my face. No sense in shaving today, it would only leave my skin too tender and easy to cut. I was willing to lose, but I didn't want to bleed to death into the bargain.

I brushed my teeth, washed my face, and combed my hair. I decided to leave the shower till later this afternoon when I was down at the gym. They had hot water down there. As I went back to my room, the sound of Papa's voice followed me through the hall. I dressed and went to the kitchen.

Papa's voice died away as I came into the room. He looked up at me coldly over the rim of his coffee cup.

Mamma hurried over to me. "Sit down and have some coffee."

Silently I sat down at the table opposite Papa. After tonight he would have nothing to bitch about, I thought. "Hi, Mimi," I said as she came into the room. Things were so bad I was even talking to her.

Her smile was warm and genuine. "Hi ya, Champ," she jested. "You going to win tonight?"

Papa's fist slammed down on the table. "Goddammit!" he shouted. "Has everybody in this house gone crazy? I don't want to hear no more fight talk, I tell you!"

Mimi turned a stubborn face toward him. "He's my brother," she said quietly. "I'll say what I want to him."

I could see Papa's jaw fall. I think it was the first time in her life that Mimi had ever spoken back to him. He sputtered for breath as Mamma's hand fell restrainingly on his shoulder.

"No arguments this morning, Harry," she said firmly. "Please, no arguments."

"B-but you heard what she said?" Papa seemed confused.

"Harry!" Mamma's voice was sharp and nervous. "Let's eat our breakfast in peace."

A tense silence fell across the room, broken only by the clinking sound of the dishes as they moved to and from the table. I ate quickly and silently; then I pushed my chair back from the table and stood up. "Well," I said, looking down at them, "I gotta go to the gym."

No one spoke. I forced a smile to my face. "Anybody here gonna wish me luck?" I asked. I knew it wouldn't make any difference, but it would be a nice thing to take with me.

Mimi grabbed at my hand, reached up, and kissed me. "Good luck, Danny," she said.

I smiled gratefully at her, then turned to Papa. His head was bent over his plate. He didn't look at me.

I turned to Mamma. Her eyes were wide and anxious. "You'll be careful, Danny?"

I nodded silently. A lump came into my throat as I looked at her. Suddenly I could see all the changes the last few years had wrought in her. She pulled my face down to her and kissed my cheek. She was crying.

I fished in my pocket. "I got two tickets for you," I said, holding them toward her.

Papa's voice rasped at me. "We don't want them!" He stared angrily at me. "Take them back!"

I still held the tickets in my hand. "I got them for you," I said.

"You heard me! We don't want them!"

I glanced at Mamma and she shook her head slightly. Slowly I returned the tickets to my pocket and started for the door.

"Danny!" Papa's voice called me back.

I spun around hopefully. I was sure he'd changed his mind. My hand was already in my pocket taking out the tickets again. Then I saw his face and knew nothing had changed. It was white and grim, and his eyes stared hollowly at me.

"You still going to fight tonight?"

I nodded.

"After what I told you?"

"I got to, Pa," I said flatly.

His voice was cold and empty. "Give me your key, Danny." He held his hand out to me.

I stared at him for a moment, then at Mamma. Automatically she turned to Papa. "Harry, not now."

Papa's voice quavered hollowly. "I told him if he fought again he would not come back here. I meant it."

"But, Harry," Mamma pleaded, "he's only a child."

Papa's voice burst into rage. It filled the small kitchen like thunder in a summer storm. "He's man enough to kill somebody! He's old enough to decide what he wants! I took enough trying to make something for him. I'm not going to take any more!" He looked at me. "You got one more chance!"

I stared at him for one blazing moment. All I kept thinking was that he was my father, that I had sprung from him, from his blood, and now he didn't care. Almost with surprise I saw the key fly from my fingers and ring crazily on the table in front of him. I stared at its shining silver brightness for a second and then turned and went out the door.

❖ ❖ ❖

I stood in front of Fields's desk as he counted out the money and dropped it on the desk. There was no smile on his lips now; the eyes, almost hidden in their rolls of fat, were crafty and cold. He pushed at the money with a pudgy finger. "There it is, kid," he said in his husky voice. "Pick it up."

I looked down at it: five crisp new one-hundred-dollar bills. I picked it up. It felt good in my hands. Papa would sing a different song when I showed him this. I folded it and stuck it in my pocket. "Thanks," I said grudgingly.

He smiled. "Don't thank me, Danny," he said quietly. "And don't cross me."

I looked at him in surprise. "I wouldn't do that," I answered quickly.

"I don't think you would either," Fields said, gesturing with his hand, "but Spit thought you might."

I looked at Spit, who was leaning against the wall, cleaning his nails with his switch knife. He met my gaze. His eyes were cold and wary.

"What ever gave him the idea he could think?" I asked Fields sarcastically.

Fields laughed loudly. His chair creaked as he got out of it. He came around the desk to me and clapped a heavy hand on my shoulder. "Bright boy," he said, geniality back in his voice. "Just don't forget that's my dough you're wearin'."

"I won't forget, Mr. Fields," I said, starting for the door.

"There's one more thing I don't want yuh to forget, Danny," he called after me.

From the doorway he looked immensely gross and powerful, standing there in front of his desk. This was the Maxie Fields I had heard about.

"What's that?" I asked.

His eyes seemed to open suddenly, revealing colorless agate irises and beady pupils. "I'll be watchin' yuh," he replied, his voice heavy and menacing.

I opened the door to the gymnasium and a sudden silence swept across the big room. Before that there had been plenty of noise, but now it was dead quiet in the East Side Boys Club.

Mr. Spritzer was standing in the corner of the room. His face turned slowly toward me. I walked across to him, conscious of every eye on me. I wished they wouldn't look at me like that, as if they were proud of me. There was five hundred dollars in my pocket that gave them nothing to be proud of.

"I—I'm here, Mr. Spritzer," I said nervously. By this time I was sure that everyone in the room had seen through me.

A bright smile flashed across his face. "Hello, Champ!"

That seemed like a signal for bedlam to break loose. Everyone in the gym crowded around me. They were all shouting at once, trying to attract my attention. I tried to smile at them, but I couldn't. My face seemed frozen into a strange sort of mask.

Then Spritzer's arm was through mine and he was clearing a path through the milling boys, leading me toward his office.

"Later, fellers, later!" he was shouting above the others. "Save your yelling till after the fight!"

Numbly I let him lead me into his office.

CHAPTER SEVENTEEN

T HE HOARSE SHOUTING OF THE CROWD CAME DOWN TO THE DRESSING-room and beat against my ears. It was a heavy monotonous sea of sound, a cry as old as time. People screamed like this in the jungle when two animals fought; they screamed like this in the Colosseum on Caesar's holidays. Five thousand years hadn't changed them.

I turned my head on the table so that my arms covered my ears and deadened the sound, but I couldn't keep it out altogether. It was there, only fainter now, just below the range of hearing, but it would come back the minute I turned my head.

A buzzer sounded sharply in the room. I felt Spritzer's hand on my back. "That's us, kid."

I sat up and swung my feet off the table. There was a lump of lead in my stomach. I swallowed hard.

"Nervous, kid?" Spritzer was smiling.

I nodded my head.

"It'll pass," he said confidently: "Every fighter gets it first time in the Garden. There's something about the place."

I wondered what he would say if he knew. It wasn't the place that threw me; it was the fight I was going to throw. We came out of the dressing-room and stood on the edge of a ramp, from which I looked out into the Garden. It was a sea of anonymous faces awaiting decision on the bout just ended. Sam was somewhere out there, Fields too. And Nellie, even she had come. Only my father and mother—they had not come.

The roar of the crowd grew louder as the verdict was announced. "Come on, Danny," Spritzer said. We started down the ramp to the white flood of light that was the ring.

I could hear them yelling. Some of them were even calling my name. I followed Spitzer stolidly, my head down, my face framed by the big white towel like blinkers on a horse. I could hear Zep's excited breathing near me. His voice rose above the roar of the crowd. "Look, Danny!" he said excitedly. "There's Nellie!"

I raised my head and saw her smiling at me, a tremulously sweet and anxious smile, and then she was lost in a sea of other faces.

I was at the ring now and climbing through the ropes. The bright white lights burned into my eyes after the dimness of the ramp. I blinked rapidly. The announcer called my name and I moved out into the center of the ring. I heard his voice, but I wasn't listening to him; I knew his little speech by heart.

"Break clean when I tell you. . . . Go on to the nearest neutral corner in event of a knockdown. . . . Back to your corner an' come out fightin', an' may the best man win."

Ha ha! That was a joke. May the best man win! I slipped out of my robe. That lump in my belly was the five hundred bucks in my pocket.

Spritzer's voice was in my ear. "Stop worryin', kid," he was saying. "The worst that kin happen is that you lose this one."

I looked up at him in surprise. He was more right than he knew. My biggest worry was somebody's clipping the five C's from my trousers back there in the dressing-room. The fight wasn't anything to worry about, I had already picked the winner.

I looked across the ring curiously. When I was out there in the center of the ring listening to the referee, I hadn't looked at the kid I was going to fight. He was staring at me with a tight nervous look on his face. I smiled at him. He didn't have a thing to be nervous about if he only knew it. He was Tony Gardella, an Italian kid fighting out of the Bronx.

The bell sounded. I moved out to the center of the ring feeling curiously lightfooted and sure of myself. Knowing that I was going to lose this fight gave me a confidence I could win it that I never really felt before. I had stopped worrying about what might happen since I already knew the answer.

I jabbed with my left to feel the kid out, wondering if he really had it. He was slow in countering and automatically I threw a fast right under his guard. The kid staggered on his feet. Instinctively I moved in for the kill. The crowd was roaring in my ears. I had him and I knew it. Then I remembered: I couldn't finish it. I was supposed to lose. I let him slip into a clinch and tie me up. I faked some light punches to Gardella's back and kidneys. As I felt his strength returning, I shoved him away, and kept him away for the rest of the round. I couldn't take any chances on hurting him.

The bell sounded and I came back to my corner. Spritzer was boiling, he was shouting at me: "Yuh had 'im, why didn't yuh follow him up?"

"I couldn't get set," I answered quickly. I would have to be more careful or he would get wise.

"Shut up!" he snarled. "Save yer breath!"

When the bell sounded, Gardella came out of his corner cautiously. I lowered my guard slightly and waited for him to come in. He hung back carefully, staying just out of range. I stared at him in amazement. How in hell did he expect to win this fight? By my knocking myself out? I moved toward him. Maybe I could lead him into it. He backed away. It was getting harder to lose this fight than to win it.

The crowd was booing by the time we went back to our corners. I sat down on the little stool, my head down, my eyes fixed on the canvas.

Spritzer was yelling again. "Rush him. Don't give him time to get away. Yuh hurt him. That's why he was bicyclin'."

At the bell I came out of my corner quickly and was more than halfway across the ring when I met him. He was throwing punches wildly. He, too, had orders to fight. I blocked a few of them by reflex. How this kid ever got to the finals I would never know; he was easy. It was a shame to let a joker like this win, but I had to. I had made a deal. Purposely I dragged my guard for a moment. His punches tore past my arm. There was a strange sweet pain in them, a kind of reward. It was as if I were two people and one of them was glad the other was taking a licking.

It was time for me to counter. I had to make it look good. I shot a wide whistling right. It was blocked easily and I was jarred by a blow in the stomach. The kid smiled confidently at me. That burned me. He had no right to feel like that. I'd give him a few shots to teach him a little respect. I stabbed with my left and tried to follow through with a right uppercut, but he got away from it easily.

I was getting sore. I followed his dancing figure. Blows were stinging me but I shrugged them off. I was going to give this baby one shot to let him know who was boss; then he could have the Goddam fight.

There was a sudden blinding explosion in my face and I felt myself go down to my knees. I tried to get up, but my legs weren't working. I shook my head savagely and caught the referee's count. Seven! I could feel the strength returning to my legs. Eight! I could get up now, my head was clear again. I knew I could. Nine! But what for? I was going to lose any way. I might as well stay down for the count.

But I was on my feet when the referee's hand started going up. What the devil did I do that for? I should have stayed down. He stepped back and Gardella came rushing at me. The bell rang and I quickly stepped aside and went back to my corner.

I slumped onto the stool. I wished Spritzer, yelling in my ear, would shut up. There was no use in it. Suddenly his words were tearing into my gut: "What d'yuh wanna be, Danny? A bum all yer life? A nobody? You kin take this boy. Shake the lead out and take 'im!"

I raised my head and stared across the ring. Gardella was grinning confidently. Me a bum, a nobody? That was just what would happen. I would be like everybody else on the East Side, nameless, faceless, another guy lost in the shuffle.

I was on my feet at the bell and moved out into the ring. Gardella came rushing at me, wide open. He had thrown all caution to the winds. I almost laughed to myself. He thought it was in the bag. To hell with you, Gardella! To hell with Fields! He could have his five hundred back and go screw himself!

I felt the jarring pain shoot up through my arm almost to my elbow. That one had steam on it. One more. If you thought the last one hurt, you son of a bitch, wait'll you feel this one.

I blocked his feeble blow almost lazily and brought my hand up in a right uppercut. My fist seemed to move jerkily in the blur of light. The kid suddenly slumped against me and I stepped back.

He was falling. I was watching him fall. It was almost in slow motion. He sprawled out at my feet. For a second I stared down at him, then I dropped my hands and jacked up my shorts and swaggered to a corner. I was in no hurry, I had all the time in the world. The kid was through fighting for the night.

The referee gestured toward me and I danced back toward him. He held up my arm. The crowd was yelling for me as I went back to my corner grinning. Champion! I was as high as a kite. The feeling stayed with me all the way down to the dressroom. I was on a jag, walking on air.

Abruptly it was all gone, the elation running out of me like air out of a pricked balloon. Leaning against the wall outside the dressing-room was a familiar figure. The roar of the crowd faded as I stared at him.

It was Spit. He was smiling at me with a peculiar smile. He had been cleaning his nails with a switch knife. Now he lifted it, still smiling, and gestured at me. I could feel the flesh on my throat crawl. Then he disappeared into the crowd. Quickly I looked around to see if anyone had noticed. No one had seen him. They were all talking. I let myself be carried along in their flow.

Sam was in the dressing-room, his face wreathed in a smile. His hand grabbed at mine. "I knew you had it, kid! I knew it! Way back that first time in school!"

I stared at him dumbly, I couldn't speak. The only thing I wanted was to get away from here. Fast.

Moving Day

MAY 17, 1934

G OOD NIGHT, CHAMP." ZEP WAS SMILING AS HE LEFT US IN THE DIMLY lit hallway and trudged up the stairs. We watched him disappear around the turn of the first landing.

We turned and looked at each other. She smiled up at me and put her arms around my neck. "First time tonight we've been alone," she whispered reproachfully, "and you haven't even kissed me yet."

I bent my head to kiss her, but as our lips met, there was a creaking sound from the staircase overhead. I drew back and stood there listening tensely.

"Danny, is something wrong?" Her voice was filled with concern.

I looked down at her. Her eyes were watching me closely. I forced a smile to my lips. "No, Nellie."

"Then what are you so jumpy about?" she asked, her arms pulling my face down to her. "Aren't you ever going to kiss me?"

"I'm still excited," I answered lamely. I couldn't tell her what was on my mind, I couldn't tell anybody.

"Too excited to kiss me?" she teased, smiling.

I tried to match her smile, but I couldn't, so I kissed her instead. I pressed my mouth to her, hard. I could feel her lips crush beneath mine. She cried in gentle pain.

"What do you think now?" I asked.

Her hands were fingering her bruised lips. "You hurt me," she accused.

I laughed wildly. "That isn't all I'll do to you!" I promised, pulling her close to me again. I pressed my mouth against her throat, along the nape of her neck, my arms crushing her against me.

"I love you, Danny!" she cried against my ear.

"I love you," I whispered back, still holding her. I felt her relax in my arms, her body close to me. Our lips met again and there was a flame in her kiss that went racing through me.

"Nellie!" I cried hoarsely, spinning her around in my grasp. Her back pressed into my waist and my arms were crossed over her breasts. I pressed my lips against her shoulder where the neck of her blouse had fallen from it.

Her face turned toward me. Her hand stroked the side of my cheek. Her voice was very low. "Danny," she murmured, "my legs are so weak I can hardly stand."

I fumbled with her blouse, and her breasts were warm in my fingers. She sighed deeply and sagged back against me, We stood like that for what seemed a long time.

At last she moved in my arms and turned her face toward me in the dimness. Her eyes were tender and loving. "My back hurts," she said in a weak apologetic voice.

I loosened my hold on her and she turned to face me, her hands holding mine to her breasts. She smiled up at me happily. "Feel better now?"

I nodded. It was true. For a little while I had forgotten about everything else.

She kissed me happily and took my hands from her blouse. Her face was flushed and warm, her dark eyes dancing, her lips curved in a gentle smile. "Now maybe you'll be able to go home and get some sleep?" she asked. "You've been so nervous all night."

I nodded again. She was right, I had been jumpy and on edge all evening. In the restaurant where Sam had taken us all for dinner I had started at every footstep. I could hardly eat. I didn't think anyone had noticed. I seized her hand and kissed its palm. "No matter what happens, Nellie," I said quickly, "don't forget I love you."

"And I love you no matter what happens," she replied earnestly. She held her face up to me to be kissed. "Good night, Danny."

I kissed her. "Good night, honey." I watched her vanish up the stairway, then I went out into the street.

I had walked only a few steps up the block when the sensation that I was being watched came over me. I stopped and looked back. The street was deserted. I started on again, but the curious feeling persisted. I paused at the street lamp on the corner to look at my watch. It was after two in the morning. Suddenly I thought I saw a movement in the shadows behind me. I spun around and my heart began to pound. I was poised for flight.

Out of the shadows came a small gray cat, and I almost laughed in relief. Next thing I knew, I'd be seeing ghosts. I went on again.

The lights of Delancey Street loomed in front of me. I stepped into the crowd, basking in their nearness. Nothing could happen to me here. Slowly I moved along with them and gradually began to feel better.

On the next corner a newsboy was yelling: "Mawnin' papers! Gloves winners!" I dropped two pennies in his hand, picked up a paper, and turned to the back page, where the sports news was. I looked closely at the fight pictures there. Mine was in the upper right-hand corner. The camera had caught me as I was standing over Gardella, sprawled at my feet. A thrill of pride ran through me. Champion! Nothing could ever take that away from me. I wondered if any of all the people passing by recognized me, if they knew that I, Danny Fisher, was standing there, smack in the middle of them.

My smile vanished suddenly. I was looking directly into the eyes of one who had recognized me: Spit. He was leaning against the window of the Paramount Cafeteria, smiling at me. The paper slipped from my nerveless fingers into the gutter. I had been right all along: they had been watching me, waiting to get me alone.

Spit was nodding to a man standing near the curb. I recognized him too. He was known to the neighborhood as the Collector. Fields used him to go after people who refused to pay up. After he got through with them they were generally glad to square accounts. If they were able.

I turned quickly into the crowd, fighting an impulse to run. I was safe as long as I could stay with them. When I looked back over my shoulder, Spit and the Collector were sauntering casually behind me, just like two ordinary men coming from a late movie. Though they seemed to be paying no attention to me, I knew their eyes were on me every second.

I turned up Clinton Street, where the crowd was thinner, but I was still safe. The next block would be the bad one. It was usually almost empty at this hour of the morning. If I could make it, I'd be just around the corner from my house.

I peered over the crowd in front of me, and my heart sank. The next block was completely empty. My steps slowed as I toyed with the idea of turning back toward Delancey Street.

A backward glance chased the thought from my mind. They were too close behind me. They would block me off. The only way I could go was straight ahead. My mind churned desperately. I was almost at the corner. A picture of that block ran through my mind. About three quarters of the way up it there was a small alley running between two houses. It was just wide enough to allow one person through at a time. If I could reach it before them, I had a chance. An outside chance, but it was the only one.

At the corner the traffic light was changing as a big trailer truck started to make its turn directly in front of me. I darted out into the street in front of it. The brakes squealed behind me as I reached the other curb, but I didn't look back. Spit was shouting at the truck, which had cut them off. I was almost halfway to the alley before I dared cast a nervous look over my shoulder.

Spit and the Collector had just reached the sidewalk and were running after me. Fear gave an added spurt to my legs. I almost ran past the alleyway in the darkness. Sharply I cut into it, my shoulder slamming against one side of the building. I bounced off the brick and fled deeper into the shadows.

It was dark in here, so dark I couldn't see where I was going. I moved more slowly now, one hand feeling along the wall beside me to guide my way. The alley ran the full length of two buildings, almost forty feet from the street, and ended in a blank wall. My hand suddenly touched the wall in front of me. I stopped, my fingers exploring it. There should be a small ledge a few feet up here. There was. Quietly I climbed up on it and turned, facing the street. I reached out in front of me, seeking a steel bar that I knew ran between the two buildings.

My eyes were getting used to the dark and I found the bar in the dim reflected glow coming from the street. My fingers grasped it firmly and I crouched there, waiting. My eyes strained through the darkness. Only one of them at a time could come after me here. My heart was bursting inside my chest. I tried to breathe quietly.

There was a murmur of voices at the end of the narrow alleyway. I tried to make out the words, but I couldn't tell one voice from another. Then they were silent and I heard footsteps scuffling slowly along the alleyway toward me.

The light from the street framed the shadow of a man. He was moving cautiously into the dark, his hand groping along the wall as mine had done. I could see another shadow up near the entrance. Good. One was waiting in the street. I wondered which of them was coming after me.

I didn't have to wonder for long. A voice hissed huskily in the dark at me. "We know yer in there, Fisher. Come with us tuh see the boss an' yuh got a chance!"

I drew in my breath sharply. It was the Collector. I didn't answer. I knew the kind of chance they would give me. He was about halfway down the alley toward me now.

The Collector spoke again, about ten feet from me now. "Yuh hear me, Fisher? Come out an' yuh got a chance!" The light behind him illumined his bulky frame. I drew myself up tensely, my hand gripping the steel bar. He was about six feet away from me. Five feet. Four. He couldn't see me hidden in the dark, but I could see him.

Three feet. Two. Now!

My feet flew off the ledge, my hands holding the bar in a tight grip. I vaulted through the air, my feet aimed at his head. Too late he sensed the sudden danger. He tried to move sideways, but there wasn't room. My heavy shoes caught him flush on the chin and face. There was a dull thud and something gave way beneath my heels. The Collector dropped to the ground.

Hanging from the bar in the air over him, I looked down trying to see him in the darkness. He was a crumpled shadow on the ground. He moaned a sighing little sound. I let go of the bar and dropped beside him. There was a stirring movement against my leg and I lashed out viciously with my foot. His head made a queer crunching sound as it snapped into the wall beside him, and then there was silence.

My fingers flew rapidly over his face. He lay there quietly, not moving. He was out.

I looked toward the entrance. Spit was still standing there in an attitude of listening. His body was framed against the light as he tried to see back into the darkness. His voice floated back to me. "Did yuh get 'im?"

I grunted as if in assent. I had to get him back in here if I wanted to get out whole. It was my only chance. I crouched low against the ground.

Spit's voice came at me again. He was moving slowly into the alley. "Hol' 'im. I wanna put my mark on the bitchin' double-crosser!"

A glint of light flashed along the wall near his hand. It was his switch knife. I crouched still lower and inched forward, holding my breath. A few more steps.

I came out of the dark ground, my fist aiming at Spit's chin. His head jerked back quickly, warned by an instinct of danger, and my fist grazed the side of his face.

Against the street light his knife flashed down at me. Desperately I lunged and caught it. He was struggling in my grasp, his free hand scratching at my eyes. A searing pain ran up my arm as Spit twisted the blade of the knife gripped in my palm. My hand jerked in reflex and I lost my grip. There was a burning pain in my side as Spit's hand flashed downward.

I gasped in sudden shock and grabbed at the knife hand. I caught it and held on tightly. Spit began twisting the knife again and the nerves in my arm screamed in agony, but I didn't dare let go. His free hand was clawing at my throat. In the dark I snapped a punch at his face. There was a sharp pain in my knuckles as they smashed against his teeth, but it was a welcome pain. I brought my knee sharply into his groin between his legs. He gasped and began to double up.

I bent his knife arm around behind him, straightening him up. I had his back against the wall, my shoulder pressing hard into his throat. With my free hand I threw punch after punch into his face. At last he slumped against me.

I let go of Spit's arm and stepped back, my breath rattling through my throat as he slid crazily to the ground. He sprawled out at my feet, lying on his stomach.

I leaned over him, searching for the knife.

I found it, its point two inches into his side. It must have happened when I held him against the wall. There was no emotion left in me. I was neither glad nor sorry. It was him or me.

I straightened up and slowly walked out of the alley. I wondered if Spit was dead. Somehow I didn't care. It didn't matter. Nothing really mattered if only I could get home and into bed. Then everything would be all right. In the morning I would wake up and find it had been nothing but a dream.

I stood in the hallway outside my door, searching my pockets for my key. It wasn't there. Nothing was there except the five hundred-dollar bills and a stub of a pencil. Wearily I tried to remember what I had done with it.

It came back to me suddenly. I had thrown it on the table in front of Papa that morning. We'd had an argument. Now I couldn't even remember what the argument was about. There was light coming from beneath the door. Somebody was still up. They would let me in. I knocked softly.

I heard a chair scuffle inside the room, then footsteps approached the other side of the door. "Who's there?" a voice cautiously asked. It was my father's voice.

A lump had formed in my throat when I first missed the key. Now I almost cried in relief. "It's me, Papa," I said. "Let me in." Everything would be all right now.

For a moment there was silence, then Papa's voice came back heavily through the door: "Go away."

Slowly the words penetrated my mind. I shook my head to clear it. I was hearing things. My father didn't say that, he couldn't. "It's me, Danny," I repeated. "Let me in."

Papa's voice was stronger now. "I said go away!"

A cold fear was running through me. I banged on the door, leaving bloody imprints from my hand. "Let me in, Papa!" I cried hysterically. "Let me in! I got no place to go!"

I could hear Mamma's voice. She seemed to be pleading with him. Then I heard Papa again. His voice was hoarse and rough and as immutable as time. "No, Mary, I'm through. I meant what I said. This time it's final!"

The sound of her sobbing came through the door, then the click of the light-switch. The light under the door had gone out. The sobbing behind it faded slowly into the house. Then silence.

I stood there a moment in shocked, frightened bewilderment. Then I understood. It was over, all over. Papa had meant what he said.

I slowly went down the stairs, feeling lonely and empty. On the stoop again, the night air was cool on my face.

I sank to the steps and leaned my head against the iron railing. I made no sound, but the tears were rolling down my cheeks. There was a burning sensation in my arm. I rubbed my hand along it. My fingers came away wet and sticky. The palm of my hand was cut and bleeding and my right sleeve was torn open. Through the rip I could see a cut on my arm in the dim light. The blood welled slowly into it, but it didn't matter. It meant nothing to me now, I was so tired. I rested my head against the railing and closed my eyes.

They were closed only a moment when I opened them suddenly. The feeling I'd had earlier that evening came back upon me. Someone was watching me. My eyes felt puffy and swollen as I peered up the street.

An automobile was parked across the way. Its lights were out but the motor was running quietly. They were after me again. Spit and the Collector must have reported back.

Without getting to my feet I rolled over on my belly and crawled back into the hallway. There I huddled for a moment, wondering what to do. Maybe I could sneak out the back and over the roof to the next house and duck them that way.

A feeling of hopelessness came over me. What good would it do? They would keep after me until they found me. They had friends everywhere. There was no place to hide.

My fingers dropped into my pocket. The money was still there. Maybe if I gave it back to them they would let me go. But even as I thought of it, I knew it wouldn't do any good. I had gone too far. I was in too deep.

But the dough was still good for what I'd got it for. The old man could still use it to buy that store. At least Mamma and Mimi would get a break that way. If they caught me with it they would only have everything. Why give them the whole pot?

On the floor near my hand there was a circular. I picked it up and looked at it. "BIG SALE AT BERNER'S DRUGSTORE." I turned it over. The back was blank. I reached in my pocket for the pencil.

The words took shape on the paper, in pencil and blood:

Dear Mamma—The money is for the store. Don't let him throw it away again. Love, Danny.

I folded the dough in the paper, got to my feet, and shoved it in the mailbox. For once I was glad the government had made the landlord put in new mailboxes, because the old ones were broken and anybody could open them. Mamma would find it there tomorrow morning when she came down for the mail.

The car was still standing out in the street, its motor purring. I brushed off my trousers. There was a dull sick feeling in my stomach as I slowly went down the steps. I turned my back on the car deliberately and started walking away. Halfway up the block I heard its gears shift and the sound of its tires rolling away from the curb. Fighting an impulse to run, I glanced back over my shoulder. The car was swerving across the street toward me.

The impulse to run grew stronger. I checked it. To hell with them! I stopped and turned to face the oncoming car. Tears were running freely down my cheeks and a freezing fear had turned my body into ice. I swallowed desperately, trying to choke back the nausea that was rising from my belly.

I moved a few steps back. My fingers felt the cold metal of a lamp-post and I sagged weakly against it. Already I could taste the bitterness of the vomit that was creeping into my mouth, and a million crazy thoughts leapt frantically through my mind.

When did you grow up, Danny Fisher?

There is a time in everyone's life when he has to answer that question. There in the cold black night of morning I found the answer.

I was afraid to die. And there, while that shapeless fear ran through my body, turning my stomach into crawling rebellion, my kidneys into a freezing lump, and my bladder into a leaking, uncontrollable faucet—I suddenly grew up.

I grew up with the knowledge that I was not immortal; that I was made of flesh that would rot and decay into dirt, and blood that would turn black in my veins when I died. Then it was that I knew I would have to face my judgment day. That my mother and father were only the mechanics of my creation and not the trustees of my soul. I was the accident of their creation.

I was alone and in a lonely world of my own. In that world I would die and no one would ever remember my name. Death would descend on me, dirt would cover me, and I would be no more.

My legs had turned to watery jelly, and despite my frantic grip on the lamp-post I sank to my knees on the sidewalk. I shut my eyes tightly, the lids squeezing out the tears from under them, as the car pulled to a stop. I heard its door open and footsteps ringing hollowly on the pavement as they hurried toward me.

I turned my face to the post and buried it in the crook of my arm. I could feel my lower lip turning into blood beneath my teeth. I began to pray. Not for life, but for death. Death to be kind and to come and take from me this terror I could not live with.

There was a soft hand on my arm, a voice was whispering in my ear. "Danny!"

I tried to bury my face deeper in my arms. A cry of fear stifled in my throat. Death's voice was gentle like a woman's, but it was so only to torture me.

The voice was insistent. "Danny!" it repeated. "I've been waiting for you. You got to get away!"

This was not the voice of death. It was a woman's voice filled with warmth and sympathy. It was a voice of life. Slowly, scarcely daring to look, I raised my head.

Her face was white in the glow of the street lamp. "I've come to warn you," she whispered quickly. "Max has got Spit and the Collector out looking for you!"

I stared at her for a moment as the words sank into my mind. Then I couldn't help it. It was Sarah called Ronnie. I began to laugh weakly, hysterically. I was still safe!

She stared at me as if I had suddenly gone mad. Her hands shook my shoulder. "You gotta hide," she whispered insistently. "They're liable to be here any minute!"

I looked up at her, the tears still running down my face. I stopped my laughter and held my hands toward her. "Help me up," I asked her, the words coming huskily from my burning throat. "They won't come."

Her arm was under my shoulder and she was lifting me to my feet. "What do you mean they won't come?" she asked.

I was standing now. Suddenly her hand came out from under me. I sagged against the post as she stared at it "You're bleeding!" she cried.

I nodded. "They caught up with me already."

A frightened look came to her face. "What happened?" she breathed.

"What happened?" I rasped. I began to laugh again. "I don't know what happened. I left them in the alley. I think Spit is dead. Maybe the Collector is too. The whole thing's very funny. They came to kill me and instead I killed them!"

The laughter gurgled in my throat as I leaned my head back against the post and closed my eyes. It was a hell of a joke on Maxie Fields.

Her hand pulled at my arm. I stumbled forward and almost fell. "You gotta get away! Fields will kill you when he finds out!"

I stared at her, still smiling. "Where can I go?" I asked. "There's no place to go. Even my father won't let me in the house."

Her eyes were staring into mine. "No place to go?" she asked.

I shook my head. "No place." I began to slide toward the sidewalk again.

Suddenly her arms were around me and she was dragging me toward the car. I followed her numbly. She opened the door and I stumbled into the back seat. The door closed and she got in behind the wheel. I felt the car begin to move beneath me. I turned my face to the seat and closed my eyes.

Once when I opened them we were on a bridge. It looked like the Manhattan Bridge, but I was too tired to see and closed my eyes again. I turned uncomfortably. I was beginning to get very warm.

She was pulling at my arm again. I woke up. There was a smell of salt air in my nostrils. I stumbled from the car wearily, my eyes trying to focus. We were parked on a dark street. A few feet from us I could see a boardwalk, and beneath it the sand was white. From beyond the beach I could hear the rolling sound of the ocean. She was leading me toward a small building just beneath the boardwalk. There was a sign on it:

BEN'S PLACE SODA HOT DOGS HAMBURGERS
CANDY

"Where are we?" I asked.

Her eyes flicked at my face. "Coney Island," she answered briefly.

She led me around behind the building to a small bungalow. I was weaving back and forth and she kept an arm around me as she knocked at the door. "Ben! Wake up!" she called softly.

A light flickered on inside the bungalow. There was a tapping sound. Then a voice came through the closed door, a man's voice, heavy and husky from sleep: "Who is it?"

"Sarah," she replied. "Hurry up, Ben, open up!"

The door swung open quickly and the light poured out on us. A man was standing there, a smile on his face. "Sarah!" he exclaimed. "I didn't expect you back so soon!" The smile left his face as soon as he saw me. "Sarah, what's this?"

"Let us in," she said, helping me over the doorway.

Silently the man stood aside. There was a small cot against the wall and she helped me to it. I sank back on it gratefully. She turned to the man. "Get some hot water," she said quickly.

I stared at her and then at him. As he started to move across the room, there was a tapping sound. From the bottom of his pajama leg protruded a stump of wood. I looked up wonderingly as he turned. One sleeve was pinned to his side. I closed my eyes. I was dreaming. When I opened them again, they were still there, Sarah and the man with one arm and one leg.

"He's hurt, Ben," she said. "We got to get some hot water and clean him up."

I pulled myself to my feet. I was very warm. The room seemed to blur in front of my eyes. The man kept it so warm in here. "I'm all right," I said. "Don't bother. I'm all right."

Suddenly the room began to spin in front of me. They were both standing on their heads. I couldn't figure it out. Maybe I hadn't got out of the alley at all. There was a ray of light way down in the corner.

"Papa! Let me in!" I cried, and pitched headlong into the light. I went through it as easily as fish through water and came out into the darkness on the other side.

All the Days of My Life

THE THIRD BOOK

CHAPTER ONE

THE JULY SUN WAS CLIMBING OUT OF THE WATER, ITS GOLDEN-RED RAYS capping the waves with a freshly laundered look as I came out from under the boardwalk. The sand beneath my feet was white and clean. Later in the day it would grow dirty and strewn with litter, but now it was fresh and cool and I liked the feel of it.

The boardwalk was deserted. Two hours from now the first of the crowd would be coming. I took a deep breath of the fresh morning air and trotted down to the water. This was the only time of the day for a swim. You had the whole Atlantic Ocean for yourself.

I dropped the towel from around my shoulders and looked down at myself. There was only a faint white scar line left along my arm where Spit had caught me. The rest was all gone, lost in the almost black tan that covered my body. I was sure lucky.

I knifed into the water and began to swim briskly toward the far pole. The bitter-sweet taste of the salt water was in my mouth and nose. It was brisk and invigorating. The beach seemed far away and small. I turned over on my back and began to float. It was almost as if I were in a world all my own.

It was hard to believe that it was almost two months since the night Sarah had brought me out here. That night had not really happened to me, it had happened to someone else living in my body, a kid with my name. But it was all behind me now. Sarah had christened me with a new name as she dipped the cotton in the warm water and washed away the dirt and crusted blood from my cut arm and side.

Danny White. That was the name she had given me as she introduced me to her brother. I smiled as I thought about it. At first I had been too weak to protest, but when I saw the papers the next day and my name under the Gloves pictures, I had been glad. The less her brother or anyone knew about me, the better off I was.

We had scanned the paper eagerly for word of what happened to Spit and the Collector. There was nothing in it. We had exchanged curious glances, but didn't dare speak until later in the afternoon when Ben went out to get something to eat.

"D'yuh think they found 'em yet?" I had asked.

She shook her head, a worried look on her face "I don't know," she answered. "I'll know more when I go back tonight."

"You're going back?" I asked incredulously.

"I have to," she answered quietly. "If I don't show up, then Maxie'll know something is wrong and come looking for me. It's the only way we have of keeping safe."

I tried to sit up in the small bed, but I was too weak and fell back against the pillows. "I'll get out of here," I muttered. "I'll bring yuh nothin' but trouble."

She looked at me curiously. "Where will you go?"

"I don't know," I answered. "I'll find some place. I can't stay here. Sooner or later they'll get wise. Then you'll get it too."

She leaned forward and her hand stroked my cheek lightly. "You'll stay here, Danny," she said quietly. "You'll stay here and work with Ben. He needs help and can't work the place by himself."

"But what if someone recognizes me?" I asked.

"No one will recognize you," she said surely. "Coney Island is a big place. Over a million and a half people come down here in the summer, and a crowd is the best place for you to hide. They'd never suspect your being down here anyway."

I stared at her. What she had said had made sense. "But what about you?" I asked. "He'll want to know where you were last night. What'll you tell him?"

"Nothing," she said flatly. "The hired help is entitled to a day off. If he asks me what I did, I'll tell him I went to visit my brother. He knows I do that every week."

It was my turn to be curious. "Does your brother know about Maxie?"

She nodded her head, her eyes looking away from me. "He thinks that I'm Maxie's personal secretary. Before that he thinks I worked as a model." She turned back to me, a pleading look in her eyes. "After his accident five years ago and he found out that his arm and leg were gone, he wanted to die. He felt there was no work left for him to do and that he would always be a burden to me. We are all the family we have. That was the year I graduated from high school. I told him not to worry, that I would work and support him until he was well enough to work again. The way he supported me after my father had died. I would go out and get a job."

She turned a mirthless smile toward me. "I was a kid then. I didn't know how much money we would need for medicine and doctors, I didn't know how little they paid stenographers and typists. The fifteen dollars a week couldn't cover even a small part of our expenses. My first job was with a vaudeville booking agent. I learned quickly, and a few weeks later when I went to the boss and asked for a raise, he just laughed at me. I didn't understand him and asked what he was laughing at.

" 'You're a bright kid,' he said, 'but I can't afford to pay you any more.'

" 'But I need more money,' I cried.

"He stood there a moment, then walked around his desk. 'If you're really that hard up,' he said, 'I can put you in the way of some real sugar.'

" 'How?' I asked; 'I'll do anything. I need the money!'

" 'There's a party going on tonight,' he told me. 'Some friends came into town and they asked me to send up some girls for the evening. They pay twenty bucks.'

"I stared at him. I don't suppose I really knew what he meant, but the twenty dollars was a lot of money, so I went to the party. I had never seen anything like it and was just about to leave when my boss came in and saw me standing stiffly against the wall. He smiled at me understandingly and brought me a drink. It made me feel good and relaxed, so I had a few more. Then I remembered going into a room with him.

"In the morning when I woke up, I was alone in a strange room and had a terrible headache. I staggered blindly out of bed looking for my clothes. They were on a chair with a white note pinned onto them: 'You can come in a little late today,' it read. Beneath the note was a twenty-dollar bill. I was a professional now. I stared at myself in the mirror. There was no change on my face that anyone could see, there was no scarlet letter on my forehead. Nothing had changed but the fact that I had found a way to make twenty dollars when I needed it. And as time wore on, I came to need it very often."

She got to her feet and looked down at me. Her face was impassive, her voice flat and emotionless. "And that is how it was. I worked and paid the doctor's bills and for medicine but it wasn't until I met Maxie Fields at a party and he liked me that I could get enough money together to fix this place up for Ben."

I didn't know what to say. My mouth was dry and I wanted a cigarette. I reached for a pack near the bed. She guessed what I wanted, our hands met on the cigarette package. I held hers and her eyes stared somberly down into mine.

"That's the way it was until the night you stayed because I asked you. Because you didn't want Maxie to think I had failed him, because you didn't want him to hurt me. Never for love, always for money. Never for myself. Always for money. Until that night. Then suddenly I realized what I had traded away. But it was too late. I had already set the price and I couldn't back out of the sale now."

She let go of my hand and held a cigarette toward me. I put it in my mouth and she lit it for me.

"You have to go back, Sarah?" I asked.

"I have to go back," she answered tonelessly. She smiled vaguely at me. "It almost seems funny to hear you call me Sarah. It's been so long since anyone but Ben called me that."

"You got no other name that I can remember," I said.

The somber look vanished from her face. "Danny," she said, a nice look coming into her eyes, "let's keep it like that between us—always. Let's be friends."

I took her hand. "We are friends, Sarah," I said quietly.

Then Ben had come back with a container of hot broth. I had some and dozed off. When I woke up again, she had gone and Ben was sitting looking at me.

"She's gone?" I asked, my eyes looking around the small room.

He nodded. "Her boss, Mr. Fields, expected her back this afternoon. He keeps her pretty busy."

I agreed with him. "He's an important man."

He hesitated a moment, then cleared his throat. "She says you want to work here this summer."

I nodded.

"I can't afford to pay very much," he half apologized. "I don't know yet how we'll make out."

"Let's not worry about the dough," I said. "It ain't what you can pay me that's important. It's what I can repay the both of you that counts."

He had grinned suddenly and held out his hand. "We'll get along, Danny," he had said.

And we had. For almost two months now. Sarah would be down to see us once a week and things began to work out all right. Business had been just fair, but Ben made expenses and was happy with that. I was happy too, because I was out of Fields's reach.

When Sarah had come down the next week, I was already back to normal. Outside the soreness in my arm I could get around all right. The first thing I had asked her when we found a moment alone was about Spit and the Collector. Nothing had appeared in the papers all that week.

They were in the private hospital of some medic that Fields knew. The Collector had a broken jaw from my kick, and Spit had nine stitches taken in his side where his knife had gone into him. Another inch and a half and he would have croaked; it would have reached his heart. In a way I was glad. I wouldn't have wanted a rap like that hanging over me.

Fields had been really burned. He had sworn that he would get me and that when he did I would be sorry. Before that night was over he had had the neighborhood gone through with a fine-tooth comb, looking for me. After a week he was still raging.

Then as the weeks went by, Sarah told me, he spoke less and less about me. Fields was convinced that I had lammed it out of town with the dough. I was happy to let him think so.

Many times I had wanted to ask Sarah if she could find out anything about Nellie and my family, but I didn't dare. I didn't even try to write them because for a long time Fields had kept a watch on them, according to Sarah. I wondered if Papa got the store with the money, if Mimi was working, how Mamma was and if they missed me and were sorry that I was gone. At night I would lie on my small cot and think about them. Sometimes when I closed my eyes I could imagine I was home again and Mamma was cooking supper and the house would be heavy with the odor of chicken soup. Then Papa would come home and a bitterness would rise in me. I would open my eyes and they would be gone.

Then I thought about Nellie. Her face would be clear before me in the night, smiling at me, her dark eyes warm with tenderness and love. I wondered if she understood, if she guessed why I had gone away. I wondered if she remembered what I had told her: "No matter what happens, remember that I love you." She would nod her head at me in the dark and I could almost hear her whispered answer: "I remember, Danny."

Then I would close my eyes tightly and the sound of Ben's snores would lull me to sleep. In the morning the sun would be shining brightly in my eyes when I woke up.

Like it was shining in my eyes now as I floated face-upwards in the water. My body felt lightly buoyant in the water and I paddled gently. The waves slipped easily past me.

"Danny!" The familiar voice came toward me from the beach.

I got a mouthful of water as I spun around toward it. Sarah was standing on the beach waving at me. I waved at her, smiling as I swam back to the shore.

CHAPTER TWO

S HE HAD FOUND MY TOWEL AND WAS DROPPING HER TERRY-CLOTH ROBE beside it by the time I reached her. I grinned at her. "What are you doing down here?" I asked. "We didn't expect you until the day after tomorrow."

"Maxie had to go out of town," she explained. "I have the whole week-end to myself."

I was curious. "What happened?"

She was tucking her hair under a bathing cap. "How do I know?" She shrugged. "It's none of my business. All I care about is that I can spend a week-end down here with you."

The meaning of her words didn't reach me until we were in the water again. She hadn't said anything about Ben. Just me. I turned my face in the water and looked at her. She wasn't a bad swimmer for a girl. She had a pretty good beat crawl stroke, which moved her through the water easily.

"Did yuh see Ben?" I called to her.

"Yeah," she replied. "He told me you were out here." She stopped swimming and treaded water. "The water is wonderful," she cried. "I'm all out of breath."

I swam over to her and put my arms under her shoulders. "Rest a minute," I said. "You'll get it back."

She weighed nothing in the water. I could feel the firmness of her body as the waves pushed us back and forth. A familiar warmth began to rise in me. Quickly I let her go.

She turned in the water and looked at me. She had felt it too. "Why did you let me go, Danny?" she asked.

"The waves were getting too much for me," I explained awkwardly.

She shook her head. "What's the reason, Danny? Don't kid me."

I stared at her. Her face was small and cute under her yellow cap, her eyes fresh and young as if the water had swept away everything she had ever known, all the hurt, all the knowledge. There was no use trying to hide anything from her. You don't hold out on a friend.

"I'm making it easy on myself," I said frankly.

"How?" she persisted.

I stared at her. "I'm not a machine," I said, "and you're beautiful."

I could see she was pleased. "Nothing else?" she asked.

"What else could there be?" I was puzzled.

She hesitated a moment. "What I am?" she asked slowly.

I shook my head emphatically. "You're my friend," I said. "Nothing else matters."

Her hands were on my arms and she was holding onto me in the water, her eyes scanning my face. "Sure, Danny?"

I nodded. "Sure." I took a deep breath. "I just don't want to louse things up, that's all."

She looked down at the water. "And if you kissed me, you think that might louse things up, is that it, Danny?"

"It might."

Her eyes turned up to mine. "Because you're in love with someone else, Danny?"

I nodded silently.

A curious hurt came into her eyes. "But how do you know if you don't even try, Danny?" she asked. "There are many kinds of love that you may not even know about."

Her lips were moving tremulously. There was a shining moisture in her eyes that hadn't entirely come from the salt water. I pulled her closer to me and kissed her. Her mouth was soft and tasted from the salt and yet was sweet and warm. She closed her eyes when I kissed her and she was limp against me. I looked down into her face.

She turned her head away and looked out into the sea. I bent my head to hear what she was saying, her voice was so low. "I know you can never love me the way you love her, Danny, and that is the way it should be. But there is something for us that we have to give each other. Maybe it's not very much or for a very long time, but for whatever it is or as long as it lasts let's make it important."

I didn't answer. There was nothing to answer.

She turned her face up to me. She looked very young. "Remember what I told you, Danny? It was: 'Never for love, always for money. Never for myself.' For once I want it to be different, for once I want it to be for me. For what I want, not for what I'm paid."

I pressed my mouth gently to her lips. "It will be as you want it to be, Sarah," I said softly. One thing I had already learned: you don't pay off friends by telling them that you haven't got for them what they want from you. And if they are willing to accept a reasonable facsimile for the real thing, you're not fooling them; they're fooling themselves.

Sarah had to find a way to repay herself for many things, and I was it.

She was drying my back with the towel. "I didn't realize it until just now,", she said, "but you're almost black and your hair is burned white from the sun. Nobody would recognize you now."

I grinned over my shoulder. "You recognized me."

"I knew where to find you," she said quickly. A puzzled expression crossed her face. " 'That reminds me. Do you know Sam Gottkin, the concessionaire?"

"Yeah," I answered. "What about him?"

She looked up into my face. "He was down to see Maxie about you the other day"

"What did he want?" I asked quickly.

"He wanted to know where you were. There was an Italian boy with him. Zep, I think his name was. You know him?"

I nodded. "He's my girl's brother. How'd they get to Maxie?"

"They had heard that Maxie was looking all over for you the night of the fight, so they came down to find out why. Sam and Maxie are old friends. Sam said he didn't know you were gone until your sister came up to see him. Why would she do that?"

"I worked for Sam before," I explained quickly. "Besides, Sam was all set to manage me when I turned pro. What did they say?"

"Maxie told them what he knew. That was nothing."

"Did he tell them why he was looking for me?" I asked.

She nodded her head. "Sam flew into a rage at that. He told Maxie that he should have kept his hands off you. He called him all kinds of names."

I looked at her wonderingly. "Maxie took it?"

"Not entirely," she answered. "Maxie felt that Sam should have given him a piece of you since you came out of Maxie's territory. They had a big argument then. Maxie said when he caught up with you, you'd be taken care of. Sam said that he should do nothing until he let him know first, that he had a score of his own to square."

I stared at her. That really did it. There was nobody I could depend on now. "Did Maxie agree to that?" I asked.

"He agreed to it then," she answered, "because afterwards they all sat down and had a few drinks and talked business. Then Sam called your sister and made a date for that night and he left. When he had gone, Maxie stamped up and down the room and swore that if he found you, Sam would never know about it until afterwards."

That was about what I expected from him. He wouldn't act any other way. Her next question really caught me by surprise.

"Is your sister engaged to Sam Gottkin?"

My mouth hung open. "Why do you ask that?" I stammered.

"Because one of the reasons Sam gave Maxie that he didn't want you touched until he saw you was that you are his fiancée's brother, and if anything happened to you it might queer all his plans." Her voice was curious. "Didn't you know that?"

I shook my head slowly. "Uh-uh. I didn't even know they had met." I wondered how that happened. It seemed stranger than anything else I had heard. Sam and Mimi—somehow I couldn't believe that.

A voice called to us from under the boardwalk. Ben was standing there beckoning to us. "Hey!" he shouted. "Aren't you ever coming back to work? What do you think this is—Christmas?"

CHAPTER THREE

I WAS SEATED BELOW THE COUNTER, BAGGING PEANUTS. BEN BEGAN TO swear. I looked up at him, surprised at his vehemence. "Goddam them kids!" he swore.

"What's the matter?" Sarah asked.

He turned to her, his good arm waving at the beach. "A customer was coming over here, but one of them damn kids got to him first. It's a wonder we can make a livin' at all with those kids around."

Sarah's voice was tolerant. "Take it easy," she told him soothingly. "It doesn't help getting all excited over it."

Ben's voice was angry. "But we're shellin' out good dough for this concession, and those kids are ruinin' it. They don't pay nothin' for takin' out boxes of ice cream and peddlin' them on the beach. There oughta be a way of stoppin' them."

"The cops chase them when they see them," Sarah said.

"But most of the time they're too busy watchin' the dames to even bother," Ben replied heatedly.

"All the same," she said, "I wouldn't want to spend a day out in that sun and hot sand peddling a carton of ice cream just to pick up a few bucks."

He stamped away from her voicelessly, his wooden leg dragging along the floor into the back room.

I got to my feet wearily and stretched. "He sounded mad," I said.

Her eyes were troubled. "He has a right to be," she answered. "This place was his big dream and he wants to make a go of it. The way things are going, he'll just clear expenses for the summer. He won't make enough to carry him through the winter. That means he'll have to come to me for money again. He doesn't like that. He's a pretty independent guy."

I didn't answer her and began to stack the peanuts up on the counter. I guess she was right. I knew how he felt. There were four of them out there on the beach right now that I could count. I could hear their hawking cries floating back toward us on the breeze.

"Hot knishes!"

"Dixie cups!"

"Fudgie-wudgies! Popsicles!"

They were mostly youngsters. Seemed like nice kids too. I had spoken to several of them from time to time. Most of them were lucky to earn more than a buck a day, because the dealers they bought their stuff from robbed them. The guy who came along and gave those kids a really square shake could clean up a fortune. There were hundreds of them on the beach.

Suddenly I was excited. What a fool I had been not to see it before! That was the only thing I had learned from Sam up in the country. Sam made a buck from his concessions up there because he cut his boys in for a fair shake. Why couldn't Ben do the same thing down here?

I turned to Sarah. She and Ben were standing at the register looking out on the beach. I tapped him on the shoulder and he turned around "The kids'll work for you same as anyone else," I said.

He looked confused. "What kids? What are you talking about?"

I jerked a thumb at the beach. "The kids out there. Why don't you take them in?"

"Don't be a jerk," he snorted. "I ain't got the time to be chasin' after them to collect what they owe."

"You don't have to chase 'em," I said. "They pay in advance for their stuff."

"Half only," he pointed out. "The rest you have to hustle 'em for. Besides, why should they do business with me? They can get the same thing from any-body."

"There must be a way to get around that," I said. "Supposin' we don't take any dough in advance? What if they left us somethin' for a deposit? Like a watch, or a bike? Then they wouldn't have to lay out any dough an' they'd come to us."

"Forget it," Ben said disgustedly. He picked up a rag and began to wipe the counter. "Besides, we haven't the room to handle them."

Sarah's voice made him look up. "You got all that room in the back that isn't being used," she said. "You could put a cold locker in there."

"But, Sarah," he protested, "where'll we get the time? I just can't go out and get the kids to come in here just because I say so."

"I'll get the kids for you," I said quickly. "I'll get all the kids you want."

She looked up at me, then turned challengingly to her brother. "Well?" she asked.

He hesitated a moment, not answering.

She smiled slowly at him. "What's the matter, Ben?" she asked. "You always said you wanted to make a real buck. This is the first good shot you can get at it. Or don't you like money any more?"

An embarrassed grin began to spread over his face. He turned gratefully toward me. "Okay, Danny," he said, "we'll try it. Sometimes I forget I don't have to do things by myself any more."

I checked my watch. It was almost dusk. Time enough for all the kids who were going to be there to have shown up. For the past hour I had been sitting on a bench watching a steady stream of boys disappear beneath the boardwalk below me.

I lit a cigarette, got up, and went down the stone steps leading to the beach. The hum of conversation came to my ears as I ducked under the boardwalk, and I smiled to myself. I had been right. The quickest way to get to a gang of kids was to find their crap game.

About twenty of them were playing on a strip of concrete just behind the rest rooms. Only a few seemed to be about my age and height, most of them were smaller. I pushed through them to the inner ring of the circle. One of the kids was getting ready to shoot. There was a lot of silver lying on the concrete around him. Casually I dropped a five-dollar bill on the concrete slab.

"I'll cover every bet," I announced.

All faces turned toward me. I watched them closely. There was no animosity in them, only curiosity. So far, so good. No trouble. It was just that a fin was a lot of bucks to these kids.

The boy with the dice in his hand rose to his feet. "Who are you?" he asked, mild resentment in his voice.

I smiled at him, my cigarette dangling loosely from my lips. "A sucker for the dice," I replied easily.

He stared at me for a moment, then at the others. Turning back to me, he said politely: "Pick up yer dough, mister. We can't go that high."

I knelt and picked up the fin, looking up at him from the ground. "What's your ceiling?"

"A cuter," he answered.

I stuck my hands in my pocket and came out with a fistful of change. "Roll 'em," I said. "I'm no snob."

He knelt again and the dice came tumbling from his hand. They hit the wall sharply and rolled to a stop. "Natural!" he breathed. His hand reached out and picked up some of the change before him.

I made a few bets and began to talk to the boy next to me. "You hustlin' the beach?" I asked.

The boy nodded, his attention on the dice.

"Makin' any dough?" I went on in a friendly voice.

He turned and looked at me. "You jokin'?" he asked.

I shook my head. "I'm not jokin'," I replied seriously. "I know there's a lot of dough in it an' I was wonderin' whether you guys got any of it."

"What are you talkin' about?" the boy asked. "All we get is twenty cents on the buck, an' we're lucky if we come out with six bits a day."

I stared at him. This was even better than I had thought. "You guys are bein' taken," I said flatly. "The Rockaways are payin' forty on the buck, and no advance dough either."

He scoffed at me. "Maybe there they do, but not on the Island."

"I know a place they do," I said quickly, my eyes on his face. "And they're lookin' for hustlers too."

He was interested. He watched me, the crap game momentarily forgotten. "Where?" he asked.

"D'yuh think your friends would be interested?" I asked evading a direct answer.

He grinned at me. "Who ain't interested in dough?" He turned from me to the crowd of boys. "Hey, fellas," he called, "this new guy here says he's got a place that pays forty on the dollar and no dough in advance."

That was the end of the crap game as they crowded around me. They were all talking at once.

I held up my hand to quiet them. "If you guys will show up at Ben Dorfman's tomorrow morning, I got twenty-five boxes for yuh to take out." I looked around, counting the heads quickly. There were about twenty of them. "Bring your friends too," I added quickly. I wanted to get all the boxes out. That way, I figured, at least enough boys would show up to put all the boxes in use.

I was only wrong about one thing. The next morning almost fifty boys showed up, and by the end of the week there were one hundred and fifty boys hustling for us.

CHAPTER FOUR

THE BATTERED OLD ALARM CLOCK ON THE SHELF READ ELEVEN WHEN Ben looked up from the table. The light from the solitary bulb glowing overhead cast weary shadows on his face. He pushed the small amount of change remaining on the table toward his sister. "Here, Sarah," he said in a tired voice, "You count the rest of it. I'm dead."

Silently she began to run the silver through her fingers and he turned to me. "What a week!" he said exhaustedly. "I never been so tired on a Sunday night before. Those kids knock hell outta you."

I smiled. "I told yuh, Pops. I figure we grossed about eight hundred bucks since we started Thursday morning. The full week oughtta be good for twelve hundred. That's four C's clear."

He nodded his head, faintly smiling. "You were right, kid," he admitted. "I gotta hand it to yuh."

Sarah finished rolling the change into small paper wrappers. She stood up. "I never saw so much change in my life," she said.

Ben looked at her meaningfully. She nodded to him and he turned back to me. "Me an' Sarah want you to know we appreciate this, Danny. You done a lot for me, an' from now on you get twenty-five per cent of the hustlers' take."

I stared at him in surprise. A lump came up in my throat. I'd never figured on anything that good. I stared helplessly at them. I couldn't speak.

He spoke quickly. "What's wrong, Danny? Ain't that enough?"

Finally I managed to shake my head and smile. "I—I didn't expect that, Ben. I just don't know how to thank you."

"Don't thank me, kid," he said. "It's Sarah here. She thought it's only fair that you should drag down a piece because if it weren't for you we would have none of it."

Sarah was smiling gently at me from the shadow just beyond the table. "It's only right," she said.

Our eyes met. I didn't speak. There are some things you just can't say, some feelings you just can't find a voice for. I owed her a lot. If it wasn't for what she'd done I might not even be around right now.

Ben's voice interrupted my thoughts. "I wish there was a hot bath in this place. I sure could use one and then a real bed to sleep on instead of this damn old cot."

Sarah looked at him. "Why don't the both of you come down to the hotel with me? We can afford it now. You can get a room and a bath there and spend the night in comfort."

"That's the best idea I heard all night," Ben said enthusiastically. He turned to me. "What do you say, kid?"

I shook my head. The Half Moon Hotel was too big a place. It drew a big crowd from all over the city. I was better off staying back here. "No, Ben," I said quickly, "you go with Sarah. One of us better stay down here to keep an eye on things."

He looked at me doubtfully, then at Sarah. "What do you think?" he asked.

She glanced at me and I shook my head slightly. She caught on quick. "I think Danny has the right idea," she said slowly. "You come along with me, Ben. Danny will watch the place."

The door closed behind them and then I went back to the cot and stretched out. I lit a cigarette and reached up over the cot and turned the switch. The glow of my cigarette was the only light in the room.

I was tired. I could just feel it now, stealing in weary waves up from my aching legs. I wished I could go with them. The hot bath sounded like home to me. But I couldn't afford the chance. If Sarah stayed down there, maybe someone else who knew me would show up in the hotel too. At least down here I knew I was safe.

I ground my cigarette out on the floor beneath the cot and put my hands behind my head, staring up through the darkness. I could hear sound of footsteps on the boardwalk over the concession. People were always walking up there. It was a monotonous, muffled sort of wooden sound and after a while seemed to keep time with the beating of your heart.

How strange it all was! Even now I found it hard to believe. I'd been away from home almost two months. I wondered if the family ever thought about me. I guessed Mamma did, but I didn't know about the rest of them. Papa would be too stubborn ever to admit to himself that he did.

I turned my face into my arms and closed my eyes. The muffled beat of the boardwalk ran into my body and loosened the tension in me. I dozed.

There was a knock on the door. I bolted upright in the dark and flipped on the light-switch. By the clock it was almost one in the morning.

The knock came on the door again and I got out of bed, rubbing my eyes sleepily as I walked to the door. I hadn't meant to fall asleep. I had just wanted to rest a little while and then go out for a bite.

"Who is it?" I called.

"Sarah," came the answer.

I opened the door and looked out. "What are you doing back here?" I asked in surprise.

Her face was luminous in the glow from the boardwalk. "I couldn't sleep," she answered, "so I went out for a walk and passed here. I wondered whether you were still awake."

I stepped back from the doorway. "I was just grabbing a nap before going out for a bite."

She came into the bungalow and I closed the door behind her. "Did Ben get his bath?" I asked.

She nodded. "And went right to sleep. He's very happy—the happiest I can remember since his accident."

"I'm glad," I said, going back to the cot and sitting down.

She sat in a small chair opposite me. "Got a cigarette?" she asked.

I fished a pack out of my pocket and tossed it to her. She caught it and took one out. "Match?" she asked.

I got up and lit her cigarette for her, then went back and sat down. She smoked silently while I watched her. At last she spoke again. "How old are you, Danny?"

"Eighteen," I said, stretching it a little.

She was silent again, her eyes blue and thoughtful. Her cigarette burned down to her fingers and she tamped it out in a plate on the table next to her. "I've got to go back tomorrow," she said slowly.

I nodded. "I know."

Her lips tightened. "I wish I didn't have to go, but he'll be back."

I watched her silently.

She stood up, almost startling me by the violence of her movement. "I hate him, I hate him," she said bitterly. "I wish I'd never seen him!"

I tried to make a joke out of it. "Me too."

There was a hurt, frightened look on her face. "What do you know about him?" she asked in a harsh voice. "What can you know about him? He's never done to you what he's done to me. He couldn't. You're a man, not a woman. All he can do is hurt or kill you. He can't do to you what he's done to me!"

The quiet sound of her tears filled the small room. I walked over to her slowly, put my arms around her shoulders, and pulled her head down against my chest.

My touch brought a fresh paroxysm of tears.

"The things he's done to me, Danny!" she cried, her voice almost muffled against my shirt. "The things he's made me do! Nobody can ever know, nobody would ever believe it. There's a perverted madness in him that you can't see. I'm so frightened to go back, I'm so afraid of him, of what he'll do to me!"

I held her shaking shoulders firmly. "Then don't go back, Sarah," I said softly. "Ben's doing all right now. You don't have to go back."

Her wide tortured eyes stared up at me. "I must go, Danny," she whispered. "I have to. If I don't, he'll come after me. I can't let him do that. Then Ben will know everything."

There was nothing I could say about that. She was crying again. I brushed my hand over her soft hair and pressed my lips against it. "Some day, Sarah," I said in a low voice, "you won't have to go back."

She turned her face swiftly and her lips pressed against mine. They clung to me with frantic desperation. Her eyes were closed tightly, the last tear hanging perilously on the fringe of her lashes. I held my breath a moment. So many things were wrong. Still, there was so much I owed her, I could never hope to pay her back. With my little finger I brushed the last tear from her eye.

Her mouth opened slightly and I could feel our breaths intermingling. The warm perfume of her came up to my nostrils. She turned her face slightly, her eyes still closed, and a cry escaped her lips. "Danny!"

I pressed my mouth harder against hers and a heat began to rise up in me. It seemed to come in heavy pulsing waves, spreading in a slow circle through my body like the ripples on the surface of water when a stone is thrown into it. Her breasts were firm, the muscles of her thighs were tense and trembling as she clung to me. "Danny!" Her voice was happy in my ear. "Danny, I can't stand on my feet!"

Quietly we moved toward the cot. I knelt beside her as her clothes fell about her, and pressed my lips to the warm soft parts of her. Then we lay together and there was only the closeness of our bodies and the excitement of our flesh.

She was agile, expert, and proficient. And yet with all the knowledge that I knew was in her, there was something about her that made me understand. And for that understanding I loved her.

It was Sarah with whom I shared my cot that night. Not Ronnie.

CHAPTER FIVE

I SNAPPED THE LOCK ON THE ICE-CREAM LOCKER AND PULLED ON IT. IT gripped tight. Satisfied, I left the back room and went into the concession. Ben was just putting down the shutters. I gave him a hand.

"Christ, what a day!" he swore, the beads of sweat running down his cheeks. "The night isn't goin' to be any better either."

I grinned at him. "I guess not." The crowds up on the board-walk were moving along slowly, searching vainly for a breath of cool air.

"It ain't goin' to do them much good comin' down here," he said. "When it's hot like this, it's hot all over."

I nodded. There wasn't even a bit of breeze coming in from the water.

Ben snapped his fingers sharply. "That reminds me, Danny," he said quickly. "Mike was looking for you. I think he wants you to help him tonight." Mike ran the Wheel of Chance concession on the boardwalk almost over our place.

"Pete drunk again?" I asked. Pete was Mike's brother. He worked the place with him except when he was on a jag. Several times before, I had given Mike a lift when that happened.

"I don't know," Ben replied. "He didn't say. He only asked for you to come up when you got through."

"Okay," I said. "I'll go up and see what he wants." I left Ben to finish closing and walked up the ramp to the boardwalk. I pushed my way through the crowds toward the concession.

Mike was there alone, a disgusted look on his face as he surveyed the crowd. His face brightened when he saw me. "Too tired to give me a hand tonight, Danny?" he called almost before I could reach him. "Pete didn't show up."

I hesitated. I was tired, but it was so hot I knew I wouldn't get any sleep down in the bungalow. Ben had done the smart thing; as soon as he had seen that the business was doing all right he moved into the Half Moon Hotel, high up where it was cool. So I had the bungalow to myself.

"Okay, Mike," I said, ducking under the counter and coming up behind it. "Wheel or spiel tonight?"

He stabbed at his face with a damp handkerchief. "Spiel, if it's all right with you," he answered. "I been buckin' the crowd both ways all day an' can't take it any more."

I nodded my head and tied a change apron around my waist. I picked up a long wooden pointer from under the counter and turned toward the crowd. Mike nodded and I began the pitch, forcing my voice into the harsh metallic cry that would carry over the hum of the crowd.

I got a great kick out of the spiel. I knew it by heart already and had heard it a thousand times, but each time it was like new. I liked being able to kid the crowd into getting rid of their nickels for no real good reason. In many ways all of living was like that. You put your dough down on something you knew sure as hell would never pay off.

"Try the Wheel of Fortune, folks. Only a nickel an' there's a winnuh evvy time she spins. Yuh can't lose, yuh kin only win. Come an' getcha money down. Try yer luck!"

I spotted a young man walking along with his girl hanging on his arm. He hesitated a moment in front of the concession. I stabbed at him with my long pointer. "Hey there, young feller!" I shouted at him so that everybody within two blocks could hear. "I mean you with the pretty girl! You get a free chance! The boss jus' tol' me any feller with a pretty girl gets a free chance for the girl along with his own! Put yer nickel down an' cover two numbers. Two fer the price of one!"

The young man looked at the girl; then, grinning embarrassedly, he stepped up to the counter and put a nickel down on one of the red numbers. I slipped the nickel off quickly and threw down two blue chips.

"There's a wise young man," I announced to the people beginning to gather round the concession. "He knows a bargain when he sees one. He knows a pretty girl too, an' all you folks can be jus' as wise as he is. Bring yer girl up to the Wheel of Chance an' get two chances fer one!"

A few nickels began to tinkle down on the counter. I had them working. I looked back over my shoulder at Mike. He nodded his dark head approvingly and reached up behind him and spun the wheel. I could see his foot catch the stirrup beneath the counter. I knew who was going to win.

"There she goes, folks!" I cried. "Round an' round she goes, an' where she stops nobody knows. Evvybody wins when the Wheel of Fortune spins." I held the long pointer ready to tap the young man's girl when the wheel stopped spinning.

Along about midnight a breeze came up and the crowd began to thin out as they beat it home for their beds. Mike came down the counter toward me. "Let's wrap it up, kid," he smiled. "There's nothin' left in 'em any more tonight."

I slipped off my change apron and handed it to Mike. He emptied it into a bag without counting the change. He pressed a switch at the wheel, and the lights went out all over the concession. Mike's face was gray and tired in the dim boardwalk lights after we had slotted in the removable doors and locked up.

"What a pisser of a day!" he exclaimed exhaustedly.

"I got some coffee downstairs," I said. "Come on."

A slow smile broke across his face. "Okay, Danny. I kin use a cup of coffee 'fore I go home."

I put the coffee on the stove to warm up while Mike sank in a chair wearily. "That's the third time in two weeks I had to call on you," he said.

I smiled silently. Mike was an all-right guy. You didn't mind helping him out because you knew he would come through if you needed him.

His voice rose slightly. "Some day I'm gonna th'ow that damn brother of mine out on his ass! Every Goddam time he gets next to a bottle he turns into a sponge."

I put two cups on the table and poured the coffee into them. It was black and steaming. I pushed some milk into it. "Here," I said, handing a cup to Mike, "drink this. You'll feel better."

He looked at me shrewdly over the rim of the cup. "I'm through foolin', Danny. This time I mean it. I know I swore it many times, but this time it'll stick." He raised the cup to his lips and sipped the coffee. "Soon's I find me a guy I can trust, he's out."

I drank my coffee silently. I'd heard this story many times already, but Mike had always taken his brother back. I dragged on my cigarette, feeling the smoke sharp and tingling in my nose.

Suddenly Mike brought his open hand down on the table in a sharp slap. "I'm a jerk!" he exclaimed. There was such a funny expression on his face as he looked at me.

"What now?" I asked.

"I'm lookin' fer a guy," he said quickly, "an' all the time here he is under my nose." He leaned forward over the table. "How'd you like to come in with me, kid?"

I looked at him in surprise. I hadn't thought about that. But I couldn't do it. "I'd like it, Mike," I said quickly, "but I can't run out on Ben now."

"The season's only got two weeks to run, Danny," he said, "I can manage that. I mean afterwards when I take the wheel south for the winter. You got any plans for then?"

I shook my head. I hadn't made any plans for the winter. I hadn't thought about it at all. But the summer had gone so quickly I just hadn't had time to think about it.

"Then come with me, kid," Mike urged. "We close down here the week after Labor Day, grab a couple weeks' rest, and catch up with Petersen's Tent Shows on October 2nd in Memphis."

"Sounds good to me," I said hesitantly. Suddenly I was homesick. Until now it had been just like many other summers. At the end of it, I suppose, I thought I would go home. But now I knew it was different. I wasn't going any place.

Mike grinned at me knowingly. "You'll like it down there, kid," he said. "The gash jumps like rabbits all through the South."

I smiled back at him, still hesitant. I'd talk it over with Sarah before I made up my mind. Maybe she had some other plans. "Can I let yuh know in a couple of days, Mike?" I asked. "There are a few things I gotta check first."

I waited until we were alone on the next evening she came down before I told her about it. She listened silently all the time I was talking. When I had finished, she lit a cigarette.

"Then you're not going home after the summer's over?" she asked.

I stared at her in surprise. "Did you think I would?" I asked.

She shook her head. "I didn't really think so," she answered slowly. "And yet I thought you might."

"Even if I could go home an' my father would let me in, how long do you think it would be before Maxie Fields found out I was back?" I asked. "Then how long do you think I would last?"

She nodded in agreement. "I guess you can't go back, then." Her eyes met mine. "But what about your girl?" she asked. "Won't you let her know what you're doing? She must be worried stiff over you."

Funny she should remember that. A peculiar lump came into my throat. "There's nothing I can do about that," I said stiffly. "I can't take any chances on anything leaking out."

A distant look came into her eyes. "I guess you might as well go, then," she said.

I walked over to her. "You sound mad," I said. "Is there anything wrong?"

She didn't look up. "Nothing's wrong," she answered, shaking her head. "You go with Mike. You'll get along. You don't need anybody."

I put my hands on her shoulders, dropped them over her breasts and around her waist. "I need you, Sarah," I said.

She spun around quickly in my grasp and broke away from me. "You don't need anybody, Danny," she snapped. "Not even me." Then she stormed out the door without looking back.

I stared after her, wondering what had got into her, and it wasn't until the next morning that I found out from Ben what it was. She was quitting her job with Maxie Fields, he told me, and they were going out west together to open up a little business.

CHAPTER SIX

I MADE UP WITH MIKE TO MEET HIM IN MEMPHIS ON OCTOBER 2ND. WE shook hands on it. He seemed very pleased. "Now my plans are all set," he said, smiling.

Sarah's plans were all set too. She had told Ben to have everything packed and ready to leave the Thursday after Labor Day. She would come down in the car and pick him up that afternoon and they would start out. I didn't have a chance to ask her if she had said anything to Maxie about it, but I knew from the way she spoke that she hadn't.

For some reason or other she kept away from me the few times she came down to the Island. She didn't seem to want to talk to me and I let her alone. I didn't see any sense in getting into an argument with her, and before I knew it the season was over.

Ben had brought everything back to the bungalow from the hotel, and by the time Thursday rolled around he was all packed and ready to go. He was as happy and excited as a kid with an all-day sucker. He could hardly wait until three o'clock, when she was due to pick him up.

"I wish you were going with us, Danny," he called from the front room of the bungalow, where he was seated amid his luggage. "At first Sarah thought you were coming with us. We were disappointed when you told her you were going with Mike."

Then the whole business was suddenly clear in my mind. I was a prize dope. She had meant to ask me to come along with them all the while, but when I had spoken to her about Mike she had changed her mind. I guess she thought that was what I wanted to do.

Before I had a chance to reply there was a knock at the door. I pulled on my trousers hurriedly and buttoned them. I heard Ben's voice as he went to the door. "Sarah must be early."

I heard the door open, then a chill ran through me. "Is Ronnie here?" It was Spit's voice.

My first impulse was to run, but the only way out was through the front door, so I froze against the wall of the room and strained my ears to the door.

Ben's voice sounded confused. "Ronnie? Ronnie who?"

Another heavy voice answered. "Don't crap us, bud. You know who we mean. Fields's girl."

A note of relief came into Ben's voice. "You must mean my sister, Sarah, Mr. Fields's secretary. Come in and wait. She's not here yet."

I heard heavy footsteps come into the bungalow and pressed my eye to the crack in the door. Spit and the Collector were standing in the center of the room. The Collector was laughing.

"Fields's secretary," he haw hawed. "That's a new name for it!"

There was a puzzled look on Ben's face. "Was there something Mr. Fields wanted?" he asked. "I know Sarah wouldn't mind if she had to stay a few extra days to help him out."

The Collector looked at him. "Why?" he asked Ben. "Was she quitting?"

Ben nodded his head. "Didn't Mr. Fields tell you?"

The Collector began to laugh again. "Maxie'll get a big boot outta that. He'll be surprised to find out his babe quit on him."

A strained look came on Ben's face. "What did you say?" he asked tensely.

"You heard me." The Collector's voice was deliberately cruel. "No whore ever powders on Maxie Fields no matter how high their price."

Ben's voice was the scream of a hurt animal. "That's my sister!" he cried, throwing himself at the Collector.

He moved out of the range of my vision and I heard a sharp crash, then a thud as Ben fell to the floor. He began to scream.

"Sarah! Sarah! Don't come here!"

I could hear the sound of several sharp slaps and muttered curses, but Ben kept on screaming. I shifted my eyes along the crack until I could see them again.

The Collector had one knee planted on Ben's chest and was slapping him on the face. "Shut up, yuh son of a bitch!" he swore at him.

Ben kept on squirming and screaming. The Collector grabbed at Ben's arm and twisted it backward viciously. "Shut up, yuh one-armed crumb," he threatened, "or I'll rip yuh other arm out of its socket!"

Ben's face went white and he lay back limply and silently on the floor, his frightened eyes staring up at the Collector. I could feel nausea gathering in the pit of my stomach. I never saw such fear in human eyes.

"Maybe yuh better take him in the back room," I heard Spit say. "If the whore sees him, she might start hollering."

The Collector nodded and lumbered to his feet, still holding Ben's arm. "Get up!" he snarled.

Ben awkwardly tried to get to his feet, but couldn't make it. The Collector yanked on his arm and Ben screamed in pain: "I can't get up! I've only got one leg!"

The Collector laughed. He let go of Ben's arm and lifted him under the armpits as you would a baby and put him on his feet. "Boy," he said callously, "you're a real mess." He poked Ben in the back and Ben stumbled toward my door.

I looked around frantically. There was a steel bar near the door that I used to prop the tiny window up on hot nights. I picked it up and, hefting it in my hand, hid behind the door.

The door opened and Ben came stumbling through, the Collector following him. The Collector kicked the door shut behind him without turning around and went after Ben.

I stepped in quietly behind him and swung the bar. There was a dull sound and blood spurted from the Collector's ear where the bar hit him. He tumbled silently to the floor. He never knew what hit him.

"I was wondering where you were," Ben whispered hoarsely.

I looked up from the Collector and met his eyes. "I was here," I whispered, "but I had to wait for a spot." My mouth had a bad taste in it.

He bought my explanation. There was something more important on his mind. "Did you hear what they said about Sarah?" he whispered.

I nodded.

"Is it true?"

I looked at him. There was a pain in his face that nothing physical had put there; this came from the heart. Sarah was his kid sister. He had put her through school after their parents died, and then she had taken care of him when he was hurt. Suddenly I knew he would believe whatever I told him. For many reasons he had to, but mostly because he wanted to. Maybe some day he would find out what she had done. But not from me.

I shook my head. "No," I said surely. "Maxie Fields is a racket boy with a lot of legit business. Sarah became his secretary, and by the time she found out what he was and wanted out, she already knew too much for him to let her go."

Some of the pain disappeared from his face, but not all of it. "Poor kid," he murmured. "What she went through all because of me." He turned his eyes to mine. "How did you meet her?"

"I got into a jam with this guy and I was hurt. She saved me." It was the first time he had ever asked me what had happened. Until now he had taken her word that I had fallen from her car that night while she was bringing me out to work for him. "She's a very square kid," I said.

His eyes held level with mine and I let him search me for the truth. Slowly his face relaxed and the rest of the pain disappeared from his eyes. "What about that guy outside?" he asked.

"We'll take care of him," I said. I bent down over the Collector. He was breathing heavily as I flipped open his jacket and pulled his gun from the shoulder holster. I straightened up, hefting it cautiously in my hand. I didn't want any accidents to happen.

Ben was staring at the gun. "That explains a lot of things," he said wonderingly. "That's why she had to get away in such a hurry. That's why she couldn't wait for me to get ready but would pick me up on the way out. That's why she always had to run right back to work. She didn't want me to know."

"Yeah," I nodded. "That's it."

The sound of an automobile stopping outside reached our ears. We turned and looked at each other. I waved Ben back to the cot and stepped behind the door. We both stood very still.

I heard the front door open. Spit's voice was very calm. "Hi yuh, Babe. Maxie sent us after you as soon as he saw yer clothes was gone."

I could almost hear her sharp intake of breath. Then she screamed: "Ben! What have you done with Ben?"

Spit's voice was anxious and reassuring. "He's okay, Ronnie. The Collector's got him in the back room just to keep him out of trouble."

I heard her quick footsteps on the floor, then the door opened. She flew into the room. "Ben! Ben!" she cried. "Are you all right?"

Ben stood up. He was smiling at her. Spit was following her into the room. I stepped in behind him and pressed the gun into his spine.

"Stand quiet, Spit," I said slowly. "I'm very nervous. I never worked one of these things before!"

I'll say this much for him. Somewhere through the summer Spit had grown up too. He'd picked up savvy. He didn't turn his head. Matter of fact, he didn't move at all. His voice was careful, yet curious. "Danny?"

I prodded him with the gun. "Over against the wall, Spit," I said. "Till your nose touches."

He stepped cautiously over the Collector. "Up to your old tricks, huh, Danny?"

he asked. "First Maxie's money, then Maxie's broad."

I reversed the gun in my hand and swiped him across the face. He staggered a little and I pushed him with my hand. He landed against the wall with a thump. I shoved the gun into his back again and pulled his knife out of its sheath.

"Maxie ain't gonna like this, Danny." Spit's voice was threatening. "You got away with it once. He ain't gonna like your hurting his boys again."

I laughed. "His boys'll like it even less if they're dead," I said coldly. "Or has Maxie got a direct phone in hell too?"

He shut up and stood against the wall. I turned slightly and looked back.

Ben's arm was around Sarah. She was crying wildly against his chest. "Don't cry, honey," he said. "You'll never have to work for that man again."

Her crying stopped suddenly and she looked questioningly at me. "Does he know, Danny?" she asked in a hushed frightened voice. "Did they—"

"I told him what kind of a man you were secretary to, Sarah," I interrupted her quickly. "I told him how he wouldn't let you quit because you knew too much about his business."

"I know all about him now, Sarah," Ben said. "Why didn't you tell me before? We would have found a way out together."

She was looking at me gratefully now. I smiled at her. She turned back to her brother. "I was afraid of him, Ben. I didn't dare."

Ben's voice was reassuring. "Well, you don't have to worry now. We'll just turn these guys over to the police and be on our way."

Fear had come back into her voice. "We can't do that, Ben!"

My voice joined hers. "They'll only hold you up and you'd never get started," I said. "You better get going. I'll turn them in after you've gone."

"Will that be all right?" Ben hesitated.

"Sure it will," I said quickly. "Now hurry. Get your stuff into the car."

Spit's voice came muffled from against the wall. "I can't stand this way much longer, Danny. Can I turn around?"

"Sure," I said, reaching for a piece of wire lying on a shelf. "In just a minute."

I pulled his hands behind him and looped the wire around them. I jerked it tight and turned him around. His eyes were flashing at me.

"Sit down, Spit. Make yourself comfortable," I said, hitting him flush on the jaw and tumbling him onto the cot.

He sat up sputtering, but he didn't say a word. I looked over my shoulder. Almost all Ben's luggage was gone. Just one small piece remained.

Ben picked it up and looked at me hesitantly. "Sure you'll be all right, Danny?"

I grinned at him. "I'll be fine, Ben. Now get outta here."

He came toward me and his hand brushed my shoulder. "So long, kid," he said. "Thanks for everything."

"Thank you, Ben," I said. "So long."

He turned and walked out the door as Sarah came in. She came up to me, her eyes looking into mine. There was a tense curious look in them.

"Sure you don't want to come with us?" she asked through stiff lips.

I managed a smile. "Can't now," I answered. "I'm a little busy."

She tried a smile at my joke, but she couldn't make it. She half turned away, then looked back at me. "Danny!" she cried, and ran back into my arms.

"Better go, Sarah," I said somberly. "This way you can leave the whole thing behind you. There'll be nothing to remind you and make you remember."

She nodded her head and looked up at me. I could see the tears standing in her eyes. She kissed me quickly on the cheek and walked back to the door. "'Bye, Danny. Good luck," she said, and she was gone before I could answer her.

I turned back to Spit. He was watching me.

"We looked every place but here, Danny," he said. "But we should have guessed it. Ronnie was out that night too. I remember now."

There was something different about him. I hadn't noticed it at first, but I did now. He'd had something done to his mouth. His lip wasn't split any more and he didn't spray saliva all over when he spoke.

He saw that I had noticed it. His eyes lighted up. "I forgot to thank you, Danny, but you didn't give me a chance. When you slugged me that night you split my lip again and the doctor had to do a plastic job on me, and while he was at it, he fixed the whole thing."

I grinned. "Don't mention it, Spit." I raised my fist threateningly. "Any time."

He shrank back on the cot. "What are you going to do now?" His voice was frightened.

I pulled down another piece of wire. "Stretch out on your belly," I said. "You'll see."

Reluctantly he stretched out on the narrow cot. Quickly I caught his ankles together with the wire and pulled his feet up behind him and ran the wire through his hands, binding them together. I straightened up and looked down at him. He ought to be good for a long time like this.

He lay there quietly and I bent over the Collector. The blood had stopped welling from his ear and he was breathing easier. I flipped open an eye and looked at it. It was dull and glazed. He would keep too.

I picked up the few things I owned and put them in the small valise I had bought, with Spit watching me all the while from the cot.

"You won't get away this time, Danny," he said.

I walked back to the cot and looked down at him. I raised the gun thoughtfully and watched the fear grow in his eyes. "How do yuh know?" I asked.

He didn't answer. Just stared at the gun with big frightened eyes. After a moment I smiled and dropped it into my pocket. A look of relief came into his face.

"It seems to me we met like this before," I said. "Last May, wasn't it?"

He nodded his head. He was too scared to talk.

"Do you love me as much in September as you did in May?" I laughed.

He didn't answer.

I bent over him and slapped his face with my open hand. "If you're as smart as I think you are, Spit," I said, picking up my bag and walking to the door, "you'll be careful not to run into me again." I opened the door. "You might not always be this lucky. They don't fix holes in your head like they do on your lip."

I shut the door behind me and walked through the front room and out of the bungalow. I snapped the padlock on the front door and jammed it tight. I walked up the ramp to the boardwalk and into the novelty store, where I left the key for the renting agent.

The small gray-haired woman who worked the store with her husband took it from me. "Going already, Danny?" she asked, smiling through her steel-rimmed spectacles. "Everything all right?"

"Sure, Mrs. Bernstein," I said with a smile. "Everything's all right now."

CHAPTER SEVEN

T HE SOUTHBOUND BUS WAS ON THE FERRY LEAVING THE DOCK AS I looked back through the window at the lights of New York. They were sparkling crazily. It had begun to rain.

That was okay with me. It was just the way I felt. I had left something behind me. I didn't know what, but whatever it was, the rain would wash it all away and it was lost. Someday I would come back. Maybe things would be different then.

I settled back into the seat and opened a morning paper. It wasn't until we were rolling through the flatlands of the New Jersey countryside that I saw the item in one of the Broadway columns. And, even seeing it there in the cold black type, I found it hard to believe.

SAM GOTTKIN, top concession and hatcheck king and former light heavy contender under the name of Sammy Gordon, was married yesterday to Miriam (Mimi) Fisher, sister of Danny Fisher, Gloves champion. After a honeymoon in Bermuda they will take up residence in a new penthouse on Central Park South that he had specially redecorated for his bride.

Automatically my hand went to the signal bell to stop the bus. My fingers rested there a moment, and then I took my hand away. It would do no good to go back. There wasn't anything I could change.

I sank back slowly in my seat and read the item again. Loneliness stole into me. Mimi and Sam. I wondered how it had happened. How they met. And what became of that guy in her office she was so crazy about? I closed my eyes wearily. It didn't matter now. Nothing that happened would matter anymore. Not to me. As far as they were concerned, I was gone as if I never was there.

The tattoo of the rain beat against the bus window and dulled my mind. I dozed fitfully. Pictures of Sam and Mimi kept flashing before me. But they were never together. Whenever one of them would come into focus, the other would disappear. I fell asleep before I could get them to stay together long enough for me to wish them happiness.

I WASN'T THERE WHEN—

She was sitting in front of the dressing-table, crying uncontrollably. Large tears were running down her cheeks, leaving long purple streaks of mascara. Her hands held a helpless handkerchief against her mouth.

Papa turned nervously. "What is she crying about?" he asked Mamma. "It's her wedding. What has she got to cry about?"

Mamma looked at him disgustedly. She took his arm and pushed him out the door into the small marriage chapel. "Go, mingle with the guests," she said firmly. "She'll be all right in time for the ceremony."

She closed the door in his protesting face and snapped the lock. Her face was calm and understanding as she waited for the paroxysm of tears to pass. She didn't have to wait long. At last Mimi stopped weeping and sat small and shrunken in her chair. She stared at the handkerchief her fingers were twisting and turning nervously.

"You don't love him," Mamma said quietly.

Mimi's head snapped up. Her eyes met Mamma's for a moment and then she looked down again. "I love him," she answered in a small, tired voice.

"You don't have to marry him if you don't love him." Mamma spoke as if she hadn't heard a word Mimi uttered.

Mimi's eyes were calm now. She looked at Mamma unwinkingly. Her voice was quietly emotionless. "I'm all right now, Mother. I was just being a child."

Mamma's face was serious. "You think maybe because you're getting married you're grown up? Don't forget I still had to sign your wedding license to give my permission."

Mimi turned and looked in the dressing-table mirror. She got out of her chair quickly and walked to the washbasin in the corner.

Mamma put her hand out and stopped her. "All your life, Miriam," she said softly, "you'll have to live with him. All your life you'll have to live with the way you'll feel. All—"

"Mamma!" A desperate note of hysteria in Mimi's voice halted Mamma's words. "Don't talk like that! It's too late now!"

"It's not too late, Miriam," Mamma persisted. "You can still change your mind."

Mimi shook her head. Her face set into determined lines. "It's too late, Mamma," she said firmly. "It was already too late the first time I went to see him when I wanted to find out where Danny had gone. What am I going to do now? Give him back all the money he spent trying to find Danny for us? Give him back the five thousand dollars he loaned Papa for the store? Give back all the clothes he bought me and the ring, and say I'm sorry, that it was all a mistake?"

The pain in Mamma's eyes grew deeper. "Better that," she said quietly, "than you should be unhappy. Don't let Papa and me do to you what we did to Danny." Her eyes began to fill with tears.

Mimi caught Mamma to her. "Don't blame yourself for anything that happened," she said swiftly. "It was all Papa's fault."

"No, I could have stopped him," Mamma insisted. "That's why I'm talking to you. The same mistake I should not make again."

Mimi's face was determined. "There's no mistake, Mamma," she said surely, as if she knew all the answers. "Sam loves me. If I don't love him as much as he loves me now, that will come in time. He's good and kind and generous. Everything will work out all right."

Mamma looked into her face questioningly.

Impulsively Mimi bent and brushed her lips across Mamma's brow. "Don't worry, Mamma," she said softly. "I know what I'm doing. This is what I want."

❖   ❖   ❖

She sat up in the bed, her body tense with anticipated fear. She could hear him brushing his teeth noisily in the bathroom. The sound of the running water stopped abruptly. She heard the click of the light-switch, lay down quickly in the darkness of the bed, and curled her body into a small huddled mass.

She heard him walking around his side of the bed in the darkness and felt the bed sagging beneath the weight of his body. She lay there quietly, her body stiff and suddenly chill, her teeth almost chattering.

There was a moment's silence, then his hand slowly touched her shoulder. She clenched her teeth tightly. Then she heard him whisper: "Mimi."

She forced herself to answer. "Yes, Sam."

"Mimi, turn around." His whisper was a pleading sound in the darkness.

Her voice was low and carefully controlled. "Please, Sam, not tonight. It hurts."

His voice was gentle and understanding. "We won't try again tonight. I just want to hold your head against my chest. I don't want you to be afraid of me. I love you, baby."

Her eyes were suddenly wet with tears. She turned around swiftly and placed her head against his breast. Her voice was very small. "Do you, Sam? Could you really love me after all I did to you?"

She felt his breath against her hair. "Sure, baby. You didn't do nothin'. All nice girls feel like that the first time."

She relaxed slowly in his arms. She lifted her face to him and kissed him lightly on the lips, much as a little girl would kiss her father. "Thanks, Sam," she whispered gratefully. She was silent a moment, then her voice came slowly through her lips. "I'll try again if you want to, Sam."

"Would yuh, honey?" He sounded pleased and happy.

"Yes, Sam," she answered in a low voice.

She shut her eyes tightly and could feel his hands stroke her hair. His lips pressed against her cheek lightly and moved to her neck. George used to do that. Angrily she pushed the flow of thought from her. Why did she have to think of that at this moment? It wasn't fair to Sam. He wasn't responsible for what had happened. It was her fault. She had wanted it this way from the very beginning when she and Nellie had gone to see him.

Contritely she raised her hand and stroked his cheek. His face was smooth. He had just shaved before coming to bed. His lips pressed to her lips. They were warm and gentle. She kissed him back.

She stiffened in momentary fright as she felt his hand, cool, light, under her nightgown. His touch was quiet, soothing; and slowly she relaxed, letting her body go limp and unresisting. His heart was pounding against her.

She began to feel warm and tingling. She used to feel like that before. . . . What was she thinking? . . . This was good and she was glad she could feel like that now.

His lips were against her bosom. She felt content and her hands held his head still as she kissed his forehead. She shut her eyes and thought of George. It would have been like this with him. It would have been easier with him. She wasn't afraid of him as she had been with. . . .

His voice was an anxious whisper in the night. "Are you all right, honey?"

She nodded her head fiercely, not trusting herself to speak.

❖   ❖   ❖

Sam was lying quietly beside her, his hand soothing on her flushed cheek. There was secret pride in his voice as he whispered: "See, darling, it wasn't anything to be afraid of, was it?"

She hid her face against his breast. "No," she whispered. But in her heart she knew she was lying. She would always have to lie to him. She would always be afraid. It wasn't his face that came before her eyes at the shattering moment of orgasm. "Oh, God," she prayed silently, "will I have to go through life like this? Always afraid?"

The answering voice was in her mind. It was rich and heavy, and its words were from the marriage ceremony: "Repeat after me, my child. 'I, Miriam, take thee, Samuel, to be my lawful wedded husband, for richer, for poorer, in sickness and in health, to love, to honor, to cherish, until death do us part.'"

He was sleeping, his breath coming deeply and contentedly. She looked at his calm face in the darkness. He was happy now. Better so.

She moved back to her pillow and closed her eyes. She had gone to him to find me, and now she would spend the rest of her days and nights beside him. But he would never know the failure. It wasn't his to know. Only she would know that she had cheated him and would cheat him in all the frenzied moments of their life together.

CHAPTER EIGHT

I STOOD IN THE CENTER OF THE DESERTED MIDWAY WITH THE RAIN POURING down over me. I pulled the collar of my slicker up around my neck so that it was snug under the brim of my soft slouch hat, and dragged at my cigarette. I looked up at the sky. This rain wasn't going to stop. I stared down the midway. The wet walls of the gray and tan tents flapped cheerlessly in the rain-swept wind.

Two years of this. It had been a long time. I'd put a large piece of time into these canvas-covered walls. There had been days so hot that the heat came baking you until you felt you were standing in an oven in some crazy part of hell, and nights so cold that the marrow in your bones seemed to freeze like the ice on a lake in winter.

Two years of this. Of the crowds pushing through the midway, gawking, their mouths filled with cotton candy, hot dogs, and ice cream. Of crowds with their eyes wary, looking upon you as they would on a vagrant, eager to purchase your wares, resentful that you were selling them.

Two years of not being at home, of not knowing what happened. Nellie. Mamma and Papa. Mimi. Sam. The names still hurt. Every time I thought I was used to it, the same lonely feeling would come back. It was buried deep, but it was always there.

And now I was almost home. Almost, but not quite. Philadelphia. I could get a train at the Market Street Station and in a little while get off at Penn Station.

It was easy when I thought about it. Only an hour and ten minutes away from home.

But things were always simple when I thought about them. They were never as simple when I started to do them. All the memories of what had happened come pouring back into me. And I am angry again. Resentful at my enforced exile. Afraid of what would happen if I were to return.

And yet I want to go home. I always want to go home. There are ties that bind me to those who are there, even when they do not want me to return. Ties that I cannot spell into words, but are emotions in me. Today I am only one hour and ten minutes away from these things. The day after tomorrow, when the tents move southward again on their annual path, I will be six hours away, a week later twenty hours away, and in a month it will be a journey of many days and I may not travel it in all my lifetime.

I look up to the sky again. The rain clouds are low and steady, the wind brushes its wetness into my face, my cigarette is sodden between my lips. The rain will spend the night on the midway.

I let the cigarette fall from my mouth and it sputters in a puddle at my feet. I could almost hear the angry hiss of its tiny fire as it vainly fights away the water. I think I am like that cigarette and I am fighting for my life against the quickly rushing rain. I cannot breathe, the air is heavy in my lungs. I must go home. I must, I must. I must see Nellie again. And Mamma and Mimi. And Papa too, whether he wants to see me or not. Even though I know I cannot stay, even if I must come back to the midway tomorrow. It may be a long time before I can go home again. I am tired of being lonely.

The inevitable card game was in progress as I came through the tent flap. The players' eyes glanced at me briefly as I swung my hat against my trousers, shaking the water from it; then they looked back at their cards.

The feeble light from the oil lamp flickered on their faces as I walked around the table. I stopped behind Mike and looked down at the cards in his hand, smiling to myself. He would never get rich trying to fill a three-card straight.

"It's gonna rain all night," I said.

"Yeah," Mike answered absently. He was concentrating on his cards.

The dealer's voice came across the table. "How many?"

Mike's voice was low. "Two."

The cards flickered across the table to him. He picked them up quickly and looked at them. A sigh of disgust crossed his lips. "I'm out," he said, dropping the cards on the table and turning to look up at me.

There was a quick showing of cards and the dealer took the pot. "Want a hand, Danny?" he asked genially.

"No, thanks." I shook my head. "You guys got enough of my dough." I looked down at Mike. "How about the night off?" I asked.

Mike grinned. "Get a dame lined up for me too and we'll both take the night off."

"Not this night, Mike. I want to run up to New York. We're not goin' to do anythin' tonight."

The dealer scoffed at me. "Playin' hard to get, Danny? Yuh better look out for these Phillie chippies. Ever' one of them has a brother on the force."

Mike's eyes turned serious. "What yuh want to go up there for?"

I had never told him very much, but he was a bright guy. He must have guessed something had gone wrong back there. But he never asked any questions and he wasn't going to get any answers now. "A vacation," I said quietly, meeting his eyes.

Mike looked down at the table. The cards were coming toward him again. He picked them up, turning each one over cautiously in his fingers. Six. Nine. Seven. Eight. Ace. All black and curly. His fingers tightened on them. I could see he had forgotten about me.

"What d'yuh say, Mike?" I prodded him.

He didn't look up from the table. "Okay," he said absently. "But be back by eleven in the morning. The papers say it's gonna clear up and we're gettin' outta here."

The rain was still beating against the windows of the train as the tired conductor came through. He tapped me on the shoulder. "Tickets, please." I gave him the ticket silently. "Bad night," he said, shaking his head. He punched my ticket and handed it back to me.

"Yeah," I answered, watching him move away. But I didn't really agree with him; I was going home. I looked at my wrist-watch. New York was only fifty-five minutes away.

CHAPTER NINE

IT WAS DRIZZLING WHEN I CAME UP THE SUBWAY STEPS, BUT THE CROWD on Delancey Street was as large as ever. Rain didn't bother them, they had nowhere else to go. It was always good to walk along Delancey Street and look in the shop windows and think about what you might buy if you had the money.

I lit a cigarette as I waited for the traffic light to change and let me cross the street. The store windows hadn't changed; they would never change. The haberdasheries still had their fire sales; the cakes and bread in Ratner's window were just as they were the last time I had been there; the hot-dog stand on the corner of Essex was just as crowded.

The traffic halted in front of me and I crossed the street. Things hadn't changed a bit. The same beggars were selling their pencils, the same whores were casing the crowds with weary disillusioned eyes. But I had changed. I knew that when one of the whores jostled me and whispered something as I passed. I looked after her, smiling. Two years ago it wouldn't have been like that. I was a kid then.

I continued down the street toward the five and ten. Nellie would be there, I was sure of it. I don't know why, but somehow I knew she would be there. The clock in the Paramount window told me it was five minutes to nine. Another five minutes and the store would close and she would be out. Suddenly I was anxious to see her. I wondered if she had changed too. Maybe she had forgotten me, maybe she had another fellow. Two years was a long time for a girl to wait, especially when she had no word. And I had never written.

I was at the store entrance. I stopped and looked in. There weren't many people in the store, but a nervous reluctance kept me from crossing the threshold. Maybe she didn't want to see me. I stood there, hesitating a moment, then I retraced my steps to the corner.

I stood under the street light—the same street light where I had always waited for her. I leaned my back against the lamp-post and smoked my cigarette, oblivious of the rain falling about me. If I closed my eyes and listened only to the night sounds in the street, it would be as if I had never been away.

The lights in the five-and-ten window went out suddenly and I straightened up. I threw my cigarette into the gutter and watched the store entrance. It should only be a few minutes now. A few minutes. I could feel a faint pulse ticking in my temples; my mouth was dry. A group of girls came chattering from the darkened store. I watched them avidly as they walked past me, still talking. She wasn't with them.

My gaze went past them to the door again. More girls were coming out. My fingers drummed nervously against my leg. She wasn't with them either. I looked at my wristwatch quickly. Almost five past nine. She had to come out soon.

I wiped my face with my handkerchief. Despite the cool chill in the air, I was sweating. I stuffed the handkerchief back in my pocket and watched the door. Girls were still coming out. I scanned each face quickly and my eyes would leap to the next. She still wasn't with them. They were coming out more slowly now, two together or singly. They came out into the street, glanced quickly up at the sky, and then hurried toward home.

I looked at my watch again. Almost twenty after. Disappointment began to course through me. I half turned, about to go away. It had been silly of me to think she would still be there. It was probably silly of me to believe that the two years hadn't mattered. Still, I couldn't walk away like that. I turned back and waited for the store to empty completely.

More of the lights in the store were going out. Another few minutes and the manager would come out and the store would be closed. I took a cigarette from my pocket and struck a match, but the wind blew it out before I could get it to my cigarette. I struck another one, this time cupping it in my hand and turning my back to shield it from the breeze. The sound of more girls' voices came to my ears, and among them I heard another voice. I froze there, holding my breath. It was her voice. I knew it. "Good night, Molly."

I stared at her. She was turned away from me as she spoke to another girl, who was starting to walk in another direction. The cigarette hung warm in my lips as I looked at her. In the dim light of the street lamp it seemed as if she hadn't changed at all. The same sweet mouth, soft white skin, rounded cheek, and wide brown eyes she always had. And her hair—there was never hair like hers, so black it was almost blue in the reflected light. I took a step toward her and then stopped. I was afraid to move, afraid to speak. I stood there helplessly, looking at her.

The other girl had walked away, and she was starting to open an umbrella. It was a gay red plaid umbrella, and as she lifted it over her head, her eyes followed it upward, she saw me. Automatically she finished opening the umbrella; there was a stunned unbelieving expression on her face. She took a tentative, hesitating step toward me and then stopped.

"Danny?" Her voice was a husky whispered question.

I was staring into her eyes. I could feel my lips move as I tried to speak, but no words came out. The cigarette tumbled from my mouth scattering tiny sparks against my clothing as it fell toward the ground.

"*Danny! Danny!*" she was screaming as she ran across the few feet separating us. The umbrella lay open and forgotten in the doorway behind her.

She was in my arms now, kissing and crying and repeating my name all at once. Her lips were warm, then cold, then warm again. I could feel her tears against my cheek, her body shivering beneath her tiny short coat.

There was a mist before my eyes that was not rain as I looked down at her. I closed them for a moment. I said her name: "Nellie."

Her fingers were on my cheek and I bent my face toward her and kissed her. Our lips clung together and melted away all the time that had come between us. It was as if nothing had ever happened. This was all that mattered—being together again.

Her eyes were searching my face. "Danny, Danny," she whispered brokenly, "why did you do it? Not a word, not a word in all this time."

I looked at her dumbly. There was no answer in me. Only now I knew how wrong I'd been in what I had done. When I could speak, my voice was hoarse and shaking. "I couldn't help it, baby, I had to."

She was crying. The sobs in her came painfully to my ears. "We tried to find you, Danny, we tried so hard to find you. It was as if the world had swallowed you up. I almost died."

I held her very close to me. I brushed my lips through her hair. It was all that I remembered. Soft and sweet-smelling and fine to touch. A peace I had not known for a long time came into me.

Her face was hidden against my breast and her voice came muffled to my ears. "I couldn't stand it again, Danny."

Then everything suddenly became very simple. I knew how it had to be, how it should be. "You won't have to, baby. From now on, we'll be together. Always."

Her face was white and childlike and trusting as she looked up at me. "Honest, Danny?"

For the first time that day I could smile. "Honest, Nellie," I answered. "D'yuh think I came back just for a visit?" It was all straight in my mind. What I wanted, all I wanted. I didn't know I was going to quit Mike when I stood there, back on the midway with the rain falling on me, but I knew it now. I would see Mike and explain it to him. He would understand. I had come home to stay.

"From now on, Nellie," I said gently, "whatever I do, we do—together."

CHAPTER TEN

THE SAME OLD SIGN WAS STILL IN THE WINDOW:

CHOW MEIN 30¢ CHOP SUEY

The same old Chinese ushered us to our seats and handed us a tired fly-dirtied menu.

Her eyes were bright and shining. "You remembered."

I smiled at her.

Her hand reached across the table toward me. "We came here the first time, remember? The first day I met you."

I clasped her hand and turned it palm upward. I studied it with a pretended concentration. "There's a tall dark man about to come into your life," I said, imitating the carny fortune-teller's heavy voice.

She laughed and squeezed my hand. "Wrong color hair." Her eyes were suddenly serious. "Danny."

I could feel the laughter fade from me as I looked at her. She was going right inside me. "Yes, Nellie."

"I hope I'm not dreaming," she said quickly. "I hope I'm not upstairs in my bed dreaming, because I'll wake up in the morning and my eyes will be red and my sister will tell me I was crying in my sleep."

I raised her hand and kissed it quickly. "That ought to prove you're awake."

Her eyes were soft and swimming. "If I'm dreaming, I never want to wake up. I just want to sleep and dream." Her voice was husky.

I was able to smile now. "You're awake."

Her hand gripped mine tightly. "I love you, Danny. I loved you the minute I saw you, I guess. Sitting at the counter with a chocolate soda." Her eyes were earnest and searching again. "I never went out with another fella. All the time you were away."

A strong guilt was in me. I couldn't meet her eyes. "Aw, go on," I said uncomfortably.

Her hand turned in mine. "Honest, Danny," she insisted. "Mamma wanted me to, but I didn't. Somehow I knew you would come back. I just knew it. Even before that girl came from Maxie Fields and told me."

I stared at her in surprise. "Girl?" I asked. "What girl?"

"Miss Dorfman," she answered quickly. "Don't you remember her? She and her brother came into the store a few days after Labor Day and said they had spoken to you and that you were all right and sent your love. They were very nice to do that on their way through New York. She said you had got into some trouble with Fields, but that you would be back as soon as things straightened out."

Suddenly I felt better. Sarah was okay. There were some people who were on the level. She had tried to help. Maybe if it wasn't for Sarah, Nellie wouldn't be here now. This way there was someone missing me, someone loving me, someone waiting for me. I wasn't altogether alone.

Her eyes were watching me earnestly. "Is it true what they said, Danny—that you took money from Fields to throw the fight that night?"

I didn't answer her question. Something else was more important. "They said?" I asked. "Who?"

"Mimi came to see me when she was looking for you. This was about a week after you'd disappeared. Zep and I took her up to Mr. Gottkin, and that's what Fields had told him." She was still watching my face. "Is it true what he said, Danny?"

I nodded slowly.

Her hand still held mine. There was a hurt echo in her voice. "Why did you do it, Danny? Why didn't you tell me?"

"There was nothing else I could do," I said in a low voice. "I needed the dough. I wanted Papa to buy a store with it, and Fields had the squeeze on me anyway. Then I couldn't lose the fight—even if I tried."

"But your father locked you out that night, Mimi told me," she said. "Why didn't you come to my house and say something?"

I stared at her. Nothing I could say to her could make anything right. I had screwed up everything. "I had to get out. Fields would have been after me."

She closed her eyes wearily. "It's all so terrible, I still can hardly believe it. Two years of not knowing what happened to you, of not knowing who to believe, what to believe."

The pain on her face made me squirm inside. "Maybe it would have been better if I hadn't come back," I said bitterly. "Then you could have forgotten about me and everything would be all right."

Her eyes were looking inside me again. "Don't say that, Danny, don't ever say that again. I don't care what has happened or what you've done so long as you don't go 'way again."

I held onto her hand tightly as the waiter took our order. This was the way I thought it should be. And it was.

I pushed the plate away from in front of me and held a match to her cigarette, then to my own. She leaned back in her chair, letting the smoke blow idly through her lips.

"You got thin," she said.

I grinned at her. "Uh-uh." I denied it. "I weigh ten pounds more now than I did two years ago."

Her gaze was thoughtful. "Maybe you do," she conceded, "but you look thinner. Your face was rounder before—more boyish."

"Maybe it's because I'm not a kid any more."

She leaned forward quickly. "Yes, that's what it is," she said in a slightly surprised voice. "You were a boy when you went away. Now you're grown up."

"Isn't that what's supposed to happen?" I asked. "Nobody stays the same forever. You've grown up too."

Her fingers reached out and touched my face slightly. They rested a moment on the corners of my mouth, then swept gently along the ridge of my nose and across my chin. "Yes, you've changed," she said reflectively. "Your mouth is firmer, your chin is stronger. What did your folks say when they saw you?"

I kept my face blank of expression to screen the hurt of her question. "I haven't seen them," I answered.

"You haven't seen them?" Her voice was wondering. "Why, Danny?"

"I don't know whether I want to," I said flatly. "I don't think they want to see me. Not after all that happened. Not after I was thrown out."

Her hand gripped mine. "In some ways you're still a baby, Danny," she said gently. "I should think they would want to see you."

"Do you?" I asked bitterly, and yet inside me I was glad she had said that.

"I know Mimi would," she said confidently, "and your mother." She smiled up at me. "Do you know that Mimi met Mr. Gottkin when we went up there and they got married? And that Mimi has a little son?"

More surprises. "I knew they were married," I said quickly, "I saw it in the papers; but I didn't know about the baby. When did that happen?"

"Last year," Nellie said. "And now she is going to have another."

"How do you know so much about her?" I asked curiously.

"We call each other every few weeks," she said. "In case either of us heard about you."

I wondered at that. In some ways I felt good; that meant Mimi missed me too. "I couldn't believe it when I read she had married Sam," I said.

"He's been very good to her," Nellie said quickly. "He's done a lot for your folks too. He's helped your father out in business."

I drew a deep breath. That was one thing that had bothered me. During the last few years I had become certain that my father needed someone to help him. Now, at least, Sam would see to it that everything would be okay. I wondered what Sam thought about me, whether he was sore at me for what I did. I guessed he was and I couldn't really blame him.

"Are you going up to see them?" she asked.

I shook my head. "No."

"But, Danny, you should," she said quickly. "After all, they are your family."

I smiled mirthlessly. "That's not what my father said."

"What difference does that make?" she asked. "I know they don't like me and what they think about me, but if I were in your place, I would go to see them."

"I'm not going!" I said flatly. "I came home to you, not to them."

CHAPTER ELEVEN

WE HUDDLED TOGETHER IN THE DOORWAY, OUR LIPS PRESSED TO-gether in a fierce, burning intensity. There were hungers in me at this time of parting that left me no peace. Suddenly she was crying. Quiet, heart-wracking sobs that shook her body.

Gently I turned her face toward me. "What's the matter, honey?"

Her arms went frantically around my neck, pulling my face close to her cheek. "Oh, Danny, I'm so frightened! I don't want you to go away again. You'll never come back!"

"Baby, baby," I whispered, holding her close and trying to make her understand, "I'm not going away this time. It's just good night. I'll be back."

Her voice was an anguished cry against my ear. "You won't, Danny! I just know you won't!"

I could feel her tears against my cheek. I kissed her. "Don't cry, Nellie," I begged her. "Please."

Her voice was more wild, more frightened than before. "Don't go away, Danny, don't leave me again. If you do, I'll die!"

"I won't leave you, Nellie," I promised. I held her still against me until her outburst of tears had subsided.

Her face was hidden against my chest and I had to strain my ears to hear what she was saying. "If there was only some place we could go, some place we would be together, so I could just sit and look at you and say to myself: 'He's back, he's back!'"

She raised her head and looked up at me. In the darkness her eyes were deep and shining. "I don't want to go home tonight and sleep with my sister and wake up in the morning and find out it was only a dream. I want to go with you and hold onto your hand so that the early light of morning doesn't take you away from me."

"I'll be back in the morning," I said softly. "I love you."

"No, you won't," she retorted desperately. "If I let you go this time, you'll never come back. Something will happen and you won't come back." The tears began to fill her eyes again. "You said that last time, Danny. Remember what you said? 'No matter what happens, remember I love you.' And then you didn't come back. But I remembered and remembered." The tears were flooding down her cheeks. Her arms held me desperately. Her voice was heavy with a pain I could not know. "I can't do it again, Danny, I can't. I'd die this time. I can't let you go."

I tried to smile, to make a joke out of the way she felt. "We can't stay in this doorway all night, honey."

"Then find a place we can stay, Danny," she said, her eyes flashing up at me suddenly. "Find a place we can stay, where, I can sit and talk and hold your hand until tomorrow comes and I believe that this is no dream."

I didn't like the look on the face of the tired desk clerk in the lobby of the run-down hotel when we walked in. I liked it less when after I had signed the register: "Daniel Fisher and Wife,", the man looked up at me, saying with a faint smile: "Two dollars, please, in advance."

I put the money on the counter and asked him for the room keys. I could feel Nellie's hand on my arm as she stood slightly behind me.

The clerk picked up the two bills and held them in his hand. He looked down at the floor near my feet. "No luggage?" he asked.

"No luggage," I replied quickly. "We didn't expect to stay in town tonight."

The clerk's eyes filled with a knowing look. "I'm sorry, sir," he said in a politely impolite voice, "but in that case the room will cost five dollars. Hotel rules, you know."

I fought down an impulse to slug him. Not because he was hijacking me for three bucks that the hotel management would never see, but for that look in his eyes. He must have read in my face something of how I felt, because he shifted his gaze and looked down at the counter. With a quick glance at Nellie, I put three more dollars beside the register.

The clerk picked up the money. "Thank you, sir," he said, pushing a room key across the counter. "That's room 402, sir. Take the self-service elevator down at the end of the hall to the fourth floor. You'll find it, second door from the elevator."

I locked the door and turned back to the room. An embarrassed silence descended upon us as we studied it. It was a small room. A washbasin stood in one corner opposite a closet door; there was a tiny dresser with a mirror to match against the wall next to it. Against the opposite wall was a small double bed. One chair stood next to the bed, and a leather-covered two-cushioned seat was placed in front of a narrow window.

Awkwardly I walked around the leather chair and looked out the window. "It's still rainin'," I said.

"Yes," she agreed in a small voice as if she were afraid it could be heard beyond the thin walls. She was watching me nervously.

I took off my hat and slicker. "I'll bed down on the club chair here," I said, walking to the closet. "You stretch out on the bed and try to get some sleep. It'll be morning soon."

I hung my coat and jacket in the closet. Quickly I slipped off my tie and draped it over one of the hangers. When I turned back to the room, she was still standing there looking at me. Her coat was still on. I smiled at her. "Don't be frightened."

"I'm not—any more," she answered softly. She crossed the room and stood in front of me. "I'm not afraid of anything when you're near me."

I kissed her lightly on the forehead. "Then take off your coat and lie down. You need the rest."

Silently she hung her coat in the closet while I sat down on the chair and slipped out of my shoes. I leaned back crossways on the couch and put my feet over one side and watched her. She was a funny kid—afraid to let me go, yet afraid to stay in the same room with me.

"Comfortable?" she asked me as she walked past the couch.

I nodded. "Yeah."

I heard her footsteps behind me. There was a faint click and the room slipped into darkness. I heard her walk to the far side of the bed. There was a faint rustle of clothing, then the sound of her shoes dropping to the floor.

I looked through the darkness, but she was only a faint white shadow on the other side of the room, sinking softly onto the bed. There was the sound of bedsprings protesting at her weight, and then the only sound in the room was the sound of our breathing.

I placed my arms behind my head and tried to fit myself into the small couch. My legs, draped over the side of the chair, began to ache. I tried to shift them quietly, but my trousers made a slithering sound across the leather.

Her voice almost startled me. "Danny."

"Yes," I answered quietly.

"Are you awake?"

"Uh huh."

"Can't you sleep?"

I shifted position again. "I can sleep all right."

There was silence for a moment; then her voice came out of the darkness again. It was very low, I could hardly hear her. "Danny, you forgot something."

"What?"

"You didn't kiss me good-night," she whispered plaintively.

I was on my knees at the side of the bed. The sheet rustled as she sat up to meet me. Her lips were soft and warm against mine. Her arms were tight around my neck, and the sweet warmth of her body came up to me through the night.

My arms tightened around her, her heart was pounding against my chest. The small cold snap of her brassiere was in my hand and I pressed my fingers against it. I felt the brassiere suddenly loose in my fingers and her breasts were free against me. I bent my head quickly and pressed my lips to them.

Her hands held my head tightly and her voice was soft against my ear. "Hold me, Danny, hold me, Never let me go."

There was a choking in my throat. "I'll never let you go, darling."

Her voice was filled with wonder. "I love you to touch me, Danny. I love the feel of you close to me. I fill with a sweet pain for the nearness of you."

I raised my head to look at her in the darkness. There was a curious inconsolable pain inside me too, a longing that I'd never known before, a strain of emotion in me that was stronger than all the physical drives my body had ever known. I tried to speak, to tell her that I loved her, but I couldn't. My voice was lost in a muscular constriction of my throat.

Her fingers explored my face in the darkness. "Danny, your cheeks—Why, Danny, you're crying!"

The tears seemed to loosen the cords that knotted my voice. "Yes, I'm crying," I answered, almost defiantly.

I could hear her draw a deep breath, then her arms tightened around my neck, drawing my face down to the pillow on which she lay. Her lips pressed lightly against my eyelids. Her voice was very low and there was a warmth and sympathy in it that no human ever had for me before. "Don't cry, darling, don't cry," she whispered "I can't bear to see you unhappy."

CHAPTER TWELVE

THE SUN POURING THROUGH THE WINDOW REACHED MY EYES. I TURNED in the bed to avoid the light, and my outstretched hand hit something soft in the bed. My eyes opened quickly.

She was lying on her side, her head resting on one hand, her eyes fixed on me. She smiled.

I stared at her for one unbelieving second, then my lips curved to match her smile. The night came back to me and an incredible warmth coursed through my body. "It's morning," I said.

She nodded and her hair cascaded down around her hand, framing her oval face in its blue-black softness. Her eyes went to the window, then back to my face. "It's morning," she agreed solemnly.

"You look even beautifuller in the morning," I said.

Her face flushed. "You look beautiful when you sleep," she replied in a low voice. "I was watching you. You look like a little boy then."

I sat up in the bed in mock anger, the sheet falling from me, leaving me naked to the waist. "You mean I don't look good when I'm awake?" I asked fiercely.

She laughed. Her fingers traced a pattern on my ribs. "You're skinny," she said. "Every bone on you sticks out. I'll have to fatten you up."

I grabbed her shoulders and pulled her face close to mine. "You can start right now," I said, kissing her. "Mmmmmh. I'm so hungry I could eat you."

Her hands framed my face. "Danny," she asked in a low voice, her eyes searching mine earnestly, "do you love me?"

I turned my head quickly and nipped at her hand. "Course I love you." I was laughing.

Her hands twisted my face back to her. Her eyes were very serious. "Danny," she said sharply, "say it like you mean it. Like you said last night."

I stopped laughing "I love you, Nellie," I said soberly.

She closed her eyes. "Say it again, Danny," she whispered. "I love to hear you say it."

My lips came down on her throat. They moved slowly down to her shoulder, my face pushing away the sheet that covered her body. I cupped her breasts lightly in my fingers, then covered them with my face. "I love you, Nellie," I whispered, resting against her bosom.

She sighed slowly, the breath escaping her lips reluctantly, her eyes still closed. I could feel her body stirring beneath my touch, striving to be closer to me. Her voice was rich and filled with happiness. "I want you, Danny. God help me, I can never get enough of you."

We were passing the open doors of the church when she stopped suddenly and looked up at me. "Danny, come inside with me."

I looked at the church, then back to her questioningly. Her eyes pleaded with me silently. "Okay," I said.

She took my hand and I followed her into the church. In the dimness she turned toward me, her voice trembling. "Danny, you're not angry with me?"

I squeezed her hand reassuringly. "What for?" I asked.

A grateful smile crossed her lips. "I wouldn't feel right if I didn't come here first."

I watched her walk down the aisle and kneel before the altar. She clasped her hands in front of her and inclined her head, closing her eyes. She remained so for a little while, then rose to her feet and came back to me. There was a radiant smile on her face.

I held out my hand to her and she took it. Slowly we walked out of the church and down the steps to the street. We walked along silently for a moment, then she turned and looked up at me.

"I feel better now," she admitted shyly.

"I'm glad," I said.

"I—I just had to go in, Danny," she explained. "I wouldn't have felt right if I didn't."

I whistled a cab to a stop in front of us. "Good," I said slowly. "I wouldn't want a bride who didn't feel right."

I opened the door and helped her in, then got in beside her. The driver's face looked back inquiringly at me. "City Hall, please," I told him.

There were several other couples in the small waiting-room outside the door marked: "MARRIAGE CHAPEL," in frosted black letters on opaque glass. They were all as nervous as we were.

I looked at my watch again. Ten o'clock. Time for the chapel to open. I smiled at Nellie. Somehow it wasn't as bad in here as it had been outside where we got the license. I guess it was because out there we had so many questions to answer. But we lied just a little and got the license with less trouble than we had expected.

The door opened and everyone in the room started nervously. A thin-lipped, gray-haired woman came into the room and looked around importantly. She consulted a list in her hand and then glanced around the room again. "Mr. Fisher and Miss Petito will please come in," she announced.

I rose to my feet and turned to Nellie, holding out my hand. I could feel the eyes of the other couples on us. Nellie's hand was trembling in mine. I squeezed it reassuringly.

The woman nodded her head and we followed her into the chapel. She closed the door behind us and led us down to a podium. "Have you the license with you, young man?" she asked in a dry matter-of-fact voice.

"Yes, ma'am," I answered quickly, giving it to her.

She glanced at it briefly. A man came silently into the room through another door and stepped up on the podium. She handed the license to him without a word.

He looked down at us. "Don't be nervous"—he smiled slightly at his own joke—"it'll all be over in a minute."

We both tried to smile with him, but I don't suppose we made it. We were too nervous.

"Did you bring any witnesses with you?" he asked.

I shook my head. I could feel my face flush.

He smiled again. "Well, no matter." He turned to the woman. "Miss Schwartz, will you ask Mr. Simpson to step in for a minute?"

"Yes, Mr. Kyle." The gray-haired woman went out the door.

Mr. Kyle looked down at the license in his hand. "You're Daniel Fisher?" he asked of me.

"Yes, sir," I said.

"Age?" he asked.

"Twenty-three," I answered quickly, hoping he would not question my word. "Like it says there."

He shot me a brief suspicious glance. "I can read," he said succinctly. He looked at Nellie. "Eleanora Petito?"

She nodded silently and he continued to read the license in front of him. The door opened again and he looked up. The gray-haired woman had returned with a small birdlike man in a single-breasted suit.

Mr. Kyle looked down at us, smiling. "We're ready to begin now," he said, pushing the paper toward us. "If you will just sign this where I indicate—"

Nellie signed first in a nervous tiny hand. Then it was my turn, and after me the witnesses and finally Mr. Kyle. He blotted the ink dry on his signature and looked down at us importantly.

"Will you please join hands," he instructed us.

Nellie placed her hand in mine. It wasn't trembling now. I could feel faint beads of moisture gathering on my forehead.

I was glad the ceremony was fast. It seemed as if it were over almost before it had begun. The only words I could remember were the last few. I don't think the whole thing took more than two minutes.

"Do you, Eleanora Petito, take this man, Daniel Fisher, to be your lawful wedded husband?"

Her eyes were fixed on me. "I do," she answered in a solemn hushed voice.

He turned to me. "And do you, Daniel Fisher, take this woman to be your lawful wedded wife?"

I was watching her. Her eyes were soft and luminous, there were faint tears in the corners of them. "I—I do," I stammered huskily.

"Then by the authority vested in me by the City of New York, I hereby pronounce you man and wife." His voice rasped dryly at my ears. "You may kiss the bride, young man, and pay the clerk two dollars on the way out."

We kissed awkwardly and turned and hurried toward the door. His voice, drier than it had ever been during the ceremony, called us back. We turned around, startled.

He was smiling. His hand held a sheet of paper toward us. "Don't you think you ought to take your marriage certificate with you?" he asked.

I could feel my face flushing heavily as I went back and took the certificate from his outstretched hand. "Thank you, sir," I said quickly. I hurried back to Nellie and we went out the door.

The couples we had left in the waiting-room looked up at us. Some of them smiled. We smiled in return and almost ran out of the building.

We stood on the steps of City Hall and looked at each other. It was the same world we had left a few minutes ago, but it was changed now. We were married.

Nellie put her hand through my arm. "First we'll go down and tell my folks," she said proudly.

"Okay," I said.

"Then we'll go and tell your family," she added.

I looked at her in surprise. "What for?" I asked. "It's none of their business. Besides, they don't give a damn."

A firm resolution glowed in her eyes. "But I do. And I want them to know."

"But they don't care about us. I don't have to tell 'em nothin'," I protested.

She squeezed my arm, smiling. "Look, Danny Fisher, we're not going to start our marriage with a quarrel, are we?"

I smiled down at her. Her face was flushed and her eyes were happy and sparkling. "N-no," I answered.

"Then we'll tell them," she said definitely, starting down the steps.

"Okay, so we'll tell them," I agreed, walking beside her. "I'll even go on the radio and tell the whole world if you want me to."

She laughed happily and looked up at me. "Say, do you think that's a bad idea?"

CHAPTER THIRTEEN

THE DOORMAN REACHED OUT HIS HAND AND STOPPED US, AN INQUIRING look on his face.

"Mr. Gottkin's apartment, please," I told him.

He nodded his head politely. "Mr. Gordon's apartment is C21. That's on the twenty-first floor."

We walked past him to the elevator and the door swung shut. The elevator man faced the front of the car stolidly. I looked at Nellie. "What's this 'Gordon' business?" I whispered.

"He changed his name legally last year," she whispered back.

I nodded my head. Logical. I guess he thought Gottkin might be good enough for Brooklyn, but in these fancy apartments on Central Park South, Gordon was more in keeping.

I looked at my watch. It was a few minutes after nine. After we had left Nellie's folks, we had gone out to dinner and then up to my folks' house. They lived in a nice place up in Washington Heights now, but nothing near as good as this. The doorman up there had told us that they usually had dinner at their daughter's house on Friday nights, so we came back downtown again.

I wondered what they would be like. A vague restlessness stirred inside me. Nellie's family hadn't been too bad.

Nellie's father had opened the door. His swarthy face looked angrily out at her. A flood of Italian poured from his lips, and in the middle of it she interrupted him with a few words in the same tongue.

Abruptly his speech came to a halt and he looked at me. I stared back at him. I couldn't tell what he was thinking because his face was still flushed from his anger. Then he silently stepped aside and let us into the apartment.

Nellie's mother descended upon us with loud shrieks. She encased Nellie in her arms and burst into tears. I stood awkwardly by the door, watching them. Nellie began to cry too. Her father and I just stood there helplessly looking at each other.

Suddenly there was a shout from the next room. "Danny!" Zep was running toward me, a broad grin on his face, his hand outstretched. Then Nellie's kid sister came into the room and began to cry too. After a while things began to quiet down and her father reluctantly brought out a bottle of wine and they all joined in a toast to our health.

By the time the bottle was almost empty we were all on fairly good terms. I couldn't imagine they were tremendously pleased at what we had done, but they recognized it and seemed to want to make the best of it. Mamma Petito even helped Nellie pack her few things so that we could go back to the hotel and wanted us to stay for supper. We begged off, saying we had to go uptown to my folks because we hadn't seen them yet.

The elevator stopped and the doors opened. The elevator operator stuck his head out the door and said: "Fourth door across the hall."

The small nameplate under the bell read: "SAM GORDON." I pressed the buzzer and somewhere in the apartment I could hear chimes ringing. "Real fancy," I murmured, looking at Nellie.

She seemed pale in the dim light of the hallway. She nodded her head silently as we waited for someone to answer the door. I took her hand. Her palms were moist.

The door opened and a small colored woman dressed in a maid's uniform looked out at us "Mrs. Gott—er, Mrs. Gordon in?" I asked.

The Negress looked at me impassively. "Who shall I say is calling, sir?" she asked in a low, pleasant voice.

"Her brother," I said.

The maid's eyes widened slightly and she stepped aside. "Will you wait here for a moment?" she asked.

We stood in the foyer and looked around the room while the maid disappeared into the apartment. The foyer was as big as all of Nellie's apartment. We could hear the quiet murmur of voices coming from another room. Suddenly there was silence and we could hear the maid's voice.

"There's a young gen'mun an' a lady to see you, Miz Gordon."

I recognized Mimi's voice. "Did they say who they were?" She sounded puzzled.

The maid's voice was stolid. "Yes'm. He say he your brother an'—"

She never finished the sentence. "It's Danny!" I heard Mimi scream. "It's Danny!" Then she was standing in the foyer looking at us.

We stood there for a moment. At first glance I didn't think she had changed, but then as we drew closer I could see that she had. Her eyes were darker than ever and there were faint bluish circles beneath them as if she didn't sleep too well. Maybe it was because she was pregnant again and her belly pushed forward in front of her, I didn't know, but there were tight small lines in the corner of her mouth that I had never noticed before.

Then her arms were pulling my face down to her and she was kissing me. "Danny," she whispered. "I'm so glad to see you." There were tears standing in the corners of her eyes.

I smiled at her. I was glad to see her too. Funny, but I hadn't known how much I'd missed her. When I had been home we fought all the time, but that was forgotten now.

She grabbed my hand excitedly and pulled me toward the other room. "Mamma and Papa are here," she said.

I cast a frantic glance over my shoulder toward Nellie. She smiled slightly at me and nodded her head; she was following us. I let Mimi lead me into the other room.

We were standing on a few steps that led down into a living-room. Mamma and Papa were sitting on a couch with its back toward us but they were turned partly around, looking at me. Mamma held one hand clutched against her bosom, her eyes almost closed. Papa's face wore a look of dull, guarded surprise, punctuated by a long cigar that hung motionless from his lips. Sam was standing facing them, holding a long drink in his hand, his back resting against a large imitation fireplace. A curious light was glowing in his eyes.

Mimi led me around the couch in front of Mamma and let go of my hand. She was staring up into my eyes as if she were trying to read in them all that had happened since we last saw each other.

"Hello, Mamma," I said quietly.

Her hand touched the front of my coat and dropped along my sleeve until she found my hand. Her eyes began to fill. She pulled me down to her, her lips pressing against my hands. "My Blondie," she whispered brokenly, "my baby."

I stood there looking at her bent head. Her hair was all gray now. This was the moment I had been afraid of. I hadn't been afraid of how they would receive me; it was really how I would feel about them. Curious how calm I was, how detached I felt. It was almost as if I were watching this from a seat in the movies. I wasn't really a part of it. It was another guy named Danny Fisher, and he had gone away two years ago and never really come back.

That was what happened. The years and the loneliness had driven a wedge between us that no surge of emotion on either side could ever heal in me. A reluctant sorrow came over me. What great thing had been lost to us, what closeness we would never know again!

I bent and kissed the top of her head. "I'm sorry, Mamma," I said. But no one really knew what I was sorry for.

I straightened up and looked for Papa. He had walked to the far end of the room and was standing there looking at me. There was a frightened, lonely look in his eyes. Slowly I withdrew my hand from Mamma and walked toward him. The only sound in the room besides that of my footsteps was that of Mamma's weeping. I held out my hand toward my father. "Hello, Papa."

His eyes wavered for a moment, then he took my hand. "Hello, Danny." His voice was shaking but reserved.

"How've you been, Papa?" I asked.

"All right, Danny," he replied shortly.

Then we ran out of words and a subtle tension began to creep into the room. I nodded to Sam. He nodded back, but didn't speak. The others stared at me silently.

Disappointment gathered in me. This was about how I thought it would be. It didn't really make any difference whether I had come back or not. Despite myself I could feel bitterness creep into my voice.

"It's been two years," I said, my eyes going slowly from face to face. "Aren't any of you going to ask what I did those two years? How I feel?"

Mamma was still weeping softly, but no one answered. Slowly I turned back to my father. I looked at him coldly. "Aren't you going to ask? Or doesn't it really matter?"

Papa didn't answer.

It was Mimi that came to me, Mimi who took my arm and said softly: "Of course it matters. It's just that we're so surprised we don't know what to say."

I was still watching Papa. I could feel an icy calm descend on me. I had been right: something had gone from us that night the door had been closed to me. It was gone and not all that the years might bring could ever bring it back. I had wanted to see them and not wanted to. Now it didn't seem important—only that I stood among them feeling like a stranger.

Mimi tried to lead me away from Papa. "Come," she was saying, "sit down and tell us what you did. We all missed you."

I looked past her across the room. Nellie was standing in the entrance, forgotten by the others, watching us with wide, pain-filled eyes. Somehow I knew that it was not her pain she felt, but mine. I smiled slowly at her and looked down at Mimi. "I can't stay," I said gently. I didn't want to hurt her; at least she had been trying. "I've got to be going. I got things to do."

"But you can't go now, Danny," Mimi protested. The tears came into her eyes again. "You just came back."

My gaze went across the room to Nellie. "I've not come back," I said quietly, "not really. I only tried."

"But, Danny—" Mimi was crying against my shoulder. I knew how she felt, what she was crying for, but it was no use. It was something that could never be again.

I put my arm around her shaking shoulder and walked back across the room with her. "Stop it, Mimi," I whispered. "You're only making it worse." I left her at the couch and went to Nellie. I took her hand and turned back to face them. "The only reason I came tonight," I said in a low voice, "was because of my wife. She thought we should tell you that we were married this morning."

I saw the expressions that appeared on their faces—my mother's pain, the grim knowing look in Papa's eyes. I writhed inside. "She was the only one that really wanted me back," I said quickly.

I waited a moment for them to speak, but they were silent. Nellie's family hadn't liked our marriage any more than mine, but at least they had acted like human beings. My family had nothing to say, no words of happiness for us. Nothing.

The pain inside me went away rapidly, leaving behind it a cold numb feeling. I kissed Mamma's cheek. She was weeping. I kissed Mimi and stopped in front of my father. His face was bitter and masklike. I passed him without a word or a gesture.

I squirmed restlessly in the bed. I was conscious that I had been crying in my sleep, but now I was awake and my eyes were dry. I tried to lie quietly so that I wouldn't disturb her.

We had undressed in silence in the small hotel room. At last I asked, smiling wryly: "You knew all the time why I didn't want to see them, didn't you?"

She nodded silently.

"And yet you made me go." My voice was almost bitter.

Her hands were on my shoulder, her eyes on mine. "You had to go, Danny," she said earnestly. "Otherwise it might have been between us all our lives. You had to find out for yourself."

I turned away from her, my shoulders heavy and sagging. "Well, I found out all right."

She came after me, her hand clutching my arm. "Now it's over and you can forget."

"Forget?" I began to laugh. There were some things she didn't know. "How can you forget? All the things we had together—the hopes, the fears, the good and the bad. It's easy for you to say forget, but how can I? Can I cut their blood out of me, let it run into the sink and down the drain and out of my life forever? Good or bad, how can I forget? Can you forget your own parents? Does right or wrong mean more than the flesh that ties you together?"

Her voice was pleading. "No, Danny, you don't understand. That's not what you forget. That's what you remember. It's the hurt that you must forget, the hurt that will turn you into something you're not. The hurt that will make you hard and bitter and angry like you are now!"

I didn't understand her. "How can I forget that?" I asked helplessly. "It's all part of it."

"It's not, Danny," she cried, pressing herself against me and kissing my lips. "It's something else altogether. I'll make you forget the hurt. I'll make you remember only the good."

My eyes widened. "How can anyone do that?"

"I can and will," she whispered, looking up at me, her eyes deep and earnest. "I have so much love for you, my husband, that you will never need for affection from anyone."

Then I understood. I caught her hands and pressed their open palms to my lips gratefully. She had made me a promise and I knew that it would be kept. I knew that in the times to come, good or bad, I would find my comfort in her, my strength in her; that no matter what might happen, I would never be alone again.

Moving Day

SEPTEMBER 15, 1936

T HE WOODEN STEPS CREAKED COMFORTABLY UNDER OUR FEET AS WE climbed the stairway. It was a friendly sound, as if these old stairs had given welcome to many a newly married couple like ourselves. I liked the sound.

The valises I carried were light and I didn't mind their weight. Not that they weighed very much anyway; there wasn't much we had to bring along in the way of clothing. Later when I got a job and made some dough we could get ourselves a few things. Right now all the dough we could scrape together went into furnishing our new apartment.

She stopped in front of a door on the fourth floor and looked over her shoulder at me, smiling. She held a key in her hand.

I smiled back at her. "Open the door, baby, it's ours."

She put the key in the lock and turned it. The door swung open slowly, but she stood in the doorway, an expectant look on her face. I dropped the valises, bent forward, and scooped her up. I felt her arms around my neck as I crossed the threshold. On the other side I looked down into her face. She kissed me. Her lips were soft and trembling, she was light in my arms.

"God bless our happy home, Danny Fisher," she whispered.

I stood there holding her and looking into the apartment. It wasn't a big place. They don't come so big for twenty-five a month. Three rooms and bath. Everything painted white. You don't get colors for that kind of dough. But it was clean.

And it had steam heat and hot water and room enough to do a lot of living.

Room enough for us to shoot nine hundred bucks of furniture: a couch and some chairs for the parlor; a big double bed and a dresser with a mirror for the bedroom; a kitchen set and some dishes, pots and pans. It was a lot of dough, but it was worth it even if it left us with next to nothing in the bank. At least we wouldn't have to worry about some collector moving in behind us.

I put her down.

"Bring the bags into the bedroom," she told me.

"Yes, ma'am," I said snappily, picking up the valises and following her. Casually I dropped them on the bed. They sank softly into the mattress.

"Danny, take those dirty bags off the bed!" she exclaimed sharply. "This isn't a hotel, this is ours!"

I laughed aloud as I looked at her. Give a woman a place of her own and the first thing she'll do is take charge. But she was right. I put the bags on the floor and sat down on the bed. "C'mere," I said, bouncing up and down on the mattress.

She looked at me suspiciously. "What for?"

"I wanna show yuh somethin'," I said, continuing to bounce on the mattress.

She took a hesitant step toward me and then stopped. I reached out a hand and pulled her toward me quickly. She fell against me and I rolled flat on the bed, her weight on top of me.

"Danny, what's got into you?" She was laughing.

I kissed her.

She pulled her face away, still laughing. "Danny!" she protested.

I pushed at the mattress with my hand. "Listen," I told her, "no squeaks. Just like the salesman said."

"Danny Fisher, you're crazy!" Her teeth were very white when she smiled.

I pulled her down on me again. "Crazy about you," I said.

"Oh, Danny," she whispered, "Danny, I love you."

My lips were against her throat. Her skin was smooth, like the satin on a dress in a Fifth Avenue window. "I love you, baby."

She was looking into my eyes. There was an expression on her face that turned my insides into mush. She could always do that—just by looking at me. "Danny, you won't be sorry," she said earnestly.

"Sorry about what?"

"That you married me," she said seriously. "I'll be a good wife to you."

I caught her face in my hands. "It's the other way round, baby. I hope you won't be sorry you married me."

I could feel her tears against my fingers "Oh, Danny," she said very softly, "I'll never be sorry."

The doorbell rang just when we had finished hanging the curtains. "I'll get it," I said walking to the door and opening it.

Nellie's mother and a priest stood there. Mrs. Petito had a small shopping-bag in her hand. She smiled at me. "Hello, Danny."

"Hello, Mamma Petito," I said. "Come in."

She hesitated a moment, embarrassed. "I brought Father Brennan with me."

I turned to the priest and put out my hand. "Please come in, Father," I said quietly.

A look of relief crossed my mother-in-law's face as the priest took my hand. His grip was firm and friendly. "Hello, Danny," he said in a professionally hearty voice. "I'm glad to meet you."

Nellie's voice came from the bedroom. "Who is it, Danny?"

"Your mother and Father Brennan are here," I called back to her.

She appeared quickly in the doorway, her face slightly flushed. She ran to her mother and kissed her, then turned to the priest and put out her hand. "I'm glad you could come, Father," she said.

He pushed her hand aside in a friendly manner. "Come now, my child," he said, smiling, "sure and ye have a better greeting for an old friend and admirer than that." He placed both hands on her shoulders and gave her a resounding kiss on the cheek.

Mrs. Petito looked at me doubtfully and placed the shopping-bag down on the floor. "I bring some things for the house," she said.

Nellie opened the bag excitedly and looked in it. She spoke excitedly in Italian, and her mother answered her. Then Nellie turned to me and explained: "Mamma brought some food to the house so that we should never be hungry."

I turned to Mrs. Petito. People may be different, but their basic concerns are the same. I remembered when we moved to the house in Brooklyn my mother had brought some salt and a loaf of bread to the house for the very same reason. "Thank you, Mamma," I said gratefully.

Her hand patted my cheek. "You're welcome, my son," she said. "I only wish we could do more."

Nellie looked at them. "How about some coffee?" she asked. "Danny will run down and get some cake and we'll have a little party."

Mamma Petito shook her head. "I gotta go home an' cook supper. Father Brennan, he come along to wish Nellie luck."

Nellie turned to the priest smiling. "Thank you, Father. I'm so glad you could come. I was afraid you might—"

The priest interrupted her. "Oh no, Nellie, nothing like that. Of course I'm disappointed that you didn't let me marry you, but this is the next best thing."

A look of doubt crossed her face. "But I thought because of him we couldn't get married in church."

The priest turned to me, smiling affably. "Would you object to being married in the true church, son?" he asked.

Nellie answered before I could. "That's not a fair question, Father," she said quickly. "Neither of us spoke about it before."

He looked at her. The smile was gone from his face now. "You realize of course, my child, that while your marriage is recognized by the church, it is not sanctioned by it."

Nellie's face was pale. "I know that, Father," she answered in a low voice.

"Have you ever thought about children?" he continued. "What religious benefits they might receive but will be deprived of?"

This time I answered. "If I understand rightly, Father, the church will not discriminate against children because of the faith of their parents."

He looked at me. "Does that mean you are willing to allow your children to be brought up within the church?"

"It means, Father," I said simply, "that my children will be free to believe in what they choose. Their faith or lack of it will be a matter of their own election, and until such time as they are old enough to decide for themselves, I am perfectly willing to allow them to attend their mother's church."

Nellie came over to me and took my hand. "I think it's a little early to be talking about things like that. After all, we've only been married a short while."

The priest looked at us. "As a Catholic, Nellie, you are fully aware of your responsibilities. Therefore it is always best to decide things like this beforehand so that no unhappiness may result."

Nellie's face was white. She spoke through motionless lips. "I appreciate your concern and your visit, Father. Please feel sure that we will do what is right for both of us, and feel free to visit us again when you're in the neighborhood."

I could have kissed her for that. In the nicest way possible she had told him to go peddle his papers somewhere else.

He knew it too, but not a sign crossed his face. "A priest's life," he sighed, "is sometimes filled with many difficult decisions. He is only a human being in the last analysis, and like all people can only pray for divine guidance in his actions. I hope and pray, my child, that my visit with you will have a good and proper effect."

"We are grateful for your prayers, Father," my wife replied politely, her hand still in mine.

I followed Father Brennan slowly to the door, where he put out his hand. "Glad to have met you, my son," he said, but there was no enthusiasm in his voice. I'm sure he thought I was the devil's child from the way he shook my hand this time.

The door closed behind him, and Nellie spoke to her mother rapidly and angrily in Italian. Her mother raised her hand in protest and answered in a stumbling fashion. Tears came to her eyes. As the argument grew hot and heavy, I stood there dumbly, not knowing what they were saying. Then as quickly as it had begun, it was over and Nellie's mother clasped her arms about her daughter and kissed her.

Nellie turned to me apologetically. "My mother is sorry she brought him here. She meant well and hopes you are not insulted."

I looked at her mother for a moment; then I smiled. "Don't be sorry, Mamma Petito," I said slowly. "I know that you meant everything for the best."

Then Mamma Petito's arms were around me and she was kissing my cheek. "You're a good boy, Danny," she said stumblingly. "All I ask is that you take good care of my Nellie."

"I will, Mamma," I promised, looking at Nellie. "You can be sure that I will."

After her mother had gone we finished straightening up the apartment. It was still early afternoon. I sat down in the parlor and turned on the radio. Soft music filled the room. It was the right kind of music to start a new day: Frankie Carle's *Sunrise Serenade*.

Nellie came into the parlor and stood next to me. "What would you like for dinner?" she asked seriously.

"You mean you can cook too?" I asked mischievously.

A reproving look crossed her face. "Don't be silly, Danny," she said quickly. "What would you like?"

"What do you want to cook for?" I asked. "We'll eat out tonight and celebrate."

"Uh-uh." She shook her head. "It's too expensive. It's time we started watching our money until you get a job. After that we can eat out if you like."

I looked at her with a new respect. It had been growing on me all day that she was a lot more grown up than I had given her credit for being. I got to my feet and turned off the radio. "Make whatever you like and surprise me," I said. "I'll take a run uptown to the agencies and see if there's anything doing."

The bright sunlight blinded me for a moment as I came out of the hallway, and I stood in front of the house for a moment. Then I started toward the subway station. A shadow fell across my path and stood in front of me. Without looking up, I started to walk around it. A hand fell on my arm and a familiar voice came to my ears.

"Now that you're back and settled down, Danny, the boss feels you owe him a visit." I didn't have to look up to know who it was. I had been expecting him ever since I had returned. I knew they would never forget.

Spit was standing there, a slight smile on his lips but none in his eyes. He looked very neat, too, in his dark expensive appearing tailored suit and freshly laundered shirt. He had so much clothing on that for a moment I almost didn't believe it was him.

"I'm in a hurry," I said, trying to step around him again.

His hand tightened on my arm. His other hand moved slightly in his jacket pocket. I could see the dull outline of the gun he held there. "You're not in that much of a hurry, Danny, are you?" he asked.

I shook my head. "No, I'm not," I agreed.

He gestured toward the curb. A car was standing there, its motor running. "Get in," he said sharply.

I opened the door and climbed into the back seat. The Collector was sitting there. "Hello, Danny," he said quietly, and hit me in the stomach.

The pain tore through my guts and I doubled up and fell forward on the floor of the car. I heard the door behind me close quickly and the car started off.

Spit's voice seemed to float in the air over me. "Cut out the rough stuff. The boss'll be sore."

The Collector's voice was sullen. "I owed the son of a bitch that."

Spit grabbed my collar and pulled me onto the seat beside him. "Don't say anything to the boss about this or next time yuh'll get worse."

I nodded my head and swallowed the vomit that threatened to rise in my throat. A few minutes passed before I was feeling good enough to realize what he had said. "Next time"—that meant, for some reason I didn't know, that I was off the hook. I wondered what had happened. I knew Maxie Fields was not the forgiving type.

The auto swung to a stop in front of his store. Spit got out of the car in front of me, the Collector behind. Together we walked into the narrow hallway beside the store and up the stairs to Fields's apartment. Spit knocked at the door.

"Who is it?" Fields's voice roared through it.

"It's me, boss," Spit answered quickly. "I got Danny Fisher with me."

"Bring him in," Fields shouted.

Spit opened the door, pushed me through it, and followed me into the room. My stomach still hurt, but I was beginning to feel better. At least I could stand up straight now.

Maxie Fields stood like a huge Gargantua behind his desk. His eyes glittered at me. "So you couldn't stay away?" he said heavily, coming around his desk toward me.

I didn't answer—just watched him coming toward me. I wasn't afraid of him this time. Spit had tipped me off without knowing it. I saw Maxie's open hand flying at my face and instinctively ducked away from it.

A sharp stabbing pain in my kidneys straightened me up. Spit, standing behind me, had jabbed me with the butt end of his knife. This time I caught Maxie's swing flush on the cheek. I rocked on my feet unsteadily, but didn't speak. Talking wouldn't do any good and it might only make things worse.

Fields grinned at me viciously. "You're not the only one who couldn't stay away." He turned and bellowed into the other room: "Ronnie, bring me a drink. An old friend of yours has come to pay us a visit."

I turned to the other door, my ears ringing. Sarah was standing there, her wide eyes fixed on mine, a drink in her hand. For a second we stared at each other, then her eyes fell and she walked slowly across the room to Fields. Silently she handed him the drink.

He was smiling maliciously at her. "Ain't you gonna say hello to your old friend?"

She turned to me, her eyes dull and vacant. "Hello, Danny."

"Hello, Sarah," I answered.

Fields looked at me, the drink still in his hand. "Just like old times, isn't it, Kid?" He took a sip of the drink and almost emptied the glass. "Nothing has changed, has it?"

I was watching Sarah's face. It was still and impassive, with no flicker of expression. "Nothing has changed," I answered quietly.

"Ronnie couldn't stay away from her sweetie. She came back all by herself, didn't she?" Fields asked.

I thought I saw a moment's fire in her eyes, but it passed too quickly to be sure. "Yes, Max," she said dully, like an automaton.

Fields pulled her close to him. "Ronnie can't live without her Max, can she?"

This time I could see her lips trembling. "No, Max."

He shoved her away angrily. "Get in the other room," he roared.

Without looking at me, she walked toward the door, paused for a moment in the doorway, then went right on through without looking back.

Fields turned to me. "No one gets away from Maxie Fields," he boasted.

I looked at him. He didn't have to tell me that; he had convinced me. I wondered what he'd done to bring her back. I wondered if anything had happened to Ben.

He went behind his desk and sat down heavily, his fat-covered eyes staring at me. "Remember that, Danny. Nobody ever gets away from Maxie Fields."

"I'll remember," I said.

He was breathing heavily as he stared at me. After a moment he raised his glass to his lips and finished the drink. "Okay," he said, putting the tumbler down on the desk in front of him, "you can go now."

I stood there unbelieving, not daring to move, wondering what was up his sleeve now. It was too easy. He wasn't going to let me off that easy—not Maxie Fields.

"You heard me!" he roared in sudden anger. "Get out and stay out of my way. The next time yuh won't be so lucky. I might not be feelin' so good!"

I stood there, not moving. I was afraid to turn around.

The telephone on his desk began to ring and he picked it up. "Yeah," he barked into it. There was a crackle of a voice, and a subtle change came across his face. "Hello, Sam," he said cordially. The voice in the phone began to crackle again and he covered the mouthpiece with his hand.

"Throw him out if he won't go by himself, Spit," he said almost cordially.

I didn't need another invitation. I got out of there in a hurry. It wasn't until I was in the familiar dirty streets again that I began to realize what had happened. I still didn't know why he had let me go, unless—there could be only one reason. Sarah had made a deal with him. That's why she didn't look at me or speak to me. That must be it. It was the only thing I could think of.

I looked at my wristwatch. It was only two thirty; I still had time to run uptown and case the agencies. No use getting back early or Nellie would wonder why I hadn't gone, and I didn't want to tell her about this. She would only worry.

I covered about four agencies, but there was nothing doing. They all told me to come back in the morning. I quit a little after four and started back downtown thinking I'd have to get an early start tomorrow if I wanted a job. There weren't many of them around.

She made chicken cacciatore and spaghetti and we had a bottle of Chianti that her mother had brought. The meal was delicious, but I had to force myself to eat, because my stomach hurt. Still, I packed enough away to make it look good.

"Yuh want help with the dishes?" I asked.

She shook her head. "Go into the parlor and turn on the radio," she said. "I'll only be a few minutes."

I went inside and sank into the club chair by the radio and turned it on. The voice of the Kingfish echoed through the room and I listened delightedly to Andy's efforts to get his friend a job.

That seemed to be everybody's worry then: to get a job. Mine too. Would be good when I got one, though. We could save a few bucks. Maybe when things got a little better and I made a little more dough, we could buy a little house. Out in Brooklyn, maybe in my old neighborhood. I liked it there. The streets were clean and the air was fresh. It wasn't like down here on East Fourth and First Avenue. But this was a better place than most in the neighborhood. The house was clean. It was a four-story, twelve-family affair, and it didn't look as run down as the others. It didn't make for a bad beginning.

I heard Nellie coming into the room and looked up. "All through?"

She nodded. "I told you I wouldn't be long," she said proudly.

I pulled her down to me. She rested her head on my shoulder, her eyes looking up at my face. We sat there quietly. I felt peaceful and happy and content.

"Danny, what're you thinking?"

I smiled down at her. "About how lucky I am," I said. "I got everything I ever wanted."

"Everything, Danny?"

"Just about," I answered, looking into her eyes. "What else is there to want? I got my girl, m' own home. All I need now is a job an' everything'll be rosy."

Her eyes turned serious. "I meant to ask you, Danny, how did things look? Was there anything?"

I shook my head. "I can't tell yet, baby," I said lightly. "After all, I did go out in the afternoon and was in only a few places. I'll know more when I get out in the mornin'."

A worried look crossed her face. "The paper says that unemployment is at an all-time high."

"The paper," I scoffed, "says anything that'll make a headline."

"But look at all the families on relief! That must mean something."

"Sure it does." I looked down at her confidently. "Those people jus' don't wanna work. You can get a job if you want to bad enough. I want to work. I'll get a job."

"But, Danny," she went on, "not all of them are like that."

"Look, Nellie," I told her. "Only bums'll go on relief. Not me. We'll never have to worry about that."

She was silent for a moment, then her face turned up to me again. "But what if you don't get a job for a while?"

I smiled at her. "We'll manage. We don't have to worry about that. You're still workin'."

"But what if I can't work, if I have to stop?" She blushed slightly and looked away. "What if I become pregnant?"

"You don't have to," I said pointedly. "There are ways to prevent that."

The blush left her face suddenly, leaving it pale and nervous. "Catholics don't believe in it. It's against the religion. It's a sin," she explained, looking down at the floor.

"Then what do they do?" I asked. "Yuh just can't go around pregnant all the time."

"There are certain times that are safe." She didn't meet my eyes.

I began to feel slightly embarrassed. There was much I had to learn. "But what if it happens some other time?" I asked curiously.

She still avoided my eyes. "It doesn't. You don't let it happen."

"That's the bunk," I said strongly. "We'll do what everybody else does." The sound of a sniffle came to my ears. "My God!" I exclaimed. "What are you crying about? I didn't say anything wrong!"

She flung her arms around my neck and pressed her cheek against mine. "I can't do it, Danny!" she cried. "I can't do it. I've done enough wrong things as it is. I can't make it any worse!"

I held her close to me. Her body was rigid with a fear I didn't quite understand. Even though she had stood up to him, that visit from the priest had loused things up for sure. "Okay, Nellie, okay," I said soothingly. "We'll do it your way."

Her tears turned into a radiant smile. "Oh, Danny," she exclaimed, kissing me with quick little kisses all over my face, "you're so good to me! I love you!"

"I love you too, baby," I said, smiling down at her, "but is it safe?"

All the Days of My Life

THE FOURTH BOOK

CHAPTER ONE

S HE WALKED PAST THE COSMETIC COUNTER, DOWN ALONG THE FOUNTAIN to my station, and climbed up on a stool. She squirmed there for a moment, getting her seat right so that her lungs showed over the counter. Out of the corner of my eye I could see Jack, the boss, watching her. I didn't blame him a bit. She had a healthy pair of lungs.

I finished mopping my face with the cold towel before I picked her up. It was one of those hot, muggy nights you hit in New York in October when the last piece of summer fights its losing battle. I leaned over the counter and smiled at her.

"Yes, miss?" I asked, checking the clock on the wall behind her.

"A short Coke with lime, Danny." Her eyes, as she smiled back, were as heavy and sultry as if she were taking me to bed.

"Comin' right up," I replied, sexing her right back. Without turning around, I reached behind me and took a glass from the shelf. Her smile grew deeper and warmer.

I held the glass under the spigot and goosed the pump. The brown syrup spurted forth and I pushed the glass under the seltzer spigot, pushing the handle back with the heel of my hand. While the glass filled, I squeezed an eighth of a lime into it, jacked it with a spoon, then cut off the seltzer.

She had an unlit cigarette in her mouth when I put the Coke down in front of her. I beat her to the match. Its dancing light flickered in her eyes as I held it for her. "Thanks, Danny." She glowed at me.

"Nothin'," I said, tapping out a straw for her.

She took the straw daintily from my fingers and stirred it slowly in the glass. "They ought to have places on the subway where you can get a Coke if you're thirsty on a night like this," she said before sipping her drink.

I grinned at her. "I wouldn' like that a' tall," I said, stretching the South in my speech. All soda jerks were supposed to be from the South. "Then I'd never get to see yuh."

She gave me an appreciative smile and pushed her lungs out a little farther. I gave them the expected, appreciative double-O before I walked up the front of the counter to Jack. It was all part of the game. The kids that sat in front of your counter expected it. It was their way of getting hunk for the way they lived. Romance at a soda fountain. Real cheap for a nickel Coke.

"After one o'clock, Jack," I said. "Clean up now?"

From the register Jack looked up at the clock. He nodded his head, his eyes going back to the girl. "Yeah, Danny," he said, grinning. "It must be that blond hair and blue eyes that gets 'em."

I waved my hand modestly. "Nuts," I answered. "It's my clean-cut red-blooded American look."

He shook his head. "I don' know what it is, but four outta five heads that come in here pass me up to set down at your station. An' the come-ons yuh get! Man, I'd be eatin' muh heart out all the time."

I grinned at him. "Don' be jealous, Jack. I may attract the dames, but you got all the dough."

"Honest, Danny?" he queried. "Yuh never bother with 'em at all?"

"You know me, Jack. A married man with a kid's got no time to fool aroun', an' besides not havin' the time I ain't got the dough." I checked the broad in the mirror behind the counter. She smiled at me and I smiled back. "On top o' that yuh keep away from these chicks. They all hold C.T.U. cards an' if yuh make a move they holler."

He grinned again and looked down at the register. "I don' believe a word yuh're saying," he said in a friendly voice. "But it's okay to start cleanin' up now."

I walked back down the counter and punched out a ticket for the girl. I dropped it on the counter in front of her just as she finished her drink. "Thank you, miss."

I pocketed the nickel she left for me as she clambered down off the stool, and turned back to the fountain. It was one fifteen but I didn't need the clock to tell me that. I was tired. My legs were weary and my back ached from the steady seven hours and fifteen minutes I had been on my feet that night since six P.M. But what the hell, I told myself as I began to pull the pumps, it was a job, and jobs weren't too easy to get this fall of 1939, even if a war was going on in Europe. I ought to know, I'd been looking long enough.

Almost three years to be exact. Sure I got some jobs, but they didn't stick. Something always happened and then I'd be hitting the streets again. It wasn't so bad while Nellie was working. We could manage then. But when Vickie came along, things were a little different. We ran head-first into something that time and economics stacked up against us.

I remembered the day Nellie came home from work and told me she was going to have a baby. There must have been a funny look on my face because she put out her hand and touched my arm.

"Danny, you don't look pleased?" she asked, a hurt deep in her dark eyes.

"I'm pleased all right," I said shortly.

She drew closer to me. "Then what's the matter?"

"I was wonderin' what we're gonna use for dough."

"You'll get a job," she said. "Things can't keep up like this forever."

I turned away and lit a cigarette. "That's what I keep tellin' myself," I said.

She turned me back to her. The hurt on her face went deeper than just her eyes. "You're not happy that we're having a baby," she said accusingly.

"Why shouldn't I be happy?" I asked, letting the smoke out through my nose. "I'm dancing in the streets. It's great. We'll be lucky if we don't wind up livin' there, the way things are going. I never been so happy in my life."

Her eyes fell from mine. "I couldn't help it, Danny," she whispered apologetically. "I—it just happened."

"Sure, it just happened," I said sarcastically. "There's a dozen ways to keep things like that from happenin', but my wife don't believe in 'em. She's gotta believe in some crackpot idea about rhythm. She's gotta—"

"Danny!"

I stopped talking and looked at her. Her eyes had filled with tears. I dragged at my cigarette silently.

Through her tears she asked plaintively: "Danny, don't you want a baby?"

The pain in her voice ran all the way through me and wound up in my heart. I pulled her to me roughly. "I'm sorry, Nellie," I said quickly. "Of course I want a baby. It's just that I'm worried. Babies cost dough, and that we ain't got."

She smiled tremblingly through her tears. "Babies don't ask for much," she whispered. "All they need is love."

But it hadn't been quite that easy. They needed a few bucks too. I remembered how, when the last buck we had saved ran out, we had gone downtown to the relief office and applied for help. The way the clerk had looked at us—at me, then at Nellie with the child big in her—as if to ask what right did we have to bear children when we couldn't take care of ourselves. There had been the endless questionnaires to fill out, and the investigators had come to the house at all hours. The endless probing until there was no part of our lives that remained private, that could be called our own.

I remembered when the investigator had brought us the first check. She was a fat woman wearing an old fur coat. "This is for food and other necessities of life," she had said as I took the check from her.

I had nodded without meeting her eyes.

"If we hear," she continued in a flat warning tone, "that you have spent any part of this on whisky or gambling or any purpose for which it is not intended, we will immediately stop further checks."

I could feel my face flaming, but I didn't look at her. I couldn't. The way I felt, I would never be able to look at anyone again.

That was before Vickie was born. The first time I saw her was when the nurse in the city hospital let me peek through the glass-paneled doors. Vickie, my daughter, my baby. Little and pink and blonde, like me. I thought I would swell up and bust. I knew than that I had done nothing to be ashamed of, nothing wrong. It was worth any humiliation, any pain, just to stand there and look at her.

Then the nurse had let me go in and see Nellie. She was in a small ward on the fourth floor of the hospital, with seven other patients in the room besides her. She watched me walk up to the bed, her dark eyes wide and steady. I didn't say anything. I didn't know what to say. I bent over her bed and kissed her lips, my hand pressing down on her arm.

As she looked up at me, I could see a thin blue vein pulsing in her throat. She seemed very tired. "It's a girl," she said.

I nodded.

"But she's got your hair," Nellie added quickly.

"And your eyes and your face," I said quickly. "I saw her. She's a beauty."

Then Nellie smiled. "You're not disappointed?" she asked in a small voice.

I shook my head violently. "She's just what I wanted," I said emphatically. "Another you."

The nurse came by. "You'd better be going now, Mr. Fisher," she said.

I kissed Nellie again and left the small ward. I had gone home and spent a restless night in the lonely apartment. Early in the morning I went out looking for a job.

As usual there had been nothing. Finally, frantic with fear that I wouldn't be able to support my child, I decided to see if Sam would help me. I remembered how I stood in the street in front of the Empire State Building, in which he had his office, for almost an hour mustering up my nerve. Then I went inside and rode the elevator up to his office.

The receptionist wouldn't let me go into the office. He didn't want to see me. I went downstairs to a public telephone and called him. His voice was gruff when he answered. His first words sent a chill through me and I slammed the receiver back on the hook with a sick feeling in my stomach as his words still echoed in my ear. "What's the matter, kid? Yuh lookin' for another handout?" It wasn't until then that I realized that all the doors had closed behind me. There was no one I could really turn to. I had made my bed.

Nellie came home with the baby and the whole summer had almost gone by before I found anything. That was just a few weeks ago, and the job didn't even pay enough to live on. It had been night work and I was so desperate for something to do that I grabbed at it. Clerk at a soda fountain, six bucks a week and tips. If I could keep it a secret from the relief people, we'd be able to get along and the few extra bucks would be a great help. The seventy-two dollars a month they doled out didn't go very far.

I flushed down the last pump and looked up at the clock. Half past two. I pulled off my apron and tucked it away beneath the counter where I could find it tomorrow night. If I hurried to the subway I could be home by three o'clock. That way at least I could get a few hours' sleep before the relief investigator came in the morning with the check. She usually got to the house by seven o'clock.

CHAPTER TWO

I COULD HARDLY KEEP MY EYES OPEN AS I SAT AT THE TABLE AND LISTENED to Miss Snyder's nasally monotonous voice. Miss Snyder was the relief investigator in charge of our case. She was one of those people who are expert at everything. Right now she was giving Nellie instructions on how to prepare a meat sauce for spaghetti without meat.

"I think that's wonderful, don't you, Danny?"

Nellie's voice snapped my eyes open. "What?" I stammered. "Yeah. Sure."

"You weren't even listening, Mr. Fisher," Miss Snyder said, coldly reproving me.

"Oh, I was, Miss Snyder," I said quickly. "I heard every word you said."

She looked at me sharply through her thin steel-rimmed glasses. "You seem very tired, Mr. Fisher," she said suspiciously. "Were you up late last night?"

I was wide awake now. "No, Miss Snyder." I hastened to relieve her suspicions. "I went to bed early, but I couldn't sleep. I was very restless."

She turned back to Nellie. I could see that I didn't impress her. "And how is the baby, Mrs. Fisher?" she asked gurglingly.

"Would you like to see her, Miss Snyder?" Nellie was on her feet already. I smiled to myself. Nellie knew how to handle her. Miss Snyder was a spinster and a sucker for babies. From now on I could fall asleep and snore at the table and she wouldn't know I was there.

I waited until Miss Snyder left; then I stumbled blindly back into bed. I didn't even bother pulling off my trousers before I was asleep. I awoke with the feeling I was alone in the house. I turned my head to look at the clock on the table next to the bed. It was noon. A small white paper propped up against the clock stared at me. It was from Nellie.

Went down to cash the check, pay the bills, and do some shopping. Took Vickie with me so that you could get some sleep. There is coffee on the stove. Will be back by three.

I dropped the note back on the night table and rolled out of bed, stood up, and stretched. The bones in my shoulders snapped gratefully. I headed for the bathroom and stared at myself in the mirror as I spread the shaving soap over my face. I looked weary and older. The skin over my cheekbones seemed taut and dry, there were faint crinkles in the corners of my eyes. I took a deep breath and began to work the lather into my skin. I felt better when my face was completely covered with fluffy whiteness.

The key rattled in the lock just as I finished shaving. I put down the razor and went to the door. Nellie was standing there, Vickie in one arm, a bag of groceries in the other. I took the baby from her and walked back to the kitchen. Nellie followed me with the groceries.

"I paid up the butcher and the grocer," she said, putting the bag down on the table, "and I've got six dollars left over after the rent, gas, and electricity is taken out."

"Good," I said. Vickie seemed curiously quiet. Usually when I held her she would squirm restlessly and playfully. "What's the matter with Vickie?"

Nellie glanced at her. "I don't know," she answered, a worried look crossing her face. "She's been like that all morning. In the store she began to cry. That's why I'm home so early."

I held Vickie up in the air at arm's length over my head. "What's with my baby girl?" I crooned, jouncing her lightly, waiting for her to gurgle happily as she always did when I held her like that.

Instead she began to cry. Her loud wails filled the room. I turned bewildered toward Nellie. I never knew what to do when the baby cried, my fingers all turned thumbs.

"Let me put her to bed," Nellie said practically, taking her from me. "Maybe she'll feel better after her nap."

I sat down at the table and had me a cup of coffee while Nellie put her to sleep. I looked through the paper idly. There was an article there about the relief bureau checking up on some people who were suspected of holding out on them. I showed it to Nellie when she came back into the kitchen.

She looked at me doubtfully. "Do you think Miss Snyder suspects anything?"

I shrugged my shoulders. "I don't see how she can. I'm always home whenever she comes up."

"Maybe some of the neighbors might have noticed and said something to her."

"They wouldn't do that. They've enough troubles of their own."

"Still, she acted peculiar this morning. As if she knew something."

"Forget it," I said, more confidently than I felt. "She knows from nothin'."

Vickie began to cry again. Suddenly in the midst of her crying she began to cough, a heavy mucousy cough. Nellie and I looked at each other for a moment, then she turned and hurried into the bedroom. I followed her.

By the time I reached her, Nellie was holding the baby in her arms and patting her back lightly. The coughing stopped. Nellie looked at me with wide, frightened eyes. "She's so warm, Danny."

I touched a light palm gently to Vickie's forehead. It felt warm and damp to my hand. "Maybe she's got a little fever."

"She was coughing last night," Nellie said. "Maybe she caught my cold."

I hadn't thought about that. Nellie had been fighting a cold for over a week now. "Let's get the doctor," I said.

The baby began to cry again. We stared at each other helplessly. Nellie looked down at the baby, then up at me. "Maybe we better," she agreed. "The medical card is on the kitchen shelf. Call right away on the phone in the hall downstairs."

The doctor turned from the baby and beckoned to Nellie. "Let me have a look at you while your husband puts the baby back in the crib," he said.

Hesitantly Nellie asked: "Is she all right?"

Out of the corner of my eye I could see the doctor nodding as I placed Vickie in the crib. "She has a cold that seems to have centered in her throat. I'll give you something for it." He held a tongue depressor in his hand. "Open your mouth and say: 'Ah.'"

Nellie opened her mouth and he put the wooden stick against her tongue. She gagged and began to cough. He withdrew the depressor quickly and waited for her coughing spell to pass, then reached into his bag for his thermometer.

"Well?" she asked.

He smiled at her. "Stop worrying, Mrs. Fisher," he said. "Let's see if you have any fever." He put the thermometer in her mouth, took out a small prescription pad, and began to write on it.

Just as I finished covering Vickie, he asked me: "Do you have your assignment number?"

"It's in the kitchen, doc," I said quickly. "I'll get it."

When I came back into the room, the doctor was studying the thermometer he had taken from Nellie's mouth. "You have a little fever too, Mrs. Fisher," he said. "Did you know that?"

Nellie shook her head.

"You better get into bed and stay there a few days," he told her.

"But, doctor," she protested, "you haven't told us what's the matter with Vickie."

He looked at her impatiently. "The same thing is the matter with both of you. You both have a sore throat and a cold. I'll give you a couple of prescriptions, one for you and one for her. Follow the directions and you'll both be okay."

"Do you think she caught it from me?" Nellie asked worriedly.

The doctor was writing again. "I don't know who caught it from who, but just

get these filled and keep warm and I'll stop by tomorrow to have a look at you."
He held out the two prescriptions and turned to me. "Do you have the number?"

Silently I gave him the small white card that the relief people had issued to
me. It was an authorization card to call for medical help at their expense.

The doctor's pen scratched quickly in his notebook. I could see that we had
already received all the time he would give us for the two dollars per visit he got
from welfare. He finished writing and handed the card and a slip of paper to me.
"Give this to your investigator when you see him," he said brusquely, picking up
his bag.

I looked at the paper in my hand. It was a Welfare Department medical-call
form. "Yes, doctor," I said.

He was already at the door. "Now do as I say," he said warningly over his
shoulder before he stepped out. "Keep in bed and take the medicine as directed
on the bottle. I'll be back tomorrow."

The door snapped shut behind him and Nellie looked at me. I stared back at
her for a second, anger filling my gorge. I crumpled the piece of paper viciously
in my hand. "The son of a bitch!" I swore heatedly. "Lookin' for a buck, that's
all. Too busy to even talk to yuh because you're on relief! I bet he don't talk to
other patients like that!"

Nellie began to cough. "Well, there's nothing we can do about it," she managed
to gasp. "At least he comes. Lots of 'em won't bother when they find out who
pays the bill."

I was still angry. "He doesn't have to act like we were dirt!"

She walked back to the bed and slumped into it. "You ought to know by now
how people are, Danny," she said wearily.

The patience in her face made me ashamed of my outburst. She was right. If
I didn't know the score by now, I would never know it. I hurried over to her and
took her hand. "Give me the prescriptions," I said. "I'll run 'em down to the
drugstore an' get them filled. I think I'll stay home tonight."

She shook her head. "No, Danny," she told me, "just get them filled. Then
you can go to work. We need the money."

"But the doctor said for you to stay in bed," I protested.

She smiled wanly at me. "They always say that, but who ever heard of staying
in bed with a lousy little cold? You go to work. We'll be all right until you get
home."

CHAPTER THREE

I RAN UP THE STAIRS AND STOPPED IN FRONT OF MY DOOR. I COULD HEAR
Nellie coughing as I slipped the key into the lock. A shaft of light coming
from the bedroom struck my eyes. I shut the door quickly and hurried to the
bedroom. "Nellie, are you up?" I called.

I stopped in the doorway. Nellie was just straightening up over the baby's crib.
"Danny!" she cried.

I crossed the room with one long stride. "What's the matter?"

She grabbed hold of my jacket. "You've got to do something!" She was coughing and trying to speak all at the same time. "Vickie's burning up!"

I looked down into the crib, my hand reaching for the baby's forehead. It was hot to my touch. I looked at Nellie.

"She has a hundred and three!" Her voice was trembling.

I was staring at Nellie's eyes. They were dark, feverish pools. I tried to keep my voice calm. "Don't get panicky," I said quickly. "Babies often have fever that high. You look like you've got some yourself."

"Don't worry about me," she said, a note of hysteria creeping into her voice. "We have to do something for Vickie!"

I gripped her shoulders harshly. "Nellie!" I whipped my voice into her ears. "Take it easy! I'll run down to the hall phone and call the doctor. I'll be back in a minute."

She was crying now, the tears running down her face. "Yes, Danny, yes." She turned and straightened the covers over Vickie. "Hurry, Danny, she's on fire!"

The spinning dial on the telephone made a loud ratchety sound in the night-ridden hallway. I heard a click and then the telephone at the other end of the wire began to ring. It rang for several seconds before the receiver was picked up. A man's sleepy voice answered: "Yes?"

"Is this Dr. Addams?" I asked.

"This is Dr. Addams speaking," the voice replied.

"Doc, this is Danny Fisher," I said quickly. "You were over to see my kid today."

His voice sounded slightly annoyed. "Yes, Mr. Fisher. I know."

"I think you better come over right away, doctor. The baby's temperature is up to a hundred and three and she's burnin' up!"

His voice came slowly through the telephone. "Is she sleeping?"

"Yeah, doc," I answered. "But I don't like her looks; she's all red an' sweatin' somethin' fierce. My wife is too. Her fever must be way up."

There was a moment's hesitation before the doctor spoke again. "Did they take the medicine as I prescribed?"

"Yes, doc."

"Then stop worrying, Mr. Fisher." The doctor's voice carried a professionally impersonal reassurance that had no conviction for me. "It's quite customary for a fever to go up at night in the case of a severe cold. Give them both something warm to drink and cover them well. They'll be better by morning and I'll come by then."

"But, doc—" I protested.

"Just do as I say, Mr. Fisher." The doctor's voice came through with firm finality, followed by a click.

I stared at the dead receiver in my hand, suddenly realizing he had hung up on me. Viciously I slammed it back on the hook.

Nellie's eyes were wide as I came back into the apartment. "Is he coming?" she asked anxiously.

"Nope," I said as casually as I could. I didn't want her to worry any more than she had to. "He said it was nothin'. It happens all the time. He said to give you both somethin' warm to drink an' cover you well."

"Danny, do you think it's all right?" Her voice was nervous.

I smiled down at her with a confidence I did not feel. "Sure, it's okay. He's a doctor, ain't he? He must know what he's talkin' about." I led her gently toward the bed. "Now you lie down an' I'll make you some hot tea. You're not feelin' so good yourself an' everything looks worse than it really is."

Reluctantly she got into bed. "Make Vickie a bottle first," she said.

"Sure, Nellie, sure," I said. "Now cover up an' keep warm."

Carefully I carried the cup of tea into the bedroom and sat down on the edge of the bed. "Come on now," I said gently, "drink this. You'll feel better."

She took the cup from my outstretched hand and slowly lifted it to her lips. I could see the warmth go through her. "This is good," she said.

I smiled at her "Of course it's good. Look who made it. Danny of the Waldorf."

She smiled faintly back at me as she held the cup to her lips again. "See how Vickie is," she told me.

I bent over the crib. The baby was sleeping quietly. "She's sleepin' like a charm," I said.

Nellie emptied the cup and handed it back to me, then lay back against the pillow, her black hair spreading over the white pillowcase.

"Baby," I said in a wondering voice, "I almos' forgot how good you look."

She smiled up at me sleepily. I could see she was very tired. "Working nights seems to do something for your eyesight, Danny," she said, trying to joke. "It even makes you see better."

I switched off the light. "Go to sleep, baby," I said, bending over the bed and pressing my lips to her temple. "Things'll be all right now."

I went back into the kitchen and rinsed out the cup. I sat down in a chair by the table and was lighting a cigarette when the sound of the baby's whimper caught my ear. I tossed the butt into the sink and hurried into the bedroom. Vickie was coughing tiny rasping coughs deep in her chest. Quickly I picked her up in her blanket and patted her little back lightly until the coughing had stopped.

Nellie was sleeping a sleep of complete and utter exhaustion. I was glad that Vickie hadn't awakened her. I touched my fingers to the baby's face. It was still warm and feverish. Vickie's head slipped toward my shoulder. She was sleeping again. Gently I put her back in the crib and covered her. "Papa'll be back in a minute," I whispered to her.

I hurried back into the kitchen and ran water over the glowing butt in the sink. Then I turned out the light and went back into the bedroom in the dark. I placed a chair next to the crib and sat down in it, then reached over the side of the crib and felt for Vickie's fingers. Instinctively her tiny hand curled around my index finger. I sat there quietly, not daring to move for fear of disturbing her rest.

Outside the window the moonlight was bright and the night itself seemed new, as if it were another world. I felt Vickie move and I turned to look down into the crib. She was sleeping on her side. In the darkness I could see her curled up into a little ball around my hand. My daughter, I thought proudly. It took a scare like this to make me realize how precious she was to me. There were so many things about her I took for granted—the way she bubbled after she ate, the way her bright blue eyes followed me when I came into the room, the cute little wrinkles on the soles of her feet.

"I'll make it up to you for havin' to live like this, Vickie baby," I promised her.

My husky whisper in the darkness startled me.

I looked nervously at the bed, but Nellie was still sleeping. I turned back to the crib, and this time I was careful that my moving lips made no sound. "Get well, Vickie baby," I whispered. "Get well and strong for your daddy. There's a whole world outside, and he wants you to share it with him. There's the sun an' the moon an' the stars an' lots of other wonderful things for your eyes to see, your ears to hear, your nose to smell. Grow big an' strong so that we can walk down the street together, so we can hold each other by the hand and feel our blood thumpin' in each other's heart. I'll buy you lots o' things, Vickie—dolls an' toys an' dresses. Anything you want, I'll get for you. I'll work hard, twenty-four hours a day, to make you happy. You're my baby an' I love you."

I felt her move again and peered down through the darkness at her. What a fool I had been all this time not to have known how rich she had made me! I looked up at the ceiling over her crib.

"Please, God," I prayed for the first time since I had been a kid myself, "please, God, make her well."

The silence of the room was broken by the sound of Nellie coughing in her sleep. I heard her move restlessly in the bed. I got out of my chair and looked at her. The blankets had fallen away from her body. I covered her again and went back to the chair and sat down.

The night seemed long and still, and gradually I began to doze, my hand dangling over the side into the crib. Several times I tried to force my eyes to remain open, but they resisted all my efforts, they were so heavy and so weary.

There was a distant small sound of coughing in my ears and the gray-white light of dawn was beating against my eyelids. My eyes opened suddenly and I was staring into the crib.

Vickie was coughing violently. Frantically I picked her up, trying to pat her back. She couldn't seem to stop coughing. Her eyes were squeezed tightly shut and tiny drops of moisture stood out on her forehead in the morning light. Suddenly she seemed to grow rigid in my arms, her little body stretching taut, her face turning a sick bluish color.

Desperately I forced her tiny mouth open with my lips. As hard as I could, I blew my breath into her, the fear and knowledge of what was happening constricting my heart.

Again and again I tried to make my breath her breath, my life her life, even long after I knew that there was nothing I could ever do for her again.

I stood there silently in the room, holding her still body against my breast, feeling the chill of the morning enter into her. This was my daughter. I could feel the salty edge of tears coming into my eyes.

"Danny!" Nellie's frightened voice cried from the bed.

Slowly I turned to look at her. I stared at her for a long and knowing moment and a thousand things were said and never spoken. She knew. Somehow she had known all along. This was what she had been afraid of. Her arms reached out toward Vickie.

Slowly I walked toward the bed, holding out our child to her.

CHAPTER FOUR

THE WOODEN STEPS CREAKED BENEATH OUR FEET AS WE SLOWLY climbed the stairs. It was a familiar sound, one that our ears had become accustomed to hearing for a long time, but there was no joy in it now. A little more than three years had passed since we first had climbed that stairway.

We were happy then. We were young and our lives were bright before us. We were laughing and excited. Somewhere in the back of my mind I remembered how I had carried her across the threshold. But even as I remembered, the memory faded and grew dim. It had been so long ago and we were young no longer.

I watched her back, stiff and straight, as she went up the stairway a step before me. She had been strong. Always she had been strong. There had been no tears, no screaming protestations of her grief. Only the hurt in her dark eyes, the twisted pain of her mouth, told me of her feelings.

She paused on our landing, swaying slightly as she turned toward our door. I reached for her quickly, afraid she might fall. Her hand found mine and gripped it tight.

We did not speak as we walked hand in hand to our door and stopped in front of it. With my free hand I reached in my pocket for my key. It wasn't there and I had to take my other hand from her in order to search the pockets on the other side. When the key was in my hand, I still did not place it in the lock, reluctant to open the door. She did not look at me. Her gaze was rigid on the floor in front of her.

I put the key in the lock, and the door swung open at my touch. I looked back at her in surprise. "I guess I didn't lock it," I said.

Her eyes were still fixed on the floor in front of her. Her voice was so low I could hardly hear her answer. "It doesn't matter," she said. "We have nothing more to lose."

I guided her through the door and closed it behind us. We stood there awkwardly in the tiny foyer, afraid to look at each other, afraid even to speak. We had no words in us.

At last I broke the silence. "Let me have your coat, darling," I said. "I'll hang it up."

She slipped out of her coat and let me take it from her hands. I put it in the closet, then hung mine next to it. When I turned back to her, she was still standing there, rigid.

I took her arm again. "Come inside and sit down. I'll get you a cup of coffee." She shook her head. Her voice was dull and tired. "I don't want anything."

"Better sit down anyway," I urged.

She let me lead her into the parlor and seat her on the couch. I sat beside her and lit a cigarette. Her eyes were fixed straight ahead, blank and unseeing though she seemed to be staring out the window. There was quiet in the room, a thick, deep, unfamiliar quiet. I found myself listening to it, listening for the familiar sounds my daughter had made in the house, little sounds of no consequence that at times had seemed so annoying.

I closed my eyes for a moment. They were beginning to burn and smart from the long hours of the day. This was a day to forget, to hide away and bury in some secret corner of your mind so that you didn't remember the empty aching loss that had come into you. Forget the solemn, quiet sounds of Mass, the tiny white coffin gleaming in the soft yellow light of the candles on the altar. Forget the metallic sounds of the shovels biting into the earth, the rain of dirt and stone pouring down on the little box of wood. Forget, forget, forget.

But how can you forget? How can you forget the kindness of your neighbors, their sympathy and gentleness? You knocked at their doors and wept in their kitchens. You had no money and your child would lie in a pauper's grave if it were not for them. Five dollars here, two dollars there, ten dollars, six dollars. Seventy in all. To pay for a coffin, for a Mass, for a grave, for a resting-place for a part of you that was no more. Seventy dollars torn from the poverty of their own lives to lighten some way the bitterness in your own.

You want to forget, but a day like this you can't forget. Some day it will be buried deep, but it will not be forgotten. Just as she will not be forgotten.

Strange, but you are reluctant to say her name, even to yourself, and in place of it you say "she." I shook my head to clear it. There was a numbing fog aching in my ears. "Say her name!" I commanded myself desperately. "Say it!"

I drew a deep breath. My lungs were bursting. "Vickie!" Its sound exploded silently in my ears. But it was a triumphant sound. "Vickie!" Again her name was glowing in my mind. It was a glad name, a glorious name for living.

But not any more. Despair crept over me. From now on, it would be nothing. Only "she" would remain, and somehow I knew it.

I took a last drag at the cigarette and put it out. "Don't you think you'd better lie down?" I asked.

Slowly Nellie turned her face to me. "I'm not tired," she replied.

I took her hand. It was cold as ice. "Yuh better lie down," I repeated gently.

Her eyes flew swiftly to the bedroom door, then back to me. There was a lonely look in them. "Danny, I can't go in there. Her crib, her toys—" Her voice trailed away.

I knew exactly how she felt. My voice was shaking when I spoke again. "It's all over now, baby," I whispered. "Yuh gotta keep on goin', yuh gotta keep on livin'."

Her hands were gripping mine fiercely. There was a wild look of hysteria spilling into her eyes. "Why, Danny, why?" she cried.

I had to answer her though I had no idea what to say. "Because yuh gotta," I replied weakly. "Because that's the way she would have wanted it."

Her fingernails were tearing into my palms. "She was a baby, Danny! My baby!" Her voice broke suddenly and she cried for the first time since it had happened. "She was my baby and she wanted only one thing: to live! And I doomed her, I failed her!" Her hands covered her face and she was weeping bitterly.

Clumsily I put my arms around her shoulders and pulled her to me. I tried to make my voice as comforting as I could. "It wasn't your fault, Nellie. It wasn't anybody's fault. It was in God's hands."

Her eyes were black with misery and they gleamed dully against the pallor of her skin. She shook her head slowly. "No, Danny," she said in a hopeless tone, "it was my fault—my fault from the very beginning. I did a sinful thing and let her become a part of it. She paid for my sin, not me. I should have known better than to think that I knew better than God."

Her eyes as she looked up at me were flaming with a fanaticism I had never seen before. "I have sinned and lived in sin," she continued dully. "I have never asked God's blessing for my marriage. I was willing to settle for man's word. How could I have expected His blessing for my child? Father Brennan told me that in the very beginning."

"Father Brennan said nothing like that!" I said desperately. "In church today he said that God would make her welcome." I held her face up to me with my hands. "We loved each other, we still love each other. That's all that God asks."

She looked at me with sad eyes, and her hand touched mine lightly. "Poor Danny," she whispered softly. "You just can't understand."

I stared back at her. She was right; I didn't understand. Love was a thing between people, and if it was real, it was a blessed thing. "I love you," I said.

She smiled slowly through her tears, got to her feet, and looked down pityingly at me. "Poor Danny," she said again in that soft whisper. "You think that your love is all you need and can't see that it is not enough for Him."

I kissed her hand. "It always has been enough for us."

There was a distant look in her eyes. She nodded her head slightly. "That's what has been wrong about it, Danny," she said in a faraway voice. "I, too, thought that it would be enough for us, but now I know it isn't." I could feel her hand brushing lightly across my head. "We have to live with God too, not only with ourselves."

She went into the bedroom and closed the door behind her. I could hear the creak of the bed as she lay down on it, and then there was silence. I lit another cigarette and turned to the window. It had begun to rain. A day to forget. The silence began to creep into my bones.

CHAPTER FIVE

A CURIOUS NUMBNESS HAD CRAWLED INTO MY BODY, BRINGING WITH IT A strange half-awake, half-asleep feeling. It was almost as if my body had fallen asleep while my mind remained awake and I had lost all sense of time. Only thoughts were with me. Half-formed and indistinct remnants of memories slipped through my mind while my body remained coldly aloof from the pain that came with them.

That was why I didn't hear the buzzer the first time it sounded. That is, I heard the sound, but didn't recognize it. The second time it rang, it was more strident, more demanding. Dully I wondered who was ringing the doorbell.

It rang again, this time piercing my consciousness. I jumped from my chair. I remember looking at my watch as I walked to the door and being surprised that it was only three o'clock. It seemed as if a year had passed since morning.

I opened the door. A strange man was standing there. "What do you want?" I asked. This was a hell of a time to be bothered by peddlers.

The stranger took his wallet from his pocket and flipped it open in front of me. He held it so that I could read the badge pinned to it: "N.Y.C. Dept. of Welfare. Investigator." "Mr. Fisher?" he asked.

I nodded.

"I'm John Morgan of the Welfare Department," he said quietly. "May I see you for a moment? I have some questions that I have to ask you."

I stared at him. This was no time for me to be answering questions. "Can't you make it some other time, Mr. Morgan?" I asked.

He shook his head. "I have to ask them now," he replied, an unpleasant tone coming into his voice. "Miss Snyder has come across some information regarding your case that must be verified. It would be for your own good to answer my questions now"

I looked at him suspiciously. "Where is she?" I asked.

A definite note of hostility had come into his voice now. "That is none of your concern, Mr. Fisher," he snapped. "All I want you to do is answer a few questions."

I began to resent this guy. A Department of Welfare badge didn't make him God. I planted my feet firmly in the doorway. I wasn't going to let him in. "Okay," I said coldly, "I'll answer your questions."

He looked around uncomfortably for a moment; then, apparently deciding I wasn't going to let him into the apartment, took out a small notebook and flipped it open. He glanced at it briefly, then at me. "You buried your daughter this morning?"

I nodded silently. The words coming from his lips, the way he spoke them, coldly and impersonally, hurt. It was profane.

He made scratches in his little book. All these investigators were the same. Give them a little notebook and automatically they begin to make scratches in it. If you ever took their little book away from them they wouldn't be able to talk. "Undertaker's services including casket were forty dollars, cemetery fees were twenty dollars, total sixty dollars for the funeral. Is that right?"

"No," I answered bitterly. "Yuh left out somethin'."

His eyes were sharp. "What?"

"We gave ten bucks to the Ascension Church for a special Mass," I said coldly. "The whole thing came to seventy dollars."

His pencil made scratching sounds in the notebook. He looked up again. "Where did you get the money, Mr. Fisher?"

"None of your Goddam business!" I snapped.

A faint smile appeared on his lips. "It is our business, Mr. Fisher," he replied snidely. "You see, you're on relief. You're supposed to be destitute. That means you have no money, that's why we help you. Suddenly you have seventy dollars. We have a right to know where you got it."

I looked down at the floor. That's where the buggers had you. You had to answer their questions or they'd cut you off. Still I couldn't bring myself to tell him where I got the dough. That was something personal between Vickie and us. Nobody else had to know where we got the money to bury our own child. I didn't answer him.

"Maybe you got the money from working nights without reporting it to us?"

he suggested smoothly, a note of triumph in his voice. "You weren't holding out on us, were you, Mr. Fisher?"

My gaze came up from the floor and fastened on his face. How could they have found out about that? "What's that got to do with it?" I asked quickly.

He was smiling again. He seemed very proud of himself. "We have ways of finding out things," he said mysteriously. "It doesn't pay to fool us. You know, Mr. Fisher, you can go to jail for something like that. It constitutes fraud against the City of New York."

My temper wore thin. I'd had enough misery for one day. "Since when does a guy go to jail if he wants to work?" I burst out angrily. "What in hell are you trying to pull anyway?"

"Nothing, Mr. Fisher, nothing," he said smoothly. "I'm just trying to get at the truth, that's all."

"The truth is that three people can't live on seventy-two bucks a month and a supplementary diet of dried prunes and seed potatoes!" I had raised my voice and it echoed in the narrow hallway. "Yuh gotta try to grab an extra buck or yuh starve!"

"Then you admit you had a job nights while pretending to us that you were totally unemployed?" he asked calmly.

"I admit nothing!" shouted.

"Yet you had seventy dollars with which to bury your child," he stated triumphantly.

"Yes, I buried the kid!" I could feel knots in my throat choking me. "That was all I could do for her. If I had any dough do you think I would have waited for your friggin' doctor to come? If I had any dough I would have called another doctor. Maybe then she would be here now!"

His eyes surveyed me coldly. I didn't know a human being could have so little feeling. "Then you were working nights?" he asked again.

Suddenly all the pain and bitterness and heartache welled up through my guts and I grabbed him by the tie and pulled his face close to mine. "Yes, I was workin' nights!" I snarled at him.

His face turned white and wriggled in my grip. "Let me go, Mr. Fisher," he gasped. "Violence isn't going to do you any good. You're in enough trouble already!"

He didn't know how right he was. A little more wouldn't make any difference now. I hit him flush on the face and he fell back against the wall on the other side of the narrow hallway. I could see a smear of blood coming to his nose as I went after him.

His eyes were frightened and he scrambled quickly along the wall to the stairway. I stood there and watched him run. At the head of the stairs he turned and looked back at me. His voice was almost hysterical. "You'll pay for this!" he screamed back at me. "You'll get thrown off relief. You'll starve! I'll see to that!"

I stepped toward him threateningly. He began to hurry down the steps. I leaned over the railing. "If yuh come back, yuh little bastard," I shouted down at him, "I'll kill yuh! Stay the hell away from me!"

He disappeared down the next landing and I went back into the apartment. I was beginning to feel sick. There was a peculiar shame in me as if I had defiled this day. I shouldn't have acted like that. Any other day all right maybe, not today.

Nellie was standing in the bedroom door. "Who was it, Danny?"

I tried to calm my voice. "Some monkey from Welfare," I said. "A wise guy, I sent him away."

"What did he want?"

She'd had enough for one day, there was no use in making it worse. "Nothin' special," I said evasively. "He just wanted to ask some questions, that's all. Go back to bed and rest, baby."

Her voice was dull and hopeless. "They know about the night job, don't they?"

I stared at her. She had heard. "Why don't you try an' get some sleep, baby?" I ducked her question.

Her eyes were fixed on mine. "Don't lie to me, Danny. It was true what I said, wasn't it?"

"What if it is?" I admitted. "It ain't important now. We'll make out on the job. The boss promised me a full trick soon."

She stood staring at me. I could see the tears welling into her eyes again. I crossed the room quickly and took her hand. "Nothing goes right for us, Danny," she said hopelessly, "not even on a day like this. Trouble, always trouble."

"It's all over now, baby," I said, holding her hand. "From now on things'll go better."

She looked up at me, her eyes dead in her face. "It will never be any different, Danny," she said futilely. "We're jinxed. I've brought you nothing but hard luck."

I twisted her face around to me. "Nellie, yuh gotta forget that idea!" I pressed my lips to her cheek. "Yuh can't go on livin' thinkin' that nothin's gonna be okay. Yuh gotta hope for better!"

Her gaze met mine levelly. "What is there to hope for?" she asked quietly. "How do you know you even have a job now? You haven't even called up there in four days."

"I'm not worried about that," I said, my heart sinking into my stomach. It was true. I had forgotten all about calling the store. "Jack will understand when I explain to him."

She looked up at me doubtingly. Some of her doubt seeped into me. But as it turned out both of us were right.

CHAPTER SIX

JACK LOOKED UP AT ME AS I WALKED INTO THE STORE. THERE WAS NO welcome in his eyes. I looked down the counter. Another man was working my station.

"Hello, Jack," I said quietly.

"Hello, Danny," he replied without enthusiasm.

I waited for him to ask me where I'd been, but he didn't speak. I could see he was angry, so I spoke first. "Something happened, Jack," I explained. "I couldn't come in."

His eyes reflected his anger. "Yuh couldn't even call in five days either, I suppose?" he asked sarcastically.

I met his gaze. "I'm sorry about that, Jack," I said apologetically. "I know I should have called, but I was so upset I forgot all about it."

"Crap!" he exploded. "For two nights I broke my back here waitin' for you to show up an' you don't even have time to call up!"

I looked down at the counter. "I couldn't help it, Jack," I said. "Something happened an' I couldn't call."

"Not even once in five days?" he said unbelievingly. "The world would have to come to an end before I'd pull a stunt like that."

I still didn't look at him. "I had trouble, Jack," I said quietly. "My ba—my daughter died."

There was a moment's silence before he spoke again. "You're not kiddin' me, Danny?" he asked.

I looked up at his face. "You don't kid with things like that," I answered.

His eyes fell. "I'm sorry, Danny. Honestly sorry."

I looked down the counter. The new man was watching out of the corner of his eyes, trying to give the impression that he wasn't interested in what we were saying, but I knew the look. He was worrying about his job. I'd had it too many times myself not to recognize it.

I looked at Jack. "I see you got a new man."

He nodded uncomfortably. He didn't speak.

I tried to make my voice sound casual, but it's hard when what you're saying is the difference between eating and not eating. "Yuh got any room for me?"

He was silent for a moment before he answered. I could see his eyes shift down the counter to the new man, then back. The new man immediately was busy cleaning the grill. "Not right now, Danny," he said gently. "I'm sorry."

I partly turned toward the door so that he couldn't see the tears I felt right behind my eyes. "That's all right, Jack," I said. "I understand."

There was a deep note of sympathy in his voice that I was grateful for. "Maybe something'll turn up soon," he said quickly. "I'll call yuh." A moment passed. "If you'd only called, Danny—"

"If a lot of things, Jack," I interrupted him, "but I didn't. Thanks anyway." I walked out of the store.

In the street outside the store I looked at my watch. It was after six o'clock. I wondered how I could tell Nellie, especially after what had happened this afternoon. The whole day had been miserable.

I decided to walk home. It was a long walk but a nickel is a lot of dough when you haven't got a job. From Dyckman Street to East Fourth took me almost three hours. I didn't mind it. It was that much more time I wouldn't have to tell Nellie.

It was nine o'clock by the time I reached home. The night had turned cool, but my shirt was damp with perspiration as I began to climb the stairs. I stood in the hallway hesitantly before opening the door. What could I tell her? I let it swing wide before I stepped in. There was a light in the parlor, but the apartment was quiet. "Nellie," I called, turning to hang my jacket in the small closet.

There was a sound of footsteps and I heard a man's voice: "That's him!"

I spun around. Nellie and two men were standing in the parlor entrance. Her face was pale and drawn. I took a quick step toward her before I recognized the man standing next to her. It was the Welfare investigator I had chased this afternoon.

There was a white bandage across the bridge of his nose and one eye was purple and swollen. "That's him!" he repeated.

The other man stepped toward me. He held a badge in his hand—a police badge. "Daniel Fisher?"

I nodded.

"Mr. Morgan has preferred charges against you of assault and battery," he said quietly. "I'll have to take you in."

I could feel my muscles tense. This was all I needed to make a perfect day: the cops. Then I looked at Nellie and all the tension seeped out of me.

"May I talk with my wife for a moment?" I asked the detective.

His eyes appraised me for a moment, then he nodded. "Sure," he said gently. "We'll wait outside in the hall for you." He took Morgan's arm and pushed him out into the hall before him, looking back at me before closing the door. "Don't be long, son." I nodded gratefully and the door swung closed.

Nellie hadn't said a word, her eyes were searching my face. At last she drew a deep breath. "No job?"

I didn't answer.

She stared at me for a moment more and then she was in my arms, sobbing violently against my shoulder. "Danny, Danny," she cried in a helpless voice, "what'll we do?"

I stroked her hair gently. I didn't know what to say. I didn't know what we could do. The walls were closing in on us.

She looked up into my face. "What do you think they'll do to you?" she asked.

I shrugged my shoulders. "I don't know," I answered. I was so tired I didn't really care. If it weren't for her I wouldn't give a damn for anything any more. "They'll probably book me and let me go until a hearing is arranged."

"But supposing they hold you?" she cried.

I tried a smile. "They won't," I answered, more surely than I felt. "It's not important enough. I'll be back in a few hours."

"But that Mr. Morgan, he was terrible. He said they were going to put you in jail."

"That louse!" I said quickly. "There's a lot of things he don't know. When they hear what has happened they'll let me out. Don't worry."

She hid her face against my shoulder. "Nothing's turning out right, Danny," she despaired. "All I've brought you is bad luck. You should never have come back."

I turned up her face and kissed her. "If I hadn't come back, baby," I whispered, "I would have missed the only thing in the world that was important to me. It's not your fault, it's nobody's fault. We just didn't get the breaks."

There was a knock at the door. "I'll be out in a minute," I called. I looked down at Nellie again. "Lie down for a while," I said. "I'll be back in a few hours."

She looked at me doubtfully. "Sure?"

"Sure," I answered, taking my jacket from the closet. "I'll be back before you know it."

Morgan's face glared at me triumphantly as we walked through the streets. "I told you I'd be back," he sneered.

I didn't answer him.

The detective between us growled at him: "Shut up, Morgan. The lad's got enough trouble without you opening up your yap."

I glanced at the cop out of the corner of my eye. I could see he didn't like Morgan. He was one of those warm Irishmen with tender eyes. I wondered how a guy like that could ever become a cop.

We had walked almost two blocks before I spoke. "What do they usually do in a thing like this?" I asked the detective.

His face turned toward me, its ruddy glow shining in the light of the street lamps. "They book yuh on charges against a hearing."

"Then they let you go until the hearing, is that right?" I asked.

The cop's eyes were sympathetic. "If yuh got the bail they do."

The surprise showed in my voice. "Bail?" I exclaimed. "How much bail?"

The cop's eyes were still gentle. "Five hundred dollars usually."

"But what if you haven't got the dough?" I asked. "What do they do then?"

Morgan answered before the cop could. "They put you in jail until the hearing," he said viciously.

I broke stride and looked at the cop. "But they can't do that!" I exclaimed. "My wife is sick. She's gone through a lot today. I can't leave her alone tonight."

The detective took my arm. "I'm sorry, son," he said gently, "but I can't help that. All I'm supposed to do is bring you in."

"But Nellie—my wife"—I could hardly speak—"I can't leave her alone. She's not well."

The cop's voice was still soft. "Don't get excited, son. You'd better just come along."

I could feel his grip tightening on my arm. I began to walk again. I had read in the papers that sometimes hearings took weeks to be arranged. Visions of myself sitting in the pokey until the hearing crept into my mind. I began to seethe. I looked at Morgan.

He was walking on the other side of the cop, a smug, satisfied look on his face. The bastard. If it weren't for him everything might have been better. Things had been bad enough, but he made them worse.

I had to do something, I didn't know what. I just couldn't let them lock me up until they were good and ready to give me a hearing. I couldn't leave Nellie alone that long. There was no telling what she might do.

We stepped out in the gutter just as the light changed. Automobiles whizzed by us as we paused in the center of the street. I felt the cop's hand fall from my arm and instinctively I jumped forward. I heard a muttered curse behind me, then a scream as a driver threw on his brakes. I didn't turn back to see what had happened, I kept running.

There was a shout: "Stop! Stop!" Then another voice took up the cry. I recognized the shrill-pitched tones of Morgan. He was screaming too.

A shrill blast of a police whistle reached my ears. But by that time I had reached the far corner and I looked back over my shoulder as I sped around it.

Morgan was lying stretched out in the gutter, and the policeman was standing over him, looking at me. The cop was waving his hand at me. I could see the glint of metal shining in his hand. He was still shouting for me to stop, but his hand was telling me to go.

I grabbed a deep chunk of air and went around the corner.

CHAPTER SEVEN

I WENT THE LONG WAY AROUND AND BACK TO MY HOUSE. I HAD TO SEE Nellie and explain to her. I had to tell her what I'd done. I had to tell her not to worry. But by the time I reached the corner I could see the white top of a police patrol car parked in front of my door. I stood stock-still on the corner staring at it, and for the first time I realized what I had done. The cops were after me now. I didn't dare show up home. I had only made things worse.

I crossed the street and went up the block slowly. There was a heavy, sunken feeling of despair in my gut. I felt sick. I had loused things up for sure. I looked at my watch. It was a few minutes after ten. I had been a fool. There was nothing to do now but go back and give myself up. If I kept on running, there would be no end to it. I would never be able to go back.

I started back for the house. Might as well get it over with. Then I remembered. The whole thing had started when I found out I would need bail in order to get out. I still had no bail.

I stopped again and thought. I would have to get the dough some place. Nellie's folks didn't have that kind of money even if they were willing to help me out. The only person I knew that could put his hands on that much dough was Sam.

I remembered the last time I spoke to him. Funny how things worked out. It had been the day after Vickie was born. He had thought I had come looking for a handout then, and I had sworn to myself that I would never go to him for anything after that. But I was in real trouble now. There was nothing else for me to do. It was either go to him or to the pokey. And I had done enough for them to lock me up and throw away the key. I had to ask him.

I went into the candy store on the corner and thumbed quickly through the telephone directory. I tried his home telephone. From the phone booth in the store I could see the police car across the street in front of my house. The cop sitting inside it was sneaking a smoke.

A woman's voice answered: "Hello."

"Is Mr. or Mrs. Gordon there?" I asked quickly, my eyes glued on the patrol car.

"Miz Gordon is away in the country," the voice replied. "Mistuh Gordon is still down at his office."

"May I have the number please?" I asked. "I must get in touch with him right away."

"Sure," the voice replied. "Just a minute, I'll get it for you."

I copied the number down and put up the receiver while I searched my pockets for another coin. I might as well have been looking for a gold mine for all the good it did me. I had just spent my last nickel.

I looked out at the patrol car. The cop had got out of it and was walking up the block toward me. I made up my mind quickly and ducked out of the candy store and around the corner before he got near enough to recognize me.

Sam's office was uptown in the Empire State Building. I began to walk quickly. With a break I could get there in little more than half an hour. I hoped he would still be there.

His name was in the directory on the Thirty-fourth Street side: "Sam Gordon Enterprises Inc., Concessions." Twenty-second floor. I went over to the white sign that read: "Night Elevators." A watchman was standing there with a registry book on a small stand. He stopped me. "Where you going, mister?" he asked suspiciously.

"Twenty-second floor," I answered quickly. "I got an appointment with Mr. Gordon there."

He looked at the register. "Okay," he said. "Mr. Gordon is still up there. He hasn't signed out since he returned from dinner. Sign here." He held a pencil toward me.

I took it and scrawled my name where he indicated. I looked up the page. About four lines above mine I saw Sam's familiar scribble. Next to his name was a circle with the numeral 2 in it.

I looked at the night watchman. "Is there anyone with Mr. Gordon?"

A faint flicker of a smile appeared on the man's face. "His secretary came back with him."

I nodded without replying. His smile had told me enough. If I knew anything, Sam's secretary would be a good-looking head, and Sam hadn't changed a bit.

I stepped out of the elevator and walked down the hall toward Sam's office. His name was spelled out in impressive gold lettering across two large glass doors. I could see clear through into the reception room. A single light glowed there. The doors were unlocked.

There was a door near the receptionist's desk in the lavishly furnished waiting-room. I opened it and found myself in a large general office. There were about twenty desks scattered through the room. On the far side of the room there was another door. I walked toward it.

Again the gold letters spelling out his name gleamed faintly at me in the dim light. I put my hand lightly on the knob and turned it. The door swung gently open. The office was dark. I put my hand out and found the light-switch on the right-hand wall. I pressed it and light poured into the room. There was a muttered curse as I blinked my eyes in the light. I heard a faint, frightened woman's cry. Then my eyes adjusted and I stood looking down at the couch. Sam was rising to his feet, his face glaring at me; the girl was trying to cover her nakedness with inadequate hands.

I stared at her and then turned to Sam with a knowing smile. His face was flushed, almost purple, as he struggled into his trousers. I didn't speak, just backed out of the door, pulling it closed after me. I sat down in a chair just outside his office, lit a cigarette, and waited for him to come out. I had been right. Sam hadn't changed a bit.

I had been waiting for almost fifteen minutes before the door opened again. I looked up expectantly.

I was disappointed. It wasn't Sam who came out, it was the girl. From the way she looked, it was hard to believe that just a few minutes ago I had caught her rocking the cradle. She looked down at me. "Mr. Gordon will see you now," she said formally.

I got to my feet. "Thank you," I deadpanned, and went into his office. I could hear the clatter of a typewriter begin as I closed the door behind me.

Sam was sitting behind his desk. "Yuh find yuh get better work from 'em if yuh relax 'em first?" I smiled.

He ignored my attempt at humor while he held a match to a cigar clamped in his teeth. The light flickered coldly in his eyes. At last he put the match down and stared at me. "What d'yuh want?" he barked.

I could feel a respect for him growing in me. This guy really had it. He was tough. Not one word about my walking in on him. There was no use playing games with him. I walked up to his desk and looked down at him. "I need help," I said simply. "I'm in trouble."

The pupils of his eyes were hard and black. "Why come to me?" he asked.

"I got nobody else," I said quietly.

He put the cigar down gently on an ashtray and stood up behind his desk. His voice was low, but it filled the office. "Blow, bum," he said flatly. "You ain't gettin' no handouts from me."

"I ain't lookin' for a handout," I said desperately. "I'm in trouble and I need help." I stood there stubbornly, staring at him. He wasn't going to chase me this time.

He walked menacingly around the desk toward me. "Get out!" he snarled.

"For God's sake, Sam, listen to me," I pleaded. "Everything's gone wrong! The cops are after me an'—"

His voice cut me off as if I hadn't spoken. "Yuh're no good!" he snapped, his flushed and angry face close to mine. "Yuh never been any good, yuh'll never be any good! I done enough fer you. Get out before I throw you out!" He raised his fist.

I went cold and hard inside. There was only one language this guy understood. "I wouldn't try that if I were you, Sam," I said coldly, watching his hands. "You ain't in condition."

"I'll show yuh who's in condition!" he growled, swinging at me.

I picked off his blow with my forearm. "Remember your own lesson, Sam?" I taunted. "Snap—don't swing like a balley dancer!" I moved away from him without trying to return his blow.

He came after me, both arms swinging. But he was heavy on his feet and I kept away from him easily. One thing I could say in favor of my diet: I never got a chance to roll up the fat around my gut like he did. For a few minutes he kept up the chase. There was only the puffing sound of his breath breaking the silence of the office. At last he sank exhaustedly into his chair, breathing heavily.

I stood on the other side of his desk and looked at him. His face was flushed with the exertion, and perspiration was running down his heavy jowls. "Now will yuh listen to me, Sam?" I asked.

He picked up his cigar and stuck it in his mouth He didn't look at me. "Go away," he said in a low, disgusted voice.

"I ain't goin' no place," I said. "Yuh're gonna help me."

"I had enough of you," he said, looking up at me wearily. "Ever since you were a kid you been putting it over on me. Up in the country with Ceil, then in the Gloves that time you made a deal with Maxie Fields. How many times you think I'm gonna bite?"

He had a memory like an elephant. He didn't forget anything. "This ain't gonna cost you no dough," I said. "All I need is a little help an' a job till I can straighten things out."

He shook his head. "I ain't got no job for you. You ain't trained for nothin'.""

"I can still fight," I said.

"Uh-uh," he answered. "Yuh're too old to start in that. You been away too long. Yuh'll never make a nickel as a pro."

There was no arguing about that. Twenty-three was too old, especially after a six-year layoff. "Then how about a job here?" I asked. "You got a big place."

"No," he answered flatly.

"Not even if I promise never to tell Mimi what I seen here tonight?" I asked shrewdly.

I knew from the expression on his face I had scored. "She wouldn't like that," I followed up quickly.

He sat there silently chewing on his cigar. I watched him patiently. This was the kind of language he could understand. I was through begging, through groveling, through asking for anything. There was only one way to get along in this world: that was to take what you wanted. That was the way he operated in everything, and if it was good enough for him, it was good enough for me.

His eyes were veiled and blank as he looked at me. "Still the same snot-nosed punk who thinks the world owes him a living, eh, Danny?" he asked coldly.

I shook my head. "Not the same, Sam," I answered bitterly. "This is a new Danny Fisher yuh're lookin' at. I been through too much to ever be the same. I put in a year an' a half on relief, crawlin' on my belly in order to have enough to eat. This afternoon I socked a Welfare agent because he wanted to know where I got the dough to bury my child an' he came after me with the cops. My wife is home sick an' wonderin' where I am. I'm not the same any more, Sam, I'll never be the—"

There was a shocked sound in his voice. "What happened, Danny?"

"You heard me," I answered, staring at him coldly. "I'll never be the same. Now do you help me or do I tell Mimi what I saw?"

His gaze dropped to his desk and he stared at it for a moment. Then he spoke without looking up. "Okay, kid," he said in a peculiarly gentle voice. "Yuh got me."

CHAPTER EIGHT

AS SOON AS I HAD PUSHED MY WAY THROUGH THE GLASS DOORS, THE receptionist looked at me and smiled. "Good morning, Danny," she said, shifting the wad of gum to a corner of her mouth. "The boss is lookin' for you."

"Thanks, baby." I smiled back at her.

I went through the other door into the large office. Everybody was at work already. The quiet hum of business came to my ears. I walked through the office to my desk, in a corner of the room near a window. I sat down behind it and began looking through some papers stacked neatly in the incoming basket on the desk.

I had been seated only a few minutes when a shadow fell across my desk. I looked up.

"Danny—" Kate started to say.

I held up an interrupting hand. "I know, baby," I said quickly. "The boss wants to see me."

She nodded her head.

"Well, I'm here," I told her.

"Then what're you waitin' for?" she snapped sarcastically. "An engraved invitation?" She turned on her heel and huffily went back to her desk.

Kate was an all-right kid even if I liked to tease her. I guess she wasn't the first secretary that had ever been jumped by the boss, and she wasn't going to be the last. But she had been edgy with me ever since the first time we met.

I smiled to myself as I thought about it. It was over three and a half years ago. A lot of things had happened in that time. A war was on. A lot of guys had gone away. I had been lucky, though. When the draft board got to me they found something I never knew I had: punctured eardrums. I was out—4 F, a highly personalized kind of abbreviation of the four freedoms.

I shuffled through the papers on my desk again and found the one I wanted. As I got to my feet the phone on my desk rang and I picked it up.

It was Nellie, calling from the war plant on Long Island where she worked. "I forgot to tell you to take the laundry down to the Chink's," she said.

"I remembered, honey," I said. She left early in the morning six o'clock, before I woke. "How are things going out there?" I asked.

"Hot, Danny," she answered. "It's over ninety in the plant."

"Why don't yuh quit that dump?" I asked. "We don't need the dough now. I'm makin' out all right."

Her voice was patient but firm. We had been through this thing many times already. "What else have I got to do?" she asked. "Stay home all day an' go nuts? I'm better off out of the house. At least I keep busy this way."

I knew better than to argue with her. Since Vickie had died, she had changed. I don't know in just what way, but she had become more silent. Some of the starlight had gone out of her eyes.

"We eatin' out tonight or home?" I asked.

"Out," she answered. "We're almost out of this month's meat points."

"Okay," I said. "I'll pick you up at the house at six."

I grinned at Kate as I opened Sam's door. She made a face at me and bent down over her typewriter, her fingers flying. I smiled to myself as I went in the door. I think Kate liked me despite everything.

Sam looked up from his desk. "So you finally got here," he growled.

I wasn't worried about what he said. I knew that in the few years I had been here, I had learned enough to carry my weight. This was a tricky business, but it was for me. It was made up of the kind of intangibles that only a few guys could turn into money. Guys like Sam and me. And Sam knew it too. "If it wasn't for the air conditioning I wouldn't have come in at all," I said, dropping into a chair in front of his desk. "You don't know how lucky you are."

Sam's face flushed. He didn't look good like that, he was packing too much weight. He had two double chins. He looked just like the Central Park South papa of three boys that he was. "Mimi says for me to ask you an' Nellie up for dinner tonight," he said.

"Okay," I said. "Was that what all the fire was about?"

He shook his head. "No," he said shortly. "I want yuh to come off that slot-machine grab."

I stared at him. "What for?" I asked. "I thought you were hot for it."

"I changed my mind," he said gruffly. "The upkeep on them machines is murder. When they go, they go, that's all there is to it. Yuh can't get replacement parts or nothin' on account a' the war."

"Is that the reason, Sam," I asked, "or is it because I hear Maxie Fields is interested in them too?"

He flushed again. I wondered whether Sam was developing a high blood-pressure. He was at the dangerous age now. "I don't give a damn about Maxie Fields!" he said. "It's just that I don't glom that racket. Give me a nice clean concession in a hotel or a night club. Checking, souvenirs, photographs—something with people running it. I can understand people, I can run 'em. But I can't figger machines."

"But I just spent a week casin' this setup," I protested. "For fifteen grand it's a steal."

"So let Maxie steal it, then," he snapped. "I ain't interested. I ain't goin' for no kick I can't savvy. Fifteen G's is too much spec."

I leaned forward. I thought Sam was missing a good thing. This was the first time I had ever really disagreed with him. "You're missin' the boat, Sam," I said earnestly. "I been all through the setup, an' what they can do with these machines is real sky stuff. Postwar they'll be sellin' everything in those machines from hot coffee to condoms."

"So let 'em," he said definitely. I could see that his mind had been made up. "Right now all they're good for is cigarettes and Coca-Cola and I ain't buyin'." He riffled through some papers on his desk. "I got somethin' else for yuh to look at. The concessions at the Trask in Atlantic City are on the block. I want yuh to run down there an' have a look-see."

I stared at him for a moment. "You mean it about them vending machines?" I asked.

"You heard me," he said angrily. "Sure I mean it. Now forget it an'—"

"I like it, Sam," I said softly, the beginnings of an idea growing in my mind.

His gaze was sharp and penetrating. "So you like it," he said sarcastically. "But it's my dough an' I say no dice. So be a good boy an' stop hokkin' me. Now, I—"

I interrupted him again. "I'd like to buy in, Sam," I said.

He let out a deep breath. "Yuh got the dough?" he asked shrewdly.

I met his eyes across the desk. He knew as well as I that I didn't have the dough. "Yuh know I can't raise that kind'a money on the big seventy-five per you pay me."

He grinned happily. He felt he was going to score. I knew the look. "But what about yer expense account on out-of-town trips? Yuh ever look at 'em? Yuh don't think I know you grab a few bucks there?"

I grinned back at him. "You're right about that, Sam," I admitted. "It's a few bucks, though. You never send me out with enough to make a real take."

"Then where yuh gonna get the dough?" Sam shot at me.

I thought for a minute. "I got about fifteen hundred dollars in our savings account. The bank ought to give me half the deal on a chattel mortgage. The rest I can get from you."

Sam was on his feet. "From me?" he roared angrily. "What kinda stupe yuh think I am? What chance I got to collect from you?"

I looked at him calmly. "Yuh got my word."

He sneered. "I sank five grand once't on your word. Yuh think I'm a sucker for that again?"

I could feel my eyes grow cold. "That was a kid you bought, Sam. That wasn't me, that was your grab outta a hat for glory. I never saw any of it. The only payoff in it for me would have been a punchin' around."

His face was red. "Well, I ain't buyin'," he said flatly, sitting down behind his desk again.

My mind was made up. "But I am," I said, "an' you're comin' in after me."

"What makes yuh think so?" he asked.

I looked at him shrewdly. "Remember how I got my job here?" I asked. "I thought I was somethin'. Since then I been around. You're the original college coxs'n. I never really knew how good you were until I ran into a certain little blonde dancer yuh got stashed in a hotel across town."

I thought he'd burst a blood vessel. His face turned a heavy purplish color. "How d'yuh know about her?" he managed to ask.

"I get around, Sam," I smiled. "I'm a big boy now."

He cleared his throat embarrassedly. His fingers picked up a pencil and toyed with it. "Yuh know how those things are, kid," he said awkwardly, not looking at me. "I'm nuts about your sister, but she's got a screwy idea that every time I come near her she's knocked up. A guy's gotta let off steam some place."

"I'm not criticizing you, Sam," I said tolerantly. "Maybe I'm even a little envious. But I don't think Mimi could appreciate that. She's an awful proud girl, you know."

Sam stared at me, then relaxed in his seat. The rancor had gone from his voice. "Ain't it enough, kid, I come through for yuh when yuh're in trouble an' got no place else to go? Ain't it enough I keep yuh out of the can, go your bail, an' square the rap against yuh, then give yuh a job to boot. Ain't yuh satisfied?"

I got out of the chair and leaned across his desk. I meant every word I said. "I owe you more'n I owe anybody in the world, Sam. Believe me, I'm very grateful for everything you done. I don't like havin' to put the boot to yuh, anymore'n you do. But there's more'n just a job to livin' in this world. A guy's gotta have a buck he can call his own. Yuh never get that on a job, Sam. There's only one way yuh can get it. That's go after the big buck for yourself. You found that out, the first year up in the country, an' you did all right by yourself. Now I want a crack at it. Sure, I'm satisfied, but now I want a chance at the big buck myself."

He looked up into my eyes for a long moment; then a smile slowly spread across his face. He knew when he was licked. But it didn't keep him from making one more try. "Supposin' Fields tries to cut in on yuh?"

"He won't," I said confidently. "I found that out while I was checkin' around for you. It's not big enough for him."

He leaned back in his chair and took out his checkbook. "Okay, Danny," he said in a quiet voice. "How much do yuh need?"

"Six grand," I answered.

"For how long?"

"A year postwar," I said quickly. "I'm not takin' any chances."

"Christ, this war may go on for ten years!" he exploded. I was smiling. "If it does, then you'll be out your dough. I figger these machines'll hold up another three years. Then I ought to be able to get new ones."

Sam was figuring. "Usual rates, Danny?" he asked shrewdly.

Usual rates in this business were usury—generally six for five. "Take it a little easy, Sam," I said. "After all, it's in the family."

"Ten percent per annum on an undated note," he said quickly.

I nodded. "Fair enough, Sam." I grinned at him. "Now yuh want me to run down to Atlantic City for yuh?"

"Hell, no!" he swore, his pen already making scratching noises in his check-book. "Kill your own swindle sheet. You're in business for yourself!"

CHAPTER NINE

I CAME OUT OF SAM'S OFFICE AND SAT DOWN AT MY DESK. I LOOKED DOWN at the check in my hand. I still couldn't believe I had done it. The thought had never entered my mind until I had gone in there. I spread the check on the desk and smoothed it down. The writing on it stared up at me: six thousand dollars. I had the strangest impulse to grab the dough and run. I had never had that much money in my life.

A temptation came over me to take the check back to Sam and return it to him. Tell him I'd changed my mind and wanted my job back. I was crazy even to think I could get away with a project as big as this. Sam was a pretty sharp apple. If he couldn't see a buck in it, maybe he was right. I had learned enough about the way he did business to realize he was generally right. Guys don't build a business as Sam had done out of nothing but hot air. Who was I to say he was wrong?

I was suddenly tired. I closed my eyes wearily. What had got into me anyway? Why the big ideas? I was making a living. I was content. A few years ago I would have given my eyeteeth for a spot like this. Now it wasn't good enough. I searched my mind for the answer. It was there somewhere, it had to be. Hidden away in some secret corner just out of reach, like a very familiar word curiously lost to your tongue. There had to be a reason. I couldn't believe it had happened just because I'd found out that Sam didn't want it.

I went over the deal again in my mind. Maybe there was something about it that had caught me. It had all started a few weeks ago when Sam sent me out to look over this vending-machine business. Until then I had covered nothing but the concessions Sam dealt in.

The first day I had come to work for him he had called me into his office. It was the first time I had realized that he had really built himself into a big business. He waited until the door had closed behind me before he spoke. From behind his desk his eyes were cold and challenging. His tone of voice was one I had never heard him use before, it was clipped and businesslike. "If you think you're gettin' a free ride here, Danny, you can get off now."

I didn't answer.

"If you think you got the job because you put something over on me, forget it," he continued in the same tone. "I'm payin' yuh thirty bucks a week because I expect you to work thirty bucks' worth." He stared at me for a moment as if he expected me to answer him. When I didn't he went on:

"You're not gettin' any favors because you're Mimi's brother either, so you can forget that too. You'll do your work or get out. There's no other way with me— nothing else counts. I don't care what you think you got on me if you don't do your job, I'll tie a can to yuh before yuh know what's happenin'!" He glared up at me. "Unnerstan'?"

I almost smiled at the familiar word. It was always a favorite of his. "I coppish," I answered. "That's the way I want it. I'm tired of favors and handouts."

He nodded his head heavily. "Good," he said. "Then we unnerstan' each other. Now get outside an' go to work."

He got busy at his desk and I was dismissed. As I went outside, his secretary's face flushed. I smiled at her and went back to my desk, which was at the front of the room then, with the other receipt clerks. My job was to record the business reported by each of the concessions and keep a perpetual check on their inventory.

I didn't see very much of Sam after that. He treated me exactly like the other employees, no better and no worse. I was in that job over a year when the first peacetime draft grabbed one of the checkers. I was promoted to his job. It paid forty-five a week and carried a car along with it. It was my job to visit the concessions and see how things were going, to see whether the company was getting a fair shake. A certain amount of holdout couldn't be avoided in a business as vague and nebulous as this, but we tried to keep it at a fair minimum.

I got pretty good at the work. It got so that I could walk into a place, hang around a little while, and instinctively I would know how we were making out. I learned what the margin was for us, what we had to do to break even. It didn't take long for Sam to catch on that I knew the business. He began to give me appraising assignments. He would send me into a joint before he took it on and I would case it for him. I spent as much time there as I needed, then I went back to the office and gave Sam the nut. I was generally within a few bucks.

I got a couple of raises and then he began to use me exclusively on appraising. I felt good about that for many reasons, mainly because we both knew I was carrying my weight. There were no favors granted on either side. I was the only person outside of himself whose word he would accept about a concession. Until then he had always appraised the new places himself.

I never thought about doing anything other than my work until Sam sent me out on the vending-machine assignment. Something about that business caught me the minute I walked into Mr. Christenson's place. It wasn't the dough either. Sam had many deals I had recommended to him that involved much more and much less money. It was just the idea in it. I could just see these machines scattered all over the city, in the best locations—restaurants, terminals, airports, every place where people stopped, congregated, went to in order to kill some time. Tremendous metal machines that stood there impersonally with their hands in everybody's pockets, appealing to everybody's tastes, to everybody's needs. Thirsty? Have a Coke. Chewing-gum, candy, cigarettes.

Maybe it was the way Mr. Chistenson had put it. I could see from the way he acted that the man didn't really want to sell. But what could the guy do when his medic told him he had a bum ticker and he had to blow the setup or croak?

How Sam heard about it I never found out; but when I got out there and saw that it ran with only a five-man crew and that the take was three grand a week, it appealed to me. It appealed to me even more when I had gone through the complete business.

Christenson had one hundred and forty-one cigarette vendors working and ninety-two Coke squirters. There were fourteen machines in the shop for which he couldn't get replacement parts, but if they were working they could bring in another three hundred bucks a week. On top of that, forty per cent of the locations were bad, but Christenson was too sick to scout up new spots for them. Relocating these machines could bring the gross up to four grand a week easy.

Christenson figured his net at about ten per cent of the gross, or about three hundred a week clear. I figured that if all the things I had thought of were done we could bring the net up to at least fifteen percent. That would mean six hundred a week on a gross of four grand. That was nice pickings. That was why I recommended the deal to Sam.

He could work a setup like that off the back of his hand, and with his connections he could probably get hold of more machines. That was the first time I had thought about it in personal terms. I had thought that if Sam didn't want to bother with it, I could make a deal to run the outfit for him. Then I went down to the manufacturers of the machines to inquire about replacements and parts. Of course there was nothing available now, they were all too busy with war work; but one of them had rolled out a booklet showing their postwar models.

My eyes had opened wide. This was a field we couldn't afford to miss. There were more real pickpockets in this booklet than at Coney Island on a crowded day. Machines that roasted a hot dog and delivered it in a toasted roll with a napkin rolled around it; machines that sold hot coffee in a disposable cardboard cup; sandwiches—anything you could think of. There was even a machine that sold you an insurance policy at the airport before you made your trip. They had figured out everything but where the locations for them would be.

Opportunity was lying around in the gutter like a two-dollar whore. It wasn't that Christenson's outfit was such a great money-maker now, for it would be just as good if it wasn't making a cent. It was the in it had on the postwar market, the edge that every business was looking for. An outfit like that could sneak around on the q.t. now while everybody was busy with other things and lock up every choice location in the country. Then it would really be big business.

But Sam was just like everybody else. He was doing good; he didn't want to strain his milk. Why go spec when the dough was pouring in like the Johnstown flood?

I looked at the check in my hand. I still hadn't answered my question. What made me want to do it? I knew now that it wasn't the business alone, it was something else. But it wasn't until I got home that night and saw Nellie that I found the answer.

❖   ❖   ❖

I came into the apartment quietly, wondering how she would take the news. I hoped she wouldn't be worried, but she was funny about things like that. She made a big thing about working and saving money; and a job was the only way she could see to do it.

Several times when I had wanted to move out of the apartment, she had refused. "Why spend the money for rent?" she had argued. "We're comfortable here."

"But, honey," I had said, "for more dough we can be more comfortable somewhere else."

"No," she had said, "we might as well hold onto it while it's coming in. Nobody can ever tell when it's gonna stop. Then we'll need every penny we ever could keep our hands on."

I stopped talking about it after a while. I could understand what she was afraid of and she had good reason for it. All we had ever known was poverty. What right did we have to expect things would ever change? It was a depression philosophy that left its roots in so deep that nothing could ever tear it out.

I closed the door quietly behind me. "Nellie," I called softly. Sometimes she was napping when I came home. She worked all day on big hot plastic molding presses and it drained her energy.

There was no answer, so I tiptoed toward the bedroom. Halfway through the parlor I saw her, curled up in a corner of the couch, all dressed to go out for dinner and fast asleep. I moved silently to her.

An outstretched hand hung alongside the couch, dangling toward the floor; her other hand was hugged tightly against her bosom. There was something clutched in it. I looked closely. It was a picture of Vickie, the one we had taken up on the roof during the short summer of her life. Nellie had held her while I snapped the shutter on the borrowed camera. I remembered how anxiously we waited for the pictures to come back to the corner drugstore where we had left them for developing, how carefully we clung to the few pennies necessary to pay the cost of printing them. Nellie had been holding the baby up in the air. The baby had been gurgling down at her and she had been smiling happily up at Vickie. I could feel a lump in my throat, Nellie looked so much like a kid herself in that picture.

I looked down at Nellie's face. Her eyes were closed and she was breathing lightly and evenly. Her long black lashes curled over the soft white of her skin. Faint lines in her makeup ran down from her eyes. She had been crying. She had been looking at the picture and crying. Suddenly I knew the answer I had been seeking. All at once I knew the answer to a lot of things.

I knew why we'd never had another child, why Nellie was so afraid to spend an extra penny, why she wouldn't let us move from here. She was afraid. She blamed herself for what had happened to Vickie and she didn't want it to happen again—neither the fear nor the poverty nor the heartbreak.

And I knew why I wanted the big buck, why I had to take the chance. It was either live in the shadow of the fear all our lives or, once and for all, break free of it and have all the things we wanted. That was the whole of it. We had to be free of the fear so that we could think of tomorrow, a tomorrow we had been afraid to look into because it looked so much like yesterday.

Now we would be able to think of ourselves again. Like other people, we could want things again, feel things again, hope things again. That was it.

You just don't die, no matter what happens; you don't quit. You go on living. That's what it is: you go on living. It's not a thing you can turn on and off like the water in a faucet, not as long as inside you the blood is running, the heart is beating, the mind is hoping. That was it. You go on living.

Lightly I took the photograph from her relaxed fingers, put it in my pocket, and sat down in the chair opposite to wait for her to wake up so that I could tell her what I had just learned.

CHAPTER TEN

I SAT THERE AWKWARDLY IN MIMI'S LIVING-ROOM AND LOOKED AT MY FA-ther. I wished that she had left well enough alone. It was one of the big things in her life to reconcile us some day, but there was no use in it. Too many things had happened between us, we had drifted too far apart. Now we sat in the same room like strangers and made small talk, each of us extremely aware that the other was near and yet never addressing ourselves to each other.

Nellie and Mamma had gone with Mimi to the children's room to watch them going to bed, and Sam, Papa, and I were left in the living-room before dinner. The only talk was when Sam spoke to either of us. Then we would answer monosyllabically, stiffly, as if we were afraid our words would lead to further conversation.

At last Sam ran out of things to say that might interest both of us and retired into the awkward silence himself. He picked up the paper and turned to the sports section. For a few seconds the only sound in the room was the rustle of the newspaper.

I had been looking out the window across the Park. It was almost dusk and the lights in the buildings were just going on, flashing like yellow topazes on purple velvet.

"Danny, you remember that kid you fought in the Gloves finals—Joey Passo?"

I turned to Sam. I remembered very well. "That was the semifinals, Sam," I corrected him. "He was the kid that almost took me. He was good."

Sam nodded his head. "That's right. I knew you had fought him, though. It says here he's just signed for a crack at the light heavy championship in the fall."

I was aware of my father's eyes on me. "I hope the kid makes it," I said. "He's a good, gutsy kid and he needs the dough."

"You could have made it," Sam said without looking up from the paper. "You were good. You were the best prospect I ever seen."

I shook my head. "Uh-uh. It was too tough a racket for me."

Sam looked up from the paper. "The only thing wrong with you was that you didn't have the killer instinct. A few more fights and you might have got the idea."

My father spoke before I could answer. "A business where a man must be a killer is not a business I should want for my son."

Both Sam and I stared at him in surprise. It was the first time we could recall that he had injected himself into a conversation between us.

Papa's face flushed. "It's a dirty business where a man has to be a killer to be successful."

Sam and I exchanged knowing looks and Sam turned to him. "That's only an expression that fighters use, Dad," he explained. "It means that when you have a man in trouble, you know enough to finish him off quickly."

"An excuse in words is just an excuse," Papa insisted stubbornly. "If it's just words, why is it all the time I read in the papers about fighters getting killed?"

"They're accidents, Dad," Sam said. "You read about people getting killed every day in automobile accidents. That doesn't make everybody who drives a car a killer."

Papa shook his head. "A different thing."

It was Sam's turn to be stubborn. "It's not a different thing, Dad," he continued. "Prize fighting is a highly skilled sport. There are very few people who have all the skills necessary for it. The mental and physical co-ordination plus the will to win. All these things basically are God-given talents, and when you see someone who has them all, you're seeing a very unusual person. Your son, Danny, was one of those people."

He turned and looked at me a moment before he spoke again. There was a respectful affection deep in his eyes. "Danny was one of those people, Dad, who come along once in a lifetime." He was speaking softly, almost as if to himself. "When I first saw him he was a tall gangling kid, big for his age, who got into a fight in school. Before that he was just one of the kids I had in the class, but after that he was something special. He had the God-given talents."

Papa grunted. "The devil's talents, I say."

Sam's eyes flashed. "You're wrong about that, Dad, like you've been wrong about many things. Just as everybody is wrong sometimes. When you know how few people there are really in this world whose arms and legs move exactly and as quickly as their brain commands, you'll know what I mean."

Papa got to his feet. "I don't want to hear about it," he said with finality. "I'm not interested. To me, fighting is a murderer's business."

Sam was getting angry. "If that was the way you felt," he snapped sarcastically, "why was it all right for Mimi to marry me? I was a fighter."

Papa looked down at him. "You weren't a fighter then," he answered.

"But I would have been if I hadn't broken my kneecap," Sam retorted heatedly.

Papa shrugged his shoulders. "Mimi wanted you. It wasn't my business to tell her what to do. She could marry who she liked, it wasn't my place to interfere."

Sam's face was flushed. By now he was thoroughly angry. "When was it your place to interfere, Dad? When it suited you? That wasn't the way you acted when Danny—"

"Knock it off, Sam," I said quickly, interrupting him. This was between my father and me; there was no point in his getting into the quarrel too.

Sam turned belligerently toward me. "Why should I knock it off?" he demanded. "I got a part in this too. I went for a barrel of dough in that fiasco." He looked stubbornly at Papa. "Everything was okay as long as the kid did what you said, but it was no good when be wouldn't listen to you. Still, you never turned down the dough he brought home for the fights. That five hundred he left for you the night you locked him out cost me five grand and almost cost the kid his life. You didn't know that, did you?"

Papa's face was pale. He looked at me almost shamefacedly. "A son has the right to listen to what his father tells him," he maintained.

"The right, yes," Sam said, "but not the obligation to do what he says. I won't ever feel like that about my kids no matter what they do, right or wrong. They didn't ask me to bring them into the world. And if I wanted them, I have to help them whether I agree or not."

Papa waved his hand excitedly. "I don't want to hear about it," he said. "We'll see what you do."

"You'll never see me close the door on my sons," Sam snapped.

Papa stared at him for a moment, his face turning very white. Then he stalked silently out of the room.

I looked at Sam. His face was still flushed. "What did you do that for?" I asked. "You're only wasting your breath."

Sam made a gesture of disgust. "I was gettin' tired of listenin' to the old man. He's so right about everything. I was getting tired of his cracks about you and what he expected from you and the disappointment you were to him."

"So what're you gettin' sore about?" I asked. "It's got nothin' to do with you. It's me he's talkin' about."

"He knows by now that I wanted you to be a fighter," Sam said, "an' it's his way of gettin' even with me because you listened to me instead of him. Some day I'm gonna make him realize that he's been wrong about a lot of things."

I stared at Sam, then turned away and lit a cigarette. "You'll never do that, Sam," I said to him over my shoulder. "You'll never get him to change his mind about anything. Take my word for it. I ought to know. After all, he's my father."

CHAPTER ELEVEN

I LOOKED AT MY WATCH AS I WALKED THROUGH THE SMALL REPAIR ROOM. The mechanic was adjusting one of the cigarette machines. He grinned at me.

"I'll have this working in a couple of hours, Mr. Fisher."

"Take your time," I told him. "There's no use in sending it out again."

An understanding look crossed the man's face. "Nothing coming in?"

I shook my head. "Not a cigarette in a carload." I continued on through the room silently.

And that was putting it mildly. For almost six months now cigarettes had been harder to get than money, and crowds lined up wherever the word got out that there were cigarettes to be had. If I hadn't been smart and guessed something like this was coming, I'd have been out of business by now. But I had guessed right and with the help of a few men who were not averse to making an extra buck I had been able to stock up on them. The way I figured it, I couldn't lose no matter what happened. I could always push the butts out through the machines. But the shortage had come and now I was one of the few guys in the business with stock. It was my turn to make a buck.

I stuck my head in the small room at the back of the shop that served as the office. "Did Sam Gordon call back yet?" I asked the girl sitting there.

She shook her head. "No, Mr. Fisher."

"Well, call me when he does," I said, and walked back into the shop. Sam would call back, I knew he would. He had to whether he wanted to or not. I felt satisfied with myself. If this shortage lasted for a little while longer I would make a bundle of dough. Then I could really set myself up after the war. I ought to be able to raise enough money out of this operation to grab up all the best locations in the city.

I went back to the repair room and watched the mechanic. There was a paper lying on the bench behind him and I picked it up. "How's the war goin'?" I asked casually, flipping the pages.

"Pretty rough," the mechanic answered. "Them Nazis are hard to knock off."

"We'll get 'em," I said, not really thinking about it. I was too busy trying to figure out if Sam would go for the price I had in mind. I took a deep breath. He had to; otherwise he'd have nothing to sell in his concessions.

I glanced at the headlines. The Germans were retreating through France, and Patton's Third Army was hot on their tail. "We'll get 'em," I repeated.

"I sure hope so, Mr. Fisher," the mechanic replied in the tone of voice that an employee uses toward his boss.

I leaned my back comfortably against the work bench and kept turning the pages. A small headline caught my eyes: "Local OPA Says No Cigarette Shortage." I grinned as I read down the column. An awful lot of people were smoking clinchers if there was no shortage.

The paper quoted the OPA as saying that the whole blame rested on the hoarders. Some unscrupulous people were piling them up in warehouses to supply a black market instead of letting them flow into normal channels of supply.

I almost laughed aloud. I wondered what they'd do if they had the same chance to grab a buck that I did. Let them go into normal channels? Like hell they would. They would do just what I did: buy them in, stock them up, and sell them for the most you can get. A guy doesn't get a break like this very often, and I wasn't going to be fool enough to shove them out where I had to sell them at the regular price when I could get double the money or better.

"It's okay now, Mr. Fisher," the mechanic called to me.

"All right, Gus," I said. "If yuh got nothin' else to do, you knock off for the day."

"Thanks, Mr. Fisher." The man grinned at me gratefully. He turned to the machine. "Too bad we can't get enough cigarettes to keep it working, though," he said.

"Yeah." I smiled back at him. "It's too bad. But maybe we're worried over nothin'. The OPA says there's no cigarette shortage."

The man nodded. "I read that," he answered vehemently. "It's them lousy hoarders. They're keepin' honest men like us from makin' a livin'."

I agreed with him. He was absolutely right. I watched him climb out of his jumper, wondering what he'd say if he knew about the butts I had socked away. He'd probably holler copper. He was that kind of an honest shnook. I felt glad I had enough brains to store them in private warehouses away from the shop. That way nobody knew what I had.

I heard the girl's voice. "Mr. Gordon returning your call."

"I'm on my way." I dropped the paper on the bench and hurried back to the office. I picked up the phone. The girl was straightening some papers on her desk, not paying any attention to me.

"Hello, Sam," I said into the telephone.

"What's the black market on butts today, Danny?" he asked.

I grinned into the phone. "Easy, Sam, easy. You know how sensitive I am. You're hurting my feelings."

"Nothin' can hurt your feelings," Sam snapped sharply, "excep' losin' a buck!"

"Is that a way for my only brother-in-law to talk?" I kidded him. "Specially when I'm tryin' to do him a favor?"

"Nuts! I know you," Sam replied in a friendly voice. "What are you gettin' for 'em today?"

"It all depends," I said evasively. "How much do you need?"

"Five thousand cartons," Sam answered.

I whistled. "That's a lot of smoke," I said. "I think you can dig it for three and a half per."

"Three and a half dollars a carton?" Sam's voice almost split the receiver.

"What are yuh bitchin' about?" I asked easily. "Your girls get a half a buck a throw or better." I knew what I was talking about. I hadn't worked those years for him for nothing. Those pretty little half-dressed babes walking around in night clubs with a cigarette tray sticking out in front of them and an almost bare fanny behind knew how to milk the suckers for a buck.

"Three and a quarter," Sam bargained. "Gimme a break. After all, if it wasn't for me you wouldn't be in that racket."

"Three and a half," I insisted. "I think the world of you, Sam, and I still owe yuh six grand, but a cuter is cuter." That was true. I hadn't repaid Sam yet because the dough that came through I was sinking in location setups.

"Danny," Sam pleaded.

"Where do you want 'em shipped?" I asked, ignoring the sound in his voice. I knew he could afford the price. Sam was making dough as he'd never made it before.

There was a moment's silence; then his voice came wearily through the phone. "The usual place."

"C.O.D."

"Yeah," Sam answered without enthusiasm. "And I hope the OPA gets yuh, yuh bastard. Good-by."

I put the phone down, smiling. That was a fast ten grand. They only cost me a buck and a half a carton. I reached into my desk and took out my little book. I studied it carefully. I had made a list of all the locations I wanted to clinch. This dough would come in handy. I was almost all through the book now. Soon I could start making arrangements to get in my machine orders.

I looked up at the calendar. It was near the end of May. A few more days and I would be twenty-seven years old. Time was running away from me; I was getting old.

I looked at the book again. I'd better start getting in the machine orders now if I wanted to be sure of a favored position on the list when the manufacturers began shipment. The whole thing wouldn't be worth a damn if I couldn't get those machines.

CHAPTER TWELVE

I CAME INTO THE APARTMENT SMILING. NELLIE WAS BENDING OVER THE stove, peering into a pot. She turned her face toward me, without straightening up, and I kissed her cheek.

"What's for dinner, baby?" I asked gaily.

"Pot roast," she answered, "with stewed white onions."

I put my head over her shoulder and sniffed at the odors coming up from the pot. "Man, that smells good!" I grinned. "How'd yuh manage it?"

"It's so close to the end of the month that the butcher took some of next month's points," she explained.

"I don't know how you do it," I said in an admiring voice. "Work out at that stinkin' plant all day, then come home an' cook a meal like that."

"So many compliments!" she kidded me. "You must be looking for something."

I shook my head. "Uh-uh. I mean it. We don't need the dough. Why don't you quit?"

"I've been thinking about it," she said, half-seriously, "but the boys are depending on us. Now more than ever."

"And I'm depending on you," I said quickly. "The boys aren't. But how'll I manage if you wear yourself out?"

"Don't be silly, Danny," she said.

"I'm not being silly. I just love pot roast with stewed little white onions."

She pushed me toward the bathroom. "Go in and wash up," she said, laughing happily. "Supper's almost ready."

I went toward the bathroom smiling. It was good to see her so happy. It had been a long time since I had seen her looking as content as that.

"Yuh want some help with the dishes?" I asked, without looking up from the evening paper.

"You pick the right time to ask," she answered dryly. "I'm all through already."

I grunted and settled back in the easy chair and turned to the sports pages. The Yankees looked like a pennant bet even this early in the season.

She came into the parlor and sank on the couch opposite me. "How'd it go today?" she asked in a tired voice.

I couldn't keep the satisfaction out of my voice. "I hooked Sam for five thousand cartons. That's a clean ten grand."

A worried look appeared on her face. "Danny," she said quietly, "I'm scared. What if they catch you?"

I shrugged my shoulders. "Stop worryin'. They ain't gonna."

"But, Danny," she protested, "I saw in the paper that—"

"The papers are full of crap," I interrupted her. "They're just fishing. Besides, what can they do to me? It ain't against the law to sell cigarettes."

The worried look remained on her face. "The money isn't worth it," she said soberly. "Nothing's worth it. It's getting so I can't sleep nights any more."

I dropped the paper and looked at her. "You'd like it better if I was like the rest of the shnooks? We had enough of that, remember? You liked being without enough dough to eat? Not me. I've had enough of it."

Her eyes met mine levelly. "I don't care about that," she said quietly. "All I want is for you to stay out of trouble."

"Don't worry about me, Nellie," I said confidently, picking up the paper again. "I'll be okay. Before this is over, baby, you'll be wearin' minks and diamonds."

"I can live without them," she said, her eyes still troubled. "All I want is for you to be around." She drew a deep breath and I could see her hands clench into tight little fists. "After all, I wouldn't like having to tell Junior that his father is in jail."

The paper slipped out of my fingers to the floor. "What did you say?" I asked incredulously.

She smiled at me calmly, with the secret pride of a woman who carries a child under her heart lurking in her eyes. "You heard me," she said matter-of-factly. "We're going to have a baby."

I was out of my chair in a second, standing excitedly over her. "W-why didn't yuh say something?" I sputtered.

Her brown eyes sparkled with amusement. "I wanted to make sure first," she answered.

I dropped to my knees beside her. "You been to the doctor already?" I asked, taking her hand.

She nodded. "This morning, on the way to work."

I pulled her toward me gently and kissed her cheek. "An' yuh went in anyway? At least you could have called me up and told me."

"Don't be silly." She laughed. "You wouldn't have been able to work."

"An' I been sittin' here like a damn fool lettin' you knock yourself out," I reproached myself. I looked at her. "When are we expectin'?"

"In about seven months," she replied. "Around the end of November."

I sank on the couch beside her. I felt good. I had been right about many things. Somehow I had known that as soon as Nellie felt secure we would have another child. I sighed contentedly.

"Happy, Danny?" she asked.

I nodded my head, remembering the last time we had been through this. Things were different now. It was a lot better this way. "Now we can get out of here," I said.

"What for?" she asked. "This place is all right."

"This ain't the right neighborhood to bring up a kid if you can afford somethin' better," I said confidently. "Let's find a place where there's some air and sunshine."

She leaned back on the couch. "A place like that is so expensive, Danny," she protested mildly. "You know they're hard to get, and you have to pay under the table for any kind of an apartment now."

"Who said anything about an apartment?" I asked. "I want to buy a house!"

"A house!" It was her turn to be surprised. "That's out altogether. Too much money. I'd rather make do here and hold onto the money."

"To hell with that!" I said defiantly. "What am I makin' the dough for, if not for you—and the kid?"

CHAPTER THIRTEEN

THE STEAMING AUGUST SUN STRADDLED MY NECK AND SHOULDERS, squeezing the last drop of perspiration out of me as I got into the car and switched on the ignition. I pressed down on the starter. The engine sputtered and gasped. I pulled the choke and hit the starter again. The engine coughed and began to turn over slowly; then it sputtered and died.

I looked at the dashboard. The ammeter needle was flickering over on "discharge." I stepped on the starter again. No use; the battery bad gone. Resignedly I turned off the ignition and got out of the car. I stood staring at the automobile as if it had betrayed me. I cursed silently. I had promised Nellie I would be home early too.

I checked my watch. Four thirty. By the time I could get the battery recharged or replaced I'd have lost an hour and Nellie would be mad as hell. I locked the car and started for the subway. The nearest station was six blocks away and I was sweating bullets by the time I reached it. I dropped my nickel into the turnstile and went down to the platform.

As soon as I reached the platform I was thirsty. I looked for a news-stand. Some of them sold cold Cokes. One would go real good the way I felt now. There was a stand down at the far end of the platform, and I covered almost half the distance to it before I noticed it was closed. I stopped, disgusted. Nothing had gone right this afternoon. First the car conked out on me, now I couldn't even get a drink. The thirst came back stronger than ever, renewed by frustration.

I fished in my pocket for a penny and threw it into a chewing-gum machine. Maybe a stick of gum would help until I could get a drink.

A train roared into the station and I boarded it, idly glancing at my fellow passengers. Their faces gleamed eerily at me in the yellow light, shining with sweat from the damp heat. After a while I began to get bored. I wished I had thought to buy a newspaper. All the faces were the same in the subway, dull and tired and blank. They were all probably as hot and thirsty as I, and just as uncomfortable.

I began to read the signs strung out on the side of the train just over my head. The first one to catch my eye was a Coca-Cola ad. There was the usual picture of the usual wholesome, pretty girl smiling. She looked fresh and cool, and behind her was the usual pale blue-green cake of ice. In her hand she held a bottle of Coca-Cola, and beneath it were the usual words: "THE PAUSE THAT REFRESHES."

My mouth watered. The chewing-gum was suddenly dry and tasteless. That was a hell of a thing to see when you were dying of thirst. Teased hell out of you.

The train had stopped again and I looked out the window. A man was dropping a coin into a chewing-gum machine. His face was red and flushed with the heat and I could hear the coin tinkling into the box as the man pulled the handle.

The doors began to close and I looked up at the Coke sign again. To hell with the gum machines, I thought wearily; what they could use on the subway was a few of my cold-drink squirters. They would really do a business. Then it hit me. I remembered something a girl had once said when I worked at a soda fountain. I remembered the girl too. She had a healthy pair of lungs and I recalled the way she pushed them over the counter at me. "They ought to have places on the subway where you can get a Coke if you're thirsty," she had said.

I stared up at the sign bewilderedly. Talk about shnooks, I could take the prize! It had been here under my nose all the time and I hadn't seen it! The best location in the world: the New York subways. All I had to do was make a deal with the city and I was on Easy Street. I wouldn't have to do another lick of work all my life.

The people in the train all looked hot and thirsty. In my mind's eye I could picture them dropping nickels into my Coke dispensers. Hell, it wasn't only cold drinks; in the winter I could serve them hot coffee.

I began to feel excited. I couldn't afford to fall asleep over this thing. This was the baby I had been looking for, the location to beat all locations. I was glad my car had stalled. It took something like that to wake a guy up. If you really wanted to grab a buck you had to get down where the people were. Where they were was where the dough was. Woolworth had the right idea: grab the nickels and dimes. If you could do that, you were set. And the nickels and dimes on the subways added up to more dough than there was in all the department stores on Fifth Avenue.

I pressed the buzzer impatiently. I looked at Nellie standing in the dull white glow of the hall light. I pressed the buzzer again and smiled at her. I liked the way she looked. Her slightly swollen frame made her look even more attractive.

"I still don't see why you had to come running up here to see Sam," she said in an annoyed voice. "You could have done it tomorrow."

I looked at her understandingly. It was hot and she was uncomfortable. Even more so than usual. "Maybe I could," I answered quickly, "but if I got the idea, it's better'n even money that somebody else got it too. An' this can't keep, we gotta—" I stopped talking as the door opened.

Mimi was standing there. A look of surprise crossed her face as she saw us. "Danny! Nellie! We didn't expect you." She smiled and stepped back to let us in.

I was in the foyer already. "I came up to see Sam on a deal," I explained, looking for him in the living-room. "Is he home?"

Sam's voice bellowing from inside the apartment gave me my answer. "Who is it, Mimi?"

"Danny and Nellie," Mimi called back. "Danny wants to see you." She turned back to us. "Go on in," she invited us. "Sam will be down in a minute."

We followed her into the living-room. "How are you feeling?" she asked Nellie sympathetically.

"Wonderful," Nellie replied happily. "If the doctor hadn't told me I was pregnant I never would have believed it, I feel so good."

"You're lucky," Mimi said. "I'm always sick as a dog." Her voice lowered to the confidential tone that women use when they discuss their pregnancies.

"What's Sam doing?" I asked, interrupting her impatiently. I had heard about

Mimi's pregnancies a thousand times since Nellie had told them the news.

"He's taking a shower," Mimi replied. "He can't take this heat, he's such a big man, you know."

I nodded and started for the stairway of the duplex apartment. "You kids go ahead and yak," I called back over my shoulder. "I can talk to Sam while he's showering."

Sam was standing in front of the mirror, a towel wrapped around his waist, combing his hair when I walked in on him. "What do you want?" he asked grumpily.

"How'd yuh like to make a million bucks?" I asked enthusiastically.

He glanced at me in the mirror. It was a suspicious look. "Not interested," he answered quickly. "Every time you come to me with an idea, it costs me money."

"Stop making with the funny cracks," I said. "I really got it this time. Yuh want to hear it or not?"

He put down the comb and turned to me wearily. "All right," he said. "So tell me. I'm gonna hear it anyway."

I grinned. "Did you ever try to buy a Coke in the subway?" I asked.

He looked bewildered. "What the hell are yuh talking about?" he asked. "You know I ain't been in the subway for years. That's for the peasants."

I dropped the cover on the toilet seat and sat down. "That's just it, Sam," I said softly. "Yuh oughtta get down there with the peasants sometimes or yuh might forget where yuh come from."

Sam was annoyed. "I ain't heard your million-dollar idea yet," he snapped.

"You heard it, Sam," I said, "but the trouble is you been away from the peasants for so long you weren't listening. I might've missed it too if my car hadn't broke down today."

"So I been away from the peasants so long," Sam said disgustedly. "So stop crappin' an tell me or get outta here an' let me dress."

I lit a cigarette and blew a gust of smoke toward him. "Remember way back, Sam," I said quietly, "remember when you were one of the six million peasants in this town who don't live on Central Park South an' you were comin' home from work? You were hot and tired and thirsty, an' when you got on the subway you realized it. You were dyin' for a drink, but when you looked aroun', there ain't none an' you gotta wait till you get off." I paused to catch my breath.

"What're you tryin' to do? Win the Accademy Award for the best performance of the year?" Sam asked caustically before I could continue.

I could feel my face flush. I hadn't realized I had been so dramatic. "You don't see it yet?" I asked. I couldn't see how he'd missed it.

He shook his head. "I don't see it," he said flatly. "I'm the Central Park type. I'm stupid. I'm not one of those smart peasants."

"Would you buy a drink if there were one of my Coke machines on the platform?" I asked quickly.

He had started to rub his face again with a towel. Now he lowered it and stared at me. There was a gleam of interest in his eyes. "Say that again, Danny," he said carefully. "And tell me slow. Now I'm listenin'!"

CHAPTER FOURTEEN

IT WAS THE BIG DEAL ALL RIGHT. EVEN SAM HAD TO SAY THAT. HE WENT for it whole hog. We formed a separate company just to handle it. He would put up the dough and take care of the arrangements, I would run the business. And there were a lot of arrangements to be made, more than I had ever thought possible. I had been so busy since I got into it that I brought Zep in with me to handle the regular business while I devoted myself to the new company.

Coke machines on the subway. Who would think such a simple thing would take so much time and effort? But there were so many people you had to see—city officials, Board of Transportation officials, engineers, Department of Health people. Approval had to come from so many places that at times I had been bewildered. And as if that weren't bad enough, when we had everything lined up, there were still the politicians.

You had to have connections for a job like this. That was why I had gone to Sam in the first place. Sam had the connections, but even there we had run into a snag: Mario Lombardi, a quiet little man who hired a press agent to keep his name out of the papers, not in them. But his name got into the papers anyway. You couldn't keep a man like that a secret. He had too much power. I found out that nothing really big could be done in the city of New York unless Mario Lombardi okayed it. That was in spite of all the honest intentions of the city government.

And there was only one way Sam knew to get to Mario Lombardi. Through Maxie Fields. I wished there had been another way to reach him—any way but through Maxie Fields. But Sam assured me there wasn't, otherwise he would prefer it himself. So we had spoken to Maxie and now we were sitting in the living-room office of Mario Lombardi's upper Park Avenue apartment and it looked as if we were going to take in two new partners at any moment.

I leaned back in the chair, the smoke curling upward from my cigarette. I looked skeptically at Lombardi, seated behind his desk. "So we cut you in, Mr. Lombardi," I said casually. "What guarantee we got that after the war the deal we make will stand up? After all, politics in this town is a tricky business. One time you're in, next time you're out."

Lombardi tapped the ashes from his cigar delicately into a tray, the big diamond in his pinky ring flashing at me. He returned my gaze steadily. "Mario Lombardi don't make promises he can't keep, Danny," he answered quietly. "I don't care who's running the city when the war is over. It's my town and I'll still be callin' the shots."

"That's right. Danny." Maxie Fields's booming voice had a fawning quality in it that made me sick. "You don't clear nothin' in this town unless Mario okays it."

I looked at Maxie coldly. I still didn't like him. There was something about him that rubbed me the wrong way.

Sam's face was inscrutable, but his head nodded impassively.

It was okay with Sam, so I turned back to Lombardi. The small, dark man, dapper in his conservative gray suit, seemed more interested in his fingernails than in our conversation. I sighed lightly this was as far as we could go; the rest was up to fate. I had already been to see every two-bit politico and they all had told me that Lombardi was the only man big enough to swing a deal like this. So we took in partners.

"Okay, Mario," I said finally. You never call a partner by his last name. "It's a deal. You get ten per cent of the profits."

Lombardi stood up and held out his hand to me. "You won't regret it, Danny," he said. "Any time you want anything, you come an' see me."

I took his hand. "Anything?" I asked smiling.

Lombardi nodded, his teeth startling white in his swarthy face. "That's what I said."

"Then get me an apartment," I said quickly. "My wife is knockin' herself out lookin' for one an' she's six months gone already." Nellie still wouldn't let me part with the dough for a house.

Lombardi's smile turned into a wry grin. He shrugged his shoulder expressively and glanced about the room, a touch of embarrassed humor lurking deep in his dark eyes. "Medium OPA approved rentals?" he asked.

I nodded. "About seventy-five to a hundred bucks a month."

The wry grin broadened on his face. He held up his hands expressively. "Ask me something easy like that, Danny, an' I'm stuck," he admitted. "This morning I spoke to a guy an' got an okay for a judge; I spoke to some other people an' fixed up a buildin' deal; I went to lunch with the Mayor an' earlier this afternoon I arranged a million-dollar loan, but you gotta come along an' ask me somethin' easy which I can't do. Tell your wife to stop beatin' her brains out, Danny. Go out an' buy a house."

"Goin' past my place, Danny?" Fields asked heavily as we stepped out into the street.

I nodded and turned to Sam. "I'll see you tomorrow?"

"Sure," Sam replied as he got into his yellow Cadillac convertible. "In the morning."

We watched Sam drive off, then turned and walked to my car. I was silent. I was figuring. Ten per cent for Lombardi and five per cent for Maxie Fields for the fix. Fields's voice cut into my thoughts.

"That Sam is a bright guy," he said, squeezing his massive bulk into the seat beside me.

I stared at him in surprise. It was the first time I had ever known Fields to say a nice word for anybody. "Yeah," I answered, throwing the car into gear and moving out into traffic.

"He's got himself a hell of a business," Maxie continued blandly. "Growin' all the time too."

I wondered what he was getting at. I confined myself to a cryptic answer. "He works." I said. "He works all the time."

"That he does," Fields agreed readily. Too readily. "I understand you're pretty hep to that racket too. You worked in very close with him."

I glanced at him out of the corner of my eye. Maxie's face was smooth; he was looking out the car window. "Yeah," I answered.

"If somethin' happened to him, I guess you'd have to take over on account of your sister," Maxie continued.

For a moment I was too surprised to even think. "Why yes," I stammered, "I—I suppose I would have to."

We stopped for a traffic light and I could feel Maxie's eyes on my face, watching me closely. "If yuh ever got any ambitions along that line, Danny," he suggested casually, "why don't yuh just talk to me? Maybe I can help you out."

There was a sick feeling in my stomach. I gripped the wheel tightly, my knuckles white against the back of my hands. I managed to keep my voice as casual as his had been. "I'm satisfied with what I got. Maxie. I'm doin' all right."

"Well, the black market in butts won't last forever, kid." His voice was bluff and hearty. "An' the war may not be over for a long time. Just remember what I said in case you should change your mind."

The rest of the ride downtown passed in silence. I couldn't wait for him to get out of the car. It was bad enough I had to do business with him; I couldn't stand havin' him around me any more than was absolutely necessary.

As I let myself into the apartment quietly, I could hear the hum of an electric fan coming from the bedroom and tiptoed toward it. Through the open door I could see a figure on the bed.

Nellie was sleeping, her head resting on one arm, the gentle breeze from the fan stirring the sheet over her. I watched her for a moment, then turned and silently began to leave the room.

Her voice called me back. "Danny?"

I turned to her. Her dark eyes were watching me. "I was so tired," she said in a small voice, "I fell asleep."

I sat down beside her on the bed. "I didn't mean to wake you up."

"You didn't wake me," she replied. "I have to make supper anyway. But I spent all day looking for an apartment and didn't find one. Then I felt so weak I just had to take a nap."

I smiled tolerantly at her. "Why don't you quit an' let's buy us a house. Even Mario Lombardi can't get us an apartment."

"But so much money, Danny," she protested, sitting up in the bed.

I leaned toward her. "Stop worrying about money, honey," I said gently. "Lombardi okayed the subway deal for us. We can afford it."

Her eyes searched mine. "Are you sure that's what you really want, Danny?"

I nodded. "All my life I wanted my own house." Even as I said it I realized how true the words were. I had never been so happy as when I was in my own house. "That's what I want," I added.

She drew in a sharp sudden breath and flung her arms around my neck. "Okay, Danny," she breathed against my ear. "If that's what you want, that's what we'll do."

CHAPTER FIFTEEN

"THE TREES ARE ALL GROWN NOW," I THOUGHT AS I TURNED THE CAR into the street. Nellie was silently looking out the window. I couldn't tell from her face what she was thinking as I let the car roll slowly up the street.

Almost twenty years had changed many things. The houses on the block had settled into homes. A little older, weatherbeaten. Some of them needed repainting badly. But one thing hadn't changed. Despite the individual differences, each house looked very much like the others.

I pulled the car to a stop at the curb in front of our house, cut the motor, and turned to Nellie. She was still sitting silently, her eyes fixed on the house. I looked at it too.

A warmth swept through me, a strong satisfaction that I had not known for a long time. Now it would really be my house. "The agent said he would be waiting for us inside," I said.

Nellie's eyes were darkly thoughtful. "Danny," she said hesitantly, "maybe we ought to wait a little while longer. Maybe we shouldn't rush into this. Something else might turn up."

"What?" I asked skeptically. "We spent a month and a half lookin' an' we seen nothin' we liked. It's the middle of September now, an' if we want a house to move into by October 1st, we gotta make up our minds."

"We don't have to rush," she said. "We can wait until after the baby comes."

I shook my-head. "Uh-uh. I want everything ready." I opened the door. "Let's go."

She got out of the car slowly and stood on the sidewalk. Her hand reached out and touched my arm. There was a deeply worried look in her eyes. She shivered slightly.

I looked at her in quick concern. There was no reason for her to shiver. It was almost hot with the sun beating down on us.

"What's the matter?" I asked. "Don't you feel well?"

She shook her head. "I feel all right."

"Then why the shiver?" I asked. "Are you cold?"

"No," she said in a low voice. "A terrible feeling just came over me. I was frightened."

I smiled at her. "What have you got to be frightened about?"

She turned and looked at the house. "Suddenly I was afraid for you, Danny. I feel something terrible is going to happen."

I laughed aloud at that. "What can happen?" I asked. "We're set now. Nothing can go wrong."

Her grip tightened on my arm. "That house means a lot to you, doesn't it, Danny?" she asked, still looking at it.

"Yeah," I said. "It was supposed to be my house from the very beginning and it never really was. Now it will be."

She turned to me, a sudden knowledge in her face. "And all your life you've been trying to get even."

I didn't understand her. "What do you mean?"

"All the time this is what you wanted. More than anything else," she explained.

I thought for a moment. Maybe she was right. But it couldn't make any difference now. It just happened that my old house was available when we were looking for one. And the way things were, there was no new housing available. Things had a way of working out. That it should be on the market just at that time seemed only right to me.

I turned toward the house without saying anything to her. Her hand pulled at my arm.

"Danny, maybe we shouldn't buy the house," she said earnestly. "Maybe it was intended that you should not live there. I got a feeling that we're tempting fate if you come back to it."

I smiled. Pregnant women were always having hunches and making gloomy predictions. Carrying children seemed to bring with it a spurious foreknowledge. "Don't be foolish, Nellie," I said. "All we're doing is buying a house."

She started for the front door, but I steered her toward the driveway and we walked between the two houses to the garden in the back. It had changed too. When we had lived there, the back yard was bare, but now it was neatly turned and filled with shrubs and bushes and plants. I looked over toward the corner near the fence and remembered the night I had come back with Rexie and buried her there. A big rosebush covered the spot. I wondered if her rest had been disturbed.

"Mr. Fisher!" a voice called.

I turned around. The real-estate agent was coming up the driveway behind us. I waved to him.

"Ready to look at the house now, Mr. Fisher?" he asked.

I nodded my head. I was ready.

The wooden floor creaked comfortably under my feet. It was a welcoming sound. "Hello, Danny Fisher," It seemed to whisper softly. The bright sun at the windows faded as a cloud crossed its face and the room grew dark.

I paused on the threshold of my old room. Nellie and the agent were in another part of the house. I entered the room quietly and closed the door behind me.

Once, long ago, I had done this. I had thrown myself on the floor and pressed my cheek against the cool wood. I was too big to do that now. Some day my son would do it in my stead.

"It's been a long time, Danny," the room seemed to whisper.

It had been a long time. I looked down at the floor. There was no dark spot there where Rexie used to lie. Many scrapings and varnishings had taken it away. The stippled wall had vanished under many layers of paint, the ceiling behind many coats of calcimine. The room seemed smaller than I remembered. Maybe it was because I remembered it when I was very small myself and saw everything in relation to me. I crossed the room and opened one of the windows. Instinctively I looked across the driveway to the next house.

Years ago, there was a girl who had that room. I tried hard to remember her name but I couldn't, I could only remember what she looked like with the electric light shining behind her. I could hear her shadowed voice calling me and I looked at the windows opposite. They were blank and the blinds were drawn.

I turned back into the room. It seemed to move with a sibilant life all its own. "I've missed you, Danny," it whispered. "Have you come home to stay? It's been so lonely without you."

There was a weariness inside me and I leaned back against the windowsill. I'd been lonely too. I'd missed this house more than I had realized. Now I knew what Nellie had meant. There was a promise here that somehow I knew would be kept. It was written everywhere I turned. "I will care for your son, Danny, as I have cared for you. I will help him grow tall and strong, happy and content, wise and understanding. I will love him as I love you, Danny, if you'll come home to stay."

There was a noise outside in the hall and the door opened. Nellie and the agent came into the room. She took one look at my face and hurried to me. Her voice echoed warmly in the empty room. "Danny, are you all right?"

Slowly I came back to her. A deep concern was in her eyes as she looked up at me. "All right?" I echoed her. "Of course I'm all right."

"But your face is pale," she said.

Just then the sun came out from behind the clouds. "It's just the light in here," I laughed, beginning to feel normal.

Her eyes were still on mine. "Sure you're doing right, Danny?" she asked anxiously. "No ghosts to bother you?"

I looked at her in surprise. I didn't believe in ghosts. "No ghosts," I said gently.

The real-estate agent looked at me curiously. "Your wife tells me you used to live here, Mr. Fisher."

I nodded.

He smiled broadly. "Well, in that case I don't have to tell you anything about the house itself. About how well it's made. Recent buildings are nowhere near as well constructed. What do you think, Mrs. Fisher?"

She looked at him for a moment, then turned back to me. "What do you think, Danny?"

I took a deep breath and looked around me. I knew what I was going to say. I had always known. And there were sounds in the house that made me feel as if it knew the answer, too.

"I think we're going to take it," I said. "Could you arrange to have the painters in tomorrow so that we can occupy on the 1st?"

CHAPTER SIXTEEN

I GOT TO MY FEET IN SURPRISE AS SAM WALKED INTO MY OFFICE. THIS WAS the first time he had ever come out here. "Sam!" I said, my surprise echoing in my voice. "What's the occasion?"

He looked meaningfully at the girl sitting at the next desk to mine in the small office.

I sent the girl out and turned back to Sam. "What's on your mind?"

Sam slipped into the chair she had vacated. "I'm gettin' a little tired of havin' to call you every week for cigarettes. I want to fix up a steady thing with you."

I smiled in relief. For a moment I had thought that he had come to complain about the orders I had placed for the subway drink dispensers. I had been spending his capital as if it were mine. "You ought to know better'n that, Sam," I said reproachfully. "Nobody can guarantee it. The stuff's hard to get."

"You can get it," he said confidently.

"I wish I could be sure," I said quickly.

"I want two hundred boxes a week," he said, his voice hardening. "You'll see that I get it."

"And what if I don't?" I challenged. I could do it all right, but I wanted to find out what had made Sam so sure of himself.

He took a folded sheet of paper from his pocket and threw it on the desk. "Glom that," he said.

I picked it up and looked at it. It was a copy of my warehouse receipts. That meant he knew where I had stashed every last pack of butts. I turned to him in bewilderment. "Where'd you get that?" I demanded.

He smiled broadly. "I got ways," he answered evasively. "Now do I get them butts?"

"Supposin' I say no anyway?" I asked.

"The OPA would love to have a copy of those receipts." He smiled.

"You wouldn't do that to me, Sam!" My voice was shocked.

He smiled again. "Of course not, Danny," he replied casually. "No more'n you'd tell Mimi about other matters."

I put a hurt, disillusioned look on my face. "I never thought you'd do a thing like that, Sam," I said mournfully, swallowing an impulse to smile.

Sam's face wore a delighted expression of triumph. "You don't like it when the shoe's on the other foot, you little blackmailin' bastard?"

That did it. I couldn't choke back the laughter any more. It echoed loudly in the tiny office.

Sam stared at me in surprise. "What's with you, Danny?" he asked in a gruff voice. "You gone off your rocker?"

I looked at him through the tears that came into my eyes. Finally I caught my breath. "I was just thinkin', brother-in-law," I gasped, "that this is a fine way for a couple of partners to act to each other!"

Then he saw the humor in it and began to laugh too.

After a while I took him out into the shop and showed him around. It seemed to open his eyes a little. He hadn't realized that the thing had turned into such a big proposition. Then when we came back into the office and I showed him the list of locations I had already signed for, I could see a new respect dawning in his eyes.

"You got almost as much here as we got in the subway deal alone," he said in surprise.

"More," I said quickly. "Before I'm through, it'll be twice as big." I offered him a cigarette and lit it for him. "Compliments of the house," I said.

He was still thinking about what he had learned. "Now I know why you're always short of dough," he said.

I nodded. "I been throwin' it back as quick as it came in."

He looked at me through the cloud of smoke coming from his nostrils. "How about puttin' the whole thing together in one package, kid?" he suggested. "It'd make it a lot easier for yuh."

I played cagey. "You throwin' your business in too, Sam?" I countered.

"Uh-uh." He shook his head. "I just mean this. I'll give yuh a fair price for half an' then supply the dough jus' like on the subway deal."

It was my turn to say no. "That was a big one I couldn't handle alone, Sam," I said. "This is mine. I built it a little brick at a time. I'm gonna keep it."

He was silent a moment. I knew that look on his face: he was figuring out an angle. When at last he looked up at me, I could tell from his expression that he had given up. "Okay, Danny," he said genially. "But if you should ever change your mind, say the word. By the way," he asked, turning to leave, "how's the house comin'?"

"Okay. We'll be in it next week, Tuesday, like we figured."

He walked back toward the desk. "You should've seen your old man's face when Mimi told him."

"What'd he say?" I asked. I couldn't conceal my interest.

"At first he didn't believe it, but when Mimi swore that it was the truth, he couldn't speak. Your mother began to cry."

I couldn't understand that. "What was she crying for?"

"She kept saying something to your father about that was what you wanted all the time and he wouldn't believe you. He couldn't speak, he just chewed away on that cigar of his and after a while he went over to the window and looked out. All through dinner he was very quiet, and toward the end of the meal he looked up at Mimi and said a very funny thing." Sam paused for breath and looked at me.

I didn't say anything.

"He said: 'So Danny's going home.' And your mother said: 'That's what he wanted all the time—to come home. And you wouldn't let him.' Then your father said: 'I'm an old man now and for me it doesn't matter any more. My mistakes I'll take with me to my grave. But happy I am that Danny found his way back.' Then they got up and your father said he was tired and they went home."

My cigarette had burned almost to my fingers and I dropped it into an ashtray.

"Y'know, kid," he said softly, "I think the old man is about ready to throw in the towel if you'll go to him."

I breathed deeply and shook my head. "It's more'n that, Sam," I replied. "He's got to square away with Nellie first. There were too many things he said, too many things he did. He's got to level all the way round."

"He will if you give him the chance, Danny."

"He's gotta do that by himself," I said. "I can't do that for him."

"You know how he is, kid," Sam said gently. "He's proud and stubborn and he's old. Only God knows how much time he's got left to—"

"I'm his son, Sam," I interrupted him wearily. "You don't have to tell me anything about him. I know him better'n you. And I'm a lot of things that he is too. I'm proud and stubborn. In a way I'm old too, older'n he is. I gone through a lot of things because of how he acted that made me older. I buried a child, Sam. She died in my arms because we didn't have anyone to turn to for help. Yuh think that can happen 'thout getting older? Yuh think yuh forget a thing like that? You can't," I answered myself. "Yuh can't forget. An' yuh can't forget that it all started when your own father locked his door on you." I shook my head. "He'll have to do it all by himself, like I had to. Then maybe we'll be able to level again and feel right with each other."

I dropped into my chair and lit another cigarette. I was very tired. When all the rush of moving and business died down and Nellie had the baby, we'd go away for a while. We both could use the rest. I couldn't ever remember feeling so tired all the time.

I looked up at Sam again and switched the subject. "Where d'yuh want the butts sent, Sam?"

He stared at me for a second before he answered. "The usual place, Danny."

"They'll be there tomorrow morning," I said.

He was still watching me. After a few moments he said: "Okay, Danny," and walked out the door.

I sat there silently for a while, thinking. Then I got up and went to the door of the little office. "Zep!" I called out into the shop.

He came running in from the workroom. "Yes, Danny?"

Time hadn't stopped for any of us. It was just a short run from the workroom, but Zep was out of breath. "Get on the other phone, Zep, an' try to scout up new warehouse space for us," I said. "We're gonna have to move everything tonight. Sam has all the places spotted."

He nodded quickly, sat down at the telephone, and began dialing. I looked at him fondly. He was okay. He knew enough not to waste any time asking questions; they could keep until after the job was done.

I picked up my phone and called Nellie. I didn't want to tell her I was going to be late again tonight, but there was nothing else I could do. She was approaching the nervous stage of her pregnancy and everything seemed to upset her. But she calmed down a little when I promised her that I would be home early every night after this and that she wouldn't be alone until the baby arrived.

CHAPTER SEVENTEEN

I PUT DOWN MY COFFEE CUP AND GOT UP FROM THE TABLE. I CAREFULLY skirted several filled cardboard cartons and walked around the table to where she was sitting, and bending, kissed her cheek. "S'long, honey," I said. "I'm off to work."

"Be home early tonight," she said, looking up at me. "I want to finish the packing."

"Stop worryin'," I told her. "We can always do a few things tomorrow before the movers come. They won't be here until eleven."

"I don't like leaving things until the last minute," she answered. "You always forget something and then you're upset. I want everything ready."

It really wasn't very much that we were moving. We were taking none of the furniture with us. We had bought everything new for the house and it was already out there. But women were like that. I remember my mother had been the same way when we had moved.

"Okay, Nellie," I said, walking to the door. "I'll be home early."

Her voice called me back. As I stood in the doorway, she came running to me clumsily and I held my arms out to her. She came running into them and rested her head against my shoulder, trembling. I kicked the door shut with my foot and stroked her hair. "Baby, baby," I whispered, "what's the matter?"

I could scarcely hear her voice, muffled by my jacket. "Danny, I'm frightened. Suddenly I'm frightened."

I held her close to me. The years had taken their toll even from her. I could notice a few tiny gray hairs under my fingers, and the closer the baby came, the more nervous she was. It hadn't been like this with Vickie; she hadn't been so nervous then. "Don't be scared, baby," I whispered. "Everything'll be all right."

She looked up into my face. "You don't understand, Danny," she whispered. "I'm not frightened for myself, I'm frightened for you."

I smiled reassuringly at her. "Don't be nervous, baby. Nothing will happen to me. I'll be all right."

She hid her face against my shoulder again. "Let's not move tomorrow, Danny, let's not move there. Let's find another place. We can wait."

"Don't talk foolish, baby," I said. "You're just nervous and upset. You'll love it, once we move in."

She was crying. "Don't go back there, Danny," she pleaded. "Please don't go back. You can't make things over again, you can't change what was meant to be. I'm afraid for you to go back!"

I put my hand under her chin and turned her face up to me. "Stop crying, Nellie," I said firmly. "It won't do any good. You're just making yourself hysterical over nothing. It's a place to live just like any other place—nothing more and nothing less. So stop trying to make it into something it's not, and try to be sensible."

Slowly she stopped weeping. "Maybe I was wrong," she admitted in a taut, controlled voice, "but I've got such a terrible premonition."

"I remember my mother saying that was one of the symptoms of her pregnancy—premonitions. Everybody has them."

She smiled doubtfully through her tears. I took out a handkerchief and wiped her eyes gently. "Forgive me, Danny," she whispered. "I was just being a woman."

I kissed her mouth. "Forgive you nothing, baby," I said, smiling. "That's the way I want you."

As the men brought in another machine, I walked out of the office and followed them back to the workroom, where they put it down. Zep and a mechanic were already examining it.

"What's wrong with this one?" I asked.

Zep looked at me. "The usual thing, Danny," he answered. "Somebody got mad because there weren't any cigarettes an' took it out on the machine."

I looked at the machine philosophically. I was getting used to it now. This made the fifteenth machine in two weeks that had come in damaged. That was a curious thing about people, how they could vent their anger on a machine.

I studied it carefully. This one was pretty well shot. I turned to Zep. "Put it in the storeroom," I said casually. "There's no use trying to do anything with it. It'll only be a waste of time."

He nodded and I started back to the office. My secretary was just coming to the door.

"There's a long-distance call from Buffalo for you, Mr. Fisher," she said.

I crinkled my brow trying to think who might be calling me from there. I didn't know anyone up that way. "Who is it?" I asked.

"He wouldn't give me his name," she answered, a puzzled look on her face. "He just insisted on talking to you."

"Okay," I said, my curiosity aroused. "I'll take it. Make out another vandalism claim for the insurance company," I told her as I picked up the phone. "You can get all the dope from Zep."

She nodded her head and went out toward the workroom. I waited until the door closed behind her before I spoke. "Fisher talking," I said.

"Danny, this is Steve Parrish," a voice crackled in the receiver.

There was a good reason for this guy not giving his name. He was a salesman for one of the big cigarette jobbers who specialized for the most part in big black-market deals. He was the first guy I had contacted when I went into the business. "Steve," I said pleasantly, "what're you wastin' your dough on long-distance calls for? Yuh got money to burn?"

Steve's voice took on a confidential tone. "I got a big deal up here," he almost whispered, "and I wanted to check with you before I let it get anywhere else."

I sat down in my chair and lowered my voice to match his. "How many boxes?" I asked.

"A full truckload," his voice answered quickly. "All standards. One thousand boxes. You interested?"

Sure I was interested. Who wouldn't be interested in a thousand boxes of cigarettes when there was hardly that many in the whole town? "What's the deal?" I asked cautiously.

"Two dollars a carton, a C note a box," he answered.

I whistled. That was a lot of dough: one hundred grand. "They hot?" I asked.

Steve laughed metallically. "Don't ask questions, Danny. Stuff like that don't come out of the icebox these days. I only found out about them by accident because these guys have to unload and grab their dough. I thought of you right away."

"All-cash deal?" I asked.

"All cash," he replied flatly. "That's why you're gettin' the two-dollar price. If they had the time they could unload for three and a half."

"Where'm I gonna get that kind of cabbage?" I asked.

There was the faintest note of challenge in his voice. "If it's too big for yuh to handle, Danny, let me know. Sam Gordon's been after me for a long time to throw some stuff his way, but I wouldn't do that. I'm not out to cut your trade an' I know he's one of your customers."

He would know that all right. I had first met him when I was working for Sam. "I didn't say that, Steve," I said quickly. "I was just wonderin' where I could raise that kind of dough. How much time have I got?"

"No time at all, Danny," he replied. "The boys want their dough tonight. Maybe I better give Sam a buzz, he's got the dough."

My watch said one thirty. The banks were still open, but all I could get there was about nineteen grand that I had socked away in a safe-deposit box. All the other money had been plowed back into the business. I stalled for time.

"Can you wait a half-hour so I can do some figurin'?"

"If yuh ain't got the dough, Danny, forget it," he answered. "There's no use humpin' around. I'll call Sam."

I snapped my fingers. I had it. And he had given me the answer without knowing. "Look," I said quickly, "I didn't say I didn't have the dough. I just said I needed a half-hour to get it. Then I'll call yuh back an' we can make up where to meet. I can hop a plane up there an' you'll have it tonight."

I heard a whispered consultation going on at the other end of the wire; then Steve's voice came back on the phone. "Okay, Danny, the boys say they'll wait a half-hour for your call."

"Good," I said quickly. "Gimme your number an' I'll call you right back." I wrote the number down on a scratch pad and put down the phone.

There was a clean fifty thousand dollars in this for me if I could pull it off, and that kind of dough didn't fall into your lap every day. I picked up the phone again and began to dial. The phone on the other end of the wire was ringing. If Steve hadn't been so quick to suggest finding another customer I wouldn't have had this idea. I owed him never-to-be-spoken thanks.

There was a click. An operator's voice sang through the receiver: "Sam Gordon Enterprises."

"Mame, this is Danny. Put me on the boss's through line."

"Okay, Danny."

I heard another click, another ring, and then Sam's voice: "Hello."

"Sam, this is Danny," I said.

"Yeah, Danny, what's up?"

"If yuh can use six hundred boxes of standards, I got a deal for yuh," I said quickly.

Sam's voice grew cautious. "I can always use 'em, but what's the deal?"

"Three bucks a carton, a hundred an' fifty bucks a box. Cash in advance. Delivery tomorrow," I said.

He hesitated a moment. "Sounds okay," he answered, still cautious. "But that's a lot of the long green. What if you can't make delivery?"

"I'll guarantee the delivery," I said confidently.

"S'posin' somethin' goes wrong?" he asked. "Then I'm out ninety grand."

I thought quickly. Sam's ninety thousand almost carried the deal by itself. I'd have to be a dope if I passed up a shot like that. "Look," I said, "you know the layout here. I got close to sixty grand worth of the stuff stashed away. The business, location options, and orders for new machines are worth another forty G's. I'll bring over the warehouse receipts and an assignment for the business an' you can hold onto that until the stuff is delivered. Then you give it back to me."

"An' if you don't deliver?" he asked carefully.

I laughed shortly. "Then the whole pot is yours. What d'yuh say?"

He hesitated a moment. "I can use the butts okay, an' I'm int'rested in the business, but not for myself. I'm out on my elbow there. I can't run it."

"So you'll give me a job"—I laughed again—"an' I'll run it for yuh."

He still hesitated. "Sure yuh want it that way, kid?" he asked slowly.

Fifty grand's a lot of dough. "You heard me, Sam," I said surely. "I'm willing to take a chance if you are."

He cleared his throat. "Okay then, Danny," he said quietly. "Come on over, the dough'll be waitin' for yuh."

I jammed my fingers on the telephone, jiggled the bar for a second until the dial tone came to my ear, then spun the long-distance operator. I gave her the Buffalo number that Steve had given me. When Steve's voice came on the wire, "I got the dough, Steve," I said quickly. "Where'll I meet yuh?"

"Good, Danny." Steve's voice sounded relieved. "Room 224, Royal Hotel. What time will you get here?"

"I'll be on the first plane I can get on," I replied. "I should be up there no later than seven tonight. Is everything ready?"

"The truck's loaded and ready to roll," he told me. "It'll leave the minute you get here with the dough."

"Okay," I said. "I'll see you tonight." I put down the phone and looked at my watch. It was almost two o'clock. I would have to hurry if I wanted to make the bank.

I went to the door of the small office and called Zep over. "Make arrangements for storage of four hundred boxes," I told him.

His eyes widened. "That's a lot of stuff, Danny. Where you gettin' it?"

In a few words I told him of the deal. He seemed worried. "You're takin' a hell of a chance, Danny," he said. "Too many things can go wrong. Maybe yuh better take me with you."

I shook my head. "Somebody's gotta stay here an' keep an eye on things. I'll be okay. You stay here. I'll call yuh as soon's I hit town with the stuff."

It wasn't until I was at the airport, waiting for the plane, that I remembered I hadn't called Nellie. I hurried to a phone booth and dialed home. She answered.

I spoke quickly before she had a chance to get in a word. "Baby, somethin' came up an' I gotta fly up to Buffalo on business. Don't wait supper for me. I'll be back in the morning."

"But, Danny," she cried, "we're moving tomorrow!"

"Don't worry," I said. "I'll be back in time."

Fear came into her voice. "Don't go, Danny, please don't go. I'm scared."

"There's nothin' to be afraid of," I said. "I'll be back in the morning."

"Then wait, Danny," she pleaded. "Wait until after we move."

"It won't keep, baby," I said hurriedly. "There's fifty grand in it for us an' there's no way of keepin' that kind of cabbage on ice. I ain't lettin' it get away from me!"

She began to weep into the telephone. "I knew something would turn up," she wailed bitterly. "I had a hunch—"

"But, Nellie," I interrupted, "it's fifty grand! Fifty thousand Uncle Sam dollars! We can do a lot with that much dough."

"I don't care!" she sobbed. "Sometimes I wish I never heard of money! Since you went into business, you're not like you used to be."

"When this is over, Nellie, I'll see that everything goes the way you want it," I promised desperately.

"You always say that," she wept accusingly. "But I don't believe you any more. You don't mean it. You'll never change! The minute there's a buck involved, you become an entirely different person. You forget everything else!"

"Don't be a fool!" I said heatedly. "This is a practical world. Without a buck, you're nothin' but crap, like everybody else! Maybe you're willin' to settle for that, but not me!"

I could hear the sharp intake of her breath through the receiver. There was a moment of shocked angry silence, then I heard a click and the phone went dead in my hands. She had hung up on me. I began to swear to myself as I searched my pockets for another nickel with which to call her back. Just then the announcer's voice came through the loudspeaker:

"Flight number fifty-four on runway three. Buffalo flight fifty-four on runway three. Taking off in five minutes."

I looked back at the phone, then up at the clock on the wall. Quickly I made up my mind and left the phone booth. She'd feel better when I saw her with the dough tomorrow. Fifty grand can cure a lot of hurt feelings.

CHAPTER EIGHTEEN

I GLANCED AROUND THE LOBBY OF THE HOTEL AS I WALKED TOWARD THE desk. It was plainly furnished but neat and clean, just the type of hotel that a salesman might stay in. The desk clerk came forward to meet me.

"Do you have a single?" I asked.

"Yes sir," the clerk answered, spinning the register toward me. "Sign there. With or without bath, sir?"

"Without bath," I said quickly as I scrawled my signature in the register.

"Yes, sir," the clerk said again. He punched a bell on the counter. "That will be three dollars, sir," he said, turning to take a key from the rack behind him.

I put the money on the counter just as a bellboy came up to the desk.

"Show Mr. Fisher to room 419," the clerk said, picking up the money and handing the key to the bellboy.

"Wait a minute," I interrupted. "Can I check an envelope here?"

"Surely, Mr. Fisher," the clerk said smoothly. "I'll put it in the hotel safe for you. Just write your name across the seal." He pushed a brown manila envelope toward me.

I took the envelope with the dough in it and placed it in the envelope that he had given me. I sealed it carefully and wrote my name across it as I had been told. I watched the clerk turn and place it in the safe, wondering what he'd do if he knew there was a hundred grand in that envelope.

He turned the lock. "It will be safe and sound here until you want it, sir," he said to me.

I thanked him and looked at my watch. It was almost seven o'clock. "I don't think I'll go to my room just yet," I said to the clerk as if an idea had just come to me. "I promised a friend of mine I'd meet him here at seven—Steve Parrish. Is he here yet?"

The clerk looked over his shoulder at the key rack. "He's in, sir," he replied. "Shall I tell him you're here?"

"Please."

He whispered a few words into a telephone, waited a few moments for a reply, then looked up at me. "He says for you to come right up, sir. Room 224."

"Thanks," I said. I was already walking to the back of the lobby where I had noticed the elevator.

The gilt numerals on the door glittered in the dimly lighted hallway. I knocked. I could hear the hum of conversation that had been coming from the room suddenly fade away into silence.

The door opened slowly and Parrish peered out. "Danny!" he said, smiling when he saw me. He stepped back from the door, pulling it open. "You're right on time. Come on in."

There were three other men in there with him. They stared up at me from their seats. I turned to Steve. Steve's face was a little pale and drawn, but he held a fairly steady hand toward me. I shook it.

"I'm glad you were able to make it, Danny," he said.

I nodded my head without answering.

Steve turned to the other men in the room. "Gentlemen," he announced, "this is Danny Fisher." Then, one at a time, he introduced them to me.

One at a time they rose and shook my hand briefly. They didn't try to make any conversation.

"How about a drink, Danny?" Steve held a bottle of whisky in his hand.

"No, thanks, Steve," I replied quickly. "Never drink while I'm workin'."

Steve nodded as he poured himself a drink. "Good policy, Danny," he said, swallowing it. "Approve of it highly."

I looked at him closely. Steve had quite a few drinks in him already. I pulled out a cigarette and lit it. "Ready to get down to business?" I asked.

Steve looked at me. "I guess so," he said hesitantly. "You bring the money?"

I nodded.

One of the men got to his feet quickly. "Let's see the color," he said.

I turned to him and smiled. "You'll see it," I replied, "after I see the stuff."

"You got it on you?" the man asked suspiciously.

"Do I look like that kind of a fool?" I retorted quietly. "Don't worry, though. If the stuff's okay, you'll get your dough. Where you got it?"

"In a garage a few blocks from here," the man replied. "Want to see it?"

"You bet."

The man picked up his hat from a chair. "Well, come on then," he said, starting for the door.

The truck was loaded just as Steve had told me it would be. I stared at the neatly piled cases skeptically. I had a feeling that something was wrong, but I didn't know what it was. Maybe it was because everything was going so smoothly. I turned to the man I had spoken to back in the hotel room. "No offense meant," I said politely, "but this is a lot of dough. I'd like to score the load."

"That'll mean unloading every box and putting it back on the truck again," the man protested.

My eyes met his levelly. "Like I said, it's a lot of dough and I'd like to check."

He looked at the others and then turned back to me, shrugging his shoulders. "It's okay with me, but you won't get out of here until two in the morning."

"I don't mind," I said.

I looked at Steve wearily, then at the others. They were standing in a semicircle around me, their faces flushed and their shirts damp with sweat. "I guess it's okay," I said. But I couldn't understand it. That feelin, still hung on. I shrugged nervously; I guess I was catching it from Nellie.

"I told you that right away, Danny," Steve said quickly. "You didn't have to check."

"For a hundred grand," I said flatly, "I check." I turned back to the others. "Who's driving the truck down?" I asked.

One of the men stepped forward. "I am," he answered.

"Okay," I said. "Then hop in the truck and drive me back to the hotel. We'll start from there."

"Now?" the man asked, staring at me.

"Now." I nodded.

"But my helper ain't due to show up till morning," he protested.

"We ain't waitin'," I said. "I'll ride down with you. This stuff's gotta be in New York by tomorrow morning."

The desk clerk turned toward me. "Yes, Mr. Fisher?"

"I had to change my plans," I said. "I'm checkin' out. If you'll give me my envelope—"

"Right away, Mr. Fisher," he answered in a tired voice. He opened the safe, tossed the envelope on the counter in front of me, and watched while I ripped open the hotel envelope and took out the smaller one that I had enclosed. "Everything all right, sir?" he asked with a yawn.

I nodded and put a dollar on the counter for him. "Fine," I said, turning away. His thanks followed me out into the street.

The truck was waiting under a street lamp. The men were standing around it. I climbed into the cab and handed the envelope down to Steve. Steve turned and gave it to the man who had done the talking in the hotel. He ripped it open quickly and peered into it. His fingers riffled the bills as he counted them.

Then he looked up at me and made a half salute toward me. I waved back at him and turned to the driver. "Okay, boy," I said. "Let's hit the road."

I glanced wearily at my watch as we came out of Newburgh. It was a few minutes after ten. I turned my eyes back to the road as my foot went down on the accelerator. Slowly the truck began to pick up speed. The road loomed white and clear before me.

I threw the engine into overdrive and looked at my companion. The man was sleeping with his head resting uncomfortably against the door. I was hungry, I hadn't eaten since yesterday afternoon, but I didn't dare stop. This load was too hot. Besides, if I kept on rolling I could make New York by noon.

The driver's voice cut into my thoughts. "I'll take over now, Danny," he said. "You get yourself some sleep. You look bushed."

"I don't mind driving a little while longer," I said. "This baby handles like a charm."

"All the same, you better knock off for a while," he said. "Your eyes are all red. You may not feel it, but you're tired."

"Okay," I answered, pressing my foot down on the brake pedal. The powerful air brakes hissed as they took hold. Slowly the big truck rolled to a stop. I pulled up the safety brake and moved out from behind the wheel.

He clambered in front of me and got in behind the wheel. "You better get some sleep," he said, lowering the safety brake. "You haven't slept since we left Buffalo an' you been up all night."

"I can sleep when this ride is over," I replied. "I'll feel a lot better then." I put my hands up behind my head and leaned back against the seat.

The truck began to move and the hum of the engine to fill the cab. I tried to take my eyes from the white line that ran monotonously down the road before us, but it fascinated me. There was something about the way it stretched endlessly before us, as far as the eye could see. A little white line running down the middle of the road. Stay on the right side of it and you were safe. Cross it and you were dead. Stay on the right side—the right side—the right side—the . . . right . . . side . . . I could feel my head lolling sleepily against the door. I shook it desperately, trying to keep my eyes open, but there was no use. I was too tired. Reluctantly I let myself slip into slumber.

I awoke with a start. The truck was standing still, its engine silent. Blinking my eyes rapidly, I turned to the driver, sitting next to me. "What's the matter?" I asked sleepily. "Is anything wrong?"

He was looking at me with a sardonic expression. He didn't answer.

A voice came from the other side of me and I snapped around. My eyes widened. I was awake now. A man was standing on the running board of the cab. There was a gun in his hand, and it pointed at my face. "Okay, sleeping beauty," the man was saying. "Rise and shine."

I started to lean forward, my hand reaching for the wrench that lay on the floor beneath my feet.

The man gestured swiftly with the gun. "Keep the hands up where I can see them, Danny boy," he said softly.

Slowly I brought my hands back to my lap. My mind was working furiously. I looked at the driver again. He was sitting absolutely motionless, his eyes fixed steadily on the road before him. Things began to add up. "You in on this?" I asked unsteadily.

The driver didn't answer. Instead the man with the gun spoke again. "What do you think?" he asked sarcastically.

I turned quietly toward him. "I got dough if you let me get this load into New York," I said desperately.

The gunman grinned at me, showing yellow discolored teeth. He spit a stream of tobacco juice toward the road. "We already got your dough," he said flatly. His hand twisted the door open and he stepped down from the running board, his gun still pointing at me. "Get out," he said. "The buggy ride is over."

"Ten grand," I said quickly, staring at him.

He gestured with his gun. "I said come down outta there."

Slowly I clambered down from the seat. The sky loomed dark and ominously gray overhead. It was going to rain. I could feel my anger rising. I had been a sucker. What a fool I had been! I should have known better.

My legs were stiff and weary and I moved awkwardly. I heard footsteps coming from the rear of the truck and turned my head. An automobile was parked directly behind us. They had probably been on my tail ever since we left Buffalo, waiting for a spot like this to jump me. The anger spilled over into my mouth and I could taste the heated bile rising from my belly. What a shnook I had been, shooting the works on a deal like this! I should have had my head examined!

The man coming from behind me called out: "Everything okay there?"

The gunman's eyes shifted from me to the man behind me. Desperately I lunged at him, my fist grazing his jaw as he instinctively jumped to the side. I shot past him and my feet slipped in the dirt on the side of the road. Frantically I tried to keep myself from falling.

A sudden pain exploded against the side of my head and I sprawled face-forward into the dirt. I tried to raise myself on my hands and knees, but there was another burst of pain in the same place and all the strength in my arms and legs ran out of me. The dirt was all around my face and a wave of darkness was rolling heavily toward me. I forced it back with my mind, but it was coming toward me inexorably. I could feel myself sliding into it.

Faintly, as if from a distance, I could hear voices. I tried to make out what they were saying, but some of the words weren't clear. One of the men was saying that Gordon wouldn't like this. Another was laughing sarcastically.

I let myself slide toward the darkness. Then a split second's thought raced through my mind before I gave myself completely up to the darkness. Crossed! Crossed right from the beginning! That was why Steve had kept talking about Sam when he called me. To make me think of him!

Then the thought was gone and I couldn't remember anything. I drew a deep breath and tried to pull myself up through the darkness. But it was no use. It was all around me now.

Moving Day

OCTOBER 3, 1944

THERE WERE HANDS POKING AT MY SHOULDERS. I MOVED SLIGHTLY, TRYing to get away from them. My head hurt.

The hands kept poking at me. I tried to curl myself into a small ball. I wished they would go away and leave me alone. Just when I was getting comfortable. I had been cold for a long, long time, but I was just beginning to warm up when the hands started to bother me. I tried to push them away and rolled over on my back.

I felt a sharp stinging smack across my face. The pain of it shot through me and I opened my eyes. There was a man kneeling beside me, his face staring into mine.

"Are you all right, mister?" he asked anxiously.

I moved my head a little to see if there was anyone with him. He was alone. Then I became aware of the rain beating down on me. I began to laugh weakly. Was I all right? I had to laugh. That was funny as hell. I tried to sit up.

A sharp, splitting pain tore through my head and I groaned. I felt his arm tighten around my shoulders to support me.

"What happened, mister?" his frightened voice asked.

"I was jumped. Hitch-hikers," I answered. I couldn't tell him what had really happened. "They stole my car," I added.

His face eased into a smile of relief as he helped me to my feet. "Lucky thing for you I got weak kidneys," he said. "I heard you groaning in the ditch at the side of the road."

I stood there, weaving slightly. I was still shaky, but I could feel the strength seeping back into my body.

"You might have got pneumonia," he said.

"Yeah," I nodded. "I was sure lucky." I looked at my watch to see the time, but it had been smashed. "What time is it?" I asked.

"Five after one," he answered, looking at his watch.

I stared at him in surprise. I had been out more than two hours. My watch had stopped at a quarter to eleven. "I gotta get back to town," I muttered. "We're movin' today and my wife'll be scared stiff. She hasn't heard from me."

The man's hand held my arm, steadying me. "I'm going to New York if that's on your way," he said.

He looked like an angel standing there with the rain pouring down on his halo. "That's the town I mean," I said.

"Come on back to the car then, mister," he said. "I'll get you into town by two thirty."

I followed him back to his small Chevvie and climbed in the front seat beside him. As soon as the door closed behind me, I began to shiver.

He took one look at my blue lips and reached over and turned on the heater. "Lean back and rest," he said considerately. "This'll warm you up and dry your clothes a little. You're soaked."

I leaned my head back against the seat and looked at him with half-closed eyes. He wasn't a young man, I could see the fringes of gray hair peeping out from beneath his hat. "Thanks, mister," I said.

"That's all right, son," he said slowly. "It's what I'd expect any human to do for another."

I closed my eyes wearily. He was wrong. Some humans didn't even have the faintest trace of what he expected them to have. The quiet clicking of the windshield wipers was a very soothing sound. My thoughts began to come slower. Sam wasn't like that. Sam didn't give a damn who you were. Sam thought only about himself.

I was getting too big. Sam didn't like that. After all, I had latched onto this racket right under his nose. He hadn't wanted it then, but that didn't matter. Now he knew what he had missed and he had made up his mind to get the whole thing back. And he had it back. There was nothing I could do about it, either.

Nothing? I began to wonder, anger seeping into me. That was where Sam was wrong. I had worked too hard to give up this easy. I was through being his patsy. He'd pay for this. I'd been a fool to sucker for a setup like this anyhow, but it wasn't over yet. He'd find out. The anger had brought a curious warmth into me and I began to doze.

I felt a hand on my arm and I woke quickly. I looked around. We were just coming onto the West Side Highway.

The man looked at me. "Feeling better?" he asked.

I nodded silently. My headache had gone.

"Where can I drop you?"

I gave him my address. "If it's not out of your way," I added.

"Its okay," he said. "I pass there on my way home."

It was a quarter after three when we pulled up in front of my house. I got out of the car and turned back to the driver. "Thanks again, mister," I said. "I won't ever forget this."

"That's okay, son," he answered. "Like I said—any human being."

Then, before I realized it, he had put the car into gear and drove off. I stared after the car. I had forgotten to even ask his name. Funny world. Someone you know all your life tries to kick your teeth in, and a man you never saw before and will never seen again comes along and saves your life.

I watched the car until it turned the corner out of sight; then I turned and walked into the house. The superintendent was sweeping out the hall. He gaped at me, his mouth open. I guess I did make a hell of a picture. My face was all cut up from the beating I had taken, and my clothes were filthy from the ditch.

"The van's gone already, Mr. Fisher," he told me. "Your wife waited around as long as she could. She was very upset, but your brother-in-law told her to go ahead."

"My brother-in-law was here?" I asked in a husky voice.

He nodded. "He came down when your wife called him. Her brother was here already, but she was still worried about you." He looked up at me curiously. "Your brother-in-law gave me a message for you if you showed up."

"What?" I asked.

"He said for you to see him, he'd be in his office." He smiled slightly. "Your brother-in-law sure is a nice guy all right. He seemed worried about you, too. Mine don't care whether I live or die."

"Thanks," I said succinctly, and left the house. Sam worried about me all right. Ninety grand worth of worry. No, two hundred grand now that he'd taken the whole pot. No wonder he showed up when Nellie called him.

I walked round the corner and grabbed a cab up to his office.

I went past Sam's secretary without waiting for her to announce me. I opened the door and stepped into his office, closing the door behind me.

He was just putting the telephone down when he looked up and saw me. He held it suspended in the air while his eyes swept over me from head to foot. "Where the hell have you been?" he finally roared, putting down the telephone. "I was just gonna put the cops on your tail."

Something in his voice hit me the wrong way; it made the hair on the back of my neck crackle. "What's the matter Sam?" I asked in a husky voice. "Didn't you expect me?"

He got up from behind his desk and came toward me. I could feel his heavy footsteps in the floor beneath my feet. "You give a guy ninety grand an' he don't show when he's supposed to, see what you think?" he said roughly. "I thought you powdered with the dough."

If it wasn't me that was catching the wrong end of the stick, I could almost admire the way he operated. This boy was tough. Right down to his toenails. He played it rough, too, adding insult to injury. He was everything I thought I could be, but now I knew I had a long way to go. I stared at him. He wasn't fooling me any more, though. I'd had enough of that.

"You know I wouldn't do that, Sam," I said softly. "You know me better'n that."

He stared at me for a moment and then turned back to his chair and sat down. His dark eyes glittered. "How would I know?" he demanded. "Ninety grand is a lot of moolah. Maybe you were getting tired of your wife and wanted to blow town. You could have a dozen reasons that I don't know about."

My eyes locked with his and stared him down. "You just don't trust nobody, do you, Sam?" I asked softly.

He looked down at his desk. "I don't make a livin' from trustin' jokers," he answered sullenly. He glanced up at me again, his eyes bright and sharp. "Where are the butts?" he asked.

I shrugged my shoulders. "I don't know," I answered simply. The wrong guy was asking the question. I'd bet he knew the answer.

He sprang to his feet angrily. "What d'yuh mean yuh don't know?" he roared. "What happened?"

I could admire this guy. He didn't miss a trick. He was the greatest. "I was tooken," I answered quietly, studying his face for any flicker of knowledge. "I got hijacked on the way and dumped in a ditch. I'm damn lucky to be alive."

He went right down the line with his act, but I thought I could detect a false note in his anger as he pounded his desk. "I should've known better'n to give yuh ninety grand like that!" he shouted.

I smiled at him bitterly. "What're you yellin' about, Sam?" I asked quietly. "You lost nothin' on the deal. It was me who got cleaned. You got the whole business now."

"Who the hell wanted it?" he roared. "I need it like I need a hole in the head. I got enough troubles. I'd rather have the ninety grand!"

That was the first false note he struck. He was hollering too much for a guy who wasn't hurt. "You sure, Sam?" I asked.

He stared at me, his eyes suddenly cautious. "Sure I'm sure," he said quickly. "Now I'm stuck with the damn thing an' you besides. I gotta have you to run it. I won't know what to worry about first. How much you're gonna be clippin' me for or how the damn thing will do? I'd've been better off doin' business with Maxie Fields instead of a punk like you. At least he's got an organization."

I stared at him for a moment before I answered. The thought kept getting bigger in my mind. That was the second idea that someone had fed me in as many days. But this one was involuntary. "That's an idea, Sam," I said gently. "That's the best idea I've heard all day."

His mouth fell open and he was staring at me as I turned and walked out of his office. I could hear him roaring for me to come back as I walked past his secretary and out the front door. There was an elevator waiting and I got in. The doors closed and we began to drop down.

By the time I hit the street, I was sure I had it figured. Sam thought he had found a way to have his cake and eat it. But he was wrong. I would turn the cake into dirt in his mouth.

The same old sign was on the window: "FIELDS CHECK CASHING SERVICE." The same old dirt was on the streets. Nothing had changed. Nothing would ever change down here. I pushed open the door and went in.

A man behind the cage looked up at me. "Yes, sir?" he asked.

"Is Maxie Fields around?" I asked.

The man's expression changed subtly. "Who wants to see him?"

"Danny Fisher," I said harshly. "Tell him I got a hundred grand wrap-up. He'll see me."

He picked up a phone and pressed a buzzer. He whispered into the phone, then looked up at me again. "Through that door," he said, pointing to the back.

"I know the way," I tossed back over my shoulder as I move toward the door. It closed behind me and I was standing in the hallway. I stared up the staircase, then began to climb it slowly.

He was standing in the doorway when I reached the landing. His hard eyes were shining blackly in his round face as he watched me. His body blocked the entrance to the apartment. "What's on yer mind, Danny?" he asked as I drew near him.

I stared back into his eyes. "Yuh still like money, Maxie?"

He nodded his head slowly.

"Then I got a bundle for yuh," I said quickly. "But let's go inside. I can't do business in the hall."

He stepped back into the room and I walked past him. The apartment hadn't changed either. It was still a lush joint. I heard the door close and turned around to face him.

"How about a drink, Maxie?" I asked.

His eyes studied my face; then he turned and roared into the next room: "Ronnie! Bring two setups." Without waiting for a reply he walked around me and sat down behind his desk. He sat down heavily. The only sound in the room was his breathing. After a moment he looked up at me. "What's the deal, Danny?"

I sat down in the chair opposite him. Footsteps came into the room behind me. I looked around.

Ronnie was carrying two glasses in her hands. For a moment she didn't see me, then an expression of surprise crossed her face. Her mouth opened as if she was going to speak, but it snapped shut quickly. Silently she placed the two glasses on the corner of Maxie's desk and started out of the room.

He called her back, his eyes glittering. "You remember our friend Danny, don't you?" he asked sarcastically.

She looked at him for a moment, then at me. Her eyes were dull and beaten. For a moment something flickered deep inside them, but only for a moment and then it was gone. Her voice was flat and lifeless. "I remember," she said. "Hello, Danny."

The years had changed her little outwardly. She looked much the same. But the spirit had gone, it had vanished and been beaten by the oppression of time.

"Hello, Ronnie," I said quietly. I remembered it had been just like this the last time I had been here, but then I hadn't been looking for him, he had been looking for me.

He wasn't content to leave well enough alone. He had to rub it in, he had to make the most of his triumph. "Danny's come back to make a deal with me," he said, a note of power showing in his voice. "Nobody can keep away from Maxie Fields, baby. That's what I always said."

There was no expression in her voice. "Yes, Maxie." She turned and started from the room again, but he called her back.

"Sit down, Ronnie," he said roughly. "Sit down and keep us company."

Obediently she dropped into a chair near him. She sat there stiffly like an automaton, no emotion visible on her face at all.

He turned to me and picked up his drink. "Now, Danny," he said heavily.

I picked up my drink and sipped at it. It tasted good and the liquor warmed my belly. I held up the glass and looked at him through it. "A hundred grand worth of butts," I said simply.

He put his drink down without having touched it and leaned forward. "What about them?" he asked.

"They're all yours," I said quietly, putting my drink down beside his. "If you do me a favor."

He drew in a deep breath. "I know you, Danny," he wheezed hoarsely. "You give ice away in the winter. Besides, where do yuh get this stuff?"

"I got it," I said. "Listen." Step by step I told him the whole story—how I latched onto the butts, how I lost them. When I was finished, I could see he was interested.

"How're you gonna get them back?" he asked.

"I'm taking over Sam's business," I said confidently.

Caution jumped like yellow traffic lights into his eyes. "How do you figger?"

"Simple," I answered. I was cold as ice. "Remember what we talked about the day I drove you down from Lombardi's? Remember what you said?"

Maxie nodded slowly. "I remember." His eyes watched me carefully. "But is anything going to happen to him?" he asked.

I picked up the drink again, shrugging my shoulders. "You tell me."

"No, Danny!" There was a terrifying sound in Ronnie's voice. I turned in surprise to look at her. Her eyes were suddenly alive in her face. "You can't do that! Sam was the only—"

Maxie's voice cut her off. "Shut up, Ronnie!" he roared fiercely.

She turned to him, a frightened expression on her face. "Maxie, you gotta tell him—"

There was a movement from behind me, and Spit was standing at her side. I hadn't even heard him come into the room.

"Get her outta here!" Maxie roared.

Spit reached quickly for her hand, but she evaded his grasp and fled from the room, her hands over her face.

Maxie was breathing heavily when he turned back to me. He waved Spit to the chair she had just left. He stared at me for a moment. There was a greedy ring to his voice when he finally spoke. "How do I know you'll pay off?" he asked. "Yuh don't even know for sure if he's got 'em."

"Let me use your phone for a minute an' we'll know," I answered.

He nodded and I picked up the phone and dialed Sam's warehouse. Good thing I had worked for him; I knew everybody there.

A voice I thought I recognized answered the phone.

"Joe?" I asked.

"Yeah," he answered. "Who is it?"

"Danny Fisher," I said quickly. "I'm checkin' if my truck got in there yet. The big trailer from upstate."

"Sure, Danny," Joe answered. "We're unloadin' it now."

"Okay, Joe. Thanks." I put down the phone and turned to Maxie. He had heard the conversation. "Satisfied?" I asked.

His eyes were shining. I could see the dollar signs in them. "I get the whole load?" he asked.

"You heard me," I answered. "The whole load."

"Fair enough," he wheezed, struggling to his feet. "Spit and the Collector and me will cover the job ourselves. Before the night is over, the whole thing'll be cleaned up."

"Stay away from this guy, boss, he's poison!" Spit's voice was angry. He was on his feet, staring at Maxie.

"What's the matter, Spit?" I asked coldly. "Chicken?"

He turned to me snarling. "I don't trust yuh. I know yuh too good!"

Maxie's voice was heavy with command. "Sit down and shut up, Spit!" he snapped. "I'm runnin' this show!"

Slowly Spit subsided into his chair, his eyes flashing angry lights at me.

Maxie's voice was still heavy, only he was talking to me now. "It's a deal, Danny," he said slowly. "But there's no backin' out now like yuh did before. This time yuh try an' run me aroun' an' yuh're deader'n hell."

In spite of myself I shivered as I got to my feet. At the doorway I turned. Spit was watching me, his eyes filled with hatred. Maxie's were cold, his face without expression. I could see him breathing heavily.

"You make up the bill, Maxie," I said quietly. "I'll pay it!" I closed the door behind me and went down the stairs.

It was a few minutes to six when I paid the cab-driver off in front of my house. As the cab pulled away, I paused on the sidewalk and looked at the house. I felt tired and old and empty. It was good to be coming home again.

Suddenly I realized that I had never thought of any place else as home. None of the other places I had lived meant anything to me. None of them were mine, none of them belonged to me the way this did. Then, as I stood there, I thought of what I had done, and all the satisfaction of coming home drained out of me. Now it didn't seem to matter.

I had gone through too much. I had come a long way. I was not the same person who had left this house so many years ago. I had lost my childish wonder. Life was too grim. You had to fight it all the time or you would be nothing. There was no peace, no friends, no real happiness. This world was a war for survival. You had to kill or be killed.

My footsteps echoed on the cement stoop. It had taken me a long time to wise up. You couldn't feel too much if you wanted to get along. You had to close your heart and lock it against people. No one must touch you, for you were alone on the day you were born and you'd be alone on the day you died.

I put out my hand to open the massive front door, but it swung open before I touched it. "Hello, Danny," the voice said quietly.

There was no surprise in me. I had heard the voice before. It was the voice of the house that had spoken to me the day Nellie and I came to buy it.

"Hello, Papa."

My father took my hand and together we walked into the house as once we had many years ago. For a moment we didn't speak, there was no need for words. Then we stopped in the living-room and looked at each other. There were tears standing in his eyes. It was the first time I had ever seen him weep. His voice was low, but filled with a tremendous pride, and I realized as he spoke that his pride was for me.

"We've all come home again, Danny," he said humbly. "If you can forgive an old man's mistakes, we'll never have to leave what we found here."

I smiled slowly, beginning to understand many things. His voice was the voice of the house. It had never really been my house at all, it had belonged to him. When I had told the house of my love, I was speaking to him, and when the house spoke to me, he was speaking to me. It would never be my house until he gave it to me, no matter how much I paid for it.

I looked around the room. Something had been missing all the time, and now that he was here, the house was warm and alive again. I was glad that he had come. I didn't have to say anything either; he seemed to know just how I felt.

"It was the most wonderful birthday present I ever had, Papa," I said.

Then for the first time he became aware of the way I looked. "My God!" he exclaimed. "Danny, what happened?"

His words snapped me back to the present. "I had an accident, Papa," I replied harshly. "Where's Nellie?"

His face stared up at me. "Mamma's got her to lie down upstairs. She was almost hysterical with worry over you."

There was a sound at the top of the stairs. Nellie was standing there, her white face looking down at me. In the harsh white light of the still unshaded stairway bulbs I must have been a hideous sight. Her lips parted in a half scream. "Danny!"

Her voice was still echoing against the walls as I started up the stairway toward her. She took a small step down toward me, then her eyes turned upward in their sockets and she fainted.

"Nellie!" I shouted, springing to catch her.

But she was falling, tumbling clumsily down half the flight before I could stop her. She was a small huddled heap near the wall and I was on my knees beside her, my hands frantically turning her face toward me. "Nellie!" I screamed at her.

Her face was the white transparency of a bottle of milk, and her eyes were squeezed tight with pain. I could see her bloodless lips whispering in her agony. "Danny, Danny, I was so worried about you."

I turned wildly toward Papa. "There's a doctor in the corner house across the street," I shouted at him. "Get him! Quick!"

I turned back to Nellie, hearing the front door slam. I rested her head against my shoulder. Her eyes were closed and she was very still. She seemed to be hardly breathing.

My mother came down the stairs, a deep world of sympathy and understanding in her eyes. Wordlessly she pressed her hand against my shoulder.

I looked at Nellie again. Why did I have to learn so many things so late? I could see the whole thing now. It was my fault. Nellie had been right. I hugged her head against my breast. It couldn't happen, it mustn't. She was all my world. I shut my eyes tightly and prayed, the tears seeping from beneath my eyelids.

"Please, God. . . . Please. . . ."

I paced nervously up and down the small hospital waiting-room. It seemed as if I had been there for days instead of only a few hours. I stuck another cigarette in my mouth and tried to light it. I broke three matches before Zep finally lit one for me and held it to my cigarette.

I looked at him gratefully. I don't know what we would have done without him that day. All day he had stayed with Nellie, calming her and helping her, and now he was here with me. "Thanks, Zep," I muttered.

Exhausted, I dropped into the chair between my father and him. "The doctor's been out an awful long time," I said.

Zep looked at me understandingly. He knew how I felt. "Don't worry, Danny," he said, awkwardly patting my shoulder. "She'll be okay. The doctor said she had a chance and I know my sister. She's a scrapper. She'll come through."

That was it. She had a chance. The doctor had said that. She had a chance. I had to keep thinking of that over and over or I would go mad—stark, raving mad. All the way down to the hospital, riding next to her, her cold limp hand in mine, as we roared through the streets in the screaming ambulance, I had to keep thinking that.

She had hurt herself inside. The baby had shifted, the doctor said. There was a pressure inside her and she was torn and bleeding. All inside where you couldn't see it. You could only know it when you looked at her face, white and bloodless.

Quickly and efficiently they had placed her on a small white table and rushed her up to the operating-room. Her eyes were still closed, she couldn't see me. Through her pale lips came a thin small sound of pain. Then she was gone through the white doors and I had to wait.

That was more than two hours ago and I was still waiting. We were still waiting. I looked over at her mother, sitting on a chair by the window, nervously twisting a handkerchief. Her eyes were puffy with tears as she listened silently to my mother trying to console her. She hadn't said anything to me, but I knew that she blamed me for what had happened to Nellie. And in a way she was right. But still, if it hadn't been for Sam none of this would have happened.

There were steps in the corridor outside. Mimi was coming toward me, an anxious look on her face. "Danny, what happened?"

I didn't answer her; my eyes were fixed on Sam, walking behind her. There was a strange uncomfortable look on his face. "What are you doing here?" I shot at him.

"Your father called and told us Nellie had an accident. Mimi was too upset to drive, so I brought her out here," he explained.

I got to my feet slowly. I could feel my legs trembling with rage. My mouth was suddenly dry. "You satisfied now?" I asked harshly. "This the way you wanted it?"

There was a peculiarly shamed look in his eyes. "This wasn't the way I wanted it, Danny," he replied in a low voice.

I stared at him for a moment, then the pent-up anger in me burst its dam and I stepped forward, my fist flying. I caught him flush on the jaw and he tumbled backward to the floor. The crash echoed through the small room as I started for him again.

Two hands grabbed at my arms. I heard Mimi's voice screaming at me. Desperately I tried to shake my arms loose. I would kill him myself. I was crying. He might as well have admitted the whole thing.

Then I heard the doctor's voice: "Mr. Fisher!"

Sam was forgotten as I turned and grasped the doctor's lapels. "How is she, doc?" I asked huskily. "How is she?"

His face, covered with weary lines, relaxed slightly as he looked at me. "She's resting comfortably, Mr. Fisher," he answered quietly. "She's in considerable pain, but she'll be all right."

I went limp, all the emotion drained out of me. I sank weakly back into a chair and covered my face with my hands. For once my prayers had been heard.

I felt the doctor's hand on my shoulder and looked up at him. "Can I see her, doc?"

"Not just yet." He shook his head, his face was grave. "Mr. Fisher, we have an outside chance to save your son's life if we can find the right type of blood."

I was on my feet again. I didn't understand him. "What d'yuh mean, doc?"

His eyes were on mine. "Your son wasn't badly hurt, maybe because he was premature and therefore small, but he has lost some blood. If we can replace it soon enough, he has a good chance of growing up."

I was pulling at his arm. "Come on, then," I said anxiously. "I got plenty."

He shook his head again. "I'm afraid your blood wouldn't do," he explained. "There was a mild Rh factor involved, and your blood would be incompatible. The type we need is one that only one donor in a thousand might have. I've put out a call for one already. It all depends on what time we can get him here."

A sinking feeling came back into me again. No luck. I slipped back into the chair. The doctor's voice continued his explanation. "The only chance your baby would have had anyway was by a Caesarean section with complete blood replacement."

That was no comfort. My son was alive now and he had a chance. That was what counted. The despair worked its way into my bones like an ache.

Zep's voice spilled into my ears like the sweetest music. "Maybe my blood will match, doctor."

I looked at him gratefully, then back at the doctor. "Maybe it will," the doctor said wearily. "Come with me and we'll see." He looked around the room. "If any of you would like to be tested, come along."

We all followed him out of the waiting-room. Mimi was helping Sam to a chair as we stepped out into the corridor. A few steps down we turned into a small laboratory, where a nurse was sitting, reading a newspaper. She got to her feet quickly as we entered.

"Check the blood type of these people right away, nurse," the doctor said.

"Yes, doctor," the nurse replied, already turning to the table behind her.

I watched her prepare the slides and place them near the microscope. When they were all finished, she deftly inserted one under the lens.

"I'll look at it, nurse," the doctor said quickly.

She stepped aside as the doctor bent and peered into the microscope. He shook his head and she slipped the next one into the rack. I held my breath until he had looked at them all. Then he straightened up, shaking his head.

"No, doc?" I asked hopelessly.

He looked around the room. My mother and father, Zep and his mother were watching him intently. He turned back to me. "Sorry, Mr. Fisher," he said sincerely. "No one here will do. I guess we'll just have to wait for the donor to get here."

"But it might be too late," I said weakly. "My son might—might—" It was the first time I had said those words: my son. But I couldn't finish the sentence.

The doctor's hand rested sympathetically on my arm. "We can only hope that he'll get here soon," he said comfortingly. "He might be here any minute."

The door opened and I turned toward it hopefully. Then I felt my heart slipping down into my shoes. It was only Sam.

Awkwardly he pushed his way into the room. There was a large bruise on his jaw, turning black. Mimi followed him. He looked at me with embarrassment for a moment, then turned to the doctor.

"Down at the blood bank, doc," he said in his rough heavy voice, "they told me I got a rare-type blood. Maybe it's the type yuh're lookin' for."

"We'll find out in a minute," the doctor said. He beckoned to the nurse.

I stared at Sam for a second, then walked past him out into the corridor. The laboratory door swung shut behind me. There was no use in hanging around; he could do me no good. All he brought me was trouble. From the first time I saw him.

"Danny! Danny!" Zep's voice echoed excitedly behind me. He was running down the corridor toward me, his dark face alive with excitement. "The doc says Sam's blood is the type!"

I stared at him, not believing my ears.

Half an hour later the doctor came into the waiting-room where we were sitting. There was a smile on his face. He came toward me, holding out his hand. "I guess you'll be passing out cigars after all, Mr. Fisher," he said. "Congratulations!"

I could hardly see his face through the blur in my eyes. "Thank you, doc," I said fervently. "Thank you."

The doctor smiled again. "Don't thank me," he said quickly. "Just thank God and your brother-in-law for being around! It's a miracle for a seven-month premature Rh to get even this far!"

My mother-in-law began to cry happily. Zep was hugging her. Mamma, Papa, and Mimi were crowding around me. Mimi's arms were about my neck, her lips against my cheek. My tears were wet on her face. Nothing else mattered—only the joy of this moment.

I turned to the doctor. "Can I see my wife now, doc?"

He nodded. "But only for a few minutes," he warned. "She's still very weak."

The nurse sitting at the side of the bed rose quickly when I came into the room, and I heard the door close softly behind me. I stared at the bed. Only Nellie's face showed above the white sheets, her bluish-black hair cascading across the pillow behind her. Her eyes were closed. She seemed to be sleeping.

I walked over to the bed and sat down beside her, scarcely daring to breathe for fear of disturbing her. But somehow she knew I was there. Her eyes fluttered open. They were dark brown and gentle. Her lips barely moved. "Danny." She tried to smile.

I put my hand on the sheet where I could see her hand beneath it. "Don't try to talk now, baby," I whispered. "Everything's all right."

"The baby too?" Her voice was faint and doubtful.

I nodded. "He's perfect," I said. "Everything's perfect. Don't worry now. Just rest and get well."

Tears gathered in her eyes. "I almost messed things up, didn't I?" she asked.

I put my face close to her cheek. "You didn't," I said. "It was me. You were right. I shouldn't have gone yesterday."

She tried to shake her head dissentingly, but it was too much effort for her. She closed her eyes wearily. "No," she whispered, "it was my fault. I should have known you would come home if something hadn't kept you. But I kept remembering how I felt the last time you went away and I couldn't bear the thought of living without you. I had such a feeling about you, Danny." The tears rolled down her cheeks silently. "That something terrible was going to happen to you—to us—and I would be alone."

"Forget it, we'll never be alone again," I said earnestly. "No matter what happens now, we'll always have Junior with us."

Her eyes opened and she looked at me. "Did you see him yet, Danny?" she asked almost shyly. "What's he like?"

I had caught a quick glimpse of him when I came upstairs with the doctor. He had stopped in front of the nursery and let me peek into the incubator.

Nellie's eyes were on my face warmly. I could see the faintest tinge of color coming back into her cheeks. I smiled at her.

"He's tiny and he's cute," I said softly. "Just like his Mamma."

An excited chatter was coming from the waiting-room as I returned to it. My hand was seized enthusiastically the moment I stepped in.

"*Mazeltov*, Danny!" my father was saying, a happy smile on his face. Everybody crowded around me, all talking at once.

My mother-in-law seized my other hand and planted a big wet kiss on my cheek. I grinned happily at her. From somewhere my father had obtained a bottle of whisky. Now we were standing in a small semicircle, the liquor in the paper cups making a small sloshing sound. My father made the toast.

"To your son!" he said, looking at me proudly. "May he ever be happy! And to your wife, may she ever take pleasure in him! And to you, may you ever take pride in him—as I do in you!"

The tears were in my eyes and they weren't put there by the whisky. I had waited a long time for my father to say that. Maybe I didn't really deserve it, but I wanted to hear the words anyway.

Papa raised his cup again. He turned to Sam. "And to my other son," he said quietly, "who made an old man see how wrong he'd been and now puts me further in his debt with his blood!"

I was bewildered. "What do you mean, Pa?" I asked.

Papa looked at me. "It was Sam that fought with me and made me realize what I had done. It was he who convinced me of what a fool I had been and made me go to you."

I stared at Sam. His face was flushing. Papa's voice in my ear seemed to be coming from a great distance: "And now he has saved your son's life with his blood. We both owe him a great deal. Me for bringing you back to me, you for giving your son life." Papa seemed to laugh a little. "A great deal," he repeated. "In the old days a man would have to repay in kind. He would have a right to our blood, even to our lives if he should want them."

I moved closer to Sam, a feeling of gratitude rising in me. My father was still talking.

"Now that you have a son, Danny, you will learn the pain of your deeds. Even those little things you think will bother no one will hurt him, and so hurt you. May you never know the pain I have known, the pain of having your child pay for your errors."

Papa was right. Maybe I would never pay for what I did, but my son might. I was still staring at Sam. He was smiling at me. Then I remembered.

Fields was waiting for him somewhere. And I had made the deal. My mind raced madly. There had to be a way to call him off.

I glanced quickly at the clock on the waiting-room wall. It was after ten. I had to reach Maxie now and cry quits. I had to. "I gotta make a call," I said wildly, and ran out of the waiting-room.

There was a telephone booth in the corridor. I ducked into it and dialed Fields's number hurriedly. The phone rang several times before anyone answered. It was a woman's voice.

"Is Maxie Fields there?" I asked harshly.

"He isn't in," the tired voice answered. "Who's calling?"

"Danny Fisher," I said quickly. "Do you know where he is? I've got to find him!"

"Danny!" the voice cried. "Yes, you've got to! This is Ronnie. You can't let him go through with it. Sam was the only friend you ever had! He was the one who made Maxie lay off you when you first came back; Sam swore he'd kill him if he ever laid a hand on you!"

I closed my eyes wearily. "And I thought it was you," I said.

"No," she answered, "he'd never listen to me. I came back because Ben got sick and I needed money for him. But it didn't do any good. He died."

"Sarah, I'm sorry."

I don't know whether she heard me, because the words kept spilling out of her like a flood. She was talking about Sam again—Sam and me. "You can't let him do anything to Sam, Danny. You mustn't! It was Sam who kept him from moving in on your business. He persuaded Lombardi to tell Maxie to lay off because he was taking it over and Maxie couldn't do anything about it. He was furious. You don't know how bad he is. You gotta stop him, Danny!"

"I want to, Sarah," I said fiercely. "Listen to me. Do you have any idea where I can find him?"

"He said something about going out to Brooklyn," she answered. "He said that Sam would probably show up at your new house tonight."

I sagged limply in the booth. That meant he was probably waiting for Sam near my house, and when we came back from the hospital he would be ready for him. I stared stupidly at the telephone. There was only one thing I could do now. That was to get home before anyone else did.

"Okay, Sarah," I said slowly, putting the receiver back on the hook. I left the booth and went back into the waiting-room.

I walked up to Sam and tried to keep my voice as casual as I could. "Can I borrow your car for a few minutes, Sam?" I asked. "I promised Nellie I'd bring a few things from the house for her, an' my car is still at the airport."

"I'll drive yuh over, kid," he offered.

"No, no," I said quickly. "You're still weak from the blood transfusion. Rest here a little while. I'll be back in twenty minutes."

His hand came out of his pocket with a car key. He held it toward me, smiling. "Okay, Champ."

I looked suddenly into his eyes. He hadn't called me that in years. I could see the warmth of his smile reach them.

"Everything okay, Champ?" he asked. Only the two of us knew what his words meant. There was a world of meaning in them.

I took his hand. "Everything's okay, Champ," I answered. His grip tightened on mine and I looked down at our hands. They were clasped together. Funny the way our hands were alike—the same shape, the same kind of fingers. I looked up into his face. His eyes were warm toward me and I loved him. He was everything I ever wanted to be. That had always been the way it was. In everything I did I tried to make myself over into him. I smiled slowly as I began to understand. "Everything's okay, Champ," I repeated. "Thanks, Sam. Thanks for everything." I took the car key from his fingers and started for the door.

My father stopped me. "Drive carefully, Danny," he admonished me. "We don't want anything should happen to you now."

"Nothing will happen. Papa," I answered. "And if it does, there'll be no regrets. I've had about everything there is to be had in life. I'll have no complaints, no kicks coming."

Papa nodded. "Good you should feel like that, Danny," he said solemnly. "But be careful just the same. You're still excited over your son."

The powerful motor beneath the hood of the canary-colored Caddy convertible hummed as I headed the car toward home. I was glad I had Sam's car. It would make it that much easier for me to find Maxie, because Maxie would be looking for the car. I wasn't worried about him. I would find a way to square him off.

I sped down Linden Boulevard to Kings Highway, then left to Clarendon. At Clarendon I made a right turn and headed toward my street. I glanced in my mirror. A car behind me was blinking its lights. It wanted to pass me. I laughed to myself and pressed my foot down on the accelerator. I was in a hurry too.

The big car responded quickly to my foot and we hurtled through the night. I looked in the mirror again. The other car was creeping up on me. Then I got the idea: Maxie must have tailed Sam out to the hospital.

I eased my foot off the gas and the car slowed down to fifty. Quickly the other car crept up alongside me. I glanced out my window. I had been right. Spit's face was staring at me from the other car. I grinned at him and waved my hand.

Then I saw the chopper resting on the window in Spit's hand. He was raising it slowly.

"Spit!" I yelled at him. "It's me! Danny! The whole thing's off!"

The chopper was still coming up. I yelled at him again: "Spit, yuh crazy bastard! It's me, Danny!"

I saw him hesitate a second. His head turned toward the back seat of his car and I saw his lips move. I stole a quick look back there, but all I could see was the faint glowing of a cigar. Then he turned back to me and the chopper kept coming up. I remembered Maxie's words: "There's no backin' out now. . . . " It was Maxie in the back seat.

There was only one thing left to do. I stepped on the gas as the chopper began to blaze. I felt a sudden pain tearing me away from the wheel. Desperately I fought the wheel, twisting it in my desire to hold onto it.

For a brief second I was blinded; then my vision cleared. The car was rocking crazily on the road in the night. I looked across at Spit. He was grinning at me. I was seized by a terrible anger. A hatred for him and all I had been spilled over into my throat, warm and hot and sticky like blood. He was raising the chopper again.

I looked past his car to the corner. It was my corner, my street. I could see my house standing there, with a light in the window we had forgotten to turn off when we left. I would be safe if I could get home. I would always be safe there. I knew that.

With all my strength I twisted the wheel toward my street. Maxie's car was in the way, but I twisted the wheel just the same. I could see Spit's white face contorted in fright. Sparks blazed from the chopper, but I didn't feel anything. He'd have to get out of my way or I'd run right through him. I could feel the wheels lock, but I didn't care. I was going home.

There was a blaze of light and I could feel the car soaring into the air. I drew a deep breath, bracing myself for the crash, but it never came.

Instead I was a kid on a van moving into a new neighborhood. I could hear the gravel crunching under the wheels. It was daylight, bright daylight, and I couldn't understand it.

Something had gone wrong. Time had run off its track. My mind wrestled crazily with the thought. It couldn't be true. Things like this just didn't happen. I was back at the beginnings of memory.

Then it was gone and I felt the steering wheel shatter. One moment I was looking stupidly at my hands holding onto the remnants of a wheel that was no longer a wheel, and the next moment I was flying crazily into a looming, leering darkness.

Somewhere deep in the silent, noiseless dark, someone was calling my name. It echoed hollowly, metallically, in my mind, the syllables rolling toward me like the waves in the sea.

"Dan—ny Fish—er. Dan—ny Fish—er." Over and over again I could hear the voice calling me. Somehow I knew that I mustn't listen to its siren song. I mustn't listen to its sound. I mustn't even hear it in my mind. Desperately I fought against it. I pushed hard and closed my mind to its echo. A sudden pain rushed through me and I tensed in the excruciating agony.

The pain grew stronger and stronger, and yet it was not a physical thing that I was feeling. It was a vague disembodied pain that floated through me like the air I used to breathe.

The air I used to breathe. Used to breathe. Why did I think that? The pain filtered into me again and permeated my consciousness, and my question was forgotten. I could hear my voice screaming in the distance. Its shout of agony was ringing in my ears. Slowly I slipped back toward the darkness again.

"Dan—ny Fish—er, Dan—ny Fish—er." I could hear the strangely soothing voice again. It was soft and gentle and held within it the promise of rest and peace and relief from agony, and yet I fought against it, with all the strength I had never used against anything before. Again the voice faded from my mind and the pain returned.

How sweet the taste of pain when all else is gone from your body! How you cling longingly to the agony that binds you to the earth! You breathe the pain as if it were the sweetest air, you drink the pain with all the thirsty fibres of your being. You long for the pain that lets you live.

It was roaring sweet and agonizingly pungent inside me. The pain I loved and held so close to me. I could hear my distant voice screaming in protest against it and I was happy in the feeling. Anxiously I reached for it with my hands but could not hold it, for once again it slipped from me and I was plunging into the quiet, restful dark.

The voice was very close to me now. I could feel it in my mind as once before I had felt the pain in my body. "Why do you fight me, Danny Fisher?" it asked reproachfully. "I only come to give you rest."

"I don't want to rest!" I shouted against it. "I want to live!"

"But to live is to suffer, Danny Fisher." The voice was deep and warm and rich and comforting. "Surely you must know that by now."

"Then go away and let me suffer," I screamed. "I want to live. There are so many things I have to do!"

"What is there for you to do?" the voice asked quietly. "Remember what you said a few short minutes ago? The words you spoke to your father: 'There'll be no regrets. I've had about everything there is to be had in life. I'll have no complaints, no kicks coming.'"

"But a man says many things he doesn't mean," I cried desperately. "I've got to live. Nellie said she couldn't go on without me. My son needs me."

The voice was as wise and as tolerant as time. It echoed hollowly through my mind. "You don't really believe that, Danny Fisher, do you?" it asked quietly. "For surely you must know that life does not cease to exist in others for any man."

"Then I want to live for myself," I wept. "To feel the firm soft earth beneath my feet, to taste the sweetness in my wife's body, to take pleasure in the growing of my son."

"But if you live, Danny Fisher," the voice said inexorably, "you will do none of these things. The body you once inhabited is smashed beyond repair. You will not see, you will not feel, you will not taste. You will be but a shell that remains a living organism, a constant burden and agony to those you love."

"But I want to live!" I screamed, fighting against the voice with all my might. Slowly I could feel the pain returning to my being.

I welcomed it as a woman would welcome a long-absent lover. I embraced it and let it enter me. I could feel the sweetly welcome agony flowing through as the blood would flow. Then suddenly there was a moment of pure clean light and I could see again.

I was looking at myself, torn and twisted and shapeless. Hands were reaching toward me, but they stopped, frozen in horror, at the sight of me. This was my body and this was the way people would look at me forevermore.

I could feel the sorrowing tears mingling with the agony that was in me. Was there nothing left of me that might bring joy to someone's heart? I looked closely down at myself. My face was clean. It was calm and still. There was even the remnant of a smile upon my lips. I looked closer.

My eyelids were closed, but I could see behind them. The hollow sockets stared vacantly at me. I turned in horror from myself. The tears were running through my mind, washing away all the strange new hurt.

The pain began to slip from me again as the light grew dim and the dark returned. The voice was once more at the gateway to my mind.

"Now, Danny Fisher," it said sympathetically, "will you let me help you?"

I pushed the tears from my mind. All my life had been a matter of bargain. Now there was time for just one more. "Yes," I whispered, "I will let you help— if only you can make my body whole that my loved ones do not turn from me in horror."

"I can do that," the voice replied quietly.

Somehow I knew that it would be done and there had been no need for me to ask. "Then help me, please," I begged, "and I will be content."

There was a sudden loving warmth around me. "Rest then, Danny Fisher," the voice said softly. "Give yourself up to the quiet, peaceful dark and do not be afraid. It's just like going to sleep."

I reached out confidently toward the dark. It was a friendly, loving kind of dark and in it I found the warmth and love of all I ever knew. It was just like going to sleep.

The dark rolled around me in gentle swirling clouds. The memory of pain was dim and far distant now, and soon even the memory had gone. Now I knew why I had never known peace before.

I was content.

A Stone for Danny Fisher

YOU PLACE THE STONE QUICKLY ON THE MONUMENT AND STAND THERE *gravely, your blue eyes wide. Within you there is a small but creeping doubt. Your father.*

I have no shape, no rounded image, in your memory. I am nothing but a word, a picture on the mantelpiece, a sound on other people's lips. For you have never seen me and I have seen you but once.

Then how can I reach you, my son, how can I make you hear me when even my voice is an unfamiliar echo in your ears? I weep, my son, I weep for all the life I gave you that I will not share. The joys, the sorrows, I will not know with you as my father has known them with me.

For though I gave you life, you have given me even more. In that short moment that we shared together, I learned many things. I learned again to love my father, to understand his feelings, his happiness, his inadequacies. For all the things I meant to him, in one short moment, you meant to me.

I never held you in my arms and pressed you close to my heart and yet I feel these things. When you are hurt, I feel your pain; when you sorrow, I share your tears, and when you laugh there is a joy in me. All the things you are were once part of me—your blood, your bones, your flesh.

You are part of the dream I was that still remains. You are the proof that once I moved and walked the earth. You are my legacy to the world, the most precious that I could bestow. All the values are as naught when compared with you.

In your time there will be many wonders. The distant corners of the earth will be a moment's journey; the deepest ocean, the highest mountain, perhaps even the stars themselves will be within the reach of your fingers. And yet all these miracles will be as nothing when compared with the miracle of you.

For you are the miracle of my continuing flesh. You are the link that joins me with tomorrow, the link in the chain that spreads from time beginning to time never ending.

And still, there is a strangeness in it all. For you, who stem from the roaring passions of my blood and strength and join me with tomorrow, know nothing of me.

We shared but a moment together, the moment of your awakening, and thus you know me not. "What are you like, my father?" you ask in the silence of your little heart. Close your eyes, my son, and I will try to tell you. Shut the bright green world from your eyes for just a moment and try to hear me.

Now you are still. Your eyes are closed, your face is pale and you are listening. The sound of my voice is the sound of a stranger in your ears, and yet, deep within you, you know who I am.

The lines of my face will never be distinct in your memory, yet you will remember. For some day, in some time, you will speak about me. And in your voice will be a sorrow that we have never known each other. And in that sorrow there will also be a contentment. A contentment that will come from the knowledge that all the things you are stem from me. The things that you will give to your son began with me, and what my father passed on to me, and his father behind him.

Listen to me, my son, and know your father.

Though the memory of man is a temporary thing because his life is but a fleeting moment, there is a quality of immortality in him that is as permanent as the stars.

For I am you and you are me, and the man that began with Adam will live forever on this earth. As I once lived.

Once I breathed the air you breathe and felt the soft give of earth beneath my feet. Once your passions raced in my veins and your sorrows wept through my eyes.

For once I was a man beside you.

I, too, had a charge account at Macy's; a bankbook at the Dime Savings; there are papers lying in some hidden vault with my signature scrawled upon them in now browning and aging ink; a social-security number buried in the mass of statistics in a government file with these strange numerical markings upon it: 052-09-8424.

These things I once had, my son. And for this and for many reasons other than this, my name will not be forgotten. For in these mere written records alone there is evidence of my immortality.

I was not a great man whose history has been recorded for children to study in school. No bells will ring for me, no flags descend upon their mast.

For I was an ordinary man, my son, one of many, with ordinary hopes and ordinary dreams and ordinary fears.

I, too, dreamed of wealth and riches, health and strength. I, too, feared hunger and poverty, war and weakness.

I was the neighbor who lived in the next house. The man standing in the subway on his way to work; who held a match to his cigarette; who walked with his dog.

I was the soldier shaking with fear; the man berating the umpire at the ball game; the citizen in the privacy of the voting booth, happily electing the worthless candidate.

I was the man who lived a thousand times and died a thousand times in all man's six thousand years of record. I was the man who sailed with Noah in his ark, who was the multitude that crossed the sea that Moses held apart, who hung from the cross next to Christ.

I was the ordinary man about whom songs are never written, stories are never told, legends are never remembered.

But I am the man who will live forever in the thousands of years yet to come. For I am the man who will reap the few benefits and pay for the many errors that are created by the great.

And the great are but my servants, for my numbers are legion. For the great lie lonely in their graves beneath their mighty monuments because they are not remembered for themselves but for what they made.

But for me, all who weep for their loved also weep for me. And every time someone mourns, he also mourns for me.

You open your eyes in slow wonder and gaze upon the six stones lying on my grave. Now you know, my son. This was your father. Your mother's arms enfold you, but still you stare at the stones. Your fingers point to the words written behind them on the monument. Her lips move gently as she reads them to you.

Listen carefully to them, my son. Are they not true?

To live in the hearts we leave behind is not to die.